ASPECTS
of MEDIEVAL *and*
RENAISSANCE
MUSIC

PHOTO DEAN BROWN

ASPECTS
of MEDIEVAL *and* RENAISSANCE MUSIC

A Birthday Offering to
GUSTAVE REESE

Edited by JAN LaRUE

Associate Editors
MARTIN BERNSTEIN
HANS LENNEBERG
VICTOR YELLIN

W · W · NORTON & COMPANY · INC · *NEW YORK*

CONTENTS

1358257

PLATES APPEAR BETWEEN PAGES 430 AND 431

PUBLISHER'S NOTE

IN THE EARLY 1930s, when Gustave Reese was assisting Carl Engel in supervising the musical publications of the house of G. Schirmer as well as holding courses in medieval and Renaissance music at New York University, it happened that M. D. Herter Norton, a colleague of his on the staff of *The Musical Quarterly*, attended some of his classes. The enthusiasm, the lucidity, and the thoroughness with which he brought that music alive to his students left no doubt that his knowledge and wisdom should be made available to many others in a book. It seemed at first that a single volume of moderate length should cover the field, but the eventual result was the two monumental works—*Music in the Middle Ages* (1940) and *Music in the Renaissance* (1954)—that are recognized throughout the world as basic in their field.

Mrs. Norton's interest in music had sparked the publication of several earlier books about music, but Gustave Reese's *Music in the Middle Ages* was the first of a long series of musicological works by American and European scholars that have appeared over the firm's imprint in the succeeding years. In selecting the material for this list the firm's aims were to help nurture and keep abreast of the remarkable growth of musicology in America; it has had the benefit of the counsel of a number of its eminent authors, whose work is inseparable from this growth. *Music in the Middle Ages*, dedicated by the author to his devoted wife Aimee, opened a new chapter in American musicography. The vigorous and fruitful venture it initiated will be continued and expanded as a younger generation of scholars joins Professor Reese and the other distinguished "elders" who not only established musical scholarship on the American scene but raised it to international eminence.

In his will William Warder Norton established a fund to be used for certain special purposes at the discretion of the Directors of the firm. This fund, the W. W. Norton Award, now fulfilling its function for the first time, has been applied toward the publication of *Aspects of Medieval and Renaissance Music* in the belief that this volume of studies dedicated to Gustave Reese eminently meets the requirements

Warder Norton had in mind. By means of a similar fund, established by Walter S. Fischer, son of the founder of Carl Fischer, Inc., that firm is also participating in this project.

In addition to his contributions to musicology, Gustave Reese has had a far-reaching influence in the development of young composers. During his twenty-year association with Carl Fischer, Inc., where he is now Director of Concert and Opera Publications, his keen discernment of budding talent among youthful musicians, his encouragement of their efforts, and his guidance along the paths he felt they were qualified to pursue with success have resulted in the writing, publication, and distribution of outstanding contemporary compositions.

Officers and staff of W. W. Norton and Company, Inc. and Carl Fischer, Inc. count it a privilege to join the distinguished company of scholars who have contributed to this publication in honoring an author celebrated wherever the study of music is alive and growing, a great scholar, teacher, and friend.

EDITORS' PREFACE

THE PLANNING and execution of a large, secret project involve many contributions performed in anonymity and never recorded on paper. For this reason it is rather more than ordinarily difficult to extend properly individual thanks to all those who aided in the preparation of this volume. At the head of the list we place our publisher, whose long and distinguished support of the field of music first attracted us to the possibility of printing the volume under the present auspices. In particular we are grateful to Mr. Robert Farlow, vice president, who at every turn—and there were many—has supported us with generosity and enthusiasm, bringing to the project a happy combination of intellect, financial ingenuity, and typographic artistry (it is he who designed the chief points of typography in the volume).

To Mr. Nathan Broder, Norton's music editor, we owe thanks too numerous and varied in nature even to present in outline. We have drawn consistently on his seemingly boundless experience and knowledge—musicological, editorial, administrative, and psychological—and very heavily on his patience. To Mr. Bruce Macomber, the Norton copy editor who coordinated the preparation and printing of the volume, we record a debt of gratitude that will be fully understood only by those who have participated in similar procedures.

At New York University all of the music faculty and advanced students contributed in some way to the project, a vast conspiracy that we believe preserved our secret more successfully than most such underground associations. Miss Jean Kessler, the department secretary during the critical period of communication with our authors, contributed many an extra hour at the end of days already long to pursue our multitudinous determinations. Her work was later ably continued by Miss Marie Gottesman. Mr. Gene Wolf followed up many problems relating to editing and production. Miss Phyllis Mason coordinated the preparation of the index by a team cited individually at the beginning of the index. Mr. Lawrence Bernstein furnished helpful expertise at several points.

Our distinguished contributors have drawn together to honor the achievement of a man who represents an unusual confluence of learning and energy, a shaping force in the history of musicology. Professor Blume has eloquently recorded his international fame and influence. For those of us who have benefited from more direct associations, this volume symbolizes the richness of his influence and the inspiration of the living example of Gustave Reese.

Jan LaRue
Martin Bernstein
Hans Lenneberg
Victor Yellin

THE GREATER WORLD
OF GUSTAVE REESE

by FRIEDRICH BLUME

WHEN AFTER the collapse of 1945 the European music historian began to inform himself of what had happened during the war in other parts of the world, his interest was seized at once by a new and extensive series under the imprint of W. W. Norton. Planned to cover the entire history of music in volumes by individual specialists, the series had begun impressively with Gustave Reese's *Music in the Middle Ages* (1940). To be sure, this was not the first comprehensive presentation of medieval music history, but it was the first of such an astonishing completeness, of such uniform mastery and penetration of the enormous mass of material, and of such conscientious and exhaustive examination of all available sources, modern editions, and scholarly commentary. The series continued equally impressively with Paul Henry Lang's *Music in Western Civilization* (1941), a seemingly impossible achievement by a single person of bringing to life the entire history of Western music against all of its cultural and spiritual background.

As precedents in modern historiography of medieval music one might mention the exposition of the Middle Ages in the first volume (1901) of the older *Oxford History of Music* or that of Hugo Riemann in the second part (1905) of his *Handbuch der Musikgeschichte;* and Ludwig's still fundamental article in Adler's *Handbuch* (1924) should be named as the initial stimulus for a total renewal of this area of research. Yet the number of studies following this pattern has remained small. The names of Besseler (1931), Prunières (1933), and Gérold (1932, 1936) mark stages along the way. Far more compendious and detailed than any of these, and at the same time of a convincing temperateness and incorruptible certainty of judgment, Reese's book has laid the worldwide foundation for all studies of medieval music. The name of the author, at that time known outside the United States mainly through several periodical articles and his contributions to the American supplement to the fourth edition of *Grove's Dictionary*, in one stroke achieved international fame; and "The Reese" became a sort of musicological Bible for students all over the world.

Originally Reese's book was intended to draw together both the Middle Ages and the Renaissance. That the state of knowledge had long since made such a plan impossible was already clear from Besseler's summary of 1931. It was therefore a blessing for both research and teaching that the original plan burst its limits; and Reese was forced into a second volume of the Norton History, *Music in the Renaissance* (1954), still more comprehensive than the first, still more detailed and exhaustive. One can but admire how the writer, with the help of his "polyphony in prose" (Foreword), has succeeded in bringing even the most remote corners to light. The investigation of sources, editions, and commentary in these two volumes can with confidence be called a sheerly superhuman performance. Small wonder that the Renaissance volume has spread equally quickly and as "Reese II" has become an indispensable foundation for both instruction and research on the period of the Renaissance. Here too the precedents were few. Since the relevant part (1907) of Riemann's *Handbuch*, there have been hardly any of the larger, all-encompassing accounts: Einstein in Adler's *Handbuch* (1924), Besseler (1931), and Pirro, *Histoire de la musique de la fin du XIVe siècle à la fin du XVIe* (1940) were the most important forerunners. Reese, however, then went far beyond.

Works of this magnitude tend to exert an almost monopolistic influence for many years; and if they succeed to the degree achieved by these two volumes, one can only wish them long life and wide distribution. A German translation of both volumes, unfortunately still lacking, would be desirable. The medieval volume appeared in Italian translation in 1960. In 1962 Reese brought out a second, revised edition of *Music in the Renaissance*, and a revised edition of *Music in the Middle Ages* will soon be in print.

Since the publication of these volumes, as far as we know, no comparable publications by a single author have come out in any country. The *New Oxford History of Music* has divided its treatment of Middle Ages and Renaissance (volumes II & III, 1954 & 1960) among a large number of authors; and as for other comprehensive treatments of music history published in the last two decades, these have as a rule been limited to individual countries (e.g. Van den Borren's *Geschiedenis van de Muziek in de Nederlanden*, I, 1959) or to tightly compressed surveys (such as Handschin's *Musikgeschichte*, 1948; Sachs's *Our Musical Heritage*, 1948; Abbiati's *Storia*, 1954; or recently Grout's more comprehensive *History of Western Music*, 1960). Among the exhaustive studies of a complete music-historical epoch, however, Reese stands alone.

For Reese himself, as he has occasionally stressed, the didactic purpose has been decisive, a statement that we can easily believe when we take in hand his *Fourscore Classics of Music Literature* (1957), a terse and expert introduction to the study of the more important musicological writings of all times. His other works reveal a noteworthy breadth of view. They extend from questions of Renaissance history to matters of music printing and music librarianship; and not less important, they demonstrate his intimate familiarity with the musical works of art themselves.

It is the greater world of musicology—the musicological interpenetration of the Old and New World—that lives in Reese and in which he so completely lives. What he has said about the relationship of Netherlandish and Italian music in the early Renaissance (*Music in the Renaissance*, page 184) calls forth a "variazione con alcune licenze" that can apply to Reese himself:

It would be difficult to overestimate the intrinsic and historical importance of much of the knowledge discussed in his books. The learned impulses of American and European musicology that had interpenetrated one another throughout the early 20th century now did so to a greater extent. A fusion has been in process that produced the underlying cosmopolitan style of Reese's books. Whatever will come afterward—let us hope there will be giants—can only be a continued treatment of what in his writings is already present in every essential feature.

[*Translated by Jan LaRue*]

ASPECTS
of MEDIEVAL *and*
RENAISSANCE
MUSIC

EARLY SPANISH MUSICAL CULTURE AND CARDINAL CISNEROS'S HYMNAL OF 1515

by *HIGINIO ANGLÉS*

T HE HISTORICAL information that we have concerning the music of Spain during the early days of Christianity indicates that this country practiced the entire gamut of secular and religious music.[1] Up to this time, we know nothing about the songs and dances of those *saltatrices* (dancing women) of the *iocosa Gades* (= Cádiz), spoken of by the poet Martial, who were so highly renowned in pagan Rome. From Martial we learn that the dancing women of Cádiz were very much imitated in the Rome of the Caesars, where music was highly cultivated in all its aspects.[2] Other information has come down to us from Pliny the Younger, who describes the attraction that the girl singers of Cádiz held for the Roman nobility.[3] This is confirmed in the writings of Juvenal.[4] In his *De bello punico,* the Roman epicurean Silius Italicus (d. A.D. 101) speaks of the love of the Galicians for dancing and popular singing, and the geographer Strabo (d. A.D. 20), in Book III, Chapter III of his *Geographica* confirms this, referring to the Basques, Asturians, and Galicians. As Spain, a Roman province, closely followed the culture, the music, and the customs of pagan Rome, so also, from the 1st to the 5th centuries, was Christian Spain profoundly Roman in its liturgy and sacred song.[5]

The Latin ecclesiastical culture, so flourishing in Africa thanks to the work of St. Augustine (d. 430), Bishop of Hippo, was spread after his death to France and Italy by his disciples. This culture, which had so flourished in Southern France and to a certain degree the *Tarraconense*

---

[1] Among other works, cf. H. Anglés, *La Música a Catalunya fins al segle XIII* (Barcelona 1935), p. 1ff (= *La Música*); and *La Música de las Cantigas de Santa Maria del Rey Alfonso el Sabio,* III/1 (Barcelona 1958), p. 1ff (= *Cantigas*).
[2] Cf. his *Epigrammae,* I, 61; III, 63; V, 78; VI, 71.
[3] Cf. his *Epistolae,* I, 15.
[4] *Satirae,* XI, 162. Cf. likewise A. Pauly, *Realenzikl. der klass. Altertum Wiss.,* new ed. G. G. Wissowa & W. Kroll, VIII (1918), col. 1965ff.
[5] Cf. *Cantigas,* III/1, p. 2ff.

(Tarragona) from the middle of the 5th to the middle of the 6th century, we see later flourishing in Spain at least from the middle of the 6th to the middle of the 7th century, the epoch of the creation and organization of the Visigothic liturgy and chant, known later, beginning in the 8th century, as the Mozarabic liturgy and chant.[6]

That the performance of sacred and secular music was widespread in the Spain of the 4th to the 7th centuries is confirmed by ecclesiastical writers such as Pacianus of Barcelona (d. latter part of the 4th century), Prudentius (d. after 405), Isidore of Seville (d. 636), Liciano of Cartagena (d. beginning of the 7th century), and by various councils—Illiberis (= Elvira, 300–03); Tarragona (516), Gerona (517), Barcelona I (540), Braga I (561), Toledo III (589), and Toledo IV (633). The religious musical practice of the 5th to the 6th centuries is demonstrated principally by the structure of the central corpus of the Visigothic liturgy and chant, the French-Tarragonese series Collectae psalmorum,[7] and the liturgical formulas of the time now known.[8]

Until now we have hardly considered that in the writings of Aurelio Prudentius Clemens, born in the Tarraconense, the greatest of the ancient Christian poets—known by the name "Christian Horatius"—there appear musical expressions which deserve to be carefully studied. It may be deduced from his writings that in his time the pipe organ was known on the Iberian Peninsula, inasmuch as in his Apotheosis, Verse 389, he writes: "Organa disparibus calamis, quod consona miscent." [9] It is worth noting that Prudentius wrote this before the time of Sidonius Apollinaris, Bishop of Clermont, France (d. end of the 5th century), who speaks of the "organa hydraulica" in the Visigothic court of Aquitaine, which ruled over a portion of Spain,[10] and much before the poet Fortunatus

---

[6] Cf. Anglés, La Música en Toledo hasta el siglo XI, in: Spanische Forschungen der Görresgesellschaft, 1. Reihe, 7. Band (Münster i.W. 1937). For more recent studies, besides the work of Dom Louis Brou, O.S.B., cf. A. A. King, Liturgies of the Primatial Sees (London 1957).

[7] Cf. Louis Brou & A. Willmart, The Psalter Collects from V–VIth Century Sources (Three Series), in: H. Brandshow Soc., 83 (London 1949).

[8] Alban Dold, Das Sakramentar in Schabcodex M.12 Sup. der Biblioteca Ambrosiana mit hauptsächlich altspanischen Formengut im gallischen Rahmenwerk, in: Texte und Arbeiten. 1. Abt. Heft 43 (Beuron 1952); and Palimpsest-Studien, ibid., Heft 45 (Beuron 1955); Joseph Jungmann, Die vormonastischen Morgenhoren im gallisch-spanischen Raum des 6. Jahrh., in: Zeitschrift für Katholische Theologie, 78. Bd., 3. Heft (1956), 306–33; Anscari Mundó, El Commicus Palimpsest Paris lat. 2269. Amb notes sobre liturgia i manuscrits visigots a Septimània, Liturgica 1. Cardinali 1. A. Schuster in Memoriam (Montserrat 1956), pp. 151–284.

[9] Migne, Patr. lat. 59, col. 955.

[10] Cf. his Epistola II, in: Monumenta germ. hist. auctorum antiquissimorum, VIII (Berlin 1887), 31.

(536–before 610), who in his *Vita Sancti Germani* speaks of organs existing in Paris.[11] A while ago I amused myself by extracting all the musical expressions from Prudentius's writings: among others, we note here, for example, Verses 152/153 of the previously referred to *Apotheosis*, "Carmina sanctorum, resonant jam sola virorum,/*Concentu triplici* regem laudantia caeli" [12] as written in two codices of the 6th century, and "concentu duplici" according to another codex of the 10th century. These expressions clearly indicate that Prudentius knew of the existence of two- and three-part polyphonic music.[13]

The royal Visigothic court of Toledo was a flourishing center for popular music ever since the 6th century, when the king Atanagildo (d. 567) chose to make this city the capital of his kingdom. This musical tradition was continued by Atanagildo's brother and successor, Leovigildo (572–586), who tried to implant the finery and splendor of the Byzantine court into the court of Toledo. On our peninsula a pre-Arab Byzantinism, in the musical sense, was much in evidence long before the Arab invasion of Spain early in the 8th century. This pre-Arab Byzantinism (beginning in the 5th to the 7th centuries—later, in the 8th through the 10th centuries, known as Mozarabic Byzantinism) contributed many elements to Visigothic-Mozarabic liturgy and music.

The permanence of Jewish communities for so many centuries on the Iberian Peninsula never ceased to be a blessing for the art of music in our country. Such communities may be traced back to the days of the Old Testament, although their more permanent establishment dates from the destruction of the Temple by Titus (A.D. 70) and the persecution by Hadrian (A.D. 125) to the year 1492. The case of the music of the *jaryas* (a kind of folksong) written in *Romance* (the peninsular language) and preserved in the Arab and Hebraic *muwaschahas* of the 10th–12th centuries, serves to illustrate another important point, namely, that an indigenous musical tradition had flourished in Spain long before the courtly music of the Provençal troubadours and the French trouvères of the 12th and 13th centuries, and had impregnated itself into the popular traditional music of the conquering people.[14]

In spite of the fact that Spain has lost in large measure the musical

[11] Cf. H. Anglés, *Die Instrumentalmusik bis zum 16. Jahrhundert in Spanien*, in: *Natalicia musicologica Knud Jeppesen* (Copenhagen 1962), pp. 143–64.

[12] Migne, *Patr. lat.* 59, col. 933.

[13] Cf. Maurice P. Cunningham, *A Preliminary Recension of the Older Manuscripts of the Cathemerinon, Apotheosis and Hamartigenia of Prudentius*, in: *Sacris Erudiri*, III (1962), 5–59.

[14] Cf. *Cantigas*, III/1, p. 37ff and 433ff, along with the bibliography that is given there.

treasure of ancient times, whatever remains is frequently of great interest for the history of universal music.[15] In studying certain facets of this remaining source of music, two unmistakable characteristics immediately appear: the type of notation and the typical character of the music. The neume notation of the Visigothic-Mozarabic chant is distinguished for its antiquity, so much so that the *horizontal* neume notation of the school of Toledo is today considered one of the oldest and most ancient of those known in Europe.[16] Similarly, the mensural notation of the ancient monody of the Sequences and of the *Cantigas de Santa Maria* of King Alfonso the Wise (13th century) offers a richness of rhythmic patterns up to this time unknown in similar repertories of other countries.[17] Both the dramaticism of the Mozarabic liturgy, with its popular-like melodies (like those of the *Pater noster*, the *preces*, the chant of the *Indulgentia*, etc. of the 7th and following centuries), and the lyricism and popular cast of the Sequences and *cantigas* of the 13th and 14th centuries, are a faithful reflection of the Spanish soul and the character of its music.

The Spanish Church stands among the first to have introduced the singing of the hymns in the liturgy, and along with the Church of Milan and the Church of Ireland was one of those where this kind of singing, intended for the community of the faithful, was most cultivated. In this respect, it is interesting to note that one of the first hymns sung with refrain, "*Ad carnes tollendas:* Alleluia, piis edite laudibus," from the Visigothic liturgy, is an exceptional case in the ancient hymnal, in that it contains the refrain *Alleluia perenne*, which was sung every two verses.

[15] Cf. among others Anglés, *Hispanic Musical Culture from the 6th to the 14th Century*, in: MQ, XXVI (1940); *Gloriosa contribución de España a la Historia de la Música Universal*, in: *Consejo Superior de Investigaciones Científicas* (Madrid 1948); *Musikalische Beziehungen zwischen Deutschland und Spanien in der Zeit vom 5. bis 14. Jahrhundert*, in: *Festschrift Wilibald Gurlitt, Archiv für Musikwissenschaft*, XVII (1959), 5–20; *Die Rolle Spaniens in der mittelalterlichen Musikgeschichte*, in: *Festschrift für Georg Schreiber, Spanische Forschungen der Görresgesellschaft*, 1. Reihe, 19. Band (Münster in W. 1962), 1–24.

[16] Cf. Dom Jacques Heurlier, *La Notation des chants liturgiques latins*, n° 12 (Solesmes 1960); Éric Werner, *Eine neuentdeckte mozarabische Handschrift mit Neumen*, in: *Miscelánea Higinio Anglés*, II (1958–61), 977–91; Anglés, *Mozarabic Chant*, in: *The New Oxford History of Music*, II (1954), 81–91, and *Cantigas*, III/1, p. 13ff. For more recent studies on the Visigothic-Mozarabic liturgy, see the work of Dom Louis Brou, O.S.B. and the already mentioned book by A. A. King, *Liturgies of the Primatial Sees*.

[17] In *Cantigas*, III/2, *Parte Musical, Sección II*, I offered a new transcription of the Huelgas Sequences, the non-modal mensural notation of which I had not understood very well in 1928–31, in spite of the help of Peter Wagner and my respected teacher, Friedrich Ludwig. When I have the opportunity, I shall re-study some aspects of the notation of the polyphonic conductus of the Huelgas Codex, a notation I did not fully understand in 1928 and for some years after. This should prove useful, in light of the fact that such studies, almost unknown at the time, have progressed so much in our day.

It appears, with Visigothic-Mozarabic neumes, in the Madrid codex B.N. MSS 1005 (= Hb 60), previously Toledo 35–1, of the 10th century, and is up to this time melodically undecipherable. According to the Romanist scholar Hans Spanke, who was so interested in these problems, the hymn was composed in Spain during the 7th century.[18]

Because of the Priscillian heretics in Portugal, it was decided, at the first (561) and second (572) Councils of Braga, to prohibit the singing of hymns; Spain, in the fourth Council of Toledo (633), agreed that "nullus nostrum ulterius improbet." [19]

The hymns of the Visigothic-Mozarabic liturgy that survive with music are very few; most of the hymns should be performed in a very simple, improvised manner, in light of the fact that all of the hymnals are lacking melodies, except for a few pieces. The codices that contain text and some hymn melody, besides the one already referred to, include Madrid, B.N. MSS 1001 (a.Hh 69) *Psalmi, cantica, hymni*, of the 9th– 10th centuries, from Toledo, which provided the texts for Cardinal F. A. de Lorenzana's *Breviarium gothicum* of 1775; London, British Museum, Add. 30.851, from Silos, texts edited by J. P. Gilson in 1905; Barcelona, Archivo de la Corona de Aragón, Ripoll 40, from the monastery of Santa María de Ripoll.[20] The texts of the hymns were studied by Faustino Arévalo in 1786 [21] and edited by Cardinal Francisco Antonio de Lorenzana, Archbishop of Toledo (1722–1814, Rome),[22] by J. P. Gilson in 1905,[23] Guido Dreves in 1894,[24] Clemens Blume in 1897,[25] and Justo Pérez de Urbel.[26] Up to now there has been no monograph on the hymns sung in Spain from the abolition of the Mozarabic liturgy in the 11th century to the days of Cardinal Cisneros in the 15th century. This monograph could help us to understand why the Spanish Church gradually replaced the old hymns of the Hispanic liturgy with a new repertory, very different from both the original Spanish and the Roman repertories. The Hymnal of the Cathedral of Huesca is precious in that it contains a complete collection of the 11th century, including the hymns *de*

---

[18] Cf. Hans Spanke, *Abhandlung der Metrik der Cantigas*, in: *Cantigas*, III/1, p. 193.

[19] Cf. José Vives-Tomás Marin-Gonzalo Martinez, *Concilios visigóticos e hispano-romanos*, in: *España Cristiana*, I (Barcelona & Madrid 1963), 78 and 197.

[20] Cf. Dom Beda Mª Moragas, *Transcripció musical de dos himnes*, in: *Miscelánea Higinio Anglés*, II, 591–95.

[21] Besides *Prudentii carmina* (1788/89), in: Migne, *Patr. lat.* 59/60, he published *Hymnodia hispanica* (Rome 1786).

[22] Migne, *Patr. lat.* 86, 885–1352.

[23] *The Mozarabic Psalter* (London 1905).

[24] *Analecta hymnica* (= AH), Vol. 16.

[25] AH, Vol. 27.

[26] *Bulletin hispanique*, XXVIII (Bordeaux 1926).

Tempore and *de Sanctis* [27] in Aquitainian notation. This hymnal, along with the hymnal of Verona, Bibl. Capitolare CIX (102), is one of the best preserved collections of its kind containing music.

In order to study the hymn melodies of Spain, besides the *Liber consuetudinum* from the monastery of San Cugat del Vallés, copied by the monk Petrus Ferrer between 1219 and 1222,[28] the different cathedral *consuetas* (customary books) of the 13th and 14th centuries, the Rituals and sacramental books both manuscript and printed, one must consider the hymnal MS from the cathedral archive of Palma, Mallorca, which I discovered about 1920. Here is a brief description of the codex: parchment, 30.6 x 22 cm, 144 folios, incomplete at the beginning and at the end, a copy from the 14th or 15th century, with square notation over two yellow and red lines. The codex has an inestimable value, for the square notation was erased on the first strophe and replaced with mensural notation, as we shall later discuss.[29]

THE HYMNAL OF CARDINAL CISNEROS

CARDINAL FRANCISCO XIMÉNES (= Jiménez)—known by the name Cisneros because of his family's place of origin—Archbishop of Toledo (1436–1517), was the Maecenas of the Spanish ecclesiastical culture of his time. It was he who founded the University of Salamanca, edited the *Biblia polyglota* of Alcalá de Henares, restored the Mozarabic liturgy in Toledo (which resulted in his publishing the *Missale* in 1500 and the *Breviarium* in 1502), and founded the Mozarabic Chapel of the Cathedral of Toledo. In addition, he published the *Intonarium toletanum* (ed. Guillermo Brocar, Alcalá de Henares 1515), the *Manuale sacramentorum* and the *Passionarium toletanum* (ed. Brocar, Alcalá de Henares 1516). The *Intonarium toletanum*, an exemplar of which is preserved in Madrid, B.N. (M. 268 = C.1ᵃ-5), is of interest for our study. The *Intonarium toletanum* is a precious volume of 119 folios, printed in black and red ink

[27] Cf. Dom Maur Sablayrolles, *A la Recherche des manuscrits grégoriens espagnols. Iter hispanicum*, in: *Sammelbände der Internationalen Musikgesellschaft*, XIII (1911–12), 427ff; H. Anglés, *La Música*, p. 184f; Dom Beda Mª Moragas, *Contenido y procedencia del himnario de Huesca*, in: *Liturgica I. Cardinali I. A. Schuster in Memoriam* (Montserrat 1956).

[28] Anglés, *La Música*, pp. 68ff and 212ff.

[29] Anglés, *La Música*, pp. 214–15, gives facsimiles of the MS of Mallorca. In the same place one finds an over-all glance at the different medieval collections of hymns performed in Tarragona and a general bibliography of the music of the hymns published up to 1935; cf. also his *Die Sequenz und die Verbeta im mittelalterlichen Spanien*, in: *Festschrift Carl-Allan Moberg* (Stockholm 1961), pp. 37–47. On the music of the hymns in general, for modern studies and editions, see among others C.-A. Moberg, *Die liturgischen Hymnen in Schweden*, I (Copenhagen 1947); Bruno Stäblein, *Hymnus*, in: MGG, VI (1957), and *Monumenta monodica medii aevi*, I:— *Hymnen*, I (Bärenreiter 1956).

on paper, with mensural notation on red five-line staves. The book is divided into six parts. What interests us in this book is the part containing the hymns. The hymnal proper forms the first part, and occupies folios II–XLIIJ^v.[30] The peculiarity of the hymnal consists precisely in the abundance of melodies, some printed in square notation, others, the majority, in mensural notation, and even some with a mixture of square and mensural notation (see the illustration).

Intonarium toletanum, fol. 2. Hymn melodies in mensural notation

As I recall, I have never seen, either in Spain or anywhere in the world, a hymnal that so lends itself to the study of mensurally notated hymns as the one under discussion. Although the Hymnal of Toledo

---

[30] Cf. H. Anglés & J. Subirá, *Catálogo musical de la Biblioteca Nacional de Madrid,* II (Barcelona 1949), p. 23ff and facs. II–VI.

dates from the beginning of the 16th century, the fact that it contains so many melodies notated mensurally and of unknown origin gives it a great importance. The mensural notation used in this collection of hymns is the same employed for the polyphony of the 15th century, and it is presented with an admirable logic and accuracy. It would be very interesting to know the identity of the expert musicians who selected and copied these pieces with mensural notation. Cardinal Cisneros's reform of the Mozarabic liturgy and chant is well known, and it was undertaken with great interest and zeal, despite the fact that at the time he could not find a man who knew how to decipher the neume notation of the Mozarabic codices in the Cathedral of Toledo. Now then, comparing the mensural notation of these hymns with the other used for the Mozarabic *Cantorales* left in manuscripts (copied around 1508) in the same Cathedral of Toledo, one guesses immediately that the musicians who prepared the mensural notation of the aforementioned *Cantorales* and of the present hymnal were not Gregorian chant singers—called "cantollanistas"—but choirmasters well acquainted with the mensural notation of the contemporary polyphony. And here is the problem: I have repeated many times that Spanish printing of the 16th century was somewhat less than generous with respect to musicians, in the sense that the Spanish presses that were so sumptuous and generous for all kinds of books about human learning were very meager, not to say stingy, for editions of music. Nevertheless, the Cisneros Hymnal demonstrates that by 1515, the print shop of the editor Guillermo Brocar of Alcalá de Henares had at its disposal splendid types to print every kind of mensural notation and consequently for printing sacred and secular polyphony. This is all the more admirable if we consider the state of music printing in Europe, and that the most famous printer at the time was Ottaviano de' Petrucci in Italy.

Another question that concerns us with respect to the Cisneros Hymnal is finding out from what source the copyists who prepared the collection took the melodies. Apart from the hymns that are printed in square notation and appear with the international liturgical chant, there are many pieces with completely unknown melodies, and sometimes with a very popular kind of melody. Is it possible that some of the latter may be a reminder of the ancient hymnodic tradition of Toledo? The very words of folio 1ᵛ, "Incipit Intonarium secundum consuetudinem alme matris ecclesie Toletane per circulum anni," seem to indicate that the *Intonarium* contained the principal pieces of the liturgical chant of the Church of Toledo. Perhaps the fact that Cardinal Cisneros expected that his chant book would be not only used in the Spanish

Church, but also imitated in foreign churches, is proof of this.

In 1926, during the course of an investigation of the musical Mozarabic codices with the illustrious Orientalist and Gregorianist Peter Wagner, I discovered, upon studying the music of the three Mozarabic *Cantorales* (put in order by decree of Cardinal Cisneros) in Toledo, that the melodies of the Proprium Missae—although not those of the intonations of the celebrant, the chant of the scriptures, a few *preces*, etc.—had nothing to do with the Visigothic-Mozarabic melodies. After transcribing some of these melodies, I arranged to have them sung at a great Mozarabic pontifical Mass in the presence of Peter Wagner. Hearing these melodies gave me reason to doubt that the melodies of the Proprium Missae kept in the Cisneros *Cantorales* could be related to the medieval Mozarabic chant performed in that ancient cathedral. It also gives me some reason now to question the age and authenticity of some of the melodies of the present hymnal. In spite of everything, this does not diminish the importance of our studying and getting to know a hymnal of this kind, which contains many melodies of a traditionally popular cast and others from the Gregorian school of an international character, all of which are printed in a mensural notation exceptionally perfect for its kind. For those interested in the problem of performing the hymns with Gregorian melodies, a few examples can be found in this hymnal which indicate how these hymns were performed in Spain during the 15th and 16th centuries. It should be noted that the mensural notation used for these hymns in the Cisneros Hymnal coincides exactly with the mensural notation that appears in certain *Processionarium, Ordinarium, Rituale,* and Spanish chant books printed both in Spain and in foreign countries.

Apparently, the Cisneros reform, musically speaking, was already far removed from the medieval musical tradition of Mozarabic chant; similarly, the hymnodic tradition of Toledo at the time of Cardinal Cisneros was very different from the Mozarabic liturgical tradition of ancient times, at least with reference to the poetic texts. I have compared the list of texts of the Cisneros Hymnal with the texts of the Mozarabic codex edited by Gilson in the British Museum, and I have only found some 28 texts that coincide with those in *The Mozarabic Psalter* of the 11th century; in AH 27 there are some 45. There are about 200 surviving texts of Mozarabic hymns, written in many different periods. These include hymns with classical meter of long and short syllables, others with rhythmic poetry based on the accent, and some written in the crude Latin of the 10th century. There are acrostic hymns that indicate the name of the author. Differing from the Roman hymnal, which is purely liturgical, the old Hispanic hymnal contained hymns for the consecration of a bishop; for the birth, consecration, and marriage of a king; for the harvest of fruits; for time of war, etc. Some were written by French and German poets, more especially French, and comprised part of the repertory of the 7th century. More than 80 texts are of foreign origin, not Hispanic. These may be subdivided into three categories: (a) 16 are by Prudentius; (b) about 40 date from before the Arab invasion; and (c) about 30 were composed after the Arab invasion.[31]

Entering more fully into the contents of the Cisneros Hymnal, we can say that it contains 316 pieces with music, of which in 91 cases only the incipit of the text and the music are printed, since these appear in complete form in another part of the hymnal. The collection is made up of 139 different texts, many of which appear with different melodies and others which are repeated with the same melodies. It is strange to find among the sung texts No. 172, *Mucro secat iberorum/Cuspide durissimus*,[32] which refers to the victory over the Arabs by the King of Castile; and another, No. 171, *Clangant coetus gloriosi/Melodie carmine/Hesperisque bellicosi*, which refers to the victory over Abu'l-Hasan Ali, who reigned from 1331–48.[33] Of the melodies, some derive from the universal liturgical heritage, and others are typical and appear only in this hymnal. The importance of the Cisneros Hymnal lies in its musical notation, which was prepared by men who were experts in the mensural notation of the 15th and the beginning of the 16th centuries. To this very day it is difficult to say if the musicians who collected these melodies and prepared their musical notation might have included a choirmaster or perhaps a professor of music in the University of Alcalá de Henares.

If we consider that in other countries no mensurally notated hymns or Sequences of ancient times have been preserved, it seems curious that in our peninsula we know of several codices appearing with Latin text and copied with mensural notation. So, for example, the Las Huelgas Codex contains 31 Sequences, 15 with two voices and 16 with one; 23 are copied in modal mensural notation. The codex of Tarragona, Archivo Diocesano, Cód. 12, of the 14th century, contains 7 Sequences copied in modal mensural notation similar to that of the Paris Codex, B.N. lat. 1343, which contains an *Officium Beate Virginis Marie*, prepared under the patronage of Charles of Anjou, brother of Louis IX of France, King of Sicily from 1266, deposed in 1282.[34] In reference to the notation of

---

[31] Cf. Justo Pérez de Urbel, *op. cit.*
[32] Cf. AH 16, No. 29, p. 41. In Toledo it was sung "In Triumpho sanctae crucis" since the 14th century.
[33] Cf. AH 16, No. 30, p. 41.
[34] *Huelgas* 91 and 178ff.

hymns in Spain we have seen that melodies of certain *Libri consuetudinum* of cathedrals or monasteries are copied in mensural notation; such is the case of the *Consueta* of the 14th and 15th centuries of San Cugat (Barcelona, Archivo de la Corona de Aragón, San Cugat, nº 20). As already mentioned, this mensural notation is also used in liturgical books printed during the 16th century. What happens in the Hymnarium of Mallorca cited above and in other printed books is surprising: the copyist who amended the Palma de Mallorca manuscript had no difficulty in changing the square notation to mensural when the hymnodic melody was syllabic, but he found that he was unable to do this when the melody was a little melismatic. The same thing happens in books printed in the 16th century, and likewise occurs in our Cisneros Hymnal. This fact is very instructive even today, for when an ancient melody cannot be sung well, it is not a defect intrinsic in the music, but rather a defect in the rhythm that we now use in transcribing.

The musical notation of the Cisneros Hymnal is on this point very instructive and teaches us to sing some of the hymns of the Gregorian repertory with mensural rhythm and others with free rhythm. For the latter, when the melody is syllabic or semi-syllabic, a mensural notation consisting of semibreves is used, resulting also in a free rhythm; but when the hymns have an adorned or melismatic melody, they are always printed in square notation, like the liturgical chant of that period. There are also hymns with Roman melodies, copied in mensural notation that indicates a ternary rhythm, as if it were a modal rhythm of the Middle Ages; in other cases a binary rhythm is indicated, which has nothing to do with the modal rhythm. Also found in the hymnal are melodies with a semi-mensural notation, indicating a more or less free rhythm. The melodies of a more or less popular strain are generally unknown, and are copied in mensural notation, indicating sometimes a binary mensural rhythm and other times a modal ternary rhythm.

The most common mensural notation in our hymnal consists of the following simple binary and ternary ligatures:

There are 102 different melodies in the hymnal, many of which
appear with several texts. In reference to the rhythm we can say that
28 appear with free rhythm, like that found in liturgical chant; 12 with
semi-free rhythm, i.e. a little mixed between mensural and almost free;
32 with ternary mensural rhythm; and 30 with binary, non-modal,
mensural rhythm. It is very important to note that at the end of the 15th
century and the beginning of the 16th, mensural notation was still used
to express a modal rhythm, even though the specialists of the time were
not familiar with the medieval theory of the six rhythmic modes. Of the
melodies with modal notation, there are 27 in the first mode, 2 in the
second mode, and 3 with a mixed rhythm combining the first and second
modes in the same melody. It is very natural that the trochaic longa-
brevis rhythm should be so abundant, considering man's natural affinity
for this rhythm and also that it is the most common rhythm of the
courtly and religious monody of the Middle Ages.

When I find it possible to publish the entire musical and literary
contents of the Cisneros Hymnal, an edition of which I am preparing for
Monumentos de la Música Española, I shall give more details on the
different points of view concerning the interpretation of the melodies,
and we shall compare these with other melodies from the Spanish liturgical books of the 16th century.

GIVEN THE LIMITATION of space on this occasion, I am restricting myself
to the seven following hymns. So that the reader may consider the
original notation of the Cisneros Hymnal, I am adding the old notation
to each piece.

Ex. 1   Fol. 3, No. 11 (Chevalier 26; AH 50:58)

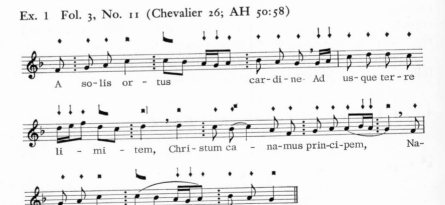

Ex. 2   Fol. 5, No. 25 (Chevalier 21481; AH 50:74)

Ve – xil – la Re – gis pro-de-unt: Ful-get cru – cis   my –
ste – ri – um,   Quo car-ne car – nis con – di – tor   Su –
spen – sus   est   pa – ti – bu – lo.

Ex. 3   Fol. 9, No. 52 (Chevalier 21204; AH 50:130)

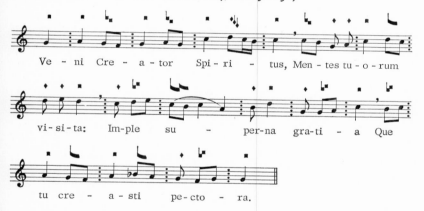

Ve – ni Cre – a – tor   Spi – ri – tus, Men – tes tu – o – rum
vi – si – ta: Im-ple   su – per-na   gra-ti – a   Que
tu cre – a – sti   pe-cto – ra.

Ex. 4   Fol. 9ᵛ, No. 58 (Chevalier 14467; AH 50:586)

Pan-ge lin-gua glo-ri – o – si   Cor-po – ris my –
ste – ri – um, San – gui – nis-que pre – ti – o – si,
Quem in mun – di pre – ti – um.

Ex. 5   Fol. 13ᵛ, No. 91 (Chevalier 9272; AH 51:40)

Jam lu‑cis or‑to   si ‑ de‑re, De‑um pre‑ce‑mur sup‑pli‑ces, Ut

in di‑ur‑nis   a ‑cti‑bus, Nos ser‑vet a no‑cen ‑ ti‑bus.

Ex. 6   Fol. 35, No. 249 (Chevalier 18607; AH 50:204)

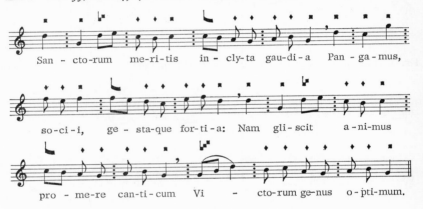

San ‑ cto‑rum me‑ri‑tis in ‑ cly‑ta gau‑di‑a Pan ‑ ga‑mus,

so‑ci ‑ i,   ge ‑ sta‑que for‑ti ‑ a: Nam gli‑scit   a ‑ni‑mus

pro ‑ me‑re can‑ti ‑ cum Vi   —   cto‑rum ge‑nus o ‑ pti‑mum.

Ex. 7   Fol. 37ᵛ, No. 266 (Chevalier 9136; AH 51:134)

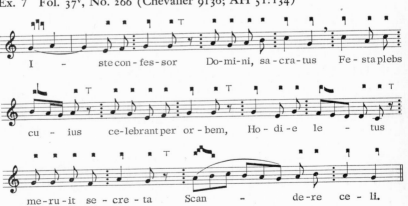

I   —   ste con ‑ fes‑sor Do‑mi‑ni, sa‑cra‑tus   Fe ‑ sta plebs

cu ‑ ius   ce‑lebrant per or‑bem, Ho ‑ di‑e le ‑ tus

me‑ru‑it se ‑ cre‑ta Scan — de‑re ce ‑ li.

NEW LASSO STUDIES

by WOLFGANG BOETTICHER

THE WORK OF Orlando di Lasso's two sons, Ferdinand and Rudolph, has still not been satisfactorily cleared up. These two extremely gifted artists, who themselves had joined their father in common publication ventures, were relatively quick in adopting the early monodic stylistic ideas; this much is certain. Recently I was able to add to our knowledge of these two some new biographical data from documents in Munich and elsewhere.[1] Some years ago, Helmuth Osthoff made references to the motets with German texts that Lasso's sons had based on German songs.[2] These were, however, only a small part of their entire output. The works of the two sons are so zealously recorded in the codices of the Munich chapel during the years 1595–1625 that, as far as the sources are concerned, a very favorable picture prevails. Ferdinand was first appointed *Sänger* at the end of March 1584.[3] Rudolph began his chapel service in 1585 and advanced to first organist in 1589 and in 1609 to *Kurfürstlicher Hofkomponist*. A more detailed bibliography shows that there must be many gaps with regard to Rudolph's works. First of all, an entire collection of Masses, which certainly contained instructive examples of parody technique (some doubtless based on the father's compositions), has most likely been lost.[4]

---

[1] In the author's publication: *Aus Orlando di Lassos Wirkungskreis, Neue archivalische Studien zur Münchener Musikgeschichte. Veröffentlichungen der Gesellschaft für Bayerische Musikgeschichte*, I (Kassel 1963), 159–63 (hereafter cited as B III).

[2] H. Osthoff, *Die Niederländer und das deutsche Lied* (Berlin 1938), pp. 293–97, to which I have added further information in *Orlando di Lasso und seine Zeit, Repertoire-Untersuchungen* . . . (Kassel 1958), pp. 724–26 (hereafter cited as B I).

[3] Recently I was able to reveal the appointment decree in B III, pp. 159–60.

[4] In a handwritten stockroom catalogue of the Antwerp publisher Plantin, *Libri venales 1555–1670* (MS Reg. latin. 795), which along with other lists from this distributor we have proved to be reliable concerning Lasso prints (B I, pp. 733–34), this collection of Masses appears in fol. 303ᵛ with the name of the publisher Nestroy (Ingolstadt) but without date. In 1607 Rudolph published two Magnificats in his *Circus symphoniacus* (Munich), one of which he based on his father's late motet for double choir *Omnia tempus habent* and the other on the 1592 setting *Aurora lucis rutilat*. One can already see in these two compositions the monodic smoothing-out of the contrasts in the sonorities of the original pieces. See B I, p. 722, fn. 8.

Another publication by this son, which escaped my attention in 1958 [5] can now, however, be mentioned: *Cygnaeum Melos, quod Rvdolphvs de Lasso, serenissimi Boiariae principis Maximiliani S.R.I. Electoris Organoedvs, svb Mortem, in Honorem vivificae Crucis, verborvmq[ue], quae Christo monenti vltima fverunt, quaternis, ternis, & binis vocibvs vnà cum Litaniis A 4 cecinit* (Munich: Georg Victorinus, 1626).[6] This print comprises five partbooks (*Vox I^a–IV^a, Bassus ad organ.*). There are in all 36 compositions, 12 each of four-part, three-part, and two-part settings, of which the two-part settings (Nos. 25–36) offer the most interest. Here one sees on the one hand how far the son has come from the *bicinia* published by Orlando in 1577, and on the other hand, how the technique of early monody destroys the autonomous two-part structure by adding a third, instrumental part. The prominent interest in the *bicinia* by most composers of early monody, particularly in Germany (*Schulgesang*), is well known and attested by numerous *exempla* in didactic publications.[7] One can see in this thin two-part structure an important link in the chain from later Renaissance to early Baroque. It is typical of this next generation that it has nothing against arrangements or even questionable adulterations (in the sense of not faithfully reproducing a work of an earlier period). Such works are sometimes deliberately veiled, which makes it extremely hard to recognize them by bibliographical data. Adam Gumpeltzhaimer printed Lasso's five-part *Cantate Domino canticum novum* in 1591 *in duas redactum* (cf. B I, p. 464), whereby the upper voice (taken from Lasso's *Quinta Vox*) is subjected to the modern concertato practice. In this case we are dealing with an artificial reduction. In another print, however (unknown either to Eitner or the editors of the *Gesamtausgabe*),[8] we find Lasso's *bicinia* of 1577 newly arranged with an added third voice, to be sure still not a textless thorough-bass, but nevertheless a monodic support that transforms the placement of the rests, the sequence of intervals, the phrasing, and the polyphonic structure of the two-part organism into a wholly new conception. In Rudolph's publication of 1626 quoted above we are obviously dealing, in the case of the *bicinia*, with compositions from the same critical period of upheaval around 1600, perhaps even with youth-

---

[5] B I, p. 721.
[6] London, Westminster Abbey Library, No. CG 1 (9), 4°.
[7] H. Albrecht, *Bicinium*, in: MGG, I (1949–51), 1839–41.
[8] *Moduli duarum vel trium vocum Orlando Lasso auctore* (Paris: Widow of Robert Ballard and Pierre Ballard, 1601). This print, which wrongly cites Lasso as composer (since the third voice is a later accretion by an unknown hand), was the subject of a contribution by the present author: *Eine französische Bicinien-Ausgabe als frühmonodisches Dokument*, in: *Festschrift für K. G. Fellerer* (Regensburg 1963), pp. 67–76.

ful works from around 1585 [9] that the composer did not consider mature enough for publication. It is significant in this respect that Rudolph depicts the famous text *Qui vult venire* (Matthew 16:24) not as his father had done in his *bicinia* of 1577 with canonic variation symbolizing an *imitatio Jesu*, but on the contrary, with four-part block harmonies, the upper voice rambling freely in configurations. Even the *tricinia* in Rudolph's print offer an instructive example of how far he has come from the models of his father.[10] In his earlier *tricinia* (1588) Rudolph was amazingly strict in following the compactness and the absolutely abstract polyphonic structure of his father's *tricinia* (even if there are a few occasional madrigalisms inserted and a freer conception of the cantus firmus). The *tricinia* in the 1626 publication, however, reveal at the very beginning broad affective melismas, implied by the exclamations of the textual incipits (*O crux venerabilis, Ecce lignum, Ecce crucem, Haec est,* etc.). We can see this modern characteristic of Rudolph's already in the broadly swinging incipits of his *Fratres* motets in an early print (1607).[11] Orlando in his late period had also set such *Fratres* motets. (They are the salutation of St. Paul's letters.) He had, however, always preserved strict diction and a pliant series of shorter motives at the beginning of a piece. The 1626 posthumous printing of Rudolph's works does not seem to be merely a gleaning of youthful pieces. As was the case in the posthumous edition of the father's motets (*Magnum opus musicum,* 1604, with Rudolph's collaboration), some of his earliest works could be included in this "Testament." It is not lacking in apparently bass-oriented composition (the four-part *Trahe me; Ascendam in Palmam*). These pieces fill an important gap; for Rudolph's late work has up to now only been known from scattered examples in *Sammelwerke* and from his four- to six-part *Triga musica,* composed (according to the title) *In Viadanae modo.* Only a fragment of one voice-part has been preserved (in Upsala). Much in these works (Munich 1612) seems to go far beyond Rudolph's late collections of motets *Ad sacrum convivium* (1617), *Virginalia Eucharistica* (1615), and *Alphabetum Marianum* (1621).

[9] These early monodic experiments must go back far beyond Viadana (1601), as the memorable work of Max Schneider and the more recent bibliographical researches of Claudio Sartori have shown. I recently referred to some newly found materials in Italian libraries (among which is an up to now unknown printed lute tablature by A. Orologio [1596]) that permit one to follow more closely the divergent process of early monodic modifications: *Zum Problem der Übergangsperiode der Musik 1580–1620,* in: *Kongressbericht Kassel 1962* (Kassel 1963), pp. 141–44.

[10] See Orlando's three-part *Ulenberg-Psalter* of 1588, a print in which Rudolph himself is represented by a considerable number of his own *tricinia.*

[11] Cf. B I, pp. 722–23.

The change in Rudolph's style is also noticeable in the madrigal sphere. From the very few manuscripts we still have in Rudolph's own hand, the MS Vienna, Nat.–Bibl., Ms. mus. 10.110 is of particular interest. Rudolph includes in this collection of works by various composers the remarkable setting by his father of *La non vol esser più mia*. Orlando's composition is a canzonetta with several stanzas. Here we see quickly shifting chordal expanses and a rigid dance-like meter that are most unusual with this classic master of the polyphonic motet.[12] This canzonetta was probably not composed until 1583. It therefore comes after the so-called "Villanellen-Krisis," which immediately followed Orlando's motets with German texts (1570s) and which the master overcame in his last German compositions (printed in 1590) with penetrating six-part writing and absolutely dogmatic treatment of the cantus firmus. The canzonetta is actually a modern experiment for Lasso, closely related to his remarkable parody-Magnificat super "un aria di un sonetto" and the canzonetta *O che vezzosa aurora*, the latter of which stems from Orazio Vecchi,[13] thereby rendering homage to a much younger artist. Among Lasso's compositions of the 1580s there is an equally remarkable parody-Magnificat on *Vola, vola pensier*, which I conjectured to be in one of the lost madrigal books by G. Caimo.[14] Caimo also belonged at that time to a much younger generation. I recently further examined his connections with the Munich chapel in correspondence documents.[15] Caimo is therein designated as "raro virtuoso con la mano assai gagliarda e velocissima."

The four-part canzonetta *La non vol*—actually an individual case in Lasso's work [16]—shows nevertheless that he had, as early as 1580–84, sought contact with the young monodists. In his last compositions, however, Lasso distinctly dissociated himself from them. On the other hand, it is revealing that Rudolph begins with these experiments of his father's and that, with all his father's works to choose from, he held fast to just this isolated canzonetta. The method of notation is also typical of the change in style. Rudolph's handwriting reads on the frontispiece: "Libro

---

[12] I was able to reproduce this piece (not available to Sandberger for the edition of Lasso's Italian works) for the first time from the publication *Continuation du mellange* (Paris 1584), now that all the partbooks have been found: *Lasso-Gesamtausgabe, Neue Folge* (Kassel 1956), I, 152–55.

[13] See B I, pp. 632–33.

[14] *Ibid.*, pp. 634 and 882.

[15] B III, pp. 130–33.

[16] The title of a Lasso publication retained in Draudius, Clessius, and several old *Messkataloge* around 1594/95, is noteworthy: *Musica nova . . . 3 voc., dove si contengono madrigali, sonetti, villanelle . . .* (Munich: A. Berg). I was not able to find this in any library (B I, pp. 583–84). For the time being nothing can be said about the publication except that it probably contained only compositions from Lasso's youth.

di partitura et intavolatura d'instrumento dove ci sono varie cose come Toccate, Napolitane, Canzonette, Madrigali, Motteti [sic] et altre diverse colsette a 3, 4, 5, 6 & 8 voci . . ." [17] The intended instrumentation for this repertoire (which contains pieces by F. Rovigo, G. Gabrieli, N. de la Grotte and anonymous composers) is therefore clear. The tablatures announced in the sub-title are missing, but it is evident that the entire collection met the demands of early monody for extracting dance movements for the orchestral suite from vocal prototypes. For this reason Rudolph only seldom underlaid the text of his father's canzonetta, since, in this borderline case of a homophonic composition with several stanzas, text indication in only the lower voice sufficed. In summary then, it can be seen that Rudolph's tendency toward monody starts wilfully from the works of his father during the years 1575–85 and then after 1620 strives for new results.

Another question that may likewise be clarified with new data is the cultivation of Lasso's works outside Munich. Here we find in the manuscripts almost exclusively sacred works: motets, Masses, litanies. The most important discoveries, which at the same time throw new light on the personal relationship with foreign chapel choirs, were made in the German language regions: in Aachen, Ansbach, Augsburg, Breslau, Brunswick, Danzig, Dresden, Ellwangen, Freising, Freiberg (Saxony), Glashütte, Graz, Grimma, Heilbronn, Karlsruhe, Kassel, Liegnitz, Lübeck, Lüneburg, Nuremberg, Pirna, Regensburg, Reichenau, Stuttgart, Vienna, Zörbig, Zwickau, and in Stockholm (the German church, St. Gertraudis). These are certainly only accidental remains of a once gigantic number of musical codices.[18] Some further supplementary information: In Regensburg there is a voluminous source in which Lasso is frequently represented.[19] In 1960 I looked for the old Liegnitz choirbooks and for the same material in Breslau, but to no avail; and yet a tenor partbook of the *Magnum opus musicum* has appeared with a handwritten registration of the Liegnitz senators with the date 1610, ordained and bound for the Liegnitz church of Sts. Peter and Paul.[20] In Brussels there is now in the possession of a private library [21] a manu-

[17] Rudolph here calls himself an employee of the stable master (*Stallmeister*) Bernardino Baron de Hermenstain, who was immediately subordinate to the electoral prince of Bavaria.

[18] B I, pp. 819–38; there will be special information concerning this in Vol. II (*Werkkatalog*), to appear shortly.

[19] Fürstlich Thurn- und Taxis'sche Bibliothek, A.R. 786–837, 857–60, 942–46, 985–86, 1011–17.

[20] I would like to thank my colleague Prof. Dr. J. Chomiński (Warsaw) for permission to study this source on the spot.

[21] Private library of Count Adrien van den Burch, transferred recently to Ecaussines-Lalaing (Prov. Hainaut, Belgium) after the death of the owner. I would like to thank my colleague Prof. Dr. Ch. Van den Borren (Brussels) for this infor-

script choirbook formerly assembled by F. Lindner *Lignicensis* with two
of Lasso's Masses *super La la maistre* and *Je prens en gré* (among other
compositions by V. Ruffo and G. Contino). The pastor rolls (*Pfarr-
matrikel*) of Meerane (1616) list *Funff theil Orlandi: Sacrae canciones*
[*sic*] *quinq. uocum . . . 1564.*[22] These can be no other than the five
partbooks from Lasso's first book of motets to be published in Germany—the so-called *Nürnberger Motettenbuch*—the oldest edition of
which we have set at 1562 (correcting Sandberger). A thorough bibliographical search actually shows that this publication found tremendous
acceptance even in Protestant Thuringia and Saxony. A total of 20
printings can be proved (by the original publisher Montanus and also
by Gardano, Scotto, Phalèse, Haultin, A. Berg);[23] and yet recently we
found still another printing in a small library of a German nobleman,[24]
this one by the original printer, which raises the number of reprints
by him up to 1586 to eight. Besides the German chapel choirs, the list
can be supplemented with reference to the Danish chapel in Copenhagen;[25] an important source was also discovered recently in Czechoslovakia.[26] It is strange that so few of the chansons composed by Lasso
have been preserved in old manuscripts. There is an excellent report
on a source that has just been discovered in France.[27] This is a 577-page
manuscript entitled *Misse in musica di diversi compositori . . . et altri
compositioni*, since 1954 in Paris, Bibl. Nat., Rés. V^{ma} 851. It was
probably already begun in 1575 in Italy and contains (along with many
Netherlands, French, and Italian composers) one madrigal and eleven
chansons by Lasso in a very early state. The first printings of some of

mation. F. Lindner wrote this Codex in Ansbach (*Onoltzbach*) in September 1574.
Cf. also Ch. Van den Borren in: *Bulletin de la classe des beaux-arts*, Académie Royale
de Belgique, tome XLV (Brussels 1963), pp. 152–53.
   [22] For this communication I am grateful to Dr. W. Hüttel, Glauchau (Saxony).
   [23] B I, pp. 172–73.
   [24] Berleburg (Westphalia), Fürstlich Sayn-Wittgenstein'sche Bibliothek, Catalogue No. T.Â.1–1 (Nuremberg: Johannes Montanus & Ulrich Neuber, 1563); the
quinta vox is missing.
   [25] *Gamle Kgl. Samling* No. 1873; Royal Libr. Copenhagen. Concordances with
the two anonymous settings *Congratulamini* and *Quare tristis*.
   [26] Levoča (ČSSR), formerly Lutheran church library. Three codices: (1) Organ
tablature with 157 compositions written by Caspar Plotz dated 1603 with *Quem
vidistis, Pater Abraham, Videntes stellam, Tibi laus, Hierusalem plantabis, Venite ad
me, Justorum animae;* (2) Choirbook, 31 compositions, written by Plotz up to fol.
159, the remainder up to fol. 306 by an unknown scribe, with *Missa quatuor vocum,
Missa super Benedicam Dominum, Missa Paschalis, Missa super Veni in hortum
meum,* 24 Magnificats, the madrigal *Nasce la pena mia;* (3) Codex Schimbracki,
20 x 31 cm., "notem Leibic 1642," latest entry 1635, with *Fili quid.* Plotz was cantor
in Levoča; Schimbracki was active in Lubici.
   [27] N. Bridgman and F. Lesure, *Une anthologie 'historique' de la fin du XVIe
siècle: le manuscrit Bourdeney,* in: *Miscelánea en homenaje a Monseñor H. Anglés*
(Barcelona 1958–61), I, 162–64.

these pieces are: 1555β (*Per pianto la mia carne*); 1559γ (*Veux-tu ton mal, Le voulez-vous*); 1560δ (*Un triste coeur*) and 1560θ (*Ardant amour, Susanne un jour, Secourez-moi, Mon coeur se recommande, J'attens le temps, Sur tout regrets, Au temps jadis, Elle s'en va*). It could be that the sole madrigal of this group was taken from the 1560β reprint —or perhaps most of it from 1560θ—a unique source now lost in which only the madrigal and *Un triste coeur* were lacking.[28]

A particular problem for Lasso research is the relatively large group of works whose authenticity is more or less doubtful. Even the post-humous *Magnum opus musicum* (1604), which served as a basis for the Lasso *Gesamtausgabe* (1894–1927), contains motets the authenticity of which I must challenge for paleographic or stylistic reasons.[29] To this, another group may be added. It is made up of compositions in older printed books (before 1650) and manuscripts which are more or less re-liably connected with the milieu of Orlando. Among the publications from the time of Orlando himself, there remain no more major collec-tions of motets, madrigals, or chansons that could have been overlooked, now that the essential gaps in our knowledge have been filled.[30] In the main, questions of authenticity are critical only for those compositions that appear in non-authorized peripheral publications or in late manu-script collections. A few of the compositions in these questionable pub-lications can be listed here (a more complete list must wait for a special study of these sources): 1609δ with *Vitrum nostrum a 6;* 1609γ with *Lobet den Herren, alle Heyden;* 1622α with *Geh deinen Weg auf rechtem Steg a 5.* (This piece is also in a MS dating before 1600: Liegnitz Nr. 34, also Berlin 40210 and Lüneburg 19, K.N. 144.) In a unique source which has been up to now not well known and since lost, the *Jubilus bethlehemiticus* (1628β), there is a *Congratulamini nunc omnes a 5* (No. XXVIII), also preserved in the MS Vienna, Nat.-Bibl. 16.704, No. XII, fol 14^v and in the handwritten appendix to a book, Augsburg, Stadtbibl. 4° 273–278 (No. XXVIII). In the latter source it

---

[28] These publications are quoted according to B I, pp. 747–818. 1560θ was in the *Preussische Staatsbibliothek*, Berlin (Mus. ant. pract. L.890).

[29] Cf. B I for the settings *Ave Maria a 5, Salve regina mater* [C] *a 6,* and further numerous contrafacta which, however, still can be traced back to original music by Lasso. In the tablatures of E. N. Amerbach (1583), S. Kargl (1571), B. Jobin (1572 and 1574), V. Galilei (1563)—and in manuscripts based on these sources—there are some compositions attributed to Orlando that are not authenticated in any other concordances. Other settings in the tablatures mentioned above are doubtless ar-rangements of Lasso's works.

[30] The author has in the *Lasso-Gesamtausgabe*, Neue Folge, Vol. I, accounted for all those publications which up to now were either unknown or incomplete: 1577θ, 1588π, 1583γ, 1575θ, $1570o$, 1576η, 1583ζ, 1587ϵ, 1559δ, 1584γ, 1596β, 1586λ, 1570ν, 1619β.

does appear anonymously, but in proximity to other authentic compositions. Finally there is the *Cantionale sacrum* (Gotha 1646), Part I,[31] with
Christe decus angelorum a 6 and *Elizabeth Zacharie a 6*. (This piece is
also in Berlin MSS 40345, 40306 and—anonymously—in Cod. Erlangen.)

There follows a survey of the MSS containing those compositions
whose authorship cannot be proved: Munich 1640 (German organ tablature from around 1596–1610, with *Averte oculos tuos a 6* next to authentic pieces from 1588α); Munich 76 (with *Benedictus Dominus Deus
a 5*, which is also in Munich 3066 from c.1714–16); Munich 516 (with
Psalmodia VIII tonorum [A] *a 4* and [D] *a 5*, also with a piece in several
movements: *Der Tag, der ist so freudenreich*, which is also in Munich
2751, Munich 71, Vienna 16.704 and Vienna 19.428); Munich 89 (with
Domine ad adiuvandum a 4, settings A and B); Munich 54 (with *Missa
ferialis* [B] *a 4*); Munich 55 (with the hymns added later: *Haec dies a 4*
and *Procul recedant* [B] *a 5*); Munich 2148 (with *Litaniae lauretanae
a 4, Psalmodia VIII tonorum* [C] *a 4* and *a 5*).

From places other than Munich: Treviso No. 29 (with *Anthoni pater
a 5, Elegit te Dominus a 5, Imola Deo a 5, O lux Italiae a 5, Qui vult
venire a 5*); Augsburg 20 (a splendid manuscript by Lasso's friend Ambr.
Mairhofer 1568, next to authentic pieces: *Ave suprema trinitas a 4*);
Genova F.VII.1 (from the circle of Marchese di San Sorlino, next to an
authentic sestina: *Chi non arde d'amor a 4*).[32] The most difficult question
concerns the partbooks that have disappeared from Breslau since 1945.
They contain motets (MSS 1–16, 18, 20, 21, 24, 28, 30, 31, 103, 106,
165b/c) and Masses (MSS 93, 96, 97–101, 165, 165a). From the Masses
it is not clear whether the name Orlando refers to the Masses or to their
models. The probability that these Breslau Masses are authentic is greater
than has been previously assumed; for one of them, *super Confundantur
a 5* (also in Breslau MSS 93 and 97), is also mentioned in a letter concerning new music for his Tyrolean chapel that Archduke Ferdinand II
sent from Prague in 1564 to Jacobus Vaet in Vienna. In this letter a work
of Lasso's—the *Missa Confundantur*—is expressly requested.[33] Moreover, this Mass has been preserved in the MS Graz, Univ.-Bibl. 11

---

[31] Not listed in RISM, Vol. I. The following examples were accessible to me:
Leipzig, II.3.2. (formerly in the possession of C. F. Becker); Munich, Liturg. 1372 c
(acquired in 1904); Berlin, Mus. ant. pract. C.140 (at present in Tübingen).

[32] Further questionable works are preserved in the following manuscripts: Munich
1503 i, 3066; Zwickau LXXIV, 1; Berlin 40272; Liegnitz 34; Brieg 19, 28, and in the
manuscript appendix to the publication 1581a also in Brieg (formerly); Vienna
16.705, 18.828, 16.704; Danzig 4013; Königsberg (Univ. Libr., formerly) 24830; Tenbury catalogue no. 389 (no. 137).

[33] Cf. B III, pp. 36–37 and W. Senn, *Musik und Theater am Hof zu Innsbruck*
(Innsbruck 1954) pp. 154–55.

(c.1590). (Many important Lasso sources are to be found in this corner of Austria.[34]) Much specialized research still needs to be done on the chronology and identification of these Masses and particularly the parody Masses bearing Lasso's name. The first step after the dissertation by Huschke and my own research in Italy and Spain has been taken with the edition of Vol. III of the new *Lasso-Gesamtausgabe* by Hermelink. One question is still unsolved: whether the volume of Masses 1570ψ that I found in Faenza (B I, pp. 313 and 765) and which is clearly designated *"liber secundus"* was preceded by another volume since lost. One can still hope for an accidental discovery, for bibliography never comes to an end. Although there are still many gaps in our knowledge, another can now be closed: of several madrigals by Lasso that cannot be edited because of missing partbooks,[35] one can now be removed from the list: *Ove d'altra montagna a 4*. The canto is available in the fragment of 1567ι,[36] and the remaining three voices have now been completed from another edition, the 20th book of chansons published by A. le Roy 1578λ (Kassel, Tübingen, and Paris, private library of the Comtesse de Chambure). This important madrigal of Lasso's and a five-part setting of *Domine, quando veneris* (see B I, p. 347f, concerning this) will shortly be edited, thus completing the corpus of authentic madrigals and motets printed during Lasso's lifetime. Finally, we can now add the missing Tenor partbook of 1569ξ (Dublin, Archbishop Marsh's Libr.), so we may also publish shortly five new madrigals by Lasso: *Al dolce suon a 5; Ben convenne*, II. pars *Solo n'andrò a 5; Spent' è d'amor*, II. pars *Ma che morta dico a 5*.

In closing, I should like to refer to the parody problem that we face when dealing with the works of Lasso's pupils and friends at the end of the 16th century. The number of parody Masses and Magnificats which stem from this circle and that paraphrase a Lasso model is considerable. This repertoire still awaits a uniform examination, for this practice betrays the direct or indirect transference of many stylistic characteristics

[34] The list of sources in B I can now be supplemented with the following sources: MSS Graz 11 (*Missa super Susanne un jour*); Graz 2064 (*Missa super Domine dominus noster*); Graz 89 (the motet *Veni pater pauperum* after 1574δ); Graz 82 (*Missa super Deus in adiutorium*, the same also in MS 22); Graz 8 (*Salve regina a 6* after 1582η); MSS 12, 22, 67, and 82 contain Magnificats. The Codex Cisterzienserstift Rein, No. 101 (choirbook, probably written for the local Abbot Barth. von Grudenegg between 1559–77) contains the Masses *super La la maistre, super Pillons*, and the *Missa venatorum* (= *Missa Jäger*) in an early version, perhaps copied from the earliest print or before.

[35] A survey of these was given in the new *Lasso-Gesamtausgabe*, Neue Folge, Vol. I, pp. XVI–XVII.

[36] This unique voice fragment of the *Terzo libro de desiderio* can be found in Bologna, Liceo Rossini, Catalogue No. R/219.

and still remains to be appreciated (beyond my occasional references to J. Vaet, A. Utendahl, J. Eccard, M. Praetorius [1611], A. Gosswin, J. Flori). Indeed, one of the most important artists from Lasso's immediate circle of pupils, Bald. Hoyoul, does not always refer to the Lasso model in his parody Magnificats.[37] At any rate, as can be seen upon closer examination, Hoyoul must have followed models other than such famous ones as *Gustate et videte* and *Timor et tremor*—perhaps the proximity of Lasso's two world-famous motets disturbed him. Only in his Magnificats *super Quid gloriaris, In me transierunt, Quis est homo,* and *Susanne un jour* can one recognize Lasso's originals, all of which, however, have been reduced from five parts to a *quattrocinium*. In the usual parody technique only the melodic incipit is copied, and yet further on one sees the ingenious transubstantiation of pregnant motives that has stamped Lasso's style. For instance, the technique of the descending fourth at the beginning of *Quis est homo*, or the concealed repeating of a motive in the bass of *In me transierunt*, or the transferring of Lasso's significant phrase symbolizing the text "praecipitationis" to the new text ". . . sanctum nomen" in *Quid gloriaris*. In such spiritual confrontation of congenial artists, the depth and limitation of Lasso's style can be seen in an age that was soon to experience a fundamental stylistic upheaval.

[37] Codex Stuttgart Ms. mus. 14, dated on fol. 38: 20. July 1577. This codex contains 17 pieces, of which numbers 1–8 list Hoyoul as the composer (Magnificats, folios 1, 12, 27, 39, 51, 64, 79, 92); Nos. 9–15 are Magnificats by Lasso (in No. 12 the author is mistakenly omitted); Nos. 16 and 17 are Magnificats by L. Daser, Lasso's predecessor and B. Hoyoul's father-in-law. In addition, there is a parody Mass by Lasso's most gifted pupil, L. Lechner, *super Domine Dominus noster a 6* (I found the model in the printed book 1577θ, Madrid, Conservatorio).

THE SYMBOLISM OF THE ORGAN IN THE MIDDLE AGES: A STUDY IN THE HISTORY OF IDEAS

by EDMUND A. BOWLES

IT IS A well-known fact that the pneumatic organ was introduced to the West via the Frankish lands from Byzantium, gaining qualified admission to the liturgical service and spreading thereafter throughout Europe as *the* ecclesiastical instrument. However, this explanation does not offer any answers to the questions as to why the organ was introduced when and where it was and why, in view of the long-standing tradition against instruments, it came to be accepted in the liturgical milieu.[1] The entire problem must therefore be re-examined in the light of far deeper historical and intellectual currents.

In order better to understand how the organ acquired its exalted, sacred connotations it is necessary to consider the instrument's role in the East. In Byzantium, where emperor-worship was pronounced, the ruler was both the living incarnation of the state and the head of the Church. By adoption he was divine, proclaimed holy at his coronation, addressed as *Sancte Imperator*, the image and representative of God. The Emperor ruled an empire that was in turn believed to be a reflection of the celestial kingdom. Asiatic pomp was used purposefully to underline imperial power and prestige, aided by a complicated ceremonial, rigorous etiquette, ostentation, and visual splendor. Within this rigid and hieratic framework developed a cycle of imperial ceremonies forming a counterpart to the series of annual liturgical feasts.[2] Both vocal and instrumental music, songs, hymns, and dances, all played important parts in these affairs, for which there evolved a whole series of so-called *acclamations*. Borrowed from ancient Roman practice, these were ad-

---

[1] A summary of these objections may be found in Edmund A. Bowles, *Were Musical Instruments used in the Liturgical Service during the Middle Ages?* in: *The Galpin Society Journal*, X (1957), 45–48.

[2] See A. Vogt, *Constantine VII Porphyrogénète: le Livre des cérémonies* (Paris 1935–39); Jacques Handschin, *Das Zeremonienwerk Kaiser Konstantins und die sangbare Dichtung* (Basel 1942), pp. 8–17; and Louis Bréhier, *Les Empereurs byzantins dans leur vies privées*, in: *Revue historique*, CLXXXVII–IX (1940), 193–217.

dressed primarily to the Emperor on various important occasions. Acclamations were also sung in church when the Emperor, as Head, made his entrance. These liturgical homages were meant to convey feelings of loyalty, devotion, gratitude, and admiration, as well as demonstrating the splendor of Constantinople and the power of the Empire.[3] The organ played a prominent part in all these affairs.[4]

Much of this ceremonial took place in the throne-room, or *chrysotriklinium*, of the imperial palace, an architectural reproduction of heaven, with painted sun, moon, and stars, "sea of glass" and garden of paradise.[5] A further consideration is the Emperor's role in the Eastern

[3] These rituals, set largely within the framework of imperial ingress and egress, paralleled the festivals and solemn ceremonies of the Church. They took place at the vestibule, pavilion, or platform fronting each section of the palace. Thrones covered with baldachins were placed at these spots where the various rites of welcome and appearance were enacted. E. Baldwin Smith, *Architectural Symbolism of Imperial Rome and the Middle Ages* (Princeton 1956), p. 133ff.

[4] Within the marble hall of the imperial palace the emperor stood under the celestial vault of heaven to receive the acclamations of the city's representatives. There were two organs here for the many ritualistic celebrations. Vogt, *op. cit.*, I, 56–67. During the triumphal entry of Theophilus into Constantinople in 831, the emperor marched through the Golden Gate and was presented with the imperial crown. Following a solemn service in Hagia Sophia he walked across the *Augusteion* to the *chalce*, or monumental entrance to the palace, in front of which was a platform with a throne and an organ, both of gold. As the emperor sat down, the populace exclaimed, "There is one Holy!" J. B. Bury, *A History of the Eastern Roman Empire* (London 1912), p. 127f. The pneumatic organ's fabrication in Byzantium is a matter of continuous record, and its use in churches appears to have begun in Constantinople itself. Al-Mas'udi (d. c. 956), referring to an oration by an earlier authority on musical instruments, Ibn Khurdadhbih (d. 912), wrote: "And they (the Byzantines) had the organ possessing bellows and iron work." Cited in: Henry G. Farmer, *Byzantine Musical Instruments in the Ninth Century* (London 1925), p. 4. According to Isho bar Bahlul (fl. 965), "they say that such [an organ] is in that church [St. Sophia] in Byzantium." R. Payne-Smith, *Thesaurus syriacus*, I (Oxford 1874), 91. Another Arabian source describes an organ at Constantinople with 60 brass pipes covered with gold, and bellows-operated. Ibn Rusta, *Kitāb al-a'lāq al-nafisa*, in: M. J. de Goeje (ed.), *Bibliotheca geographorum arabicorum* (Leyden 1870–94), VII, 123. On the use of the organ in Byzantine imperial ceremonies, see *De caeremoniis*, in: J. P. Migne, *Patr. gr.*, CXII, 73f; Constantine Manassis, *Compendium chronicum*, in: Migne, CXXVII, 400 ("imperial organ trees"); Georgios Codinus, *De officiis cosmopolitanis*, in: Migne, CLVII, 86 (an organ sounding during the imperial presence at the Christmas festivals); also G. Reese, *Music in the Middle Ages* (New York 1940), p. 76f; Anselm Hughes (ed.), *Early Medieval Music up to 1300*, New Oxford History of Music, II (Oxford 1954), 32–35; and Egon Wellesz, *A History of Byzantine Music and Hymnography* (2nd ed. Oxford 1961), pp. 98–107.

[5] On the ceremonial purpose and heavenly symbolism of the *sacrum palatium* at Constantinople, see Smith, *op. cit.*, p. 179f, and Lars Ringbom, *Graltempel und Paradies* (Stockholm 1951), pp. 57–85. The famous throne-room of Khosraus II, an important influence on both ecclesiastical architecture and literature, was described by the Byzantine chronicler Georgios Kedrenos. The image of the emperor was on a heavenly throne, under a spherical dome on which were painted sun, moon, and stars. Here Emperor Theophilus I (829–42) had a pneumatic organ constructed with carved birds for pipes, supplied with air from bellows: "a golden tree upon which everywhere birds were seated which gave forth a sweet-sounding melody." Michael

rite. There was a close interrelationship between the so-called court "liturgy" and the main ecclesiastical festivals. The Byzantine service actually provided for recognition of the sacerdotal character of the Emperor, in which he appeared as a Christ-like high priest (*defensor, deputatus*), making the oblation at the altar himself.[6] Although the organ was not permitted to accompany the liturgy, it sounded on high holidays, when the curtains around the imperial dais were drawn aside, revealing the Emperor to the populace, as well as upon the entry of the ruler in church and during his processional to and from the altar between Mass movements.

A fundamental point to keep in mind concerning the transmission westwards of both the organ and its sacred, imperial connotations is the continuous relationship between the Franks and Byzantium. As with most other Western princes, the Frankish rulers were encouraged by the Eastern Empire to think of themselves as nominal dependencies, members of the imperial family, followers of Augustus and Constantine. This worked to their mutual advantage, giving the aura of legitimacy and power to the Franks while preserving an important line of communication and control for the Empire.[7] On the part of the West, Charlemagne's avowed aim was to consolidate his kingdom, re-create Roman *imperium*, and reform political and ecclesiastical administration, the calendar, art, letters, and the liturgy.[8]

The center of gravity within which this so-called rebirth took place was the royal court; and of the several important by-products of this movement, Carolingian culture was the outcome of basically political and religious forces, looking both to Early Christian Rome and to the

Glykas, *Annalium*, in: Migne, *Patr. gr.*, CLVIII, 537. Similar instruments were installed in the palace by Constantine Porphyrogenetos. Fashioned of gold and silver respectively, they were shaped in the form of gilded trees and placed near the throne. The sounds issued forth from birds perched on their many branches. Luitprand of Cremona, *Antapodosis*, in: *Mon. germ. hist., Scrip. rer. germ.*, III, 338. See also Jean P. Richter, *Quellen zur byzantinischen Kunstgeschichte* (Vienna 1897), p. 317.

[6] This subject is treated in detail by Otto G. von Simson, *Sacred Fortress: Byzantine Art and Statecraft in Ravenna* (Chicago 1948), pp. 24–38.

[7] The Merovingian and Carolingian rulers accepted the impressive titles bestowed upon them by Byzantium: *vir inluster* (i.e. *viri inlustres*), consul, *patricius magnus*, all implying imperial recognition of sorts. In their correspondence, the Franks even adopted the custom of addressing the emperor as *patrem nostrum*, who reciprocated in kind. This father-son relationship was a conscious political symbol of paternal protection on the one hand and filial devotion on the other. A. Gasquet, *L'Empire byzantin et la monarchie franque* (Paris 1888), pp. 134–58.

[8] A good study of this whole subject is P. E. Schramm, *Kaiser, Rom und Renovatio* (Leipzig 1929), I, 21–27 and II, 17–33; also L. Duchesne, *Christian Worship*, transl. M. L. McClure (London 1904), p. 102; and T. Klauser, *Die liturgischen Austauschbeziehungen zwischen der römischen und deutschen Kirche vom 8. bis 11. Jahrhundert*, in: *Historisches Jahrbuch der Görresgesellschaft*, LII (1933), 169ff.

East. The competition of these opposing elements furnished a stimulus to this *renovatio*.[9] However, of the two major influences, the Byzantine is of principal concern here as regards the symbolism of architecture and music, for Carolingian theocracy borrowed much from the East.[10]

It was in part out of the Byzantine concept of God-King, with its sacred physical environment, that Western ecclesiastical architecture developed. Both the church building and *sala regalis*, containing a throne-room and palatine chapel, reflected a melding of ideas and forms at once sacred and secular, including many of the oriental iconographic features.[11] Their transfer onto Frankish soil was brought about as a direct result of this revival, with its Eastern contacts.

Charlemagne's palatine chapel at Aachen (c. 790–805) was derived from San Vitale at Ravenna, the imperial chapel in the last capital of the Roman emperors of the West. Its vaulted, octagonal plan, resembling an Eastern basilica, was dominated by a strong westwork with two towers flanking a western entrance reminiscent of a Roman city gate. Inside the west façade was a throne-room and raised gallery, or tribune, from which the monarch could either take part in the service at a private altar or, along with his entourage, witness the liturgical observances.

[9] See Erwin Panofsky, *Renaissance and Renascences in Western Art* (Stockholm 1960), I, 44–50.

[10] During the complex power-plays involving the Franks, the Papacy, and the Empire, Charlemagne deliberately employed the various avenues to the East, pursuing his dream of union of the two empires and his own legitimization by Byzantium, the traditional font of law, its senate the source of imperial recognition, its capital the customary seat of all such coronations. As contemporary chronicles record, a steady stream of legates and ambassadors plied between Aachen and Constantinople on a succession of political and religious matters. In addition, plagued by a series of military catastrophes and palace revolutions, a humiliated Byzantium called for a pact of friendship and solidarity. Signed in 813 by Charlemagne and the Emperor Michael, it accorded the first official and unprecedented recognition by the East of Charlemagne's title of *basileus* and gave it official sanction. The Frankish monarch, far from wishing to seal off or destroy the Greek empire, desired to unite it with the West, finally combining once again the two halves of the Christian world (*foederanda atque adunanda haec duo*). P. Jaffé (ed.), *Bibliotheca rerum germanicarum* (Berlin 1864–73), IV, *Ep. carol.*, XXIX. The visible manifestation of this would be the two emperors ruling together, a Christian fraternity under the Kingdom of God, mediated by the Pope. Gasquet, *op. cit.*, pp. 290–318. In this way was the iconography of empire and sacerdotal kingship transmitted from East to West. "From the remote time when men began to visualize their deities as like themselves in need of shelter, and then began to see in their rulers either priest-kings or god-kings, the palace and the temple developed as interrelated forms of architecture." Smith, *op. cit.*, p. 180f.

[11] For example, the Early Christian churches of Aquileia (312–20) and Trier (324–48), with their two cult chambers reserved respectively for the celebration of the Eucharist and imperial ceremony. In both buildings there was a tendency to fuse the two areas. Günter Bandmann, *Mittelalterliche Architektur als Bedeutungsträger* (Berlin 1951), pp. 171–74. The emperor's residence at San Lorenzo included a sacred chapel in which both sacred and secular were fused like the complex of St. Sophia, a veritable *Augusteion* or *Caesareum*.

These Carolingian tower-fortresses were deliberate symbols of imperial power (iconographical reminders of Rome and Jerusalem, the two most important Christian cities), within which stood the Frankish potentate, the new protector of the Church. In confirming his authority Charlemagne had marble columns and pavement slabs brought from Ravenna, as well as an equestrian statue of Theodoric. In fact, Byzantine stone masons and mosaicists may have assisted in the chapel's construction. Its fittings included an organ, also a sacred, imperial accouterment. Thus Aachen symbolized the celestial throne-room in which Christ ruled with his angels. It was the link between Christ and the new Caesar, between the ancient world and the early Middle Ages.[12] Charlemagne had become a priest-king.[13]

Within this multi-faceted environment the concept of liturgical homage to the ruler played an important part. Following the ancient tradition of acclamations sung in the form of prayers during the litany, scores of laudes came to be performed on important occasions, and gradually, almost every official appearance of Charlemagne became liturgized with a fixed ceremonial.[14] The formulas for these acclamations reflected the new concepts of imperium and were modeled after Byzantine prototypes. When Charlemagne made a ceremonial entry into a city or a church on high feast-days, Byzantine symbology and form again prevailed. According to the *Ordines ad regnum suscipiendum*, the reception recreated both Christ's entry into Jerusalem, with the new Emperor playing the role of savior, and the welcoming of souls in the Heavenly City. *Laudes hymnidicae* and antiphons (e.g. *Blessed is he that cometh in the name of the Lord*) were sung.[15] On the great church festi-

[12] See L. Kitschelt, *Die frühchristliche Basilika als Darstellung des himmlischen Jerusalem* (Munich 1938), pp. 51–68; Bandmann, *op. cit.*, Chap. II, Part I (*Der Kaiser und die Baukunst*); and A. Stange, *Das frühchristliche Kirchengebäude als Bild des Himmels* (Cologne 1950). On Aachen, see Kenneth J. Conant, *Carolingian and Romanesque Architecture* (London 1959), Chapter II, p. 14f; Richard Krautheimer, *The Carolingian Revival of Early Christian Architecture*, in: *Art Bulletin*, XXIV (1942), 1–38; H. Thümmler, *Die karolinginische Baukunst* (Wiesbaden 1957), pp. 84–108.

[13] At the Synod of Frankfurt in 796 the assembled bishops had proclaimed Charlemagne *rex et sacerdos*.

[14] Ernst Kantorowicz, *Laudes Regiae: A Study in Liturgical Acclamations and Medieval Ruler Worship* (Berkeley 1946), p. 25f. When the Frankish potentate visited Rome in 774 his welcoming ceremony, including the singing of laudes, followed the Eastern form appropriate for an exarch or imperial viceroy. *Ibid.*, p. 75, fn. 33. In 812 the traditional *laudes regiae* were accorded Charlemagne by the Byzantine legates who at the same time recognized his claim to the title of *Imperator et Basileus. Annales Einhardi*, in: Migne, *Patr. lat.*, CIV, 477.

[15] Literary sources from the Carolingian milieu (for example, Walafrid Strabo, Theodulf of Orleans, Notker of St. Gall) describe these receptions at which the emperor, crowned and adorned in full regalia, set forth to the royal church. Bandmann (fn. 11 above), p. 184; and Kantorowicz, *op. cit.*, pp. 72 and 211.

vals these acclamations to the ruler were inserted within the Mass between the first Collect and the Epistle. They invoked a victorious God,
the ruler, and acclaimed him directly or through his royal vicars on
earth: the pope, the king, the bishops and princes.[16] As such, the laudes
represented a fusion of both celestial and terrestrial, of divine and earthly
powers, in which heavenly figures were merged with ecclesiastical and
temporal in glorious acclaim, with Charlemagne as *Christus domini*,
linked to the angelic intercessors.

The extremely close link between these Frankish acclamations and
their Byzantine models suggests a similarity in basic performance practices.[17] The use of the organ in connection with Eastern ceremony has
already been mentioned. Furthermore, like the imperial acclamations
themselves, this instrument was transmitted to the Franks from the East,
along with the ceremonial and symbolic concepts discussed above. In
757 the Emperor Constantine Copronymus VI sent among other gifts an
organ to Pippin, Mayor of the Palace. The advent of this new instrument
was duly observed by the various Frankish chroniclers with the remark
venit organa in Franciam.[18] Michael I dispatched a similar instrument as
a gift to Charlemagne in 812, along with musicians who set it up at
Aachen and then instructed the Frankish clerics.[19] Fourteen years later
another organ was built in the royal palace for Louis the Pious by a
Venetian priest named Georgius Veneticus.[20] Considering both the
economic and cultural ties of this city-state to Byzantium, and the fact
that two organs had been installed recently in St. Mark's, itself patterned
after the Church of the Apostles at Constantinople, the continuity with
Eastern usage and symbolism seems even more obvious. Furthermore, as

[16] Thus, *Carolo excellentissimo et a Deo coronato atque magno et pacifico regi Francorum.* Kantorowicz, *op. cit.*, p. 27.

[17] At the court of Constantine Porphyrogenetos the two silver organs at each side of the throne room sounded during the antiphonal singing of the polychronions for the emperor. Egon Wellesz, *Byzantinische Musik* (Breslau 1927), p. 17ff. In the West, according to Manfred Bukofzer (Kantorowicz, *op. cit.*, p. 87), the soloists intoned *alta voce* while the responded passages were sung by the chorus. At the Cathedral of Metz, as well as other Frankish churches, Greek chants and prayers were customarily sung on certain occasions. See Schramm, *op. cit.*, I, 99.

[18] *Annales alemannici*, in: *Mon. germ. hist.*, SS, I, 29; *Annales nazariani*, SS, I, 29; *Annales Lauresbamenses*, SS, I, 28 ("Venit organus in Franciam"); *Annales Lauris-senses*, SS, I, 140; *Annales Einhardi*, SS, I, 141 ("Constantinus imperator misit Pipino regi multa munera, inter quae et organum").

[19] Notker of St. Gall, *Gesta Karoli*, in: *Mon. germ. hist.*, SS, II, 751; *Annales Einhardi*, SS, I, 199.

[20] This organ was constructed "in the Greek [i.e. Byzantine] manner." *Vita Hludovici imperatoris*, SS, II, 629 (". . . qui se promitteret organum more posse componere graecorum"); *Einhardi translatio, Marcellini et Petri*, SS, XV, 260; *Annales Einhardi fuldensis*, SS, I, 359. This is the only source that uses the term *organum ydraulicum*, the basis no doubt for the errors of both Degering and Farmer that this was not a pneumatic organ.

if stressing the organ as an imperial status symbol, Ermoldus Nigellus spoke of this latest achievement ("Now the court of Aachen holds it"), laying to rest the boast that only the Eastern Empire possessed such an instrument.[21] Strabo, too, mentioned this organ, observing that heretofore Byzantium had been boasting of its instruments.[22]

It was a short step from the musical practices at the Frankish court to those of the entire realm. Thanks to the efforts of Bishop Chrodegang of Metz among others, Charlemagne was able to promulgate his many reforms, and indeed the Frankish bishops took their cue from the imperial and religious ceremonial at Aachen. The so-called palace rite was followed faithfully by the clergy.[23] The acclamations employed in the cult of emperor worship with its organ music served as important influences on the evolving Mass-forms, such as the Kyrie, Gloria and Amen.[24] Since the success of Charlemagne's grandiose plans depended in a large measure upon the active support of his domestic clergy, a broad base of ecclesiastical support was sought. One outcome of this policy was the establishment of many religious houses by the Carolingian ruler and his successors. The corresponding rise of monasticism led to the expansion of these centers both as disseminators of culture and focal-points of liturgical chant. It was at these large centers that the organ first appeared as an adjunct to the growing religious pomp.

In its liturgical use, however, the organ was limited to high feast days.[25] The extremely crude and clumsy nature of the instrument's mechanism at this early stage, together with its well-documented noise and clatter, scarcely made it suitable for extended vocal accompaniment. In all probability, the organ was limited to what might be called para-liturgical contexts, such as intonations or fragments in sacred processions and during movements of the clergy during the service, as well as the very acclamations discussed above. At Reichenau, for example, one monk gave a rather complete report on contemporary musical prac-

---

[21] In hon. Hludovici, SS, I, 513.

[22] De imagine Tetrici, in: Mon. germ. hist. poet. lat. aevi carolini, II, 374.

[23] For example, Bishop Leidrade of Lyon: secundum ritum sacri palatii. Jaffé, op. cit., IV, 420f.

[24] See the article Akklamation, ed. T. Klauser, in: Reallexikon für Antike und Christentum (Stuttgart 1950), I, 227. Certain antiphons, too, were actually acclamations, such as Magnus Dominus. See also F. Cabrol & Henri Leclercq (eds.), Dictionnaire d'archéologie chrétienne et de liturgie (Paris 1907), I, col. 253f.

[25] See Presbyter Theophilus, Schedula artium (Prologue to Book III): ". . . quae adhuc desunt in utensiliis domus Domini, ad exemplum aggredere toto mentis conamine, sine quibus divina mysteria et officiorum ministeria non valent consistere"; English transl. R. Hendrie, An Essay upon Various Arts (London 1847); also Vita S. Oswaldi, in: Acta sanctorum, scl. V. 756: "Triginta libras ad fabricandos organorum calmos erogavit qui . . . diebus festis . . . praedulcem melodiam . . . ediderunt."

tices during the early 9th century, relating that monastic students had both to sing and play, and that many formerly at the abbey performed on the organ.[26] Walafrid Strabo, in a letter reporting a visit of Charles the Bald to the same abbey in 829, also noted the presence of an organ.[27] The many treatises written systematically by the monks of this period attest to the fact that organ-building lay in their capable hands.[28]

It was only natural that this environment proved fertile for the type of symbolism to which the organ was susceptible. Like the fascination with numbers or colors, musical instruments, in spite of their negative position in the eyes of the church, were favorite vehicles for symbolic and allegorical interpretations by the theoreticians. According to them, God had availed himself of both mankind and instruments in order to reveal his being or essence as well as his power.[29] The Greek church was the first to have developed this mystical vocabulary, and instrumental symbolism was soon transplanted westwards, where it grew into an elaborate form.[30] Origen, for example, called the organ "the Church of the Lord made up of active and contemplative souls." [31] Arnobius worked out an elaborate allegory in which the instrument's pipes were related to chastity.[32] For Pope Gregory I the organ symbolized the praise of God, the voices of the preachers heard through its pipes.[33] However, until the Carolingian period the instrument was seldom if ever mentioned in such symbolic contexts in the West.

Following the introduction of the organ to the West, precedent was established, and the writers of liturgical exegesis produced a variety of religious connotations.[34] Indeed, there is a striking parallel between the

[26] H. Jacob, *Die Kunst im Dienste der Kirche* (4th ed. Berlin 1882), p. 420.

[27] *Mon. germ. hist. poet. lat. medii aevi*, II, 406. On the efflorescence of organ-building during the Carolingian period, see Norbert Dufourcq, *Esquisse d'une histoire de l'orgue en France* (Paris 1935), p. 21.

[28] See Notker (d. 912), *Tractatus de musica*, in: Migne, *Patr. lat.*, CXXXI, 1175; Hucbald (d. 931), *De harmonia institutione*, Migne, CXXXII, 935; Odo of Cluny (d. 942), *Opuscula de musica*, Migne, CL, 1333; and Aribo Scholasticus (d. c. 980), *Musica Aribonis Scholastici*, Migne, CL, 1334.

[29] For example, Justin Martyr, *Paraenes.*, p. 61; Athenagoras, *Legatio pro christianis*, in: Migne, *Patr. gr.*, VI, 970f; Clement of Alexandria, *Paedagogi*, Migne, VIII, 439ff.

[30] On this, see Hermann Abert, *Die Musikanschauung des Mittelalters* (Halle 1905), pp. 211–15; also Théodore Gérold, *Les Pères de l'église et la musique* (Paris 1931), pp. 123–34.

[31] *Selecta in psalmos*, Lib. CL, in: Migne, *Patr. gr.*, XII, 1682f.

[32] *In psalmos*, Lib. CL, in: Migne, *Patr. lat.*, LIII, 369ff. Cf. Prosper of Aquitaine, *Liber de promissionibus* (c. 400), Migne, LI, 856, wherein the organ pipes are filled with the word of God.

[33] *Moralium*, Lib. XX, Migne, LXXV. See also G. Frotscher, *Geschichte des Orgelspiels und der Orgelkomposition* (Berlin 1935), I, 51.

[34] One of the first examples of this is Athanasius, *Epistola ad Marcellinum*, in Migne, *Patr. gr.*, XXVII, 39f. See Abert, *op. cit.*, p. 221; and Robert Haas, *Aufführungspraxis der Musik* (Potsdam 1931), p. 50.

allegorizing surrounding the Mass as symbolic of the heavenly liturgy, a symphonic song of praise, and the organ, through its multitude of pipes a composite, sonorous expression of both the Word and man's paeans to the Lord.[35] In late Merovingian and Carolingian sources the organ is nearly always associated with the religious or spiritual, calling attention to its exalted rank.[36] Rhabanus Maurus likened it to the Gospel of Christ.[37] Further enlarging the organ's symbolic vocabulary, the English churchman Wulstan called it the *Ecclesia tonans*.[38] Later, the theorist Guido d'Arezzo wrote that the organ, along with bells, was the means by which the whole church sang praises to God.[39] Bishop Baudri of Dôle (c. 1125) compared the number of pipes to the diversity of mankind, asking if their tones did not represent a similar symphony of sound.[40] Richard of St. Victor, too, wrote that the organ's sounds symbolized human utterances in praise of God.[41] It was associated with the choir of angels by Gulielmus Durandus (c. 1230–96). He noted particularly that the organ was used in the Sanctus of the Mass.[42] This is especially interesting in view of the symbolical connections between this particular section of the liturgy and the instrument itself.[43]

[35] An excellent discussion of this is to be found in Reinhold Hammerstein, *Die Musik der Engel* (Munich 1962), pp. 30–46.

[36] For example, *Vita episcopi carnoteni*: "magna nobis organa hodie religiosaque canent auspicia . . . ," *Mon. germ. hist., Scrip. rer. merovingicarum*, VII (Hanover 1919), 316; *Vita caesarii episcopi*: "Spiritualis et sanctus organarius . . . ," SS, III, 496; *Vita Desiderii episcopi*: "cum spiritalibus cymbalis et organis," SS, VII, 644; *Vita Landiberti episcopi*: ". . . psallentium cymbalisque spiritualibus peristrentibus, canora organis suavis . . . ," SS, VI, 380.

[37] *De universo*, in: Migne, *Patr. lat.*, CXI, 497.

[38] *Vita S. Swithuni*, in: J. Mabillon, *Acta sanctorum ordinis S. Benedicti* (Venice 1733–39), V, 630.

[39] *Regulae rythmicae*, in: Martin Gerbert, *Scriptores ecclesiastici de musica sacra* (St. Blasien 1784), II, 27.

[40] *Descriptio monasterii fiscannensis*, ed. P. du Moustier (Rouen 1663), p. 230.

[41] *Adnotatio mysticum in psalmum*, in: Migne, *Patr. lat.*, XCVI, 373.

[42] *Rationale divinorum officiorum*; English transl. J. Neale and B. Webb, *The Symbolism of Churches and Church Ornaments* (London 1843), p. 9. Cf. also p. 97: "Moreover, in this symphony of angels and men, the organs do from time to time add their harmony." See also Haas, *op. cit.*, p. 51.

[43] Keeping in mind the liturgy as a symbol of the "Heavenly Liturgy," as well as the loud, rather crude sonorities of contemporary instruments, there is a parallel with the Old Testament (Isaiah, VI, 3–4) where one Seraphim calls to another the words of praise in such a loud voice that the threshold of the Temple trembles. See U. Bomm, *Hymnus seraphicus: Das Sanctus als Zugang zum Choralverständnis*, in: F. Tack (ed.), *Der kultische Gesang der abendländischen Kirche* (Cologne 1950), p. 36ff. The *Te Deum*, too, came very early to use the organ, since it was a song of praise in which, according to tradition, the whole universe took part, appearing as a tonally-overwhelming communal song which, with organ accompaniment, obtained a massive and colorful sound. On this point see Walter Krüger, *Die authentische Klangform des primitiven Organum* (Kassel 1958), p. 23. Very possibly the apparently awesome sonorities of these early instruments was one of the reasons it was so easy to view the organ as a reflection of heavenly music, a multitudinous symphony of praise. See for example St. Jerome (?), *Epistola ad Dardanum:*

Not only architecture and musical instruments showed a pronounced didactic intent, but liturgical reforms as well, emphasizing both the cult of the Savior and the correspondence between celestial and terrestrial order. In keeping with the new focus in the Mass upon Christ's sacrifice rather than on a communion of the redeemed, the mysterious elements of the liturgy came to the fore. There developed numerous explanations of the Mass, intended both to instruct the faithful and assist the Carolingian clergy in passing the yearly examinations in liturgy. The churchman's delight in symbolism found an outlet in the *expositio*, an allegorical interpretation first applied to the Mass by Alcuin, head of the palace school and later Abbot of St. Martin, Tours.[44] His pupil, the liturgist Amalarius of Metz, Abbot of Fulda, was an even greater innovator, setting the standard for the more or less continuous series of liturgical explanations that followed.[45] Amalarius, incidentally, represented Charlemagne as ambassador at the time a treaty with the Eastern Empire was negotiated. During his visit to Constantinople he witnessed the ritual and ceremony at the Byzantine court, as well as the celebration of the liturgy at Hagia Sophia.[46] It was after this long journey that Amalarius wrote his extended treatise concerning the divine office and ecclesiastical calendar.[47]

Occasionally the Heavenly City served as a model for the temporal state. The author of the *Vita Ansberti* saw in the sacred music of the Frankish court a reflection of the songs of the angels.[48] This concept of similarity of order extended to the priests and monks, "angelic choirs

"Through twelve brazen pipes it emits a grand sound like thunder . . ."; Cassiodorus, *De artibus ac disciplinis liberalium litterarum*, in: Migne, *Patr. lat.*, LXX, 1052: "The organ's pipes which . . . produce a grand and most charming music"; Aldhelm, in: J. H. Pitman, *The Riddles of Aldhelm* (New Haven 1925), p. 10: "My mighty voice makes mute the sounding strings" (of the harps); Wulstan, *Vita S. Swithuni*, in: Mabillon, *loc. cit.*: "Like thunder the iron voice batters the ear . . . ," *Vita Landeberti episcopi*, SS, VI, 380: ". . . the organ rang out . . ." An organ brought from Byzantium to Aachen in 812 produced sound which "equalled the voice of thunder." *Mon. germ. hist.*, SS, II, 751. Later comments on the organ's loud noise may be found in Helen Bitterman, *The Organ in the Early Middle Ages*, in: *Speculum*, IV (1929), 408. See also Aelred of Rievaulx, *Speculum charitatis*, in: Migne, *Patr. lat.*, CXCV, 571: ". . . this awful noise which expresses more the sound of thunder than the sweetness of the human voice."

[44] A. Franz, *Die Messe im deutschen Mittelalter* (Freiburg 1902), p. 361f; J. Jungman, *The Mass of the Roman Rite: Its Origins and Development*, transl. F. A. Brunner (New York 1950), I, pp. 74–86.

[45] Amalarius of Metz, *De ecclesiasticis officiis*, in: Migne, *Patr. lat.*, CV, 1104–55.

[46] *De ordine antiphonarii*, XXI, 4: ". . . audivi Constantinopoli in ecclesia Sanctae Sophiae . . . ," in: J. M. Hanssens (ed.), *Amalarii episcopi opera liturgica omnia* (Rome 1950), III, 57.

[47] See Alan Cabaniss, *Amalarius of Metz* (Amsterdam 1954), pp. 31–42; also Eleanor Duckett, *Carolingian Portraits* (Ann Arbor 1962), p. 96.

[48] *Mon. germ. hist., Scrip. rer. merov.*, V, 621.

in human garb." [49] Their music symbolized the link with the celestial. The Gloria, for example, was a common song of praise, according to Strabo annexed from above by the wise Church Fathers in order to laud the marvels of God.[50] Even the voices of the populace were to join forces with the angels in the Sanctus, according to Charlemagne's famous capitulary.[51] This was the environment into which the organ was placed.

It remains only to carry the organ's symbolic role through the Middle Ages, considering as well the further development of this very environment. It is not surprising to find that the church building came to symbolize the House of the Lord, and that it was believed God was mysteriously present within its walls.[52] Equally important was the notion of the universe as a symphonic composition, the concept of a balanced world created by measure in certain proportions, found in the metaphysics of Plato and those who followed his path.[53] The transition from musical to architectural symbolism was accomplished by the Platonic schoolmen from Chartres, who followed the *Timaeus*, with its description of the world's elements as building materials, put together in the same proportions as the universal soul. To these scholastics God was the master-builder who created by means of an architectural science based

[49] See St. John Chrysostom, in: Migne, *Patr. gr.*, LVII, 547. The *Historia monachorum* related that the monks were so filled with grace that when they entered a church they resembled the eternal choirs of angels, whose hymns and songs of praise they imitated. Migne, *Patr. lat.*, XXI, 4–7. Cf. Fulgentius of Ruspe, Migne, LXV, 817; St. Ambrose, Migne, XVI, 724; St. Jerome, Migne, XXIV, 575; Rhabanus Maurus, Migne, CX, 58.

[50] *De rebus ecclesiasticis*, Migne, CXIV, 944.

[51] *Mon. germ. hist.*, *Legum sectio*, II, 59: "et ipse sacerdos cum sanctis angelis et populo Dei communi voci 'Sanctus . .' decantet." Later Gulielmus Durandus wrote that in the Sanctus, the prayer sung in common by both angels and man alike, they were united in praise of the Lord. *Rationale divinorum officiorum*, IV, 66.

[52] At the dedication of the new choir of Canterbury Cathedral in 1130, the assembly chanted the liturgical, "Awesome is this Place, Truly it is the House of God and the Gate of Heaven, and it will be called the Court of the Lord." Henry R. Luard (ed.), *Annales monastici* (London 1869), IV, 19. After the dedication of the choir of St. Denis in 1144, Abbot Suger wrote in his *De consecratione* of the ceremony as having been a spectacle in which heaven and earth, angels and men, seemed to merge. Erwin Panofsky, *Abbot Suger on the Abbey Church of St. Denis* (Princeton 1946), p. 115.

[53] Plato's *Timaeus* (XL–XLVI) saw the universe divided according to Pythagorean ratios. Boethius (*De musica*, I) pointed out the division accomplished by ratios of musical harmony. Macrobius (*Commentarius*, II) wrote that cosmic order was based upon the harmony of musical consonances. These ideas were fused with the Augustinian concept of a universe created "in measure, number and weight." For example, the greatest theologian of the 9th century, Johannes Scotus Erigena, in his *De divisione naturae*, described the entire Creation as a symphonic composition. Migne, *Patr. lat.*, CXXII, 602, 630f, and 965. See also Jacques Handschin, *Die Musikanschauung des Johan Scotus Erigena*, in: *Vierteljahrsschrift für Literaturwissenschaft und Geistesgeschichte*, V (1927).

upon mathematics.[54] From this point of view it was but one short step
to the concept of the church building as the image of heaven.[55]

During the Gothic period there was an enrichment of ceremonial,
a multiplication of elements, a repetition of detail, and an emphasis upon
ornament. Following the tradition of Amalarius of Metz, every ceremony, every element was subjected to further allegorizing.[56] Within
this context a new esthetic developed concerning beauty and its place
in the sanctuary. All stimuli appealing to the senses were employed in
the service of God, so that man's spirit might raise itself from the
temporal to the spiritual realm. The eye and ear became the basis of
this new point of view, and the arts in turn became at once more appealing and alive.

This new esthetic spread from art-form to art-form, including the
liturgy.[57] The formerly simpler, more austere music of the church was
vitalized by florid passages, melismas, and an extended use of polyphony.
The service, in other words, began to take on the magnificence of its
new milieu. Even more important was the relationship to the celestial
liturgy of the Heavenly Jerusalem, following the visions in *Revelations,
John*, and other Biblical texts that mentioned the *musica coelestis*. This
sacred music was thought to be a reflection of theological truth, since the
laws of music formed the basis for cosmic order.[58] Liturgical music,
as a symbol of this divine liturgy, as part of this symphonic praise of
God's work, assumed a mystical role. The Gloria and Sanctus unified
heaven and earth in acclaiming the Lord, while the polyphony employed

[54] Allan of Lille, in his *De planctu naturae*, portrayed God as the artful architect
who built the cosmos as his regal palace, composing and harmonizing via musical
consonances. Migne, *Patr. lat.*, CXX, 453.

[55] Abelard, for example, symbolically interconnected the cosmos and the Heavenly
City of Jerusalem with the terrestrial sanctuary. He suggested that, as Solomon's
temple was pervaded by the divine harmony, the proportions were the same as
those musical consonances used by God the Creator; and that it was this "symphonic"
perfection which made the cathedral the image of heaven. The foregoing is drawn
largely from von Simson (fn. 6 above), pp. 11, 28–32, and 38.

[56] See Gulielmus Durandus, *Rationale divinorum officiorum*, transl. C. Barthélemy
(Paris 1854), I, 215 and II, 21f, 49f, 101, 147, 177, and 310; Honorius of Autun,
Gemma animae, in: Migne, *Patr. lat.*, CLXXII, 541ff. Also Franz, *op. cit.*, p. 315f;
Jungman (fn. 44 above), pp. 107–12; J. Sauer, *Symbolik des Kirchengebäudes und
seiner Ausstattung in der Auffassung des Mittelalters* (2nd ed. Freiburg 1924).

[57] The effect of the new esthetic was vividly described in Suger's *De administra-
tione*, Chap. XXXIII: "Thus, when . . . the loveliness of the many-colored gems
has called me away from eternal cares, and worthy meditation has induced me to
reflect, transferring that which is material to that which is immaterial, . . . (then)
by the grace of God I can be transported from this inferior to that higher
world . . ." Panofsky, *op. cit.*, p. 63f.

[58] Abbot Suger wrote, concerning the liturgical observances at his new abbey-
church of St. Denis, that the spectators "believed themselves to behold a chorus
celestial rather than terrestrial, a ceremony divine rather than human." *De consecratione*, Chap. VI, in: Panofsky, *op. cit.*, pp. 54 and 115.

on solemn feast-days represented the heavenly organum: *Celeste organum hodie sonuit in terra.*[59] Thus, throughout the Middle Ages, the liturgical service was closely connected to the music of heaven, reflecting the duality of visible and invisible, celestial and terrestrial: a double community of angels and men. All this served to conjure up the image of the medieval congregation joining the heavenly hosts of angels, archangels, apostles, martyrs, and virgins in that "great Sabbath without evening" when suddenly God was revealed to all the faithful.[60]

Thus it was that the great Abbot Suger of St. Denis described the Mass as a "symphony angelic rather than human," adding that the brightness of an artifact brightened the mind of the beholder—and the listener, too—by a spiritual illumination.[61] It followed that just as the blazing lights, radiant colors, precious stones, magnificent vestments, and artifacts of all sorts within the church helped to uplift man's soul closer to God, the multicolored harmonies of the liturgy joined forces with the new sonorities of the "heavenly" instrument in a joyous burst of praise.

[59] Ulysse Chevalier, *Repertorium hymnologicum* (Louvain 1892), I, No. 3413. See St. Ambrose, *Hexaemeron*, III, 5, in Migne, *Patr. lat.*, XIV, 178. Maximus the Confessor spoke of liturgical chant symbolizing the heavenly symphony of the angels and elect souls in praise of God. Migne, *Patr. gr.*, XIC, 665f. Similarly Fulbert of Chartres, in his *Philomela*, characterized the twitter of birds, the roar of the ocean, the voices of angels, and liturgical chant as part of a hymn of praise. Migne, *Patr. lat.*, CXLI, 348. Cf. Walter Krüger, *Aufführungspraktische Fragen mittelalterlicher Mehrstimmigkeit*, in: *Die Musikforschung*, XI (1958), 188.

[60] St. Augustine, *Civitas Dei*, XVIII, 18. Pope Gregory I referred to the opening of the heavens, when the choir of worshipping angels was revealed. Migne, *Patr. lat.*, LXXVII, 425. Above and below, heaven and earth united, and the invisible and the visible became as one. This text was frequently cited during the Middle Ages, cf. Gerbert, *op. cit.*, II, 91.

[61] *De consecratione*, Chap. VII, in: Panofsky, *op. cit.*, p. 121. This whole concept was profoundly influenced by Dionysius the Pseudo-Areopagite's *De coelesti hierarchia*, wherein was stated that man, relying upon his sensory perceptions and his imagination, could transcend the physical world by absorbing it, rising from the material to the immaterial. This was possible inasmuch as all visible things were "material lights" which reflected God, "The Father of all Lights." *Ibid.*, pp. 19–23.

SOME UNIFYING DEVICES IN THE RELIGIOUS MUSIC DRAMA OF THE MIDDLE AGES

by ROSE BRANDEL

THAT THE 11th- or 12th-century liturgical drama was unconcerned with elaborate stage props, virtuoso soliloquy, or Verdian elephants is quite definite. The austere suggestiveness of *mise-en-scène*—this being the church altar—the barest indication of physical movement, such as a nod, an extended arm, as well as the mystic potency of the occasion itself (one of the ecclesiastic feast-days) sufficed to transfer to the listener all the necessary subject matter of the drama, the communication symbols being in this respect highly familiar and well understood, despite their esoteric and formalized nature.

Although a tendency toward more extended "production," even a certain lavish carelessness in scenic extension and addition, as well as the growth of an audience-conscious actor species, emerged a bit later on, the adoption of these elements did not swerve the drama away from the generally static, non-integrated pattern it assumed throughout this period (and even in the early Renaissance).[1] The conviction of dynamic drama, with its concomitants of facial-gestural expressiveness, psychological connective tissue, and structural cohesiveness, was on the whole lacking in these early plays. Thus, play directives point to a modicum of naturalistic aids and dramatic continuity, the latter conspicuously absent in the seriated grafting on of scene after scene. The metric prologue of a 12th-century Tours *Resurrection* drama,[2] for example, mentions 13 *simultaneous* scenes, or *mansions* (*domus*) as they were called, placed at a certain distance from each other and hence obviously necessitating disjunct, episodic movement from the first to the last, on the part of the actors. In the 10th-century Easter trope *Quem queritis*, which "may be

---

[1] The later, more elaborate plays were not as closely aligned with the liturgy as were the earlier ones.

[2] *The Resurrection*, MS 927, Bibliothèque de Tours. Text of the prologue is quoted in Edmund K. Chambers, *The Mediaeval Stage* (London 1903), II, 82.

considered," states Gustave Reese, "one of the earliest, if not *the* earliest, of the liturgical dramas," [3] the dramatic "action" is hardly conceded any personality of its own, but is as limited and unobtrusive as possible, in fact quite static, carried on, according to the description by Bishop Ethelwold, "in imitation" of the various biblical figures and performed "without attracting attention." [4] Of facial expression there is no mention, and of bodily position the barest suggestion, such as "stepping delicately as those who seek something."

Impersonal, stylized, and narrational rather than truly dramatic, the early religious dramas were actually a kind of revitalized prayer-form, even when severed from the liturgy proper and even when containing texts in the vernacular.[5] Dramatic unity and dimension, naturalistic portrayal, the immediate and personal were hardly the goals of these dramas. In fact, the characterizations *tragoedia* and *comoedia* were avoided, no doubt because of their secular and personal connotations; instead, the religious drama was significantly designated as *officium, ordo, ludus, miraculum, repraesentatio,* terms quite impersonal and noncommittal in their meanings. Even in the 14th century of Dante, when the terms *tragoedia* and *comoedia* became more prevalent, they rarely referred to the personal conflicts of a single human, his inner workings, strivings, and failures, but more broadly, were intended to specify the *pattern* of a play, i.e. the happy or unfortunate ending and the "legends" leading up to this ending. In other words, the terms covered certain narrativistic formulas or devices and not the cross-sectional exposure of an individual and his personal dynamics.

Dramatic probing, however, gained some impetus in the later plays. Thus, for example, in the *Planctus Mariae* (one of the famous "Laments" of the three Marys, short representations of the Easter sorrows) of the 14th-century Cividale MS,[6] the simple pointing of the earlier plays is now superseded by extensive breast-striking (*hic se percutiat pectus*) [see Plate 1a, miniature rubrics on staves 2, 5, 7, and 8], theatrical raising and striking of hands (*hic manus elevet, hic percutiat manus*), timely weep-

---

[3] G. Reese, *Music in the Middle Ages* (New York 1940), p. 194.

[4] From the *Concordia Regularis*, c. 970, by Ethelwold of Winchester, as given in Reese, MMA, pp. 194-95.

[5] The vernacular was introduced into these dramas somewhere in the 12th century; cf. two plays of this century, *The Wise and Foolish Virgins,* or *Sponsus* (Bridegroom), of the St. Martial of Limoges MS, Paris, Bibliothèque Nationale, lat. 1139, which was partly in French and partly in Latin, and *Ordo Repraesentationis Adae* of the Tours MS 927, which was entirely in French with merely Latin rubrics. Text of the latter play is edited by Alfred Jeanroy in *Le Théâtre religieux en France, du XIe au XIIIe siècles* (Paris 1924).

[6] *Planctus Mariae,* Cividale MS CI, fols. 74ʳ-76ᵛ, Museo Archeologico Nazionale, Cividale del Friuli.

ing (*suas lacrimas ostendendo*), and sympathetic embracing (*hic amplectetur unum Mariam ad collum*).

Although much of the static, non-dramatic character of the religious drama derived from the piecing together of texts and music, taken mainly from liturgical and allied sources, paradoxically enough, the almost formula-like patterning of these plays served as a kind of unifying agent. Some level of structural cohesiveness was achieved through the use of recurrent germ motifs or melody formulas. Such formulas are to be expected in a music derived essentially from a body of chant with a partly Oriental heritage. In the religious dramas, the melody formulas, while not used, to be sure, in the developmental or variational sense of the Wagnerian music drama, often served to weld together a seemingly dissociated, insubstantial dramatic production. Although frequently tied to textual formulas and special scenes, which generally appeared in plays according to the ecclesiastic occasion, the melody motifs were often skilfully woven throughout the entire dramatic texture of a play, thus functioning not only as scenic-textual carriers, but also as religious symbols and at times as expressionistic devices.

In the Cividale *Planctus* mentioned above, the recurrent motif forms an important part of the drama, which also shows signs of some basic attempt to portray the emotional declamations of the text by appropriately vivid musical phrases. The most important recurrent theme, first sung by one of the Marys and then by various characters, appears no less than nine times, in whole, in part, in extension, and in variation. Ex. 1 shows the first statement of the theme (sung by Maria Major); Plate 1a contains two other statements, on staff 4, *Quis est hic* (sung by Maria Jacobi), the text of which is adapted from verse 5 of the Sequence *Stabat Mater dolorosa*,[7] and on staff 5, *O vos omnes* (sung by Maria Major), the text taken from portions of the Feast of the Seven Dolours of the Blessed Virgin Mary—namely, from the verse of the Tract *Stabat sancta Maria*, from an Alleluia verse, and from a short Responsory.[8] Some other occurrences of the theme in the Cividale *Planctus* may be found on the passages *Munda caro* (sung by Maria Jacobi), *Mi Johannes* (by Maria Major), and *O Maria* (by Johannes):

[7] *Liber Usualis* (Amer. ed. pr. Tournai 1961), p. 1635. (*Note:* all further *Liber* references in the present paper are to the 1961 edition.) The connection of *Quis est hic* with the *Stabat Mater* was noted both by Fernando Liuzzi, *L'Espressione musicale nel dramma liturgico*, in: *Studi medievali*, New Series, II (1929), 100, and by Karl Young, *Drama of the Medieval Church* (Oxford 1933), I, 513.

[8] *O vos omnes* portions from Feast of the Seven Dolours of the B.V.M., *Liber*, pp. 1634, 1634^v, and 1632. Some of the text also appears in a Holy Saturday antiphon *O vos omnes* (*Liber*, p. 776B).

Ex. 1 From Cividale *Planctus Mariae* [9]

Maria Major:

Er - go qua - re fi - li   cha - re pen - des i - ta cum

sis   vi - ta ma - nens an - te se - cu - la?

In addition to the recurrence of this theme throughout the play, a significant melismatic fragment of the melody, actually a formula-like turn, is subtly threaded through the entire work. The motif, which appears on the words *fili chare* (and also *cum sis vita*) in Ex. 1, tightens the drama considerably and makes for a kind of microhomogeneity, acting almost as a small "leading motif" recalling the larger melody of Ex. 1. Maria Major dramatically introduces her theme of Ex. 1 with the miniature motif on the words *O dolor* (Ex. 2), and in addition to its expected appearances in the larger recurrent melody, the germinal fragment appears (always melismatically) on such phrases as *solvis penas, Marie (vulnera), flete (sorores), Crucifixi, lancee, gladius, matertere, (peccatricem) respice, amor meus,* and *(linguas) duplices,*[10] among others.

Ex. 2 From Cividale *Planctus Mariae*

Maria Major (while striking her hands):

O do - lor proh do - lor

Basically the same melismatic fragment and some other portions of the whole melody may also be found in two related Cividale dramas of the 14th century, *The Sepulchre* and *The Resurrection*, on the passages *(Quem) queritis, Jhesum Nazarenum,* and *sed cito* (see especially *ejus* in the last passage).[11]

[9] Transcribed by the present author from photographs of the original MS obtained from the Museo Archeologico Nazionale (see fn. 6 above). This *Planctus* and other liturgical dramas are printed in plainsong notation in C. de Coussemaker, *Drames liturgiques du moyen âge* (Paris 1861). The present author has avoided rhythmic interpretations in this paper (all notes are given equal value), since the emphasis is on melody types, and themes invariably recur with new texts and shifted accents, suggesting a variety of rhythmic contours for the same tune.

[10] In Coussemaker, *Drames*, these phrases appear on pp. 285, 286, 287, 288, 290, and 291, respectively.

[11] *The Sepulchre*, Cividale MS CII, fols. 77ʳ-79ᵛ, and *The Resurrection*, Cividale

The theme of Ex. 1 seems to be a melody type, or at least a variant of a melody type. Some resemblance may be seen in the Easter Monday Magnificat antiphon *Qui sunt hi* [12] (Ex. 3a), as well as in two other examples pertaining to Mary, the famous *Regina coeli* [13] (Ex. 3b) and the Christmas Magnificat antiphon *Hodie Christus natus est* [14] (Ex. 3c). Other related examples [15] are the Gloria Patri of the Introit in Mode 6, the psalm *In te Domine speravi* (for the Introit of Quinquagesima Sunday), and what may perhaps be considered the archetypes of the melody, namely, Gregorian psalm tones 1, 6, and the *Tonus peregrinus*.

Ex. 3   From the *Liber Usualis*

a) Antiphon *Qui sunt hi*

b) Antiphon *Regina cœli*

c) Antiphon *Hodie Christus natus est*

MS T.VII, at Museo Archeologico Nazionale, Cividale del Friuli. Both dramas are printed in plainsong in Coussemaker, *Drames;* the passages cited are on pp. 299, 307, 308.

    [12] *Liber*, p. 788.
    [13] *Ibid.*, p. 278.
    [14] *Ibid.*, p. 413.
    [15] *Ibid.*, pp. 15, 512, 113, 116, 117. Cf. also the melodies of the chant texts (from Seven Dolours of the B.V.M.) cited in fn. 8 above, as well those of the Short Responsories *Defecerunt* and *Fasciculus*, the Sequence *Inviolata*, and the Responsory *Virgo parens Christi* (*Liber*, pp. 1638, 1861, 1862).

There are numerous appearances of this melody type, in one form or another, in dramas other than the Cividale *Planctus*. An interesting elaboration, assuming the secular ballade form *aabC* (Ex. 4), may be found in the 12th-century Tours *Resurrection* drama,[16] in the scene involving the Marys purchasing spices from the merchants.[17] With its mundane overtones, the scene well lends itself to *forme-fixe* adaptation and is constructed around eight four-line strophes, the fourth line being a refrain which is sung by all the Marys after the first three verses:

Ex. 4 From Tours *Resurrection*

ⓐ Om-ni - po-tens   pa-ter al-tis-si-me, ⓑ Quid fa-ci-ant   i - ste
ⓐ an-ge-lo - rum   re-ctor mi-tis-si-me,

mi-ser-ri - me? ©He   —   u! quan-tus est no - ster do-lor!

The same scene in *The Three Marys*, a play of the 14th-century Origny MS,[18] is given in French translation (the play is partly in French and partly in Latin) and makes use of the same ballade tune.[19] Repeated through 16 strophes, the melody starts a whole tone higher than that of the Tours drama. Later on in the same Origny play, the ballade melody is again repeated with slight alteration, this time in a dialogue between Mary Magdalene and the Angel, at the sepulchre.[20] The eight stanzas are in French, of which numbers 1, 3, 5, and 7 are not in ballade form but in strophic *lai* form, viz., *aaba* (without refrain), while stanzas 2, 4, 6, and 8 are again in ballade form *aabC*. The refrain melody, C, is quite different from either of the two settings cited above (Ex. 4 and that of the Origny merchant scene).

Since this last scene is actually in the nature of a *planctus*, the dance-like, tight symmetry and immediate repetitions of the ballade melody seem rather badly placed and non-dramatic in effect. In a sense these long ballade sections function as patchwork arias, adding little and in fact interrupting the dramatic action. The section itself is, of course, unified

---

[16] See fn. 2 above. Plainsong and text of the drama are in Coussemaker, *Drames*, pp. 21–36; the ballade is on pp. 22–23.

[17] This is one of the scenes glued on to the *Quem queritis* trope.

[18] *The Three Marys* (written by the nuns of Origny Sainte-Benoîte), MS 75, Bibliothèque de St. Quentin; reproduced in Coussemaker, *Drames*, pp. 256–70. The play is probably not earlier than 1286, since the *Ordinarium* in the MS, *ibid.*, p. 338, mentions this date.

[19] Coussemaker, *Drames*, pp. 257–61.

[20] *Ibid.*, pp. 265–67.

through immediate recurrence of the entire melody, but it is not the type of unification such as is achieved in the Cividale *Planctus* by the weaving through the play of both a tune (Ex. 1) and its fragments.

The melody type thus far discussed occurs in fixed, song-like form in other religious dramas, among them the 12th-century *Sponsus* play of the Limoges MS [21] and a 12th-century play about the three Marys from the Ripoll monastery in Catalonia.[22] In the former, the music of the prologue, constructed in tight, four-line strophes in the melodic form *abac* (or two-line strophes in a_ba_c), strongly resembles the first two parts (*a* and *b*) of the ballade theme of Ex. 4. In the Ripoll play, an allied version of the ballade melody is very prominent throughout. Another important example is found in the 12th-century *Son of Gedron*,[23] a St. Nicholas play of the Orléans MS; the same ballade melody, slightly modified, is again apparent, repeated almost identically through the numerous strophes of the play.

The problem of derivation and chronology should, of course, not be overlooked, with respect to these secular-like versions of the melody type in question. It is possible that the melody type may be secular rather than liturgical in origin, and that the ballade tune and even the liturgical examples given above (e.g. Ex. 3) all derive from some secular prototype, whether on the art or folk level. The melody's contour and basic character are not unknown to European medieval art music (see, for example, *Robins m'aime*, said to be by the 13th-century trouvère Adam de la Halle [24]) and to some European folk music (especially with respect to the melody's triadic and "major-like" structure). On the other hand, further information is required on the secular music of the very early Middle Ages, to evaluate more precisely the relationship of this music to the liturgical psalm-tones, some of which were mentioned above as being possible archetypes of the melody in question. The influence on the liturgy of Oriental melody-formulas cannot be disregarded, and although formulas have also been found in European secular music, these have generally not displayed the strict patterning of Oriental formulas with respect to note-clusters in special turns, leaps, and other configurations.

[21] Limoges *Sponsus*, see fn. 5 above. The play in plainsong is reproduced in Coussemaker, *Drames*, p. 1ff. See also Otto Ursprung, *Das Sponsus-Spiel*, in: *Archiv für Musikforschung*, III (1938), 80–95.
[22] The play is given in Higini Anglès, *La Música a Catalunya fins al segle XIII* (Barcelona 1935), p. 276ff.
[23] *The Son of Gedron*, MS 201 (originally from the monastery of Fleury-sur-Loire, near Orléans), Bibliothèque d'Orléans; see Coussemaker, *Drames*, and Otto E. Albrecht, *Four Latin Plays of St. Nicholas* (Philadelphia 1935).
[24] The piece is given in Reese, MMA, p. 223.

Before proceeding to some other recurrent melodies in the religious dramas, I should like to give a few more examples of the first melody, this time in its freer, more liturgical forms, comparable to the treatment in the Cividale *Planctus* (e.g. Ex. 1). As mentioned above, the recurrent motifs generally (but not always) appear with recurrent texts and scenes which are incorporated within plays of the same liturgical intent. It should be emphasized, however, that the association of a motif with a particular text does not prevent utilization of the melody with other texts. This is evident from all the citations, thus far, of our particular melody type. That it *has* a particular text is in fact not clear, although its scenic association (the Easter sepulchre) and psychological association (the sorrows of Mary and others) are to some degree fairly uniform.

The melody is associated with the same text or fragment of text in perhaps one or two instances. *Qui sunt hi sermones*, the text of the antiphon (see Ex. 3a), appears with the melody (substantially the melody of the antiphon itself) in a 12th-century play, *The Appearance at Emmaus;* [25] in a Christmas play of this time, *The Adoration of the Magi*, some semblance of the melody runs through two successive passages, the first of which begins with the words *Qui sunt hii* (not the antiphon text).[26] The *Emmaus* play, incidentally, displays some interesting variation and fragmentation of the melody, somewhat like the procedure in the Cividale *Planctus*. The recurrent fragment this time comes from the second part of the melody, namely, the triadic rise, $f^1-a^1-c^2$, on the word *ambulantes* (Ex. 3a), which is allied to the rises on *pendes* in Ex. 1, *Quia* in Ex. 3b, the second *hodie* in Ex. 3c, and *Quid faciant* in Ex. 4. The triadic rise occurs frequently in the *Emmaus* play, especially in the following passages, most of which are set to variations of the larger melody as it first appears on *Qui sunt hi* at the beginning of the play: *Tu solus* (the rise is on *peregrinus* and *his diebus*), *De Jesu Nazareno* (on *coram* and *Quomodo; summi sacerdotes* in this section recalls the opening of the melody), *O stulti* (on *tardi*), *Sol occasum* (on *placet;* the opening of this section is, however, related to another melody type), *Thoma* (on *vidimus*), *Nisi videro* (on *manibus*), *Thoma fer digitum* (on *vide*), and *Mitte manum* (on *Et noli*).[27]

As in the Origny *Three Marys*, the melody appears again in the sepulchre scene of the Tours *Resurrection* drama. The angel's *Nichil tibi* passage [28] is very similar in outline (although beginning on c^1 instead of f^1) to the ballade form of the melody as it occurred earlier in the same

[25] *The Appearance at Emmaus*, Orléans MS 201; Coussemaker, *Drames*, p. 195.
[26] *The Adoration of the Magi*, Orléans MS 201; Coussemaker, *Drames*, p. 154.
[27] Coussemaker, *Drames*, pp. 195–97, 201, 202.
[28] *Ibid.*, p. 32.

play (Ex. 4), while something of the opening of the theme introduces his *Non est hic* statement to the Marys.[29] A *Non est hic* passage, sung by two angels in another drama, *The Night of Easter*, of the 13th-century Bigot MS,[30] is an almost exact musical duplicate of the corresponding section in the Tours *Resurrection*. (However, an earlier statement of *Non est hic* in the *Night of Easter* has an entirely different melody.) To reiterate, the melody type seems to be associated not with any distinct text, but rather with scenic-psychological material.

A second recurrent theme in the religious drama may best be illustrated by *Venite et videte* (see Ex. 5 and also the original on Plate 1b, staff 5), sung by the angel in the Cividale *Sepulchre* drama: [31]

Ex. 5   From Cividale *Sepulchre*

The vigorous opening immediately brings to mind the Lutheran Reformation hymn *Ein feste Burg ist unser Gott* and especially J. S. Bach's cantata (see Ex. 6a) and chorale prelude of the same name (as well as his chorale prelude *Erstanden ist der heil'ge Christ*, which is based on a somewhat similar hymn tune).

There are numerous occurrences of the essentials of the *Venite* melody, obviously a melody type, in the Roman liturgy. Some of the strongest resemblances are found in the St. Thomas antiphon *Quia vidisti* (Ex. 6b),[32] the *Agnus Dei I* (Ex. 6c),[33] which is listed under *ad libitum*

---

[29] *Ibid.*, p. 30.

[30] *The Night of Easter*, Bigot MS (originally from Rouen), Paris, Bibliothèque Nationale, lat. 904; see Coussemaker, *Drames*, p. 251. *Non est hic* in this portion of the play is incorporated within a *Quem queritis viventem* section. Another *Non est hic*, with a different melody, appears earlier in the same drama; see *ibid.*, p. 250 and Chart I below in the present paper.

[31] Cividale *Sepulchre* examples (5 and 9) transcribed by the present author from photographs of the original MS obtained from the Cividale Museum (see fn. 11 above). The *Venite* passage is in Coussemaker, *Drames*, p. 299.

[32] *Liber*, p. 1326.

[33] *Ibid.*, p. 94.

chants, the *Kyrie I, Lux et origo* (Ex. 6d),[34] and the Lenten antiphon *Audite et intelligite* (Ex. 6e):[35]

Ex. 6

a) Chorale excerpt, Bach Cantata No. 80, *Ein feste Burg*

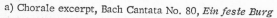

b) Antiphon *Quia vidisti*

Qui-a vi-di-sti me, Tho-ma, cre-di-di - sti: be-a-ti qui non vi-de-runt,

et cre-di - de-runt, al - le - lu - ia.

c) *Agnus Dei I, ad libitum* chant

A - gnus De - i qui tol - lis

d) *Kyrie I, Lux et origo*

Ky - ri-e e - le-i-son. Chri - ste

e - le - i - son.

e) Antiphon *Audite et intelligite*

Au-di-te et in-tel-li-gi-te tra-di-ti-ones quas Dominus de-dit vo-bis.

The *Venite* melody, together with the text (Ex. 5), is duplicated almost exactly in the Cividale *Resurrection*, where it is sung by the angel.[36] In two other Easter dramas, the Tours *Resurrection* and the Bigot *Night of Easter*, the *Venite* text appears with a variation of the melody, transposed a fifth lower and again sung by the angel.[37] Also

[34] *Ibid.*, p. 16.

[35] *Ibid.*, p. 1090. Cf. also the Easter week Communion *Christus resurgens* (*Liber*, p. 795); the Lenten Introit *Invocabit me* (*Liber*, p. 532); and the Christmas antiphon *De fructu* (*Liber*, p. 412).

[36] Coussemaker, *Drames*, p. 308.

[37] *Ibid.*, pp. 27, 250. In both dramas the *Venite* text is part of a passage opening with *Non est hic* set to a different melody type (see *Ad monumentum* in the present paper).

present in the Tours *Resurrection* is the St. Thomas antiphon *Quia vidisti* (sung by Jesus) [38] in the version of the melody belonging to the antiphon itself (Ex. 6b). The "composer-compiler" has made an interesting little attempt just before the *Quia vidisti* to anticipate the melody with a fragment (Ex. 7) [39] derived from the notes of [*credi-*] *disti* . . . *et* (Ex. 6b) (comparable to *locum* . . . in Ex. 5):

Ex. 7   From Tours *Resurrection*

Tho-mas mit - te ma-num tu -am   et co - gno - sce

A *Quia vidisti* section sung by Jesus in the Orléans *Appearance at Emmaus* [40] makes especially evident the piecing together of texts and music borrowed from the liturgy. Two successive statements of the melody (substantially that of Ex. 6b) on the antiphon texts *Quia vidisti* and *Data est mihi* [41] (the latter, incidentally, has the same melody in the liturgy), are followed by a quite free variation on the text of the Pentecost antiphon *Non vos relinquam;* [42] highlights of the variation are the fragments $c^2–b^1–g^1$ and $g^1–c^2–g^1$, which in one way or another are prominently featured in the melody type.

None of the plays mentioned thus far in connection with the second melody type make use of it as consistently as does the Cividale *Annunciation* drama.[43] It appears here at least nine times in various forms, eight of which are knit together by the characteristic open fourth, and all by the chasmatonic (i.e. gapped) tetrachord $c^2–a^1–g^1$ of the melody type. (The major-third chasmatonic tetrachord $c^2–b^1–g^1$ or $g^1–b^1–c^2$ seems to be lacking here, although it exists in diatonic form, viz. $c^2–b^1–a^1–g^1$.) The most typical motion may be seen in the opening (Ex. 8) of the angel's *Ne timeas* passage, at the beginning of the play, the text and music of which are taken from the Advent and Annunciation antiphon of the same name.[44]

[38] *Ibid.,* p. 35.

[39] *Ibid.,* p. 34. The text is from the Communion *Mitte manum tuam* (*Liber,* pp. 811, 1328). This has a melody somewhat like Ex. 7, although without the distinctive tetrachord between c^2 and g^1, which is important to the *Quia vidisti* melody and is used diatonically in Ex. 7.

[40] Coussemaker, *Drames,* p. 203.

[41] *Liber,* p. 803, bottom of page.

[42] *Ibid.,* p. 862. This antiphon (in the liturgy) has an entirely different melody.

[43] Coussemaker, *Drames,* pp. 280–82.

[44] *Liber,* pp. 326, 1417. *Note:* In the *Liber* the *Ne timeas* antiphon *does* contain the chasmatonic tetrachord $c^2–b^1–g^1$, on the syllables (*gra*)*tiam*. In his classification, according to melody types, of the antiphons in the tonary of Regino of Prüm,

Ex. 8   From Cividale *Annunciation*

Angel:

Ne ti - me - as Ma - ri - a,   in - ve - ni - sti gra - ti - am

a - pud Do - mi - num.

The same melody appears later in the Cividale *Annunciation* on lines beginning with *Et ecce Helisabeth* and *Et hic mensis*, sung by the angel, and on *Et unde hoc, Ecce enim*, and . . . *et beata*, sung by Elizabeth. Mary herself sings three passages, which although slightly different from the *Ne timeas* melody seem to belong to the same melodic category. Both the characteristic open fourth and tetrachordal descent are strongly prominent in two of her passages. One of these, especially, points (as do other clues) to a possible archetype of all the examples cited under our second category, namely, the Magnificat Tone 8G. In the drama, Mary sings the Magnificat on the *Solemn* Tone 8G.[45]

IT IS impossible within the limited space of this paper to deal adequately with the many recurrent motifs (large and small) in the religious drama. Hence, some of the findings appear in condensed chart form, below.

One of the most common root melodies is found to be associated with the text *Ad monumentum* . . . , sung by one or all three of the Marys when describing their meeting with the angel at Christ's tomb. Not only is this text-melody pair an integral part of many Easter dramas, but the melody itself is often used in a variety of ways—in whole, in variation, in fragmentation—within the same play. The returning musical signal, particularly in interwoven fragment form, does much, as stated earlier, to cement the psychological as well as purely formal structure of the play. The plan, evident in the Cividale *Planctus* (cf. Exx. 1, 2, and discussion above), is also characteristic of the Cividale *Sepulchre*, this time with respect to the *Ad monumentum* theme (Ex. 9a), sung by all the Marys. (It ought to be emphasized, incidentally, that there may be

Gevaert sets up two types for what the present author considers as one. The difference between the tetrachords c^2-b^1-g^1 and c^2-a^1-g^1 apparently is the basis for his reasoning, although actually both tetrachords appear somewhere in his examples, if not at the openings. See François A. Gevaert, *La Mélopée antique dans le chant de l'église latine* (Ghent 1895), pp. 281–82.

[45] *Liber*, pp. 212, 218.

several recurrent motifs in a play, not merely one.) Although the bold open fifth at the beginning of the melody commands attention, it is interesting to see that the favored recurring fragment, as was the case with respect to Ex. 2, is a melismatic turn. Derived from the notes on the words *venimus gementes* (Ex. 9a), the turn occurs some 13 times and may be illustrated by the following excerpts (Exx. 9b, 9c, 9d, 9e—see especially the brackets), the first of which appears at the beginning of the play, as well as by *Scio, cujus,* and *non creditis* (see Plate 1b, staves 2, 3, and end of 4 and beginning of 5), among others:

Ex. 9   From Cividale *Sepulchre*

a) *Ad monumentum*

phrase I   phrase II   phrase III

Ad mo-nu - men-tum ve-ni - mus ge-men-tes an-ge - lum Do-mi-ni

b) *Pastore*

Pa - sto - re   o - ves   er -rant mi - se - re.

c) *Ite*

I - te   ad   di - sci - pu - los

d) *Mulier*

Mu - li - er,quid plo -

-              -   ras?

e) . . . *ascendo*

. . . a-scen-do ad   Pa -trem me - um,

Chart I lists some examples of the *Ad monumentum* melody as it occurs in several other dramas and with other texts (the page numbers in parentheses in both Charts I and II are references to Coussemaker's *Drames,* see footnote 9 above). Unless otherwise described, the examples have essentially the same melody as Ex. 9a; the designations "phrase I," "phrase II," etc. also pertain to Ex. 9a.

CHART I—*Ad monumentum* Melody

Play   *Text and Description of Melody*

Bigot *Night of Easter: Non est hic* (p. 250)—phrase I only; . . . *vade autem* and . . . *Deum meum* (p. 252)—phrase I only, modified and transposed fifth higher

Bigot *Three Kings:*[46] *Que regem* (p. 242)—modification, as in Orléans *Adoration of Magi* below (p. 148)

Cividale *Resurrection: Ad monumentum* (p. 308); *et corpus* (p. 308)—phrase I

Cividale *Sepulchre:* (see Ex. 9 and discussion above)

Origny *Three Marys: Ad monumentum* (p. 268)

Orléans *Adoration of Magi: En Magi* (p. 148)—modification; . . . *querimus en regem* (p. 149)—modification; *Regem, quem queritis* (p. 149)—modification; *Illum natum* (p. 149)—modification; *Illum regnare* (p. 149)—modification; *Contra illum* (p. 152)—phrases I and III only, modified; *Ite* (p. 152)—variation and free treatment; *Quem non prevalent* (p. 153)—slight modification

Orléans *Appearance at Emmaus: Surrexit Dominus et apparuit* (p. 198); (*Surrexit Dominus de sepulchro*) *qui pro nobis* (p. 199)

Orléans *Saintly Women at Tomb: Sed nequimus* (p. 180)—hint of melody, with Bb instead of B♮; *Ad monumentum* (p. 181)—modification, beginning in middle of melody with a¹-c²-d² as in Ex. 9e; *Imo* (p. 182); *Ista qui* (p. 182)—like Ex. 9e; *Congratulamini michi* (p. 184)—some modification; (*Surrexit Dominus de sepulchro*) *qui pro nobis* (p. 185)—slight modification; *Alleluia* (p. 186)—open fourth instead of fifth at beginning

Tours *Resurrection: Non est hic* (p. 27)

In the Gregorian liturgy, the *Ad monumentum* melody has many close relatives, among them the *Kyrie Summe Deus II* (an *ad libitum* chant); *Credo IV*, on the sections *Genitum, Qui propter*, and especially *Confiteor;* the Easter Tuesday Gradual verse *Surrexit Dominus de sepulchro* (cf. the Orléans *Saintly Women* and *Appearance at Emmaus,* in Chart I); *Gloria XIII* on *Et in terra* (Ex. 10); and the Lenten antiphon *Vadam ad patrem.*[47]

Ex. 10   *Gloria XIII*

Et in   ter-ra   pax ho-mi - ni - bus   bo-nae vo-lun - ta-tis. Lau - da-mus   te.

[46] *The Three Kings,* Bigot MS, see fn. 30 above.
[47] *Liber,* pp. 80, 71–73, 790, 51, and 1088, respectively.

The secular world enters the picture again with the alba *Reis glorios* [48] by the troubadour Guiraut de Bornelh (d. c. 1220), which is similar in many ways to the *Ad monumentum* melody. And again one reflects on the devious paths traveled somewhere in the remote past by the root melody on which all of these examples are based.

Our final melody is that of the famous *Quem queritis*. Most sepulchre scenes in the Easter dramas derive textually from the 10th-century Winchester trope *Quem queritis*, and many of them make use of the same root melody on the angel's prime question to the three Marys, "Whom do you seek in the sepulchre?" The vital features of this melody may be seen in the typical version appearing in the Bigot *Night of Easter* (Ex. 11a); [49] a free variation on a different text, sung by Jesus, is found in the Orléans *Appearance at Emmaus* (Ex. 11b).[50] Even some Christmas plays, such as the Bigot *Shepherds* [51] and the Orléans *Adoration of the Magi*, make use of the melody (see Chart II). Of the numerous thematic parallels in the liturgy, one of the closest is that of the antiphon *Paraclitus autem* (Ex. 11c),[52] sung within the octave after Pentecost. Among other examples featuring this melody type are the Communion *Spiritus Sanctus docebit vos*, the Introit *Accipite jucunditatem* (the *Accipite Spiritum Sanctum* of Ex. 11b is from the antiphon of the same name), and the

Ex. 11

a) From Bigot *Night of Easter*

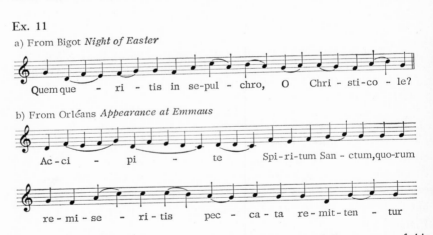

b) From Orléans *Appearance at Emmaus*

[48] The piece is given in Reese, MMA, p. 215; Reese notes the appearance of this alba in the 14th-century play of St. Agnes, *ibid.*, p. 196.

[49] See fn. 30 above and Coussemaker, *Drames*, p. 250. A very early version (c. 1100) of the *Quem queritis* melody and text, from Einsiedeln MS 367, is given in Arnold Schering, *Geschichte der Musik in Beispielen* (Leipzig 1931), p. 5.

[50] See fn. 25 above and Coussemaker, *Drames*, p. 200.

[51] *The Shepherds*, Bigot MS, see fn. 30 above.

[52] *Liber*, p. 900.

c) Antiphon *Paraclitus autem*

Pa - ra-cli - tus au - tem . . . il -le vos do - ce-bit, et sug-ge-ret

vo - bis o -mni - a

Introit *Deus, dum egredereris*—all belonging within the octave after Pentecost, as well as the Lenten antiphon *Ego sum* and the antiphon *Refulsit sol.*[53]

CHART II—*Quem queritis* Melody (some examples)

Play   Text and Description of Melody

Bigot *Night of Easter: Quem queritis* (p. 250); *Jhesum Nazarenum* (p. 250)—variation, beginning in middle of melody

Bigot *Shepherds: Quem queritis in praesepe* (p. 237)

Origny *Three Marys:* . . . *quem queritis esse dolentes* (p. 262)—hint of melody on *esse dolentes; Jhesum crucifixum* (p. 263)—hint of melody; . . . *venite et videte* (p. 263)—hint of melody

Orléans *Adoration of Magi: Quem queritis, pastores* (p. 144); *Ecce stella* (p. 152)

Orléans *Appearance at Emmaus: Accipite* (p. 200)—free variation

Orléans *Saintly Women: Quem queritis* (p. 180)—descending fifth instead of fourth at beginning; *Jhesum Nazarenum* (p. 180)—begins in middle of melody; *Quid, Christicole* (p. 180)—descending 5th instead of 4th

Tours *Resurrection: Quem queritis* (p. 26); *Jhesum Nazarenum* (p. 26)—begins in middle of melody; *Dicite* (p. 23)—fragment, beginning on 2nd note of melody; *Ecce Deus* (p. 33)

More might be said about such matters as the merging of one melody type with another (the blurred results of which often defy classification), or the ingenious abscissions and subtle insertions of the Easter Sequence *Victimae paschali* (apart from its block attachments to the "finale" of many dramas). Suffice it to say here that the religious music drama, despite its borrowed material, was often a model of artful planning in the ways of melodic recurrence, fragmentation, blending, and unification, which not infrequently resulted in some measure of dramatic depth and expressiveness.

[53] *Ibid.*, pp. 889, 890, 892, 568, and 994, respectively.

CHANSONS FOR THE PLEASURE OF A FLORENTINE PATRICIAN:

FLORENCE, BIBLIOTECA DEL CONSERVATORIO DI MUSICA, MS BASEVI 2442

by HOWARD MAYER BROWN

THE FIRST 25 years of the 16th century were crucial for the history of secular music in the Renaissance. During that quarter century an old order ended, and a new one began. Secular music to a 15th-century musician, wherever he lived, meant, above all, the refined and delicate art of the chanson, the history of which can be traced in a relatively straight line from Dufay and Binchois to Busnois and Ockeghem. About 1500, however, the hegemony of this "classic" Burgundian chanson was successfully challenged, and the way left open that would eventually lead to the Parisian chanson of the '30s, the Netherlandish chanson of the '40s, and the Italian madrigal.[1]

The predominance of the chanson in the 15th century may be likened to the use of one universal language that had, to be sure, various accents, depending on the individual composer, and the time and place in which he worked. But after 1500 a number of disparate dialects, each one quite separate and distinct, replaced the one universal language. Even the nature of the sources that preserve early 16th-century music reflects the new heterogeneity. The three volumes of chansons printed by Ottaviano Petrucci between 1501 and 1504, the *Odhecaton, Canti B,* and *Canti C,* are both a beginning and an end: a beginning in that they herald the flood of printed polyphonic music that was soon to engulf Europe, but an end in that they are the last of the great 15th-century chansonniers, those vast miscellanies presenting a true cross-section of

[1] I should like to express my gratitude to the John Simon Guggenheim Memorial Foundation, for awarding me a fellowship for travel in Italy; to Villa I Tatti, The Harvard University Center for Italian Renaissance Culture, in Florence, for allowing me the use of their facilities; and to the director and staff of the Biblioteca del Conservatorio di Musica in Florence, for innumerable kindnesses shown me during the preparation of this essay. Owing to limitations of space, the concluding section of the discussion and list of contents in Florence 2442 could not be included here; they will shortly be published elsewhere.

contemporary activity. After Petrucci, collections of chansons are apt to be much smaller, and more restricted and specialized in scope. For example, the two most important printed sources of the chanson between *Canti C* (1504) and the first of Pierre Attaingnant's volumes in the late 1520s are both collections emphasizing one particular style to the exclusion of all others: double canons (RISM 1520³) and "three-part popular arrangements" (RISM 1520⁶).[2]

The subject of this essay, the set of partbooks now in Florence, Biblioteca del Conservatorio di Musica Luigi Cherubini, with the call number MS Basevi 2442, contains a similarly unified repertoire of French chansons. Most but not all of its 55 compositions are settings *a 4* of pre-existing melodies in a style I have elsewhere called the "four-part popular arrangement."[3] This very limitation on the repertoire increases the importance of the manuscript, for one of the new styles of the new century is thus much more clearly exposed than would be the case in a more miscellaneous collection. And Florence 2442 is important also in helping to fill the still somewhat mysterious gap between Petrucci and Attaingnant. It is curious, therefore, that the manuscript has never been the subject of a separate study. Perhaps its neglect can be explained partly by the frankness of some of the texts—their obscenity is striking even by 16th-century standards—and partly because one of the partbooks, the bassus, is now missing. Although many of the chansons can be reconstructed through concordances, some of them remain, alas, incomplete.

The three surviving partbooks, cantus, altus, and tenor, measure 20 by 14 centimeters, or approximately 5½ by 7¾ inches, an extremely convenient size if only one person was to sing a part. All of the books have exactly the same number of folios.[4] The first of the two parchment leaves that begin each volume is glued to the inside of the front cover. Four blank paper folios follow these guard sheets; then come 96 paper folios with the music, and four more blank ones. Two parchment sheets end every volume, the second glued to the inside of the back cover. The

[2] Complete titles for the two volumes are given in François Lesure, ed., RISM: *Recueils imprimés XVIᵉ–XVIIᵉ siècles* (München-Duisburg 1960). The term "three-part popular arrangement" is discussed in Howard M. Brown, *The Genesis of a Style: The Parisian Chanson, 1500–1530*, in: James Haar, ed., *Chanson and Madrigal* (Cambridge, Mass. 1964). Helen Hewitt and Isabel Pope have published a modern edition of the *Odhecaton* (Cambridge, Mass. 1942).

[3] Brown, *Genesis*. The first chanson in the manuscript, Josquin's *Faulte d'argent*, is the only one *a 5*. I shall hereafter refer to the manuscript simply as Florence 2442. An index of its contents is included in R. Gandolfi, C. Cordara, and A. Bonaventura, eds., *Pubblicazioni dell'associazione dei musicologi italiani. Catalogo delle opere musicali*, Series IV, Vol. I: *Città di Firenze. Biblioteca del R. Conservatorio di Musica* (Parma 1929), p. 246.

[4] Fol. 96 of the altus partbook has been torn out.

96 folios with music consist of twelve gatherings of eight folios each; in all three partbooks the first folio in each gathering is numbered (1-12) in the upper left corner, doubtless as a precaution to ensure that the binder assembled the gatherings in their proper order. All of the folios are numbered in a modern hand in the lower left corner. The cantus partbook has as well page numbers and Roman numerals for each composition, both also in a modern hand.

The moroccan leather binding, with simple but elegant tooling in early 16th-century style, points to a Florentine origin for the manuscript. The two decorated rectangles stamped with a stylized leaf pattern and framed by tooled straight lines, the discreet gilding that includes the four dots just inside the larger rectangle, the designation of the voice part, and the four half-moons at the corners (see Pl. 2b), and the gilt gauffered edges of the paper, are all characteristics of the symmetry and grace of the Florentine art of bookbinding in the 15th and early 16th centuries.[5]

As parchment guard sheets, the Florentine binder took loose leaves from the "Co-" section of a dismembered manuscript Latin dictionary, apparently of the early 15th century, a dictionary similar to but not the same as Johannes de Janua's *Catholicon*.[6] Originally glued to the front and back covers of each partbook, these parchment folios have now come loose, revealing that the covers of the volumes were stiffened with pages from a discarded printed book. In the cantus part the parchment from the front cover has been torn away enough to expose one complete stanza of verse in *ottava rima*, beginning "Falseron che havea tanto disiato," stanza 66 of Canto XXVI of Luigi Pulci's comic epic *Morgante*.[7] By rummaging carefully through the covers of Florence 2442, it is not difficult to see that the same profusely illustrated edition of *Morgante* was used in place of bookboards in the binding of all three partbooks. A comparison of these visible fragments with the early 16th-century editions listed by Max Sander [8] reveals that the manuscript contains pages from

[5] See Tammaro De Marinis, *La Legatura artistica in Italia nei secoli XV e XVI* (Florence 1960), I, 89-123.

[6] I should like to thank Prof. Renato Piattoli of Florence for dating the handwriting on the parchment sheets, and for confirming the dates of the other handwriting in the manuscript. The *Catholicon* was finished in 1286, but first printed in Mainz in 1460. I consulted a copy of the Venetian edition printed by Peter Liechtenstein of Cologne in 1506, presently in the Biblioteca Nazionale Centrale in Florence.

[7] Luigi Pulci, *Morgante*, ed. Franca Ageno (Milan & Naples 1955), p. 952.

[8] *Le Livre à figures italien depuis 1467 jusqu'à 1530* (Milan 1942), II, 1031-32. See also Paul Kristeller, *Early Florentine Woodcuts* (London 1897), I, 135-36. I am greatly indebted to Dr. E. Trenkler of the Oesterreichische Nationalbibliothek in Vienna, who very kindly compared the page from Florence 2442 with the 1500 *Morgante* in Vienna, and also to François Lesure of the Bibliothèque Nationale in Paris, and M. J. Faigel of Houghton Library, Harvard University, who checked other editions for me.

the *Morgante* printed in Florence by Antonio Tubini "ad petitione & instantia di Ser Piero Pacini da Pescia," and dated 22 January 1500, copies of which were hitherto known only in Vienna and Berlin. The book must have been at least 20 or 25 years old before being discarded —a binder would hardly dismember a new book for such a purpose—and therefore, Florence 2442 cannot have been bound before the third decade of the 16th century.

The binding does not reveal the exact date of the manuscript, and neither do the watermarks, although they do tend to confirm the approximation suggested by the pages from *Morgante*. Two different watermarks are found in each partbook. The first, a set of scales within a double circle surmounted by a bird, appears on the paper of the main portion, the 96 folios that contain music. The blank pages inserted before and after the music have the second, a plant with a three-pronged fruit or flower, and two leaves. Both Briquet and Zonghi list watermarks similar to but not identical with the set of scales.[9] The one that most closely resembles it is listed as Briquet, No. 2480, found on papers used in Venice and Udine between 1490 and 1493, demonstrably too early for the set of partbooks. Briquet does, however, list the second watermark, the plant, as No. 7388, found on papers used in Tuscany between 1529 and 1540. As a preliminary working hypothesis, a starting point for further investigation, the years between 1525 and 1540 seem most likely to have been the time when Florence 2442 was compiled and bound.

The 96 folios that contain music each have four five-line staves. Music and text are written in one hand throughout, an exceptionally clear and simple humanistic hand, which seldom causes a modern reader any difficulty (see Pl. 2a). Indeed, if the scribe was an Italian, and everything seems to indicate that the manuscript was copied in Italy by an Italian, he has taken pains unusual in those days of orthographical indifferencè to preserve the French texts uncorrupted by Italianisms. Moreover, he was exceptionally careful about placing the text beneath the music. Although each syllable is not fitted exactly to the note to which it was meant to be sung, the scribe always begins each new stave of music with the proper syllable of text (see Pl. 2a). And even in the course of a phrase he sometimes divides a word into its syllables, an uncommon procedure for the time. Since the text is set in a syllabic style, with short melismas normally only at the ends of phrases—as we shall see this is one of the new features of this style—these partbooks present unusually clear examples of the practice of text underlay for the first

---

[9] See Charles Briquet, *Les Filigranes* (Leipzig 1923), and *Zonghi's Watermarks, Monumenta chartae papyraceae historiam illustrantia*, III (Hilversum 1953).

quarter of the 16th century. Each chanson begins with a rather elaborate calligraphic initial, from which quite often fanciful faces, like the two heads of Pl. 2a, peep out. The initial letters were all added after the text was copied under the music, for invariably the letter that is elaborated calligraphically is repeated just beneath and to the left of the clef sign (see the lower-case L in Pl. 2a), doubtless as a guide to the calligrapher.

The music is as finely written and easy to read as the texts, presenting almost no problems of transcription. Only the notation of the fairly frequent sections of music in triple meter is apt to trap the unwary student. The sections in duple meter are invariably notated in alla breve with the mensuration sign C. Triple meter is indicated in one of four ways: by coloration or by the signs 3, C3, or $\frac{0}{3}$. Coloration signifies *proportio sesquialtera*, three black minims being equal in value to two white minims. The proof of this relationship, if proof is needed, can be found in Nos. 10 and 25, in those sections where two voices have coloration while the other two voices rest, the rests being indicated in normal values. Having determined the meaning of coloration, we can deduce the significance of two of the proportional signs by examining those compositions in which the same music is notated in two different ways. In both Nos. 14 and 21 a refrain is repeated at the end of the chanson, notated in coloration, that had previously been notated with a proportional sign. If the repeated music is to have the same time values both times it is sung—and that is the only musically acceptable solution—then the relationship of the proportions to *integer valor* (that is, to C) can be demonstrated. In No. 14 the music following the sign 3, in breves and semibreves, is identical with the music in blackened semibreves and minims. Therefore the sign 3 must indicate *proportio tripla*, three semibreves being equal in time to one semibreve of *integer valor*. Similarly in No. 21, the sign C3 is used to indicate *proportio tripla*. That 3 and C3 mean exactly the same thing is confirmed by No. 23, where one voice has 3, and the others C3, for the same measures in triple meter. Similarly 3 and $\frac{0}{3}$ are used together to signify *proportio tripla* in Nos. 15 and 26. Moreover, the sense of the music demands my solution; interpreting all three signs, 3, C3, and $\frac{0}{3}$, to mean exactly the same thing, *proportio tripla*, even when *integer valor* is represented by an *alla breve* mensuration sign, C, is the only way to achieve a balance between the two meters, in which the music is neither too slow nor too fast.[10]

[10] This solution contradicts statements in Willi Apel, *The Notation of Polyphonic Music, 900–1600* (4th ed. Cambridge, Mass. 1953), pp. 193–94, and Apel, *Harvard Dictionary of Music* (Cambridge, Mass. 1961), p. 749.

There can be little doubt, from what I have written already, that Florence 2442 was planned and executed as a unit: the manuscript is written in one hand throughout, none of the initial letters is missing, as is so often the case with 15th- and early 16th-century miscellanies, the gatherings are all neatly numbered for the binder, and, most important, the music is unified stylistically. One glance at the table of contents, which does not appear in any of the partbooks, confirms the impression that Florence 2442 was conceived as a whole, for the plan of the manuscript is extremely clear. The compositions are arranged by composer, whose names appear only in the cantus part. Three composers take the lion's share. Almost half of the manuscript is devoted to Josquin Des Prez (6 chansons), Ninot le Petit (13 chansons), and Antoine Bruhier (6 chansons). Following these "stars" 14 composers: Jean Braconnier dit Lourdault, Rogier, Marbriano de Orto, Loyset Compère, Antoine Brumel, Antoine de Févin, Henricus Morinen[sis] (Henri de Thérouanne?),[11] Pierre de La Rue, Heinrich Isaac, Holain, Gaspar van Weerbecke, Jean Mouton, Jacob Obrecht, and N. Beauvoys, are each represented by one, two, or three compositions.

For whom and when was the manuscript prepared? The only written indication of ownership in the three partbooks is the legend on one of the blank pages of the tenor part: "Ex Liberalitate Bernardi Renuccini," repeated in the same early 16th-century hand on the back cover. The man responsible for Florence 2442 was, then, a member of one of Florence's best-known patrician families, the same Rinuccinis that produced Ottavio, so important in the early history of opera. The Rinuccini family tree [12] includes five Bernardos in the 16th century:

1. Bernardo di Giuliano Maria (b. 1473), who became a monk ("Frate dell'Osservanza"),
2. Bernardo di Alessandro (1515–1582), who became a Dominican and took the name "Fra Alessio,"
3. Bernardo di Bartolommeo (1544–1620),
4. Bernardo di Neri, whose father was born in 1436 and died in 1508, and
5. Bernardo di Jacobo, who was a captain in the Florentine army, and whose father was born in 1465.

The first two men, having taken up the religious life, are not likely to have had such a collection of ribald songs assembled, for even 16th-century clerics must have had some residual traces of piety. The third Bernardo can be eliminated immediately as a candidate since he was not

[11] See Alfred Franklin, *Dictionnaire des noms, surnoms et pseudonymes latins de l'histoire littéraire du moyen âge* (Paris 1875), p. 403.

[12] G. Aiazzi, ed., *Ricordi storici di Filippo di Cino Rinuccini dal 1282 al 1460 colla continuazione di Alamanno e Neri suoi figli fino al 1506* (Florence 1840), following p. 108 and pp. 130–31.

yet born when the manuscript was compiled. Before deciding which of the last two Bernardos is more apt to have had Florence 2442 prepared, however, the phrase "Ex Liberalitate" should be considered, for it suggests that the set of partbooks was presented as a gift by Bernardo to a friend or patron. If the person who received the manuscript can be identified, then the identity of the giver will be easier to discover.

The first clue to this puzzle appears on the bindings of the manuscript. Four gilded crescents decorate the corners of the covers of all three part-books (see Pl. 2b), the same crescents that appear in the coat of arms of the Strozzis, one of the wealthiest and most powerful families in Renaissance Florence.[13] More significantly the same crescents are scattered over the covers of the account books of the Strozzis during the early 16th century.[14] And the fact that a Strozzi owned Florence 2442 explains why the manuscript begins and ends with settings of "Faulte d'argent, c'est douleur non pareille," a sentiment most fitting for a member of one of Florence's leading banking families.

But which Strozzi was Bernardo's friend? They were a large and famous family. Litta reports that during the early years of the 16th century the Strozzis included some 80 heads of families, and in 1524 presented 120 candidates eligible for office in the Florentine government.[15] A man like Lorenzo Strozzi (1482–1549), for example, would seem to be an ideal recipient for Florence 2442. As a poet of *canti carnascialeschi* he would have had a certain susceptibility to boisterous music, an impression confirmed by his biographer, Francesco Zeffi, who reports that Lorenzo was a passionate music lover who sang his own part with much grace, and especially liked to sing mocking love songs to the lute.[16] In all probability, however, the manuscript was presented not to Lorenzo, but to his brother, Filippo.

The historian, Benedetto Varchi, gives the final clue to this puzzle of identities in his *Storia fiorentina*.[17] Varchi, reporting the events sub-

[13] See Conte Pompeo Litta, *Celebri famiglie italiane* (Milan n. d.), VII, 66, and Luigi Passerini, *Sommario storico delle famiglie celebri toscane* (Florence 1864), III, art. "Strozzi."

[14] See De Marinis, *La Legatura*, Pls. D6, D7, and p. 116.

[15] Litta, *Celebri famiglie*, VII, 66.

[16] See Pietro Stromboli, ed., *Le Vite degli uomini illustri della casa Strozzi, commentario di Lorenzo di Filippo Strozzi, con ragionamento inedito di Francesco Zeffi sopra la vita dell' autore* (Florence 1892), pp. xiii–xiv: "E Lorenzo non solo della poesia fu sempre studioso, ma ancora mirabilmente si dilettò della musica, e nel cantare adempiva con molta grazia la parte sua, tanto che alcuna volta pareva lascivo, massime quando col suo liuto conferiva i suoi amori: ai quali, oltrechè naturalmente pareva inclinato; essendo ancora dalle madame de'suoi tempi provocato; parve, che in questo trapassasse il segno: talchè in certi sonetti, dove si tassavono li vizi de'più nobili, a lui fu dato il titolo dell'Amore."

[17] Benedetto Varchi, *Storia fiorentina*, in: *Opere* (Trieste 1858), I, 46 (Book III, par. 9). See also Cecil Roth, *The Last Florentine Republic* (London 1925), pp. 87–88.

sequent to the restoration of the last Florentine Republic in 1527, explains the rebels' concern to keep some members of the Medici family in the city, to prevent any rash move on the part of Pope Clement VII, unlikely to endanger the safety of a kinsman. Therefore, Filippo Strozzi, the leader of the rebels, had the young Catherine de' Medici brought back from her family's villa at Poggio a Caiano to the city, where she was installed for safekeeping in the nunnery of Santa Lucia. To lead Catherine back to Florence, says Varchi, Filippo Strozzi sent, among others, one of his agents, Bernardo Rinuccini, called Il Braciaiuolo, the same Bernardo, son of Jacopo, we learn from another passage in Varchi,[18] who was a captain in the Florentine army, the fifth in my list of five. And it was surely this Captain Bernardo di Jacopo Rinuccini who presented to Filippo Strozzi the set of partbooks now in the Conservatory library in Florence.

Filippo Strozzi, born in 1488, first achieved notoriety in 1508 when, at the age of 20, he decided to marry Clarice de' Medici, granddaughter of Lorenzo the Magnificent, and niece of Giovanni, later Pope Leo X. At that time the Medicis were banished from Florence; since there was a law against marrying into rebel families, Strozzi's action was punished by a fine and several years banishment to Naples. But when the Medicis were restored to power in 1512, Strozzi was in a very strong position indeed. He played an important political role in papal circles as well as in Florence throughout the reign of Leo X, and for much of the reign of the second Medici pope, Clement VII. For some time, however, he had become increasingly disillusioned with Medici rule, and, in 1527, a few days before the sack, he and his wife fled Rome, and made their way back to Florence, where Filippo became the leader of the rebellion that restored the republic, an action that Clement VII never forgave. After only a few days of popular leadership Filippo seemed to vacillate—through no fault of his own his maneuvers to secure Florentine control over Pisa and Leghorn were indecisive—and the Florentines, with their usual fickleness, deserted him. Humiliated, he disappeared from public view for a few years, first retiring to his villa at Orti Rucellai near Ripoli, and then, in 1528 and 1529, moving to Lyons to pursue his business interests there. After the siege and capitulation of Florence he returned to his native city, was forgiven his past sins by the Medici party, and even helped to plan governmental reforms. But before long he had made an enemy of the despotic Duke Alessandro de' Medici. Strozzi's trips to France, in 1533 to accompany Catherine de' Medici to her wedding with the Duke of Orléans, later Henri II, and again in 1535 to rejoin

[18] Varchi, *Storia*, p. 237 (Book X, par. 73), where Bernardo is incorrectly said to be the son of Francesco Rinuccini.

Catherine, were motivated at least partly by his desire to escape the oppressive atmosphere of Florence. Events following the assassination of Duke Alessandro in 1537 quickly led to Strozzi's final downfall. Once more he plotted against the Medicis, this time unsuccessfully. He was arrested by Cosimo, and died in prison in 1538, whether by his own hand or not remains uncertain.[19]

What manner of man was he? The chroniclers agree in describing him as a swashbuckling man of the world. Well endowed by nature, Filippo was gracious, generous, and a superb conversationalist. But even my short summary of his career reveals his fondness for intrigue. Apparently he was vain and dissolute as well; Varchi stresses this latter quality, explaining that in matters of love he had regard neither for the age nor the sex of his partners.[20] Like so many well-born Florentines of the time, Strozzi combined a life of action, as banker, *bon vivant*, and statesman, with a genuine devotion to the humane world of letters. After he retired to Orti Rucellai in 1527, for example, he devoted himself to correcting after Ermolao Barbaro the manuscripts of Pliny the Elder, assisted by none other than Bernardo Pisano, the Florentine composer.[21] A document from the time when Strozzi was enjoying high favor in papal circles suggests that he also took some interest in music, and specifically French music, and gives us a hint of the exchange of compositions between France and Rome during the reign of Leo X. On 6 May 1514, Balthassare Turini in Rome, writing to Lorenzo de' Medici, later Duke of Urbino, in Florence, reports that he has received the song recently sent from France, and forwarded by Lorenzo. Turini goes on to say that Strozzi had already taken it, intending to give it to Leo for performance.[22]

One chanson in Florence 2442 may refer to a historical event actually

---

[19] The summary of Strozzi's career and personality is taken from F.-T. Perrens, *Histoire de Florence* (Paris 1890), III, *passim*; Roth, *The Last Florentine Republic, passim*; Stromboli, *Le Vite, passim*; and Varchi, *Storia, passim*.

[20] Varchi, *Storia*, p. 325 (Book XII, par. 29).

[21] Varchi, *loc. cit.* On Pisano, see Frank A. D'Accone, *Bernardo Pisano. An Introduction to His Life and Works*, in: *Musica disciplina*, XVII (1963), 115-35, esp. p. 125.

[22] The letter, in Florence, Archivio di Stato, Medici avanti il Principato, Filza CVII, c. 18, reads:

"Mag.^{ce} patrone mi obser.^{me} commen.

. . . Il canto venuto di Francia et mandato da V. S. Philippo Strozzi me lo ha tolto et dice che lo vuole presentare ad N. S.^{re} [Leo X] quando S. Sta canterà . . . Roma, die. VI Maii. MDXIIII

Humill. Sor Balth.^{ar} "

I am indebted to Frank D'Accone for pointing out to me the existence of this letter, as well as for many valuable suggestions made in the course of preparing this essay.

witnessed by Strozzi. The quodlibet by Gaspar van Weerbecke beginning "Bontemps je ne te puis laissier" (No. 49), contains the lines:

> Sonnez, chantez du bon cueur fin,
> Sonnes la bienvenue de monsigneur le dauffin,
> Sonnez trompette, sonnes bonbardez, sonnes falcons,
> Sonnez, chantez, soir et matin,
> Sonnez la bienvenue de monsigneur le dauffin.[23]

There were only two dauphins between 1493 and 1536: Charles-Orland (1492–96), son of Charles VIII, and François (1518–36), son of Francis I. The song quoted by Gaspar is unlikely to have been written in honor of Charles-Orland, since his short life ran its course slightly before most of the chansons in Florence 2442 were composed. François, on the other hand, was born in February 1518, and baptized in April of that year at Amboise, only a few days before Lorenzo de' Medici, Duke of Urbino, married Madeleine de la Tour d'Auvergne, an event already famous in music history as the occasion for the preparation of the so-called Medici Codex.[24] At the baptism the Duke of Urbino, representing his uncle, the Pope, held the baby, and the King's sister, Marguerite of Navarre, was godmother. Filippo Strozzi also attended, in the entourage of Lorenzo. Shortly after the wedding, the French court left Amboise for a tour of Brittany, at least partly so that the dauphin could take up his heritage there. At Angers there were "mommeries, esbatemens et gorgiastez." And both Nantes and Paris arranged elaborate entertainments to celebrate the entry of the king, and to welcome the new dauphin.[25] Is it possible that *Sonnez, chantez* was commissioned for one of these *joyeuses entrées?* Perhaps Filippo heard the song then, and its inclusion in Florence 2442 was to remind him of this trip to France.

If my conjecture is correct, the manuscript was not prepared until after 1518. In any case the evidence of the bindings and the watermarks

---

[23] The text is reproduced from the cantus part; the manuscript incorrectly reads "chantrez" in the fourth line. The other voices consistently have "daulfin" rather than "dauffin." The other songs quoted in the quodlibet are:
Adieu mes amours (See Hewitt, ed., *Odhecaton*, p. 134)
Bontemps je ne te puis laissier
Bontemps ne viendra tu jamais (See Howard M. Brown, *Music in the French Secular Theater, 1400–1550,* Cambridge, Mass. 1963, p. 194, No. 38)
Hélas, hélas, dessulz ton lict, et la demourrez
Il est de bonne heure né (See Brown, *op. cit.,* p. 226, No. 165)
Levez vous, hau, Guillemette (complete chanson in Florence 2442, No. 10 and elsewhere)
Tu m'a donné merencolie.
[24] Edward E. Lowinsky, *The Medici Codex,* in: *Annales musicologiques,* V (1957), 61–178.
[25] On the baptism of François see Pierre Jourda, *Marguerite d'Angoulême* (Paris 1930), I, 53–54. I am indebted to Prof. Myron Gilmore for giving me advice about dauphins.

point to a slightly later date. Nor is the set of partbooks likely to have been compiled later than 1528. For in that year Filippo left Florence, and by the time he returned, he had already begun to intrigue in a way not apt to endear him to a Florentine patriot, if we can assume Bernardo Rinuccini to have remained faithful to those ideals of liberty so dear to most Florentines. In searching for a likely date for Florence 2442, I see no reason to look beyond the year for which we have evidence of a connection between Bernardo and Filippo, namely, 1527. Perhaps Bernardo presented it to Filippo to celebrate his triumphal entry into Florence in 1527, or, more probably, gave it to Filippo to solace him in his semi-retirement later in the same year. It is not difficult to imagine this proud, vain man, temporarily humbled, sitting with three of his friends around a table in his sumptuous villa at Orti Rucellai, forgetting his troubles for an hour or two with a lusty song.[26]

[26] The range of most of the voice parts does not exceed an octave and a tone, and there are no other musical difficulties that would prevent these chansons from being sung by amateur singers.

MUSICIANS OF THE NORTHERN RENAISSANCE

by *HENRY LELAND CLARKE*

EPOCHE Dufay—Epoche Ockenheim—Epoche Josquin." These designations still stand out as clear and useful although introduced 130 years ago by R. G. Kiesewetter, Viennese Imperial Councilor, in his *Geschichte der europäisch-abendländischen oder unsrer heutigen Musik* (1834).[1] The Dufay period, the period of Ockeghem, Josquin's generation—such expressions surpass in reasonableness the confused and conflicting national terms that have obscured even the latest discussions of 15th- and early 16th-century music.

To be sure Kiesewetter's nominations for some of the other periods would find few to second them today. Furthermore by singling out any one man he gives encouragement to the Great Man Theory. Not without reason Warren D. Allen asserts, "For Kiesewetter, the great man dictated the epoch." [2] If an individual is named in this way, he must be put forward explicitly as a representative man, not proposed for canonization. Assistance in this matter is given by Sir John Stainer's happy and widely adopted phrase, "Dufay and his Contemporaries." [3] Naming an epoch for even two outstanding men instead of just one helps to dispel any impression of one giant among pygmies. Thus Gustave Reese speaks of "The Period of Busnois and Ockeghem" as well as of "Josquin des Prez and his Contemporaries." [4]

Reese does explore the possibilities of national labels. "But perhaps it is just as well," he writes, "to avoid all the hairsplitting to which historians' use of national names for the successive generations has given rise, and simply to name them after their leading composers." [5] These judicious words should have been taken to heart by writers of the past ten years. *The New Oxford History of Music* follows well along this

---

[1] R. G. Kiesewetter, *Geschichte der europäisch-abendländlischen oder unsrer heutigen Musik* (Leipzig 1834), chapter headings.
[2] W. D. Allen, *Philosophies of Music History* (New York 1939), p. 87.
[3] J. F. R. Stainer, *Dufay and his Contemporaries* (London 1898).
[4] G. Reese, *Music in the Renaissance* (rev. ed. New York 1959), in chapter headings.
[5] *Ibid.*, p. 9.

path with *Dufay and his School* by Charles Van den Borren and *The Age of Ockeghem and Josquin* by Nanie Bridgman.[6] Proceeding along similar lines, the present discussion will divide Northern Renaissance music into "The Generation of Dufay and Binchois" (early 15th century), "The Generation of Busnois and Ockeghem" (late 15th century), and "The Generation of Josquin and Obrecht" (surviving into the 16th century).

But with most writers, unfortunately, the turmoil of nationalistic naming and counternaming continues unabated. The opening gun of this nationalistic epoch making was touched off by the same Councilor Kiesewetter in his very first published work, *Die Verdienste der Niederländer um die Tonkunst*, written expressly for (and receiving) the gold prize-medal of the Royal Netherlands Academy in Amsterdam in 1828.[7] From this work the classification, First Netherlands School, Second Netherlands School, and Third Netherlands School, has been handed down to students of music history right into our own day. Kiesewetter's effort could scarcely have been more poorly timed. Within two years, so musicians tell the story, the opera lovers at La Monnaie in Brussels transformed themselves effortlessly into a mob, rushed out into the streets, and throwing off the rule of the Royal Netherlands government, established the freedom of Belgium. What this meant for music history was that the only place associated with any of the Netherlands Schools that remained in Netherlands hands was Bergen op Zoom, home of Jacob Obrecht of Bergen. As will be emphasized further on, Obrecht was not so alien to the other composers of our chosen six as calling him "the only Netherlander" makes it appear.

Even before Belgian independence, the expression "Netherlands Schools" failed to indicate that the composers involved spoke French, at least professionally, and that they were deep recipients of French culture. Now that Belgium was a separate kingdom, the word *Netherlands* became more and more restricted to the northern provinces that remained loyal to King William I. And using it in the broader sense to include both countries became more and more misleading.

Music historians took some time to realize that the unadorned designation of Netherlands was obsolete in referring to leading composers of the 15th century. Waldo Selden Pratt, writing in 1907, still divides the "Netherlanders" into the three "groups of masters." But he is uneasy about it and adds:

---

[6] *Ars Nova and the Renaissance, 1300-1540, The New Oxford History of Music,* III, ed. Dom Anselm Hughes & Gerald Abraham (London 1960), chapter headings.
[7] R. G. Kiesewetter, *Die Verdienste der Niederländer um die Tonkunst* (Amsterdam 1829).

The period is here called that of the Netherlanders. It has also been called Flemish or Belgian, neither of which is quite satisfactory. It might also be called Burgundian, since from 1363 for over a century it owed much to the four great dukes, Philip the Bold (d. 1404), John the Fearless (d. 1419), Philip the Good (d. 1467), and Charles the Bold (d. 1477), all of whom were friends of culture, especially music and painting.[8]

Pratt's mild suggestion turned out to be prophetic. The vogue of the Burgundian begins innocently enough with Wilibald Gurlitt's publication, *Burgundische Chanson und deutsche Liedkunst* (1924).[9] Like the adjective "Scotch," "Burgundian" is much less objectionable applied to a thing—such as a song—than it is to a person. But in *Die Musik des Mittelalters und der Renaissance* (1931) Heinrich Besseler conjures up a "Burgundian School" composed of Dufay, Binchois, and their contemporaries. The later generations he continues to label "Netherlanders." [10] Once more the timing could not have been worse. Within two years of this formulation, the Western world became suddenly very sensitive about racial generalizations. In response to the irresponsible racism that had overtaken Berlin, group labels of every kind were thoroughly scrutinized by scholars in a position to do so.

It was precisely because he thought of Burgundian as dynastic—less racial than other possible terms—that Paul Henry Lang put forward the expression so forcefully in his teaching and writing.[11] In a special article on *The So-Called Netherlands School* (1939), he declares, "With our present knowledge of political and artistic history, we cannot retain the old designation and will substitute 'Burgundian School,' this term being more appropriate, as it does not refer to any specific 'racial' or national music but stands for a culture group of which the components are many and varied." [12] In spite of himself, however, Lang plunges deeper into the racial morass when, after pronouncing the generation of Dufay and Binchois "Burgundian," he grants the generation of Ockeghem and Busnois a "Flemish monopoly," emerging only in the generation of Josquin with "Franco-Flemish," a comparatively sane characterization of all these composers from the oldest to the youngest.[13]

Returning to the expression "Burgundian," are the "many and varied components" sufficiently represented by an appellation which, if ducal, is also provincial? On the one hand it fails to suggest French culture as a

[8] W. S. Pratt, *The History of Music* (New York 1907), p. 94.
[9] Wilibald Gurlitt, *Burgundische Chanson und deutsche Liedkunst* (Basel 1924).
[10] Heinrich Besseler, *Die Musik des Mittelalters und der Renaissance* (Potsdam 1931), pp. 184–227.
[11] P. H. Lang, *Music in Western Civilization* (New York 1941), pp. 181–83.
[12] P. H. Lang, *The So-Called Netherlands Schools*, in: MQ, XXV (1939), 53.
[13] *Ibid.*, p. 56.

whole, and on the other it fails to suggest the North, where this culture was enhanced and carried into life.

If workable alternatives can be found, it would be better to do away with the term "Burgundian School" altogether. The most urgent reason for abolishing it is to liberate students—and scholars—from what can only be called the Dijon Complex. Mention of Burgundy inevitably conjures up a vision of Dijon, on the route from Paris to Geneva, where Philip the Good's ancestors lived from the 11th century on and where his father and grandfather are magnificently buried. The ancient citadel outlined against the low vine-covered slopes of the Côte d'Or cannot be forgotten. Referring to the seizure of the old duchy of Burgundy by Louis XI in 1477, Nanie Bridgman writes, "Dijon, the musical centre of the previous generation, reverted to the kingdom of France." [14]

Admittedly Dijon was an intellectual center in the days of Philip the Good's predecessors: art historians even speak of the sculptor Claus Sluter (d. 1406) as founding the "Burgundian School of Dijon." But serious music was no more cultivated in Dijon than was fine painting. These arts were concentrated in the northern provinces. The only great musician Dijon produced was Rameau, who was not born until 1683.

The magic of Dijon transmuted André Pirro's simple statement that Dufay, as a canon of Cambrai Cathedral, was intrusted with a mission to the Court of Burgundy in October 1446.[15] Embroidering Pirro, Guillaume de Van, editor of Dufay's works, asserts, "Dufay was *at Dijon* in October 1446, on a *diplomatic* mission." [16] All Dufay had to do was to go down to Brussels where Philip was ensconced in his palace during that entire month. Indeed from June, when he was briefly in Ghent, to November 18, when he began to stay in Louvain, the Duke scarcely set foot outside Brussels for anything more demanding than an outing to the Bois de la Cambre (November 6). Furthermore his last visit to the old family seat in Dijon had been three years earlier, and he would not get there again until eight years later. Herman Vander Linden, to whom we are indebted for these details, has traced the itineraries of the Duke throughout his entire reign (1433–67) and shows him at Dijon only in 14 out of the total of 34 years.[17]

The Court of Burgundy under Philip the Good was peripatetic, his

[14] *New Oxford History of Music*, III, 240.
[15] André Pirro, *Histoire de la musique de la fin du XIVe siècle à la fin du XVIe* (Paris 1940), p. 87, citing Cambrai, MS 1058, fol. 80.
[16] Guglielmus Dufay, *Opera Omnia*, edidit Guglielmus de Van, II (Rome 1948), xxiii. (Emphasis added.)
[17] Herman Vander Linden, *Itinéraires de Philippe le Bon, duc de Bourgogne (1419–1467), et de Charles, comte de Charolais (1433–1467)* (Bruxelles 1940), index, p. 514.

favorite residences being the respective capitals of French Flanders, West Flanders, East Flanders, and Brabant: Lille, Bruges, Ghent, and, especially in the latter half of his reign, Brussels. Choice, business, war, and bloody conflicts with his own prosperous, rebellious burghers kept Philip on the move, but as much as possible within the ambit here described. As for Charles the Bold, while born in Dijon, he seldom went back. Brussels was definitively the chief dwelling place of Charles and of his daughter, Mary of Burgundy, whose marriage turned her House over to the Habsburgs. Therefore to call an exclusively Northern group of Philip's subjects Burgundian seems from this distance almost quixotic. No one has seriously proposed that J. S. Bach be called a Polish composer because his sovereign, Frederick Augustus II, Elector of Saxony, bore a still higher title, Augustus III, King of Poland.

Granting, however, that service at the ducal court made one a "Burgundian," which of our composers was eligible? The musical counterpart of Jan van Eyck (c. 1390–1441), founder of Flemish painting and *valet de chambre* of Philip the Good, was Gilles Binchois (c. 1400–60), chaplain of the Burgundian court chapel from 1430 to 1456. In the next generation, Antoine Busnois was in the service of Charles the Bold even before his accession as Duke in 1467 and continued at the Burgundian chapel under Mary of Burgundy until her death in 1482. But there is no record of any regular position at the court held either by Binchois's contemporary, Dufay, or by Busnois's contemporary, Ockeghem. Even by this definition then the "Burgundian School" is shadowy and certainly no criterion for distinguishing one generation from another.

Few patrons of the arts have been more colorful than Philip, Grand Duke of the West, Grand Master of the Order of the Golden Fleece. His prosperity, based on the trade and industry of the Northern towns, encouraged painting and music that combined appeal with technique as never before. But he paid for his art, rather than generating it. As a matter of record he regarded musicians as suitable ingredients for a pasty. At the *Banquet du voeu,* it will be remembered, one course was "a pie within which were 28 live persons, playing various instruments, each when his turn came." [18]

The flamboyant and itinerant Burgundian court was no wellspring of serious education. The Duke of Burgundy was a consumer of musicians; we must look elsewhere for institutions capable of producing them. First and foremost among these were the choir schools of the two great dioceses east of the Scheldt, Liège and Cambrai. The cathedral choir-

[18] Translated from Jeanne Marix, *Histoire de la musique et des musiciens de la cour de Bourgogne sous le règne de Philippe le Bon* (Strasbourg 1939), p. 38.

masters discovered youngsters and made musicians out of them. They provided singers not only for the ducal choir across the Scheldt in Flanders, but also for the papal choir across the Alps in Rome.

The diocese of Liège provided Rome with predecessors and colleagues of Dufay and later gave Jacob Obrecht his start. If, however, we look for ecclesiastical patrons to match the dukes of Burgundy, we find them only in the bishops of Cambrai. It is not too much to say that the two foci of Northern Renaissance music were the Cathedral of Cambrai and, to the north of it, the Court of Burgundy, moving like a pendulum from Bruges to Ghent to Brussels with periodic digressions to Lille, capital of *la Flandre gallicante*. Association with either the Court or the Cathedral was sufficient guarantee of some contact with both French and Flemish culture.

The term "Franco-Flemish," therefore, fits the chief Northern Renaissance musicians with a snugness that is out of the question for either "Netherlandish" or "Burgundian." If any cultural delimitation is to be used at all, this is it.

French was the language of the Court, but it sat in Lille, which was Flemish geographically; in Brussels, which was Flemish linguistically; and in Bruges and Ghent, which were Flemish in every sense of the word. Thus while its manners were French, its setting was Flemish.

As for the other focus, the ancient Cameracus, seat of a bishop since the 4th century, became the Flemish Kamerik on the Schelde. When the English named the fine, woven cloth they imported from the town "cambric," they showed their familiarity with the name in Flemish. As time went on it became Cambrai on the Escaut, French-speaking but still a part of the Holy Roman Empire of the German Nation.

The Bishop of Cambrai presided over a diocese mixed in population and sweeping in extent. Until 1559 it stretched down the right bank of the Scheldt, to use the English name of the Franco-Flemish river, from source to mouth. It reached the North Sea beyond Antwerp but stopped short of Bergen op Zoom, which belonged to its eastern neighbor, the diocese of Liège.[19] The diocese of Cambrai can claim as natives Dufay, Binchois, and Ockeghem, not to mention Hayne van Ghiseghem, Tinctoris, Heinrich Isaac, Cipriano de Rore, and Roland de Lassus. And Josquin and Obrecht also made their contributions to its musical activity.

Cambrai played a vital role in transmitting Parisian civilization northward. In 1398 Pierre d'Ailly, who had been chancellor of the University of Paris (1385-95), became Bishop of Cambrai. This man's influential

[19] Théo Luykx, *Atlas historique et culturel de la Belgique* (Bruxelles 1959), map facing p. 26.

Places associated with musicians of the Northern Renaissance

ideas gave Columbus support in his contention that the world was round and led the authorities to reform the calendar into its present shape. His actions were decisive factors in condemning Jan Huss to the stake and in healing the Great Schism of the West. Such a man must have left a permanent stamp on the cathedral of which he was bishop.

Under his regime, Nicolas Malin, master of the choirboys, secured the services of a promising young musician, Wilhelmus named Dufay. The words "natus est ipse Fay" in Dufay's motet *Salve flos Tuscae gentis* certainly convey the impression that Fay was his birthplace, not just the name he was born with.[20] It is widely asserted that he was born in the county of Hainaut. Close examination of a detailed map of France, Belgium, and Holland discloses no Fay in Hainaut, but it does show one Fayt, now a separate commune named Fayt-lez-Manage in the canton of Seneffe and provostship of Binche.[21] If Dufay (also known as du Fayt and Doufayt) was born here, near the ancient priory of Saint-Nicolas-au-Bois,[22] his birthplace is only 6 miles from Binche and 12 miles from

---

[20] *Dufay*, in: *Riemann Musik Lexikon*, 12th ed., Wilibald Gurlitt, ed. (Mainz 1959), I, 427; musical score in Dufay, *Opera Omnia*, I² (1948), 68.

[21] United States Board on Geographical Names, *Gazetteer to Maps of France, Belgium, & Holland* (Washington, D. C. 1944), *5/J51, Lat 50 30 N, Long 4 14 E.

[22] Léopold Devillers, *Cartulaire des comtes de Hainaut* (Bruxelles), V (1892), 503n; VI (1896), index, p. 812.

Mons, where his colleague Binchois was born. On this basis they were
boyhood neighbors long before the familiar miniature depicted them
together in Martin Le Franc's *Champion des dames* (1440)[23] and long
before the particular reunion they had as canons of Saint-Waudru in
Mons, recorded as taking place in 1449.[24] The presence of the silent *t* in
Fayt is outweighed by the fact that it is two syllables, as verses about the
composer show the "fay" in his name should be. When old records spell
the name with an i, a dieresis is placed over the *i* to show the syllabifica-
tion: *Le faït.*[25]

Of course it is still possible that Dufay came from one of the French
communities actually spelled Fay. If so, the one likely spot is Fay just
south of the Somme River between Amiens and Saint-Quentin.[26] The
musical importance of the latter city will be commented on later, and
this Fay is actually a bit closer to Dufay's destination, Cambrai, than
Fayt-lez-Manage. But the decision surely goes to Fayt-lez-Manage, fulfilling the generally accepted view that Hainaut was his native county.
Among musicians Dufay was supreme at the cathedral and Binchois at
the court. While Dufay was no doubt well known to the Duke and his
establishment he was more closely associated with another member of
the Duke's family—at least officially.

There is a nice symmetry about the fact that the three leading composers of the early 15th century were in the service of the three most
prominent offspring of John the Fearless, Duke of Burgundy. And here
we include with Dufay and Binchois, their somewhat older colleague
from whom they learned so much, John Dunstable, also a musician of
the Northern Renaissance if Northern can be stretched across the English Channel. John Dunstable was in the entourage of Anne of Burgundy, the first lady of Paris, and her husband, John, Duke of Bedford,
who ruled France north of the Loire as regent for the English child
king Henry VI. Binchois served Philip of Burgundy. And for the last
34 years of his life (with some leaves of absence) Dufay served as
canon of the Cathedral of Cambrai while Philip's bastard brother, John
of Burgundy was bishop.[27] Thus Dufay was not unconnected with the

[23] Reproduced in D. J. Grout, *A History of Western Music* (New York 1960),
p. 143; standard cover for *Revue belge de musicologie*.
[24] *Binchois,* in: *Grove's Dictionary of Music and Musicians* (5th ed. London
1954), I, 710.
[25] M.-A. Arnould, *Les dénombrements de foyers dans le comté de Hainaut,*
XIVe–XVIe siècle (Bruxelles 1956), pp. 680–81.
[26] *Gazetteer,* *5/N45, Lat 49 53 N, Long 2 48 E.
[27] Pius Bonifacius Gams, *Series episcoporum ecclesiae catholicae* (Graz 1957),
p. 527. "Joannes VI de Bourgogne" was bishop from 1440 to 1479.

House of Burgundy. Above all, however, he must be regarded as the "Cambrai master."

More is known about the origins of Gilles Binchois (c. 1400–60). His father, Jean de Binch, was named after Binche, the town where the family came from. At his birth they must have been living in the capital city Mons, where Jean was councilor to Duke William IV of Bavaria, Count of Hainaut. After the Duke's death in 1417 Jean retained the same functions for Marguerite of Burgundy, the dowager Duchess, and was especially attached to Jacqueline of Bavaria, now Countess of Hainaut.[28]

From this it can be seen that young Gilles was brought up close to weighty affairs of state—weighty indeed since serious consequences resulted from the unhappy Jacqueline's flight from her husband and her country to become the bride of Humphrey, Duke of Gloucester, Bedford's brother and then the ruler of England. When Gloucester attempted to take over Hainaut, Philip's fury was one of the causes of his switching from the English to the French side in the Treaty of Arras (1435).[29] In the meantime Gilles had been a soldier, serving the Duke of Norfolk—a commander in action in France who probably did not have time to take him home to England with him as has been suggested.[30] Binchois became a priest and entered the service of Philip the Good in time to compose a motet in honor of Philip's short-lived son Anthony, born not long after Philip's marriage to Isabella of Portugal in 1430.[31] Most faithfully Burgundian in length of service of the musicians of his generation, Binchois, like the rest, was a man of French culture in a Flemish environment.

In the next generation, Busnois was the Frenchman going to spend his life in Flanders, and Ockeghem the Fleming going to spend his life in France. There is only one Busne, and it must be the town of origin of our composer, who was called Antoine de Busne. This little market town is located near the Aire Canal between Béthune and St. Omer,[32] two places where the Count of Charolais stopped with some frequency be-

---

[28] Devillers, *op. cit.*, IV (1889), 83.

[29] *Philip the Good*, in: *Encyclopaedia Britannica* (11th ed.), XXI, 387.

[30] *Binchois*, in: *Riemann Musik Lexikon*, I, 166; *Suffolk, William de la Pole, Duke of*, in: *Encyclopaedia Britannica*, XXVI, 27. Suffolk "returned to England in November 1431, after fourteen years' continuous service in the field."

[31] Giving 30 September 1430 as the date of Anthony's birth is an error handed down from Enguerrand de Monstrelet (c. 1390–1453), Provost of Cambrai (Monstrelet, *Chronicles*, transl. Thomas Johnes, 1809, II, 398). Anthony was actually born at the palace in Brussels on 30 December 1430 and baptized across the square in the church of Saint-Jacques-sur-Caudenberghe on 18 January 1431. (Devillers, *op. cit.*, V [1892], xii, fn. 3.)

[32] *Gazetteer*, *2/H33, Lat 50 35 N, Long 2 31 E.

fore he became the Duke of Burgundy.[33] Where young Antoine, who was a poet as well as a musician, got his education is unknown; but it is not surprising to find him already in the employ of Charles the Bold at the time of his accession (1467).[34]

Johannes Ockeghem on the other hand was surely born in Flanders, if on the extreme eastern edge of it and within the diocese of Cambrai. Again there is only one Okegem (as it is now spelled), a village about 13 miles due west of Brussels.[35] This must be where the family came from, although so many members of it lived in Termonde (about 13 miles north of Okegem, but still on the right bank of the Scheldt River) that there is a strong supposition that our Ockeghem was born there.[36] A choirboy in Antwerp in 1443–44 and a pupil of Dufay at Cambrai in 1449, he became the chief musical figure in France, chaplain and composer to Charles VII, Louis XI, and Charles VIII. Thus in opposite directions Busnois and Ockeghem are strictly and literally Franco-Flemish.

Josquin Desprez (c. 1445–1521) has been called French. He has been called Flemish and one of the Netherlanders. In his own day the Italians called him French, using expressions like "da Francia," "francese," and "gallus." A St. Gall manuscript styles him "belga veromanduus"; a passport of the court of the Sforzas, "picardus." [37] These last two point in the direction of Saint-Quentin, capital of the ancient county of Vermandois, which had by that time been absorbed as part of Picardy.

The earliest specific information we have about Josquin places him as a choirboy at the collegiate church in Saint-Quentin.[38] The only further clue we have to his birthplace is his name and the acrostic on it in his motet *Illibata Dei virgo*.[39] With nice and perhaps intentional ambiguity the first stanza yields two possible spellings of his name. By taking strictly the first letter only of each line of verse, it reads JOSQVIN-DPREZ—so one would pronounce "Josquin de Prez." But by adding the second and third letters of the line beginning with D, it becomes JOSQVINDESPREZ, that is, "Josquin Desprez." In either case the Z is distinctive and is confirmed by the spelling "Desprez" in a communication to Margaret of Austria written in 1507.[40]

From this it would seem that Josquin, or at least his family, might

[33] Vander Linden, *op. cit.*, index, pp. 526, 532.
[34] Reese, *op. cit.*, p. 101.
[35] *Gazetteer*, *2/J45, Lat 50 52 N, Long 4 04 E.
[36] Dragan Plamenac, *Ockeghem*, in: MGG, IX (1961), 1826.
[37] Helmuth Osthoff, *Josquin Desprez*, MGG, VII (1958), 191.
[38] *Loc. cit.*
[39] Written out in Caldwell Titcomb, *The Josquin Acrostic Re-examined*, in: JAMS, XVI (1963), 50 and 54.
[40] According to Héméré, Richelieu's librarian, quoted by Reese, *op. cit.*, p. 228.

have come from a village named Prez. Since he is first heard of at Saint-Quentin, a picture presented itself of finding the word Prez in the vicinity of that musical city. The detailed map of France, Belgium, and Holland revealed no De Pres, Des Pres, Du Pres, Le Pres, or Pres. There was one Les Pres about 40 miles south of Grenoble. Of two places with the distinctive spelling of Prez, one is a remote spot on the Marne surely irrelevant to the geography in hand.[41] The other turned out as predicted to be near Saint-Quentin, about 48 miles east and a little to the south, 17 miles almost due south of Chimay in Hainaut, but clearly a hamlet whose inhabitants would regard Saint-Quentin as their metropolis.[42]

Either his birth in Prez or his upbringing in the choir school at Saint-Quentin would be enough to explain Josquin's designations as "belga veromanduus" and "picardus." But it is not regarded as an accident that some lines in the second stanza of the famous acrostic produce the combination ESCAU. The puzzle seems to be trying to communicate something about his connection with the river Escaut, known in English as the Scheldt.

This irresistibly obscure acrostic leads every imaginative student to produce an interpretation that tends to satisfy himself and few others. The words that the initial letters yield in the clear are all in French. This is one reason for resisting the macaronic intrusions from the Flemish suggested by Charles Van den Borren and from the Latin by Caldwell Titcomb.[43] By a procedure involving the initials of half-lines and some manipulation, the latter comes out with *Ad caput fluvii Escau* ("At the head of the river Escau"). The derivation is shaky, but the conclusion is hospitable to the idea that Josquin came from the region containing the headwaters of the Scheldt, namely, Vermandois.

For what it is worth, an all-French alternative is offered here. The initial letters of the stanza in question, ACAVVESCAVGA, may be read

à C(ondé), au V, Escau(t) ga(llicant)

The proposed interpretation is: "at Condé at the V, or junction, of the river Escaut in its French part" as opposed to its Flemish part lower down. Perhaps the word "gallicant" is too recondite—but the Flanders around Lille is called "la Flandre gallicante"[44] to distinguish French Flanders from Flanders proper. Any other GA word meaning French,

[41] *Gazetteer*, 17/Z 09, Lat 48 34 N, Long 5 03 E.
[42] *Gazetteer*, *5/0 53, Lat 49 48 N, Long 4 21 E.
[43] Titcomb, *op. cit.*, pp. 54–55, 57–59.
[44] Arnould, *op. cit.*, p. 4.

such as "gallois," would do to provide a putative family ZIP code. As for the V, the one important confluence in the French-speaking part of the Scheldt valley is at Condé—with the river Haine after which the county of Hainaut is named. This is "Gallic" as opposed to the Flemish forks down river.

The way is still open for more convincing interpretations, but all agree that the acrostic appears to connect Josquin at some point with the Escaut. He might have been born in Condé and somehow snatched off to Saint-Quentin to be a choirboy there instead of at the closer and greater choir school at Cambrai. More likely his birthplace, or at least his family home, was at Prez, and that as a Vermandois boy he began his musical career at its capital, Saint-Quentin. Residence on the banks of the Escaut would come later, perhaps not until he was provost at Condé and often went up to the cathedral at Cambrai to "verify" his compositions.[45]

Our information concerning Josquin's connection with the Flemish-speaking world is confined chiefly to his nickname and to what appears to have been largely a non-resident appointment as canon of St. Gudule in Brussels.[46] Condé-sur-Escaut, like the rest of Hainaut, spoke a Picard dialect of French.[47] And this, Josquin's final resting place, is now a part of France proper. But the county of Dufay and Binchois is Flemish in the broader sense, and like them Josquin may be regarded without question as Franco-Flemish.

Into Josquin's generation—where he belongs—recent writing has put Jacob Obrecht of Bergen (c. 1450–1505), usually with the label "the only true Netherlander" among musicians of his age. But there is no reason to exaggerate Obrecht's Dutchness. To be sure, his town, Bergen op Zoom, is inside the boundaries of the present-day kingdom of the Netherlands. Yet its associations were not with the northern lowlands, but with Antwerp, some 25 miles up river along the mouth of the Scheldt, where Obrecht later served at Notre-Dame. The original dialect form of his name, Hobrecht, is strikingly close to that of Jan van Eyck's older brother Huybrecht. Both were namesakes of Hubert, 8th-century Bishop of Liège, patron saint of the hunt. The painter brothers came from Liège itself, some now believe, and Bergen op Zoom was the northern outpost of the diocese of Liège. It was also the northern outpost of the duchy of Brabant, in the capital of which, Brussels, the House of Burgundy held court.

[45] Vladimir Fédorov, *Cambrai*, MGG, II (1952), 704
[46] Reese, *op. cit.*, p. 229.
[47] Arnould, *op. cit.*, p. 4.

If Obrecht of Bergen was not born in Bergen op Zoom (there is some thought that he was born in Sicily where his father stopped on a pilgrimage), at least it was his cradle. He must have received excellent musical instruction, perhaps as a cathedral choirboy at either Cambrai or Liège. He became a priest and sang his first Mass at Bergen op Zoom in 1480,[48] the very year that his lord, Henry of Bergen, was appointed Bishop of Cambrai.[49]

In strong contrast to John of Burgundy, a rather absent bishop, Henry was a man of force, authority, and culture. He served as Chancelor of the Golden Fleece, performed the marriage ceremony for Philip the Fair and Joanna of Spain, and persuaded all warring parties to respect the neutrality of his church lands around Cambrai.[50] He brought Obrecht from his own domain to take charge of the choirboys at the Cathedral in 1484. He engaged Erasmus of Rotterdam as his secretary and in 1495 sent him to the University of Paris.[51]

In the spring of 1496 these two brilliant but erratic protégés of the Bishop, one a singing priest in Antwerp, the other a student in Paris, fell ill and came back to Bergen op Zoom to recuperate.[52] Obrecht had long since been dismissed from his position in Cambrai, charged with negligence in looking after the choirboys. Erasmus had found the rigors of student life in Paris too much for him. This convalescent summer in Bergen op Zoom provides the obvious locale for Obrecht's teaching Erasmus as attested by the latter's pupil Glarean in his *Dodecachordon*. No need to postulate a meeting in Utrecht, Cambrai, or Bruges. Undoubtedly the two ailing prodigals had much in common, and Erasmus could be counted on to learn all he could from a gifted older contemporary.

Like the other composers discussed, Obrecht had his French side and his Flemish side. When French Cambrai dismissed him, it was Flemish Bruges that took him up. And like his contemporary Josquin he carried the music of the North to foreign parts—in his case to Ferrara where he was swept away by the plague in 1505.

The musicians we have discussed are only six out of a whole galaxy of men north of Paris whose creative musical activity spread throughout Western Europe during the 15th and 16th centuries. Neither the six nor

[48] *Obrecht*, in: *Grove's Dictionary*, VI, 169.
[49] Gams, *loc. cit.* (fn. 27 above).
[50] J. J. Mangan, *Life, Character, & Influence of Desiderius Erasmus of Rotterdam* (New York 1927), I, 49.
[51] *Ibid.*, I, 54.
[52] *Obrecht*, in: *Grove's Dictionary*, VI, 170; Johan Huizinga, *Erasmus* (New York 1924), p. 31.

the many can be divided into generations on cultural or regional grounds. Each generation may be named chronologically or by its representative figures. Calling these musicians Netherlandish distorts their image to the north; Burgundian distorts it to the south. If they are French, they are also Flemish. If they are Flemish, they are also French. Call them—but call all of them—"Franco-Flemish." Or, better still, let them be the musicians of the Northern Renaissance.

Unhappily the habit of calling early 15th-century music "Burgundian" is so entrenched that writers who dare to challenge it arm themselves with interrogation points. "Peut-on parler d'une école bourguignonne?" inquires Vladimir Fédorov.[53] "École bourguignonne, école néerlandaise ou début de la Renaissance?" demands Floris Van der Mueren.[54] Surely the last of these alternatives is the most congenial. Let us divide the musicians of the Northern Renaissance into Early Renaissance and Late Renaissance. For this, something more than history and geography is needful. If these stylistic concepts are to be applied meaningfully to music, they must justify their position in time and space by the nature of the music itself.

The chief criterion for musical periodization is texture, the most stable element in the procession of music through the years. Renaissance texture is incontrovertibly polyphonic texture. In its broadest sense, however, polyphony embraces all music for more than one voice from the *Musical Handbook* of the 9th century to the *Musical Offering* of the 18th. To narrow it down, this Polyphonic Age can be divided into five periods. The word *diaphonic* describes the note-against-note writing of the Romanesque Period; *metaphonic*, the music added to a cut-and-dried cantus firmus in the Gothic Period; and *amphonic*, the music of opposed outer voices that distinguishes the Baroque Period. These are the first two and the last periods of the Polyphonic Age.

The third period, Early Renaissance (some would say Ars nova or late Gothic), and the fourth period, Late Renaissance, divide the interval from 1300 to 1600 between them. The former is the period of *independent polyphony*, in which each voice is separate but equal. If there is a cantus firmus, it is no longer a structural, mathematically conceived ingredient, but a melody among melodies.[55] This *Allophonic* Period ("sounding different") has its experimental phase in the freer writings of

[53] Vladimir Fédorov, *Peut-on parler d'une école bourguignonne de musique au XVᵉ siècle?*, in: *Les Cahiers techniques de l'art*, II (1949), 29.
[54] Floris Van der Mueren, *École bourguignonne, école néerlandaise ou début de la Renaissance?*, in: *Revue belge de musicologie*, XII (1958), 53.
[55] Cf. E. H. Sparks, *Cantus Firmus in Mass and Motet, 1420–1520* (Berkeley 1963), p. 2.

Machaut and the Florentine *trecento* and its established phase, at its best, in the chansons of Dufay and Binchois. The Late Renaissance is signalized by the advent of systematic *imitative polyphony*. This *Periphonic Period* ("sounding around") begins in the experimental imitation of Ockeghem's generation and establishes itself in the pervading imitation of Josquin and his contemporaries. Periphony prolongs its established phase in the Epoche W i l l a e r t, Generation of Willaert and Festa, and reaches its elaborate culmination in the Epoche P a l e s t r i n a, Generation of Lassus and Palestrina. As the arbiter of music in Venice, Willaert symbolizes the diffusion of Franco-Flemish musicians throughout Europe. Lang's map in *Music in Western Civilization* has demonstrated unforgettably how overwhelming that diffusion was.[56] Festa marks the rise of native Italians capable of winning back the leading musical positions from Franco-Flemish competitors. Lassus speaks for the moment when the outstanding Northern musician has to share top place with an Italian of equal stature, Palestrina.

While music grew great in Italy, the Low Countries were in the hands of Philip II of Spain. Alarmed at the spread of Lutheranism, he determined to establish an unshakable center of Roman Catholic power in the North. At his instance, Paul IV reorganized the bishoprics and installed Antoine Perrenot de Granvella as archbishop of the new province of Malines (1559).[57] The diocese of Cambrai, immemorially Franco-Flemish, was shorn of its Flemish-speaking territory.[58] Though the Bishop of Cambrai was advanced to archbishop in compensation, the Archbishop of Malines assumed and held the real ecclesiastical power.

The sees of Cambrai and Liège sank into insignificance, and the humanist traditions established by bishops like Pierre d'Ailly and Henry of Bergen were a thing of the past. As prime minister of the regent, Margaret of Parma, Granvella infuriated all Northern patriots, whatever their religion, by imposing the Spanish Inquisition and quartering Spanish troops upon the inhabitants.[59] Repression and conflict settled on the land.

The Roman Catholic North was no longer in a position to bring forth creative geniuses for export. When Lassus died in 1594, the end had come for musicians of the Northern Renaissance.

[56] Lang, *Music in Western Civilization*, between pp. 240–41.
[57] *Granvella*, in: *Encyclopaedia Britannica*, XII, 361.
[58] M. Cartier, *Cambrai (Diocèse)*, in: *Dictionnaire d'histoire et de géographie ecclésiastiques*, XI, 554.
[59] *Granvelle*, in: *The Columbia Encyclopedia* (2nd ed.), p. 806.

SURVIVALS OF
RENAISSANCE THOUGHT
IN FRENCH THEORY 1610–1670:
A BIBLIOGRAPHICAL STUDY

by ALBERT COHEN

USICAL THOUGHT in 17th-century France was dominated by the work of two important theorists: Marin
Mersenne (1588–1648) and Sébastien de Brossard (1655–
1730). Mersenne, steeped in humanistic doctrine, was an encyclopaedist
with a universal outlook, a neo-Platonist who sought to bring discipline
and order to knowledge of music—not as a distinct, separate art but (to
use the words of Tyard) as an "image of the whole encyclopaedia." [1]
As such, "Mersenne's works provide . . . the most certain of all our
links between seventeenth-century thought and the sixteenth-century
academies." [2] Brossard, on the other hand, was a practitioner of the art
of music. He was a composer and lexicographer whose major works
reveal him to be a traditionalist with an interest in cataloguing musical
thought and practice rather than in seeking to form them.

The distinction made is a significant one, for it characterizes the
difference in the underlying philosophies of the periods dominated by
these men. The abstract, idealized music that formed the theoretical
basis for the first part of the century (until about 1660–70)—founded
upon Renaissance practice—reflected not only "an age that turned to
geometry for an expression of truth and beauty," [3] but also one during
which theory and practice were often divorced from each other.

---

[1] Pontus de Tyard, *Discours philosophiques* (Paris 1587), quoted in Frances A.
Yates, *The French Academies of the Sixteenth Century* (London 1947), p. 285. See
further Kathleen M. Hall, *Pontus de Tyard and his Discours Philosophiques* (London 1963), p. 81ff. Concerning Mersenne's interest in a *"dictionnaire international de
musique,"* see Robert Lenoble, *Mersenne, ou la naissance du mécanisme* (Paris 1943),
p. 592.
[2] Yates, *The French Academies*, p. 284. See also D. P. Walker, *Musical Humanism
in the 16th and Early 17th Centuries*, in: *The Music Review*, II (1941), 10ff.
[3] Arthur W. Locke, *Descartes and Seventeenth-Century Music*, in: *The Musical
Quarterly*, XXI (1935), 426.

82

Indeed, for some theorists, the philosophy and aesthetics of music were of more significance than was music itself. Mersenne, as *Question IV* of his *Questions harmoniques* (Paris 1634), debates: "A sçavoir si la pratique de la musique est préférable à la théorie; et si l'on doit faire plus d'estat de celuy qui ne sçait que composer, ou chanter, que de celuy qui ne sçait que la raison de la musique." [4] He does, finally, conclude: "la spéculation d'un art est inutile . . . si l'on ne la réduit en pratique," [5] but not without deliberation.

Annibal Gantez, concerning the "différence qu'il y a entre les Théoriciens & les Praticiens," writes: "Toutesfois je voy beaucoup de choses que Messieurs les Théoriciens déffendent que néantmoins sont les meilleurs," [6] ridiculing theorists who write about music without having composed any themselves. He also derides "Astrologiens, Mathématiciens, Arithméticiens, & autres qui disent que la Musique est une partie de toutes celles-là." [7]

For theorists of the period, composers whose works served as ideal models for composition were those of the Renaissance, the most favored being Josquin Des Prez, Orlando di Lasso, Claude Le Jeune, and Eustache Du Caurroy. To Du Caurroy, perhaps the most celebrated French composer of the early 17th century, music was a "science faisant partie des mathématiques," which could be understood only "par la lecture des bons autheurs & pratique des anciens," [8] a humanistic view taken by many composers of the period, some of whom were theorists as well as composers.[9]

The most honored of theorists was Gioseffo Zarlino, from whom (notes Mersenne) "Du Caurroy & tous les autres [compositeurs], médiatement, ou immédiatement, ont puisé tout ce qu'ils sçavent de pratique." [10] Extended discussions of ancient Greek music [11] and of the

[4] Mersenne, *Questions harmoniques*, p. 226.

[5] *Ibid.*, p. 227.

[6] Annibal Gantez, *L'Entretien des musiciens* (Auxerre 1643, ed. E. Thoinan 1878), p. 109.

[7] *Ibid.*, p. 106.

[8] Eustache Du Caurroy, *Preces ecclesiasticae* (Paris 1609), dedication.

[9] See, for example, Charles Guillet, *Institution harmonique* (Vienna, Österreichische Nationalbibliothek, MS Sm 2376), p. 2; Antoine Du Cousu, *La Musique universelle* (Paris 1658), p. 2; Guillaume-Gabriel Nivers, *Traité de la composition de musique* (Paris 1667), p. 7; Jean Titelouze, *Hymnes de l'église* (Paris 1623), *au lecteur*, and in letters to Mersenne, in: *Correspondance du P. Marin Mersenne*, I (1932 & 1945), 72ff and *passim*. It would be interesting to know if Jacques Mauduit—whom we may likewise regard as a composer-theorist (see entry below)—shared this view also.

[10] Marin Mersenne, *Harmonie universelle* (Paris 1636–37), *Livre cinquiesme de la composition de musique*, p. 283.

[11] Of interest among editions of Greek theorists current during the period are those by Artus Thomas (Sieur d'Embry), *Philostrate de la vie d'Apollonius*

teachings of Guido d'Arezzo are commonplace in this theory, and there are at least as many non-musicians writing on music as there are musicians (indeed, from about 1610 to 1640, seemingly more). Considerations of musical acoustics were basically thought to belong to the realms of physics and mathematics.[12]

In volume and depth of study, but often not in subject matter, the treatises from the period under discussion contrast sharply with those that appeared in France during the 16th century (a slight production devoted principally to elementary instruction manuals and abstract essays).[13] Manuals dealing with the basic elements of music continue to appear, as do tutors in the art of singing and dancing. But as in the 16th century, so in the 17th, there is little intended for the practicing musician, at least until about 1660. A distinct literature devoted to the modes also appears, reflecting general confusion in regard to modal organization and terminology.[14] Sets of pieces organized by modes—serving as both collections of music and treatises dealing with the modes—are not uncommon in France at this time.[15] Concern with simplification of musical notation and of methods of solmization is likewise apparent during this period, a concern that seems to have occupied French theorists as well into the 18th century.[16]

Thyanéen (Paris 1611), which includes a *Discours sur les douze modes* (Ch. 16), excerpts from which are found in Paris, Bibl. Nat., fonds fr. n. a. 4673, fols. 41–46; and Ismaël Boulliau, *Theonis Smyrnaei Platonici, eorum, quae in mathematicis ad Platonis lectionem utilia sunt, expositio* (Paris 1644), in which the second of two treatises, entitled *De musica* (p. 73), is supplied with extensive notes by the author (p. 247).

[12] Mersenne frequently conferred with scientist friends in solving acoustical problems. For example, the division of the octave into 12 equal parts, which had been of concern to both Zarlino and Salinas and was the subject of much controversy among Mersenne and his correspondents (see *Correspondance*, IV, 149), was a problem that the theorist set before the mathematician Jean de Beaugrand and the astronomer Ismaël Boulliau. He employed their findings in his own publications. (These findings, as well as other solutions to the problem, are reviewed in *Correspondance*, IV, 435–37.)

[13] A brief description of a sampling of French treatises from the 16th century is given in *Exposition de la musique française*, publ. by the Bibl. Nat. (Paris 1934), pp. 36–39. See also Åke Davidsson, *Bibliographie der musiktheoretischen Drucke des 16. Jahrhunderts* (Baden-Baden 1962), *passim*.

[14] That contemporary theorists realized this confusion is evident in Denis Dodart's *De la musique* (Paris, Bibl. Nat., MS fonds fr. 14,852), fol. 75, where after discussing the differing modal organizations, the author writes, "toute cette distribution est fort arbitraire." See further Jacques Chailley, *L'Imbroglio des modes* (Paris 1960), pp. 7off.

[15] For example, Charles Guillet, *Vingt-quatre fantasies à quatre parties disposées suivant l'ordre des douze modes* (Paris 1610); Arthus Auxcousteau, *Les Quatrains de Mathieu mis en musique à trois parties, selon l'ordre des douze modes* (Paris 1636); Charles Racquet's *Douze modes à deux parties*, printed in Mersenne, *Harmonie universelle, Livre cinquiesme de la composition de musique*, pp. 284–89.

[16] See George Lange, *Zur Geschichte der Solmisation*, in: *Sammelbände der Internationalen Musikgesellschaft*, I (1899–1900), 586ff. Philippe-Joseph Caffiaux,

About 1670, the musical climate of France changed in an important way. Supported by Louis XIV, Lully had become the dominant musical force at the court; the French Académie de Musique (the *Opéra*) was formally established in 1669, shortly after the Académie de Danse (1661); and interest in court music and concerts spread, generally. The role of theory changed, too. No longer dominated in production by academicians, treatises written by leading practitioners of the day began to reflect matters of practical significance and value. They dealt with theory in terms that were not merely extensions of Renaissance thought, but rather were expressions of the unique contribution to music of the French Baroque.

A Bibliography of French Theory 1610–1670

"French theory" as interpreted here includes works appearing in France during the period indicated that deal with music in specific terms and that primarily serve pedagogical, philosophical, or scientific purposes. Editions of earlier treatises, in particular the many of ancient Greek and medieval Latin theorists, are not included, nor are introductions to publications of music. Some foreign writers who published works in France, or whose writings specifically reflect French thinking of the period, are included in the listing.

Citations of current bibliography are limited to editions of sources mentioned, to items which provide pertinent information immediately relevant to the discussion, and to references having adequate bibliographical listings relative to the source, when available (such as those in MGG). MS copies of printed sources are not referred to, except where the original is lost or where copies help to clarify points made. Spellings, punctuation, and forms of proper names have been standardized so far as possible.

Symbols used in Bibliographical References

BrenetL   Michel Brenet, *La Librairie musicale en France de 1653 à 1790, d'après les Registres de privilèges*, in: *Sammelbände der Internationalen Musikgesellschaft*, VIII (1906–07), 401–66.

BrossardC   Sébastien de Brossard, *Catalogue des livres de musique théorique et prattique* (1724). Paris, Bibl. Nat., Rés. Vm^8 20.

Nouvelle méthode de solfier la musique, 1756 (Paris, Bibl. Nat., MS fonds fr. 22,538) fol. 7ff, discusses different methods of notating music as they evolved in France during the 17th and early 18th centuries.

FétisB   François-Joseph Fétis, *Biographie universelle des musiciens* (2nd ed. Paris 1860–65).
MersenneC   *Correspondance du P. Marin Mersenne*, ed. Cornélis de Waard (Paris 1932—).
MersenneHU   Marin Mersenne, *Harmonie universelle* (Paris: Sébastien Cramoisy & Pierre Ballard, 1636–37).
MGG   *Die Musik in Geschichte und Gegenwart*, ed. Friedrich Blume (Kassel 1949—).

ANONYMOUS

Méthode facile et assurée pour apprendre le plain-chant sans gamme et sans muances (Paris: Trichard, 1670).

Méthode facile pour apprendre à chanter la musique par un maistre célèbre de Paris (Paris: Robert Ballard, 1666; 2nd ed. 1670).

This source has been ascribed to both Jean Le Maire (c. 1581–c. 1650) and Guillaume-Gabriel Nivers (1632–1714). The attribution to the former is based on the authority of Sébastien de Brossard as found on the title page of the 1st ed. of the source in Paris, Bibl. Nat., Rés. V. 2554 (see Pl. 3a), and in BrossardC, pp. cliv and 41; that to the latter is suggested by FétisB, V, 263 (founded partly on some unsubstantiated information). It should be observed, however, that besides chronology, which is in Nivers's favor, his *Méthode certaine pour apprendre le plein-chant de l'église* (Paris: Christophe Ballard, 1699) appears to be an expansion and later ed. of the source (in some places the texts read identically). Also, in C. Ballard's ed. of *Rituel du chant ecclésiastique* (Paris 1725), p. 85, and in the catalogue to Jean-Philippe Rameau's *Traité de l'harmonie* (Paris 1722), Nivers is referred to as author of a treatise called *La Gamme du Si* (without date), a name by which the system described in the source in question became commonly known. (FétisB, *ibid.*, does refer to a treatise by Nivers with this title, but cites a publication date of 1646, which is hardly possible in view of Nivers's birth date.) In Jean Rousseau's *Méthode claire, certaine et facile pour apprendre à chanter la musique* (5th ed, Amsterdam: Pierre Mortier, n.d.), *Préface*, p. 5, for example, the author writes, "La Nouvelle Méthode pour apprendre à chanter la Musique, que l'on appelle la Méthode du Si, a esté si clairement expliqué, et si solidement establie dans le livre que l'on vend sous le nom d'un Maistre célèbre de Paris."

Qu'est ce que contrepoint et de ses espesses (Paris, Bibl. Nat., MS fonds fr. n. a. 4671, fols. 2–49ᵛ).
See BrossardC, p. 294.

Traicté de musique, contenant une sommaire instruction pour méthodiquement pratiquer la composition (Paris: Pierre Ballard, 1616; reissued 1617).

Essentially a re-edition of *Traicté de musique, contenant une théorique succincte pour méthodiquement pratiquer la composition* (Paris: Adrian Le Roy & Robert Ballard, 1583; reissued by *la veufve R. Ballard, & son fils Pierre Ballard*, 1602). MS 3042 at the Bibl. de l'Arsenal in Paris, fols. 32–41ᵛ, paraphrases the ed. of 1602. See the listing of the original ed. in

François Lesure & Geneviève Thibault, *Bibliographie des éditions d'Adrian Le Roy et Robert Ballard* (*1551-1598*) (Paris 1955), p. 213.

B., P. M.

Le Chant ecclésiastique dans les livres de choeur, 1619 (Paris 1620).
   The source is cited in Paris, Bibl. Nat., MS fonds fr. 20,002, fols. 1–4^v, but is otherwise unknown.

BACILLY, BÉNIGNE DE (c. 1625–1690)

Remarques curieuses sur l'art de bien chanter, et particulièrement pour ce qui regarde le chant françois (Paris: *chez l'autheur . . . et chez monsieur [Robert] Ballard* [pr. Claude Blageart], 1668). 1st ed. also issued *chez monsieur Ballard et chez Pierre Bienfait,* and *chez l'autheur & P. Bien-fait.* 2nd ed. *Traité de la méthode ou art bien chanter* (Paris: Guillaume de Luyne, 1671). 3rd ed. *L'Art de bien chanter de M. de Bacilly, Augmenté d'un Discours qui sert de réponse à la critique de ce traité* (Paris: *chez l'autheur* [Claude Blageart], 1679). This ed. is usually found with an extra, engraved title-page: *Remarques curieuses sur l'art de bien chanter.*
   See Henry Prunières, *Bénigne de Bacilly, un maître de chant au XVIIe siècle,* in: *Revue de musicologie,* VII (1923), 156–60.

[BALLARD, ROBERT?] (d. 1673)

Instruction pour comprendre en bref les préceptes et fondemens de la musique (3rd ed. Paris: Robert Ballard, 1666). [Earlier eds. unknown.]
   Author attribution is suggested in BrossardC, p. 41.

BARTOLOTTI, ANGELO MICHELE (c. 1615–c. 1680)

Table pour apprendre facilement à toucher le théorbe sur la basse-continuë. (Paris: Robert Ballard, 1669).
   Author's name is spelled "Bartolomi" in the source. See Henri Quittard, *Le Théorbe comme instrument d'accompagnement* in: *Revue musicale mensuelle, Société Internationale de Musique* (Section de Paris), VI/4 (1910), 231–35.

BASSET, JEHAN (d. 1636)

L'Art de toucher le Lut, in: MersenneHU, *Traité des instruments,* Book II, Props. IX–XI.
   English transl. Roger E. Chapman, *Marin Mersenne, Harmonie universelle, The Books on Instruments* (The Hague 1957), pp. 104–16. See Lionel de La Laurencie, *Un maître de luth au XVIIe siècle, Jehan Basset,* in: *La Revue musicale,* IV/9 (1923), 224–37.

BERGIER, NICOLAS (1567–1623)

La Musique spéculative. Paris, Bibl. Nat., MS fonds fr. 1359.
   See D. P. Walker, *Musical Humanism in the 16th and Early 17th Centuries,* in: *The Music Review,* II (1941), 113. The reference to a treatise by Bergier in Mersenne's *Quaestiones celeberrimae in Genesim* (Paris 1623), col. 1681, appears to relate to *La Musique spéculative,* and not to

another, unpublished work, as suggested in FétisB, I, 357. See MersenneC, I, 117, where the passage in question is quoted.

[BOUILLON, FRANÇOIS]

Instruction ou Méthode facile pour apprendre le plain-chant (Paris: Robert Ballard, 1654; 2nd ed. 1660).

Author attribution is indicated in contemporary hand on title-page of copies of both eds., Paris, Bibl. Ste.-Geneviève, Rés. V. 4.° 603 and 604.

BOURGOING, FRANÇOIS

Brevis psalmodiae ratio, ad usum presbyterorum congregationis oratii (Paris: Pierre Ballard, 1634).

Le David françois ou Traité de la saincte psalmodie (Paris: S. Huré, 1641). See BrenetL, p. 406.

BRICEÑO, LUIS DE

Método muy facilissimo para aprender a tañer la guitarra a lo español (Paris: Pierre Ballard, 1626).

See François Lesure, *Trois instrumentistes français du XVIIe siècle*, in: *Revue de musicologie*, XXXVII (1955), 186; José Subirá, in: MGG, II (1952), 318–19.

CAUS, SALOMON DE (1576–1626)

Institution harmonique, divisée en deux parties; en la première sont monstrées les proportions des intervalles harmoniques, et en la deuxiesme les compositions dicelles (Frankfurt: Jan Norton, 1615).

Les Raisons des forces mouvantes: Livre troisiesme traitant de la fabrique des orgues. (Frankfurt: Jan Norton, 1615; reissued in Paris: Charles Sevestre, 1624). In German transl. *Von gewaltsamen Bewegungen* (Frankfurt: A. Pacquart, [1615]).

FétisB II, 222, indicates a 2nd German ed. 1620. Occasional copies of the *Institution harmonique* occur with an appended *Livre troisiesme* from *Les Raisons*.

CHAVENEAU, LOUYS (LOUIS)

Déffinitions nécessaires de sçavoir pour l'intelligence de la musique (Nancy 1631). Paris, Bibl. Nat., MS fonds fr. 19,099, pp. 1–22 (the source continues with a description of the monochord, pp. 24–54); MS fonds fr. 19,100, pp. 2(2)–32(2), contains much of the same material.

Traité de musique contenant une théorique géneralle pour méthodiquement pratiquer la composition. Paris, Bibl. Nat., MS fonds fr. 19,100, pp. 1(3)–62(3).

COCQUEREL, ADRIEN

Méthode universelle très brieve et facile pour apprendre le plein chant sans maistre (2nd ed. Paris: Jean de La Caille, 1647).

BrenetL, p. 407, cites November 1645, from the *Registre des permissions d'imprimer*, as applying to "*un livre intitulé Méthode pour apprendre le plain-chant sans maître par Adrien Cocquerel.*" Since such permission would ordinarily follow the granting of the royal privilege, the Cocquerel work cited probably refers to the 1st ed. The privilege for the ed. of 1647 is dated "25 May 1646" in the source, and the completion of printing, "23 Novembre 1646."

COSSARD, JACQUES

Méthode pour apprendre à lire, à escrire, chanter le plain chant, et compter (Paris: *l'auteur,* 1633).

That a 2nd ed. might have been published is suggested by references to this work in BrenetL, p. 407, from the *Registre des permissions d'imprimer* for the year 1646.

Pour apprendre à chanter (Paris: *l'auteur,* n.d.).

DENIS, JEAN (d. 1671)

Traité de l'accord de l'espinette, avec la comparaison de son clavier à la musique vocale (Rev. ed. Paris: Robert Ballard, 1650).

See Norbert Dufourcq, *Une dynastie française: Les Denis,* in: *Revue de musicologie,* XXXVIII (1956), 151–55.

DESARGUES, GIRARD (GÉRARD, GASPARD; 1593–1662)

Méthode aisée pour apprendre et enseigner à lire et à escrire la musique. Printed in MersenneHU, Part I, Book VI, *L'Art de bien chanter,* Prop. I, pp. 332–42.

See Armand Machabey, *Gérard Desargues, géomètre et musicien,* in: *XVIIᵉ Siècle,* Nos. 21–22 (1954), 396–402.

DESAUGES, DENIS (b. 1598)

L'Esclaircissement du plain-chant, ou le vray thrésor des choristes (Paris 1664).

The work is listed in FétisB, III, 1, but is otherwise unknown. However, in Brossard's *Dictionnaire de musique* (3rd ed. Amsterdam: Estienne Roger, n.d.), p. 360, there is a "Denis des Auges" listed among *"Auteurs qui ont écrit en François."*

DESCARTES, RENÉ (1596–1650)

Musicae compendium (1618). Leyden, Universiteitsbibliotheek, MS Huy. 29.a. First publ. in Utrecht: Gisbert Zijll and Theodor van Ackersdijck, 1650. Reissued in Amsterdam: Johannes Jansson, Jr., 1656; Amsterdam: Blaviana, 1683; Frankfurt: Friedrich Knochius, 1695. English transl. *Excellent compendium of musick: with necessary and judicious animadversions thereupon. By a person of honour* [William Viscount Brouncker] (London: "printed by Thomas Harper for Humphrey Moseley," 1653). In French transl., with notes by Nicolas-Joseph Poisson, *Traité de la méchanique, composé par Monsieur Descartes. De plus l'Abrégé de musique* [found also as Part II of *Discours de la méthode*] (Paris: Charles Angot, 1668; re-ed. Paris: Compagnie des libraires, 1724). Latin ed. *N. Poisonii Elucidationes physicae in Cartesii*

Musicam, Part III of *Opuscula posthuma physica et mathematica* (Amsterdam: "Janssonio-Waesbergios, Boom & Goethals," 1701).

In modern English transl. by Walter Robert, American Institute of Musicology, *Musicological Studies and Documents,* Vol. 8 ([Rome] 1961). See Rudolf Stephan, in: MGG, III (1954), 209–11.

DU COUSU, ANTOINE (d. 1658)

La Musique universelle, contenant toute la pratique et toute la théorie (Paris: [Robert Ballard], 1658).

See Ernest Thoinan, *Antoine De Cousu et les singulières destinées de son livre rarissime: "La Musique universelle"* (Paris 1866); André Verchaly, in: MGG, III (1954), 864–65.

DUMANOIR, GUILLAUME (1615–c. 1690)

Le Mariage de la musique avec la dance (Paris: Guillaume de Luyne, 1664). Re-ed. Paris: Jules Gallay, 1870. See Eugène Borrel, in: MGG, III (1954), 926–28.

EVEILLON, JACQUES (1572–1651)

De Recta ratione psallendi liber (La Flèche: Gervasius Laboe, 1646).

FLEURY, NICOLAS

Méthode pour apprendre facilement à toucher le théorbe sur la basse continuë (Paris: Robert Ballard, 1660).

See André Verchaly, in: MGG, IV (1955), 310–11.

FORNAS, PHILIPPE (b. 1627)

Nouvelle méthode pour apprendre le plain chant en fort peu de iours (Lyons: "La veufve de Pierre Muguet," 1657). Later ed. as *L'Art du plain-chant* (Lyons: Michael Mayer, 1672 & 1673).

FRANÇOIS, RENÉ (pseud. of ÉTIENNE BINET, 1560–1639)

Essay des merveilles de nature et des plus nobles artifices [Ch. LIII: *La Musique;* Ch. LIV: *La Voix*] (Rouen: R. de Beauvais, 1621). The work had more than 20 eds., of which the following have been traced: 2nd ed. Rouen: R. de Beauvais, 1622; also issued by Jean Osmont, same place and year. 4th ed. Rouen: R. de Beauvais, 1624. 5th ed. Rouen: J. Osmont, 1625. 6th ed. 1626. 7th ed. 1629. 8th ed. 1631. 9th ed. 1632; 9th ed. also issued in Lyons: I. Jacquemetton, 1636; Paris: J. Dugast, 1632; Rouen 1644. 12th ed. Paris: J. Dugast, 1646; also Paris 1657. 13th ed. Paris: M. Bobin, 1657; also issued by H. Legras, same place and year.

GANTEZ, ANNIBAL (d. after 1668)

L'Entretien des musiciens (Auxerre: Jacques Bouquet, 1643).

Re-ed. Ernest Thoinan (Paris 1878). See Denise Launay, in: MGG, IV (1955), 1362–63.

GASSENDI (GASSEND, GASSENDUS), PIERRE (1592–1655)

Manuductio ad theoriam seu partem speculativam musicae. Paris, Bibl. Nat., MS fonds lat. n. a. 1636, pp. 817ff. First pr. Paris 1654. Found among complete works: *Opera omnia* (Lyons: Laurent Anisson & Jean-Baptiste Devenet, 1658–75), V, 629–58. Re-ed. Florence: "Joannem Cajetanum Tartini, & Sanctem Franchi," 1727, V, 575–99.

Du son, Ch. XII of *Des qualitez,* in: F. Bernier (ed.), *Abrégé de la philosophie de Gassendi* (2nd ed. Lyons: Laurent Anisson, Jean Posuel, & Claudin Rigaud, 1684), III, 181–208.

See *Pierre Gassendi 1592–1655, sa vie et son oeuvre* (Paris: Centre international de synthèse, 1955).

GUILLET, CHARLES (d. 1654)

Institution harmonique, divisée en trois livres. Ier livre (1642–47). Vienna, Österreichische Nationalbibliothek, MS Sm 2376.

Although the MS is undated, there is a reference to 1642 on fol. 8ᵛ, and the approval for printing added to the title-page is dated "*à Bruges le 20. de Septembre. 1647.*" See Ant. Schmid, *Eine Handschrift von Charles Guillet,* in: *Caecilia,* XXIV (1845), 252–56; Albert Van der Linden, in: *MGG,* V (1956), 1097–98.

LA MOTHE LE VAYER, FRANÇOIS DE (1588–1672)

Discours sceptique sur la musique, in: Marin Mersenne, *Questions harmoniques* (Paris: Jacques Villery, 1634), pp. 84–165. Repr. in: *Petit discours chrestien de l'immortalité de l'âme, avec le corollaire et un discours sceptique sur la musique* (Paris: J. Camusat, 1637). 2nd ed. Paris: *veuve* J. Camusat, 1640. 3rd ed. Paris: A. de Sommaville, 1647. Also found among complete works: *Oeuvres* (Paris: A. Courbé, 1654 and later eds.).

See Florence L. Wickelgren, *La Mothe Le Vayer, sa vie et son oeuvre* (Paris 1934).

[LANCELOT, CLAUDE] (c. 1615–1695)

Nouvelle méthode pour apprendre parfaitement le plein-chant en fort peu de temps (Paris 1660). 2nd ed. *Nouvelle méthode très seure et très facile pour apprendre parfaitement le plein chant en fort peu de temps* (Paris: Charles Savreux, 1669). Rev. ed. slightly expanded, Paris: Guillaume Desprez, 1683.

The attribution to Lancelot is by Antoine-Alexandre Barbier, *Dictionnaire des ouvrages anonymes,* III (Paris 1875), col. 557. See Louis Cognet, *Claude Lancelot, Solitaire de Port-Royal* (Paris 1950), p. 109.

LAUZE, F. DE

Apologie de la danse et la parfaicte méthode de l'enseigner tant aux cavaliers qu'aux dames (n.p. 1623).

Re-ed. in French with English transl. on parallel pages by Joan Wildeblood (London 1952).

Traité de musique pour bien et facilement apprendre à chanter et à composer
(Paris: Robert Ballard, 1656). 2nd ed. *"reveu et augmenté de nouveau d'une
quatriesme partie,"* 1666. In Italian transl., *Trattato di musica* (Paris: Robert
Ballard, 1659).
     See Robert Siohan, in: MGG, VIII (1960), 389–90.

De la musique harmonique spéculative. Paris, Bibl. Nat., MS fonds fr. 19,102,
fols. 3–21; MS fonds fr. 19,103, fols. 29–31ᵛ, 52, 64–65ᵛ.

Deux méthodes pour apprendre le plein chant (1660). Paris, Bibl. Nat., MS
fonds fr. 19,103, fols. 12–14ᵛ.

*Méthode facile et accomplie pour apprendre le chant de l'église sans l'aide
d'aucune gamme* (1665). Paris, Bibl. Nat., MS fonds fr. 19,103, fols. 2–3ᵛ,
7–11ᵛ, 21–28, 56–63, 66–107, 174–81, 183–84ᵛ; MS fonds fr. 20,001, fols. 1–40.

Traitté des gammes du chant et des alphabets des langues Grecque et Latine.
Paris, Bibl. Nat., MS fonds fr. 20,002, fols. 23–38.

Traitté des tons et de la quantité du chant et de la grammaire. Paris, Bibl. Nat.,
MS fonds fr. 20,002, fols. 62–208ᵛ.
     These appear to be incomplete sketches for the most part. Philippe-
Joseph Caffiaux mistakenly refers to Le Clerc as the author of a *Théorie
et pratique du plainchant*, in Paris, Bibl. Nat., MS fonds fr. 22,538, fol.
3ᵛ, and of *La Science et la pratique du plainchant*, in MS fonds fr. 22,536–
37, II, 179ᵛ. The work in question is *La Science et la pratique du plainchant* (Paris: Louis Bilaine, 1673) by Pierre-Benoit de Jumilhac. See the
2nd ed. of this work (Paris: Théodore Nisard & Alexandre Le Clercq,
1847), pp. 3–5, concerning this point.

*Méthode nouvelle pour apprendre en fort peu de temps la musique, tant pour
la spéculative que pour la pratique.*
     This work, seemingly lost, might have included *Méthode pour la musique
almérique*, London, Brit. Mus., MS Harl. 6796, fols. 175–77, and Paris,
Bibl. Nat., MS fonds fr. 19,103, fol. 128. See the author's *Jean Le Maire
and La Musique Almérique*, in: *Acta musicologica*, XXXV (1963), 178f.

Reigles très-faciles pour apprendre en peu de temps le plein-chant (Paris:
Robert Ballard, 1664).

*Les Tons, ou discours sur les modes de musique, et les tons de l'église, et la
distinction entre iceux* (Tournay: Charles Martin, 1610).
     See Jumilhac, *La Science et la pratique du plain-chant*, 2nd ed., p. 168.

MAUDUIT, JACQUES (1557–1627)

Traitez de la rhythmique.
Listed among unpublished works of Mauduit, in: MersenneHU, *Traité des instruments*, VII, 65.

MAUGARS, ANDRÉ (c. 1580–c. 1645)

Responce faite à un curieux sur le sentiment de la musique d'Italie escrite à Rome le Ier Octobre 1639 [Paris 1639 or 1640]. Ed. as *Discours sur la musique d'Italie et des opéra*, in: Pierre de Saint Glas (ed.), *Divers traitez d'histoire, de morale, et d'éloquence* (Paris: veuve Claude Thiboust and Pierre Esclossan, 1672), VI, 154–79. Re-ed. 1697 and 1700.
Modern ed. Ernest Thoinan, *Maugars, célèbre joueur de viole* (Paris 1865). German transl. W. J. v. Wasielewski, *Eine französischer Musikbericht aus der ersten Hälfte des 17. Jahrhunderts*, in: *Monatshefte für Musikgeschichte*, X (1878), 1–19, 17–23. See André Verchaly, in MGG, VIII (1960), 1828.

MENESTRIER, CLAUDE-FRANÇOIS (1631–1705)

Remarques sur la conduite des ballets, in: *L'Autel de Lyon* (Lyons: J. Molin, 1658).

Traité des tournois, joustes, carrousels, et autres spectacles publics [*De l'harmonie*, pp. 167–80] (Lyons: Jacques Muguet, 1669). Re-ed. 1674.
See Denise Launay, in: MGG, IX (1961), 99–100.

MERSENNE, MARIN (1588–1648)

Quaestiones celeberrimae in Genesim (Paris: Sébastien Cramoisy, 1623).

La Vérité des sciences (Paris: T. Du Bray, 1625).

Traité de l'harmonie universelle (Paris: Guillaume Baudry, 1627).
See John B. Eagen, *Marin Mersenne, Traité de l'Harmonie Universelle: Critical Translation of the 2nd Book* (Diss. Indiana 1962), unpublished.

Les Préludes de l'harmonie universelle ou Questions curieuses (Paris: Henry Guenon, 1634).

Les Questions théologiques, physiques, morales et mathématiques (Paris: Henry Guenon, 1634).

Questions harmoniques (Paris: Jacques Villery, 1634).

Questions inouyes ou récréation des sçavans (Paris: Jacques Villery, 1634).

Harmonicorum libri, in quibus agitur de sonorum natura (Paris, Guillaume Baudry & Pierre Ballard, 1635). Re-ed. 1636; in augmented form, as *Harmonicorum libri XII* (G. Baudry, 1648; later ed. Thomas Jolly, 1652).

Harmonicorum instrumentorum libri IV (Paris: Guillaume Baudry, 1636).

Harmonie universelle (Paris: Sébastien Cramoisy and Pierre Ballard, 1636–37).
Mersenne's personal copy of this ed., with autograph marginal notes,

has been issued in a facsimile edition by the Centre National de la Recherche Scientifique, 3 vols. (Paris 1963). A 17th-century copy of the notes is at the Bibl. Nat., MS fonds fr. 12,357, fols. 4–24. The *Traité des instruments* is available in English transl. Roger E. Chapman (The Hague 1957).

Cogitata physico-mathematica (Paris: Antoine Bertier, 1644).

Novorum observationum physico-mathematicorum, III (Paris: Antoine Bertier, 1647).

Livre de la nature des sons. Paris, Bibl. de l'Arsenal, MS 2884.

MersenneC I, 195f, indicates that this source is part of an unfinished *Sommaire des seize livres de la musique,* the first two of which were published in *Traité de l'harmonie universelle* of 1627. (The source is probably a portion of the third part of the *Sommaire.*) The projected study was never completed, but the unfinished material was recast for use in *Harmonicorum libri.* For discussions of Mersenne's works and for bibliographical references, see Robert Eitner, *Die Druckwerke P. Marin Mersennes über Musik,* in: *Monatshefte für Musikgeschichte,* XXIII (1891), 60–68, 164; Hellmut Ludwig, *Marin Mersenne und seine Musiklehre* (Berlin 1935); Hans-Heinz Dräger, in: MGG, IX (1961), 131–34; François Lesure, in: *Encyclopédie de la musique,* III (Paris 1961), 187.

MILLET, JEAN (c. 1620–1684)

Directoire du chant grégorien (Lyons: Jean Grégoire, 1666).

La belle méthode ou l'Art de bien chanter (Lyons: Jean Grégoire, 1666).

Despite the similarity of publisher, place, and date of issuance, the two works by Millet are distinctively different. (FétisB VI, 145, and later writers who base their views on his observations suggest that the works are the same.) The *Directoire* is an extensive study of liturgical chant, whereas *La belle méthode* is a short tutor dealing with vocal ornamentation.

NIVERS, GUILLAUME-GABRIEL (1632–1714)

Traité de la composition de musique (Paris: *chez l'autheur . . . et Robert Ballard,* 1667). Re-ed. Christophe Ballard, 1712. Ed. with Flemish transl. by Estienne Roger (Amsterdam: Jean-Louis de Lorme and E. Roger, 1697).

MS 3042 at the Bibl. de l'Arsenal in Paris, fols. 1–29^v, is a copy of the 1st ed. of 1667 (marked clearly in the source) and not of "1664," as indicated in Henry Martin, *Catalogue des manuscrits de la Bibliothèque de l'Arsenal,* III (Paris 1887), 201, and in Lionel de La Laurencie & Amédée Gastoué, *Catalogue des livres de musique de la Bibliothèque de l'Arsenal à Paris* (Paris 1936), p. 158. The source is available in English transl. by the author, Institute of Mediaeval Music, *Musical Theorists in Translation,* Vol. 3 (Brooklyn, N.Y. 1961).

OUVRARD, RENÉ (1624–1694)

Secret pour composer en musique par un art nouveau (Paris: *la veuve Gervais Alliot & Anthoine Clement,* 1658). Reissued 1660.

See Denise Launay, in: MGG, X (1962), 501–02. In Åke Davidsson, *Catalogue critique et descriptif des ouvrages théoriques sur la musique imprimés au XVIe et au XVIIe siècles conservés dans les bibliothèques suédoises* (Upsala 1953), p. 26, the first ed. is attributed to "Du Reneau," which is a pseud. of Ouvrard. For clarification of this point, see BrenetL, p. 413.

PARRAN, ANTOINE (1587–1650)

Traité de la musique théorique et pratique, contenant les préceptes de la composition (Paris: Pierre Ballard, 1639). 2nd ed. Robert Ballard, 1646.
See André Verchaly, in: MGG, X (1962), 834.

PASCHAL, LOUIS

Briefve instruction pour apprendre le plain-chant tiré des meilleurs autheurs (Paris: Jean de La Caille, 1658).

PURE, MICHEL DE (1634–1680)

Idée des spectacles anciens et nouveaux (Paris: Michel Brunet, 1668). [Book II, Ch. 9: *Du Balet*, pp. 209–306.]

ROBERVAL, GILLES PERSONNE DE (1602–1675)

Elementa musicae (1651). Paris, Bibl. Nat., MS fonds fr. 9119, fols. 374–407^v.

SAINT-HUBERT, DE

La Manière de composer et faire réussir les ballets (Paris: François Targa, 1641).

SOUHAITTY, JEAN-JACQUES

Nouvelle méthode pour apprendre le plain-chant et la musique (Paris: 1665).

TRICHET, PIERRE (1586 or 1587–1644)

Traité des instruments (c. 1640). Paris, Bibl. Ste.-Geneviève, MS 1070.
Partial modern ed. by François Lesure, *Le Traité des instruments de musique de Pierre Trichet*, in: *Annales musicologiques*, III (1955), 283–387; IV (1956), 175–248; also issued separately for the *Société de musique d'autrefois* (Neuilly-sur-Seine 1957); supplements in: *The Galpin Society Journal*, XV (1962), 70–81; XVI (1963), 73–84.

ARISTOXENUS AND
GREEK MATHEMATICS

by RICHARD L. CROCKER

EVER SINCE Ptolemy's account of Greek music theory, Aristoxenus has been seen as the irreconcilable opponent of the Pythagoreans. The grounds of the opposition, however, have been often misunderstood. It has been assumed that because Aristoxenus ignored the interval ratios set forth by the Pythagoreans, he was a practical empiricist. But Aristoxenus was not just an empiricist; rather, he was proposing an entirely new kind of theory, as theoretically rigorous as that of the Pythagoreans, but founded on a new mathematical method. This method was thought out by Greek mathematicians of the 4th century B.C.; Aristoxenus, working in the latter half of that century, applied the method to music in order to describe more accurately the current musical style, whose development—what little we know of it—shows us that there was an urgent need for the kind of theory Aristoxenus proposed. Stylistic change demanded, while philosophical growth allowed, the very special form in which Aristoxenus cast his thought.[1]

Up until the beginning of the 4th century (400 B.C.), Greek mathematics was basically Pythagorean, developed by that shadowy group of 5th-century thinkers called "the Pythagoreans" by Plato and Aristotle.[2] Pythagorean mathematics dealt exclusively with whole numbers, in-

---

[1] Aristoxenus's works on music are preserved in three fragments, *The Harmonics of Aristoxenus*, ed. & transl. H. S. Macran (Oxford 1902). In spite of certain questionable or obsolete features, Macran makes clear the basic nature of Aristoxenus's theory, providing in his notes valuable elucidation of many points. See also R. da Rios, *Aristoxeni Elementa harmonica* (Rome 1954); L. Laloy, *Aristoxène de Tarente et la musique de l'antiquité* (Paris 1904); R. Westphal, *Aristoxenus von Tarent* (Leipzig 1883); a very useful, cautious account by R. P. Winnington-Ingram, *Greek Music (Ancient)*, in: *Grove's Dictionary of Music and Musicians*, ed. E. Blom (5th ed. London 1954); R. P. Winnington-Ingram, *Aristoxenus and the Intervals of Greek Music*, in: *The Classical Quarterly*, XXVI (1932), 195; another very useful account, marked by refreshing scepticism, by I. Henderson, *Ancient Greek Music*, in: *New Oxford History of Music*, I: *Ancient and Oriental Music*, ed. E. Wellesz (London 1957), 336–403.
[2] See P. H. Michel, *De Pythagore à Euclide* (Paris 1950); R. L. Crocker, *Pythagorean Mathematics and Music*, in: *Journal of Aesthetics and Art Criticism*, XXII (1963), 189–98, 325–35.

tegers; the Pythagoreans expressed quantity in terms of units in such a way that any quantity could be compared to any other quantity in terms of that unit. The quantities 9 and 17, for example, can be compared as 9 units and 17 units; they are comparable, "commensurable," on this basis, for they are measured by the same unit. The Pythagoreans thoroughly explored the various kinds of relationships, or ratios, between integers; the results of their investigations constituted the kind of mathematics that was called arithmetic.

Even before 400 B.C., however, certain quantities appeared that arithmetic could not handle, quantities that could not be expressed in terms of integers or of the ratios of integers. The Greeks gradually became aware of another world of quantity lying in the interstices of the integer system; arithmetic had, as it were, barely scratched the surface. The first such quantity to come to the Greeks' attention seems to have been the hypotenuse of an isosceles right triangle.

Fig. 1   Theorem of Pythagoras applied to an isosceles right triangle

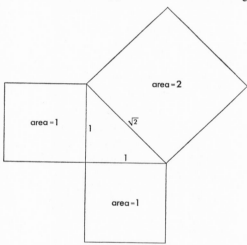

The Pythagoreans already knew that a certain relationship held between the hypotenuse of a right triangle and its sides—the square on the hypotenuse is equal to the sum of the squares on the other two sides—but they knew it only as the few special cases in which this relationship could be expressed in integers, as in the case of the 3–4–5 right triangle. But as they became aware that this relationship held in all cases, they realized that this relationship involved real quantities that could not be expressed as integers; for if the two sides were each one unit long, then the sum of their squares was 2, and since 2 was not a square number, its side—the length of the hypotenuse—could not be determined by arithmetic. Here was a quantity that inescapably existed; you could draw a picture of it, but you could not give it a number. Hypotenuse and side were measured by no common unit: they were "irrational"—without a ratio—when compared to each other. Their relationship could be analyzed only by lines, not numbers.

Throughout the 4th century, Greek mathematicians were increasingly involved with these irrational quantities, first in demonstrating their existence, then in finding ways to deal with them.[3] These mathematicians, no longer identifiable as Pythagoreans, belonged to a new phase of mathematics that went under a new name, "geometry." There had been for a long time an art called geometry which "measured the earth" in a literal sense: it provided precepts for laying out lengths and areas on the ground. The "new geometry" of the 4th century used these traditional methods of construction, but gave them a new, theoretical significance they never had before; they became tools for gaining some of the most sophisticated insights ever attained in the history of mathematics.

The culmination of the new geometry came in Euclid's *Elements* at the end of the 4th century (300 B.C.). Much of Euclid's work was not original: he summarized Pythagorean arithmetic (books VII–IX); then welded together the geometric methods and theorems worked out by his 4th-century predecessors into a uniquely consistent system. (There are, we are told, only two minor inconsistencies in the whole 13 books.) The layman knows Euclid through high-school diagrams, but is not usually aware of the purpose of these diagrams. By representing quantity with lines instead of numbers, geometry made possible a comparison of *all* quantities and types of quantities, commensurable or incommensurable, rational or irrational. In books X–XIII Euclid goes far beyond ordinary school constructions to solve—with the help of very special constructions—problems of quadratic equations taken up after his time only through algebra. Mathematicians usually feel that Euclid's solution of these problems is unnecessarily roundabout, which is obviously true from an abstract point of view, but seen historically the remarkable thing is that Euclid was able to solve them at all. Such was the power of the new mathematics.

The music theory of Aristoxenus—part of it called *Elements*—was conceived around 320 B.C., shortly before Euclid, just at the time when the new geometry was being given definitive form. Aristoxenus, it should be noted, was a Pythagorean by heritage: he came from Tarentum in

[3] Michel, *De Pythagore*, pp. 412–522.

Italy, where the Pythagoreans traditionally held forth, and he even studied with a Pythagorean named Xenophilus. But then he also studied with Aristotle at the Academy in Athens; he was a candidate to succeed as head of the Academy after Aristotle's death. Much of what we imagine to be "geometric method" is really Aristotelian logic—the format of definitions, axioms, problems, and proofs is derived from Aristotle's concern for systematic method. It appears in Euclid not as an essential feature of geometry, but rather as the most highly developed form Euclid knew for presenting his materials. This format could just as well be used to expound Pythagorean arithmetic—in fact was used in a thoroughly Pythagorean treatise on music attributed for a long time to Euclid on the basis of its "Euclidian" method.[4] This method, this format, is found in Aristoxenus too, but does not by itself constitute what is "geometric" about Aristoxenus. There is a much more profound relationship between Aristoxenus and the new geometry: Aristoxenus's new kind of music theory was designed—like the new geometry—to handle intervals without reference to numbers or ratios.

Aristoxenus refers only once to the measurement of intervals by ratios: "For some of these [my predecessors] introduced extraneous reasoning, and rejecting the senses as inaccurate fabricated rational principles, asserting that height and depth of pitch consist in certain numerical ratios and relative rates of vibration—a theory utterly extraneous to the subject and quite at variance with the phenomenona."[5] In other words, Aristoxenus felt that Pythagorean music theory was two centuries of wasted effort. His contempt expressed in this passage is matched by his total neglect of the results of Pythagorean theory; refusing to analyze musical intervals with integer ratios, he sought a way to discuss irrational intervals on the same basis with the rational ones treated by the Pythagoreans.

While Aristoxenus simply ignored the Pythagoreans, he argued at length (he is not the most ingratiating writer on music) with another group of predecessors; these, as far as we can tell from Aristoxenus's own account, were concerned only with practical things like scales. Aristoxenus's criticism of them is that their work lacked rigor and system: they had no reasons for what they did, he says; they found no way to demonstrate their conclusions. We may assume that Aristoxenus made full use of their empirical solutions, but transformed them, with his distinctive thoroughness, into a consistent, comprehensive theory.

[4] The *Sectio canonis*, ed. C. Jahn, *Musici scriptores graeci* (Leipzig 1895); French transl. C. E. Ruelle, in: *Collection des auteurs grecs relatif à la musique*, III (Paris 1894).
[5] *Harmonics*, p. 188.

Aristoxenus was able to go beyond purely empirical solutions because he began with a careful analysis of basic concepts, which he derived from Aristotle's *Physics*. Aristoxenus's discussion of "movement of the voice according to place" can be compared to Aristotle's definitions of motion and place in books III and IV of the *Physics*, and to his classification and continuity of movement in books V and VI.[6] In particular, Aristoxenus's discussion of continuity and consecution is a direct application to music of chapter 3, book V of the *Physics*, "Succession, Contact, Continuity, and Related Distinctions." Aristoxenus, like his teacher Aristotle, was trying to grasp what was "natural" about his subject; this was the starting point of his disagreement with the Pythagoreans. One of Aristotle's powerful tools had been the concept of continuity, as in the continuity of an infinite number of points on a line, each occupying a position but no space—a concept that when applied to quantity led to the new geometry. Aristoxenus applied it to music. He began with a well-known distinction between speaking and singing, the one involving continuous, siren-like movement of the voice, the other involving discrete pitches of song. What is important is not so much the distinction itself, which a Pythagorean could also make, but rather the fact that Aristoxenus made continuous sound the foundation of all that was to come. From it he carefully disengaged the notion of discrete sound, then just as carefully sought a way of distinguishing one discrete sound from another. This involved him in subtle and perhaps tedious distinctions— but the subtlety is essential to avoid any contact with the discrete quantities associated with numbers and ratios by the Pythagoreans. Aristoxenus avoided string lengths to define pitch or interval, using instead string tension as the best way to keep the discussion in the realm of continuous quantity. Even here his procedure was circumspect: first, he made sound a function of tension-relaxation; then he described the resulting sounds as acute or grave (or better, if less grammatical, as acuter and graver); then, very carefully, he called a single instance of acute or grave sound a pitch. By beginning with continuous, rather than discrete sound, Aristoxenus made it possible to deal with *all* musical intervals regardless of whether these intervals could be represented by ratios between integers. The greater generality of Aristoxenus's approach comes out clearly in his definition of interval, "a space capable of containing pitches greater than the lesser pitch and lesser than the greater." [7]

The radical difference between Aristoxenus and the Pythagoreans also makes itself felt, if less patently, in the definition of concord and

---

[6] *Aristotle's Physics*, transl. R. Hope (Lincoln, Nebraska 1961).
[7] *Harmonics*, p. 176.

discord.[8] The definition goes by so fast that the reader must stop to search for it—and only then realizes that the whole foundation of Pythagorean theory, the primacy of small-number ratios, has been quietly finessed. Aristoxenus considers some intervals to sound consonant, others dissonant. No reason is given; the distinction is made as a self-evident fact of music. A fourth is the smallest consonance. Why? Because the ear perceives no smaller one. There are no consonances between fourth and fifth, or between fifth and octave, for the same reason. It is one thing to assert this as an item of practical musicianship, but quite another to incorporate it, as Aristoxenus did, into a severely logical theory.

The definition—or better, postulation—of basic concords marks a critical phase in Aristoxenus's argument. On the one hand there was great pressure from the realities of musical style for a kind of theory that would account for all sizes of intervals; such a theory could only be based on the concept of continuity derived from Aristotle and shared with the new geometry. On the other hand, musical style as it actually existed used not continuous pitch, but discrete pitches, separated from each other by intervals which, however variable they might be, still tended to assume certain conventional sizes and orders. The Pythagoreans, dealing with discrete quantity *only*, could and did account for the more standardized intervals (the basic concords), but ran into difficulty with the more variable ones. An approach based merely on continuity, however, could not account for standard intervals such as concords and conventional orders such as scales. Aristoxenus's problem was to find a way, based on continuity, that would permit him to deal with all sizes of intervals, rational as well as irrational, but also to describe and analyze these standard intervals and scales. His solution to this dilemma—a solution that is more than merely pragmatic—was to refer the standard intervals and scales to universal categories of perception, as in the case of consonances. We perceive a fifth as consonant, argues Aristoxenus, so what further qualification is necessary? It does not make it more consonant to analyze it as a small-number ratio (2:3) as the Pythagoreans do. Why not simply accept it as a given fact? A system is made rigorous, Aristoxenus would continue, not by referring its elements to other elements (like numbers) outside the system, but rather by selecting the system's most basic elements, reducing them to an absolute minimum, then deducing the others from them. Aristoxenus was quite aware of the arbitrary nature of his undefined terms (such as consonance), their dependence on cultural habit; he wistfully compared such

[8] *Harmonics*, p. 198.

Fig. 2   The Genera of Archytas and Aristoxenus compared

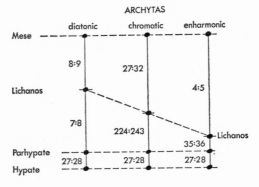

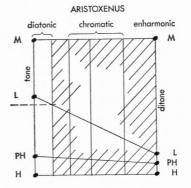

concepts, requiring the close attention of an educated ear, to the undefined terms of the geometer, whose straight lines and circles could
be universally and objectively grasped without reference to sense perception.[9] But the relativity of Aristoxenus's terms was necessary if his
theory was to correspond completely and comprehensively to the facts
of musical practice.

Perhaps the clearest, most convincing example of Aristoxenus's new
method is his treatment of the genera, or kinds of tetrachord—diatonic,
chromatic, enharmonic. These three genera were apparently first sys-
tematized by Archytas, a Pythagorean, around 400 B.C., using a carefully
constructed set of integer ratios.[10] A direct comparison of Archytas's
genera with those of Aristoxenus reveals the nature of the latter's new
theory, as well as suggesting something about the stylistic changes that
might have gone on during the early 4th century.

Archytas differentiated his three genera solely by the position of the

[9] *Harmonics,* p. 189.
[10] Crocker, *Pythagorean,* pp. 189–98.

lichanos ("indicator"). The ratios used in the three genera suggest that while he fixed the position of the lichanos very carefully in the diatonic and enharmonic, he considered its position in the chromatic genus somewhat arbitrary. Aristoxenus, then, simply made explicit what was already present in Archytas's system, but did so by concentrating on the movement of the lichanos rather than on its positions. He set the positions of the lichanos in diatonic and enharmonic as "limits" to the movement of the lichanos, then allowed it to assume an infinite number of positions in between; the lichanos was now defined as a "locus" rather than as a point corresponding to a ratio. Since Aristoxenus set the limits of this locus in terms of the whole tone, which in turn was defined as the difference between the undefined consonances fourth and fifth, the entire description of the behavior of the lichanos was independent of integer ratios, hence accounted for all possible values, rational and irrational alike.

Unlike Archytas, Aristoxenus allowed the *parhypate* to move too, but gave it a locus much smaller than lichanos. This movable parhypate probably reflects an increase in variability of the tetrachord during the 4th century. Also in response to musical practice, Aristoxenus singled out for discussion six kinds of tetrachords from the infinite number of possible ones (one enharmonic, three chromatic, and two diatonic). He describes these by means of fractions such as half tone, quarter tone, third of a tone and so forth—a procedure that has been the scandal of theoreticians from his day to ours. For every Pythagorean knew that a whole tone 8:9 cannot be divided in half—at, least, the result cannot be expressed in integer ratios; nor can any of the other fractional values Aristoxenus used be so expressed. But Aristoxenus was not at all interested in expressing these intervals in integer ratios, only in expressing them in some way that permitted definition of their relative position and function within the tetrachord. He was willing, in other words, to sacrifice absolute knowledge of some intervals to gain relative knowledge of all. The whole tone 8:9 can, in fact, be divided "in half"; we express the result as $\sqrt{8:3}$, an irrational number, while Aristoxenus, using geometric operations, merely represented the whole tone by a line, then bisected the line. In the same way he could divide any interval into any fraction he wished, without regard for whether the result was rational or irrational. The same approach that made the new geometry more general, more powerful than the old arithmetic, was here used by Aristoxenus to create a new description of the genera.

Hence the long, elaborate descriptions of the *chromai* in fractions. These fractions serve only to make clear the relative arrangements of intervals within the genera—the relative positions of points on a line. Since Aristoxenus considered all intervals within the tetrachord to be dissonant (the fourth being for him the smallest consonance), one tetrachord was no more "consonant" than another. If Aristoxenus designated several tetrachords as the conventional ones, he ended up by reaffirming the infinite number of possible tetrachords, bounded at either extreme by the diatonic and enharmonic.

Aristoxenus treated the two lower intervals of the tetrachord as a unit—perhaps because of a tradition of an older type of tetrachord (or rather, trichord) that had only one very large interval at the top, and one very small interval at the bottom, a shape preserved in Archytas's enharmonic.[11] In Aristoxenus's enharmonic, the pair of small intervals at the bottom added up to a semitone, obviously much smaller than the ditone above them; in his diatonic, the lower two intervals added up to tone-plus-semitone, obviously larger than the tone above them. At some point on the continuum between these tetrachords, then, the sum of the lower intervals must be exactly equal to the single interval above. Aristoxenus used this point, easily defined by geometric procedures, to distinguish diatonic from chromatic genera. In all tetrachords lying within the shaded area on Fig. 2, which includes all chromatic and enharmonic tetrachords, the sum of the lower two intervals is called the pyknon, whose value, obviously, is less than the upper interval, mese to lichanos.

It is essential to observe that no tetrachord contains more than two inner movable notes, lichanos and parhypate. Within any given tetrachord, then, the intervals are defined solely by the actual position of these two notes. All intervals so defined Aristoxenus calls "simple," regardless of their size. The crucial case is the interval from lichanos to mese in the enharmonic tetrachord: the size of this interval is two whole tones, but it is not a "compound" interval made of two simple intervals, for the reference to ditone is only to fix the locus. Basing his definitions once more on stylistic reality, Aristoxenus defines a simple interval as one that occurs between two adjacent notes, like mese and lichanos, not on the theoretical units used to measure intervals. It is as if we said, "The interval between C and D, in C major, is a simple interval a whole tone in size." There is, to be sure, a note C♯ on the keyboard, but this note has no function in simple C major. The tetrachord described above has only four notes, mese, lichanos, parhypate, and hypate, in spite of the fact that lichanos and parhypate may assume an infinite number of pitches. The

---

[11] This tradition is explored in an interesting study by M. Vogel, *Die Enharmonik der Griechen* (Düsseldorf 1963).

names mese, lichanos, parhypate, and hypate, then, describe the *functions* of these notes, not their position—which is defined only by locus. Aristoxenus's theory is a theory of functions, of mutual relationships within a system; this kind of theory was made possible by the concept of continuous quantity basic to the new geometry.

In analyzing relationships outside the tetrachord, Aristoxenus proceeded with the help of the assumptions and procedures we have studied so far; he used the consonances of fourth and fifth as basic, undefined terms, the whole tone as their difference. He added one more fact of stylistic reality: while it was possible to sing the two consecutive quarter tones, *dieses,* in the pyknon of the enharmonic genus, it was not possible to sing three such dieses in succession. Aristoxenus formulated this musical fact as a general law, saying that the next interval in succession after the pyknon had to be either the remainder of the tetrachord (lichanos-mese) or a whole tone. This implied that the pyknon could only be conceived as part of a tetrachord; in effect, it postulated that systems larger than a tetrachord would be constructed out of tetrachords joined together.

Then Aristoxenus gave us another general law that in two similar tetrachords following one after another, the notes of one must be a fourth or a fifth away from their counterparts in the other; hypate must be a fourth from hypate, parhypate from parhypate, and so on, or hypate must be a fifth from hypate, parhypate from parhypate. If the condition was fulfilled by the fourth, then the two tetrachords were what was commonly called "conjunct," the hypate of the upper tetrachord coinciding with the mese of the lower. If the condition was filled by the fifth, then the two tetrachords were "disjunct," the hypate of the upper being a whole tone higher than the mese of the lower—exactly a whole tone, the difference of fourth and fifth, not some other interval. The terms conjunct and disjunct, as well as the structures they referred to, seem to have been in existence before Aristoxenus; he is showing what they mean by reasons that can be incorporated into a rigorous system. He is showing that the normal succession of notes in the scale can be rigorously deduced from the undefined terms of fourth and fifth, and from the impossibility of singing three dieses in succession. The goal of his theory is to demonstrate such succession; he refers often in the first two fragments to "continuity and consecution in scales." The demonstration really takes place, however, in the third fragment, in the format of propositions and proofs familiar to us from Euclid's *Elements.* The end result of Aristoxenus's theory as it unfolds in the third fragment is the Greek scale known to us as the Greater Perfect System.

What is the point, you ask, to this demonstration of the obvious? There are several answers. First, it is by no means certain that this *was* the normal form of the scale until Aristoxenus made it so. He may actually have constructed the Greater Perfect System as a standard to replace or synthesize various conflicting systems whose nature we can only surmise. Second, even if he did not invent this standard scale, it seems certain that he was the first (as he claimed) to show how its structure was logically derived from a few simple principles—and that without Pythagorean arithmetic, but rather by a system that not only had greater theoretical generality but also was able to account better for increasingly varied musical practice. He was the first, in other words, to show that even the most intricate musical construction could be the object of systematic, scientific knowledge. Finally, by defining a normal scale, Aristoxenus opened the door to a clearer understanding of the abnormal scales encountered in the process of modulation.

Modulation is the most important and most neglected aspect of Greek music. We know it existed simply because theorists from Aristoxenus on speak of it; from these references we can form a reasonably clear, if incomplete, idea of what it involved. In the early 5th century it was apparently not possible to change from one *harmonia* (whatever kind of tonal organization that might be) to another in the course of a composition; but it became possible to do so sometime around 400 B.C.[12] Simultaneously, however, the *harmoniai* disappeared, replaced in Aristoxenus by *tonoi* of similar names—Dorian, Phrygian, Lydian. The tonoi are transpositions of the basic scale, Aristoxenus's Greater Perfect System: Phrygian is a position of the Greater Perfect System a whole tone above Dorian, Lydian another position a whole tone above Phrygian. All this is well known; what has been neglected is the fact that transposition took place within a work, being called "change" or modulation. It is this use of tonal change within a piece that gives substance to the idea that tonoi sounded different, for even if a difference of absolute pitch was not perceptible, the effect of transposition or modulation within a piece obviously was.

Aristoxenus mentions the tonoi as if they were familiar. Unfortunately his own theory of tonoi is not preserved. We have only the testimony of Cleonides, a later writer (2nd–3rd century A.D.) who reproduces in textbook form the outlines of Aristoxenus's theory.[13]

[12] Evidence for this comes mostly from the "Pherecrates" fragment; see Henderson, NOHM, I, 394.

[13] Transl. O. Strunk, *Source Readings in Music History* (New York 1950), pp. 34–46. Aristeides Quintilianus (2nd–3rd century A.D.) ascribes 13 tonoi to Aristoxenus, but his witness is doubtful; R. Schäfke, *Aristeides Quintilianus, Von der Musik* (Berlin 1937), p. 194.

Cleonides includes a clear, complete account of 13 tonoi or transpositions, a semitone apart. The only question is, was this Aristoxenus's theory? Although a definite answer cannot be given, I suspect the answer is "no." Aristoxenus provides two indirect reasons against the use of 13 tonoi. On several occasions he severely criticizes certain predecessors who used a system of 28 consecutive dieses—a system apparently designed as a common basis for all scales in all tonoi.[14] Aristoxenus says this system suffers from *katapyknosis*, a term sounding like some dread disease and meaning a succession of pykna, which Aristoxenus said could not occur. The system of 12 tonoi separated by semitones clearly suffers from the same fault: in Aristoxenus's view it would not correspond to a musical reality.

In the same passage Aristoxenus also speaks of the seven forms of the octave, each an octave segment starting on a different note of the scale. He admits his predecessor Eratocles used these seven octave forms, but (he says) not rigorously. It is clear that Aristoxenus himself intended to use the seven forms in a more rigorous way. Now a theorist speaks of seven octave forms only because that is all there are. Although we do not know how many tonoi Aristoxenus used, we can reasonably assume he intended seven, relating them to each other through the seven octave forms in the way familiar to us from later writers, especially Ptolemy.[15] At any rate, to use fewer than seven tonoi would have been unsystematic and hence quite uncharacteristic, but to use more than seven would have been not only unsystematic, but would have involved something similar to katapyknosis. For while it is clear that there are no more than seven octave forms in the Greek seven-toned system, it is just as clear that there can be as many transpositions as you please; transpositions in excess of seven, however, can only be described in terms of the seven octave forms. Ptolemy, criticizing the 13 tonoi, asked, how can there be 13 tonoi, since each must correspond to an octave form?[16] A good question; if we ask, what octave form corresponds to the Dorian octave nete-hypate in Cleonides's Iastian tonos (lying a semitone above Dorian) we find that it is either the Dorian octave form itself, a semitone too high, or else the Phrygian octave form paranete-lichanos a semitone too low. It can be referred to, then, either as "high Dorian" or "low Phrygian"; Cleonides chose the latter. Hence the extra tonoi are theoretically redundant. Aristoxenus, I think, would have preferred seven tonoi, one for each octave form.

[14] *Harmonics*, p. 170, and Macran's footnote, pp. 229–32.
[15] Henderson, NOHM, I, 352–58.
[16] I. Düring, *Ptolemaios und Porphyrios über die Musik*, in: *Göteborgs Högskolas Årsskrift*, XL (1934), 79–80.

Fig. 3   The Iastian, or Low Phrygian tonos of Cleonides

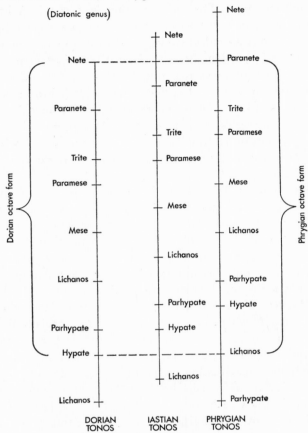

The obscurities surrounding the harmoniai, tonoi, and octave forms have often made an understanding of Greek music seem impossible. There is no denying that these topics are of central importance, or that we lack the very material—the music itself—needed to understand them fully. But a careful reading of Aristoxenus gives us a better perspective on the whole problem. In the first place, there are other aspects of Greek theory: the tonoi form only the concluding part of Aristoxenus's discussion. The remainder of his thought, leading up to the tonoi, is more or less intact, quite comprehensible, and very enlightening—the treatment of genera being perhaps the best. Then, even though we can only guess at the relationship of tonoi and octave forms in Aristoxenus, our guess can be a good one, for their relationship is inherent in their very nature—and that is the point. It is the relationship of tonoi and octave forms that is important for music theory. The long-debated question—which existed for the sake of the other—need not obstruct our understanding of the theory, for it pertains rather to the way these concepts were applied to practical music. Did the octave forms provide a way of changing from one tonos, one position of the basic scale, to another, or did the tonoi provide a way of filling a certain space (the "central octave") with a variety of octave forms? This is a matter that concerns the application of theoretical concepts to musical practice and musical style. It is easy to imagine that both alternatives were true at various stages of Greek musical development. The more drastic kind of modulation achieved by simple transposition of the scale upwards or downwards presumably represents an earlier practice, followed later by the more subtle modulation brought about by rearranging intervals within a fixed space (modern analogies might be the strong 17th-century modulation upwards by whole tones, called "Rosalia," and the *Liebestraum* device). Such matters, however, remain speculative in the absence of the musical repertory forever lost. But we do know how tonoi and octave forms were related, and through this relationship we can come to an understanding of Greek theory.

Furthermore, even though we do not—perhaps cannot—know what the 5th-century harmoniai were, what they sounded like, what their ethos was, or how it was achieved, still we can see in the 4th-century constructions of tonoi and octave forms the analogs of at least two aspects of the harmoniai. The transpositions represented by the tonoi seem to reproduce, in systematic form, the effect of "high" and "low" described in such tantalizing terms by writers like Plato, while the varying arrangements of intervals in the octave forms seem to reproduce—if only in principle—the varied harmoniai. As far as we can gather, the 5th-century harmoniai were not systematic; at least, if they were, we can not discover what the system was. But the 4th-century system of tonoi and octave forms is entirely accessible to us—owing largely to the work of Aristoxenus. This system does not, of course, tell us what the music sounded like; but it does tell us something about the space within which the music moved and had its being. Definition of that space, description of how notes could function within it, was the special achievement of Aristoxenus. As Macran put it, Aristoxenus was concerned with a system "each member of which *is* essentially what it *does*." This was a new kind of music theory, as different from Pythagorean theory as the new geometry was from Pythagorean arithmetic—and in exactly the same way. The construction of a purely functional system in which elements were related only to each other, not to external units of measurement, was made possible by the new-found ability to deal with all types of musical intervals on the same basis without reference to number. Aristoxenus's theory of music was one of the most modern developments in 4th-century Greek mathematics.

MUSIC IN BIOGRAPHIES
OF EMPEROR MAXIMILIAN

by LOUISE E. CUYLER

GERMANY WAS late in joining the cultural surge known today as the Renaissance. Even as late as the second half of the 15th century, when music and painting were flourishing in Italy and the Low Countries especially, the German provinces showed negligible concern for culture and learning. This was especially true in the Eastern Reich of the sadly diminished Holy Roman Empire. That region, which would enjoy the greatest flowering music has ever known some three centuries later, was remote from the great trade routes between Flanders, the Hanseatic cities, and Italy. Vienna, the natural capital of this district, lay perilously close to the always troubled Hungarian and Bohemian frontiers; she was, moreover, especially vulnerable to the Turkish hordes that threatened Europe for many years after the fall of Constantinople in 1453.

Vienna's low estate in the dawning Renaissance is attested by the fact that she remained under the ecclesiastical jurisdiction of the bishop of Passau until 1469. During this year, two bishoprics were set up—for Vienna and Wiener–Neustadt—at the insistence of Emperor Friedrich III. That Wiener–Neustadt remained the more important for some 20 years was to be expected, since this military bastion about 60 kilometers south of Vienna was the imperial residence throughout Friedrich's reign. The Viennese were notably unfriendly toward Friedrich, who retaliated by ignoring them as much as possible.

Aeneas Sylvius Piccolomini, the future Pius II (1458–64), has left vivid pictures of Vienna in his day scattered throughout his *Commentaries*.[1] This scholar, humanist, traveler, as well as churchman was secretary to Friedrich III for several years. He came to know the Austrians better than they knew themselves, albeit he viewed them with an Italian's somewhat prejudiced eyes. He saw Vienna as a cultural wasteland, her university fallen on evil days, her erstwhile scholars departed

---

[1] *Memoirs of a Renaissance Pope*, transl. Florence A. Gragg, ed. Leona C. Gabel (New York 1959).

for greener pastures, her citizens too busy carousing, drinking, de-
bauching to manifest any interest in the classics or culture in general.

Aeneas Sylvius was probably prejudiced; but his remarks are partly
confirmed by other circumstances, and the likelihood is that most of
central and eastern Austria resembled Vienna.

By contrast, towns closer to Flanders or Italy, as well as those on the
trade routes from north to south, were, by mid-century, having the first
stirrings of a cultural awakening. Augsburg, Munich, Regensburg in
Bavaria, and Innsbruck, capital of the Tyrol, on the direct route to the
Brenner Pass, were important German cities in this nascent Renaissance.
Organ building and the science of wind instrument making had found a
natural habitat, furthermore, among the dextrous, inventive men of
central and southern Germany; and Nuremberg was a veritable cradle of
the printer's craft.

A dramatic change of attitude which transformed the whole temper
of the Empire may be perceived in the closing years of the 15th century.
This was accomplished largely through the enthusiasm for all the arts
and learning engendered by the new Emperor, Maximilian I, who succeeded his father in 1493. Few monarchs have influenced their people
more profoundly; the foundation for Germany's magnificent cultural
future was firmly laid in his reign (1493–1519).

Easy to perceive is the reason this young German prince had become
a man so strikingly different from his bumbling father and most of his
compatriots. When he was but 18, Max went to Flanders to wed Mary
of Burgundy, daughter and granddaughter of the music-and-art-loving
dukes of Burgundy. In 1477, the year of their marriage, Bruges and
Ghent were filled with the music of Binchois, Dufay, Busnois; the
lovely paintings of the Van Eycks and Memling were to be seen everywhere; the celebration of Mass, processions and festivals were carried
out with a grandeur equaled only in Italy. Little wonder that the im-
pressionable young Max was won over quickly to the cult of the arts.

When Mary of Burgundy died suddenly and tragically after only
five years of marriage, she left a grieving young husband who mourned
her for the remainder of his life. Her bequest to him, besides their children Philip and Marguerite, was an abiding love of beauty. That Max,
as Emperor, was able to transmit this to his German people is a vital fact
of cultural history.

Maximilian assembled his musical household during the ten years
between 1486 and 1496. For his coronation as King of the Romans,[2]

---

[2] This was a preliminary title, which would, he hoped, be followed in due course
by the more prestigious one of Holy Roman Emperor. Maximilian became Emperor-

four years after Mary's death, he reassembled the fine *chapelle* that had served the dukes of Burgundy so well. Jean Molinet has described this restoration and the subsequent coronation ceremonies at Aachen (Aix-la-Chapelle) in vivid detail.[3] The year after he became Emperor-elect, Max founded his *Hofmusik* by combining the Burgundian musicians with the remnants of his father's more modest *Kapelle*. In 1496, he established the *Hofkapelle* in the Hofburg at Vienna. An early product of its splendid choir school, which would train so many of music's future great men, was Ludwig Senfl, who served his monarch as singer, then chief court composer for 23 years.

Paul Hofhaimer, greatest organist of his day and a principal ornament of the Kaiser's *Hofmusik*, came into Max's household when the Tyrol was given over to his custody in 1490. Hofhaimer, who, like the Emperor, was born in 1459, had been in the service of Duke Sigmund at Innsbruck. He was faithful to the Kaiser throughout Max's lifetime, sharing his fortunes and peripatetic existence. The life of a musician in the 16th century was a strenuous one, for most monarchs carried their musical households along when they traveled, even when they made war. The pictures of Kaiser Max's musicians in the *Triumphzug*, on horseback or crowded into various animal-drawn vehicles, are by no means entirely fictitious.

Heinrich Isaac, a Fleming and the third illustrious musician in the Kaiser's service, was hired when Max was encamped before Pisa in one of his many abortive attempts to subdue some of the towns of northern Italy. Many details of Isaac's life, obscure until recent times, are now being disclosed. He first emerges from the shadows in the records of the Innsbruck court for 1484, when he probably passed through that town on his way to the Brenner and Italy.[4] After this time, he served Lorenzo the Magnificent at Florence for some ten years and worked also at Ferrara. That he was teacher to Lorenzo's children, among them Giovanni, the future Pope Leo X, might have implications as yet undiscovered, with regard both to his own later life and the affairs of Emperor Max's *Hofkapelle*.

Surprise has been expressed that Isaac was hired by the Kaiser so promptly after Lorenzo's death. An obvious explanation is that Maxi-

---

elect at his father's death in 1493. Fifteen years later he received formal permission to use the title of Emperor, although he was never crowned. An important aid in dating items of Maximiliana is his use of the single eagle, emblem of the King of the Romans, until 1508 and his adoption of the double eagle of the Empire from that year on.

[3] *Chroniques de Jean Molinet*, ed. J. A. Buchon (Paris 1827).

[4] Walter Senn, *Musik und Theater am Hof zu Innsbruck* (Innsbruck 1954).

milian had probably known and admired Isaac in Flanders. This composer must have been about 32 years old when the Burgundian musicians were scattered far and wide after Mary's death. That he was a mature, gifted artist at the time is attested by the distinguished Italian patrons who appear to have employed him immediately. Thus Maximilian could scarcely have failed to know his talents. The time of Isaac's probable departure from his native land was soon after Mary's unfortunate death.

By the end of Emperor Maximilian's life in 1519, a strong musical tradition had been emplanted in the Empire. Despite bitter religious strife, partition, and other vicissitudes, the German states never faltered, advancing steadily in musical prowess through the years. All the world knows the glorious flowering in the 18th and 19th centuries.

Fortunately for future historians, Emperor Max possessed another trait just as strong as his love of the arts. This was a magnificent conceit that impelled him to project his own glory, along with that of his Habsburg line, into posterity. Self-aggrandizement was an obsession of most Renaissance princes, but few were able to satisfy their ambitions in so complete and impressive a manner.

Portraying himself as he wished future generations to know him seemed eminently sensible to the Kaiser, as he attests in *Weisskunig*.[5]

[The man] who achieves no remembrance for himself during his lifetime has none after death, and will be forgotten with the sound of a bell. Thus the money I spend for my remembrance is not lost; but the money saved on my remembrance is a suppression of future remembrance; and what I do not bring about for my memory during my life will not be accomplished by you or any other person.

The exact role Kaiser Max played in compiling his numerous biographical works is still a controversial matter. That he inspired, examined, and corrected most of them is established fact; that he planned and dictated at least three is the opinion of most scholars today. There are some 16 quasi-biographical books which, along with two contemporary histories of his reign (Cuspinian, *De Caesaribus* and Grünpeck, *Die Historia Federici et Maximiliani*), paint a vivid and imperishable picture of life at the court of a German Emperor in the early Renaissance. Most of these

---

[5] "Wer sich in seinem Leben kein Gedächtnis macht, der hat nach seinem Tode kein Gedächtnis, und desselben Menschen wird mit Glockenton vergessen. Darum ist das Geld, das ich für mein Gedächtnis ausgebe nicht verloren; sondern das Geld das erspart wird an meinem Gedächtnis, das ist eine Unterdrückung meines kunftigen Gedächtnisses; und was ich in meinem Leben zu meinem Gedächtnisse nicht vollbringe, das wird nach meinem Tode weder durch dich noch durch andere dazugetan werden." *Weisskunig*, II, 24.

accounts are wonderfully illustrated by the best artists of the realm, with the result that the pictorial record is even more revealing than the verbal one.

Music permeated the life of the Emperor's court, as these illustrations attest so graphically. It is the purpose of the remainder of this article to cite the principal sources of musical information among Emperor Max's books and to comment briefly upon them.

WEISSKUNIG

Weisskunig [6] is the work most intimately connected with Kaiser Max. It is thought to be largely of his planning, probably even of his dictation, since one of the illustrations shows Treitzsauerwein, the faithful secretary, kneeling before his monarch as he writes.

This work seems to have been undertaken formally around 1506, after the Emperor had dabbled with several lesser ones. It underwent constant alteration during the next few years, but was completed in a format of several folios by 1514. The subsequent reassembling of these parts from many corners of the Reich and from several different owners is itself a fascinating saga. The first printed edition was not issued until 1775, a full 260 years after Max gave it his stamp of approval.

Weisskunig is the life story of Friedrich III—the Old Weisskunig—and Maximilian I—the Young Weisskunig. Sixty years in the history of the Empire are recorded in its pages. Especially valuable are the 251 superb woodcuts, of which 118 are the work of Hans Burgkmair, the great artist of Augsburg. It will be recalled that this same master created the splendid murals of the Ladies' Court at the Fugger Palace, along with many of the other art treasures that were Augsburg's glory. The descriptive texts match in no way the quality of the illustrations. They are, in fact, written in so naive a style that they might be considered strong testament to the Emperor's authorship.

Seven of the woodcuts have musical allusions or are based on musical subjects. Illustration 14 is the first of these; it lacks a descriptive paragraph, but is entitled *Meerfahrt der Königen Leonora*. Leonora (Eleanor of Portugal) was the wife of Friedrich III and Maximilian's mother. The scene depicted is the waterfront of a city with studiedly oriental architecture, presumably a town in Portugal. Two ships bearing pennants with the double eagle of the Holy Roman Empire are anchored offshore. In the one to the left, which is being approached by a small skiff bearing the bride-to-be, Leonora, a trio of trumpeters is sounding a

---

[6] *Kaiser Maximilians 1 Weisskunig,* Kohlhammer ed. (Stuttgart 1956).

flourish. Their instruments are the folded military or field trumpets used during the 15th and 16th centuries for salutes and fanfares to embellish all ceremonial occasions.

Illustration 14 is not in correct sequence in the narrative, since it follows the 12 that recount the betrothal and marriage of the Old Weiss-kunig with Leonora—this ceremony took place after Eleanor's departure from her native land.

Illustration 33 (see Pl. 4a) holds the greatest musical interest and is, fortunately, among those drawn by Burgkmair—his familiar autograph "H.B." may be seen on the organ post. The Young Weisskunig (Maximilian), shown as a comely youth bearing a laurel-wreath, stands in the midst of a room filled with instruments and performers. The caption— "Wie der junge weisse König das Spielen aller Saiteninstrumente erlernte" is belied by the variety of the instruments scattered about the room.

In the left foreground is an organ with 52 pipes arranged in two rows, and a pedal-board. The top octave of the manual is visible, showing the usual three black notes of the period—F$\sharp$, C$\sharp$, and B$\flat$. The top limit of the keyboard is not clear, but could be d^3, if the highest black key is c$\sharp$. If the compass of the manual is estimated on the basis of the measurement of this top octave, it would seem to be about four octaves. Thus the full range might be C to d^3, although such a conclusion is, obviously, a tenuous one. Not enough of the pedal-board is in sight to permit any conclusions about it; but if each key of the manual governed a single pipe, the pedal compass could have been 10 or 12 notes, which is close to the average for German organs of the time. The usual *Blasebalgtreter*, gay in his feathered headdress, is operating the bellows, his sobriquet a reminder that the wind machines for the great church organs literally needed a *Treter*—one who operated the huge bellows by what must have been very intricate footwork.

Opposite the organ, beneath the casement windows to the right, is a table on which a harpsichord (*clavicymbalo*) is placed. Two performers are sitting before it, but the keyboard is not visible. Surrounding the keyboard instrument are, from left to right, a viol with the backward-slanted head adopted from the older rebec, C-shaped sound holes, and six strings; five flutes and recorders of various sizes, along with a cromorne; and three books. At the end of the table, a tromba marina, lute, sidedrum, kettledrum, and trumpet are to be seen. Between the organ and the table, a harpist is fingering his 16-stringed instrument.

A second table is to be seen back of the Young Weisskunig and in front of a rear window. Around it are grouped four singers and a flutist, performing, probably, a polyphonic *Lied*, the most popular type of secular composition in Maximilian's Germany.

Illustration 33, along with its descriptive paragraph, is intended to carry the inference that Maximilian had, as a youth, the advantage of a fine musical education. This must have been mere wishful reminiscing on the Emperor's part, since neither Cuspinian nor Grünpeck mentions that he played any instrument, although they do stress his important role as a lover and patron of music.

Illustration 35 shows the Young Weisskunig directing a group of mummers in bird masks. They are wearing (according to the descriptive text) Hungarian costumes, and are preceded by a herald with a torch. Eight ladies, seated at a table in the rear, are enjoying the show. Three musicians—two flutists and a drummer—stand behind a table on which a lute, several pipes, and a cromorne are clearly seen. The drummer appears also to be playing the one-handed flute or tabor-pipe, although this instrument is not actually visible. This kind of musical group was used for most performances of mummers, as will be seen quite convincingly in the discussion of *Freydal*. The "H.B." of the artist appears this time on the musicians' table.

Illustration 48, one of many showing a joust, has two mounted trumpeters behind a barrier.

Eighty-seven woodcuts intervene before musicians again appear. Illustration 136 shows the rescue of the Young Weisskunig by his father, who "mit zahlreichen Schiffen und vielem Volk auf dem Rhein zu Hilfe kam." Presumably this rescue is symbolic of the one carried out by old Friedrich when the Flemish burghers had Max locked in a tower at Bruges. Four ships appear, the foremost one with the Reich double-eagle on a pennant held at the prow by a *Landsknecht*. Aside from this standard-bearer, a helmsman, and rowers, the ship is filled with musicians: four trumpeters behind the *Landsknecht*, then several pipers and a drummer. A second ship shows the Spanish arms, and all are loaded with pikemen. Truly wars and fetes were as one to the Renaissance lords.

Illustration 160, which has neither caption nor descriptive matter, shows a similar but less festive scene. Here a small craft to the left bears only a single piper and a drummer.

Illustration 186 depicts the storming of the fortress of Monselice, which crowns a hill and is surrounded by a great wall. Pikemen, swarming up the slope, have reached the very door of the fortress, while at the foot of the hill and outside the wall a piper and a drummer seem to be urging the attack with their brisk strains.

Aside from the facts to be learned from the *Weisskunig* illustrations showing music, a suggestion of considerable significance comes by negative inference. A number of woodcuts present the scene of a funeral Mass; Illustration 57 shows that for the King of Feuereisen, Illustration 87 that for the wife of the Young Weisskunig (Mary of Burgundy), for example. Although each of these Requiem Masses is being said for a person of royal blood, with full pomp as is attested by the ceremony and display, musicians do not appear in a single one. This seems to imply that Masses for the Dead were generally celebrated as Low Masses in Maximilian's time. If this be true, it explains the scarcity of composed Requiems until quite late in the Renaissance.

TEUERDANK

A WORK closely akin to the *Weisskunig* is *Teuerdank*,[7] which was printed in 1517 and must have enjoyed a considerable vogue for many years, since it was reprinted in numerous later editions. This work is Maximilian's apologia for the five-month delay in reaching Mary of Burgundy, his betrothed, after her father Charles the Bold was slain in battle. The knight Teuerdank is, of course, Max himself; and the lady he seeks to reach—Princess Ehrenreich—is none other than Mary. The 118 wonderful colored woodcuts relate the adventures and misadventures of the hapless Teuerdank, including one which is the source of the famous *Martinswand* legend. The knight appears to have had little solace from music during his troubled journey, because only three illustrations, all of them picturing the joust, show musicians. Illustration 101 has a piper and a drummer accompanying the fray from a window behind the barrier. Illustration 102 shows three trumpeters who have just lifted their folded, military instruments. Illustration 105 places a piper, a trumpeter, and a drummer close behind the barrier.

FREYDAL

LITERARY scholars now hold that *Freydal*,[8] like *Weisskunig*, was planned, directed, perhaps actually dictated by Kaiser Max himself. It depicts him as the gallant knight he wished posterity to remember, a dashing fellow who gallops from joust to joust, pausing by night to make merry with the ladies.

The unpublished original, from which the facsimile edition was

---

[7] *Teuerdank*, abbreviation for *Die geuerlicheiten und einsteils der geschichten des loblichen streytparen und hochberümten helds und Ritters herr Tewrdannckhs.* (Nuremberg: Schonsperger, 1517). The first edition, a copy of which is owned by the Library of the University of Michigan, is the basis of these comments.
[8] *Freydal des Kaisers Maximilian I: Turniere und Mummerein* (Vienna 1880–82).

made, is corrected in the Kaiser's own hand, and has his own list of the men and women with whom he had "gerennt, gestochen, gekämpft und gemummt."

The illustrations, numbering 255 in all, are extraordinarily fine. Except for a few instances, they are presented in groups of four: three depicting tournaments or jousts, then a fourth showing some kind of mummery. None of the jousting scenes shows musicians, which is surprising in light of the just-cited illustrations in *Teuerdank*. Most of the representations of mummery do have musicians, however, and the relative consistency of instruments used is clear indication of the kind of music preferred in the early 16th century for such entertainments.

A total of 49 plates in *Freydal* show music. Of these, more than half—28—have only a transverse flute or pipe and a drum. Three more have the common alternative to this: the tabor-pipe and drum performed by a single player. Four illustrations use flutes alone, three of them showing a single performer, the last, two players.

Three plates depict bladder-pipes, both straight and curved. These primitive relatives of the bagpipes apparently carried no drone pipe. Another plate has a bladder-pipe used with the one-man drum-tabor-pipe combination. Two scenes have three S-trumpets, another three long pommers.

Instruments or combinations appearing only once are these: drum and pommer; a single S-trumpet; the one-man drum-tabor-pipe with a viola da braccio; recorder and rattle; a single vielle; flute and S-trumpet; an instrument resembling a primitive English horn—like the cromorne in shape, but with the wind-chest close to the bell.

To judge from the *Freydal* illustrations, mummery was almost always accompanied by music of some sort.

TRIUMPHZUG

The best known of all Emperor Max's works, and the one holding the greatest interest for musicians is the mighty *Triumphzug*,[9] which was completely planned by the Kaiser himself. Only the final editing was carried out, in 1512, by Max's faithful secretary, Marx Treitzsauerwein. A number of artists participated in preparing the drawings for the woodcuts: Burgkmair, Albrecht, Altdorfer, Hans Springenklee, Leonhard Beck, Hans L. Schäufelein, even the great Albrecht Dürer himself. Of

---

[9] *Triumphzug des Kaisers Maximilian I* (Vienna 1883–84). The captions and commentary appear in *Jahrbuch der kunsthistorischen Sammlung des allerhöchsten Kaiserhaus*, I (Vienna 1883), pp. 154–81.

the 137 woodcuts, 14 are concerned entirely with music, and through them the magnificence of Emperor Maximilian's musical household is recorded in vivid and imperishable form.

The first illustration shows a naked (but feathered!) man—Preco—astride a *Greyfen* and blowing a highly ornate *Waldhorn* from the bell of which flames are leaping. Preco and most of the subsequent musicians wear the laurel crown.

After an intervening title plate, woodcuts 3 and 4 appear, carrying a single title: *Pfeyffer und Trumlslager*. In the first of these, three mounted players of the transverse flute (military pipe) are preceded by a mounted standard bearer. The leader is Anthony of Darmstadt, Max's favorite piper. Although the flute of the early 16th century is said to have had only six holes—none for the small finger—Anthony's flute appears to have one under his poised little finger. In the second of these plates, five mounted drummers are shown.

After 15 illustrations depicting hunting scenes for the greater part, the most important musical illustrations, five in all, appear. Drawn in minute, loving detail, they are a veritable goldmine of information. At this point in the procession the illustrations occur in pairs, the first in each case showing the animals that draw the car and the shafts, the second the actual vehicle with its lovely musical burden.

Illustrations 17 and 18, entitled *Musica Lauten und Rybeben*, show a low, moderately ornate car (see Pl. 4b) carrying three lutenists and two viola da gamba players. The playing positions of all are interesting. The two lutenists in the outside positions hold their instruments up and pointed over the left shoulder, whereas the middle man points his lute downward toward the floor of the car. The lutenist farthest to the right, in the center of the car, is Artus, a prime favorite at the court. One of the viol players is bowing with his left hand, the other with his right. If their positions in the car were reversed so that the bow arm of each was outside and free, this arrangement might seem purposeful. At it is, the ambidextrousness may be a mere caprice of the artist. Two reindeer are the beasts drawing the car.

Illustrations 19 and 20, entitled *Musica Schalmeyen, pusaunen, krumphörner*, were drawn by Burgkmair. The low, buffalo-drawn car carries a trombonist (probably Neyschl, master of the court wind-band), and two players each of the shawm and cromorne. The shawms face each other on the inside, the cromornes are side-by-side at the right, and the trombone is farthest left, outside.

Illustrations 21 and 22 show the great Hofhaimer in solitary glory on the *Orgelwagen* drawn by a camel. This picture of the first

German organ virtuoso is perhaps most familiar of all, and has been re-produced numerous times. He is seated at an instrument designated in the text as a *Schalmeyenpossetif*, that is, a positive organ with reed pipes —a rather small one, since the pipes number only 13. Behind Hofhaimer are two other organs—regals, by the caption. The case of the first bears the imprint of the Imperial double-eagle.

Illustrations 23 and 24 depict a more ornate car (see Pl. 5a) drawn by a dromedary. The caption *Musica süess Meledey* might suggest prefer-ence for the kind of mixed band crowded into this car. At the left, under the canopy, are players of viola da gamba, harp, and *Fydel;* in front, legs over the side of the car, are a very jolly man with a large lute and another, dour one with a quintern (guitar). In front is a single player of the one-man drum-tabor-pipe combination. Two Rauschpfeifen are at the rear, behind the lute and guitar. The inference to be drawn from this plate is that, if Burgkmair is depicting a real situation, there was no limit to the mixture of instruments used together in Max's day.

The bison-drawn car of Illustrations 25 and 26 (see Pl. 5b) is of great interest, because it shows the Kaiser's *Hofkapelle* in a mixed vocal-instrumental performance of sacred music. It indicates, moreover, the proportion of singers used. Directly back of the great lectern with the choirbook stand six boy singers. On their left are Augustin playing the zink and Stewdl the trombone. Seven adult male singers surround the boys. Seated at the rear of the car, beside another, unnamed cleric, is Georg Slakonia, Bishop of Vienna and master of the music at St. Stephen's Cathedral. The zink may have been used for some of the un-vocal and peripatetic alto parts in music like the motets of Isaac's *Choralis Constantinus*. The trombone probably reinforced the cantus-firmus parts.

The remaining musical subjects in the *Triumphzug* are of much less interest than those just cited. Illustration 30, entitled *Natürlich Narren*, shows one of the "fools" with a tabor-pipe. Much later, Illustrations 115, 116, and 117 show the trumpeters of the Reich, all mounted and, pre-sumably, five drummers, also mounted—although only the instrument of the outside player is in sight. Both the single eagle of the King of the Romans and the Imperial double-eagle appear on the pennants.

And so Emperor Max's memory has been kept green these many years through the works he planned, even as he asserted in *Weisskunig* that he hoped would happen. He was wrong on one count, however: the greatest monument of all, the colossal *Grabmal* in the Innsbruck Hofkirche, was brought to fulfillment full 30 years after his death, "durch andere"—his grandson Ferdinand.

THE LOST FRAGMENTS OF A NOTRE DAME MANUSCRIPT IN JOHANNES WOLF'S LIBRARY

by LUTHER A. DITTMER

OF ALL THE manuscripts of 13th-century polyphony, the manuscript known to us by Friedrich Ludwig's symbol Mü A appears to have been the most comprehensive; it contained French and Latin motets, polyphonic and monophonic conductus, trouvère music, and (if the assumption regarding its affiliation with the leaves of organa is correct) a version of the two-part Magnus Liber. Thus, it combined within itself all of the important genres of musical creativity of the central developmental area of France during the early 13th century; only a separate fascicle devoted to substitute clausulae is lacking in the fragments known to have existed. Unique to this collection is the arrangement of the motets according to musical considerations: the succession of motets follows that of the tenors in the Magnus Liber (but see below, note 25). While the arrangement of clausulae according to the succession of the organa (*Choralbearbeitungen*) is important for their orderly inclusion as substitute settings *ad libitum* for comparable passages in the main versions, a similar arrangement of motets serves no like purpose, since the motet, especially the pastoral and convivial motets in French, essentially played no such comparable external rôle. The presence of a cycle of motets arranged according to the succession of tenor sources and polyphonic models strengthens the conviction that motet composition, at least in the first half of the 13th century, involved an organized setting of entire series of such works comparable to the various groups of substitute clausulae; furthermore, it provides further justification for the method used by Ludwig for the classification of motets according to the order of the tenors in the Magnus Liber. Our knowledge of this lost manuscript of the 13th century has been gained from two sets of fragments used as binding material in other codices; one set is preserved in Munich, Bayerische Staatsbibliothek, gallo-rom. 42 (or Mus. Ms. 4775) and was therefore assigned the symbol

Mü A by Ludwig; [1] the other set became a victim of the destruction in World War II of Johannes Wolf's library in Berlin.

The parts of this manuscript now preserved in Munich were purchased in 1873 by the present Bayerische Staatsbibliothek from the Leipzig antiquarian Kirchoff and Wigand; nothing is known about their previous ownership or history. The Munich fragments have been discussed by C. Hofmann,[2] J. J. Maier,[3] and A. Stimming,[4] and they were thoroughly inventoried and discussed by F. Ludwig in his *Repertorium;* [5] facsimiles of these fragments have been published in my study, hereafter referred to as the *Reconstruction.*[6]

The parts of this manuscript formerly preserved in the library of Johannes Wolf formed part of the *Nachlass* of Gustav Jacobsthal, who died in 1912. Although Ludwig had dedicated the half-volume of the *Repertorium* appearing in 1910 to his teacher Jacobsthal, he did not know of the existence of these fragments until 1913, when he was first able to examine Jacobsthal's *Nachlass.*[7] Evidently they had already passed into the hands of Wolf by this time, and it was only after World War I that Ludwig was able to study the fragments. Two pages from the fragments were printed in Wolf's *Musikalische Schrifttafeln,* 1923 (Heft 1, No. 3). On the basis of a handwritten copy by F. Ludwig,[8] I undertook to reconstruct the lost fragments.[9] Two isolated events have subsequently combined to permit further study of the lost Berlin fragments.

Following my published reconstruction, Mlle. Solange Corbin was able to draw my attention to the presence in the music division of the Bibliothèque Nationale in Paris of photographs of Wolf's fragments that Y. Rokseth had used for her commentary to the edition of the Mont-

[1] Friedrich Ludwig, *Repertorium organorum recentioris et motetorum vetustissimi stili* (referred to hereafter as *Repertorium*), Vol. I, pt. 1 [all that was published] (2nd ed. New York & Hildesheim 1964), p. 279; see also F. Ludwig, *Die Quellen der Motetten ältesten Stils,* in: *Archiv für Musikwissenschaft,* V (1923), 187–90, reprinted in Friedrich Gennrich (ed.), *Friedrich Ludwig, Repertorium,* Vol. I, pt. 2, page numbers according to the original (Darmstadt 1961).

[2] C. Hofmann, *Bruchstücke eines altfranzösischen Liederbuches (Chansonnier) aus dem 13. Jahrhundert,* in: *Sitzungsberichten der philosophisch-philologischen und historischen Klasse der königlichen bayerischen Akademie der Wissenschaften zu München* (1873), pp. 349–57.

[3] J. J. Maier, *Die musikalischen Handschriften der kaiserlichen Hof- und Staatsbibliothek in München,* I (Munich 1879), No. 201, p. 109.

[4] A. Stimming, *Die altfranzösischen Motette der Bamberger Handschrift* (Halle 1906), pp. 102–13.

[5] Pp. 279–85.

[6] L. Dittmer, *Eine zentrale Quelle der Notre Dame-Musik—A Central Source of Notre-Dame Polyphony* (New York 1959), pp. 21–22 & 27–28.

[7] Gennrich, *Ludwig, Repertorium,* Vol. I, pt. 2, preface.

[8] Göttingen, Niedersächsische Landes- und Universitätsbibliothek, Nachlass Friedrich Ludwigs, Fascicle VII/8.

[9] *Reconstruction,* pp. 21–36.

pellier manuscript.[10] It is thus possible now to reprint in facsimile the lost fragments formerly in Wolf's library from photocopies supplied by the Bibliothèque Nationale.

Furthermore, Heinrich Besseler has kindly provided me with the manuscript copy of the unprinted portion of Ludwig's *Repertorium*, together with printed proofs of parts of Vol. I/2 and Vol. II that extend beyond those printed by F. Gennrich.[11] As a supplement to Vol. I/1, Ludwig includes as section XI (the same section devoted to Mü A in the published part of the *Repertorium*) an inventory of the Wolf fragments.[12] While this catalogue does not add much to our knowledge of the contents of these fragments, it does furnish us with certain information otherwise not available. Rather than review the information provided in my *Reconstruction*, I wish here to discuss only the further information pertaining to these fragments that has come to light through the discovery of the facsimiles and through the information provided by Ludwig in the manuscript of his *Repertorium*. Corrections of the transcriptions and renderings of the texts as far as the motets are concerned will be contained in the edition of 13th-century motets prepared by H. Tischler,[13] whom I wish to thank for having provided me with an early photographic copy.

Ludwig's inventory lists 9 fragments corresponding to the indicated pages in my *Reconstruction*, as follows:

> 1) und 2) Reste von 2 weiteren Doppelblättern dieser Lage [Ludwig had just discussed the 2 bifolios in Munich], durch die die in München fragmentarischen Motetten No. 4 und 11 vervollständigt und 9 weitere überliefert werden. Von einem sind 3 bzw. 4, vom anderen 2 Streifen erhalten . . . , zusammengesetzt etwa 10 (vorderes) bzw. 7,5 (hinteres Blatt): 10,5 (Streifen 1–3) bzw. 7 (Streifen 4) und 6:11 bzw. 4,5 und (der Streifen 2 des hinteren Blattes:) 6 cm, so dass das 1. knapp 4/5 des vorderen und etwa die Hälfte des hinteren Blattes und das 2. etwa ein Drittel des alten Doppelblattes überliefert;" [These correspond to Plates 6–8, see also the *Reconstruction*, Complex A, pp. 23–26.]

---

[10] Y. Rokseth, *Polyphonies du XIIIe siècle*, IV (Paris 1939), p. 68, fn. 3; whereas the Munich fragments were consulted for the transcription volumes (II–III, published in 1936), Rokseth (IV, 274) indicates "Je n'avais pas encore les photographies du fragment de *MuA* appartenant à M. Johannes Wolf quand j'ai publié ce motet [No. 140]." Accordingly, II, 118, fn. 1 should read only: "Musique et texte manquent dans *Mo*."

[11] Gennrich, *Ludwig, Repertorium*, II (Darmstadt 1962); actually, the music was engraved to p. 114 and the text set to p. 87, see the introduction to Vol. I, pt. 1 of the second edition of the *Repertorium*.

[12] Part of the information contained in this inventory was published by Ludwig in: *Archiv für Musikwissenschaft*, V (1923), 189 (see above fn. 1).

[13] H. Tischler, *A Complete Edition of the Earliest Motets, c. 1190–1270* (in preparation).

3) und 4) 2 Doppelblätter aus einer späteren Lage des Motetten-faszikels mit 11 Motetten;" [These correspond to Plates 9–12, see also the *Reconstruction*, Complex B, pp. 29–32.]

5) 1 Doppelblatt aus dem Conductusfaszikel;" [This corresponds to Plates 15–16, see also the *Reconstruction*, Complex D, pp. 35–36.]

6) 2 Streifen eines Blattes eben daher, etwa 5:11 cm;" [This corresponds to Plate 17, see also the *Reconstruction*, Complex E, pp. 35–36.]

7) etwa 2/5 eines Doppelblattes aus einem Organafaszikel, etwa 6:11,5 cm; obwohl mindestens der Text von anderer Hand geschrieben ist und auch die Einrichtung der Notensysteme in den Massen abweicht, kann der Faszikel doch der gleichen Handschrift entstammen;" [This corresponds to Plates 13–14 (top), see also the *Reconstruction*, Complex C, pp. 33–34.]

8) ein kleiner Rest eines Blattes eben daher, etwa 7,5:5 cm;" [This corresponds to Plates 13–14 (bottom), see also the *Reconstruction*, Complex C, lower portion, pp. 33–34.]

9) über ein weiteres kleines Fragment, das anscheinend nicht zu Mü A gehörte . . . [See the *Reconstruction*, Complex F, pp. 35–36.]

Concerning the final item, I was able to give no further information except its size and shape in the *Reconstruction*. Furthermore, this small remnant is missing from among the photographs in Paris, thus our only additional information about this scrap is afforded by Ludwig's further description:

Bei den Berliner Fragmenten von Mü A liegt weiter ein kleiner Pergamentrest, etwa 1,6 cm hoch und 4,2 cm breit, der unterste Teil eines Blattes; auf der einer Seite das Bruchstück eines französischen Textes mit Notation enthaltend (2 Systeme, deren Anfang fehlt darüber einige weitere Textreste; auf der anderen Seite frei), von anderer Hand geschrieben und, wie schon aus den Massen hervorgeht, wesentlich kleiner als Mü A. Das Erhaltene beginnt: loee par sa grant soloi; es bricht ab: dites amerez mi. Es ist anscheinend ein Motettenfragment; "dites amerez mi" beginnt wie ein Refrain in einem Mot.; doch kann ich es anderwärtig noch nicht nachweisen. Über die Zugehörigkeit des Fragments zu Mü A ist nichts sicheres bekannt. [Such a refrain is apparently not known in Gennrich's listing.[14]]

Although this last fragment was not included among the remnants photographed for Rokseth, two other fragments were included that are not listed by Ludwig. The first of these measures 5 x 4 cm, and the second 5.6 x 3.2 cm, see Plate 17; each formed a lower part of a leaf (perhaps of

---

[14] F. Gennrich, *Rondeaux, Virelais und Balladen*, II (Halle 1927); the listing of refrains is continued in the *Zeitschrift für romanische Philologie*, LXXI (1955), 379–90. This composition is transcribed in *Reconstruction* (p. 269) and should have been included under the discussion of Complex F (not E, see *Reconstruction*, p. 19).

the same leaf). The notation shows rhomboid figures, either semibreves or English breves. The leaves were apparently glued on both sides to provide a binding for a codex of other contents; in the removal of the scraps, the text of the contingent leaf has adhered to the present fragment; one can read ". . . eri in cenentās . . ./ . . . mo cū sūmo . . ./ . . . iā cando celes . . ." While these fragments undoubtedly contained compositions with rhythmic texts, possibly motets, there is no reason to believe that they had once formed part of Mü A, although their source may have suffered the same destructive fate simultaneously with Mü A. We recall in this regard that the Worcester Fragments [15] are known only from the remnants reclaimed from the bindings and fly-leaves of further codices of Worcester origin.

Although the hand that wrote the texts for the organa differs from the hand that wrote the texts for the compositions with rhythmic text, there are several reasons for considering the leaves containing the liturgical compositions to have issued from the same codex as the leaves from the other fascicles. First of all, the leaves apparently reached Jacobsthal as a unit. Secondly, the rather small size of the various complexes of leaves is common to all. Finally, the arrangement of the tenors of the motets according to the liturgical succession of the organa would have additional purpose if a cycle of organa were present. In accord with Ludwig, therefore, I shall assume the likelihood of a common origin for these leaves.

The manuscript Mü A is the smallest of the four Notre-Dame manu-

[15] L. Dittmer, *The Worcester Fragments* (Rome 1957). Some doubt has been cast on the relationship between the Willelmus de Winchecumbe at St. Andrews in Worcester in 1283 (*Musica disciplina*, VIII, 1954, 35) and the "W. de Winc." and "W. de Wīc." in the index of a lost manuscript now bound in London, British Museum, Harley 978, fols. 160ᵛ-161 (or according to other foliations 158ᵛ-159 or 181ᵛ-182)—see A. Hughes, *The Topography of English Mediaeval Polyphony*, in: *In Memoriam Jacques Handschin* (Strasbourg 1962), p. 138. It is, of course, difficult to identify individuals solely on the basis of abbreviations; Ludwig (*Repertorium*, pp. 270–71) read "Wincestre" from the abbreviation, and indeed he may be right. In any event, there is an *n* in the one abbreviation and an *n*-stroke in the other to suggest that Winchecomb alone on this basis is to be preferred to Wycombe. Of course, we are not sure of the provenience of that section of the manuscript containing this index, nor for that matter are we sure that the *Reading Rota* really does spring from this center at all. What is important is that this individual wrote two rotulae containing music that are apparently preserved in part in Oxford, Bodleian Library, Rawlinson C 400*, and that these compositions are of the same kind as those among the Worcester Fragments. This would then indicate that the organa in the Harleian source are of the same sort as those of the Worcester Fragments *inter alia*, which differed markedly from the Notre-Dame type (see *Musica disciplina*, VII, 1954, 19ff). The identity of "W. de Winc." with Willelmus de Winchecumbe is important only for what light it sheds on the dating of the Worcester Fragments; and the meager relationship of this individual (or individuals) with Winchecomb or Wycombe, certainly gives no reason for placing either of these cities on a map showing distribution of references to mediaeval music (Hughes, p. 128).

scripts; F [16] is the largest and measures 23.2 x 15.7 cm, W1 [17] is 21.5 x 15, W2 [18] is 18 x 13, whereas Mü A measures only 15.5 x 11.5 cm, a handy pocket size. The organa issue from the end of the Mass settings of the Magnus Liber and include settings of the *Alleluia* $\bar{V}$ *Veni electa* (M 54), an unidentified Alleluia, . . . the *Alleluia* $\bar{V}$ *Posui adiutorium* (M 51), and the Gradual *Domine* $\bar{V}$ *Vitam*. Since the order of compositions for the *Commune sanctorum* was less fixed than for the *Proprium sanctorum*, no such definite conclusions can be drawn as to the possible source of the liturgical tradition for these compositions.[19] The version of these compositions is identical for the most part with the version found in W1 and only occasionally follows the other manuscripts, when F and W2 have differing versions. Thus, the apparently older forms of the organa, such as have been attributed to Leonin, finally are found in a central source, assuming that the entire manuscript springs from a French source.

The rediscovery of the organa bifolio permits an important revision of the disposition of the compositions on the page. The original size of the bifolio appears to have been 15.5 cm high x 23 cm wide, or 15.5 x 11.5 cm for each folio; instead of being contingent to each other, the larger

[16] Florence, Biblioteca Mediceo-Laurenziana, pluteo 29.1.
[17] Wolfenbüttel, Herzog August Bibliothek, 677; facs. ed. J. H. Baxter, *An Old St. Andrews Music Book* (London 1931). This manuscript has both an older and a more recent foliation; the more recent foliation is easier for the modern researcher to read but has no other advantages, since it fails to compensate for folios now lost but present at the time of the older foliation. Moreover, the older foliation has become standard through Ludwig's *Repertorium*. It is thus not quite clear why J. Knapp, in JAMS, XVI (1963), 211, fn. 1, has chosen to confuse us in reference to foliation. For example, p. 218, fn. 18, refers to E. Gröninger, *Repertoire-Untersuchungen zum mehrstimmigen Notre Dame-Conductus* (Königsberg 1939), which study lists the conductus according to their older folio numbers in the manuscript; thus *Trine vocis tripudio* is listed in W1 in fols. 75ᵛ–77 not in fol. 68ᵛ, the new foliation.
[18] Wolfenbüttel, Herzog August Bibliothek, 1099; facs. ed. L. Dittmer, *Wolfenbüttel 1099* (Brooklyn 1960).
[19] See H. Husmann, *The Enlargement of the Magnus liber organi*, in: JAMS, XVI (1963), 176–203; this and related articles of this indefatigable scholar present a new approach to the appraisal of the Notre-Dame organa in attempting to justify and localize the liturgical order of the series of compositions according to the varying traditions of usage and succession of pitches in Northern France. It is reasonably possible that this method, combined with the investigation of the borrowing back and forth of sections from one version of an organum to one or more versions of a different organum, will finally elucidate the significant details attendant upon this most important body of music. This study, like most recent studies, has overlooked the relevant material in Mü A. The newly discovered fragment and sixth Notre-Dame source, Marburg, Staatsbibliothek, Stiftung preussischer Kulturbesitz (see Fischer, *Acta musicologica*, XXXVI, 1964, 80), also presents a double leaf with two-voice organa from the *Commune sanctorum* including versions of *Alleluia* $\bar{V}$ *Nativitas* and *Alleluia* $\bar{V}$ *Veni electa* as in Mü A. These settings, however, are quite similar to the versions in F and W₂ and undoubtedly represent a more recent stage of development than those in Mü A.

fragment (6.3 x 23 cm) and the smaller fragment (7.2 x 5 cm) lack a strip approximately 2.1 cm high between them (see Plates 13–14). As a result, a system of two lines is missing between these two parts of the same leaf, and thus there were 4 accolades instead of 3 to the page. This compares with 6 in W1 and F, and 5 in W2 for comparable sections. For the missing section, [in thronu]m, measures 127–49, Mü A had sufficient space to contain the organal version found in W1 (fol. 41 I–II) rather than the clausula found in F (fol. 142), W2 (fol. 85ᵛ), and the clausula F 203 (fol. 170ᵛ). For the verso side, however, matters are somewhat different; the verso II breaks off with the penultimate note of the tenor succession in measure 194,[20] and the notes on the smaller fragment IV begin in measure 203. The versions of the setting in F and W2 have no melisma at all for measures 194–202, and present only two measures (203–04) over the penultimate C, which passage parallels rhythmically, but not melodically, the comparable section in Mü A. The version in W1 has a long melisma, but its final two measures are related to those preserved in Mü A only to the extent that they move toward the lower D (instead of the higher D as in F and W2) to form the final cadence. Nevertheless, there are only enough notes in the melisma in the version in W1 to fill half of the upper line of system III. It is possible that the scribe merely did not fill the entire length of the system, as in the case of the second leaf recto II; but in that case, he did not quite finish the line, because the next section (℣ Vitam) then could not begin the new system. If the system is complete, then the melisma was probably about twice as long as the comparable melisma present in W1. It is not possible that the composition ended with a second setting of the Alleluia, since the final note in the tenor is D, the ending of the verse, not G, the ending of the Alleluia. On the other hand, my assumption—that the new Alleluia which begins on IV of the verso of the first leaf ends on the second leaf recto I—must be revised. The setting of the Alleluia ℣ Posui adiutorium (M 51) requires 5 systemata in W1, or roughly the equivalent of one page in Mü A; this would leave at least three pages unaccounted. Concerning this new composition, Ludwig wrote, "Ebendort: Ale (Alleluia?) mit Noten E F im Tenor und 11 Töne im Duplum (E beginnend). Der Tenoranfang passt zu keinem Alleluia des Notre Dame—Repertoires: auch das All. Hodie Maria (M 34), das E F beginnt, zeigt die Silbe le erst dem 5. Ton unterlegt und dessen 2st. Kompositionen W1 f. 39', F f. 124' und f. 125' abweichend beginnen, kommt wohl nicht in Betracht." It is not that passages like that of the duplum are lacking in the various main versions of the Magnus Liber; for example, in the Alleluia ℣ Iustus germinabit (M 53), related

[20] Reconstruction, p. 200.

passages occur on the syllable *ut* (from *sicut*, W1 fol. 47ᵛ III), and the second syllable *li* (from *lilium*, W1 fol. 47ᵛ IV), but a comparable section at the beginning of an Alleluia has eluded me so far in the other extant versions of the Magnus Liber.

The new Alleluia (provided it is the beginning of such a composition) commencing on leaf 1 verso III does not correspond to any of the known beginnings of compositions in the Magnus Liber. For one thing, no setting of an organum in W1 (the closest related, extant source to Mü A) begins on a unison, and only two internal sections (℣ *Adiuvent nos*, O 24, and ℣ *Catervatim ruunt*, O 25) start on this interval. Most compositions begin on the octave above the tenor, preceded by its lower neighbor; a few begin on the fifth; a fourth is found in the ℣ *Hodie Maria* (M 34), and ℣ *Sicut audivimus* (M 11), ℣ *Notum fecit* (M 1). The beginning E F is also quite unusual for an Alleluia, occurring in the Notre-Dame repertory only for the *Alleluia* ℣ *Hodie Maria* (M 34); here no identity is possible because, as Ludwig has pointed out, the syllable *le* does not come until the fifth tone. The beginnings F G on the one hand, and C D on the other, however, are quite common among the tenors used in settings of the Notre-Dame repertory. For F G, there are the *Alleluias* ℣ *Nativitas gloriose* (M 38) and ℣ *Letabitur iustus* (M 49); for C D, there are the *Alleluias* ℣ *Post partum* (M 35), ℣ *Dilexit Andream* (M 45), ℣ *Per manus autem* (M 46), and ℣ *Veni electa* (M. 54). The sequence C D is much more probable, requiring as it does a change of clef by a third.[21] There is some similarity between the final eight notes of the preserved section of the duplum in Mü A and the 12th to 18th notes of the *Alleluias* ℣ *Post partum* (M 35) and ℣ *Per manus autem* (M 46), which compositions have identical tenors for larger sections. Of these two Alleluias, the *Alleluia* ℣ *Post partum* is not particularly important in the Notre-Dame repertory and is restricted almost to the main setting in F, although it is much more significant in the parallel Worcester repertory.[22] Furthermore, this Alleluia is less closely related to the *Commune sanctorum* than is *Alleluia* ℣ *Per manus autem*. Accordingly, the *Alleluia* ℣ *Per manus autem* is the most likely candidate for this composition, provided that this setting really is an Alleluia and is known elsewhere among the Notre-Dame manuscripts. This composition (M 46), like many of

[21] Although infrequent in the Notre-Dame sources, there are passages written with the clef too high or too low, as in W1 fol. 47, where the tenor and duplum are written a third too low for the first two tenor notes on the syllable *Po-* (from *Posui adiutorium*); see W. Waite, *The Rhythm of Twelfth-Century Polyphony* (New Haven 1954), p. 141.

[22] The *Alleluia* ℣ *Post partum* (Worcester No. 19) is one of the sources for the Stimmtausch motet *Ave magnifica Maria*, which was included in the MS Montpellier, Faculté de Médecine, H 196 (No. 339) with text *Alle psallite cum luya*.

those dealing with the *Commune sanctorum*, is out of order in the succession of the main settings of W1 (placed at the end after M 58), and in the fifth group of clausulae in F (between M 49 and M 53).

Accordingly, the fragments of organa from Mü A present a bifolio, not the middle of a gathering, from the settings for two voices of Alleluias and Graduals destined for use in the *Commune sanctorum;* these settings give essentially the version of the Magnus Liber found in the manuscript W1, but unlike that codex issue from a central source. The order of compositions was either M 54 (?M 46), x, M 51, and M 48; or M 51, M 48, x, M 54, and (?M 46).

The Berlin fragments present the inner two bifolios of the first gathering of the motet fascicle immediately adjacent to those in the Munich fragments, as well as two consecutive double leaves, not the middle of a gathering, of a later part of the fascicle. In the first complex (A), corresponding to pp. 21–28 of the *Reconstruction* (see also Plates 6–8), there are 26 motets completely or partially preserved (numbered A 1–8, 10, 12–20, and 22–28); the reasons for leaving place for possible motets 9, 11, and 21, which undoubtedly had been written on the missing parts of fol. 3 recto and verso and fol. 6 verso (pp. 25 and 26 of the *Reconstruction*, see also Plates 6–7) are given on pp. 51, 52, and 59 of the *Reconstruction;* similarly, place has been left in the second complex (B), corresponding to pp. 29–32 of the *Reconstruction* (see also p. 67), for at least one missing motet, No. 7; accordingly, the motets of the second series are numbered 1–6 and 8–12, a total of 11 motets partially or completely extant. It is hoped that this numbering will remain standard at least until other parts of this manuscript may have been discovered. In Tischler's edition of 13th-century motets,[23] these compositions will be found transcribed as follows:

No. A 1—241	A 8—250	A 17—257
A 2—242	A 10—251	A 18—258
A 3—204	A 12—252	A 19—243
A 4—72	A 13—67	A 20—244
A 5—247	A 14—255	A 22—60
A 6—248	A 15—140	A 23—245
A 7—249	A 16—256	A 24—246

[23] *A Complete Edition of the Earliest Motets, c. 1190–1270.* F. Gennrich, *Aus der Frühzeit der Motette,* I (Langen 1963), gives a transliteration of the motets A 17 *Tot le premier jor* (p. 21), B 11 *Doce nos hac die* (p. 33), and B 10 *Selonc le mal* (p. 35); the latter two have the syllable *bit* erroneously under the final tenor note, and are incorrectly attributed to the Munich (p. XII) instead of to the Berlin fragments.

A 25—197	B 2—22	B 8—261
A 26—13	B 3—22	B 9—200
A 27—263	B 4—259	B 10—37
A 28—254	B 5—186	B 11—37
B 1—22	B 6—260	B 12—25

Actually, only seven of these motets are completely unknown in other sources: A 5, A 6, A 10, A 15, A 16, A 23, and A 26; and even some refrains from these compositions are textually (or both textually and musically) known elsewhere. Seven further compositions are otherwise known to us only as clausulae, two of these in St. V,[24] A 1, A 2, A 8, A 17, A 27 (St. V), B 1, and B 8 (St. V). As contrafacta, we have sources for B 1, B 3, and B 10, which compositions are included in successions with a motet that is musically identical and whose text is known elsewhere. This rather high incidence of compositions using clausulae from the Notre-Dame and St. Victor manuscripts as models and known to us as motets only in Mü A suggests that an even higher proportion of such clausulae was used for motets than has heretofore been known.

The versions of the motets in Mü A show in relationship to those in the other sources certain details of notation and repertory that are sometimes conservative, sometimes innovative. For example, as concerns the preservation of the separation of notes belonging to successive syllables, a syllable stroke is utilized in the motetus of *Factum est salutare* (A 7, measures 40–41), and the tenor of the musically identical motets *Selonc le mal* and *Doce nos hac die* (B 10–11, and measures 1–2) divide the initial ternaria into a single note plus binaria; on the other hand, no such division is found in the tenors of *Dame, vostre doz regart* (A 25), *Maniere esgarder* (A 26), and *En doce dolor* (A 27), all set to the tenor *Manere*, nor in *Au departir plourer* (B 9) to the tenor *Docebit*. Further, Mü A preserves the additional texts in the strophic motets *Qui servare puberem* (A 20) and the unique *Celi semita* (B 3), as well as in the only known French strophic motet that is not an adaptation of a chanson, *. . . qe soions* (B 1); and it maintains three-voice composition only for *Doce nos optime* (B 12), the three-voice motet with one motet text in F for which no clausula source has been identified;[25] where there is a two-

[24] Paris, Bibliothèque Nationale, lat. 15139 (previously St. Victor 813); facsimile edition of the musical part of the manuscript (fols. 255–293ᵛ) available in E. Thurston, *The Music in the St. Victor Manuscript, Paris lat. 15139* (Toronto 1959).
[25] Ludwig, *Repertorium*, Vol. I, pt. 1, p. 109ff, as well as in the discussion of the individual motets in the unpublished addition, represents the view that for those motets in the first motet fascicle of F (fols. 381–386) the three-voice form with a common rhythmic text for the upper parts was the original disposition of such a motet, even though all of the first 23 compositions (the main collection, arranged

voice clausula, as in *Qui servare puberem* (A 20) or *Scandit solium* (B 2, see also B 1 and B 3), Mü A has only a two-voice, F a three-voice setting without additional text. Irregularities in the succession of ligatures, however, is undoubtedly indicative of further development; thus, *Dame cui j'aim* (A 5) normally notates the tenor as groups of 2 2 3 (the standard notation for the third *ordo* of the second mode) but has 3 2 2 (the standard notation for the third *ordo* of the first mode) in measures 19–22; a similar confusion exists in *Au departir* (B 9) in that the ternaria often begins the group (as in first mode), but ends it (as in second mode) in measures 3–4 and again with the repetition of the tenor in measures 27–28.[26]

From among the conductus and *chansons pieux*, the lai *Flour ne glais* has been ascribed to Gautier de Coincy by the editors of *Lais et descorts français du XIIIe siècle*,[27] but the attribution apparently is otherwise not substantiated. The version in Mü A is the only extant copy of this composition in which the text is underlaid to the music; it begins in the seventh musical section, strophe 3, verse 2 with the words *Nos desenseigne de pectrier de trichier* (*Reconstruction*, p. 253). If we assume that this composition was complete in Mü A, it would have required approximately 21 lines of music prior to the extant part; this would leave three lines on the previous recto available for the end of a preceding composition.

The following composition is the conductus *O Maria virginei*, of which only the first two verses are present. This three-voiced composition is present in the newly discovered manuscript Châlons-sur-Marne, Archives de la Marne, apparently without number.[28] The manuscript,

somewhat like Mü A according to liturgical usage) with the exception of the series 15–17 have clausulae as models, and only 9–10 and 22 have 3-part clausulae as models. This may, however, represent a special development of the repertory of F. It is just such motets for which sources have not been identified that are present in 3-voice settings with one motet text in Mü A and Ch (see below, fn. 28); thus F 1,25 *O Maria maris stella* is Ch No. 13, and F 1,26 *In veritate comperi* is Ch No. 11, each from the appendix to the fascicle in F; only Ch No. 9, *O quam sancta*, is based on a clausula and has a 3-voice setting with one motet text, but here the composition has two texts in the upper parts in F (fols. 411ᵛ–412 with different texts; is *O quam sancta* the original text of this composition?).

   [26] The first 12 notes of the tenor are foreign to the *Alleluia ⅂ Paraclitus* (M 26) and conceivably *Do* was sung to the first four notes of the tenor, and *ce* beginning with the fifth note. Such a possibility is strengthened by the presence of a stroke after the fourth note in the motetus; this stroke appears otherwise to be unnecessary. Of course, this would mean that the syllable *ce* is underlaid in the incorrect position. The ligating of the initial phrase, however, might be repeated in measure 25, where the tenor begins its second *cursus*.
   [27] A. Jeanroy, L. Brandin, and P. Aubry; see p. 29.
   [28] The non-liturgical religious compositions are discussed by J. Chailley, *Fragments d'un nouveau manuscrit d'Ars antiqua à Châlons-sur-Marne*, in: *In*

which Dom Hourlier [29] believes to originate from Marchiennes after 1224, is similar in size to Mü A, and likewise includes monophonic and polyphonic compositions with rhythmic text in succession. The conductus, both polyphonic and monophonic, as well as the motets,[30] however, are all in Latin. *O Maria virginei* is listed by Chailley as No. 12. Since this composition is common to the two different sets of fragments, it is unlikely that they ever formed part of the same manuscript.

Thus, the fragments Mü A, like the Worcester fragments, found their way to the bindery and have been recovered from the bindings of at least two different codices. It is hoped that further parts of this most important, central source will come to light in the future.

Memoriam Jacques Handschin (Strasbourg 1962), pp. 140–50, who gives the manuscript the symbol Ch.

[29] In *Mémoires de la Société d'Agriculture, Commerce, Science et Arts de la Marne*, XXX (1956).

[30] The source Mü A was apparently unknown to Chailley in his discussion of *O Maria virginei* (p. 148), as well as for the edition *Les Chansons à la vierge de Gautier de Coinci* (Paris 1959), pp. 35 & 59.

THE ENGLISH MUSICAL ELEGY
OF THE LATE RENAISSANCE

by *VINCENT DUCKLES*

Lamenting is altogether contrary to reioising, euery man saith so, and yet is it a peece of ioy to be able to lament with ease, and freely to poure forth a mans inward sorrowes and the greefs wherewith his mind is surcharged. This is a very necessary deuise of the Poet, and a fine, besides his poetrie to play also the Phisitian, and not onely by applying a medicine to the ordinary sicknes of mankind, but by making the very greef it selfe (in part) cure of the disease.

The Arte of English Poesie (1589) [1]

RATHER SURPRISINGLY, the motif of death as a stimulus to musical composition has attracted little attention from music historians. Perhaps the scope of the subject has discouraged investigation. It offers an abundance of material for study. Musicians of all times and places have responded to the theme of human mortality with some of their most serious and profound expressions, and they have had at their disposal a multitude of formulae in which to memorialize the ending of human life: the planh, déploration, tombeau, lament, dirge, threnody, epicedium, and elegy, to name only the most familiar. All these are secular forms; the liturgical celebration of death has a history of its own descending from equally remote beginnings. But apart from the funeral music of the Western church, a long line of commemorative composition can be traced from such works as Gaucelm Faidit's plaint for the death of Richard Coeur de Lion at the end of the 12th century to Igor Stravinsky's *In Memoriam Dylan Thomas*, a representative 20th-century example.[2]

Of that vast funeral procession, one small segment has been selected

---

[1] George Puttenham is usually credited with the authorship of this masterpiece of Elizabethan literary criticism. References in this study are made to Edward Arber's edition of the work (London 1869). The quotation above comes from Chapter 23, p. 61, under "The forme of Poeticall Lamentations."

[2] One of the few scholars to address himself to the subject of musical tributes to deceased persons is Charles Van den Borren. See his recent *Esquisse d'une histoire des "tombeaux" musicaux*, in: *Festschrift für Erich Schenk, Studien zur Musikwissenschaft*, L (1962), 56–67. Although described as a "sketch," the author's rich store of humanistic knowledge and musical insight make this paper a substantial starting point for future investigations of this topic.

for consideration here, the musical elegy of the closing years of the English Renaissance. The time span is concentrated in the late 16th and early 17th centuries, but no student of English music will underestimate the productivity of that period, associated as it is with the flourishing of the English madrigal and the school of lutenist song writers. Two noble deaths, those of Sir Philip Sidney in 1586 and of Prince Henry in 1612, provide a kind of inner symmetry for the period, the one emphasizing the Elizabethan and the other the Jacobean side of the picture. No public funerals prompted greater response from the poets and musicians of the time. For the rest, the occasions that produced elegies were as varied as the persons celebrated, ranging from deaths in the royal family to the loss of colleagues among the ranks of court musicians. A careful but by no means exhaustive search has brought to light some 75 compositions by English musicians inspired by the loss of some renowned figure or personal friend. One might question whether a selection of musical samples based on the accidental events of history can lead to observations of more than sociological interest. But an examination of these works reveals an unexpected coherence, a common quality which in England seems to be the result of a native tradition in elegiac composition.

A starting point for any discussion of the English elegy is the recognition that it involves a blending of literary and musical elements. What the Elizabethan poet understood by the term was anything but a simple concept; it presented him with a diversity, not to say confusion, of meanings.[3] A search for classical antecedents is not very helpful. As J. C. Bailey disarmingly remarks in the introduction to his anthology of *English Elegies* (1900), "the conception of an elegy was, in fact, left somewhat undefined by the Greeks; and so it still remains."[4] For theorists of prosody such as Campion and Webbe, the term recalled a species of quantitative meter inherited from Greek and Latin verse. It could also be applied to poetry of an epistolary nature, or to verse with a didactic content. It could even, on occasion, be extended to light, epigrammatic verse. But a long humanistic tradition, stemming from Horace through Petrarch, supported the idea of the elegy as the poetic expression of unhappy love. Melancholy, grief, exaggerated despair were its prevailing tones. Puttenham cites the love elegy among his "forms of poetical lamentations":

[3] See Francis W. Weitzmann, *Notes on the Elizabethan Elegie,* in: *Publications of the Modern Language Association,* L (1935), 435–43. Weitzmann cites at least eight different uses of the term current during the period under consideration.

[4] J. C. Bailey, *English Elegies* (London 1900). Bailey's anthology was one of the first to give special attention to the elegy as a literary genre.

The third sorrowing was of loves, by long lamentation in Elegie; so was their song called, and it was in a pitious maner of meetre, placing a limping Pentameter after a lusty Exameter, which made it go dolourously more than any other meeter.[5]

Elsewhere he instructs the would-be poet how to modify his metrics in keeping with the subject-matter of his verse:

If ye use too many Dactils together ye make your musicke too light and of no solemne grauite such as the amorous Elegies in court naturally require, being always either very dolefull or passionate as the affections of love enforce . . .[6]

From this position on the dark side of the emotional spectrum, it was an easy step to an identification of the elegy with any lyric of a solemn, grave, or mournful character, and particularly with a song inspired by the death of some well-loved individual. In the latter case, however, the term was rarely used without some qualifying adjective or phrase: "Funerall Elegie," "Elegy on the death of . . ." Or one might add a list of verbal equivalents: "Mourning Song," "Funeral Teares for . . . ," "A Passion on the death of . . ." This points to an obvious distinction that must be made between the elegy as a conventionalized poetic expression of grief prompted by disappointment in love, and the funeral elegy, a work memorializing a specific tragic event. Elegies of the second type are the subject of the present study, yet it goes without saying that erotic and funereal melancholy shared a common vocabulary. It was an easy passage from terms expressing unrequited love to laments for the death of a particular individual.

No Elizabethan needed to be convinced that music offered an appropriate, even a necessary, medium for the expression of grief. Music served as a means of heightening the quality of experience, however painful, "of putting life into the dead'st sorrows." Its purpose was not to obliterate melancholy but to render it more exquisite:

Musicke though it sweetens paine
Yet no whit empaires lamenting:
But in passion like consenting
Makes them constant that complaine:
And enchantes their fancies so,
That all comforts they disdaine,
And flie from joy to dwell with woe.[7]

[5] *The Arte of English Poesie* (Arber ed.), p. 64.
[6] *Ibid.*, p. 140.
[7] This is the second strophe of the first elegy in Coperario's *Funeral Tears for the Earle of Devonshire* (1606).

John Case, in his famous apologia, *The Praise of Musicke* (1586), amplifies the view that music has powers to intensify feeling, and he draws upon classical authority to demonstrate that grief was one of the three major territories within the domain of the art:

> With musick no times are amisse. For we know that life is, as it were, put into the dead'st sorrows by inflection and modulation of the voice. And they whose heartes even yearne for very greefe sometimes fall on singing, not to seek comfort therein (for the best seeming comfort in such cases is to be comfortless) but rather to set the more on float that pensiveness wherewith they are perplexed. *Similitudo parit amicitiam*, saith Boetheus, and sorrowe findes somewhat in Musick worthie his acquaintance. If not, how chance they (the Ancients) have specified three originals or causes of Musick?—the first pleasure of which there is no question, the next grief, and the last Enthusiasm some divine and heavenly inspiration.[8]

Since music could express *dolour* so effectively, it was recognized as an adjunct of that melancholia which infected late Renaissance life and thought, not in England alone but throughout Europe. A self-conscious affection indulged by the intellectuals of the time, melancholy was made up, in part, of the Petrarchan love convention, of a residue of the medieval physiology and psychology of the humors, and of a general dismay at the breakdown of old mores and institutions. Its imprint can be observed in almost every form of art, perhaps most clearly in certain stock characters of the drama—Malvolio and his tribe. In music it can be traced to the Tudor partsong of the mid-16th century, in settings such as Tallis's *When shall my sorrowful sighing slack*, or *Like as the doleful dove alone delights to be*, both found in *The Mulliner Book*, and it lasts through the production of the lutenist song writers, well into the 17th century. The subject of Elizabethan-Jacobean melancholy is too large for consideration here except in so far as it provided a milieu within which the English musical elegy developed. Most writers on the subject have called attention to the subtle but clearly discernible shift in the melancholic spirit that took place after the death of Elizabeth I. At the risk of overgeneralization, one might say that melancholy was for the Elizabethan a positive thing, an expression of his insatiable appetite for life, while for

---

[8] John Case, *The Praise of Musicke* (London 1586). The excerpt is quoted in a useful anthology of encomiums directed toward music by Charles Sayle: *In Praise of Music* (London 1897), p. 85.
The same triumvirate of "causes" is stressed by Thomas Ravenscroft almost 30 years later in his *Brief Discourse* (1614). "I have heard it said that *Love* teaches a man Musick, who ne'er before knew what pertayned thereto: and the Philosopher's three *Principall Causes of Musick*, 1. *Dolour*, 2. *Joy*, 3. *Enthusiasm or ravishing of the Spirit*, are all found by him within Love's territories." From Ravenscroft's discussion of "Enamouring," one of the "five usuall Recreations which can be sought in music." Also quoted in Sayle, p. 126.

the Jacobean mind it led to a resigned and sometimes bitter commentary on the futility of existence.[9]

From Italy the English poets imported a full-blown vocabulary of *dolour:*

> Dolorous mournefull cares, ruthless tormenting,
> Hatefull guyves, cursed bonds, sharpest endurance . . .
> *Musica transalpina,* II, No. 9

Phrases of this kind played their part in shaping the English madrigal, but the English funeral elegy, in essence, was neither derived from, nor submerged by, literary or musical conventions from below the Alps. The funeral lyric set to music was not a characteristic Italian genre, and few collections of Italian madrigals contain elegies.[10] On the other hand, most of the English sets, and to a lesser extent the books of the lutenist song writers, contain one or more memorial compositions. The customary place for such works was at the end of the collection.

The immediate forerunners of the English musical elegy can be found in the work of Richard Farrant, Robert Parsons, Nicholas Strogens, and others of their generation. These musicians provided dramatic songs for the choirboy players of Blackfriars Theatre in the 1570s, chiefly in the form of laments, or as Peter Warlock aptly designated them, "death songs." *Abradad, Pandolpho, Awake, ye woeful weight, Alas, alack my heart is woe*—all belong in this category.[11] So does the famous lament, *O Death, rock me asleep.* In style these settings display characteristics that distinguish them sharply from the Italian-inspired madrigal. They are *consort songs,* solo settings in which the voice is suspended in a web of abstract instrumental polyphony supplied by a consort of viols.[12] Their contrapuntal interest is slight; the supporting instrumental voices supply what Joseph Kerman has characterized as "animated homoph-

[9] The literature on Elizabethan-Jacobean melancholy is impressive. The most thorough study from the literary point of view is Lawrence Babb's *The Elizabethan Malady* (East Lansing 1951); see also E. K. Chambers's *The Disenchantment of the Elizabethans,* in: *Sir Thomas Wyatt and Some Collected Studies* (London 1933). Musical applications of the theme have been suggested by Wilfrid Mellers in *La Mélancolie au début du XVIIe siècle et le madrigal anglais,* and by Jean Jacquot in *Lyrisme et sentiment tragique dans les madrigaux d'Orlando Gibbons,* both in: *Musique et poesie au XVIe Siècle* (Paris 1954).

[10] Philippe de Monte's elegy on the death of a child, *Carlo che in tenerella e acerba etade,* in his *Secondo Libro delli Madrigali à 5* (1598), is an exception. See Alfred Einstein, *The Italian Madrigal* (Princeton 1949), II, 508.

[11] Many of these songs were edited by Warlock in his *Elizabethan Songs* (London 1926).

[12] The clearest description of the style of the consort song is given in a paper by Philip Brett, *The English Consort Song, 1570–1625,* in: *The Proceedings of the Royal Musical Association* (1961–62), p. 73–88. Apart from his published writings in this field, I am indebted to Mr. Brett for numerous suggestions in the course of this study.

ony." [13] They are by no means deficient in expressive effect, but they achieve pathos by means other than that employed in the madrigal. There is little word painting, chromaticism, or dissonance. The mood of the lyric is sustained throughout the work as a whole, created by the use of somber sonorities, a wide-ranging vocal line moving characteristically by skip rather than by step, interrupted by dramatically placed rests and instrumental interludes.

These are features that link the "death songs" of Tudor drama with the elegies of William Byrd, although he lifts the form to higher powers of skilfulness and refinement. All of Byrd's elegies are consort songs, although those that appear in his printed collections have the text adapted to all the voices. Even so, the character of "the first singing part," usually the soprano but sometimes an alto or medius, is never obscured. Only three elegies, identified as such, appeared in print during Byrd's lifetime. These comprise two funeral songs to Sir Philip Sidney (*Come to me, grief* and *O that most rare breast*) printed at the end of *Psalms Sonets and Songs* (1588); and in the same collection, Henry Walpole's epitaph for the Catholic martyr, Edmund Campion (d. 1581), *Why do I use my paper, ink and pen*, not so much an elegy as a bit of sententious religious propaganda. *Songs of Sundrie Natures* (1589) contains a setting on the Dido and Aeneas theme (*When first by force of fatal destiny*), which elsewhere was associated with a text commemorating the death of Elizabeth I (*I that sometime a sacred Mayden Queen*). Fellowes printed three additional elegies from manuscript sources in Volume 15 of the *Collected Vocal Works: Crowned with flowers and lillies*, for Queen Mary Tudor (d. 1558); *Ye sacred Muses*, for Thomas Tallis (d. 1585); and another hidden elegy that appears in a Christ Church manuscript as *When Phoebus used to dwell* and in the British Museum as *The noble famous Queen*, an elegy for Mary Queen of Scots. Finally, there remain three as yet unpublished elegies probably by Byrd although the attributions have not been firmly established.[14] These are *In Angells weede*, another elegy for Mary Queen of Scots; [15] *Fair Britten Ile*, for Prince Henry (d. 1612); and the setting of a text beginning "With lillies white,"

---

[13] Joseph Kerman, *The Elizabethan Madrigal* (New York 1962), p. 105, footnote. Although the elegy is incidental to the main purpose of his study, Kerman's appraisal of its role in Elizabethan music is a model of stylistic insight.

[14] A discussion of a number of these settings that are probably by Byrd is found in *Songs by William Byrd in Manuscripts at Harvard*, by Thurston Dart & Philip Brett, in: *Harvard Library Bulletin*, XIV (1960), 343–65. The study also prints the lyrics of several Byrd elegies.

[15] According to Philip Brett, in a communication to the author, it is possible that *In Angells weede* was originally an elegy for Sidney, with a text beginning "Is Sidney dead."

commemorating the death of "fair Mawdlyn," The Lady Magdalen Montague, who died in 1608. This brings to ten the number of elegies within the Byrd canon, more than any other composer's for the period under consideration with the exception of Coperario, who wrote two complete collections of such works.[16]

Each of Byrd's elegies is a musical accomplishment of great interest and deserves a closer study than this general survey will permit. The two elegies to Sidney represent contrasting expressions of the consort song style.[17] *Come to me, grief* is a short, deceptively simple setting tailored to the dimensions of its lyric quatrain. The declamatory rhythm of the first line of verse, with its prolonged feminine cadence, is imposed on the succeeding lines with a deliberately archaic rigidity suggesting those experiments in the use of quantitative meter that Sidney and Watson delighted in.

$$— \; \smile \; \smile \quad — \; — \quad — \; —$$

Come to me,	grief, for	– ev – er,
Come to me,	tears day	and night
Come to me,	plaint, ah	help – less . . .

The "first singing part," in this case the superius, engages in antiphonal exchange with the supporting voices. *O that most rare breast* is constructed on a much larger scale, in keeping with the requirements of its lyric, an awkwardly contrived, unrhymed fourteener. Here the text is given a modified strophic setting, the first 8 lines are broken into 2 sections of 4 lines each and set to the same music, lines 9 to 12 form a third section with new musical materials, and the last couplet is expanded by repetition to balance the whole: *A A' B cc*. There are traces of patterned declamation similar to that found in the preceding elegy, but here treated in a more spacious context. Queen Mary's elegy, *Crowned with flowers and lillies*, is a sonnet likewise calling for extended treatment. Byrd gives it a rich, abstract setting for soprano and bass voices with supporting strings. It is through-set except for the repetition of the last couplet. The mood is one of objective commemoration, not personal grief of the kind expressed in *Ye sacred Muses*, written in memory of Thomas Tallis, the composer's fellow musician and business partner.

[16] There may be other unspecified elegies among Byrd's songs. The duet *Delight is dead* (*Complete Vocal Works*, XV) could well be a piece commemorating Sidney. With its repeated refrain and motif of tolling bells, it is obviously modeled on Sidney's lyric, *Ring out your bells, let mourning shows be spread, for Love is dead.*

[17] Philip Brett, on evidence from the Dow manuscripts at Christ Church, suggests that the lyrics for these two elegies were by Sir Edward Dyer. Dyer supplied two other texts set by Byrd in the 1588 volume. See *The English Consort Song*, pp. 82–83.

> Ye sacred Muses, race of Jove,
>   Whom Music's lore delighteth,
> Come down from crystal heavens above
>   To earth where Sorrow dwelleth
> In mourning weeds, with tears in eyes;
>   Tallis is dead, and Music dies.

Yet even here the tone of the setting is elevated, restrained, and has the remote quality of a motet. Not all of Byrd's elegies are laments. The song addressed to Edmund Campion has been mentioned as somewhat outside the pattern. So also is *The noble famous Queen*, which treats the execution of Mary Queen of Scots as a moral lesson for those in high places.

> The noble famous Queen
>   Who lost her head of late,
> Doth show that kings as well as clowns
>   Are bound to fortune's fate.

In discussing the elegies of Byrd's contemporaries, one can treat them conveniently according to the extent to which they remain within the consort song tradition or verge toward the characteristic madrigal style. It may be said that the older practice of consort song remained the dominant one throughout the period, and that composers who were fully at home in the new idiom reverted to consort song when they wrote memorial compositions. This is true of Gibbons, for example, whose great three-part elegy for Prince Henry, *Nay let me weep*, is in a style not far removed from that of Byrd. It has the texture of a Netherlandish motet, with the melodic interest centered in the top voice. Pilkington's *Weep, sad Urania*, for Thomas Purcell, is a viol-accompanied duo for two soprano voices, as is Vautor's *Weep, mine eyes, salt tears*. Likewise the unpublished elegies of Cobbold and Ramsey, and the five-voice memorial to Fulke Greville by Martin Peerson, partake of the earlier style.[18] Even Thomas Morley, most Italianate of English musicians, in his setting of *O grief, even on the bud* in *Canzonets to 5 and 6 Voices*, employs a texture which, as Kerman points out, is much more akin to accompanied song than to the canzonet.[19] I take this work to be an elegy for an unknown young woman, and it must be admitted that the conservative style of the piece is contributing evidence for that assumption. Similarly, Morley's six-voice "memorial of that honorable true gentlemen Henry Noel" (*Hark, Alleluia*) in the same collection makes strange

[18] Peerson wrote both a five-voice and a six-voice setting of *Where shall a sorrow*, an elegy for Fulke Greville. The six-voice setting has more features in common with the madrigal style.

[19] *The Elizabethan Madrigal*, p. 166.

company for the light Italianate settings which precede it. The distinction comes not merely from the gravity of its subject matter, but because it stands out as an English bloom in an Italian garden. Morley's lament for the death of Bonny-Boots, that mysterious member of the inner circle of Elizabeth's court, lies quite outside the elegiac pattern.[20] It is clear that when English composers wrote elegies they tended to adopt a style at variance with that of the madrigal, a style based on their own native tradition of accompanied solo song.

There were exceptions, of course. At the extreme Italian side of the continuum were those memorials to Astrophill and Meliboeus (Sidney and Walsingham) that Thomas Watson grafted on Marenzio's music in his *Italian Madrigals Englished* (1590).[21] But these are not properly English elegies at all, rather the hybrid products of literary experiment. The three Oriana elegies: Bateson's *Hark, hear you not*, Vautor's *Shepherds and nymphs that trooping*, and Pilkington's *Where Oriana walked*, are true madrigals, as one might expect, since their composers had the image of *The Triumphs* in mind when they set their texts. Michael East's *Fourth Set of Books* (1618) contains two interesting pastoral elegies, *Fair Daphne, gentle shepherdess*, and *Come, shepherd swains*, which seem effectively to bridge the gap between the old and the new. The identities of the deceased are not specified, but the events of death are explicit enough, personified in the first instance by the shepherd, Thyrsis, and in the second by an unnamed shepherdess. These works are actually secular verse anthems, with viol-accompanied duos at the start, leading to choral sections in five-voice polyphony at the close. A similar treatment is employed in Vautor's impressive ceremonial elegy for Prince Henry. The work is in two parts. Part I, *Melpomene, bewail thy sisters' loss*, is a lament sung by two sopranos with accompanying strings; Part II, *Whilst fatal sister held the bloody knife*, shifts the tone from lament to commemoration, and ends in a triumphant six-voice chorus extolling the joys of the Prince's life in Heaven:

> Such joy he hath to hear the heavenly choir
> No earthly music doth he more desire.

[20] Bonny-Boots was the pseudonym for a court figure whose identity has not been established conclusively. Sir Henry Noel has been suggested as a possibility. Reference to Bonny-Boots is made in two madrigals from *The Triumphes of Oriana*, in a madrigal in Holborne's *The Cittharn Schoole*, as well as in Morley's *Canzonets*. The matter is discussed by Roy C. Strong, *Elizabeth I as Oriana*, in: *Studies in the Renaissance*, VI (1959), 255–56.

[21] *How long with vain complaining* is matched to the music of Marenzio's *Questa di verd'herbette* from the first book of five-voice madrigals (1580). *The fates, alas, too cruel* is set to the music of *Questa ordi il laccio* from the fourth book *a 6* (1586); *When Meliboeus' soul*, to the music of *Di nettare amoroso* from the same book. The English texts are obviously not translations from the Italian.

Mention of anthem-like settings such as these may serve as a reminder that the separation of the funeral anthem from the secular elegy is, after all, a fairly arbitrary one. Most of the composers concerned were as active in the royal chapel as in the court. Thomas Tomkins's *Know you not*, found in several Christ Church College manuscripts, is described as "Prince Henry, his Funerall Anthem." The Prince's death also inspired a number of settings of the Absalom text (*When David heard* and *O my son, Absalom*) that served to symbolize the grief of James I for his son. East, Weelkes, and Tomkins all contributed works to this repertory.[22]

One might expect to find in the polyphonic elegy abundant evidence of the use of musical pictorialism, word painting suggested by the various attitudes of bereavement. The evidence is there, but not as plentiful as might be anticipated. The English madrigal never inclined toward the exaggeration of detail or the use of extremes in chromaticism and expressive dissonance that can be found in its Italian counterpart. And those few English works that can be singled out as most experimental or advanced in this respect (Weelkes's *O Care, thou wilt despatch me*, or Tomkins's *Weep no more, thou sorry boy*) are not to be counted among the elegies. Even in works in which the Italian influence is unmistakable, the English retain their concern for the total musical impression to be conveyed. Devices used to achieve an effect of solemnity are integrated into the texture by means of imitation or sequence; the repetition of declamatory patterns often plays a part in unifying the whole. Thus, while it can be said that the precepts advocated by Morley under his *Rules to be observed in dittying* [23] were observed ("Likewise when any of your words shall express complaint, dolour, repentance, sighs, tears, and such like let your harmony be sad and doleful"), the result was never a nervous, discontinuous display of verbally stimulated effects, but a carefully controlled expression of the prevailing mood. The elegies of Thomas Weelkes are among the best representatives of the mature English madrigal style in which Italian influences have been fully assimilated. Weelkes's collections contain three such works: for Lord Borough (c. 1598), for Henry Noel (d. 1600), and for Thomas Morley (d. 1608).

[22] Charles Butler had special praise for Tomkins's setting, which he refers to as "that passionate Lamentation of the good musical King, for the death of his Absalom: Composed in 5. parts by M. Th. Tomkins, now Organist of his Majesties Chappel. The melodious harmoni whereof, when I heard in the Musik-schoole, wheither I shoolde more admire the sweet wel governed voices (with consonant instruments) of the Singers; or the exquisit invention, wit and Art of the composer, is hard to determin." *The Principles of Musik* (1636).

[23] Thomas Morley, *A Plain and Easy Introduction to Practical Music* (1597), ed. Alec Harman (London 1952), p. 290.

The Borough elegy is the least impressive of the three and shows some evidence of being an early work. All three employ a rich six-voice texture with the polyphonic activity shared by all the voice parts. They are also alike in using a sestet stanza form. The elegy to Henry Noel is an extended work, running to some 142 measures (as edited by Fellowes). Its design is based on the alternation of passages in quick motion with slow sections marked by chains of suspensions. Key words are touched with harmonic color, as in Example 1, below, where the voices converge on an augmented triad at the word "dead."

Ex. 1

In Example 2, the word "death-bed" is singled out by means of one of the most poignant uses of the simultaneous cross relation found in the madrigal literature.

Ex. 2

Death hath deprived me, Weelkes's "remembrance of my friend M. Thomas Morley," besides being a work of great artistry, presents a subtle example of word-music relationship that seems to have escaped the notice of scholars in this field. The elegy employs a six-line pentameter stanza identical in form to that of the lament for Noel. Musically, however, the setting is almost exactly half as long as Noel's elegy. This observation is explained by the fact that the structure of the lyric is based on a rhetorical device of overlapping phrases; each line of verse, except

the first, begins with a repetition of the closing words of the preceding
line.[24]

> Death hath deprived me of my dearest friend,
>   My dearest friend is dead and laid in grave,
> In grave he rests until the world shall end,
>   The world shall end, as end must all things have.
> All things must have an end that nature wrought,
> That nature wrought, must unto dust be brought.

The verbal overlay is reflected in the musical setting. Every ending becomes a beginning; each cadence sets the stage for a new development.
The result is a foreshortened, symbolic, highly concentrated expression
of personal grief, unlike any other example among the English elegies
studied. A work of similar stature, but without the subtlety of organization, is Ward's elegy on Prince Henry, *Weep forth your tears*. It contains much expressive dissonance and makes its effect by means of a
carefully planned dramatic development. Where Weelkes's lines tend
to descend to suggest pathos, Ward builds toward higher levels of intensity by mounting one entry on another in a series of ascending
statements.

Elegies by the lutenist song writers are comparatively fewer in number, in spite of the fact that the names of Dowland and Daniel come first
to mind in connection with the music of Jacobean melancholy. Did the
composer of *Lachrimae*, that prime example of musical lamentation,
write elegies in the specific sense? [25] The question requires a qualified
answer. Dowland did set a lyric in 1610, in Robert Dowland's *Musical
Banquet*, which had been set four years earlier by Coperario as one of
the *Funeral Teares* for the Earl of Devonshire. This song is one of his
supreme accomplishments, *In darkness let me dwell*. Also in the *Musical
Banquet* there is a Dowland setting of a lyric by Sir Henry Lee, Queen
Elizabeth's champion in the Court of Chivalry, which has the ring of a
funeral lament. In *Far from the triumphing court*, the aged Lee pictures
himself as "Time's prisoner," desolate because "that goddess who he
served to heaven is gone, and he on earth in darkness left to moan."
Oddly enough, this is not a typical late Renaissance lament but is one of

---

[24] The device is one which Puttenham refers to as *Anadiplosis*, or *The Redouble*,
and he defines it as "another sort of repetition when with the worde by which you
finish your verse ye begunne the next verse with the same;" see *The Arte of English
Poesie* (Arber ed.), p. 210.

[25] Reference to Dowland raises the question as to whether or not certain of his
instrumental works were conceived as elegies. One of the pavans in the *Lachrimae*
set bears the title, *Sir Henry Umpton's Funerall*. Very likely some of the named
pavans by Dowland and his contemporaries are in fact memorial pieces.

the songs in which Dowland anticipates most clearly the techniques of Baroque declamation and harmony.

In the lute-song elegies, two trends are discernible. There is, on the one hand, a reëmergence of the older English song style that had been displaced by the current taste for the Italian madrigal. In the lute ayres of this type, consort song achieved a fulfilment of the kind paralleled in English poetry after it had freed itself from the confinements of the Petrarchan formulae. Thus Dowland and Byrd can be said to pursue the same artistic ends, however much they differed in the means they employed. On the other hand, one can observe the beginnings of a new cycle of Italian influence culminating in the declamatory air, the characteristic English adaptation of Baroque continuo song. The two tendencies are closely intermingled and can often be found within the works of a single composer. Campion's only known elegy, *All looks be pale*, on Prince Henry, is an odd mixture of the old and the new. The song is printed in the composer's *First Book of Ayres* along with other "Divine and Morall Songs," with an archaic text that suggests a bardic lament, yet it is one of the clearest examples of declamatory air to be found in all of Campion's works. For an elegy that stands at the culmination of late Renaissance developments, there is no better example than John Daniel's *Grief, keep within*, a song described as "Mrs. M. E., her Funerall teares for the death of her husband." This piece could be regarded as a consort song if the lute accompaniment were replaced by a group of viols. But in the rich quality of its pathos, its melodic chromaticism, aspirate rests, and chains of suspensions, it reveals its close kinship to the serious madrigal style.[26]

If Daniel can be said to represent the main stream of late Renaissance song in England, Giovanni Coperario (John Cooper) is the fountainhead of the new Baroque spirit. His work prefigures most of the characteristics of the declamatory air. In the quantity of his output, Coperario stands as the leading composer of elegies for the Jacobean period. His two collections, *Funeral Teares* (1606) and *Songs of Mourning* (1613), contain a total of 14 commemorative songs. As special collections of elegies these two volumes form a pair of publications unique in early English music.[27]

[26] This is the only specified elegy in Daniel's book, but it is tempting to regard the highly expressive "Chromatic Tunes" (*Can doleful notes to measured accents set*) as belonging to the same category.

[27] At least one other book of elegies seems to have been projected. In Thomas Hamond's partbooks in the Bodleian Library there is a group of pieces by Robert Ramsey identified as *Dialogues of sorrow, upon the death of the late Prince Henrie, 1615 . . . Composed by Robert Ramsey, Bachelor of Musicke.* No copy of this book has survived, if indeed it ever was published. The Bodleian manuscripts contain one

Peerson's *Mottects or Grave Chamber Musique* (1630) is a memorial volume, but not in quite the same sense; only two of the settings are elegies, the rest are settings of poetry by the deceased, Fulke Greville. *Funeral Teares* contains seven songs, with lyrics by an anonymous poet, to the memory of Charles Blount, Earl of Devonshire. His wife of a few years, and mistress for many more, was Penelope Rich, a lady whom the poets and musicians of the time held in particular affection.[28] The songs are scored for a solo voice, lute, and bass viol, with an optional alto or *meane* part "that may bee added, if any shall affect more fulnesse of parts." *Songs of Mourning: bewailing the untimely death of Prince Henry* appeared seven years later, settings of lyrics by Thomas Campion. Five of these songs are addressed to individual members of the royal family, the sixth "To the most disconsolate Great Brittaine," and the seventh "To the World." There was no optional voice part provided for this set.

Already in the songs of 1606 there are features that take them out of the category of the typical lute ayre. As Bukofzer has observed, there is in Coperario's style an "unmistakable shift of emphasis from contrapuntal to harmonic combinations which are sought for their own sake." [29] His melodic writing is characteristically disjunct, made up of triadic progressions and wide skips (he does not hesitate to use the leap of a diminished octave on occasion). Unlike Daniel, he rarely exploits the doleful device of melodic chromaticism; his lines do not droop or wail. There is a kind of masculine dignity in his expression of grief that is refreshing in contrast to the mannered lamentations of some of his contemporaries. One of his finest elegies is No. 2 in the Prince Henry set, addressed *To the most Sacred Queene Anne, Tis now dead night* [30] (see Example 3).

long five-voice elegy, *O tell me, wretched shape of misery,* and six other Ramsey works copied by Hamond, serious songs but not elegies. See Margaret Crum, *A 17th-century collection of music belonging to Thomas Hamond, a Suffolk landowner,* in: *Bodleian Library Record,* VI (1957), 373–86.

[28] Her name is mentioned in Byrd's *Weeping full sore,* in: *Songs of Sundry Natures* (1589), and there are other references in a song, presumably by Byrd, in Harvard MS Mus. 30 (*My mistress had a little dog*).

[29] In the introduction to Bukofzer's edition of Coperario's *Rules How to Compose* (Los Angeles 1952), p. 3.

[30] This setting came to the attention of Max Schneider as an anonymous work bound into a copy of Rossiter's *Book of Ayres* (1601). Schneider printed it in the supplement to his *Die Anfänge des Basso Continuo* (Leipzig 1918), pp. 160–62. Through Schneider's study the song became known to Charles Van den Borren, who cites it as an anonymous work in his *Esquisse d'une histoire des "tombeaux" musicaux, op. cit.,* p. 64. Van den Borren conjectured that the setting might have been a work by Coperario. Both of Coperario's volumes of elegies have been edited by G. Hendrie & T. Dart, *English Lute Songs,* First Series, XVII (London 1959).

Ex. 3

'Tis now dead night, and

not a light on earth or star in heav'n doth shine

The non-polyphonic lute part that interrupts its motion along with the voice, the strong, harmony-supporting bass, and the sharp dissonance at the cadence are all characteristic of a style developed in the songs of John Wilson, William and Henry Lawes, and other musicians active in the reign of Charles I.

A focal point for the comparison of Coperario's song style with that of his greater contemporary, John Dowland, is offered in the two settings of *In darkness let me dwell*, mentioned above. From the striking similarity in the opening phrases of the two settings it is obvious that the two works are related, but the problem of their relationship is not a simple one. We are not even certain that the Dowland setting is later in actual date of composition, although it did not appear in print until four years after Coperario's publication. One curious discrepancy in the texts must be mentioned, apart from the fact that the Coperario version introduces a second strophe. The climax of the lyric resides in the bitter paradox of its last line:

> O let me living die, till death do come!

Dowland sets it in a passionate recitative that breaks into the smooth flow of the preceding phrase and then sinks back as if in resignation to

the inspired repetition of the opening line—"In darkness let me dwell."
In Coperario's setting the paradox is inverted. His last line reads:

O let me dying live, till death doth come!

There is no question of a printer's error involved here. Coperario sets the
text with a deliberately rising leap of a fifth to the word "live." The
sequential repetition of the figure gives a false sense of triumph to an
otherwise tragic piece. There may be some difference of opinion as to
which of these versions makes the best poetic sense, but by musical
standards the Dowland song remains unchallenged in its position as one
of the finest songs of its time. In any other company the Coperario setting
would be recognized as a skilful and creditable piece of work. The setting is also distinguished by the use of a subtle device worthy of special
notice. In the short instrumental prelude before the voice enters, the bass
viol gives a clear quotation of one of Ophelia's best known songs from
Hamlet.[31] It is the popular melody that begins with the text, "How
should I your true love know," but most vividly remembered from the
play by the words which begin its second stanza:

He   is dead and   gone, la - dy

Here is an allusion that no contemporary courtier could miss, an elegy
within an elegy, linking the sorrow of Devonshire's widow with the
pathetic grief of Polonius's daughter. If the quotation is an authentic one,
and there seems little reason to doubt it, we have here the earliest record
of a melody long associated with the Shakespearean tradition but never
fully documented in early 17th-century sources.[32]

As Coperario's work moves in a direction that leads outside of the
period we designate as the Renaissance, it may serve to remind the reader
that the remaining years of the 17th century produced further chapters
of great interest in the history of the English elegy.[33] The execution of
Charles I in 1649 found numerous royalist composers ready to pay

[31] Act IV, Scene 5.
[32] The tune is found in *The Beggar's Opera* with the words, "You'll think ere
many days ensue." It was also printed by Charles Knight in his *Pictorial Edition of
Shakespeare* (1839–42) and by William Chappell. Its connection with Shakespeare
production has been based largely on oral tradition.
[33] A study of the English elegy, concentrating on its later 17th-century developments, has been completed by Judith M. Hudson as a Master's Thesis at the University of California (Berkeley 1962), under the title, *The Musical Elegy in 17th-
century England*.

tribute to his memory. The death of a well-loved musician, William Lawes, at Chester in 1645, prompted eight of his colleagues to compose elegies for publication in *Choice Psalms* (1648). The genius of Henry Purcell enriched the genre with elegies to Charles II, Queen Mary, Matthew Locke, and John Playford; and Purcell was in turn the subject of an impressive memorial composition by John Blow. And so the procession continues. In the musical elegy one is confronted with the responses of poets and musicians to one of the great ceremonial occasions of human life. Death engenders emotions shared by all men, but their modes of expression are stamped with the peculiar lineaments of an age or of the individual artist. Because of the heightened quality of feeling such works possess, the elegy serves as a rich field for the study of a national or a personal style of composition.

English Musical Elegies of the Late Renaissance

Abbreviations: EMS = English Madrigal School
LSW = School of Lutenist Song Writers
CVW = Complete Vocal Works (Byrd)

COMPOSER	TEXT INCIPIT	SOURCES	EDITION	NOTES
Amner, John	"With mournful music"	*Sacred Hymns* (1615)		On Master Thomas Hynson
Bartlett, John	"If ever hapless woman"	*Ayres* (1606)	LSW 2, vol. 10	By Mary, Countess of Pembroke, on Philip Sidney, d. 1586
Bateson, Thomas	"Hark, hear you not a heavenly harmony"	*First Set of Madrigals* (1604)	EMS vol. 21	"Orianaes farewell"; on Elizabeth I, d. 1603
Byrd, Wm.	"Come to me, grief"	MSS: Chr. Ch. 984–88; Add. 29401–05; Eger. 2009–12 (1588)	CVW, vol. 12	On Sidney, d. 1586
	"Crowned with flowers"	MSS: Add. 18936–39 & 29401–05; Eger. 2009–12; Harvard Mus 30	CVW vol. 15	On Queen Mary, d. 1558
	"Fair Brittan Ile"	MS Add. 29401–05		On Prince Henry, d. 1612; probably by Byrd
	"I that sometime" (When first by force)	MSS: Add. 29401–05 Harvard Mus 30 (1589)	CVW vol. 13	On Elizabeth I, d. 1603
	"In Angells weede"	" "		On Mary Queen of Scots, d. 1587; probably by Byrd
	"The noble famous Queen" (When	" "	CVW vol. 15	On Mary Queen of Scots, d. 1587;

COMPOSER	TEXT INCIPIT	SOURCES	EDITION	NOTES
	Phoebus used to dwell)			probably by Byrd
	"O that most rare"	MS Chr. Ch. 984–88 (1588)	CVW vol. 12	On Sidney, d. 1586
	"With lillies white"	MS Add. 29401–05		On Lady Magdalen Montague, d. 1608 ; probably by Byrd
	"Why do I use my paper, ink and pen"	MSS : Add. 29401–05 ; Eger. 2009–12 ; Harvard Mus 30	CVW vol. 12	On Edmund Campion, Jesuit, d. 1581
	"Ye sacred muses"	MS Add. 29401–05	CVW vol. 15	On Thomas Tallis, d. 1585
Campion, Thomas	"All looks be pale"	*First Book of Ayres* (1613?)	LSW 2 vol. 1	On Prince Henry, d. 1612
Carlton, Rich.	"Sound, saddest notes"	*Madrigals* (1601)	EMS vol. 27	On Sir John Shelton
Cobbold, Wm.	"For death of her"	MS Add. 18936–39		On Mary Gascoygne, "dying in travell of child", 1588
	"Ye mortal wights"	" "		"Venus her Lamentation for Adonis"
Cranford, Wm.	"Weep, Brittans, weep"	MS Chr. Ch. 56–60		"A Passion on the death of Prince Henry"
Coperario, Giov.	"Oft thou hast"	*Funeral Teares* (1606)		On the Earl of Devonshire, d. 1606
	"O sweet flower"	" "		" "
	"O the unsure hopes"	" "		" "
	"In darkness let me dwell"	" "		Also set by John Dowland
	"My joy is dead"	" "		On the Earl of Devonshire, d. 1606
	"Deceitful fancy"	" "		" "
	"Foe of mankind"	" "		" "
	"O grief, how divers"	*Songs of Mourning* (1613)		On Prince Henry, d. 1612 ; lyrics by Campion
	"Tis now dead night"	" "		Also set by Ford
	"Fortune and glory"	" "		On Prince Henry, d. 1612
	"So parted you"	" "		" "
	"How like a golden dream"	" "		" "
	"When pale famine"	" "		" "
	"O poor distracted world"	" "		" "
Daniel, John	"Grief, keep within"	*Songs* (1606)	LSW 2, vol. 12	"Mrs. M.F., her Funeral tears for the death of her husband"

COMPOSER	TEXT INCIPIT	SOURCES	EDITION	NOTES
	"Can doleful notes"	" "	LSW 2, vol. 12	"Chromatic Tunes," not specified as an elegy
Deering, Rich.	"Sleep quiet, Lee"	MS Chr. Ch. 747–49		Possibly on Sir Henry Lee, d. 1610
Dowland, John	"Far from the triumphing court"	Musical Banquet (1610)	LSW 1, vol. 14	Lyric by Sir Henry Lee; possibly on Elizabeth I, d. 1603
	"In darkness let me dwell"	" "	LSW 1, vol. 14	Set by Coperario as an elegy to Earl of Devonshire, d. 1606
East, Michael	"Come, shepherd swains"	4th Set of Books (1618)	EMS vol. 31	Unspecified pastoral elegy
	"Fair Daphne, gentle shepherdess"	" "	EMS vol. 31	Unspecified pastoral elegy
Ford, Thomas	"'Tis now dead night"	MS Chr. Ch. 56–60		A Passion on Prince Henry; also set by Coperario
Gibbons, Orlando	"Nay, let me weep"	First Set of Madrigals (1612)	EMS vol. 5	On an unknown young man, possibly Prince Henry
Ives, Simon	"Sad clouds of grief"	MS Chr. Ch. 736–38		On William Austin of Lincoln's Inn
Jenkins, John	"No, he is not gone forever"	" "		On a musician named Marks
Johnson, Edw.	"Come, blessed bird"	Triumphs of Oriana (1597)	EMS vol. 32	Laments the death of "Bonny-boots", possibly Henry Noel, d. 1597
Kirbye, George	"Up then, Melpomene"	First Set of Madrigals (1597)	EMS vol. 24	Unspecified elegy; lyric from Spenser's Shepherd's Calendar
Morley, Thomas	"Fly Love, that art so sprightly"	Canzonets to 5 & 6 voc. (1597)	EMS vol. 3	Lament for "Bonny-boots", possibly Henry Noel.
	"O Grief, even on the bud"	" "	EMS vol. 3	Unspecified elegy to a young woman
	"Hark, Alleluia"	" "	EMS vol. 3	On Henry Noel, d. 1597
Peacham, Henry	"Awake softly with singing"	MS Harl. 6855		Commemorates Eliz. I and celebrates James I
Peerson, Martin	"Wake, sorrow, wake"	MS Add. 29372–77		In memory of the Lady Arabella Stewart, d. 1615. Also set by Porter
	"Arbella . . . sole paragon"	" "		" "
	"Where shall a sorrow"	Mottects or Grave Chamber Musique (1630)		5-pt. setting, on Fulke Greville, d. 1628
	"Where shall a	" "		6-pt. setting, on

COMPOSER	TEXT INCIPIT	SOURCES	EDITION	NOTES
	sorrow"			Fulke Greville, d. 1628
Pilkington, Fr.	"Come, all you that draw"	*First Book of Songs* (1605)	LSW 1, vol. 15	On Thomas Leighton
	"Come, shepherd's weeds"	*2nd Set of Mads.* (1624)	EMS vol. 26	Pastoral elegy from Sidney's *Arcadia*
	"Wound, woeful plaints"	*First Book of Songs* (1605)	LSW 1, vol. 15	On William Harwood
	"Weep, sad Urania"	*2nd Set of Mads.* (1624)	EMS vol. 26	On Thomas Purcell of Dinthill, Salop
	"When Oriana walked"	*First Set of Mads.* (1613)	EMS vol. 25	On Elizabeth I, d. 1603
Porter, Walter	"Wake, sorrow, wake"	*Mads. and Airs* (1632)		On Lady Arabella Stewart, d. 1615; also set by Peerson
Ramsey, Robt.	"O tell me, wretched shape of misery"	Bod. MS Mus. fols. 20–24		On Prince Henry, d. 1612
	"What tears, dear Prince"	Bod. MS Don. c. 57		Probably on Prince Henry
Tomkins, Thos.	"Know you not"	Chr. Ch. MSS		"Prince Henry, his Funerall Anthem"
Vautor, Thos.	"Melpomene, bewail thy sisters' loss"	*Songs of divers Natures* (1619)	EMS vol. 34	On Prince Henry, d. 1612
	"Shepherds and nymphs"	" "	EMS vol. 34	On Elizabeth I, d. 1603
	"Weep, mine eyes, salt tears"	" "	EMS vol. 34	On Sir Thomas Beaumont, d. 1614
Ward, John	"If Heav'ns' just wrath"	MS Chr. Ch. 56–60		On Sir Thomas Fanshaw
	"No object dearer"	MS Chr. Ch. 56–60; 61–66		"Passions on the death of Prince Henry," d. 1612
	"Weep forth your tears"	*First Set of Mads.* (1613)		On Prince Henry
Watson, Thos. (adap. Marenzio's music)	"How long with vain complaining"	*First Set of Ital. Mads.* (1590)		Elegies on Sidney, d. 1586, and Sir Francis Walsingham, d. 1590
	"When Meliboeus' soul"	" "		" "
	"The fates, alas, too cruel"	" "		" "
Weelkes, Thos.	"Cease now, Delight"	*Balletts & Mads.* (1598)	EMS vol. 10	On Lord Borough, d. 1597
	"Death hath deprived me"	*Airs or Fantastic Spirits* (1608)	EMS vol. 13	On Thomas Morley, d. c. 1604
	"Noel, adieu thou court's delight"	*Mads. of 6 pts.* (1600)	EMS vol. 12	On Henry Noel, d. 1597
Anonymous	"How short a time of breath"	Bod. MS Don. c. 57		Possibly on Prince Henry

DIDACTIC EMBELLISHMENT LITERATURE IN THE LATE RENAISSANCE: A SURVEY OF SOURCES

by ERNEST T. FERAND

THE ANCIENT ART of ornamentation in music, in all probability as old as the art of music itself, entered a crucial phase of its long history in the second third of the 16th century. After many centuries of free and spontaneous, truly creative embellishment —still alive to a certain extent in parts of the Oriental world, where the borderline between composition and performance, so strictly observed in the later Western music, is hardly distinguishable—the stage of rationalization and standardization had been reached.

This development is clearly recognizable in the appearance of numerous manuals and textbooks of ornamentation and collections of embellished compositions as well as in the growing space allotted to the discussion of embellishment practices in special chapters of theoretical treatises of counterpoint and composition. They all serve the practical pedagogical purpose of systematically instructing singers and instrumentalists—professionals as well as lay musicians, virtuosos as well as choirboys—in the art of embellishment.

In the theoretical and didactic literature of the second half of the 16th and the early 17th century—which latter still often reflects Renaissance practices—this art is demonstrated in a very great number of practical examples. They consist of one or more voices, taken either complete or in more or less extended portions from polyphonic compositions of the time and presented in ornamented versions by expert and experienced teacher-virtuosos—singers and instrumentalists—with the pedagogic aim of providing performers with models of ornamentation and ornamented compositions, to save them the trouble of inventing the embellishments themselves.

The following survey is concerned only with the literature of embellished polyphonic compositions; those of the monodic type are excluded. In listing the ornamented versions, all types of tablatures—lute and keyboard—are disregarded; not only because they are too numerous to be dealt with in the space at our disposal but first of all for the reason that they do not serve primarily didactic purposes; they are genuine transcriptions with predominantly, or exclusively, artistic, technical, and virtuoso aims.

A quick glance at the terminology of embellishment reveals that the following verbs may be encountered to denote the technique of ornamentation: *diminuir(e)* (*disminuir, desminuir, sminuir*), *passeggiare* (*passaggiare*), *rompere, glosare, kolorieren*, etc. The corresponding nouns are: *diminutione, minuta, passaggio, rottura, glosa, coloratura* (*Koloratur*); also *gorga* (*gorgia*), *fioretti, division* (Latinized: *minuritio*), *agrémens*, etc. The term *diminutio* appeared as early as the first half of the 14th century in the theoretical literature of counterpoint or composition; and the term *passaggio* acquired a specific meaning in the early 17th century when it was used to denote a variation, especially of a dance (e.g. *Balleto Piemontese . . . Il suo Passagio*).

The didactic literature was not limited to the field of vocal or to that of instrumental music. In line with Renaissance and Baroque performance practices the art of embellishment was applicable to both media, as consistently stressed in the titles of the manuals and collections. Instruments especially favored for ornamentation were members of the viol family, including the bass viol (violone) and the viola bastarda (lyra viol), the flute, and all kinds of plucked and keyboard instruments.

A survey of the sources and their contents permits a good insight into the range and the methods of embellishment practices; at the same time it also reveals the preference some of the compositional types and certain composers enjoyed or the neglect others suffered by contemporaries or following generations from the viewpoint of ornamentation pedagogy. It is well known that the most favored types of polyphonic composition for that purpose were chansons, madrigals, and motets; on the other hand, polyphonic settings of sections of the Ordinary of the Mass were never used.

Among the composers preferred for exemplifying the art of embellishment were masters of such widely differing styles as Crecquillon, Willaert, Rore (the most popular of all), Palestrina, Striggio, and Marenzio; favorite compositions were Rore's *Anchor che col partire* and Palestrina's *Io son ferito* and *Vestiva i colli*. On the other hand it is surprising to learn from our survey that other outstanding masters like Josquin (who seems to have been the first to attach special importance to the systematic teaching of embellished song and embellished composition), Festa, Verdelot, or La Rue, are conspicuous by their absence in the didactic embellishment literature, while other prominent composers, like Lasso or Monte, are represented by but one single example. One explanation of this curious fact may have been the commercial interest of the publishers, especially those of Venice (Gardano, Vincenti, Amadino, Scotto), but also of Paris and Antwerp (Attaingnant, Le Roy & Ballard, Susato, etc.), so efficient in promoting the output of their authors. This accounts also for the fact that no German or English composer, and only one Spanish, is represented in the diminution literature of the 16th century, although they show up abundantly in that of the lute and keyboard music. As a consequence, among the languages one encounters French, Italian, and Latin, but not German, Spanish, or English.

In attempting to find a clue to the seemingly haphazard and arbitrary selection of compositions for demonstrating the technique of diminution it is interesting to note that the examples are often taken over "wholesale" from particularly successful collections of works by one or more composers (among them by Rore, Palestrina, Renaldi, Marenzio, and many others), and sometimes also "second hand" from collections of instrumental transcriptions of vocal music, such as the *Musica de diversi autori*, published by Gardano [RISM 1577[11]] or *Canzon di diversi per sonar*, published by Vincenti [1588[31]]; a considerable portion of their contents can be encountered again in the manual of dalla Casa (1584) and the collection of Bassano (1591), respectively.

The earliest embellishment manual, Ganassi's *Fontegara* (1535), contains only rules and patterns of diminution but no embellished compositions. The first ones used to demonstrate the *ars eleganter canendi* for didactic purposes—allegedly based on the teaching method of Josquin—were two chansons whose top and bottom voices appeared anonymously in A. Petit Coclico's treatise of 1552; they can be identified as four-voiced compositions of Claudin de Sermisy, originally published unembellished 24 years earlier (cf. RISM 1528[8] and 1529[3]). At the other end of the line there still appeared, as late as 1620 (F. Rognone) and 1626 (Bonizzi), instrumental transcriptions (for the viola bastarda) of chansons and madrigals by Sandrin, Crecquillon, Willaert, Rore, Lasso, Palestrina, and others, some of the earlier ones published unembellished nearly one century before. The last embellished versions of polyphonic compositions, other than in lute or keyboard tablatures, were madrigals of Marenzio, Giovanelli, and G. M. Nanino, all published originally in the year 1585; to these may be added a "self-embellished" canzone (da sonar) by Antonio Mortaro. Thus the phase and the aspect of the embellishment pedagogy under consideration in the present study extend over approximately three quarters of a century, from 1528 to 1600, as far as the composers are concerned; and from 1552 to 1626, with regard to the arrangers and compilers, a phase which also includes the all-important one of the transition from the Renaissance to the Baroque.

The following tables list:

I. Sources of the didactic embellishment literature (treatises, manuals, collections) in the 16th and 17th centuries, arranged chronologically.

II. Collation of original and embellished versions of individual pieces, arranged in parallel columns: (1) Consecutive numbers; (2) Names of composers represented in the literature, in alphabetical order; (3) Incipits or titles of compositions contained in the literature either complete or incomplete; (4) Types of compositions and number of voices; (5) Source(s) of embellished version(s); (6) Principal source of the original (unembellished) version.

III. Text incipits or titles in alphabetical order, followed by names of composers.

TABLE I
Chronological List of Manuals, Treatises, and Collections of Embellished Compositions [1]

Silvestro Ganassi, *Opera intitulata Fontegara* (Venice 1535), chaps. 9, 13–22.
Silvestro Ganassi, *Regola Rubertina* (Venice 1542–43), chaps. XVII–XVIII.
Adrian Petit Coclico, *Compendium musices* (Nuremberg 1552), *De elegantia et ornatu . . . in canendo*.
Diego Ortiz, *Tratado de glosas sobre clausulas* (Rome 1553), Lib. I–II.
Nicolò Vicentino, *L'antica musica ridotta alla moderna prattica* (Rome 1555), p. 88 (recte 94).
Hermann Finck, *Practica musica* (Wittenberg 1556), Lib. V.
Gioseffo Zarlino, *Le Istitutioni harmoniche* (Venice 1558), Pt. III, chap. 46.
Gio. Camillo Maffei, *Delle lettere . . . Libri due* (Naples 1562), I, 3–81.
Fray Tomás de Sancta Maria, *Libro llamado arte de tañer fantasia* (Valladolid 1565), I, chap. 23.
Girolamo dalla Casa, *Il vero Modo di diminuir* (Venice 1584), I–II.
Giovanni Bassano, *Ricercate, passaggi et cadentie* (Venice 1585) [1585³⁸].
Girolamo dalla Casa, *Il secondo libro di madrigali a cinque voci, con i passaggi* (Venice 1590).
Giovanni Bassano, *Motetti, madrigali et canzoni francese . . . diminuiti . . .* (Venice 1591).[2]
Richardo Rogniono, *Passaggi per . . . diminuire . . .* (Venice 1592).
Lodovico Zacconi, *Prattica di musica* I (Venice 1592), chaps. 66, 78.
Gio. Luca Conforto, *Breve et facile maniera . . . a far passaggi . . .* (Rome 1593 [1603?]).
Girolamo Diruta, *Il Transilvano . . .* (Venice 1593) [1593⁹], pp. 18–21.

Gio. Batt. Bovicelli, *Regole, passaggi di musica, madrigali e motetti passeggiati* (Venice 1594).
Adriano Banchieri, *Brevi documenti musicali* (Venice 1599), pp. 49–50.
Aurelio Virgiliano, *Il Dolcimelo*. MS Bologna, Civico Museo Bibliografico Musicale (c. 1600).
Gio. Luca Conforti, *Passaggi sopra tutti li salmi* . . . (Venice 1607).
Ottavio Durante, *Arie devote* (Rome 1608).
Gio. Batt. Spadi, *Passaggi ascendenti, et descendenti* . . . (Venice 1609, 1624) [1609³⁵].
Girolamo Diruta, *Seconda parte del Transilvano* . . . (Venice 1609), *Primo libro*, pp. 10–13 [1609³³].
Giovanni Coperario, *Rules How to Compose* [c. 1610] Part III, *Of Division*. MS, San Marino, California, Huntington Library.
Girolamo Kapsberger, *Libro primo di motetti passeggiati a una voce* (Rome 1612).
Girolamo Kapsberger, *Libro primo di arie passeggiate a una voce* . . . (Rome 1612).
Girolamo Montesardo, *I Lieti giorni di Napoli* . . . *arie gravi passagiate* . . . (Naples 1612) [1612¹²].
Pedro Cerone, *El Melopeo y maestro* (Naples 1613), *Libro octavo*.
Adriano Banchieri, *Cartella musicale* (3d ed. Venice 1614), pp. 216–19.
Antonio Brunelli, *Varii esercitii* . . . *per il cantare con passaggi* . . . (Florence 1614).
Bartholomeo Barbarino da Fabriano (detto il Pesarino), *Spartitura con la parte passeggiata. Del secondo libro delli Motetti* . . . (Venice 1615).
Francesco Severi, *Salmi passeggiati* . . . *sopra Falsi-Bordoni* (Rome 1615).

TABLE II: Alphabetical List

(1) NO.	(2) COMPOSER	(3) INCIPIT (TITLE) [3]	(4) TYPE OF COMPOSITION, NUMBER OF VOICES	(5) EMBELLISHED VERSION [4]
1.	Animuccia, P.	*Nasce la gioia*	Madr. *a 6*	Bassani 15ᵛ
2.	Anon. (I) [Willaert?]	*D'amour me plains*	Chans. *a 4*	Bonizzi 30
3.	Anon. (II)	*Domine quando veneris*	Motet *a 4* (?)	R. Rogniono 41
4.	Anon. (III)	*Tendit ad artua virtus*	Fuga quatuor vocum ex una	Coclico fol. I iijᵛ
5.	Anon. (IV)	*Vago augelleto*	Madrigal	Maffei I, 71–76
6.	Arcadelt, J.	*O felici occhi*	Madr. *a 4*	Ortiz II, 37–40
7.	Bovicelli, G. B.	*Dixit Dominus Domino*	Falso bordone *a 4* and Salmo passeggiato	Bovicelli 83–87
8.	Clemens	*Frais et gaillard*	Chans. *a 4*	Casa II, 5, 6; Bassano No. 27
9.	"	*Mais languirai je*	Chans. *a 4*	Casa II, 17

Michael Praetorius, *Syntagma musicum*, tom. III (Wolfenbüttel 1619), II. Theil, Cap. IX, pp. 229–40.

Michael Praetorius, *Polyhymnia caduceatrix et panegyrica* (Wolfenbüttel 1619).

Francesco Rognone Taegio, *Selva de varii passaggi I–II* (Milan 1620).

Francesco Maria [and Orazio] Bassani, *Lezioni di contrapunto* (c. 1622). MS Bologna, Civico Museo Bibliografico Musicale.

Giovanni Nauwach, *Libro primo di arie passeggiate* (Dresden 1623).

Vicenzo Bonizzi, *Alcune opere di diversi auttori . . . passaggiate . . .* (Venice 1626) [1626¹⁵].

Francesco Severi, *Arie . . . a una, due, et tre voci, Lib. I, op. 2.* (Rome 1626). [Lost: cf. O. Chilesotti in: RMI, XX (1913), 527ff.]

Marin Mersenne, *Harmonie universelle . . .* vol. II (Paris 1637), *Livre sixième*, pp. 440–44.

Tobias Michael, *Musicalischer Seelen-Lust Ander Theil* (Leipzig 1637), *Praefatio* to *Quinta vox.*

Johann Andreas Herbst, *Musica moderna prattica . . .* (Frankfurt 1653).

Christopher Simpson, *The Division Violist* (London 1659); 2nd ed.: *The Division Viol. Chelys, minuritionum artificio exornata* (London 1665).

Tomaso Marchetti, *Il primo libro d'intavolatura della chitarra espagnola . . . sonate passeggiate . . .* (Rome 1660) [1660⁶].

Wolfgang Caspar Printz, *Compendium musicae* (Leipzig-Dresden 1668 ff).

Wolfgang Caspar Printz, *Phrygnis mitilenaeus* (Leipzig-Dresden 1676–77, 1696).

John Playford, *The Division-Violin . . .* (London 1685, 1695) [1685¹⁰, 1695¹⁵].

Georg Falck, *Idea boni cantoris* (Nuremberg 1688).

of Composers and Works

---

(6)

UNEMBELLISHED ORIGINAL

(1) Original unknown. Lute transcription in V. Galilei, *Fronimo* (Venice 1584), p. 45 [1584¹⁵].

(2) *Trente et huyt chansons musicales . . .* (Paris 1529), fol 14ᵛ [1530⁵].

(3) Unknown.

(4) A. Petit Coclico, *Compendium musices* (Nuremberg 1552), fol. I iijᵛ.

(5) Unknown.

(6) *Il primo libro de i madrigali d'Archadelt a quatro* (Venice 1541), p. 47 [1541⁶].

(7) Gio. Batt. Bovicelli, *Regole, passaggi . . .* (Venice 1594), pp. 83–87.

(8) *Le huitiesme livre des chansons . . .* (Antwerp 1545), fol. 13 [1545¹⁶].

(9) *L'unziesme livre . . .* (Antwerp 1549), fol. 16 [1549²⁹].

(1) NO.	(2) COMPOSER	(3) INCIPIT (TITLE)	(4) TYPE OF COM- POSITION, NUMBER OF VOICES	(5) EMBELLISHED VERSION
10.	Clemens	*Rossignolet qui chantes*	Chans. *a 4*	Casa I, 34
11.	Courtois, J.	*Petit Jacquet estoit*	Chans. *a 4*	Casa II, 9, 22
12.	Crecquillon, T.	*Alix avoit aux dents*	Chans. *a 4*	Casa II, 8
13.	"	*Content désir*	Chans. *a 4*	Casa II, 16
14.	Crecquillon [Clemens?]	*Oncques amour*	Chans. *a 4*	Casa II, 10, 11
15.	Crecquillon	*Petite fleur*	Chans. *a 4*	Casa II, 7
16.	"	*Puis ne me peult venir*	Chans. *a 5*	Bonizzi 57
17.	"	*Un(g) gay bergier*	Chans. *a 4*	Bassano No. 24; Casa II, 19; R. Rogniono 48, 50, 51
18.	Finck, H.	*Te maneat semper*	Motet *a 4*	Finck fol. V u- X ij
19.	Gabrieli, A.	*Amor mi strugge'l cor*	Madr. *a 6*	Casa I, 40
20.	"	*[Amor rimanti]* [5]	Madr. *a 6*	Casa I, 41
21.	"	*Caro dolce ben mio*	Madr. *a 5*	Bassano No. 39
22.	"	*Ringratio e lodo il ciel* [6]	Madr. *a 6*	Casa I, 40
23.	Gabucci, G. C.	*Magnificat (2° tono)*	Falso bordone *a 4*	Bovicelli 73, 74
24.	Giovanelli, R.	*Ahi che farò ben mio*	Madr. *a 4*	Bassano No. 16
25.	"	*Et exultavit (1° tono)*	Falso bordone *a 4*	Bovicelli 78, 79
25a.	Gombert, N. (?)	*Le rose* (cf. No. 122)		Casa I, 44; Bassano No. 48
26.	Guami, G.	*Soavissimi baci*	Madr. *a 5*	Bassano No. 37
27.	Janequin, C.	*Le Chant des oiseaux [= Canzon delli uccelli*	Chans. *a 4*	Casa II, 1–4
28.	"	*Martin menoit son porceau*	Chans. *a 4*	Casa II, 25
29.	Lasso, O. di	*Susanne un jour*	Chans. *a 5*	Casa II, 12, 13; Bassano No. 25; F. Rognone II, 61, 63
30.	Layolle, F.	*Lasciar il velo*	Madr. *a 4*	Maffei I, 42–57
31.	Marenzio, L.	*Cosi morirò* [7]	Madr. *a 5*	Bassano No. 36
32.	"	*Dissi a l'amata mia*	Madr. *a 4*	Bassano No. 17

(6)
UNEMBELLISHED ORIGINAL

(10) *Le huitiesme livre des chansons* . . . (Antwerp 1545), fol. 15 [1545[16]].

(11) *Musica de diversi autori* . . . (Venice 1577), p. 19 [1577[11]].

(12) *Le huitiesme livre des chansons* . . . (Antwerp 1545), fol. 12 [1545[16]].

(13) *Canzon di diversi per sonar* . . . (Venice 1588), p. 9 [1588[31]].
(14) *Le tiers livre de chansons* . . . (Antwerp n.d.), fol. 16 <[1544[11]]>.
(15) *Cinquiesme livre des chansons* . . . (Louvain 1555), p. 28 [1555[21]].
(16) *Mellange de chansons* . . . (Paris 1572), fol. 25 [1572[2]].

(17) *Premier livre des chansons à quatre* . . . (Antwerp 1543), fol. 16 [1543[16]].

(18) MS destroyed.

(19) *Il primo libro de madrigali a sei voci* (Venice 1574), p. 12.

(20) *Ibid.*
(21) *Musica di XIII. autori illustri a cinque voci* (Venice 1576), p. 28 [1576[5]].

(22) *Il primo libro de madrigali a sei voci* (Venice 1574), p. 1.

(23) Bovicelli, pp. 73–79.

(24) *Di Gio. Batt. Moscaglia, Il secondo libro de madrigali* . . . (Venice 1585), p. 16 [1585[20]].
(25) Bovicelli, pp. 78–83.

(25a) Same as No. 122.

(26) *Di Gioseffo Guami da Lucca Il terzo libro de madrigali a cinque voci* (Venice 1584), p. 6.
(27) *Musica de diversi autori* . . . (Venice 1577), p. 7 [1577[11]].

(28) Same as No. 27, p. 24.

(29) *Livre de Meslanges* . . . (Paris 1560), fol. 15.

(30) *Il primo libro de i madrigali d'Archadelt a quatro* . . . (Venice 1541), p. 22 [1541[9]].
(31) Luca Marenzio, *Il primo libro de madrigali a cinque voci* (Venice 1580), p. 5.
(32) *Di Gio. Batt. Moscaglia, Il secondo libro de madrigali a quattro voci* (Venice 1585), p. 18 [1585[20]].

(1) NO.	(2) COMPOSER	(3) INCIPIT (TITLE)	(4) TYPE OF COMPOSITION, NUMBER OF VOICES	(5) EMBELLISHED VERSION
33.	Marenzio, L.	*Freni Tirsi il desio* [8]	Madr. *a* 5	Bassano No. 33
34.	"	*Liquide perle Amor*	Madr. *a* 5	Bassano No. 41
35.	"	*Madonna mia gentil*	Madr. *a* 5	Bassano No. 36
36.	"	*Quando i vostri begli occhi*	Madr. *a* 5	Bassano No. 38
37.	"	*Tirsi morir volea* [9]	Madr. *a* 5	Bassano No. 32
38.	Martin Peu d'Argent	*Canzon [Il n'est plaisir ne des batemens]*	Chans. *a* 6	Casa I, 27
39.	Merulo, C.	*Assumpsit Jesus*	Motet *a* 6	Bovicelli 68
40.	"	*In te Domine speravi*	Motet *a* 6	Bovicelli 64
41.	"	*Mirami vita mia*	Madr. *a* 5	Bassano No. 31
42.	Monte, F. de	*Cantai un tempo*	Madr. *a* 6	Casa I, 15
43.	Mortaro, A.	*La Porcia [= La Portia]*	Canzon *a* 4	F. Rognone II, 57
44.	Nanino, G. M.	*Amor deh dimmi*	Madr. *a* 5	Bassano No. 35
45.	"	*Lego questo mio core*	Madr. *a* 4	Bassano No. 15
46.	Palestrina, G. P. da	*Ave Maria*	Motet *a* 4	Bassano No. 2
47.	"	*Ave verum corpus* [10]	Motet *a* 5	Bovicelli 42
48.	"	*Benedicta sit sancta Trinitas*	Motet *a* 4	Bassano Nos. 1, 20
49.	"	*Cosi le chiome mie* [11]	Madr. *a* 5	Casa II, 36; Bassano No. 29; F. Rognone II, 59, 65; Bassani 20[v]
50.	"	*Fuit homo missus*	Motet *a* 4	Bassano No. 19
51.	"	*Hodie beata Virgo*	Motet *a* 4	Bassano No. 3
52.	"	*Introduxit me*	Motet *a* 5	Bassano No. 50
53.	"	*Io son ferito* [12]	Madr. *a* 5	Bassano No. 30; Bovicelli 38, 42; F. Rognone I, 30, 48; II, 55; Bassani 17[v]
54.	"	*Pulchra es amica*	Motet *a* 5	Bassano No. 51; F. Rognone I, 45, 46
55.	"	*Tota pulchra es*	Motet *a* 5	Bassano No. 49
56.	"	*Veni, veni dilecte mi*	Motet *a* 5	Bassano No. 52

(6)
UNEMBELLISHED ORIGINAL

(33) Same at No. 31, p. 7.

(34) Same as No. 31, p. 1.

(35) Same as No. 31, p. 10.

(36) Same as No. 31, p. 5.

(37) Same as No. 31, p. 6.

(38) *Second livre des chansons a cincq et six parties* (Louvain 1553), p. XXIII
[1553²⁵].

(39) Claudio Merulo, *Il primo libro de motetti a sei voci* (Venice 1583).
(40) Same as No. 39.

(41) *Li amorosi ardori . . . libro primo . . .* (Venice 1583), p. 6 [1583¹²].
(42) *Di Filippo Monte Il secondo libro delli madrigali a sei voci* (Venice 1576), p. 2.
(43) *Primo libro de canzoni da sonare a quattro voci Di Antonio Mortaro . . .*
(Venice 1600), p. 13.
(44) *Madrigali a cinque voci . . .* (Venice 1581), p. 8 [1581¹⁰].
(45) Same as No. 32, p. 4.

(46) *Motecta festorum totius anni . . . quaterius vocibus a Joanne Petro Aloysio
praenestino, liber primus* (Rome 1563).
(47) Cf. No. 53.

(48) Same as No. 46.

(49) *Il Desiderio secondo libro de madrigali a cinque . . .* (Venice 1566), p. 8
[1566³].

(50) Same as No. 46.
(51) Same as No. 46.

(52) *Joanni Petraloysii Praenestini Motettorum quinque vocibus liber quartus*
(Rome 1584).
(53) *Il terzo libro delle Muse a cinque voci* (Venice 1561), p. 9 [1561¹⁰].

(54) *Joanni Petraloysii Praenestini Motettorum quinque vocibus liber quartus*
(Rome 1584).

(55) Same as No. 54.
(56) Same as No. 54.

(1) NO.	(2) COMPOSER	(3) INCIPIT (TITLE)	(4) TYPE OF COMPOSITION, NUMBER OF VOICES	(5) EMBELLISHED VERSION
57.	Palestrina, G. P. da	Vestiva i colli [13]	Madr. a 5	Casa II, 36; Bassano No. 28; F. Rognone II, 59, 65; Bassani 20ᵛ
58.	Pathie, R.	Doulce memoire	Chans. a 4	Casa II, 28
59.	Renaldi, G.	Amor io sento	Madr. a 4	Bassano No. 14
60.	"	Chi fia che dal mio cor [14]	Madr. a 4	Bassano No. 11
61.	"	Dolci rosate labbie	Madr. a 4	Bassano No. 13
62.	"	Madonna il mio desio	Madr. a 4	Bassano No. 12
63.	"	Vaghi leggiadri lumi [15]	Madr. a 4	Bassano No. 10
64.	Rore, C. de	A la dolc' ombra [16]	Madr. a 4	Casa I, 22–23; Casa II, 38–49
65.	"	Amor, ben mi credevo	Madr. a 4	Spadi 22
66.	"	Anchor che col partire [17]	Madr. a 4	Casa II, 20, 35; Bassano Nos. 4, 21, 22; Bovicelli 46; R. Rogniono 42, 43, 45, 46; Spadi 28
67.	"	Angelus ad pastores [18]	Motet a 4	Bovicelli 50
68.	"	Beato me direi [19]	Madr. a 4	Casa II, 31
69.	"	Ben qui si mostra'l ciel	Madr. a 4	Casa II, 24
70.	"	Charità de Signore	Madr. a 4	Casa I, 12; Bassani 19ᵛ
71.	"	Com' havran fin	Madr. a 4	Casa II, 29
72.	"	Dalle belle contrade	Madr. a 5	Casa I, 21
73.	"	Dall' estremo oriente	Madr. a 5	Casa I, 20
74.	"	Datemi pace [20]	Madr. a 4	Casa II, 31
75.	"	Di tempo in tempo mi si fa	Madr. a 4	Casa I, 19, 29
76.	"	Di virtù di costumi	Madr. a 5	Casa I, 46
77.	"	E nella face [21]	Madr. a 4	Bassano No. 9
78.	"	En vos adieux, dames	Chans. a 4	Bonizzi 43, 50
79.	"	Era il bel viso suo [22]	Madr. a 4	Bassano No. 8
80.	"	Hellas comment voulez vous	Chans. a 4	Bonizzi 74
81.	"	Io canterei d'amor	Madr. a 4	Casa I, 7; Bassano No. 5

(6)

UNEMBELLISHED ORIGINAL

(57) *Il Desiderio secondo libro de madrigali a cinque voci* . . . (Venice 1566), p. 8 [1566³].

(58) *Musica de diversi autori* . . . *per sonar* . . . (Venice 1577), fol. 23 [1577¹¹].

(59) *Di Giulio Renaldi Padovano Il primo libro de madrigali a quatro voci* (Venice 1569), p. 20 [1569³²].

(60) Same as No. 59, p. 9.

(61) Same as No. 59, p. 10.

(62) Same as No. 59, p. 11.

(63) Same as No. 59, p. 8.

(64) *Il primo libro de madrigali a quatro voci di M. Cipriano de Rore* (Ferrara 1550), pp. 1–4.

(65) *Di Cipriano de Rore Il primo libro de madrigali a quatro voci* (Venice 1551), p. 12.

(66) *Primo libro di madrigali a quatro voci di Perissone Cambio* . . . (Venice 1547), p. 28 [1547¹⁴].

(67) Cf. No. 66.

(68) *Di Cipriano de Rore il secondo libro de madrigali a quatro voci* (Venice 1571), p. 4.

(69) *Di Cipriano et Annibale madrigali a quatro voci* . . . *Libro quinto* (Venice 1561), p. 1 [1561¹⁵].

(70) Same as No. 65, p. 6.

(71) Same as No. 66, p. 27.

(72) *Il quinto libro di madrigali a cinque voci* (Venice 1568), p. 2 [1568¹⁹].

(73) Same as No. 72, p. 23.

(74) *Il secondo libro de madregali a quatro voci* (Venice 1557), p. 7 [1557²⁴].

(75) Same as No. 66, p. 16.

(76) *Il quarto libro d'i madregali a cinque voci* (Venice 1557), p. 12 [1557²⁸].

(77) Same as No. 69, p. 2.

(78) Same as No. 65, p. 21.

(79) Same as No. 69, p. 2.

(80) Same as No. 65, p. 22.

(81) Same as No. 64, p. 13.

(1)	(2)	(3)	(4)	(5)
NO.	COMPOSER	INCIPIT (TITLE)	TYPE OF COMPOSITION, NUMBER OF VOICES	EMBELLISHED VERSION
82.	Rore, C. de	La bella netta ignuda e bianca mano	Madr. a 4	Casa I, 9; Bassano No. 23; Bonizzi 66 (= Bassani 22^v)
83.	"	Lasso che mal accorto fu	Madr. a 5	Bassani 10^v
84.	"	Ma poi che vostr' Altezza [23]	Madr. a 5	Bassano No. 43
85.	"	Non è ch'il duol mi scem'	Madr. a 4	Casa I, 8; Bassano No. 6
86.	"	Non gemme non fin' oro	Madr. a 4	Casa II, 26, 34; Bassano No. 7
87.	"	Non vidde'l mondo [24]	Madr. a 4	Casa I, 22–23; Casa II, 38–49
88.	"	O sonno, o della queta humida [25]	Madr. a 4	Casa II, 32
89.	"	Ove'l silentio [26]	Madr. a 4	Casa II, 33
90.	"	Però più ferm' ogn' hor [27]	Madr. a 4	Casa I, 22–23; Casa II, 38–49
91.	"	Qual è più grand', o Amore	Madr. a 4	Casa II, 18
92.	"	Quando fra l'altre donne [28] (La terza vergine II)	Madr. a 5	Casa I, 25
93.	"	Quando Signor lasciaste [29]	Madr. a 5	Bassano No. 42
94.	"	S'amor la viva fiamma	Madr. a 5	Casa I, 21
95.	"	Selve, sassi, campagne [30]	Madr. a 4	Casa I, 22–23; Casa II, 38–49
96.	"	Signor mio caro	Madr. a 4	Casa I, 11; Bassano 19, 20; Bassani 16^v
97.	"	Tanto mi piacque [31]	Madr. a 4	Casa I, 22–23; Casa II, 38–49
98.	"	Un lauro mi diffese all' hor [32]	Madr. a 4	Casa I, 22–23; Casa II, 38–49
99.	"	Vergine bella (La prima vergine)	Madr. a 5	Casa I, 15
100.	"	Vergine chiara (La seconda vergine)	Madr. a 5	Casa I, 23
101.	"	Vergine pura (La quarta vergine)	Madr. a 5	Casa I, 17
102.	"	Vergine, quante lagrime (La terza vergine I) [33]	Madr. a 5	Casa I, 24

(6)
UNEMBELLISHED ORIGINAL

(82) *Madrigali de la fama a quattro voce* (Venice 1548), p. 4 [1548[8]].

(83) *Di Cipriano Rore et di altri . . . il terzo libro di madrigali a cinque voce* (Venice 1548), No. 9 [1548[9]].
(84) Same as No. 76, p. 8.

(85) Same as No. 64, p. 6.

(86) Same as No. 64, p. 19.

(87) Same as No. 64.

(88) Same as No. 74, p. 5.

(89) Same as No. 74, p. 5.
(90) Same as No. 64.

(91) Same as No. 65, p. 19.

(92) *Musica di Cipriano Rore sopra le stanze del Petrarcha . . . Libro terzo* (Venice 1548), Nos. 1–10 [1548[10]].

(93) Same as No. 76, p. 8.

(94) Same as No. 92, p. 34.

(95) Same as No. 64, pp. 1–10.

(96) Same as No. 65, p. 6.

(97) Same as No. 64, pp. 1–10.

(98) Same as No. 64, pp. 1–10.

(99) Same as No. 92.

(100) Same as No. 92.

(101) Same as No. 92.

(102) Same as No. 92.

(1) NO.	(2) COMPOSER	(3) INCIPIT (TITLE)	(4) TYPE OF COMPOSITION, NUMBER OF VOICES	(5) EMBELLISHED VERSION
103.	Rore, C. de	Vergine saggia (La nona vergine)	Madr. a 5	Casa I, 16
104.	"	Vergine santa (La quinta vergine)	Madr. a 5	Casa I, 18
105.	"	Vergine sol al mondo (La sesta vergine)	Madr. a 5	Casa I, 20
106.	Sandrin, P.	Doulce memoire	Chans. a 4	Ortiz II, 43–46
107.	Sermisy, C de	C'est à grand tort	Chans. a 4	Coclico I ij^v–Iiij
108.	"	Languir me fault	Chans. a 4	Coclico I^v–I ij
109.	Stabile, A.	La bella bianca mano	Madr. a 4	Bassano No. 18
110.	Striggio, A.	Anchor ch'io possa dire	Madr. a 6	Bassano No. 45; Casa I, 39
111.	"	Dolce ritorn' amor	Madr. a 6	Casa I, 25
112.	"	I dolci colli	Madr. a 6	Casa I, 14
113.	"	Invidioso Amor	Madr. a 5	Bassano No. 40; Bonizzi 12
114.	"	La ver l'aurora	Madr. a 6	Casa I, 16
115.	"	Nasce la pena	Madr. a 6	Casa I, 13; Bassano No. 44
116.	"	Questi che inditio fan	Madr. a 6	Bassano No. 46
117.	Vittoria, T. L. de	Dilectus tuus candidus [34]	Motet a 6	Bovicelli 59
118.	"	Vadam et circuibo [35]	Motet a 6	Bovicelli 53
119.	Willaert, A.	A la fontaine du prey	Chans. a 6	Casa I, 42; Bassano No. 47
120.	"	Helas ma mère	Chans. a 5	Casa I, 29
121.	Willaert [Sermisy?]	Joyssance vous donneray	Chans. a 5	Casa II, 14; Bonizzi 22
122.	Willaert [Gombert?]	Le Rose	Chans. a 6	Casa I, 44; Bassano No. 48
123.	Willaert	Se la gratia divina	Madr. a 5	Casa I, 16
124.	Willaert [Crecquillon?]	Si me tenez tant de rigueur	Chans. a 6	Casa I, 32
125.	"	Voulez ouir	Chans. a 5	Casa I, 36

(6)
UNEMBELLISHED ORIGINAL

(103) Same as No. 92.

(104) Same as No. 92.

(105) Same as No. 92.

(106) *Le Parangon des chansons* . . . (Lyons 1538), fol. 19 <[1538][15]>.
(107) *Trente et quatre chansons musicales à quatre parties* (Paris 1528), fol. 15 [1529][3].
(108) *Trente et sept chansons musicales à quatre parties* (Paris c. 1528), fol. 3ᵛ [1528][8].
(109) *Di Gio. Batt. Moscaglia Il secondo libro de madrigali a quattro voci* (Venice 1585), p. 7 [1585][29].
(110) *Il primo libro de madregali a sei voci* (Venice 1560), p. 4 [1560][22].

(111) *Secondo libro delle fiamme* (Venice 1567), p. 6 [1567][13].

(112) Same as No. 110, p. 1.
(113) *Il secondo libro delle Muse a cinque voci* (Venice 1559), p. 15 [1559][16].

(114) Same as No. 110, p. 11.
(115) Same as No. 110, p. 3.

(116) Same as No. 111, p. 22.

(117) *Thomae Ludovici a Victoria abulensis motecta* . . . (Rome 1583).

(118) Same as No. 117.

(119) *Le sixiesme livre contenant trente et une chansons* . . . (Antwerp 1545), fol. 4ᵛ [1545][14].
(120) *Selectissimae* . . . *cantiones* . . . (Augsburg 1540), No. 44 [1540][7].
(121) *Mellange de chansons* . . . (Paris 1572), fol. 1ᵛ [1572][2].

(122) *Canzon di diversi per sonar* . . . (Venice 1588), p. 13 [1588][31].

(123) *Di Cipriano Rore et di altri eccellentissimi musici il terzo libro di madrigali a cinque voce* . . . (Venice 1548), p. 23 [1548][9].
(124) Same as No. 121, fol. 59ᵛ.

(125) Same as No. 121, fol. 27.

TABLE III

Alphabetical List of Incipits or Titles

1. *Ahi che farò* (Giovanelli)
2. *A la dolc' ombra* (Rore)
3. *A la fontaine* (Willaert)
4. *Alix avoit* (Crecquillon)
5. *Amor, ben mi credevo* (Rore)
6. *Amor deh dimmi* (Nanino)
7. *Amor io sento* (Renaldi)
8. *Amor mi strugge* (Gabrieli)
9. [*Amor rimanti*] (Gabrieli)
10. *Anchor che col partire* (Rore)
11. *Anchor ch'io possa dire* (Striggio)
12. *Angelus ad pastores* (Rore) [= No. 10]
13. *Assumpsit Jesus* (Merulo)
14. *Ave Maria* (Palestrina)
15. *Ave verum corpus* (Palestrina) [= No. 59]
16. *Beato me direi* (Rore)
17. *Benedicta sit sancta Trinitas* (Palestrina)
18. *Ben qui si mostra'l ciel* (Rore)
19. *Cantai un tempo* (Monte)
20. *Canzon delli uccelli* (Janequin)
21. *Caro dolce ben mio* (Gabrieli)
22. *C'est à grand tort* (Sermisy)
23. *Charità di Signore* (Rore)
24. *Chi fia che dal mio cor* (Renaldi)
25. *Com' havran fin* (Rore)
26. *Content désir* (Crecquillon)
27. *Cosi le chiome mie* (Palestrina)
28. *Cosi morirò* (Marenzio)
29. *Dalle belle contrade* (Rore)
30. *Dall' estremo oriente* (Rore)
31. *D'amours me plains* (Anon. I) [Willaert?]
32. *Datemi pace* (Rore)
33. *Dilectus tuus candidus* (Vittoria)
34. *Dissi a l'amata mia* (Marenzio)
35. *Di tempo in tempo mi si fa* (Rore)
36. *Di virtù di costumi* (Rore)
37. *Dixit Dominus Domino* (Bovicelli)
38. *Dolce ritorn' Amor* (Striggio)
39. *Dolci rosate labbie* (Renaldi)
40. *Domine quando veneris* (Anon. II)
41. *Doulce memoire* (Pathie)
42. *Doulce memoire* (Sandrin)
43. *E nella face* (Rore)
44. *En vos adieux, dames* (Rore)
45. *Era il bel viso suo* (Rore)
46. *Et exultavit* (Giovanelli)
47. *Frais et gaillard* (Clemens)
48. *Freni Tirsi il desio* (Marenzio)
49. *Fuit homo missus* (Palestrina)
50. *Helas ma mère* (Willaert)
51. *Hellas, comment voulez-vous* (Rore)
52. *Hodie beata Virgo* (Palestrina)
53. *I dolci colli* (Striggio)
54. [*Il n'est plaisir ne des bate-*

mens] Canzon (Martin Peu d'Argent)

55. *In te Domine speravi* (Merulo)
56. *Introduxit me* (Palestrina)
57. *Invidioso Amor* (Striggio)
58. *Io canterei d'amor* (Rore)
59. *Io son ferito* (Palestrina) [= No. 15]
60. *Joyssance vous donneray* (Willaert) [Sermisy?]
61. *La bella bianca mano* (Stabile)
62. *La bella netta ignuda e bianca mano* (Rore)
63. *Languir me fault* (Sermisy)
64. *La Porcia* (= *Portia*) (Mortaro)
65. *Lasciar il velo* (Layolle)
66. *Lasso che mal accorto fu* (Rore)
67. *La ver l'aurora* (Striggio)
67a. *Le Chant des oiseaux* (= No. 20)
68. *Lego questo mio core* (Nanino)
69. *Le rose* (Willaert) [Gombert?]
70. *Liquide perle amor* (Marenzio)
71. *Madonna il mio desio* (Renaldi)
72. *Madonna mia gentil* (Marenzio)
73. *Magnificat* (Gabucci)
74. *Mais languirai je* (Clemens)
75. *Ma poi che vostr' Altezza* (Rore)
76. *Martin menoit son porceau* (Janequin)
77. *Mirami vita mia* (Merulo)

78. *Nasce la gioia mia* (Animuccia)
79. *Nasce la pena mia* (Striggio)
80. *Non è ch'il duol mi scem'* (Rore)
81. *Non gemme non fin' oro* (Rore)
82. *Non vidde'l mondo* (Rore)
83. *O felici occhi miei* (Arcadelt)
84. *Oncques amour* (Crecquillon) [Clemens?]
85. *O Sonno* (Rore)
86. *Ove'l silentio* (Rore)
87. *Però più ferm' ogn'hor* (Rore)
88. *Petite fleur coincte et jolie* (Crecquillon)
89. *Petit Jacquet estoit en la cuisine* (Courtois)
90. *Puis ne me peult venir* (Crecquillon)
91. *Pulchra es amica mea* (Palestrina)
92. *Qual è più grand', o Amore* (Rore)
93. *Quando fra l'altre donne* (Rore)
94. *Quando i vostri begli occhi* (Marenzio)
95. *Quando Signor lasciaste* (Rore)
96. *Questi che inditio fan* (Striggio)
97. *Ringratio e lodo il ciel* (Gabrieli)
98. *Rossignolet qui chantes* (Clemens)
99. *S'Amor la viva fiamma* (Rore)
100. *Se la gratia divina* (Willaert)

101. *Selve, sassi, campagne* (Rore)
102. *Signor mio caro* (Rore)
103. *Si me tenez* (Willaert) [Crecquillon?]
104. *Soavissimi baci* (Guami)
105. *Susanne un jour* (Lasso)
106. *Tanto mi piacque* (Rore)
107. *Te maneat semper* (Finck)
108. *Tendit ad artua virtus* (Anon. III)
109. *Tirsi morir volea* (Marenzio)
110. *Tota pulchra es* (Palestrina)
111. *Un(g) gay bergier* (Crecquillon)
112. *Un lauro mi diffese all'hor* (Rore)
113. *Vadam et circuibo* (Vittoria)

114. *Vaghi leggiadri lumi* (Renaldi)
115. *Vago augelleto che cantando vai* (Anon. IV)
116. *Veni, veni dilecte mi* (Palestrina)
117. *Vergine bella* (Rore)
118. *Vergine chiara* (Rore)
119. *Vergine pura* (Rore)
120. *Vergine, quante lagrime* (Rore)
121. *Vergine saggia* (Rore)
122. *Vergine santa* (Rore)
123. *Vergine sol al mondo* (Rore)
124. *Vestiva i colli* (Palestrina)
125. *Voulez ouir* (Willaert)

[1] Limitations of space have required radical shortening of titles and similar curtailment of bibliographical references and details of reprints and facsimile reproductions. RISM numbers appear in square brackets, with the addition of < > to show numbers already bracketed in RISM.

[2] No copy of the original print is extant. For the contents of a complete handwritten copy by F. Chrysander see my contribution in *Festschrift Helmuth Osthoff* (Tutzing 1961), pp. 75–101.

[3] References to names of authors of texts have been omitted for reasons of space.

[4] The following abbreviations are used in col. 5 (for full citations see Table I): Bassani = F. M. (Orazio) Bassani, *Lezioni* . . . (c. 1622).—Bassano = Gio. Bassano, *Motetti, madrigali* . . . (1591).—Bassano 1585 = Gio. Bassano, *Ricercate, passaggi* . . . (1585).—Bonizzi = V. Bonizzi, *Alcune opere* . . . (1626).—Bovicelli = G. B. Bovicelli, *Regole, passaggi* . . . (1594).—Casa = Gir. dalla Casa, *Il vero modo di diminuir* (1584).—Coclico = A. P. Coclico, *Compendium musices* (1552).—Finck = Hermann Finck, *Practica musica* (1556).—Maffei = Gio. Camillo Maffei, *Lettere* . . . (1562).—Ortiz = Diego Ortiz, *Tratado de glosas* . . . (1553).—R. Rogniono = Richardo Rogniono, *Passaggi* . . . (1592).—F. Rognone = Francesco Rognone, *Selva* . . . (1620).—Spadi = Gio. Batt. Spadi, *Passaggi* . . . (1609).

[5] = No. 22, Seconda parte.
[6] Cf. No. 20.
[7] = No. 37, Terza parte.
[8] = No. 37, Seconda parte.
[9] Cf. Nos. 31 and 33.
[10] Contrafactum = No. 53.
[11] = No. 57, Seconda parte.
[12] Cf. No. 47.
[13] Cf. No. 49.
[14] = No. 63, Seconda parte.
[15] Cf. No. 60.
[16] Cf. Nos. 87, 90, 95, 97, 98.
[17] Cf. No. 67.
[18] Contrafactum = No. 66.
[19] Cf. No. 74.
[20] = No. 68, Seconda parte.
[21] = No. 79, Seconda parte.
[22] Cf. No. 77.
[23] = No. 93, Seconda parte.
[24] = No. 64, Seconda parte.
[25] Cf. No. 89.
[26] = No. 88, Seconda parte.
[27] = No. 64, Quarta parte.
[28] Cf. No. 102.
[29] Cf. No. 84.
[30] = No. 64, Quinta parte.
[31] = No. 64, Sexta parte.
[32] = No. 64, Terza parte.
[33] = No. 92, Seconda parte.
[34] = No. 118, Secunda pars.
[35] Cf. No. 117.

ORGANAL AND CHORDAL STYLE IN RENAISSANCE SACRED MUSIC: NEW AND LITTLE-KNOWN SOURCES

by KURT von FISCHER

I T IS A GENERALLY known fact that toward the end of the 15th century a new note-against-note style came into being in several areas of sacred and secular music. In Italy the new style is found primarily in the *frottola*, the *lauda*, and in the simple liturgical psalm settings called *falsobordone*. In Germany the style arose in the humanist ode and in certain Protestant *Lied* settings of the early Reformation, such as those, for example, of Johann Walter in 1524 and especially in 1544 and 1551. Shortly before the middle of the century the style is found in some of the Huguenot psalms of Loys Bourgeois (1547). The two last-named types of composition are of basic importance to the development of the Protestant chorale.[1]

The history of this style known as *Kantionalsatz*[2] has been quite fully explored from the time of the Reformation to that of Bach, especially in its relationship to the Protestant chorale. Its origin and pre-Reformation history, on the other hand, have not yet been clarified.[3] The following exposition represents an attempt to trace connections with music discovered in some manuscripts that are either unfamiliar or not known at all.[4]

---

[1] Gustave Reese, *Music in the Renaissance* (Rev. ed., New York 1959).

[2] See the article *Kantional*, in: MGG, VII (1958), 611–30. (Translator's note: *Kantionalsatz* is used throughout this essay as a term meaning a four-part, note-against-note syllabic setting of sacred songs with the melody in the highest voice or in the tenor.)

[3] Reese, *op. cit.*, p. 705 discusses the possible relationship between humanist ode, Latin school dramas, and the *Kantionalsatz* of Osiander (1586) previously mentioned by von Liliencron in *Die Chorgesänge des lateinisch-deutschen Schuldramas im XVI. Jarhundert*, in: VfMW, VI (1890), 309–87. See also Max Zulauf, *Zur Entwicklung des Kantionalsatzes*, in: *Musik und Gottesdienst* (1960), pp. 6–19, for a somewhat imperfect attempt to portray these relationships.

[4] This is a good place to acknowledge the cooperation of the following libraries and institutions, which made a study of the sources possible by allowing me access directly and by supplying microfilms: Aosta, Biblioteca del Seminario Maggiore;

The first source to be briefly described here is one so far unknown to musical scholarship: [5]

Cologne, Historisches Archiv der Stadt Köln, Ms.W75, is a collection compiled very early in the 16th century in a Franciscan monastery in Mechlin, Belgium consisting of 75 paper folios and measuring 13.6 x 10 cm. The codex contains rules of the order, theological tracts, and prayers. The following two-part musical compositions are found on fol. 39 as well as fol. 46ᵛ–51:

(1) fol.39–39ᵛ   *Philomena praevia temporis ameni* (*Devotissimi fratris Bonaventurae carmen de mistica Philomena*) [6]

(2) fol.46ᵛ–47   *Ave pulcerrima regina* (2nd part, *Mira res angelorum*) [7]

(3) fol.47ᵛ–48   *Te rex regum deus deorum* (the music is the same as part 1 of number 2 above) [8]

(4) fol.47ᵛ–48   *O gloriosa domina excelsa* [9]

(5) fol.48ᵛ   *Cantum epithalamum*

(6) fol.50   *Ad festum leticie* (this composition bears the heading *Te deum laudamus* in the margin above) [10]

Cologne, Historisches Archiv der Stadt Köln; Cracow, Biblioteka Polskiej Akademii Nauk; Munich, Handschriftenabteilung der Bayerischen Staatsbibliothek; Nijmegen, Library of the Redemptorist Monastery Nebo.

[5] I should like to thank Dr. G. Göller of Cologne for calling my attention to this manuscript.

[6] See Cyr Ulysse Chevalier, *Repertorium hymnologicum* (Louvain 1892–1921), No. 14898, and Wilhelm Bäumker, *Das katholische deutsche Kirchenlied in seinen Singweisen von der frühesten Zeit bis gegen Ende des 17. Jahrhunderts* (Freiburg i.B 1883–91), I, No. 310, which has the same text set to a different melody.

[7] The same two-part composition is also found in a late 15th-century MS from the Netherlands (Utrecht), Berlin, Deutsche Staatsbibliothek, Cod. germ. 8° 190, fol. 32ᵛ (now in Tübingen). For the most recent publication referring to this MS see *Het geestlijk lied van Noord Nederland in de vijftiende eeuw*, *Monumenta musica neerlandica*, VII (Amsterdam 1963). The strange position of the clefs in the Berlin MS results in an exchange of voices in the first part. It must be considered an error. See Wilhelm Bäumker, *Niederländische geistliche Lieder nebst ihren Singweisen aus Handschriften des XV. Jahrhunderts*, in: VfMW, IV (1888), 231–33. See further in this article (p. 229) a monophonic setting of the lowest, the main voice, but with Dutch text. See also Arnold Geering, *Die Organa und mehrstimmigen Conductus in den Handschriften des deutschen Sprachgebietes vom 13. bis 16. Jahrhundert* (Bern 1952), p. 17, Nos. 38/39.

[8] In the MS Berlin, Cod. germ. 8° 190, the text *Te rex regum* is appended under *Ave pulcherrima regina*.

[9] Chevalier, No. 13042. This text is found throughout a large geographical area. See Bäumker, *Das katholische Kirchenlied*, II, No. 47, set to another melody. The rhythm of the setting ♩ ♩ ♩ ♩ ♩ ♩ found in the MS

O   glo - ri - o - sa   Do - mi - na

Cologne W75 is remarkable for the fact that only the first and last syllables are given long values, a practice that survived primarily in the Huguenot Psalter.

[10] Compare the text in *Analecta hymnica*, XX, 80. There are variants *Ad cantum leticie* and *Ad cantus leticie*. For other two-part settings see Jacques Handschin, *Angelomontana polyphonica*, in: *Schweizer Jahrbuch für Musikwissenschaft*, III (1928), 93–94. To the sources listed by Handschin the following should be added: Karlsruhe, Landesbibliothek, Codex St. Georgen 31, fol. 128ᵛ; Cividale, Museo

(7) fol.50ᵛ–51   *Dies est leticie in ortu regali* (headed in the margin by
Gracias agimus tibi propter magnam gloriam tuam) [11]

The first five and the seventh compositions are written in white
mensural notation. They are simple, almost entirely in note-against-note
style, with a texture predominantly in thirds or sixths. For example:

Ex. 1   Cologne, Hist. Archiv, MS W75, 46ᵛ/47[12]

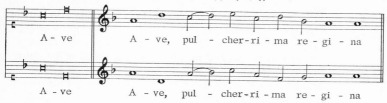

No. 6, on the other hand, is written in older square notation and may be
described as being in organum style.

Ex. 2   Cologne W75, 50

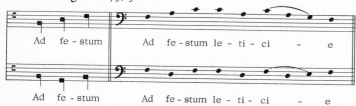

The juxtaposition of these compositions which, while not always written
by the same scribe, surely date from the same time, shows that in the
area of the lower Rhine, old and new polyphonic styles existed side by
side about 1500. Since the newer style predominates numerically, however, it may be concluded that the old organum-like practice was about
to die out.

A similar coexistence of styles is found some decades later in another
hitherto neglected manuscript of the late 16th century. This is now in

Archeologico, Cod. LVI, fol. 242ᵛ; Aosta, Biblioteca del Seminario Maggiore, Cod.
9-E-17, fol. 64 and Cod. 9-E-19, fol. 78. Regarding the last two sources see Frank
Ll. Harrison, *Benedicamus, Conductus, Carol, Study in the Ancestry of Forms*, to
be published in: *Acta musicologica*, XXXVI or XXXVII, and Kurt von Fischer,
Neue Quellen zur Musikgeschichte des 13., 14. und 15. Jahrhunderts, in: *Acta musicologica*, XXXVI, 87–90.

[11] The same composition is found in Gothic plainchant notation in Berlin 8° 190,
fol. 4ᵛ (See Geering, *op. cit.*, p. 16, No. 1). Further on the melody, i.e. the lower
part of the two-part setting, see Bäumker, *Das katholische Kirchenlied*, I, No. 43, as
well as the same author's *Niederländische geistliche Lieder*, in: VfMW, IV, 184,
with a Dutch text. See further, Chevalier, No. 4610.

[12] See fn. 7 above.

the library of the Redemptorist Monastery Nebo near Nijmegen, Holland, where it is known as MS Cabinet P, No. 3. Before 1928 the codex was located in Roermond. It contains 14 Latin and Dutch songs, for the most part in two voices, as well as two-voiced settings of the 8 psalm tones in notation which is a mixture of white mensural, Gothic plainchant, and black square notation.[13] The following is a list of polyphonic compositions contained in the manuscript:

(1) fol.5   *Patrem omnipotentem* (two-part, square notation with mensural elements)

(2) fol.8ᵛ   *Ave verum corpus* alternating with verses of *Adoro te devote* (two-part in mixed white mensural and Gothic plainchant notation)

(3) fol.11ᵛ   *O salutaris hostia* (three-part, white mensural notation)

(4) fol.15   *Ave maris stella* (two-part, Gothic plainchant notation)[14]

(5) fol.15ᵛ   *Kyrie Godt is gecomen* [*Kyrie magne Deus*] (two-part, Gothic plainchant notation)[15]

(6) fol.17ᵛ   *Nu laet ons singen* (two-part, white mensural notation)[16]

(7) fol.20ᵛ   *In hoc festo blijdelijcke* (two-part, white mensural notation)

(8a) fol.23ᵛ   *Jhesum corde colite pie* with the refrain *Ons is gheboren een wtuercoren* (two-part, white mensural notation)

(8b) fol.26ᵛ   *Jesu dulcis memoria* with the refrain *Ave Jesu* (white mensural notation)[17]

(9) fol.28ᵛ   *Enixa es puerpera* (two-part, white mensural notation)[18]

(10) fol.29ᵛ   *Jubilemus singuli* (two-part, white mensural notation)

(11) fol.30ᵛ   *Laet ons met harten reyne* (two-part, white mensural notation)[19]

---

[13] See A. Geering, *op. cit.*, p. 21, No. 69 (referred to as MS Roermond). Geering assumes the provenance to be a Cistercian monastery. He obviously knows only one composition from this MS (No. 5), however. See the recent article by Jop Pollmann, *Iets over tekstplaatsing in oude liederen*, in: *Mens en Melodie*, XVII (1962), 178–82.

[14] The music of this composition is not identical with that for the same text in MS Berlin, Cod. germ. 8° 190, fol. 40ᵛ.

[15] Reprinted in Bäumker, *Niederländische geistliche Lieder*, 322–26. The composition from the Berlin MS (fol. 66) reprinted on p. 320 of this article is not monophonic, as the author maintains; it is a two-part piece. The second part differs from the one in Nijmegen, however. For other settings of the Latin text see Geering, *op. cit.*, p. 24.

[16] See Bäumker, *Das katholische Kirchenlied*, I, No. 152 for a monophonic version.

[17] None of the melodies given by Bäumker and Zahn (*Die Melodien der deutschen evangelischen Kirchenlieder*, Gütersloh 1889–93) corresponds with that in the Nijmegen MS. I have assigned the numbers 8a and 8b to the pieces on fols. 23ᵛ and 26ᵛ on the assumption that they belong together as one composition.

[18] See Bäumker, *Das katholische Kirchenlied*, I, 132, where the German text "Die edle Mutter hat geborn" is given as the fifth verse of *Christus wir sollen loben schon*. The melody differs from the one in the Nijmegen source, however. The same statement applies to the monophonic setting of the text in the MS Berlin, Cod. germ. 8° 190, fol. 71.

[19] Found in a monophonic non-mensural setting in the MS Berlin, Cod. germ. 8° 190, fol. 35. See *Het geestelijk lied van Noord Nederland*, p. 168.

(12) fol.30ᵛ   *Jesus natus de virgine* (two-part, white mensural notation)

(13) fol.31ᵛ   *Venit quem pater miserat* (two-part, white mensural
notation, same music as No. 12 above)

(14) fol.32ᵛ   *Ave Maria, O suijver maecht van Israel* (two-part, mixed
square and white mensural notation) [20]

(15) fol.138ᵛ   *Gloria Patri et Filio* (two-part Gothic plainchant notation through all 8 psalm tones) [21]

The mixed notation of this manuscript suffices to suggest the simultaneous presence of old and new styles even without examining the
prevailing compositional techniques that confirm the impression. In the
following example parallel fifths, conductus-like crossings of the parts,
and parallel thirds are all found together:

Ex. 3   Nijmegen, 32ᵛ

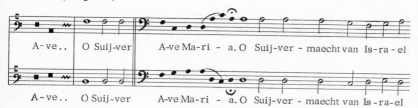

A most unambiguous and precisely dateable demonstration of the
change from organum-like composition to a style dominated by thirds
—in this case chordal as well—is found in a manuscript from Cracow
written at the end of the 15th century. On fol. 5ff of Cracow, Academy
of Fine Arts, Ms.1706 [22] we find a *Liber generationis* setting in Gothic
plainchant notation with the inscription, "hic reperies tres voces scilicet
tenor, medium et discantus." Above it stands the date "Anno domini
MCCCC nonagesimo sexto." Of the compositions under this heading
the following are polyphonic: the opening *Dominus vobiscum*, a *Secundum Mattheum*, and every third name of the ancestral table of Christ,
Jacob, Esrom, Naasom, etc. The rest of the text is set for one voice. In
the three-part compositions the tenor or lowest part contains the cantus

[20] A monophonic *O suijver maecht van Israel* found in the MS Berlin, Cod. germ.
8° 190, fol. 37, has only the text of the first verse in common with the present MS.
[21] Compare the polyphonic setting of the psalm tones in Georg Rhau's *Enchiridion
utriusque musicae practicae* (Wittenberg 1536; facs. in: *Documenta musicologica*,
ed. Hans Albrecht, Kassel 1951).
[22] See Reese, *op. cit.*, p. 745, where further literature about this source is cited. In
Reese as well as MGG (X, 1393), however, the MS is erroneously referred to as
MS 2216. The error has been rectified by Dragan Plamenac, *Music Libraries in
Eastern Europe*, in: *Notes*, XIX (1962), 227. He is mistaken, however, in stating
(as does MGG, *loc. cit.*) that the source contains polyphonic lamentations beginning
on fol. 49. They are all monophonic.

firmus. The style of these compositions is anachronistically organum-like.

Ex. 4   Cracow, Akad. Nauk, MS 1706, 5

Do - mi - nus vo - bis - cum.

Beginning on fol. 9ᵛ we find the same text from the *Liber generationis* in the hand of the same scribe set for four voices headed by the inscription, "Hic est liber generationum quatuor vocum scilicet discantus, tenor, contratenor et altus qui est notatus MCCCCLXXXXVII.[23] An example of a setting of the same text as above now reads as follows:

Ex. 5   *Ibid.*, 9ᵛ

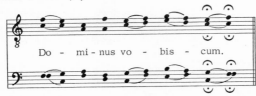

Do - mi - nus vo - bis - cum.

This version alternates between one-, three-, and four-voiced sections. These parts, which in the 1496 version had been for three voices, are now for four: the solo sections of the earlier version have been either maintained or replaced by three-voiced settings. While the cantus firmi are still in the tenor in the later setting, that voice is now the second from the bottom. Although, as we pointed out, the lowest voice is called contratenor in the heading, the term has been replaced by "bassus," a more modern term, in the margin. This bass moves in the fourths characteristic of the period around 1500. Also noteworthy is the fact that the tenor often forms thirds with the lowest voice, a feature clearly indicative of polyphonic Italian *lauda* and *falsobordone* influence, the latter having been much used for declamatory and other simple liturgical compositions since the late 15th century.[24] In the second version of the *Liber generationis*, which is only one year younger than the first, the archaic monastic style has been largely replaced by the more modern manner of Italian church and secular settings. This should not surprise

---

[23] The same four-part setting is found in Cracow, Archiwum Kapituly Metropolitalnej, MS 58.

[24] See among others Kurt von Fischer, *Zur Geschichte der Passionskompositionen des 16. Jahrhunderts in Italien,* in: AfMW, XI (1954), 192.

us, considering that Italian influence in Poland can be traced as far back as the Council of Constance (1414–18).[25]

As recent research has shown, certain peripheral areas, even in Italy, also maintained old-fashioned organal elements until late into the 15th century,[26] while at the same time the newer chordal style—stimulated perhaps by the Continental *fauxbourdon* of the Franco-Flemish masters —generally prevailed elsewhere. In the peripheral church music of northern Italy, however, a change from organal style dominated by fifths toward a texture governed by sixths may be found as early as c. 1400. An example attesting to this transformation exists in a heretofore ignored manuscript dating from the late 14th century, MS 9-E-17 of the Seminario Maggiore in Aosta.[27] (The fact that Aosta belonged to the House of Savoy and that its church belonged to the Tarantaise See, not to Milan, must be acknowledged here.) Beside an organal *A[d] cantus leticie* (mentioned in footnote 10) there is, between other pieces on fol. 67[r/v], an Introductory Verse to the *Benedicamus* of the Vespers of St. Ursus (patron of the Collegiale S. Orso in Aosta):

Ex. 6   Aosta, Sem. maggiore, MS 9-E-17, 67

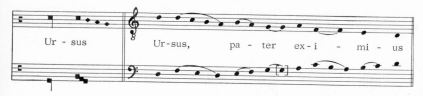

In this composition fifths and sixths are used side by side. Admittedly there is some question about the manner in which the first few notes were sung.

Ex. 7   Excerpt from Ex. 6

---

[25] See the MS Warsaw, Biblioteka Narodowa Zaklad Muzyczny 52, and the now missing MS Leningrad F I 378 (the so-called "St. Petersburg MS").

[26] As, for example, in sources from the second half of the 15th century, Venice, Biblioteca Nazionale Marciana IX 145 and the MSS in Cividale recently discovered by L. Lockwood and P. Petrobelli. See M. L. Martinez, *Die Musik des frühen Trecento* (Munich 1963), pp. 117–28.

[27] MS 9-E-19 discovered by Frank Ll. Harrison is presumably a later copy of MS 9-E-17. I cannot agree with Harrison's dating of the former in the early 14th century. Regarding the MS from Aosta, see Harrison, *op. cit.* and my own *Neue Quellen.*

According to the old rule of the long final note in organum, the first solution is the most likely one while the third is more generally consistent with organum style. Perhaps such passages in parallel sixths explain how it was that *fauxbourdon* was so readily accepted in Italy. The same music (which, incidentally, is constructed on the old principle of *Stimmtausch*) is found again further back in the same manuscript as the Vespers *Benedicamus* for Easter, *Voce digna, corde pio*.

The examples cited so far permit us to draw the conclusion that within the limits of simple liturgical or sacred compositions, two-part music dominated by thirds and sixths as well as full chordal style may be regarded as descending directly from organum. The repertoire for both types was the same in the Netherlands, Germany, Poland, in some North Italian, and possibly in French areas. Both unpretentious styles were used as part of the simplest or monastic liturgies.

There is still another source, ignored until now, relevant to the development of the *Kantionalsatz*, a source that strengthens the hypothesis that the religious *Kantionalsatz* was influenced by the humanist ode.[28] Apparently a university student's notebook, the manuscript Munich, Bayerische Staatsbibliothek Clm 24506, contains dates indicating that it was written in the first two decades of the 16th century. Aside from predominantly literary texts such as Lucian and Terence it has some musical entries as well. Of these the most important for our purposes is a four-part composition on fol. 79:

Ex. 8   Munich, Bayer. StB., Clm. 24506, 79

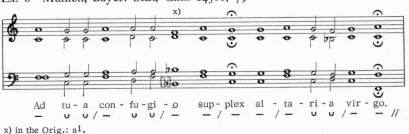

x) in the Orig.: a¹.

The heading for the piece, which is written in open score, reads: *Elegiaca carmina hisce notulis possunt decantari* [*per*] *omnes versos* [*sic*] *ut iam sequitur*. Below the music we find the date 1507.[29] The

---

[28] See fn. 3 above.

[29] Another polyphonic composition, however without text, is found on fol. 90ᵛ of this MS with the note "Huiusce generis carmina hoc numero [meaning "rhythm" or "meter"] possunt cantari." On fol. 91 the text *Jucundissime Martialis hec sunt* is given with the same rhythm as the preceding music. It bears the inscription, *Carmen*

composition's note-against-note style is the familiar one of the humanist ode. The text, which is in hexameter, is cited by H. Walter (*Initia carminum*, Göttingen 1959, No. 467) as *Baptistae Mantuani ad B.M.V.*[30] We must consider the piece a *Kationalsatz* in which, however, the almost constant movement of tenor and superius in octaves, as well as the appearance of parallel fifths between superius and altus, show traces of organum style. It is a *Kantionalsatz* having the melody (possibly a cantus prius factus) in the tenor, just as in certain settings by Johann Walter and Loys Bourgeois. The fact that the superius ends on the third of the chord in the cadence—as it does again at the end of the entire composition—points clearly to Italian influence.[31]

This example serves to show that already before the Reformation, Latin sacred texts as well as classical ones were set as odes. Until the discovery of this source, no sacred compositions and certainly no hymns were believed to have existed before the third decade of the 16th century. (Of the outstanding early ones, Agricola's *Melodiae scholasticae* published in 1557 but obviously begun in the 1530s should be mentioned.) [32] The step from such songs to the chordal setting of the chorale in the vernacular was thus but a small one, with both types of setting sharing the aim of textural clarity achieved by syllabic chordal writing.

By way of summarizing the results of this investigation we may say that the chordal song style, i.e. *Kantionalsatz*, which became very important in the course of the 16th century, especially in the Protestant chorale, may be regarded, at least in part, as a continuation of organal style that had survived on the periphery of the main stream of music. The survivals of organum came under the influence of the new style originating in Italy around 1500. A further influence exercised over this cumulation of elements was that of the humanist ode as is evident in the above notebook from Munich. All these factors combine in simple set-

---

phalentium [*sic*] *de vita tranquillori Martialis,* which indicates that this is a so-called *carmen phalaeceum* having the following meter $--/- \cup \cup -/\cup -/\cup --$. The text is apparently related to that given by Chevalier, *op. cit.,* as No. 9860, in connection with St. Martial, Bishop of Limoges, *Jucundis panget mentibus.*

[30] According to Walther, *op. cit.,* who does not know the Munich MS, the text is found in Berlin, Deutsche Staatsbibliothek, lat. fol. 39, and Cambridge, University Library H. h. 18.

[31] See among others, the author's *Zur Geschichte der Passionskompositionen,* p. 204.

[32] See Arthur Prüfer, *Untersuchungen über den ausserkirchlichen Kunstgesang in den evangelischen Schulen des 16. Jahrhunderts* (Diss. Leipzig 1890), p. 14ff, and especially Heinz Funk, *Martin Agricola* (Diss. Würzburg 1933), pp. 21 & 137. The statement that *Melodiae scholasticae* was published in 1512 is based on an error in Gerber's *Tonkünstlerlexikon;* see also M. Jenny, *Christoffel Wyssgerber alias Christophorus Alutarius,* in: *Basler Zeitschrift für Geschichte und Altertumskunde,* XLIX (1950), p. 69.

tings with the aim of serving the comprehensibility of the text, an aim corresponding with the then prevailing popular desire for simple piety as well as humanistic tendencies, thus completely expressing the spirit and the musical ideals of the Reformation.

[*Translated by Hans Lenneberg,*
University of Chicago]

INDEX OF FESTSCHRIFTEN AND SOME SIMILAR PUBLICATIONS

by WALTER GERBOTH

PREFACE

THE TERM *Festschriften* has been variously defined.[1] As applied in this index it includes publications issued to honor scholars on the occasion of an important anniversary or birthday, or as a memorial shortly after death. The publications included are at least 25 pages in length, and they contain articles on diverse subjects by diverse authors. Certain closely related types of publications have also been included. Because of their diversity of either subject matter or authorship, volumes consisting of collections of articles written by the person being honored and volumes honoring composers and performers have been included. In addition a few publications honoring institutions and publishers were deemed sufficiently diverse to require indexing. They have been included although most *Festschriften* for places, institutions, and business establishments as such have not. Musical articles appearing in *Festschriften* honoring persons and institutions in other fields have also been included. Because these publications are less likely to be familiar to musical scholars, all those located have been included regardless of the occasion for which they were prepared or the person or institution being honored.

The process of compilation uncovered a number of references to musical *Festschriften* that were never published. These include collections in honor of Ludwig Schiedermair (70th birthday), Max Schneider (75th), Hermann Stephani (70th), Willi Kahl (50th), Karl Gustav Fellerer (50th), Antoine-Elisée Cherbuliez (70th), and Richard Münnich (70th). Whenever it was possible to obtain microfilm copies of the typescripts and place them in an institutional library they have been

---

[1] See Dorothy Rounds and Sterling Dow, *Festschriften*, in: *Harvard Library Bulletin*, VIII (1954), 283–98; S. Griswold Morley, *The Development of the Homage Volume*, in: *Philological Quarterly*, VIII (1929), 61–68; Alfred Gudemann, *The Homage Volume once more*, in: *Philological Quarterly*, VIII (1929), 335–38; Ernest C. Krohn, *Musical Festschriften and Related Publications*, in: *Music Library Association Notes* 2nd ser., XVIII (1963–64), 94–108.

indexed. Conversely, published *Festschriften* which could not be located in an institutional library, and which could not be obtained and placed in one, have not been indexed.

The index is organized in three sections: A) a list of the *Festschriften*, B) a classified list of the musical articles and complete musical compositions in the *Festschriften*, and C) an index by author and subject to the articles in section B.

A typical entry in section A contains the following information: name of the person being honored (initials if it is an institution); title and editors of the publication; if it is part of a series, title and volume of the series; place of publication, publisher, and date of publication; number of pages; the term "bibliog" if the publication contains a bibliography of the works of the person being honored, and the names of the compilers of the bibliography if they are given; the term "biog" if the publication contains articles about the life or work of the person being honored, and the names of the authors of such articles. The following is a sample entry.

SCHENK   Festschrift für Erich Schenk. (*Studien zur Musikwissenschaft, Beihefte der Denkmäler der Tonkunst in Österreich* 25) Graz: Böhlau, 1962 ❖ 652p bibliog   biog (G. Roncaglia)

The number of pages, and the bibliographical and biographical information are given only for the musical *Festschriften*. The editors, authors, and compilers listed there are not listed anywhere else in the index.

A typical entry in section B contains the following information: item number; author; title; symbol for the *Festschrift* and page numbers; information about publication of the articles in other sources, summaries in other languages, etc. The following is a sample entry.

86   Handschin, Jacques. Der Geist des Mittelalters in der Musik. HANDSCHIN 70–81; orig. in *Neue Schweizer Rundschau* 20 (1927)

Most of the articles in section B are grouped according to the standard historical eras. Each article is listed only once. Articles that could appropriately appear in several different categories are placed in a historical era whenever possible. An article about wind instruments in the Renaissance, for example, would be found under the heading "Renaissance era: Instruments and instrumental music." Cross references are made for articles about several individuals, for historical articles about several eras, and for articles that give equal emphasis to several of the categories used. Complete musical compositions, whether included in the *Festschriften* separately or as part of an article, have been listed individually with the identifying symbol ♪.

For the compilation of the index many references were consulted.

There were, however, five chief sources of information: 1) A basic list of musical *Festschriften* was compiled from existing bibliographies such as Willi Kahl's and Wilhelm-Martin Luther's *Repertorium der Musikwissenschaft* (Kassel 1953) and James B. Coover's *Festschriften, a Provisional List of those Proposed for Indexing* (1958). 2) The catalogues of Columbia University Library, New York Public Library, and the Library of Congress were searched under various catchwords. 3) Lists of current publications, especially those in *Jahrbuch der Musikbibliothek Peters* and *Music Library Association Notes*, were scanned. 4) Printed indexes of *Festschriften* in other fields were also used. The most important are Herbert H. Golden and Seymour O. Simches, *Modern French Literature and Language, a Bibliography of Homage Studies* (Cambridge, Mass. 1953) and *Modern Iberian Language and Literature, a Bibliography of Homage Studies* (Cambridge, Mass. 1958); International Committee of Historical Sciences, *Bibliographies internationales des travaux historiques publiées dans les volumes de mélanges, 1880–1939* (Paris 1955); Dorothy Rounds, *Articles on Antiquity in Festschriften* (Cambridge, Mass. 1962); Harry F. Williams, *An Index of Medieval Studies Published in Festschriften* (Berkeley 1951). 5) The bibliographies in the *Festschriften* also yielded many references to additional articles. Persons who are subjects of *Festschriften*, it would seem, write busily for those of their colleagues.

Many persons assisted me in the preparation of this index. Professor Reese gave me much helpful advice and encouragement when the index was in its formative stages (although he had no notion then where it would be published). Mr. Thor E. Wood's assistance and generosity must be especially mentioned. For a time we worked jointly on the index. When this was no longer possible, he continued to supply useful information and advice. I am equally grateful to the many others who have been helpful. While the index is infinitely better for their assistance, the responsibility for its present form, its idiosyncrasies and limitations, and any errors, is solely mine.

A. LIST OF FESTSCHRIFTEN

AALL Festskrift til Anathon Aall på 70-årsdagen hans 15. August 1937. Oslo: H. Aschehoug, 1937

ABERT Gedenkschrift für Hermann Abert von seinen Schülern; hrsg. von Friedrich Blume. Halle/Saale: M. Niemeyer, 1928 ❖ 189p bibliog (E.t Laaff) biog (F. Blume)

ABRAHAMS Jewish Studies in Memory of Israel Abrahams by the Faculty and Visiting Teachers of the Jewish Institute of Religion. New York: Jewish Inst. of Rel., 1927

ADLER   Studien zur Musikgeschichte. Festschrift für Guido Adler zum 75. Geburtstag. Wien: Universal, 1930 <> 224p bibliog

ADN   Festschrift zum 15. Neuphilologentage in Frankfurt am Main, 1912 [Im Auftrag des Vorstandes des Allgemeinen deutschen Neuphilologen-Verbandes hrsg. von M. Banner, F. J. Curtis, M. Friedwagner] Frankfurt/Main: Knaver, 1912

ALBRECHT   Hans Albrecht in memoriam. Gedenkschrift mit Beiträgen von Freunden und Schülern; hrsg. von Wilfried Brennecke und Hans Haase. Kassel: Bärenreiter, 1962 <> 290p bibliog (M. Geck)   biog (A. A. Abert, H. Haase)

ALONSO   Homenaje a Amado Alonso. (*Nueva revista de filología hispánica* 7) Colegio de México, 1953

AMMANN   Ammann-Festgabe; besorgt vom Seminar für vergleichende Sprachwissenschaft an der Universität Innsbruck anlässlich der Feier d. 25jähr. Dienstjubiläums . . . (*Innsbrucker Beiträge zur Kulturwissenschaft* 1 & 2) Innsbruck: Sprachwiss. Seminar d. Univ., 1953–1954

ANDERLUH   Lied und Brauch aus der Kärntner Volksliedarbeit und Brauchforschung. [Anton Anderluh, dem Volksliedforscher und -pfleger, zur Vollendung seines 60. Lebensjahres dargebracht] (*Kärntner Museumsschriften* 8) Klagenfurt: Landesmuseum für Kärnten, 1956 <> 167p bibliog (F. Koschier)   biog (G. Graber, G. Mittergradnegger, H. Pommer, E. Zenker-Starzacher)

ANDERSON   Holberg blandinger; udg. af Holbergsamfundet af 3. december 1922. [Vilhelm Anderson, 75th Birthday] København: Gyldendal, 1939

ANDLER   Mélanges offerts à M. Charles Andler par ses amis et ses élèves. (*Publ. de la faculté des lettres de l'université de Strasbourg* 21) Strasbourg: Librairie Istra/ London: Oxford, 1924

ANDREAE   Volkmar Andreae. Festausgabe aus Anlass seines Rücktrittes nach 43jähriger erfolgreicher Tätigkeit als künstlerischer Leiter der Tonhalle-Gesellschaft Zürich und verantwortlicher Chef des Tonhalle-Orchesters, 1906–1949; hrsg. vom Vorstand der Tonhalle-Gesellschaft Zürich. Zürich: Tonhalle-Gesellschaft, 1949 <> 109p biog (H. v. Gonzenbach, W. de Boer, R. Wittelsbach, C. Vogler, M. Auer, H. Odermatt, F. Brun, B. Walter)

ANGLÉS   Miscellánea en homenaje a Monseñor Higinio Anglés. Barcelona: Consejo Superior de Investigaciones Científicas, 1958–1961 <> 1054p in 2 v   bibliog

ANSERMET   Hommage à Ernest Ansermet. Lausanne: Marguerat, 1943 <> 138p

ASAF'EV   Pamiati akademika Borisa Vladimirovicha Asaf'eva. Sbornik statei o nauchno-kriticheskom nasl'edii. [In Memory of Academician Boris Vladimirovich Asaf'ev. Collection of Articles on the Scientific-Critical Heritage] Moskva: Izdat'elstvo Akademii Nauk SSSR, 1951 <> 94p biog (R. Glière, I. E. Grabar, D. Kabalevsky, T. N. Livanova, V. A. Vasina-Grossman, E. M. Orlova)

ATL   Thüringische Studien. Festschrift zur Feier des 250jährigen Bestehens der Thüringischen Landesbibliothek Altenburg; hrsg. von deren Leiter Dr. Franz Paul Schmidt. Altenburg: O. Bonde, 1936

AUBIN   Syntagma Friburgense. Historische Studien Hermann Aubin dargebracht zum 70. Geburtstag am 23. 12. 1955. (*Schriften des Kopernikuskreises* 1) Lindau, Konstanz: Thorbecke, 1956

AUBIN/T   Deutscher Osten und slawischer Westen. Tübinger Vorträge; hrsg. von Hans Rothfels und Werner Markert. [Hermann Aubin zum 70. Geburtstage 23. Dezember 1955] (*Tübinger Studien zur Geschichte und Politik* 4) Tübingen: J. C. B. Mohr, 1955

BADT   Festschrift Kurt Badt zum siebzigsten Geburtstage; Beiträge aus Kunst- und Geistesgeschichte. Berlin: W. de Gruyter, 1961

BAG   Festschrift zur Vierhundertjahrfeier des Alten Gymnasiums zu Bremen, 1529–1928. Bremen: G. Winter [1928]

BIANCHI Studi in onore di Lorenzo Bianchi. Bologna: Zanichelli, 1960

BIEHLE Festschrift Johannes Biehle zum sechzigsten Geburtstage überreicht; hrsg. von Erich H. Müller. Leipzig: Kistner & Siegel, 1930 ◇ 107p bibliog biog (H. Biehle, D. H. Schöttler)

BINZ Festschrift Gustav Binz, Oberbibliothekar der Öffentlichen Bibliothek der Universität Basel, zum 70. Geburtstag am 16. Januar 1935 von Freunden und Fachgenossen dargebracht. Basel: B. Schwabe, 1935

BJØRNDAL Norsk folkemusikk; utg. som festskrift til 70-årsdagen Arne Bjørndal. Bergen: Nord- og Midnordland sogelag, I komm. hja A.s Lunde, 1952

BJØRNSON Bjørnstjerne Bjørnson. Festskrift i anleding af hans 70 års fødelsdag. København: Gyldendal, 1902

BLECH Leo Blech, ein Brevier; anlässlich des 60. Geburtstages hrsg. und eingeleitet von Walter Jacob. Hamburg, Leipzig: Prismen [1931] ◇ 64p bibliog biog (W. Jacob, K. Holy, H. Rüdel, R. Albert, F. Schorr)

BLUME/F Festschrift Friedrich Blume zum 70. Geburtstag; hrsg. von Anna Amalie Abert und Wilhelm Pfannkuch. Kassel: Bärenreiter, 1963 ◇ 426p bibliog

BLUME/S Syntagma musicologicum, gesammelte Reden und Schriften; hrsg. von Martin Ruhnke. Kassel: Bärenreiter, 1963 ◇ 904p

BOAS Boas Anniversary Volume. Anthropological Papers Written in Honor of Franz Boas . . . Presented to Him on the Twenty-fifth Anniversary of His Doctorate, Ninth of August, 1906. New York: G. Stechert, 1906

BÖMER Westfälische Studien; Beiträge zur Geschichte der Wissenschaft, Kunst und Literatur in Westfalen. Alois Bömer zum 60. Geburtstag gewidmet. Leipzig: K. W. Hiersemann, 1928

BOLLERT Festschrift Martin Bollert zum 60. Geburtstage. Dresden: W. Jess, 1936

BOLLERT/80TH Festschrift Martin Bollert zum achtzigsten Geburtstag am 11. Oktober 1946; dargebracht von Freunden und Mitarbeitern. Dresden: [VEB Landesdruckerei Sachsen] 1956

BORREN Hommage à Charles van den Borren. Mélanges. Anvers: N. V. de Nederlandsche Boekhandel, 1945 ◇ 360p bibliog (R. Wangermée) biog (S. Clercx)

BORREN/80TH Hommage à Charles van den Borren à l'occasion de son quatre-vingtième anniversaire. (Revue belge de musicologie 8, 1954, 61–140)

BOYER Mélanges publiés en l'honneur de M. Paul Boyer. (Institut d'études slaves. Travaux 2) Paris, 1925

BREITKOPF Breitkopf & Härtel. Gedenkschrift und Arbeitsbericht von Oskar von Hase. 4. Aufl. Leipzig: Breitkopf & Härtel, 1917–1919

BRITTEN Tribute to Benjamin Britten on His Fiftieth Birthday; ed. by Anthony Gishford. London: Faber & Faber [1963] ◇ 195p biog (M. Rostropovich, C. Curzon, A. Copland)

BRODY Geist und Werk aus der Werkstatt unserer Autoren zum 75. Geburtstag von Dr. Daniel Brody. Zürich: Rhein-Verlag, 1958

BROWN Essays and Studies in Honor of Carleton Brown. New York: New York Univ. Press, 1940

BRUUN Kristendom og norskdom. Festskrift til Christopher Bruun . . . Oslo: Steen, 1920

BU Festschrift zur Feier des 450jährigen Bestehens der Universität Basel; hrsg. von Rektor und Regenz. Basel: Helbing & Lichtenhahn, 1910

BURCKHARDT Dauer im Wandel. Festschrift zum 70. Geburtstag von Carl J. Burckhardt; hrsg. von Hermann Rinn & M. Rychner. München: G. D. W. Callweg [1961]

BUSH Tribute to Alan Bush on his Fiftieth Birthday, A Symposium. London: Workers' Music Assn., 1950 ◇ 63p bibliog biog (J. Ireland, H. Murrill, R.

Boughton, W. Mellers, H. Eisler, W. Sahnow, E. H. Meyer, M. Rostal, T. Russell, D. Ellenberg, E. J. Dent)
CAIX In memoria di Napoleone Caix e Ugo Angelo Canello. Miscellanea di filologia e linguistica per G. Ascoli, C. Avolio . . . ; Firenze: Successori Le Monnier, 1886
CARÍAS Homenaje tributado por el pueblo hondureño por medio del soberano Congreso Nacional, al . . . Tiburcio Carías Andino. [Tegucigalpa, 1945]
CASADESUS Hommage à Francis Casadesus, pour ses quatre-vingts ans, 2 décembre 1870–2 décembre 1950. [Paris, 1950] ◇ 79p
CASE Studies in the Literature of the Augustan Age. Essays Collected in Honor of Arthur Ellicott Case. Ann Arbor: Augustan Reprint Society, 1952
CASELLA [Special number for his 60th birthday] (Rassegna musicale 16, 1943, 129–208) ◇ bibliog biog (G. de Chirico, M. Mila, G. Gavazzeni, A. Mantelli, G. Rossi-Doria, E. Zanetti, F. d'Amico, D. Alderighi, M. Labroca)
CASTIGLIONI Studi in onore di Carlo Castiglioni, Prefetto dell'Ambrosiana. (Fontes Ambrosiani 32) Milano: A. Giuffrè, 1957
CHABANEAU Mélanges Chabaneau. Festschrift Camille Chabaneau zur Vollendung seines 75. Lebensjahres 4. März 1906. (Romanische Forschungen 23) Erlangen: Junge, 1907
CHAMARD Mélanges d'histoire littéraire de la renaissance offerts à Henri Chamard, professeur honoraire à la Sorbonne, par ses collègues, ses élèves et ses amis. Paris: Nizet, 1951
CHWOLSON Recueil des travaux rédigés en mémoire du jubilé scientifique de M. Daniel Chwolson (1846–1896). Berlin: S. Calvary, 1899
CHYBIŃSKI/50TH Księga pamiątkowa ku czci profesora Dr. Adolfa Chybińskiego ofiarowana przez uczniów i przyjaciół z okazji pięćdziesiątej rocznicy urodzin i dwudziestej piątej rocznicy jego pracy naukowej (1880–1905–1930). [A Memorial Volume in Honor of Prof. Dr. Adolf Chybiński, Offered by his Friends and Pupils on the Occasion of his 50th Birthday and the 25th Anniversary of his Scholarly Activity) Kraków: Nakładem Autorów, 1930 ◇ 187p
CHYBIŃSKI/70TH Księga pamiątkowa ku czci Prof. Adolfa Chybińskiego w 70-lecie urodzin. Rozprawy i artykuły z zakresu muzykologii [A Memorial Volume in Honor of Prof. Adolf Chybiński on his 70th Birthday. Studies and Articles in the field of Musicology] Kraków: Polskie Wydawnictwo Muz., 1950 ◇ 380p bibliog (K. Michałowski) biog
CLOSSON Mélanges Ernest Closson. Recueil d'articles musicologiques offerts à Ernest Closson à l'occasion de son 65e anniversaire. Bruxelles: Société Belge de Musicologie, 1948 ◇ 210p bibliog (A.-M. Regnier, A. van der Linden) biog (C. van den Borren)
COHEN Mélanges d'histoire du théâtre du moyen-âge et de la renaissance offerts à Gustave Cohen . . . par ses collègues, ses élèves et ses amis. Paris: Nizet, 1950
CORBINIANUS Wissenschaftliche Festgabe zum zwölfhundertjährigen Jubiläum des heiligen Korbinian; hrsg. von D. Dr. Joseph Schlecht. München: A. Huber, 1924
CRESCINI Miscellanea di studi critici in onore di Vincenzo Crescini. Cividale: Stagni, 1927
CU Cologne. Universität. Concordia decennalis, deutsche Italienforschung. Festschrift der Universität Köln zum 10jährigen Bestehen des Deutsch-Italienischen Kulturinstituts Petrarcahaus 1941. Köln: Balduin Pick [1941]
CU/F Festschrift zur Erinnerung an die Gründung der alten Universität Köln im Jahre 1388. Köln: K. Schroeder, 1938
CUYPERS Hubert Cuypers 80 jaar. [Amsterdam: Huldigingscomité Hubert Cuypers, 1953?] ◇ 93p biog

ČYŽEVŚKYJ Festschrift für Dmytro Čyževśkyj zum 60. Geburtstag am 23. März 1954. (*Berlin, Freie Universität, Osteuropa-Institut, Slavistische Veröffentlichungen* 6) Wiesbaden: Harrassowitz, 1954

DAVISON Essays on Music in Honor of Archibald Thompson Davison by His Associates. Cambridge, Mass.: Harvard Univ., Dept. of Music, 1957 ◇ 374p bibliog (J. M. Coopersmith)

DEBUSSY Numéro spécial consacré à la mémoire de Claude Debussy. (*La Revue musicale* 12, Dec. 1920, 97–216, suppl. 1–32) ◇ biog (A. Suarès, A. Cortot, L. Laloy, E. Vuillermoz, R. Peter, D. E. Ingelbrecht, R. Godet, G. J. Aubry, H. Lesbroussart, M. de Falla, L. Dunton-Green, A. Casella, L. Saminsky)

DEGERING Mittelalterliche Handschriften, paläographische, kunsthistorische, literarische und bibliotheksgeschichtliche Untersuchungen. Festgabe zum 60. Geburtstage von Hermann Degering. Leipzig: K. W. Hiersemann, 1926

DENYN Gedenkboek Jef Denyn, stadsbeiaadier en meester van den toren. Mechelen: Beiaardschool [1947] ◇ 329p bibliog biog (P. Verheyden, K. Lefévere, S. Nees, J. Casparie, J. Rottiers, A. Geudens, G. Clement, N. Johnston, L. Reypens)

DEUTSCH/80TH Festschrift Otto Erich Deutsch zum 80. Geburtstag am 5. September 1963; hrsg. von Walter Gerstenberg, Jan LaRue und Wolfgang Rehm. Kassel: Bärenreiter, 1963 ◇ 392p bibliog (O. Schneider)

DRUMMOND Studies in Speech and Drama in Honor of Alexander M. Drummond. Ithaca, N.Y.: Cornell Univ. Press, 1944

DUKAS Hommage à Paul Dukas. (*La Revue musicale,* numéro spécial, May/June 1936, 321–456, suppl. 1–32) ◇ bibliog (G. Samazeuilh) biog (P. Valéry, R. Brussel, G. Samazeuilh, E. Dujardin, J. G. Ropartz, M. Emmanuel, O. Messiaen, E. Schneider, G. Marcel, A. George, R. Dumesnil, J. Rouché, A. Boschot, A. Boll)

DUSSAUD Mélanges syriens offerts à Monsieur René Dussaud . . . par ses amis et ses élèves. Paris: P. Geuthner, 1939

EINSTEIN [Essays for Alfred Einstein and Curt Sachs on their 60th Birthdays] (*Musical Quarterly* 27, 1941, 263–413) bibliog & biog (E. Hertzmann)

EINSTEIN/C Collectanea historicae musicae I. (*Biblioteca historiae musicae cultores* 2) Florentiae: L. S. Olschki, 1953 ◇ 210p bibliog

EMANUELE Studi pubblicati dalla regia università di Torino nel IV centenario della nascita di Emanuele Filiberto, 8 Luglio 1928. Torino: F. Villarboito [1928]

EMMANUEL Maurice Emmanuel. (*La Revue musicale,* numéro spécial 206, 1947, 1–128) ◇ bibliog biog (R. Bernard, E. Estaunié, R. Jardillier, R. Dumesnil, R. Schwab, L. Aubert, V. Basch, G. Migot, C. Koechlin, S. Demarquez, P. Le Flem, G. Samazeuilh, J. Chailley, M. B. d'Harcourt, F. Raugel, S. Baud-Bovy, O. Messiaen, E. Jacques-Dalcroze, A. Fornerod, H. Classens)

ENGEL A Birthday Offering to Carl Engel; comp. and ed. by Gustave Reese. New York: G. Schirmer, 1943 ◇ 233p bibliog biog (P. L. Atherton, J. Erskine, N. Peterkin, H. Spivacke)

ERDMANN Minnesskrift af forna lärjungar tillägnad professor Axel Erdmann på hans sjuttioårsdag den 6. febr. 1913. Upsala: Almquist & Wiksell, 1913

FABRA Miscellània Fabra; recull de treballs de lingüística catalana i romànica dedicats a Pompeu Fabra pels seus amics i deixebles amb motiu del 75e aniversari de la seva naixença. Buenos Aires: Coni, 1943

FALLETTI Studi di storia e di critica dedicati a Pio Carlo Falletti dagli scolari celebrandosi il XL anno del suo insegnamento. Bologna: N. Zanichelli, 1915

FAURÉ Gabriel Fauré. (*La Revue musicale,* numéro spécial, Oct. 1922, 193–308, suppl. 1–47) ◇ bibliog biog (E. Vuillermoz, M. Ravel, R. Chalupt, C. Koechlin, F. Schmitt, J J. Roger-Ducasse, A. Cortot, N. Boulanger)

GEIGER Beiträge zur Literatur- und Theatergeschichte. Festschrift Ludwig Geiger. Berlin: B. Behr, 1918

GESSLER Miscellanea J. Gessler. 's-Gravenhage: Martinus Nijhoff, 1948

GEWANDHAUS Festschrift zum 175jährigen Bestehen der Gewandhauskonzerte, 1781–1956. Leipzig: Deutscher Verlag für Musik, 1956 ◇ 107p hist (O. Gerster, R. Fischer, M. Butting, F. Konwitschny, H. J. Moser, W. Vetter, H. Keller, R. Petzoldt, D. Wolf)

GILDERSLEEVE Studies in Honor of Basil L. Gildersleeve. Baltimore: Johns Hopkins Press, 1902

GRAT Mélanges dédiés à la mémoire de Félix Grat. Paris: Pecquer-Grat, 1946

GRÉGOIRE Pankarpeia. Mélanges Henri Grégoire. (*Annuaire de l'Institut de Philologie et d'Histoire Orientales et Slaves 9–12*) Bruxelles, 1949–1953

GREGOR Zum 65. Geburtstage von Hofrat Prof. Dr. Joseph Gregor. (*Das Antiquariat 9/15–18, 1953, 225–242*)

GRÜNWALD Festschrift zur Feier des 50. Geburtstags Richard Grünwalds; hrsg. von der deutschen Zitherkonzert-Gesellschaft. Düsseldorf: D. Zitherk.-Ges., 1927 ◇ 66p biog (F. Stichenoth, J. Brandlmeier, W. Gfeller, J. Schletter, J. Baltes, K. Lohmann, W. Altmann)

GSHG Festschrift 75. Jahre Stiftliches Humanistisches Gymnasium M. Gladbach. M. Gladbach, 1952

GUGITZ Kultur und Volk, Beiträge zur Volkskunde aus Österreich, Bayern und der Schweiz. Festschrift für G. Gugitz zum 80. Geburtstag; hrsg. von Leopold Schmidt. (*Veröffentlichungen des Österreichischen Museums für Volkskunde 5*) Wien: Horn, Berger, 1954

GURLITT Festheft Wilibald Gurlitt zum siebzigsten Geburtstag. (*Archiv für Musikwissenschaft 16/1–2, 1959, 1–259*)

HAAS Festgabe Joseph Haas von seinen Schülern, Mitarbeitern und Freunden, nebst einem Verzeichnis seiner Werke, zum 60. Geburtstag am 19. März 1939; hrsg. von M. Gebhard, O. Jochum und H. Lang . . . Mainz: Schott [1939] ◇ 131p bibliog biog (K. Laux)

HAAS/75TH Joseph Haas-Heft. (*Zeitschrift für Musik* 115, 1954, 129–149) ◇ biog (K. G. Fellerer, W. Zentner, H. Lang, E. Valentin)

HAEBLER Wiegendrucke und Handschriften. Festgabe Konrad Haebler zum 60. Geburtstage; dargebracht von Isak Collijn. Leipzig: K. W. Hiersemann, 1919

HALPHEN Mélanges d'histoire du moyen âge dédiés à la mémoire de Louis Halphen. Paris: Presses Universitaires, 1951

HAMMARSTEDT Etnologiska studier tillägnade Nils Edvard Hammarstedt. (*Föreningen för svensk kulturhistoria, Böcker 2*) Stockholm, 1921

HANDSCHIN Gedenkschrift Jacques Handschin. Aufsätze und Bibliographie; [hrsg. von der Ortsgruppe Basel der Schweizerischen Musikforschenden Gesellschaft; zusammengestellt von Hans Oesch] Bern, Stuttgart: Paul Haupt [1957] ◇ 397p bibliog

HANDSCHIN/I In memoriam Jacques Handschin; ediderunt H. Anglés, G. Birkner, Ch. van den Borren, Fr. Benn, A. Carapetyan, H. Husmann, C.-A. Moberg. Argentorati: P. H. Heitz, 1962 ◇ 200p bibliog (C. Stroux)

HANSELMANN Festschrift zum 60. Geburtstag von Professor Dr. phil. Heinrich Hanselmann. Erlenbach/Zürich: Rotapfel Verlag, 1945

HANSEN Festskrift til museumsforstander H. P. Hansen, Herning, på 70-årsdagen den 2. oktober 1949. København: Rosenkilde og Bagger, 1949

HARNACK Fünfzehn Jahre Königliche- und Staatsbibliothek dem scheidenden Generaldirektor Exz. Adolf von Harnack überreicht von den wissenschaftlichen Beamten der preussischen Staatsbibliothek. Berlin: Preuss. Staatsbibl., 1921

HASKIL Clara Haskil; mit Beiträgen von Pierre Fournier, Ferenc Fricsay, Rafael

Kubelik, Igor Markevitch, Peter Rybar. Bern/Wien/Stuttgart: Scherz [1961] <> 169p discog biog (R. Wolfensberger)

HAUVETTE Mélanges de philologie, d'histoire et de littérature offerts à Henri Hauvette. Paris: Presses Françaises, 1934

HELD Festschrift für Hans Ludwig Held; eine Gabe der Freundschaft und des Dankes zum 65. Geburtstag dargebracht 1. August 1950. München: K. Alber, 1950

HERRLIN Festskrift tillägnad Axel Herrlin den 30. mars 1935. Lund: C. Blom, 1935

HERRMANN Hugo Herrmann, Leben und Werk. Festschrift zum 60. Geburtstag am 19. 4. 1956 . . . ; hrsg. von Armin Fett. Trossingen: M. Hohner, 1956 <> 85p bibliog biog (A. Fett, H. J. Moser, B. Stürmer, R. Sonner, W. M. Berten)

HERTZ Philologische Abhandlungen. Martin Hertz zum 70. Geburtstage von ehemaligen Schülern dargebracht. Berlin: W. Hertz, 1888

HEWARD Leslie Heward, A Memorial Volume; ed. by Eric Blom. London: Dent, 1944 <> 89p bibliog discog biog (S. H. Nicholson, E. Warr, W. D. Suddaby, B. Johnson, A. Boult, V. Hely-Hutchinson, H. Costley-White, S. Goddard, C. Armstrong-Gibbs, E. J. Moeran, J. Harrison, W. H. Bell, M. Mukle, B. Marx, A. Goldsbrough, J. Barbirolli, P. Jones, H. Proctor-Gregg, A. N. Harty, G. D. Cunningham, M. Tookey, N. Stanley, E. Ansermet, H. Unger, E. de Selingcourt, W. K. Stanton, C. Gray, M. Johnstone, E. Irving, G. Sharp, E. Blom)

HEWITT Essays on German Language and Literature in Honor of Theodore B. Hewitt; ed. by J. Alan Pfeffer. (*Buffalo University Studies* 20/1) [Buffalo, 1952]

HILBER J. B. Hilber. Festgabe zu seinem 60. Geburtstage 2. Januar 1951 überreicht von seinen Freunden. Altdorf: Schweizer Kirchenmusikverlag, 1951 <> 100p bibliog biog (A. Schönenberger, P. Schaller, H. Lemacher, O. Eberle, F. A. Herzog, W. Hauser)

HIRTH Festschrift für Friedrich Hirth zu seinem 75. Geburtstag. Berlin: Oesterheld, 1920

HOBOKEN Anthony van Hoboken. Festschrift zum 75. Geburtstag; hrsg. von Joseph Schmidt-Görg. Mainz: Schott, 1962 <> 162p biog (J. Schmidt-Görg)

HOEPFFNER Mélanges de philologie romane et de littérature médiévale offerts à Ernest Hoepffner . . . par ses élèves et ses amis. (*Publications de la faculté des lettres de l'université de Strasbourg* 113) Paris: Société d'Édition Les Belles Lettres, 1949

HOFMANN [Special number in honor of Dr. Josef Hofmann's golden jubilee] (*Overtones* 8, Nov. 1937, 5–31) Philadelphia: Curtis Inst., 1937

HOFMEISTER Tradition und Gegenwart. Festschrift zum 150jährigen Bestehen des Musikverlages Friedrich Hofmeister. Leipzig: VEB F. Hofmeister, 1957 <> 102p hist

HOLMES Holmes Anniversary Volume. Anthropological Essays presented to William Henry Holmes in Honor of His Seventieth Birthday, December 1, 1916, by his Friends and Colaborers. Washington: [J. W. Bryan] 1916

HOLTZMANN Kritische Beiträge zur Geschichte des Mittelalters. Festschrift für Robert Holtzmann zum sechzigsten Geburtstag. Berlin: E. Ebering, 1933

HORACE Études horatiennes, recueil publié en l'honneur du bimillénaire d'Horace. (*Travaux de la faculté de philosophie et lettres de l'université de Bruxelles* 7) Bruxelles, 1937

HOWARD Festschrift zum 50. Geburtstag Walther Howard's am 8. Mai 1930; hrsg. vom Walther Howard-Bund. Berlin-Hermsdorf: Verlag für Kultur und Kunst, 1930 <> 62p biog (E. Ulrich, A. Heymann, W. Schönberg, H. Pflieger-Haertel, M. Scholle)

HOYOS SÁINZ Homenaje a Don Luis de Hoyos Sáinz. Madrid: 1949

HUBER Kurt Huber zum Gedächtnis. Bildnis eines Menschen, Denkers und Forschers dargestellt von seinen Freunden; hrsg. von C. Huber. Regensburg: Habbel, 1947 <> 172p bibliog biog (K. Vossler, C. Huber, O. Ursprung, W. Riezler, A. Wenzl, H. Maier, G. Schischkoff, T. Georgiades, K. Pauli, I. Köck, M. Li, C. Orff)

HUC Hebrew Union College Jubilee Volume (1875-1925). Cincinnati: Hebrew Union College, 1925

HUGUET Mélanges de philologie et d'histoire littéraire offerts à Edmond Huguet par ses élèves, ses collègues et ses amis. Paris: Boivin, 1940

JAHNN Hans Henny Jahnn. Im Auftrag der Freien Akademie der Künste in Hamburg aus Anlass von Hans Henny Jahnns 60. Geburtstag von Rolf Italiaander zusammengestellt. Hamburg-Wandsbek: Hanseat. Druckanst., 1954

JAKOBSON For Roman Jakobson. Essays on the Occasion of his Sixtieth Birthday, 11 October, 1956; [ed. by Morris Halle & others] The Hague: Mouton, 1956

JASPERS Offener Horizont. Festschrift für Karl Jaspers. München: R. Piper [1953]

JBMV Aus der Welt des Barock, dargestellt von Richard Alewyn . . . Stuttgart: J. B. Metzlersche Verlagsbuchhandlung, erschienen im 275. Jahr ihres Bestehens [1957]

JEANROY Mélanges de linguistique et de littérature offerts à M. Alfred Jeanroy. Paris: E. Droz, 1928

JENKINSON Essays presented to Sir Hilary Jenkinson; ed. by J. Conway Davies. London: Oxford, 1957

JEPPESEN Natalicia musicologica Knud Jeppesen septuagenario collegis oblata; redig. curaverunt Bjørn Hjelmborg & Søren Sørensen. Hafniae: Wilhelm Hansen, 1962 <> 318p bibliog (J. P. Jacobsen)

JÖDE Fritz Jöde, Leben und Werk; eine Freundesgabe zum 70. Geburtstag im Auftrage der Fritz Jöde-Stiftung zusammengestellt und hrsg. von Reinhold Stapelberg. Trossingen: Hohner; Wolfenbüttel: Möseler [1957] <> 221p bibliog biog (R. Stapelberg, H. Mersmann, W. Burmeister, H. R. Franzke, L. Kestenberg, H. Scheel, E. Zuckmeyer, H. Erpf, J. Müller-Blattau, H. M. Sambeth, W. Jansen, K. Lorenz, G. Maasz, J. Thiel, F. Wartenweiler, H. Alm, C. Bresgen, E. Österreicher, A. Junge, E. Auwärter, H. J. Moser, E. Valentin)

JOHNER Der kultische Gesang der abendländischen Kirche; ein gregorianisches Werkheft aus Anlass des 75. Geburtstages von Dominicus Johner; in Verbindung mit zahlreichen Mitarbeitern hrsg. von Dr. Franz Tack. Köln: J. P. Bachem, 1950 <> 126p biog (H. Lemacher)

JUCHOFF Aus der Welt des Bibliothekars. Festschrift für Rudolf Juchoff zum 65. Geburtstag; hrsg. von K. Ohly und Werner Krieg. Köln: Greven [1959]

KAHL Festgabe zum 60. Geburtstag von Willi Kahl. Köln: [Unpublished typescript] am 18. Juli 1953 <> 146p bibliog (J. Hein)

KAHLE Studien zur Geschichte und Kultur des Nahen und Fernen Ostens. Paul Kahle zum 60. Geburtstag überreicht von Freunden und Schülern aus dem Kreise des orientalischen Seminars der Universität Bonn; hrsg. von W. Heffening und W. Kirfel. Leiden: E. J. Brill, 1935

KALLEN Aus Mittelalter und Neuzeit. Gerhard Kallen zum 70. Geburtstag dargebracht von Kollegen, Freunden und Schülern; hrsg. von Josef Engel und Hans Martin Klinkenberg. Bonn: P. Hanstein, 1957

KARABECEK Festschrift Josef Ritter von Karabecek zum siebzigsten Geburtstage gewidmet von seinen Schülern . . . Wien: Hälder, 1916

KIENZL Festschrift zum sechzigsten Geburtstage des Meisters Wilhelm Kienzl; hrsg. von Hilde Hagen [Hermann Schilling, pseud.] 2. Aufl. Graz: Leuschner & Lubensky, 1917. <> 63p biog (F. Weingartner, J. Schuch, F. Hirth)

KINKELDEY [. . . Otto Kinkeldey in Honor of His Seventieth Birthday, November 27, 1948] (*Music Library Assn. Notes*, ser. 2/6, Dec. 1948, 27–121) ⟨⟩ biog (C. S. Smith)

KINKELDEY/80TH   A Musicological Offering to Otto Kinkeldey upon the Occasion of His 80th Birthday. (*Journal of the American Musicological Society* 13, 1960, 1–269)

KLOSE   Friedrich Klose zum 80. Geburtstag 29. November 1942; hrsg. von der Bibliothek Walter Jesinghaus, Lugano. [Lugano, 1942] ⟨⟩ 114p bibliog biog (G. Becker, G. Geierhaas, H. Suter, F. Grüninger, M. Hohl, F. de Quervain, H. Knappe, A. Oetiker)

KML   Festschrift zum 75jährigen Bestehen des Königl. Konservatoriums der Musik zu Leipzig am 2. April 1918. Leipzig: C. F. W. Siegel, 1918 ⟨⟩ 80p

KOCZIRZ   Festschrift Adolph Koczirz zum 60. Geburtstag; hrsg. von Robert Haas und Joseph Zuth. Wien: E. Strache [1930] ⟨⟩ 56p

KODÁLY/60TH   Emlékkönyv Kodály Zoltán hatvanadik születésnapjára/Mélanges offerts à Zoltán Kodály à l'occasion de son soixantième anniversaire; szerk. Gunda Béla/Réd. par Béla Gunda. Budapest: Kiadja a Magyar Néprajzi Társaság/Edition de la Société Ethnographique Hongroise, 1943 ⟨⟩ 372p bibliog (J. Bartók)   biog (S. Veress)

KODÁLY/70TH   Emlékkönyv Kodály Zoltán 70. születésnapjára; szerk. Szabolcsi Bence és Bartha Dénes. (*Zenetudományi Tanulmányok* 1) Budapest: Akadémiai Kiadó, 1953 ⟨⟩ 766p bibliog (A. Szöllösy)   biog (F. Szabó, A. Tóth, L. Vargyas, B. Szabolcsi)

KODÁLY/75TH   Zenetudományi tanulmányok Kodály Zoltán 75. születésnapjára; szerk. Szabolcsi Bence és Bartha Dénes. (*Zenetudományi Tanulmányok* 6) Budapest: Akadémiai Kiadó, 1957 ⟨⟩ 763p biog (A. Molnár, B. Szabolcsi, J. Kovács)

KODÁLY/80TH   Zoltano Kodály octogenario sacrum. Budapest: Akadémiai Kiadó, 1962; also appeared as *Studia musicologica* 3. ⟨⟩ 399p bibliog (L. Eösze, F. Bónis)   biog (L. Eösze, E. Martinov, A. Molnár, B. Szabolcsi, C. Mason)

KONWITSCHNY   Vermächtnis und Verpflichtung. Festschrift für Franz Konwitschny zum 60. Geburtstag. Leipzig: Deutscher Verlag für Musik, 1961 ⟨⟩ 94, 32p discog biog (H. Pischner, H. Heyer, E. Krause, F. Zschoch) incl. a 45rpm phonodisc of *Fidelio* & *Egmont* overtures conducted by K.

KORRODI   Freundesgabe für Eduard Korrodi zum 60. Geburtstag. Zürich: Fretz & Wasmuth [1945?]

KRÁL   Sborník prací filologických dvornímu radovi professoru Josefu Královi k šedesátým narozeninám. V Praze: B. Stýblo, 1913

KRETSCHMER   Festschrift für Univ.-Prof. Hofrat Dr. Paul Kretschmer. Beiträge zur griechischen und lateinischen Sprachforschung. Wien: Deutscher Verlag für Jugend und Volk, 1926

KRETZSCHMAR   Festschrift Hermann Kretzschmar zum siebzigsten Geburtstage überreicht von Kollegen, Schülern und Freunden. Leipzig: C. F. Peters, 1918 ⟨⟩ 184p bibliog (G. Adler)

KRISTENSEN   Festskrift til Evald Targ Kristensen på hans halvtredsårsdag son mindesamler den 31. december 1917; udg. af foreningen Danmarks folkeminder ved Gunnar Knudsen. (*Danmarks Folkeminder* 17, 1917) København: Schønberske, 1917

KROHN   Juhlakirja Ilmari Krohn'ille 8. XI. 1927. Helsinki; 1927 ⟨⟩ 183p

KROYER   Theodor Kroyer. Festschrift zum sechzigsten Geburtstage am 9. September 1933 überreicht von Freunden und Schülern; hrsg. von H. Zenck, H. Schultz, W. Gerstenberg. Regensburg: G. Bosse, 1933 ⟨⟩ 182p

KUHNERT   Von Büchern und Bibliotheken. Dem ersten Direktor der Preussischen Staatsbibliothek geheimen Regierungsrat Dr. Phil. Ernst Kuhnert als Abschiedsgabe dargebracht von seinen Freunden und Mitarbeitern. Berlin: Struppe und Winckler, 1928

LACH   Robert Lach, Persönlichkeit und Werk, zum 80. Geburtstag überreicht von Freunden und Schülern . . . Wien: [Musikwissenschaftliches Institut der Univ. Wien] 1954 ◇ 31p bibliog biog (E. Schenk, W. Graf, L. Nowak, R. Meister, H. Jancik)

LAMPRECHT   Studium Lipsiense. Ehrengabe Karl Lamprecht dargebracht aus Anlass der Eröffnung des Königlichen Sächsischen Instituts für Kultur- und Universalgeschichte bei der Universität Leipzig von Schülern aus der Zeit seiner leipziger Wirksamkeit. Berlin: Weidmann, 1909

LAMPROS   Eis mnemen Spyridonos Lamproy. Athenais: 1935

LAURENCIE   Mélanges de musicologie offerts à M. Lionel de la Laurencie. (*Publ. de la Société Française de Musicologie* 2/3 & 4) Paris: E. Droz, 1933 ◇ 294p

LEEMANS   Etudes archéologiques, linguistiques et historiques dédiées à M. le Dr. C. Leemans à l'occasion du cinquantième anniversaire de sa nomination aux fonctions de Directeur du Musée Archéologique des Pays-Bas. Leiden: E. Brill, 1885

LEFORT   Mélanges L. Th. Lefort. (*Le Muséon, revue d'études orientales* 59, 1946) Louvain, 1946

LEFRANC   Mélanges offerts à M. Abel Lefranc par ses élèves et ses amis. Paris: E. Droz, 1936

LEIDINGER   Festschrift für Georg Leidinger zum 60. Geburtstag am 30. Dezember 1930. München: H. Schmidt [1930]

LEIP   Hans Leip, Leben und Werk; [aus Anlass von Hans Leips 65. Geburtstag am 22. Sept. 1958 von R. Italiaander zusammengestellt] Hamburg: Freie Akademie der Künste, 1958

LEMACHER   Musikalisches Brauchtum. Festschrift für Heinrich Lemacher; hrsg. von seinen Freunden und Schülern. (*Schriftenreihe des Allgemeinen Cäcilien-Verbandes für Deutschland, Österreich und die Schweiz* 1/3) [Köln, 1956] ◇ 93p bibliog biog (W. Hammerschlag, A. Schneider)

LEMONNIER   Mélanges offerts à M. Henri Lemonnier par la Société de l'Histoire de l'Art Français, ses amis et ses élèves (*Archives de l'art français*, nouv, période 7) Paris: E. Champion, 1913

LEVY   Mélanges Isidore Levy. (*Annuaire de l'Institut de Philologie et d'Histoire Orientales et Slaves* 13, 1953) Bruxelles, 1955

LEXA   Diatribae quas amici, collegae, discipuli Francesco Lexa, quinque et septuaginta annos nato, DDD; ed. curavit Zbyněk Žába (*Archiv orientálni* 20) Praha, 1952

LGR   Festgabe zum 25jährigen Jubiläum des Gymnasiums und Realgymnasiums zu Landsberg a. W. dargebracht von ehemaligen Lehrern und Schülern. Landsberg a. W.: F. Schoeffer, 1885

LICHTENBERGER   Mélanges Henri Lichtenberger; hommage de ses élèves et ses amis, juin 1934. Paris: Stock, 1934

LILIENCRON   Festschrift zum 90. Geburtstage Sr. Exz. des Wirklichen geheimen Rates Rochus Freiherrn von Liliencron überreicht von Vertretern deutscher Musikwissenschaft. Leipzig: Breitkopf & Härtel, 1910 ◇ 463p

LIPATTI   Hommage à Dinu Lipatti. Genève: Labor et Fidés, 1951 ◇ 95p bibliog discog biog (M. Lipatti, E. Ansermet, N. Boulanger, C. J. Burckhardt, J. Chapuis, A. Cortot, H. Gagnebin, A. Honegger, W. Legge, N. Magaloff, I. Markevitch, F. Martin, R.-A. Mooser, P. Sacher, B. Siki)

LÖFSTEDT   Eranos Löfstedtianus. Opuscula philologica einaro Löfstedt, A. D. XVII Kal. Iul. anno MCMXLV dedicata (*Eranos; Acta philologica Suecana* 43, 1945) Gotoburgi, 1945

LOTH   Mélanges bretons et celtiques offerts à M. J. Loth. Rennes: Plihon, 1927

Vereine für jüdische Geschichte und Literatur in Deutschland. Berlin: Poppe-
lauer, 1929
MENÉNDEZ PIDAL Homenaje ofrecido a Ramón Menéndez Pidal. Miscelánea de
estudios linguisticos, literarios e históricos. Madrid: Hernando, 1925
MENÉNDEZ PIDAL/E Estudios dedicados a Menéndez Pidal. Madrid: Consejo Su-
perior de Investigaciones Científicas, 1952–1957
MENÉNDEZ Y PELAYO Homenaje a Menéndez y Pelayo en al año vigésimo de su
profesorado. Madrid: Suárez, 1899
MENGELBERG Willem Mengelberg. Gedenkboek 1895–1920. 's-Gravenhage: Nijhoff,
1920 <> 290p bibliog biog
MERCATI Studi storici in memoria di Mons. Angelo Mercati, Prefetto dell' Archivio
Vaticano; raccolti a cura della Biblioteca Ambrosiana. (Fontes Ambrosiani 30)
Milano: A. Giuffrè, 1956
MERSMANN Musikerkenntnis und Musikerziehung. Dankesgaben für Hans Mers-
mann zu seinem 65. Geburtstage; hrsg. von Walter Wiora. Kassel: Bärenreiter,
1958 <> 224p bibliog
MICHAËLIS DE VASCONCELLOS Miscelânea de estudos em honra de d. Carolina
Michaëlis de Vasconcellos, professora da faculdade de letras da Universidade de
Coimbra. (Revista da Univ. de Coimbra 11) Coimbra, 1933
MIES Beiträge zur Musikgeschichte der Stadt Köln. Zum 70. Geburtstag von
Paul Mies in Verbindung mit Heinrich Hüschen, Willi Kahl und Klaus Wolf-
gang Niemöller; hrsg. von Karl Gustav Fellerer. (Beiträge zur rheinischen
Musikgeschichte 35) Köln: Volk, 1959 <> 80p
MILFORD Essays Mainly on the Nineteenth Century Presented to Sir Humphrey
Milford. London: Oxford, 1948
MIRBT Begegnungen und Wirkungen. Festgabe für Rudolf Mirbt und das deutsche
Laienspiel; hrsg. von Hermann Kaiser. Kassel: Bärenreiter [1956]
MOBERG Studier tillägnade Carl-Allan Moberg 5 juni 1961. (Svensk tidskrift
för musikforskning 40, 1961) Stockholm, 1961 <> 407p bibliog (M. Tegen)
MOHLBERG Miscellanea liturgica in honorem L. C. Mohlberg. (Bibliotheca ephe-
merides liturgicae 22, 23) Roma: Edizioni Liturgiche. 1948–1949
MOMMSEN Commentationes philologiae in honorem Theodori Mommseni scrip-
serunt amici. Berolini: apud Weidmannos, 1877
MONTE CASSINO Casinensia. Miscellanea di studi cassinesi pubblicata in occasione
del XIV centenario della fondazione della Badia di Monte Cassino. Sora: [Stab.
tipogr. P. C. Camustro] 1929
MONTEMEZZI Omaggio a Italo Montemezzi; a cura di Luigi Tretti e Lionello
Fiumi. (Numero unico ed. a cura del Comitato onoranze a Italo Montemezzi in
collaborazione con la rivista mensile Vita veronese) Verona, 1952 <> 79p biog
(G. Silvestri, L. Fiumi, L. Tretti, L. Ceolari, U. Cattini, L. Spezzaferri)
MORNET Mélanges d'histoire littéraire offerts à Daniel Mornet, professeur hono-
raire à la Sorbonne, par ses anciens collègues et ses disciples français. Paris:
Nizet, 1951
MOSER Festgabe für Hans Joachim Moser zum 65. Geburtstag 25. Mai 1954; hrsg.
von einem Freundeskreis. Kassel: Hinnenthal, 1954 <> 170p bibliog (H. Wege-
ner)
MOSER/70TH Musik in Zeit und Raum, ausgewählte Abhandlungen. Berlin: Merse-
burger, 1960 <> 358p
MÜLLER VON ASOW Festschrift Erich H. Müller von Asow, Dr. Phil., Ritter des
Ordens der Krone von Rumänien, zum fünfzigsten Geburtstag überreicht von
Hermann Ambrosius. Salzburg: [Unpublished typescript] 1942 <> 307p bibliog
(H. Müller von Asow) biog (J. Pilz)
MÜLLER-BLATTAU Festgabe für Joseph Müller-Blattau zum 65. Geburtstag. (An-

Hoffmann-Erbrecht und Helmut Hucke. Tutzing: H. Schneider, 1961 ◇ 237p
bibliog (W. Osthoff)

PANOFSKY De artibus opuscula XL. Essays in Honor of Erwin Panofsky; ed. by
Millard Meiss. [New York] New York Univ. Press, 1961

PAULER Gedenkschrift für Ákos von Pauler; mit Unterstützung der Ungarischen
Wissenschaftlichen Akademie und der P. Pázmány-Universität Budapest, hrsg.
von der Ungarischen Philosophischen Gesellschaft; unter Mitwirkung von
Julius Kornis zusammengestellt von Ludwig Prohászka. Berlin/Leipzig: W. de
Gruyter, 1936

PAUMGARTNER Wissenschaft und Praxis, eine Festschrift zum 70. Geburtstag von
Bernhard Paumgartner. [Die Herausgabe besorgte Dr. Eberhard Preussner]
[Zürich, Freiburg i. Br.] Atlantis Verlag, [1957?] ◇ 160p bibliog biog (O. F.
Schuh)

PEDRELL Al maestro Pedrell, escritos heortásticos. Tortosa: Orfeó Tortosí, 1911
◇ 332, 60p in 2v bibliog biog (J. J. de Urríes, R. Chabás, M. Urgellés, C.
Rofas, A. Gasco, R. Catarineu, G. E. Campa, M. D. Calvocoressi, A. Galli, E. L.
Chávarri, R. Goberna, A. Serrano, V. Ripollés, R. Ortiz, R. Mitjana, M. Morera
y Galicia, F. Lliurat, A. Amorós, S. Guinot, F. de P. Viñaspre, A. Bonaventura,
J. J. Nin, F. Ortiz y San Pelayo, H. Collet, F. Mestre y Noé)

PEDROLLO Per Arrigo Pedrollo. [Vicenza] La scuola di Arzignano [1953] ◇
47p bibliog (R. Cevese) biog (R. Cevese)

PETERSON-BERGER Wilhelm Peterson-Berger. Festskrift den 27. februari 1937 [red.
av E. Arbman, S. Beite, G. Morin, E. Rosenborg. Stockholm] Natur och Kultur
[1937] ◇ 302p bibliog (T. Fredbärj) biog (B. Bergman, O. Rabenius, S.
Beite, I. Oljelund, C. Berg, J. A. Selander, H. G. Pihl, F. Ege, F. H. Törnblom,
J. Norrby, G. Berg, S. E. Svensson, T. Fogelquist, B. Carlberg, R. G. Berg, E. W.
Olson, L. Wahlberg)

PEUCKERT Festschrift für Will-Erich Peuckert zum 60. Geburtstag dargebracht
von Freunden und Schülern. [Berlin] E. Schmidt [1955]

PFITZNER Hans Pfitzner, ein Bild in Widmungen anlässlich seines 75. Geburtstages
im Auftrag seiner Freunde und Verehrer; hrsg. von Walter Abendroth. Leipzig:
Heling [1944] ◇ 126p biog (W. Abendroth, F. Schütz, J. Marx, W. Matthes,
Z. Diemer, V. Junk, O. Krauss, L. Schrott, W. Preetorius, E. Ernst, M. Fischer,
V. v. Falkenhayn-Groeben, H. v. Besele, H. Unger, M. Brockhaus, H. Franck,
G. Frommel, J. Müller-Blattau, E. Betz, W. Gieseking, M. Strub, F. Wührer,
J. Ritt, R. Ockel)

PHILIPP Franz Philipp 70 Jahre. Das Bild eines deutschen Musikers in Zeugnissen
von Zeitgenossen [hrsg. von der Franz-Philipp-Gesellschaft e. V.] Gedruckt als
Gabe seiner Freunde zum 70. Geburtstag, 24. August 1960 ◇ 202p bibliog
biog (J. Amann, H. A. Berger, H. Berl, W. M. Berten, M. Ganter, F. Grüninger,
J. Hatzfeld, F. Hirtler, J. Lechthaler, O. zur Nedden, K. Preisendanz, H. E.
Rahner, F. Ruh, H. Ruh, H. Schorn, W. Schwarz, B. Steinert, K. E. Wiemann,
E. Zimmermann)

PIZZETTI La Città dannunziana a Ildebrando Pizzetti, saggi e note; [a cura di
Manlio La Morgia. Pescara, Comitato Centrale Abruzzese per le Onoranze a Ildebrando Pizzetti, dist. Milano: G. Ricordi] 1958 ◇ 338p

POPPEN Weg und Werk, eine Festgabe zum 70. Geburtstag von Prof. Dr. Hermann Meinhard Poppen, geb. 1. Jan. 1885; unter Mitwirkung von H. Haag
hrsg. von O. Riemer. (Evangelische Kirchenmusik im Baden, Hessen, Pfalz. 32/1,
Jan. 1955, 1–31) ◇ bibliog biog (C. Mahrenholz, K. Dürr, W. Lieb, H. Haag,
G. Hees, W. Fortner, S. Hermelink, K. M. Ziegler, O. Riemer)

PUSTET Bohatta, Hanns. Liturgische Drucke und liturgische Drucker. Festschrift
zum 100jährigen Jubiläum des Verlages Friedrich Pustet, Regensburg: Kösel &
Pustet [1926] ◇ 74p

PUTNAM   Essays offered to Herbert Putnam by His Colleagues and Friends on His Thirtieth Anniversary as Librarian of Congress, 1 April 1929; ed. by William Warner Bishop and Andrew Keough. New Haven: Yale Univ. Press, 1929

QC   Twenty-fifth Anniversary Festschrift (1937–1962); ed. by Albert Mell. Flushing, N.Y.: Queens College Department of Music, 1964 <> 91p

RAABE   Von deutscher Tonkunst. Festschrift zu Peter Raabes 70. Geburtstag; in Gemeinschaft mit dreiundzwanzig Fachgenossen hrsg. von Alfred Morgenroth. Leipzig: Peters [1942] <> 247p bibliog biog (Alfred Morgenroth)

RAMUZ   Hommage à C.-F. Ramuz. Lausanne: Porchet, 1938

RASPE   Festschrift zum 50jährigen Amtsjubiläum Gustav Heinrich Carl Raspes, vom Lehrer-Collegium des Friedrich Franz-Gymnasium zu Parchim gewidmet. Parchim, 1883

RAVEL   Maurice Ravel. (La Revue musicale, numéro spécial, Apr. 1925, 1–112, suppl. 1–4) <> bibliog biog (A. Suarès, T. Klingsor, R. Manuel, E. Vuillermoz, A. Casella, H. Gil-Marchex, A. Hoérée, R. Chalupt, A. Coeuroy, H. Prunières, Colette)

RAVEL/H   Hommage à Maurice Ravel. (La Revue musicale, numéro spécial, Dec. 1938, 1–284, 4p) <> biog (H. Bidou, A. Suarès, E. Vuillermoz, A. Boll, A. Honegger, G. Marnold, S. Lifar, G. Marcel, H. Gil-Marchex, A. Hoérée, M. Babaian, A. Mirambel, D. E. Ingelbrecht, T. Klingsor, R. Dumesnil, R. Chalupt, P. Landormy, R. Allard, V. Jankélévitch, F. Goldbeck, B. Crémieux, M. Dauge)

REFARDT   Musik in der Schweiz, ausgewählte Aufsätze [zum] 75. Geburtstag Edgar Refardts; hrsg. im Auftrag der Ortsgruppe Basel der Schweizerischen Musikforschenden Gesellschaft von Hans Ehinger und Ernst Mohr. Bern: P. Haupt, 1952 <> 160p

REGER   Max Reger. Festschrift aus Anlass des 80. Geburtstages des Meisters am 19. März 1953; hrsg. vom Max-Reger-Archiv Meiningen in Verbindung mit dem Rat des Bezirkes Suhl. Leipzig: F. Hofmeister [1953] <> 90p biog (J. Haas, K. Hasse, H. Unger, H. J. Moser, A. Kalkoff, G. Wehmeyer, H. Poppen, H. Grabner, F. Stein, A. Schmid-Lindner)

RENIER   Scritti varii di erudizione e di critica in onore di Rodolfo Renier. Torino: Bocca, 1912

RICORDI   . . . R. stabilimento Tito di Gio. Ricordi e Francesco Lucca, G. Ricordi & C., Mailand . . . (Internationale Musik- und Theaterausstellung, 1892, Wien) [Milano] G. Ricordi, 1892 <> 168p

RICORDI/C   Casa Ricordi, 1808–1958; Profile storico a cura di Claudio Sartori. Itinerarie grafice editoriale. Milano: Ricordi, 1958 <> 116p

RIDGEWAY   Essays and Studies presented to William Ridgeway . . . on his Sixtieth Birthday, 6 August 1913; ed. by E. C. Quiggin. Cambridge: Univ. Press, 1913

RIEMANN   Riemann-Festschrift. Gesammelte Studien; Hugo Riemann zum sechzigsten Geburtstage überreicht von Freunden und Schülern. Leipzig: M. Hesse, 1909 <> 524p bibliog (H. Sočnik) biog

RIEMANN/70TH   [Hugo Riemann zum 70. Geburtstag] (Zeitschrift für Musikwissenschaft 1/10, July 1919, 569–628) Leipzig: 1919 <> biog (A. Einstein, W. Gurlitt, R. Steglich, G. Becking)

ROBINSON   Studies Presented to Daniel Moore Robinson on his Seventieth Birthday; ed. by George E. Mylonas. St. Louis: Washington Univ., 1951

RÖDER   1846–1896. Festschrift zur 50jährigen Jubelfeier des Bestehens der Firma C. G. Röder, Leipzig. Leipzig: Röder, 1896 <> 16, 88p

RÖDER/75TH   Zur Westen, Walter von. Musiktitel aus vier Jahrhunderten. Festschrift anlässlich des 75jährigen Bestehens der Firma C. G. Röder, Leipzig. [Leipzig: Röder, 1921] <> 115p

ROMAGNOLI Omaggio alla memoria del Romagnoli. (*Dioniso, bollettino dell'* *Istituto Nazionale del Dramma Antico*, n.s. 11, 1948, 65–141) Siracusa, 1948

ROSENFELD Paul Rosenfeld, Voyager in the Arts; ed. by Jerome Mellquist and Lucie Wiese. New York: Creative Age, 1948 ⬦ 284p biog (W. Schuman, M. Graf, A. Frankenstein, C. Chávez, E. Carter, C. Ives, A. Copland, C. Mills, E. Bloch, E. Varèse, R. Harris, D. Diamond, L. Engel)

ROSENHEIM Festschrift für Jacob Rosenheim anlässlich der Vollendung seines 60. Lebensjahres. Frankfurt/Main: J. Kauffmann, 1931

ROTHACKER Konkrete Vernurft. Festschrift Erich Rothacker; hrsg. von Gerhard Funke. Bonn: H. Bouvier, 1958

ROUSSEL Albert Roussel. (*La Revue musicale*, numéro spécial, Apr. 1929, 1–112, suppl. 1–32p) Paris, 1929 ⬦ biog (R. Chalupt, M. Brillant, G. Aubry, A. George, P. Le Flem, H. Prunières, P.-O. Ferroud, H. Gil-Marchex, A. Hoérée, N. Boulanger)

ROUSSEL/M A la mémoire d'Albert Roussel. (*La Revue musicale*, 18, Nov. 1937, 289–374, suppl. 1–4) ⬦ biog (R. Bernard, A. Cortot, M. Emmanuel, G. Samazeuilh, C. Delvincourt, R. Chalupt, R. Dumesnil, J. Weterings, P. Collaer, F. Goldbeck)

ROY Essays in Anthropology Presented to Rai Bahadur Sarat Chandra Roy; ed. by J. P. Mills, K. P. Chattopadhayay, B. S. Guha . . . Lucknow: Maxwell [1941?]

RUBIÓ I LLUCH Homenatge a Rubió i Lluch. (*Estudis universitaris catalans* 21–22; *Analecta sacra Tarraconensia* 12) Barcelona, 1937

RUDBECK Rudbeck studier. Festskrift vid Uppsala Universitets minnesfest til högtidlighållande av 300-årsminnet av Olof Rudbeck d. Ä:s födelse. (*Upplands fornminnesförening Uppsala, tidskrift* 44 Bilaga, 1930) Uppsala: Almquist & Wiksell, 1930

SACHS see EINSTEIN

SACHS/C The Commonwealth of Music, in honor of Curt Sachs; ed. by Gustave Reese and Rose Brandel. Glencoe: The Free Press, 1964 ⬦ 374p biog (L. Schrade, H.-H. Draeger)

SALÉN Strandblomster, en bukett överräckt till Sven Salén med anledning av hans sextioårsdag den 7 november 1950. [Stockholm] Fågel [1950]

SAMUEL Bingkisan budi; een bundel opstellen aan Dr. Philippus Samuel van Ronkel door vrienden en leerlingen aangeboden op zijn tachtigste verjaardag, 1. Augustus 1950. Leiden: A. W. Sijthoff, 1950

SANDBERGER Festschrift zum 50. Geburtstag Adolf Sandberger überreicht von seinen Schülern. München: Ferdinand Zierfuss, 1918 ⬦ 295p

SANDVIK Festskrift til O. M. Sandvik, 70 års dagen 1875–9. Mai 1945. Oslo: H. Aschehoug, 1945 ⬦ 268p bibliog (Ø. Gaukstad) biog (S. Olsen, A. Sandvold)

SARMIENTO Homenaje a Domingo Faustino Sarmiento en el cincuentenario de su muerte. (*Humanidades, filosofia y educación* 26) [La Plata] Universidad Nacional de La Plata, 1938

SCHÄFER Ter herinnering aan Dirk Schäfer, 25. November 1873–16. Februari 1931. Amsterdam-Sloterdijk: Maatschappij tot verspreiding van goede en goedkoope lectuur, 1932 ⬦ 112p bibliog discog biog (J. Koning, H. van Loon, W. Zonderland, M. J. Brusse, H. Mooy, A. de Wal, L. Couturier)

SCHAEFER Festschrift zum 70. Geburtstage vom Moritz Schaefer zum 21. Mai 1927; hrsg. von Freunden und Schülern. Berlin: Philo, 1927

SCHAUINSLAND Festschrift zum 70. Geburtstage 30. Mai 1927 und 40jährigen Dienstjubiläum 31. Mai 1927 des Herrn Professor Dr. H. H. Schauinsland. Bremen: Heilig & Bartels, 1927

SCHENK Festschrift für Erich Schenk. (*Studien zur Musikwissenschaft, Beihefte der Denkmäler der Tonkunst in Österreich* 25) Graz: Böhlau, 1962 ❖ 652p bibliog biog (G. Roncaglia)

SCHERING Festschrift Arnold Schering zum sechzigsten Geburtstag; in Verbindung mit Max Schneider und Gotthold Frotscher hrsg. von Helmuth Osthoff, Walter Serauky, Adam Adrio. Berlin: A. Glas, 1937 ❖ 274p bibliog (K. Taut)

SCHEURLEER Gedenkboek aangeboden aan Dr. D. F. Scheurleer op zijn 70sten verjaardag. Bijdragen van vrienden en vereerders op het gebied der muziek. 's-Gravenhage: Nijhoff, 1925 ❖ 396p bibliog (A. J. de Mare) biog (W. N. F. Sibmacher Zijnen)

SCHIEDERMAIR/60TH Beethoven und die Gegenwart. Festschrift des Beethovenhauses Bonn. Ludwig Schiedermair zum 60. Geburtstag; hrsg. von A. Schmitz. Berlin/ Bonn: Dümmler, 1937 ❖ 342p

SCHIEDERMAIR/80TH Studien zur Musikgeschichte des Rheinlands. Festschrift zum 80. Geburtstag von Ludwig Schiedermair; in Verbindung mit der Arbeitsgemeinschaft für rheinische Musikgeschichte und dem Verein Beethovenhaus, Bonn; hrsg. von Willi Kahl, Heinrich Lemacher und Joseph Schmidt-Görg. (*Beiträge zur rheinischen Musikgeschichte* 20) Köln: Volk, 1956 ❖ 155p bibliog (E. Wagner)

SCHLOSSER Festschrift für Julius Schlosser zum 60. Geburtstage. Zürich: Amalthea, 1927

SCHMALZ Oskar Friedrich Schmalz und der heimatliche Jodelgesang; hrsg. Eidgenössischer Jodlerverband und Bernisch-Kantonaler Jodlerverband. [Oskar Friedrich Schmalz zu seinem siebzigsten Geburtstag, 1881–1951]. Thun: F. Weibel, 1951 ❖ 124p biog (B. Kaiser, H. Holzer, K. Grunder, J. Berger)

SCHMID In memoriam Ernst Fritz Schmid, 1904–1960; ein Gedenkblatt für seine Angehörigen und Freunde. [Recklinghausen: Bauer, 1961] ❖ 42p bibliog biog (H. Endrös, W. Fischer, W. Gerstenberg, L. Nowak)

SCHMIDT Festschrift; Publication d'hommage offerte au P. W. Schmidt; hrsg. von W. Koppers. Wien: Mechistaristen-Congregation, 1928

SCHMIDT-GÖRG Festschrift Joseph Schmidt-Görg zum 60. Geburtstag; Gemeinsam mit seinen Kollegen, Schülern und Freunden im Auftrag des Beethovenhauses hrsg. von Dagmar Weise. Bonn: Beethovenhaus, 1957 ❖ 408p bibliog biog (L. Schiedermair)

SCHNEIDER/60TH Festschrift Max Schneider zum 60. Geburtstag überreicht von Kollegen, Freunden und Schülern; hrsg. von H. J. Zingel. Halle, Eisleben-Lutherstadt: E. Schneider, 1935 ❖ 160p bibliog (H. Ludwig) biog (A. Schering, H. Hoffmann)

SCHNEIDER/80TH Festschrift Max Schneider zum achtzigsten Geburtstage; in Verbindung mit Franz von Glasenapp, Ursula Schneider und Walther Siegmund-Schultze hrsg. von Walther Vetter. Leipzig: Deutscher Verlag für Musik [1955] ❖ 363p

SCHÖNBERG/50TH Arnold Schönberg zum fünfzigsten Geburtstage 13. September 1924. (*Musikblätter des Anbruch* 6, Sonderheft Aug./Sept. 1924, 269–342 ❖ bibliog biog (W. Klein, P. Bekker, E. Stein, R. Kolisch, P. von Klenau, H. Eisler, H. Scherchen, D. J. Bach, P. A. Pisk, A. Berg)

SCHÖNBERG/60TH Arnold Schönberg zum 60. Geburtstag, 13. September 1934. [Wien: Universal, 1934] ❖ 75p biog (H. Jone, H. Jalowetz, E. Buschbeck, A. Webern, A. Hába, T. Wiesengrund-Adorno, E. Wellesz, E. Stein, E. Steuermann, O. Adler, A. Zemlinsky, J. Koffler, P. Stefan, W. Reich, K. Schulhofer, J. Polnauer, H. Brock, A. Berg, D. J. Bach)

SCHÖNBERG/70TH Homage to Schönberg. (*Modern Music* 21, 1944, 131–145) biog (E. Krenek, L. Harrison, K. List)

SCHÖNBERG/75TH   [Arnold Schönberg Jubilee Issue.] (*The Canon, Australian Journal of Music* 3, Sept. 1949, 83–96) ⋄ biog (D. Newlin, R. Leibowitz, F. Stiedry, P. A. Pisk, O. Klemperer, R. Kolisch, K. McIntyre)

SCHOLTE   Verzamelde opstellen geschreven door oud-leerlingen van professor Dr. J. H. Scholte. Amsterdam: J. M. Meulenhoff, 1947

SCHRADE   Musik und Geschichte. [Leo Schrade zum sechzigsten Geburtstag]/ Music and History [Leo Schrade on the Occasion of His Sixtieth Birthday] Köln: Volk [1963] ⋄ 206p

SCHREIBER   Volkstum und Kulturpolitik, eine Sammlung von Aufsätzen gewidmet Georg Schreiber zum 50. Geburtstag; hrsg. von H. Konen und J. P. Steffes. Köln: Gilde, 1932

SCHREKER   Franz Schreker zum 50. Geburtstag, 23. März 1928. (*Musikblätter des Anbruch* 10, Sonderdruck aus dem Märzheft 1928, 81–118) Wien: Universal, 1928 ⋄ biog (A. Maril, F. L. Hörth, O. Erhardt, R. St. Hoffman, W. Gmeindl, G. Schünemann)

SCHREMS   Musicus—Magister. Festgabe für Theobald Schrems zur Vollendung des 70. Lebensjahres; hrsg. von Georg Paul Köllner. Regensburg: F. Pustet, 1963 ⋄ 226p biog (G. P. Köllner, R. Mauersberger, J. Stadler, H. Schrems)

SCHRIJNEN   Donum natalicum Schrijnen. Versameling van opstellen door oudleerlingen en bevriende vakgenooten opgedrangen aan Mgr. Prof. Dr. Jos. Schrijnen bij gelegenheid van zijn zestigsten verjaardag, 3. Mei 1929. Nijmegen-Utrecht: Dekker & Van de Vegt, 1929

SCHÜTZ   Festschrift Julius Franz Schütz; unter Mitwirkung der Steiermärkischen Landesbibliothek hrsg. und redig. von Berthold Sutter. Graz, Köln: Böhlau, 1954

SCHWARBER   Festschrift Karl Schwarber. Beiträge zur Schweizer Bibliotheks- Buch- und Gelehrtengeschichte zum 60. Geburtstag am 22. Nov. 1949 dargebracht. Basel: Schwabe, 1949

SCHWEITZER/60TH   Albert Schweitzer, mannen och hans gärning. Vänners hyllning till Lambarenesjukhusets 25-åriga tillvaro; utg. av Greta Lagerfelt. Uppsala: Lindblads, 1938 ⋄ biog (E. Bangert, H. Ekman)

SCHWEITZER/70TH   Albert Schweitzer Jubilee Book; ed. by A. A. Roback with the Cooperation of J. S. Bixler and George Sarton. Cambridge, Mass: Sci-Art Publishers [1945] ⋄ biog (A. Ehlers)

SCHWEITZER/80TH   Ehrfurcht vor dem Leben. Albert Schweitzer, eine Freundesgabe zu seinem 80. Geburtstag. Bern: Haupt [1955] ⋄ biog (E. Bangert)

SCHWEITZER/80F   Hommage à Albert Schweitzer [pour son quatre-vingtième anniversaire le 14 janvier 1955. Paris] Diffusion Le Guide [1955] ⋄ biog (P. Casals, A. Cortot, A. Honegger, R. Minder)

SEEBACH   Ehrengabe dramatischer Dichter und Komponisten Sr. Exzellenz dem Grafen Nikolaus von Seebach zum zwanzigjährigen Intendanten-Jubiläum. [Leipzig: K. Wolff] 1914.

SEIDL/AN   Anton Seidl, A Memorial by His Friends. New York: Scribner, 1899 ⋄ 259p biog (H. T. Finck)

SEIDL/AR   Musik und Kultur. Festschrift zum 50. Geburtstag Arthur Seidls; hrsg. von Bruno Schuhmann. Regensburg: G. Bosse [1913] ⋄ 273p biog (B. Schuhmann)

SEIFFERT   Musik und Bild. Festschrift Max Seiffert; in Verbindung mit Fachgenossen, Freunden und Schülern hrsg. von Heinrich Besseler. Kassel: Bärenreiter, 1938 ⋄ 160p bibliog (T. Schneider)

SIEBS   Festschrift Theodor Siebs zum 70. Geburtstag 26. August 1932; hrsg. von Walther Steller. (*Germanistische Abhandlungen* 67) Breslau: M. & H. Marcus, 1933.

SIEVERS Germanica. Eduard Sievers zum 75. Geburtstage 25. November 1925. Halle/Saale: M. Niemeyer, 1925

SILVA Studi in onore di Pietro Silva. Firenze: F. Le Monnier [1957]

SINGER Festgabe Samuel Singer überreicht zum 12. Juli 1930 von Freunden und Schülern; hrsg. von Harry Maync unter Mitwirkungen von Gustav Keller und Marta Marti. Tübingen: Mohr, 1930

SJÖGREN Emil Sjögren in memoriam. Stockholm: Lundholm [1918] ◇ 90p biog (B. Sjögren, S. Elmblad, W. Peterson-Berger, G. Norlén, N. Söderblom)

SMEND Festschrift für Friedrich Smend zum 70. Geburtstag dargebracht von Freunden und Schülern. Berlin: Merseburger [1963] ◇ 100p bibliog (R. Elvers)

SÖHNGEN Gestalt und Glaube. Festschrift für Vizepräsident Professor D. Dr. Oskar Söhngen zum 60. Geburtstag am 5. Dezember 1960; hrsg. von einem Freundeskreis. Witten: Luther-Verlag/Berlin: Merseburger [1960]

SPG Festschrift zur Feier des 350jährigen Bestehens des protestantischen Gymnasiums zu Strassburg; hrsg. von der Lehrerschaft des protestantischen Gymnasiums. Strassburg: Heitz, 1888

STEIN Festschrift Fritz Stein zum 60. Geburtstag überreicht von Fachgenossen, Freunden und Schülern; hrsg. von H. Hoffmann und Fr. Rühlmann. Braunschweig: H. Litolff, 1939 ◇ 213p bibliog (K. von Pein)

STEUBEN Festschrift zur Feier des zweihundertjährigen Geburtstages von Baron Friedrich Wilhelm von Steuben. (*Deutsch-amerikanische Geschichtsblätter, Jahrbuch der deutsch-amerikanischen historischen Gesellschaft von Illinois* 30, 1930, 4–181) Chicago, 1930

STRAUBE Karl Straube zu seinem 70. Geburtstag; Gabe der Freunde. Leipzig: Koehler & Amelang, [1943] ◇ 387p biog (F. A. Beyerlein, J. N. David, W. Furtwängler, W. Gurlitt, K. Matthaei, H. Mitteis, F. Münch, G. Ramin, M. Schneider, B. Schwarz, K. Thomas)

STRAVINSKY/70TH Igor Strawinsky zum siebzigsten Geburtstag. (*Musik der Zeit, eine Schriftenreihe zur zeitgenössischen Musik*) London/Bonn: Boosey & Hawkes, 1952 ◇ 78p bibliog discog biog (H. H. Stuckenschmidt, G.-F. Malipiero, A. Honegger, W. Grohmann, T. Karsavina, I. Markevitch, F. Ballo, H. Boys, G. von Einem, C. Stuart, A. Cortot, E. Ansermet, W. Egk, E. W. White, F. Fricsay, P. Sacher, E. Zanetti, M. See, H. Mersmann)

STRAVINSKY/75TH [In Honor of Stravinsky's 75th birthday] (*The Score & I.M.A. Magazine* 20, June 1957, 1–76) ◇ biog (R. Craft, H. Boys, R. Sessions, R. Gerhard, M. Perrin, D. Drew)

STRAVINSKY/80TH Special Issue for Igor Stravinsky on His 80th Anniversary. (*Musical Quarterly* 48, 1962, 287–384) ◇ bibliog (C. D. Wade) biog (P. H. Lang, B. Schwarz, E. T. Cone)

STRAVINSKY/80TH/W Igor Strawinsky, eine Sonderreihe des Westdeutschen Rundfunks zum 80. Geburtstag; hrsg. von Otto Tomek. Köln: Westdeutscher Rundfunk, 1963 ◇ 86p biog (L. Schrade, P. Souvtchinsky, H. Kirchmeyer, A. von Milloss, K. H. Ruppel, J. Cocteau, H. Lindlar, H. Curjel, R. Schubert, R. Vlad, P. Boulez, P. Sacher, O. F. Schuh)

STRECKER Studien zur lateinischen Dichtung des Mittelalters. Ehrengabe für Karl Strecker zum 4. September 1931; hrsg. von W. Stach und H. Walther. Dresden: W. und B. v. Baensch Stiftung, 1931

STRICH Weltliteratur. Festgabe für Fritz Strich zum 70. Geburtstag; im Verbindung mit W. Henzen hrsg. von W. Muschg und E. Staiger. Bern: Francke, 1952

STUMMVOLL Festschrift für Josef Stummvoll, Alois Kisser, Ernst Trenkler zum 50. Geburtstage dargebracht von Kollegen, Freunden und Mitarbeitern; zusam-

mengestellt von Michael Stickler und Bruno Zimmel in Zusammenarbeit mit
Walter Krieg. (*Das Antiquariat* 8/13–18, Aug. 15 1952, 1–94)

STUTEN   In memoriam Jan Stuten 15 Aug. 1890–25. Febr. 1948; im Auftrag von
M. Steiner hrsg. durch W. Teichert und F. Wörsching. Dornach, Schweiz, 1949
◇ 56p bibliog (F. Wörsching) biog (L. F. Edmunds, F. Wörsching, W. Teichert, H. O. Proskauer)

SUCHIER   Forschung zur romanischen Philologie. Festgabe für Hermann Suchier
zum 15. März 1900. Halle: M. Niemeyer, 1900

SUFL   Mélanges 1945. (*Publications de la faculté des lettres de l'université de
Strasbourg* 104–108) Paris: Les Belles Lettres, 1946–1947

SUIDA   Studies in the History of Art Dedicated to William E. Suida on His
Eightieth Birthday. New York: Phaidon, 1959

SWINDLER   [Dedicated to Mary H. Swindler] (*American Journal of Archeology*
50/2, 1946, 217–340)

THOMPSON   Studies in Folklore in Honor of Distinguished Service Professor Stith
Thompson. (*Indiana University Publications, Folklore Series* 9) Bloomington:
Indiana Univ. Press, 1957

TIEMANN   Libris et litteris. Festschrift für Hermann Tiemann zum 60. Geburtstag
am 9. Juli 1959; hrsg. von C. Voigt & E. Zimmermann. Hamburg: Maximilian
Gesellschaft, 1959

TITCHENER   Studies in Psychology, Contributed by Colleagues and Former Students of Edward Bradford Titchener. Worcester, Mass.: L. N. Wilson, 1917

TODD   Todd Memorial Volumes. Philological Studies ed. by John D. Fitzgerald
and Pauline Taylor. New York, Columbia Univ. Press, 1930

TRIER   Festschrift für Jost Trier zu seinem 60. Geburtstag am 15. Dezember 1954;
hrsg. von Benno von Weise und Karl Heinz Borck. Meisenheim: A. Hain, 1954

TYLOR   Anthropological Essays Presented to Edward Burnett Tylor in Honour
of His 75th Birthday, Oct. 2, 1907. Oxford: Clarendon Press, 1907

UNIVERSAL   25 Jahre neue Musik. Jahrbuch 1926 der Universal-Edition; hrsg. von
Hans Heinsheimer and Paul Stefan. Wien: Universal [1926] ◇ 279p

UUTF   Festskrift utgiven av Teologiska fakulteten i Upsala, 1941, till 400-årsminnet
av Bibelns utgivande på svenska, 1541. Upsala: A.-B. Lundquist/Leipzig: O.
Harrassowitz [1941]

VARONA Y PERA   Homenage a Enrique José Varona y Pera en el cincuentenario de
su primer curso de filosofía. La Habana: Molina, 1935

VECCHIO   Studi filosofico-giuridici dedicati a Giorgio del Vecchio nel XXV anno
di insegnamento, 1904–1929. Modena: Società Tipografica Modenese, 1930–1931

VERMEYLEN   Gedenkboek A. Vermeylen. 's-Gravenhage: Nijhoff [1932]

VIANEY   Mélanges de philologie, d'histoire et de littérature offerts à Joseph Vianey.
Paris: Presses Françaises, 1934

VIRGIL   Virgilio nel medio evo. (*Studi medievali*, n.s.5) Torino: G. Chiantore, 1932

VNB   Festschrift der Nationalbibliothek in Wien; hrsg. zur Feier des 200jährigen
Bestehens des Gebäudes. Wien: Österreichische Staatsdruckerei, 1926

VORSTIUS   Bibliothek, Bibliothekar, Bibliothekswissenschaft. Festschrift Joris Vorstius zum 60. Geburtstag dargebracht; unter Mitarbeit von W. Göber, H. Kunze
und E. Paunel hrsg. von H. Roloff. Leipzig: Harrassowitz, 1954

WAESBERGHE   Organicae voces. Festschrift Joseph Smits van Waesberghe ange-
boten anlässlich seines 60. Geburtstages 18. April 1961. [Amsterdam: Instituut
voor Middeleeuwse Muziekwetenschap, 1963] ◇ 180p bibliog

WAGNER   Festschrift Peter Wagner zum 60. Geburtstag gewidmet von Kollegen,
Schülern und Freunden; hrsg. von K. Weinmann. Leipzig: Breitkopf & Härtel,
1926 ◇ 237p

WAHLE   Funde und Forschungen. Eine Festgabe für Julius Wahle zum 15. Februar 1921, dargebracht von Werner Deetjen, Max Friedlaender . . . Leipzig: Inselverlag, 1921

WALEY Arthur Waley Anniversary Volume. (*Asia Major* 7, London 1959, 1–227)

WALZEL Vom Geiste neuer Literaturforschung. Festschrift für Oskar Walzel; hrsg. von Julius Wahle und Viktor Klemperer. Wildpark-Potsdam: Athenaion [1924]

WARTENWEILER Gespräch und Begegnung. Gabe der Freunde zum 70. Geburtstag von Fritz Wartenweiler; hrsg. von den Freunden schweizerischer Volksbildungsheime zum 20. August 1959. Zürich: Rotapfel, 1959

WEBERN Anton Webern zum 50. Geburtstag. (*23, eine wiener Musikzeitschrift* 14. Feb. 1934, 1–25) ◇ biog (W. Reich)

WEBERN/R Anton Webern. (*Die Reihe* 2) Wien: Universal [1955]; [English edition] Bryn Mawr: Presser [1958] ◇ 100p bibliog biog (F. Wildgans, H. Eimert, K. Stockhausen, P. Boulez, C. Wolff)

WEINGARTNER Festschrift für Dr. Felix Weingartner zu seinem siebzigsten Geburtstag; hrsg. von der Allgemeinen Musikgesellschaft, Basel, 2. Juni 1933. [Basel: H. Oppermann, 1933] ◇ 167p bibliog (I. Schaefer) biog (E. Bienenfeld, R. Petit, A. Cortot, O. Maag, L. D. Green, E. von Sauer, C. B. Oldman, A. Botstiber, F. Hirt, A. Müry, B. Paumgartner, J. Homberg, W. Merian, H. Oppermann)

WILMANNS Beiträge zur Bücherkunde und Philologie, August Wilmanns zum 25. März 1903 gewidmet. Leipzig: O. Harrassowitz, 1903

WILMOTTE Mélanges Maurice Wilmotte. Paris: Champion, 1910

WK Festschrift zur 900-Jahr-Feier des Klosters [Weingarten] 1056–1956; ein Beitrag zur Geistes- und Gütergeschichte der Abtei. Weingarten: Abtei, 1956

WLH Kirchenmusik, Vermächtnis und Aufgabe, 1948–1958. Festschrift zum zehnjährigen Bestehen der westfälischen Landeskirchenmusikschule in Herford; hrsg. von Wilhelm Ehmann. [Darmstadt-Eberstadt: K. Merseburger, 1958?] ◇ 109p bibliog (W. Ehmann) discog hist (H. Henche, W. Ehmann, F. Ehmann)

WÖLFFLIN Festschrift Heinrich Wölfflin zum siebzigsten Geburtstage. Dresden: W. Jess, 1935

WOLF Musikwissenschaftliche Beiträge. Festschrift für Johannes Wolf zu seinem sechzigsten Geburtstag; hrsg. von W. Lott, H. Osthoff und W. Wolffheim. Berlin: M. Breslauer, 1929 ◇ 221p

WOOD Sir Henry Wood; Fifty Years of the Proms . . . London: British Broadcasting Corp. [1944] ◇ 64p biog (W. W. Thompson, T. Burke, C. B. Rees, A. Bax, B. Shore, Solomon, G. Baker, R. Hill, F. Dobson, C. E. M. Joad, J. Agate, S. Sitwell)

WOSSIDLO Volkskundliche Beiträge. Richard Wossidlo am 26. Januar 1939 zum Dank dargebracht von Freunden und Verehrern und dem Verlag. Neumünster: K. Wachholtz, 1939

WROTH Essays honoring Lawrence C. Wroth. Portland, Maine: [Anthoensen] 1951

ZAHN Festgabe für Theodor Zahn. Leipzig: A. Deichert 1928

ZODER [Raimund Zoder zum 75. Geburtstag] Geleitet von Karl M. Klier, Leopold Nowak, Leopold Schmidt. (*Jahrbuch des österreichischen Volksliedwerkes* 6) Wien, 1957 ◇ 227p bibliog (M. Kundegraber) biog (K. Lugmayer)

ZUCKER Festschrift für Friedrich Zucker zum 70. Geburtstag. Berlin: Akademie-Verlag, 1954

ZWEIBRÜCKEN Zweibrücken, 600 Jahre Stadt, 1352–1952. Festschrift zur 600-Jahrfeier; im Auftrag der Stadtverwaltung Zweibrücken hrsg. Zweibrücken: Historischer Verein, 1952

B. SUBJECT LISTING OF ARTICLES

GENERAL HISTORY

1 Borren, Charles van den. Musique expérimentale à travers les âges. HANDSCHIN/I 186–190
2 Dent, Edward J. The Universal Aspect of Musical History. ADLER 7–11
3 Einstein, Alfred. Die deutsche Musiker-Autobiographie. FRIEDLAENDER 57–66
4 Hutschenruyter, Wouter. Componeerende gekroonde hoofden. SCHEURLEER 169–175
5 Kamieński, Lucian. Musikhistorische Grenzforschungen. SEIDL/AR 223–233
6 Liess, Andreas. Prolegomena zu einer Weltmusikgeschichtsschreibung. OREL/70TH 103–111
7 Łobaczewska, Stefania. Z zagadnień metodycznych historii muzyki. [Concerning a Methodical History of Music] CHYBIŃSKI/70TH 120–145
8 Lorenz, Alfred. Neue Gedanken zur Klangspaltung und Klangverschmelzung. SCHERING 137–150
9 Mersmann, Hans. Zur Stilgeschichte der Musik. FRIEDLAENDER 67–78
10 Moser, Hans Joachim. De mari interno quasi vinculo musico gentium accolentium. MOSER/70TH 252–254; orig. in *Atti del Congresso Internazionale di Musica Mediterranea e del Convegno dei Bibliotecari Musicali* (Palermo 1959)
11 ——. Historie, Historik, und Historismus. MOSER/70TH 8–9; orig. in *Musik und Kirche* 23 (1953)
12 ——. Ist Tradition Schlamperei? MOSER/70TH 244–247
13 ——. Neuralgische Punkte der Musikgeschichte. MOSER/70TH 9–12; orig. in *Neue Musikzeitung* 4 (1950)
14 Mueren, Floris van der. Pourquoi l'histoire universelle se désintéresse-t-elle de l'histoire de la musique? FELLERER/60TH 368–376
15 Ochlewski, Tadeusz. Z dziejów pracy wydawniczej prof. A. Chybińskiego [From the Published Works of Prof. A. Chybiński] CHYBIŃSKI/70TH 380–389
16 Orel, Alfred. Der Wandel der Musik im Spiegel ihrer Niederschrift. OREL 23–32
17 Pannwitz, Rudolf. Betrachtung über den Wert der Geschichte. SEIDL/AR 137–151
18 Siegmund-Schultze, Walther. Zum Problem Wort und Ton. BESSELER 465–474
19 Westphal, Kurt. Französische und deutsche Musikentwicklung. MERSMANN 164–170
20 Wolff, Hellmuth Christian. Geschichte und Wertbegriff. BLUME/F 398–405
21 Wustmann, Rudolf. Individualismus als musikgeschichtlicher Begriff. LAMPRECHT 214–224

ANTIQUITY: GENERAL

22 Bielefeld, Erwin. Ein boiotischer Tanzchor des 6. Jh. v. Chr. ZUCKER 27–35
23 Gerlach, Hermann. Die musikalische Proportion. RASPE 1–7
24 Kraiker, W. Aus dem Musterbuch eines pompejanischen Wandmalers. ROBINSON I, 801–807
25 Landsberger, Benno. Die angebliche babylonische Notenschrift. OPPENHEIM 170–178
26 Stauder, Wilhelm. Zur Frühgeschichte der Laute. OSTHOFF 15–25

ANTIQUITY: EGYPT

27 Baillet, Auguste, & Jules Baillet. La Chanson chez les Egyptiens. MASPERO I/i, 121–135
28 Borchardt, Ludwig. Die Rahmentrommel im Museum zu Kairo. MASPERO I/i, 1–6.
29 Closson, Ernest. Une nouvelle série des hautbois égyptiens antiques. ADLER 17–25
30 Sainte-Fare Garnot, Jean. L'Offrande musicale dans l'ancienne Egypte. MASSON I, 89–92
31 Hickmann, Hans. L'Essor de la musique sous l'Ancien Empire de l'Egypte pharaonique (2778–2423 av. J.–C.) ORTIZ II, 831–836
32 ——. Le Jeu de la harpe dans l'Egypte ancienne. LEXA 449–456
33 ——. Musikerziehung im alten Ägypten. MERSMANN 55–63
33a ——. Pharaonic jingles. SACHS/C 45–70

miges Organum aus Sens unter den Notre-Dame Kompositionen. BLUME/F 200–203
287 ——. St. Germain and Notre-Dame. JEPPESEN 31–36
288 ——. Zur Stellung des Messpropriums der österreichischen Augustinerchorherren. SCHENK 261–275
289 Ludwig, Friedrich. Die liturgischen Organa Leonins und Perotins. RIEMANN 200–213
290 ——. Mehrstimmige Musik des 12. oder 13. Jahrhunderts im Schlettstädter St. Fides-Codex. KRETZSCHMAR 80–84
291 ——. Über den Entstehungsort der grossen Notre-Dame Handschriften. ADLER 45–49
292 Machabey, Armand. Remarques sur le Winchester Troper. BESSELER 67–90
293 ♪ O miranda/Salve Mater salutifera/Kyrie. HANDSCHIN/1 168[a]
294 ♪ Pato linis oculum/In seculum. HANDSCHIN/1 168[b]
295 ♪ Plus joliment/Quant li douz/Portare. HANDSCHIN/1 168[a]
296 ♪ Psallat chorus/Eximine Pater/Aptatur. HANDSCHIN/1 168[c]
297 ♪ Reple sacro flamine/Reple tuorum corda. HANDSCHIN/1 168[a]
298 ♪ Res nova mirabilis/Virgo decus castitatis/Alleluia. HANDSCHIN/1 168[b]
299 Rokseth, Yvonne. Le Contrepoint double vers 1248. LAURENCIE 5–13
300 ——. Danses cléricales du XIIIe siècle. SUFL III, 93–126
301 ♪ Rondeaux, 13th-century SUFL III, 120–126
302 ♪ Se je chant/Bien doi/Et sperabit. HANDSCHIN/1 168[d]
303 ♪ Serena virginum/Manere. HANDSCHIN/1 168[d]
304 Spiess, Lincoln Bunce. An Introduction to the Pre-History of Polyphony. DAVISON 11–15
305 Stäblein, Bruno. Modale Rhythmen im Saint Martial Repertoire? BLUME/F 340–362
306 Stimming, Albert. Altfranzösische Motette in Handschriften deutscher Bibliotheken. CHABANEAU 89–103
307 Wagner, Peter. Ein versteckter Discantus. WOLF 207–213
308 Wallin, Nils L. Hymnus in honorem Sancti Magni comitis Orchadiae: Codex Upsaliensis C 233. MOBERG 339–354
309 ♪ Winchester Troper. Dies sanctificatus. BESSELER 82–83

310 ♪ ——. Fulgens praeclara. BESSELER 86–90
311 ♪ ——. Ymera/Dies. BESSELER 84–96
312 Wolf, Johannes. Eine neue Quelle zur mehrstimmigen kirchlichen Praxis des 14. bis 15. Jahrhunderts. WAGNER 222–237

MIDDLE AGES: POLYPHONY AFTER 1300
See also nos. 273, 274, 312

313 ♪ Alanus, Johannes. Sub Arturo/Fons citharizancium/In omnem terram. BESSELER 169–174
314 Anglés, Higinio. Els Cantors i organistes Franco-Flamencs i Alemanys a Catalunya els segles XIV–XVI. SCHEURLEER 49–62
315 ——. El Músic Jacomí al servei de Joan I i Martí I durant els anys 1372–1404. RUBIO 613–625
316 ——. Una nueva versión del credo de Tournai. BORREN/80TH 97–99
317 ♪ Bartolino da Padua. La Biancha selva. ANGLÉS I, 277–280
318 Borren, Charles van den. Le Fragment de Gand. WOLF 198–206
319 ♪ Ciconia, Johannes. Regina gloriosa. BORREN/80TH 68–70
320 Dart, Thurston. Une Contribution anglaise au manuscrit de Strasbourg? BORREN/80TH 122–124
321 Fischer, Kurt von. Drei unbekannte Werke von Jacopo da Bologna und Bartolino da Padua? ANGLÉS I, 265–281
322 ♪ Ballade (Gent fragment). WOLF 203–206
323 Ghisi, Federico. Gli Aspetti musicali della lauda fra il XIV e il XV secolo, prima metà. JEPPESEN 51–58
324 Günther, Ursula. Das Wort-Ton-Problem bei Motetten des späten 14. Jahrhunderts. BESSELER 163–178
325 Haapanen, Toivo. Dominikanische Vorbilder im mittelalterlichen nordischen Kirchengesang. SCHEURLEER 129–134
326 ♪ Jacopo da Bologna. Gridavan tuti: viva sachomano. ANGLÉS I, 266–267
327 ♪ ——. Nel prato pien de fiori. ANGLÉS I, 269–272
328 Krings, Alfred. Zur Rhythmik einiger Balladen der Handschrift Chantilly 1047. KAHL 35–42
329 Machabey, Armand. O potores. MASSON I, 149–153

442   Winternitz, Emanuel. The Curse
of Pallas Athena: Notes on a *Contest
between Apollo and Marsyas* in the
Kress Collection. SUIDA 186–195
443   Wolff, Hellmuth Christian. Die
Musik im alten Venedig. BESSELER
291–303

RENAISSANCE ERA:
LOW COUNTRIES, FRANCE, & ITALY.
15TH CENTURY
See also no. 314

444   Becherini, Bianca. Musica italiana
a Firenze nel XV secolo. BORREN/80TH
109–121
445   Bridgman, Nanie. Fêtes italiennes
de plein air au quattrocento. ALBRECHT
34–38
446   ♪ *Brunette ie vous ay amée/
Brunette au foral noir.* BRESSELER 199–
201
447   Droz, Eugénie. Les Chansons de
François Villon. LAURENCIE 29–32
448   ——. Les Formes littéraires de la
chanson française au XVe siècle.
SCHEURLEER 99–102
449   ♪ *Et in terra* (Copenhagen. Königl.
Bibl. Ny kgl. Saml. *1848*fol.) JEPPESEN
81–86
450   ♪ *Faulx envieux tenez vous/()e qui
vous ame.* BESSELER 195
451   Fédorov, Vladimir. Des Russes au
concile de Florence, 1438–1439. ALBRECHT
27–33
452   Feldmann, Fritz. Alte und neue
Probleme um Cod. *2016* des Musikalischen Instituts bei der Universität
Breslau. SCHNEIDER/80TH 49–66
453   ♪ *Filles a marier* (Sevilla. Bibl. Col.
Cod. *5-1-43*). BESSELER 201–202
454   ♪ *Funde preces* (Copenhagen.
Kgl. Bibl. Ny kgl. Saml. *1848*fol.)
JEPPESEN 95–97
455   Gerber, Rudolf. Die Hymnen des
Apelschen Kodex (Mus. Ms. *1494* der
Universitätsbibliothek, Leipzig).
SCHERING 76–89
456   Gerson-Kiwi, Edith. Sulla genesi
delle canzoni popolari nel '500.
HANDSCHIN/I 170–184
457   Ghisi, Federico. Strambotti e
laude nel travestimento spirituale della
poesia musicale del quattrocento.
EINSTEIN/C 45–78
458   Glahn, Henrik. Ein kopenhagener
Fragment aus dem 15. Jahrhundert.
JEPPESEN 59–100

459   Gmelch, Joseph. Unbekannte
Reimgebetkompositionen aus Rebdorfer
Handschriften. WAGNER 69–80
460   Gülke, Peter. Das Volkslied in der
burgundischen Polyphonie des 15.
Jahrhunderts. BESSELER 179–202
461   Handschin, Jacques. Zur Musikgeschichte des 15. Jahrhunderts.
HANDSCHIN 113–116; orig. in NEUE
ZÜRCHER ZEITUNG 2376 (1934)
462   Helm, Everett B. Heralds of the
Italian Madrigal. EINSTEIN 306–318
463   Hoppin, Richard H. A Fifteenth-
Century *Christmas Oratorio*, DAVISON
41–49
464   Jeppesen, Knud. Népi dallam-
elemek Octavio Petrucci frottolaki-
adványaiban (1504–1514)/Das
Volksliedsgut in den Frottolenbüchern
des Octavio Petrucci (1504–1514).
KODÁLY/60TH 265–274
465   ——. Die Textlegung in der Chan-
sonmusik des späteren 15. Jahrhunderts.
KROHN 82–90
466   ——. Ein venezianisches Laudenmanuskript. KROYER 69–76
467   Linden, Albert van der. La
Musique dans les chroniques de Jean
Molinet. CLOSSON 166–180
468   Parrish, Carl. A Curious Use of
Coloration in the Pixérécourt Codex.
DAVISON 83–90
469   Plamenac, Dragan. Browsing
through a Little-Known Manuscript.
KINKELDEY/80TH 102–111
469a   ——. The Two-part Quodlibets in
the Seville Chansonnier. SACHS/C
163–181
470   ♪ *Rolet ara la tricoton/Maistre
Piere/La tricotée.* BESSELER 198–199
471   ♪ *Salve Regina* (Copenhagen.
Kgl. Bibl. Ny kgl. Saml. *1848*fol.).
JEPPESEN 77–81
472   Schwartz, Rudolf. Zum Form-
problem der Frottole Petruccis. KROYER
77–85
473   Wolf, Johannes. Eine neue Quelle
zur Musik des 15. Jahrhunderts. KROHN
151–162

RENAISSANCE ERA:
LOW COUNTRIES, FRANCE, & ITALY.
16TH CENTURY
See also no. 314

474   Albrecht, Hans. Ein quodli-
betartiges Magnificat aus der Zwickauer
Ratsschulbibliothek. BESSELER 215–220

RENAISSANCE ERA: GERMANY, SWITZERLAND, & SCANDINAVIA
See also no. 2146

BAROQUE ERA: ITALY

BAROQUE ERA: GERMANY & AUSTRIA

791 ——. Die Musik des Barock in Deutschland. BLUME/S 187–209; orig. in *MGG* 3, col. 303

792 Federhofer, Helmut. Alte Lieder- drucke in der Universitätsbibliothek Graz. ZODER 39–45

793 ——. Zur Musikpflege im Benedik- tinerstift Michaelbeuern (Salzburg). FELLERER/60TH 106–127

793a Geiringer, Karl. *Ed ist genug, so nimm Herr meinen Geist;* 300 Years in the History of a Protestant Funeral Song. SACHS/C 283–292

794 Gotzen, Joseph. Über die Trutz- Nachtigall von Friedrich von Spee und die Verbreitung ihrer Melodien. KAHL 60–85

795 Haas, Robert. Dreifache Orchesterteilung im Wiener Sepolchro. KOCZIRZ 8–10

796 Hamel, Fred, & Albert Rodemann. Unbekannte Musikalien im Braun- schweiger Landestheater. ALBERT 72–79

797 Klaus, Gregor. Zur Orgel- und Musikgeschichte der [Weingarten] Abtei. WK 230–253

798 Löffler, Hans. Thüringer Musiker um Joh. Seb. Bach. ATL 105–122

799 Moser, Hans Joachim. Die andere Kaffeekantate. SCHNEIDER/80TH 173–176

800 ——. Eine augsburger Liederschule im Mittelbarock. Aus einer Geschichte des mehrstimmigen Liedes im 17. Jahr- hundert. KROYER 144–148

801 ——. Brauchtümliches im Thüringer Chorlied des Frühbarock. STEIN 48–56

802 ——. Eine pariser Quelle zur wiener Triosonate des ausgehenden 17. Jahrhunderts: der Codex Rost. FISCHER/W 75–81

803 ——. Zur älteren Musikgeschichte des Burgenlandes. RAABE 114–118

804 ——. Zwischen Schütz und Bach. MOSER/70TH 106–118; orig. in *Wissen- schaftliche Zeitschrift der Karl-Marx- Univ., Leipzig, Gesellschafts- und Sprachwissenschaftliche Reihe* 5 (1954/1955)

805 Müller von Asow, Erich H. Die alte Orgel in der evangelischen Pfarrkirche zu Hermannstadt. BIEHLE 31–35

806 Nettl, Paul. Eine wiener Tänzehandschrift um 1650. KOCZIRZ 23–25

807 Paulke, Karl. Die Kantorei- Gesellschaft zu Finsterwalde. SCHEURLEER 241–249

808 Pietzsch, Gerhard. Dresdener Hoffeste vom 16.–18. Jahrhundert. SEIFFERT 83–86

809 Pirro, André. Remarques de quelques voyageurs sur la musique en Allemagne et dans les pays du nord de 1634 à 1700. RIEMANN 325–340

810 Pisk, Paul A. Die melodische Struktur der unstilisierten Tanzsätze in der Klaviermusik des deutschen Spätbarock. SCHENK 397–405

811 Schenk, Erich. Österreichisches im Klavierbuch der Regina Clara Imhoff. ZODER 162–167

812 Schmidt, Gustav F. Die älteste deutsche Oper in Leipzig am Ende des 17. und Anfang des 18. Jahrhunderts. SANDBERGER 209–257

813 Schmitz, Arnold. Arbeiten zur mittelrheinischen Musikgeschichte. SCHIEDERMAIR/80TH 118–123

814 Schneider, Max. Ein braun- schweiger Freudenspiel aus dem Jahre 1648. SEIFFERT 87–94

815 Seiffert, Max. Die Orgel der Stadtkirche zu Delitzsch. KRETZSCHMAR 149–151

816 Süss, C. Die Manuskripte protestantischer Kirchenmusik zu Frankfurt am Main. LILIENCRON 350–357

817 Ursprung, Otto. Die Chorordnung von 1616 am Dom zu Augsburg; ein Beitrag zur Frage der Aufführungs- praxis. ADLER 137–142

818 Wolffheim, Werner. Mitteilungen zur Geschichte der Hofmusik in Celle (1635–1706), und über Arnold M. Brunckhorst. LILIENCRON 421–439

BAROQUE ERA: LOW COUNTRIES, FRANCE, & SPAIN
See also nos. 565, 575

819 Barwick, Steven. Puebla's Requiem Choirbook. DAVISON 121–127

820 Gérold, Théodore. Das Lieder- album einer französischen Provinzdame um 1620. ADN 92–129

821 Kastner, Santiago. Harfe und Harfner in der iberischen Musik des 17. Jahrhunderts. JEPPESEN 165–172

822 Keyzer, Berten de. Bijdrage tot de geschiedenis van het muziekleven in onze kerken. Instrumentisten in de St.-Baafs-Kathedraal te Gent (XVIIe en XVIIIe eeuw). MUEREN 75–83

823 Lancaster, H. Carrington. Comedy versus Opera in France, 1673–1700. BROWN 257–263

CLASSICAL ERA: GENERAL

See also nos. 74, 82, 198, 443, 507, 752,
787, 793a, 797, 813, 826, 2562

d'après les spectacles de Paris.
MASSON II, 9–15
1121 ——. Un Paradoxe musical au
XVIIIe siècle. LAURENCIE 217–221
1122 ——. La Strumentazione della
sinfonia francese del sec. XVIII.
MARINUZZI 7–22
1123 Engelke, Bernhard. Neues zur
Geschichte der Berliner Liederschule.
RIEMANN 456–472
1124 Falvy, Zoltán. A Linus-féle
XVIII. századi táncgyüjtemény
[The Linus Dance Collection of the 18th
Century] KODÁLY/75TH 407–443,
German summary 756–757
1125 Fédorov, Vladimir. Lettres de
quelques voyageurs russes du
XVIIIe siècle. BLUME/F 112–123
1126 Feicht, Hieronym. Musikalische
Beziehungen zwischen Wien und
Warschau zur Zeit der wiener
Klassiker. SCHENK 174–182
1127 Fellerer, Karl Gustav.
Thematisches Verzeichnis der
fürstbischöflichen freisingischen
Hofmusik von 1796. DEUTSCH/80TH
296–302
1128 ——. Zur Melodielehre im 18.
Jahrhundert. KODÁLY/80TH 109–115
1129 Frotscher, Gotthold. Ein
danziger Musikantenspiegel vom
Ende des 18. Jahrhunderts.
SCHERING 68–75
1130 Gálos, Rezső. Erdélyi
hangversenyek a XVIII. században
[Transylvanian Concerts in the 18th
Century] BARTÓK/E 489–499, summary
556
1131 Gérold, Théodore. Le Réveil
en France au XVIIIe siècle de
l'intérêt pour la musique profane
du moyen âge. LAURENCIE 223–234
1132 Glasenapp, Franz von. Eine
Gruppe von Symphonien und
Ouvertüren für Blasinstrumente
von 1793–1795 in Frankreich.
SCHNEIDER/80TH 197–207
1133 Gottron, Adam. Musik in sechs
mittelrheinischen Männerklöstern
im 18. Jahrhundert. SCHENK 214–230
1134 Haas, Robert. Über das wiener
Dilettanten-Konzert 1782. OREL/70TH
77–80
1135 ——. Von dem wienerischen
Geschmack in der Musik. BIEHLE 59–65
1136 Heyer, Hermann. Vermächtnis
und Verpflichtung. KONWITSCHNY 9–21
1137 Hoffmann-Erbrecht, Lothar.

Der galante Stil in der Musik des
18. Jahrhunderts; zur Problematik
des Begriffs. SCHENK 252–260
1138 Johansson, Cari. Studier kring
Patrik Alströmers musiksamling.
MOBERG 195–207
1139 Klein, Herbert. Nachrichten
zum Musikleben Salzburgs in den
Jahren 1764–1766. OREL/70TH 93–101
1140 LaRue, Jan. Major and Minor
Mysteries of Identification in the
18th-Century Symphony.
KINKELDEY/80TH 181–196
1141 Lesure, François. Le Manuscrit
Lavergne et le répertoire des maîtrises
du Sud-Ouest de la France vers 1750.
FELLERER/60TH 315–320
1142 Lindfors, Per. Musik för en
Barmhärtighetsinrättning [Music for
a Charitable Institution] MOBERG 239–248
1143 ♪ Linus dance book. KODÁLY/75TH
420–431
1144 Murányi, Róbert Árpád.
Két XVIII. századi iskoladráma
dallamai [The Songs of Two 18th-
Century School Dramas] BARTÓK/E
501–507, summary 557
1145 Nowak, Leopold. Ein Druck
mit Melodien für Theophilanthropen.
STUMMVOLL 61
1146 Rodriguez-Moñino, A. Instrumentos músicos para el Infante Don
Gabriel (Doce documentos inéditos de
1777–1784). ANGLÉS II, 723–724
1147 Schering, Arnold. Das
öffentliche Musikbildungswesen in
Deutschland bis zur Gründung des
leipziger Konservatoriums. KML 61–80
1148 Schoenbaum, Camillo. Die
böhmischen Musiker in der Musikgeschichte Wiens vom Barock zur
Romantik. SCHENK 475–495
1149 Schünemann, Georg. Ein Sing-
und Spielbuch des 18. Jahrhunderts.
WOLF 179–183
1150 Subirá, José. Conciertos
espirituales españoles en el siglo XVIII.
FELLERER/60TH 519–529
1151 Szabolcsi, Bence. Kleine Beiträge
zur Melodiegeschichte des 18.
Jahrhunderts. SCHENK 532–538
1152 Wieder, Joachim. Bickham's
Musical Entertainer in der englischen
Buchkunst des 18. Jahrhunderts.
JUCHHOFF 147–158
1153 Wolf, Werner. Die Gewandhauskonzerte im Spiegel der Kritik.
KONWITSCHNY 72–86

CLASSICAL ERA: OTHER INDIVIDUAL
COMPOSERS, PERFORMERS, ETC.

ROMANTIC ERA: GENERAL
See also nos. 82, 143, 557, 793a, 805,
908, 1136, 1147, 1148, 1153, 1161, 1166,
1220, 1233, 2708a

1403 Adams, Nicholson B. French
Influence on the Madrid Theatre in
1837. MENÉNDEZ PIDAL/E VII, 134–151
1404 Altmann, Wilhelm. Über einige
mit Unrecht vergessene Streichquartette
KROHN 1–5
1405 ♪ Baron Steuben's American
March. STEUBEN 165
1406 Bernet Kempers, Karel P. Iso-
metrische Begriffe und die Musik des
19. Jahrhunderts. BLUME/F 34–49
1407 Böckmann, Paul. Klang und Bild
in der Stimmungslyrik der Romantik.
BENZ 103–125
1408 Bónis, Ferenc. Magyar
táncgyüjtemény az 1820-as évekből
[A Hungarian Dance Collection from
the 1820s] KODÁLY/70TH 697–732
1409 Branscombe, Peter. Some Viennese Hamlet Parodies and a Hitherto
Unknown Musical Score for One of
Them. DEUTSCH/80TH 337–344
1410 Broeckx, Jan L. Muziekhistorische
feiten als kultuurhistorische symptomen.
Muzikale stijl als spiegel van de
levenshouding in de XIXe eeuw.
MUEREN 53–62
1411 Bücken, Ernst. Romantik und
Realismus; zur Periodisierung der
romantischen Epoche. SCHERING 46–50
1412 Chávarri, Eduardo L. El
Nacionalismo en la música española.
PEDRELL 199–200
1413 Dannemann, Erna. Musikpflege
und Musikerziehung in einer englischen
Provinz. BESSELER 505–508
1414 Ehinger, Hans. Die Rolle der
Schweiz in der Allgemeinen musikalischen Zeitung, 1798–1848. NEF 19–47
1415 Fournol, Etienne. De l'entrée des
slaves dans l'histoire de la musique.
BOYER 75–82
1416 Gurvin, Olav. Ja, vi elsker dette
landet; et essay om utførelsen [Ja, vi
elsker . . . ; An Essay on Interpreta-
tion] MOBERG 163–170
1417 Hafner, Johannes. München als
Ausgangspunkt der regensburger
kirchenmusikalischen Restauration.
SCHREMS 153–156
1418 Handschin, Jacques. Die
europäische Rolle der russischen Musik.

HANDSCHIN 275–286; orig. in Neue
Zürcher Zeitung 2501, 2509, & 2513
(1930)
1419 ——. Das russische Lied.
HANDSCHIN 287–290; orig, in Neue
Zürcher Zeitung 220 (1927)
1420 Hill, Richard S. The Melody of
The Star-Spangled Banner in the
United States before 1820. WROTH
151–193 (also issued separately Wash.,
D.C.: Lib. of Congress, 1951)
1421 Kahl, Willi. Musik als Erbe; von
der Aufklärung zur Romantik.
MERSMANN 64–68
1422 ——. Zur musikalischen Renais-
sancebewegung in Frankreich während
der ersten Hälfte des 19. Jahrhunderts.
SCHMIDT-GÖRG 156–174
1423 Loth, Peter. Ein Jahrhundert
Chorschaffen in Zweibrücken.
ZWEIBRÜCKEN 288–291
1424 Malen, Aarne. Eräs yritys
suomalaisaiheisen laulunäytelmän teke-
miseksi v. 1829 [An Essay concerning
an Operetta with Finnish Motives from
the Year 1829] KROHN 108–111, German
summary v
1425 Mersmann, Hans. Sonatenformen
in der romantischen Kammermusik.
WOLF 112–117
1426 Niemann, Walter. Charakter-
köpfe norddeutscher Schumannier in
der Klaviermusik. [Ernst Haberbier,
Friedrich Wilhelm Markull, Heinrich
Steil, Karl Lührs, Hugo Ulrich, Albert
Dietrich, Louis Ehlert, Robert Radecke,
Constantin Bürgel] SEIDL/AR 199–222
1427 Norlind, Tobias. Adatok a
keringő és a polka történetéhez/Zur
Geschichte des Walzers und der Polka.
KODÁLY/60TH 189–194
1428 Nowak, Leopold. Ländler,
Walzer und Wienerlieder im Klavier-
buche einer preussischen Prinzessin.
ZODER 133–148
1429 Prahács, Margit. Zene a régi
óvodákban (1828–1860) [Music in the
Old Nursery Schools (1828–1860)]
KODÁLY/70TH 515–566
1430 Rebling, Oskar. Kleine Beiträge
zur Musikgeschichte der Stadt Halle.
SCHNEIDER/80TH 271–276
1431 Refardt, Edgar. Männerchöre
und Männerchorkomponisten in der
Schweiz. REFARDT 75–78; orig. in Neue
Zürcher Zeitung 1588 (1926)
1432 ——. Die Musik in den
Alpenrosen. NEF 202–209

ROMANTIC ERA: FRANZ SCHUBERT
See also no. 1233

1468 ♪ [Waltzes] Waltz in G, piano.
WAHLE 11–12
1469 Werner, Theodor W. Schuberts
Tod; Versuch einer Deutung. WOLF
214–216

ROMANTIC ERA: RICHARD WAGNER
See also nos. 1220, 1521
1470 Abraham, Gerald. Wagner's
Second Thoughts. NEWMAN 9–28
1471 Burch, Gladys. The Literary
Taste of Richard and Cosima Wagner.
ENGEL 53–59
1472 Ferran, André. Baudelaire et la
musique. HUGUET 387–393
1473 Krech, Hans. Richard Wagner
als Sänger und Sprecher.
SCHNEIDER/80TH 255–264
1474 [Liebesverbot] Engel, Hans.
Über Richard Wagners Oper Das
Liebesverbot. BLUME/F 80–91
1475 [Parsifal] Valentin, Erich. Wagners Parsifal in Braunschweig 1882,
mitgeteilt nach dem Briefwechsel
Ludwig Schemanns und Hans Sommers.
MÜLLER VON ASOW [208–221]
1476 Prod'homme, Jacques-Gabriel.
Trois lettres inédites de Cosima Wagner. LAURENCIE 282–286
1477 Prüfer, Arthur. Richard Wagner
und Jakob Grimm. SEIDL/AR 234–259
1478 Riesenfeld, Paul. Die Aus-
wanderung vom heiligen Gralsberge,
Variationen zu dem Thema: Ergo
vivamus. SEIDL/AR 152–179
1479 [Siegfried] Stephani, Hermann.
Der Wanderer im Siegfried. SEIDL/AR
269–273
1480 Stephani, Hermann. Felix
Draesekes Aufenthalt bei Richard
Wagner in Luzern 1859 nach Draesekes noch unveröffentlichten Leben-
serinnerungen. MÜLLER VON ASOW
[171–175]
1481 Sternfeld, Richard. Die zwei
Reiche in Wagners Dramen. SEIDL/AR
260–268
1482 [Tannhäuser] Ferran, André.
Tannhäuser à l'opéra de Paris en 1861,
caricatures et parodies. MORNET 189–197
1483 —— Sandberger, Adolf. Zu den
literarischen Quellen von Richard
Wagners Tannhäuser. SCHEURLEER
267–269
1484 —— Tonnelat, E. Richard Wagner et Wolfram von Eschenbach.
LICHTENBERGER 257–266
1485 Vermeil, Edmond. Le Génie con-

structif de Richard Wagner.
LICHTENBERGER 267–293
1486 Viotta, H. A. Richard Wagners
verhouding tot de muziekgeschiedenis.
SCHEURLEER 359–365
1487 Wagner, Cosima. [Letters to
Anton Seidl]. SEIDL/AN 199–202
1488 Wagner, Richard. [Letters to
Anton Seidl]. SEIDL/AN 187–198

ROMANTIC ERA: OTHER INDIVIDUAL
COMPOSERS, PERFORMERS, ETC.

1489 [Albéniz] Jankélévitch, Vladimir.
Albéniz et l'état de verve. MASSON II,
197–209
1490 [Arnold] Refardt, Edgar. Gustav
Arnold. REFARDT 33–46; orig. in
Schweizerische Musikz. 90 (1950)
1491 [Augundson] Bjørndal, Arne.
Myllarguten på det Norske Teater i
Bergen 1850 [Møllarguten (i.e.,
Augundson) at the Norwegian Theatre
in Bergen] BJØRNDAL 175–182
1492 [Becker] Tappolet, Willy.
Georges Becker, 24 Juli 1834 bis 18.
Juli 1928. SCHENK 539–544
1493 ♪ Becker, Reinhold. Albumblatt.
SEEBACH 26
1494 [Berlioz] Handschin, Jacques.
Hector Berlioz. HANDSCHIN 213–222;
orig. in Vereinsblatt der Basler
Liedertafel 10 (1931/1932)
1495 [Berwald] Brandel, Åke. Släkten
Berwald, dess tidigare historia och
dess verksamhet i Ryssland. [The
Berwald Family, its Early History and
its Activity in Russia] MOBERG 89–97
1496 ♪ Bezeredj, Amalia. Flori könyve.
KODÁLY/70TH 528–542
1497 [Bizet] Dean, Winton. Bizet's
Ivan IV. NEWMAN 58–85
1498 [Borodin] Handschin, Jacques.
Borodin und sein Fürst Igor.
HANDSCHIN 238–241; orig. in Die
Tribüne, hrsg. v.d. Bühnen der Stadt
Köln, 22 (1952/1953)
1499 [Bosret] Montellier, Ernest. Li
bia bouquet et son auteur, Nicolas
Bosret. CLOSSON 145–152
1500 [Brahms] Bernet Kempers, Karel
P. Die "Emanzipation des Fleisches"
in den Liedern von Johannes Brahms.
SCHENK 28–30
1501 —— Kross, Siegfried. Brahms
und der Kanon. SCHMIDT–GÖRG 175–187
1502 —— Moser, Hans Joachim. Zur
Sinndeutung der c-moll Symphonie

Henri Vieuxtemps an W. A. Mozart Sohn. SCHENK 389–390
1671 [Weber] Köhler, Karl-Heinz. Carl Maria von Webers Beziehungen zu Berlin. BESSELER 425–435
1672 —— Schnoor, Hans. Stufen des 19. Jahrhunderts. STRAUBE 233–260
1673 —— Schünemann, Georg. Carl Maria von Weber in Berlin; sein erster Besuch im Jahre 1812. RAABE 78–94
1674 —— Wirth, Helmut. Natur und Märchen in Webers *Oberon*, Mendelssohns *Ein Sommernachtstraum* und Nicolais *Die lustigen Weiber von Windsor*. BLUME/F 389–397
1675 [Widmann] Refardt, Edgar. Die Musiktexte J. V. Widmanns. REFARDT 134–139; orig. in *Der Bund* 447 (1938)
1676 [Widor] Handschin, Jacques. Charles-Marie Widor. HANDSCHIN 242–245; orig. in *Neue Basler Zeitung* 18 (Mar. 1937)

POST-ROMANTIC AND MODERN ERA:
GENERAL
See also nos. 793a, 1136, 1153, 1165, 1413, 1423, 1431

1677 Abeele, G. van den. Bij de herleving van oude muziek. MUEREN 167–176
1678 Altmann, Wilhelm. Die Ur- und Erstaufführungen von Opernwerken auf deutschen Bühnen in den letzten 25 Spielzeiten. UNIVERSAL 247–275
1679 Bartók, Béla. The Influence of Peasant Music on Modern Music. BARTÓK/T 71–76
1680 Baur, Jürg. Das kurze Klavierstück und seine Stellung in der modernen Musik. FELLERER 63–66
1681 Berg, Alban. Verbindliche Antwort auf eine unverbindliche Rundfrage. UNIVERSAL 220–225
1682 Berten, Walter. Musikpolitik-Musiksoziologie-Musikdramaturgie, Begriffsbestimmungen und Zielsetzungen. RAABE 52–58
1683 Bie, Oskar. Der Tanz. UNIVERSAL 125–129
1684 Biehle, Herbert. Das Institut [Biehle] BIEHLE 101–103
1685 Binder, Julius. Der Staat der Musik. VECCHIO 31–37
1686 Cogni, Giulio. Il Problema dell' interiorità nella musica contemporanea. SCHENK 89–95
1687 Collaer, Paul. La Composition musicale, de 1939 à 1945. CLOSSON 81–87

1688 ——. Poésie et musique dans la mélodie française contemporaine. BORREN 149–162
1689 Cross, Joan. The Bad Old Days. BRITTEN 175–184
1690 Daisne, Johan. Zur Geschichte von Lili Marleen. LIEP 68–71
1691 Egk, Werner. Musik als Ausdruck ihrer Zeit. RAABE 23–28
1692 Engel, Hans. Der Musiker, Beruf und Lebensformen. RAABE 187–211
1693 Engelbrecht, Christiane. Die Psalmvertonung im 20. Jahrhundert. SÖHNGEN 153–161
1694 Fellerer, Karl Gustav. Alte Musik im Musikleben der Gegenwart. MERSMANN 44–50
1695 ——. Europäisches Musikschaffen. HILBER 60–66
1696 50 Komponisten: Porträts, Lebensdaten, Werke in der Universal-Edition. UNIVERSAL 285–332
1697 Gruenberg, Louis. Vom Jazz und anderen Dingen; Rückblick und Ausblick. UNIVERSAL 229–236
1698 Handschin, Jacques. Die alte Musik als Gegenwartsproblem. HANDSCHIN 338–341; orig. in *Neue Zürcher Zeitung* 786 (1927)
1699 ——. Musikalisches aus Russland. HANDSCHIN 263–274; orig. in *Basler Nachrichten* 332 & 333 (1920)
1700 ——. La Naissance d'une musique russe d'orgue vers 1914. MASSON II, 189–193
1701 ——. Das Problem der modernen Oper. HANDSCHIN 342–347; orig. in *Neue Zürcher Zeitung* 1074 & 1081 (1928)
1702 ——. Die Stellung der Musik im Rahmen der Gesamtkultur. HANDSCHIN 355–358; orig. in *Schaffhauser Nachrichten* (Oct. 17, 1947)
1703 Hasse, Karl. Grundlagen einer bodenständigen Musikpflege. STEIN 104–111
1704 Hauer, Josef M. Wende der Musik? UNIVERSAL 237–240
1705 Hausegger, Siegmund von. Kunst und Öffentlichkeit. SEIDL/AR 56–57
1706 Hope-Wallace, Philip. Meditation. NEWMAN 124–129
1707 Hürlimann, Martin. Was ist Wahrheit? Bemerkungen eines Liebhabers zur heutigen Situation der Musikkritik. PAUMGARTNER 70–80
1708 Jenkner, Hans. Wir brauchen die Oper der Zeit. BOTE 51–56
1709 Kaminski, Heinrich. Evolution oder Revolution. UNIVERSAL 60–62

POST-ROMANTIC AND MODERN ERA: HOUSE AND YOUTH MUSIC

à *Albert Roussel. Berceuse.* ROUSSEL
suppl. 17–19
2012 ♪ Unger, H. *Kukuks Tod.*
MÜLLER VON ASOW [268–269]
2013 ♪ ——. *Menuett.* HASS 130–131
2014 ♪ Wagenaar, Johan. *Het vinnich
stralen van de son.* SCHEURLEER 367–368
2015 [Wagner, P.] Handschin, Jacques.
Peter Wagner. HANDSCHIN 395–397;
orig. in *Neue Zürcher Zeitung* 2021
(1931)
2016 [Webern] Eimert, Herbert.
Interval Proportions. WEBERN/R 93–99
2017 —— Jone, Hildegard. A Cantata.
WEBERN/R 7–8
2018 —— Klammer, Armin. Webern's
Piano Variations, op. 27, 3rd movement.
WEBERN/R 81–92
2019 —— Kolneder, Walter. Klang-
technik und Motivbildung bei Webern.
MÜLLER-BLATTAU 27–50
2020 —— Metzger, Heinz-Klaus.
Analysis of the Sacred Song, op. 15, no.
4. WEBERN/R 75–80
2021 —— ——. Webern and Schönberg.
WEBERN/R 42–45
2022 —— Pousseur, Henri. Webern's
Organic Chromaticism. WEBERN/R
51–60
2023 —— Spinner, Leopold. Analysis
of a Period. WEBERN/R 46–50
2024 —— Stockhausen, Karlheinz.
Structure and Experiential Time.
WEBERN/R 64–74
2025 ♪ Wenzel, Eberhard. *Vespera
iam venit.* SÖHNGEN 133–136
2026 ♪ Wolpert, F. A. *Lied eines
theokritischen Ziegenhirten.* MÜLLER
VON ASOW [270–272]
2027 ♪ Zöllner, Heinrich. *Strophen-
liedlein.* SEEBACH 172

ETHNOMUSICOLOGY: GENERAL
See also nos. 101, 566, 571, 1679, 2474,
2491, 2496–2498, 2547, 2570, 2590, 2598,
2599, 2602, 2604

2028 Belaiev, Victor M. A népi
harmóniarendszer [The System of
Folk Harmony] KODÁLY/70TH 75–86
2029 Bimberg, Siegfried. Über die
Bedeutung der Volksmusik für die
Entwicklung der Musikkultur.
HOFMEISTER 58–61
2030 Brailoiu, Constantin. Un
Problème de tonalité: la métabole
pentatonique. MASSON I, 63–75
2031 Chailley, Jacques. Incidences

pédagogiques des recherches
d'ethnologie musicale. KODÁLY/80TH
65–71
2032 Danckert, Werner. A félhang-
nélküli pentatónia eredete/ Der
Ursprung der halbtonlosen Pentatonik.
KODÁLY/60TH 9–18
2033 Graf, Walter. Neue Möglich-
keiten, neue Aufgaben der
vergleichenden Musikwissenschaft.
SCHENK 231–245
2034 Groven, Eivind. Det naturs-
varande i musikk-kjensla vår. [The
Natural Variety in our Musical
Sensibility] SANDVIK 32–38
2035 Kertész, Gyula. A népdal gépi
felvétele. [The Recording of Folksong]
KODÁLY/70TH 659–662
2036 Keyser, P. de. Enkele losse
beschouwingen over volksliedkunde.
MUEREN 85–92
2037 Kodály, Zoltán. Eine Vorbedin-
gung der vergleichenden Liedforschung.
BARTÓK/S 7–8
2038 Krohn, Ilmari. Psalmengesang in
der Volkssprache. WAGNER 118–123
2039 Kunst, Jaap. Fragment of an
Essay on *Music and Sociology.*
BARTÓK/S 143–145
2039a ——. Fragments from Diaries
Written During a Lecture Tour in the
New World (October 4, 1955–March 3,
1956) and a Trip to Australia (May 15–
August 28, 1959). SACHS/C 328–342
2040 Lach, Robert. Vergleichende
Sprach- und Musikwissenschaft.
KRETSCHMER 128–139
2041 Molnár, Antal. A népzenekutatás
kérdéseiből [On the Problems of
Folkmusic Research] KODÁLY/70TH
331–338
2042 Myers, Charles S. The Ethno-
logical Study of Music. TYLOR 235–253
2043 Nef, Karl. Zur Geschichte des
Volksliedinteresses. KRETSCHMAR 105–
109
2044 Rajeczky, Benjamin. Népdaltör-
ténet és gregorián-kutatás/Storia del
canto gregoriano e le ricerche sul
canto popolare. KODÁLY/60TH 308–
312
2045 Riemann, Ludwig. Die Beziehungen der heutigen Volksmusik zur
Kunstmusik. LILIENCRON 203–214
2046 Schaeffner, André. Primitív,
exotikus zene és modern nyugateurópai
muzsika/Musique primitive ou exotique
et musique moderne d'Occident.
KODÁLY/60TH 213–218

2080 Bhaduri, M. B. Hindu Influence on Munda Songs. ROY 256–260

2081 Collaer, Paul. La Musique des Protomalais. KODÁLY/80TH 71–88

2082 Eckardt, Hans. Zur Frage und Bedeutung der Rangô. BESSELER 35–42

2083 Farmer, Henry G. Zenei kölcsönhatások Kelet- és Kozépázsia között/Wechselwirkungen mittel- und ostasiatischer Musik. KODÁLY/60TH 32–42

2084 Fujii, Seishin. A buddhizmus és a zene/Der Buddhismus und die Musik KODÁLY/60TH 139–142

2085 Gerson-Kiwi, Edith. Musiker des Orients, ihr Wesen und Werdegang. KODÁLY/80TH 125–132

2085a ——. Women's Songs from the Yemen; Their Tonal Structure and Form. SACHS/C 97–103

2086 Graf, Walter. Zur Ausführung der lamaistischen Gesangsnotation. KODÁLY/80TH 133–147

2087 Handschin, Jacques. Indische Musik. HANDSCHIN 306–309; orig. in Neue Zürcher Zeitung 2040 (1932)

2088 Holst, Imogen. Indian Music. BRITTEN 104–110

2089 Hurgronje, C. S. Een arabisch minnelied met luitbegleiding. MENGELBERG 141–143

2089a Kishibe, Shigeo. A Chinese Painting of the T'ang Court Women's Orchestra. SACHS/C 104–117

2090 Kaufmann, Walter. Folksongs of the Gond and Baiga. EINSTEIN 280–288

2091 Lach, Robert. Orientalistik und vergleichende Musikwissenschaft. KARABACEK 155–193

2092 Land, J. P. N. Essais de notation musicale chez les Arabes et les Persans. LEEMANS 315–316

2093 Marçais, Georges. Les Figures d'hommes et de bêtes dans les bois sculptés d'époque fâtimite conservés au Musée Arabe du Caire; Etude d'iconographie musulmane. MASPERO III, 241–257

2094 Müller, F. W. K. Ikkaku sennin, eine mittelalterliche japanische Oper, transkribiert und übersetzt . . . nebst einem Exkurs zur Einhornsage. BASTIAN 515–537

2095 Myers, Charles S. The Beginnings of Music. RIDGEWAY 560–582

2096 Picken, Lawrence. Twelve Ritual Melodies of the T'ang Dynasty. BARTÓK/S 147–173

2097 Ránki, György. Indokínái dallamok [Indochinese Melodies] KODÁLY/70TH 413–422

2098 Roy, Trina. Outlines of Tagore's Music. SCHMIDT-GÖRG 235–266

2099 Schermann, L. Musizierende Genien in der religiösen Kunst des birmanischen Buddhismus. HIRTH 345–353

2100 Tegethoff, Wilhelm. Lili Rabaulenses. FELLERER 73–104

2101 Twitchett, D. C. & A. H. Christie. A Medieval Burmese Orchestra. WALEY 176–195

2102 Wang, Kwang-Chi. Musikalische Beziehungen zwischen China und dem Westen im Laufe der Jahrtausende. KAHLE 217–224

2103 Wellesz, Egon. Die orientalische Musik im Rahmen der musikgeschichtlichen Forschung. KRETZSCHMAR 172–174

2104 Wolff, Hellmuth Christian. Rabindranath Tagore und die Musik. FELLERER/60TH 590–593

2105 Yuen Ren Chao. Tone, Intonation, Singsong, Chanting, Recitative, Tonal Composition and Atonal Composition in Chinese. JAKOBSON 52–59

ETHNOMUSICOLOGY: EUROPE (GENERAL)

See also nos. 460, 464, 884, 1383

2105a Bachmann, Werner. Die Verbreitung des Quintierens im europäischen Volksgesang des späten Mittelalters. SCHNEIDER/80TH 25–29

2105b Bartók, Béla. Népdalkutatás keleteurópában. KODÁLY/70TH 73–74

2105c Maróthy, János. Az európai nepdal születése. KODÁLY/75TH 503–626

1205d Ortutay, Gyula. Az "europai" ballada kérdéséhez. KODÁLY/70TH 125–132

2105e Suppan, W. Bi- bis tetrachordische Tonreihen im Volkslied deutscher Sprachinseln Süd—und Osteuropas. KODÁLY/80TH 329–356

ETHNOMUSICOLOGY: EUROPE (INDIVIDUAL COUNTRIES)

See also nos. 460, 464, 884, 1383

2106 [Austria] Commenda, Hans. Aus dem Notenbüchl vom Urähnl; Volksmusik aus Bad Ischl. ZODER 8–15

2107 —— Holaubek-Lawatsch, Gundl, & Ernst L. Uray. Hochzeitslieder aus der Weststeiermark. ZODER 54–60

svenska folksmusiken; en materialsam-
ling ur protokollen från 1840-talets
början till 1870-talets slut [The Royal
Music Academy and Swedish Folk
Music; Documents from 1840 to 1870]
MOBERG 321–337
2246 [Switzerland] Refardt, Edgar.
Wie ein stolzer Adler. REFARDT 143–146;
orig. in *Schweizer Volkskunde* 28
(1938)
2247 —— Wiora, Walter, Alpen-
ländische Liedweisen der Frühzeit und
des Mittelalters im Lichte vergleichen-
der Forschung. MEIER/85TH 169–198
2248 [Turkey] Bartók, Béla. On
Collecting Folksongs in Turkey.
BARTÓK/T 19–23
2249 —— Reinhard, Kurt. Zur
Variantenbildung im türkischen
Volkslied, dargestellt an einer Hirten-
weise. BESSELER 21–34
2250 [Yugoslavia] Lord, Albert B.
The Role of Sound Patterns in Serbo-
Croatian Epic. JAKOBSON 301–305
2251 —— Širola, Božidar. Horvát népi
hangszerek/Kroatische Volksmusikin-
strumente KODÁLY/60TH 114–127
2252 —— ——. Die Volksmusik der
Kroaten. BARTÓK/S 89–106
2253 —— Žganec, Vinko. Die Ele-
mente der jugoslawischen Folklore-
Tonleitern im serbischen liturgischen
Gesange. BARTÓK/S 349–363

BIBLIOGRAPHY
See also no. 995

2254 Adler, Guido. Ein Musikkatalog
aus unserer Zeit. SCHEURLEER 39–41
2255 Autographen ausgestellt in der
Internationalen Musik-und Theater-
Ausstellung in Wien, 1892. RICORDI
159–162
2256 Autographen von Opern,
Operetten, Oratorien, Cantaten, u.s.w.,
Eigenthum der Firma G. Ricordi & Co.
RICORDI 145–155
2257 Bach, Ursula. Bemerkungen zur
Fachbibliographie der Musikwissenschaft. VORSTIUS 17–19
2258 Badura-Skoda, Eva. Eine private Briefsammlung. DEUTSCH/80TH
280–290
2259 Bush, Helen E., & David J.
Haykin. Music Subject Headings.
KINKELDEY 39–45
2260 Ciceri, Angelo. L'Archivio della

Veneranda Fabbrica del Duomo di
Milano. MERCATI 165–183
2261 Clasen, Theo. Die musikalischen
Autographen der Universitäts-
Bibliothek Bonn. SCHMIDT-GÖRG 26–65
2262 Dagnino, Eduardo. L'Archivio
musicale di Montecassino. MONTE-
CASSINO I, 273–296
2263 Dreimüller, Karl. Musikerbriefe
an einen rheinischen Musikliebhaber
aus der Sammlung Ludwig Bisschopinck
in München-Gladbach. HOBOKEN 29–49
2264 Engel, Carl. Concert, A.D. 2025,
in the Library of Congress. PUTNAM
140–145
2265 Goff, Frederick R. Early Music
Books in the Rare Books Division of the
Library of Congress. KINKELDEY 58–74
2266 Grasberger, Franz. Katalogisie-
rungsprobleme einer Musikbibliothek.
VORSTIUS 172–181
2267 Hofmann, Gustav. Musikpflege
und wissenschaftliche Universitätsbibliothek. STUMMVOLL 41–43
2268 Kahl, Willi. Musikhandschriften
aus dem Nachlass Ernst Bückens in der
Kölner Universitäts- und Stadtbibliothek. JUCHOFF 159–171
2269 King, A. Hyatt. The History and
Growth of the Catalogues in the
Music Room of the British Museum.
DEUTSCH/80TH 303–308
2270 Lach, Robert. Aus dem Hand-
schriftenschatze der Musikalien-
sammlung der Wiener Nationalbibliothek. WN 553–574
2271 Lindberg, Folke. Sveriges Radios
musikbibliotek; en undersökning om
dess tillkomst och förste år [The
Swedish Radio Music Library; An
Examination of its Early Years]
MOBERG 227–237
2272 Lunelli, Renato. Di alcuni
inventari delle musiche già possedute
dal coro della parrocchiale di Merano.
SCHENK 347–362
2273 Luther, Wilhelm M. Der
Komponist und seine Eigenschrift.
JUCHHOFF 172–186
2274 Mertens, C. Proeve eener docu-
mentatie over onze belgische toonkunstenaars, musicologen en instrumen-
tenbouwers. BORREN 216–239
2275 Meyer, Kathi. Über Musikbibliographie. WOLF 118–122
2276 Mies, Paul, & Klaus W. Niemöller. Bibliographie zur Musikgeschichte der Stadt Köln. MIES 55–80

2277 Mörner, C. G. Stellan. Rariteter
ur en akatalogiserod notsamling i
Kungl. Biblioteket i Stockholm
[Curiosities from an Uncataloged
Collection in the Royal Library,
Stockholm] MOBERG 273–281
2278 Moser, Hans Joachim. Im
Zeitalter des Schallbandarchivs.
MOSER/70TH 247–252 (orig. 3 separate
studies: *Im Zeitalter des Schallbandarchivs; Gefährdung des Lebendigen
durch die Technik; & Wider den
Missbrauch der Perfektion*)
2279 Pérez Gómez, Antonio. Graba-
ciones en discos microsurco de
música y canciones españolas hasta
fines del siglo XVI. ANGLÉS II, 623–645
2280 [Ricordi] Brief-fac-simili.
RICORDI 69–141
2281 Riedel, Friedrich W. Die Bibliothek des Aloys Fuchs. ALBRECHT
207–224
2282 Schmieder, Wolfgang. Aphoris-
men zur Musik-Dokumentation.
ALBRECHT 285–288
2283 ——. "Menschliches Allzumen-
schliches" oder einige unparteiische
Gedanken über Thematische Verzeich-
nisse. DEUTSCH/80TH 309–318
2284 Schneider, Max. *Denkmäler der
Tonkunst* vor hundert Jahren.
LILIENCRON 278–289
2285 Schulz, Gottfried. Musikbibliographie und Musikbibliotheken.
SANDBERGER 129–134
2286 Versyp, J. De muziekbibliotheek
van de St-Salvatorskerk te Gent in
1754. MUEREN 217–225
2287 Verzeichnis der grösstentheils
von Sigismund Streit dem grauen
Kloster geschenkten Musikalien.
BGGK 5–18
2288 Wackernagel, Peter. Aus glück-
lichen Zeiten der Preussischen Staatsbibliothek. SMEND 61–65
2289 Weinmann, Alexander. Die
Wiener Zeitung als Quelle für die
Musikbibliographie. HOBOKEN 153–160
2290 Weinmann, Karl. Die Proskesche
Musikbibliothek in Regensburg.
LILIENCRON 387–403
2291 Zehnter, Hans. Die handschrift-
lichen Nachlässe von schweizer
Komponisten in der Universitätsbibliothek Basel. SCHWARBER 297–315
2292 Die zeitgenössischen Komponisten der Salzburger Festspiele in
Faksimile-Wiedergaben ihrer Opern.
PAUMGARTNER 41–55

MUSICOLOGY AS A DISCIPLINE
See also nos. 98, 2033, 2040–2042, 2052

2293 Bartha, Dénes. Bemerkungen zum
New-Yorker Kongress der I.G.M.W.,
1961. KODÁLY/80TH 53–64
2294 Blume, Friedrich. Musikforschung und Musikpraxis. STEIN 13–25
2295 Dehnert, Max. Wert und Unwert
des Anekdotischen; ein Beitrag zur
biographischen Methodik.
SCHNEIDER/80TH 357–364
2296 Demuth, Norman. A propos des
voyages de Ch. Burney. MASSON II,
33–42
2297 Felber, Erwin. Die Musikwissenschaft. UNIVERSAL 139–154
2298 Goslich, Siegfried. Gedanken
zur geisteswissenschaftlichen Musik-
betrachtung. SCHERING 90–95
2299 Grainger, Percy A. The Special-
ist and the All-Round Man. ENGEL
115–119
2300 Handschin, Jacques. Der Arbeits-
bereich der Musikwissenschaft.
HANDSCHIN 23–28; orig. in *Basler Nachrichten*, Sonntagsblatt 26 (July 6, 1952)
2301 ——. Belange der Wissenschaft.
HANDSCHIN 60–69; orig. in *Schweizer
Annalen* (1936)
2302 ——. Gedanken über moderne
Wissenschaft. HANDSCHIN 51–59; orig.
in *Annalen* 2 (1928)
2303 ——. Humanistische Besinnung.
HANDSCHIN 376–384; orig. in *Neue
Zürcher Zeitung* 797 & 813 (1932)
2304 ——. Über das Studium der
Musikwissenschaft. HANDSCHIN 38–50;
orig. in *Mitteilungen der Schweizerischen Musikforschenden Gesellschaft*
3 (1956)
2305 ——. Vom Sinn der Musikwissenschaft. HANDSCHIN 29–37; orig. in *Neue
Zürcher Zeitung* 903 & 919 (1929)
2306 Lenaerts, René. Wegen en doel-
stellingen van de muziekwetenschap.
CLOSSON 139–144
2307 Linden, Albert van der. Gloses
sur l'étymologie du mot *musique*.
GESSLER 735–741
2308 Lissa, Zofia. Uwagi o metodzie
marksistowskiej w muzykologii [Notes
on the Marxist Method Applied to
Musicology] CHYBIŃSKI/70TH 50–119
2309 Meyer, Ernst H. Künstlerisches
und wissenschaftliches Denken.
SCHNEIDER/80TH 303–310
2310 Moberg, Carl-Allan. Musik-

2424 Neal, Heinrich. Lehrer und Schüler. GRÜNWALD 19–22
2425 Nuffel, J. van. L'Histoire de l'art à l'université. BORREN 327–335
2426 Oberborbeck, Felix. Grundzüge rheinischer Musikerziehung der vergangenen fünfzig Jahre (1900–1956). SCHIEDERMAIR/80TH 77–96
2427 ——. Musikerziehung als Gegenstand wissenschaftlicher Forschung. MERSMANN 97–99
2428 Pfannenstiel, Ekkehart. Aus der Wendezeit der Musikerziehung. JÖDE 46–52
2429 Preussner, Eberhard. Bild einer neuen Musikschule; Utopie und Wirklichkeit. MERSMANN 100–110
2430 ——. Musik und Menschenerziehung. PAUMGARTNER 87–101
2431 Reichenbach, Hermann. Zur Frage: Musik und Jugend. JÖDE 53–58
2432 Schäfer, Dirk. Het klavier. SCHÄFER 81–88
2433 Schneider, Albert. Die Kölner Musikhochschule nach dem zweiten Weltkrieg. MERSMANN 123–128
2434 Schneider, Norbert. Zur Situation der Musikerziehung an höheren Schulen. MERSMANN 133–134
2435 Schroeder, Hermann. Der Kompositionslehrer in unserer Zeit. LEMACHER 27–29
2436 Schumann, Heinrich. Jugendmusik und Blockflöte. JÖDE 109–118
2437 Siukohen, Wilho. Erilaisia käsityksiä koulun laulunopetuksen peruskysymyksistä [Different Views concerning the Fundamentals of Teaching Vocal Music] KROHN 116–142 German summary p.
2438 Steinitzer, Max. Über den Nutzen des Gymnasialbetriebs. SEIDL/AR 97–117
2439 ——. Zur Methodik des Anfangsunterrichts für die Frauenstimme. RIEMANN 76–100
2440 Stone, David. Scholar-Musician as Teacher. DAVISON 337–340
2441 Thamm, Joseph. Carl Thiel—Theobald Schrems; zur Entstehung des Regensburger Musikgymnasiums. SCHREMS 170–185
2442 Thomas, Kurt. Zur Chorleiter- und Dirigentenerziehung. STEIN 129–134
2443 Übersicht der JALE-Schriften. MÜNNICH 152
2444 Waldmann, Guido. Einfluss auf die Privatmusikerziehung. JÖDE 99–109
2445 Wittelsbach, Rudolf. Zum

Problem der Tonsprache im Theorieunterricht. MERSMANN 197–205
2446 Wölper, Ernst-Otto. Über den Sinn des Studiums an Musikhochschulen. MERSMANN 206–212
2447 Zepf, Josef. Die Mundharmonika in der Jugend. JÖDE 172–175

THEORY & ANALYSIS: GENERAL
See also nos. 92, 274, 299, 337, 639, 1302, 1425, 1446, 1726, 1782, 1846, 2030, 2032, 2053, 2053a, 2322, 2345, 2351, 2357a, 2382, 2386, 2445, 2530

2448 Bengtsson, Ingmar. On Relationships between Tonal and Rhythmic Structures in Western Multipart Music. MOBERG 49–76
2449 Besseler, Heinrich. Musik und Raum. SEIFFERT 151–160
2450 Blessinger, Karl. Versuch über die musikalische Form. SANDBERGER 1–20
2451 Blume, Friedrich. Fortspinnung und Entwicklung; ein Beitrag zur musikalischen Begriffsbildung. BLUME/S 504–525; orig. in Peters Jahrbuch 36 (1929)
2452 ——. Die musikalische Form und die musikalischen Gattungen. BLUME/S 480–504; orig. in MGG 4, col. 523
2453 Bücken, Ernst. Zur Frage des Stilverfalls. KROYER 164–168
2454 Chomiński, Jósef. M. Z zagadnień analizy formalnej [Concerning Formal Analysis] CHYBIŃSKI/70TH 146–197
2455 Fischer, Kurt von. Zur Theorie der Variation im 18. und beginnenden 19. Jahrhundert. SCHMIDT-GÖRG 117–130
2456 Flothuis, Marius. Twaalf overwegingen. BERNET KEMPERS 35–37
2457 Fox, Charles W. Modern Counterpoint, a Phenomenological Approach. KINKELDEY 46–57
2458 Graf, Max. Musikkritik. UNIVERSAL 198–203
2459 Greissle, Felix. The Composer as Thinker. ENGEL 120–127
2460 Güldenstein, Gustav. Die Gegenwart in der Musik. NEF 72–101
2461 Handschin, Jacques. Der Begriff der Form in der Musik. HANDSCHIN 332–337; orig. in Neue Zürcher Zeitung 1088 (1932)
2462 Hartmann, Friedrich H. A Return to the Question of Atonality. SCHENK 246–251
2463 Herrmann, Joachim. Gibt es

2498 Saygun, A. A. La Genèse de la mélodie. KODÁLY/80TH 281–300
2499 Szabolcsi, Bence. Dallamtörténeti kérdések [Problems concerning the History of Melody] KODÁLY/70TH 743–764
2500 Wiora, Walter. Älter als die Pentatonik. BARTÓK/S 185–208

THEORY & ANALYSIS: HARMONY
See also nos. 67, 693, 763, 770, 2028, 2331

2501 Bimberg, Siegfried. Notwendiges Vorwort zur Harmonielehre. MÜNNICH 46–57
2502 Borris, Siegfried. Hindemiths harmonische Analysen. SCHNEIDER/80TH 295–301
2503 Moser, Hans Joachim. Neapolitana. MOSER/70TH 324–328
2504 Münnich, Richard. Von Entwicklung der Riemannschen Harmonielehre und ihrem Verhältnis zu Oettingen und Stumpf. RIEMANN 60–76
2505 ——. Zur Theorie des Leitklangs. KRETZSCHMAR 101–104
2506 Piston, Walter. Thoughts on the Chordal Concept. DAVISON 273–278
2507 Reuter, Fritz. Über die Lage des musiktheoretischen Unterrichts an den Ausbildungsstätten für Musik. MÜNNICH 58–65
2508 Riemann, Hugo. Giebt es Doppel-Harmonien? PEDRELL 315–319
2509 Schmiedel, Peter. Einiges über Konsonanz und Tonverwandtschaft. BESSELER 489–494
2510 Tirabassi, Antonio. Complément à la note présentée au Congrès de Musicologie de Bâle en 1924. Histoire de l'harmonisation, les trois règles. BORREN 292–307

THEORY & ANALYSIS: OPERA
See also nos. 1678, 1701, 1708, 1742, 1745

2511 Abert, Hermann. Vom Opernübersetzen. KRETZSCHMAR 1–5
2512 Albright, H. Darkes. Musical Drama as a Union of All the Arts. DRUMMOND 13–30
2513 Auden, Wystan H. Reflexion über die Oper. STRAVINSKY/70TH 59–64
2514 Hassall, Christopher. Words, Words. NEWMAN 108–123
2515 Hörth, Franz L. Der Wende-

punkt der Opernregie. UNIVERSAL 114–124
2516 Hoffmann, R. S. Die Operette. UNIVERSAL 204–211
2517 Middleton, Robert E. Opera Is Not What It Should Be. DAVISON 293–301
2518 Moser, Hans Joachim. Sciocchezze e saviezze del melodramma viste dal podio del direttore. MARINUZZI 113–138
2519 Vatielli, Francesco. L'Opera coi burattini. MÜLLER VON ASOW [222–225]

PERFORMANCE PRACTICE
See also nos. 175, 187, 402, 421, 573, 579, 746, 817, 851, 1012, 1121, 1201, 1230, 1361

2520 Daniel, Friedrich. Die Improvisation, eine versiegende Kunst. HILBER 70–75
2521 Fischer, Wilhelm. Die sogenannte Werktreue. PAUMGARTNER 12–16
2522 Gieseking, Walter. Intuition und Werktreue als Grundlagen der Interpretation. RAABE 154–157
2523 Göthel, Folker. Zur Praxis des älteren Violinspiels. SCHERING 96–105
2524 Grout, Donald J. On Historical Authenticity in the Performance of Old Music. DAVISON 341–347
2525 Gui, Vittorio. La Funzione dell'esecutore. MARINUZZI 47–68
2526 Haas, Joseph. Über die Kunst der Improvisation in der Musik. RAABE 158–159
2527 Handschin, Jacques. Über das Improvisieren. HANDSCHIN 327–331; orig. in Neue Zürcher Zeitung 991 (1926)
2528 Hoffmann, Hans. La Pratica dell'esecuzione musicale. MARINUZZI 69–111 (Italian translation of his article Aufführungspraxis in MGG without the bibliography and many of the illustrations)
2529 Koczirz, Adolf. Über die Fingernageltechnik bei Saiteninstrumenten. ADLER 164–167
2530 Kornauth, Egon. Theorie und Praxis. PAUMGARTNER 128–133
2531 Kroyer, Theodor. Zur Aufführungspraxis. SCHEURLEER 191–200
2532 Langner, Thomas M. Darstellungs-und ausdrucksbetonte Werkbilder. MERSMANN 83–90
2533 Laux, Karl. Dirigent, Diener oder Diktator? KONWITSCHNY 53–56

A. A. Heldal] BJØRNDAL 130–134; orig.
in *Fra Fjon til Fusa* (1949)
2568 ——. Nasjonalinstrumentet
hardingfela, 1651-1951. BJØRNDAL
33–38; orig. in *Univ. i Bergen Arbok*
(1950) Hist. Antikv. Rekke 3
2569 Boyden, David. The Tenor
Violin, Myth, Mystery, or Misnomer.
DEUTSCH/80TH 273–279
2570 Corrêa de Azevedo, Luis-Heitor.
La Guitare archaïque au Brésil.
BARTÓK/S 123–124
2571 Duhamel, Maurice. Les Harpes
celtiques. LOTH 178–185
2572 Emsheimer, Ernst. Die Streich-
leier von Danczk. MOBERG 109–117
2573 Fryklund, Daniel. Einige deutsche
Ausdrücke für *Geige*. ERDMANN 120–
125
2574 Handschin, Jacques. Das Klavi-
kord. HANDSCHIN 323–326; orig. in
Neue Zürcher Zeitung 258 (1929)
2575 Lorentz, H. A. De tonen van
de aeolusharp. MENGELBERG 143–151
2576 Luithlen, Victor. Klaviere von
Anton Walter in der Sammlung alter
Musikinstrumente des Kunsthistorischen
Museums in Wien. MÜLLER VON
ASOW [128–131]
2577 Meyer, Josef. Über die
physikalischen Grundlagen des
Grünwaldischen Volltonsystems zur
Resonanzverstärkung bei Saiteninstrumenten. GRÜNWALD 30–34
2578 Sachs, Curt. Der Ursprung der
Saiteninstrumente. SCHMIDT 629–634
2579 Salazar, Adolfo. La Guitarra,
heredera de la kithara clásica. ALONSO
118–126
2580 Schaeffner, André. Note sur la
filiation des instruments à cordes.
LAURENCIE 287–294
2581 Seewald, Otto. Die Lyredarstel-
lungen der ostalpinen Hallstattkultur.
OREL/70TH 159–171
2582 Simon, Alicja. Na drodze
historycznego rozwoju gęśli
słowiańskich; na marginesie odkrycia
wczesnohistorycznego w Gdańsku
1949 r. [The Historical Development
of the Slavic Gusle; On a Marginal
Discovery in 1949 of its Early
History in Gdańsk] CHYBIŃSKI/70TH
347–353
2583 Szulc, Zdzisław. Lutnicy polscy
od XVI wieku do czasów najnowszych
oraz ich karteczki rozpoznawcze;
zbiór materiałow do słownika lutników
polskich [Polish Violin and Lute

Makers from the 16th Century to
the Present Time and their Labels; A
Collection of Materials Leading to a
Dictionary of Polish Violin and Lute
Makers. CHYBIŃSKI/70TH 354–379
2584 Väisänen, A. O. Eräs
kanteletutkimus [A Kantele Study]
KROHN 163–183, German summary vi
2585 ——. A vepsze kantele/Die
Kantele der Wepsen. KODÁLY/60TH
337–342
2586 Viski, Károly. Hegedü/Hegedü,
Geige. KODÁLY/60TH 43–54
2587 Zingel, Hans J. Wandlungen im
Klang- und Spielideal der Harfe; zur
Geschichte des Instruments im 19.
Jahrhundert. SCHNEIDER/60TH 147–153

INSTRUMENTS: WIND
See also nos. 29, 45, 64, 77, 397, 827,
2192, 2224, 2447

2588 Closson, Ernest. Un Facteur
belge oublié, Nicolas-Marcel Raingo
de Mons. BORREN 140–148
2589 Ehmann, Wilhelm. Neue
Trompeten und Posaunen. WLH 58–63
2590 Kollmann, J. Flöten und Pfeifen
aus Alt-Mexico. BASTIAN 559–574
2591 Schmitz, Hans-Peter. Über die
Verwendung von Querflöten des 18.
Jahrhunderts in unserer Zeit.
SCHNEIDER/80TH 277–284
2592 Schneider, Marius. Bemerkungen
über die spanische Sackpfeife.
MERSMANN 129–130
2593 Stumpf, Carl. Trompete und
Flöte. KRETZSCHMAR 155–157

INSTRUMENTS: PERCUSSION
(INCLUDING CARILLONS)
See also nos. 28, 389, 397, 827, 2055,
2058

2594 Chapouthier, Fernand. Cybèle
et le tympanon étoilé. DUSSAUD II,
723–728
2595 Denyn, Jef. Beiaardklavieren.
DENYN 203–229
2596 ——. Technique et mécanisme
du carillon/Inrichting en behandeling
van het klokkenspel/Structure and
Handling of the Carillon. DENYN 123–
137/139–153/157–171
2597 ——. Wat zal de beiaard spelen?
DENYN 67–79
2598 Graiule, Marcel. Symbolisme des
tambours soudanais. MASSON I, 79–86

2632 ——. 75 Jahre Verband evangelischer Kirchenchöre Deutschlands. MAHRENHOLZ 262–283; orig. in *Musik und Kirche* 29 (1959)
2633 ——. Ich danke meinem Gott allezeit. MAHRENHOLZ 3–10
2634 ——. Die Kirchenmusik in der neuen Lutherischen Agende. MAHRENHOLZ 239–262; orig. in *Musik und Kirche* 25 (1955)
2635 ——. Kompendium der Liturgik zur Lutherischen Agende I. MAHRENHOLZ 295–405
2636 ——. Die Liedauswahl des Evangelischen Kirchengesangbuches. MAHRENHOLZ 545–564; orig. in his *Das Evangelische Kirchengesangbuch; ein Bericht* . . . (Kassel 1950)
2637 ——. Liturgiegeschichtliches aus dem Lande Hadeln. MAHRENHOLZ 521–542; orig. in *Stat crux dum volvitur orbis* (Berlin 1959)
2638 ——. Die Melodien des Evangelischen Kirchengesangbuches. MAHRENHOLZ 592–608; orig. in his *Das Evangelische Kirchengesangbuch; ein Bericht* . . . (Kassel 1950)
2639 ——. Orgel und Liturgie. MAHRENHOLZ 13–27; orig. in *Bericht über die dritte Tagung für deutsche Orgelkunst* (Kassel 1928)
2640 ——. Die Textfassung des Evangelischen Kirchengesangbuches. MAHRENHOLZ 564–592; orig. in his *Das Evangelische Kirchengesangbuch; ein Bericht* . . . (Kassel 1950)
2641 ——. Zum Kirchenmusikergesetz 1932. MAHRENHOLZ 643–649; in *Begründung des Kirchenmusikergesetzes im Landeskirchentage. Protokolle* . . . (Nov. 24 & 25, 1932)
2642 ——. Zur Begründung des Agendengesetzes vor der Hannoverschen Landessynode. MAHRENHOLZ 421–430
2643 ——. Zur musikalischen Gestaltung von Luthers deutscher Litanie. MAHRENHOLZ 169–195; orig. in *Lutherjahrbuch* (1937)
2644 ——. Zur neuen Gottesdienstordnung der Agende I vor der Generalsynode in Braunschweig. MAHRENHOLZ 405–421; orig. in *Nachrichten der evangelisch-lutherischen Kirche in Bayern* (1954)
2645 Mauersberger, Erhard. Thuringia cantat. MAUERSBERGER 76–83
2646 Mudde, Willem. Brief aus Holland. SÖHNGEN 169–171

2647 Reindell, Walter. Gregorianik und evangelische Liturgie. JOHNER 101–104
2648 Schönian, Hans G. Das kirchenmusikalische Aufbauwerk. SÖHNGEN 162–168
2649 Schröder, Rudolf A. Die Kirche und ihr Lied. SÖHNGEN 61–74
2650 Smend, Julius. Was ist evangelische Kirchenmusik? SCHEURLEER 303–312
2651 Söhngen, Oskar. Die Entwicklung der neuen evangelischen Kirchenmusik seit dem Fest der deutschen Kirchenmusik 1937. MAUERSBERGER 32–41
2652 ——. Kirchenmusik und Theologie. SCHNEIDER/80TH 335–342
2653 Straube, Karl. Kirchenmusikalisches Vermächtnis. MAUERSBERGER 132–134
2654 Thamm, Hans. Vererbung des Knabenchor-Ideals; Erziehung, Ausbildung, Leistung. MAUERSBERGER 138–141
2655 Voll, Wolfgang. Kirchenmusik und Schallplatte. WLH 53–57
2656 ——. Die Schallplatte im Dienste der Kirchenmusik. MAUERSBERGER 122–131
2657 ——. Das Wochenlied in katechetischer Sicht. WLH 67–75

CHURCH MUSIC: CATHOLIC
See also nos. 1417, 1737

2658 Drinkwelder, Erhard. Der musikalische Aufbau des Hochamtes. JOHNER 12–14
2659 Fellerer, Karl Gustav. Katholische Kirchenmusik und Musikforschung. SCHREMS 100–109
2660 ——. Kirchenmusik als Brauchtumsmusik. LEMACHER 30–37
2661 Jammers, Ewald. Choral und Liturgie. WAESBERGHE 89–99
2662 Köllner, George P. Der Mainzer Domchor als Träger der regensburger Tradition. SCHREMS 157–169
2663 Lueger, Wilhelm. Die geistige Situation der neuen katholischen Kirchenmusik. MERSMANN 94–96
2664 Moissl, Franz. Von neuer Kirchenmusik, Reaktionäres und Fortschrittliches. UNIVERSAL 169–191
2665 Overath, Johannes. Die Enzyklika *Musicae sacrae disciplina* vom 25. Dezember 1955 und der Komponist. LEMACHER 9–19
2666 ——. Erwägungen über das

C. AUTHOR AND SECONDARY-SUBJECT INDEX

A

Aarburg, Ursula, 243
Abeele, Gab. van den, 1677
Abert, Anna Amalie, 1465, 1995
Abert, Hermann, 40, 41, 844, 867, 2511; *1766*
Abraham, Gerald, 1470, 1641, 1663
Abraham, O., 2065
Abrégé alphabétique, Le Cocq, 995
Absolute pitch, 2338
Achilleus, Bruch, 1510
Ackere, J. van, 1944
Acoustics, 1561, 2322–2335, 2368, 2480, 2553, 2575, 2593; see also: Organs; Singing technique
Adam, Theo, 2620
Adam de la Halle, 233, 234
Adams, Nicholson B., 1403
Adams, S. M., 42
Adler, Guido, 399, 502, 2254; *1767*
Adolfs, Eug., 2336
Adorno, Theodor W., *1750*
Adrio, Adam, 991, 1012, 1038, 2621
Aebischer, Paul, 219
Aeolian harp, 2575
Aeschylus, 42
Aesthetics, 100, 103, 424, 1421, 1478, 2298, 2328, 2336–2396; H. Cohen, 2343; Heinse, 2354; Huber, 2357; Schweitzer, 1985; Stravinsky, 2002; Volkelt, 2389, 2390
Affections, doctrine of, 1110
African music, 2053a–2064
Agrippa of Nettesheim, 586
Ahle, Johann Rudolf, 793a
Aichinger, Gregor, 587
d'Alayrac, Nicolas, 1578
Albéniz, Isaac, 1489
Albenses, Codex, 220
Albert, Franz Joseph, 1262
Albrecht, Hans, 474, 611, 715
Albrechtsberger, Johann Georg, 1332
Albrici, Vincenzo, 923, 924
Albright, H. Darkes, 2512
Album für die Jugend, Schumann, 1655
Alceste, Floquet, 1350
Aldrich, Putnam, 746
Alexandru, Tiberiu, 2224
Alexis, Georges L. J., 1525a
Alewyn, Richard, 747
Alfonso X, The Wise, 266, 267
Alleluias, plainchant, 72, 159, 201, 202, 207,
218, 288; *Christus resurgens,* 186; *Dies sanctificatus,* 214, 215
Allgemeine Cäcilien Verband, Der, 2666
Allgemeine musikalische Zeitung, 1414
Allorto, Riccardo, 1369
Alsace (France), 1053
Alströmer, Patrik, 1138
Altmann, Wilhelm, 1172, 1346, 1375, 1404, 1678
Amades, Joan, 2685
Ambrosian chant, 123, 124, 1369
Ameln, Konrad, 918
Amerbach, Bonifacius, 515
American music, 1420, 1581
Amorós, José, 2337
An den Mond, Schubert, 1457
Analysis; see: Theory and analysis
Anchor che col partir, Rore, 718
Andel, G. G. van den, 244
Anderson, Emily, 1277, 1278
Andersson, Otto, 1065, 1116a, 2241, 2566
Andorfer, Eduard, 1154
Andrez, Benoît, 1333
Andries, M., 2397
Andromeda, Baumgarten, 927
Anglés, Higinio, 79, 80, 121, 132, 228, 229, 271, 272, 314–316, 347, 372, 388, 530, 565, 624, 683
Antica musica ridotta alla moderna prattica, L', Vicentino, 739
Antico, Andrea, 497
Antiphonaries, 165, 166
Anton Reiser, Moritz, 1372
Anton von Ysenburg, 429
Apel, Nikolaus, 455
Apel, Willi, 273, 274, 964
A poste messe, Lorenzo da Firenze, 329a
Apologie de la danse, de Lauze, 992
Arabian music, 2083, 2089, 2092, 2093
Ariane et Barbe-Bleue, Dukas, 1539
Aribo Scholasticus, 349, 366
Arlt, Wulf, 954
Arme Spielmann, Der, Grillparzer, 1568
Armide, Lully, 1003
Arnaud, François, 1046
Arnheim, Amalie, 1090
Arnold, Gustav, 1490
Aron (= Aaron), Pietro, 590
Ars perfecta (Coussemaker III, 28–35), 347
Arsunar, Ferruh, 2078
Art and music, 24, 222, 389, 392, 394, 397, 402, 410, 442, 543, 566, 569, 571, 584b, 764, 808, 1288, 1295, 1553, 2089a, 2093,

Fischer, Kurt von, 281, 321, 374, 570, 1238, 2455
Fischer, Pieter, 1024
Fischer, Wilhelm, 50, 145, 887, 2521
Fistula, 395
Flade, Ernst, 942
Flath, Walter, 2346
Flecha, Mateo, 624
Fleischauer, Günter, 126
Floquet, Etienne–Joseph, 1350
Florence (Italy), 444, 482
Florentius de Faxolis, 625
Floros, Constantin, 903
Flothius, Marius, 2456
Flutes, 397, 2121, 2224, 2590, 2591, 2593
Folk music, 571, 2029, 2030, 2035, 2038, 2041, 2043–2045, 2049, 2105a–2253, 2491; and "art" music, 169, 218, 464, 884, 1679, 2044, 2045, 2049, 2142, 2196; Austrian, 811, 2106–2126; Bulgarian, 2127–2130; Canadian, 2065, 2066, 2067; Danish, 2131, 2244; Egyptian, 2063; English, 2, 132, 2133; European, 1383, 2105a–2253; Finnish, 512, 1424, 2134, 2135; French, 607, 2136, 2137, 2157; Gaelic, 2230; German, 963, 1438, 2138–2156; Greek, 2157, 2158; Hungarian, 129, 562, 841, 842, 1429, 1881, 2136, 2161–2196, 2499; Italian, 2197–2202; Mexican, 2236; Norwegian, 1524, 1565, 1567, 1618, 2203–2217; Polish, 560, 2218-2222; Portuguese, 2223; Rumanian, 2170, 2224–2228; Russian, 2585; Scandinavian, 2566; Scottish, 2207, 2229, 2230; Slovakian, 2231, 2232; Spanish, 267, 535, 538, 2233–2240; Swedish, 2241–2245; Swiss, 2246, 2247; Turkish, 2078, 2248, 2249; United States, 2073; Yugoslavian, 2250–2253
Forbes, Elliot, 1326
Forelle, Die, Schubert, 1463
Forkel, Johann Nikolaus, 1074
Form, 872, 1973, 2221, 2450, 2452, 2454, 2461; see also names of individual forms
Formula missae et communionis, Luther, 672
Fornari, Matteo, 775
Fortassier, Pierre, 1822
Fortner, Wolfgang, 2404
Fournol, Etienne, 1415
Fox, Charles Warren, 591, 2457
Franceschi, Alfredo, 2347
Franck, Melchior, 962, 963
Fraternal organizations, 90
Frau Musica, Hindemith, 1845
Freemasonry and music, 1142
Freiberg (Germany), 2152
Freiburg (Switzerland), 569
Freising (Germany), 106, 1127
Freistedt, Heinrich, 146, 2405
Frescobaldi, Girolamo, 964
Frey, Michael, 1166
Fricke, Jobst Peter, 2326
Friedenssieg (1648), 814
Friederike Louise, Princess of Prussia, 1428
Friedlaender, Max, 1254, 1454, 1455, 1458, 2142
Friedrich, Wilfried, 2406
Friemann, Witold, 1947
Fritzius, Joachimus Fridericus, 626
Fritzsche, Gottfried, 627
Froberger, Johann Jakob, 966
Fröhlich, Friedrich Theodor, 1555
Frosch, Johannes, 501

Frotscher, Gotthold, 571, 1129
Frottola, 431, 456, 462, 464, 472, 669, 737
Frühlingsglaube, Schubert, 1461
Frye, Walter, 469
Fryklund, Daniel, 2573
Fuchs, Aloys, 2281
Fuchs, Carl, 2626
Fuchs, Ignaz Josef, 1351
Fuchs, Johannes, 2407
Fürnberg, Louis, 1825
Fugues, 845, 867–869, 906, 907, 1339, 1531; see also: Ricercars
Fujii, Seishin, 2084
Fuller-Maitland, John Alexander, 606
Furtwängler, Wilhelm, 1686
Fux, Johann Joseph, 898, 967

G

Gabrieli, Giovanni, 968
Gaforio, Franchino, 629–632
Gaisser, Hugo Athanas, 147
Galathea, Rist, 1057
Galimathias musicum, Mozart, 1222
Galitzin, Nikolas, 1278
Gallant style, 1137
Galley, Eberhard, 148
Gallican chant, 130
Gallicano, Prince of, 969
Gallico, Claudio, 737
Gálos, Rezsö, 1130
Garcia Matos, M., 2234
Gárdonyi, Zoltán, 868, 1592, 2169
Garms, J. H., 2495
Garros, Madeleine, 1023
Garsi, Santino, 780
Gassenhawerlin und Reutterliedlin, Egenolff, 518
Gastoué, Amédée, 950
Gatti, Guido, 1829
Gaubier de Barreau, 1164
Gaudeamus omnes in Domino, plainchant, 170
Gaultier, Ennemond, 970
Gavel, H., 412
Geburt unsers Herren Jesu Christi, Die, R. Michael, 679
Geck, Martin, 1609
Geering, Arnold, 282, 505, 647
Geiger, Albert, 619
Geiringer, Karl, 793a, 1192 1335, 1354
Geisslerlieder, 263
Geistliche Chormusik, Schütz, 1077
Gelats, Joan Amades, 2235
Generali, Pietro, 1557
Geneva (Switzerland), 1402
Gennrich, Friedrich, 149, 235
Georgiades, Thrasybulos, 1460
Georgius Anselmi, 393, 630
Gerber, Rudolf, 455, 670, 1078
Gerlach, Hermann, 23
Gérold, Théodore, 820, 1131
Gershwin, George, 1833
Gerson-Kiwi, Edith, 72, 456, 2085, 2085a
Gerstenberg Walter, 375, 413, 507, 728, 1223, 1239, 1459
Gestalt psychology, 2355, 2457
Geyer family, 971
Ghisi, Federico, 323, 457, 593, 1016, 2197, 2198
Giazotto, Remo, 600
Gibert, Vincents M. de, 1634
Gieseking, Walter, 2522
Gil, Bonifacio, 2236

AN ANGEL CONCERT IN A
TRECENTO SIENESE FRESCO

by FEDERICO GHISI

THE MUSICAL sources of the 14th century pertaining to Italian *Ars nova* that we know today are in codices and fragments that have been thoroughly studied and transcribed, although it is still possible that new material may turn up in addition to that uncovered in recent recades. The dearth of collections of music—in spite of the considerable amount composed in that period—may be somewhat mitigated by the paintings, about which art historians have written at length but not from a musical aspect. Indeed, 14th- and 15th-century Renaissance paintings on walls, wood, or canvas offer many examples of this sort, usually summarily described as "groups of angel musicians."

An important instance of this was brought to my attention by Giulio Cogni in the apse of the romanesque church of San Leonardo al Lago near Siena.[1] It is a superb 14th-century fresco of a choral and instrumental ensemble. Only ruins remain of this 12th-century Augustinian monastery that overlooks a plain that was a lake in ancient times (hence the name "al Lago"). The Blessed Augustine Novello, knight at the court of King Manfredi, retired to this monastery where he died and was buried in 1309. His miracles are the subject of Simone Martini's triptych in the sacristy of the Sienese church of San Agostino.

The fresco in the apse of the ancient church of San Leonardo al Lago shows various scenes from the life of the Virgin, among them the Annunciation, the Presentation in the Temple, and the Marriage. Encircling these are angel musicians holding instruments. So superb a Marian allegory deserves a closer examination and a more fitting description because of its specific relationship to music.

These frescoes have already been the subject of a study by Eve Borsook,[2] but purely as regards their place in Sienese paintings of the *tre-*

---

[1] I wish to express my most sincere gratitude to my friend, Giulio Cogni, who, because of my particular interest in the *Ars nova*, brought me to this place to see and to admire such an imposing figurative document of that period during the last Sienese Musical Week.

[2] Eve Borsook, *The Frescoes at San Leonardo al Lago*, in: *The Burlington Magazine*, Vol. 98 (October 1956).

cento. Despite lack of documentary evidence, they have been attributed to Lippo Vanni, a disciple of Ambrogio Lorenzetti. This attribution was recognized and confirmed by Bernard Berenson as well, and more recently by Enzo Carli, Superintendent of Monuments and Galleries of Siena,[3] because of some miniatures known to be Vanni's work and dating from 1345–72, the period of the frescoes of San Leonardo al Lago.

Eve Borsook compares the quality of their painting and their imposing majesty to the style of Simone Martini in the famous *Coronation of the Virgin* in the town hall of Siena. They are also comparable, in their architectural perspective and foreshortening, to those angel singers and musicians painted in the chapel of San Martino in the basilica of St. Francis in Assisi. The colors are especially typical of the Sienese school, ranging in delicate nuances from pale pink to a pastel yellow, and from madonna blue to an aquamarine green.

This concert of angels fills the four vaults of the apse of the church. In the foreground an angelic company sings and plays, absorbed in the majesty of a harmonious exaltation and jubilation dedicated to Mary; red- and blue-winged seraphim form the background. Such an ensemble, magnificent in number and variety, is like a modern arrangement of voices and orchestral instruments.

At the back (Pl.18a) is a group of singers and players of plucked, bowed, and keyboard instruments; in front (Pl.18b) are three soloists singing together in parts. To the right (Pl.18c) and left (Pl.18d) are still more instrumentalists, playing woodwind instruments, brasses, and a considerable number of drums. A more detailed description of each part may facilitate the allocation of this wonderful musical painting to its correct position in its historical period.

The triangular lunette shown in the background (Pl.18a) has six angels who sing as they play and a seventh who only sings. The instruments are those that made up the ensembles of the *trecento*. In the middle is a small portative organ, an instrument made famous by Landini in Florence, and played (as here shown) with the right hand on a keyboard of about two octaves, while the left hand works a bellows that blows air into the pipes. To its right, and at the left end of the performing group, are two players of the psaltery, a plucked instrument that appeared in Europe about the 13th century and was made in two different styles. The first is in the form of a symmetrical trapezoid with two straight and two concave sides, while the second is a rectangular trapezoid shaped like a wing,

[3] I am indebted to the kindness of Prof. Enzo Carli for the photographs that he reproduced, and I thank him sincerely for having given me permission to make these the objects of study and publication.

a form we later find repeated in the bodies of harpsichords and pianos. The players pluck the strings with the index and middle fingers of the right hand, while in the left is held a plectrum made like a tiny hammer, showing the polyphonic character of the instrument.

The second and sixth figures in the row (from left to right) are playing lutes: the former holds a large lute exquisitely decorated in arabesques, and the latter a similar but smaller one, equally ornamented, which is a *mandora*, an instrument of Moorish origin in use in the West after the 13th century. Both are plucked instruments: the index finger is used with the first one, and the thumb and index with the second, where also the position of the left hand on the neck of the lute may be clearly seen.

The next angel is the only one playing a *fidula*, the ancient vielle with flat elongated body and played with a curved bow. The fingers of both hands are quite distinct, those of the right holding the bow, while those of the left press the strings against the fingerboard of the instrument. The four tuning pegs are easily discernible too. The mouths of six of these angelic musicians are open as they sing, while the seventh singer—arms crossed on breast—holds no instrument.

The triangular lunette in front (Pl.18b) holds three angels singing together polyphonically. Each of the two groups on either side of them is made up of one angel swinging a thurible of incense and two others carrying torches, the whole giving the painting a proper air of mysticism.

Studying the two flanking lunettes, we find the one on the right of particular interest because of its instrumental ensemble. A double straight oboe (the double *aulos*, which still existed in Europe after the 5th century) may be distinguished among the wind instruments, played by the second angel from the left. The second angel on the right plays a shawm or bombard (*chalemie*), a sort of primitive oboe with conical wooden bore, whose joyful sound was similar to that of the *piffero*, a folk instrument still used in southern Italy.

As for the brasses in the center, the angel on the left blows a long straight trumpet (which he holds in the right hand), conical in form and ending in a bell: such trumpets are associated with heralds or with the Day of the Last Judgment. The angel on the right plays a shorter trumpet, cylindrical in form, whose bell is turned up.

The large percussion section is made up of a singing angel (on the left) who also plays a tambourine having small jingles around its circumference, another angel (on the extreme right) who clashes together two brass cymbals, and two others (on either side of the trumpeters) who beat kettledrums, holding a heavy drum-stick in each hand.

There is a similar scene in the lunette on the left (Pl.18d) where an angel in the middle beats a kettledrum with sticks that are thicker at the held end than at the end that strikes the drum's surface. Flanking him are angels holding long, straight trumpets to their mouths. At each end of this row of musicians is an angel in a meditative pose, arms crossed on breast, and next to them stands still another musician: the one on the right plays a bombard, such as we have seen in Plate 18c, while the one on the left clearly shows his instruments to be the pipe and tabor, or one-handed drum and flute. The pipe (held in one hand) has three holes, two in front and one in back, and the range of an octave. The other hand is thus free to wield a stick (which is larger at the held end) against the leather head of a small round drum (called "tabor" in England and "tambourine" in Provence). As may be seen in the fresco, the drum is fastened with a strap to the player's waist or left arm, and so here is partially hidden.

In the description of this ensemble the absence of the harp will be noticed: it was much more used in northern Europe, but was also well known among the Italian *Ars nova* musicians, as is proved through the *Saporetto* of Prodenziani and other writings of the *trecento*, where it is mentioned.

Instruments like those described here are to be found in the famous *Manesse* manuscript (Heidelberg), delineated to show their characteristic shapes. Here are the psaltery, fidula, and bombard, to name only a few, such as are in the *Trionfo della morte* in the Campo Santo at Pisa and held by angelic musicians in the *Incoronazione di Maria* (1335) by Taddeo Gaddi (school of Giotto) in the church of Santa Croce. The double oboe and the mandora are depicted in Simone Martini's *Consacrazione a cavaliere di San Martino* in the church of St. Francis at Assisi (1330), and the portative organ in Andrea da Firenze's *Trionfo della Chiesa* in the Spanish Chapel (1360-70) of Santa Maria Novella, Florence. Musical ensembles such as those that figure in Italian frescoes of the *trecento* were also painted during the 15th century (but with a greater number of instruments) by Flemish and German artists. Of the end of the *quattrocento* is the admirable painting by Girolamo di Benevento (Sienese school) in the parish church of the Nativity in Montalcino (Siena), in which angels play the double oboe, lute, psaltery, fidula, and mandora. It seems that the painters of that time must have felt obliged, when depicting a scene of praise and thanksgiving to the Virgin, to encircle it with an angelic choir playing on instruments. In fact, the Italian *quattrocento* abounds in such tributes to Mary. To mention only a few of the more famous ones containing angelic musicians: those of Fra Angelico da Fiesole and of Sano di Pietro in the *Incoronazione di Maria* at the Louvre in Paris and also in Siena; the *Madonna Enthroned* at Siena by Giovanni di Paolo, and those by Bernardino Butinone and Bernardino Zenale in San Martino at Treviglio. Others, on the theme of the Assumption or the Madonna and Child, are the paintings by Signorelli in the Cathedral of Perugia, works of Bartolomeo Montagna and Giovanni Bellini, always remembering the sumptuous angel concerts by Giovanni Boccati da Camerino at Perugia, and by Sassetta in Berlin.

Did the artist paint these musical instruments purely from his imagination, or do they correspond to actual instruments of the period? Their forms as shown are certainly of instruments that were played. Were they all played at the same time in those stately concerts?

What we know of the *trecento* musical repertory lets us attempt an interpretation of the four frescoes of the complete Marian cycle described above. Actually, Plate 18a offers a clear contrast between vocal and instrumental polyphony, except for one single part that is sung in monophony. This would lead one to suppose that in chanting the Litany of Loreto in honor of the Madonna, with antiphons such as *Ave Maria* and *Ave Regina coelorum*, the solo voice would alternate with a choir singing in unison, while the instruments accompany the singing.

Plate 18b suggests a three-part polyphonic lauda of three voices sung by a trio of angels. At least fifteen such Marian lauds are in the 13th-century monophonic *Laudario 91* of Cortona. Later documents (of the 14th century) attest that sacred texts were set to secular melodies, an example of which is the lauda *Creata fusti o Vergine Maria* sung by three voices (as in the fresco) to Landini's ballata, *Questa fanciulla amor.*[4] Then there is the lauda to the Virgin, *Appresso al volto chiaro*, which was sung to the music of the well-known madrigal by Giovanni da Cascia, *Appresso a un fiume chiaro*, and also Jacopo da Bologna's lauda in praise of the Virgin, *Nel mio parlar di questa donn'eterna*, which has two instrumental parts that harmonize with the singing, just as we see in these frescoes.

Musical compositions in honor of Mary are not numerous in the *trecento*, but gradually increase from the beginning of the 15th century along with a growing iconographical documentation. Petrarch's *Vergine bella* was set by several composers, beginning with Dufay, and so were Latin hymns in praise of the Virgin. At the same time, the instrumental repertory *ad modum tubae* was growing, using woodwinds and brass along with percussion, as is shown in this very fresco, which was painted

[4] Federico Ghisi, *Gli Aspetti musicali della lauda fra il XIV e il XV secolo*, in: *Natalicia musicologica Knud Jeppesen* (Copenhagen 1962), pp. 51–54.

at a time when very few musical documents were in existence that contained this repertory.[5]

In Plate 18c, trumpets, double oboes, bombards, cymbals, and kettledrums accompany a solo singer who is playing a tambourine. Such an unusual and varied combination of sounds would seem to be that of the music of *Ars nova;* or would it be merely an allegorical representation of religious texts such as the hymns glorifying God and His exalted Mother, sung to the accompaniment of organ, kettledrums, triangles, cymbals, flutes, and psaltery in a song of hallelujah? In any case, the section in Plate 18d without doubt anticipates an instrumental composition *ad modum tubae,* the percussion underlining the rhythm.

In its entirety, the fresco at San Leonardo al Lago portrays a truly superb orchestra whose startling sound effects would surely be those of an *Ars nova* concert. Polyphonic singing, brasses, and drums provide sharp differences in rhythm and timbre, contrasting strongly with a single singing voice accompanied by only the light plucking of stringed instruments. This sound must have had a truly modern flavor.

[Translated by Elizabeth Hunter Merrill]

---

[5] See, for example, the Tuba Heinrici de Libero Castro, *Virgo dulcis atque pia,* with two instrumental "contratenor and tenor tube" ("Laudate cum in sono tube") in Charles Van den Borren, *La Musique pittoresque dans le Ms. 222 C 22 de la Bibliothèque de Strasbourg,* in: *Bericht Musikwiss. Kongress* (Basel 1924), pp. 93–100.

EARLY MUSIC
PERFORMANCE TODAY

by NOAH GREENBERG

SURELY I MAY speak for all performers of early music in the
United States, both professional and amateur, when I say that
Gustave Reese's lifelong and monumental work in the music
of the Middle Ages and the Renaissance has served, and continues to
serve, as our basic and trusted guide to the musical literature of these two
great eras in European history. In my own case, when I first came to his
publications, I was a mere enthusiast; but it was the extraordinary impact
of his work that persuaded me to devote my entire life to the study and
performance of this music.

The two volumes that summarize Reese's work, *Music in the Middle
Ages* and *Music in the Renaissance*, not only opened up six or seven centuries of music hitherto known only to certain scholars in the United
States, but also gave us insight into almost every aspect of the creation
and making of music in European civilization. There is no problem of
any kind associated with the music of these two periods that cannot be
usefully approached through the comments, direct or oblique, that Reese
has made on it, as well as via the references, accurate and detailed, that
his publications so abundantly supply.

Indeed, it is in supplying these very references to the primary and
secondary sources of the musical literature that his two works have perhaps been of the greatest help to American performers. In the past, unfortunately, there has been a traditional fear of rigorous scholarship among
practical musicians, a fear that has often led them to ignore scholarly
work and its products altogether, or to be satisfied with the few "samples" of Renaissance music that made their tired and repetitious appearances in the traditional "collections." Rare was the practical musician
who studied his score directly from the scholarly edition. Reese's publications, I think, have helped change this situation by constantly directing
the reader to the sources and encouraging him to go see for himself. This
attitude has been of enormous service to both scholars and performers.
It has, in some cases, served to introduce one to the other and persuaded

both to shake hands and start to talk. It is therefore no longer so uncommon, for example, for a choral conductor to go directly to the *Opera omnia* of Dufay to study a motet or a Mass. Certainly the "collections" no longer exert the influence they once did; certainly performers feel much less inhibited about going directly to the "complete works" of a given composer.

The results of this are plain to see throughout the United States today. There are now hundreds of small choirs, madrigal groups, and vocal and instrumental ensembles that perform a great deal of medieval and Renaissance music. The programs given, and given very often in public, are very impressive in content. A decade ago, and earlier, one would have been happy to find any piece of earlier music represented at a concert. Now, by contrast, programs may be entirely drawn from this literature, and their contents carefully planned to produce a cohesive grouping:

Music for the Medici	An Elizabethan Concert
Burgundian Court Music	A Monteverdi Program
Machaut and His Contemporaries	

Since, in most cases, this music is not now available in practical editions, the inference is clear: the performers have gone for their programs directly to the scholarly sources.

Because a goodly number of musicians have become seriously—and in more and more cases professionally—interested in earlier music, we are happily being made increasingly aware of the dozens of styles contained in this repertory, styles that differ radically from those heard in the music of the "standard" repertory. This awareness has had, I believe, an important effect on the listening habits of the concert public as well as on the nature of the demands it is beginning to make on those who draw up programs.

Amusingly enough, it was not the givers of conventional concerts who opened up their programs to the repertory of early music, but the record companies—and, for the most part, not the large record companies (who could have easily afforded to do it) but the small ones, who could not afford to hire the virtuoso ensembles and artists needed to sell recordings of the standard repertory. Given the LP record and a restricted operating budget, the small companies were drawn to the modest (and modestly priced) ensembles of the practitioners of earlier music. The partnership was an extraordinarily happy one. Not only is the general public now familiar with sonorities and repertory both of which were largely unknown two decades ago, but what began as a curious interest in new music and timbres has now broadened and deepened into a cultivated awareness of musical styles. Today there is a new tolerance in public listening and understanding, a tolerance that may even be extending itself into a demand for the curious novelties of contemporary sounds. Certainly the tyrannical monopoly of the standard repertory has been seriously weakened.

The unexpected blossoming of the performance of medieval and Renaissance music, welcome and refreshing as it is, has come with striking suddenness, a suddenness that has produced a new set of problems arising out of new relationships of performance and scholarship. The developments in the field of musical performance have been so numerous and have happened so quickly that certain aspects of scholarly work have not kept pace. Whereas performers for decades felt free to ignore the patient and adventurous labors of musical scholars, today it is the performers who are making adventurous demands upon scholarship, without whose guidance their undertakings are unduly perilous. Before our performers journey too far, I think the scholarly world should be apprised of their course.

Musicians, especially musicians who are willing to seek out new music and prepare it for performance, are an imaginative group. Those who have undertaken to prepare works of Josquin Des Prez, for instance, are now naturally interested in doing his works as "correctly" as possible. In most cases, they know how to find the available editions and identify the acceptable ones. They schedule many rehearsals, and they bring a great deal of energy and enthusiasm to their work. But beyond the bare transcription of the notation and (perhaps) a few tentative suggestions for performance, what guidance does the scholar give? Sad to say, the answer is very little. The performer has seen a few references to the use of instruments around 1500, but how does he apply the available information to the cases at hand? He has heard that the sizes of most court and chapel choirs were "small," but how small? He has heard that sections of these works were sometimes sung with solo voices that may have alternated with the choir, but which sections and what solo voices? He has been led to believe that the singers of Josquin's day ornamented their melodies, but where can he hope to learn how this might have been done? He is confronted with the staggering problem of adding accidentals, or he puzzles over relationships of tempos within one movement that is partly in duple, partly in triple time. All of these are important matters, and for performers very urgent ones, and there are many more. Perhaps there can never be definitive answers; but it is obvious that much scholarly work can be profitably devoted to questions such as these, questions that performers are asking, and asking now.

Lacking help, the imaginative performer will have no choice but to experiment and seek his own answers. The pity is that without scholarly guidance many of the solutions he will find may have more grace than wisdom.

Experiment without direction can produce two opposite sets of results. On the one hand, the performer's enthusiasm for experimenting with sonorities may lead him too far astray. As a case in point, let me mention a performance of a Fayrfax motet from the Eton choir manuscript that the New York Pro Musica gave a few years back. The work was executed by ten musicians—five singers, and five instrumentalists doubling the vocal lines in unison. A scholar who was acquainted with the Eton choir manuscript made a helpful criticism of our performance based on his firm belief, after careful study of available evidence, that instruments had not originally been used in these works. I then restudied the piece in the light of this scholar's comments and became convinced that the motet should have been performed by a small choir and a group of five solo voices.

On the other hand, the performer may find himself far too conservative. Years ago, I studied a *Salve Regina* of Francisco Guerrero and was persuaded at the time that the texture of this polyphonic antiphon implied an *a cappella* rendition. It therefore came as quite a shock to me recently to read Guerrero's rules for performance as they have been found in the Seville Cathedral archives.[1] One of the instructions states that "at Salves, one of the three verses that are played shall be on shawms, one on cornetts, and the other on recorders; because always hearing the same instrument annoys the listener." Obviously, therefore, it was Guerrero's practice in Seville to perform the *Salve Regina* with instruments as well as voices.

I believe that scholars could, to the benefit of all performers, profitably undertake work in two directions. There is, first, an urgent need for articles and books on a host of subjects. Besides those I have already mentioned, we need, for example, a great deal more study of early instruments. We must have detailed investigations into their history, construction, and manners of tuning. We need to know much more about the techniques of playing them and about the circumstances under which the various instruments were used. Far too often, research into matters of this sort has been left as the province of amateur scholars, who lack the background and the experience to give us precise and reliable scholarly information.

[1] Robert Stevenson, *Spanish Cathedral Music in the Golden Age* (Berkeley & Los Angeles 1961), p. 167.

I also think it is pressingly important for us to learn a great deal more about the singers of medieval and Renaissance times. How were they trained? What kind of sounds did they produce? What, exactly, were the choral organizations to which they belonged, and what were the sizes of these groups? A small beginning on research in this field has been made, to be sure; but much remains to be done before the practical musician can be assured of being able to give a performance that comes closer to the original conditions.

To some scholars, of course, knotty matters like musica ficta and proportion may seem purely theoretical problems; but to the performer they are burning issues, and I think it is fair to say that most of us who try to face them are equipped only to dabble in their solutions.

Besides articles and books on these and many other matters (and I should like to see them appear with much greater frequency and in much greater quantity during the coming decades), there is another kind of publication I think scholars must now undertake. I speak of the practical edition, prepared by the professional scholar. On no account, of course, would such an edition be a substitute for the scholarly one, for which the continuing need is self-evident and beyond challenge. But I believe that scholars should accept the responsibilities of preparing practical editions for at least two reasons. First, practical editions are currently being prepared by people whose knowledge, background, and experience do not fully qualify them for the tasks. Second, the preparation of practical editions would offer scholars the chance to put forward many suggestions for performance that could not—and should not—properly be included in the scholarly edition, suggestions that would greatly assist the practical musician and that would be received by him with enthusiasm.

If this kind of research and publication is now necessary and timely, that fact can, in my opinion, largely be attributed to the stimulus the work of Gustave Reese has given to the development of vast and radical changes in the American musical scene. Now that his enthusiasm and guidance have made it possible for the performance of medieval and Renaissance music to take its proper place in our musical life, I hope that he, and others, will find the time, energy, and resources to continue the work which they have so well begun.

TRADITION AND INNOVATION IN INSTRUMENTAL USAGE 1100–1450

by *FRANK Ll. HARRISON*

INTRODUCTION

WHILE musicologists continue to discuss in meticulous detail the written records of medieval music, they seldom have anything to say about its realization in sound. Such information as the possibilities and alternatives of medium, tempo, style and treatment, instrumental techniques, numbers of performers, preferred acoustical conditions—in short, the kind of information considered essential to the performance of later and more familiar music—is thought not to be in the normal province of the medievalist. Orthodox tradition in medieval musicology has long since determined its requirements for establishing musical texts by collation of manuscripts and study of their notation, though it is still not unanimous about the kinds of transcription into modern notation that communicate the meaning of the original with the minimum of distortion. Unlike musicologists concerned with some later eras, however, medievalists have as yet barely broached the subject known in Germany as *Aufführungspraxis*. The results of the absence of even the most elementary notions of performance practice may sometimes remind one of Angela Thirkell's headmistress Miss Sparling, who countered her history mistress's objections to anachronistic costumes in a proposed show with the words: "*Anything* looks nice in a pageant; why shouldn't Boadicea wear green tights and a yellow wig?"

Though the term "Middle Ages" has value as a pedagogical convenience, it needs to be stressed, particularly in the context of musical instruments, that there is no such entity as "medieval music." We have come to expect a certain degree of historical precision on such subjects as modal notation, the style of the Italian *trecento*, and the evolution of the cantus-firmus Mass. Nevertheless, the history of instruments is too often dealt with as if there were indeed an entity that could be called medieval organology—an idea just as invalid as the supposition that the history of post-1500 instruments could be treated as an undivided whole.

319

Likewise, when the name of a particular instrument crops up at various points over a period of half a millennium, comparison with the instrumental history of the past four centuries and a half should warn us that it would be misleading to assume that the same concept of sound and technique was still operative at the end of the period as at the beginning.

The shyness of historians of medieval music on questions to do with the practice of their material is due in large part to the difficulty of giving a clear answer to two related questions: (1) How did instruments participate in written music, both monophonic (apparently) and polyphonic? and (2) What assumptions about performance are to be derived from the partial absence of words in polyphonic music? It is not the object of this paper to make definitive pronouncements on either of these questions. Complete answers to them would certainly be as complex as would the answers to similarly sweeping questions about performance in later centuries. The sort of evidence that ideally we should like to have about performance—intelligent and detailed description by a musical observer (like Berlioz) whose presuppositions and standpoint are ascertainable, exact information about tone quality, balance, ornamentation, improvisation, and so on—does not exist for any period anterior to the age of recording. Nor is it completely communicable in words even by the most practiced observer. Of the kinds of evidence that exist for our period—written music, archives and chronicles, iconography and imaginative writing—only the first has as yet been investigated systematically in depth. In particular cases musical historians have drawn on the accounts of states, households, and religious communities, and on descriptions by contemporary chroniclers, often with notable results. However, not nearly enough has been done to enable these instances to be added up to a coherent account of the changing musical activities of the various levels of society to which they refer. Research in musical iconography has still many serious gaps in its coverage; in addition, the difficulty of estimating its documentary as distinct from artistic value limits its application to many questions concerning the instrumental usage both of written and unwritten musical tradition. It is rarely taken into account that the written music of any time represents only the top of the iceberg that stands for musical events as a whole. We are accustomed to considering music as sacred or secular, polyphonic or monophonic, vocal or instrumental, texted or untexted, but scarcely at all as written or unwritten. For the centuries under discussion, it is particularly instrumental practice outside the church that belongs to the invisible part of the iceberg. Evidence about it cannot be direct, but indirect evidence may be drawn from comparable practices of the unwritten traditions where they still exist, as well as from documents and depictions, properly evaluated. The purpose of this essay is to discuss the chief elements of continuity and change in instrumental usage between 1100 and 1450, and to relate them to musical style and practice as found in ascertainable records, and in unwritten tradition as far as this may be deduced.

INSTRUMENTS AND THE ECCLESIASTICAL TRADITION

ALL ECCLESIASTICS of whatever rank had as their first duty the daily rehearsing of the liturgy. This was both an act of worship and an act of ritual, self-validating in the degree to which it conformed to a pre-ordered pattern. The performance of music in ritual, as distinct from in a concert hall, is to some degree analogous to performance of popular music, the nature of which is succinctly put by Jacques Chailley: "La musique populaire, dans de nombreuses circonstances, est comme ces discours officiels dont le but n'est pas d'être écoutés, mais prononcés." [1] Organized religion, provided it has a compact priesthood concerned to conserve its ritual tradition, has no more need for written texts than popular tradition, which admits of infinite variation. However, Western monasticism and the Carolingian reorganization brought such an increase in the number of communities practicing a more or less uniform Christian rite (i.e. in the number of its consumers) as to necessitate written authorities for text, music, and ritual action. In such communities musical instruments found acceptance only in two clearly defined contexts. In the context of ceremonial the organ was associated with certain new interpolations in the ritual (it was an essential concomitant in the performance of the Sequence); monochord, organistrum, and tuned bells [2] were adjuncts to the teaching that was so important a function of many of the larger institutions. Throughout the period with which we are concerned it was the ritual function of a relatively large organ, placed always on a screen in a gallery (see Pl. 19a), to alternate with the choir in festive choral—not solo—plainsong,[3] generally monophonically with

---

[1] *Journal of the International Folk Music Council,* XVI (1964), 48.

[2] On the David page in the Hunterian Psalter in Glasgow University Library (reproduced in *The New Oxford History of Music,* III, London 1960, Pl. VII) fifteen bells are arranged in two series—a hexachord running from left to right marked *Ut* to *La* and another from right to left similarly marked; in the middle are three bells, two marked *Fa* and *Mi,* with an unnamed one between which would be *Sol* or *La* depending on the direction from which it was approached.

[3] The 13th-century encyclopedist Bartholomaeus Anglicus said of the term *organum:* "specialiter cum appropriatum est de instrumento ex multis composito fistulis cui folles adhibentur; utitur iam ecclesia in prosis sequentibus [*sic:* other versions have "et in"] sequenciis et ymnis, propter abusum ystrionum reictis aliis fere instrumentis." (Bodleian Library, MS Bodley 749, fol. 280ᵛ) The *histriones* had probably been actors in liturgical plays. The forms Bartholomaeus specifies as those

probably some recognized forms of ornamentation. In the clausula, the new category of non-ritual music for solo ensemble around 1200, a small positive organ was almost certainly used to play the tenor under one or two vocalized parts. Following the process which turned a set of clausulae into a motet—merely a matter of words in place of vocalization —it may be assumed that the organ continued to be used, though not necessarily always, to play the tenor until the isorhythmic cantus-firmus motet ceased to be cultivated just about 1450. In the meantime the earlier "teaching" instruments had given way by about 1400 to instruments with keys that not only activated the sound but also represented visually the formation of the hexachords. Unlike the monochord, the organistrum has possibilities as a means of musical expression. It seems also to have been used in secular circles at least until the advent of stringed keyboards. Since then it has survived vigorously in rural France, and to some extent in Spain and in Eastern Europe.

SECULAR INSTRUMENTS IN THE 12TH CENTURY

IN THE 12TH CENTURY for the first time some of the fashionable domestic music of one particular group in Western society—the great seigneurs of the Midi—was written down, presumably when the possession of a *chansonnier* became one of the marks of a household with cultivated and sophisticated pursuits. (The prestige value of a house *chansonnier* may also be connected with the fact that many of the troubadours were high-born amateurs.) The instrument most likely to have been used by troubadours and their jongleurs in performing dances and dance-like songs is the three-stringed short-necked oval fiddle.[4] The degree of use in music played before aristocrats in the 12th century of instruments such as the mandora and psaltery, derived from middle Eastern types, is unknown, as is also that of indigenous instruments like fipple flutes and bagged and mouth-blown reeds. On the evidence of the late troubadour romance *Flamenca*, both of these kinds were played at a princely wedding banquet where some 1,500 musicians are said to have assembled.[5] It may be assumed that both types were also played by traveling jongleurs at great commercial congregations such as the fairs held in the Champagne towns. Panpipes always appear in the rustic or pastoral

in which the organ was used are precisely those specified in some ordinals of the time; see F. Ll. Harrison, *Music in Medieval Britain* (London 1958), pp. 205–06.
    [4] See, e.g., F. Ll. Harrison and Joan Rimmer, *European Musical Instruments* (New York 1965), Pl. 45; the term "fiddle" will be used here instead of "viol," which is properly reserved for the post-1500 instrument with frets.
    [5] Quoted in Harrison & Rimmer, *European Musical Instruments*, pp. 14–15.

context with which they were already associated in classical times.[6] The northern European lyre-forms (e.g. the *rotta*) were well known in mid-European monastic circles from at least the 8th century, notably along the routes of Irish missionary monasticism. Judging from the number of remains of lyres found in graves, the instrument was also in use among Germanic tribes, who probably already possessed it for many centuries. The application of the new sound-producing principle of the bow to this most ancient stringed instrument (seen in the David of one of the St. Martial tropers)[7] was not in the long run a successful one. Its only place of survival today is in some Baltic countries.

The spread of monastic learning from the north, with its strong elements of classical and new secular poetry, may also have given an important impetus to the development of the harp into the relatively wide-range instrument of the 12th century, with its rigid frame and large soundbox.[8] Its traditional use was to bring musical dignity to the recitation of epics. In the *Flamenca* banquet heroic lais were told with harp, fiddle, or other instrument, and *l'us diz los motz e l'autrels nota*.

The strong resemblance of such percussion instruments as clappers and cup-shaped cymbals to classical depictions suggests copying from antique models rather than representation of current practice.

SECULAR INSTRUMENTAL PRACTICE IN THE 13TH CENTURY

HALF A CENTURY before the suppression by successive religious crusades (1209–40) of the civilization that had cultivated lyric poetry in the Provençal language, the new courtly romances and epics of the trouvères were already being written in the Angevin empire, especially in the court that Eleanor of England and Aquitaine set up on her return to Poitiers about 1170. The trouvère poet-composers who in the 13th century poured out the smaller forms of lyric song on courtly themes included the noble of birth, the worldly cleric, the professional musician, and the cultured burgher, as did their clientèle. A cross-section of written music of trouvère provenance and influence would include, besides the lyric song, the secular motet and the polyphonic chanson. The instrument which most evidence points to as having been associated with performance of these genres is the large five-stringed oval fiddle, which is quite evidently a 13th-century development. This is certainly the instrument John of Grocheo, writing about 1300, had in mind when he

---

[6] In the Ivrea Psalter (11th c.) David as shepherd is depicted playing panpipes.
[7] Paris, Bibliothèque Nationale, MS lat. 1118, fol. 109.
[8] Harrison & Rimmer, *European Musical Instruments*, Pl. 46.

observed that "a good artist introduces every song or dance tune and every kind of music generally on the *viella*."[9] Jerome of Moravia's information on the tuning and fingering technique of the two-stringed *rubeba* and the five-stringed *viella*[10] unfortunately cannot be checked, since there is nothing else on this subject in the whole of our three centuries and a half. Jerome first described an instrument with a re-entrant tuning, the off-the-fingerboard bourdon string (d) being a fifth higher than the lowest fingered string. The three others were tuned to g and duplicated d^1. He pointed out that e and f were supplied an octave higher on the doubling fourth and fifth strings. Although he held that this instrument fulfilled every modern need, it is obvious that with its gapped scale it would not have done for the tenor of most motets. His second "tuning" is not merely another tuning but another instrument, with five strings on the fingerboard and the full compass of the Guidonian hand (Γ to d^2)— a good multipurpose instrument, which the other is not. On the other hand, just such an instrument is shown as one of the "song-school" instruments in the upper part of a David page in a manuscript of the theorist Lambertus[11] and in an *Exultate* initial of about the same time (Pl. 19b). In both, the player has his thumb on the inside of the bourdon string as if in the act of plucking it. Perhaps this form of *viella* was useful for demonstrating intervals, as the organistrum may have been earlier. In general, however, Jerome's first instrument seems right for certain tunes, played as he described with the bourdon string bowed (or plucked with the thumb) only when it made a consonance with a note played on another string, while the instrument with five fingered strings and a completely contiguous range could play all kinds of music, from dance tunes at the high pitch of earlier smaller fiddles to the low-pitched written dances and sustained-note tenors. Its long bow and large body must have given it the substantial tone needed for part playing. It seems the right choice for pieces like the five three-part wordless "motets"— clausulae out of due time, on the assumption that the earlier clausulae were self-sufficient instrumental or vocalized pieces—in the Bamberg manuscript, one of which is inscribed "In seculum viellatoris." On such a fiddle (or on an organ with appropriate range) would have been played the tenor of secular motets, whereas in a sacred motet in church only the organ would have done this.

---

[9] *Der Musiktraktat des Johannes de Grocheo*, ed. E. Rohloff (Leipzig 1943), p. 52.
[10] E. de Coussemaker, *Scriptorum de musica*, I (Paris 1864), 152–53.
[11] In the upper right hand corner of fol. A^v in Paris, Bibl. Nat., MS lat. 6755 (2); the page is reproduced in MGG, VIII (1960), Tafel 3.

The new instrumental sounds that must have been more and more heard in the West in this century were the result of the infiltration of Arab musical usage. In the Seventh Crusade (1250) St. Louis already had his trumpets and drums, as Jean de Joinville related.[12] Matthew Paris (d.1259) illustrated his account of the reception of Richard Earl of Cornwall and King of the Romans (younger brother of Henry III of England) at Cremona in 1241 with a drawing of one of the sights of the occasion. This was an elephant going before Richard by order of the Emperor Frederick II of Hohenstaufen carrying two trumpeters, a drummer, and a player of double pipes, while the driver of the elephant ("magister bestie") sounded a large handbell.[13] The early use of trumpets and drums in the West was for heralding the ceremonious movements and occasions of royalty and high nobility. The particular instrument of heralds was the high-pitched clarion (clairon), while the long trumpet (busine) seems to have been played at such court events as tournaments and banquets. With the increasing use of the imperious sound of clarions to punctuate events of high social ritual, players of these instruments became indispensable to the entourage of persons of high rank. They and the trumpeters were the most highly regarded and the best paid of the growing new class of "minstrels"—properly so called because they were paid members of the retinue (*ministerium*) of great personages. Playing individually or in groups—in contrast to the earlier competitive individualism of jongleur and harper—the *ministralli*, a term that included heralds, trompours, nakerers, harpers, pipers, tabourers, etc., etc., formed themselves into guilds. They thus became the *organized* keepers and transmitters of an unwritten repertory and the art and craft of playing it.

Other instruments with known Arab antecedents which were domesticated in the West in the 13th century were the psaltery (sometimes made in trapezoid form but usually in the uniquely European pig's-head shape) and the mandora, both plectrum plucked.

INSTRUMENTAL PRACTICE FROM 1300 TO 1450

IN CONTRAST to the feudal civilization of the Atlantic northwest the civilization of northern Italy was manifested in independent cities which still carried on the city culture of late antiquity. Their prosperity may

---

[12] "Là où j'estoie à pié et mi chevalier, aussi bleciez comme il est devant dit, vint li roys à toute sa bataille, à grant noyse et à grant bruit de trompes et nacaires, et se aresta sur un chemin levei," from: Jean Sire de Joinville, *Histoire de Saint Louis*, ed. N. de Wailly (Paris 1868), p. 80; and *ibid.*, p. 82: "A l'esmouvoir l'ost le roy, rot grant noise de trompes, de nacaires et de cors sarrazinnois."

[13] Harrison & Rimmer, *European Musical Instruments*, Pl. 51.

be judged from the forest of towers, 180 of them, which were built by the more affluent citizens of Bologna in the 12th and 13th centuries. However, it was not the music of the wealthy families but that of the other half of their mercantile society, the small citizens and manual workers who provided the membership of the *compagnie de' laudesi*, which was first put into writing. While the lyric songs of troubadours and trouvères were recorded in writing because they were a fashionable possession, the vernacular laudi of the *joculatores Dei* were recorded presumably because they were in wide demand for the evangelistic work of the Franciscans, and because it was important to guard their orthodoxy. Nothing of the music of the well-off citizenry before c.1325 has survived, though Marchetto of Padua clearly intended his treatise on mensural music, the *Pomerium* of 1318, for the professionals who catered to that class. For unlike most French theorists, whose methods of notation he contrasted strongly with his own, Marchetto wrote in this work for practitioners of secular music. In his treatise on the theory of sound and Gregorian chant, the *Lucidarium* of 1317–18, Marchetto cited the use of horns (*cornui*), trumpets (*tubae*), and other instruments in battle, as part of daily experience. In a section on instrumental music (*musica organica*) he mentioned *tubae, cymbala, fistulae, organa, monocordum*, and *psalterium*.[14] He made no specific reference to the large fiddle, but a contemporary depiction of it may be seen in Giotto's *Return of the Virgin and St. John from the Temple* at Padua. It would be hazardous to attempt a precise identification of the instruments named by Prodenzani in his sonnets and by Villani in his encomium on Florentine musicians.[15] However, Prodenzani's reference to the lute in Sonnet 33 ("Con lo liuto fè ballo amoroso") agrees with a mass of iconographical evidence that until the second half of the 15th century the lute was an instrument whose function was chiefly to play dance music and dance-like songs, not to participate in part-music or to play polyphony. It belonged particularly with popular entertainers. Prodenzani's *chitarra, cetera*, and *pifar sordi*, which according to this sonnet played the tenor of various pieces, must (if one assumes accuracy in his observation) be of tenor range and might possibly be harp, cittern (going down to g or f), and large, and therefore relatively soft, transverse flute, respectively. For this last there is little other evidence in this century; it may be the *traversayne* in Eustache Deschamps's lament for Machaut. Prodenzani's *rubebe, rubechette*, and *rubecone* in Sonnet 34 cannot but be generic terms

----

[14] Ed. by M. Gerbert in *Scriptores*, III (St. Blasien 1784), 66, 68.
[15] See L. Ellinwood, *The Works of Francesco Landini* (Cambridge, Mass. 1939), pp. xli, 302.

for three sizes of bowed stringed instrument—or simply rough coverage of the great variety of form, size, and detail of these instruments that existed in the 14th century. The variable pitch-range of the written instrumental dances also seems to imply the use of various sizes of bowed strings. To judge from contemporary accounts of Landini's prowess on the *organetto*, this was primarily a solo instrument.

There is probably enough reliable evidence here to establish the participation of certain instruments in Italian secular polyphony of the *trecento*. With the caveat that absence of words in a part is not necessarily to be taken as an indication of instrumental performance, the parts most often without words are the tenor of *cacce* and the tenor and contratenor of three-part *ballate*. Since none of Landini's tenors have a written lowest note higher than g and most go down to d or c, the only possible candidates for these parts are the five-string fiddle, harp, psaltery, cittern (to g or f), and perhaps large transverse flute. In any event the use of any slide brass, double reed, or enclosed reed instrument in music of this period would not only be anachronistic but also inappropriate in terms of social usage.

The earliest written polyphonic chansons in France, those of Adam de la Halle, were put in score with one text below three parts, presumably for vocal performance. With Machaut, and for a century after him, chansons were written in separate parts, most often three, and most often with wordless tenor and countertenor with the same clef and identical range. The probabilities of instrumental participation are in general the same as with the Italian three-part *ballate*. John of Grocheo, writing particularly about Paris, gave most musical importance to string instruments, and in addition to the *viella* cited the *psalterium, cithara* (harp), *lyra* (possibly lira), and *quitarra sarracenica* (lute or guitar).

During the 14th century there was a great development in the position of court and household musicians. Bishops and abbots maintained households that emulated those of the secular nobility,[16] while kings and dukes kept private chapels for daily services with music. The musicians of such a royal or ducal establishment comprised two distinct groups, concerned respectively with unwritten and written music: (a) the minstrels, with the clarioners, trumpeters, and drummers as a special group; and (b) the chapel clerks, who could be laymen, unlike the vicars and clerks of a cathedral or collegiate church. Only the latter group was trained in the increasing intricacies of polyphonic notation.

[16] See W. Salmen, *Zur Geschichte der Ministriles im Dienste geistlicher Herren des Mittelalters*, in: *Miscelánea en homenaje a monseñor Higinio Anglés*, II (Barcelona 1961), 811.

In courts within the orbit of the French language they performed both sacred and secular polyphony. It must be assumed, therefore, that most were equally competent in singing and playing one or more of the instruments used in the performance of chansons. However, another possibility, vocalization, should not be entirely ruled out.

No evidence has yet been adduced that instruments other than the organ were played in church under any but exceptional circumstances. These circumstances were of two kinds: (1) at a coronation, a reception of a noble person, or the installation of a high ecclesiastic, when the heraldic musicians of his household and of the receiving institution would both participate—not however in the sacred music but with reverberating fanfares; (2) on the feast of Corpus Christi, especially in Italy and Spain, when the players of instruments from the town or region who had walked in the sacred procession continued with it into the church and played at suitable points in the service.

This brings us to one of the most problematical of the questions about performance of written music in this period. For a century after c.1350 much polyphonic church music was cast in the same form and written down in the same manner as were the secular chansons of the time. How were the wordless tenor and countertenor parts performed? The chanson manner of writing certain genres of church music was practiced not only in France but also by English composers from the period of the Old Hall manuscript (c.1400) to shortly after the death of Dunstable in 1453. Initially English composers imitated directly this French style, for they themselves had no written secular polyphonic tradition. (There is no possibility that such a tradition could have been sunk without trace; there simply was no musical usage in 14th-century England corresponding to the polyphonic ballade, rondeau, and virelai in France.) Nevertheless, neither in France nor in England is there the slightest indication that "secular" instruments were brought into normal use in cathedrals, collegiate churches, or household chapels during the time in question.

The only possible hypothesis is that wordless tenor and countertenor parts in sacred music in chanson style were vocalized. This is a possibility that the musical traditions of the past three hundred years, with their bias toward instrumental music and an artificial style of singing, have made it difficult for musicologists to accept. But thinking has been moving that way, and it is now rarely held, for example, that the wordless *caudae* of vocal conducti were played on instruments. The usage of plainsong before the "reform" of the 16th century is full of instances of vocalization in the festal *neumae*, in the *jubilus*, and in the choral repeats of troped Kyries and proses. In the modern practice of vocalization two kinds of situation provide suggestive analogies to our hypothesis. One occurs where instruments are rare because of expense, as in the "mouth-music" of Gaelic Scotland and Ireland. The other happens when vocal virtuosi take material from or make material comparable with that of instrumental practice, as in the superb Bach performances by "Les Swingles Singers" and the jazz vocalizations of Annie Ross. Around 1400 vocal technique in terms of rhythmic device was at a highly sophisticated level.

The chief innovations in instruments used in the sphere of secular written music concern the fiddle and the harp. It is known that fiddles were made with built-up ribs and separate back and front from fairly early in the 14th century. Their crafting as delicately and elegantly made objects is iconographically documented, however, only from the 15th. The "Renaissance" harp had a shallow sound-box and an almost straight forepillar. A somewhat puzzling feature was the jarring quality deliberately given to its sound by the right-angled wooden pegs with which the strings were secured to the box. It seems clear that it was somewhat larger than the earlier "Romanesque" harp; its larger size would indicate that this harp had a wide range and powerful tone. The Irish harp, which was a different type, had its own sphere of musical activity and seems not to have been in use on the continent.[17] There is clear iconographical evidence for the existence of curved cornetts before 1450,[18] but not enough other evidence to suggest their place in musical usage. An early iconographical evidence for the big bore straight flute (the pre-Baroque recorder) is its depiction, being played by a shepherd, on an embroidered chasuble dated 1390–1420.[19] The English name of the instrument has an early use in the household accounts of John of Gaunt for 1388 ("i fistula nomine Ricordo").[20] This enlargement of the originally stone-age fipple flute into a comparatively sizeable art instrument must have been accomplished during the 14th century.

The use of instruments in the unwritten music of this period was governed by an elaborate but flexible code of socio-musical functions; within this pattern, however, there were some proliferations of size and

[17] See Joan Rimmer, *The Morphology of the Irish Harp,* in: *Galpin Society Journal,* XVII (1964), 39.

[18] Harrison & Rimmer, *European Musical Instruments,* Pl. 67.

[19] *Opus anglicanum; English Medieval Embroidery* (Victoria and Albert Museum Exhibition 1963), Exhibit No. 103, from Abegg-Stiftung Bern, Thun.

[20] See *Music in Medieval Britain,* p. 221, fn. 3.

Fig. 1   Procession of Florentines at the Council of Constance (1414–18) on
the feast of St. John the Baptist. (*Concilium Constantiense*, 1874,
Pl. 26)

some extensions of basic techniques. Players of heraldic trumpets, for
example, seem to have added to their resources the technique of "close"
playing. An early instance of this is shown in a drawing in a near-
contemporary manuscript of Ulrich von Richental's chronicle of the

Council of Constance (see Fig. 1). (There is evidence for the terminology and meaning of "open" and "close" ceremonial trumpet playing also in the 16th and 17th centuries.) Iconographical sources also
show that from the late 14th century, trumpets were made in S and
later in folded shape for greater length and therefore lower pitch, or with
a sliding mouthpiece section to make it possible to fill gaps between the
natural notes of the instrument. (The combining of loop-shape and
slide-mechanism to make the *saqueboute* was brought about in the second
half of the 15th century.) The use of shawms of different sizes, with
the implication of part-playing, can be documented from the second
half of the 14th century, for example, in an illustrated manuscript of the
Roman de la Rose showing a *carole* danced to treble and alto shawms
and bagpipe.[21] Around 1400 some great households would have had a
group of shawm players; mounted shawm and clarion players are shown
attending the Emperor Sigismund in the Constance Chronicle. Before
1450 we have depictions of court musicians playing banquet music on
treble and alto shawms and long trumpet with loop or slide (or both),
a clear implication of some mode of playing in three parts.

An occasional feature of the written polyphonic music of this period
is a part which is marked *trompette, tuba,* or something of the sort. The
seven pieces with some such express indication [22] are a version of Pierre
Fontaine's *J'ayme bien,* in which the *Contratenor Trompette* replaces
an earlier contratenor part; the *Introitus* of Jo Franchois's isorhythmic
motet *Ave virgo lux Maria;* the brief opening section of a Gloria by
Arnold de Lantins; sections of a four-movement Mass by Grossin;
Dufay's *Gloria ad modum tubae;* Henry of Lauffenberg's antiphon *Virgo
dulcis;* and an anonymous three-part wordless piece with the title *Tuba
gallicalis*—a total of one secular piece, one textless, and the rest sacred.

It has been generally assumed that parts indicated in this way were
written for slide trumpet; only in the two "tuba" parts of Dufay's Gloria
and in the middle part of *Tuba gallicalis* are the notes restricted to those
of the natural trumpet. This assumption has not hitherto been questioned
on technical grounds.[23] However, it is demonstrable that the number
of slide positions on a trumpet with sliding mouthpiece could not have
been more than four. The following example shows the notes which
would then be playable on trumpets in C, D, E♭, and F respectively:

[21] Harrison & Rimmer, *European Musical Instruments,* Pl. 60.
[22] They are listed by H. Besseler, *Die Entstehung der Posaune,* in: *Acta musicologica,* XXII (1950), 13, who also gives references to transcriptions.
[23] I am greatly indebted to Don Smithers for formulating this technical evidence.

Ex. 1

The lowest available note is A; this alone rules out the possibility
of playing the *trompette* part of *J'ayme bien* at the written pitch.
With each instrument there is an inescapable gap of a major third
in the first octave. This eliminates the *trumpetta* part of Franchois's
Introitus, the relevant section of Grossin's Sanctus, the two lower parts
of *Virgo dulcis* and the tenor of *Tuba gallicalis*. Only the Gloria and
Credo of Grossin's Mass (which begin at f) and the opening of de
Lantins's Gloria (which begins at c but has no d) are possible, and
these only on a C trumpet. Hence the idea that the words *trompette* and
tuba indicated parts for slide trumpet seems untenable. Dufay's piece is
of course suited to natural trumpets, and may have been performed with
them on occasions of high ceremonial.

Why then are these parts so indicated? For reasons that cannot be
detailed here, tenor parts and (more especially) contratenor parts of
pieces in the chanson manner had inescapably a high proportion of leaps.
(In this way they were markedly different from the lower parts of
cantus-firmus compositions.) At times these leap patterns resembled, even
if originally unintentionally, those of trumpet music, and this resemblance was in some cases intentionally exploited. Occasionally, though
certainly not in the majority of cases, the written parts bear a term that
was probably in common usage for this kind of part. A good analogy
would be the horn idioms in Haydn's piano sonatas, which it would be
quite superfluous to indicate, since they are among our normal musical
associations. As to the performance of such parts, as far as the sacred
pieces are concerned there is again no other normal possibility than
vocalization.

The instances in both sacred and written secular music in this period of imitation of instruments by voices are not confined to trumpet pieces. An English motet [24] of the mid-14th century was composed on this tenor:

Ex. 2

This kind of imitation of instruments is well known in the unwritten tradition, and is found in many folksongs.[25] The late 14th-century chanson *Or sus vous dormez trop* [26] has an imitation of bagpipes and drums:

Ex. 3

[24] The work referred to will be published under the writer's editorship in a forthcoming volume of English motets of the 14th century.

[25] See R. Pinon, *Philologie et folklore musical: les chants de pâtres avant leur émergence folklorique*, in: *Journal of the International Folk Music Council*, XIV (1962), 7.

[26] Paris, Bibl. Nat., MS ital. 568, fols. 122ᵛ–124; printed in W. Apel, *French Secular Music of the Late Fourteenth Century* (Cambridge, Mass. 1950), p. 117.

And it may not be too fanciful to hear in some passages of Paolo da Firenze's madrigal on the taking of Pisa by Florence in 1406 [27] suggestions of the sound of pipe and tabor:

Ex. 4

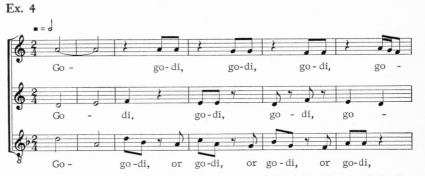

[27] *Ibid.*, fols. 56ᵛ–57; quoted in Besseler, *Die Musik des Mittelalters und der Renaissance* (Potsdam 1937), p. 164 and in *The New Oxford History of Music*, III (London 1960), 31f.

-            -   -   -   -   di,

-    -   di,   go - di Fi-ren-ze,poi che se'   si   gran-(de)

go-di,   go-di,   or

which Uccello depicted leading the pikemen at precisely that event (Pl. 19c). This is a rare piece of iconographic evidence for the use of pipe and tabor in a military context.

Writing on the history of reed instruments from early Christian times to 1540, Gerald Hayes has remarked: "It is in examining these that we notice the only real weakness of instrumental music before the 15th century." [28] This not untypical attitude betrays a fundamental misconception of musical practice, here expressed in the misapplication of a post-medieval criterion to the instrumental usage of the times we have been considering. It is one of the chief functions of musicology to remove misconceptions about musical practice in the past before recording, and to suggest at least general criteria for performance in the inevitably different circumstances of today. The anything-looks-nice-in-a-pageant-ism that too often foists a rag-bag of sounds from pseudo-Renaissance instruments on the music of two or three centuries earlier is largely due to the failure of medieval musicologists to give a positive lead to would-be performers of the music they discuss.

[28] *The New Oxford History of Music*, III (London 1960), p. 477.

THE HYMNS OF
JACOBUS DE KERLE

by GLEN HAYDON

WHEN OTTO URSPRUNG discussed the hymns of Kerle in his introduction to the *Preces speciales*,[1] he had at his disposal only six of the hymns contained in Kerle's first published set of hymns. Of the early editions (there apparently were two—1558 and 1560) only the tenor and bassus books were known to have survived (in Heilbronn and Barcelona). Ursprung identified six of the early hymns in manuscripts in German libraries. Wilfried Brennecke (MGG, VII, 848f) apparently follows Ursprung's listings and also refers to the hymns as having been preserved in incomplete form. In 1955 I came across a complete set of the partbooks of 1560 in the library of the Conservatorio G. Verdi, Milan, in the *Fondo di Santa Barbara*. The present study is based upon the transcriptions of these hymns and of the other hymns found in German sources. An examination of the several existing partbooks has turned up a number of interesting discrepancies, but the evidence is not all in yet so that further discussion will have to be deferred to another article.

Jacobus de Kerle, according to Ursprung, went to Orvieto, a small town not far from Rome, late in 1555. The dedication of his *Hymni totius anni* carries the date of 25 March 1558. The Milan partbooks are dated Rome: Ant. Barre, 1560, both on the title page and at the end of each book. Table I gives an inventory of the 23 hymns contained in this collection.

Kerle's polyphonic style as evidenced in the Orvieto hymns may be characterized as a smooth-flowing, imitative contrapuntal style based upon the given chant melodies associated with the various hymns. The treatment of the cantus firmus falls into three main types. First, there is the type in which the cantus firmus appears in all the voices in various kinds of imitative treatment. This is by far the most common procedure since some 27 of the 54 settings begin with a point of imitation based

---

[1] Jacobus de Kerle, *Preces speciales*, ed. O. Ursprung, in: *Denkmäler der Tonkunst in Bayern*, XXVI (1926).

TABLE I

Jacobus de Kerle, *Hymni totius anni* (Orvieto)

TEXT AND STROPHE	KEY SIGNATURE MENSURAL SIGN NO. OF VOICES		CONCORDANCES, VARIANTS, AND REMARKS
1. In Adventu Domini			
1. Conditor alme	C	4	Cantus ₵. Stuttgart 24, fols. 149ᵛ–161
3. Vergente mundi	C	3	
5. Te deprecamur	C3	5	Heilbronn has C $\frac{3}{2}$
2. In Nativitate Domini			
(1. Christe Redemptor)			
2. Tu lumen	♭ C	4	Augsburg 27, 1; ₵. Stuttgart 24, 171ᵛ–180;
4. Hinc presens	♭ C	3	2,₵; 4,C; 6,C
6. Nos quoque	♭ C	5	
3. In Epiphania Domini			
(1. Hostis Herodes)			
2. Ibant Magi	C	4	Augsburg 27, 3a; ₵
4. Novum genus	C	5	
4. In Dominicis Diebus			
(1. Lucis creator)			
2. Qui mane	C	4	
4. Caelorum pulset	C	5	
5. Temp. Quad. in Domini Die			
1. Aures ad nostras	C	4	
3. Crimina laxa	C	3	
5. Christe, lux	C	4	
7. Tu nobis	C	6	Texts for strophes 7 & 9
9. Gloria Deo			
6. Dominica in Passione			
1. Vexilla Regis	♭ C	4	Texts for strophes 1 & 5
3. Impleta sunt	♭ C	3	
5. Beata, cujus			
7. Te summa	♭ C	5	
7. Temp. Pasc.			
(1. Ad coenam Agni)			
2. Cujus corpus	♭ C	4	
4. Jam Pascha	♭ C	3	
6. Consurgit Christus	♭ C	5	Texts for strophes 6 & 8
8. Gloria tibi			
8. In Ascensione Domini			
(1. Jesú nostra red.)			
2. Quae te vicit	C	4	
4. Ipsa te cogat	C	5	"Parody" in *Sacrae cantiones* 5,4
9. In Festo Pentecostes			
(1. Veni Creator)			
2. Qui Paraclitus	C	4	
4. Accende lumen	C	3	
6. Per te sciamus	C	5	

	KEY SIGNATURE		
	MENSURAL SIGN		CONCORDANCES, VARIANTS,
TEXT AND STROPHE	NO. OF VOICES		AND REMARKS

10. In Festo Sanct. & indiv. Trinitatis
    (1. Adesto, sancta)
    2. Te caelorum   C   4
    4. Unum te lumen   C   5

11. In Festo Corporis Christi
    (1. Pange lingua)
    2. Nobis datus   C   4
    4. Verbum caro   C   5
    6. Genitori, Genitoque   C   6

12. In Nativitate S.Io. Baptistae
    (1. Ut queant laxis)
    2. Nuntius celso   ♭ C   4
    4. Ventris obstruso   ♭ C   5

13. In Festivitate Apost. Petri & Pauli
    (1. Aurea luce)
    2. Janitor caeli   C   4

14. In Festo S.Mariae Magdalenae
    (1. Nardi Maria)
    2. Honor decus   ♭ C   4

15. In Dedicatione Ecclesiae
    (1. Urbs beata)
    2. Nova veniens   C   4   A¹A²TB
    4. Tunsionibus   C   5   A¹A²QTB

16. In Exaltatione Sanctae Crucis
    (1. Tibi Christi)
    7. Te summa, Deus   C   4   Setting of 7th strophe only

17. In Dedicatione Beati Michaelis Archangeli
    (1. Tibi Christi)
    2. Collaudemus   C   4   Augsburg 27, 18, mens. sign ₵
    4. Gloriam Patri   C   4

18. In Festivitate B.M.V.
    (1. Ave maris stella)
    2. Sumens illud   C   4
    4. Monstra te esse   C   3
    6. Vitam praesta   C   5   with canon in subdiapente

19. De Apostolis
    (1. Exsultet caelum)
    2. Vos saecli   C   4
    4. Quorum praecepto   C   3
    6. Deo Patri   C   4

20. In Festo Unius Martyris
    (1. Deus tuorum)
    2. Hic nempe   C   4
    4. Ob hoc precatu   C   4

TEXT AND STROPHE	KEY SIGNATURE MENSURAL SIGN NO. OF VOICES		CONCORDANCES, VARIANTS, AND REMARKS
21. In Festivitate Plurimorum Martyrum			
(1. Sanctorum meritis)			
2. Hi sunt quos	C	4	Augsburg 27, 17, mens. sign ¢
4. Caeduntur gladiis	C	3	
6. Te summa Deitas	C	4	
22. De uno Confessore			
(1. Iste Confessor)			
2. Qui pius, prudens	C	4	Augsburg 27, 19, mens. sign ¢
4. Unde nunc noster	C	4	
23. De Virginibus			
(1. Jesu, corona)			
2. Qui pascis	♭ C	4	Changes to C$\frac{3}{2}$ in cantus and bassus, C3
4. Te deprecamur	♭ C	5	in altus, tenor

on the chant melody and running through all the voices. However, in this kind of treatment there is constant variety—variety in the order of entrance of the voices, in the pitch interval of the imitation, in the time interval of the various entrances, and even in the time values of the notes, as in imitation by diminution or augmentation. In fact, of the 27 settings checked, only three followed the same order of voice entrances (alto-tenor-cantus), and yet these were varied in both pitch and time intervals. Six patterns of voice entrances occurred twice each, but, again, with a similar amount of variety. It seems the composer made a conscious effort not to repeat his procedures.

The second type of contrapuntal treatment, one closely related to the first, is one in which the cantus firmus, or elements of it, appear imitatively in 2, 3, or 4 voices while one or more voices move in free, non-imitative counterpoint or in independent points of imitation, or in a combination of the two. Although it is difficult to make a very meaningful generalization because, even in a given setting, the technique is frequently shifting, nevertheless, we may venture to say that type two occurs in at least a dozen of the settings. Most of these features may be seen in the opening of the doxology of *Ave maris stella* (18,6), the only instance in the hymns in which Kerle makes use of the canon. It will be seen that the tenor and bassus are built on an independent point of imitation, while the three upper voices derive their material from the cantus firmus. Then the bassus, after a brief rest, makes a reference to the cantus firmus, while the cantus and tenor continue, also after rests, with entrances in free, non-imitative counterpoint. The *dux* and *comes*, in the altus and quintus, continue their points of imitation,

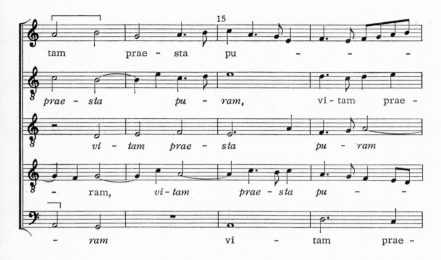

this time with material only slightly related to the cantus firmus, while the cantus gives a fairly full statement of the cantus firmus, although it is freely elaborated in the middle portion. The two following sections show other variations of this type of treatment, but the last line returns to the style of the first in that the cantus firmus is introduced successively in the three upper parts, this time in simple semibreve movement, while the tenor and bassus continue with free, non-imitative counterpoint.

Type three, which occurs less often than the other two types, yet often enough to constitute a separate category, is one in which the cantus firmus appears in one voice only while the other voices move independently or with points of imitation not derived from the cantus firmus. This type is particularly effective in settings *a 3* in which the melodically stylized cantus firmus appears in the cantus, while the alto and tenor develop their independent play. Again, this technique never seems to be carried out pedantically, for the composer quite regularly shifts from one style to the other from line to line in the same setting.

Ex. 2   Orvieto 1, 3,   1–7

Pronounced homophonic sections are rare. One occurs in 2, 6, 13–16, and No. 14, 2, 1–5 begins in chordal fashion, but that is about all. There is one setting (5,1) in which the cantus firmus in long notes in the tenor is accompanied by a florid countermelody in the bass and the pair is then imitated in the cantus and alto. But already at the caesura of the first line of this Sapphic meter the style shifts to points of imitation based on the cantus firmus and running through all the voices. Three of the settings, all of them doxologies, present the chant melody in un-adorned semibreves in the *quinta* or *sexta pars*, the individual lines of the melody in each case being separated from each other by long rests.[2]

The beginning of the doxology of the Corpus Christi hymn *Pange lingua* may serve as an illustration of Kerle's polyphonic resourceful-

Ex. 3   Orvieto 11, 6,   1–12

[2] 5,7 & 9; 9,6; and 11,6.

ness. The altus begins with the first part of the cantus firmus in augmentation (breves), and the cantus enters after five and a half measures rest
and in imitation at the unison in *integer valor* (semibreves). Meanwhile
the tenor and *quinta pars* enter in stretto in the first measure on an independent, flowing point of imitation at the unison and proceed, after
the entrance, mostly in parallel thirds until the first cadence. The bassus

enters in measure two with skips of the fifth in supporting bass fashion, but soon changes to a more flowing, stepwise movement. The cantus firmus, in the *sexta pars*, makes its entrance in the middle of the eighth measure, being neatly woven into the polyphonic fabric and psychologically well prepared through its overlapping with the final chord of an intermediate half-cadence. Against the cantus firmus, the other parts move on in a rather thick web of free polyphony interspersed with some independent points of imitation and intermittent entrances of the supporting bass. This treatment continues after the end of the first line of the cantus firmus for six measures before the appearance of material from the second line of the text. The tenor and *quinta pars* are the most active parts at this point, and they continue their free contrapuntal movement some nine measures into the second section with constant repetition of the last word of the first line of text. The second section is quite varied in its treatment from the first, the frequent points of imitation (derived from the first notes of the cantus firmus), the thinning out of the texture, and the build-up to a strong cadence at the end of the line—all evidently conceived as being an appropriate musical expression of the text *Laus et jubilatio*. The remaining four sections continue in a generally similar, though continually varied, manner to produce one of the longest of Kerle's hymn settings—83 measures.

In the treatment of dissonance, Kerle comes very close to the style of Palestrina. Probably the most noticeable remnant of early 16th-century practice is his frequent use of the échappée. In the use of passing dissonances, suspensions, cambiata, and other dissonant idioms, Kerle was quite conventional. Three unusual uses of the suspension dissonance should probably be mentioned in passing. In one instance (Ex. 4a) the dissonance has the duration of a breve while the note of preparation has the value of a semibreve. In the second instance (Ex. 4b) a four-three $\left(\begin{smallmatrix}5-\\4\ 3\end{smallmatrix}\right)$ semibreve suspension dissonance occurs on the second half of the measure, with the resolution on the first of the next measure.[3] In the third instance the suspension dissonance of the seventh resolves by skipping up to the third of the chord. In similar instances in the works of other composers, the skip down to the third is more common.[4]

Another substantial collection of hymns by Kerle is contained in Augsburg, *Staats- und Stadtbibliothek*, MS 27, a choirbook entitled

---

[3] The parallel octaves in measure 23 of this setting may be the result of a typographical error. There is a definite typographical error in the first four measures of the tenor of this strophe, which has been partially (though incorrectly) amended, apparently by hand, in the Heilbronn partbook.

[4] For examples in the hymns of Festa, cf. Glen Haydon, *The Hymns of Costanzo Festa: A Style Study*, in: JAMS, XII (1959), 116.

Ex. 4a   Orvieto 6, 7,   10–12

b   Orvieto 6, 7,   38–39

c   Orvieto 13, 2,   19–20

Solemnium vespertinarum precum responsoria et hymni. This vesper
cycle contains responses and hymns for 23 of the more important feast
days of the church year (cf. Table II). In the manuscript, which is
written in a bold clear hand, the music for each feast day is normally
prefaced by a full page on which is given the pertinent information
with regard to the feast day, the music, the composer, and the date of
the manuscript (1577). Hymns Nos. 18, 19, 22, and 23 have the composer's name omitted from the introductory page, but three of the four
are identifiable from other sources as may be seen from the table of
hymns. Ursprung attributes some of the hymns (3b, 4, and 16) to a
composer whom he identifies as the Augsburg Benedictine Anonymous.
He also states that Kerle emended some of the compositions of the
Anonymous, with no further explanation than the phrase "as may
readily be seen" (*wie sich wohl einwandfrei ergibt*). He then lists the
settings that may be identified from our table as 4,2; 13,2 and 4; 22,2;

TABLE II

Jacobus de Kerle, Hymns in Augsburg MS 27 (1577)

FOLIO	TEXT AND STROPHE	KEY SIGNATURE MENSURAL SIGN NO. OF VOICES	CONCORDANCES, VARIANTS, AND REMARKS
1.	**In Vigilia Sacratissimae Nativitatis Christi**		
	(1. Christe Redemptor)		
14ᵛ– 16	2. Tu lumen	♭ ¢ 4	Orvieto no. 2 with mens.
15ᵛ– 17	4. Hic presens	♭ ¢ 3	sign C throughout. Stutt-
17ᵛ– 20	6. Nos quoque	♭ ¢ 5	gart MS 24 171ᵛ–180 with 2,¢; 4,¢; 6,¢
2.	**In Festo Circumcisione Domini**		
	(1. A solis ortus)		
26ᵛ– 28	2. Beatus Auctor	¢ 4	
27ᵛ– 29	4. Domus pudici	¢ 3	
29ᵛ– 31	6. Foeno jacere	¢ 4	Tenor must be read octave
31ᵛ– 33	8. Gloria tibi	¢ 5	higher to correct errors in dissonance treatment.
3a.	**In Festo Epiphaniae Domini**		
	(1. Hostis Herodes)	¢ 4	Orvieto 3; mens. sign C
39ᵛ– 41	2. Ibant Magi	¢ 5	Variant at cadence—
41ᵛ– 43	4. Novum genus		Orvieto 3,4 probably right.
3b.			
44ᵛ– 46	2. Ibant Magi	¢ 4	Attributed by Ursprung to
46ᵛ– 47	4. Novum genus	¢ 4	Augsburg Anonymous
4.	**In Festo Purificationis BMV**		
	(1. Quod chorus)		
56ᵛ– 57	2. Haec Deum coeli	♭ ¢ 4	Attributed by Ursprung to
57ᵛ– 59	4. Tu libens voti	♭ ¢ 4	Augsburg Anonymous
5.	**In Festo Sanctissimi Patroni Sancti Benedicti**		
	(1. Christi favente)		
65ᵛ– 67	2. Vir vite	¢ 4	
66ᵛ– 68	4. Reiecta secularium	¢ 3	
68ᵛ– 69	6. Regula vitae	¢ 5	C.F. in tenor in square notation
6.	**In Festo Annunciationis BMV**		
	(1. Ave maris stella)		
76ᵛ– 78	2. Sumens illud ave	¢ 5	
78ᵛ– 80	4. Monstra te esse	¢ 4	CCAA
80ᵛ– 82	6. Vitam praesta	¢ 6	
7.	**In Die Sancto Paschae**		
	(1. Ad coenam agni)		In *Sacrae cantiones*, 1575, with all 8 strophes set
85ᵛ– 87	2. Cujus corpus	¢ 5	S.c., 6,1
87ᵛ– 89	4. Jam Pascha	¢ 4	S.c., 6,2
89ᵛ– 91	6. Consurgit Christus	¢ 6	S.c., 6,6
91ᵛ– 94	8. Gloria tibi	¢ 8	S.c., 6,8
8.	**In Dedicatione Ecclesiae**		
	(1. Urbs beata)		
102ᵛ–104	2. Nova veniens	♭ ¢ 4	
103ᵛ–106	4. Tunsionibus	♭ ¢ 4	CCAA
106ᵛ–109	5. Gloria tibi	♭ ¢ 5	

FOLIO	TEXT AND STROPHE	KEY SIGNATURE MENSURAL SIGN NO. OF VOICES	CONCORDANCES, VARIANTS, AND REMARKS
9.	In Ascensione Domini		
	(1. Festum nunc celebre)		Same music as 12b
115ᵛ–116	2. Conscendit jubilans	¢ 4	Changes to φ $\frac{3}{2}$
116ᵛ–117	4. Oramus, Domine	¢ 4	CCAT
117ᵛ–119	6. Praesta hoc	¢ 6	
10.	In Festo Pentecostes		
	(1. Veni Creator Spiritus)		
126ᵛ–127	2. Qui Paraclitus	¢ 4	
127ᵛ–129	4. Accende lumen	¢ 4	
129ᵛ–130	6. Per te sciamus	¢ 5	
11.	In Festo Sanctissimae Trinitatis		
	(1. O lux beata)		
137ᵛ–139	2. Te mane laudum	¢ 4	
12a.	In Festo Corporis Christi		
	(1. Pange lingua)		
146ᵛ–148	2. Nobis datus	¢ 4	Changes to φ$\frac{3}{2}$
148ᵛ–150	4. Verbum caro	¢ 3	
150ᵛ–152	6. Genitori, Genitoque	¢ 6	
12b.			
	(1. Sacris sollemniis)		Same music as 9
153ᵛ–155	2. Noctis recolitur	¢ 4	Changes to φ $\frac{3}{2}$
155ᵛ–157	4. Dedit fragilibus	¢ 4	CCAT
157ᵛ–159	6. Panis angelicus	¢ 6	
13.	In Festo Sanctis: Patroni nostri Udalrici Episcopi		
	(1. Gaude, Sion, sub-limata)		Ursprung: "nachgebessert"
165ᵛ–167	2. In Salutem	¢ 4	Same music as 20,2
167ᵛ–169	4. Praesul sanctus	¢ 3	" " " 20,4
169ᵛ–172	6. Praesta Pater	¢ 5	" " " 20,8
14.	In Festo Sanctae Affrae Martyris		
	(1. Gauda civitas Augusta)		
177ᵛ–178	2. Narcissus primo	¢ 4	
178ᵛ–180	4. Damon clamavit	¢ 4	
180ᵛ–182	6. O Narcisse cum	¢ 3	
182ᵛ–184	8. Praesta, Pater	¢ 5	
15.	In Festo Assumptionis BMV		
	(1. Quem terra, pontus)		
190ᵛ–192	2. Cui luna, sol	¢ 4	
192ᵛ–194	4. Beati caeli nuncio	¢ 3	
194ᵛ–196	6. O gloriosa Domina	¢ 4	(CCTB) or CCAT
196ᵛ–198	8. Gloria tibi Domine	¢ 5	
16.	In Festo Nativitatis BMV		
	(1. Sanctorum meritis)		Attributed by Ursprung to
206ᵛ–207	2. Cuius magnifica	♭ ¢ 4	Anonymous
207ᵛ–210	4. Felix multiplici	♭ ¢ 5	Changes to φ $\frac{3}{2}$ last line
17.	In Festo Sanctorum nostrorum hic quiescentium		
	(1. Sanctorum meritis)		Orvieto 21, mens. sign C
225ᵛ–227	2. Hi sunt quos	¢ 4	
227ᵛ–229	4. Caeduntur gladiis	¢ 3	
229ᵛ–231	6. Te summa Deitas	¢ 4	

| | | KEY SIGNATURE MENSURAL SIGN | |
| FOLIO | TEXT AND STROPHE | NO. OF VOICES | CONCORDANCES, VARIANTS, AND REMARKS |

18. In Dedicatione Beati Michaelis Archangeli
            (1. Tibi, Christe)

			Feast day not given in Augsburg
234ᵛ–236	2. Collaudamus	¢ 4	Orvieto, 17 mens. sign C
236ᵛ–238	4. Gloriam Patri	¢ 4	

19. In Festo Sancti Simperti Episcopi
            (1. Iste Confessor)

| 245ᵛ–248 | 2. Qui pius, prudens | ¢ 4 | Orvieto 22, mens. sign C |
| 248ᵛ–250 | 4. Unde nunc noster | ¢ 4 | |

20. In Festo Sancti Narcissi Episcopi et Martyris
            (1. Gauda civitas Augusta)

			Same text as 14
257ᵛ–259	2. Narcissus primo	¢ 4	Same music as 13,2
259ᵛ–261	4. Damon clamat	¢ 4	" " " 13,4
261ᵛ–263	6. O Narcisse	¢ 4	New music
263ᵛ–265	8. Praesta, Pater	¢ 5	Same music as 13,6

21. In Solemni Festo Omnium Sanctorum
            (1. Christe, qui virtus)

271ᵛ–273	2. Ecce solemnis diei	¢ 4	
273ᵛ–275	4. Haec dies festum	¢ 3	
275ᵛ–277	6. Gloria sanctae piae	¢ 4	

22. In Festo Conceptionis BMV
            (1. Ave maris stella)

			All 7 strophes set in *Sacrae*
283ᵛ–285	2. Sumens illud Ave	¢ 5	*cantiones* 7,2
285ᵛ–287	4. Monstra te esse	¢ 4	S.c. 7,4; CCAT
287ᵛ–290	6. Vitam praesta puram	¢ 6	S.c. 7,6

23. De Sanctis infra Pasca
            (1. Vita sanctorum)

			Author not given
297ᵛ–299	2. Tu tuo laetos	♭ ¢ 4	Anonymous (Ursprung)
299ᵛ–301	4. Nunc in excelsis	♭ ¢ 4	
301ᵛ–303	6. Hoc Pater tecum	♭ ¢ 4	

and 23,2. Finally, there are, according to Ursprung, two hymns (9; and 20,2 and 4) that either stem from an earlier time in Kerle's career, or have fallen into an old (*historisierenden*) style, "certainly unconsciously on the part of Kerle and only induced by his preoccupation with the compositions of the Anonymous." Although there is some confusion in these statements,[5] Ursprung is probably right in assuming that most of the questionable settings mentioned are not by Kerle. One setting (2,6), not mentioned by Ursprung, is obviously incorrectly notated in the manuscript. A literal transcription gives rise to numerous flagrant errors in the treatment of the dissonance. If the tenor is transcribed an octave higher, everything falls into place and the dissonance treatment becomes perfectly normal. However, the resulting setting for three cantus parts and

[5] For example, 13,2 & 4 of the second list are the same musical settings as 20,2 & 4 of the last mentioned hymn; and 22,2 appears in Kerle's *Sacrae cantiones* of 1575.

an alto is unique among Kerle's hymn compositions. Placing the alto an octave lower also gets rid of the faulty dissonances but leaves numerous inordinately wide spacings among the voices. The arrangement for high voices does not seem too incongruous for Kerle's style, since he does occasionally set an intermediate strophe for two cantus and two alto parts (cf. 6,4 and 8,4).

As will be seen from the table, five of the hymns are taken over from the Orvieto publication (2, 3a, 17, 18, and 19). It is interesting to note in passing that the mensuration sign in each case is changed from *tempus imperfectum* to *tempus imperfectum diminutum* without change of note values. The Stuttgart *Landesbibliothek* MS 24 has the first hymn with the mensuration sign ₵ for the first strophe and C for the other two, again without change of note values. Apparently these differences in the mensural signs had no particular significance. For the period, of course, the sign used in the Orvieto publication is rare.

The music for two of the Augsburg hymns (7 and 22) is obviously taken over from Kerle's *Sacrae cantiones* published in Munich by Adam Berg in 1575 (cf. Table IIIa). There is, however, an important difference

TABLE IIIa

Sacre cantiones

TEXT AND STROPHE	KEY SIGNATURE MENSURAL SIGN NO. OF VOICES	CONCORDANCES, VARIANTS, AND REMARKS
5. De Resurrectione Domini		
1. Jesu nostra redemptio	₵ 5	
2. Quae te vicit clementia	₵ 4	AQTB. Coloration last line
3. Inferni claustra penetrans	₵ 3	
4. Ipsa te cogat pietas	₵ 5	Parody on Orvieto 8,4
5. Tu esto nostrum gaudium	$\phi\frac{3}{2}6$	Change to ₵ at third line
6. De Ascensione Domini		
1. Ad coenam agni	₵ 5	Music = Aug. 7,2
2. Cujus corpus	₵ 4	Music = Aug. 7,4
3. Protecti Paschae	₵ 5	
4. Jam Pascha	₵ 3	
5. O vere digna	₵ 5	
6. Consurgit	₵ 6	Augsburg 7,6
7. Quaesumus Auctor	₵ 7	
8. Gloria tibi	₵ 8	Augsburg 7,8
7. De BMV		
1. Ave maris stella	₵ 5	
2. Sumens illud Ave	₵ 5	Augsburg 22,2
3. Solve vincla, reis	₵ 4	ATQB
4. Monstra te esse matrem	₵ 4	Augsburg 22,4
5. Virgo singularis	₵ 5	
6. Vitam praesta puram	₵ 6	Augsburg 22,6
7. Sit laus Deo Patri	₵ 7	

in that in the *Sacrae cantiones* Kerle provides a new polyphonic setting for each strophe of the hymn, rather than for the alternate strophes. The implication is that they were intended for independent performance rather than for their normal liturgical use in the vespers service. In the Augsburg hymn number 7, the musical settings for strophes number 1 and 2 of the *Sacrae cantiones* are used for strophes 2 and 4 respectively, while the music for strophes 6 and 8 is taken over as it stands. Number 22 uses the music of the even-numbered strophes of the setting in the *Sacrae cantiones*. In this hymn the melody of the chant is used as a cantus firmus in semibreves, laid out in the second cantus. In each strophe the cantus firmus enters after five measures rest, and each of the succeeding lines enters after a rest of two and a half measures. Exactly the same procedure is followed in the *Sacrae cantiones*, except that the cantus firmus in the odd-numbered strophes appears in the second tenor. Kerle used the same method in his setting of the seven strophes of *Vexilla regis, Liber*

TABLE IIIb

Liber modulorum sacrorum

TEXT AND STROPHE	KEY SIGNATURE MENSURAL SIGN NO. OF VOICES			CONCORDANCES, VARIANTS, AND REMARKS
6. (Ad Completorium)				
1. Christe, qui lux es et dies	♭	C	5	
2. Precamur, sancte Domine	♭	¢	4	
3. Ne gravis somnus irruat	♭	C $\frac{3}{2}$	4	
4. Oculi somnum capiant	♭	¢	4	
5. Defensor noster	♭	¢	3	
6. Memento nostri, Domine	♭	¢	5	
7. Deo Patri sit gloria Amen	♭	¢	6	
7. (Dominica in Passione)				
1. Vexilla Regis	♭	¢	5	
2. Quo vulneratus	♭	¢	5	
3. Impleta sunt	♭	¢	4	
4. Arbor decora	♭	¢	4	
5. Beata, cujus	♭	¢	5	
6. O Crux ave	♭	¢	6	
7. Te summa, Deus	♭	¢	7	
11. (De sacro foedere contra Turcas)				
1. Gaudentes gaudeamus omnes		¢	8	
2. Cantemus Domino		¢	4	
3. Confitemini Domino		¢	4	
4. Videbimus gloriam		¢	4	
5. Gaudentes gaudeamus omnes		¢	8	Repeats first strophe

modulorum sacrorum (Munich: Adam Berg, 1572, No. 7; cf. Table IIIb). Here again the cantus firmus in semibreves alternates between the second tenor and the second cantus in the successive strophes. The cantus firmus enters after a rest of four breves, and the subsequent rests are each of two breves duration. These two hymns, with the rigid layout of the cantus firmus, are extreme examples of what Sparks has referred to as the structural cantus firmus.[6] The other voices are worked out in free contrapuntal style using material from the cantus firmus as well as independent points of imitation, in addition to the usual free entrances.

Of the ten hymn texts common to the Orvieto and Augsburg collections, five occur with the same music, two make use of different chant melodies, and three that are based on the same chants are newly composed, one of them twice. As will be seen from the table of hymns, the other hymns in the Augsburg collection are for the most part either those in honor of locally important saints or hymns not common in Italian usage.

Probably the most pronounced over-all difference in Kerle's style in the Augsburg hymns as compared with those of the Orvieto collection is the substantial increase in the number of settings that are mostly homophonic. Whereas in the Orvieto settings only one (14,2) begins with all voices entering in block-chordal style, in the Augsburg settings there are at least five (5,6; 9,2; 9,4; 14,4; and 15,6). In addition, there are several settings *a 5* in which four of the voices participate in a chordal beginning while the fifth voice enters in imitation (10,6; 12a,6; and 13,6). The several *sesquialtera* ($\mathbb{Q}\frac{3}{2}$) sections are all treated in chordal fashion.

In one of the hymns (5,2) in which the last line of the chant melody is a repetition of the first, Kerle repeats the music of the first line with a modification only for the final cadence. The tenor in the last strophe of this hymn (5,6) has the chant throughout in square notation with no mensural sign or rests. In the first setting of *Ave maris stella* (6,2) the bass is made up of an ostinato figure six notes in length, with alternate entrances on *d* and *a*. The figure appears first in the alto at the very beginning, followed by entrances in the second and first tenor, respectively, before the entrance of the bass in measure seven. It occurs twice more in each of the tenor voices alternating with the entrances in the bass. The cantus firmus, in moderately stylized form, appears in the cantus throughout, with the middle voices taking up occasional points of imitation based either on elements from the cantus or on independent figures.

[6] Cf. Edgar H. Sparks, *Cantus Firmus in Mass and Motet, 1420–1520* (Berkeley 1963), Chap. 3 *et passim.*

Ex. 5   Augsburg 6, 2,   1–16

The most radical departure from Kerle's normal hymn style occurs in the second setting of *Ave maris stella* (22,6) at the last line of the sixth strophe with the words *semper collaetemur* ("that we may rejoice with Him forever"). The example speaks for itself.

Ex. 6 Augsburg 22, 6   24–31

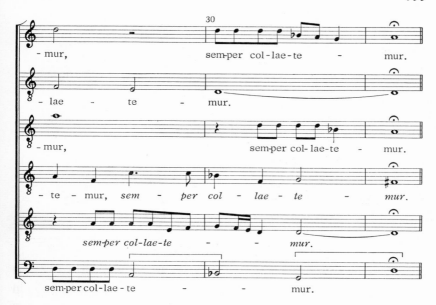

Other instances of text setting with syllables on semiminims occur in middle sections of the doxology of *Ad coenam agni* (7,8). Here the style becomes quite declamatory with some quasi-antiphonal interplay among different voice groupings. Both of these settings appeared in the *Sacrae cantiones* of 1575.

The hymn, *Jesu nostra redemptio*, the first of the three hymns included in the *Sacrae cantiones*, has polyphonic settings for all five strophes. The first two strophes are set in a fairly conventional imitative style (*a 5* and *a 4*, respectively), but the third strophe (*a 3*) breaks off at the word *victor* into a brief section of motivic interplay involving sequential patterns in contrary motion. The remainder of the setting returns to a more normal style, although melodically there are a half dozen instances of ascending skips from accented, or relatively accented, semiminims, an idiom foreign to the Palestrina style and otherwise rare in the hymns of Kerle. The fourth strophe (*a 5*), *Ipsa te cogat*, may perhaps best be described as a parody treatment of the corresponding setting in the Orvieto collection (8,4). The general layout of the parts is followed with remarkable faithfulness throughout, but there is an obvious attempt to add rhythmic interest. An idea as to the success of the attempt may be gained from a comparison of the first line of the bass:

Ex. 7a   Orvieto 8, 4,   1–8

b *Sacrae cantiones* 5, 4,   1–9

The only new material added is the entrance at the very beginning of the *quinta vox* with four measures of rather florid free counterpoint filling in the rests that the corresponding voice had in the Orvieto setting before its entrance with a free part in semibreves. The style of the new material seems out of keeping with that of the original setting, but, in a way, it is a foretoken of the type of elaboration that takes place throughout the strophe. Often longer note values are broken up into repeated notes and there is a decided increase in the amount of text repetition. In the succeeding sections, as the movement of the voices increases, the setting adheres more closely to the original, except for continued text repetition and some changes in the movement of the parts at the final cadence. After a fairly normal setting of the doxology (except for a brief flurry of semiminims and fusas in the middle section), there follows an Amen that is rather ingeniously worked out, but seems far removed from Kerle's normal style. In this ten measure section a motive in three parts (consisting of a dotted minim followed by two fusas and several semiminims in parallel sixths in the upper voices, and a bass with essentially the same rhythm, but in contrary motion), begins on *c* and is echoed antiphonally by the three other voices. Then the bass moves down to *A*, and the motivic structure is repeated with the upper voices now in parallel thirds. This, in turn, is echoed antiphonally by the three other voices, but with a tenth between the two upper parts. The last *A* in the bass of the motive then descends to the low *E* for the final Phrygian cadence. Unfortunately, however, for the purity of the style, the motive in the upper

Ex. 8 *Sacrae cantiones* 5, 5, 39–48

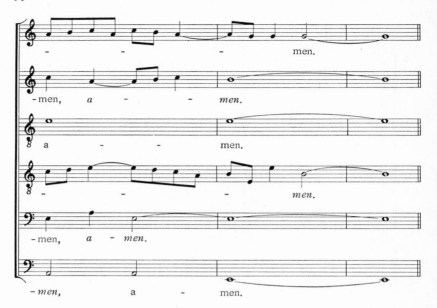

voices has an ascending skip of a fourth from an accented semiminim. Further, one of the continuing parts has a descending skip of a third followed by another descending leap of a fifth in semiminims, a progression that is immediately echoed by the antiphonal voice.

In the matter of dissonance treatment, Kerle remains quite consistent to his early period with, perhaps, one notable exception. The échappée, which was quite common in the early hymns, is not found in the hymns of the later period. The cambiata, however, continues to be quite common.

For the most part, Kerle's style does not differ in the later hymns from that in the earlier. The most pronounced over-all change is perhaps in the increase in the number of homophonic settings, with a tendency for a generally thicker texture. In several instances there is an increased use of motivic material (including the ostinato bass), and there are occasional sequential passages. It may be significant that some of the most radical departures from the style of the earlier period occur in the hymns apparently composed originally for the motet collections, that is, in works not specifically conceived for liturgical use. In his normal style, Kerle shows himself to be a competent master of the polyphonic technique of the period.[7]

[7] For a more comprehensive discussion of Kerle's style in all his works, the reader is referred to Otto Ursprung's introduction to his edition of the *Preces speciales*, DTB, XXVI.

A 15th-CENTURY BALLO:
Rôti Bouilli Joyeux

by DANIEL HEARTZ

BLOCKHEAD: I spy some open books over there,
Let's see if we know them or not.
Have you by chance the *Danse macabre?*
BUMBLER: You bother with the likes of that?
FEATHERBRAIN: If you have anything new
For God's sake don't hide it.
BUMBLER: I have the new *Basse dance.*
BLOCKHEAD: And you?
TRIFLER: I have this *Rosty boully.*

A PRINTER'S SHOP provides the setting for this scene from a 15th-century *sottie.* The characters are taxing their brains to find some amusing and untried diversion. At the mention of "Rosty boully" the anonymous playwright evidently expects a knowing response from his audience—whether the rough crowd in the streets where farces were performed, or the literate public buying the play from the presses of Jean Trepperel in Paris. And indeed, no one would miss a reference to the dance that was making the rounds of Europe, from royal court to barnyard. *Rôti bouilli* was no longer new about 1485, at least not new enough to satisfy the foppish Featherbrain, goat of the above scene, who goes on to demand something that "really swings" ("Chose qui monte"—see the original text in Appendix A).

The "roasted-boiled" dance had in fact been circulating for quite a few years, as is apparent from a document no less remarkable for content than for having survived at all. One Anthonius Girardi, a student at the University of Avignon, requested *rostit bollit* among other tunes in a contract drawn up with his music teacher, Mosse de Lisbonne, and signed on 19 November 1449 (Appendix B). A "citara sive arpa" (meaning probably a lute) and its case went along in the bargain. In exchange for the pupil's diligent and frequent practice the *maître* promised painless and honest instruction with a particular emphasis, it seems, on correct rhythm. Specifically, the tunes were to be learned in two mensurations: "en Basse dance" and "en Pas de Brébant."

359

South of the Alps, *Rôti* was no less a favorite. About 1454 Gaugello Gaugelli described the celebrations following the feast of San Secondo, patron of his native Pergola, a tiny town in the Marches (Appendix C). Even here, among the petty bourgeois, one danced *Rostoboli*, as well as *Lioncello* and *Gelosia*, all three familiar from the aristocratic dance treatises of the time. For the festivities in 1459 upon the passage of Pius II through Florence, a whole string of dances were played by shawms and trombone, the usual dance-band for great occasions (Appendix D). The student will easily identify them from contemporary dance treatises. Of interest here is that "the master" (i.e. young Galeazzo Sforza, the star of the occasion) "led two ladies to dance *gli arrosti*."

On into the following century the piece persisted, becoming quite literally a "potboiler." In 1521 G. G. Alione published a Piedmontese dialect play, *Comedy of Man and His Five Senses* in which one of his characters, The Feet, makes a speech allowing that they have led man many a time through *Rôsti bôgli* and other dances (Appendix E). A few later writers cite *Gioioso* (by which single word the dance is frequently known in the dance treatises), and they probably refer to the old tune—mention of other old choreographies at the same time suggests as much (Appendix F). Ruzzante in one of his comic dialogues has the amorous old fool Andronico declare that "his legs are still good for four measures of *Zogioso*." When G. G. Trissino and Andrea Calmo refer to *Gioioso* the context indicates that they are recommending a return to the songs and dances of "the good old days."

Rôti was by no means confined to the central musical axis of the Low Countries, France, and Italy. The dance was at home even in the British Isles, as several writers have pointed out. We find it in swineherds' company in the Scottish dialect poem, *The Tale of the Colkelbie Sow:*

> At leser drest to daunce
> Sum *Orfute*, sum *Orliance*
> Sum *Rusty Bully* with a bek

("Bek" cannot be the Scottish term "brook," as has been suggested, but is surely the French *bec*, "mouthpiece," which is to say that the tune was tooted on a wind instrument.) In England no less a poet than Skelton, laureate to Henry VII, found *Rôti* useful to his purposes. His satirical *Against a comely coistrum* (1495–96) inveighs against some simpleton of a music teacher, a Fleming of low birth but all the rage at court:

> He lumbreth on a lewd lute *Roty buly joys*
> Rumble down, tumble down, hey go, now now!

Similarly, in the morality play *Magnificence* (1516), Skelton has the character Courtly Abusion enter singing "Rutty bully, joly rutterkin, hey da!," another satire on a Fleming, as Nan Cooke Carpenter has shown.[1] With a pleasant faculty for speculation Miss Carpenter guesses that the lost text of *Rôti* went back to some incident in the Hundred Years' War, the French mocking the English for their love of "jolly roast beef." By bringing beef into the stew she has unwittingly concocted a *pot au feu*. Her point might better be supported, on the other hand, by noting that the dance title implies a fatal amount of overcooking.

Many dances of the late Middle Ages are no more than names, because neither choreography nor music survives. Hundreds of choreographies are extant—especially of basses dances—for which the music is lost. *Rôti* belongs to the fortunate few that by chance come down to us with music as well as steps. But its rare distinction is to have survived in both the Italian treatises and the Northern sources—the Brussels MS and *L'Art et instruction de bien dancer* printed at Paris by Michel Toulouze sometime before 1496. Geneviève Thibault was the first to point this out in the commentary she supplied to Eugénie Droz thirty years ago elucidating the scene quoted in Appendix A. Not long thereafter Margaret Dean Smith in her lively article on the Toulouze incunabulum again observed that *Rôti* furnished a major link between the two repertories, but, unable to overcome what still seemed an enigmatic notation, she could not reconstruct the dance.[2] Artur Michel included a facsimile of both the Brussels and Toulouze *Rôti* in his fine monograph, *Die ältesten Tanzlehrbücher*,[3] but he offered no transcription. Not until Ingrid Brainard's dissertation of 1956 was a serious comparative study attempted.[4] More recently, Otto Kinkeldey devoted some attention to

---

[1] Nan C. Carpenter, *Skelton and Music: Roty bully joys*, in: *Review of English Studies*, New Series, VI (1955), 279–84. Another poem of Skelton's, *Jolly Rutterkin* with its refrain *Hoyda, jolly rutterkin, hoyda* "reinforces the idea of the Flemish knight ('rutterkin') who made his money in the wool trade and aped his betters at court," according to Miss Carpenter. This poem was set to music by William Cornysh, Master of the Children in the first quarter of the 16th century, which piece was included by Hawkins in *A General History of the Science and Practice of Music* (London 1776), III, 3–14. The poem was set again by Ralph Vaughan Williams in his *Five Tudor Portraits*. "Rutters" appeared as torchbearers in a Masque for Queen Elizabeth I in 1579; see Enid Welsford, *The Court Masque* (Cambridge 1927), p. 151.

[2] Margaret D. Smith, *A Fifteenth Century Dancing Book*, in: *Journal of the English Folk Dance and Song Society*, III (1937), 100–10.

[3] Artur Michel, *Die ältesten Tanzlehrbücher* (Brünn n.d.) The study appeared in English translation, without the facsimiles, as *The Earliest Dance Manuals*, in: *Medievalia et humanistica*, III (1945), 117–31.

[4] Ingrid Brainard, *Die Choreographie der Hoftänze in Burgund, Frankreich und Italien im 15. Jahrhundert* (Diss. Göttingen 1956), p. 334.

the music, if not the choreography, and gave a parallel transcription of the different versions.[5] It remains to put together steps and music, compare the reconstructed versions, and draw the consequences of this unusual meeting-ground between the dance practices of North and South.

Rôti is that rare thing in the Northern sources, a figure dance (it has passages executed by one or the other partner and by both). According to the introductory dance instructions in Brussels and Toulouze it also belongs to a special category of basse dance called *mineure*, because it begins with a *Pas de Brébant* and concludes with the basse dance proper. The *basse dance majeure*, on the other hand, begins with the basse dance, we are told, with the implication that it concludes with the *Pas de Brébant*—the instructions neglect to mention this fact, perhaps because it was so well known. The relationship of the two parts *en basse dance* and *en pas de Brébant* may be studied in *Rôti* (Example 1a), for which the Brussels MS was used as the main source, the less reliable Toulouze having been called upon only for those additions in parentheses. For the first part, marked "en pas de breban," a transcription in $\frac{6}{2}$ meter (*Tempus imperfectum cum prolatione maiori*) seemed to offer the best solution to the difficult passage from mm. 9–16. The original lacks barlines and mensural signs. In the concluding part *en basse dance*, the same tenor was made to serve; and although freely treated, it corresponds in all essentials to the first statement, as the parallel lay-out of Example 1a is intended to show. Where scribal omissions obscure the choreography, additions have been made in brackets according to the rules of Northern dance-theory—the *simple* (*s*) never occurs singly; the choreographical unit of the *mesure* should terminate with a *reprise* and a *branle* (*r b*).

As an Italian ballo, *Rôti* occurs in several dance treatises and is attributed to Domenico of Piacenza (or of Ferrara), the founder of a Northern Italian school which dominated the entire *quattrocento*. Only one treatise includes the music, that of Domenico's pupil Giovanni Ambrosio (Paris, BN f. ital. 476), where the piece is called *El gioioso* (shortened from *Rostibuli gioioso*). With Kinkeldey's literal transcription of *El gioioso* easily available, a schematic reconstruction along the lines of Brussels suggested itself as a means of facilitating comparison. Thus the longs in the first section of Example 1b were written out in the original as six semibreves, being repetitions of the same tones except for occasional ornamental tones. The second part (second line of music)

---

[5] Otto Kinkeldey, *Dance Tunes of the Fifteenth Century*, in: *Instrumental Music*, ed. David G. Hughes, *Isham Library Papers*, I (Cambridge, Mass. 1959), 3–25; for the transcription see pp. 102–06.

Ex. 1a *Rôti bouilli joyeux* (from the Brussels basse dance MS with additions from Toulouze, *L'Art et instruction de bien dancer*)

continues with the groups of six semibreves, but this part is preceded by the sign for cut time, which produces breves rather than longs in the transcription. As in Brussels, the same tenor suffices for both sections. But here the basse dance comes first, the saltarello (equivalent to the *Pas de Brébant*) second. This is clear from the choreography, which has been restored in Example 1b using the letter symbols as in the French fashion. (See Appendix G for the original.) Kinkeldey's comparison of the two versions misses the mark, because this inverted order was not taken into account. Comparing the *Pas de Brébant* and saltarello sections, note that both move by the brevis, and that both adhere to a four-plus-four periodic structure, even if they disagree on a few melodic details. The sections *en basse dance* and *in bassadanza*, on the other hand, depart from regular periodic structure in their long first parts, one offering fourteen units, the other ten. Periodic structure had never been essential to or characteristic of the basse dance, musical length having been determined by the choreographies. And so it is here, where the tenor is stretched or abbreviated to fit a different though recognizably related sequence of steps. A striking notational difference is that Brussels (and Toulouze) offer a colored brevis for what the Italian scribe writes out to the worth of a long. Gombosi's theory that the blackening of the breves in the Northern sources indicated augmentation receives hereby a substantiation in the practical realm that he was unable to lend it when

Ex. 1b *El Gioioso* (Schematic version reconstructed from Paris, BN f. ital. 476)

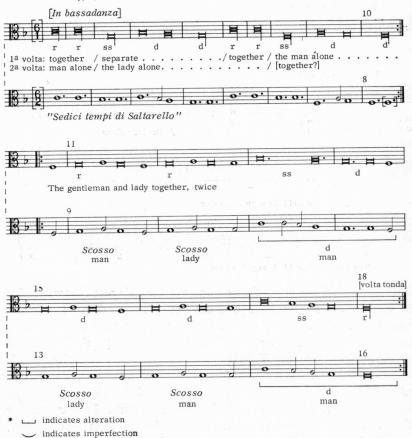

[*In bassadanza*]

1ª volta: together / separate . . . ./ together / the man alone . . . .
2ª volta: man alone / the lady alone. . . . . / [together?]

"*Sedici tempi di Saltarello*"

The gentleman and lady together, twice

Scosso
man

Scosso
lady

d
man

[volta tonda]

Scosso
lady

Scosso
man

d
man

* ⌣ indicates alteration

⌣ indicates imperfection

he summed up a lifetime's preoccupation with these matters in his chapter, *The Cantus Firmus Dances* in the *Capirola Lute-Book*.[6]

El gioioso occurs in the section of Ambrosio's treatise devoted to *Balli*. In whatever treatise this dance appears it is always called a *Ballo* or *Balletto*, by which the Italians understood those creations, usually figure dances, that freely and frequently mixed steps from the different metric and choreographical categories. Among the several score balli described in the treatises, the dance on *Rôti* cuts a relatively plain and sober figure. In the Northern sources only one other piece, *L'Esperance de Bourbon*, joins *Rôti* in the category of the *Basse dance mineure*. On

[6] Otto Gombosi, *Compositione di meser Vicenzo Capirola* (Neuilly-sur-Seine 1955), pp. xxxvi–lxiii.

the face of it, and considering the rarity of the genre, this category would appear to be something patched up to explain a foreign element. This is the conclusion of Mrs. Brainard, who feels that *Rôti* shows "the direct influence of the Italian masters on the Northern practice." [7] *El gioioso* has in its favor a more complete choreography to oppose to the Brussels version, where the first section lacks some steps (not to mention Toulouze, where the steps are omitted altogether). *Rôti bouilli joyeuse* is musically defective also, as is evident in particular from the section in the first part from mm. 9–16, which can be made to come out only with considerable arbitrariness and by invoking the aid of the parallel passage in *El gioioso*. Besides the inverted order of the sections, there is the matter of Ambrosio's F major against the D minor of Brussels, suggesting that some Northern scribe misplaced a clef. The picture that begins to emerge is of a bumbling and none too careful imitator, who transplanted an Italian creation into a Northern setting where it was ill adapted.

The most carefully executed of the Italian sources is Paris, BN. f. ital. 973, a presentation copy of the Guglielmo treatise for Galeazzo Sforza dated 1463; it preserves a choreography identical with *El gioioso* in the Ambrosio treatise. Close to this manuscript in authority and date and much larger in size is the Siena Codex, likewise a version of Guglielmo's teachings. This source presents a *Ballo chiamato Rotibolo* that resembles the others and is also attributed to Domenico, but differs from them in one vital respect: the saltarello section stands first, that is, the order of the sections resembles the *Basse dance mineure*. Here is the closer link between the Italian and Northern practices, and one that precludes a simple explanation of the inverted order in the latter as being either error or caprice. But was this the version of what was copied in the North? Or did Domenico adapt a Northern creation, which then became reordered in its parts upon subsequent diffusion?

The dates of the various dance treatises help very little in deciding questions of priority, because most are second-hand compilations representing several masters and more than one generation. A case in point is the Brussels MS, formerly believed to have been written about 1450 or even as early as the first third of the 15th century but now placed around 1500, although many of its tenors are demonstrably related to chansons of the mid-15th century and at least one can be traced back as far as c. 1420.[8] On the Italian side, we should recall that people were dancing

---

[7] Brainard, *Choreographie*, p. 4. In her later discussion, p. 326ff, the author qualifies this position by suggesting that the piece may have traveled back and forth.

[8] Daniel Heartz, *The Basse Dance. Its Evolution circa 1450 to 1550*, in: *Annales musicologiques*, VI (1958–63), 287–340. On the dating of Brussels see pp. 317–19; concerning the age of some tenors, see p. 288, fn. 2.

Rotibolo in the 1450s. From the standpoint of the treatises, Domenico's choreography can be no later than the Paris Guglielmo treatise of 1463. This does not tell us when Domenico is likely to have "arranged" *Rôti*. Nor is the life of this master-choreographer sufficiently well documented to be of aid. Domenico would appear to have been born early in the 15th century at Piacenza. He became known as Domenico of Ferrara as a result of serving the Este family, to which some of his creations bear witness (e.g. his *Leoncello*, which seems to honor the reigning Marquess of Ferrara from 1441 to 1450, Leonello d'Este.) Domenico passed into Milanese service sometime after 1450, the year in which Francesco Sforza took possession of Lombardy. At the marriage of Tristano Sforza in 1455 Domenico presided as the court's dancing master, in which capacity he is still mentioned in the Guglielmo treatise of 1463. Guglielmo says that he was present himself for the festivities of 1450 when Francesco Sforza entered Milan, and for the reception the same year of Duke John of Cleves, a representative from Philip the Good of Burgundy—the latter occasion suggestive as to how dances might have traveled between the Lombard and Burgundian courts. It may be of significance that the treatise most directly connected with Domenico (Paris, BN f. ital. 972) lacks his choreography of *Rôti* as a ballo (it does contain at the very end the steps for a *Bassadanza* called *Zoglioxa* written in an almost illegible hand and lacking music). This treatise is dated about 1450 by Artur Michel, which would seem correct because it contains the balli with Este connections, but none suggesting Sforza connections; however, a fly-leaf inscription in Latin gives the name of the (first?) owner as "Duke of Milan, Count of Pavia and Angera, etc.," helping to situate the MS in the latter part of the master's career, or as a compromise, somewhere between Este and Sforza service, i.e. about 1450.[9] When Antonio Cornazano, another Domenico pupil, compiled the second and only surviving version of his dance treatise c. 1465 he left out many balli, among them *El Zoioso*, because they were "o troppo vecchi o troppo divulgati." [10] In sum, *Rôti* was widely current in Italy soon after 1450, but there appears no way of proving that Domenico's choreography was earlier than this, and indeed its absence among the balli in Paris, BN f. ital. 972, suggests that it was not.

The solution to the puzzle is complicated by another kind of evidence. *Rôti bouilli* as a title, possibly as the beginning of a lost text, has meaning

---

[9] The date "1416" written in Roman numerals at the top of folio 1 must be a later addition. Besides the work of Michel the most reliable and extensive guide to the Italian treatises is to be found in the articles of Gino Tani on the various dancing masters for the *Enciclopedia dello spettacolo* (1954–62); the article *Guglielmo Ebreo* in MGG is not free of errors and inconsistencies.

[10] Ed. Mazzi in: *La Bibliofilia*, XVII (1915–16), 1–30.

in French. More than this, in common parlance the two words formed a pair to the extent of providing something of a standing joke. They occur in 16th-century authors, for example in Amyot: [11]

> Mais celuy là qui jamais n'est content
> Que son rosty ou bouilly le soit tant

or in Montaigne:

> Bouilly ou rosty, beurre ou huyle, tout m'est un

A century later Molière plays on this same difference between Tweedle Dee and Tweedle Dum, as we might say, in a scene from his *Malade imaginaire* (I,vi):

DIAFOIRUS: . . . il vous ordonne sans doute de manger force rosty.
ARGAN: Non, rien que du bouilly.
DIAFOIRUS: Eh ouy! rosty, bouilly, mesme chose.

To have seen lots of *Rôti bouilli* also occurs, in the sense of having lived through many experiences. Thus in Noel Du Fail (16th century): "Eutrapel donc alla a la cour, ou il vit bien du rosti et du boulli"; similarly in the *Commentaires* of Blaise de Monluc from the same period: "Il ne devoit pas traiter ainsi, j'avai veu trop de rosty et de bouilly en ma vie." From a syntactic point of view, the combinations of two participles in a single expression is especially characteristic of French and of Provençal.[12]

Regarded from south of the Alps, the situation now takes on a different aspect. To say "roasted-boiled" in Italian would require "arrosto bollito," or at the least, "rosto bollito." But the Italian treatises give us nothing close to a translation, only transliterations such as "rotibolo," "rostibulli," "rostiboli," etc.—phrases that are quite without any meaning. The conclusion seems inescapable that *Rôti* was originally a French tune. This does not mean that the dance arranged on the tune was necessarily of Northern origin, of course, yet such an argument has simplicity to speak for it. The other sequence, from North to South as a tune, then back to the North as a dance, involves a lot of traveling.

Rôti is not a unique case of a "foreign" melody in the Italian treatises. As Kinkeldey has pointed out, Domenico composed two balli on the French ballata *La figlia Guilielmino;* his ballo entitled *Franco cuore gentile* suggests Dufay's *Franc cueur gentil.* The index of the Ambrosio

---

[11] This and the following quotations were derived from Huguet, *Dictionnaire de la langue française au xvie siècle* (1924–) and from Littré, *Dictionnaire de la langue française,* s.v. "*bouilli.*"

[12] The writer is indebted to Professor A. H. Schutz of the Ohio State University for answering his queries and furnishing this information.

treatise reveals such titles as: *Ballo francese chiamato "amoroso," Ballo francese chiamato "petit riens," Bassadança chiamata "flandesca," Bassadança chiamata "danes," Ballo chiamato "petit rose."* Of his pupil and patroness Ippolita Sforza (Duchess of Calabria by her marriage in 1465 to the son of King Ferrante) Ambrosio wrote from Naples back to Sforza *mère* that "your daughter is very skilled in the dance; she has devised two new balli on two French chansons" ("ave facto duy balli novi supra duy cansuni francese.") [13] At the end of his treatise while describing the many occasions at which he had presided as dance-master he mentions one at which the Duke of Calabria "facta bally francese con madona duchessa [Ippolita] e con madona Lionora [daughter of King Ferrante]." Dances made on French tunes hardly surprise in an Italy teeming with *oltremontani* singers and instrumentalists. Some of the cases just mentioned show that dances as well as tunes were often imported from abroad, particularly from France and Flanders, surely not surprising either at a time when the many little courts of the peninsula looked to Burgundy for fashions in costume and courtly etiquette.[14] A few more details in this general picture are furnished by the Italian treatise recently acquired by Walter Toscanini and on loan to the New York Public Library. This New York codex, as it may be called, must date like the others from the third quarter of the century and includes numerous bassadanze and balli, including a *Gioioso in dua* and *in tre* (see Appendix G). Its first section concludes with a *Danza chiamata bassa franzesse in dua* that would be identifiable from its choreography alone as a French basse dance, and a *Ballo chiamato "franza mignion," franzese, in dua*. Both creations are anonymous, unlike the bulk of the other dances, attributed to one or the other of the dance masters such as Domenico, Guglielmo Ebreo, and Giovanni Ambrosio (appearance of the last two names in the same treatise argues against the supposition of Michel and others that Ambrosio is merely a name that Guglielmo assumed after his conversion). The very terminology of the Italian treatises betrays an awareness of the Northern practice, e.g. the use of the term *Pas de Brébant* (often in some garbled form such as *passo barbante*) which invariably attends any explanation of the saltarello. Brussels and Toulouze on the other hand offer no hints of an awareness

[13] Emilio Motta, *Musici alla corte degli Sforza*, in: *Archivio storico lombardo*, Second Series, IV (1887), 61–63.

[14] Daniel Heartz, *Les Goûts Réunis, or, The Worlds of the Madrigal and the Chanson Confronted*, in: *Chanson and Madrigal 1480–1530*, ed. James Haar, *Isham Library Papers*, II (Cambridge, Mass. 1964), 90. Analogies might be pursued in art with the movement which Panofsky calls the "International Style" of the earlier 15th century: *Early Netherlandish Painting* (Cambridge, Mass. 1953), I, 51–74.

of the Italian dance either in terminology or in repertory.[15] Admittedly they constitute a scanty record of what the Northern practice really was. It is significant nevertheless that, with the dubious case of *Rôti* left aside, borrowed dances are lacking altogether, whereas in Italy they abound. Thus when Bukofzer states flatly that the "French Basse dance is dependent on Italian models," [16] he ignores the little specific evidence on the point and also contradicts what is known of cultural movements in general during the early and middle 15th century.

All attempts to relate *Rôti* to a polyphonic piece had failed before the discovery of a correspondence in a little-expected place—the keyboard pieces which Hans Kotter copied for the use of his pupil Bonifacius Amerbach, the humanist of Basel, between c. 1513 and 1530; among the several settings of the basse dance *La Spagna*, one by Hans Weck is followed by a *Hopper dancz*,[17] the superius of which is nothing other than the *Rôti* tenor (Example 2). Note that *Hopper dancz* means literally "saltarello" and that the mensural relationship of main dance in longs and after-dance in breves applies to Weck's pair, making it a proper basse dance—*Pas de Brébant*. (Since German tablature quartered the value in relation to mensural notation, the original note-values have been doubled twice in Example 2.) The old tune offers not a few surprises in this new guise. The tune that Weck knew resembles the saltarello in Example 1b in such a prominent detail as the descent of a second in the first two measures, rather than the descent of a fourth in Brussels, which stands corrected again for its carelessness. But the mode according to Weck was not Ambrosio's F major but the D minor of Brussels and Toulouze. Thus if someone made a mistake in copying it was

[15] Kinkeldey believed that the French symbol *r* for *démarche* furnished an exception to this general rule, having been borrowed from the Italian word for the same thing, *ripresa;* see his study on Guglielmo, *A Jewish Dancing Master of the Renaissance,* in: *A. S. Freidus Memorial Volume* (New York 1929), p. 350. The point loses its force when we note that *reprise* as a synonym for *démarche* was in use as early as the Nancy choreographies of 1445 and that both terms persisted until the 16th century; in 1521 Robert Coplande, translating a lost treatise into English, says "in some places of Fraunce they call the repryse desmarche." On the terminology in the Northern sources see the study cited in fn. 8 above.

[16] Manfred Bukofzer, *A Polyphonic Basse Dance of the Renaissance,* in: *Studies in Medieval and Renaissance Music* (New York 1950), p. 198. Gombosi questioned the statement in his review of the book in JAMS, IV (1951), 144, taking the position that we do not know enough to say in which direction influences went. The claims made for *La Spagna* as a unique bridge between the northern and southern repertories (and between monophonic and polyphonic practices) demonstrate once again how little studied the treatises have remained and how unassimilated the secondary literature concerning them.

[17] Wilhelm Merian, *Der Tanz in den deutschen Tabulaturbüchern* (Leipzig 1927), pp. 48–49. Weck died about 1515, according to Merian; see his *Bonifacius Amerbach und Hans Kotter,* in: *Basler Zeitschrift für Geschichte und Altertumskunde,* XVI (1916), 167.

likely to have been Ambrosio with his major version. Used as a discant and ornamented as Weck has done, *Rôti* appears to be out of its element. The normal place for it would be a low voice. That is, it is really a tenor like *La Spagna*, both by reason of its notation in a middle range with tenor or alto clefs, and by reason of the skeleton-like cantus firmus quality—long notes of equal value (with the exception of the more animated ending). If the "point" of the Weck *Tanz-Nachtanz* combination of *La Spagna* and *Rôti* were not precisely that of placing what is usually a tenor cantus firmus in the discant and disguising it with coloration, we should have had a *Spagna* setting of the "normal" type, as elsewhere in the Kotter MS, with the cantus firmus in the middle or lowest voice, and a *Rôti* setting that followed suit. Let us pursue this point for a moment and consider Ambrosio's *16 tempi di Saltarello* as a bass. A rather startling perspective emerges in the resemblance these measures bear to the famous family of passamezzo antico, passamezzo moderno, romanesca, folia, etc.—the favorite ground basses of 16th- and 17th-century dance music or, more accurately, the formulae progressions that gave rise to thousands of dance pieces (not necessarily called by these names). It is not merely the isometric structure, the balancing four-measure units, the prominence of certain intervals such as the fourth, that are so reminiscent of later dances. Ambrosio's *16 tempi di Saltarello* actually duplicate tone for tone throughout six of the eight measures the bass of the progression that will later be identified by the name of passamezzo antico. When the *quattrocento* instrumentalists improvised discants above this bass they must have produced a kind of music that sounded very much like some of the pieces existing in written form—the best examples are those given as a demonstration on how to improvise by Diego Ortiz, in whose *Tratado de glosas* (1553) all the prominent grounds (called "Tenori"!) are treated. The Northern musicians whose musical practice and repertory are reflected, however imperfectly, in Brussels and Toulouze help complete the picture. When improvising discants above *Rôti en Pas de Brébant* they too must have made music close in spirit to the later grounds, the cardinal feature of which was their rigidly four-square character and their repetitiveness. Not the basse dance with its irregular periods, but the saltarello and like dances where music was master, opened the way to the future—to the variations and grounds of the 16th century and to that *carrure* wherein lay the course of instrumental music. The part *Rôti bouilli* played in this process may be surmised by recalling that it outdistanced all of its companions by far to become the most widely diffused ballo of the 15th century.

Ex. 2 Johannes Weck: *Hopper dancz* [*Rôti bouilli*] (from Merian, *Der Tanz in den deutschen Tabulaturbüchern*)

Appendices

A. French Play, 15th century, *Sottie a cinq personnages des coppieurs et lardeurs qui sont copiez et farcez:*

SOTIN: Je voy la des livres ouvers,
                Scaichons se les congnoissons point . . .
                N'aves vous point ceans la Dance
                De Macabre par personnaiges?
MALOSTRU: Vous meslez vous de telz ouvraiges? . . .
TESTE CREUSE: Se vous avez rien de nouveau,
                Pour Dieu, que point on ne le celle.
MALOSTRU: J'ay la *Basse dance* nouvelle
SOTIN: Et vous?
NYVELET: J'ay ce *Rosty boully* . . .
TESTE CREUSE: Vous n'avez point chose qui monte?

From: Eugénie Droz, ed., *Le Recueil Trepperel* (Paris & Geneva 1935–62), I: *Les Sotties*, 162–63. Droz dates the play "before 1488." In *Music in the French Secular Theater, 1400–1550* (Cambridge, Mass. 1963), p. 157, Howard Mayer Brown draws the implication that all the items mentioned were to be found in one of the open printed books and says that talk of single dances suggests that dance tunes and steps were available in broadsides, although none have survived.

B. Avignon Contract, 19 November 1449: "Mosse de Lisbonne . . . judeus promisit et convenit dicto Anthonio ipsum Anthonium docere et instruere ad ludendum de citara sive arpa carmina sive cantinellas sequentes: et primo *joyeux [e]spoyr.* Item *sperance, rostit bollit, joyeux acontre, la bone volunté que j'ey,* a deux mesures, contenant *l'aubedance* [*sic*, for basse dance] et *le pas de breban.* Deux *bergeres* [i.e. bergerettes or branles?] c'est assavoir *le joly vertboys* et *Jauffroit* et l'entrée acostumée a toutes dances." From: Pierre Pansier, *Les Débuts du théâtre à Avignon à la fin du xve siècle,* in: *Annales d'Avignon et du Comtat Venaissin,* VI (1919), p. 42. Pansier read the dance title as *roscit bollit,* which was corrected by Pirro to *rostit bollit* in his study, *L'Enseignement de la musique aux universités françaises,* in: *Bulletin de la Société Internationale de Musicologie,* II (1930), 45.

C. Festival Poem of Gaugello Gaugelli, c. 1454 (Cod. Vatic. Urbin. 692):

                Udirai melodia del bel sonare
                  De vantaggiosi pifari e trombecti
                  Arpe e leuti, con dolce cantare,
                Viole, dolcemele et organecti,
                  Con citare salterio e canterelle:
                  Tu poderai danzar se te 'n dilecti.

E vederai queste mie donne belle
Danzare a *bassadanza* e *lioncello*
A doi a doi con l'altre damigelle,
Quale *a la piva* e quale *a saltarello*
E chi a *rostoboli* e chi al *gioyoso*
E chi a *la gelosia*, novo modello.

From: Guido Vitaletti, review of Santorre Debenedetti's *Il "Sollazzo," Contributi alla storia della novella, della poesia musicale e del costume nel trecento* (Turin 1922), in: *Archivum romanicum*, VIII (1924), 199.

D. Anonymous account of festivities at Florence in 1459 (Florence, BN Magl. VII, 1121, fols. 66ᵛ–69ᵛ):

In questo tempo i pifferi e'l trombone
cominciaro a sonare un saltarello
fondato d'arte d'intera ragione . . .

Ballato quella danza *peregrina* . . .

E doppo questo il conte stette poco
che si rizzò e due dame invitava
le qual fecian la guancia lor di foco . . .

E ballato gran pezza al *saltarello*
ballaron poi a danza variata
come desiderava questo e quello
Feron la *chirintana* molto ornato
e missero amendue *gli arrosti* in danza
con *laura, communia* e *carbonata,*
Lioncel, bel riguardo e *la speranza*
L'angiola bella e *la danza del re.*

From: Vittorio Rossi, ed., *Un Ballo a Firenze nel 1459* (Bergamo 1895). (Nozze Fraccaroli-Rezonico).

E. Giovan' Giorgio Alione, *Comedia de l'homo e de soi cinque sentimenti* (printed in 1521):

I PE: L'hom, mi sì ve faren baler
ôtôrdiôn, la *giranzana,*
rôsti bôgli, fois, la *pavanna*
e altre dançe d'ogni sort
per tenir vostr coeur an desport
che l'hom an balant sta jojôx,
ch'el va sul galle e sta amorôx,
e, per tenirve exerçità,
e' ve menreu per la çità,
là nd' se fan feste e bônne ciere,
pr'i bosch, campagne e per rivere,
a derve mille spasament.

From: Enzo Bottasso, ed., *L'Opera piacevole di Giovan' Giorgio Alione* (Bologna 1953), p. 11.

F. Uses of *Gioioso* in the 16th century

1. *Bilora*, comic dialogue by Ruzzante, c. 1525:

> ANDRONICO: Digo che son sì in su la gamba,
> che me basterave l'animo
> de ballar quattro tempi del *zogioso*
> e farlo *strapassao* anchora
> e anche la *rosina* . . .

From: *Due dialoghi di Ruzzante in lingua rustica, sentenziosi, arguti et ridiculosissimi*. On the date of *Bilora*, see Carlo Grabher, *Ruzzante* (Milan 1953), pp. 96–97, footnote.

2. G. G. Trissino, *La Poetica, Quinta divisione* (c. 1530): "Ancora è cosa manifesta . . . che alcuni imitano i buoni, altri i cattivi. Verbi grazia nel ballare, alcuni ballando *Giojosi, Lioncelli*, e *Rosine*, e simili, imitano i migliori, altri ballando *Padoane*, e *Spingardò, imitano i peggiori*." From: Alfred Einstein, *The Italian Madrigal* (Princeton 1949), I, 112.

3. Letters of Andrea Calmo, c. 1540: "Al far de le feste, i homeni con le so veste longhe serai devanti, senza far strepiti, ni romor, ni frape, se sonava el so tamburin e altabasso un clavicimbano o do liuti, o una baldosa con la so violeta, balando *passo e mezo, rosina, tentalora, anella*, [g]*uanti di Spagna, torela mo vilan, zoioso, padoan, saltarello, bassadanza*." From: Vittorio Rossi, ed., *Le Lettere di messer Andrea Calmo* (Turin 1888), p. 232.

It is convenient to dispose here of some further "posthumous" appearances. Musically speaking, *Rôti*, or the last part of it, lived on as the melody of *Pacientia*, a four-part Italian secular song of c. 1500; see Nanie Bridgman, *Un Manuscrit italien du début du xvie siècle*, in: *Annales musicologiques*, I (1953), 200, No. 11; to the concordances cited, add J. Dalza, *Intabolatura de lauto Libro quarto* (Venice 1508), fol. 54. *Pacientia* betrays the duple meter of a *Quarternaria* but corresponds otherwise quite closely to mm. 9–12 of Example 1a above, with which it shares the same D-minor tonality. A related tune, now in F major, turns up in 1530 as the *Pavanne "La Rote de Rode,"* published in several versions by Attaingnant, for one of which and for concordances see D. Heartz, ed., *Preludes, Chansons and Dances for Lute* (Neuilly-sur-Seine 1964), No. 102.

From the choreographic point of view the basic "programmatic" idea of the dance with its separate, then joint, passages for man and woman seems to have survived as a *Gioioso* figure, in evidence as late as Caroso's *Ballarino* of 1581. See the *Bassa et alta* transcribed by Mabel Dolmetsch in her *Dances of Spain and Italy from 1400 to 1600* (London 1954), pp. 34–51.

G. Giovanni Ambrosio's treatise (Paris, BN f. ital. 476): *Ballo chiamato rostiboli composto per messer Domenico* [Tavola, fol. 4^v]:

BALLO CHIAMATO ROSTIBULI GIOIOSO IN DOI [Fol. 37–37ᵛ]

Imprima doi rimprese l'una sul sinestro e l'altra sul drecto, e poi l'homo se parta da la donna con doi sempii e doi doppii cominciando col pe sinestro, e poi faccia doe rimprese, una sul sinestro e l'altra sul dricto; e in quel tempo la donna anchora faccia le rimprese insieme con l'homo; e poi l'homo faccia ancora doi sempii e doi doppi, e poi doe rimprese l'una sul sinestro e l'altra sul dricto e l'omo se fermi; e poi la donna faccia tucto quello che ha facto l'omo; e poy se piglieno per mano e facciano doe rimprese l'una sul sinestro e l'altra sul dricto; e poi faciano doi sempii e tre doppii cominciando col sinestro; e poi dagano una volta tonda con doi sempii cominciando col drecto e una rimprese sul drecto; e tucto questo facciano un altra volta. E poi facciano sedice tempi di saltarello cominciando col pie sinestro e poi se fermino. E l'omo faccia un scosso e la donna glie arisponda e l'omo vada innanci con un doppio partendose col sinestro e la donna faccia un schosso e l'homo glie arisponda e vada da la donna. Appresso l'omo partendose col pe sinestro e faccia un passo doppio, e li schossi altri tanto con un doppio chome e dicto. Finis.

The text has been modernized by the addition of punctuation and capitalization; contractions in the original have been rendered as complete words. The same choreography is found in the Paris Guglielmo codex, BN 973, fol. 34–34ᵛ; in the Florence codex, BN Magl. XIX, 9.88; and on p. 47 of the New York codex, the MS owned by W. Toscanini on loan to the New York Public Library; it occurs with the sections reversed (the saltarello at the beginning) in the Siena codex, fol. 62, ed. Mazzi in: *La Bibliofilia*, XVI (1914–15), 201. The Modena codex gives substantially the same sequence of steps in an arrangement for three dancers and is called *Ballo chiamato Zojoso in terzo—tre ballano*. See Messori-Roncaglia, ed., *Della virtute et arte del danzare* (Modena 1885), p. 42. The same choreography *a tre* appears in the Siena codex where it is attributed to Domenico, ed. Mazzi, p. 206, and in the New York codex, where it is more elaborately described and bears the attribution: *Baleto chiamato gioioso in tre composto per m. Giovanni Ambruogo*. The New York codex also contains a *Balo chiamato goioso spangnuolo in dua*, p. 59, which may be related to the *Joyos* that figures twice in the Cervera MS; for a facsimile reproduction of the two pertinent pages, see A. Michel, *Die ältesten Tanzlehrbücher* (Brünn n.d.), p. 8; and Aurelio Capmany, *El Baile y la danza*, in: Fr. Carrera y Candi, *Folklore y costumbres de España* (Barcelona 1931), II, 303.

A *CHANSON RUSTIQUE* OF THE EARLY RENAISSANCE: *Bon temps*

by HELEN HEWITT

S HIS FIRST venture into the art of printing music, Ottaviano de' Petrucci published a series of three anthologies of secular polyphony by composers of the Franco-Flemish school. Much of the music included in these volumes was, at its time of origin, associated with poetry of either courtly or popular derivation. Yet Petrucci supplied only a short verbal incipit by way of identification. Recovery of the missing texts, to enable us to perform these polyphonic settings as conceived by their composers, presents a challenge to the modern editor. The task may be an easy one if words and music are found together in a contemporary source; it may prove impossible when the words cannot be traced in the extant literature; yet between these two extremes occur situations of varying degrees of difficulty and complexity.

Uncertainty becomes most acute when the composer has arranged a popular song of the day, a *chanson rustique*.[1] Deriving from the middle classes, these tunes were also enjoyed in court circles, and today many of them are known only through polyphonic arrangements made by serious composers for their more sophisticated audiences. We cannot name the composers of these tunes nor can we be certain of their "original" forms. As Brown states, "an original did exist, but no one will find it, for probably a ménétrier himself would not have been able to reconstruct it exactly."[2] A similar judgment might be passed concerning the words of these chansons rustiques.

A search for the missing text of *Bon temps*,[3] the popular melody ar-

---

[1] Howard Mayer Brown, *The Chanson rustique: Popular Elements in the 15th- and 16th-Century Chanson*, in: JAMS, XII (1959), 16–26.

[2] Howard Mayer Brown, *Music in the French Secular Theater, 1400–1550* (Cambridge, Mass. 1963), p. 116.

[3] Randle Cotgrave, *A French and English Dictionary* (London 1673), s.v. "Bon temps," defines this term as "prosperity; also merriment, or time spent in merriment."

ranged by an anonymous composer and appearing on folios 17^v–18^r of Petrucci's *Canti B Numero Cinquanta*,[4] provides a perfect example of the futility of a quest for the "original"—either words or melody. Yet whether we succeed in attaining this narrower objective or not, an acquaintance with available contemporary evidence pertaining to these chansons should make for fuller understanding of them and enhance our enjoyment of this music of the Early Renaissance.

This essay proposes to trace the steps taken in an effort to recover the words sung to the melody *Bon temps*. A number of polyphonic settings preserve the melody, but in themselves are only incidental to the main line of thought: to establish the identity or relationship of the melodies and texts at hand.

A. CANTI B, FOLS. 17^v–18^r, *Bon temps*

IN THIS four-part setting of *Bon temps* an unknown composer has placed the popular melody in the tenor, neither extending its phrases nor interspersing any passages of his own invention. The composer's treatment of the melody is uneven, for while he anticipates each of the first two phrases of the cantus firmus by rather long sections starting in imitation (mm. 1–30), he compresses his arrangement of the last two phrases into 12 measures.

The c.f. itself (see "Variant A" in the Table of Variant Cantus Firmi)[5] consists of four phrases of equal length (six measures) which together form a double period: ABAB'. Phrase 2 cadences on the dominant of the mode, whereas the other phrases all come to rest on the final. Phrases 1 and 3 are identical in every respect, and all four phrases start with a repetition of the dominant tone. The melody is a minor one, and its mode may be thought of as Aeolian, once transposed, or as Dorian with the B♭, often needed in this mode, here placed in the signature. The *Canti B* setting shows a signature of one flat in each voice.

Petrucci supplies no text beyond the incipit *Bon temps*.

Gaston Paris and Auguste Gevaert, eds., *Chansons du xve siècle* [MS f. fr. 12744] (Paris 1875; reissued 1935), p. 15, fn. 1, comment that "*Bon temps*, sans article, est aux quinzième-seizième siècles une personnification très-aimée."

[4] Venice 1502. This anthology was followed by the *Canti C Numero Cento Cinquanta* (Venice 1504) and preceded by the *Harmonice Musices Odhecaton A* (Venice 1501). See Gustave Reese, *The First Printed Collection of Part-Music* (*the Odhecaton*), in: MQ, XX (1934), 39–76.

[5] Agreeing with Brown's idea, I am assuming an imaginary "original," of which the versions of the melody discussed in this essay then become variants, not excepting the c.f. of the work in the *Canti B*.

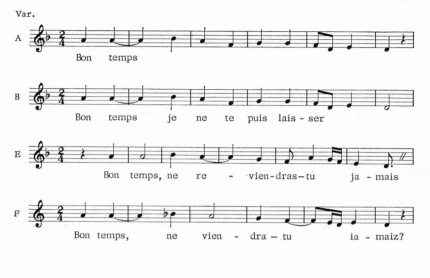

B. COPENHAGEN, P. 376, *Bon temps, je ne te puis laisser* [6]

THIS IS a three-part setting of only 24 measures—exactly the length of the c.f. in the tenor. All three voices start and stop together, and in their course proceed without pause. Although the phrases of the c.f. are not

[6] Copenhagen, Det Kongelige Bibliotek, Ny. kgl. S. 2°. 1848. The codex is paginated. This MS was discovered independently by Henrik Glahn of Copenhagen and Dragan Plamenac of the University of Illinois. Dr. Glahn read a communication about the MS before the Danish Musicological Society in November, 1956, and Dr. Plamenac read a paper about it at the annual meeting of the American Musicological Society held in Urbana in December, 1956. Glahn then wrote an article, published in a Danish periodical, an organ of the Association of Danish Libraries, in which he stated that he wished merely to acquaint Danish librarians with the newly discovered source, but that a full study would be published by Plamenac. This study

IANT CANTUS FIRMI

A

B

E
Por main - te - nir   tou - jours   en   paix

F

C
Tu m'as   fait cou - cher au son -   ger

D
Kyrie II

G
Sou - vent   m'as faict   la   soif   pas - ser,

separated by the usual rests, they are clearly marked by the progression
of the voices as they produce cadential formulas of the period. (Three
of these cadences are of the "octave leap" variety.) Elsewhere, the outer
parts move mainly in parallel tenths, an interesting feature of this short
work. Although the c.f. again has D as final, only the tenor is given a
signature of one flat.

The c.f., Var. B, shows minor deviations from Var. A at the ends

Plamenac also promised in *A Postscript to "The 'Second' Chansonnier of the
Biblioteca Riccardiana,"* in: *Annales musicologiques,* IV (1956) 261–62. I am deeply
indebted to Dr. Plamenac for his generosity in permitting me to study the pieces on
"Bon temps" in the new Copenhagen MS and to use the various cantus firmi in the
present article.

A ta   no - ble puis - san   -   ce

Tu   m'a don - né me - ren-co - li - e.

Je t'ay   m'a - mors don - né   -   e.

Je t'ay   m'a - mour don - né   -   e.

of phrases. (Throughout the Table one notices much variety in the
ornamentation of cadences. These differences need not be described in
detail.) More significant is the change at the beginning of phrase 4, where
the values of the repeated notes (Var. A: quarter, half) are now reversed
(half, quarter), thus eliminating the syncopation. In this same phrase
the characteristic upward leap of a fourth is also suppressed. Yet even
these variants seem not to destroy the essential "identity" of these two
cantus firmi.

In this work we become acquainted with one complete line of verse,
identically worded and spelled under each of the three voices: "Bon
temps, je ne te puis laisser."

C. COPENHAGEN, P. 2 1 3, *Bon vin, je ne te puis laisser*

THIS ARRANGEMENT is like the preceding in that it is for three voices, that the c.f. lies in the tenor, and that all voices start and stop together. Here, however, the phrases are set off by rests, and some attempt is made in the later phrases to employ anticipatory imitation. The pitch of the c.f.—the final is G—is a fourth higher than that of Vars. A and B, yet only one flat appears in the signature. The rules of musica ficta require the insertion of an E♭ several times.[7]

The most striking feature of the work is its metric signature. Although both the preceding compositions were written in *tempus imperfectum*, this one shows the sign of *tempus perfectum*. If the music is transcribed

---

[7] This c.f. and all others requiring it appear in the Table transposed to bring the final on D for easier comparison.

in this meter and barred so that cadential tones fall on the first beat of the measure, all phrases of the c.f. begin with an anacrusis (see Var. C). The notation, however, lacks the rests that would normally appear at the beginning of the work, if an anacrusis were desired.[8] A curious disturbance of the triple rhythm occurs near the end, requiring irregular barring by insertion of measures of $\frac{4}{4}$. Questions also arise concerning musica ficta.

Attention may now be called to the fact that the preceding setting (Copenhagen, p. 376) will sound not only as well, but perhaps better, if barred in $\frac{3}{4}$ with an anacrusis of one beat.[9] Is this, then, an example of triple meter masquerading in the guise of duple meter? One is now led to re-examine the arrangement in the *Canti B;* although the c.f. itself could be barred successfully in triple meter (see Var. A), the polyphonic work as a whole could not.

Melodically, Var. C alters the first phrase so that a member of the tonic triad always falls on the accent in triple meter (*A, A, F, D*); in phrase 2 it restores the dotted rhythm occurring in Var. A; in phrase 3 it uses the syncopated cadence heard in Var. B, but now involving a cambiata; while in phrase 4 it shows features of both the preceding cantus firmi: it has the upward leap of a fourth in common with Var. A and the ornamented syncopated cadence in common with Var. B. We cannot know, of course, which variant may have borrowed from another; but, by virtue of their sharing these common elements, the three c.f. are all the more closely linked together despite their differing meters.

An examination of the textual situation reveals that the first line of text in Var. C differs in only one word from the one line given with Var. B. One complete stanza beginning "Bon *vin,* je ne te puis laisser" accompanies Var. C. We shall return to it later.

D. ANTOINE BRUMEL, *Missa Bon temps*

BRUMEL USES the melody *Bon temps* in all the movements of his Mass. In most of the sections he manipulates it rhythmically in such a way that

---

[8] Since no perfect breve occurs in this work, a signature of *tempus imperfectum* would have produced all the values needed. Furthermore, at the point where the third phrase ends and the fourth begins, two semibreve values between breves call for alteration of the second; this rule cannot be followed, however, since the outer parts lack equivalent values.

[9] Particularly in m. 1, where the dominant-tonic progression in the bass is intolerable in $\frac{2}{4}$. *Le grant desir* (*Canti B* No. 51) also approaches the tonic chord through the dominant tone in octaves (twice repeated). It is written in *tempus imperfectum* but opens: $\frac{2}{4}$ ♩♪♫|♩ . (Only at the beginning of phrase 4 of Var. B would (V) I the c.f. not sound well in $\frac{3}{4}$.)

it is useless for our purpose here. At times he uses only a part, not all, of the melody in a particular movement. The complete melody can be reconstructed, however. In the "Tu solus altissimus" (from the Gloria) the first two phrases appear quite simply—possibly the "purest" version of them seen thus far.[10] To complete the melody we may take the third and fourth phrases from the second Kyrie.[11] It will be noticed how closely this c.f. (Var. D) resembles Var. C without, however, being identical in every detail. Like Var. C it is pitched a fourth higher than Vars. A and B, yet uses a signature of only one flat.

The secular words do not accompany the secular melody, but Brumel acknowledges the presence of a *cantus prius factus* and identifies it for us in naming his work *Missa Bon temps*.

E. COPENHAGEN, PP. 392 (D, T) AND 411 (C), *Bon temps, ne reviendras-tu jamais;* ST. GALL, MS 461, PP. 38–39, *Bon tamps*

THIS COMPOSITION, appearing in both the Copenhagen and St. Gall manuscripts, has been published in a performing edition by Giesbert.[12] It is not a c.f. composition in the usual sense of the term, for no single voice presents the c.f. consecutively. At the beginning the tenor announces the first phrase of the melody, the contra accompanying (mm. 1–6); the superius then quotes the same phrase at the fourth above, the other voices having unthematic counterpoints; the contra then gives out the first phrase in the lower octave (fifth below).[13] A similar procedure is then followed for the remaining phrases. The composer varies the order in which the voices present the fragments of the melody, but he does not vary their melodic features from one voice to another. Var. E shows the four phrases as they appear in the tenor. Again we find essential melodic agreement with the c.f. of the *Canti B* setting (Var. A). Perhaps it bears the closest resemblance to Var. C (*Bon vin*), however.

The most noteworthy feature of this work, for our study, is the composer's rhythmical treatment of the c.f. The work as a whole is in duple meter, yet the c.f. itself could be felt in $\frac{3}{4}$ with an anacrusis.[14]

---

[10] The ends of phrases 2 and 4 are lengthened by one measure since each closes one section of the Mass.

[11] For these c.f. I am indebted to the detailed study of this Mass by Lloyd Biggle in his doctoral dissertation (University of Michigan 1953), *The Masses of Antoine Brumel* (Ann Arbor: University Microfilms No. 5760), pp. 84–97.

[12] F. J. Giesbert, ed., *Ein altes Spielbuch: Liber Fridolini Sichery* (*um 1500*) (Mainz 1936), I, 40–41.

[13] My terminology (superius, tenor, contra) names the voices from highest to lowest. Giesbert, in his edition, gives *Sopran, Diskant,* and *Tenor* with these same voices. His terms, however, refer to members of the recorder family to which he assigns these parts.

[14] Except at the end of phrase 4.

Of the 12 phrase-quotations, 8 show the phrase beginning with an anacrusis—in duple meter. The other four shift the phrase so that it begins on the first beat of the measure. It may be noted that the second phrase is so shifted in the tenor, traditionally the bearer of the cantus firmus. The impossibility of identifying the "original" form of a chanson rustique when it survives embedded in polyphony becomes increasingly apparent.

In the St. Gall manuscript only the words "Bon tamps" appear—and only in the superius. In the Copenhagen codex, however, both superius and tenor continue with the words to the end of the line, "Bon temps, ne reviendras-tu jamais," while the contra supplies a complete stanza of four lines (to be discussed below). We have now discovered that a second text was associated with our melody.

F. FLORENCE, BIBLIOTECA DEL CONSERVATORIO, MS 2442, NO. 49: QUODLIBET

THIS MS was originally a set of four partbooks, of which the bass partbook has not survived. In this MS appears a quodlibet attributed to "Gaspart," possibly Gaspar van Weerbecke.[15] It begins by quoting fragments of popular songs of the day, among them *Adieu mes amours* (of which a setting occurs as No. 14 in the *Odhecaton*), *Il est de bonne heure né* (see the *Canti C*, No. 59), *Et levez vous hau, Guillemette* (MS 2442, No. 10; *Canti C*, No. 62)—and *Bon temps*. Following these quotations the three extant voices (and presumably the missing bass) assist each other in singing the following refrain, a composite of the words found in the three partbooks:

> Sonnez, chantez du bon cueur fin,
> Sonnez la bienvenue de Monsigneur le Dauffin;
> Sonnez trompettez, sonnez falcons; [16]
> Sonnez bonbardez et clairons;
> Sonnez, chantez, soir et matin,
> Sonnez la bienvenue de Monsigneur le Dauffin.[16a]

It is regrettable that the Dauphin's name was not given,[17] but his identity is not our chief concern here; the quodlibet offers a more perti-

---

[15] See MGG, s.v. "Gaspar."

[16] In addition to its normal meaning of falcon or hawk, "faucon" was used c.1500 for a piece of artillery. (See Littré, *Dictionnaire*, s.v. "faucon.")

[16a] Since no two of the voices give identical readings of the refrain, each selecting only what is needed by the musical phrases, I have tried to shape the quotations into a stanza; the last two lines appear in all three voices. See Howard Brown's article earlier in this volume for the refrain as it appears in the superius.

[17] As it was by the poet Clément Marot, who wrote a ballade "de la naissance de feu Monseigneur le Daulphin Françoys (1517)," the refrain of which reads: "Le beau

nent problem. The alto voice starts by singing the first two phrases of our melody (see Var. F) to the words:

> Bon temps, ie ne te puis laissier;
> Tu m'a donné merencolie.

Simultaneously the superius sings an unfamiliar melody to the lines:

> Bon temps, ie ne te puis laissier;
> Tu m'a t'amors donné.

We have already learned that two different texts were used with our melody. It now appears that "Gaspart" was also aware of this fact and wished to include both in his quodlibet; ingeniously, he contrived to do this by placing one of the texts with the melody itself (alto) and writing a suitable counterpoint (superius) to which the second text could be sung. The two voices start out together, in duet-fashion, thus emphasizing the relationship of both texts to the melody. The melodic line of the superius has not been found elsewhere; furthermore, its shorter note-values, contrasting with the longer values used for quotation of known melodies (not only the alto *Bon temps* but also *Adieu mes amours* when it enters) suggest its purely accompanimental function. Lastly, we may infer that the text "Bon temps, ne viendra-tu iamaiz" was the original text, since it is placed with the cantus prius factus, and that "Bon temps, ie ne te puis laissier" was an alternative text.

G. *Le Manuscrit de Bayeux*,[18] NO. XLIII, *Bon vin, je ne te puis laisser*

THIS MANUSCRIPT gives a monophonic version of *Bon vin*. It consists of nine phrases and seems, at first glance, to have no connection whatsoever with our melody. Gérold, the editor of the MS, has already pointed out, however, that the basic stanza of this drinking-song is composed of only four lines. Through a scheme of repetitions (both verbal and musical) and by the insertion of a refrain [musical notation: A - ne hau - voy!] [19] the

Daulphin tant desiré en France"; or by Jean Molinet in his two poems on "La Naissance de tres illustre enfant, Charles, archiduc d'Austrice." For the ballade, see *Oeuvres complètes de Clément Marot*, ed. Pierre Jannet (Paris 1883), II, 68–69; for the two poems see *Les Faictz et dictz de Jean Molinet*, ed. Noël Dupire (Paris 1936–39), I, 352ff and 359ff.

[18] *Le Manuscrit de Bayeux*, ed. Théodore Gérold (Strasbourg 1921). See also Gustave Reese and Theodore Karp, *Monophony in a Group of Renaissance Chansonniers*, in: JAMS, V (1952), 4–15.

[19] Gasté explains this expression as "l'ancien évohé grec" in *Chansons normandes du xv*e *siècle*, ed. Armand Gasté (Caen 1866), p. 69, fn. 2; i.e. it was an "exclamation used in the cult of Dionysus" (*A Greek-English Lexicon*, comp. Henry G. Liddell and Robert Scott, rev. ed. Oxford 1940, s.v. "εὐοῖ"); or, in its Latin equivalent,

song was greatly expanded. Actually the melody shows only two different (complementary) phrases in addition to the refrain. If the three phrases are lettered A, B, and R, the Bayeux melody may be analyzed as: ABRBAABRB. Since the two phrases A and B are also used for the third and fourth lines of text, the musical setting of the stanza would then be: ABAB. The four phrases are placed in the Table as Variant G.

In this form (ABAB) the melodic material seems to have certain features in common with Vars. A–F. It begins with a repeated note, rises one degree, and then takes a downward course (cf. Vars. A–F); its first and third phrases are identical. It is also interesting that Gérold publishes the melody in $\frac{3}{4}$ meter, starting it with an anacrusis; the Bayeux MS, however, shows the mensuration symbol for *tempus imperfectum diminutum* (cf. Var. C). Gérold's interpretation seems justified. (The rhythm of the words also supports this interpretation.) Curt Sachs gives considerable attention to this phenomenon in his *Rhythm and Tempo*.[20] Space does not permit a summary of his remarks, but in the section entitled "Pitfalls of Time Signatures," after stressing that, in conducting, the *tactus* (or "beat") merely "maintained the even pulsation of units," and that "as a consequence, the time signature, reflecting the *tactus*, does not, and cannot, reflect the rhythm of a piece," he comments that "the simplest case of clash of rhythm and time signature is ternary rhythm under the disguise of binary notation." Our dilemma, however, is not caused by the monophonic form of the melody, but by the fact that in certain compositions it appears with a background frankly binary and in others in a ternary framework.

The Bayeux melody differs from *Bon temps* in being in a major mode —Ionian. It is entertaining to speculate whether it could have developed as a major "answer" to the minor melody. Possibly the brighter mode was desired for the drinking-song. The first phrase of the minor melody starts on the dominant and closes on the tonic; the first phrase of the major melody starts on the tonic and ends on the dominant. If one attempts to convert the minor melody into major by inserting a signature

"a shout of joy at the festival of Bacchus" (*A New Latin Dictionary*, comp. Charlton T. Lewis and Charles Short, rev. ed. New York 1907, s.v. "euhoe"). This expression was therefore particularly appropriate for a drinking-song, but found its way into other chansons of whatever content. A more nearly homophonous French equivalent of the Greek, "Et hauvée," is used as a refrain in No. 130 of the MS edited by Gaston Paris. Cf. also derivative refrains in the Bayeux MS: "Hauvoy" (Nos. 21, 28, and 65), "Enne (*or* Ene) hauvoy" (Nos. 69 and 103), "Et (*or* Eh) ho!" (No. 46), and "Et hoye!" (Nos. 30 and 25, the latter being the chanson used in *Canti B* No. 51, *Le grant desir*).

[20] Curt Sachs, *Rhythm and Tempo* (New York 1953), pp. 241–43.

of two sharps, phrase two will not "convert," since the hypothetical ascent to the leading tone would be intolerable in this period. Omission of this phrase would leave but three phrases for the stanza of four lines. Since we find that phrase 3 is, in both melodies, a repetition of phrase 1, we need only consider how the second (= the fourth) phrase of the major melody evolved. Since the major form substitutes tonic for dominant of the minor form, phrase 2 would need to start on the tonic. Instead of a repeated tonic (= repeated dominant of phrase 2 of the minor melody) we find leading tone, tonic, which at least suggests the more vigorous rise in phrase 2 of the minor melody (*F-A-C*, Vars. A–F). Since either melody would be required to close on its tonic, the major form could descend through the scale to the lower tonic, while the minor melody would either have to "break back"—upward leap of a fourth (as in phrase 4 of Vars. A, C, D, E)—not to arrive at the tonic too soon; or "hover about" the third of the tonic triad as in Var. B. (Actually, the major melody also does a bit of both: note the upward leap, *F♯-A*, and the repetition of the tones *A-G-F♯* in phrase 2.) [21] Note also how the second "major" phrase touches the tones of the tonic triad on the first beat of each measure: 8–5–3–1.[22] A minor melody has now taken on a major form. With the repetition of these two phrases the major melody will now accommodate the four-line stanza. (The brief refrain was doubtless inserted to ease the rise from the end of phrase 2, lower tonic, to the beginning of its repetition, upper leading-tone —BRB.)

The Bayeux MS gives four stanzas of the drinking-song to be sung to the major melody. These run as follows:

1 Bon vin, je ne te puis laisser,
2   Je t'ay m'amour donnée,
Souvent m'as faict la soif passer,
Ne soir ne matinée.

Tu es plaisant à l'emboucher:
J'aymes tant la vinée,
Je prens plaisir à te verser,
8   Tout au long de l'année.

Soubz la table m'as faict coucher 9
Maincte foys ceste année.
Et si m'as faict dormir, ronfler, 11
Toute nuit à nuitée.

Et ma robe à deux dedz jouer,
Chanter mainte journée,
A la maison d'ung tavernier,
Passer ma destinée.

It may now be recalled that Var. C (the minor melody) also has a text beginning "Bon vin." The lines appearing in Copenhagen, p. 213, read as follows:

[21] In its four statements in the Bayeux MS, this phrase closes as follows: 1) as in Var. G, phrase 2, or Var. E, phrase 1; 2) as in Var. C, 3rd phrase; 3) and 4) as in Var. G or B, 4th phrase.

[22] Cf. Vars. C and D, first phrase, which similarly place 5-5-3-1 of the tonic chord.

Bon vin, je ne te puis laisser,	(= Bayeux, line 1)
Je t'ay m'amors donnée.	(= Bayeux, line 2)
Tu m'as fait coucher au songer	(cf. Bayeux, lines 9, 11)
Tout au long de l'année.	(= Bayeux, line 8)

These lines may have resulted from the composer's effort to compress the general sense of the Bayeux chanson into one stanza. On the other hand, possibly it was all of the poem he could remember. Whatever the truth may be, we may now assume that the drinking-song was sung to both the major and minor melodies.

Since the "identity" of Vars. B and C has been established, and since the one line of text found with Var. B differs from the first line of the stanza accompanying Var. C only in reading "temps," not "vin," it would appear that the two words were used interchangeably in the text represented most fully in the Bayeux MS. Of this hypothesis there is insufficient proof at hand, but if there was once another set of verses beginning "Bon temps, je ne te puis laisser," to our present knowledge they have not survived.

Let us now examine the second of the two lines sung by the superius in the Florentine quodlibet:

Bon temps, ie ne te puis laissier;
Tu m'as t'amors donné.

This line seems to be nothing more than a textual variant of the second line of the Bayeux MS. Could it have been a scribal error? Or was it possibly a reading especially contrived for a meeting with the Dauphin? Was it intended as a reminder of past patronage? An investigation of the extant texts of the other chansons cited in the quodlibet uncovers little that might suggest *double entendre*. "Adieu, mes amours," seeming at first inappropriate for a "bienvenue," continues as follows, however:

A Dieu, mes amours, à Dieu vous commant
A Dieu, mes amours, jusques au printemps.
Je suis en soucy de quoy je vivray;
La raison pourquoy, je vous la diray:
Je n'ay point d'argent, Vivray je de vent?
Se l'argent du roy ne vient plus souvent,
A Dieu, mes amours, à Dieu vous commant.[23]

One of the best loved of the chansons rustiques of the period, its first lines would have been sufficient to recall its theme. Was the composer hoping for a monetary reward for his musical homage?

[23] *Le Manuscrit de Bayeux*, p. 100.

The second stanza of *Il est de bonne heure né* [24] also contains two plaintive lines (not used in the quodlibet) that the composer may have had in mind:

> Je vous ay servy
> Bien et loiamment.

The other text beginning "Bon temps" was also cited in the quodlibet:

> Bon temps, ne viendra-tu iamaiz?
> Tu m'a donné merencolie.

Again no extant source confirms the reading of the second line, and again one is led to suspect that this line was substituted for the usual line for this particular occasion. Was the composer hinting at his state of dejection because of loss of the Dauphin's favor? In the Copenhagen MS (see Var. E) appears a stanza which tends to support this presumption:

> Bon temps, ne reviendras-tu jamais
> A ta noble puissance
> Por maintenir toujours en paix
> La réaulme de France?

Again we find that, after establishing the identity of a song by its first line, Gaspart continues his text as he wishes.

While the stanza from Copenhagen is complete, its first line has one syllable too many, so that the reading in the quodlibet is in this respect preferable. We find another alternative reading, however, in one of the stage plays of the period, *Farce Nouvelle a cinq Parsonnages*.[25] The cast is composed of only five players: "Faulte d'Argent," [26] "Bon Temps," and "troys gallans." As the curtain rises, according to a stage direction "les troys gallans commencent en chantant":

> Bon temps reviendras-tu jamais
> A ta noble puissance
> Que nous puissions tous vivre en paix
> Au royaulme de France?

We now have three alternative readings for the first line: "ne viendra-tu," "ne reviendras-tu," and "reviendras-tu." Of these, the third seems the

[24] See Howard Mayer Brown, *Theatrical Chansons of the Fifteenth and Early Sixteenth Centuries* (Cambridge, Mass. 1963), Nos. 25 and 26, for two polyphonic settings of this melody; see p. 78 for the two lines of text quoted here.

[25] See Gustave Cohen, ed., *Recueil de farces françaises inédites du xvᵉ siècle* (Cambridge, Mass. 1949), Farce No. XLVII, pp. 379–83. See also Brown, *Music in the French Secular Theater*, pp. 194–95 and *passim*, for other references to "Bon Temps" in the theater of the time.

[26] It is interesting that the Florentine MS 2442 (which contains the quodlibet discussed above) both opens and closes with settings of *Faulte d'argent*. It contains no complete setting of *Bon Temps*, however.

best both metrically and grammatically. We also have two versions of the full stanza, though with similar meanings.

The last composition in the Copenhagen MS to use the words "Bon temps" (found on pp. 170–73) seems to stand apart from all the material discussed above. Musically it has nothing in common with any of the *Bon temps* cantus firmi, and its stanzas are not known to exist elsewhere. Only its subject matter and part of its rhyme-scheme seem to link it with the poetry given above. The music is attributed to "Johannes de Sancto Martino." Although this ascription could not possibly refer to the distinguished Johannes Ockeghem of the Abbey of St. Martin at Tours, it may be a clue to the identity of the amateur who composed the various settings of *Bon temps* in the Copenhagen MS. The work is alternatively homophonic and polyphonic, and begins by setting off the words "Bon temps" by two simple chords (iv—i of the Phrygian mode), of which the second bears a fermata in each voice. Of all the settings discussed here, this is the only one that seems to be trying to give expression to the sadness occasioned by the absence of "Bon Temps." Two lines beginning "Bon Temps" are used as a refrain, and their musical setting is identical (and written out) each time it recurs: the first line in homophony, the second in polyphony. The complete text reads:

> (Ref.) Bon Temps, las ques-tu devenuz,
>   Mais ou fais-tu ta residence?
>   1. Chascun te quide, grans et menus.
>   Je te prieus, viens et t'avance.
> (Ref.)   Bon Temps, *etc.*
>   2. Il fault que soyt detenuz.
>   Pourquoy nous perdons patience?
> (Ref.)   Bon Temps, *etc.*
>   3. Tout malheur nous est advenu
>   Despuis que non mes ta presence.
>   4. Reviens, Bon Temps, et bienvenue
>   Seras au royaume de France.
> (Ref.)   Bon Temps, *etc.*

Let us now summarize our findings. The minor melody appearing as a c.f. in the *Canti B* is also found elsewhere in variant forms (Vars. A–F), but which of these is closest to the "original" will forever remain unknown. Var. G, the major melody, differs so greatly from the minor melody, not alone in its mode but also in its contour and structure, that its derivation from the minor melody is very doubtful. Two quite different texts seem to have been sung to the minor melody. One stanza of *Bon temps, reviendras-tu jamais* has come down to us, possibly better preserved in the *Farce*.[27] We have no absolute proof that *Bon temps, ie ne te puis laissier* and *Bon vin, je ne te puis laisser* were the same text; but if they were, this second text was sung to both the minor and major melodies. Since the reading "Bon vin" occurs only with the variants in triple meter (Vars. C and G), and since the first text is found only with the minor melody in duple meter, it seems probable that the text beginning "Bon temps, reviendras-tu jamais" was the one sung to the melody appearing in the *Canti B*. That locally other texts were written on this same subject, and variants of the original texts and melodies improvised at will, seems certain from the evidence at hand.

Whatever form, melodic or poetic, the "original" may have taken, it appears that the various strata of French society—both "grans et menus"—found a common ground in their love of music and of

"Bon temps."

[27] The allegorical treatment of "Bon Temps" continued well into the 16th century. An even more fascinating play entitled *Satyre pour les habitans d'Auxerre*, in: *Recueil général des sotties*, ed. Émile Picot (Paris 1902–12), II, 347–72, has a cast of five players, of whom "Peuple François" and "Bon Temps" are two. A number of historical personages are mentioned. A third character relates, "J'ay veu le roy,/ Aussi la royne Alienor/ Qui est richement paree d'or,/ Voire vrayment qui est bien fin/ Et aussi monsieur le dauphin/ Et le petit duc d'Orleans." (The play was written in 1530.) After "Bon Temps" has arrived and been greeted, "Peuple François" comments that "C'est assez pour fouyr Soucy/ D'avoir Paix et Bon Temps ensemble." Neither of our songs is quoted in this play, however.

EXULTANTES COLLAUDEMUS:
A SEQUENCE FOR
SAINT HYLARION

by RICHARD H. HOPPIN

AFTER THE INTENSE musicological activity of recent decades, one is astonished to discover a wide, and widely cultivated, field of musical composition still remaining virtually
unexplored. Yet monophonic settings of late medieval and Renaissance
liturgical poetry do constitute such a field. In part, at least, neglect of
this later plainchant may be blamed on the antiquarian fallacy that what
is oldest is necessarily best. The Golden Age of Plainchant is followed
by the Silver Age, which leads in turn to the (lower case) age of debase-
ment.[1] Liturgical reforms, by excluding virtually all late additions to
the repertory, officially sanctioned this curious evolution *à rebours*. With
all too few exceptions, unfortunately, musical scholars have accepted on
faith that what was excluded must therefore be unworthy of their attention. Literary scholars made no such mistake, and the enormous collections of hymns, Sequences, and rhymed Offices published in the *Analecta
hymnica* bear witness to the continuing creation of liturgical poetry
throughout the 14th and 15th centuries.[2] In contrast, only a negligible
fraction of the music that necessarily accompanied this poetry has been
made available for study. For the texts of over 850 rhymed Offices in
the *Analecta hymnica*, almost no musical settings are to be found in
modern editions, and even hymns and Sequences are far too sparsely
represented. Studies of the latter form have concentrated largely on its
origins, and interest in its development generally ceases with the 12th-
century compositions of Adam de St. Victor. But Sequence composition
did not end with Adam. Written over 200 years after his death in 1192,
Exultantes collaudemus carries on the tradition. Quite obviously the
later history of the form cannot be projected on the basis of a single

---

[1] Anselm Hughes, *Anglo-French Sequelae, edited from the papers of the late
Dr. Henry Marriott Bannister* (London 1934), p. 10.
[2] *Analecta hymnica medii aevi* (hereafter AH), ed. G. M. Dreves, C. Blume,
H. M. Bannister (Leipzig 1886–1922).

work, but the Sequence for St. Hylarion serves notice that further investigation of that history should prove both interesting and fruitful.

The Office and Mass for St. Hylarion, source of *Exultantes collaudemus*, can be dated with considerable exactitude, for they received official approval from Pope John XXIII in a bull issued at Bologna on 23 November 1413.[3] Interestingly enough, the *ad hoc* examining committee consisted of Cardinals Pierre d'Ailly and Francesco Zabarella, men whose concern with musical matters has long been recognized. On their recommendation, permission was granted for the Office to be sung (*decantari*) with reverence, devotion, and honor, each year for all future time.[4] We may assume, therefore, that the music, as well as the text, was in existence when the bull was issued and that both had been composed within the preceding one or two years.

The text of the Hylarion Sequence was published long ago by H. M. Bannister, who remarked that, although it was often incomprehensible, it constituted a "kulturhistorischen Kuriosität" to which he would not willingly deny a place.[5] Actually, *Exultantes collaudemus* is curious only by virtue of its subject and its presumed Cypriot origin. Nothing could be more traditional than its poetic form. With only minor deviations, the pattern $A_8\ A_8\ B_7\ C_8\ C_8\ B_7$ is used for each of the 12 stanzas.[6] This rigid adherence to a form favored by Adam de St. Victor and all later liturgical poets clearly places the unknown author of the text in the mainstream of Sequence composition.

In both its form and style, the melody of the Hylarion Sequence proves to be equally traditional. The two halves of each stanza are sung to the same melody in a setting that is almost completely syllabic.[7] Twelve simple melodies thus follow one another to create the standard Sequence form *aa bb cc dd* etc. But this description, with which the form is too often casually dismissed, gives no indication whatsoever that a high degree of creative skill has produced a structure of great musical interest.

---

[3] *Reg. Lateran. Joann. XXIII*, No. 172, fols. 134–138. The bull, addressed to Janus, King of Cyprus, contains the complete text of the service for St. Hylarion. The same service with music is found in the Turin MS, Bibl. Naz., J. II. 9 (hereafter Tu B), fols. 1–13. The Sequence itself begins on fol. 10ᵛ, after the rubric *sequitur sequentia*.

[4] From Wilhelm Meyer's copy of the bull preserved in the Niedersächsische Staats- und Universitätsbibliothek Göttingen (*Nachlässe Wilhelm Meyer XXXIII—Turiner Liederhandschrift*). I am deeply grateful to the Göttingen Library for making these papers available to me on interlibrary loan.

[5] AH XL (1902), 205f.

[6] Variety is introduced in stanza 10 by means of internal rhyme and retention of the same rhymes throughout. The third lines of stanzas 7b and 12a have only six syllables. These irregularities evidently preceded composition of the music, for in each case the melody is adapted by combining two notes into a ligature.

[7] Apart from the adaptations in stanzas 7b and 12a, two-note ligatures occur only in melodies 2 and 4.

Perhaps the most unexpected architectonic feature of *Exultantes collaudemus* is its organization by tonal means into four groups of three melodies each. The Sequence as a whole is in Mode 7, which is strictly adhered to in all but three melodies. These three drop down to the plagal range (Mode 8) and occur in strategic positions as Nos. 3, 6, and 10. The irregular placement of the third plagal melody becomes immediately explicable when the distribution of cadential notes is examined. Corresponding with its three lines of poetic text, each melody naturally subdivides into three phrases, the final notes of which are shown in Table 1.

TABLE I

Cadential Notes in *Exultantes collaudemus*

GROUP			FINAL	NOTES	OF	PHRASES			
		A	B	C	A	B	C	A	B	C
I. Melodies	1–3	g	d′	g	g	d′	g	g	g	g
II. ″	4–6	g′	g	d′	g	d′	g	g	g	g
III. ″	7–9	g	d′	g	d′	d′	g	d′	d′	d′
IV. ″	10–12	d	a	g	d′	g	d′	d′	g	g

Establishment of the formal subdivisions is accomplished in part through the use of the same note to end all three phrases only in melodies 3, 6, and 9. In the first two, the finality of the endings on *g* is enhanced by the use of the plagal range. In melody 9, however, the three endings on *d′* call for a tessitura near the top of the authentic range.[8] With use of the plagal mode thus precluded in melody 9, its reappearance in melody 10 produces a new and dramatic effect. Although still signaling the division of the whole into groups of melodies, the plagal mode is now introductory rather than conclusive. At the same time it reaffirms the final of the mode after the incomplete ending of Group III. This reaffirmation, be it remarked, is not accomplished until the only phrase that does not end on *g* or *d* has been introduced. The different treatment of phrase endings in melody 10 thus reflects and subtly emphasizes the plagal mode's different structural function.

The quadripartite division of the Sequence, effected by the adroit distribution of phrase endings in combination with the plagal mode, is further emphasized by even subtler contrasts of range. After the plagal melody 3, with its three cadences on *g*, phrase 4A rises to *g′* for the first time in the sequence. In addition, this phrase stresses the only cadence

[8] The complete melodies may be seen in Ex. 1.

on g' by using the cadential formula g' f' g' g' to be discussed shortly. Exactly the opposite contrast of range occurs between melodies 9 and 10. After the high range of melody 9, with its three cadences on d', phrase 10A introduces the only cadence on d, the pattern d e d d being an inversion of the standard cadence formula. Such parallelism at corresponding structural points, far from being accidental, provides unimpeachable evidence of a carefully planned and skilfully executed musical form.

From the cadential notes as shown in Table 1, it is quite obvious that the composer of *Exultantes collaudemus* was as fully aware of the organizing power of the first and fifth degrees of the scale as any 18th-century musician. Within the limits of Sequence style, and without recourse to later methods of melodic repetition, he has created a tonal structure comparable to the Classical A A B A form. It should be noted, however, that the tonal procedures in the Hylarion Sequence also look back to the early practice of ending Sequences a fifth above the level of the beginning. The origin of this curious practice has yet to be satisfactorily explained,[9] but its faint echo within a balanced and sophisticated tonal structure constitutes part of the charm, as well as the originality, of *Exultantes collaudemus*.

The objection might be made, and with some validity, that more than cadence points is needed to create a sophisticated musical structure and that it is time to examine the complete Sequence melody. To counter this objection, therefore, the 12 melodies of *Exultantes collaudemus* are presented in Ex. 1. Although no two of these melodies are identical, it will be seen that thematic, or at least motivic, repetitions are by no means absent. A systematic and complete discussion of all these repetitions would be both wearisome and futile, but a few may be mentioned briefly.

Only rarely do the motivic repetitions seem designed to reinforce the quadripartite structure of the Sequence as a whole. This is the case, however, with phrase 3C. The complete phrase, with a note prefixed, has already appeared as phrase 3A, and its first four notes are anticipated at the close of phrase 3B. Its identity with the final melody of Group I being thus firmly established, phrase 3C is peculiarly fitted to return intact as the closing phrase of the Sequence (12C).[10] Much more often, scattered repetitions or successive modifications of a phrase diversify and disguise the rigid outlines of the tonal structure. Phrase 1C, for

---

[9] For discussions of this question see: A. Hughes, *Sequelae*, p. 13ff.; E. Misset and P. Aubry, *Les Proses d'Adam de Saint-Victor* (Paris 1900), p. 119ff.; and C. A. Moberg, *Über die schwedischen Sequenzen* (Uppsala 1927), I, 175ff.

[10] In the repetition of melody 3, the final phrase begins d f g a instead of f g a g. Since this is the only instance when the repeated melodies are not identical, it may be assumed that the first version is correct and the variant merely a scribal error.

Ex. 1 *Exultantes collaudemus*

instance, reappears as phrase 5C and then undergoes various additions and subtractions to form phrases 6B, 6C, 7A, and 7C. Phrase 1B is accorded a different treatment. Varied in phrase 4C, it is transposed down a fifth in phrase 6A and returns to its original position in phrase 12A with the change of only one note.

Even more than complete phrases, four-note motives appear with astonishing frequency throughout the Sequence. The pattern c' d' e' d', for instance, forms the first half of phrases 1B, 2B, 4C, and 12A. Transposed down a fifth, the same motive opens phrases 3C, 6A, and 12C. In addition, phrases 6B, 10C, and 11C begin with the motive inverted, phrase 9A with the retrograde form, and phrases 6C, 7A, and 8C with the retrograde inversion. Various forms of the motive also occur within phrases 3A, 10B, 11B, and 12B, and the original form, either on c' or f, appears at the end of phrases 3B, 5A, and 5B. While the use of this original form to open seven phrases and to close three cannot have been wholly unpremeditated, it is not to be believed that the inverted and retrograde forms, or those appearing within a phrase, resulted from a deliberate manipulation of the motive. Nevertheless, its presence in some form in 21 of the 36 phrases certainly contributes to the stylistic unity that is as satisfying now as it must have been to its creator.

Other motives recur somewhat less frequently throughout the Sequence, but their various appearances need not be detailed here. The cadential formula g f g g, however, cannot go unmentioned any more than it can pass unnoticed in the Sequence itself. Leaving aside for the moment the historical significance of this formula, we may briefly survey the manner of its use in *Exultantes collaudemus*. In the first place, all 12 melodies close with some form of this rising cadence, the complete formula being used for melodies 1, 3, 5, and 12. With a different first note, the variant x f g g closes melodies 2, 8, and 10, and, in transposition up a fifth, melodies 4, 9, and 11. The remaining melodies, 6 and 7, use a shortened form, g f g, which drops the final repeated note. But this is not all. The complete pattern also appears in five A phrases (melodies 2, 3, 4, 7, and 11) and is inverted in phrase 10A. Moreover, the first variant is used in the opening phrases of melodies 6 and 8, and in the middle phrases of melodies 1, 4, 9, and 10. The complete formula concludes middle phrases only in melodies 6 and 7. All in all, then, the complete formula or one of its variants appears in 8 first, 6 middle, and all 12 final phrases.

That the distribution of this cadence formula and its variants was not fortuitous may be seen in the unique characteristics of melodies 6 and 7. It is surely significant that these melodies, the only ones to use the complete formula for their middle phrases, are also the only ones to close with the shortened variant g f g. By following the complete pattern in the middle phrase with a less decisive close, the composer may have deliberately softened the effect of finality in melody 6, with its three cadences on g in the plagal mode. Melody 7 contributes to the feeling of continuity by beginning with a repetition of phrase 6C in which an added final note produces the complete cadence formula. The relationship between the two melodies is then established unmistakably by the parallel cadential patterns of their middle and final phrases.

These subtle connections between the final melody of Group II and the first melody of Group III illustrate once again the composer's careful articulation of the subdivisions within his total musical structure. Every aspect of the Hylarion Sequence, indeed, attests to its composer's intelligence, sensitivity, and skill. Using the simplest and most restricted of materials, he has produced a work of the highest artistic order, perfect in structural balance and symmetry, unified and subtly diverse. After analyzing the early Sequence *Observanda* (*Adorabo major*), Bruno Stäblein remarked: "*Das ist Hohe Schule melodischer Kunst.*" [11] The remark may be applied with equal right to *Exultantes collaudemus.*

It is not merely by its artistic quality, however, that the Hylarion Sequence worthily prolongs the traditions of Sequence composition. However advanced its architectonic structure may be, much of its thematic and motivic material derives from a melodic vocabulary as old as the genus itself. A complete study of that derivation remains an impossibility until many more Sequence melodies become available in modern editions. Enough material is at hand, however, to make a preliminary investigation into the origins of two motives in the Hylarion Sequence: its opening phrase and its already discussed cadential formula.

To deal with the latter first, we may note that its persistence throughout the history of the Sequence is so obvious as to need only the slightest documentation here. Of the Sequences remaining in the liturgy, *Lauda Sion* uses the cadential formula *g f g g* most conspicuously.[12] This leads us back to Adam de St. Victor, since *Lauda Sion* took over almost intact the melody of *Laudes crucis*, which was also used for seven more of his Sequence texts.[13] But the formula did not originate with Adam, and its prominence in his Sequences is merely an indication that they too are using a traditional melodic vocabulary. Appearances of the cadential formula in some of the earliest Sequence melodies may be studied in the *sequelae* published by Anselm Hughes,[14] or in the partially texted Sequences analyzed by Bruno Stäblein.[15]

---

[11] Bruno Stäblein, *Zur Frühgeschichte der Sequenz,* in: *Archiv für Musikwissenschaft,* XVIII (1961), 14.

[12] *The Liber Usualis with Introduction and Rubrics in English* (Tournai 1952), p. 945 (hereafter LU).

[13] Misset and Aubry, *Proses,* p. 130, *timbre* 61. See also Hans Spanke, *Die Kompositionskunst der Sequenzen Adams von St. Victor,* in: *Studi medievali, nuova serie,* XIV (1941), 22ff.

[14] Hughes, *Sequelae:* see especially Nos. 2, 4, 5, and 6 among others.

[15] Stäblein, *Frühgeschichte:* see p. 8ff.

A formula that thus persisted through more than four centuries of Sequence composition must have had special significance for those who used it, and we may well ask whence that significance derived. Only an origin in the earlier plainchant repertory, it would seem, could account for the introduction and continued use of the cadential formula as an essential element of the Sequence's melodic style. While descending cadences are generally regarded as being characteristic of Gregorian chant,[16] the rising cadential formula is by no means an innovation. It occurs, in fact, in exactly the same pattern as in the Sequences, as the mediant cadence of the first, sixth, and seventh psalm tones when the antepenultimate syllable is accented.[17] Considerably more pertinent, given the origin of the Sequence, is the frequent appearance of the cadential formula in Alleluia melodies, where the penultimate syllable is often set to an *epiphonus* that anticipates the final note.[18] An example from which a known Sequence was derived is the *Alleluia: Mirabilis Deus.*[19] In the cadence before the *jubilus,* the characteristic *epiphonus* followed by a single note produces the pattern *ga a.* This Alleluia melody is repeated exactly as the first phrase of the *sequela,* whose second phrase is derived from the beginning of the *jubilus* but extends its cadence on *d* by means of the well-known *d c d d* formula. This formula also concludes the next two phrases, and only the final, unrepeated phrase has a descending cadence.[20]

Of the many other examples that might be cited, one is particularly suggestive. The partially texted *Gloria victoria* is a Sequence to the *Alleluia: Adorabo ad templum* that is still in use for the Dedication of a Church.[21] Sung to the word *alleluia,* the first phrase of the Sequence corresponds at its beginning with the original Alleluia. The close of the phrase on *g,* however, is again extended by the standard cadence formula. Thereafter, melodies 2–4 close with the same cadence on *g,* while melodies 5–14 transpose the pattern up a fifth to end on *d'.* Again only the

---

[16] See Hughes, *Sequelae,* p. 12f.; and Willi Apel, *Gregorian Chant* (Bloomington, Ind. 1958) p. 263ff.

[17] LU, pp. 113 and 116.

[18] Cf. LU, p. 786, the *Alleluia: Angelus Domini* for Easter Monday. The repetitions of the formula in the Verse are noteworthy. The last seven notes of the Alleluia before the *jubilus* are identical with phrases 3C and 12C in the Hylarion Sequence (*f g a g f g g*). The same phrase ends *timbre* 166 in Aubry's catalogue of melodies in the sequences of Adam de St. Victor. (Misset and Aubry, p. 152.)

[19] *Graduale sacrosanctae Romanae ecclesiae* (Rome 1948), p. 364.

[20] Hughes, *Sequelae,* p. 57. *Mirabilis Deus* in its syllabic form, without the opening, unrepeated phrase, may be seen in the 13th-century *Prosaire de la Sainte-Chapelle* published in facsimile by Dom Hesbert in: *Monumenta musicae sacrae* (Macon 1952), I, 280.

[21] Stäblein, *Frühgeschichte,* p. 19ff.

15th and final melody ends with a descending cadence. The parallel between this use of musical rhyme and the custom of ending verses or half stanzas with the vowel *a* is obvious, although the interrelationship between the two procedures calls for further study.[22] It is interesting to recall that both introductory Alleluias and rhymes ending in –*a* are generally to be found in Sequences of French origin. Perhaps the use of musical rhyme will also prove to be an essentially French characteristic. In any case there can be little doubt that the origin of the genre is deliberately recalled in both the poetic and the musical procedure.

Even more obvious than the ancestry of the cadential formula is the derivation of some opening phrases from Alleluia melodies. Early Sequences, as is well known, quite commonly began with the first phrase of the parent Alleluia. With the frequent use of old melodies for new texts, however, Sequences often lost their connection with specific Alleluias. The initial phrase was thereby freed of liturgical limitations and could be absorbed into the common vocabulary of Sequence composition. Only such a development can account for the phrase that opens the St. Hylarion Sequence. Far from being original, this is the initial phrase of *timbre* 63 in Aubry's catalogue, the first melody in four Sequences of Adam de St. Victor.[23] Whether the phrase can be traced back still farther has yet to be determined, but there can be little doubt that it is merely a variant of the even more common initial phrase of *Laudes crucis*. With only a change of the first note from *g* to *e*, this phrase begins the popular melody that was used for eight of Adam's texts.[24] In addition, it begins the four-phrase melody of Adam's Sequences *Virgo mater singularis* and *Ave virgo singularis*.[25] Spanke comments that these two Sequences borrow tunes from the famous old Sequence *Verbum bonum et suave* for their first three stanzas.[26] However, he does not remark on the close connection between their opening *timbre* and that of the *Laudes crucis* family.

The complex genealogy of these Sequence melodies cannot be disentangled here, but it is obvious that the common source of their opening phrases is the *Alleluia: Dulce lignum*.[27] The earliest Holy Cross Sequence reproduces both the initial phrase and the *jubilus* of this *Alleluia*. Later Sequences, whether on the same or a different subject,

---

[22] Both the partially and completely texted versions of this Sequence may be seen in H. Husmann, *Sequenz und Prosa*, in: *Annales musicologiques*, II (1954), 81ff. The coincidence of musical rhyme with lines ending in –*a* is particularly striking.
[23] See Ex. 2, Nos. 5 and 7.
[24] *Timbre* 61, Ex. 2, No. 4.
[25] *Timbre* 121, Ex. 2, No. 3.
[26] Spanke, p. 11.
[27] LU, p. 1456.

Ex. 2   Alleluia Melodies

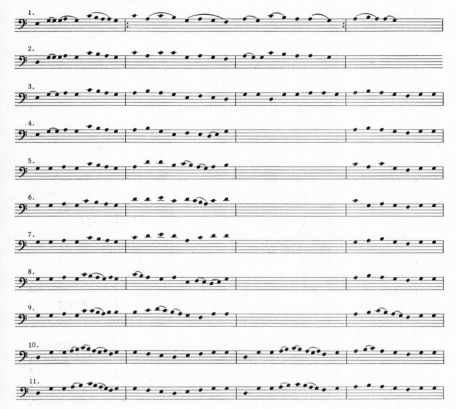

generally retain only the initial phrase. These relationships may be clearly seen in the melodies assembled in Ex. 2. The ensuing comments on each melody do not pretend to be a complete and chronological history of the Sequences involved. They are intended, rather, as an illustration of the complex interrelationships existing in a group of melodies characterized by a common derivation of their initial phrases.

1. *Alleluia: Dulce lignum* (*Liber Usualis*, p. 1456).
2. *Salve crux sancta* (A. Hughes, *Anglo-French Sequelae*, p. 37; and C. Moberg, *Uber die schwedischen Sequenzen*, II, No. 61).
3. *Verbum bonum et suave* (Moberg, II, No. 7). This melody is used without change for the Sequences *Ave virgo* and *Virgo mater* by Adam de St. Victor (*timbre* 121). Two characteristic variants of melodies 2, 3, and 4 should be mentioned. The first note is often *d* instead of *e*, not only in German and Swedish, but also in French sources. The *bistropha* on the second syllable is sometimes reduced to a single note; e.g. in Adam's Sequences. The same melody, beginning *d gg*, appears with the text

Verbum bonum et jocundum (*S. Corona Domini*) in the 13th-century *Prosaire de la Sainte Chapelle.*[28]

4. *Laudes crucis* (*Sainte Chapelle*, facs. p. 134). As given by Aubry (*timbre* 61), the second syllable has only a single note. Despite the return to the subject of the Holy Cross, the complete first melody of *Laudes crucis* resembles *Dulce lignum* and *Salve crux* less than it does the opening of *Verbum bonum*. The first and last phrases of 3 and 4 are identical, and the second phrase of the earlier melody (3) has been modified in *Laudes crucis* to accommodate the reduction from four to three phrases and to achieve a smoother transition to the common final phrase. This latter, incidentally, may have been derived from the end of the Alleluia *jubilus* by the characteristic addition of the standard cadence formula. The connection between 3 and 4 is confirmed by a curious variant in two versions of *Heri mundus*. As printed by Aubry, this Sequence begins with the melody of *Laudes crucis*.[29] In *Sainte Chapelle*, however, the middle phrase of *Heri mundus* is the second phrase of *Verbum bonum*.[30]

5. *Gaude Roma* (Misset and Aubry, *Les Proses, timbre* 63).

6. *Lux advenit* (*Sainte Chapelle*, facs. p. 101).

7. *Exultantes collaudemus*. In Nos. 5–7, only the first phrases and the cadential pattern of the final phrases are identical. In all three melodies, moreover, the second and third phrases differ strikingly from the corresponding phrases of Nos. 3 and 4. Perhaps the higher range of the middle phrases in Nos. 5–7 induced the change of the first note from *e* to *g*. The resulting modal purity, at any rate, contributes to the melodies' strongly tonal organization.

8. *Roma Petro* (*Prosaire d'Aix-la-Chapelle*, facs. p. 33).[31] This sequence further confirms the close relationship of all these melodies. It is sung to the melody of *Laudes crucis* (No. 4) in *Sainte Chapelle*. This ornamented version from Aix-la-Chapelle also introduces the variant of the first note that characterized melodies 5–7. The St. Victor version of *Roma Petro*, incidentally, is a totally different melody.[32]

9. *Gaude Roma* (*Sainte Chapelle*, facs. p. 146). This Sequence, sung to No. 5 in the St. Victor sources, provides another example of elaboration on a simpler, and presumably earlier, melody.

10. *Ave virgo*. (*Sainte Chapelle*, facs. p. 187).

11. *Virgo mater*. (*Sainte Chapelle*, facs. p. 19). That these two versions are the same melody with minor variants is obvious. Less so is their derivation from No. 3, the melody to which they both are sung in the St. Victor sources. The opening phrase has been highly ornamented, a new second phrase has been introduced, and the more sophisticated musical form A B A C has been created. The final phrase, however, except for the minor variant in No. 10, corresponds exactly with the original.

---

[28] Facs. p. 177.
[29] Misset and Aubry, p. 229.
[30] Facs. p. 70.
[31] Dom Hesbert, ed., *Monumenta musicae sacrae*, III (Rouen 1961).
[32] *Ibid.*, p. 72. Hesbert gives the opening melodies of all three versions.

ONE GENERAL comment on the melodies in Ex. 2 remains to be made. Unlike final phrases, which reappear in many melodies, initial phrases seem not to have been used in subsequent melodies within a Sequence. This cannot be verified for the entire repertory, but it holds true for the St. Victor settings of Adam's texts and for the Hylarion Sequence. The exclusively introductory function of these phrases not only provides final confirmation of their origin but also implies recognition of that origin by their composers. As far as can be ascertained, the composer of *Exultantes collaudemus* did not borrow a complete melody from any other Sequence. By his choice of an opening phrase, however, he could have made no more obvious bow to tradition.

The foregoing inquiry into the origins of an initial phrase and a cadential pattern suggests that much remains to be discovered with regard to the common melodic vocabulary used by composers of Sequences. Aubry proposed that the melodic origin of the "proses adamiennes" was to be found in popular melodies that are "inconnus par ailleurs," a hypothesis he claimed to be both "commode et vraisemblable." [33] While it may still be the most convenient hypothesis—since it is incapable of proof—even the meager evidence offered here makes it no longer seem probable. Part of the difficulty arises from the uncertain implications of the word *popular*. If, by troping, we define it as 'popular in ecclesiastical circles concerned with the composition and performance of Sequences' —which Aubry seems not to have meant—then we can agree that Adam chose his melodies, or created them, from "le trésor mélodique de son temps." [34] But that treasure, originating in the Alleluia melodies and augmented by later generations of composers, was a magnificent inheritance from the past. We must be careful, however, not to push too far the derivation from plainchant melodies. Very few Sequences exhibit the extended borrowing of *Dulce lignum*, and Willi Apel, with reason, has characterized as "unconvincing" the efforts of Besseler and Gennrich to derive other complete Sequences from specific Alleluias.[35] The present study suggests the hypothesis that Alleluias and their earliest extensions in the form of untexted Sequences provided a fund of motives and phrases—introductory, internal, and cadential—which later composers adapted, modified, and rearranged to suit their own needs. Tracing the development of this fund from its beginnings should be a fascinating bit of detective work.

Equally promising should be an investigation of the different ways in

[33] Misset and Aubry, p. 119.
[34] *Ibid.*
[35] Apel, *Gregorian Chant*, p. 449 and fn. 12.

which composers organized their thematic material into complete and unified musical structures. Previous studies of sequence structure—and they have been few indeed—have not really attacked this problem. Aubry's catalogue of the *timbres* in the Sequences of Adam de St. Victor groups together melodies with the same internal structure and lists the Sequences in which each melody appears.[36] But Aubry's study gives no idea whatsoever of the over-all designs to be found in Adam's Sequences. Hans Spanke made a valuable beginning in this direction by showing in tabular form the distribution of *timbres* in all the Sequences of each family or group.[37] Spanke does consider the ways in which *timbres* were expanded or contracted to accommodate different texts, but his analyses ignore the tonal organization of Sequences and give only the sketchiest indications of motivic relationships between one *timbre* and another. Like most students of the later Sequence, Spanke seems to have been impressed chiefly by the frequent adaptation of one Sequence to a large number of different texts. He thus arrived at the conclusion that the compositional technique of the St. Victor musicians was more mechanical than artistic.[38] While this judgment may be valid for the adaptations, it is manifestly unjust to the creator of the model. *Exultantes collaudemus* clearly proves that the use of traditional materials and procedures does not preclude the creation of a new and artistically satisfying musical entity. Such composition is no more mechanical, no less artistic, than the work of the architect who combines the traditional shapes of stone and glass to create a new cathedral.

[36] Misset and Aubry, pp. 120–59.
[37] Spanke, pp. 8–25.
[38] *Ibid.*, p. 28.

EXULTANTES COLLAUDEMUS
Original Text *

1a. Exultantes collaudemus,
Mira sancti personemus
Eiusque solennia.

1b. Hic vocatur Ylarion,
Quem duxit tethagramaton
Regna in perennia.

2a. Paternis ab erroribus
Ne pravaretur, sordibus
Destitit ab ydolis.

2b. Audiens hic Anthonium
Reliquit patrimonium
Puer bone indolis.

3a. Hic descendit a prophanis
Flevit puer non inanis
Pro baptismi gloria.

3b. Artem hausit scripturarum
Querens lumen doctrinarum
Mox in Alexandria.

4a. Mox, ut se fecit monacum
Hic tempus post bimensium,
Ad propria meavit.

4b. Defunctis iam parentibus,
Datis rebus pauperibus,
Monacos cumulavit.

5a. Primus hic in Palestina
Fulsit, in quo lux divina,
Monacus in Syria.

5b. Duodenum hic agebat,
Christum scire cum querebat,
Quadam in cemeria.

6a. Cella, stratus et vestitus,
Vicens vanus, sal et ficus,
Huius sunt delicie;

6b. Cellibantes facit vivos,
Sanat dentes, haurit rivos:
Eius sunt divitie.

7a. Regia fit hic camuca
Qui vult nobis sed tunica
Sancti Ylarionis,

7b. Qui sanat energuminos,
Depellit spiritus malos,
Proficit in donis.

8a. Abicit mulierculam,
Dicit oratiunculam
Dando Deo gratias,

8b. Accensis quinque digitis,
Et ait cum iniuriis:
Cede retro sathanas.

9a. Cella huius fuit bustum,
Lentes, aqua scedant bustum
Semper post crepusculum,

9b. Panis, radix, ficus, olus,
Sextus illi fuit bolus
Sepe post quatriduum.

10a. Cecam curat,
Stuprum fugat,
Pauper durat,
Celum mirat
Unus ex lapidibus.

10b. Deum orat,
Cyprum rorat,
Quando plorat
Tunc honorat
Christum cum virtutibus.

11a. Extraxit ortum parvulum,
Quo suum stat corpusculum
Alma continentia.

11b. Quod flagrat in odoribus
Cum toga fert Hieronimus
Sanctaque constantia.

12a. Sancte pater, tende manum,
Salva cetum Ciprianum
In pace prospera.

12b. Regni fructus da fecundos
Aufer pestes, et iocundos
Omnes duc ad supera.

* In presenting this text, I have followed Bannister's form and punctuation (AH, XL, 205), but I have retained the spelling and the mistakes of the original source (Tu B).

◈◈◈◈◈

FUGUE AND MODE IN
16th-CENTURY VOCAL
POLYPHONY

by IMOGENE HORSLEY

B Y USING "IMITATION" as the equivalent of fugue in speaking of 16th-century polyphony, we misconstrue an important
structural element in the music. For fugue had then a particular
meaning, and if it did not mean a "form," still it had an important function in the creation of polyphonic form. It is true that, especially from
the time of Gombert and Willaert, the text largely determined the
form, which reinforced the grammatical structure of the text, using
cadences [1] and rests [2] as a means of punctuation. The text was also
primary in the choice of the mode used and the departures from that
mode,[3] and musical figures pointed up the rhetorical figures in the text.[4]
But while the text was clearly primary, an abstract tonal form based upon
the modal system can be found, which the *fugae*, along with the cadences,
have an important part in defining.

The consciousness of a definite mode as characteristic of a total
polyphonic complex was of serious interest to theorists and composers
from the late 15th century. The modal structure of a single melodic line
was clearly defined in contemporary theory books [5] and pedagogical

---

[1] Stephano Vanneo, *Recanetum de musica aurea* (Rome 1533), fol. 93ᵛ; Angelo da
Picitono, *Fior angelico di musica* (Venice 1547), Bk. II, Chap. 39; Gioseffo Zarlino,
Istitutioni harmoniche (Venice 1558, 1562, 1573, 1589), Bk. III, Chap. 51. Zarlino is
the first to suggest using imperfect cadences for a *distintione mezana* (Chap. 51,
1562 and later editions), and avoiding a cadence when one arrives at one in the
wrong place in the text.
[2] Zarlino, *Op. cit.*, Chap. 50.
[3] The first rule in every discussion of composition; for a detailed analysis of this
in specific works see: Bernhard Meier, *Bemerkungen zu Lechners "Motectae Sacrae"*
von 1575, in: *Archiv für Musikwissenschaft*, XIV (1957), 83–101.
[4] Hans-Heinrich Unger, *Die Beziehungen zwischen Musik und Rhetorik im*
16.–18. Jahrhundert (Würzburg 1941); Arnold Schmitz, *Figuren, musikalisch-*
rhetorische, in: MGG, IV (1955), 176ff.
[5] Johannes Tinctoris, *Liber de natura et proprietate tonorum*, ed. E. de Coussemaker, *Oeuvres théoriques de Jean Tinctoris* (Lille 1875), pp. 39–103; Franchino
Gafori, *Practica musicae* (Milan 1496, Venice 1512), Bk. I; Vanneo, *Recanetum*,
Bk. I; Pietro Aaron, *Compendiolo di molti dubbi, segreti et sentenze* (Milan n.d.),

treatises,[6] and a precise and detailed knowledge of the modes was basic to musical training. Each mode was defined by the scale species of the fifth and fourth included in its octave ambitus, and by its beginning tones, its *repercussio*, and its final. The formulas for the psalms were memorized, along with the *differentiae* (settings of the *Seculorum amen*) which ended on notes other than the regular finals. Great stress was placed upon each mode as the determinate of a characteristic melodic type focused around the outer notes of its fifth, fourth, and octave, and to a lesser extent, its *repercussio*. Indeed, this characteristic structure, which most writers related to the species of the mode, and which Glareanus called its *phrasis* and Zarlino, its *forma*, was considered the most important element in judging the mode of a melody—more important than its initial or final note. An examination of the examples given in these texts, whether in chant or in figural notation, shows that the fifth common to each pair of modes (Dorian and Hypodorian, *d–a*), the fourth that belonged to each particular mode (Dorian, *a–d* [1]; Hypodorian, *A–d*), plus its characteristic octave (Dorian, *d–d* [1]; Hypodorian, *A–a*), were used as the main large skips in the melody. In a Dorian melody, no skips of a fifth or octave except *d–a* and *d–d* [1] are found; in some, however, skips of fourths other than *a–d* [1] appear. Apparently the fourth was less important than the fifth in determining the *phrasis*. Furthermore, the main notes of the mode (Dorian, *d, a, d* [1]) were always the notes upon which the melody centered.

If, however, a melody was not limited to the characteristic octave of its mode, but included also the range of its related authentic or plagal mode, and centered about the characteristic tones of both its authentic and plagal forms, the melody was in a mixture (*mixtio*) of the two forms of the mode. The introduction of a "foreign" species or *phrasis* into a

---

Chaps. 1–50; Heinrich Glarean, *Dodecachordon* (Basel 1547); Picitono, *Fior angelico*, Bk. I, Chaps. 30–59; Hermann Finck, *Practica musica* (Wittenberg 1556), Bk. IV; Illuminato Aiguino, *Il Tesoro illuminato* (Venice 1581); Pietro Pontio, *Ragionamento di musica* (Parma 1588), pp. 99–121; Oratio Tigrini, *Il Compendio della musica* (Venice 1588 & 1602), Bk. III; Scipione Cerreto, *Della prattica musica vocale* (Naples 1601), Bk. II; and, in less detail: Nicola Vicentino, *L'antica musica ridotta alla moderna prattica* (Rome 1555), Bk. III; and Zarlino, *Istitutioni*, Bk. IV.

[6] Johannes Cochlaeus, *Tetrachordum musices* (Nuremberg 1511; six more printings to 1526); Georg Rhaw, *Enchiridion utriusque musicae practicae* (Wittenberg 1520; nine more printings to 1553); Johann Spangenberg, *Quaestiones musicae* (Nuremberg 1536; five more printings to 1560); Nicolaus Listenius, *Musica* (Nuremberg 1537; twenty-five more printings to 1583); Martin Agricola, *Rudimenta musices* (Wittenberg 1539); Sebald Heyden, *De arte canendi* (Nuremberg 1540); Johann Vogelsang, *Musicae rudimenta* (n.p. 1542); Gregorius Faber, *Musices practicae* (Basel 1553); Luca Lossio, *Erotemata musicae practicae* (Nuremberg 1563; six more printings to 1590); Gallus Dressler, *Musicae practicae* (Magdeburg 1571, 1575, 1584, 1601); Gallus Dressler, *Practica modorum* (Jena 1561).

melody (such as *e–b*, the Phrygian fifth, into a Dorian melody) produces a mixture (*commixtio*) of two different modes.[7]

Ex. 1[8]
(a) Tinctoris: *Commixtio*—Dorian and Mixolydian

(b) Vicentino: *Commixtio*—Dorian Fifth with Phrygian Fourth

(c) Aiguino: *Commixtio*—Dorian and Phrygian

These concepts remain basic to melodic analysis and composition, subject only to more precise refinement as the century moves on. The investigation of the chromatic and enharmonic genera, both in regard to a more analytical approach to the use of altered notes in the diatonic system and as a means to experimental composition, was one aspect of this refinement. Glarean's clarifying of extant modal practice by adding two new pairs of modes in the "natural" series—Ionian and Hypoionian on C and Aeolian and Hypoaeolian on A—was another.[9] These modes had long been a part of musical practice as the result of using B♭ in the Lydian and Dorian pairs on F and D, and by pointing this out he was bringing about a more precise definition of scale species. Even though his system of 12 modes was not universally accepted during the 16th

---

[7] For an analysis of this technique in Josquin, see: Bernhard Meier, *The Musica Reservata of Adrianus Petit Coclico and its Relationship to Josquin*, in: *Musica disciplina*, X (1956), 67–105.

[8] (a) Tinctoris, *Liber de natura*, p. 61; (b) Vicentino, *L'antica musica*, Bk. III, Chap. 33; (c) Aiguino, *Il Tesoro*, fol. 31.

[9] *Dodecachordon*.

century, his precision was a strong force in the clarifying of modal ideas. His differentiation between the use of occasional B♭s in Dorian—a temporary change in species—and the constant use of it, so that the species of the upper fourth is changed, transforming it to transposed Aeolian, is a case in point. Succeeding theorists who rejected his 12-mode system did it with a clear idea of the problem involved, arguing that these were not new modes, but mixtures of old ones. Aeolian, for example, they explained as a *commixtio* of the species of fifth found in Dorian (half step between the second and third tones) with the Phrygian fourth (half step between the first and second tones).

A parallel clarification of mode as polyphonically defined takes place at the same time. In polyphonic music the modal form of each part was judged according to melodic considerations, according to *phrasis, mixtio* and *commixtio*, initial, and final notes.[10] Ambitus was less important, since the lines commonly went one or two notes above or below the octave of the mode,[11] but the species of fourth, fifth, and octave around which the melody centered were stressed. A work might be made up of melodic lines each in a different mode, or of melodic lines all in the same mode.[12] Yet, throughout the period, there is a consistent effort to arrive at a single mode by which each piece could be identified, both by prescription (directions as to the proper way of writing in each mode) and analysis (rules for deciding the mode in which a given composition is written).

Throughout the period, it was generally agreed that the mode of the tenor was the mode to be assigned to the whole polyphonic piece.[13] Composers were warned to be particularly careful in composing the tenor, to be sure that it clearly established the mode.[14] By mid-century it was generally accepted, too, that the soprano and tenor would be in the same mode, the dominating mode of the piece, and that the alto and bass would be in the corresponding authentic or plagal mode.[15] A work in Dorian would have a soprano and tenor in Dorian, a bass and alto in Hypodorian; in a work in Hypodorian, the soprano and tenor would be in that mode, the bass and alto in Dorian. The idea of different parts being in entirely different modes was not discussed after Glarean, but there may be

---

[10] Detailed analysis of particular compositions according to all these only in Glarean, *Dodecachordon*, but these terms are used in all general discussions of mode, whether in chant or in figural music.

[11] Zarlino, *Istitutioni*, Bk. III, Chap. 31.

[12] See particularly: Tinctoris, *Liber de natura*, p. 74; Glarean, *Dodecachordon*.

[13] Only Hermann Finck, *Practica musica*, Bk. III, and Vicentino, *L'antica musica*, fol. 48, disagree. Vicentino feels the bass determines the mode.

[14] Zarlino, *Istitutioni*, Bk. III, Chap. 31.

[15] Zarlino, *Ibid.*; Seth Calvisius, *Exercitationes musicae duae* (Leipzig 1600), p. 39f.

later works constructed in this way. Certainly in a work in one mode, the individual parts could be temporarily in other modes, and the whole *concentus* often moved temporarily into another mode, or even another *genus*.

Theorists of the late 15th century show an awareness of the problems of writing contrapuntally within a particular mode—the problem of writing correct and interesting counterpoint and yet keeping the individual lines in the mode established by the tenor. Ramos de Pareja mentions this in his *Musica practica* (1482).[16] He gives an example in his section on counterpoint—a tenor with two different countermelodies. The tenor is in Dorian, and he rejects the first countermelody because it stresses the Phrygian structural tones, and shows by the second how to adjust the line so that it emphasizes the basic tones of Dorian. Tinctoris,

Ex. 2   Ramos de Pareja, *Musica practica* [17]

in his treatise on counterpoint (1476), gives as his fifth general rule that a cadence must not be made on any note that denies the mode.[18] Throughout the whole period, cadences were one way of indicating the mode of a polyphonic work. The other control exercised by the mode over the total complex of parts was in the initial notes of the different parts.

In the late 15th and early 16th centuries, a large number of initial and cadence tones were listed for each mode, and these were mostly derived from analysis of church chants in the modes. For Dorian,[19] Tinctoris lists *c d e f g a;* [20] Gafori, *c d f g a;* [21] Aaron,[22] Vanneo,[23] and

[16] Johannes Wolf, ed., *Musica practica Bartolomaei Rami de Pareia*, in: *Publikationen der IMG, Beihefte*, II (Leipzig 1901).

[17] *Ibid.*, p. 72; original notation in letters.

[18] *Liber de arte contrapuncti*, transl. & ed. Albert Seay, in: *American Institute of Musicology, Musicological Studies and Documents*, V (Rome 1961), 135-36.

[19] Most theorists identify the modes by numbers, but since Zarlino renumbers them in the 1573 edition of *Istitutioni*, Bk. IV, listing Ionian rather than Dorian as No. 1, I use the Greek names throughout.

[20] *Liber de natura*, Chap. 9.

[21] *Practica musicae*, Chap. 8.

[22] *Trattato della natura et cognitione di tutti gli tuoni di canto figurato* (Venice 1525), Chap. 21.

[23] *Recanetum*, Chap. 38.

Picitono,[24] *c d e f g a d*[1]. Vanneo, however, remarks that the most common *initiae* are the final of the mode, and the fifth and third above it. For Aaron these are also the preferred beginning tones.

Tones listed for regular cadences in Dorian likewise vary from theorist to theorist. Aaron gives *d f g a*, with the principal cadences made upon *d* and *a*.[25] His lists as *distonati* in Dorian, those on *e* and *c*.[26] Picitono gives *c d f g a d*[1],[27] but Vanneo does not list any in his section on polyphonic cadences,[28] and Aaron often uses the *differentiae* in his analyses of liturgical works. Despite these disagreements, all agree that the final cadence of a work is not a sufficient guide to the mode. And certainly with the great number of possible cadence and initial tones listed, there is a great overlap in the cadences and beginnings allowed for all the modes, and a problem exists in trying to identify the mode of a work by these means alone.

The many German texts teaching music fundamentals do not discuss polyphonic composition in the modes, though single-line examples of the modes are often taken from choral works. Glarean's analyses are meticulous, detailed, and illuminating, but based solely upon a melodic analysis of each part separately. Hermann Finck is the first German theorist to devote a chapter to the problem of mode in polyphonic music.[29] His approach is analytical, not prescriptive; and after stating that figural music does not adhere strictly to rules and is therefore less easy to analyze modally than plainchant, he gives three general rules for discovering the mode in which a piece is written.[30] First, one should examine the beginning fugue, to see what mode it can be in, then examine the remaining *fugae* and cadences to see what modes they agree with. The mode to which the majority of the fugues and cadences belong is the one to which the piece can be assigned. Second, one must know the recitation notes of the psalms and their tropes and *differentiae*, though only the *differentiae* are found often in figural music. Third, one must examine the final cadence, although the final cadence of a work is often not on the final of the mode, so that this is not a sure indication. This discussion is particularly interesting because of the stress on *fugae* in their relation to establishment of mode. Finck was a great admirer of

[24] *Fior angelico*, Chap. 40.
[25] *Op. cit.*, Chap. 9.
[26] *Ibid.*, Chap. 17.
[27] *Fior angelico*, Chap. 39.
[28] *Recanetum*, Chap. 40.
[29] Frank Kirby, *Hermann Finck's "Practica Musica"* (Diss. Yale 1957), p. 214f.
[30] *Practica musica*, fol. Rriii–Rriii[v].

Gombert, and fugal sections are an essential part of Gombert's forms. But it is clear also that the regulation of polyphonic music by *initiae* and cadences is not sufficiently codified to give modal identification by purely polyphonic means.

A more regulated prescription for polyphonic modal control comes with Zarlino.[31] As a follower of Glarean, he accepts the 12-mode system and particularly the mathematical rationalization that accompanies it —the division of the octave harmonically (fifth at bottom, fourth at top) to form an authentic mode, and arithmetically (fourth at bottom, fifth on top) to produce a plagal mode. Zarlino applies this principle also to the division of the basic fifth of each pair of modes, arriving by harmonic division at the major triads of Ionian, Lydian, and Mixolydian and their plagals, and by arithmetic division, at the minor triads of Dorian, Phrygian, and Aeolian, with their plagal forms. The notes of this triad become the only regular notes to be used for *initiae* and cadences in each mode,[32] and these are the same for each pair of modes so that, as far as polyphonic control was concerned, there was no difference between the plagal and authentic forms of a mode. There was, of course, still a clear difference as far as the ranges of individual parts were concerned, and thus in the range of the total texture. Zarlino shows a strong feeling for the establishment of mode over a larger span strengthened by limiting the regular *initiae* and cadences of each mode. He prefers ending a work in the chord of the final, though agrees that the *confinalis* is often used, particularly for the end of the first part of a madrigal or motet. He also admits that there are many works with irregular *initiae* and in *modi misti* (his term for *commixtio*), but shows a strong preference for the clear establishment of a single dominating mode. This is, of course, a reflection of musical practice in the works of Willaert, Gombert, and their followers. The logic of his rationalization, as well as the general musical trend, helped to further his views. In Italy the theorist-pedagogues Pietro Pontio,[33] Oratio Tigrini,[34] and Giovanni Maria Artusi accepted and preached, in even more dogmatic form, his doctrines. In Germany, Seth Calvisius,[35] Joachim Burmeister,[36] and Johann Lippius [37] used them as a springboard for their teachings. Toward the close of the 16th century the influence is especially strong in religious

---

[31] *Istitutioni*, Bk. IV.
[32] *Ibid.*, Chap. 18.
[33] *Ragionamento di musica.*
[34] *Il Compendio.*
[35] *Exercitationes* (Leipzig 1600).
[36] Joachim Burmeister, *Musica poetica* (Rostock 1606).
[37] Johann Lippius, *Synopsis musicae* (Strasbourg 1612).

music, where the opening of a work clearly establishes a mode, and the final chord and inner cadences reinforce it.

BOTH THESE aspects of modal pattern—melodic and polyphonic—are closely bound up with 16th-century fugue. At the time when Zarlino pointed out the difference between the *fuga sciolta* (strict imitation of a short melodic fragment with free continuation) and *fuga legata* (strict imitation from beginning to end, later called canon), the two techniques had long been in use. By his time, the *fuga sciolta* had taken definite precedence over the *legata* as a form-building technique. Both types had originally, in theory and practice, been limited to imitation at the unison, fourth, fifth, and octave, since it was at these intervals that exact imitation naturally took place. But from the time of Ockeghem "canons" began to appear at other intervals at which strict intervallic imitation did not take place; shorter points of imitation were also used at other intervals. Zarlino clarified terminology here also, by calling these *imitazione legata* ("canon" at the second, third, sixth, and seventh) and *imitazione sciolta* (short points imitated at these intervals). In these, the same generic intervals would be followed in the imitations, but a particular interval such as a major second might be answered by a minor second, for example. To Zarlino's followers, then, imitation and fugue had precisely defined meanings. By the 17th century, *fuga* came to mean what Zarlino meant by *fuga sciolta* and, by association, also the subject of a fugue. Canon, however, came to include within its scope both *fuga legata* and *imitazione legata*. It is with these meanings that the terms will be used in this paper.

At the beginning of the 16th century, fugue at the fourth and fifth included much more than our experience with 18th-century fugue would lead us to expect. It implied the possibility of the *comes* starting at both the fourth and fifth above the opening note of the *dux* (like the opening entries on *f c bb*, and *c*[1] in the first Kyrie of Josquin's *Missa Allez regretz* [38]) or the *comes* starting in two succeeding fifths above the *dux* (as in the entries *Bb, f*, and *c*[1] that open Obrecht's motet *Salve crux*,[39] or the entries on *c g d*[1] and *g* in the beginning of the *Esurientes* from Josquin's *Magnificat tertii toni* [40]). And the initial notes do not necessarily imply the mode in which a composition was written.

By the time of Gombert and Willaert, the opening fugue of a piece

[38] A. Smijers, ed., *Werken van Josquin des Près; Missen,* XX (Amsterdam 1956), p. 61.
[39] A. Smijers, ed., Obrecht, *Opera omnia,* Vol. II, Fasc. I (Amsterdam 1956), p. 17.
[40] *Werken: Motetten, Bundel* XXI (Amsterdam 1958), p. 58.

usually had the first entry on the final of the mode in which it was written, or on the fifth or third above it; and, especially in the works of Gombert, the mode and the final chord of a work can be anticipated by looking at the opening fugue. But the *comes*, even though following at the proper interval for fugue—as in the case of the *dux* starting on the note a third above the final imitated at the fifth above, the seventh note above the final—may suggest another mode.[41] This type of entry, found often at the beginning of the century, is still found in Zarlino's time, but had practically disappeared in fugues (of a single subject) by the end of the century. The only entrance pattern that really establishes a mode within the limitations set by Zarlino is the use of the final and the fifth above it (or the fifth above the final followed by the final) in the *dux* and *comes* pair. It is significant that Zarlino, who does not mention anywhere the relation between modal *initiae* and fugue, uses this combination in all his duets showing the proper polyphonic use of the modes except those where the entering fugue is at the unison or octave.[42] By the end of the century the only *dux-comes* pair not limited to the final and fifth above it is the answering of the final on the fourth degree above it. In 18th-century terminology this would be the "subdominant," but at this time it was only one of the irregular tones, one of the *peregrinae* in the mode. However, the answer on the subdominant is found, particularly in Mixolydian and Phrygian and their plagals, until the advent of the major-minor system.

An examination of the half steps in the authentic modes shows some of the problems involved. (True Lydian was so rarely used that it is omitted here.)

D E F G A B C D

E F G A B C D E

C D E F G A B C

G A B C D E F G

A B C D E F G A

When the patterns of the tetrachords are examined it can be seen that if fugue with the *comes* starting on the fifth note is desired, this will

[41] This type of entry is found often in Josquin; in later composers, less commonly at the beginning, but often starting the second part of a work, or as an entry in the middle of a work.

[42] *Istitutioni*, Chaps. 18–29, in Bk. IV.

take place naturally only in Dorian, Phrygian, and Ionian. In Mixolydian and Aeolian, exact imitation will by nature occur only on the fourth degree, the tetrachords with the same pattern occurring only by conjunct division. In all cases the available scale material for exact imitation can be expanded to six notes (the two natural hexachords) by extending each of the tetrachords above and below.

The diagram explains nicely the reasons for the "subdominant" answer in certain modes, but in these same modes the answer on the fifth is also common. According to modal tradition it is this fifth that confirms a mode. In practice, composers, with their usual skill in circumventing difficulties, often omit the note or notes that would make the answer at the fifth inexact. A *dux* such as G A C in the Mixolydian, for example, could be answered exactly at the fifth by D E G; and the Aeolian A C D E at the fifth by E G A B.

But the musical practice was at times even freer. Zarlino and his followers defined fugue as exact imitation but, as the theorist and composer Pietro Pontio points out, practice is more subtle and difficult than theory.[43] He defines as the real answer that which conforms "di nome, di figure, e d'intervalli" to the subject, but lists two other ways in which the answer is made—keeping everything exact but the rhythm ("simili di nome e d'intervalli ma non già di figure"), or keeping the rhythmic and melodic pattern, but not the precise intervals ("similitudine delle figure + delli intervalli ma non già del nome").[44] These last two ways are certainly common in this period, and his example for the third way—A B C D E answered by E F G A B—is interesting as an inexact answer in Aeolian at the fifth.

The basic fifth of each mode being by tradition the determining factor in defining that mode, the theoretical explanation of the "subdominant" answer demands some sort of rationalization. The two most common of these, the "subdominant" answer in Phrygian and Mixolydian, clearly come under Zarlino's description of the two most used combinations of modes found in *modi misti*, or of a work ending not on the final but on the *confinalis*.[45] These commonly found mixtures—Hypomixolydian with Ionian, and Hypoaeolian with Phrygian—would easily give what sounds to us like a "subdominant" answer, if thought of as Hypomixolydian basically, but mixed with Ionian, with the answer starting on C; or as primarily Phrygian, but mixed with Hypoaeolian, with the answer

[43] Pietro Pontio, *Dialogo . . . ove si tratta della theorica, e prattica di musica* (Parma 1595), p. 57.
[44] *Ibid.*, pp. 49, 50.
[45] *Istitutioni*, Bk. IV, Chap. 30.

starting on A. Likewise, they could be conceived of as Ionian ending on
G, the *confinalis*, or Hypoaeolian ending on the *confinalis* E. Aeolian
with the subdominant answer, of course, would be thought of as Dorian
ending on the *confinalis*. From our point of view, looking backward
from major and minor instead of forward from the 12-mode system,
they appear as indications of the amalgamation of the minor modes
moving toward a single harmonic ordering expressed in the minor of
the 18th and 19th centuries.

Another point of interest is the fact that in fugal practice there is no
differentiation between plagal and authentic modes insofar as the interrelation of entries is concerned, although certainly the range and species
of each individual part did present a particular mode type. Here is one
of the conflicts inherent in 16th-century polyphony between melodic
and polyphonic aspects, and one that is brought clearly into focus in the
study of fugue. Although not all points used as material for fugue define
a mode precisely by their melodic contour, a point skipping a fifth or
fourth or strongly outlining one of these intervals clearly projects some
one mode. A real answer to one of these just as clearly defines another
mode. For some reason, transposition of a mode is never suggested in
this context, or in relation to melodic analysis; transposition is discussed
only in regard to the pitch location of an entire melody, or an entire polyphonic work in a particular mode. The fifth A–E in answer to the Dorian
fifth D–A projects Aeolian, and the fourth D–G in answer to the Dorian
fourth A–D defines Mixolydian. In 16th-century practice this was not
objected to, since any melodic line could be temporarily out of mode.
Zarlino, in fact, wants enough statements of the "foreign" species to
really establish that mode before he will designate a part as in *modi
misti*.[46] The initial notes of the entries, D and A, were all that were needed
to define the Dorian mode of the beginning, reconciling the melodic lines
to the over-all mode of the work. The tonal answer, which had appeared
but rarely in the 15th century, was used more and more frequently as
the 16th century moved on. Zarlino himself, who never mentions it in
his section on fugue, uses it in the beginnings of three of his duets illustrating the polyphonic treatment of the modes. Pontio describes it in his
Dialogo in a casual way, when describing a four-part fugal example where
A C D E is answered by E F G A, pointing out that though the two are
not exact, each has "gli intervalli suoi proprij del tuono; perche và
modulando per le Quinte, e per le Quarte forme di tal tuono" and useful
because either form of the theme can be used as a first entry without dis-

[46] *Ibid.*, Chap. 14.

turbing the mode (*tuono*) since each form expresses the mode so clearly.[47] He adds that it is a conception worthy of much thought!

The insistence upon the tonal answer as the only correct answer comes first in 17th-century Italy, when it is felt that the entire subject and answer, not just the initial notes, should establish the mode at the beginning of a work. At the turn of the century, Scipione Cerreto gives a list of possible *fughe* (subjects for fugue) that can be made within the characteristic fifth, fourth, and octave of each mode.[48] Girolamo Diruta considers the tonal answer to be the only correct one, insisting that the subjects and answers should be based on the proper fourth and fifth of the mode used.[49] If one is composing a fantasia in Dorian, the fifth D–A must be answered by the fourth A–D. The answer A–E cannot be used because it belongs to the Aeolian, not the Dorian mode, nor should the fourth D–G be used because it implies Mixolydian. He allows more liberty in the middle of a piece, but at the beginning and end, only the correct fifth and fourth of the basic mode should be used.

Giovanni Maria Trabaci writes no pedagogical works, but as a composer he is careful that his subjects and answers stress the fifth and fourth of their mode. To him a real answer where a tonal one was required was so far from normal that in his *Secondo libro de ricercate* (Naples 1615) he justifies the "wrong" answer, the fifth G–C in answer to the fifth D–G in the ricercar *Settimo tono con tre fughe,* by explaining that Luzzasco Luzzaschi answers it thus in his third book of ricercars.

The third edition of Banchieri's *Cartella musicale* adds a new section, *Altri documenti musicali.*[50] In it he includes duos in each of the twelve modes and also for each mode he includes a table of the *Fughe, corde, cadenze & finale* for each mode. The *fughe* are simply the fifths, fourths, and octaves of each mode into which the subjects and answers must fit. Each duo except those in which the *fuga* is answered at the octave has a tonal answer and, furthermore, the subjects are all of the type that would require a tonal answer.

We must conclude, then, that the 16th-century composers were aware of the tonal (modal) effects of the tonal answer, but that it was not felt essential to emphasize the mode in all parts, since the initial notes of the entries would establish it. And, further, that a variety of

---

[47] *Dialogo,* pp. 55–57.

[48] *Della prattica musica,* pp. 212–18; he emphasizes this as particularly important in sacred music.

[49] *Seconda parte del transilvano* (Venice 1609; 2nd ed. 1622), Bk. III, pp. 2, 3.

[50] Adriano Banchieri, *Cartella musicale* (Venice 1614); *Altri documenti musicali* has a new title page, but is paginated as a continuation of the *Cartella.*

answer types was not only allowed, but was perhaps desired. Certainly melodic invention is limited by the tonal answer, and the interest of variety in treatment is sacrificed to the expression of tonal unity.

The musical nature of the tonal answer in the modal system differs in certain significant ways from the tonal answer in the major-minor system. The first, which is particularly characteristic of the early 17th century, is that not just the head, but the entire subject is adjusted to fit the proper fifth or fourth.

Ex. 3a   Trabaci: Ricercar, *Primo tono contre fughe* [51]

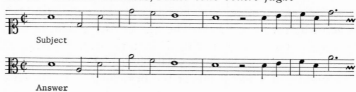

The second is that a subject built on the basic triad of a mode will often have the third answered by the sixth above the final, rather than the seventh as in major and minor.

Ex. 3b[52]   Zarlino: Duo in Lydian

The third is that a direct scale filling in the fifth or fourth of the mode was usually given a real answer, even though this outlined the fifth or fourth of another mode. The adjustment of the answer by using a repeated note (in adjusting the fourth of the answer to the fifth of the subject) or other adjustments which would change the direct scale pattern were not used until the advent of the major-minor system, when harmonic considerations were stronger than melodic. One thing we can be sure of, and that is that the composers were well aware of what they were doing within the framework of their conventions.

[51] Trabaci, *Secondo libro: Primo tono con tre fughe*, first subject.
[52] Zarlino, *Istitutioni*, Bk. IV, Chap. 22; Banchieri, *Cartella*, p. 76.

THE OTHER important aspect of fugue in its relation to the modes in the 16th century concerns form. The initial notes and final cadence defined the mode of a complete composition. But within a work, particularly after Gombert, whose use of a series of fugal sections articulated by cadences to create a form had such a strong influence on choral form, the successive fugal subjects, with their initial pitches, were important in establishing the mode, moving away from it and returning to it. Their entries, limited by tradition to the unison, fourth, fifth, and octave, gave emphasis to intervals with modal significance, an emphasis that was enhanced by the fact that most of these entries were preceded by a rest. Often there are a number of entries to a section, and a shift of the entry notes to new pitches—imitations, or in fugues, outlining the species of other modes. Cadences, as well, are important in defining these modes, though some ambiguity must always exist, as even the regular cadences of a mode on the fifth or the third above the final could often be interpreted as being in other modes. Also, not always are all the sections fugal; familiar style, and many shades between familiar and fugal style, are found. Entries may also involve inverted themes, play on invertible counterpoint, double fugues, or a combination of several free melodies. All these are important elements in the structure, and a concentration on fugues alone does not by any means give the whole picture. But they are a major factor in the polyphonic establishment of mode; and a diagram of the entries and cadences is, in many instances, illuminating in the study of a single work and in discovering the habits and skills of individual composers.

There follows such a diagram of Gombert's four-part motet, *Domine, si tu es* [53] starting at the beginning of the *secunda pars, Cumque vidisset.* The exact pitches of entrances are indicated by measures. Letters indicate the heads of themes. Where two versions appear, the number following the letter indicates the interval changes in the different versions; though this may only indicate a tonal answer, this is used because the two different forms sometimes occur on other pitches. A note in parentheses stands for a free entry—an entrance after a rest, but unrelated thematically. Chords in parentheses show beginnings of sections in familiar style. All of the cadences here are indicated by symbols used for the major-minor key system, for convenience only. The cadences here indicated are all in the regular *sincope* form of the 16th century, and occur at a stop in at least two parts. Many of these do not have the

[53] From Joseph Schmidt-Görg, ed., *Nicolai Gombert, Opera omnia*, Vol. V: *Cantiones sacrae* (Rome 1961), 101–06; first published 1538.

Ex. 4   Gombert: *Domine, si tu es*, secunda pars: *Cumque vidisset*

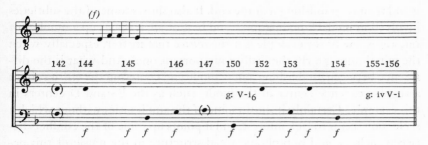

raised leading tone added by the editor; nevertheless they are true cadences both in form and function.

A pattern emerges that shows at least a part of the structure. The whole motet is in Dorian transposed to G. E♭s are concentrated in a few sections, but are not used consistently enough to make it Aeolian. The *prima pars* ends with a cadence on the final, G, and the *secunda pars* begins with entries affirming the mode. The entries in measures 85 and 86 outline the Mixolydian fifth (Mixolydian with B♭), and a deceptive cadence in D, the fifth of the basic mode, moves to a chord on B♭, the third of the mode, a regular cadence. A full pause emphasizes the sudden appearance in measure 91 of the C-minor chord, a chord on a note not considered a regular chord in the mode, and this accomplishes a break in structure, dramatizing the word *timeunt*.

The chord of the third degree, however, returns, and the next entries on a new point emphasize this new tonal center, but in such a way that the last four entries can also be related to D, the *confinalis* which is emphasized in the next cadence. The next section, in familiar style, centers around the regular triad of the mode of the work, settling back on the final. In measures 112–13 and 114–15 come a set of paired fugal entrances, using within each pair a tonal answer, in such a way that the first pair establishes Hypomixolydian melodically *and* polyphonically, while the second pair reëstablishes Dorian by the same means. These two modes are related by having the same octave ambitus, and this is a typical modal-fugal play, emphasizing the two melodically related modes.

Later on, the *initiae* in measures 124–28 emphasize the fifth D–A, perhaps anticipating the half-cadence on D in measures 131–32. Then follows a firm reëstablishment of the mode, by a series of entrances centering on G and D, the basic notes of the mode, and the final cadence is on the regular final of the mode.

An analysis of this type is necessarily incomplete. Yet it shows the part that fugues and cadences play in establishing mode, departing from it and then reëstablishing it at the end. It also shows some of the subtleties involved in modal "modulation," and best of all, it opens up a number of questions—why for example is it the *initiae* that matter, especially when the initial note is a rhythmically unimportant one? And what is the difference between establishing a new mode and centering the entries about a regular cadence-center in the mode, such as the B♭ and D centers in this example? Certainly it shows some of the ambiguities without which a style soon seems to lack interest, and it points up some of the conflicts between melodic and polyphonic tonal structure in the music of this period.

THE SOURCES OF
CHRISTUS MANENS

by *DAVID G. HUGHES*

I T IS WELL KNOWN that the composers of Parisian organa preferred as the bases of their polyphonic settings the responsorial chants of the Mass and Office. The presence in the sources of a piece that does not set such a chant is thus a clear sign of special circumstances, and invites investigation. On fol. 20ᵛ of the manuscript Florence, Biblioteca Laurenziana, Pluteus 29.1, there is a three-voice setting, in organal style, of the text *Christus manens quod erat,* obviously not a responsorial chant. It has long been suggested that this work is not Parisian in origin —that it may have been written at Sens or Beauvais.[1] But study of the sources of the piece yields somewhat more information, and also presents an interesting picture of text-transmission in the 12th and 13th centuries.

Christus manens appears in three manuscripts: that of Florence (hereafter *F*); the Circumcision Office of Sens (Sens, Bibliothèque de la Ville 46 and Musée 276, fol. 2; hereafter *S*), monophonically; and the Circumcision Office of Beauvais (British Museum, Egerton 2615), where it appears three times (fols. 3, 71ᵛ, and 83ᵛ), the first time monophonically, the other two in the three-voice organum of *F* (these three appearances will be referred to as *A, B,* and *C*).[2] The two monophonic versions are accompanied by rubrics calling for performance *cum organo.* From the rubrics of *S,* we learn that *Christus manens* is a versus of the prosa *Letemur gaudiis. Letemur* was originally a prosula—a texting of a melisma—of the verse *Mirabilis* of the Offertory *Deus enim firmavit.*[3]

---

[1] Friedrich Ludwig, *Repertorium organorum recentioris et motetorum vetustissimi stili* (Halle 1910), I¹, 233; Heinrich Husmann, *Die Offiziumsorgana der Notre-Dame Zeit,* in: *Jahrbuch der Musikbibliothek Peters,* XLII (1935), 42; and the same author's *Die drei- und vierstimmigen Notre-Dame-Organa,* in: *Publikationen älterer Musik,* XI (Leipzig 1940), xxiv.

[2] The entire Sens manuscript was edited by Henri Villetard, *Office de Pierre de Corbeil* (Paris 1907). *Christus manens* appears (monophonically) on p. 133. The organum is printed (from all three sources) in Husmann's *Notre-Dame-Organa,* pp. 46–48.

[3] See C. Ott, *Offertoriale, sive versus offertoriorum cantus Gregoriani* (Paris 1935), pp. 16–18. The melisma appears on p. 18 at the words "in longitudine dierum." The nature of *Letemur* was observed by Villetard (p. 88, fn. B). See also Ulysse Chevalier, *Repertorium hymnologicum* (Louvain & Brussels 1892–1921), No. 10087;

Like a few other prosulae, it acquired a certain independence from its parent chant, and was occasionally used by itself. In the Sens and Beauvais Circumcision Offices, *Letemur* (with *Christus manens*) is used at first vespers. At Paris, *Letemur* was similarly used, but there is no mention of *Christus manens*.[4]

Why a piece such as *Letemur* should have acquired a versus is not at all clear. The connection is not, however, a casual one, as the end of *Christus manens* repeats the last word (with its music) of *Letemur*. But the fact remains that we have here an organum composed to a melody that is an appendage to a piece already extraneous to the liturgy. The assumption of a non-Parisian origin of such a work seems entirely justified.

Before considering the relationship of the five extant versions of *Christus manens*, it will be necessary to devote a few words to the dates of the manuscripts. *F* is too well known to require extended comment. It is generally regarded as relatively late, and even Apel, who inclines towards early dates for this and the other Notre Dame sources, does not place it before 1250.[5] *S* is dated by Villetard,[6] on the advice of the palaeographer Quantin, as early 13th century, and this seems reasonable enough. Egerton 2615 has already been shown to be composite.[7] Versions *A* and *B* of *Christus manens* appear in the original body of the Office (consisting of the Office proper and a polyphonic supplement to it, all in the same hands), datable 1227–34.[8] Version *C* appears in a second

Analecta hymnica, XLIX (Leipzig 1906), 313; Hubert Sidler, *Studien zu alten Offertorien mit ihren Versen*, *Veröffentlichungen der Gregorianischen Akademie zu Freiburg-in-der-Schweiz*, XX (Freiburg 1939), 52; Léon Gautier, *Histoire de la poésie liturgique au moyen âge. Les tropes* (Paris 1886), p. 162. *Letemur* originated, to judge by the sources, in the 10th century. The attribution to Notker (e.g. by Kehrein, *Lateinische Sequenzen des Mittelalters*, Mainz 1873, No. 85) is unlikely, to say the least.

[4] This information cames from the celebrated ordinance of Eudes de Sully, dated 1199. The text is printed in M. Guérard, *Cartulaire de l'église Notre Dame de Paris* (Paris 1850), I, 73ff, and has often been cited from that publication. Other references to the use of *Letemur* (without mention of *Christus manens*) may be found in Hermann Daniel's *Thesaurus hymnologicus* (Halle 1841–56), II, 329 (Tours; the citation is after Martène); and Chevalier, *Ordinaires de l'église cathédrale de Laon*, *Bibliothèque liturgique*, VI (Paris 1897), 49.

[5] *The Notation of Polyphonic Music* (4th ed. Cambridge, Mass. 1949), p. 200 and fn. 1.

[6] *Op. cit.*, p. 14. Villetard's attribution of the compilation of this Office to Pierre de Corbeil (pp. 51–53) is not wholly conclusive. Thus the fact that Pierre died in 1222 does not necessarily constitute a terminus for the manuscript.

[7] See my *Liturgical Polyphony at Beauvais in the Thirteenth Century*, in: *Speculum*, XXXIV (1959), 184ff, discussing the specific functions of the various parts. The generally composite nature of the manuscript was already recognized by Ludwig.

[8] The date is supplied by the names of rulers mentioned in the *laudes* (fols. 41ʳ–42). See my *Liturgical Polyphony*, p. 186, fn. 13. The name of the queen is not, as

polyphonic supplement, not originally part of the Office manuscript, and hence not necessarily sharing its date or place of origin. We can only suggest a North French provenance in the 13th century, adding that this section seems later than the Office proper. The probable chronological order of the sources is, then: *S, A, B* (the latter two roughly at the same time, although *A* must have been written before *B* was inscribed), *C,* and *F.*

We may now turn to the textual and musical divergencies among the five versions. We shall for the moment consider only the tenor melody, since only this is present in all the sources, and since it is less subject to arbitrary alteration than the upper voices of an organum. Example 1 gives the reading of *A*, with the textual and musical variants [9] of the other sources, numbered and aligned below it. In the example, all divergencies are reckoned from *A*, and the absence of any notation in one of the lower staves indicates that at that point the source in question agrees with *A*.

The variations are as follows:

1.	F:ABCS	7b.	(music) AS:BCF [10]
2.	B:ACFS	8.	S:ABCF
3.	A:BCFS	9.	AB:CFS
4.	C:ABFS	10.	AS:BCF [11]
5.	ABS:C:F	11.	AS:BC
6.	AS:BCF	12.	A:BCS
7a.	(text) C:ABFS	13.	A:S:BCF [12]

This list indicates that no version could have acted as an intermediary between any other two—or, in Dearing's language, that all states are terminal. This is shown by the fact that each source stands alone against all the others at least once. To be noted are the variations in which *A* and

I there stated, indecipherable. Consultation of the original shows that the space was left blank.

[9] I use "variant" here for the varying reading, "variation" for the entire textual situation at the point of variance. In this, as in other matters relating to textual transmission, I am indebted to Vinton Dearing's valuable work, *A Manual of Textual Analysis* (Berkeley & Los Angeles 1959).

[10] *B, C,* and *F* do not agree exactly, but are much closer to each other than to *A* and *S* (which are identical here). Here and in variation 10 I have reduced a complex variation to simple form on the grounds of close similarity among the readings. The ultimate result would be the same if the variation were recorded in its more complex form.

[11] Here *A* has a liquescent virga (descending), and *S* the clivis on the corresponding pitches. Since manuscripts of the period (especially Egerton 2615) often make this sort of substitution—even in parallel places in different stanzas of a strophic piece—I have regarded the two readings as equivalent. This is the more justifiable in that the other sources agree here on a different note.

[12] *S* adds a long melisma to "collocaret," as well as the words "in celum."

Ex. 1

S agree against *B*, *C*, and *F* (Nos. 6, 7b, and 10). Against them stands
variation 9, with the pattern *AB:CFS*. In the first group, the monophonic
sources stood together against the polyphonic; in variation 9, the two
readings from the Beauvais Office stand together—both being natural, if
conflicting groupings.

   Variation 9 is not merely a textual variant: it involves an actual error.
A and *B* have the clearly incorrect text "erectos," as against the "ereptos"
of the other sources. As a result, neither *A* nor *B* can be the original
ancestor. If we try making *S* the ancestor (*C* and *F* being definitely too

late), we find that there is no way of accounting for both *AB:CFS* and *AS:BCF*. Any solution that satisfies one condition conflicts with the other. Even if we were to propose conflation or emendation as a solution for the troublesome variation 9, we should be no further along, since the placement of *S* at the top of the tree prevents effective use of these expedients.

Thus none of the extant states can be the original ancestor. In Diagram 1, a provisional stemma, deriving all of the extant states from a lost ancestor by means of hypothetical intermediaries, is proposed.

In the diagram, X represents the lost ancestor. Y (a hypothetical intermediary) is the point at which the incorrect "erectos" entered the text. At variations 7 and 10, Y has the readings of A and S, permitting these sources to agree against the rest. W (also a hypothetical source) perpetuates the "erectos" error, but introduces the BCF reading in variations 7 and 10 (it is reasonable to assume that the extant organum, to which we shall return shortly, entered at W). Z, the last hypothetical intermediary, is the work of a scribe who, perceiving the weakness of the text at "erectos," either deduced the correct version by himself, or took the trouble to get the correction from X or S (in the latter case, a conflation line would run from X or S to Z).

Diagram 1

The diagram fulfills the conditions set by the variations, but, in postulating no less than four hypothetical sources, it offends against one's sense of economy. Could not some of these be eliminated, or else substantiated by actual evidence of their existence?

We may begin with W. This is necessary solely because B cannot serve as intermediary. If this condition could be set aside, B could replace W in the line of descent between Y and Z. The variation requiring the terminality of B is No. 2 in the list preceding Example 1. Here B omits a g at the end of the first "quod" found in all other sources. The polyphonic context is shown in Example 2.

Ex. 2

Quod

In purely monophonic transmission, the probability against the restoration of a dropped note such as this would be overwhelming. But the situation is not quite the same in polyphony: the relation among the voices may suggest emendation. In the example, the upper voices strongly suggest that a *g* (given in brackets from the other sources) ought to appear in the tenor (this is true also of Husmann's rather different transcription, based primarily on *F*). As in the case of the "erectos" error, an intelligent scribe might have made the correction himself—or, merely suspecting that something was wrong, he might have turned to *A* (present in the same manuscript, and hence right at hand) and got the correction from there.

As far as the tenor is concerned, then, it is possible that *B* stood as intermediary between *X* and *Z*, although no evidence can be produced showing that it definitely did. But, before accepting this interpretation even as a hypothesis, we must examine the variants in the heretofore neglected upper voices, to see whether such a transmission is possible in this respect. Note that we here consider the polyphonic sources as a unit, with the result that a source terminal with respect to the polyphony might still be intermediary in the larger diagram. The importance of this point becomes immediately apparent, for we discover that the variations occurring (too numerous to list here [13]) take all of the possible forms: B:CF; C:BF; F:BC; and B:C:F, with the first type by far the most numerous. Thus all three are terminal as far as the polyphony is concerned, although *B* is not thereby prevented from standing between *Y* and *Z*. On the basis of the variations, and taking into account the fact that *B* is the earliest of the polyphonic sources, the schemes in Diagram 2 are possible.

---

[13] Almost all are indicated by Husmann in his edition of the piece (see fn. 2, above). Note that Husmann's "W_1" and "W_2" (p. 47, system 3) should be "L_1" and "L_2" (corresponding to our *B* and *C*).

Diagram 2*b* would restore the fourth hypothetical source *W*, at the junction of the lines from *B* and *Z*. Otherwise it seems at first sight the more attractive, since the version of *B* is generally the poorest. Its notation is inelegant and not always clear, and it contains some obvious errors (e.g. the last measure of Ex. 2). *B*, according to this diagram, would be merely a corrupt copy, without issue.

Diagram 2

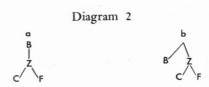

But the alternative (Diagram 2*a*) is by no means impossible. As we have said, polyphony offers excellent clues for emendation (the error just mentioned is an obvious case), and there is certainly ample precedent for scribal revision in the Notre Dame epoch. It is quite possible that a sophisticated copyist, working from a rather primitive exemplar, would have felt impelled to make improvements as he went along (note that in each case where scribal initiative is assumed, it is the scribe of *Z* that is involved). And, in any case, there are several variations of the type *B*:*CF* in which not corruption but revision—whether by *B* or *Z*—must be involved. Thus, near the beginning of "patris" (Husmann, mm. 145–147), *B* writes both voices as simplex, ternaria, simplex. *C* and *F* write all five notes as simplices. In such cases, it seems better to ascribe deliberate revision to *Z*, rather than to the obviously inexperienced *B*.

There is, then, an excellent chance that the hypothetical *W* may not have existed, and that its place in Diagram 1 should be taken by *B* (the sources below it remaining as in Diagram 1). Whether or not *W* be eliminated, however, the composition of the organum must have taken place at that point of the Diagram (i.e. at the source immediately above *Z*, whichever is chosen). *Y* can hardly have contained the extant polyphony. It must have had the tenor version of *A* and *S*, as we have seen. If it did, however, *B* (or *W*) must have introduced variants in the tenor part of the organum—a procedure that could result in serious difficulties in the fitting together of the parts. At variation 10, for example, the polyphony definitely requires the *c* of *BCF*, not the *b* of *AS* (Husmann, mm. 126ff).

When we turn from *W* to the other hypothetical sources, we find that the position of *Z*, at least, appears unassailable. It is the only place for the correction of "erectos" to "ereptos" (independent correction by both *C* and *F* is scarcely likely); and, if *W* is eliminated, *Z* is the only

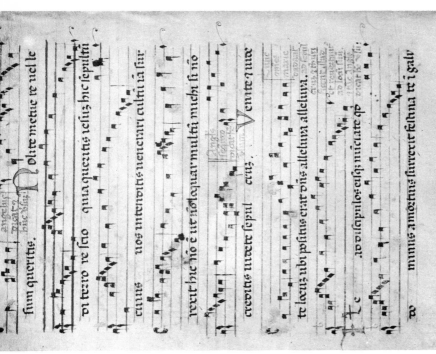

PLATE 1a Fol. 76ʳ from *Planctus Mariae*, Cividale MS CI, Museo Archeologico Nazionale, Cividale del Friuli

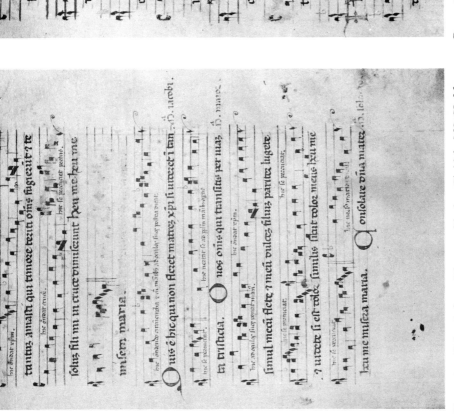

PLATE 1b Fol. 77ᵛ from *The Sepulchre*, Cividale MS CII, Museo Archeologico Nazionale, Cividale del Friuli

PLATE 2a   Fol. 84 of the cantus partbook of Florence 2442

PLATE 2b   Cover of the altus partbook of Florence 2442

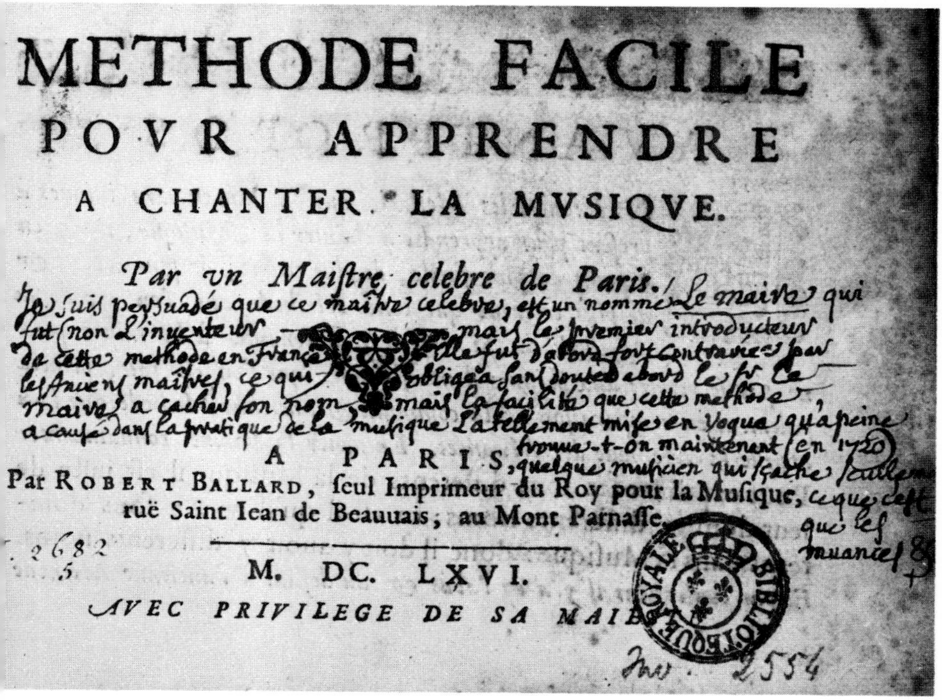

MÉTHODE FACILE
POVR APPRENDRE
A CHANTER LA MVSIQVE.

Par vn Maiſtre celebre de Paris.

A PARIS,
Par ROBERT BALLARD, ſeul Imprimeur du Roy pour la Muſique,
ruë Saint Iean de Beauuais, au Mont Parnaſſe.

M. DC. LXVI.

AVEC PRIVILEGE DE SA MAIE

E 3a   Title-page of anonymous *Méthode facile pour apprendre à chanter la musique*
is 1666), with identification of the author in the hand of Sébastien de Brossard
is, Bibl. Nat., Rés. V. 2554)

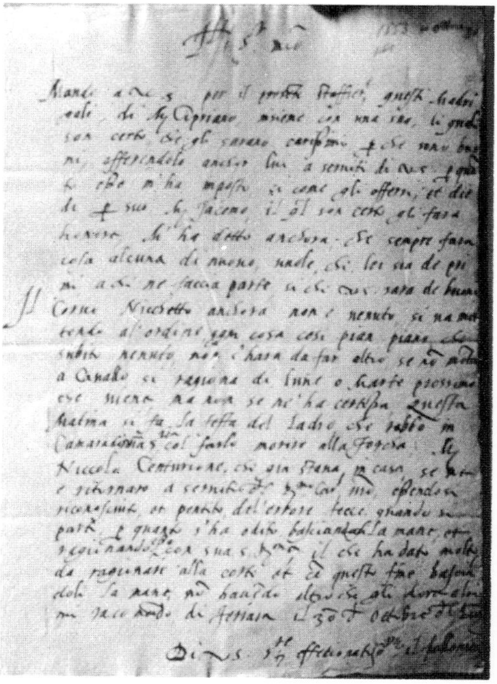

PLATE 3b Letter from Pollonice to Count Alfonso di Novellara, dated Ferrara, 30 October 1553. "Cipriano" can be clearly seen in the second line, and "Jacomo" in the sixth (Novellara, Archivio del Municipio)

PLATE 4a How the young Weisskunig learned all (string) instruments

PLATE 4b Music of lutes and viols, with Artus, principal court lutenist

PLATE 5a   Music of a mixed band

PLATE 5b   Maximilian's *Hofkapelle* with Georg Slatkonia, Bishop of Vienna and Choirmaster at St. Stephen's Cathedral

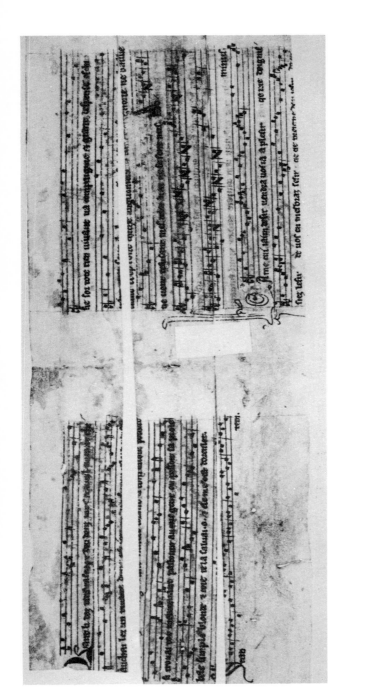

PLATE 6 Notre-Dame fragments formerly in the private library of Johannes Wolf (Berlin), Complex A, fols. 7ᵛ and 2ʳ (Dittmer, *Reconstruction*, p. 23)

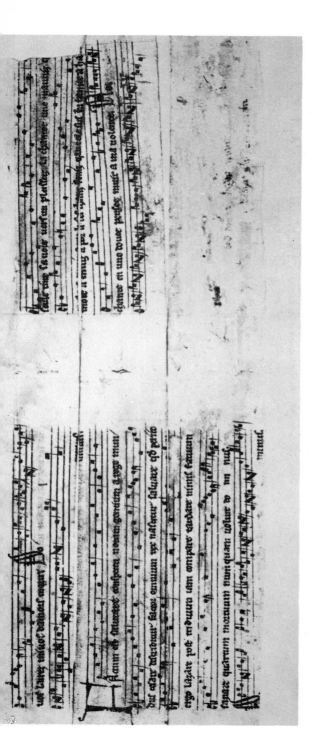

PLATE 7 Notre-Dame fragments, Complex A, fols. 2ᵛ and 7ʳ
(*Reconstruction*, p. 24)

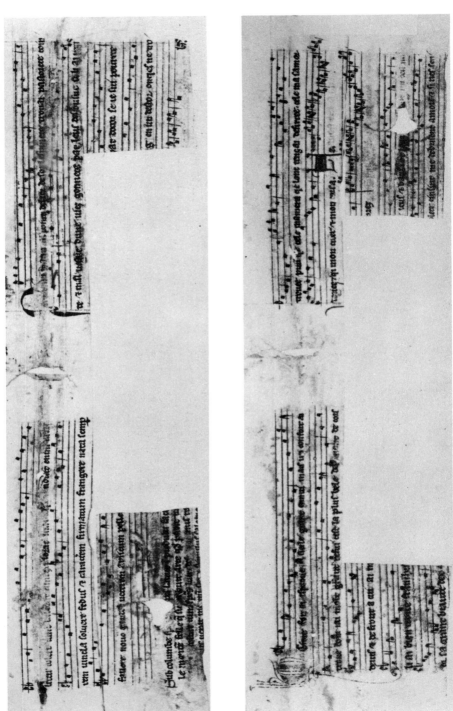

PLATE 8   Notre-Dame fragments, Complex A, fols. 6ᵛ and 3ʳ (*Reconstruction*, p. 25); fols. 3ᵛ and 6ʳ (*Reconstruction*, p. 26)

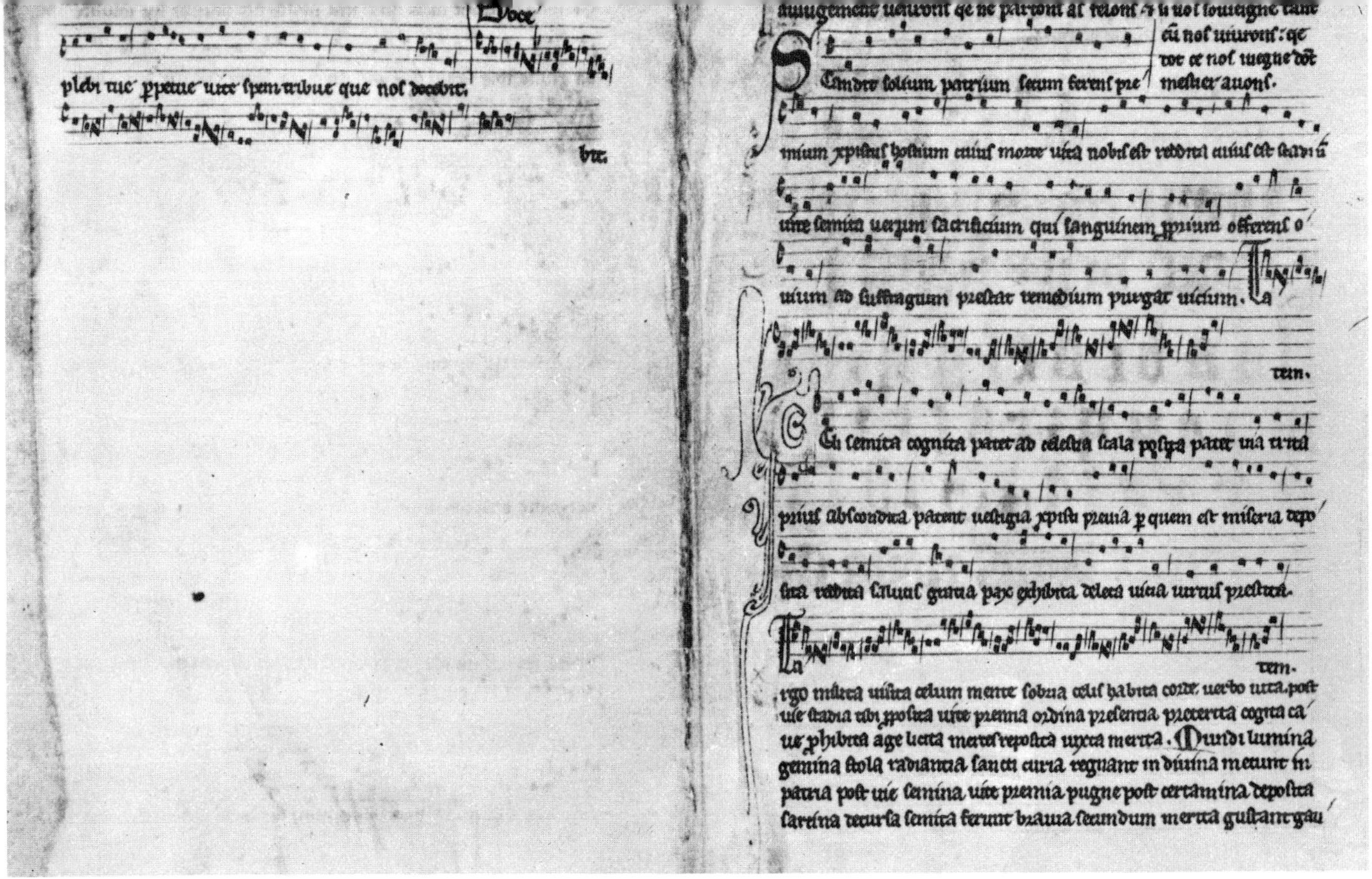

PLATE 9 Notre-Dame fragments, Complex B, fols. 6v and 1r (*Reconstruction*, p. 29)

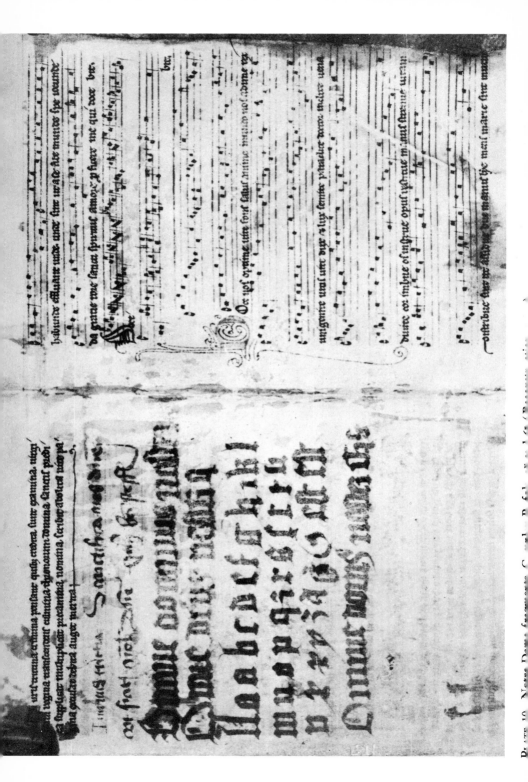

PLATE 10. Notre Dame fragments. Cambridge, Pembroke College, fol. 61 (Reproduced, actual size).

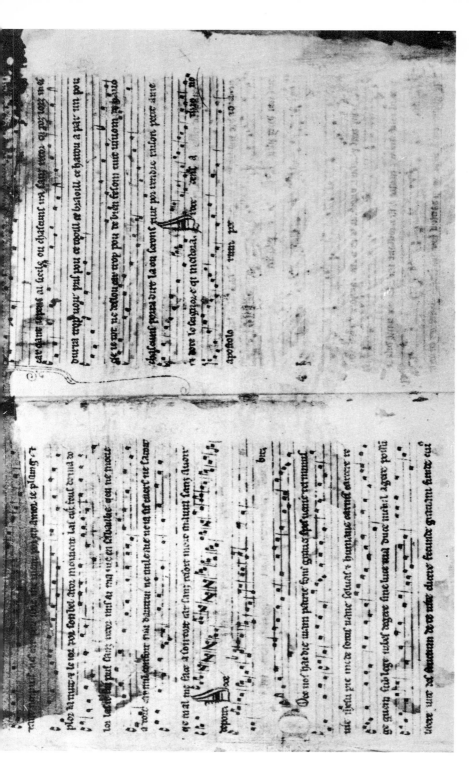

PLATE 11   Notre-Dame fragments, Complex B, fols. 5ᵛ and 2ʳ (*Reconstruction*, p. 31)

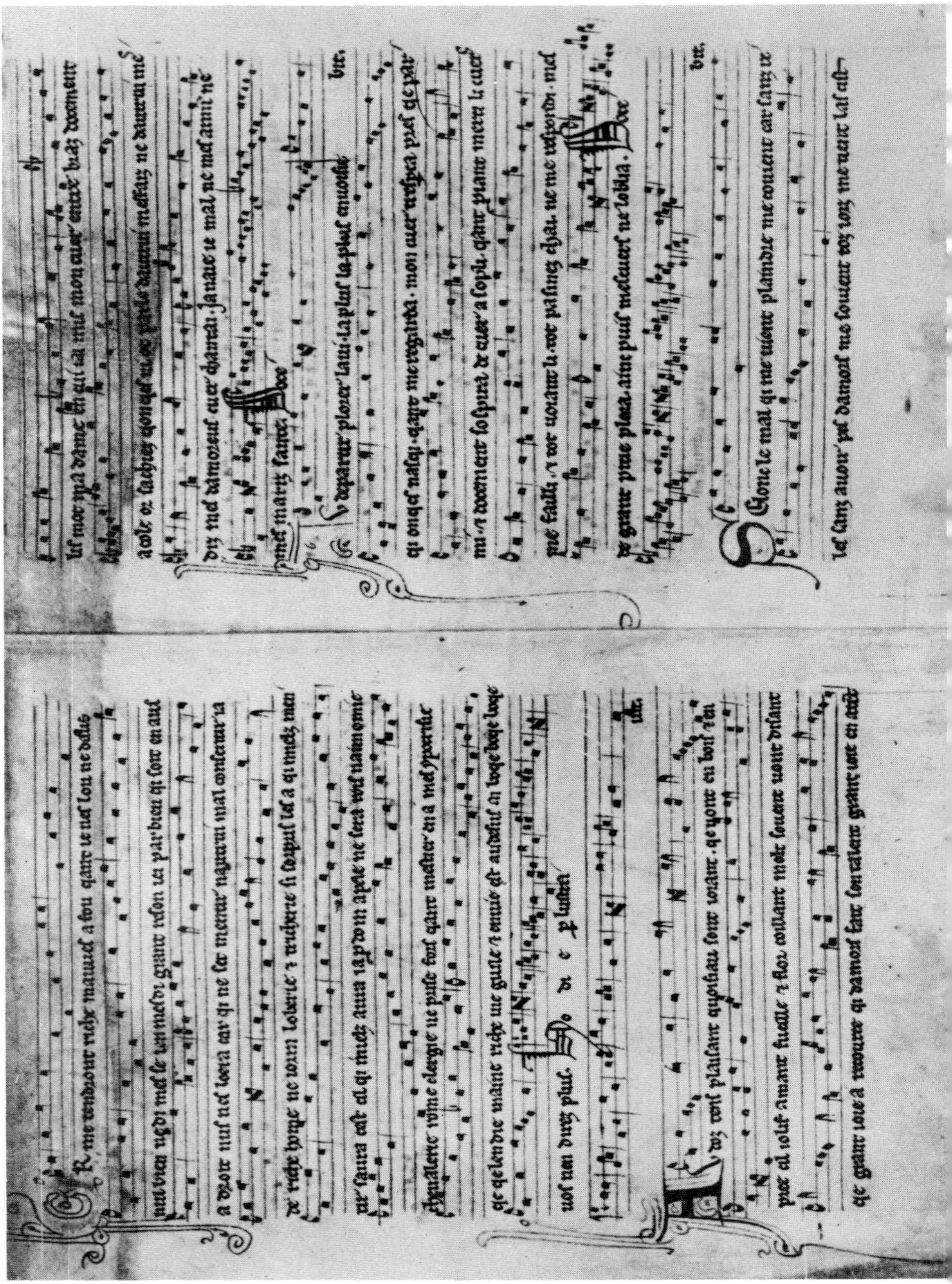

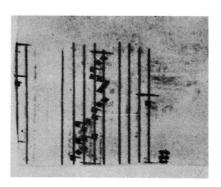

PLATE 13 Notre-Dame fragments, Complex C, fols. 4ᵛ and 1ʳ
(*Reconstruction*, p. 33)

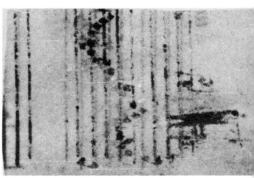

PLATE 14   Notre-Dame fragments, Complex C, fols. 1ᵛ and 4ʳ
(*Reconstruction*, p. 34)

PLATE 15 Notre-Dame Fragments, Complex D, fols. 6ᵛ and 11ʳ (*Reconstruction*, p. 35)

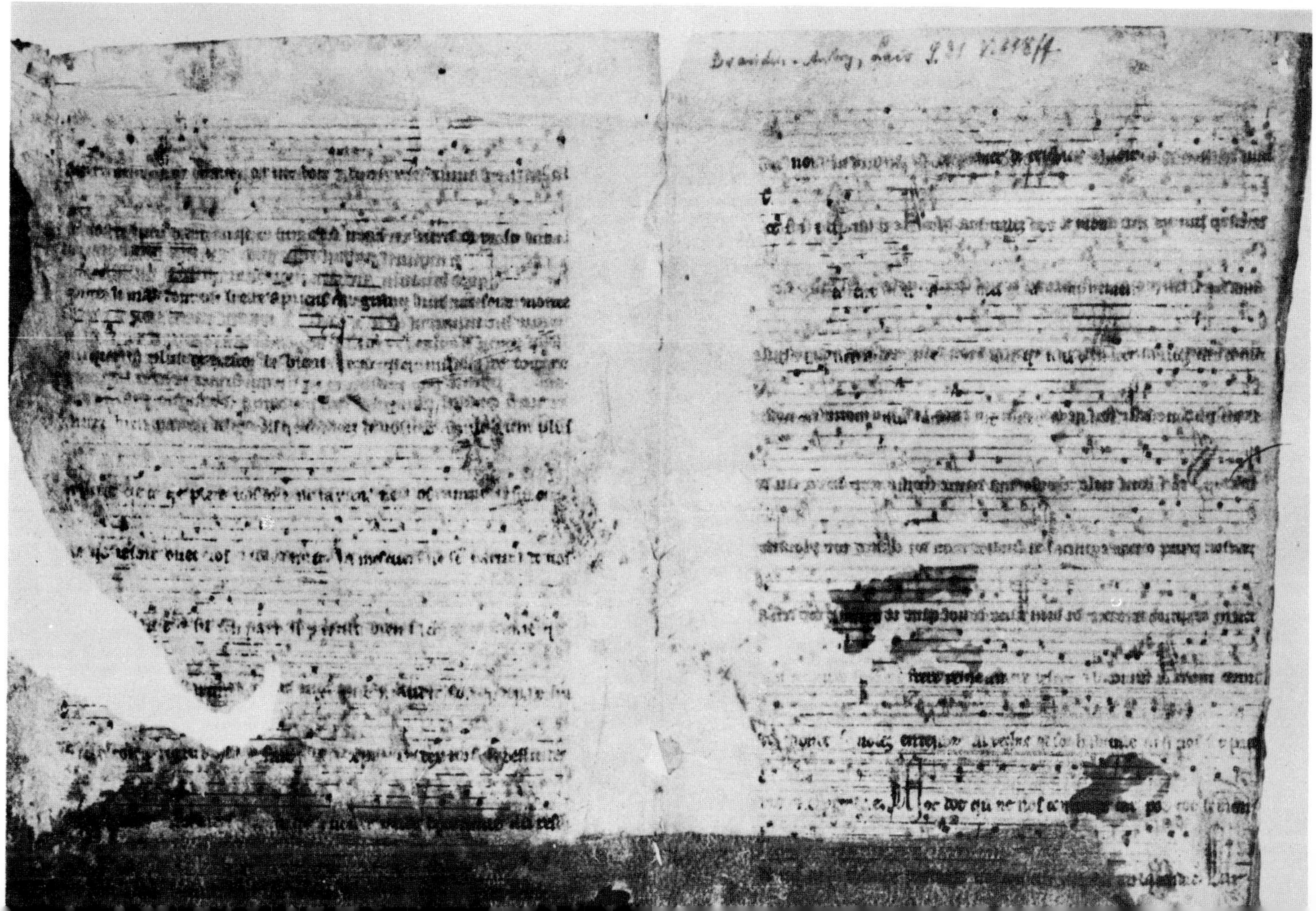

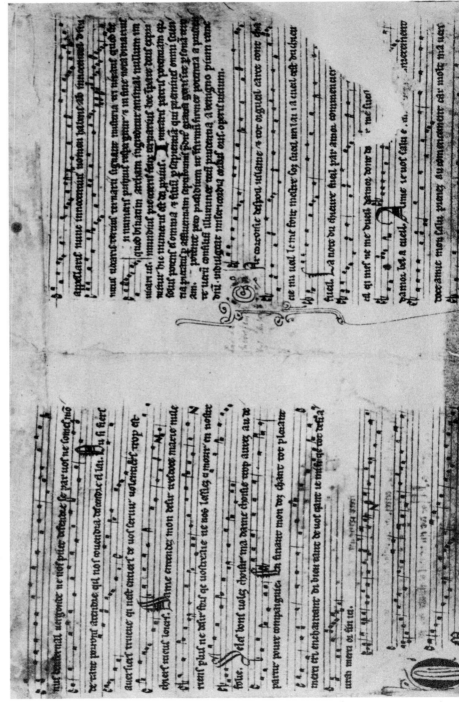

PLATE 16 Notre-Dame fragments, Complex D, fols. 1v and 6r (*Reconstruction*, p. 36)

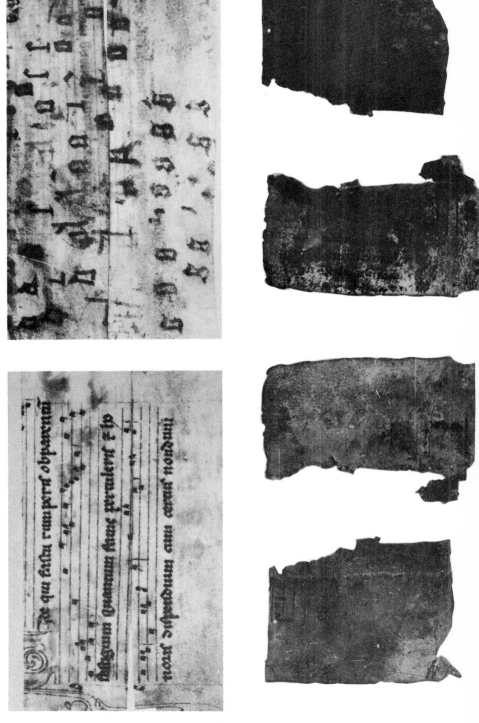

PLATE 17 Notre-Dame fragments, Complex E, fols. 1ᵛ, 1ʳ (*Reconstruction*, pp. 35, 36), and unidentified fragments

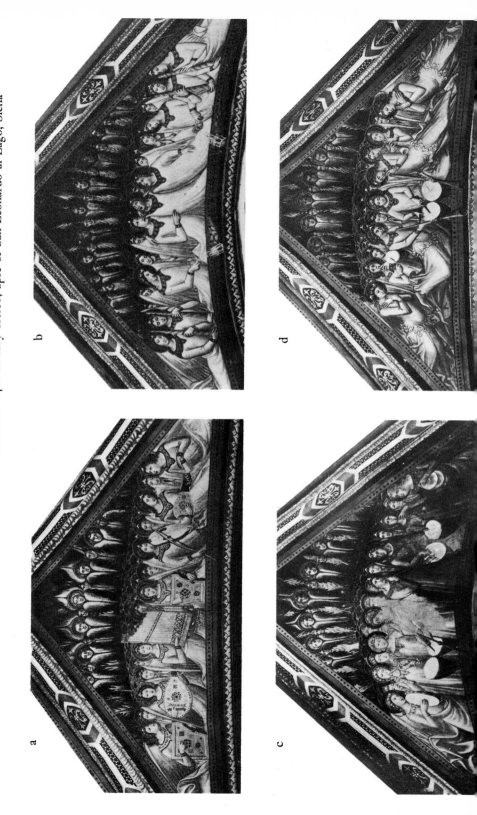

PLATE 18 14th-century fresco, apse of San Leonardo al Lago, Siena

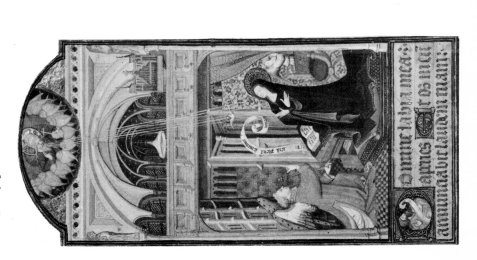

PLATE 20a Anonymous, *A[dri]ano Willaert*, 18th century ([Bo]logna, Liceo Musicale)

PLATE 20b "L.C." (unidentified artist), *Adrian Willaert*, in: *Musica nova* (Venice 1559)

PLATE 21a Jan Stevensz van Calcar (?), *Portrait of a Bearded Man*, c. 1536 (Rome, Galleria Spada)

PLATE 21b Anonymous, *Hadrianus Wilhart*, late 16th century (Vienna, Kunsthistorisches Museum)

PLATE 21c Anonymous, *Adria.ˢ Wilaert*, 17th century (Leipzig, University Library)

PLATE 22a   Jacopo Bassano (
Portrait of a Bearded Man,
1560 (Courtesy of the Art In
tute of Chicago)

PLATE 22b   "L. C.," *Adrian Willaert* [reversed], in: *Musica nova*
(Venice 1559)

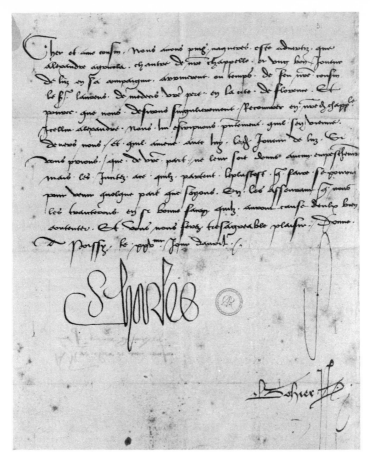

PLATE 23a   Letter of Charles VIII of France concerning Alexander
Agricola (Pierpont Morgan Library, VR/R, F/Box I/Charles VIII/
No. 4)

PLATE 23b   Title-page of the *Frottole intabulate* (1517) of A. Antico,
(Prague, Dobrovský Library Gg. 19)

PLATE 24a King David and musicians, San
Isidoro of Leon, main portal

PLATE 24b Fid-
dle, San Isidoro of
Leon, main portal

PLATE 24c King David, Santiago de Co
stela, Puerta de las Platerías

PLATE 24d King David and musicians, Cathedral of Jaca, south porch

PLATE 25a Stele in museum at Mérida

PLATE 25b Detail of capital, Cathedral of Jaca, south porch

PLATE 25c Double psaltery, Church at Artáiz (Navarre)

f) Lute type and
portative organ

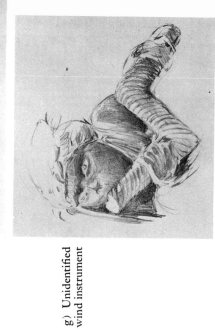

g) Unidentified
wind instrument

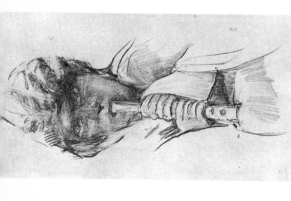

d) Shawm type (*caramillo*)

PLATE 26   Cathedral of Jaca

e) Harp and horns

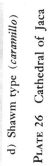

a) Fiddle and
psaltery

b) Horn

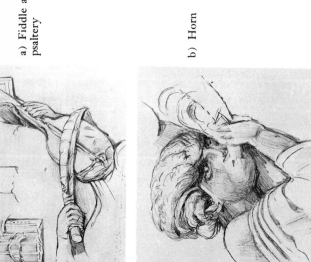

b) Panpipes

c) Panpipes

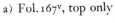

a) Fol. 167ᵛ, top only

b) Fol. 168, top only

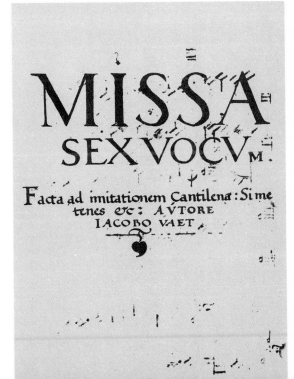

c) Fol. 167ʳ

PLATE 28a   Oxford, Bodleian Library, Arch. Selden B. 14, fol. 312ᵛ (d, e)

PLATE 28b   Brussels, Bibliothèque Royale, II. 266. 10, fol. 1ᵛ (ii)

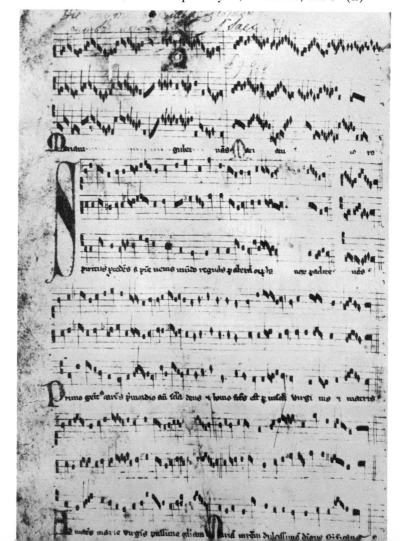

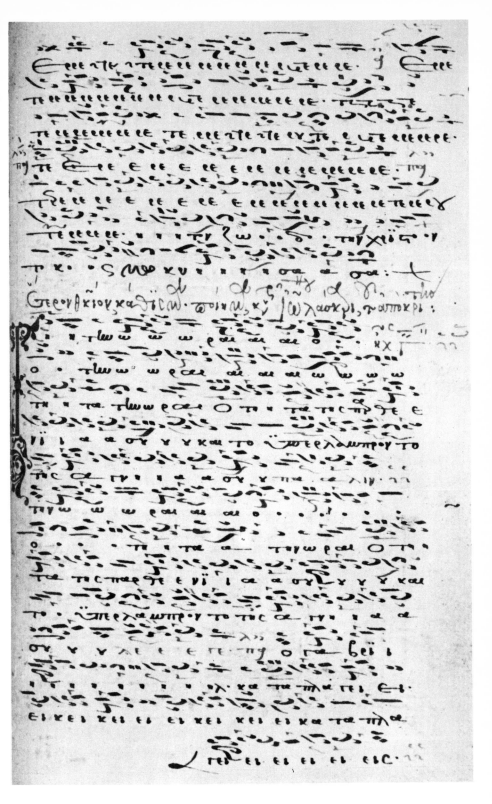

PLATE 29 Beginning of the Theotokion, Τὴν ὡσαιότητα (Mode III) by John Laskaris (Athens, National Library, MS 2406, fol. 422ʳ)

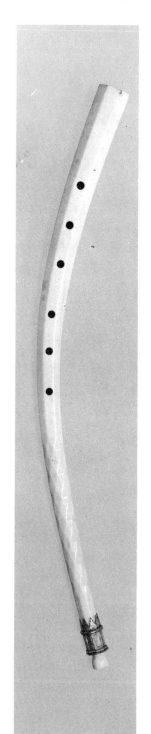

PLATE 30a *Cornetto curvo* of wood covered with leather. France, early 17th century (New York, Metropolitan Museum of Art, Crosby Brown Collection)

PLATE 30b *Cornetto curvo* of ivory, c. 1600, with gilded mounting and original mouthpiece (New York, Metropolitan Museum of Art, Crosby Brown Collection)

PLATE 30c Silver flute made by Theobald Boehm, Munich, 19th century (New York, Metropolitan Museum of Art, gift of Mrs. J. J. Canning 1911)

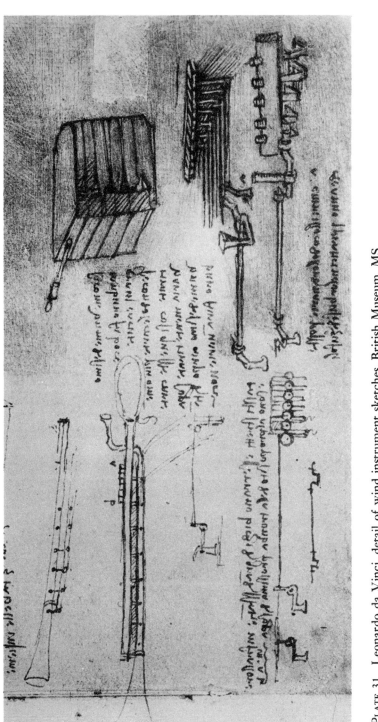

PLATE 31 Leonardo da Vinci, detail of wind instrument sketches, British Museum, MS Arundel 263, fol. 175ʳ

PLATE 32a Giotto, *Coronation of the Virgin,* detail showing trumpets (Flor«
S. Croce)

PLATE 32b Luca della Robbia, *Cantoria,* detail showing trumpets (Florence, Oper«
Duomo)

explanation for the preponderance of $B:CF$ variations in the polyphony. Unfortunately, we can do no more than speculate on the nature of Z. It was inscribed by a person of some intelligence, and was apparently well regarded, if the scribe of F elected to copy from it. Its approximate date can be derived only from the dates of its ancestor and of its descendants. A suggestion regarding its provenance will be made below.

For X and Y, the situation is rather different. They cannot be eliminated from the Diagram, but we can present evidence giving some substance to their claim to existence. The 17th-century Beauvais historian Pierre Louvet describes, in his *Histoire et antiquités du diocèse de Beauvais* (Beauvais 1631–35),[14] a lost manuscript of the Office of the Circumcision at Beauvais that differs in a number of particulars from Egerton 2615. The description is not as detailed as we might wish,[15] but it is enough to show that a Beauvais Circumcision Office other than Egerton 2615 once existed, that it was written (on the evidence of the names of the rulers given in the *laudes*) between 1160 and 1162, and that it was, on the whole, remarkably similar to Egerton 2615, for which it may well have served to a large extent as a source—either immediate or remote. But did Louvet's manuscript (hereafter L) contain *Christus manens?*

On this point, Louvet is silent. He lists the pieces beginning first vespers, which are almost the same as those of Egerton 2615;[16] but when he comes to the point where *Letemur* and *Christus manens* appear in the latter, he merely says that "two proses were sung." The description then resumes with the first antiphon of vespers, as in Egerton 2615. Louvet's nomenclature is by no means precise, and he, like other writers of the period, uses "prose" for almost any kind of interpolation.[17] Thus the two

[14] Not to be confused with the same author's *L'histoire de la ville et cité de Beauvais, et des antiquitez du pays de Beauvaisis* (Rouen 1613–14), which contains much of the same matter, but not the passage in question here.

[15] The account by Dom Grenier in his *Introduction à l'histoire générale de la province de Picardie, Mémoires de la société des antiquaires de Picardie, Documents inédits*, III (Amiens 1856), 362–63, while more ample, is not, as it claims to be, a description of Louvet's manuscript, but a confusing conflation from Louvet, Egerton 2615, and other sources as well. It is thus of no value.

[16] The one difference, apart from a textual variant in the first piece (which has no significance for this study), is the inclusion of the *Veni creator* in L, as opposed to the *Veni sancte* or *Veni doctor previe* in Egerton 2615. The last piece is a motet (appearing in Egerton 2615, fols. 69 and 84^v, and in F, fol. 390^v). Such a piece would doubtless not have existed as early as the 1160s.

[17] For example, Louvet says that 19 proses were sung at matins. It is hardly likely that all of these would have been "proses" in the modern sense. Louvet probably counted versiculi, smaller interpolations (like responsorial prosulae), and perhaps even conductus in the total.

Earlier writers quite generally apply the term "prose de l'âne" to the conductus *Orientis partibus*. The word is thus anything but specific.

"proses" may well have been *Letemur* and *Christus manens*, especially in view of the otherwise almost complete agreement between *L* and Egerton 2615. If this should be the case, it cannot have been the extant three-voice setting that was used, partly because the piece must be considerably later,[18] and partly because Louvet elsewhere remarks on pieces sung *cum organo*, and does not do so here.

It is thus possible that *L* is one of our hypothetical sources. There is, moreover, evidence of the existence of yet another lost manuscript. In the Bibliothèque Municipale of Beauvais there is a vast assemblage of notes, copies of documents, and the like, known as the Collection Bucquet-Aux Cousteaux, made by 18th-century Beauvais historians for a projected history of the city.[19] Volumes XXXI and XXXII [20] of this collection deal with liturgical and ecclesiastical matters, and contain, among other things, a number of copies of and extracts from Circumcision Offices—all but one of which turn out to derive directly from Egerton 2615. The one exception (Vol. XXXII, pp. 399ff) is of interest. It is a synopsis of a Circumcision Office (headed "Ancien antiphonier in festo stultorum" [21]), giving titles of most of the pieces sung,[22] and a few complete texts (it contains no music). It cannot be a résumé of *L*, since it differs from it in many particulars. Nor can it derive from Egerton 2615, since the writer of the synopsis carefully points out pieces present in that manuscript, but absent from his source ("manque après l'invitatoire la prose A rea virga primae matris"; ". . . manque aussy le conductus Ex adae vitio").[23] It represents, then, yet another lost manuscript. This one

[18] Husmann, *Die drei- und vierstimmigen Organa*, p. xxii, dates the *Christus manens* organum as one of a later group, postdating 1200. In any event, there is no evidence of *tripla* as early as 1160.

[19] There is a valuable inventory by Victor Leblond, *Inventaire sommaire de la collection Bucquet-Aux Cousteaux* (Paris 1907).

In point of fact, the Bucquet-Aux Cousteaux collection represents only a part of the literary remains of these historians. Another part, the Collection Danse, formerly a part of the Collection de Troussures, was destroyed in World War II. The third part, the Collection Borel, remains in the hands of the Baron de Bretizel, Château de Vieux-Rouen (Seine-inférieure), who kindly made it available for my consultation in the summer of 1960.

[20] These volumes have deteriorated badly, and can no longer be consulted at the library. I am much indebted to M. R. Lemaire, librarian of the Bibliothèque Municipale, for providing me with microfilms of them.

[21] The "festum stultorum" or "Feast of Fools" was often celebrated on January 1, properly the Feast of the Circumcision. The relation of Egerton 2615 and the lost manuscripts to this festivity will be discussed in my edition of Egerton 2615. The literature on the subject is enormous, and I shall cite here only Villetard, *Office*, pp. 61–73; and E. Chambers, *The Mediaeval Stage* (Oxford 1903), I, 274–336.

[22] The writer omits certain minor matters, such as the incipits of psalms, or of subsequent members of a series of antiphons, when the first makes clear what is to follow.

[23] There are also enough divergencies to show that the writer was not copying a defective late copy of Egerton 2615.

specifically includes *Christus manens* (only the text incipit is given) at its usual place at first vespers. Unfortunately, however, the source (hereafter *Q*) cannot be dated. It entirely lacks the Mass, and hence the *laudes*, which were our guide in dating *L* and the Office of Egerton 2615. The Office of *Q* agrees closely with Egerton 2615 (as did *L*), with the omission of a number of conductus and other interpolative pieces, and of all reference to polyphonic performance. It does, however, contain several pieces in the developed rhythmic style of 12th-century poetry, and hence is not likely to be earlier than *L*.[24] Its close agreement with the other Beauvais Offices—extending even to identical series of matins responsories—and its presence in the Bucquet-Aux Cousteaux collection indicate that it derives from Beauvais.

We have, then, evidence of the existence of two lost Circumcision Offices, one of which definitely contained *Christus manens*, and the other of which probably had it.[25] Since the exact version of the text and music has not come down to us in either case, we cannot be certain what part they may have played in the transmission of *Christus manens* but, in the interests of economy, it is reasonable to give to them the places originally occupied in our Diagrams by *X* and *Y*. Since *L* is known to have been an early source, we may equate it with *X*, leaving the undatable *Q* to take the place of *Y*. The results are shown in Diagram 3 (*3a* supposes the retention of the hypothetical *W*, *3b* its elimination).[26]

Diagram 3

In both Diagrams, *Christus manens* shows deep roots in the Circumcision liturgy of Beauvais. In Diagram *3b*, the organum appears without question as a local Beauvais composition. In *3a*, the matter is not quite so

---

[24] *Q* may be a reworking of the normal Beauvais Circumcision Office (whether from *L* or Egerton 2615) for the use of a smaller church. Its tendency towards abbreviation and its omission of polyphony suggest this. Such a reworking could, of course, have been made at any time.

[25] The evidence of *Q*, which confirms the stability of the Circumcision tradition at Beauvais, tends to increase the likelihood that Louvet's "two proses" were the same as those of the other sources.

[26] Naturally, there must also have been the original autograph of the composer of the organum. But this is not a "source" in the same sense as the others: it would presumably have been turned over to the copyist of *B* (or *W*), and then destroyed.

simple. We have no direct evidence of the provenance of W. But, since it stands between two Beauvais sources—Q and, eventually, C—it is extremely likely that it, too, was a local product (the same reasoning, incidentally, applies to Z).

Also interesting is the proof offered by the Diagrams that the *Christus manens* melody existed prior to the composition of the extant organum. Heretofore, since all known sources had either been polyphonic, or had prescribed polyphonic performance, this could only be surmised— although, given the habits of the organum composers, it was a natural guess. Now, since Q does not mention organal performance, and since it could not in any case have contained the extant organum, we can be certain that in this case as in all others, the composer of the organum worked from a pre-existent tenor melody.

It will not have escaped the reader that our final Diagram leaves unanswered one question: the nature of the organum in S. We should naturally be inclined to suppose that this was the same as the surviving piece, especially since Pierre de Corbeil was acquainted with the Parisian style of polyphony.[27] But there is simply no way of fitting S into the stemma in a place where it might receive (or give) the organum in the normal way. If Sens used the organum we have, it must have got it by conflation from B or W (i.e. S took the chant from L, but the lost source for the Sens organum took the piece from B or W).[28] If B is selected, S must be dated rather later than is usual, since the Sens organum source cannot postdate S (owing to the fact that S, in prescribing polyphony, takes for granted its availability). There is nothing impossible in this, but it may be that the Sens organum was merely a local product that failed to survive.[29]

[27] He was one of the signers of the ordinance of Eudes de Sully (above, fn. 4), being then *canonicus Parisiensis*. The ordinance gives regulations regarding the singing of certain chants "in organo, vel triplo, vel quadruplo"; Pierre surely knew what these terms stood for.

[28] The relation between the Sens and Beauvais Offices will be treated exhaustively in my edition of Egerton 2615. For the present, I shall point out only that there is little evidence of direct transmission from one to the other, and that, on the whole, the Beauvais tradition appears to have influenced that of Sens more than the reverse (as already suggested by Chambers, *Mediaeval Stage*, I, 288). It may well be that Q or L served as a model for the Sens Office—not, to be sure, in its strictly liturgical content, which was naturally regulated by diocesan tradition, but in its choice and use of para-liturgical pieces.

[29] On the rather meager evidence of polyphonic compositions at Sens, see my *Liturgical Polyphony*, pp. 185, 199, and the literature there cited.

THE PRACTICE OF ORGANUM IN THE LITURGICAL SINGING OF THE SYRIAN CHURCHES OF THE NEAR AND MIDDLE EAST

by HEINRICH HUSMANN

URING MY first visit to the oriental churches, where I heard the boys of the Syrian Orthodox college and orphanage of Beirut singing the evening prayer called *ramsha*, I observed that a few boys often sang a fourth lower than the rest of the choir. They followed this practice for longer parts of the service but returned to the pitch of the other singers for the shorter portions. At first I attached no significance to this observation, because in any school choir some boys who do not have good musical ears sing fourths, fifths, or octaves above or below the others, especially during the period when their voices are changing. It was the famous Carl Stumpf who made this phenomenon the basis of a psychological theory of consonance: the more consonant an interval is, the more often nonmusical singers believe it to be the unison. Yet, after so often hearing the singing in parallel fourths it seemed possible that it could be related to the old practice of organum: perhaps the Syrian-Orthodox boys have retained, in the modern world, the last remnants of an antique and medieval type of singing. With this in mind, I spoke to the Deacon of the church, who also conducts the choir, and tried to explain to him that his boys were singing at two different pitch levels. But he had not the slightest idea of musical intervals, not to mention theory of composition, scales, etc. His only answer was that his boys were all singing the same melody, and that they therefore were absolutely right—and I could not question his statement, because in a literal sense it, too, was correct. Therefore I gave up, concluding that the boys were as nonmusical as their teacher, yet retaining some doubt, because the teacher was really an intelligent and musical person, instructing people in the Syriac language and being one of the very few persons in the Near East to know the complete repertory of the liturgical melodies by heart.

435

When, during my second journey to the Orient, I came to India and studied the musical practice of the wonderful Carmelite monastery of Ernakulam in Kerala, the See of the Prior General of the Indian Carmelites of Maria Immaculata (C.M.I.), I was immediately reminded of my experience in Beirut: the 25-year-old Brother Kuriakose Elias was singing parallel organum in fourths with the choir. The Prior General, the Very Reverend Father Maurus (C.M.I.), had given to me as musical adviser the General Economist of the order, the Rev. Father Amos, the musical authority of his house, who then sang for me with unsurpassable precision the melodies of the Indian-Chaldean repertory. The tempo was controlled by a watch lying beside his breviary. He, as well as all the monks of the house, were highly educated persons, many of them having spent years in Europe for theological or other studies and having earned European doctoral degrees. I thus hoped that he would understand my question and asked him about the parallel fourths of the young brother. He understood instantaneously and said with smiling charm: "But this is the right of youth, each age has its own musical range, young men singing of course higher than old ones." (Brother Kuriakose Elias had indeed sung his fourths *above* the level of the choir.) This explanation not only gave a confirmation of the fact itself, but also a psychological theory concerning its origin. A bridge from the present era to the antiphony of Christian antiquity, when boys or virgins sang alternately with the monks of the other half of the choir, can easily be constructed. In former publications I have already suggested for etymological reasons that the old antiphony was not sung in unison, but at the octave ("antiphonia"), to which interval the fourth now could be added. In this way, antiphony and organum would come into a close connection.

These speculations, however, could not be definitively confirmed merely by the performance of Brother Kuriakose Elias, since he was the only one singing in parallel fourths in his half of the choir, all the other monks singing at the same pitch as those in the other half of the choir. In this other half there was also a young brother, but he had a bass voice and therefore sang in unison with the older fathers. This fact immediately shows that the problem is more complex: it is not only difference in age that determines the interval of singing but also the vocal range of the singer. Furthermore, in responsorial performance a real alternation of pitch levels very often occurred: Brother Kuriakose Elias was the leader of his choir-half and therefore sang the intonations and shorter phrases ("Let us pray," for example), to which the whole choir then answered a fourth lower. In other cases I found that a priest in the Mass was reciting his part a fourth higher than the choir sang. Once also I heard the leader of a group of coolies singing a fourth higher than the boys who answered. But these cases of alternating fourths were only exceptions; normally the two halves of a choir had the same composition, i.e. when there was organum, then it occurred in both halves and also in the combined choir.

While studying the musical practice of the Carmelite Prior General's House intensively for three weeks, I observed a number of musical facts that were able to cast more light on the musical and psychological side of the phenomenon. First, concerning Brother Kuriakose Elias: he was markedly *un*musical—a wonderful example of Stumpf's theory of consonance and "Verschmelzung." Very often he could not find the most consonant interval between his voice and the voice of the other fathers, but dropped beneath the interval of the fourth by a half or whole tone. Then he was singing parallels of major or minor thirds. After some time he became aware of this and then slowly raised his pitch until he had reached the interval of the fourth, which he then maintained. Occasionally he also sang in parallels a fifth higher, apparently not by intent but rather because the composition of the choir, which was continually changing, had been influenced by deeper voices, and consequently the whole choir was singing a tone lower than normal. Obviously Brother Kuriakose Elias had a relatively good instinct for absolute pitch: he started with wrong intervals such as major and minor thirds because these fell within the natural range of his voice. Then, however, he corrected himself in order to reach more consonant intervals.

Brother Kuriakose Elias also performed the same kind of temporary parallel singing that the Beirut orphans used. In his case the real reason for the practice was clear: he used the parallels when he was reciting psalms, but when there were more complicated chants to be sung, in the first notes he tried to observe the parallels, but afterwards he obviously found it too difficult and had to return to the pitch of the other singers. His ideal was certainly to observe the parallels throughout; but when the musical pieces became somewhat complex, his musicality was not sufficient for continuing the practice.

Not only did this one young brother sing parallel intervals, but also the others of the choir, though singing unison in psalmody and in melodic pieces, used a very much freer practice when praying together. Then each monk was allowed to recite in his own range; and normally the result was not a musical chaos, for the monks regulated the range so that third-, fourth-, or (rarely) fifth-parallels emerged. In this manner they prayed the rosary each day after vespers, and on Friday evening also the special prayer of the five wounds of Christ. In the same way also, the boys of the institution prayed their afternoon and evening prayers in the church. Furthermore, the whole community prayed in this manner also during the Mass, for instance during the Creed; and the same practice occurred in the prayers at home. When walking in the dark evening through the streets of Ernakulam it was pleasant to hear the sisters of the hospital, the children of a school, or the parents and children of a family saying the good-night prayer in third- or fourth-parallels. And, of course, there was no difference in this practice between the different rites: my Carmelite monks belonged to the Syro-Malabar church (i.e. East-Syrian Catholic), but I observed the same style of singing also in the Jacobite church of Ernakulam (i.e. West-Syrian Orthodox) and when visiting the orphanage of the same church in Perumbavur. After returning from India to Beirut, I found the same tradition in the singing of the communities of the Syrian-Orthodox (Jacobite) church and the Chaldean church (East-Syrian Catholic), for instance when singing the *Pater noster*. Since the children sing an octave higher than the adults, there is thus a real four-part organum of the Guidonian type. As the musical practice of the Arabic and Indian peoples among whom these Christians live is an absolutely different one, namely the use of heterophony—singing and playing the same melody in different variations at the same time, but in unison and octaves—it is therefore clear that the practice of parallel singing described above is a peculiarity of the Eastern Syrian Christians.

I found the finest form of parallel fourths when visiting the Syro-Malankar Bishop of Tiruvalla (in the south of Ernakulam), the Syro-Malankar Church being the Indian Catholic branch of the West-Syrian church. Here I attended the noon service of the theological seminary. The young seminarians, together with their professors and the bishop, sang—in both halves of the choir—such perfect parallel fourths, not only in the psalmody, but also throughout the melodic chants, that it was a pleasure to hear this divine consonance of musical sound.

These experiences show all forms of reciting and singing in parallel intervals. The cruder examples used seconds, thirds, and fourths together; the more elevated communities sang in either thirds or fourths; and the highest style practiced only parallel fourths (very rarely fifths). These different types of parallel singing obviously demonstrate the psychological origin of organum at the fourth: in the most primitive style each person sings in his normal range, but when the musical ear controls the polyphonic result, the principle of consonance puts the intervals in order. Persons trying to sing at the same pitch may sing at first in parallel seconds, thirds, or fourths (the interval of the fifth is already too wide), but they will gradually adjust to parallel fourths: those singing in parallel seconds will join those at the unison, and those singing parallel thirds will combine with those singing at the fourth. When this result is once reached, the musically well-educated communities sing the pure form of organum at the fourth, the less privileged groups remaining at more primitive stages. This ancient performance tradition thus survives today in the practice of organal singing in the Syrian churches.

Certainly the Syrian practice is very old. We may conjecture that it is as old as antiphony and the liturgical singing of bigger choirs. Obviously, organum is the original form of singing in the ancient Eastern brotherhoods—the Eastern churches having also preserved to the present the original language in which Christ celebrated the Easter feast with his disciples. Thus, we may infer that organum in parallel fourths is of Syrian origin and with antiphony found its way to Western Christianity, to the paraphony of the Papal court and to the organum of the antiphons and sequences of early medieval polyphony. Also, the mixed timbres of the Byzantine organ may derive their construction from the same origin. Thus, by extension of our hypothesis, even the European organ with its fifth-and-octave registers (neglecting for a moment that there are also third registers) may be a last instrumental remainder of the old Syrian vocal practice of singing parallel fourths.

THE MANUSCRIPT FLORENCE BIBLIOTECA NAZIONALE CENTRALE, BANCO RARI 230: AN ATTEMPT AT A DIPLOMATIC RECONSTRUCTION

by KNUD JEPPESEN

THE FAMOUS manuscript of our title (formerly known as Magliabecchiana XIX, 141) must be considered the central source of secular Florentine polyphony of c. 1500. Unfortunately it has been preserved quite incompletely, and the remains do not tell us directly just how large or small the missing portions were. Written on paper, apparently by a single scribe, the codex—hereafter referred to as F230—dates from the beginning of the 16th century. In its obviously reduced present state it contains 151 folios and is approximately 22 cm high by 15.5 cm wide. It has been known since the middle of the 19th century, when it was seemingly discovered by Adrien de La Fage,[1] who continued to take an interest in it. Roberto Gandolfi,[2] Eugenia Levi,[3] and Johannes Wolf[4] were next in dealing with our manuscript, but the first and so far unique modern edition of a large portion of its contents we owe to Paul-Marie Masson, who published 20 of its canti carnascialeschi in *Chants de carnaval florentins*.[5] Of more recent publications concerning our manuscript the following should be singled out: Federico Ghisi's *I Canti carnascialeschi*[6] and *Poesie musicali italiane;*[7] Alfred Einstein's *The Italian Madrigal;*[8] and the index of its contents included

---

[1] Adrien de La Fage, *Canti carnascialeschi*, in: *Gazzetta musicale di Milano*, VI-XII (1847-52).
[2] Roberto Gandolfi, *Illustrazioni di alcuni cimeli concernenti l'arte musicale in Firenze* (Florence 1892).
[3] Eugenia Levi, *Lirica italiana antica* (Florence 1905).
[4] *Denkmäler der Tonkunst in Österreich*, Jahrg. XIV/1, Vol. XXVIII (Vienna & Leipzig 1907), 171.
[5] Paris 1913.
[6] Florence 1937.
[7] In: *Note d'archivio*, XVI (1939), 40-67.
[8] (Princeton 1949), I, 59.

in Bianca Becherini's catalogue of manuscripts in the Biblioteca Nazionale Centrale.[9] A more detailed description based on the physical aspects of the codex, clearly warranted by its importance, has not yet been attempted, and I shall take this occasion to remedy the lack by means of a hypothetical reconstruction based essentially on external criteria.

When I first had the opportunity to see the codex in the spring of 1929, I found the folios to have been numbered in pencil by a modern hand in the upper right-hand corner of the recto side of each leaf. In front and back of the manuscript there were two modern blank sheets used as protective covers as well as the two old blank sheets at the beginning. Returning some years later for a closer look at the manuscript, I found that it had been restored meanwhile. It was now newly bound in white parchment and had been renumbered, again in pencil, in the lower left-hand corner of each recto. While the new numbering came out correctly to a total of 151 folios this time, fol. 121 was erroneously placed between fols. 131 and 132. Many leaves in a poor state of preservation had been reënforced with silk, which does not exactly improve their legibility, never very good to begin with. At the time of my first visit I had found the order of the codex difficult enough to analyze, since many leaves stuck together, but I believed it to have consisted of 9 gatherings. This order had been altered in the course of the restoration. At the same time the volume's call-number was changed as indicated above. Unfortunately there is no index. The original ink foliation found on the bottom left-hand corner of the versos, however, is still legible in part and, although it is frequently quite unclear, if not faded altogether, is still of considerable value in reconstructing the book.

The following comparative table lists the modern foliation in column A (in italics), while B contains the original numbering. The large brackets connecting several folio numbers indicate that their belonging together can be deduced from their musical context while > means that incomplete compositions indicate that folios are missing. The letter "m." stands for the absence of an original folio number.[10]

So UNIQUE a source deserves to be studied from as many sides as possible. Aside from an analysis based on the completeness of its compositions shown in the above table, we should examine external criteria such as paper, watermarks, the sewing of leaves into gatherings, etc., and espe-

---

[9] Bianca Becherini, *Catalogo dei manoscritti musicali della Biblioteca Nazionale di Firenze* (Kassel 1959), pp. 60–68.

[10] The foliation reported here does not always correspond precisely with that given by Ghisi in *Poesie musicali italiane* or by Becherini, *op. cit.*

TABLE I

A	B	A	B	A	B
1	m.	52	53?	103	130
2	(2?)	53	54	104	131
3	(3?)	54	55	105	133
4	(4?)	55	56	106	134
5	5	56	57	107	135
6	(6?)	57	m.	108	136
7	8	58	m.	109	137
8	(9?)	59	m.	110	138
9	(10?)	60	m.	111	140
10	(11?)	61	(74?)	112	142
11	m.	62	75	113	143
12	13	63	76	114	144
13	14	64	77	115	145
14	15	65	79	116	146
15	16	66	81	117	147
16	17	67	82	118	148
17	18	68	85	119	149
18	19	69	86	120	m.
19	20	70	m.	*121	(150)
20	21	71	m.	122	151
21	22	72	94	123	152
22	23	73	95	124	153
23	24	74	96	125	154
24	25	75	97	126	155
25	26	76	100	127	156
26	27	77	101	128	157
27	28	78	102	129	158
28	29	79	103	130	159
29	30	80	104	131	160
30	31	81	105	132	161
31	32	82	(107?)	133	162
32	33	83	108	134	163
33	34	84	109	135	164
34	35	85	110	136	165
35	36	86	111	137	166
36	37	87	113	138	167
37	38	88	114	139	168
38	39	89	115	140	169
39	40	90	116	141	?
40	41	91	117	142	181
41	m.	92	118	143	183
42	m.	93	120	144	184
43	44	94	121	145	186
44	45	95	122	146	187
45	46	96	123	147	188
46	47	97	124	148	189
47	48	98	125	149	194
48	49	99	126	150	197
49	50	100	127	151	199
50	51	101	128		
51	52	102	129		

* Misplaced in rebinding

cially, the legible remains of the original foliation. The sewing of the gatherings is not last in order of importance. Nearly all the original threads are still present. New sewing is found only after fols. 76, 85, and 132, while that between fols. 5/6, 15/16, 25/26, etc. is original. From the grouping of the latter the original make-up of the codex in gatherings of five sheets is apparent. By means of this evidence as well as the matching of watermark fragments (always found in the center of a sheet and therefore usually cut in half) one can reconstruct the order in which the gatherings were most likely put together when the volume was compiled.[11]

IT THUS BECOMES apparent that the manuscript originally consisted of at least 20 five-fold gatherings, six of which are still intact, namely, II–V, XIII, and XVI. In seven further gatherings—I, VI, XI–XII, XIV–XV, and XVII—one or two leaves are missing, while the remaining ones are often very defective. Gathering I lacks fol. 7 (the right-hand leaf of the fourth sheet), and in VI the right-hand leaves of sheets 1 and 2 (fols. 59 and 60) are gone. In gathering VII sheets 1 to 4 are lacking (fols. 61/70, 62/69, 63/68, and 64/67) with only the center sheet (fols. 58/59) surviving, recognizable as such on the basis of its musical content as well as by its paper: fols. 58/59 being the only ones in this part of the manuscript bearing watermark 2, an anchor. In gathering VIII the first and third sheets are missing (fols. 71/80, 73/78) while fol. 60 is most probably the left-hand leaf of the second sheet, since it shares its paper and watermark with fol. 65. Gathering IX lacks the right-hand leaf of the first sheet as well as sheets 3 and 4 (fols. 83/88, 84/87). Fol. 70 may be the right-hand leaf of the second sheet, the left-hand leaf of which is fol. 67. The way in which gatherings X–XII, XIV–XV, and XVII–XX are incomplete can be seen in Table II above. It needs only to be added that the presence of the thread in gathering XI between fols. 104 and 105

[11] There are altogether six different kinds of paper in F230 and the following three different watermarks, two of them having variants: (1) Ladder in a circle surmounted by a six-pointed star very similar to No. 1550 (Fabriano 1497) in Aurelio Zonghi's *Watermarks* (Hilversum 1953). (2) An anchor in a circle surmounted by a star: This watermark occurs frequently in 15th- and 16th-century Italy, although neither Briquet in *Les Filigranes* (Paris 1907) nor Zonghi reproduces an identical one. Our watermark most closely resembles Zonghi's Nos. 1584 and 1588 (Fabriano 1456 and 1511). (3) A crowned eagle in a circle: Two variants of this watermark are found (see Briquet, *op. cit.*, Nos. 203 and 204, Lucca 1504 which, however, differ somewhat from F230). Besides these our manuscript also has a similar eagle but without the circle.

Although these watermarks do not correspond exactly with those found in either Briquet or Zonghi, they are types very common to 15th- and 16th-century Italy, as we pointed out.

TABLE II [12]

Gathering	A	B	Gathering	A	B
I	*1*	(1)	VI	*50*	51
	2	(2)		*51*	52
	3	(3)		*52*	53
	4	(4)		*53*	54
	5	5		*54*	55
	6	(6)		*55*	56
	>	[7]		*56*	57
	7	8		*57*	58
	8	(9)		>	[59]
	9	(10)			[60]
II	*10*	(11)	VII		[61]
	11	(12)			[62]
	12	13			[63]
	13	14			[64]
	14	15		*58*	(65)
	15	16		*59*	(66)
	16	17		>	[67]
	17	18			[68]
	18	19			[69]
	19	20			[70]
III	*20*	21	VIII		[71]
	21	22		*60*	(72)
	22	23		>	[73]
	23	24		*61*	(74)
	24	25		*62*	75
	25	26		*63*	76
	26	27		*64*	77
	27	28		>	[78]
	28	29		*65*	79
	29	30		>	[80]
IV	*30*	31	IX	*66*	81
	31	32		*67*	82
	32	33			[83]
	33	34			[84]
	34	35		*68*	85
	35	36		*69*	86
	36	37		>	[87]
	37	38			[88]
	38	39		*70?*	(89)
	39	40		>	[90]
V	*40*	41	X		[91]
	41	42			[92]
	42	43		*71*	(93)
	43	44		*72*	94
	44	45		*73*	95
	45	46		*74*	96
	46	47		*75*	97
	47	48		>	[98]
	48	49			[99]
	49	50		*76*	100

[12] Column A contains the numbers of the most recent penciled foliation in italics, while B gives the original numbers. Parentheses denote leaves which have no foliation but which can be assigned a place with some certainty on the basis of musical or external evidence. Small square brackets represent missing folios, while the large

Gathering	A	B		Gathering	A	B
XI	77	101		XVI	122	151
	78	102			123	152
	79	103			124	153
	80	104			125	154
	81	105			126	155
	>	[106]			127	156
	82	(107)			128	157
	83	108			129	158
	84	109			130	159
	85	110			131	160
XII	86	111		XVII	132	161
	>	[112]			133	162
	87	113			134	163
	88	114			135	164
	89	115			136	165
	90	116			137	166
	91	117			138	167
	92	118			139	168
	>	[119]			>	[169]
	93	120			140	170
XIII	94	121		XVIII	>	[171]
	95	122				[172]
	96	123			⌐120	[173]
	97	124			▷	[174]
	98	125				[175]
	99	126				[176]
	100	127				[177]
	101	128			└141	[178]
	102	129			>	[179]
	103	130				[180]
XIV	104	131		XIX	142	181
	>	[132]			>	[182]
	105	133			143	183
	106	134			144	184
	107	135			>	[185]
	108	136			145	186
	109	137			146	187
	110	138			147	188
	>	[139]			148	189
	111	140			>	[190]
XV	>	[141]		XX	>	[191]
	112	142				[192]
	113	143				[193]
	114	144			149	194
	115	145			>	[195]
	116	146				[196]
	117	147			150	197
	118	148			>	[198]
	119	149			151	199
	121	(150)			>	[200]

brackets connect folios belonging to the same sheets. Horizontal lines in the middle of each gathering represent the sewing, with broken lines standing for missing threads. The three threads added later are found, as we pointed out already, after fols. 76, 85, and 132.

can be explained by the loss of fol. 106 in consequence of which the loose left-hand leaf of the center sheet (fol. 105) was later glued to 107. A similar explanation applies to gathering XIX, in which the left-hand leaf of the center sheet is now missing. Gathering XVIII is lost entirely, although perhaps fols. 120 and 141, to which we cannot assign any other place (and which were probably once a sheet), are remnants of this gathering.

It is evident on the basis of this explanation that F230, as already mentioned, consisted exclusively of five-fold gatherings. Only in the case of the last part of the codex, in respect to gatherings XVIII–XX, will this assumption seem overly conjectural. The fact that such organization is typical of the frottola codices originating in Florence at this time should lend support to such a hypothesis, however. It is particularly noteworthy that the three sources most closely related to F230 on the basis of their concordances are all made up of five-fold gatherings.[13] It should further be pointed out that, while the 156 compositions listed by Becherini [14] correspond with my count, there are certain discrepancies between her catalogue and mine. For example, fols. 6ᵛ–8 contain not merely a single composition, as she and Ghisi [15] state, namely, *Se mi lassi in tanto felle* (the last word being an obsolete form of *fièle*, "gall" or "ire," not *fallo* as given by both the above). Instead, fol. 7 contains the incomplete beginning of another composition, as can be seen from a concordance in Paris, Bibliothèque Nationale, Ms. Rés. Vm⁷676, fols. 106ᵛ–107, where we find *Tropo e grave il mio dolore.* Fols. 7ᵛ–8 of F230 contain the complete second part of this frottola *P[er] te son legato e preso.* Ghisi [16] mentions this; Becherini does not. On the other hand, when Becherini lists fols. 71ᵛ–72 as two incomplete compositions, they turn out to complement one another and together make the frottola *Alla fe ch[e] la tuo fe.* The incomplete composition on fol. 93 is listed by both Becherini and Ghisi without a text incipit. Basing his conclusions on later stanzas, Ghisi assumed that the piece constitutes a "canto artigiano." [17] In actuality the fragment of text is the close of *Canto delle buttagre* of Pietro Cimatore. Its beginning reads, "Dragomanni siam, donne levantini." [18] A similar situation applies in the case of a piece

[13] The three manuscripts, all originating in Florence, are: Florence, Bibl. Naz. Cent. B. R. 337 (Palat. 1178), with 39 concordances; Florence, Istituto Musicale Cherubini 2440, with 13 concordances; and British Museum, Egerton 3051, with 8 concordances.

[14] *Op. cit.*

[15] *Poesie musicali italiane,* p. 43.

[16] *Ibid.,* p. 48; Ghisi, however, reads the title as *"A te son . . . "*

[17] *I Canti carnascialeschi,* p. 202.

[18] See A. F. Grazzini (called "Il Lasca") in the most important Florentine col-

found on fol. 111, of which F230 preserves only the cantus and bassus. While it, too, is listed without text incipit by both Becherini and Ghisi, it turns out to be the fourth stanza of *Canto di ninfe cacciatrice*.[19] Another piece listed by Becherini as an independent composition, fols. 83–84, *Perche ne dogni stato en tuttol mondo*, is the second part of the preceding frottola, *Udite quantol ciel ben si provede*. The reverse is true of *Labito donne leffigie el colore* on fols. 104ᵛ–105, believed by Becherini to be a complete composition. In reality the two textless voices (altus and bassus) on fol. 105 belong to another piece, the text of which, however, cannot be found. The bass part of this composition exists textlessly in Florence, Bibl. Naz. Centrale, B.R. 337 (Palat. 1178) on fol. 48ᵛ (59ᵛ). The two missing voices for *Donne sel cantar nostro ascolterete* on fol. 119 can be found on fol. 121, which therefore makes the piece complete. The reader will see that despite these disagreements the total number of compositions in the remains of the codex accidentally corresponds to the number given by Becherini.

Closer musical examination of the volume reveals that 40 of the compositions found in its pages are incomplete for lack of one or two voices. This circumstance is caused by the fact that F230, in which each composition usually takes up two sides, has lost at least 20 folios. Altogether, however, I calculate that 49 folios are missing. This means that besides the incomplete compositions a total of up to 29 pieces may be lost in their entirety. Among these a considerable number are likely to have belonged to the especially interesting forms of the *carri* and *canti carnascialeschi*, since these categories seem to have been concentrated in the back of the volume, from fol. 82ᵛ to the end. In fact, these species occupy this part of the codex exclusively, the same part to which about half the missing sheets belong.

Unfortunately, F230 is not likely to share the rare good fortune of manuscripts such as the glorious chansonnier Seville, Colombina 5-I-43, two parts of which were reunited with the main part from separate places across the Pyrenees. Whether fragments of F230 exist elsewhere is not known, but it is not likely. While this reconstruction is thus a Platonic one, it is to be hoped that, in accordance with our heading, it is also a diplomatic one—in both senses of the word, I may add!

lection of texts, *Tutti i trionfi, carri, mascherate e canti carnascialeschi* (Florence 1559, 2nd ed. Lucca c. 1750), p. 166.
[19] *Ibid.*, p. 200.

A MUSICAL OFFERING
TO HERCULES II,
DUKE OF FERRARA

by ALVIN JOHNSON

THE PURPOSE for which Mass compositions were ordained was not always circumscribed by their liturgical function. Josquin wrote the Mass, *Hercules Dux Ferrariae*, as much to the honor of Hercules I, Duke of Ferrara, as to the Supreme Being. Josquin's Mass not only introduced a device, the *soggetto cavato*, as a means of inventing a cantus firmus, but the *Hercules Mass* inaugurated in Ferrara a series of Masses dedicated to the ruling duke of the house of Este. Following in the path laid out by Josquin are the Hercules Masses by Lupus, Jachet da Mantua, and Cipriano de Rore (two), all presented to Hercules II, the grandson of Hercules I, Josquin's patron. To this list should be added another composition written in honor of Hercules II which has heretofore remained unnoticed and is the subject of this essay.

Hercules II was born in 1508, the eldest son of Alfonso I and Lucrezia Borgia. Educated and trained for the position he was to inherit upon his father's death, he grew up to be a typical Renaissance prince. He was an effective orator, an accomplished writer of Latin verse, skilled in the arts of diplomacy and war, and naturally gifted for music. In 1528 Hercules traveled with a large and princely retinue to Paris, where his marriage to Princess Renée of France, daughter of Louis XII, was consummated. The political alliance with France, symbolized by this marriage, was a part of the skilful diplomacy Hercules's father, Alfonso, was forced to carry on throughout his reign in order to maintain the independence of his small state, caught as it was in the cross-currents of conflicting interests on the part of the great powers—France, Venice, the Papacy, and the Empire. In 1534, when Pope Clement VII died and was succeeded by Paul III, Alfonso could look forward to a period of peace and tranquillity for his duchy and for himself. But he did not live to enjoy the bright future he foresaw. After three days of illness Alfonso died on the last day of October 1534.

On 1 November Hercules succeeded his father and became the fourth duke of Ferrara. In honor of his elevation to the head of the house of Este he was presented with a book of music which today survives in the Estense Library at Modena. It is a large, paper choirbook, measuring 718 by 465 millimeters. The original leather cover is in poor condition now, but the paper has for the most part been well preserved; on only a few pages has the corrosive effect of the ink made the music difficult to read. The folios were not numbered by the scribe, and they remain unnumbered at the present time. There are about 200 folios in the volume, and of these only 12 are blank. The manuscript is without interest to the art historian; illuminated initials and decorative designs found in parchment manuscripts are absent from this plain but neat choirbook.[1]

The manuscript, whose present call number is α N.1.2., was copied by Joannes Michael of France, singer in the ducal chapel. Inside the front cover the copyist has inscribed the following dedicatory poem and on the verso of the first folio a Latin inscription from which we learn that the manuscript was copied in the first year of the reign of Hercules II and presented as a token of the singer's loyalty and devotion to the new duke:

Hercules secundus dux ferrarie iiii

> Le premier an et second de ce nom
> De ta duche tresillustre seigneur
> Ce livre ycy a ton veu et renom
> Je tay escript et note de bon cueur
> Et sil nest tel que merite ung greigneur
> De si hault prix pardonne a lingnorance
> Plus hault ne peult attaindre ma science
> Accepte donc mon labeur et ma paine
> Et le voloir qui a mis sa puissance
> A t[e servir] dune amour souveraine

Joannes michael de francia Cantor Ill*m* ducis ferrarie
pro Copia

fol. 1 verso:

Divo Herculi Atestino ii Duci iiii Cui vix edito quod maximum habuit: corpus animusque dicavit Jo. Michael gratiss: operam hanc suam servitii monumentum primo regni an: offert.

Joannes Michael was not a newcomer to Ferrara, nor was this manuscript the first example of his skill as a copyist. He was, however, principally employed as a singer at Ferrara, and as a singer received wages

---

[1] The manuscript has been described and its contents listed in *Bollettino dell' Associazione dei Musicologi Italiani*, Series VII: *Catalogo delle Opere Musicali Città di Modena R. Biblioteca Estense*, p. 18 and A. Smijers, ed., *Werken van Josquin des Prez, Deel III: Missen* (Amsterdam 1952), p. xliv.

commensurate with those of the highest paid musicians at the court.[2] He is specifically named among the singers who entertained the court during a banquet at the Belfiore in Ferrara on the 20th of May 1529.[3] From 1533 until his name disappears from the account books in 1556, the wages he received mark him as one of the most valuable musicians in the choir.

The only composition in the manuscript that relates directly to Hercules II and to the occasion that prompted the copyist to make his presentation is the work that appears at the beginning of the volume: *Missa Omnes sancti et sancte Dei.* The composer of this work, Maistre Jan, was at the time the maestro di cappella in Ferrara. Maistre Jan entered the service of the court in February 1522 along with Adrian Willaert, but although Willaert soon moved on, Maistre Jan remained in Ferrara until 1541.[4] In the latter year Jan published a book of madrigals in which he is named "maestro di Capella," [5] but his name is missing from the court records in 1542. Yet, in the following year a collection of motets bears his name on the title page. In this publication his full name and title are given: *Symphonia quatuor modulata vocibus excellentissimi musici Joannis Galli alias chori Ferrariae magistri quae vulgo (Motecta Metre Jehan) nominantur, nuper in lucem edita.*[6] The identity of the composer beyond the period of his stay in Ferrara has been dealt with by Charles Van den Borren in two entries in MGG under the names Maître Jean (VI, 1821–23) and Jean Lecocq (VIII, 448–50).

Maistre Jan, as maestro di cappella, was not negligent in duly noting the festive occasion of Hercules's promotion to the seat of power in Ferrara. The Mass that opens our manuscript celebrates the occasion and the new duke. It would be rash to claim that this composition was sung at the service Hercules attended on the day he succeeded his father to the throne. That event occurred on the day following Alfonso's death and the composer could hardly have anticipated the former duke's death, since it came suddenly after a very short illness. Furthermore, as will be demonstrated, the Mass is directly associated with the Feast of All Saints, the day of Hercules's coronation. Thus, the Mass is a memorial to an event that had already taken place, not a composition to be sung on the day of celebration.

Maistre Jan's Mass, entitled *Omnes sancti et sancte Dei* in the table of

---

[2] Walter Weyler, *Documenten betreffende de muziekkapel aan het hof van Ferrara,* in: *Vlaamsch Jaarbock voor Muziekgeschiedenis,* I (1939), 81–116 *passim.*
[3] MGG, IV, 60.
[4] Weyler, *op. cit.*
[5] RISM 1541[15].
[6] RISM 1543[4].

contents, might be described as another *Hercules Mass*. It follows in the tradition begun by Josquin des Prez's *Missa Hercules Dux Ferrariae*. Josquin's composition was constructed upon a subject drawn directly from the title—in Zarlino's words, a "soggetto cavato dalle vocali" in which the vowels in the title are equated with the solmization syllables to form a musical subject. Thus, the words "Hercules Dux Ferrariae" produce a melody: *re ut re ut re fa mi re*. The invention of a musical subject by this means is ingenious and interesting, but were it not for the fact that the subject is sung with the text from which it is drawn, it would be of little importance to the end product—the Mass as a completed work of art. As a result, however, we now hear a Mass with a text in one voice which acclaims a secular prince, while the remaining voices sing the liturgical text of the Ordinary of the Mass. The importance of Josquin's invention lies not in the method of inventing the subject, but rather in the employment of the Mass as an instrument of homage to a secular prince rather than the glorification of God.

Maistre Jan follows the basic plan of Josquin's Mass, in that one voice, the first tenor, sings a subject bearing the words that direct our attention to the new duke. The text sung by the tenor is a paraphrase of an acclamation from the Litany of the Saints. In its liturgical form the text is: "Omnes Sancti et sanctae Dei intercedite pro nobis." The melody to which this text is sung is also drawn from the Litany. It is an embellishment and extension of the prolix version of the melodic formula of the litany.[7] Since Hercules's coronation took place on All Saints' Day, the choice of this text and melody as the point of departure for Maistre Jan's subject is most appropriate. The original melody of the Litany is clearly in the Dorian mode, more specifically, Dorian with the B♭ consistently added. Maistre Jan, during the course of the Mass, sometimes retains the B♭, sometimes demands B♮. Because of its length and phrasing, the melody lends itself to a natural division into two parts. In some sections of the Mass the subject is stated as a single unit, in others it is divided. The determining factor in each case is the musical material in which the subject is embedded. The tenor melody, howsoever it appears, functions as a structural foundation for the entire Mass. It is the one repetitive element that binds the Mass together.

In Josquin's *Hercules Mass* the subject in the tenor remains an independent voice; that is to say, the remaining voices do not draw upon the tenor as a fund of melodic ideas—rather they are freely invented voice parts which imitate each other but remain aloof from the tenor subject. Certainly this is a matter of design and intention on the part of the com-

[7] MGG, VIII, 996.

poser, for by keeping the tenor, which proclaims the name of the duke, independent and separate from the other voices, Josquin succeeds in making the tenor acclamation stand out in bold relief.

Maistre Jan maintains the same separation of melodic material between the tenor and the voices surrounding it. But the surrounding voices in Maistre Jan's Mass are not, as in Josquin's Mass, the free invention of the composer. Without identifying the source of his melodic material, it is abundantly clear that Maistre Jan has turned to the chant as the source of his melodic ideas. The chant Maistre Jan uses is identified in the modern Gradual as Gregorian Mass IV—*in Festis Duplicibus Primus*. Again the choice of this Gregorian Mass is completely appropriate to the day of Hercules's coronation, 1 November, the Feast of All Saints, which is ranked in the liturgy as a Double Feast of the first class.

The problem of combining the melodic substance of the Gregorian Mass with the melody of the tenor produces two basic problems for the composer. First is the problem of counterpoint, the fitting of the two melodic ideas together; and second, the problem of modal agreement. The first problem is quite simply solved by avoiding it. That is to say, Maistre Jan usually develops the material of the Gregorian Mass while the tenor is silent, and then relaxes or gives up completely his dependence upon the chant when the tenor enters with its subject. Since the tenor is always the last voice to enter in each movement, and usually at a considerable distance after the other voices, the composer has ample opportunity to develop in polyphonic imitation the melodic material of the Gregorian Mass. Furthermore, there are sections of the composition in which the choir is reduced from five to four, three, or even two voices; and in each of these instances the tenor drops out.

A more difficult problem arises from the fact that the Gregorian Mass is not uniform in mode, while the tenor subject remains Dorian throughout. The Kyrie is in the Dorian mode, the Gloria and Credo in the Hypophrygian, the Sanctus in the Hypomixolydian, and the Agnus Dei in the Hypolydian mode. Yet throughout the Mass, whenever the tenor enters with its subject, the Dorian mode will be present. Now of course it is important to recognize that modality in its very essence is compromised in a polyphonic composition. But to say that it is compromised is not to suggest that it is abandoned. The composer, after all, deliberately chose certain material cast in a form and mode he was bound to respect to some extent.

The aspect of the Gregorian chant that Maistre Jan is careful to respect in his polyphonic setting is invariably the finalis. And since the tenor subject is always in use at the end of a movement, it is evident

that its finalis must either coincide with the finalis of the chant or come
to rest on the fifth or third of the final chord. This fact suggests the basic
approach to the problem, but there are other special problems that arise
in individual cases. For example, the Dorian mode of the chant in the
Kyrie would seem to fit well with the Dorian of the tenor subject. Yet
the problem of modal agreement is as acute here as elsewhere in the Mass,
for the Dorian of the Mass is pure Dorian without the B♭, while the mode
of the tenor subject demands B♭. At any rate, this seems to be the problem; and when we observe that Maistre Jan has transposed the tenor
subject up a fifth, thereby removing the flat, we seem to be confirmed
in our estimate of the problem. But apparently the transposition of the
tenor was not for that reason. Later on in the Mass, the composer has
altered his tenor subject by removing the flat. If he were willing to make
that alteration later, why not in the Kyrie? The correct reason for the
transposition of the tenor lies in the finalis of the concluding Kyrie,
which ends, not on D, as do the first Kyrie and the Christe, but on A,
the dominant. Obviously, in the final chord of the second Kyrie, the
tenor subject must come to rest on A, C, or E, but certainly not on D,
as it would if it were sung in its untransposed position. On the other
hand, the A finalis of the tenor is easily accommodated as the fifth of the
D chord at the end of the first Kyrie. In these two Kyrie movements
(the tenor is silent in the Christe) the finalis A of the transposed tenor is
the fifth of the cadential chord on D of the first Kyrie and coincides with
the tonic of the final chord on A of the second Kyrie. Thus it is
really the finalis of the chant that has governed the composer in the
placement of the tenor subject.

I won't insist on an exposition of the solution to this problem of modal
agreement in each of the movements of the Mass. The procedure is much
the same in all the movements except the Agnus Dei, which poses a special problem. The Gregorian Mass of the Agnus Dei is in the Hypolydian
mode, with its finalis on F. In this chant all the B's are flatted, a feature
characteristic of many chants in the sixth mode. In previous movements
of the Mass the composer found it possible to limit himself to placing
the Dorian tenor subject in three positions: (1) resting on D in its
original untransposed position; (2) on G transposed up a fourth; and
(3) on A transposed up a fifth. Transposition to any other position
would require the addition of an impossible number of flats or sharps in
order to maintain the essential Dorian character of the subject. That is
certainly the situation that faced the composer in the Agnus Dei, where
he was confronted with the necessity of embedding the Dorian tenor in
a polyphonic web constructed out of melodic material in the Hypo-

lydian mode. Of course, the transposition to A would be acceptable, since the tenor would then come to rest on the third of the final chord of F. But Maistre Jan desired to have the tenor sung in canon during the final Agnus Dei; therefore, the transposition of the tenor to A was not an acceptable solution unless the canon was at the octave or unison. What he has chosen to do instead is to transpose the material of the Agnus Dei chant from F to G. Since the Hypolydian of the chant demanded B♭ instead of B♮ the transposition to G necessitated the addition of only one sharp. But since that sharp is the leading tone and supplied at sight by the singers, he omits it from his signature. Now, with the Hypolydian mode transposed to G, the tenor melody may take its original untransposed position on D or the transposed position on G. Either one will satisfactorily fit the harmony of the transposed Hypolydian. And furthermore, the canon in the final Agnus Dei takes a normal form with the subject sung on D and G, a canon at the fourth.

The occasional character of Maistre Jan's Mass as a memorial of the coronation of Hercules II is proved by the direct relationship of the musical material of the work to the Feast of All Saints. Its position at the very beginning of the manuscript further supports our argument. Yet, the main interest in the composition as a work of art must reside in the practical solution the composer has given to the problem of conflicting modality.

THE SECULAR WORKS OF
JOHANNES MARTINI

by THEODORE KARP

JOHANNES MARTINI: colleague of Josquin, Compère, and Agricola; friend of Hofhaimer; teacher of Isabella d'Este. Thus might one describe one of the lesser-known musicians of the late 15th century. Martini's name is of course familiar to those who have more than a passing knowledge of this period. But only a tiny proportion of his music has yet been published. The two best treatments of his music—the pertinent section of Gustave Reese's *Music in the Renaissance* [1] and Ludwig Finscher's article on Martini in *Die Musik in Geschichte und Gegenwart* [2]—each make use of unpublished transcriptions. Because the composer's surviving output is considerable, and because he had a high reputation within his circle, it is desirable that we reach a critical evaluation of Martini's stature, based on a knowledge of his complete output. This brief survey of Martini's secular works is offered as a first step toward this goal.

Unusually eloquent evidence of Martini's prestige is furnished by Florence, Bibl. naz. cen. MS XIX.59 (Banco Rari 229), which opens with a piece by Martini and alternates works by Martini and Isaac until fol. 19ᵛ. The first opening to contain music is a blaze of color, staves and notes being written in gold against a blue-green background on the verso,[3] and in gold against a red background on the recto. Each page is adorned by a miniature, frieze, and elegant floral borders, the miniature on the left representing Tubal-cain, that on the right, Martini.[4] It is quite possible that Gherardo and Giovanni di Monte, who prepared these magnificent pages, were acquainted with our composer and have presented a good likeness. The fact that Gherardo died in 1497 [5] furnishes a

---

[1] Gustave Reese, *Music in the Renaissance* (New York 1954), pp. 220–23.
[2] Ludwig Finscher, *Martini*, in: MGG, VIII (1960), 1724–26.
[3] A color reproduction of this page is to be found in Mario Salmi, *Italian Miniatures*, 2nd ed. transl. Elisabeth Borgese-Mann (New York 1956), Pl. XLVI.
[4] Black-and-white reproductions of the miniature are given by both Reese (Pl. III) and Finscher.
[5] For further information concerning the two artists and their work, see Salmi, *Italian Miniatures*, p. 51f.

useful *terminus ad quem* for the works contained in the MS. Twenty works by Martini, including one *opus dubium*,[6] are to be found in Banco Rari 229.

The second of the two major sources for Martini's secular works is the Rome, Casanatense MS 2856, which ascribes 23 pieces [7] to Martini, and contains also the opus dubium referred to above. Martini is represented in the Verona, Bibl. Cap. MS 757 by at least six works.[8] This is a large number for a source of modest size; apparently only Agricola is better represented. The Segovia MS and *Canti C* may be mentioned here because they each contain three works by Martini not to be found in either of the two main sources.

Altogether, 37 pieces are attributed to Martini without known conflict. Those with text incipits are as follows: *Biaulx parle tousjours, De la bonne chiere, Des biens d'amours, Fault il que heur soye, Fortuna desperata, Fortuna d'un gran tempo, Fuge la morie, Groen vint, Helas coment, Il est tel, Il est tousjours*, two versions of *J'ay pris amours, J'espoir mieulx, La Fleur de biaulté, La Martinella, La Martinelle pittzulo, Le Pouverté, Nenciozza mia, Non per la, Non seul uno, O di prudenza fonte* (known also as *Per faire tousjours*), *Que je fasoye, Sans siens du mal, Se mai il cielo* (known also as *Je remerchi Dieu*), *Tant que Dieu vosdra, Tousjours bien, Tousjours me souviendra, Tout joyeulx*, and *Vive, vive*. A textless *Fuga ad quatuor* is preserved in Casanatense 2856. Six textless pieces not identical with any of the above are attributed to Martini in Banco Rari 229. (Another six textless pieces attributed to Martini in this source have been identified by means of concordances.[9])

The authorship of two works—*Cayphas* and *Malheur me bat*—is problematical. The former apparently survives only in the Segovia MS. The page on which it is located gives two names: Compère and Martini.

[6] This work is *Malheur me bat*.

[7] Of these, ten are concordant with works in Banco Rari 229.

[8] As is well known, most works in this codex are given without either attribution or text incipit. *Le Pouverté* (fols. 9ᵛ–10ʳ), by Martini, is one of the two works that are fully identified in the MS. Other pieces by our composer included in Verona 757 are *Tant que Dieu vosdra* (fols. 10ᵛ–11ʳ), *Se mai il cielo* (= *Je remerchi Dieu;* fols. 11ᵛ–12ʳ), *La Martinella* (fols. 17ᵛ–18ʳ), and *O di prudenza fonte* (= *Per faire tousjours;* fols. 27ᵛ–28ʳ). The anonymous, textless piece on fols. 25ᵛ–26ʳ is the same as the textless piece attributed to Martini on fols. 143ᵛ–44ʳ of Banco Rari 229. This piece is given in *Le Frottole nell' edizione principe di Ottaviano Petrucci*, ed. Gaetano Cesari, Raffaello Monterosso, and Benvenuto Disertori, *Instituta et Monumenta*, I (Cremona 1954), XLIIf; for bibliographical information concerning other works by Martini in modern publications, see either *Music in the Renaissance* or the Finscher article (fns. 1–2 above).

[9] Cf. Albert Smijers, *Vijftiende en zestiende eeuwsche muziekhandschriften in Italië met werken van Nederlandsche componisten*, in: *Tijdschrift der Vereeniging van Nederlandsche Muziekgeschiedenis*, XIV (1935), 165–81.

Certain stylistic traits, in particular the use of sequences, indicate that the work is more likely to be by Martini than by Compère, but it is safest to treat the piece as an opus dubium. *Malheur me bat* is attributed to Martini in Banco Rari 229 and Cappella Giulia XIII.27, to Malcort in Casanatense 2856, and to Ockeghem in the *Odhecaton* and in St. Gall, Stiftsbibl. MS 461. Pietro Aron refers to the work as by Ockeghem.[10] The likelihood that Malcort composed *Malheur me bat* seems quite small. When Johannes Wolf and Otto Gombosi [11] judged the work to be by Ockeghem, the attribution to Martini in Banco Rari 229 was apparently unknown. It is possible to give reasonable and yet opposite interpretations of the evidence of this MS as well as of that of the *Odhecaton*.[12] Although external evidence may slightly favor Ockeghem's claim to authorship, it is not conclusive. No stylistic traits inconsistent with present knowledge of Ockeghem's style and of Martini's style are discoverable. Lacking a significant balance favoring either of these composers, I would suggest that *Malheur me bat* be treated as an opus dubium, to be studied in conjunction with works by both composers.

The high proportion of space devoted to Martini in certain MSS is a fair index of the esteem he enjoyed. Yet, among his 37 genuine works, only two—*La Martinella* and *Des biens d'amours*—survive in more than three MSS; the former is found in ten sources, the latter in at least eight. One may therefore conclude that Martini's fame was largely of local nature.

Mention of *La Martinella* calls for a brief digression because six compositions by that title are presently known, two by Martini, two by Isaac, and two anonymous.[13] Five of the six are to be found in Banco Rari

[10] In the *Trattato della natura e cognizione di tutti gli toni di canto figurato* (1525); a part published in translation in Oliver Strunk, ed. *Source Readings in Music History* (New York 1950): see p. 214.

[11] Cf. Wolf, *Jakob Obrecht, Werken: Missen* (Amsterdam and Leipzig, n.d.), I, 189; Gombosi, *Jacob Obrecht, eine stilkritische Studie, Sammlung musikwissenschaftlicher Einzeldarstellungen*, IV (Leipzig 1925), 85.

[12] If one seeks to confirm Martini's claim to the piece, one may point out that Petrucci lacked direct access to Ockeghem's works since the latter was not employed in Italy, and that, by contrast, the compiler of Banco Rari 229 was particularly familiar with Martini's work and perhaps with the composer himself. If one seeks to confirm Ockeghem's claim to the piece, one may stress the fact that Petrucci's attributions are usually accurate and disclaim the evidence of Banco Rari 229 on the ground that the compiler was simply displaying favoritism toward Martini.

[13] The source of the title, *La Martinella*, remains something of a problem. It is conceivable that some reference to Martini himself was intended. A more likely interpretation was suggested by Friedrich Ludwig (*Joh. Wolf's Ausgabe der Weltlichen Werke H. Isaac's*, in: *Sammelbände der Internationalen Musikgesellschaft*, X [1908–9], 322), who reminded music historians that *La Martinella* was the name of the Florentine alarm bell of Martini's day. This bell, which hung in the arch of the Porta Santa Maria (near the Ponte Vecchio), was sounded regularly when it was necessary to recruit men for the Florentine army and was taken down and

229. The composition referred to above is located on fols. 12^v–13^r. The other *Martinella* by our composer is given as anonymous on fols. 219^v–220^r; its authorship is established by the Casanatense MS, where it is labeled, *La Martinelle pittzulo*. This work, and the anonymous setting in Banco Rari 229, fols. 44^v–45^r, apparently have nothing in common either with the first *Martinella* or with each other. In view of the fact that the word "pittzulo" is associated with only one composition, it would be best to retain this association to distinguish between the two Martini settings. The Isaac setting of *La Martinella* in the Segovia MS borrows the two upper voices of Martini's famous work; Isaac furnishes a new bass concerned chiefly with the elaboration of an ostinato-like motive.[14] The anonymous *Martinella* in Banco Rari 229, fols. 141^v–142^r (also in Cappella Giulia XIII.27, fols. 75^v–76^r) may be described as a free paraphrase of selected material from Martini's upper voices. (The possibility of divergent usage of pre-existent material cannot be entirely ruled out.) The freedom of this paraphrase permits the hypothesis that the Isaac setting of *Martinella* in Banco Rari 229, 207^v–208^r, also took the Martini work as a point of departure. The opening motives of the two works are similar, as are certain structural highlights, but close resemblance in centrally located motivic material is lacking. In his *Missa La Martinella*, Martini employs his own chanson tenor as a cantus firmus.

Any investigation of Martini's secular works must contend with two obstacles, a vagueness of chronology, and a lack of texts for the majority of pieces. Neither Martini's birth-date nor death-date is known. Available documents pertaining to our composer cover only the period, 1474–92. The roster of the Sforza chapel in 1474 places Martini's name between those of Compère and Josquin, and it has been customary to treat our composer as one of the Josquin generation. He is dealt with in such fashion by Reese. Finscher, on the other hand, strongly suggests that Martini be considered among the composers of Ockeghem's generation.

mounted on the carriage on which the Florentine banners were mounted, so that it might lead the way for the army's festive exit from the city. The examination of the various pieces for programmatic clues that might help verify the soundness of this interpretation has unfortunately produced only negative results.

[14] One may conclude that Martini's composition served as Isaac's model, rather than vice-versa, for two reasons. Isaac's work survives only in the Segovia MS, and it is unlikely that a composer would borrow two voice-parts from a little known work. If he were to do so, his audience would be unaware of the nature of his contribution. More important, the style of Isaac's bass would indicate that this piece belongs to a rather sizable group, wherein each composer develops a special technical device within the framework provided by the pre-existent material. Frequently, the technical device is canon, as in Josquin's setting of *De tous bien plaine* and Martini's setting of *J'ay pris amours* in Banco Rari 229.

He points out that an anonymous treatise of 1480 names Martini together with Dufay, Dunstable, Ockeghem, Binchois, and Faugues, and that Martini's name does not appear in documents after 1492. Finscher also suggests that Martini may have died before the turn of the century.

If one examines Martini's secular music to find stylistic affinities that will help fix a chronological framework, conflicting evidence will be unearthed. Several features might be cited in support of Finscher's hypothesis:

1. Twenty-nine works (including the two opera dubia) are written for three voices, only ten for four.

2. Pervading imitation does not obtain. On the whole, imitation is employed more sparingly than one might expect for a composer of the Josquin generation.

3. The normal combined range of the various voices is comparatively restricted. The middle and lowest voices are customarily intertwined, while the middle voice frequently crosses above the highest. Occasionally (e.g., in *O di prudenza fonte* and in *Tout joyeulx*) the highest voice may cross below both lower parts.

4. Octave-leap cadences are fairly frequent, and occasional examples of under-third cadences may be found.

On the surface, this assemblage of evidence seems quite persuasive. Nevertheless, Finscher's hypothesis is contradicted by one particularly strong piece of evidence: Among all 39 secular works, there is not a single piece written in *tempus perfectum!* Moreover, the use of *tempus perfectum* in Martini's Masses is usually quite restricted.[15] The normal mensuration sign employed by Martini is that of *tempus imperfectum diminutum*. When he wishes to write in triple meter, he uses the symbol for *proportio tripla. Fortuna d'un gran tempo, Que je fasoye*, and *Sans siens du mal* are written entirely in that mensuration, while several works employ it for brief passages in the middle or at the end. To be sure, *tempus perfectum* was being used less and less by composers of the Ockeghem generation, but its complete absence from Martini's secular works is striking. Because the archaic traits enumerated above are to be found in various compositions by composers known to belong to the Josquin generation, I am inclined at present to place reliance on the rhythmic evidence and to continue to treat Martini as a conservative

---

[15] Among the Masses I have examined, only the *Missa Io ne tengo* uses *tempus perfectum* with any consistency. This mensuration does not appear at all in the *Missa Orsus, orsus,* the *Missa Dio te salvi,* or the *Missa Ma bouche rit.* It appears in the second Kyrie of the *Missa La Martinella* and in the first section of the Sanctus, as well as in the first (= third) Agnus of the *Missa Dominicalis.*

composer of the Josquin generation. Tentative dates of c. 1445–c. 1495 would seem to be in keeping with such evidence as is presently known. Most of Martini's works are preserved with text incipits only. Reproductions of sources available to me yield only three texts, those of *Fortuna d'un gran tempo*, *J'ay pris amours*, and *Nenciozza mia*. A preliminary search for other texts among literary sources—the *Jardin de plaisance*,[16] the MS of the Cardinal de Rohan,[17] the Lachèvre bibliography,[18] etc.—has proven nearly fruitless. It is possible that Martini's *Des biens d'amours* is based on Jean d'Auton's rondeau, *Des biens d'amours quiconcques les depart*. No other leads have come to light. Obviously very little can be said concerning Martini's treatment of text. One may perhaps add slightly to Edward Lowinsky's findings concerning the symbolism associated with the figure, Fortune.[19] Lowinsky demonstrates various ways in which the relentless motion of Fortune's wheel was represented by musical means. In examining Martini's *Fortuna d'un gran tempo*, one's attention is drawn to the greater than usual number of skips and the unusual undulations of pitch in the lowest voice. Is it not possible that Martini was seeking to depict in terms of pitch the rising and falling stations on Fortune's wheel?

Assuming that the majority of Martini's secular works were composed to texts, one may inquire whether the musical structures shed any light on the possible structures of the texts. The majority of Martini's works are divisible into two nearly equal sections, the first being slightly the longer of the two. The point of division is generally marked in the MSS by a *corona* or a *signum congruentiae*. Among the *formes fixes*, the ballade and the virelai may undoubtedly be excluded from consideration. The proportions between the two parts of the individual musical works are not those one would expect from the construction of a virelai text. Sometimes, too, the cadence ending the first part—the final cadence of a virelai structure—is not suitable as a final cadence. Usually the proportions between the two parts are consistent with the proportions of a *rondeau cinquain*, and, in view of the conservative features of Martini's style pointed out previously, it is quite likely that many of our assumed texts were cast in such a form. One may also suggest that some texts

[16] *Le Jardin de plaisance et fleur de rethoricque* (Paris c. 1501); issued in facsimile by the *Société des anciens textes français* (Paris 1910), *Introduction et notes* by Eugénie Droz and Arthur Piaget (Paris 1925).
[17] *Die Liederhandschrift des Cardinals de Rohan*, ed. Martin Löpelmann, *Gesellschaft für Romanische Literatur*, XLIV (Göttingen 1923).
[18] Frédéric Lachèvre, *Bibliographie des recueils collectifs de poésies du XVIe siècle* (Paris 1922).
[19] *The Goddess Fortuna in Music*, in: MQ, XXIX (1943), 45–77.

were written in the freer style that began to come to the fore in the late
15th century.

Up to this point we have touched upon several features of Martini's
style without, however, reaching the most vital ones. What manner of
composer are we dealing with? That Martini was no melodist is obvious
after browsing through a handful of his pieces. His interests and abilities
lay elsewhere. The phrases that one would consider as characteristic are
short, the opening motive proceeding quickly to one of several standard
cadences. Usually longer stretches uninterrupted by rests are made up
of two or more fragments, a fragment sometimes consisting of nothing
more than a cadential formula. The forward impulse of the music is
preserved—despite the high proportion of cadences—by rhythmic and
harmonic means.

Ex. 1   The phrase construction of *Vive, vive;* breves 29–37

The study of these pieces affords valuable insights into the working
methods of competent composers lacking genius. The music seems to be
constructed in the manner of a kaleidoscope; that is, a number of standard
bits continually appear in new constellations, the composer being judged

in terms of the imaginativeness of his presentation, rather than in terms
of startling originality. Variations of a few basic cadences reappear frequently in Martini's works and even more florid passages may be found
more than once.

Ex. 2   Variants of a standard closing formula

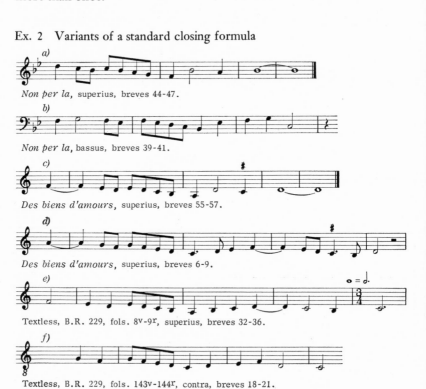

Non per la, superius, breves 44-47.

Non per la, bassus, breves 39-41.

Des biens d'amours, superius, breves 55-57.

Des biens d'amours, superius, breves 6-9.

Textless, B.R. 229, fols. 8ᵛ-9ʳ, superius, breves 32-36.

Textless, B.R. 229, fols. 143ᵛ-144ʳ, contra, breves 18-21.

Fragments such as the above were the composer's stock in trade, to be
manipulated according to the demands of the occasion.

   And Martini does manipulate his material with considerable dex-
terity, displaying a fine sense of structure. This concern for musical
architecture—for proportion and climax within both small and large
forms—makes itself felt in numerous ways. Although the general trend
during the late 15th century was toward the delineation of form by
means of a clearly articulated series of points of imitation, imitation is
only one of the structural devices employed by Martini. Frequently
sequences are of at least equal, if not greater, structural importance. (The
following descriptions of Martini's music will be stated in terms of
breves rather than of measures.) Turning to *Fuge la morie,* we find a

work based on a set of seven sequential figures stated in the lowest voice. The piece opens with a point of imitation beginning in the superius, followed by the tenor and contra, each voice an octave lower than the preceding one, and each following the other at the distance of 2½ breves. The motive on which the imitation is based is then treated sequentially in the lowest voice, being repeated at the upper fifth and then at the upper octave. This motive, as well as the succeeding one, which follows after a semibreve rest, is three breves long. There then follows a systematic reduction in the length of the remaining sequential figures, the third and fourth being 2½ breves long, the fifth being two breves long, and the sixth and seventh being only one breve long. The second, third, fourth, and fifth motives are each presented twice, the first time on the tonic, the second on the dominant. The last two motives are presented five times each, the sixth sequence descending in scalewise fashion, the seventh reversing this direction, using a scalewise progression interrupted once by a skip of a third. In the second part of the piece, which contains the last three motives, there is a steady increase in pace through the use of smaller time-values. Having reached a rhythmic peak with the 50th breve, Martini proceeds with his final cadence, which is independent of previous material. Imitation occurs between the upper two voices at the end of the 10th breve, and at the opening of the second part (breve 32).[20] A similar over-all plan based on sequences is to be found also in *Groen vint*. *Le Pouverté* makes extensive use of sequence without, however, submitting to an over-all plan of equal consistency. In general, in Martini's secular works, sequences are used more often to shape the lowest voice than any other, and they are frequently used near the end of a work as a means of achieving climax.

At this point we shall digress briefly to consider a few of the larger structural features of Martini's *Missa La Martinella*. Here a sense of climax is achieved through the handling of the cantus firmus, and, at the end, through a distinctive use of imitation. Unification is achieved by the imitative presentation of material from the chanson opening at the openings of each of the five sections of the Ordinary. As indicated on the following table, the first four of these are each based on different segments of the chanson tenor, while the Agnus serves as a final summary, presenting in two sections the first 80 of the 90 breves of the chanson tenor.

[20] A tenor imitation of the second sequential motive in the bass is suggested in the middle of the 18th breve, the illusion being produced by paralleling the sequence itself at the distance of a third. There is an echo of this motive in the superius at the end of the 22nd breve.

MASS SECTION	CHANSON COUNTERPART	NUMBER OF STATEMENTS
Kyrie I	3–12	1
Christe	Free [21]	
Kyrie II	13–17	2
Et in terra	18–41	1
Qui tollis	18–27	2
Cum sancto spiritu	29–39	1
Patrem omnipotentem	44–66	1
Et incarnatus est	44–66	2
Crucifixus	67–79	4
Sanctus	82–90	2
Pleni	Free	
Osanna	82–90	2
Benedictus	Free	
Osanna	As above	
Agnus I	1–41	1
Agnus II	Free	
Agnus III	44–80	1

The first presentation of each cantus firmus segment is in augmentation, while later repetitions of these segments are more rhythmically compact. Thus Martini is able to achieve both unity and a sense of climax within the individual sections. The Agnus contrasts with earlier movements in that the cantus is stated entirely in normal values, creating the sensation of a heightened pace. Among the significant points of imitation in the first four movements of the Mass, the more characteristic ones are at the distance of two breves or more. When, towards the end of Agnus III, Martini reaches a half-cadence, cancels out several voices, and then presents a point of imitation involving *all* voices with only a breve's distance between successive entries, he creates the effect of a striking stretto.

In his secular works too, Martini may seek to define the high point of his musical structure through special imitative treatment. The quick succession of entries at breves 47–48 of *Des biens d'amours* achieves on a much smaller scale the effect described with regard to the above Agnus. Each of the two parts of *J'espoir mieulx* reaches a climax through close imitation appearing near their respective conclusions.

[21] The Christe derives from material presented in the chanson, and is free only in the sense that it does not employ a cantus firmus in long notes. (The cantus-bearing voice is omitted in this movement.)

In *Fault il que heur soy*, which, together with *La Martinella*, is one of the longer of Martini's chansons, one may sense an over-all structure governed in terms of imitative technique. Following an opening based on paired imitation between the two lower and two upper voices, Martini presents a series of three imitations involving only two voices each. At the 50th breve, he foreshadows in the superius the first of a pair of motives that appear in ascending alternation at a breve's distance each, thus providing an intermediate climax. The following point of imitation involves only two voices. The final point is the first to carry out a single motive in all four voices. The tenor, bassus, superius, and contra enter at a breve's distance from each other, providing a significant high point before reaching the final cadence.

In general, however, imitative technique is not employed to obtain over-all architectural definition. On the contrary, imitation is often used inconsistently, some phrases being built without reference to the device, while others consist of several points of imitation. Sometimes imitation is quite concealed, as in the superius entries of the 34th and 19th breves of *J'espoir mieulx* and the textless opening work of Banco Rari 229, respectively.

Often Martini will handle a given point of imitation in some unexpected fashion. The voices of *Se mai il cielo*, for example, enter one by one, the tenor imitating the contra at the distance of two breves. One expects that the superius entry at the 8th breve will cap the set of three, but instead a new motive is presented, to be imitated by the lower voices in descending order. The second part of *Il est tousjours* opens with the simultaneous presentation of two motives, which are then developed successively, the lower one being treated first. *O di prudenza fonte* begins with an ascending point of imitation in all three voices; the tenor repeats the imitative motive sequentially, producing the effect of a redundant entry. Later in this work, three brief points of imitation are presented in quick succession. The spacing of the entries is such that the third motive enters in the contra before the presentation of the second of the tenor entries.

One is frequently impressed by the long spans covered by individual imitative pairs. Passages covering six breves in the individual voices are commonplace, and passages of approximately twice that length are by no means rare. Examples of the latter are furnished in *Tant que Dieu vosdra*, *Il est tel*, *Biaulx parle tousjours*, and *Le Fleur de biaulté*, among others. Occasionally, as in the textless pieces in Banco Rari 229, fols. 173^v–174^r and fols. 235^v–236^r, imitation between a pair of voices is carried out to such an extent that one might almost speak of free canon.

In longer imitations, Martini does not hesitate to take liberties with the imitating voice. He may change either the pitch interval or the time interval within a given passage; notes of the original pattern may be embroidered or otherwise altered, or even omitted.

In view of Martini's penchant for long imitative spans, it is curious that only two of his surviving pieces are canons in the modern sense of the word.[22] Neither the *Fuga ad quatuor* nor the Banco Rari 229 setting of *J'ay pris amours* is representative of Martini at his best.

Paired imitation, mentioned previously in connection with *Fault il que heur soy*, occurs in several other works, both for four voices and for three. In the opening duet of *Tant que Dieu vosdra*, the tenor and contra participate in an exchange of motives.

Despite a certain variety of technique, one may single out as characteristic of Martini's normal style those works that employ imitation between tenor and superius over a non-imitative contra. Among the more prominent characteristics of Martini's harmonic norm are close adherence to primary tonal centers and non-quartal harmony (i.e. an avoidance of essential fourths between any two voices of a three-voice structure). In many chansons, both entries and cadences are predominantly, if not exclusively, on the final and fifth degree. The sense of clear-cut tonality is also enhanced by a preference for imitation at the unison or octave. Imitation at the fourth or fifth is frequent, but other intervals are employed only rarely. About a third of Martini's three-part works are written in a strict non-quartal style. Well over half the remainder admit of one or two essential fourths, these occurring chiefly at cadential points. Charles Warren Fox, in his pioneering article on this technique, listed Martini among composers contributing non-quartal compositions; [23] we may now place our composer among those—including Busnois—who exhibit a definite predilection for this style.

Passages in parallel thirds or tenths—a usual concomitant of a non-quartal style—are frequent in Martini's work. The cloying sensation they produce is, however, often counterbalanced by other sections in a mildly dissonant style. Martini enjoys dissonant semiminims on the second and fourth quarters of the breve, these being used in passing function. Consecutive dissonances may occur, either as a result of passing

---

[22] The "canon" provided for the Segovia setting of *J'ay pris amours* directs that the borrowed voice (the altus) be performed in contrary motion to the written notes; since no added voice is involved, this work is *a 4*, rather than *a 5*, as stated elsewhere.

[23] C. W. Fox, *Non-Quartal Harmony in the Renaissance*, in: MQ, XXXI (1945), 32–53.

functions in different voices or as a result of movement in one voice during the resolution of a suspension in another.

Also contributing to the mild pungency of Martini's style is his occasional willingness to permit a dissonant entry on the second or fourth quarter of a breve.

Ex. 3 *Non seul uno;* breves 35–40

Had Martini considered the momentary clash in the 37th breve offensive, he could easily have avoided the dissonance by postponing the re-entry of the altus until the third quarter of the breve. His chosen version, however, is superior to the alternative in terms of rhythmic development.

Concern for rhythmic structures is another of the major features of Martini's style. His music furnishes countless examples of the Renaissance delight in rhythmic interplay, both within the single voice-part and between the different voice-parts of the polyphonic complex. Imitation at the minim is one of the more obvious devices producing this interplay. The notes of the *dux* that fall on the harmonically strong part of the breve are pushed onto the weak part in the *comes,* while those that are in weak position in the *dux* are in strong position in the *comes.* In *Sans siens du mal,* which is in triple meter, each of the three entries occurring in breves 31–33 begins on a different part of the breve.

More frequently, rhythmic interplay arises from the development of patterns that proceed in groupings other than those suggested by the mensuration sign. The pieces in *proportio tripla* exhibit the simplest and most direct rhythms. They achieve variety primarily through the use of hemiolia, indicated in the notation by coloration. Works in *tempus imperfectum diminutum* are apt to be more complex. The duple patterns that one might expect of this mensuration are often set aside temporarily in favor of patterns three minims long; obviously, these patterns run counter to whatever impulses might be conveyed by the tactus. At their strongest, with all voices proceeding in parallel fashion, they may briefly obscure the effect of the tactus. It is quite tempting, for example, to bar the opening of *Il est tel* in triple meter, the mensuration sign notwithstanding.

Ex. 4   *Il est tel;* the opening barred according to the agogic stresses

Even when one voice resists the primary trend, the effect of these counter-patterns can be quite powerful.

Ex. 5   *Non per la;* breves 23–27

The close of *De la bonne chiere* is particularly daring. A climax is provided by a sequential figure of five minims that occurs in the two upper voices; in this sequence, the agogic stresses of the two voices are not simultaneous, but a minim apart.

Ex. 6 *De la bonne chiere* (Rome, Casanatense MS 2856, ff. 132ᵛ–133ʳ)

Of somewhat different nature is the following passage from *Il est tousjours*. Here, for a short space, Martini provides agogic stresses on the sections of the breve treated as weak from the harmonic standpoint, while the sections normally perceived as strong are rhythmically weak.[24]

Ex. 7 *Il est tousjours;* breves 12–16

How are we to interpret such conflicting patterns, and how are they to be presented in transcription? Otto Gombosi advocated irregular barring of individual voices. His method reveals the great variety of rhythmic configurations in Renaissance music, but—at least visually—ignores the tactus. Gombosi's suggestions are vigorously rejected by Edward Lowinsky, who points out that such transcription practices are both visually distracting and misleading.[25] They ignore the steady harmonic rhythm of late Renaissance music and the fact that dissonance was regulated according to the tactus. Further, they imply that the Renaissance composer was unaware of syncopation in the modern sense. One may inquire whether Lowinsky's conclusions, reached with regard to 16th-century music (including that of Josquin), are also valid for slightly earlier music with marked irregularities of harmonic rhythm. This writer would answer in the affirmative.

Not only do we find that Martini's polyphony was governed in terms of the tactus—namely through the regulation of dissonance—but also that the individual voice-parts reveal the tactus' shaping influence. This influence is made manifest in two ways, through the disposition of long notes, and through the disposition of cadences.[26] As a rule, both in

---

[24] The passage in Example 7 is unique among Martini's secular works from the standpoint of consistency. However, instances in which all voices are tied over the barline are fairly frequent (cf. Ex. 1); as a result, the harmonic rhythm is often irregular.

[25] Edward E. Lowinsky, *Early Scores in Manuscript*, in: JAMS, XIII (1960), 126–73; cf. esp. pp. 156–60.

[26] A further influence of the tactus concerns the writing of rests. If, for example, a phrase ends in the middle of a breve, and the next phrase begins some time later, also in the middle of a breve, one normally finds a semibreve rest, followed by rests for the requisite number of breves, and, finally, another semibreve rest. Had the

Martini's music and elsewhere, breves and longs begin only on the first and third quarters of the breve. Exceptions to this rule, such as those brought on by the quintuple patterns in the *Qui tollis* of Obrecht's *Missa Je ne demande*, are rare. Lowinsky has already pointed out that cadence endings too are restricted to the first and third quarters of the breve. His discussion is oriented from the standpoint of harmony, but it is obvious that cadential functions are equally important from the melodic standpoint. If the conflicting patterns created by agogic stresses were actually evidence to the effect that the tactus had little role in shaping the individual voice-part, then—in view of the irregularity of these patterns —one would expect to find both long notes and cadential endings on the second and fourth quarters of the breve. I would assume that, at some time, in transcribing the initial voice-part of a polyphonic complex, many of us have experienced a premonition that something had gone wrong, owing either to an error in the MS or to a momentary lapse of attention. Usually the accuracy of such premonitions is borne out when the other voice-parts are added. Surely the basis for this "sixth sense" is the conscious or unconscious awareness of the shaping power of the tactus. It is entirely fitting, therefore, that this regulative force be acknowledged through regularly spaced barlines. If the transcriber wishes to draw attention to the numerous ways in which this force is challenged, and even temporarily submerged, ways other than irregular barring must be employed. It is entirely possible that the shortness of phrase in Martini's secular music—an irritating quality at times—was calculated as a means of counterbalancing the frequent and forceful rhythmic challenges to the tactus. That is, the cadences are used to reaffirm the tactus' basic role. A review of the relationship between rhythmic variety and phrase length in other late 15th-century secular music could prove quite illuminating.

An impartial assessment of Martini's secular works must reckon with weaknesses as well as with strong points. As a group, these pieces lack the range and depth exhibited in the secular music of a Josquin or a Pierre de la Rue. Nor is the material employed of consistent quality;

tactus been of no importance, the two semibreve rests flanking the group could have been combined into a single symbol. A detailed study of rest patterns in Renaissance musical sources is offered by Knud Jeppesen in *Et Par notationstekniske Problemer i det 16. Aarhundredes Musik og nogle dertil Knyttede Iagttagelser* (*Taktinddeling-Partitur*), in: *Svensk Tidskrift för Musikforskning*, XLIII (1961), 171–89. (A summary in German is given on pp. 190–93.) Jeppesen indicates that 16th-century theoretical writings substantiate the fact that configurations of rests were to be written in a manner to help the performer keep his place with regard to the tactus.

there are passages that are clumsy and tedious. But Martini's better works are full of grace and elegance. He is, furthermore, a fascinating craftsman to observe. A closer study of his work promises to yield worthwhile insights into the music of his period.

A "DIATONIC" AND
A "CHROMATIC" MADRIGAL
BY GIULIO FIESCO

by HENRY W. KAUFMANN

RGUMENTS ABOUT the nature of the diatonic, chromatic,
and enharmonic genera enlivened much of the theoretical
writing of the later 16th century in Italy. The central event
dealing with this problem certainly must have been the famous debate
between Nicola Vicentino and the Portuguese musician Vincente Lusitano held before the Papal Choir in the spring of 1551.[1] This controversy
was sparked by a performance of a composition based on the "Regina
coeli" that was sung at a private academy held in Rome at the home of
Bernardo Acciaioli, or Rucellai, as he was otherwise known.[2] In the
discussion that followed, Vicentino asserted that few composers really
understood the gender of the compositions that were written or sung
in his day.

Vicentino's argument was premised on a particular interpretation
of the genera. For instance, instead of considering the diatonic, chromatic, or enharmonic tetrachord as a unit, he felt that the use of any *one*
of its component members was sufficient to identify the gender. Thus,
chromatic could be represented by (a) the series: minor third, half step,
half step; (b) the minor third alone; (c) a half step alone. Similarly,
the major third alone could be interpreted as evidence for the existence
of the enharmonic gender. In essence then, the music commonly sung
was in reality a mixture of the three genera, a "musica participata &
mista," [3] since the mere presence of a minor third or a major third in the

---

[1] The first portion of the fourth book of Vicentino's treatise is completely devoted to the question. Cf. Nicola Vicentino, *L'antica musica ridotta alla moderna
prattica*, facsimile ed. Edward E. Lowinsky, in: *Documenta Musicologica*, Series I,
No. XVII (Kassel 1959), fols. 95–98ᵛ. A brief summary of the debate, including
English translations of pertinent passages from the treatise, may be found in John
Hawkins, *A General History of the Science and Practice of Music*, with a new
introduction by Charles Cudworth (New York 1963), I, 392–95. For full details of
the controversy, see the present author's forthcoming book, *The Life and Works of
Nicola Vicentino*, now in press, American Institute of Musicology, Rome.

[2] Giuseppe Baini, *Memorie storico-critiche della vita e dell'opere di Giovanni
Pierluigi da Palestrina* (Rome 1828), I, 343.

[3] Vicentino, *op. cit.*, fol. 48.

musical context indicated the invasion of the diatonic by the chromatic and enharmonic species respectively.[4]

Lusitano, in return, offered to prove, in the name of all musicians, that he *did* know the gender of the pieces written in his day, and that it was the tried and true diatonic.[5]

Though the difference now seems merely semantic, the viewpoints expressed by the two contestants actually led in diametrically opposed directions. The "diatonicists" were not only fighting for the retention of the ecclesiastical modes, but also for all the traditional rules of composition. The "mixturists" were trying to justify the more progressive contemporary tendencies in composition within the framework of a rational system that allowed for chromatic and even enharmonic "aberrations."

Unfortunately for Vicentino, who lost the debate, his system was so complex and involved that for all practical purposes it proved unwieldy. Since the "musica participata & mista" that he favored was in reality a combination of the species of all three genera, it premised, in order to be understood intelligently, the existence of "pure" diatonic, chromatic, and enharmonic modes. In effect, Vicentino constructed a network of modes that not only included the eight diatonic modes known traditionally, but also eight chromatic and enharmonic variants,[6]

[4] *Ibid.*, fol. 95. This type of interpretation was not limited to Vicentino alone, although he was practically the only theorist to include the enharmonic in his consideration of mixed genera. Bermudo, for example, speaks of a semichromatic gender that combines the diatonic and chromatic. Cf. Juan Bermudo, *Declaración de Instrumentos musicales 1555*, facsimile ed. Macario Santiago Kastner, in: *Documenta Musicologica*, Series I, No. XI (Kassel 1959), fol. 22, col. 1. This opinion is repeated in the treatise of a less well-known Spanish theorist, [Martin de] Tapia in his . . . *Vergel de Musica* . . . (Burgo de Osma 1570), fol. 44^v. Morley similarly remarks that a point used by organists, consisting of the notes e, f, f$\sharp$, g, g$\sharp$, a "is not right Chromatica, but a bastard point patched up of half Chromatic and half Diatonic. Lastly it appeareth . . . that those virginals which our unlearned musicians call Chromatica . . . be not right Chromatica but half Enharmonica . . ." Thomas Morley, *A Plain and Easy Introduction to Practical Music*, ed. R. Alec Harman (London 1952), p. 103. Morley also remarks that the "kind of music which is usual nowadays is not fully and in every respect the ancient Diatonicum . . . so that it must needs follow that it is neither just Diatonicum nor right Chromaticum."

[5] Lusitano's staunchest supporter was Ghisilino Danckerts, one of the judges in the debate who, in a treatise written shortly thereafter, not only defended the purity of the diatonic gender, but excoriated those who included chromatic "distortions" in their works. Cf. Ghisilino Danckerts, *Trattado . . . sopra una differentia musicale* (Rome, Vallicelliana, MS 56), *passim*. This argument may well have inspired Zarlino's diatribe against certain chromaticists that first appeared with the publication of his *Le Istitutioni harmoniche* in 1558. These opinions remained basically unchanged in the subsequent editions of this work; for instance, cf. the chapter entitled "Opinioni delli Chromatici ributtate," Gioseffo Zarlino, *Istituzioni harmoniche* (Venice 1573), Bk. III, ch. lxxxx, pp. 357-58.

[6] For a more complete discussion of this system of modes see this author's *Vicentino and the Greek Genera*, in: JAMS, XVI (1963), [325-]46.

all conceived in terms of pure scales no longer employed in actual practice. In the examples he wrote to illustrate the modes of his more modern "musica participata & mista," Vicentino kept the name of each mode as well as its dominant and final as before, but because an actual melody was shown with a variety of leaps and steps instead of the previous exposition of the mode by means of scalewise segments, he felt justified, on the basis of his broad concept of gender, to label this music with the new term and to relate it to contemporary practice.

Most of his contemporaries, including Vicentino himself, found a more simple explanation for their deviations from High Renaissance practice. As long as the art of composition developed on purely musical grounds, it was based on a fairly strict adherence to modal principles, the concepts of consonance and dissonance laid down by medieval and early Renaissance theorists, and the established "rules" of counterpoint. With the 16th century, however, there arose a new interest in the relationship of word to tone, inspired by humanistic studies, that led to extra-musical considerations in the development of musical forms. These developments involved abrogation of many of the "rules" because of the growing dependency of music on textual influences. As a result, the principles of High Renaissance musical composition tended to be replaced by creativity on the basis of natural instinct, inspired by the meaning of the words. This subjective approach dominates many pages of *L'antica musica*, and although its musical grammar still derives its impetus from High Renaissance sources, its syntax reveals new patterns and formations that result from an obedience to the demands of the text, the "soggetto delle parole." The demands of the text became the excuse for all sorts of musical "deviations" and in effect obviated the necessity of a complex apparatus, such as that erected by Vicentino, to explain them.

Nonetheless, questions concerning the nature of the genera continued to permeate the thinking of the theorists [7] and composers who followed Vicentino. In several madrigal collections, for instance, there appeared occasional compositions specifically marked "Diatonico" or "Cromatico," thereby implying that the rest of the collection was written as "musica participata & mista." [8] Two such works by Fiesco,

---

[7] Cf. note 4, *supra*.

[8] In addition to the pieces by Fiesco mentioned in the title of this article, similar designations can be found as follows. Cf. Theodor Kroyer, *Die Anfänge der Chromatik im italienischen Madrigal des XVI. Jahrhunderts,* in: *Publikationen der internationalen Musikgesellschaft,* IV (Leipzig 1902), 46–47:

　　a) Cesare Tudino, *li Madrigali a Note Bianche et Negre Cromatiche . . . a 4 voci* (Venice 1554), containing two madrigals designated "cromatico."

　　b) Francesco Orto, *I° libro de Madrigali con due Madrigali cromatici nel fine* (Venice 1567).

one designated "Diatonico" and the other "Cromatico," [9] have been selected for special study because of the composer's connection with Ferrara and possible direct relationship to Vicentino.

Little is known of the life of Giulio Fiesco. Most of the standard reference works indicate that he was born in Ferrara c. 1519 and died there c. 1586,[10] thus making him a contemporary of Vicentino. He supposedly worked at the d'Este court,[11] but his name does not appear in any known document relating to the music chapel of that court.[12] The earliest biographical reference to Fiesco appears in a work published in 1620 in which he is described as "non solo musico, ma degno suonatore de varij instromenti." [13] Since the musicians of the court are usually designated in this work as "Musico Ducale," and no such appellation is attached to Fiesco's name, it is apparent that his role in the court music must have been only peripheral to his other duties in Ferrara. Nevertheless, the dedication of his works to Alfonso II, Lucrezia, and Leonora d'Este indicate some relationship to the personalities of the Ferrara court.

Fiesco's extant works consist chiefly of a first book of four-part madrigals (1554), a second book of five-part madrigals (1567), and another collection of five-part madrigals entitled *Musica nova* (1569). In addition, there exist isolated pieces in the collections of other madrigalists.[14] The "diatonic" and "chromatic" madrigals under discussion are both found in the first book.[15]

The diatonic *Nov'angioletta* (Ex. 1) is based on an eight-line *madrigale* by Petrarch with the rhyme scheme aab aab cc. The first six lines of the text are set to continuous music, each line unfolding like a point of imitation, primarily because of the rhythmic similarity of the initial notes of the different entries, but more oriented toward harmony than polyphony. Some text repetition occurs, but without a concomitant

c) Ludovico Agostini, *Il I° libro di Madrigali à 4* (Venice 1570), also including two madrigals inscribed "Chromatico."

d) Rocco Rodio, *Il II° libro di Madrigali à 4* (Venice 1587), containing one madrigal "Del Genere cromatico."

[9] The theorist Artusi considered these two pieces by Fiesco to be a mixture of diatonic and chromatic. Kroyer, *op. cit.*, p. 94.

[10] Cf. MGG, IV (1955), 172–73 and *Dizionario Ricordi della musica e dei musicisti* (1959), p. 466, col. 2. The fifth edition of *Grove's Dictionary of Music and Musicians*, III (1955), 88, suggests Modena as the probable place of death.

[11] Cf. in addition to the above, Nando Bennati, *Musicisti ferraresi* (Ferrara 1901), p. 25.

[12] Cf. Walter Weyler, *Documenten betreffende de muziekkapel aan het hof van Ferrara*, in: *Vlaamsch Jaarboek voor Muziekgeschiedenis*, I (1939), 81–113.

[13] Agostino Superbi, *Apparato degli huomini illustri della città di Ferrara* (Ferrara 1620), p. 130. The spelling of his name is here given as Fies.

[14] MGG, IV, 172–73.

[15] Giulio Fiesco, *Il primo libro di madrigali a quattro voci* (Venice 1554). The madrigal marked "Diatonico" appears on fol. 7, the one called "Cromatico" on fol. 25.

melodic repetition. The last two lines, separated from the first part of the text by a simultaneous rest in all parts, are set as a unit culminating in a definite cadence, and then are immediately repeated. The resultant musical structure emerges as ABB.

Ex. 1 *Nov' angioletta* ("diatonico")

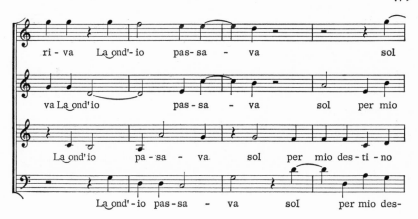

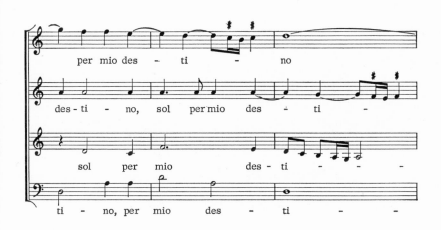

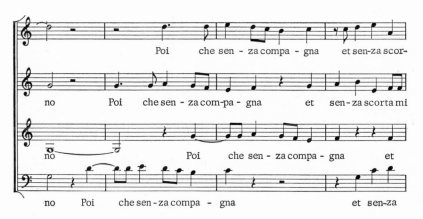

te Mi vidd' un lac - cio che di se - ta or-di -

vidd'   un   lac-cio che di se - ta or-di -

sen - za scor - ta Mi vidd' un lac - cio che di se - ta or-

scor - ta Mi vidd' un lac - cio che di se-ta ordi -

va. Te - se fra l'herb' ond'   e

va Te - se fra l'herb'   ond'   e

di   va   Te - se fra l'herb ond'   e verd'

va   Te - se fra l'herb   ond'   e

verd'   il   ca - mi - no   All' hor   fui

verd' il   ca - mi - no   All' hor fui pre-so

il   ca -   - mi - no   All' hor   fui

verd'   il   ca - mi - no   All' hor   fui

pre - so e non mi spiacque po - i, e non mi

e non mi spiacque po - i, e non mi

pre - so e non mi spiacque po - i·

pre - so e non mi spiacque po i

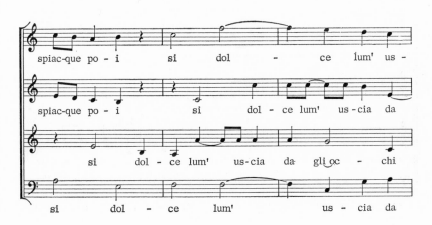

spiac-que po - i si dol - ce lum' us -

spiac-que po - i si dol - ce lum' us -cia da

si dol - ce lum' us-cia da gli oc - chi

si dol - ce lum' us - cia da

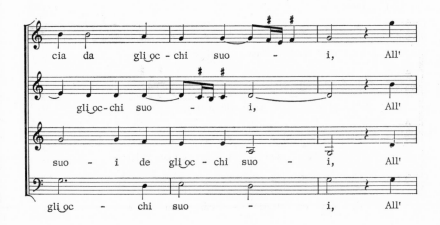

cia da gli oc - chi suo - i, All'

gli oc-chi suo - i, All'

suo - i de gli oc - chi suo - i, All'

gli oc - chi suo - i, All'

hor fui pre - so e non mi spiacque po - i,

hor fui pre so e non mi spiacque po i,

hor fui pre - so e non mi

hor fui pre - so e non mi

(e non mi spiacque po - i) si dol -

e non mi spiacque po - i si dol -

spiac-que po - i si dol - ce lum' us-cia

spiac-que po - i si dol - ce lum'

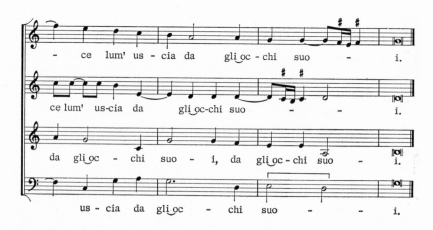

- ce lum' us - cia da gli oc - chi suo - i.

ce lum' us-cia da gli oc-chi suo - - i.

da gli oc - chi suo - i, da gli oc - chi suo - i.

us - cia da gli oc - chi suo - - i.

As befits the diatonic gender, most of the melodic intervals are written stepwise, consisting of either the major or the minor second. The outer framework of the tetrachord, forming the interval of the perfect fourth, or its inversion the perfect fifth, is most frequently used for skips. Similarly, the leap of the octave can be found on occasion.[16]

Contrary to the theory of the "pure" diatonic gender, this composition includes a few leaps of the major or minor sixth, mostly in the upper voices.[17] The major sixth in both cases occurs after a rest. According to Vicentino, any such "forbidden" interval can be obviated by the insertion of a rest between its component notes.[18] The minor sixths cannot, however, be explained on any such basis, and must be considered as aberrations from the theoretical problem that this composition purports to solve. Since they are so few in number, they do not seriously affect the "diatonicism" of the piece.

The diatonic concept is a purely melodic one and does not pertain to the intervallic relationships between the various parts. Harmonically, the over-all effect wavers between modality and tonality. Although the piece begins and ends on G, this tone is not concretely established as the center of gravity despite its prominence. The very beginning of the madrigal sets up an ambivalence between G and C that makes it difficult to decide which is to serve as "tonic." There are many clear cadences in G, but these are almost immediately followed by a passage that is definitely in C so that the ambivalence of "key" permeates most of the piece. This is also aided in part by the frequent use of "modal" degrees of the scale,[19] as well as chords that can be interpreted as "minor" dominants. The text, moreover, is of no help in explaining this duality of function, since it is fairly direct and straightforward.

The "chromatic" madrigal, *Bacio soave* (Ex. 2), based on an unidentified text, is through-composed in a basically homophonic style, animated on occasion by rhythmic points of imitation. The four-part texture is relieved near the end of the piece by writing for paired voices, as if

[16] The "immobile" perfect fourth of the tetrachord is common to all three genera; hence, any leap of a perfect fourth, or its inversion the perfect fifth, or the interval of the octave that results when the varied fourths and fifths are superimposed to produce the different modes may be used freely in compositions purporting to be diatonic, chromatic, or enharmonic respectively. Only the inner notes of the tetrachord, the "mobile voices," have any specific meaning in terms of gender.

[17] Cf. the major sixth: alto, measures 32 and 42, and the minor sixth: soprano, measure 23 and alto, measures 9 and 13.

[18] Vicentino, *op. cit.*, fol. 52.

[19] The introduction of editorial accidentals may serve to "tonalize" some of these modal harmonies, but do not destroy the essential diatonicism of the piece, since the only changes made altered a major to a minor second, both intervals within the context of the diatonic gender.

Ex. 2 *Bacio soave con ch'il cor* ("cromatico")

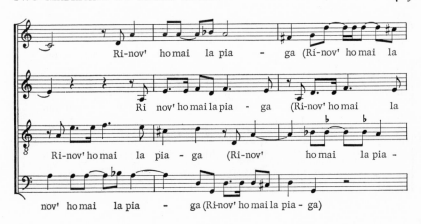

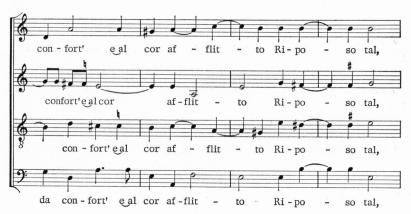

con - fort' e al cor af - flit - to Ri - po - so tal,

confort' e al cor af - flit - to Ri - po - so tal,

con - fort' e al cor af - flit - to Ri - po - so tal,

da con - fort' e al cor af - flit - to Ri - po - so tal,

Ri - po - so tal

Ri - po - so tal

Ri - po - so tal che l'un' e l'al-tro sen -

Ri - po - so tal che l'un' - e l'al-tro sen - te,

che l'un' e l'al-tro sen - te,

che l'un' e l'al-tro sen - te,   che l'un' e

te,   che l'un' e l'al-tro sen - te

che l'un e l'al-tro sen - te

hearkening to the message of the text, "che l'un' e l'altro sente."

Most of the melodic intervals adhere to the theoretical limits set for the chromatic gender: the minor third and the two semitones. Leaps common to all the genera, such as the perfect fourth, perfect fifth, and octave, are also employed. One unauthorized interval, the minor sixth, occurs several times.[20] Since this interval is the inversion of the major third, normally belonging to the enharmonic gender, it theoretically has no justified place in this composition. Vicentino himself, however, in one of his chromatic compositions,[21] admits that he has included in this piece "gradi lunghi dell-Enarmonico," that is, major thirds, in several places, "fatti per incitatione delle parole," which the singer may modify if he

---

[20] Cf. tenor, measure 13; soprano, measure 14; bass, measure 20; tenor, measure 21 (this one may be excused on the ground that it occurs between the end of one phrase and the beginning of another); bass, measure 29; alto, measure 30.

[21] The "Motettino" based on the words of the Easter Gradual, "Haec dies." A transcription of this work can be found in Luigi Torchi, *L'Arte musicale in Italia*, I (Milan 1897–1908?), 147–48.

wishes by the use of a flat.[22] In Fiesco's composition, the alteration of the minor to the acceptable major sixth would produce untenable cross-relations. Since the forbidden interval occurs most often on words of great emotional import, such as "afflitto" or "ardersi," the text may supply in most cases the reason for the use of the minor sixth.

The composition is basically "tonal" in effect since the progressions are guided by a principle that presages the circle of fifths of later theory. The rate of modulatory change is so rapid, however, that it approaches the concept described by Lowinsky as "floating tonality" or "triadic atonality" because of the constant shifting of the tonal center from one area to another within a triadic texture of harmony.[23]

Fiesco's music has significance beyond the purely theoretical. His few extant compositions reveal a sensitivity and refinement of style that make him a worthy member of that company of 16th-century composers who combined technique and imagination to produce a "new" music. The innovations, so ardently cultivated and so furiously defended, led directly to the great masters of the Baroque.

[22] Vicentino, *op. cit.*, fol. 62. The freedom of the singer to alter at will the given pitch offers another mite of support to Lowinsky's theory of a "secret chromatic art."

[23] Edward E. Lowinsky, *Tonality and Atonality in Sixteenth-Century Music* (Berkeley 1961), pp. 38–39.

IN PRAISE OF THE LAUDA

by SYLVIA W. KENNEY

A SONG-MOTET, it seems, is innocent until proved guilty. That is to say that a certain type of 15th-century composition can be called a "song-motet" or "chanson-motet" with impunity unless a version of it is discovered with a secular text. Then it usually becomes known as a contrafactum. Many of these pieces that would normally have been called song-motets by modern scholars have been known to be contrafacta because they are accompanied in the Trent codices by the textual incipits of the chansons from which they were derived.[1] Others, such as Ciconia's *O beatum incendium* (*Aler m'en veus*), Binchois's *Virgo rosa venustatis* (*C'est assez*), Frye's *O sacrum convivium* (*Alas, alas*) and *Sancta Maria succurre* (*So ys emprentid*), were thought to be song-motets at one time, but their identity with secular songs was eventually revealed.

There is one curious case of a so-called song-motet that was neither composed as such originally nor made into a contrafactum in the usual manner. The first version of Compère's *O vos omnes*[2] was most probably a motet chanson. Although the piece appears in several sources with the Latin text (from the Lamentations of Jeremiah) in all voices, the Brussels MS 228 (Bibliothèque Royale) presents it with the Latin text only in the lowest voice, while the upper two parts have a French text, *O devotz cueurs* (fols. 59ᵛ–60). There is no known source for the melody accompanying the Latin text, although *O vos omnes* was a well-known Alleluia verse.[3] Besseler assumes that Compère's melody was a cantus prius factus, however,[4] and he seems justified, particularly since there is another setting two folios earlier in the same manuscript. This anonymous piece (fols. 57ᵛ–58) has a different rhythmic formulation of the *O vos omnes* melody and the upper parts have the text *Mes chants sont*

---

[1] See, for example, Trent 90, Nos. 988, 1009, 1012, 1072, 1139, 1140, 1141, and 1142. Thematic index in *Denkmäler der Tonkunst in Österreich*, VII (Vienna 1900).
[2] Attributed to Obrecht in *Jacob Obrecht: Werken*, ed. Johannes Wolf (Amsterdam 1912–21), IV, 173.
[3] *Graduale sacrosanctae Romanae ecclesiae* (Tournai 1948), p. 597.
[4] *Altniederländische Motetten*, ed. Heinrich Besseler (Kassel 1929), *Quellen und Texte*.

de deuil. Compère himself seems to have had a marked predilection for the motet chanson, as can be seen by his three examples in the *Odhecaton, Royne de Ciel/Regina Coeli* (No. 84), *Le corps/Corpusque meum* (No. 67), and *Male bouche/Circumdederunt me viri mendaces* (No. 46) as well as his *Plaine d'ennuy/Anima mea.*[5] Through an odd confusion of terminology, this type of composition is called a motet chanson when in fact it has the strongest claim of any 15th-century form to the designation "motet" as the term was originally used in the 13th century, particularly when, as in most of Compère's pieces, the vernacular texts are troping or paraphrasing the sense of the Latin. But the motet chanson is primarily governed by the secular forms of its French text, usually the rondeau or virelai, at a time when the term "motet" usually referred to Latin sacred pieces. Hence in spite of its Latin cantus firmus the motet chanson stands apart from the main line of development among 15th-century forms. The fact that *O vos omnes* was converted into a song-motet by elimination of the French texts indicates its somewhat ambiguous position.

Pieces called "song-motets" fall into two categories. One group reflects clearly the bipartite structure of any one of the chanson forms in which there is a medial cadence about halfway through (and in some cases, the musically rhymed endings between the two sections so characteristic of the ballade), while the other is made up of freely composed, generally formless pieces. The first group appears suspect, mainly because so often pieces of this type have proved to be contrafacta. Scholars continue to call them song-motets, however. Sparks, for example, designates Compère's *O vos omnes* as such,[6] and Besseler published it with the Latin text only, even though acknowledging the Brussels version. Frye's *Ave Regina* too will probably continue to be cited as a classical example of the song-motet, in the absence of the secular model, despite this author's strenuous efforts to prove it guilty.[7] The second group, however, cannot be so easily discredited. Thus there remain many 15th-century song-motets whose status as bona fide motets remains unchallenged.

Johannes Touront is frequently mentioned as one of the foremost exponents of the song-motet with his two small compositions *O florens*

---

[5] Brussels, Bibliothèque Royale, MS 228. See Charles Van den Borren, *Inventaire des manuscrits de musique polyphonique qui se trouve en Belgique,* in: *Acta musicologica,* V (1933), 125.

[6] Edgar H. Sparks, *Cantus Firmus in Mass and Motet* (Berkeley 1963), p. 461, fn. 9.

[7] Sylvia W. Kenney, *Contrafacta in the Works of Walter Frye,* in: JAMS, VIII (1955), 187–90.

rosa and *O gloriosa regina*. But he is by no means the only one, nor even
perhaps the most significant. There are numerous examples throughout
the 15th century, from Binchois's *Ave Regina coelorum* earlier in the
century, to Ockeghem's *Ave Maria*, Tinctoris's *Virgo dei throno*,
Regis's *Ave Maria*, Gaspar van Weerbecke's (or Josquin's) *O Venus
bant*, Obrecht's *Parce domine* and *Si sumpsero*, Josquin's *Pace in idipsum*,
Agricola's *Si dedero*, and De Orto's *Ave Maria*. All these pieces do not
seem consistently characterized by anything except the fact that they
are short, simple, generally three-voiced, and generally lack a cantus
firmus. Regis's *Ave Maria* and Binchois's *Ave Regina*, however, both cite
some of the plainsong at the beginning. Thus even the absence of a
motet-like cantus firmus does not seem to be a criterion for the song-
motet.

Many of these pieces appear in predominantly secular collections.
The Mellon chansonnier, for example, includes Tinctoris's *Virgo dei
throno* (fols. 80ᵛ–81), while Frye's *Ave Regina* invariably appears in
chanson collections. Even as late as 1501 the *Odhecaton* includes song-
motets by De Orto, Agricola, Josquin, and Brumel. Frequently a song-
motet is placed at the very beginning, perhaps to sanction the entire
collection. Petrucci placed De Orto's *Ave Maria* at the beginning of the
Odhecaton and Compère's *Virgo coelesti* at the beginning of *Canti B*,
while Frye's *Ave Regina* is the first piece in the Wolfenbüttel chansonnier (Landesbibliothek MS 287 extravag.). Their inclusion in chansonniers suggests that the function of the song-motets was probably
different from that of the loftier tenor motet and that they served for
private devotions rather than in the liturgy, even though the texts are
frequently liturgical.

Whatever the function of the song-motet, it is apparent that by the
second half of the 15th century, when nearly all the outstanding composers are represented by the genre, the song-motet was an eminently
legitimate form. Furthermore, the question of whether a piece is a
song-motet or a contrafactum seems to have very little importance. The
more significant point is that motets were created, even though sometimes artificially by text substitution, in the style and small form of a
chanson. There is, of course, no binding definition of the motet in the
15th century. Tinctoris describes it vaguely as a piece of moderate size,
on any text, though frequently sacred.[8] Thus it need not have a cantus
firmus, it need not be liturgical nor even sacred. The manuscript indices
themselves frequently announce a series of motets with the phrase "Hic

---

[8] *Diffinitorium musicae*, in: E. de Coussemaker, ed., *Scriptorum de musica medii
aevi* (Paris 1864–76), IV, 185.

incipiunt motetti" and follow this supposedly elucidating statement with both liturgical and non-liturgical works.[9] By and large, however, the pieces called "motets" were sacred and Latin, varying only in their liturgical or paraliturgical functions. Purely occasional pieces like Busnois's *In Hydraulis* are relatively rare, as are the hybrid forms like the motet chansons.

Nevertheless, musical compositions of the 15th century that are sacred and composed to Latin texts do not appear to be the exclusive property of the motet. They are most certainly related to the lauda. Petrucci, in 1507 and 1508, published two volumes of laude, the first made up of compositions by one Innocentius Dammonis, and the second of pieces by various frottola composers, including Tromboncino and Cara and even Josquin. While the lauda was originally a vernacular sacred form, it was no longer restricted to the vernacular in the 15th century, and by Petrucci's time there was quite a large proportion of Latin laude. In Petrucci's Book I there are 15 Latin and 51 Italian laude, and in Book II the proportion of Latin texts doubles, for there are 31 Latin pieces among the 56 compositions.[10] The texts of these Latin laude are not merely sacred; many of them are well-known liturgical texts such as *Ave Maria, Tenebrae factae sunt, Verbum caro factum est,* and *O sacrum convivium.* Thus the lauda, at least in its Latin forms, is no longer composed exclusively to freely devised devotional texts. It draws from the same sources as the motet and hence appears to usurp to a considerable extent the functions of the motet.

The lauda, on the other hand, had been closely associated with secular forms. By the time of Petrucci it was primarily the frottola that was the counterpart of the lauda (with some contrafacta between them), but earlier in the century the lauda drew on French chansons as well. Monophonic laude frequently used melodies of French chansons such as *Jamais tant que je vous revoye* (*Giammai laudarti quanto degna se*), *Mon seul plaisir* (*Nessun piacere ho senza se*) and *Pour prison* (*Ben venga Gesù l'amor mio*).[11] A number of polyphonic laude in the Panciatichi MS are actually contrafacta of French chansons and include the French text incipits, as do the contrafacta in Trent 90. The piece *Canti zoiosi* on fol. 41[v], for example, is the same as the chanson *Jay pris amours* of Japart.[12]

The tradition of setting Latin texts in secular forms and styles, a tra-

[9] G. Reese, *Music in the Renaissance* (New York 1954), p. 21.
[10] See Knud Jeppesen, *Die mehrstimmige italienische Laude um 1500* (Leipzig 1935), p. XXV.
[11] *Ibid.,* p. XVIII.
[12] *Ibid.,* p. XIX.

dition which has considerable relevance for the song-motet, had appeared early in Italy, probably because the cantus firmus technique had been foreign to Italian polyphony from the time of its origins in the 14th century. Thus it seems very likely that the original concept of the song-motet and/or contrafactum can be attributed to Italy. Many 15th-century contrafacta of French chansons appear in Italian or Italian-influenced sources, i.e. Trent; Florence, Bibl. Naz. Magliab. XIX, 112bis; and the Schedel Liederbuch. One of the earliest contrafacta is Ciconia's O beatum incendium,[13] and many of Ciconia's other motets, while not contrafacta, are composed in the style and form of the madrigal.[14] There are also to be found quite a few miscellaneous Latin pieces set in vernacular forms among Italian sources around 1400. These have been referred to vaguely as Latin ballades, chanson motets or motet ballades.

In the Modena MS α.M.5.24 (L 568) there are five Latin ballades and a Latin virelai. The Chantilly MS contains one of the same ballades as Modena, plus another one and a Latin virelai, all three of which have been described as being "paraliturgical" pieces. The Oxford MS Canonici 213 includes three Latin pieces termed "laude," one of which reappears in the Bologna MS Q 15 with eight other Latin pieces designated as laude.

The works in Modena appear to be predominantly secular except for the one piece by Mayshuet, Inclite flos and possibly Bartolomeo da Bologna's Arte psalentes. The six pieces are:

No. 15 (fol. 12ᵛ) Sumite carissimi a 3, Zacharias. (ballade)
No. 25 (fol. 16ᵛ) Inclite flos a 3, anon., but attributed to Mayshuet in Chantilly (No. 62). (ballade)
No. 63 (fol. 34) Ore pandulfum a 3, anon. (ballade)
No. 71 (fol. 37ᵛ) Veri almi pastoris a 3, Corrado da Pistoia. (ballade)
No. 72 (fol. 38) Quae pena a 3, Bartolomeo da Bologna. (virelai)
No. 73 (fol. 38ᵛ) Arte psalentes a 3, Bartolomeo da Bologna. (ballade) [15]

Zacharias's Sumite carissimi has all the appearances of a pure French ballade, with two lines of text under the first part and a resulting form of AAB. Furthermore, it has an extensive rhymed ending between the

[13] Suzanne Clercx, Johannes Ciconia, un musicien liégeois et son temps (Brussels 1960), II, 85 and 151.
[14] Ibid., I, 61–63.
[15] Fabio Fano, Le Origini e il primo maestro di cappella: Matteo de Perugia; La cappella musicale del duomo di Milano (Milan 1956), pp. 109–38; Johannes Wolf, Geschichte der Mensural-Notation (Leipzig 1904), I, 335–39.

music of A and B of ten and one half measures.[16] Corrado's piece has
exactly the same structure and text placing but without the pronounced
rhymed musical endings.[17] Of the other three ballades, Mayshuet's
Inclite flos has a tenor designated "Pro Papa Clemente" (Clement VII)
and thus appears to be a tenor motet written in the form of a ballade,
though it does not have the rhymed endings. *Ore pandulfum* and *Arte
psalentes* both do have rhymed endings of about four and eight measures
respectively. The one virelai, *Quae pena* of Bartolomeo, also has a
rhymed ending of four measures, though this is less typical of the
virelai.[18] All six pieces are three-voiced and in a generally treble-
dominated style (i.e. while the lower two parts are rhythmically active,
they are decidedly unmelodic, having wide leaps).

Mayshuet's *Inclite flos* reappears in Chantilly (No. 62) along with
two other cantilena style pieces with sacred Latin texts: No. 10, a four-
voiced virelai entitled *Laus detur multipharia*, of which the triplum is
attributed to Petrus Fabri, and No. 77, a two-voiced ballade, *Angelorum
psalat tripudium* by S. Uciredor.[19] All three of these pieces Reaney describes as "paraliturgical," but he does not call them "laude." [20]

In the Oxford Canonici MS, however, Reaney singles out three
Latin pieces as laude and an Italian one as a lauda motet.[21] Bukofzer calls
the three Latin compositions "cantilenae" but also says that such pieces
are "related to the Italian lauda." [22] The three laude-cantilenae are
Arnold de Lantins's *In tua memoria* (No. 109) and two settings of
Verbum caro factum est (Nos. 15 and 16, the first of which is incomplete and in a later hand). Both of the two complete laude are built like
the virelai, although the ripresa and volta of *Verbum caro factum est* are
identical musically.[23] Bukofzer has observed that the melody of this
latter piece is carried in the tenor and that this same tenor recurs in three

[16] Published in Johannes Wolf, *Geschichte*, III, 168. See also II, 127.
[17] *Ibid.*, III, 161. See also II, 120.
[18] *Ibid.*, III, 164. See also II, 122.
[19] See Gilbert Reaney, *The Manuscript Chantilly, Musée Condé 1047*, in: *Musica
disciplina*, VIII (1954), 88, 91, and 92. Reaney assumes that S. Uciredor is an inversion of the name Rodericus (see p. 78).
[20] *Ibid.*, pp. 61–62.
[21] Gilbert Reaney, *The Manuscript Oxford, Bodleian Library, Canonici misc. 213*,
in: *Musica disciplina*, IX (1955), 87, 92, and 103. Reaney describes Dufay's *Vergine
bella* (No. 312) as a lauda motet (p. 103). Dufay's piece, however, seems like a typical example of a pure Italian lauda in many respects. It is strikingly similar to the
vernacular lauda from the Venice MS published by Jeppeson in *Laude*, p. XXII,
Padre del cielo.
[22] Manfred Bukofzer, *Studies in Medieval and Renaissance Music* (New York
1950), p. 149, fn. 59.
[23] Published in Charles Van den Borren, ed., *Polyphonia sacra* (London 1932),
pp. 267 (No. 109) and 290–91 (Nos. 15 and 16).

settings of the text in Venice, Bibl. Marc. MS Ital. IX, 145.[24] Thus the melody of *Verbum caro factum est* seems to serve as a cantus firmus, functioning very much like those of the tenor motets.[25]

Certainly at this point the lauda and motet begin to be confusable. The laude had not originally been cantus firmus compositions, but from now on they appear to borrow melodies associated with certain texts quite frequently. *Verbum caro factum est* is a particularly interesting case. The text was a popular one in the 15th century (other settings are found in Florence, Bibl. Naz. Magliab. XIX, 112bis, fols. 47ᵛ–49, 59ᵛ, and 60, i.e. three settings, and Trent No. 1374) and Gaspar van Weerbecke's setting was published by Petrucci as a motet (*Motetti B*) and then had its text changed when part of it appeared in the second book of laude.

By the mid-15th century, polyphonic Latin laude begin to appear in increasing numbers. In the earlier part of the century they are still scattered in various manuscripts, principally Bologna, Conservatorio Q 15 (olim 37); Bologna, Biblioteca Universitaria 2216; London, B.M. Add. 29987; and Rome, Vatican Urb. lat. 1419. But by the second half of the century they are amply represented in Venice, Bibl. Marc. MS Ital. IX, 145.[26]

The Bologna MS Q 15, dated around 1430, contains a setting of *Verbum caro factum est* by Lymburgia (No. 283) but one which is totally unrelated to the melody of the Oxford and Venice versions. It has also the Arnold de Lantins *In tua memoria* from Oxford and four other laude by Lymburgia, three of which are Latin (No. 166 *Recordare frater pia*, No. 170 *Salve salus mea*, and No. 266 *Salve virgo regia*). In addition there are four Latin laude which are anonymous: No. 172 *Ave fuit prima salus*, No. 180 *In nataly domini gaudent*, No. 269 *Dilecto Yhesu Christi*, and No. 285 *Gaude, flore virginali*.[27]

Both Arnold de Lantins and Lymburgia seem to be key figures in this fusion of the Netherlands motet with the lauda traditions. Both were probably Netherlanders from the province of Liège, and while nothing is known about Lymburgia, de Lantins is known to have been in the Papal chapel for a few months in 1431–32.[28] Lymburgia is the more widely represented by laude in the Bologna manuscript, but de Lantins appears in both Oxford and Bologna. The lauda of de Lantins, *In tua memoria*,

---

[24] Fol. 1, fols. 104–104ᵛ and fols. 116–118ᵛ. See Bukofzer, *Studies*, p. 149, fn. 59.
[25] Jeppesen mentions several monophonic laude, *Verbum caro factum est* among them, which were frequently used as cantus firmi. See *Laude*, p. XX.
[26] *Ibid.*, p. XXI.
[27] Guillaume de Van, *Inventory of Manuscript Bologna, Liceo musicale Q 15* (*olim 37*), in: *Musica disciplina*, II (1948), 231–57.
[28] Reese, MR, p. 39.

does not differ markedly in style from his two motets on texts from the Song of Solomon in Oxford, *Tota pulchra es* and *O pulcherrima mulierum*,[29] although the form of the lauda is that of a virelai, while the two motets are through-composed.

The Bologna University MS 2216 contains ten Latin laude which Besseler designates as "lauda motets," among which are three concordances with Bologna Q 15.[30] The ubiquitous *Verbum caro factum est* appears here, as does the text *O quam suavis est*, which later became so popular for polyphonic settings.

The Venice MS IX, 145 contains the largest number of laude, those in the first part of the manuscript being from the earlier half of the 15th century while the second section, which appears to be a later addition, is in an Italian hand of the later 15th century.[31] One rather surprising feature of the Venice MS is the apparently retrogressive tendency toward reduction of voices, since a great many of them are for only two, whereas earlier sources had a majority of three-voiced laude. Among the pieces in the first section are Dufay's *Ave Regina*, a setting of *Benedicamus Domino*, and Binchois's *Ut queant laxis à fauxbourdon*. Thus it appears that hymn texts as well as antiphons have invaded the realm of the lauda. The later part of the manuscript also has a *Benedicamus Domino* (fol. 93), a *Pange lingua gloriosi* (fols. 91^v–92), and two settings of *Verbum caro factum est*. The lower voice of one of these (fols. 104–104^v) provides the upper voice of the next Latin lauda in the manuscript, *Ave fuit prima salve* (fols. 108^v–109). These compositions were all called "laude" by the compiler of the first part of the Venice MS, or at least by the binder, for the volume actually bears the inscription "22/ Laudi sacre/ antiche." [32] Possibly the Italians simply used the term "lauda" to designate what others called "motets," but if so, one wonders why Petrucci made a distinction in his publications between books of laude and books of motets.

Certainly by the end of the century the Latin lauda does not seem to have any textual or stylistic features that distinguish it unmistakably from the motet. Many of the same texts, often strictly liturgical, were used for both lauda and motet, and stylistically the Latin laude in Petrucci's publications are far more contrapuntally ornate than the simple chordal frottole to which they are so often related. They are

[29] *Polyphonia sacra*, pp. 262 and 269.
[30] Heinrich Besseler, *The Manuscript Bologna biblioteca universitaria 2216*, in: *Musica disciplina*, VI (1952), 51.
[31] Knud Jeppesen, *Ein venezianisches Laudenmanuskript*, in: *Theodor Kroyer-Festschrift* (Regensburg 1933), 69–76.
[32] *Ibid.*, p. 70.

actually much closer to the motet, and in fact the same music sometimes appears as a motet in one Petrucci publication and as a lauda in another: note the five concordances between *Motetti B* (1503) and the lauda books (1507 and 1508).[33] Possibly the so-called frottola influence on the Netherlandish motet was accomplished through the lauda, but it must be equally true that the lauda was influenced by the contrapuntal style of the motet. In any case, the exchange of music from motet to lauda publications is striking. The first part of Josquin's motet *Tu solus qui facis mirabilia* appears in Petrucci's second book of laude with the text *O mater dei et homines*.[34] Two pieces of Gaspar van Weerbecke that appeared originally in Petrucci's *Motetti B* reappear, at least in part, among the laude of the second book: the motet *Verbum caro factum est* becomes the lauda *O inextimabilis dilectio caritatis*,[35] and his *Panis angelicus* from *Motetti B* becomes *Ave panis angelorum* in *Laude II*.[36] In almost all cases of motets being changed into laude, only part of the motet is preserved. Curiously enough, the same text is not used for both lauda and motet with the same music, even though at least one of the texts involved had been used interchangeably (i.e. *Verbum caro factum est*).[37] One other example of identical motet and lauda settings suggests that the lauda was the original and the motet a contrafactum. *Lauda Sion* (No. 6 in Jeppesen), from the second book of laude, paraphrases the very beginning of the chant melody belonging to that text, while the version in *Motetti B* has an entirely different text, *Gaude virgo mater Christi*.[38]

In the matter of priority it is also interesting to note in a comparison of lauda and motet using identical texts but different music that the lauda is more authentic with regard to the liturgical text. Gaspar's setting of the responsory for Good Friday, *Tenebrae factae sunt*, in *Motetti B*, has a rather free treatment, with interpolations in the text, while Spartarius's lauda adheres faithfully to the text.[39]

A surprising number of the laude around 1500 drew on cantus firmi, although never in the traditional manner of citing the entire chant. Usually only a fragment of the beginning is quoted, as in the *Lauda Sion*

[33] Jeppesen, *Laude*, p. LX.
[34] *Ibid.*, No. 25, p. 40. For the motet see Albert Smijers, ed., *Josquin des Pres: Werken* (Amsterdam 1921–), *Motetten* (1926), I, 35. See also Reese, MR, p. 258.
[35] Gerhard Croll, *Gaspar van Weerbecke, An Outline of His Life and Works*, in: *Musica disciplina*, VI (1952), 72. For the lauda see Jeppesen, *Laude*, No. 52, p. 90. For the motet see Albert Smijers, ed., *Van Ockeghem tot Sweelinck* (Amsterdam 1951), p. 174. See also Reese, MR, pp. 218–19.
[36] Croll, *Gaspar*, p. 71. For the lauda see Jeppesen, *Laude*, No. 9, p. 15.
[37] See Jeppesen, *Laude*, p. LX.
[38] *Ibid.*, pp. XLVI and LXI.
[39] For Gaspar's motet see Smijers, *Van Ockeghem tot Sweelinck*, p. 178. For the lauda see Jeppesen, *Laude*, No. 3, p. 4.

mentioned above. Foglianus's *Ave Maria* (No. 96 in Jeppesen) also makes a clear reference to the chant melody at the beginning, while *Sancta Maria* (No. 18 in Jeppesen), attributed to both Tromboncino and Cara, quotes the litany formula exactly. It is stated like a migrant cantus firmus, first in the tenor, then alto, bass, and soprano and provides an ostinato-like framework for the entire piece.[40] The litany formula also appears in many other settings, specifically those of the *Ave Maria*, of which the second part of the text is "Sancta Maria, ora pro nobis." [41] One *Ave Maria* (No. 46 in Jeppesen) also appears to have a plainsong intonation at the beginning, although no such melody for that text has survived. There are, finally, two settings of *Salve Regina*, although both are macaronic texts, merely starting with the Latin phrase and then continuing in Italian. One of these (No. 79 in Jeppesen) clearly refers to the chant melody at the beginning. Jeppesen thinks that No. 80 is also a paraphrase of that melody, but if so it is a very obscure one.[42]

Brief quotations of chant melodies at the beginnings of these laude suggest the technique used in Binchois's *Ave Regina* and Regis's *Ave Maria*, both of which state the cantus firmus melody only in part. Perhaps this was one respect in which the motet influenced the lauda. In any event, there was apparently a great deal of interaction between lauda and song-motet, for they have a strong resemblance in technique, style, form, and perhaps in function as well.

In the fusion of international styles that took place during the 15th century the role of Italy is not always clear. But it seems probable that with regard to the song-motet Italian musicians, and particularly lauda composers, were highly influential. The hitherto clear distinction between chanson and motet in French circles of the 14th and early 15th centuries was no longer maintained, and the same music, or type of music, was used indiscriminately for motet and chanson, just as in the lauda.

Probably it was this breaking down of stylistic boundary lines between 15th-century categories that was responsible for the very vagueness, or absence, of definitions of the motet. The cyclic Mass is generally clear; it was a new form based on techniques of the isorhythmic motet. The chanson is generally clear, for it remained essentially unchanged in form until the end of the century. But the motet, after losing its former

---

[40] Jeppesen, *Laude*, pp. XLVI and LXI. The music of *Sancta Maria* (No. 18) also appears as that of a frottola, *Me stesso incolpo*, in Petrucci's 4th book of frottole. Jeppesen assumes, with good reason, that the lauda was the original, since it refers to the chant melody (p. LXI).

[41] *Ibid.*, pp. XLVI and LXI. See Nos. 34, 46, 95, and 96.

[42] *Ibid.*, p. XLVII.

identity as a polytextual isorhythmic composition, became a very ill-defined form when it reached out toward both sacred and secular elements during the 15th century. Certainly the 13th- and 14th-century motet, with sacred cantus firmus and secular texts, partook of both elements, but its form and style transcended that dichotomy. The song-motet of the 15th century, on the other hand, appears to be a real stylistic anomaly and by its very contradictions is perhaps one of the most characteristic manifestations of the spirit of transition from the Middle Ages to the Renaissance.

A FADED LAUREL WREATH

by EGON KENTON

THIS PAPER is concerned with a hardly known manuscript collection of five- and six-part Italian madrigals, originally in the cupboards of the Accademia Filarmonica of Verona, now in those of the Biblioteca Capitolare of the same city. There is little doubt that they must have been written in the early years of the penultimate decade of the 16th century and that through some unrecorded and probably trivial circumstance the collection remained unpublished. The existence of the collection has been known for over 25 years, for the learned curator of that library has made available the tool so indispensable and so rare: a printed catalogue of the library's contents.[1]

Generous though the catalogue may be with information on background and history of some items, it is, nevertheless, very uncommunicative in the case of the present manuscript.[2] This is all the more frustrating as both its background and history—the purpose for which it was assembled—as well as its content, are highly interesting. The latter can be seen and described. The former must be inferred.

The inferences, as repeatedly set forth in plentiful detail by Alfred Einstein, are quite easy to draw.[3] Curiously, Einstein did not refer to this manuscript (or any other manuscript, for that matter, excepting rare cases), either in his *magnum opus* or in his scattered articles on the Italian

---

[1] G. Turrini, *Catalogo descrittivo dei manoscritti musicali antichi della Società Accademia Filarmonica di Verona*, in: *Atti e memorie della Accademia di Agricoltura, Scienze e Lettere di Verona*, Serie V, vol. xv (1937).

[2] There is, however, a reference to it in the same author's history of the Academy, in connection with the report on the salaried musician Alessandro Sfogli, a contributor to our manuscript: *L'Accademia Filarmonica di Verona dalla fondazione (Maggio 1543) al 1600, e il suo patrimonio musicale antico*, in: *Atti e memorie della Accademia di Agricoltura, Scienze e Lettere di Verona*, Serie V, vol. xviii (1941), 123, fn. 1. From this reference we quote the following: "This collection [MS 220] is not a musical anthology, but a magnificent wreath (*corona*) of madrigals in praise of a *Laura*, living glory of Mantua, who in one of the madrigals declares herself born of a *Margherita* (pearl). The wreath was probably prepared by the composition of poetic texts which then were distributed to many of the best-known and greatest composers of the times . . ."

[3] A. Einstein, *The Italian Madrigal* (Princeton 1949), mainly Vol. II, 825ff. and 844f., but also on most of the pages referred to in the Index, under the headings Bendidio, Lucrezia; Molza, Tarquinia; and Peperara, Laura.

500

madrigal. To be sure, he had left the Continent by the time Turrini's *Catalogue* appeared. On the other hand, there can be no doubt that on his very first *Italienreise* in 1904 he visited the Capitolare, and perhaps even scored some of these madrigals.[4] But the present writer, who struggled through the ink blotches of this manuscript and tortured his eyes guessing the lines of the staves or the words written in ink now yellowed and frequently disappearing, can understand if Einstein chose rather to work with prints. He had enough printed examples of the great and near great composers without having to resort to manuscripts difficult to read.

The present manuscript [5] refers to an event recorded in a printed collection that gave Einstein the opportunity for his remarks referred to above,[6] and the duplication of effort our manuscript represents is what makes it really interesting. The event was the wedding on 22 February 1583, of the highly gifted soprano, Laura Peperara.[7] The life and the extraordinary talents and charm of this young lady, daughter of a wealthy Mantuan merchant and dilettante but accomplished harpist have been described by Angelo Solerti.[8] She seems to have been taken to Ferrara by Margherita Gonzaga (daughter of Guglielmo, Duke of Mantua; sister of Vincenzo, his successor; and third and last wife of Alfonso d'Este) as a *damigella* (lady-in-waiting), and she was welcomed by the music-loving prince as an excellent addition to his ensemble of virtuoso singers. She soon became the star of the trio, and fired the imagination of poets and composers alike as much by her youthful charms and blond hair as by her beautiful voice and accomplished singing.

Two printed collections are closely related to our manuscript, both evidently assembled in honor of Laura Peperara. But while our manuscript was surely copied at about the same time as the two prints, it must be a matter of conjecture at the present time—since it bears no date—whether it followed them or was assembled at the same time as either one.

[4] Of the 22 madrigals in this collection, only three appear in his manuscript scores now in the Smith College Archives. All three were printed in 1582–83.

[5] MS 220. See Turrini, *L'Accademia Filarmonica*, pp. 194–96.

[6] *Il Lauro verde, madrigali a 6 voci di diversi autori* (Ferrara: per Vittorio Boldini, 1583). See Vogel-Einstein, *A Bibliography of Italian Secular Vocal Music*, 1582² and 1583². A collection of five-part madrigals, issued by the same printer under the title *Il Lauro secco* in the preceding year, naturally attracts attention and prompts conjectures.

[7] The event, which seems to have attracted the attention of chroniclers interested in the affairs of the courts of Mantua and Ferrara, and given an importance out of all proportion to its historical significance, was recorded in numerous letters and memoirs. It is described by Urbani, the ambassador of the Medicean court, in letters dated July 1582, and 7, 19, and 21 February 1583; in a letter of the Provost of Ferrara to the Cardinal Ercole d'Este, of 23 February 1583, and by biographers of Torquato Tasso.

[8] *Ferrara e la corte estense nella seconda metà del secolo decimosesto* (Città di Castello 1891), Cap. IX.

The chronological order of the two prints is clear not only because the dates of publication prove it, but because there is the following passage in the preface of *Il Lauro secco:* ". . . di corto porremo un'altra scielta di Madrigali, composti sopra un nuovo et verde Lauro . . ." *Il Lauro verde* can therefore be regarded as a sequel to *Il Lauro secco.*

The poets and composers of the two printed collections were recruited mainly, though not exclusively, in upper Italy by the Ferrarese Accademia dei Rinnovati. But the 1583 collection already contains a madrigal by Philippe De Monte, who sent two two-part madrigals to the Verona Filarmonica's manuscript collection from Prague. It is an open question whether the collection *Il Lauro secco* is an homage to her; [9] but there is no doubt that Verona MS 220 was assembled as a compliment to Laura Peperara. And, while all three collections contain some only more or less locally known composers, the *Lauro secco* boasts a rarity, a madrigal by Giovanni Bardi, "dei conti di Vernio"—a clear indication that the "editorial committee" was intent on making it socially glamorous, in spite of the protestations of the preface *Ai virtuosi lettori:* "In tanto noi confidati nella candida et sincera nostra intentione, per fuggir il morso degl'invidi, non la abbiamo voluto ammantarsi della protettione di alcun Prencipe, come ricerca il costume d'hoggidi, tanto più che non bramiamo altro premio della nostra fatica che la buona vestra universal gratia; in cui ci raccomandiamo." [10]

It is only natural that the Rinnovati, while clearly wishing to flatter not one prince but two—Alfonso d'Este and Vincenzo Gonzaga—wished at the same time to avoid the somewhat awkward circumstances behind the scenes, the real motive for assembling at least *Il Lauro verde:* the intense interest of the recently married Vincenzo Gonzaga in the young musician Laura Peperara. [11]

There seems to be no reason to quote here the relevant passages from the second volume of Einstein's *Italian Madrigal* referring to Laura. But a few salient facts should be mentioned to make the background of Verona MS 220 clear. Solerti relates that Alfonso d'Este took care to

[9] Solerti writes in connection with *Il Lauro verde* (1583) known to be gathered and published in her honor: "Non me è riuscito di capire in quale relazione stia [*Il Lauro verde*] con questa [*Il Lauro secco*], un'altra raccolta pubblicata poco prima," in: *Vita di Torquato Tasso* (Turin 1895), p. 364 (5).

[10] G. Gaspari, *Catalogo della biblioteca del liceo musicale* (Bologna 1905), III, 27. (There is no dedication in this print.)

[11] Cf. the Urbani correspondence (in the Biblioteca Nazionale in Florence) quoted in Solerti, *Ferrara e la corte estense*, letter of 19 March: "A secretary of the prince of Mantua came here, it is believed, for certain family affairs of that Mantuan lady who is so excellent in singing, and who enjoys the favors of the Duke so much . . ."

assure not only the present but also the future of his singing ladies by providing well-situated husbands for them. Thus, Anna Guarini was married off to a member of the noble family of the Trotti, Livia d'Arco was given as a spouse to the Marquess Alfonso Bevilacqua, and Laura Peperara became Countess Annibale Turchi. Lucrezia Bendidio became the wife of Count Paolo Macchiavelli. (She was a sister-in-law of the poet Guarini.) Only Tarquinia Molza was denied a similarly smooth and comfortable life, though not through Alfonso's negligence. This artist, perhaps the strongest talent and certainly the strongest character among her colleagues, is well known for the tragic passions she roused in Tasso and Wert, as well as for her long and stormy career.

Laura's wedding was set for as early as July 1582. And perhaps it was for this occasion that the *Lauro secco* was published. (It is a fact that the *Lauro verde* was assembled mainly through the efforts of Vincenzo.) The wedding was postponed, however, and contemporary writers—the primary sources of Solerti—openly conjectured that the reason for the postponement was the interest the young Vincenzo had in her. He was almost constantly in Ferrara and, furthermore, occupied much of his time in enriching Laura's repertory by prompting poets and musicians to write for her. Finally, the wedding was set so as to fall in the Carnival season, and Vincenzo was tireless in organizing ever new amusements in which she was entertained, while she herself kept entertaining the noble company. Concerts, balls, ballets, games, falconry, and tournaments followed each other ceaselessly, and Vincenzo himself rode in a bout in her honor.[12] All this was "the talk of the town" at princely courts as far away as Venice, Florence, and Milan. And Urbani, the Medicean ambassador, reported in his letter of 7 February 1583, that "the rumor is afoot, and I have it on good authority, that the Duke gives her ten thousand scudi as dowry; provides for her, her husband and her mother-in-law, and gives her an apartment at the court [of Mantua] that used to

[12] Solerti, *Ferrara*, p. lxxiv, quotes Urbani's letter of 21 February, according to which the prince of Mantua, who returned home for a few days, arrived again in Ferrara, bringing with him Don Ferrante Gonzaga, and "enjoying with him now the final developments of this carnivalesque intrigue which is indeed a great intrigue among those that go usually with such an occasion. There was another tournament yesterday, with the usual extravagances that make so much effect and cost so little, and tomorrow, for the conclusion of the festivities, there will be the wedding of the Lady Laura Peperara, with a tournament, the program of which I enclose, showing the ostentation and the honors done to this lady, and also the text of a grand ballet led and performed with 11 other ladies by the Duchess [Margherita], for the composition of which the Cavaliere Guarino was recalled from Venice, where he went for the negotiation of some private business of his and for some financial matters. Although the Este princes usually honored and assisted their courtiers at the occasion of their wedding, that which was done for 'la Peverara' is indeed extraordinary."

be that of Madama Leonora of happy memory," i.e. of Archduchess Leonora of Austria, Vincenzo's mother.[13]

This was the high point in the glamorous but, alas, brief life of the beautiful Laura, for she died in 1601—the same year in which Luzzaschi's madrigals, composed for her and her two colleagues Lucrezia and Tarquinia and dedicated to the Cardinal d'Este (whom Einstein calls the grave digger of Ferrara's splendor),[14] were published. In 1597 Alfonso d'Este had already died childless and his widow returned to Mantua when the duchy was joined to the Papal States. Laura, however, remained, and was buried in the Jesuit church of Ferrara. The shower of laurels she received made her immortal, and her immortality was well deserved on three grounds: her beauty, her accomplished artistry, and the love of a glamorous prince that she roused. We are left with only one riddle. For what reason did the Accademia Filarmonica of Verona, a provincial city on Venetian territory, decide to commission a score of famous composers to help it join Ferrara and Mantua in honoring this lady? Sometimes a writer of historical fiction with the divination of a poet offers a plausible hypothesis. Such a writer of history is Maria Bellonci. But her books [15] offer no clue.

Not all the members of the two ducal families were pleased about these events and rumors. But Duke Alfonso was now mainly preoccupied with the disappointment that not even his third wife was able to provide him with an heir, while Duke Guglielmo, who suffered all his life from the humiliation of being a hunchback, now retired almost completely into a solitary life.

The influence of Alfonso's famous *tre grazie* is seen throughout the late phase of the Italian madrigal. From 1580 on, the madrigal literature is full of pieces written with them in mind.[16] Marenzio wrote virtuoso parts unsingable by amateurs, such as in the six-part *Lucida perla* on Guarini's text, written for Alfonso's wedding with Margherita Gonzaga, and *La dove sono i pargoletti amori*, and the echo *O verde selvi* on Tasso's texts. Both are in the high register, and all three were published

[13] The day after the wedding the Provost of Ferrara reported about the event to Cardinal d'Este in these terms: "Yesterday morning Count Annibal Turco married Signora Peverara in the chambers of His Highness, in the presence of all the nobility. Later a beautiful tournament was held, and in the evening a most beautiful ballet, with Her Highness, the Duchess, and 11 other ladies dressed similarly, partly in white and gold, partly in tan and gold, and after supper a bout, and the feasting continued almost until daybreak." (Solerti, *Ferrara*, p. lxxv.)

[14] Einstein, *The Italian Madrigal*, II, 825.

[15] *Segreti dei Gonzaga* (Milan 1947); *idem: A Prince of Mantua, The Life and Times of Vincenzo Gonzaga*, Eng. transl. by Stuart Hood (New York 1956).

[16] Einstein, *The Italian Madrigal*, II, 829.

in his sixth book of six-part madrigals, in 1595.[17] Monteverdi also wrote for the three ladies (published in his third book [1592] and dedicated to Vincenzo; and in his fourth book [1603] No. 13).[18] Wert's eighth book (1586) is dedicated to Alfonso's "three young noblewomen." Luzzaschi's famous madrigals "*a uno, doi, e tre soprani (e cembalo)*" were written of course for them, as well as several pieces by Striggio, who not only stated the fact but described the singing style of these artists in 1584 in a letter to Grand Duke Francesco. Philippe De Monte dedicates his fourteenth book of madrigals to Alfonso and refers in the dedication to the *angeliche voci*, thus showing that the influence of these famous singers extended far beyond the narrow confines of Ferrara.[19]

II

The Ms 220 of the Accademia Filarmonica of Verona is simply entitled *De diversi a mano à 5 et 6. Madrigali*. It is complete, and to the best of the writer's knowledge, unique. It is written on paper, 282 by 210 mm. There are five partbooks, each consisting of 24 leaves, plus two flyleaves. The books are bound in robust, yellow-colored parchment, reinforced by a sheet of strong paper, in turn covered by another sheet of paper, over which horizontal, alternately rose and yellow ribbons are glued so as to bind the cover to the spine. The conservation of the books is perfect.

The calligraphy shows the typical humanistic style of the late 16th century. The text writing is characterized by the very tall *l*-s and very short *t*-s; by the well-known shortening of the diphthong *ch;* by the appendix of the letter *e'*, and by the substitution for most of the nasals of a long acute accent on the preceding vowel (só : son). The entire manuscript is the work of one single scribe, although he is not always consistent, as, for example, in the shape of the F clef.

The notation is also typically late 16th century, with the note shapes drop-like rather than oval. There are numerous ligatures, although only of one variety, *sine proprietate et cum perfectione*. Only flats (♭) and sharps (♯) are used. The latter serves as well for canceling a B♭ at the clef (the only accidental at the clef). The clefs employed are G2, C1, C2, C3, C4, F3, and F4. Time signatures are ₵ and C, with very few instances of *tempus perfectum*. Marenzio uses the latter with the sign O^3_2 or C^3_2, and also *prolatio major* with a stemless black note, and

[17] *Ibid.*, p. 675.
[18] *Ibid.*, p. 723.
[19] *Ibid.*, p 829.

the 3 after rather than before the first note. Although the copying was done carefully (there are corrections by the copyist), a few errors did slip in. Since with a few exceptions the pieces were written with virtuoso singers in mind, numerous fiorituras occur. When they are notated in eighth notes, these are tied by beams broken to follow the melodic curve. In madrigals in two *parti* the clefs are the same in both parts, except in one instance. Guami used for the *prima parte* of his madrigal G2, C2, C3, C3, F3, for *seconda parte* G2, C1, C2, C3, F3. It is to be noted that Ingegneri and Merulo set the same text.

The contents of the collections are as follows:

Verona MS 220: Thematic Index

5. Fol. 4ᵛ
a5
L. Marenzio

La   ne   l'Au - ro -   ra ap-par'

Fol. 5ʳ
2.P.

Ma   là   Ma   là   dov' è LAVR' o - ra

6. Fol. 5ᵛ
a5
L. Marenzio

Ri   -   de - an   già per le piagg'herbet - te

Fol. 6ʳ
2.P.

Piag - ge   her - be fio   -   ri

7. Fol. 6ᵛ
a5
G. Guami

LA - VRA   ch'a   l'au   -   ra

Fol. 7ʳ
2.P.

Voi   bea   -   ta Si - re - na

8. Fol. 7ᵛ
a5
C. Merulo

Men   -   tre LA - VRA gen - til

Fol. 8ʳ
2.P.

El - la gli spir - ti al-tru - i

9. Fol. 8ᵛ
a5
V. Ruffo

Tra quant-un-que il sol gi - ra   il mar cir-con   -   da

Fol. 9ʳ
2.P.

Ch'in   quel pon - to   la   men-te in gom-bra i sen - si

10. Fol. 9v

T. Massaino

Ar - bor gen- til   da le cui bel   -   le fron - de

Fol. 10r
2.P.

Man - dan per tan - te   me-ra - vi-glie ogn'ho - ra

11. Fol. 10v

(sic)   H. Vecchi

Pas - sa il pen-sier che rio mon - te ne cam- pi

Fol. 11r
2.P.

In - di mill' al-me in tor   -   -   na

12. Fol. 11v

O. Lasso

Chi non sa co - me spi - ra

Fol. 12r
2.P.

Ma quel ch'u - na sol vol - ta

13. Fol. 12v

M. A. Ingegneri

Te - ne - ra pian- t'an - cor   di ver-de Lau - ro

Fol. 13r
2.P.

A cui d'in-tor - no   i par-go- let-ti a - mo - ri

14. Fol. 13v

M. A. Pordenone

Vid' io di pre - ti - o - sa Mar-ghe - ri - ta

Fol. 14r
2.P.

Con faccia essangue chia - mai mer - cè

15. Fol. 14ᵛ   A. Gabrieli

a5

Se   per la-sciar di   te me-moria e- ter - na

Fol. 15ʳ

2.P.

Che   d'un bel LA -VRO   le do-ra- te chio-me

16. Fol. 15ᵛ   G. Gabrieli

a5

Quan - do LA - VRA c'hor tan-to il-lu- str'e be - a

Fol. 16ʳ

2.P.

Que - ste fu - ron bel - lez - ze et ho - nes - ta - te

17. Fol. 16ᵛ   M. Asola

a5

Lu - me di-vin a cui vo-land' in-tor -   -   no

Fol. 17ʳ

2.P.

E   fuor de l'al - ga

18. Fol. 17ᵛ   V. Bell'Haver

a5

Spi - ra dal va -   go sen' del Min -   cio LA - VRA

Fol. 18ʳ

2.P.

Ster- po herba ram'   o fron - de

19. Fol. 18ᵛ   P. Valenzola

a5

Nel   gior - no ch'el - la nac - que

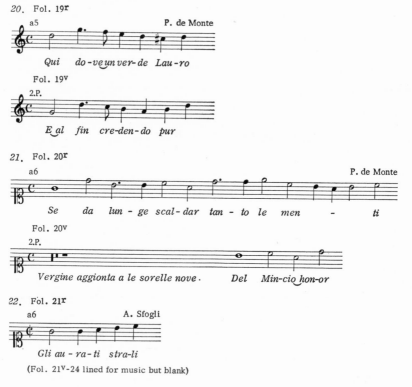

20. Fol. 19ʳ

a5   P. de Monte

Qui   do-ve un ver- de Lau -ro

Fol. 19ᵛ

2.P.

E al   fin   cre-den- do   pur

21. Fol. 20ʳ

a6   P. de Monte

Se   da   lun - ge scal- dar tan - to le   men   -   ti

Fol. 20ᵛ

2.P.

Vergine aggionta a le sorelle nove .   Del   Min-cio hon-or

22. Fol. 21ʳ

a6   A. Sfogli

Gli au - ra- ti stra-li

(Fol. 21ᵛ-24 lined for music but blank)

This is as they appear in the cantus part. The other parts follow this order—only one part appears on a page, the bottom of the page left empty if the part is short—except in the quintus part, in which the sextus parts of the two six-part madrigals are included, thus making this part three pages longer.

The manuscript, then, contains 22 madrigals by 18 composers. Seven of the composers—Andrea Gabrieli, Ingegneri, Marenzio, Massaino, Merulo, Striggio, and Vecchi—contributed to the *Lauro secco*, and five—Andrea Gabrieli, Marenzio, De Monte, Striggio, and Vecchi—to the *Lauro verde*.

Of the 22 madrigals six can be found in contemporary prints:

Guami, *Laura ch'a laura—Voi beata*, in: *Il terzo libro di madrigali a 5 voci* (Gardano 1584)

Ingegneri, *Mentre Laura—Ella gli spirti* and *Tenera pianta—A cui d'intorno*, in: *Quarto libro di madrigali a 5 voci* (Gardano 1583). Modern edition in Cesari, *La musica in Cremona nella seconda metà del secolo XVI, Istituzioni e monumenti dell'arte musicale italiana* VI (1939).

Lasso, *Chi non sa—Ma quel ch'una*, in: *Quinto libro di madrigali a 5 voci* (Gardano 1585); and *Madrigali a quattro, cinque et sei voci* (Gerlach 1587). (Vogel ignores the 1585 print.)

Marenzio, *Ridean già—Piagge herbe*, in: *Terzo libro di madrigali a 5 voci* (Gardano 1582).

De Monte, *Qui dove un—E al fin credendo*, in: *Undicesimo libro di madrigali a 5 voci* (Gardano 1586).

The others may be considered at the present time as unpublished.

Except for Merulo's *S'è ver Donna gentile*, Valenzola's *Nel giorno ch'ella nacque*, and Sfogli's *Gli aurati strali*, all the madrigals have a *seconda parte*. These three are interspersed among the others, the succession of the madrigals being determined by the clefs of the voices, so that those with the same, or similar, voice-groupings might easily be found by the performers, and the necessity of turning several pages avoided.

This grouping of the madrigals will be clearly seen in the following table.

Ingegneri	Mentre Laura	C1 C3 C4 C4 F4
	Ella gli spirti	C1 C3 C4 C4 F4
Merulo	S'è ver Donna	C1 C2 C3 C4 F4
Striggio	Alma città	C1 C3 C4 C4 F4
	Ma dov'è	C1 C3 C4 C4 F4
Carteri	Pianta cara	C1 C3 C4 C4 F4
	Felice agricoltor	C1 C3 C4 C4 F4
Marenzio	La ne l'Aurora	C1 C3 C3 C4 F4
	Ma la dov'è	C1 C3 C3 C4 F4
	Ridean già	G2 G2 C2 C3 C4
	Piagge herbe	G2 G2 C2 C3 C4
Guami	Laura ch'a l'aura	G2 C2 C3 C3 F3
	Voi beata Sirena	G2 C1 C2 C3 F3
Merulo	Mentra Lavra	G2 C1 C2 C3 F3
	Ella gli spirti	G2 C1 C2 C3 F3
Ruffo	Tra quantunque	G2 C2 C3 C3 F3
	Ch'in quel ponto	G2 C2 C3 C3 F3
Massaino	Arbor gentil	G2 G2 C2 C3 F3
	Mandan per tante	G2 G2 C2 C3 F3
Vecchi	Passa il pensier	C1 C2 C4 C4 F4
	Indi mill'alme	C1 C2 C4 C4 F4
Lasso	Chi non sa come	C1 C2 C4 C4 F4
	Ma quel ch'una	C1 C2 C4 C4 F4
Ingegneri	Tenera piant'ancor	C1 C1 C3 C4 F4
Pordenone	A cui d'intorno	C1 C1 C3 C4 F4
	Vid'io	C1 C3 C4 C4 F4
	Con faccia essangue	C1 C3 C4 C4 F4

A. Gabrieli	Se per lasciar	G_2 C_2 C_3 C_3 C_4
	Che d'un bel	G_2 C_2 C_3 C_3 C_4
G. Gabrieli	Quando Laura	G_2 C_2 C_2 C_3 F_3
	Queste furon bellezze	G_2 C_2 C_2 C_3 F_3
Asola	Lume divin	G_2 C_2 C_3 C_3 F_3
	E fuor de l'alga	G_2 C_2 C_3 C_3 F_3
Bell'Haver	Spira del vago	G_2 G_2 C_2 C_3 C_4
	Sterpo herba	G_2 G_2 C_2 C_3 C_4
Valenzola	Nel giorno	G_2 C_2 C_3 C_3 F_3
De Monte	Qui dove un	G_2 G_2 C_2 C_3 C_4
	E alfin credendo	G_2 G_2 C_2 C_3 C_4
	Se da lunge scaldar	C_1 C_1 C_3 C_3 C_4 F_4
	Vergine	C_1 C_1 C_3 C_3 C_4 F_4
Sfogli	Gli aurati strali	C_1 C_1 C_3 C_4 F_4 F_4

INGEGNERI auspiciously opens the collection. He was a native of Verona and a pupil of Vincenzo Ruffo, likewise Verona-born. He was, in turn, the teacher—or acknowledged teacher—of Marenzio and Monteverdi, two of the greatest exponents of the madrigal. His *Mentre Laura gentil —Ella gli spirti altrui* shows him as a master of the "classic" madrigal, in which melodic invention and technical manipulation of the material (imitation and counterpoint) are equally perfect. Although the beginning is imitative, the alto and quinto voices open the piece in thirds, and set the stage for a "harmonic" treatment. The virtuosity of the *tre dame* is ignored, and the sole aim is the sensitive musical setting of the text. The same mood pervades his second piece, *Tenera piant' ancor—A cui d'intorno.*

Merulo's *S'è ver Donna gentile* perhaps suffers from its juxtaposition to Ingegneri and he possibly found the exaggerated praise of the text heaped on Laura a little too much. At any rate, he did not set a *seconda parte.*

Anyone unacquainted with the type of talented and well-educated Italian dilettante of the Renaissance period—or for that matter with his modern counterpart, still abounding in Italy—should read Einstein's pages devoted to Alessandro Striggio,[20] a nobleman born in Mantua and in the service of Cosimo, later of Francesco, de' Medici. He was a frequent guest at the courts of Mantua and Ferrara, and wrote for the three ladies, whom he describes in a letter to Grand Duke Francesco as *queste signore dame, anzi angioli del paradiso,* not only in Ferrara, but even in Florence when, in 1586, Alfonso d'Este sent them there to sing at the

[20] *Ibid.*, pp. 761–72. See also Ray J. Tadlock, *Alessandro Striggio, Madrigalist,* in: JAMS, XI (1958), 29.

wedding of Don Cesare d'Este and Virginia de' Medici. Striggio was a Renaissance man, i.e. versatile. Basically, he was serious. And his second offering to the "angels," *Alma città—Ma dov'è quel che già di Troia*, is serious, and to be taken seriously.

Bartolomeo Carteri is as good as unknown outside Verona. We find first mention of him in the contract drawn up on 31 December 1564, between the old Accademia degli Incatenati and the Accademia Filarmonica (founded in 1543), that set the terms for the union of the two academies. Carteri is mentioned in Article 8, which refers to the status of individual members, and which names him as *Compagno esente* (exempt member).[21] He ran a music school in Verona, and became a "factotum" of the Filarmonica, acting toward the end of his life as its treasurer, custodian of its house, and general counsel and manager.[22] Carteri, in his *Pianta cara e gentil—Felice agricoltor*, refers to the laurel tree rather than to Laura. Nevertheless, he favors the upper three voices, even though he sets them in soprano, alto, and tenor clefs. He evidently chose Ruffo and Ingegneri as models, but his music is timid rather than classic, with its tone repetitions and frequent fifth steps.

Marenzio's close connections with the court of Ferrara, with Tasso, and even with the three ladies are too well known to need repeating. He composed for the three ladies long before the social event celebrated in our manuscript, simply on order of his master, Cardinal Luigi d'Este.[23]

Giuseppe Guami is one of those many fine Italian composers whose fame suffers from neglect. We know next to nothing of his music. Yet, if we read Giovanni Gabrieli's recommendation,[24] which was perhaps the basis of his having been appointed in 1585 as organist at San Marco in the place of the recently deceased Vincenzo Bell'Haver, we feel we should at least have a dissertation on it. His madrigal *LAVRA ch'a l'aura —Voi beata Sirena* is a beautifully serene piece, wistful and nobly elegiac, from the expressive initial apostrophizing in descending major thirds with an ensuing pause that makes it sound like a sigh, to the sad and resigned ending. Guami disregards the opportunity offered by the virtuosity of the lady singers and spreads the sound as well as the fio
rituras

[21] Turrini, *L'Accademia Filarmonica*, p. 142.

[22] *Ibid.*, p. 145.

[23] Hans Engel, in his monograph, *Luca Marenzio* (Florence 1956), does not mention the madrigal *La ne l'Aurora—Ma la dov'è LAVR'ora* in his list of works, nor does it appear in the bibliography of Vogel and in the revision by Einstein. It is, therefore, missing in the Complete Works as well. *Ridean le piagge—Piagge herbe* is to be found in Vol. II of the Complete Works.

[24] See E. Kenton, *Giovanni Gabrieli, His Life and Works*, Chapter II, now in press, *American Institute of Musicology in Rome, Studies and Documents*.

evenly from soprano to basso. His style is classic, but the harmony is spiced with the Venetian cross-relations. The texture inclines to Venetian homophony.

Merulo's second, and this time two-part, madrigal *Mentre LAVRA gentil—Ella gli spirti altrui* immortalizes Laura without restraint.

> Mentre LAVRA gentil che'l Mincio honora,
> Immortal Donna, anzi pur vera Dea,
> Con le candide man l'arpa premea
> Sparger fior per lo ciel parea l'Aurora.
>
> Fra perle uscian note amorose all'hora
> Dagl'occhi un lampo che d'intorno ardea,
> Onde con mille modi amor tessea
> Meraviglie tra noi non viste ancora.

Merulo was 24 years older than Giovanni Gabrieli, but the homophonic texture of his madrigal and its chordal declamation are very much like those found in the motets of his successor at the organ of San Marco. There is even a hint at divided choirs. We should like to compare the styles of the two. But where are the collected works of Merulo? It is also interesting to compare this madrigal with Ingegneri's on the same text. It is surprising to find that Ingegneri, Merulo's junior by 12 years, seems to belong to a preceding generation. The reason may be seen in Ingegneri's conservative temperament and in the progressive atmosphere of Venice, which carried away all those who breathed its soft and tangy sea breeze and saw its incredible pastel-colored air. That atmosphere influenced music as much as painting and gives the clue to Merulo's sensitive music.

A negative proof of the influence of Venice may be seen in the following piece, Vincenzo Ruffo's *Tra quantunque il sol gira—Ch'in quel ponto*, a serious madrigal with imitative beginning and rather dense texture which leaves the emotions, so frequently moved in these madrigals —and generally in madrigals—untouched. The texts naturally play an important, although not exclusive, role in stirring the emotions of singers as well as of listeners.[25]

Since these 22 madrigals were assembled for one common purpose, even though it will probably never be known precisely which texts were composed expressly for this collection, it would seem appropriate to look at their subjects and character. They may be divided into two cate-

---

[25] We have not advanced very much beyond the point Einstein described in his short note on Ruffo's *Opera nova di musica*, in: JAMS, III (1950), 233. Again one must sadly note that, in spite of the many articles published yearly, we are rather poorly enlightened on the Italian music of the late 16th century, principally because of the paucity of *Opere complete* of the Italian composers of that period.

gories, those that have Laura as a subject, and those that concentrate on either the laurel tree, or the Mincio, as attributes of Laura (much as the attributes of saints would be exploited by the Renaissance painter) in order to wax philosophical or allegorical about them in a poetically exaggerated way. Thus, the large lake formed around Mantua by the Mincio would become a sea, and even the sun and the stars would appear to have the sole purpose of being reflected in Laura's blond tresses.

Massaino's *Arbor gentil—Mandan per tante* is an example of the madrigal with narrative rhythm—we shall return to this point—and sprightly elegance. And Massaino himself is another example of an Italian whose work is hardly known today, although he appears in print in the best company—Wert, Andrea Gabrieli, Vecchi, Bell'Haver, Merulo—in celebrating Bianca Capello (Vogel-Einstein, 1579[2]).

If there is one man among the great figures in the history of the madrigal whose still-outstanding up-to-date collected works we miss most, it is Orazio Vecchi. In spite of an excellent monograph on him,[26] and in spite of Einstein's enthusiastic description of his creative nature and merits,[27] we have only a spotty picture of his total *oeuvre*. On his connections with Venice and Mantua we learn a great deal from Einstein. His talent in entertaining, his sense of humor and virtuosity in composing appear clearly in the lively piece *Passa il pensier—Indi mill'alme* he contributed to our collection.

Lasso's beautiful contribution, *Chi non sa come spira—Ma quel ch'una sol volta*, was printed in 1585, in his fifth book of five-part madrigals. It was also printed in 1587 in Nuremberg, by Katharina Gerlach. Sandberger published it in his sixth volume of Lasso's *Werke*, where he remarks that there is no reference in the Gerlach print to the fact that it was previously printed in a *Libro Quinto*. Although Lasso by this time was an elderly man and, as Einstein states, the specific master of the Counter Reformation who now confined himself to religious madrigals, and who even in his "newly composed" madrigals (1585) uses the poems of two ascetic poets—Petrarch and Gabriel Fiamma—exclusively,[28] his *Chi non sa* is far from being religious or ascetic. To be sure, it is serious. Lasso's mastery appears at the very beginning—chordal, wistful, and chromatic—with a diminished fourth on the word *soavemente*. As usual, Lasso translates the text into music briefly and expressively.

Not much is to be said of Pordenone, a minor master on the periphery

---

[26] T. C. Hol, *Horatio Vecchis weltliche Werke* (Leipzig-Zürich 1934). See also T. C. Hol, *Horatio Vecchi*, in: *Rivista Musicale Italiana*, XXXVII (1930), 59.
[27] *The Italian Madrigal*, I, 455-71.
[28] *Ibid.*, II, 494.

of the Venetian orbit who succeeded in publishing a respectable number of compositions. His madrigal *Vid'io di pretiosa Margherita—Con faccia essangue* is clear and limpid.

In contrast, Andrea Gabrieli's contribution, *Se per lasciar di te memoria eterna—Che d'un bel LAVRO le dorate chiome* is sheer pleasure. Although 11 of the 18 composers start their pieces with a subject of dactylic beginning, Andrea widens this characteristic of the instrumental canzona throughout his madrigal in a gay mood, to include the canzona's texture and its very spirit. Indeed, the score almost gives the impression of an instrumental piece, *buono da cantare et sonare*. Andrea was of course a master of music in a gay mood. (It can be said to be in the Ionian mode.) One may even detect three almost distinct sections in each part, and a close relationship between subjects and developments of the two parts. The whole so resembles material, texture, and development found in Giovanni's works that it can be accepted as one of the models the nephew took to emulate.

The nephew's contribution, *Quando LAVRA—Queste furon bellezze*, follows that of the uncle. Giovanni—if he composed the piece toward the end of 1582 (the wedding took place on 22 February 1583) —was 25 years of age and, as can safely be surmised, an accredited substitute organist at San Marco, who regularly played there if his uncle or Merulo were indisposed or otherwise occupied. He was given a text that clearly speaks for Vincenzo Gonzaga:

> Il Mincio e le sue rive imperla e inostra
> La ve' con desio ardente io l'attendea
> . . . . fu ogni
> Mio ardir c'humile a lei la chiave
> Donai de la mia cara libertate.

The text mentions also the *honorata giostra*, the noble joust; Laura's beauty and fame—*tanto illustre e bea*—and her attainments, *dolce e soave voce e d'un arpa insolito concento*. (Since other texts refer to the harp, it seems not only her father but she also played this instrument.) The music itself is not as glamorous as the occasion—or some other madrigals of Giovanni. It is a *madrigale chromatico*, gay and nimble as Andrea's. And just as tightly knit. The initial bouncing subject appears in three voices in imitation, with a countersubject in two of the voices. The related subject of the *seconda parte*, however, appears chordally. The end brings the final repetition so characteristic of Giovanni.

Perhaps one may be pardoned the liberty of mentioning in one breath the madrigals of Asola and Bell'Haver, two respectable masters. The reason is that both illustrate so perfectly Einstein's theory on the narrative rhythm in the madrigal.[29] Einstein's contention, in brief, is that up to 1542, when De Rore's revolutionary madrigals were printed, the madrigal was formalistic. It adhered strictly to the poetic form of *octave* and *sestet*. After 1542 every idea and every image and emotional value in the text was exploited. The reason for the formalism was the narrative beginning of the text. And Palestrina's *Vestiva i colli* became so popular because it was not formalistic. In fact, it has an instrumental setting, i.e. instrumental from the Italian point of view, since it follows the pattern of the *canzon francese*—originally vocal of course. The madrigals of Asola and Bell'Haver in this collection are canzoni francesi also, and so is Andrea Gabrieli's *Se per lasciar*. Andrea followed Palestrina's model also, and so did Ingegneri in his *Tenera piant'ancor*.

Valenzola's *Nel giorno ch'ella nacque* belongs to the same category. This Spaniard, composer and singer, scored a great success in Verona in September 1569. He was immediately engaged by the Filarmonica, but only as a *salariato*, not as a *maestro*. He may have had higher designs, however, for he left after only a few months, even though his salary was doubled after one month.[30]

De Monte, the great counterpart of Lasso, and the most prolific madrigal composer, is represented here by two madrigals, the five-part *Qui dove un verde LAVRO—E alfin credendo pur*, and the six-part *Se da lunge scaldar—Vergine aggionta alle sorelle*.[31] De Monte was in touch with Italy until his death and published in Venice madrigals composed in Vienna and Prague. He dedicated his 11th book of five-part madrigals to Count Mario Bevilacqua, the great patron of the Accademia Filarmonica of Verona, and knew of and composed for the *angeliche voci* in Ferrara. Yet, it is an open question whether he knowingly contributed to our collection. True, these madrigals are rather melismatic, but this is a general characteristic of his madrigals of the 1580s. He does not let all the voices participate in the imitation; but neither does he favor the upper three voices. It is incontestable that these two madrigals are among the most elegant compositions of the collection.

The rear is brought up by the six-part madrigal *Gli aurati strali* by Alessandro Sfogli. The very name of this composer is unknown outside Verona, and we are indebted to Turrini for the following:

"Alessandro Sfogli (Sfoi, Sfoil), magiaro, autore e forse certamente

---

[29] Einstein, *Narrative Rhythm in the Madrigal*, in: MQ, XXIX (1943), 485.
[30] Turrini, *L'Accademia Filarmonica*, p. 159 .
[31] The first one was printed in Monte's 11th book of five-part madrigals (Gardano 1586); the second is not listed in any of the eight books of six-part madrigals in the bibliography of G. van Doorslaer, *La Vie et les oeuvres de Philippe De Monte* (Brussels 1921), pp. 92ff.

anche scrittore del Ms. 222, madrigali a 5 voci, fu assunto come musico dell'Accademia il 25 maggio 1560 e vi rimase fino al termine del secolo, prestando un servizio intelligente e fedele." [32]

Turrini supplements this information in his history of the Academy: "Il 25 maggio 1560 entrava come musico 'suonatore di strumento di tasto,' propriamente di arpicordo, Alessandro Sfogli (Sfoi, di Fois), magiaro (o ungherese) con salario di 12 scudi all'anno. Compositore eccellente a fecondo, serve fedelmente, devotamente la Compagnia sino alla morte, avvenuta qualche giorno dopo la metà di maggio del 1591." [33]

To this information may be added that among the Italian musicians imported by King Matthias (Corvinus) of Hungary (1458–90) to his court, there was a singer Michelangelo Sfogli, employed in the choir of the Church of Our Lady (now commonly known as the Matthias or Coronation Church). Possibly he may have returned to Italy after the debacle of 1526, perhaps with a son and grandson born in Hungary.[34] Turrini mentions another Hungarian, Francheschin Maggiar, *musico popolano*, employed in certain solemnities on 1 May 1570, in Verona.[35]

IN THE foreword to his catalogue of the treasures of the Biblioteca Capitolare of Verona—as distinct from that of the Accademia Filarmonica [36]—Turrini states that Italy has large and small libraries, ecclesiastic and secular ones, the great ones of the Academies and Conservatories, the little ones of the chapels, and the numberless private collections—and that they are sources of frequent and happy discoveries.

This writer takes the liberty to add that if Turrini's many colleagues would emulate his example in publishing catalogues, the *lauro*, the *arbor gentil* that is the music in the Renaissance, would forever truly remain *verde*.

[32] Turrini, *Catalogo* (see fn. 1), p. 162.
[33] Turrini, *L'Accademia Filarmonica*, p. 122. There follow details about his work, his duties, and his compositions.
[34] The writer is indebted for this information to Prof. Antal Molnár in Budapest.
[35] Turrini, *op. cit.*, p. 162.
[36] Turrini, *Il patrimonio musicale della Biblioteca Capitolare di Verona dal secolo XV al XIX*, in: *Atti e memorie della Accademia di Agricoltura, Scienze e Lettere di Verona*, Serie VI, vol. ii (1950-51).

BYRD, TALLIS, AND THE
ART OF IMITATION

by JOSEPH KERMAN

THE HISTORY OF imitation is a key topic in Renaissance musicology. Our understanding of "the central musical language" owes a great deal to analyses of minutiae of imitative technique, to hypotheses about its evolution, and to interpretations of its changing structural role. In England, away from the center, imitation like everything else developed in its own fitful way, with one eye on older Continental practice, and the other eye turned insular-inward. "The English were in no haste," as Gustave Reese puts it, "to adopt the main musical characteristic of the Late Renaissance." [1] Laggard or not, however, the development must presumably be well charted before any serious stylistic exploration can be made of Tudor music. The groundwork has been laid in *Music in the Renaissance*. More recently details have been filled in by Frank Ll. Harrison, in the later chapters of *Music in Medieval Britain*— English historians are in no haste to terminate their Middle Ages—and in his admirable chapters for Volumes III and IV of *The New Oxford History of Music*.

Around 1500, Fayrfax and the composers of the Eton Manuscript were not employing much imitation in their most important compositions. These were elaborate Masses, Magnificats, and votive antiphons for five, six, or even more voices, composed with or without cantus firmus in alternating sections for full choir and for semi-choir *a 2, a 3, a 4,* etc. Taverner, who is said to have quit music by 1530, employed the technique more freely, but in "full" sections imitative writing is still only incidental. The large votive antiphons of Tallis, however, and those of William Mundy, recently published by Harrison,[2] come to drop the cantus firmus altogether and rely on imitation almost constantly both in "full" and in semi-choir sections. Heir to the great votive antiphon in the 1550s and 1560s was the extended psalm setting. Composed first of all in the very same prolix sectional form, this was gradually shortened and

---

[1] Gustave Reese, *Music in the Renaissance* (New York 1954), p. 778.
[2] Frank Ll. Harrison, ed. *Early English Church Music*, II (London 1963).

homogenized into a moderately-scaled motet *a 5* or *a 6* characterized by "continuous full treatment in imitative style." Such works are—at last—directly comparable to Continental motets of the same time, in text, form, scope, and, at least in a general way, in style.

Imitation in "full" sections of the votive antiphons tends to be flexible and unsystematic. Individual lines often run into long melismas, and no scheme controls the spacing or pitch-placement of the entries. Imitation does not seem to have been viewed yet as an architectural device, but rather as another form of rich decoration to the leisurely flow of alternating sections—as though an invisible cantus firmus were still assuming structural responsibility. With the psalm settings, however, a very marked change takes place towards terseness of material and towards regularity, even squareness, of imitative technique. A probable impetus for this came from much smaller, simpler four-part motets, which circulated increasingly during Henry VIII's reign, and which absorbed something from the Franco-Netherlandish tradition. Tallis and Mundy, in any case, tightened their imitative style as they turned from the votive antiphon to the psalm and to the smaller motet. When they thought that imitation had to bear the weight of the structure, they could only think to make it as rigid as possible. Or so one is tempted to suppose: these composers extend phrases by means of strict, symmetrical repetitions of one kind or another; very rarely indeed do they significantly *develop* a contrapuntal idea within the course of an imitative section.

As an example, the beginning phrase of Tallis's motet *Salvator mundi* [3] may be quoted. (See Example 1.) This is the first of two settings of these words in the *Cantiones quae ab argumento sacrae vocantur*, 1575, an important joint publication by Tallis and Byrd which marked the first appearance in print for both composers. Some of the music it transmits must have been written a good deal earlier.) The construction of Tallis's phrase is simplicity itself. The subject imitates tonally, forming a contrapuntal unit five semibreves long (half notes, in the transcription; let us say "beats"); this unit repeats itself systematically down through the five voices, without transposition. No effort is made to provide a sixth entry to fill out the third unit, which remains a single one. Perhaps on this account, and in any case to good effect, a beat is skipped, and then the entire contrapuntal complex returns voice by voice, with only an occasional light alteration of the opening note of the subject or the answer.

Tallis even stresses the symmetry by leaving the bass silent in measure

[3] Tallis's motets are published in Volume VI of *Tudor Church Music, Salvator mundi* on pp. 216-18.

9, so that this measure corresponds exactly with measure 4; though in adding new lower voices in measures 6–7, he shows himself excellently sensitive to potentialities of variation. Notice the beautiful new E♮ and B♮ sonorities. The phrase does not cadence firmly, but tapers punctually to a close in the last measure of the repetition. Here new imitations on the next text-fragment enter overlapping.

A crude line-diagram may be devised to show the spacing and placement of these entries at a glance:

$$G_2\,D_4 \qquad G_2\,D_4 \qquad G_5 \qquad G_2\,D_4 \qquad G_2\,D_4 \qquad G$$

Letters refer to the initial note of the entry, subscript numbers denote the number of beats between the entry and the next one, and the spaces between letters are kept roughly proportional to the length of time between entries. Much is ignored in a diagram of this type—tonal answers, octave registers, the individual voices involved in the imitations, and the delicate variations introduced during the counter-exposition or second set of entries (indicated on the diagram by italics). Nevertheless, with the aid of such diagrams one can readily grasp the determined regularity of the opening phrases of those Tallis motets in the *Cantiones sacrae* which involve "continuous full treatment in imitative style": [4]

a 7: *Suscipe, quaeso*
$$GC_9 \qquad F_{11} \qquad C_{11} \qquad GC_9 \qquad F$$
2ᵃ pars: *Si enim*
$$GC_4 \qquad GC_4 \qquad GC_4 \qquad GC$$
(The subscript number "1" is omitted from the diagrams)

a 5: *In manus tuas*
$$GD_7 \qquad GD \text{ (the tenor does not really imitate)}$$
Salvator mundi (I)
$$G_2\,D_4 \qquad G_2\,D_4 \qquad G_5 \qquad G_2\,D_4 \qquad G_2\,D_4 \qquad G$$
O sacrum convivium
$$G_2\,DDGG_2\,D_2\,DG_2\,DDGG$$
Absterge, Domine
$$G_2\,CGDGG_2\,CGD$$
Mihi autem
$$D_3 \quad D_3 \quad D_3 \quad D_3 \quad G_7 \qquad d_2\ d_2\ d_2\ d_3\ g$$
Derelinquat impius
$$G_4 \quad E_4 \quad C_4 \quad A_6 \qquad ¢D_2¢$$

[4] The fine motet *In ieiunio et fletu* is not included here, since the opening in declamatory stretto cells, almost homophonic in feeling, seems to me rather different in principle. The diagram would go $B♭E♭G_7 \qquad AFD_5 \qquad A♭A♭C$

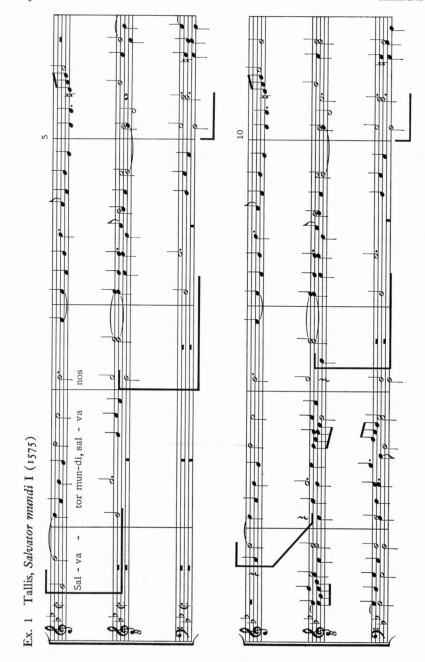

Ex. 1 Tallis, *Salvator mundi* I (1575)

Sal - va - tor mun-di, sal - va nos

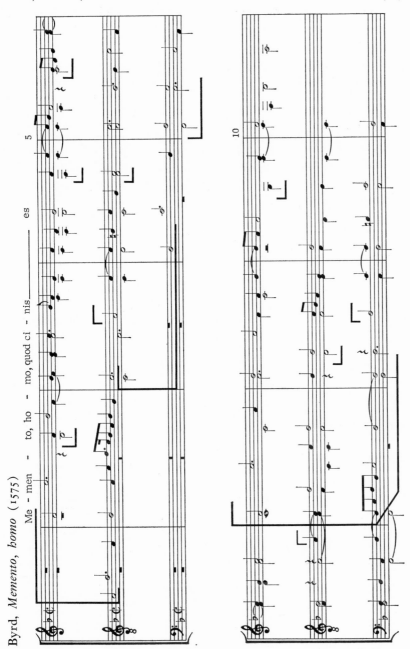

Byrd, *Memento, homo* (1575)

In *Mihi autem,* a slightly sophisticated case, the small letters on the diagram denote a free diminution of the original subject, but the counter-exposition in diminution follows almost the same strict pattern as that of the first exposition, even down to the order of the voices. Only *Derelinquat impius* is anomalous, very obviously; not only do as many as five different notes figure as initials for the entries, but symmetry is knocked out by two *very* free syncopated stretto entries (shown by "₵" and "₵" on the diagram). Quaintly enough, these unique features are associated with the words "Let the wicked forsake his way," from one of the Lenten responsories. This point of imitation is quite literally—even didactically—the exception that proves the rule.

The rule, or rather, the general principle of regularity in imitation, was followed by Tallis in his other continuously imitative motets, not printed in the *Cantiones sacrae. O salutaris hostia* affords a very striking example. The principle was also followed in one way or another by Tallis's younger contemporaries, such as Robert White, active from the late 1550s until his death in 1574, and William Mundy, active from the 1550s until his death in 1591.

The fearful symmetry of much of White's writing has been recognized ever since his music was published in Volume V of *Tudor Church Music.* "At times," the editors remarked, "we feel that he is composing by specific, mechanically, even pompously," and they went so far as to single out certain compositions in which White's "formal instinct is shown at its coldest and most calculating." [5] Mundy, who was presumably closer to Tallis and Byrd, since all three men were in the Chapel Royal, writes with only a little more variety. One of his motets opens with an imitative phrase rather along Tallis's lines:

a 6: *In aeternum*

$$A_4 \quad E_5 \quad A_2 A_3 \quad A_4 \quad E_5 \quad A_4 \quad E_5 \quad A_2 A_3 \quad A_4 \quad E$$

one shows a different but even more aggressive sort of regularity—the lower-case letters here referring to a free inversion of the brief opening subject:

a 6: *Adolescentulus sum ego* e_2 $eEeEe_2$ $eEeEe_2$ eb_3 b

one is very short, skipping a counter-exposition and therefore precluding large-scale symmetry:

a 6: *Domine, non est exaltatum* CF_4 $FB\flat_5$ F_3 C

[5] P. xv.

and one is very long, with strong hints of regularity (but the tenor voice of this piece is lost; the starred entries have been fitted in by Harrison):

a 6: *Domine, quis habitabit*

C_4 F_8 *CF_9 CF_9 *CF_6 $G_2 CF_9$ CF

All this looks very different from the practice of William Byrd, even in his earliest motets.

Born in 1543, some 35 years after Tallis, Byrd joined him on an equal basis in the *Cantiones sacrae* of 1575, and enjoyed along with him the pompous compliments of such important persons as Richard Mulcaster and Sir Ferdinando Heybourne in the prefatory matter of the publication. Byrd had obviously made a great impression in London in a period of only three years after arriving there from Lincoln Cathedral. That Byrd's music for the print is vastly different from Tallis's goes without saying; one might not have expected it to differ so strongly from that of White or Mundy, who were no more than 10 or 15 years his senior. Of the 17 numbers that he contributed, 8 of which are continuously imitative motets, only one shows any concern for the symmetry that preoccupied his contemporaries:

a 6: *Laudate, pueri* [6] $F_2 C_2 F_2 C_2 F_2 CF_3$ $F_2 C_2 F_2 C_2 F_2 CF$

This runs the "principle of regularity" into the ground. However, *Laudate, pueri* stands in a class by itself. It is not originally a motet but an adaptation of a Fantasia; hard pressed, perhaps, to supply as many as 17 numbers, Byrd fell back on an instrumental piece to which he added (none too skilfully) a pastiche of various cheerful psalm verses.[7] The lockstep structure, so reminiscent of the *canzona*, characterizes the remaining phrases of the composition also.

The Fantasia shows, of course, that Byrd was perfectly aware of the symmetrical tendencies in contemporary English polyphony. But he seems to have considered them applicable to a major vocal work only as a makeshift; in the other seven motets, the imitations are kept studiously *irregular* in their spacing and in the pitches employed, at least within the conspicuous opening phrases. The simplest motet, *Memento, homo* [8] (see Ex. 1), bears a similarity to Tallis's *Salvator mundi*. At the back of Byrd's mind, I believe, was a two-voiced unit consisting of subject and

---

[6] Byrd's motets of 1575 are published in Volume IX of *Tudor Church Music* and in Volume I of *The Collected Works of William Byrd*, edited by E. H. Fellowes. *Laudate, pueri* appears on pp. 181–93 of the latter edition.

[7] See JAMS, XIV (1961), 361.

[8] Byrd *Works*, I, 194–98.

tonal answer, to be repeated down through the other voices—as is the case with the older composition. But the following differences are to be noted. (1) Byrd reverses and compresses his unit from seven beats to six to five. (2) He complicates the second unit with a full-fledged stretto entry, at the end of the fourth measure of the example. (3) So far from writing a counter-exposition mirroring the exposition proper, Byrd instead introduces one more unit constructed not of subject plus tonal answer, but of answer plus answer, so arranged that a new note B♭ appears in the bass as the initial of the last true entry. This being the subdominant, and being reinforced by another B♮ in the top voice, it provides a cumulative strength to the section as a whole which is altogether different in spirit from Tallis's level ideal. A diagram would run as follows:

a 6: *Memento, homo* C₃ F₄   C₃ F₂ FF₅   F₃ B♭

However, a diagram of this type is helpless to indicate (4) the remarkable number of very free syncopated entries which Byrd jammed in, it would seem, at every possible occasion. (On the score, these are marked with small brackets.) They have a distinct tendency to group themselves in pairs (measures 3 and 4: A or F—C; measures 5 and 6: C—F; measures 8 and 9: A or G—C). The three free strettos in measures 8 and 9 seem calculated to add to the sense of climax imparted by the harmonic weight of the B♭ in the bass, and by the strongly cadential urge of the concluding measures.

If an artistic judgment were in question, one would not hesitate long between the two phrases that have been quoted. Tallis is sober, assured, deeply individual; Byrd is coarse, busy, brash, and rather anonymous in feeling. But his piece is more advanced in many ways—in the brilliance (or intended brilliance) of contrapuntal action; in the harmonic lucidity; and in the clear concern for climax, which is to say in the dramatic shaping of the phrase. More fundamentally, whereas with Tallis the contrapuntal structure is the be-all and end-all of the phrase, with Byrd other considerations determine the form. The imitative units serve rather as underpinning to a guiding polarity of the outer voices. Yet as a whole *Memento, homo* is one of the more awkward of Byrd's early compositions; and it is most curious to see the second and last phrase of this little motet ruled by symmetrical contrapuntal thinking.

In the first phrase, it should be observed that although the complete text handled is "Memento, homo, quod cinis es," only the first two words are articulated thematically. The second text-fragment, "quod cinis es," though sung more than a dozen times, never attaches itself to a consistent musical idea; clarity in this matter was sacrificed, evidently, to the rather excessive joy in strettos. Tallis, when dealing with a text-phrase of some length, ordinarily defines it clearly enough:

Ex. 2   Tallis, *Suscipe, quaeso, Domine* [9]

This imitates almost canonically all the way through in all seven voices. But when any one of the voices subsequently repeats the second text-fragment "vocem confitentis," free counterpoint is used; what Tallis does not do is divide his long subject in two and develop the two parts in flexible conjunction. One would speak of a single long subject, not of a first and second subject treated as a "double imitation" of any sort.

In certain of Byrd's imitative motets of 1575, he works deliberately—if not always successfully—with independent second subjects within his imitative phrases. At the beginning of the large six-part motets *Da mihi auxilium* and *Domine, secundum actum meum*, for example, clearly separate subjects are used together for the text-fragments "Da mihi auxilium/ de tribulatione" and "Domine/ secundum actum meum." Something similar appears to be evolving at the opening of the *secunda pars* of *Libera me, Domine, et pone me juxta te* for the words "Dies mei/ transierunt." And although the effort seems rather to have defeated the composer, *Aspice, Domine* actually involves three subjects at once, for the text-fragments "Aspice, Domine,/ quia facta est/ desolata civitas." Examples can be multiplied from later phrases within many of the 1575 motets. By the time of Byrd's own individual *Cantiones sacrae* of 1589 and 1591, the technique of "double imitation" has been normalized and is employed with a power and variety that precludes any thought of technical difficulties.

In the *Plain and Easy Introduction to Practical Music* of 1597, Byrd's pupil Thomas Morley actually states that the best way to begin a song is with "two several points in two several parts at once, or one point foreright and reverted," preferably the former alternative: "this way of

[9] *Tudor Church Music*, VI, 222.

two or three several points going together is the most artificial kind of composing which hitherto hath been invented either for Motets or Madrigals, specially when it is mingled with reverts, because so it maketh the music seem more strange."[10] However, the example that so awes Philomathes and Polymathes is less "strange" in Morley's sense than plain clumsy, and in any case stylistically much more like an instrumental fancy than a madrigal, let alone a motet. In going about his example—like all his other examples—without any consideration of the words, Morley effectively disqualifies himself on this topic. For of course the technique arose not from any purely musical impetus, but from the desire to differentiate, articulate, and contrast successive fragments of a text-phrase within the unity of a single musical section. This explains the staple role of double imitation in the Continental and especially in the Italian madrigal and motet; a fine example would be the opening of Palestrina's famous seven-part motet *Tu es Petrus* (published in 1567). It is natural to enquire whether foreign influence had anything to do with Byrd's introduction of double imitation into English music.[11]

Some time ago the present writer worked through the madrigals of Alfonso Ferrabosco, a minor Italian composer active at Queen Elizabeth's court on and off between 1562 and 1578, in the hope that they would throw some light on the English madrigal development.[12] They throw some, but not much—in spite of the abnormally wide circulation of Ferrabosco's madrigals in Elizabethan England, and in spite of Morley's recommending him in the same breath as Marenzio as a "guide" for madrigal composition. By the time native musicians began writing madrigals and reading Morley, in the 1590s, they had more up-to-date models than the rather humdrum works of a man who had long since disappeared from the local scene. The case was quite other in the 1570s, when Ferrabosco was very much in evidence, and when the style of his music must have struck London musicians such as White, Mundy, Tallis, and Byrd as extremely radical, or perplexing, or suggestive—depending on their individual temperaments. It is possible that Morley's pious attitude towards Ferrabosco traces back to Byrd, for there can be little doubt that on Byrd Ferrabosco's influence was a good deal more telling than on madrigalists of a later generation. Certain of Byrd's more singular experiments in the 1575 *Cantiones sacrae* derive from Ferrabosco;[13] and

---

[10] Thomas Morley, *Introduction*, ed. by R. Alec Harman (London 1952), p. 276.
[11] The best discussion of double imitation I have found occurs in H. K. Andrews, *An Introduction to the Technique of Palestrina* (London 1958), Chap. VIII.
[12] *The Elizabethan Madrigal*, American Musicological Society: *Studies and Documents*, IV (Philadelphia 1962), Chap. 3.
[13] Pointed out by the present writer in JAMS, XIV (1961), 377f, *Studies in the*

his usual, normal contrapuntal style, notably in this technique of double imitation, also owes much to the example of "Master Alfonso."

A pair of motet openings by Byrd and Ferrabosco illustrates the technique well (see Example 3).[14] The melodic figures for the words "non secundum" (Ferrabosco) and "secundum actum meum" (Byrd) were conceived from the start as separate or separable elements, so much so that they are chiseled out of the texture by means of preliminary rests. These figures enjoy rich imitative life of their own independent of and simultaneously with the "Domine" figure, both in the passages shown and even more extensively in the concluding parts of the phrases, which are not quoted here because of their considerable length. In both pieces, a voice may make its very first entrance not with the opening words and the opening subject, but with the second subject. In measure 11 of Ferrabosco's motet, he is even beginning to treat a third subject independently, for the words "peccata mea."

The imitative ground-plans are, of course, irregular. Even if the composers had desired symmetry—which they did not—symmetry would hardly allow the kind of contrapuntal complexity which they did desire. The following diagrams cover the entire opening phrases, but are able to indicate only *full entries* of the first plus the second subject:

FERRABOSCO

$A'D_9$ A'_3 D_{11} $A'A'D_8$ DD'_{12} $D'_2 G_2 G$

BYRD

$B'E'_7$ $E'_2 E'_8$ $E'A'_{11}$ A'_{12} $A_3 E_3 E'_6 A_{11}$

The first (un-italicized) expositions are still built out of units combining two entries each, but neither composer cares to standardize the stretto interval within his units, nor the length of time between units, and Byrd moves restlessly through various different notes to begin his subject. The counter-expositions (italicized) are unsystematic to the point of omitting one of the six voices. Both composers introduce heavy, deliberate strettos before cadencing in the subdominant 31 measures (in each case) from the beginning.

In the above diagrams certain letters have been provided with prime marks: these indicate those entries in which the second subject involves

Renaissance, IX (1962), 289f, *Musical Quarterly*, XLIX (1963), 448f, and by Harrison in the forthcoming Volume IV of the *New Oxford History of Music*.

[14] Byrd's motet appears in the *Works*, I, 218-31. Sources for the Ferrabosco are St. Michael's College, Tenbury, Ms. 389, pp. 53-54 (a single part) and the "Sambrooke Book," New York Public Library Drexel 4302, pp. 173-76 (a contemporary score without words and with a faulty incipit: "*Domine, non secundum* iniquitates"). A lute arrangement appears in British Museum Add. MS 31992, f. 97[v].

Ex. 3   Ferrabosco, *Domine, non secundum peccata mea*

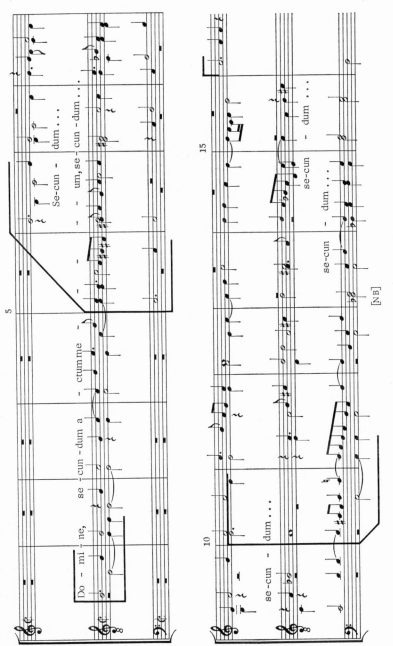

Byrd, *Domine, secundum actum meum* (1575)

a semitone step above the note of the "Domine" monotone. This is more typically the case with Byrd, who is working with a real answer, than with Ferrabosco, who builds his "unit" with a free answer substituting the interval of a third for a second (D—F answering A—B♭). At his eighth entry, however, Ferrabosco moves from his customary D not to F but to E♭. This carefully calculated introduction of a new affective interval finds a parallel in Byrd's sixth entry, where A—B♭ is added to the previous semitone arsenal B—C and E—F. Although both composers have concocted themes dwelling on a semitone by repetition, Byrd certainly seems more in love with the interval. Still, he finds a use for the alternating second and third suggested by Ferrabosco's "unit"—though at the end of his total phrase, not at the beginning. Expansion of the subject "secundum actum meum" from A—B♭— to A—C— and from E— F— to E—G— gives the ending stretto (which is not quoted, but whose letters *lack* prime marks in the diagram) an appropriate rugged touch.

Subjects hinging on an expressive semitone step are important in Byrd's work, and decidedly rare in earlier English music. Sooner or later Byrd always brings in a third semitone, a B♭ or an E♭ which artfully lacerates the modal purity. Ferrabosco's *Domine, non secundum peccata mea* may seem to provide a model for the procedure—for of the two motets I should not hesitate to accord his the priority. Still, deliberate manipulation of an impressive subject featuring a semitone occurs already in Byrd's *De Lamentatione*, a work which on other stylistic evidence one would date earlier than the 1575 motets, presumably from before Byrd's association with Ferrabosco in London after 1572.[15]

Whether Ferrabosco "guided" Byrd or whether he simply confirmed his prejudices is unimportant compared to what emerges as the central historical fact here: the wonderful widening of horizons in British music of the 1570s at the hands of the young composer from Lincoln. There is a new freedom of imitative counterpoint, along with a new variety and expressivity of melodic material; also a remarkable series of experiments in affective homophony, in which Tallis seems to participate; and at just the same period a new personal attitude begins to be assumed towards the choice of words for a motet. (See *The Elizabethan Motet: A Study of Words for Music*, in: *Studies in the Renaissance*, IX, where I have examined this matter at some length.) In a very short time Byrd attained the mastery fulsomely attributed to him by Mulcaster and Heybourne, and amply forecast by many of the motets of 1575. Though imitative technique is only one element of that mastery, it remains a central one

---

[15] This stylistic evidence is discussed in my article *Byrd's Motets: Chronology and Canon*, in JAMS, XIV (1961), 379–81.

for Byrd through the period of the Masses and the two later volumes of *Cantiones sacrae*, in 1589 and 1591. Only with the *Gradualia* in 1605 and 1607 does imitation start to recede as the principal driving force of his work.

The opening phrase of Byrd's motet *Domine, praestolamur adventum tuum* [16] (1589), shown in Example 4, employs means similar to those of *Domine, secundum actum meum* more freely, more concisely, and more dramatically. The irregular ground-plan would appear in a diagram as follows:

a 5: *Domine, praestolamur* E_4 $\quad A_3 \quad A_5 \quad A_{10} \qquad AEA_4 \quad A_{12}$

But it is time to throw out these diagrams (and throw out bland Alfonso Ferrabosco, too); they and he no longer take account of the essentials. The second subject, "adventum tuum," is not merely a separable element with contrapuntal potential of its own, but an element that takes powerful control of the phrase both at its center and at its conclusion. Which is only just: in a dramatic reading of the text, emphasis ought to fall not on "Lord we await" but on "Thy advent." The two themes cleave admirably to the words, too, though the treatment is less obvious than that of *Domine, secundum actum meum*, with its monotone apostrophe and its guilt-ridden semitones. "Lord we await" mounts rockily up the Phrygian scale, conspicuously *minore* in sonority; "Thy advent" makes a delicate lyric contrast by the relatively sudden descent of a fourth curling back on itself, suggesting a major sonority. Anticipation is a somber matter for Byrd; we greet the Advent with something like an intimate gesture of gratitude and release, not with jubilation, rapture, complacency, triumph, humility, or whatever.

The first exposition counts as quite free, for the soprano does not even sing the first subject, entering directly with the second instead (as we have also seen happen with some voices in the related pair of motets by Ferrabosco and Byrd). The ecstatic stretto rush of the second or counter-exposition is superbly lifted up by a free version of the second subject (measures 13–14). Fourths and fifths leap up to a held A which seems to be stretched higher yet by the held F above it (measures 14–15, across the barline), the climax of an almost perfect syncopated entry.

As for the second subject, "adventum tuum," that is handled throughout with the greatest flexibility and imagination. Inverted and syncopated entries occur, but the chief device seems to be repetition in and around the same note (measures 4, 6, and 8: E—F; measures 9, 10 *bis*, and 11:

[16] Byrd, *Works*, II, 14–28.

Ex. 4 Byrd, *Domine, praestolamur adventum tuum*

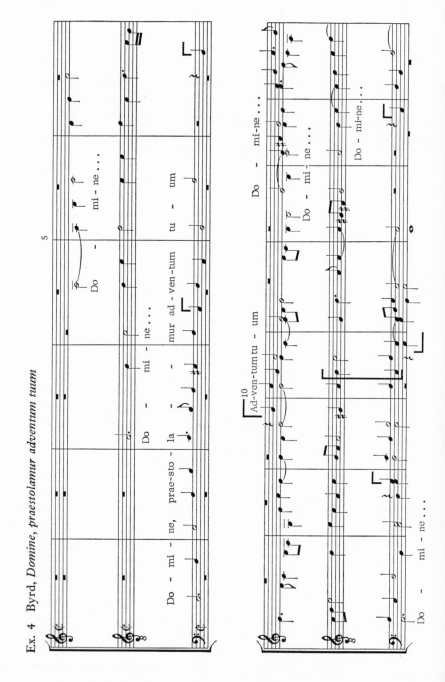

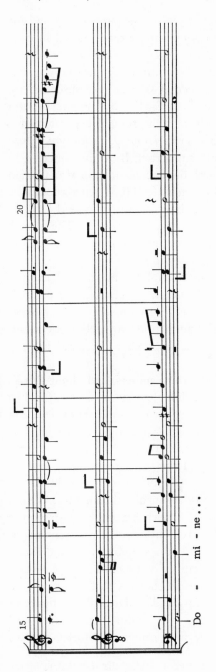

B or A—C; measures 16, 17, and 18: G or B—C; measures 18, 19, and 20: E or D—G). This tendency towards ostinato, already noted in connection with the untidy strettos of *Memento, homo*, is very characteristic of Byrd, and evidently an inheritance from earlier English polyphony. Interestingly, the final form of the second subject (measures 18, 19, and 20) replaces the original semitone step E—F— by the interval of a third, E—G—: a modification that recalls the rugged expansion of a subject involving the step E—F in Byrd's *Domine, secundum actum meum*. The new note G is elegantly supported. Byrd introduces it in measure 18 over a G triad which stands out because it is the first G triad in the piece, and because it is rhythmicized so freshly. Then at the end he dissolves his insistent motivic G by clashing it away against the G♯ of the cadence—the sharp being expressly marked in the print. The famous old cadential cross-relation is turned to aesthetic capital; how carefully, too, the dissonance level is released in measure 21.

Paradoxically, Byrd finds the leisure to duplicate measures 7–10 quite closely in measures 15–18. Yet the distance traveled from the parallelisms of Tallis's day is immeasurable: this repetition sounds not like retracing ground, but like touching ground prior to a climactic vault. Craft and expression, in the motets of 1589 and 1591, stand in very sophisticated equilibrium.

There is much more to say about these motets, and about Byrd's contrapuntal style in general. Perhaps, though, enough has been said to clarify some not unimportant points about the development of imitation into Elizabethan times. In the later Middle Ages, imitative writing was essentially a decorative or a special device. Then when imitation came to be the guiding structural principle in large-scale composition, English musicians tended to work with stiff, schematic patterns which still recall, in a dim curious way, something of the medieval mentality. Within seventeen years [17] after the accession of Queen Elizabeth, contrapuntal structure had grown a great deal more subtle and was beginning to serve more dramatic, imaginative goals in the shaping of the individual phrase. The technique of double imitation, determined by the words, goes hand in hand with a new interest in subjects that "express" the words. The great figure here is William Byrd, and a shadowy figure in the background is Alfonso Ferrabosco, with whom Byrd entered into a "friendly æmulation" not only in devising canons, as Morley tells us,

---

[17] To Denis Stevens we owe a pleasant conceit linking the regnal date of the Tallis-Byrd *Cantiones sacrae*—XVII Elizabeth—to the number of pieces contributed by each composer (*Tudor Church Music*, London 1961, p. 43 note).

but also in composing complex expressive motets, as we have been able to see.

That Byrd was now exercising much more personal choice in taking texts for his motets is certainly no accident. One way or another, the text is the new guiding principle in late Tudor music. "In sacred words," Byrd observes in a much-quoted preface, "as I have learned by trial, there is such a profound and hidden power that to one thinking upon things divine and diligently and earnestly pondering them, all the fittest numbers occur as if of themselves." [18] Like so much else in late Renaissance music, the maturing of the art of imitation in England stemmed from a passion to make music match the quality of the word, phrase, sentence, sonnet, or psalm: to make music rhetoric.

[18] *Gradualia*, 1605; see Oliver Strunk, *Source Readings in Music History* (New York 1950), p. 328.

SOME MINOR FRENCH
COMPOSERS OF THE
16th CENTURY

by FRANÇOIS LESURE

WITH DICTIONARIES of musicians rapidly multiplying, several years ago Emile Haraszti and I conceived the idea of a "dictionary of musicians who are not in any dictionary," a kind of lexicon of the forgotten and of the *refusés*. Here is a trifling slice of this imaginary work for 16th-century France.

There still remains a significant number of French musicians of this epoch on whom we have no information, among them composers of the importance of Maillard and Passereau. In the introduction to the bibliography of the musical publications of Nicolas Du Chemin and in various dictionaries I have already furnished guideposts that may direct future investigations towards some of them. For a score of new names, I am grouping below some analogous data. Experience shows that the interest of musicologists hardly extends to these lesser masters, if we have not succeeded in attaching them to a cadre, to a region, or to a milieu.

The notes that follow serve to bring into relief, despite their documentary bareness, the vitality of French provincial choir-schools in the Renaissance epoch. It is therefore quite natural that music printers from Paris went off to seek new repertory in Poitiers, Bourges, Reims, Amiens, Dijon, Angers, Beauvais, Chartres, Nancy, and Troyes, as we will be able to verify here. In the 50th edition of Gustave Reese's *Music in the Renaissance* we can therefore hope that, given the progress of musicology, these centers may be assigned their proper place!

JEAN BASTARD

This author of two chansons published respectively by Attaingnant (1547) and Du Chemin (1550), as well as of a motet *a 5* (1550), can be identified thanks to a poem that was dedicated to him in 1549. In *Le Temple de chasteté* (Fezandat, 1549, fol. F vi^v), François Habert, a poet from Berry and rather a mediocre rival of Clément Marot, dedicated to

538

him the following epigram, which tells us not only his place of activity, but in praising his reputation as a musician, also indicates his concern for poetry:

A Monsieur Bastard
maître des enfants de la Saincte Chapelle de Bourges

Bastard de nom, mais enfant légitime
Du père grand, qui est recteur des cieulx,
Je te supply tousjours d'Habert estime
Que tu es l'un de ceulx qu'il ayme mieulx,
Car j'ay congneu ton esprit curieux
Non seulement de ton art de musique,
Mais des couleurs de phrase poétique,
En quoy si grand est ton auctorité
Que Pallas dict sans aucune réplique
Qu'estre son filz tu as bien mérité.

The archives of Bourges inform us that as vicar of Ste-Chapelle, he succeeded Jean Le Boutillier (see below) and was master of the boys' choir from 1 April 1536 to 1552. On 13 February of this latter year, he asked the chapter for a leave of absence of five or six weeks in order to visit his father. He undoubtedly never returned, for on 4 May the chapter discharged his servants.[1]

LAURENT BONNARD (BONARD)

A priest, on 4 October 1547 he became master of the boys' choir of the cathedral of Amiens and remained so at least until 1553.[2] There survive four of his chansons a 4, published by Du Chemin between 1550 and 1552, one of which is based on a poem by Gilles d'Avrigny (*Amour et mort*). We must avoid confusing him, as R. Eitner did, with the Italian musicians, authors of madrigals and motets, Francesco and Iseppo Bonardo.

JHERONIMUS DE CLIBANO

Native of Bois-le-Duc ('s-Hertogenbosch), he was choirmaster at St-Donatien in Bruges from 1491, but his negligence led the chapter to replace him on 16 August 1497. On 11 October following, he refused reinstatement and left Bruges.[3] We find him again at Chartres, where he became master of the boys' choir of the cathedral; on 22 October he sold a horse to a local merchant.[4] He probably did not remain long in this

---

[1] Archives du Cher, 8 G 1516, fol. 279ᵛ; 1519, fol. 114; 1520.
[2] Archives de la ville d'Amiens, FF 92, fol. 43; Archives de la Somme, G 1053; G. Durand, *La Musique de la cathédrale d'Amiens avant la Révolution*, in: *Bulletin de la Société des Antiquaires de Picardie* (1922), p. 362.
[3] A. C. de Schrevel, *Histoire du séminaire de Bruges* (1895), I, 165–66.
[4] Archives d'Eure-et-Loir, G 180, fol. 30ᵛ.

place, for in 1499 we note his visit to the brotherhood of Bois-le-Duc,[5] and in 1501, with Pierre de La Rue, Agricola, and others, he was among the choristers who accompanied Philip the Handsome to Spain.[6] He left one motet and one Mass *a 4*.

RICHARD CRASSOT

This Huguenot musician was probably a native of Nantes. In 1556 he was accepted as master of the boys' choir at Troyes. He fled from this city on 29 March 1560, without even paying his respects to the master at whose house he had lived—and he left behind some debts.[7] In 1564 at Lyons, his collection of psalms *a 4* appeared. He was not a victim of Saint Bartholomew, as is often written, for in 1572 we find him master of the boys' choir of Ste-Croix in Orléans,[8] and on 8 December 1581, master of the precentorships of the cathedral of St-Martin in Tours.[9]

JEAN DOUBLET

Author of two chansons published in 1536 in two collections by Attaingnant, in 1532 he was organist of the cathedral of Beauvais.[10]

PHILIPPE FROMENTIN (FOURMENTIN)

Clericus from the diocese of Noyon, in 1558 Fromentin was vicar and master of the boys' choir of the cathedral of Reims. In addition, on 17 August he received the advowson [the right of presentation to a vacant ecclesiastical benefice] of the canonship of St-Calixte Chapel in the same church.[11] The following year Le Roy & Ballard published a chanson *a 6* and a "quarillon de cloches" *a 5* under the name of "Fourmentin."

JEHAN FRESNEAU

Between 1470 and 1475 he was ordinary chaplain of the king's chapel. A list of his works, one Mass *a 4* and six chansons *a 3*, has been established by N. Bridgman.[12] The presence of Fresneau in the choir school of the cathedral of Chartres in 1494 has been briefly noted by André

---

[5] A. Smijers, *De Illustre Lieve Vrouwe Broederschap te 's-Hertogenbosch* (Amsterdam 1932), p. 211.

[6] E. Van der Straeten, *La Musique aux Pays-Bas avant le XIXe siècle* (1867–88), VI, 164; VII, 105.

[7] A. Prévost, in: *Mémoires de la Société académique de l'Aube*, LXIX (1905), 243.

[8] P. Leroy, in: *Réunion des sociétés des beaux-arts des départements*, XXI (1897), 766.

[9] Archives d'Indre-et-Loire, G 320.

[10] G. Desjardins, *Histoire de la cathédrale de Beauvais* (1865), p. 75.

[11] Archives de la Marne, G 419.

[12] N. Bridgman, *Fresneau*, in: MGG, IV (1955), 926–27.

Pirro.[13] The musician was acting that year as procurator of the canon-ships of St-Martin in Tours with the title of "canon and provost of Mayet in the church of said S. Martin." [14] On 9 February 1500 he was still in Chartres as "notary and procurator in the church's court"; and in February 1505 he was acting there as executor of a canonship of the town.[15]

NICOLAS GROUZY (NICOLE GROUSIL, GROUSSY)

He is the author of 11 chansons (one on a poem by Pierre Danche, *Argent prend ville*) published between 1549 and 1567, the majority by Le Roy & Ballard. In 1563 he was master of the boys' choir of the cathe-dral of Chartres, where he died on 8 June 1568. As canon of St-Piat, he had requested to be buried in the church of the Jacobins in Chartres.[16] The arguments for attributing to this musician the ricercar and the chan-son from the lute manuscript of the Upsala Library (MS 87) seem rather fragile.[17]

RAIMOND DE LA CASSAIGNE (CASSAGNE)

This meridional [person from southern France] is known as a com-poser only from a chanson *a 5* (*Ayant fait de mes pleurs*), published in the *Rossignol* of 1597, and a motet *a 5* (*O Jesu flos Mariae*), which ap-peared in the *Florilegium musicum motectorum*, edited by J. Degen (Bamberg: A. Baals, 1631). Coming from the choir school of Toulouse, on 15 July 1575 he became master of the boys' choir of Notre-Dame de Paris. He had just obtained the silver harp prize in the musical competi-tion of the Puy d'Evreux. In 1577 his prolonged absence caused him to be replaced as the head of the choir school of Notre-Dame, but he was reinstated in 1579.[18] His fame was widespread, as we can see from a passage in one curious "Hymn to music," published in 1582 in the *Nouvelles oeuvres* of the poet Jean-Edouard Du Monin:

> . . . Boëce prend tout pour soi l'honneur du présent âge
> En laissant un rameau au Zarlinois visage,
> Au merveilleus Orlande, au doucereus Bonin,[19]

---

[13] A. Pirro, *Gilles Mureau, chanoine de Chartres*, in: *Festschrift J. Wolf* (1929), p. 166, fn. 3.
[14] Archives d'Eure-et-Loir, G 179, fol. 126.
[15] *Ibid.*, G 180, fols. 151ᵛ and 597.
[16] *Ibid.*, G 321, 236 and 596; Clerval, *L'ancienne maîtrise de Notre-Dame de Chartres* (1899), p. 81.
[17] B. Hambraeus, *Codex carminum gallicorum* (Upsala 1961), p. 53.
[18] F. L. Chartier, *L'ancien chapitre de Notre-Dame de Paris* (1897), pp. 82–83.
[19] Guillaume Boni.

A Bertrand, à Caurrois, à Cassagne, à Clodin,[20]
Et à quelque autre encor dont et l'encre et la plume
Je n'ai encor batu au dos de mon enclume . . .

In 1587 he was again crowned in the Puy d'Evreux, and afterwards we lose track of him.

MATHIEU LASSON

He was the author of four motets *a 4* and of one *a 2* as well as four chansons *a 4* that appeared between 1529 and 1549. As early as 1533, H. Gerle transcribed *En l'ombre d'un buissonet* for lute. His entire career was spent in the duchy of Lorraine, where he was canon and treasurer of the collegiate church of St-Georges in Nancy from 1528 to 1529, and master of the ducal chapel; in 1543 the rectory of the hospital of Notre-Dame in Pont-à-Mousson was created for him.[21] He died before 1595, on which date an obituary was solemnized for him in St-Georges in Nancy.

BARTHÉLEMY LE BEL

Of a family originally from Montlhéry, he was born about 1483 in Anjou, a little town of the Dauphiné (Isère). Becoming a priest, he was for six years "master of the boys of the vestment" in the cathedral of St-Pierre in Geneva, no doubt shortly after Antoine Brumel's visit to this choir school. At the close of 1552, he entered Ste-Chapelle in Dijon, where he performed the same function. The atmosphere of the Dijon choir school pleased him but little, and being, it seems, of a rather vindictive temperament, he aspired to succeed one of his enemies, Thiebaut Le Jay, at Langres. He also tried to have himself hired by the Duke of Guise. It was on the morrow of the battle of Pavia, and the musician, apparently little interested in politics, publicly announced that Charles V would be heartily welcomed at Dijon; in other words, he said that he was in favor of merging Burgundy with the Empire. He was arrested and turned over to the municipal judge on 17 March 1525 and interrogated on the following days. Parliament sent him back before the judge of the chapter. Unfortunately we are unaware of the conclusion of this curious affair. What is known is that in 1552 Le Bel was in Geneva, where he requested that he be received as a resident of the Calvinist town, and there pursued his musician's calling. He died there on 16 October 1553 at the age of seventy. Although he seems not to have

---

[20] We can recognize Antoine de Bertrand, Eustache Du Caurroy, and Claude Le Jeune.

[21] Archives de Meurthe-et-Moselle, B 1040, 1073, 1092; G 643; A. Jacquot in: *Réunion des sociétés des beaux-arts des départements* (1903), p. 683.

published any work during his lifetime, in 1554–55 the publishers Du Bosc and Guéroult printed at Geneva four prayers *a 4* in the form of motets and one Latin motet *a 4*.[22]

JEAN LE BOUTEILLER (BOUTILLIER)

He was the author of two motets and of three chansons published by Attaingnant between 1534 and 1542. From November 1530 to October 1535 he was master of the boys' choir of Ste-Chapelle in Bourges,[23] then performed the same function in the following years at the cathedral of Chartres.[24]

JEAN LE SAINTIER

The description by E. Lowinsky of the Medici Codex has revealed to us the name of a musician unknown before this time: "Le Santier," author of an *Alma Redemptoris a 5* in canon.[25] Investigations must now be directed toward an old and important family in Tours, whose representatives are encountered in this city from the 14th to the 18th century. At the time of the Codex, we can identify the musician with Jean Le Saintier who, up to about 1513, was almoner and guardian of the seal of St-Martin of Tours.[26]

SIMON MAGDELAIN (MADELIN)

Organist of the cathedral of Rouen in 1524,[27] he was author of a chanson published in 1538 and twice reprinted.

CLÉMENT MOREL

He was in 1552 master of the boys' choir of the church of Nevers. The chapter of Ste-Chapelle in Bourges, which Jean Bastard had just left (see above), tried to attract him that year, but in vain.[28] We have two of his motets and 11 chansons published between 1539 and 1552 (one on a text by Clément Marot).

VULFRAN SAMIN

Author of a Mass *Sancti Spiritus* (1558) and of 16 chansons published by Attaingnant and Le Roy & Ballard between 1546 and 1559 (often

---

[22] Archives de la Côte-d'Or, G. 1152; Pierre Pidoux, *Le Psautier huguenot du XVIe siècle* (1962), II, 175.

[23] Archives du Cher, 8 G 1515, fols. 132 and 235ᵛ.

[24] Clerval, *L'ancienne maîtrise de Notre-Dame de Chartres* (1899), p. 81.

[25] E. Lowinsky, *The Medici Codex*, in: *Annales musicologiques*, V (1957), 111 and 150.

[26] Archives d'Indre-et-Loire, G 423.

[27] Collette et Bourdon, *Notice historique sur les orgues et les organistes de la cathédrale de Rouen* (1894).

[28] Archives du Cher, 8 G 1520, fol. 30ᵛ.

under the single name of "Vulfran"), in 1543–44 he was chorister extraordinary of the Notre-Dame brotherhood of Puy d'Amiens.[29]

PIERRE SANTERRE

On Santerre, Fétis has furnished a piece of the most unexpected information: "born in Poitiers," he writes, "of Protestant parents." [30] If, as one can suppose, he was born not later than 1530, the said parents were astonishing forerunners in the history of the Reformation. Limiting ourselves to the actuality of the sources, we are able to accept that Santerre was in 1555 the organist of the cathedral of Poitiers. On 11 April he rented part of a house situated on the main street of this town to Louis Rogier, counselor.[31] It is known that he died before 1567, for in that year his edition of *150 Psalms* [*a 4*] appeared (of which today no copy remains), preceded by a preface by Logerois, the printer from Poitiers, explaining that this was a posthumous work.[32] There remain eight of his chansons published between 1536 and 1556, the first among them (*Faict elle pas bien*) having earlier appeared anonymously (RISM 1536⁴). Four of these chansons are styled "poitevines," of which one rather long piece in local dialect is *Le Procès de Tallebot*.

JEAN SEVIN (SÉVAIN)

Author of a chanson *a 4* issued in 1556 by Fezandat, from 1561 he resided at Angers and between 1570 and 1577 was organist to the Dames du Ronceray, a powerful abbey, where interest in music had already been manifested at the time of Clément Janequin's sojourn in the region.[33]

JEAN WAUQUEL

In 1551 he was organist to the keeper of the seals, Jean Bertrand, and on 2 July accepted the advowson of a canonship at St-Florent in Roye.[34] Between 1541 and 1545 five chansons *a 4* appeared under his signature in collections by Attaingnant.

[*Translated by Elaine Brody, New York University*]

[29] Archives de la Somme, E 932.

[30] F. J. Fétis, *Biographie universelle des musiciens* (1833–44), VII, 394.

[31] *Inventaire des autographes de B. Fillon* (Paris 1879), pp. 171–72, No. 2295. In 1570 Nicolas Santerre was organist of St-Germain l'Auxerrois in Paris. (Bibl. Nat., nouv. acq. fr. 12184.)

[32] O. Douen, *C. Marot et le psautier huguenot* (1879), II, 53; P. Pidoux, *Le Psautier huguenot* (1962), II, 157.

[33] C. Port, *Les Artistes angevins* (1881), p. 287; J. Levron, *C. Janequin* (1948), p. 69.

[34] Bibl. Nat., MS fr. 5128, p. 392.

THE PLACE OF MUSIC
IN THE SYSTEM OF
LIBERAL ARTS

by EDWARD A. LIPPMAN

I N THE medieval system of liberal arts, music has its place as one of
the quadrivial sciences—arithmetic, geometry, music, and astronomy; but its position in the group shows a curious variability. It is
the last of the four disciplines in the definitive scheme of Martianus
Capella around 400 A.D., but more often it appears as the second or third
study; in reduced formulations, when arithmetic is omitted and only
three sciences are mentioned, it can appear as the first.[1] To the extent
that this variability is not due to chance, its explanation must be sought
in the internal structure of the quadrivium and in the interrelationship
of the constituent studies. This quest will take us to Pythagorean and
Platonic sources, for it was within these traditions that the quadrivial
concept of the branches of mathematics was formulated and developed.

According to the Pythagorean Archytas of Tarentum, a pupil of
Philolaus and a friend of Plato, the mathematical sciences are related
because they all deal with the two primary forms of being (which we
can take to be multitude and extension).[2] In listing these sciences,
Archytas puts music in the last place, a position that may point to its
culminating status, for it is in the field of music that he expresses his
special admiration for the work of mathematicians. He affirms also that
the arithmetic, geometric, and harmonic means all belong to the subject
of music, so that arithmetic and geometry would appear to be presupposed and more basic studies. If we consider music to be the science
of relative quantity, it will obviously comprehend both arithmetic and
geometric relationships; thus it will logically occupy the third or fourth
place in the quadrivium. But actually music is restricted in principle to
rational ratios; it is the science of relative *multitude*, and although ra-

---

[1] The different arrangements of the liberal arts are examined in Karl Wilhelm
Schmidt, *Quaestiones de musicis scriptoribus romanis inprimis de Cassiodoro et
Isidoro* (Darmstadt 1899).
[2] The Archytas fragments can be found in Hermann Diels and Walther Kranz,
Die Fragmente der Vorsokratiker, I (5th ed. Berlin 1934-37), Ch. XLVII.

tional relationships can always be stated geometrically, geometry has a peculiar interest in incommensurable line segments and thus possesses a greater generality than music. Since it is closely connected with arithmetic in particular, music will become the second quadrivial study, or—fused with arithmetic—the first of a group of three. It would seem, alternatively, that the rational ratios of music might be considered a special case of the more general geometric study of proportion, and that music might consequently be placed after geometry; but this would be an arrangement suggested by a modern rather than an ancient perspective.

Astronomy is somewhat different from geometry in its relationship to music, for while it also makes use of musical proportions, these become a peculiarly characteristic part of the science; unlike line segments, the heavens bear an inherent resemblance to the world of consonance and musical intervals, and for this reason, even apart from the factor of rhythm and motion that is common to both spheres, music is frequently placed either directly before or directly after astronomy in the quadrivium.

A closer inspection of the actual subject matter of the discipline of music confirms its complex interconnection with the other branches of mathematical science. As one of the *mathemata* music was represented by harmonics, and Archytas was one of the major figures in its development. His work in harmonics, explained in part by both Ptolemy and Boethius, can be represented fairly by the Euclid *Section of the Canon*, written about 300 B.C., just as the arithmetic known to Archytas can be represented by the arithmetic and harmonic books of the Euclid *Elements* (Books VII–IX). Considered not as the whole study of proportion but more accurately as the study of proportion in so far as it relates to musical intervals, ancient harmonics depends directly on arithmetic. It deals with the compounding and dividing of consonances in accordance with the postulate that they correspond to multiple and superparticular ratios. The ratios of the consonances are determined and then used as a basis for deriving the ratios of the entire tonal system. The central concern of the science is the insertion of arithmetic, harmonic, and geometric means between two given quantities. Archytas is responsible for the basic proof that neither one nor more geometric means can be inserted in a superparticular ratio, so that by and large, and except for the fundamental articulation of the tonal range into octaves, the division of intervals must proceed on the basis of the arithmetic and harmonic means.

But more fundamental for the broad ramifications of music than its close dependence upon arithmetic was the fact that the consonant ratios which were known to Philolaus and Archytas in terms of the comprehensive progression 12, 9, 8, 6, were all contained in the integers 1, 2, 3, 4 —the holy tetractys of the Pythagoreans—which had basic ontological importance. In addition, the Pythagoreans conceived the very constitution of number, and thus of the world, as resting on the harmony of two fundamental constituents, the monad and the dyad (or the limited and the boundless). In spite of his opposition to the Pythagorean and Platonic hypostasis of number, even Aristotle acknowledged paired contraries and their harmonic combination as basic principles in philosophy and science; but it is Plato who most fully appreciates the general role of music, and who at the same time deepens the theoretical basis of the interconnection of the *mathemata*. Music becomes the final discipline because it is the most general and it best explains the whole nature of mathematics. Its position as the last discipline emphasizes not only its concern with relation but also its connection with motion: it becomes the counterpart of astronomy, as the motion of both number and figure. Plato insists upon the universal relevance of music, writing in the *Laws:* "Moreover, as I have now said several times, he who has not contemplated the mind of nature which is said to exist in the stars, and gone through the previous training, and seen the connection of music with these things, and harmonized them all with laws and institutions, is not able to give a reason of such things as have a reason." [3] Indeed it may very well be music that is responsible both for the unity of mathematics and for its ethical value. A vibrating string is an audible unity of number and length, of arithmetic and geometry, while the moral and emotional influence of music suggest that its corresponding mathematical study may possess ethical powers of its own.

In the *Republic*, Plato emphasizes the ethical value of the *mathemata*,[4] a view that was of vital importance in defining the function of the liberal arts. The ethical concept is incidentally reinforced by the introduction of a fifth science; stereometry is inserted between geometry and astronomy, obscuring the significant symmetry of the four-fold Pythagorean scheme in favor of a different systematic concept. Of each of the disciplines Plato stresses the abstract and ideal character; they are not concerned with practical use, nor with experienced objects at all. In the case of music, it is not only a concern with actual tones that Plato discards, but also what he takes as the interest of the Pythagoreans—the study of harmonic numbers and proportions. Harmonics is to deal instead with the problem of why certain numbers are harmonic, the problem of the

[3] *Laws* 967e. The translation is by Jowett.
[4] *Republic* 521c–32a.

nature of harmony. Music becomes the most typical representative of the *mathemata*, the last and most general science. Numbers are succeeded by plane figures, plane figures by solids, solids by the motion of solids, and this motion by the motion of sounds. The Pythagorean classification—although it may originally have been connected with a notion of cosmogonical succession—is in fact a static analysis of being; but this is transformed by the introduction of stereometry and by the pedagogical and propaedeutic function of the Platonic system. At each step, abstraction is made from sensory phenomena to principles. Then, after a study of the interrelationships of the principles of all the disciplines, which is an investigation itself harmonic in nature, the ascent of dialectic begins.

But dialectic too, if we treat the *Republic* as an example, is largely the study of harmony, in man and state and world. And when we are told that the preliminary sciences are the handmaids and helpers of dialectic, the intention seems to be not only that their help is preparatory, but also that they are continuous adjuncts. Again the *Republic* provides its own confirmation: much more than the proposal of a curriculum, it is an actual instance of the philosophical use of the principles of the preparatory disciplines.

The *Timaeus* also reveals the cooperative function of the quadrivial sciences, but as adjuncts to the study of being and the cosmos; the *mathemata* are at once ontological and scientific in importance, and the unity of mathematics derives from the nature of the world and of thought. Still more strongly here, however, the interrelation of the component disciplines is shown to be grounded in harmonics; the arithmetic, geometric, and astronomical structure of the cosmos is harmonic in nature throughout, and harmony is again associated with ethical value, but in a cosmic sense rather than a human or social one. Commentaries on the *Timaeus* understandably become compendiums of the quadrivial studies, with harmonics in the commanding role. But the concept of cosmic harmony, which ensures the relevance of music to astronomy, is kept alive not only by the tradition of the *Timaeus*, but also by that of the *Republic*. In this regard, Cicero's *Somnium Scipionis* and the commentary on it by Macrobius are of outstanding importance. With the commentary of Macrobius, Plato's myth of Er is transformed into a new focal point of mathematical knowledge, and the cosmic harmony of the *Republic*—originally quite different in its concept—comes to resemble that of the *Timaeus*.

Standing at the head of the quadrivial studies, the arithmetic treatise more than any of the others may be expected to furnish evidence concerning the role of music in mathematics. In his important *Introduction to Arithmetic*,[5] which is carried over into Latin as the *Arithmetic* of Boethius, Nicomachus discusses the nature of the quadrivium in detail. Science is characterized as dealing with limited multitude and limited magnitude, or with quantity and size. Arithmetic treats of absolute quantity and music of relative quantity, while geometry treats of size at rest and astronomy of size in motion and revolution. Arithmetic is the source of all the studies, and the only one that can exist alone; music depends upon it because the absolute is prior to the relative and the harmonies are named after numbers. But astronomy in turn is dependent upon music, for the motions of the stars proceed in perfect harmony. Logically, then, music should follow arithmetic and precede astronomy, thus occupying either the second or third position in the mathematical series. But in fact, music would seem to be entitled also to the first place, for Nicomachus's treatise reveals that arithmetic is thoroughly harmonic in nature. Number is formed from the harmony of the limited and the boundless, and odd and even thus become a harmony extending throughout the numerical domain. Harmonic conceptions enter again in the consideration of perfect numbers, those which are "equal to their own parts," like 6, the sum of 1, 2, and 3. Compared to superabundant and deficient numbers, not equal to their own parts, the perfect number appears as a mean. "For the equal," Nicomachus tells us, "is always conceived of as in the mid-ground between greater and less, and is, as it were, moderation between excess and deficiency, and that which is in tune, between pitches too high and too low." Finally the study of ratio and proportion—the subject matter of music in its most general sense—takes up a surprisingly large part of the treatise and is found most suitable to bring it to a close. Proportions are held to be most essential "for the propositions of music, astronomy, and geometry." The three basic types of proportion—arithmetic, geometric, and harmonic—are actually illustrated in terms of music. They can be produced in the division of the canon, Nicomachus says, "when a single string is stretched or one length of a pipe is used, with immovable ends, and the mid-point shifts in the pipe by means of the finger-holes, or in the string by means of the bridge." As the concluding topic of the *Arithmetic* the proportion 12, 9, 8, 6 is introduced: "It remains for me to discuss briefly the most perfect proportion, that which is three dimensional and embraces them all, and which is most useful for all progress in music and in the theory of the nature of the universe. This alone would properly and truly be called harmony rather than the others."

Since Plato's *Timaeus* is the *locus classicus* not only for the philosoph-

[5] The passages cited are given in the translation by M. L. D'Ooge.

ical role of the quadrivium but also for the interrelation of its component disciplines, it is not surprising that the clearest explanation of the varying place of music can be found in a work based on this dialogue—the pedagogical treatise of Theon of Smyrna,[6] which seeks to prepare the student mathematically for the reading of Plato. We have no need of instrumental music, Theon says at the outset in close dependence on Plato; what we desire is to comprehend harmony and celestial music. We cannot examine this harmony, however, until we have studied the numerical laws of sound. Thus when Plato remarks that music occupies the fifth position in the study of mathematics, he is speaking of celestial music, which results from the movement, the order, and the concert of the stars moving in space. But to harmonics, Theon continues, we must assign the second place, setting it after arithmetic, as Plato wished, since we can understand nothing of celestial music if we do not know its foundation in numbers and in reason, and the numerical principles of music are attached to the theory of abstract numbers. Here we have come upon the chief cause of the variable place of music in mathematics; in addition to its general diffusion throughout the quadrivial sciences, it has especially powerful ties to both arithmetic and astronomy; thus as a distinct discipline, music has a legitimate claim to two well defined positions in the quadrivium. In compendiums of the liberal arts it appears variously in either the second or the last place, but when separate treatises are written the Pythagorean rather than the Platonic tradition is decisive. For the history of musical thought this becomes on occasion a fortunate circumstance accounting for the existence of arithmetical and musical tracts where geometrical and astronomical ones are absent, since the writers in question did not succeed in realizing the projected cycle in its entirety. Thus we possess only an *Arithmetic* and a *Music* of Nicomachus, works on the same two subjects by Boethius, only an *Arithmetic* of Iamblichus, and only a *Music* of Augustine.

To understand fully the place of music in the liberal arts we must also examine the trivium, which consists of grammar, dialectic, and rhetoric. Here music as a mathematical study clearly has no place; but curiously enough, the origins of the trivium in ancient Greek education are closely connected with music in another sense—with musical practice and the theory of performance, and traces of this connection can still be found in the medieval trivium. Liberal education was originally not a process of imparting knowledge but of fashioning and cultivating the character; thus the trivium, frankly ethical in nature throughout its

---

[6] *Expositio rerum mathematicorum ad legendum Platonem utilium,* edited by E. Hiller (Leipzig 1878).

history, is actually the older of the two divisions of the liberal arts. But education was initially centered in music, in the leisured musical pursuits of an aristocracy to which was added the civic ceremonial of the polis; preparation for participation in symposium and choral dance was the basic motivation. And this concern with sonorous music, which has already become evident in the Homeric world, is in effect a group of studies rather than one, for musical composition and performance meant ability in dance, song, and lyre playing. Although they were connected with dance, gymnastics stood somewhat apart because of their connection with military prowess and later increasingly with athletics and sport. Grammar was more completely a part of the musical complex, which consequently can be thought of as dealing with a linguistic composite of meaning, melody, and rhythm, plus the additional manifestation of rhythm in dance. Evidently the traditional compact description of the lower education as consisting of music and gymnastics is an accurate representation of its content. It was also conceived of as an *enkyklios paideia*,[7] a cultivation that would seem to pertain to the *kyklios*, or circle, of the choral dance, and the meaning of the term may have been reinforced by the coincidence that the skolion, too, involved a circle as the singing passed around the table to each guest in turn. Thus the *enkyklios paideia* had an aristocratic and specifically ethical connotation, designating education for a cultivated and urbane way of life and in particular for the chief manifestation of this life in music. But the *enkyklios paideia* is certainly not the trivium; the historical course of events subjected it to radical changes in which its musical nature was largely lost. With the decline of the ancient musical institutions and their society, philosophy and rhetoric fought over the right of succession. We can see in Plato's *Theaetetus* [8] how the whole musical conception with its class prerogative of leisure and its scorn for the servitude of practical occupations is taken over by philosophy. Rhetoric becomes the antithesis, representing illiberal employment for gain. A specific terminology based on music embodies the contrast of the two social classes, and this is also adopted by philosophy. Conscious of its role as a successor of music, philosophy even invades the symposium and supplants song, while the Platonic Academy similarly replaces the music of the poetic school with discussion. But in terms of educational trends and the whole temper of society, it is rhetoric that conquers; grammar grows in importance and becomes the cornerstone of education, and eventually the *enkyklios*

---

[7] See the study by Hermann Koller, *Enkyklios Paideia*, in: *Glotta*, XXXIV (1955).
[8] *Theaetetus* 172c–77c.

paideia is transformed into the trivium of the encyclical studies, dialectic and rhetoric joining grammar in the service of oratory. Gymnastics and music, almost invisible but still present, make a modest contribution to the same end. This process begins during the course of the 5th century B.C.; the disintegration of the composite art of music, accompanied by political ferment and the growth of a rhetorically minded culture, brings about the demusicalization of education. With these changes, the *enkyklios paideia* begins to expand its scope, and the term itself is used in a more general and preparatory sense, as we can find it in Aristotle, to mean usual or customary; the ethical significance also fades. The quadrivial studies as well, to which rhetoric already had laid claim even in the time of Socrates, come to be included in the Hellenistic concept of encyclical education. At the same time, the Roman interpretation of *enkyklios paideia* as a "circle," or group, of studies (*orbis doctrinae*) left the limited and specific selection of the subjects unaccounted for; new ethical aims could easily be set for the whole, and the most prominent of these, apart from rhetoric, was supplied by theology. Ultimately the term became "encyclopedia"; the "circle" was gradually widened to comprise the universality of encyclopedic knowledge. But that the term and the concept absorbed the *mathemata* and not vice versa, and indeed eventually absorbed all of knowledge, confirms the essentially ethical nature of sonorous music and education. Science extended and deepened the ethical goals by adding new ones of a metaphysical nature, but neither science nor education as a whole was ever concerned in ancient and medieval times with knowledge for its own sake.

If the departments of the *enkyklios paideia*, like those of the *mathemata*, are tied together by musical factors, the possibility suggests itself that the two large divisions of the liberal arts may be importantly interconnected, perhaps by some bond of a musical nature. The higher education might even turn out to contain the theory of the lower. If this were so, the Greek concept of the identity of doing and knowing would find confirmation, and education as a whole would have the strongest possible unity, even if that unity—as Plato believed—could be fully realized only by a few superior people. Now the theoretical study of music and dance can be fairly represented by grammar, harmonics, and rhythmics; metrics and orchestics might even have existed as distinct divisions of rhythmics. Other musical studies must have been known also, such as those of composition and performance, and of the function and utility of music. The theory of composition and performance would remain closely united to practice even if it was formalized, and its rudiments would doubtless have been taken up as part of the *enkyklios paideia*, along with the fundamentals of grammar, harmonics, and rhythmics. Theories of the ethical value of music might also have been touched upon, although properly speaking, since Plato places them in philosophy, they were above liberal education rather than within it. But the detailed study of composition and performance, and of ethics in its relation to music, clearly belongs to the sphere of professional education. The same would seem to be true of the basic disciplines of grammar, harmonics, and rhythmics: their rudiments would belong to the *enkyklios paideia*, their full and adequate treatment to the field of professional or technical training. They are certainly not the sciences constituting the *mathemata*, which apparently have a different source and grow out of the conception of harmony rather than out of practical music, so that they have from the start a metaphysical and cosmological interest. But harmonics has a double attachment: it is the theory of melos but it is also part of the quadrivium; its equivocal position is of particular interest in pointing to the existence of various types of theory, differing in degree of practicality. Thus there may very well have been two harmonic disciplines, one more practical in orientation and one more speculative; it is too much to expect that these interests will coincide, so that the details of musical structure, for example, will be of purely theoretic value in mathematics or philosophy; the theories of Plato undoubtedly represent a remarkable rapprochement in this respect. To some extent the same considerations apply to rhythmics, for this study too has some claim to membership in the quadrivial sciences; the mathematical discipline of harmonics is so general and so abstract that it can be taken to include a theoretical form of rhythmics implicitly. In any event, it has become apparent that the larger relationship between practical and theoretical education cannot be described as a simple correspondence. An additional factor of importance is that studies may arise not only through the reflective examination of practice, but also through the application of theory. It is in this sense that Aristotle treats harmonics as an instance of applied mathematics rather than as a department of mathematics itself, and he places it between mathematics and physical science. The harmonics of Aristoxenus, on the other hand, seems to conform to our picture of the theoretical studies derived from musical practice. Finally there is also a mystic pseudo-science of harmonics that comes into prominence in Neopythagorean times. Descended from an ancient and universal sphere of harmonic thought, speculative notions about harmony in man and the world found themselves unrepresented in the era of specialized and defined sciences. Their persistence helps to explain the wide variety of subject matter found in the harmonic treatises of late antiquity as well as the innumerable links between harmonics and other studies.

To help elucidate the ambivalence of harmonics we can turn briefly to the somewhat similar situation of astronomy, for this is not only one of the *mathemata*, or in Aristotle's view a branch of physical mathematics, but is also one of the Muses. In the developed classical system of the nine Muses, there are comprised the various forms of *mousike*, including epic and lyric poetry, drama, history, dance, and astronomy. Evidently the classification represents a sophisticated point of view in which the original *mousike* has been elaborated and in part dissected into component arts. The presence of astronomy can be explained by the mathematical and synesthetic connections between the cosmos and music; it is present where arithmetic and geometry are absent because it deals with time and motion even more essentially than harmonics does. The heavens are a complete work of art, even though they can be subjected to scientific analysis. Astronomy can become a Muse, which is to say it can become sonorous, because motion connects it with sonority; just as harmony—not harmonics—can be the Mother of the Muses because its broad domain comprises temporal manifestations as well as static. Like the *enkyklios paideia*, the Muses testify to a musical conception of culture, and they represent the sphere of artistic practice, in contrast to that of mathematical cosmology and scientific theory.

That grammar, harmonics, and rhythmics were indeed associated with the *enkyklios paideia* as rationalizations of musical practice is strongly suggested by certain passages in Plato's *Cratylus, Theaetetus,* and *Philebus*.[9] Socrates compares the letters, syllables, words, and articulate speech of grammar to the tones, intervals, systems, and melody of harmonics, and also to the durations, feet, meters, and poetic form of rhythmics. Here we have exactly the divisions of an empirically oriented harmonics and rhythmics, as these studies are known in the writings of Aristoxenus. But in the very element of the comparison—the letter, tone, and basic duration—there is contained something more than a simple correspondence; the relationship is closer than one resulting from a single system of analysis applied to three different fields. The element of grammar was not the *gramma*, or letter, but the *stoicheion*,[10] a sonorous entity, a vowel sound; speech and melody both involved the organization of tone, one according to verbal reason and the other according to pitch. Rhythm was the organization of durational form, and also followed harmonic principles. The identity of vowel sound and tone is clearly shown

[9] *Cratylus* 424b–25b; *Theaetetus* 201e–06c; *Philebus* 16c–18d.
[10] See the study by Hermann Koller, *Stoicheion*, in: *Glotta*, XXXIV (1955).

by solmization; the vowel was the only way to realize the vocal tone, but still more, it revealed the serial position of the tone in the tetrachord, and was thus directly coordinated with pitch. Thus the grammatical *stoicheia* were measured tones capable of serial arrangement, and not simply elemental constituents indifferent in nature. This new concept of element can have originated only in music, although it soon developed into a general word for elements of any type. If in their search for first principles the Pythagoreans turned from the notion of primitive material constituents to formal ones, if they found their *arche*, as Aristotle reports, in number, then the concept of *stoicheion* can with some probability be attributed to them, especially since such serial constituents were both numerical and harmonic and could very well have been durational also. The numbers they found in all things would here have been concrete tones of defined pitch and duration, possibly thought of in addition as the bearers of conceptual meaning. Again it is in the 5th century, shortly after the term *stoicheion* itself appears, that the *stoicheion* of grammar begins to change into the *gramma;* the sonorous and tonal "element" becomes identified with its symbol, a visual and purely linguistic "letter." But its original significance argues persuasively that grammar, harmonics, and rhythmics all arose from the unity of music. The parallel of grammar and harmonics persists for centuries within the sphere of Neoplatonic thought; it is found in the commentary of Calcidius on Plato's *Timaeus* (4th century A.D.), and in various musical treatises starting in the 9th century.[11] From a purely structural point of view, the detailed correspondences between various disciplines are produced by an analytical method that has a numerical basis. The *Philebus* emphasizes the role of number in grammar, harmonics, and rhythmics, and Socrates observes humorously that "he who never looks for number in anything will not himself be looked for in the number of famous men." In the *Theaetetus* also, where the same method of division is illustrated, grammar is used in conjunction with arithmetic, and letters are expressly coupled with the elements of all things. Indeed all the relevant Platonic passages point to a Pythagorean origin for this analytical conception. The generality of the method and its metaphysical significance again can be found in the Middle Ages, in the *De divisione naturae* of John Scotus (9th century), where all the sciences are conceived as proceeding from unity, and the tonus of music is expressly

---

[11] *Timaeus a Calcidio translatus commentarioque instructus,* edited by J. H. Waszink (London 1962), pp. 92–93. The examples in musical treatises can be found conveniently in Martin Gerbert, ed., *Scriptores ecclesiastici de musica* (St. Blasien 1784), I, 152, 275–276; II, 14–15.

compared with the monas, signum, and atom of arithmetic, geometry, and astronomy.[12] If the application of quantitative thought to the external world and to being in general gave rise to the quadrivial sciences, a similar process applied to musical practice created the formal subjects of the *enkyklios paideia*. The coincidence that music was the major determinant of both spheres of knowledge produced a confusing overlap of subject matter, our chief source of difficulty in attempting to understand the system of liberal arts.

As the arts of the Muses drew apart, the specifically verbal aspect of music became an object of study in its own right. But it was only natural that the trivium should preserve remnants of the earlier comprehensive art. We have seen that the fundamental divisions of grammar—vowel sounds, syllables, words, and so on—mirror the fundamental divisions of harmonics and rhythmics. But this basic science of the trivium also literally includes the musical disciplines of rhythmics and metrics, elaborate discussions of which are to be found in the treatise of Donatus, perhaps the most important grammatical source for compendiums of the liberal arts. Isidore describes 124 kinds of rhythmical feet, as well as various meters and types of poetry such as bucolic, elegiac, and so forth—all within the scope of his discourse on grammar. He tells us, for example, that the hexameter "excels the rest of the meters in authority, being alone fitted as well to the greatest tasks as to the small, and with an equal capacity for sweetness and delight," and that David the prophet "was the first to compose and sing hymns in praise of God," while Timotheus "wrote the first hymns in honor of Apollo and the Muses." [13]

But it is not only grammar that contains musical material. In a more impressive fashion, rhetoric appears to have taken up every feature of music into its province; and although the literally musical character of oratory is often inconspicuous in manuals of the liberal arts, the specialized treatises from which these are derived—most importantly, the writings of Cicero and Quintilian—reveal the true importance of music in rhetorical practice and theory. The delivery of a speech demands attention to the quality and pitch of the voice, to bodily movements of all kinds, and to emotional expression, while rhythmics and metrics assume considerable importance in the discussion of rhetorical style, especially in connection with clausulae. Indeed the study of prose style in general, which grew out of oratory, is centrally concerned with euphony and rhythm; composition and its musical properties are its

---

[12] *Patrologiae cursus completus, Series latina*, edited by J. P. Migne (Paris 1865), CXXII, 869.
[13] *Etym.* I. 39.

main themes. The orator of late antiquity can with justice be called the leading practitioner of music, even in respect of his ethical mission, his social role, and his powerful influence on the feelings of the audience; he was the positive counterpart of the musical virtuoso of the theater.

Important as they are, the musical components of grammar and rhetoric are by no means the only musical constituents of lower education, for with the change from rhetorical motivation to religious utility, the conventional trivium was replaced by a new group of studies: music, grammar, and computational arithmetic. In this "Carolingian trivium," music once again became the controlling interest, just at it had been in earliest antiquity. Education was transformed by the inherent powers of music, now manifested in the vital musical practice of liturgical singing. Whether attached to a cathedral, a church, or a cloister, the medieval lower school was concerned primarily with the *cantus ecclesiasticus*. The pupils were essentially singing students; they studied musical notation along with their letters, and even grammar and the computation of the church calendar were approached through song. The obvious values of the curriculum stood in contrast to the older justification of the classical liberal arts, which had been admitted by Augustine and Cassiodorus only in so far as they served the understanding of scripture. Thus the *ars musica* had been an adjunct, while the *cantus ecclesiasticus* was an integral part of the Christian world. In a process reminiscent of the ancient evolution of the *enkyklios paideia*, a new body of theory was gradually derived from medieval musical practice, but the development was complicated by the necessity of harmonizing the novel science with the traditional one.[14] The tracts of the Carolingian era were in part devoted to the elementary pedagogy of the *schola cantorum*, but they were also concerned with a more elaborate theoretical elucidation of contemporary music, a speculative interest that was doubtless of value in the professional training of the cantor. A knowledge of the heritage of Greek theory was decisive in this connection, and while the liberal ideal of Cassiodorus had been counteracted first by asceticism and then by an exclusive concentration on liturgical song, the secular learning of Irish monks was transported to the continent as early as the 7th century and gradually brought the liberal arts into prominence, achieving its greatest influence and diffusion through the work of Alcuin and his pupils. In the larger monastic schools before the Cluniac and Cistercian reforms, in the episcopal schools, and later

[14] See the article by Joseph Smits van Waesberghe, *La place exceptionelle de l'Ars musica dans le développement des sciences au siècle des carolingiens*, in: *Revue grégorienne*, XXXI (1952).

in the *studium generale* and the university, medieval scholars and professors accomplished an impressive rationalization of musical practice. The science they created was specifically medieval, and it successively examined every current technical problem of polyphony and rhythm in systematic detail; but it had its basis in the reinterpretation of Greek concepts and its procedure was characteristically mathematical. Tracts would often open with a series of traditional topics borrowed from the hortative or introductory vein of the quadrivial science of music, and the spirit that informed the musical speculum or summa belonged more to the quadrivium than to the trivium. Indeed the scientific dignity of practice had its reflection in the very style of Gothic polyphony and its corollary in the fact that composer and theorist were often one and the same person.

But if treatises on practical music were shaped by the rational attitude of the quadrivium and even found their way into the university curriculum, an opposite change had taken place long before in the earlier quadrivial study of music, for this had assimilated many of the conceptions that arose in the sphere of practice. The subject explicitly designated as "music" (or "harmony") in the system of liberal arts was by no means a strictly mathematical study of ratios and scales, but to a considerable degree was also humanistic and historical. The duality of the sources of the medieval notion of *ars musica* is clearly reflected in the diverse definitions found in the treatises; the two main traditions can even be represented side by side in the same compendium. The science of music is defined variously as treating of proper movement, of relative quantity, or of measurement in relation to sound; by way of contrast, practice rather than theory accounts for the definition of music as the science of poems and songs, or as the science of melody and singing. The former group of definitions closely parallel those of the other divisions of the quadrivium, while the latter group duplicate the form and phraseology of the definitions of grammar and rhetoric.

The contents of the scientific musical tract were initially liberalized by Aristotle, who freed harmonics from its subservience to philosophy and gave it a new relationship to sense; this process was continued by his pupils and given its final impetus by rhetoric, which discovered important expressive values in musical sonority. Music in the quadrivium of the liberal arts combines Aristoxenian and Pythagorean theory; harmonics can be based almost entirely on Aristoxenus or the first book of Aristides Quintilianus. And rhythmics is also included, again in a form combining empiricism and mathematics. But throughout the Middle Ages the mathematical conception, nourished by the constant influence of Neoplatonism, remained the dominant one; while the contrition of the laity was appropriately fostered by the concrete moral force of song, theology was better served by the transcendent tendency of mathematical speculation.

A final constituent of the *ars musica* was a traditional stock of ethical material, legends of the effects of music and theories of its value, all obviously associated with musical practice rather than mathematics. To be sure, Pythagorean harmonics itself represented a final and general stage in the process of purifying the soul from the world of sense; but the more conspicuous ethical values of sonorous music reinforce this superiority and become responsible for a continuing emphasis on the worth of music. "Of the four mathematical disciplines," Boethius says, "the others are concerned with the pursuit of truth, while music is related not only to speculation but also to morality." [15] Music is preferred for a property the other quadrivial sciences obviously cannot claim to possess, for their sensible and applied forms have a purely utilitarian character.

[15] *De inst. mus.* I. I.

ON "PARODY" AS
TERM AND CONCEPT IN
16th-CENTURY MUSIC

by LEWIS LOCKWOOD

FEW TERMS can be more common coin in studies of 16th-century music than "parody" and its compounds ("parody technique," "parody Mass," etc.), yet few are more urgently in need of elucidation. In the introductory stages of definition all goes smoothly, for the distinction between the conventional and technical meanings of the term is easily made. Indeed, there is scarcely a more familiar procedure in accounts of older polyphony than to introduce the term, to divest it of its connotations of travesty and burlesque, and to reduce it to the neutral function of denoting—however loosely—the class of polyphonic compositions derived to some extent from polyphonic antecedents. The barriers arise when one attempts to reach more refined shades of meaning and more exact prescriptions of usage. The purpose of these remarks is to try to clear away a few of these obstacles, first by examining the basis for the authority of the term itself, and then by considering what some early sources tell us about the concept for which it normally stands.

Although a number of music historians have tried to dislodge "parody" from the professional vocabulary, on the grounds of possible confusion of its technical with its ordinary meaning, none has yet had the slightest success in curbing its use. Doubtless this is due in part to the force of habit and inertia, but it must also be due to inherent weaknesses in the substitutes thus far proposed. These have been either cumbersome or ambiguous, or have seemed to evoke new associations more misleading than those abandoned; for example, such substitutes for "parody Mass" as "elaboration Mass," "second-hand Mass," "polytranscription," or "derived Mass." [1] But the solid hold of "parody" has also

[1] For these terms and for comments on them see the following: W. Rubsamen, *Some First Elaborations of Masses from Motets*, in: *Bulletin of the American Musicological Society*, IV (1940), 6–9; R. B. Lenaerts, *The 16th-Century Parody Mass in the Netherlands*, in: MQ, XXXVI (1950), 410–21; Knud Jeppesen in: MQ, XLI (1955), 388; Frank Ll. Harrison, *Music in Medieval Britain* (London 1958),

been due to quite general acceptance of the claims advanced for *parodia* and *Missa parodia*, namely, that of the terms so far introduced in this category, only these two have a historical foundation in the technical parlance of the 16th century. It is therefore cause for some surprise when a close look at the available evidence discloses that the factual basis for this use of *parodia* is virtually non-existent, and that the widespread belief that *Missa parodia* was a familiar term among Renaissance musicians has so little documentary support that it can scarcely be maintained.

What may well be considered a major myth of terminology seems to have originated almost by accident in the 19th century, and to have gained wide acceptance since then. The first music historian to use the term in reference to Renaissance polyphony seems to have been Ambros, in the masterly third volume of his *Geschichte der Musik*,[2] and it is no coincidence that he was also the first to describe the practice at all adequately. But what later writers seem to have overlooked is that Ambros never really claimed that *parodia* and *Missa parodia* were terms widely employed in the 16th century. All he did was to offer one sober and objective reference to *one* use of the term that he had run across in the title of a single Mass by Jacob Paix (a relatively obscure German organist and composer of the second half of the century), published in 1587 as a separate composition.[3] Yet by the time of Peter Wagner's *Geschichte der Messe* (1913), this isolated bit of evidence had somehow grown significantly in importance. Although Wagner too cited only this one Mass by Paix, his use of the term encouraged the inference that it had been quite familiar in Paix's time: "Im 16. Jahrhundert nannte man solche Messen Missae parodiae."[4] And from Wagner's deservedly authoritative monograph it was but a short step, or series of steps, through the labyrinthine chain of German, French, and English reference books, to "Parodiemesse," "Messe parodie," "parody Mass," and thence to "parody technique" and other derivatives.

p. 283; Ludwig Finscher, *Parodie und Kontrafaktur*, in MGG, X (1962), 815 *infra*. The term was unfortunately not discussed in Hans Heinrich Eggebrecht's pioneering *Studien zur musikalischen Terminologie* (Mainz 1955).

[2] Ambros, III (1868), 45. That the term was not known to earlier music historians in this meaning is apparent from its absence in the 16th-century sections of the histories of Burney and Hawkins, in Forkel's description of Mass-types in his *Allgemeine Geschichte der Musik*, II, 562, in Baini's *Palestrina* (1828), Winterfeld's *Gabrieli* (1834), and in Kiesewetter's *Geschichte der Musik* (1834).

[3] Ambros, III, 45, writes: "Eigenthümlich ist jene Gattung von Messen, die der Organist Jacob Paix von Lauingen mit dem Namen Missa parodia bezeichnet." Peter Wagner, *Geschichte der Messe*, p. 69, refers to Ambros, III, 45, and also to a supposed reference to *Missa parodia* in Ambros, III, 218; but I am unable to find any mention of it on that page.

[4] Wagner, p. 69. See the further references in Wagner's book given in the index under the entry "missa parodia."

The term has thus gained international currency and continues in ever-widening use, even though no one since Ambros has produced a scrap of evidence showing the use of the designation *Missa parodia* by any 16th-century musician other than Jacob Paix in this one Mass of 1587.[5] Paix was then a church organist in the provincial town of Lauingen on the Danube, and while his organ works and transcriptions have received considerable attention, neither this Mass nor any other of his vocal compositions has ever been reprinted or even described. This is unfortunate, for had they been, the isolated and artificial character of Paix's one use of this term would have stood out sharply against the background provided by the 1587 publication as a whole, as well as by a parallel Mass print of his, brought out three years before, and by his own references to these two Masses.

Moreover, a glance at the broadly dispersed linguistic conventions by which Masses were designated in the 16th century makes the adventitious character of *parodia* in Paix's title all the more apparent. That there were such linguistic conventions across the century becomes clear from a scrutiny of primary and secondary sources, and while the present remarks can scarcely claim to be utterly exhaustive, they are nevertheless as complete as such a scrutiny can make them. Their burden is that the established conventions were more nearly uniform at the beginning of the century, more diverse at the end; that they tended to divide along regional lines; and that the term *parodia*, so far as can now be told, was unknown in this meaning, or as a musical designation, before Paix used it in 1587.

There appear to have been three principal ways in which 16th-century Masses were designated: (1) simply as *Missa*, followed directly by the name of the source, whatever its origin (e.g. *Missa Di dadi*, *Missa Ecce sacerdos magnus*, etc.); (2) as *Missa super* . . . (or using the vernacular prepositions "sopra" or "sur"; (3) as *Missa ad imitationem moduli* . . . (or *cantionis* or *motetae*), with designation of the source. Of these three means of denomination, the first is found uniformly in the earliest Mass publications of the century (those of Petrucci, Antico, and Giunta, and of the first French printers, Attaingnant and Moderne).[6]

[5] Paix, born at Augsburg in 1556, passed his career at Lauingen (1576–1601) and Neuburg (1601–c.1617), and died sometime after 1623. See the article on Paix by Manfred Schuler in MGG, X (1962), 647–49 and the bibliography given there. The best-known of Paix's publications was his organ tablature of 1583, on which see especially W. Merian, *Der Tanz in den deutschen Tabulaturbüchern* (Leipzig 1927), pp. 114–66.

[6] See C. Sartori, *Bibliografia delle opere musicali stampate da Ottaviano Petrucci* (Florence 1948); R. Eitner, *Bibliographie der Musik-Sammelwerke* (Berlin 1877); G. Gaspari, *Catalogo . . . Bologna*, II, 17–155 and other bibliographies. I am also indebted to Professor Daniel Heartz for access, prior to publication, to his forthcoming bibliography of the prints of Attaingnant.

It is also found in many manuscripts of this period. At about mid-century two distinct conventions emerge: the first method continues to be used in Italian publications down to the end of the century, with an occasional preference for the closely related second method.[7] In France, however, the Parisian publisher Du Chemin seems to be the first to systematically introduce the third method, with its more refined, more classical, more humanistic turn of phrase. From 1552 to 1568, Du Chemin produced some 22 Mass publications (mainly of single works by French and Flemish composers), and in every one of these the Mass and its antecedent are named in the title by means of the formula *Missa ad imitationem* . . . with the name of the model. The pattern is established by Goudimel's *Missa ad imitationem cantionis Il ne se treuve en amitié* of 1552.[8] The distinctive feature of this French convention is that it makes the polyphonic relationship explicit in the title for the first time, and that the operative term for this relationship is *imitatio*, a term richly laden with associations for literary-minded musicians and patrons of music in the Renaissance.

While there is no sign at present that the rubric *ad imitationem* ever passed from France to Italy, there is no doubt of its exportation to Germany. The first German Mass anthologies, the retrospective collections of Petreius, Ott, and Rhaw (1539 and 1541) still use the older means of designation. But by 1568, the year of an important anthology published by Schwertel at Wittenberg, the French formula is in use, and is adopted for every Mass in the collection.[9] From about the 1560s on, a strong

[7] E.g. Mauro Palermitano, *Missarum . . . quinque vocum* (Venice: R. Amadino, 1588) entitles three of four Masses *Missa super* . . . , and gives the name of the model's composer; e.g. *Missa super Susanna un giour. Orlandi Lassus.* An exceptional case is Claudio Merulo's *Misse Due* . . . as published at Venice in 1609: these combine the first and second conventions, such as *Missa Cara la vita mia . . . sopra il madrigale di Jaches Vuert.* See Gaspari, *Catalogo . . . Bologna,* II, 104, 106. Compare also the title of Monteverdi's Mass of 1610 (*Opere,* XIV, 57ff.): *Missa da Capella . . . fatta sopra il motetto In illo tempore del Gomberti* . . .

[8] See F. Lesure and G. Thibault, *Bibliographie des éditions musicales publiées par Nicolas Du Chemin,* in: *Annales musicologiques,* I (1953), 269–373: Nos. 26, 35, 48, 49, 50–58, 60–63, 80, 88–91. The same formula was then adopted by Le Roy & Ballard in prints extending from 1557 to 1587; see F. Lesure and G. Thibault, *Bibliographie des éditions d'Adrian Le Roy & Robert Ballard* (Paris 1955): Nos. 24–25, 28, 38–40, 42–47, 51–52, 258, 284–85. Since it appears at present that this formula began with Goudimel's Mass of 1552, it seems well worth noting that precisely at this time Goudimel, then a student at the University of Paris, was in effect "artistic director" for the musical publications of Du Chemin. See Lesure and Thibault in *Annales musicologiques,* I (1953), 274f.

[9] E.g. *Missa quinque vocum Ad imitationem cantilenae surrexit pastor, composita: autore Lupo.* Other Masses in the volume are labeled *Ad imitationem psalmi, cantionis,* and *modulationis.* In the light of Jacob Paix's choice of model and title for his Mass of 1587, it is noteworthy that this collection of 1568 contains a direct antecedent in a Mass by Crecquillon himself: *Missa sex vocum ad imitationem cantionis, Domine da nobis auxilium, formata, autore Thoma Crequilone.* For the full title of the entire collection see the *Répertoire international des sources musicales,* Vol. I, No. 1568¹.

vein of German humanism seems to have encouraged the wide use of the formula,[10] and it is precisely this wording that is used by Jacob Paix when he himself refers to his published Masses of 1584 and 1587 in letters of dedication he wrote for the two works. The contextual meaning of *parodia*, as Paix uses it in the 1587 title, will be clear if we simply place side by side his titles for both of these Masses, which were published at Lauingen by the same local printer and are further parallel in being based on motets by Mouton and Crecquillon that had been published in German collections [11] (see Figs. 1a, 1b for facsimiles of the title pages):

Mass of 1584:
Missa./Ad Imitationem Mottetæ In illo tempore./Ioan[nis] Moutonis, Quatuor Vocum./. . .

Mass of 1587:
Missa:/Parodia/Mottetæ Domine/da nobis auxilium, Thomæ Cre-/quilonis, senis Vocibus, ad/Dorium./. . .

The first publication, of 1584, follows the French convention to the letter, adding the name of the composer of the model to the usual formula. On the title page of the 1587 Mass, the term *Missa* is all but buried in the upper decorative border of each partbook and is separated from what follows by a colon, so that one might well question whether the

[10] Perhaps the earliest use of the formula in a German source is that in Berg & Neuber's *Thesaurus musicus*, I (1564), in which a *Salve regina* by Jacob Vaet is labeled *ad imitationem iay mys mon coeur;* quoted by M. Steinhardt, *Jacobus Vaet and his Motets* (East Lansing 1951), p. 56. Some other instances of its use in German publications of the period are those by Andreas Crappius, in a Mass published by Schwertel at Wittenberg in 1573; see Á. Davidsson, *Catalogue . . . des imprimés de musique . . . dans les bibliothèques suédoises* (Upsala 1952), p. 103; by the Nuremberg publisher Friedrich Lindner in his *Missae quinquae* of 1590; see RISM I, 1590[1], and Eitner, *Sammelwerke*, 1590a; and by Jacob Regnart in Mass prints of 1602 and 1603 published at Frankfurt; see R. Mitjana, *Catalogue . . . d'Upsala*, I (Upsala 1911), Nos. 179–81. Noteworthy too is the way in which what we would call the "parody" relationship is referred to in letters of the 1550s from Bavarian archives, published by A. Sandberger, *Beiträge zur Geschichte der bayerischen Hofkapelle unter Orlando di Lasso*, III (Leipzig 1894), 304f: Maximilian II refers to "ain Mess, die mein capellmeister *aufs* dissimulare . . ." [note the German equivalent of the Italian "sopra"]; and Dr. Seld, the Bavarian Vice-chancellor, writes to Albrecht V: "Und sollen E.F.G. wissen, dass der Rö. M. Capellmaister ain Motet mit 6 gemacht, nemlich *Vitam quam faciunt beatiorem*, darinnen hatt er des Orlando *Tityre tu patulae* wellen *Imitiren* [again the same term!]. Also ist die Mess *auf* beide die selben Moteten gemacht." (My italics in both quotations.)

[11] Although Paix's choice of a motet by Mouton might be taken to imply a broad acquaintance with music of a considerably earlier generation and quite distant from his own milieu, the bibliographic facts support the assumption that to know these two motets Paix needed nothing more than fairly recent German publications. The Mouton model is the motet *In illo tempore accesserunt: Propter hoc dimittet*, 4 v., which is indeed known *only* from Ott's *Novum et insigne opus musicum*, 1537[1]; and Berg & Neuber's *Magnum opus musicum*, III, 1559[2]. Rolf Dammann, *Studien zu den Motetten von Jean Mouton* (Diss. Freiburg 1952), *Nachtrag*, expresses doubt that this motet is by Mouton. As for the Crecquillon motet, it was published at Nuremberg in Berg & Neuber's *Tomus quartus psalmorum selectorum*, 1554[11]; and at Antwerp by Waelrand & Laet, *Sacrarum cantionum . . . liber tertius*, 1555[7]. See also fn. 9 above.

Fig. 1a Title page of tenor of Jacob Paix's Mass of 1584, based on Mouton's motet *In illo tempore accesserunt*

MISSA·

Ad Imitationem Mottetæ In illo tempore.
Ioan. Moutonis, Quatuor Vocum.

A

IACOBO PAIX, ORGANICO LAVINGANO.

TENOR

Lauingæ imprimebat Leonhardus Reinmichælius.
Anno M. D. LXXXIIII.

words *Missa* and *Parodia* form a direct grammatical unit at all. But even granting that they do, it is perfectly obvious that the formula is the same as that of 1584 with the single exception of one element: the insertion of *parodia* (from the Greek Παρῳδία: "counter-song" or "Nebengesang") as an elegant, classical replacement for *ad imitationem*.[12] Evidently, Paix is merely indulging the humanistic habit of substituting a classical Greek word for a Latin one. That the two titles meant the same thing to him is further evident not only in the two compositions themselves, but in the letters of dedication he prefixed to each, in which he refers to them as follows (italics mine):

Mass of 1584:
Cum igitur . . . Ecclesiae cantionem quae Kyrie, & vulgò Missa appellatur . . . nuper *ad imitationem mottetae* In illo tempore praestantissimi artificis Iohannis Moutonis composuissem . . .

Mass of 1587:
Composui igitur senis Vocibus cantionem eccliasticam, quae Κύριε & vulgò Missa vocatur, *ad imitationem Mottetae* Domine da nobis auxilium, à praestantissimo Musico Thoma Crequilone factae.

---

[12] There are other instances of this sort of "classicization" involving Greek, or Latin-Greek mixtures, in titles of German musical publications of this period, e.g.: Christoph Walliser's *Ecclesiodiae, Das ist Kirchen Gesang* (Strasbourg 1614); or Praetorius's collections, *Missodia sionia* [Masses], *Hymnodia sionia* [Hymns], *Eulogodia sionia* [Antiphons], and *Megalynodia sionia* [Magnificats] of 1611. The last is especially interesting in this connection, since it consists of what we would now call "parody Magnificats" but makes no use of the term *parodia;* rather,

Fig. 1b   Title page of discantus of Jacob Paix's Mass of 1587, based on
Crequillon's motet, *Domine da nobis auxilium*

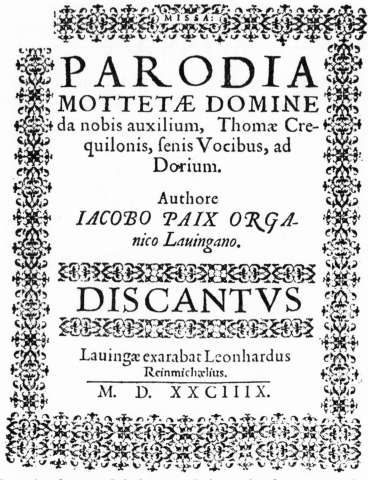

MISSA:

PARODIA
MOTTETÆ DOMINE
da nobis auxilium, Thomæ Cre-
quilonis, fenis Vocibus, ad
Dorium.

Authore
IACOBO PAIX ORGA-
nico Lauingano.

DISCANTVS

Lauingæ exarabat Leonhardus
Reinmichælius.

M.   D.   X X C I I I X.

When, therefore . . . I had com-	I have therefore composed this
posed this sacred composition,	sacred composition for six voices,

When, therefore . . . I had composed this sacred composition,
called "Kyrie," or, more commonly,
"Missa," . . . in imitation of the
motet *In illo tempore* by the most
famous and most skilful Jean Mouton . . .

I have therefore composed this
sacred composition for six voices,
called "Kyrie," or, more commonly,
"Missa," in imitation of the motet
Domine da nobis auxilium, by the
most famous musician, Thomas
Crecquillon.

In both letters the pedantic lingering over "Kyrie" and "Missa" reflects
a sense of exactitude unusual even for a German humanist, and it is even
more strongly in evidence when Paix goes so far as to print the texts of

Praetorius uses the formula "super . . ." See M. Praetorius, *Gesamtausgabe der
musikalischen Werke*, Band XIV.

the Kyrie-Christe-Kyrie, in both Masses, *entirely in Greek* in every partbook. (See Fig. 2 for the superius of the 1587 Kyrie.) Other publications of his reveal the same bent for the display of classical learning, now mixed with some pride in knowledge of theory. In a motet anthology he compiled for practical use he quotes extensively from Gafori and Zarlino; and in an organ tablature of 1583 he intersperses proverbs and quotations among intabulated dance compositions.[13] It scarcely seems surprising, then, that a musician of such leanings should have been the man to use the term *parodia* for polyphonic imitation of this kind, thus choosing a term that had originally been taken over from Greek by direct transliteration. Paix could possibly have seen it in its Latin form (and in reference to music) in Quintilian's *Institutiones oratoriae*, or in a commentary on it; Quintilian's famous compendium was not only enormously influential in the formation of Renaissance theories of education, but has been described as "for many centuries an authority on matters of literary composition second only to Cicero; and in actual influence even greater than Cicero."[14] Had there been any historic justice, however, it would not have been *parodia* that has come down to us as the term representing the practice of polyphonic borrowing, but rather *imitatio*, the term actually used in innumerable other cases and even in this very one in which *parodia* itself uniquely appeared.

WHAT little theoretical discussion of this concept one finds in the 16th century confirms the evidence of the practical sources. Very few theorists devote any attention to the practice of polyphonic derivation, despite its manifest importance as a contemporary procedure of com-

---

[13] The motet anthology is his *Selectae . . . fugae . . .* (Lauingen 1594); see Eitner, *Sammelwerke*, 1594. On the tablature see Merian, *Tanz* (fn. 5 above), and A. G. Ritter, *Zur Geschichte des Orgelspiels*, II (Leipzig 1894), 126–28.

[14] W. L. Bullock, *The Precept of Plagiarism in the Cinquecento*, in: *Modern Philology*, XXV (1927/28), 296. The possible relevance of this use of the term by Quintilian was first pointed out for music historians by L. Finscher in MGG, X (1962), 815. The question of the relationship between the term and the practice of borrowing in 16th- and 17th-century literatures—and the connection of these to music, if any—is so complex and difficult that it is impossible to deal with it at all adequately here. Some very valuable observations have recently been offered by Rosamond Tuve, *Sacred 'Parody' of Love Poetry, and Herbert*, in: *Studies in the Renaissance, Publications of the Renaissance Society of America*, VIII (1962), 249–90. It should be noted, however, that the present evidence tends to undermine Miss Tuve's contention that the word "parody" as a literary term, in 17th-century England, denoting transformation in poetry, could have been derived from a common use of *missa parodia* as a musical term. What remains to be investigated is the possibility that musicians of the 16th century recognized in their own manipulations of antecedents something akin to the transformations practiced in contemporary literature (neutral or serious rather than satiric), and that the prevalent term *imitatio* may reflect such a connection.

Fig. 2 End of dedicatory letter by Jacob Paix for his Mass of 1587, and discantus part for Kyrie I and Christe (texts in Greek)

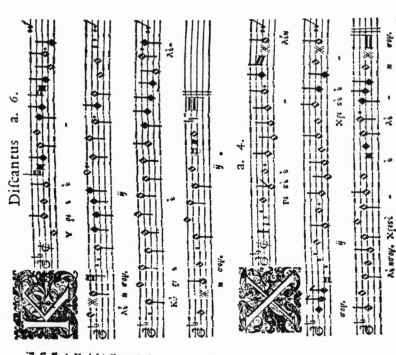

Discantus a. 6.

a. 4.

PRÆFATIO.

voluptate & commendatione eorum omnium, quibus audiendi data fuit potestas. Quod suum erga diuinam hanc artem studium C. T. illustrissima nobis quoque non obscurè declarauit, cum nuper Lauingam transiret, & tenui nostræ Musicæ aures tam benignas præberet. Quæ res me mouit, & tantum non impulit, vt aliquod obseruantiæ erga C. T. meæ testimonium ederem, Composui igitur senis Vocibus cantionem ecclesiasticam, quæ κύριε & vulgò Missa vocatur, ad imitationem Motetæ Domine da nobis auxilium, à præstantissimo Musico Thoma Crequilone factæ. Quantum verò præstiterim, rectius iudicabunt artifices, qui eam secundum artis præcepta accuratè examinabunt, quàm ij qui obiter tantum inspicient aut canent. Quem meum laborem C. T. humiliter offero dedicoque, & vt eam hilari fronte solitaque clementia suscipiat, ea qua possum & debeo animi humilitate & submisione rogo & obsecro. Cui etiam felicem gubernationem & diuturnam rerum omnium tranquillitatem à Deo Opt. Max, precor, & me artemque Musicam humilimè commendo. Lauingæ Dominica Trinitatis, Anno M. D. LXXXVII.

Celsitudini tuæ

deditissimus

Iacobus Paix Augusta-nus, Organicus La-uinganus.

position, and those who do discuss it appear well after the practice had become established: we can find brief passing allusions to the practice in the treatises of Vicentino (1555) and Zarlino (1558); more extended references by Pietro Ponzio in writings of 1588 and 1595; and a still more extended though far from exhaustive discussion by Cerone, in his *Melopeo y maestro* of 1613.[15]

The terminology used by all these theorists fully corroborates what we see in the practical sources: the term *parodia* is unknown to any of them. Vicentino merely alludes to the practice of basing Masses on madrigals and chansons in a passage bearing on the mingling of secular elements in sacred music, and he uses the expression "alcuni comporranno una Messa *sopra* un Madrigale, & *sopra* una Canzone Franzese, o *sopra* la battaglia . . ." [16] (italics mine). Zarlino, in Book III of the *Istituzioni*, makes passing mention of this type of borrowing when he says that the *soggetto* may consist of more than one part from a polyphonic antecedent.[17] Ponzio, in his *Dialogo* of 1595, offers two passing references to polyphonic borrowing, and the point of interest in both is again the use of *imitatione* as a term referring to two interrelated compositions, in contradistinction to *fuga*, the familiar alternative 16th-century term for contrapuntal "imitation," as later understood.

[15] Recently, Hellmuth Christian Wolff has contributed a brilliant find, in a hitherto unnoticed passage from a treatise by Johann Frosch that can be dated 1532 (Frosch was a German theorist of the Luther circle): see Wolff, *Die aesthetische Auffassung der Parodiemesse des 16. Jahrhunderts*, in: *Miscelánea en homenaje a Mons. Higinio Anglés* (Barcelona 1958-61), II, 1011-19. In this passage, Frosch advises the tyro (to whom the whole treatise is addressed) to learn through imitation (again the Latin term *imitatio*) of the best composers, to copy down well-constructed passages in their works, and to use these passages (*commissurae*) at opportune moments in his own compositions. Frosch supplies highly enlightening examples, one of which is given in its entirety by Wolff. It may be questioned, however, whether the passage from Frosch really bears on "parody technique" as we know it, or whether Frosch is merely suggesting a means of generally acquiring skill in composition. The difference is that neither his text nor his examples have to do with the problem of deriving a *single* composition from a single antecedent, but are concerned rather with the presentation of a variety of passages (all cadential ones, be it noted) that can be inserted in compositions generally. For this reason I do not at the moment count Frosch among those who write *directly* of "parody" in the sense of compositions having a one-to-one relationship. (The 1535 edition of Frosch's treatise is available, incidentally, from the Deutsches Musikgeschichtliches Archiv, Kassel, No. 1/447.)

[16] *L'antica musica ridotta alla moderna prattica* (Facs. ed. Edward Lowinsky, *Documenta musicologica*, XVII), fol. 84ᵛ (wrongly numbered 79ᵛ).

[17] Zarlino, *Istituzioni armoniche* (Venice 1589 edition), III, 211. Translated in O. Strunk, *Source Readings in Music History* (New York 1950), p. 229 (a passage which admirably restates for musicians one meaning of the Renaissance theory of *imitatio*) and p. 231 (in which Zarlino specifically refers to the borrowing of the *soggetto* and its re-working).

Ponzio, *Dialogo* (1595)

Et in questo proposto voglio dire, che, trouandosi una cantilena simile di figure, & d'intervalli à quella di qualche altro Compositore, esso sarebbe giudicato huomo di poca scienza, & di niun valore; eccetto però, se non fosse per qualche imitatione di Messe ouer Ricercarij; che in tal caso vien lecito al Compositore il pigliar l'istessa inuentione & Harmonia propria di detta compositione . . .[18] (p. 45)	And in this connection I wish to say that, when one finds a composition similar in figures and intervals to one by another composer, the borrowing composer would be considered a man of little ability and of no value— unless it were a case of imitation in a Mass or ricercar, in which case the composer is permitted to borrow the inventions and harmony themselves from the other composition . . .
L'imitatione sarà questa, che imitarà un Motetto, Madrigale, ò Canzone con gli istessi movimenti; ma non servarà il valore delle figure del Motetto, ò Madrigale, od altra cosa, che si sia; nè tampoco alle volte gli stessi Tuoni, e Semituoni. Questo modo adunque si dirà imitatione; e questa è la differenza, che si trova tra la fuga, & l'imitatione. (p. 106)	Imitation will consist in this: that one will imitate a motet, madrigal, or chanson, with the same elements of movement; but one will not use the temporal values of the figures of the motet, madrigal, or whatever it may be; nor, at times, the same successions of tones and semitones. This procedure will be called "imitation"; and this is the difference between "fugue" and "imitation."

In his earlier treatise, the *Ragionamento* of 1588, Ponzio discourses on the general procedures that should be followed in the composition of various types of pieces: motet, Mass, psalm, magnificat, lesson, ricercar, madrigal (pp. 154–60). Since the entire treatise is now readily available in facsimile reprint,[19] details need not be cited here. Pertinent again, however, is the absence of the term *parodia*, and also of interest is the relationship between this part of Ponzio's *Ragionamento* and the better-known discussion of methods of composition in Cerone's *El Melopeo y maestro* of 1613.[20]

---

[18] It may be observed that Ponzio's derogation of borrowing in this passage is also picked up by Cerone: *El Melopeo y maestro*, Book XII, Chap. 6, p. 675: "Haziendo Missas, le es permitido al Componedor servirse de un subiecto, que sea de otro autor, por una vez sola, y no mas . . . Uno quiere componer una Missa a 4 bozes ò a mas, puede tomar el thema de un Motete, ò Madrigal etc., y sobre della Componer su Missa; serviendose en todo el curso della de las invenciones, Fugas, y passos del Motete elegido . . . Fuera desta occasion el servirse de los passos inventados de otras Composidores es vicio, y atribuyese à hurto . . ."

[19] Edited by Suzanne Clercx, *Documenta musicologica*, XVI (Kassel 1959).

[20] Cerone, Book XII, Chaps. 12–19; chaps. 12–16 are available in translation in O. Strunk, *Source Readings in Music History* (New York 1950), pp. 263–73. The passages on the Mass are quoted in the original by Knud Jeppesen, *Marcellus-Probleme*, in: *Acta musicologica*, XVI/XVII (1944/45), 20ff.

Book XII of Cerone's gigantic compendium has long been singled out as one of the most enlightening sections in that vast mélange of lore and learning that he brought together into a volume of more than a thousand dense pages. Writing like a man who had managed to educate himself far beyond his natural capacities, Cerone must have assembled an immense store of material from assiduous reading of his predecessors. He offers many incidental annotations and postils; a long list of his "authorities" (Lib. II, Cap. 84, pp. 335–36) which supplies no particulars as to the parts he used or where he used them; and a general acknowledgment in the *Preambulo* that he has based much of his work on earlier sources.[21] So far as I have found, however, the only specific confession of dependence made by Cerone is offered at page 935, where he admits, with his usual prolixity, that he has borrowed extensively from Zarlino. Indeed, it has been observed already that much in Cerone's chapters on counterpoint and modality is little more than translation of Zarlino into Spanish;[22] in addition, there are at least some instances in which Cerone, clumsily and without acknowledgment, plagiarized from Zarlino with mere changes of names and dates.[23] No doubt a truly exhaustive comparison of Cerone with earlier writers—a task no one has yet had the patience or temerity to undertake—would yield a far clearer picture of what is old and what is new in this vast sea of information and opinion.

At all events, the dependence of Cerone's Book XII, Chapters 12–19, on Ponzio's *Ragionamento*, pp. 154–60, is self-revealing.[24] Cerone follows exactly Ponzio's ordering of subjects in discussing, a chapter at a time,

[21] See Cerone's *Preambulo* in Libro I, 3. His list of "authorities" is briefly discussed by K. G. Fellerer, *Zur Cerones musiktheoretischen Quellen*, in: *Spanische Forschungen der Görresgesellschaft*, Erste Reihe, Band 11 (1955), 171–78, but without any detailed comparison.

[22] See O. Strunk, *Readings*, p. 229, fn. 2.

[23] Thus, in Libro I, 173, Cerone tells an anecdote about the French composer Dominique Phinot (whom he evidently admires) and sets the story in Savona, near Genoa. But the whole story is lifted straight from Zarlino's *Sopplimenti musicali* (Venice 1589), Lib. 8, Cap. xiii, p. 326, where Zarlino tells it about his own master, Willaert, and places it in Venice.

[24] The reader can compare for himself the following passages ("*l.*" = line on page): Cerone, p. 685, *l.* 40–46, 49–50 / Ponzio, p. 153, *l.* 23–29 & p. 154, *l.* 4–5; Cerone, p. 686, *l.* 1–9, 10¹, 11², 12–14, 19–20, 21–22, 23–29 / Ponzio, p. 154, *l.* 6–16, 23–29 & p. 155, *l.* 1–2. Here and there Cerone shuffles the order of a few sentences. Similarly (to give pages only), Cerone, p. 687 / Ponzio, pp. 155–56; Cerone, p. 688 (parts of sections ix and xii) / Ponzio, p. 156; Cerone, p. 690 / Ponzio, pp. 157–58. With these dependences in mind, I looked through Cerone's and Ponzio's discussions of contrapuntal technique for any further similarities. And, sure enough, it is very clear that a good deal in Cerone's often-praised discussions of counterpoint is also derived from Ponzio's *Ragionamento*, including many musical examples, lifted note for note or altered very slightly. The relevant part of Cerone is Book XI; see, for example, Cerone, p. 618, Exx. 2, 4, 5, 6 / Ponzio, pp. 29–30; also Cerone, p. 623 / Ponzio, pp. 34–36; Cerone, p. 624 / Ponzio, pp. 37, 38, 40.

the "proper method of composing" the motet; Mass; psalm; canticles; hymns and lamentations; ricercari and tientos; and madrigals. To this he adds an evidently original chapter covering the "Chanzoneta, Frotolas y los Estrambotes." Since each category of composition is given a chapter of its own, Cerone's discussion is in every case longer and more elaborate than Ponzio's. Yet in each chapter there are at least some important observations which are nearly verbatim translations from Ponzio, fitted out with slight interpolations, adjustments, and modifications. Here is a sample from Chapter XII, concerning the Mass:

Ponzio (1588), p. 155, lines 15ff.

Cerone (1613), p. 687, lines 5ff.

Lo stile, ouer modo, come vogliamo dire, di Messe è conforme à quello del Motetto, intendendo però il far movimento con le parti; ma quanto all' ordine, esso è diverso; poiche nel Motetto il principio della seconda parte potrete voi fare, come vi piace; mentre sia appropriato al Tuono; ma nel far una Messa la inventione del suo primo Kyrie, cioè il principio, & quello della Gloria, & del Credo, & del Sanctus, & del primo Agnus, conuiene, che siano simili . . .

La manera y el estilo, que se ha de tener para componer una Missa, es conforme la del Motete, enquanto al mouimiento grave, que han de tener las partes; mas no enquanto à la orden, que es muy differente. Porque el principio de la primera parte, y el principio de la segunda y mas partes del Motete, son differentes el uno do lo otro; y la inuencion esta hecha à voluntad y aluedrio del Compositor, mientras apropriada sea al Tono. Mas en el componer una Missa . . . conviene que la Inuencion en el principio del primero Kyrie, y en el de la Gloria in excelsis Deo, del Credo, del Sanctus, y en el del primero Agnus Dei, sea una misma . . .

Although Cerone's discussion of this type of Mass is the most detailed we have by a contemporary theorist, it falls far short of providing a theory of polyphonic borrowing adequate to the immense variety of procedures visible in even the relatively limited body of material thus far available in reprint. Like Ponzio before him, Cerone concentrates mainly on the larger framework of the Mass and on the general distribution of borrowed material among its major divisions. His prescriptions for the practice of borrowing amount to these: (1) the beginnings of the five major divisions should correspond to the beginning of the model, though their contrapuntal treatment of this material should vary; (2) the Christe may be based on a subsidiary motive from the model; (3) the Kyrie II and the second and third Agnus Dei may be based on freely invented material or on other subsidiary material from the model; (4) the ending of the Kyrie II and of the other major divisions should use, though in diverse ways, the ending of the model; (5) the endings of the interior divisions may conclude on the confinal of the tone; (6) the more use that is made of internal motives from the model, the more praiseworthy the elaboration will be.

Cerone has other valuable comments to offer on Mass composition, but they do not relate specifically to the practice of borrowing. And while we recognize that his specific prescriptions, taken by themselves, scarcely supply more than a stereotyped framework of procedure, it does not seem to have been emphasized sharply enough that they nevertheless offer, at least by implication, important clues to the concept of "parody" in the 16th century and thus to an eventual theory of this practice that might serve effectively to restrict and elucidate the term.

One of the major barriers to the definition of "parody" has arisen from its loose application to many instances and types of musical interrelationship remote from the 16th-century polyphonic styles for which the term was first used (or applied) by Ambros. Because the term provides a useful short-hand means of designating the broad class of polyphonically interrelated compositions, it has been permitted to spread far afield to other categories in other periods, some of which have little or nothing in common with the procedures of 16th-century music. In some extreme cases, "parody" has even been applied to compositions in which merely fractional citation occurs, or in which mere verbal substitution of text takes place, with no musical transformation whatever—a relationship properly restricted to the category of *contrafactum*.

A further problem arising from the wide diffusion of the term is that mere recognition of the *fact* of musical interrelationship between two works (even, to take a relevant case, two polyphonic works) has too often been allowed to take the place of distinguishing the *degree* and *type* of interrelationship between them and of discerning the principle of derivation at work. The loose extension of "parody" has tended to diminish the force of the term and the directness with which its more traditional and narrower use conveyed the meaning, not only of a set of procedures but also of a specific historical period within which these procedures functioned; a period of whose habits of musical thought such procedures were not merely congenial by-products but also direct and characteristic symptoms, part and parcel of the musicality of the time. For the narrower definition of "parody" this period was (and ought to be) pre-eminently the 16th century; its major area of cultivation (though by no means its only one) was the Mass, within whose development the category of fully developed "parody" seems to extend roughly from the works of the younger contemporaries of Josquin

(Févin, Mouton, and their peers) to the end of the century—with a convenient point of delimitation in the well-known Monteverdi Mass of 1610, based on a Gombert motet.

The element in Cerone's discussion that furnishes an important guide towards clarification of the concept is not only his emphasis on transformation rather than mere use of the borrowed material, but also his reference to *fugas y passos* ("imitations and motives") as the operative units of elaboration and composition. The second point is at least as important as the first, for it helps to focus attention on a major problem of musical history, namely, where and how to draw a line in the evolution from cantus firmus composition to "parody" composition. What Cerone's reference reconfirms is what many recent studies of "parody" technique have also tended to show: that a distinctive and essential feature of 16th-century "parody" is that its unit of procedure is the motive, and that the skill and art of "parody" lay in the manifold transformations that composers could wrest from previously formed motivic constructions. To put it another way, it seems reasonable to suggest that it is necessary but insufficient to regard "parody" as elaboration upon a known polyphonic model, or even as the type of such elaboration that makes use of all voices, or most voices, of the polyphonic source.[25] For it is possible to use all voices, but to transform nothing—or nothing but text—or, on the other hand, to rework material that is present in literal form in only one voice of a thematic complex, and to do this in what might well be considered the fashion of "parody," thanks to the nature of the material. An apparently essential historical condition for "parody" would seem to have been the development of means of contrapuntal organization based *primarily* on the manipulation of congeries of motives, each distributed to all voices in consequence of the principle of imitation and rhythmic complementation, and thus involving, as a matter of necessity, a drastic change in the concept of composition itself. And that this coincides with the decline of cantus firmus composition— of larger linear borrowing—is scarcely coincidental.[26] Admittedly, to trace the stages through which this approach to composition developed,

[25] Cf. G. Reese, *Music in the Renaissance* (New York 1954), p. 202; also Howard M. Brown, *The Chanson Spirituelle, Jacques Buus, and Parody Technique*, in: JAMS, XV (1962), 163.

[26] I am indebted here to Professor Oliver Strunk. I have attempted to deal with some specific instances that I take to be representative of early stages of this process, in an essay, *A View of the Early Sixteenth-Century Parody Mass*, to be published in a volume celebrating the 25th anniversary of the founding of the Music Department at Queens College, New York. I might add, in conclusion, that despite my own attempt to show that "parody" has little or no historical basis, I am quite prepared to continue using it—as others will do, needless to say—insisting, however, on the importance of recognizing the need, not merely to repeat the term and to apply

in short, to grasp fully the complex development from the 15th- to the 16th-century processes of polyphonic elaboration, is one of the major goals towards which more and more published transcriptions and studies are presently tending. Yet in the present state of knowledge there seems to be no reason to doubt that the rise of the motivic process of organization played a decisive role in shaping and determining the concept of "parody"—or *imitatio*—as the 16th century knew it.[27]

it with the customary looseness, but to make its multiple meanings and fields of reference progressively more exact and more significant.

[27] After this article had gone to press, there appeared an essay by Werner Braun, *Zur Parodie im 17. Jahrhundert*, in: *Bericht über den Internationalen Musikwissenschaftlichen Kongress Kassel, 1962* (Kassel 1963), 154–55, containing several interesting references to uses of the term "parody" by German musicians in the earlier 17th century. These are:

1) A motet by Sethus Calvisius based on Josquin's *Praeter rerum seriem* and published in Bodenschatz's well-known *Florilegium Portense*, 1603, is labeled "Parode ad Josquini."

2) A treatise by Georg Quitschreiber, partially described by Braun, is entitled *De Parodia* (1611) and deals with various types of musical transformations of antecedents.

3) Braun cites his earlier reference in *Archiv für Musikwissenschaft* XV (1958), 300, to a piece by the Eisenach Cantor Theodor Schuchardt which adds several voices to a 5-voice composition by Melchior Franck, and is entitled, in a source described by Braun, ". . . *In den Armen dein.* a 8. Th. Sch. Parodia ex 5. M[elchior] F[ranck] . . ."

It is especially noteworthy that all of these appear in works by German musicians of the generations immediately after that of Jacob Paix. In the meantime I have run across two further uses of the term in German treatises on poetic theory of the same period: Johann Peter Titz, *Zwey Bücher von der Kunst hochdeutscher Verse und Lieder zu Machen* (Danzig 1642), Erste Buch, Cap. XVI; and G. P. Harsdörffer, *Poetische Trichter* . . . , 2nd ed. (Nuremberg 1660), Fünffte Stund, p. 98. I hope to deal with these elsewhere, especially in connection with the implications of the terms *parodia* and *imitatio* in music, literature, and the fine arts in this period.

༄༅༔

PROBLEMS IN
ADRIAN WILLAERT'S
ICONOGRAPHY*

by EDWARD E. LOWINSKY

TWO YEARS AGO, during one of my first explorations of the Art Institute of Chicago, not long after my arrival in that city, the portrait of a bearded man in the wing dedicated to the old masters arrested my attention. I had never before seen it, yet I was certain I had seen the sitter. I did not know, nor care at the moment, who the painter was. I stood transfixed before the figure of an altogether unusual man whose furrowed features and faraway look suggested a thinker and an artist of uncommon depth and concentration. Slowly, the realization dawned upon me that I was standing before a portrait of Adrian Willaert. I stepped closer. The description named the painter as Jacopo Bassano, the sitter was unidentified: "Portrait of a bearded man," the legend said. The date was given as c. 1560, and the painting was described as coming from the collection of Charles H. and Mary F. S. Worcester.[1] The date as well as the circumstance that the painter was, like Willaert, a Venetian, seemed to favor my first impression.

I went home and began to look into the iconography of Adrian Willaert. Soon it became painfully clear that musicology offered no systematic help in the field of iconography; that, in particular, no bibliographical tool was available in the field of the iconography of

* I am indebted to a number of art historians with whom I discussed or corresponded about the problems involved in the present study. I should like to mention in particular Professor Erwin Panofsky (Institute for Advanced Study, Princeton), Professor H. W. Janson (New York University), Professor W. R. Rearick (Johns Hopkins University). I am grateful to John Maxon, Director of the Art Institute of Chicago, for his continued help and interest in regard to the Jacopo Bassano portrait at the Art Institute. Dr. Frank W. Newell, Professor of Ophthalmology (University of Chicago), gave freely and generously of his time and expert knowledge in a detail of the anatomical aspect of the eyes in some of the portraits. I owe the photo of the *Musica nova* woodcut to the kindness of Professor V. Duckles, University of California, Berkeley. Finally, I wish to express my thanks to my assistant, Miss Bonnie J. Blackburn, for valuable help in matters of bibliography.

[1] *Catalogue of the Charles H. and Mary F. S. Worcester Collection of Paintings, Sculpture and Drawings*, comp. Daniel Catton Rich (Chicago 1938), p. 11. *Paintings in the Art Institute of Chicago* (Chicago 1961), p. 18.

Renaissance musicians; that portraits of Willaert had been discussed by some scholars, but that a list of his portraits was nowhere to be found; and that those portraits that were known and mentioned had never been subjected to a critical examination and comparison.

Surely, confronted with such a situation, one must agree with Otto Erich Deutsch that "iconography, as portrait study, is no exact science." [2] We hope, however, that the present study, though no more than an introduction to the problems of portrait study in the case of Adrian Willaert, will illustrate that iconography can become a *more* exact science. At the same time it is well to remember that iconography, like all other humanistic disciplines, will always be both less and more than an exact science; less, in that it will rarely reach the status of objective verification by experiment that characterizes exact science; more, in that imponderable elements such as perception, sensitivity to artistic values, critical judgment, the art of translating facial features into facets of a personality, and, least but not last, human empathy, are as indispensable to its study as exactness in the search for dates and data.

René Lenaerts, in his valuable archival study on Willaert,[3] presents the portrait from the Liceo Musicale of Bologna (Pl. 20a) and deduces from its inscription [4] the composer's approximate date of birth. He reasons that the age of the composer in this portrait must be between 45 and 50 and that one may therefore assume him to have been born around 1480. Most dictionaries give his date of birth as between 1480 and 1490. The latter date seems to me the more likely one in view of Willaert's career and his first appearances in manuscripts and prints (1518 and 1519); the main period of his publications, which extends from 1539 to 1559; and his trips home to Flanders in 1542 and particularly in 1556. It would seem, however, that the composer's age according to this portrait would rather be between 55 and 60. It is hard to imagine that he would have started his career at San Marco at that age.

Lenaerts did not raise the question of the authenticity of the Bologna portrait. Neither did Geo. Pistarino who, in an essay entitled "Portrait of Adrian Willaert," writes of this likeness: "Willaert appears . . . at the age of circa 40 to 50 years, with hair thinning at the temples, high forehead, penetrating eyes, a beard *alla cappuccina*, long and lean face, marked lines, a thoughtful and austere expression." [5]

[2] "Ikonographie, in der Bedeutung Bildniskunde, ist keine exakte Wissenschaft"; see Otto Erich Deutsch, *Was heisst und zu welchem Ende studiert man Ikonographie?* in: *Schweizerische Musikzeitung*, C (1960), 230.

[3] *Notes sur Adrien Willaert maître de chapelle de Saint Marc à Venise de 1527 à 1562*, in: *Bulletin de l'Institut historique belge de Rome*, XV (1935), 107-17.

[4] "D. Adriano Willaert. mae° di cap. di S. Marco in Venezia 1527."

[5] *Ritratto di Adriano Willaert*, in: *Rivista musicale italiana*, LVI (1954), 117.

Pistarino compares this portrait with the woodcut in Willaert's *Musica nova* of 1559 (Pl. 20b) and says of the latter: "It recalls in the general pose the painting of the Conservatory of Bologna. The likeness of the celebrated musician, who was then between 70 and 80 years old, naturally seems older, above all in the face furrowed by deep wrinkles." [6]

Now the woodcut of *Musica nova* is the only authenticated portrait of Willaert.[7] It is, in any iconographic study of the master, the one certain point of reference and comparison. It appeared in Venice, place of his residence, in 1559, three years before his death, in an edition prepared by Francesco Viola, a pupil of his, an edition done with the greatest care, comprising a huge corpus of both secular and religious music, and dedicated to Alfonso d'Este II, who probably financed it, who fought with the Roman censorship, successfully, to have Willaert's madrigals on texts by Petrarch included,[8] and who, incidentally, succeeded Ercole II as duke of Ferrara in the same year 1559.

The woodcut shows an old man of Socratic ugliness: a mighty, large forehead, as of granite, more wide than high, marked by strong horizontal lines and vertical wrinkles between the tense eyebrows, the fore-

---

[6] *Ibid.*, p. 118.

[7] At the bottom of the page, not included in our photograph, the woodcut bears the initials "L. C." in the lower left corner, followed by "In Venetia appresso di Antonio Gardano. 1559." The reproduction of the woodcut in Georg Kinsky, *A History of Music in Pictures* (London 1929), p. 88, No. 1, includes this line of print. I have been unable to find an "L. C." who might fit these initials. Perhaps another scholar will be luckier. Among others, the following books were consulted: G. K. Nagler, *Die Monogrammisten* (Munich & Leipzig n.d.); Louis Lampe, *Signatures et monogrammes des peintres de toutes les écoles* (Brussels 1895); O. E. Ris-Paquot, *Dictionnaire encyclopédique des marques et monogrammes* (Paris n.d.); Paul Kristeller, *Kupferstich und Holzschnitt in vier Jahrhunderten* (Berlin 1922); Mary Pittaluga, *L'Incisione italiana nel cinquecento* (Milano 1928); Arthur M. Hind, *An Introduction to a History of Woodcut* (n.p. 1935; New York 1963). Pittaluga excludes book illustrations; the other authors include them.

It may be of interest to mention that Venice in the 15th and 16th centuries had almost a monopoly in the field of the Italian woodcut. Paul Kristeller (*op. cit.*, p. 284) writes:

> Aus der derb schraffierenden Manier, die im Anfange des XVI. Jahrhunderts meist mit ganz handwerksmässiger Sorglosigkeit ausgeübt wurde, entwickelt sich in der Buchillustration ein eleganter glatter und glänzender Holzschnittstil, der in Feinheit und Schärfe der regelmässigen und stark gerundeten Taillen, in der Weichheit der Modellierung und in der Abstufung der Töne mit der Kupferstichtechnik in Wettstreit tritt.

It is probably this finesse of technique that prompted Kinsky (*op. cit.*, p. 88, No. 1) to speak of the woodcut of 1559 as of an "engraving." We learn furthermore from Kristeller's account (p. 285ff) that Venice excelled from the 1530s on in the art of authors' portraits in the books printed by great Venetian publishing houses such as Gabriel Giolitto de' Ferrari and Vincenzo Valgrisi. Antonio Gardano was certainly influenced by this Venetian tradition.

[8] See the correspondence between Ferrara and Rome on this matter in Edmond van der Straeten, *La Musique aux Pays-Bas* (Brussels 1882), VI, 208ff.

head of a hard, indefatigable, intellectual worker; an immense, fleshy, broad, aquiline nose; hair receding at the temples; and a rather large, grizzly beard with prominent streaks of white in the middle—neither hair nor beard trimmed, groomed, or showing the slightest sign of care. Obviously this man paid little attention to his appearance, a trait that seems more in accord with his Flemish ruggedness than with Italian love of external beauty. Nor is there any attribute in Willaert's dress that betrays the slightest trace of vanity: a simple gown, held together in front by a bow, a collar of the same material, neither starched nor smooth —that is all. Out of the enormously strong face look two pensive eyes, the eyes of a dreamer, a thinker, an artist, who draws his inspiration from inside rather than from the outside world. These eyes have one very characteristic feature, aside from their fixed stare into an uncertain distance: the drastically lowered eyelids. Also, they seem slightly asymmetrical.

A careful comparison with the Bologna portrait shows that the latter is nothing more than a prettified copy of the woodcut. Telltale are the hair, the facial wrinkles, the eyebrows, the gown, the bow in front. To beautify Willaert, the painter has given him a higher forehead, a longer face, a more bony and slender nose; in particular, he has smoothened the eyelids and rendered the eyes symmetrical. He succeeded in robbing the composer's face of its monumental strength and its unflattering truth and integrity. The art historians whom I have consulted agree that this is an 18th-century painter's "hack work"—an expression used by my friend H. W. Janson. A similarly insipid, "romanticized," portrait of Willaert appears in Francesco Caffi's *Storia della musica sacra*.[9]

Where does this portrait come from? It forms part of the portrait gallery housed in the Liceo Musicale of Padre Martini. I do not know of any study dealing with this collection. Francesco Vatielli, in his account of the Padre's great library, has merely in passing enumerated among its treasures the *quadri di soggetto musicale*.[10] In a letter of 2 September 1962 from Bologna, Luigi Ferdinando Tagliavini kindly answered my inquiry concerning the origins of this collection and the authenticity of the portraits. I translate: "The collection of musicians' portraits of Padre Martini is still conserved and forms the nucleus of the great iconographic collection now residing in the halls of the Con-

[9] (Venice 1854), I, frontispiece to the chapter on Willaert, p. 81ff. The portrait carries the frank admission: *Adriano Willaert tratto dalle di lui opere musicali stampate in Venezia per cura del Duca di Ferrara.*

[10] *La Biblioteca del Liceo Musicale di Bologna* (Bologna 1917), Biblioteca de "L' Archiginnasio," Serie II—N. XIV, p. 8.

servatory of Music (formerly 'Liceo Musicale'). It consists not only of copies, but also of originals, often of notable artistic value, aside from their iconographic usefulness (as examples may serve Gainsborough's portrait of Johann Christian Bach and Reynolds's portrait of Burney). This aspect of Padre Martini's activity is documented in his great correspondence preserved in the library that carries his name; there one learns of his various requests for portraits of musicians."

A historical account of the erudite Padre's collection of portraits with a transcription of all documents bearing on it would be highly welcome. From a passage in Burney's accounts of his travels in France and Italy, one may surmise that one of the reasons that might have prompted the Padre's decision to collect musicians' portraits was his plan for an "illustrated music history." Burney reported that the fifth volume of Padre Martini's comprehensive *Storia della musica*—which, unfortunately, never grew beyond three—was designed to contain "some account of the lives and writings of the most famous musicians and in-gravings of their heads." [11]

While a historical account of this collection is missing, a critical examination of Padre Martini's collection has not been undertaken either, as far as I can see. No doubt, many of the 18th-century composers pre-sented in this collection are genuine portraits by fine masters done from life. But there can be no reasonable doubt either that many, if not all, portraits of 16th-century composers were simply copies commissioned by Padre Martini, copies done by second-rate painters from likenesses probably supplied by Padre Martini himself.

A hint is provided by the inscriptions on these paintings. They are obviously written at a later time, and must have been phrased by Padre Martini himself, the only one in Bologna at the time to have the required knowledge. This, we believe, is true of the Bologna portrait of Willaert. But other Bologna portraits of 16th-century masters carry inscriptions worded in a manner leaving no possible doubt that they were later, "historical" additions rather than 16th-century inscriptions of such authenticity that one could deduce biographical information from them. The portrait of Giovanni Animuccia, for example, carries the legend: "Giovanni Animuccia Fiorentino m͞ro di cappella di S. Pietro in Vaticano di Roma morì nell'anno 1569." Soriano's portrait is inscribed: "Francesco Soriano m͞ro. di cappella e fiorì nel 1590." [12]

---

[11] Charles Burney, *The Present State of Music in France and Italy* (2nd ed. London 1773), p. 199.

[12] Kinsky, *op. cit.*, reproduces the Bologna portraits of Animuccia (102/4) and

But there are other, more solid, proofs for the derivative character of the portraits of 16th-century composers in Padre Martini's collection. In the case of Costanzo Porta's portrait in Bologna—and Padre Martini was particularly fond of Porta [13]—we have the model from which the copy was made. The Bologna portrait is reproduced in *Die Musik in Geschichte und Gegenwart*.[14] It carries the inscription "P. Costanzo Porta Cremon. Min. Conv. di S. Franc. celebre composi[tore] di musica fiorì dal 1555 al 1578." The painting that I believe to be the model for the Bologna portrait is reproduced as frontispiece of Antonio Garbelotto's work *Il Padre Costanzo Porta da Cremona*.[15] It now hangs in the Museo Civico of Padua. Again, a forceful 16th-century original has been watered down and prettified in the Bologna copy and robbed of its magnificent virility. The give-aways are the position of the sitter, agreeing precisely with the Padua portrait; the general features; and the scroll in Porta's hand containing the same canon on the text *Quis infirmatur* as does the scroll in the painting at Padua, except that the Bologna scroll carries below the canon the name of the composer and of the order to which he belonged.[16]

Whereas the authenticity of Porta's Bologna portrait has not been challenged by the authors and editors of *MGG*, the Bologna portrait of

Soriano (104/5) and adds with the sureness of touch and the accuracy that characterize all of his work: "(18th century)" without giving any reasons. Unfortunately, he gives these and other Bologna portraits only as details, omitting the inscriptions. The portraits are reproduced in their entirety in Franco Abbiati, *Storia della musica* (Milano 1939), I, 503 (Animuccia), 511 (Soriano); see p. 408 for Zarlino.

[13] Evidence of the Padre's predilection for Porta's music may be found in Edward E. Lowinsky, *Early Scores in Manuscript*, in: JAMS, XIII (1960), 150.

[14] X, Pl. 88.

[15] (Roma 1955), Pl. 1.

[16] Garbelotto, in a chapter entitled *Iconografia Portiana* (*op. cit.*, pp. 102–08), fails to recognize the dependence of the Bologna portrait on that in Padua. He is further confused by the fact that the Bologna likeness is preserved in a portrait of the Arca di S. Antonio in Padua (*ibid.*, p. 103). I do not know the latter portrait, and I cannot judge whether it is, as Garbelotto believes, the original of which the Bologna work is the copy. But it seems likely that both paintings, if they indeed agree, depend on the Padua portrait. Curiously enough, Garbelotto reports that the Bologna portrait carries, at the end of the above quoted inscription, the words: "In Bol. a F.C.F. 1801" which are not visible in the otherwise very good reproduction in *MGG*. Of course, Padre Martini died in 1784. Should this portrait in Bologna be one of those commissioned by Padre Martini—and in view of his admiration for Porta this is very likely—then the possibility arises that the portrait in the Arca di S. Antonio was the "original" and the Bologna painting was the copy done by a Bolognese painter in 1801 for the Arca and that in the process the two paintings were exchanged, understandably enough because the "copy" carried the place name of Bologna. Incidentally, Garbelotto, notwithstanding the date of 1801 that, he says, might perhaps be a later addition or might be a note of the later proprietor of the picture, thinks it possible that the Bologna portrait was painted in the 16th century (*ibid.*, p. 104).

Claudio Merulo in that same encyclopedia [17] stands next to one from Naples. The two pictures appear with the following critical remarks:

1) concerning the Bologna portrait: "Das im 18. Jahrhundert, vermutlich im Auftrage des Padre Martini nach dem Bildnis in den posthumen Merulo-Drucken (Venedig 1606 und 1607) entstandene Porträt Claudio Merulos. Bologna, Bibl. G. B. Martini."

2) concerning the Naples portrait: "Annibale Carracci, Porträt Claudio Merulo (?). Neapel, Galleria Nazionale (vorher Parma, Palazzo del Giardino). Ob dieses 1587 datierte Bildnis tatsächlich Merulo darstellt, wird nach neuestem Stand der Wissenschaft als wahrscheinlicher angesehen als die Echtheit des Bologneser Bildes."

Another example of a Bologna portrait of a 16th-century master painted in the 18th century is the painting of Adrianus Petit Coclico. Van Crevel has pointed out that the inscription was of 18th-century origin, since the 16th-century version of the theorist-composer's name was Coclico, whereas the Bologna portrait calls him *Adrianus Petit Coclicus*.[18] Van Crevel also shows the indisputable dependence of the Bologna portrait on the woodcut in Coclico's *Compendium musices* of 1552.[19] In Coclico's case the painter of the Bologna portrait made not the slightest attempt to change the features presented in the 16th-century original, whereas it is hard to reject the suspicion that the changes made in the portraits of Willaert and Porta from their recognizable models may be due not only to a tendency to idealize, but also to the wish to make these portraits appear as "originals" by concealing their derivation.

In sum, the Bologna portrait of Willaert is not an authentic portrait made from life, nor can the inscription be used for biographical purposes. Are there other portraits of the Venetian master? René Lenaerts, in the aforementioned essay, writes:

L'on connait le magnifique portrait de Willaert au Palazzo Venezia à Rome. Le maître, vêtu d'un ample manteau bordé de fourrure et coiffé d'une large toque, y est représénté, âgé d'environ 35 à 40 ans. Dans un coin du portrait se trouvent deux livres de musique; devant lui, on remarque une couronne, qui doit sans doute symboliser le titre de "prince de la musique." Le portrait n'étant pas daté, il ne nous fournit donc aucun détail biographique.[20]

Lenaerts names no painter and gives no reference. To locate the painting, to procure a photograph, to trace its attribution to a painter and the identification of the man portrayed to Willaert, was no small task.

---

[17] IX, Pl. 7.

[18] M. van Crevel, *Adrianus Petit Coclico* (The Hague 1940), p. 261, frontispiece.

[19] See the facsimile reprint by Manfred F. Bukofzer in *Documenta musicologica*, IX (Kassel 1954).

[20] *Loc. cit.*, p. 110, fn. 1.

The only book on music in which I could find the portrait, reduced to a size of 3" x 2.2", was the *Atlas historique de la musique* by Paul Collaer and Albert Vander Linden,[21] where it is provided with the following identification: "Adrien Willaert, Peinture anonyme. Rome, Palazzo di Venezia." Inquiries at the Museum of the Palazzo di Venezia in Rome having remained fruitless, I sent a copy of the photograph in the *Atlas historique* for easier identification to the Gabinetto Fotografico Nazionale in Rome.[22] The painting was finally traced to the Galleria Spada in Rome whence it had gone temporarily to the Museum of the Palazzo di Venezia and where it is again at this time, the Galleria Spada being its lawful and permanent home.

The painting (Pl. 21a) is a masterly portrait, and it presents a highly interesting personality. That it is the portrait of a musician is made clear by the harp in the left and the flute in the right corner, and the open music books, seemingly handwritten partbooks of vocal music. But is it a portrait of Willaert? If so, how are we to reconcile the portrait of Bologna, in which the sitter is described by Lenaerts as of 45 to 50 years, with that of Rome, in which, he says, the artist is 35 to 40 years old, when in reality the difference in age between the two faces seems more like 20 to 25 than 10 years? But let us first try to trace the history of the identification of the sitter. Federico Zeri, in his illustrated catalogue of the Galleria Spada,[23] refers to an article by T. H. Fokker and attributes to him the suggestion that the figure represents Willaert. He takes no sides on the question, being more interested in the problem of the authorship of the painting, which he ascribes, with reservations, to Jan Stevensz van Calcar, a Netherlandish painter born in 1499, living in Venice c. 1536–37, and in Naples between 1546 and 1550. His work has often been taken for that of Titian.[24] The date of the painting is therefore assumed to be 1536–37, and while art historians differ on the attribution, they do not object to the date. Of course, this makes Lenaerts's position even more untenable inasmuch as the Bologna portrait signed "1527" shows a Willaert considerably older than the Rome portrait done presumably a decade later.

T. H. Fokker on the other hand does not accept the attribution to van Calcar. But with regard to the identity of the man portrayed he

[21] (Paris 1960), p. 54, No. 223.
[22] I wish to thank its Director, Dr. Giorgio Castelfranco, for sending me a photograph of the painting.
[23] *La Galleria Spada in Roma* (Florence 1954), pp. 48–49.
[24] Thieme-Becker, *Allgemeines Lexicon der bildenden Künstler* (Leipzig 1911), V, 376. Professor Panofsky believes that "Calcar was probably in Venice for several years after 1537, since he made the woodcuts not only for Vesalius's *Tabulae Sex* (1538) but also for Vesalius's *Fabrica* (1543)" (letter of 13 July 1964).

writes: "It is, however, not easy to resist the temptation to guess the name of this 'prince of musicians' and to see in this Venetian work a portrait of Adrian Willaert, who at that time dominated the musical life of the city of lagoons." [25]

Again, no reference to the origin of the identification with Willaert. In rereading Einstein's account of Willaert I finally found that he also knew this portrait. Apparently, he had neither seen it in Rome nor found it in a catalogue, but had come across it in the book of the man who claims to have discovered, or rather rediscovered, it. He, too, accepted the painting as authentic. [26]

The late Dutch art historian, one time professor at the University of Utrecht, G. J. Hoogewerff, who attributed the portrait to Jan Stevensz van Calcar, writes in a work on Flemish art and the Italian Renaissance in which he identifies the man portrayed with Willaert: "He was reported to be the 'king' of the composers of his day, and in a portrait recently rediscovered by this writer one sees him portrayed with a crown beside him on a table." [27]

[25] De "Galleria Spada" te Rome, in: Mededeelingen van het Nederlandsch Historisch Instituut te Rome, Tweede Reeks, Deel II ('sGravenhage 1932), 132.

[26] After quoting Calmo's description of Willaert as "such a tiny little man," he goes on to say: "Another portrait of him, by his compatriot Jan Stevensz van Calcar [?], certainly gives him a more imposing appearance. It represents him at the age of about forty-five, wearing a sort of turban which suggests Hungary . . . Calcar was in Venice about 1530, where he seems to have been a pupil of Titian. This fits in perfectly." (The Italian Madrigal, Princeton 1949, I, 324.) We should not omit to mention that Einstein, in the title to the painting of Morto da Feltre (ibid., facing p. 159) of a group of four musicians, identifies the older man to the right holding a scroll of music in his left hand with "Adrian Willaert(?)"—a tempting identification, since the younger man on the left is Verdelot—but one that I find hard to accept on pure physiognomical evidence.

[27] G. J. Hoogewerff, Vlaamsche Kunst en Italiaansche Renaissance (Amsterdam n.d.), p. 99: "Hij gold als de 'koning' der toenmalige toonkunstenaars en op een portret van hem, dat onlangs door schrijver dezes werd teruggevonden, ziet men hem dan ook afgebeeld met een kroon naast zich op tafel."

Incidentally, Zeri believes that the harp in the background and the crown resting on the base of the socle (rather than on a table, as Hoogewerff says) suggests that the name of the musician portrayed was David. Professor Panofsky finds this explanation not very convincing and proposes—as a mere hypothesis—that "perhaps the famous relationship between Alexander the Great and his Timotheus might be alluded to. Then the crown would say that, as it says in all those stories about Alexander, music is more powerful than even the greatest king the world has ever known, and the flute would be a fitting attribute for a musician thus compared with Alexander's 'court flutist.' The harp, on the other hand, would be intended to show that the person in question was a master of both the wind and the stringed instruments (the latter, of course, being superior to the former); and that is not irreconcilable with the Timotheus idea, because Alexander's Timotheus and my Timotheus, the composer and lyre-player from Miletus, could easily be confused in later writing" (letter of 13 July 1964). On the two ancient musicians by the name of Timotheus, see Erwin Panofsky, Early Netherlandish Painting (Cambridge, Mass. 1954), I, 435–36, note to p. 197.

Hoogewerff does not present the evidence on which he based his identification. It was, as far as I can discover, a hypothesis based on three elements, none of which is certain:

1) that van Calcar painted the portrait in Venice;
2) that the greatest musician in Venice being Willaert, the figure must represent that composer;
3) that the crown in the painting symbolized Willaert's status as "king" of musicians.[28]

When I showed the portrait together with the woodcut and the Bassano portrait to John Maxon, Director of the Art Institute of Chicago, during an interview on 9 August 1963, he rejected the possibility that the man portrayed in the van Calcar portrait might be the same person who is presented in the woodcut and the Bassano portrait. He pointed out that the ear, which does not change with age, is entirely different from the Bassano portrait, and that the nose differs essentially from both Bassano and woodcut. He made some further observations with regard to the original form of the portrait. He thought that the turban was a later elaboration of an original beret such as was worn by many Venetian noblemen at the time, as could be seen in portraits by Paris Bordone or Lorenzo Lotto. He surmised further that the harp on the left as well as the socle of the pillar on the right were later additions. He thought the portrait might possibly represent a nobleman who was a musical amateur. H. W. Janson, during a visit to Chicago, confirmed the view held by Maxon on the inadmissibility of identifying the figure in van Calcar's (?) work with Willaert.

To the observations adduced one might add that the person in the Bassano portrait and the woodcut is dressed with extreme simplicity, whereas the man from the Galleria Spada is dressed in a rich and luxurious manner, not to speak of the crown on the table. Moreover, the flute would hardly be a fitting attribute of Willaert. In the many descriptions that we have of him no mention is made that he played the flute. If the Bassano portrait were to be identified with Willaert—and this we shall not assert with certainty—then one might also point out that the thumb of the man in the Rome portrait grows broader, rounder, fleshier, that of the Chicago portrait instead more slender and pointed. In sum,

---

[28] I wrote a letter to Professor Hoogewerff who, as Professor Emeritus of the University of Utrecht, resided in Florence, Italy. The absence of an answer was explained when I heard that the Utrecht scholar had died just a few months earlier. His successor, Professor William S. Heckscher, obliged me by having his assistant, Miss Karla Langedijk, search Hoogewerff's files and bibliography to confirm that he "never published his discovery of this portrait" (letter of Miss Langedijk of 1 June 1964).

the portrait of the Galleria Spada must be eliminated as a likeness of Willaert.

There exists, however, a portrait of Willaert unknown to most of his biographers although mentioned in various books, a portrait on which Willaert's name is written by a contemporary hand (Pl. 21b).[29] It hangs now in the Kunsthistorisches Museum in Vienna; it belonged in the 16th century to the portrait collection of Archduke Ferdinand II of Tyrol.[30] The portrait bears the inscription: "Hadrianus Wilhart Componista."

By now our eye is trained enough to determine at once that this portrait cannot be authentic either; it cannot have been painted from life. While the composer appears to be about the age of the woodcut, the painter has made every effort to present a handsome, but unfortunately lifeless, likeness. Eyes, forehead, nose, beard—everything has been changed according to a standard of empty, stereotyped beauty. The

[29] This portrait is mentioned in Walter Senn, *Musik und Theater am Hof zu Innsbruck* (Innsbruck 1954), p. 346. Senn refers to inventories of 1665 and 1741 in which the portrait is still listed as presenting Willaert. The portrait is listed, together with the woodcut, in the *A. L. A. Portrait Index* (Washington 1906), p. 1558. This work, a very useful bibliographical tool, is limited to portraits in printed books and periodicals. The two portraits are mentioned because they appear, one in a periodical (see n. 30), the other in a book. Finally, the portrait appears in Franco Abbiati, *Storia della musica* (Milano 1939), I, 353, but with attribution to the "Bibl. Marciana, Venezia." This attribution is erroneous according to the Director of the Biblioteca Nazionale di San Marco in Venezia, Signora Lia Sbriziolo, who writes in a letter of 21 June 1964: "The portrait referred to by you is not preserved in this institution. Abbiati's attribution must therefore originate in a confusion. We have undertaken accurate investigations also at the Archive of San Marco, attached to the Basilica, and at the Civico Museo Correr without being able to discover any trace of Willaert's portrait."
I am grateful to Dr. Erwin M. Auer, Director of the Kunsthistorisches Museum in Vienna, for his kindness in sending me a photograph of the painting.

[30] Here is what Fr. Kenner, in his study on *Die Porträtsammlung des Erzherzogs Ferdinand von Tirol*, in: *Jahrbuch der Kunsthistorischen Sammlungen des allerhöchsten Kaiserhauses*, XIV (1893), 37, writes on this collection:

Der am wenigsten bekannte Bestandtheil des grossen Kunstbesitzes, der vormals im Schlosse Ambras vereinigt war, bildet eine Sammlung kleiner Bildnisse von regierenden Fürsten des 15. und 16. Jahrhunderts und ihren Ahnen, von Feldherren, Staatsmännern, Gelehrten, Künstlern und Dichtern derselben Zeit und aus verschiedenen Ländern Europas, unter denen Deutschland und Italien obenan stehen. Man pflegt sie als Porträtsammlung des Erzherzogs Ferdinand von Tirol († 1595) zu bezeichnen, was in der Hauptsache richtig ist. Doch finden sich in ihr auch Bildnisse aus dem 17. Jahrhundert bis zum Ende desselben. Diese zeigen, dass deren auch noch später in einer wenngleich nicht grossen Zahl nach Ambras gekommen sind, also zwischen einem alten Bestande und späteren Erwerbungen unterschieden werden muss.

Kenner describes the portraits numbered 1–913 as

Bildnisse von gleicher Grösse, im Durchschnitte 13.5 cm. hoch, 10.5 cm. breit, rechteckig, in Oel auf Papier gemalt und auf dünne Täfelchen aus Fichtenholz aufgezogen, fast alle vorne mit aufgemalten Bezeichnungen in Lapidarbuchstaben versehen.

simple vesture, too, had to be replaced by a gown made of precious material, probably velvet, with a ruffled collar; moreover, the composer is made to wear a double golden chain around his neck.

Our impression is confirmed by the history of Ferdinand's portrait collection. Kenner proves that its earliest beginnings go back to the year 1576, when Willaert had been dead for 14 years.[30] Willaert's portrait appears to be a copy made by a Northern painter of mediocre skills. At any rate, it is unlikely that an Italian painter would have spelled Willaert's name in this fashion.[31] In particular, "Wilhart" seems a Germanization of the Flemish name. And the word *componista*, which does not occur in classical Latin, seems to be a Latinization of the German word *Komponist*. The Italians say *compositore*. Tinctoris, in his *Terminorum musicae diffinitorium* of c. 1475, uses the term *compositor* (whom he defines as *alicujus novi cantus editor*) and Glareanus follows him in this usage; but in German one finds the term *Komponist*.[32]

A hardly known portrait of Willaert hanging in the Library of the University of Leipzig (inventory no. 551 of the catalogue of paintings) was brought to my attention through a German portrait catalogue.[33] I am indebted to Heinrich Besseler of that University for his kindness in ordering a photograph and to Dr. Debes, Curator of Manuscripts, for sending it to me. This 17th-century painting of unknown origin, c. 60 cm high and c. 49 cm wide, presents a copy made after the Vienna portrait or, perhaps, after its presumed Bavarian model. Gown, collar, double chain around the neck, the angle of the head, and the general features agree with the Vienna portrait. But something new is added: the composer holds in a large, long-fingered, carefully painted hand a book of music which seems bound in parchment with chorale

---

[31] *Ibid.*, p. 41. In a later instalment of the same study (*Jahrbuch*, XV [1894], 249) Kenner surmises that the Willaert portrait in Ferdinand's collection is a copy of a Willaert portrait in Duke Albrecht V's collection of portraits, now lost. If this were true, the German character of the style and the spelling of the name would be even more understandable. Franz von Reber, in his study on *Die Bildnisse der herzoglich bayerischen Kunstkammer nach dem Fickler'schen Inventar von 1598*, in: *Sitzungsberichte der philosophisch-philologischen und der historischen Classe der k. b. Akademie der Wissenschaften zu München*, I (1893), 2–56, enumerates the painters who worked for Albrecht; they are for the most part Germans.

[32] For example, in the well-known letter of Dr. Seld to Albrecht V of Bavaria (22 September 1555), Monte is "der pest Componist, der in dem ganzen land ist"; see A. Sandberger, *Beiträge zur Geschichte der bayerischen Hofkapelle unter Orlando di Lasso* (Leipzig 1894), I, 55.

[33] Hans W. Singer, *Neuer Bildniskatalog* (Leipzig 1938), V, 118, refers under No. 38758 to a 17th-century painting of Willaert in the University Library of Leipzig, designated as a copy. It should be mentioned that Singer lists paintings only very exceptionally, limiting himself on the whole strictly to the graphic arts and photography.

notation. Above is written: ADRIA.[s] WILAERT. The face shows the transformation from a Manneristic concept of Willaert as a melancholic introvert of an almost haggard appearance to a powerful, self–confident Baroque expression (Pl. 21c).

The unauthentic portraits are significant in that they not only attest to the lasting interest in Willaert through the centuries but also offer the changing images of the great chapel master of San Marco: a late 16th-century Manneristic, a 17th-century Baroque, an 18th-century Bologna, and a 19th-century Romanticized Venetian (Caffi) interpretation. They are all connected, by more or less tenuous threads, with the woodcut from *Musica nova*.

Having now eliminated four portraits as unauthentic, there remains the portrait of the Art Institute of Chicago attributed to Jacopo Bassano (Pl. 22a). The painting shows an altogether unusual figure, a man of advanced age, of slight build, with a face of extraordinary spiritual intensity, quietness, nobility, and thoughtfulness, a face deeply furrowed and wrinkled, the face of a man whose battles were waged in the realm of ideas, the face of a thinker, a visionary, an artist, with the beautiful hand, the long, slender fingers of an artist. The head is shown in three-quarter profile, revealing a finely fashioned pointed ear. It is held as in a position of listening. Notwithstanding the atmosphere of quiet and contemplation, there is an element of liveliness and tension provided by the head moving in countermotion to the left hand which, in an eloquent gesture, points to the scroll held in the right hand. The contrapuntal play between head and hand dominates the portrait visually; it may also stand as a symbol of the artist, whose mental vision is executed by his hand.

Are the persons portrayed in the woodcut and the Bassano painting identical? Art historians are well aware of the pitfalls besetting the road on which the scholar preoccupied with problems of portrait identification must travel. It is only with trepidation, therefore, that a music historian proceeds on the path that art historians fear to tread. Both portraits show a man with rugged features, a highly individualized face, heavily marked with lines and wrinkles, with high cheekbones, sunken cheeks, the low-lidded eyes and the distant look of a thinker, and an immense, outspoken, aquiline nose. The mantle is hardly visible under the full beard, which has streaks of white in the middle. The forehead, not particularly high, but broad and worked out, is strongly wrinkled, and the hair recedes at the temples in both likenesses, but more so in the woodcut. Neither hair nor beard is well groomed; indeed, both portraits show a man who is singularly lacking in vanity, indeed, in any attention to externals of any kind. And this is a feature worth emphasizing. Sixteenth-century men—not to speak of women—when sitting for a portrait are ordinarily very sensitive about their appearance. The utter simplicity of dress and the complete lack of interest in details of his appearance in Willaert's portrait in *Musica nova* are striking: no fur, no lace work, no silken collar, no precious materials, no decorative buttons, no gloves, no head gear, no ring or golden chain, no jewels, no armchairs, no marble columns, no curtains—such austerity is exceedingly rare in contemporary portraits, particularly so in Venetian portraits; it was surely a characteristic peculiar to Willaert. The almost ascetic plainness of dress in the woodcut is the more astonishing if we consider the traditional splendor of Venice, the outstanding position of San Marco's chapel master, Willaert's fame radiating all over musical Europe, the importance of the publication, its dedication to an illustrious Italian prince. None of this could affect Willaert, who was posing for this portrait in his simplest daily dress.

The dress of the man in the painting is different in color, material, and cut; it looks like a black choir gown,[34] with a loose outer garment falling from the shoulders. But it is likewise conspicuous for the absence of any decorative attribute whatever. A study of other Venetian portraits of the period will confirm our impression that such simplicity in a famous Venetian citizen holding the highest musical office the Republic could bestow—and it should not be forgotten that Willaert was not a monk, he was married—is in itself an important characteristic that merits consideration in any comparison of the two portraits. The simplicity of Willaert, his modesty and gentleness, are praised in contemporary accounts [35] and shine through in the immense popularity that he enjoyed in an age and in a country torn by furious jealousies in politics and in art.

Both portraits seem to present a man of an outspoken melancholic temperament which, since antiquity, has been believed to be the mark of men of extraordinary gifts—a notion revived in the Renaissance by

---

[34] Similar choir gowns are worn by other composers of the time: see portraits of Cipriano de Rore, Felice Anerio, Adam Gumpelzhaimer, in: K. M. Komma, *Musikgeschichte in Bildern* (Stuttgart 1961), ills. 264, 273, 288.

[35] Parabosco, for example, in his comedy *La Notte* (1556) calls him "tanto cortese, tanto gentile, et così piacevole, et modesto, che si può porre per un essempio di tutte queste altre virtuti"; see G. Bianchini, *Girolamo Parabosco* (Venice 1899), 43–44. Andrea Calmo, in his letter to Willaert written in Venetian dialect (parts of which were already printed by Einstein) finds him "saveu zentil mio modesto, e imbalsamao de pacientia . . ."; see *Supplimento delle piacevoli, ingeniosi, et argutissime lettere* . . . (Venice 1552), fol. 28bis verso; modern ed. Vittorio Rossi, *Le Lettere di messer Andrea Calmo* (Turin 1888), p. 199.

Marsilio Ficino.[36] The eyes, in both likenesses, have the faraway look of a man more concerned with his inner, than his outer vision; they could well be the eyes of a musician. Moreover, there are certain peculiarities in the physical shape of the eyes that led me to consult an authority in eye research. I am grateful to Frank W. Newell, Chief of the Section of Ophthalmology, School of Medicine of the University of Chicago, for his kindness in studying the two portraits, consulting with two of his colleagues about them, and formulating his views in the following letter of 22 May 1964:

> The woodcut and the painting each illustrate an individual with puffy or baggy eyelids. This is more marked in the woodcut than in the painting. The right eye in the painting is displaced downward and the lid droops over the globe. The right eye in the woodcut does not show this abnormality. However if the woodcut is reversed it would appear that there is an abnormality of the eye corresponding to the painting. Unfortunately in the woodcut this eye was not clearly delineated; the lid does does not appear to droop as it does in the painting. However the eye appears more prominent than the fellow eye and appears to be displaced downward. Generally the pattern of wrinkles and attachments of the skin to the bone surrounding the eyes appears comparable in the woodcut and the painting.
>
> It was the opinion of Professor Potts, Director of Research, that the woodcut is not distinct enough to allow a comparison. Assistant Professor Krill believed that the width from the inner corner to the outer corner of each eye was quite different in the woodcut and the painting. It was Dr. Newell's opinion that these were the same individual.

In several conversations in 1962 Maxon had pointed out that the woodcut, in accordance with the ordinary techniques employed, shows Willaert's face in reverse, and that a comparison with the painting should take this into account. Newell now arrived at the same conclusion on the basis of his study of the eyes, the peculiar shape of which had already attracted Maxon's attention. During my conversation with Newell the idea came up to have a photo taken of the woodcut in reverse (Pl. 22b). The reader may determine for himself whether the photo in reverse aids the comparison. I believe it does. It shows the head slightly turned to the right (from the onlooker's viewpoint), the same direction in which the head in the painting is turned. It also reveals the right ear—but only partly, since the turn is not so energetic—and the similarity of the heavy

[36] Erwin Panofsky and Fritz Saxl, *Dürers "Melencolia I,"* in: *Studien der Bibliothek Warburg,* II (Leipzig & Berlin 1923), 32ff and 49ff, trace this idea back to the Pseudo-Aristotelian Problems and regard Ficino as its chief representative in the Renaissance. P. O. Kristeller, in his *Il Pensiero filosofico di Marsilio Ficino* (Florence 1953), p. 224ff, confirms and elaborates on this view.

lines under the right eye and of the lines from nose to mouth on the right side of both portraits.

Of course, there are also dissimilarities in the two heads that should be taken into consideration. Erwin Panofsky, in a letter of 20 March 1964, wrote: "There is certainly a marked similarity between the Chicago painting and the woodcut accompanying Willaert's *Musica nova;* but there are also marked differences, particularly in the conformation of the cranium, not to mention the volume of the beard." During my recent visit to Johns Hopkins University, W. R. Rearick, a Bassano expert, had the kindness to discuss the two portraits at length with me. He had already years ago formed the opinion that the Chicago portrait was not by Jacopo Bassano [37] and was considerably later than 1560. Nevertheless, he conceded that there were striking similarities between the painting and the woodcut of 1559. He mentioned in particular "the high domed forehead, the prominent cheekbones, the slightly down tilted nose, the deep-sunk eyes (in general only), the heavily lined, knit eyebrows." But he felt that the head in the woodcut was "more solidly boned" than in the painting, where it had a "more delicate structure"; he found the nose in the woodcut "rather flat, in the painting slightly aquiline, the deep-sunken eyes in the woodcut reasonably regular, whereas the two eyes in the painting are markedly different." [38] Here it may be remarked that Newell did observe some irregularity in the eyes also in the woodcut and that they are perhaps a bit easier to see in the reverse photo which Rearick did not have at his disposal. It is also possible, and Rearick is as much aware of this as I, that some of these differences may be due to the cruder technique of the woodcut, to the immense difference in artistic skill, and to the different angle at which the head is portrayed.

The only attribute in the painting is the scroll held in the right hand. It is obvious that in a picture so completely devoid of any accessories the scroll held by the sitter would be of significance. This belief is reinforced by the gesture of the left hand pointing toward the scroll. A scroll with musical notation is a frequent symbol of a musician in portraits of the period.[39] It had been my hope that in view of the poor state

---

[37] See fn. 41 below.

[38] The quotations come from notes taken during my conversation with Professor Rearick.

[39] See Piero di Cosimo's portrait of the Florentine architect and musician Francesco Giamberti (Kinsky, *op. cit.*, p. 67, No. 4), the Leonardoesque portrait of Franchino Gafori (*ibid.*, p. 108, No. 1), the portraits of Melchior Newsidler (*ibid.*, p. 134, No. 2), Claude le Jeune (*ibid.*, p. 94, No. 1), and Adam Gumpelzhaimer (*ibid.*, p. 85, No. 4). Orlando di Lasso holds a music book, both pages of which are open (*ibid.*, p. 89, No. 3). Adrian Petit Coclico, in addition to the musical device on top of

of conservation of this part of the painting, an infrared photograph of the scroll might provide a clue to the identity of the sitter. Unfortunately, an infrared photograph taken on instruction by Maxon revealed only abrasions and the presence of later additions, a state of affairs already surmised by Maxon and confirmed by the professional restorer of the Art Institute of Chicago. Maxon had the kindness to formulate his findings on the scroll and his views on the identity of the sitter in the Bassano portrait in the following letter of 14 December 1962:

> That part of the picture in which the scroll appears is a modern extension of the painting, that is, the canvas has been pieced out at a much later date and the material of the scroll added. It is quite impossible to tell whether the hand originally held a scroll or not, as the old part is quite missing. It is possible, of course, that a scroll did exist, but it is equally possible the hand held something else. The canvas has been extended all around and in the reframing of the picture, we have adjusted the frame to hide the extension.
>
> As I said before to you, the identification of subjects from prints is exceedingly difficult, especially in the period under consideration. There are some problems about the date of the picture on stylistic grounds. However, I do, for once, think that the subject of the picture does bear a strong resemblance to the subject of the print and may be supposed to represent the same person.

We are not yet at the end of the problems obstructing an identification of the sitter in the painting with Adrian Willaert. Two further difficulties are the uncertainty of attribution to Jacopo Bassano and the date of the painting, issues completely beyond the competence of the writer. There is no need to trace here the whole history of changing attributions and dates of this painting, the less so since research on Giacomo da Ponte, better known as Jacopo Bassano, seems to enter its most critical phase only now. Suffice it to say that of 13 portraits assembled for the last great exhibition of paintings by Jacopo Bassano in 1957 in Venice, only one has been accepted by all critics as authentic, and that because it carries the autograph signature of the master.[40]

his portrait, is further characterized by a scroll that he holds in his left hand rolled up and showing no musical notation (*ibid.*, p. 84, No. 5). Marenzio holds a scroll with notes (Komma, *op. cit.*, p. 115, No. 266), Samuel Scheidt has lying before him, but facing the spectator, a canon (*ibid.*, p. 129, No. 296), Monteverdi (*ibid.*, p. 125, No. 286) and Michael Praetorius (*ibid.*, p. 127, No. 291) have open music books and Heinrich Schütz holds in both hands a long sheet on which no writing can be discerned (*ibid.*, p. 131, No. 301). Finally, I should like to recall the astonishing identification of the Rembrandt portrait of 1633 in the Corcoran Gallery of Art in Washington with Heinrich Schütz; see Otto Benesch, *Schütz und Rembrandt*, in: *Festschrift Otto Erich Deutsch* (Kassel 1963), pp. 12–19. The sitter holds in his left hand a scroll which, though folded, reveals music notes in its upper left corner.
[40] *Jacopo Bassano. Catalogo della mostra a cura di Pietro Zampetti. Venezia,*

All critics agree that the portrait is of extraordinary power, a work worthy of a great master. Whereas the Art Institute of Chicago dates the work c. 1560, other critics tend to date it decades later, some even as late as the early 17th century.[41] Now if the portrait were indeed of Willaert one would have to assume—this was also Rearick's estimate—that it was done a few years before the woodcut, perhaps in 1555. Yet, considering the difference in the artistic media and the caliber of the artists involved, it is perhaps not impossible that the two likenesses come from the same time, more or less. The notion that it might have been done after Willaert's death from a drawing is not very convincing because its immense liveliness suggests its having been painted from life. But even this possibility, in the case of a great painter, should perhaps not be ruled out altogether.

That the work of Jacopo Bassano is full of surprises has been pointed out by Michelangelo Muraro, a leading Bassano scholar, who writes in an article on the great Bassano exhibition in 1957:

The unwary visitor may be disconcerted by the startling fluctuations, from picture to picture, both in source of inspiration and in technique. But every one of these changes in style is no more than a stage in the relentless research that Bassano undertook throughout his life. 'Nil mihi placet,' Jacopo noted on a drawing of 1569, almost a confirmation of this state of perpetual unrest.[42]

Palazzo Ducale 29 giugno—27 ottobre 1957 (Venice 1957), pp. 212–37. The title page to the portraits (p. 211) carries the following note:
N.B. I ritratti sono stati reuniti in un gruppo a sè stante data l'estrema incertezza della critica circa la ritrattistica bassanesca. Unico certo, perchè firmato, è "l'Uomo con barba" che apre la serie, subito dopo il presunto "Autoritratto" degli uffizi.

[41] Bernard Berenson, in his *Italian Pictures of the Renaissance, Venetian School* (New York 1957), I, 17, attributes the work to Jacopo da Ponte, called Bassano, and dates it 1590. Edoardo Arslan, *I Bassano* (Milan 1960), I, 336, says of it: "Opera notevole, ma di primo Seicento; forse del Bassetti." Professor W. R. Rearick expressed to me his belief that the portrait was painted by Palma il Giovane at the end of the 16th century.

[42] *The Jacopo Bassano Exhibition*, in: *The Burlington Magazine*, XCIX (September 1957), 292. A letter sent to Dr. Muraro containing the photographs of the Bassano portrait and the woodcut was answered by him after the present study was completed in a note of 30 June 1964, in which he made the following points—and I translate from the Italian:
"1) This portrait is not by Jacopo Bassano.
2) It does not seem to me to represent the same person (see the different shape of the cranium).
3) If it were by Bassano, it would have to be from circa 1546–1547."
Grateful as I am for Dr. Muraro's judgment in a matter where he is highly competent, I hope I may be forgiven for confessing a logical difficulty. I find it hard to see how the possibility of an attribution to Bassano can be denied categorically (1), while a possible place in the artist's stylistic development is conceded (3). Of course, a separation of approximately ten years between painting and woodcut would fit the visual evidence better than any other hypothesis.

And viewing *Lazarus and the Rich Man* from the Cleveland Museum, Muraro writes:

> In the presence of the Cleveland masterpiece we have the sensation that all the works considered so far belong to a prehistory which, however rich in inventiveness and possibilities for the future, did not prepare us for the outburst of such overflowing genius.[43]

Is it not possible that a similar state of affairs might obtain in the case of the "portrait of a bearded man"? If, as I believe, the painting presents Willaert, would not the fact alone that Bassano, himself highly musical,[44] was confronting the most famous musician of Venice and perhaps, at that point, the most famous master of Europe, stimulate him to an extraordinary effort?

We should not forget that the Venetian publisher Antonio Gardano in accompanying *Musica nova* with the portrait of the composer also did something out of the ordinary. Whereas it was not unusual for books on theory to go out into the world graced with pictures of their authors,[45] it was not the habit to do the same in printed partbooks of vocal or instrumental music. Indeed, the whole undertaking of publishing *Musica nova* is so extraordinary in its size, its combination of secular and religious music, the significance and excellence of the selections, the beauty of the publication, and, of course, the composer's portrait, that one suspects that the year of publication may have been of very special significance in Willaert's life. Was 1559 perhaps the 70th anniversary of Willaert's birth? Was *Musica nova* perhaps published as an act of homage to the composer? Was it perhaps the first instance of a *Festschrift* in the form of a "Collection of Essays" edited by an admiring student of the master?

[43] *Ibid.,* p. 295.

[44] John Maxon drew my attention to the following passage in Carlo Ridolfi's biography of Jacopo da Ponte da Bassano in his work on Venetian painters, published originally in 1648, *Le Maraviglie dell'arte ovvero le vite degli illustri pittori veneti e dello stato,* ed. Detlev Freiherr von Hadeln (Berlin 1914–24), I, 402—I translate:

> He entertained himself and his friends at times with music, in which he was very experienced, particularly in wind instruments; thus it was that his house became a noble home of painting and of the Muses.

Professor Rearick has discovered very interesting evidence of the young Jacopo's practice of music which, in good time, he will publish himself.

[45] Aside from works such as Franchino Gafori's *Angelicum opus musicae* (Milan 1508) or Pietro Aron's *Trattato della natura di tutti gli tuoni del canto figurato* (Venice 1525) in which the composer appears more as an ornamental symbol than as an individual person, treatises by Nicola Vicentino (1555), and by Diego Ortiz have life-like portraits of their authors (all of these and others may be found in Kinsky, *op. cit.,* pp. 108, No. 3; 109, Nos. 2 and 3; 145, No. 2). Tablature books, too, have portraits (*ibid.,* pp. 132, No. 4; 134, No. 2). After Willaert's example in 1559 others followed in 1570 (Guillaume Costeley, *ibid.,* p. 94, No. 2), in 1603 (Claude le Jeune, *ibid.,* p. 94, No. 1), 1604 (Claudio Merulo, *ibid.,* p. 107, No. 1).

NEW LIGHT ON
GIACHES DE WERT

by CAROL MacCLINTOCK

T HE RECONSTRUCTION of a biography is difficult at best; it is doubly so when attempted from a distance of several hundred years. One of the most vexing problems is that of tracing the subject's movements prior to the time he began to achieve some renown. Particularly is this true of 15th- and 16th-century musicians, for whom documentary sources are generally either non-extant or so fragmentary and inconclusive as to be of little help. In the case of Giaches de Wert,'so little has been known about his youth that such a reconstruction has seemed an impossible task. Nevertheless, during a recent sojourn in Italy [1] I felt that yet another attempt to clarify, if possible, the circumstances of Giaches's life before he went to Mantua as maestro di cappella in 1565 should be made. The Mantuan records are copious, and from 1565 on there are numerous reports of his life and activities in the service of the Gonzaga princes. However, from the time of his arrival in Italy until he accepted the charge in Mantua very little has been known with certainty, and a great many wrong guesses have been made. Eitner thought that he arrived in Italy only about 1550, following in the steps of his famous compatriot Rore and seeking, like him, to make his fame and fortune in Italy.[2] Ramazzini correctly stated that Wert served as "ragazzo da cantare" to Maria di Cardona, but had him in the service of Alfonso di Novellara for many years, placing him in Mantua only in 1568.[3] Fétis said nothing at all about his early years, but suggested that he came to Italy to serve as maestro di cappella at Ferrara, basing this opinion on Wert's dedication of his eighth book of madrigals to the Duke and Duchess of Ferrara.[4] I will not attempt to recount here all the misinformation that has been printed. Suffice it to

---

[1] This period of research was made possible through the generous assistance of a Fellowship for 1962–63 from the John Simon Guggenheim Foundation.
[2] Robert Eitner, QL, X, 235.
[3] A. Ramazzini, *I musici fiamminghi alla corte di Ferrara*, in: *Archivio storico lombardo*, VI (1879), 116.
[4] François-Joseph Fétis, *Biographie universelle des musiciens* (2d ed. Paris 1860–65), VI, 454.

say that only two facts have been certain; all the rest has been conjecture. These are: 1) that Wert came to Italy to be a singer in the cappella of Maria di Cardona, Marchesa della Padula; 2) that he had been in the service of Alfonso di Novellara before coming to Mantua in 1565. Assuming that he came to Italy at about the age of eight, this leaves a period of some twenty-odd years to be accounted for.

The logical place to start seemed to be Maria di Cardona, Wert's first patron. The Marchesa della Padula, Maria di Cardona, was a poetess and singer of some renown. It is most likely that she was the daughter of Ramón de Cardona (d. 1522), Viceroy of Naples from 1509–22, but this point is not entirely clear. Investigations revealed that her first marriage was to her cousin, Artale di Cardona, son of Pietro di Cardona, Conte di Colisano.[5] Further investigation revealed that three years after Artale's death in 1537, she married en secondes noces Don Francesco d'Este,[6] natural son of Alfonso I and half-brother to the Duke of Ferrara—a point that seems to have been overlooked by all previous biographers. Now the connection between Padula and the North began to be apparent, and further searching in the Archivio di Stato at Modena was indicated. Knowing that Padula was in the south of Italy, near Naples, I expected to be told that certain archives in Naples should also be consulted. Instead, existing letters and records concerning the Marchesa were in Modena, being part of the Estense documents, since all her property and papers passed into the hands of the Este family at her death in 1563. The complete file of her letters from 1538 to 1562 was made available—almost all of them written from Avellino, where she kept her residence, for she was Contessa d'Avellino as well as Marchesa della Padula. Avellino is very near Salerno and Naples, and the correspondence contains many references to visits to Salerno (she was related to the Principessa di Salerno, Isabella Villamarino e di Cardona) and to Naples, especially Pozzuoli, a favorite resort even today. There are no references to music or to a musical cappella, or to a certain "ragazzo da cantare"; nevertheless we know now where Giaches spent his youth. The next question, or perhaps it should have been the first question, is: how did he

---

[5] Pietro di Cardona (d. 1522), "Grande Ammiraglio e gran Conestabile del regno," had three children by his wife Susanna Gonzaga: Antonia, Diana, and Artale. After Don Pietro's death Charles V bestowed the father's titles on Artale. His marriage to Maria di Cardona took place in deference to his father's wishes, for it appears that Artale was a somewhat reluctant bridegroom. (See Francesco Flamini, ed., *Tansillo: L'Ecloga e i poemetti* [Naples 1893], Introd.)

[6] In 1540 the Prince of Salerno, Ferrante Sanseverino, gave a *festa* for Maria di Cardona, in honor of her marriage with Don Francesco d'Este. On this occasion two comedies, *Il Beco* and *Il Calando* (*La Calandria?*), were performed by Sienese comedians. See Benedetto Croce, *I Teatri di Napoli* (4th ed. Bari 1947), p. 21.

get to Avellino, and when? Knowing what we now do, it is reasonable to assume that he was originally brought, or caused to be brought, from Flanders in 1543 or 1544 by Don Francesco d'Este, who was a renowned *capitano di guerra* [7] serving His Majesty the Emperor in Flanders during those years under the leadership of Ferrando Gonzaga, Conte di Guastalla, then Viceroy of Sicily as well as commander of Charles V's army. That the little Giaches was brought to Italy by his protector Francesco d'Este, just as the little Orlando di Lasso was brought by *his* protector Ferrando Gonzaga in 1544, is the only plausible explanation. Giaches would at this time have been about eight years old.

Maria di Cardona, the gifted musician, singer, and poetess, was undoubtedly pleased to have a Flemish chorister in her cappella, for such was the fashion at the time. Giaches was thus placed in a sophisticated artistic and literary milieu; Naples and Salerno were flourishing cultural centers with literary interest and activity at its height. The Marchesa was a member of the group that counted Vittoria Colonna; Bernardo Tasso, secretary of the Prince of Salerno; Luigi Tansillo, secretary to Don Pietro di Toledo, Viceroy of Naples; the Duke of Sessa; and the Marchese della Terza among the many brilliant poets and writers. The academies of the *Incogniti* and *Ardenti* at Naples and the *Sereni* at Sessa were in full flower. Theatrical performances in the Prince of Salerno's palace in Naples, where a permanent theater was maintained, were famous throughout Italy for the splendor and magnificence of the *rappresentazioni* and the excellence of the music. In particular *Gl'Ingannati*, given in 1545 with Giulio Cesare Brancaccio, Luigi and Fabrizio Dentice (father and son), and Scipione della Palla taking parts, and with the music directed by Lo Zoppino, was judged by connoisseurs to have surpassed anything previously given. The following year *La Philemia*, by A. Mariconda, performed by much the same group, with the assistance of Scipione della Palla and the "divinissimo Signor Dentice," and with music by Vincenzo Venafro, received equally enthusiastic praise. Comedies and eclogues with musical intermedii presented by Consalvo

[7] As a youth, Francesco d'Este (1516-78) served Charles V in Spain and also at Nice in 1538. In 1539 he went to serve Pope Paul III and helped to conclude an accord with the Pope that gave Ferrara to the Este family. He later returned to service with Charles V and was sent to Flanders to put down the rebellion of Ghent, then to Africa, and finally returned to Flanders as a general of light cavalry. He distinguished himself in these campaigns. Taken prisoner in 1543, he was freed by the King of France and placed in the custody of Cardinal Ippolito d'Este, who was then at the French court. He fought also in Piedmont and in Germany in religious wars. He married Maria di Cardona in 1540. There was no issue from this marriage, but Don Francesco had two natural daughters, Bradamante (m. Conte Ercole Bevilacqua, 1575) and Marfisa (m. Alfonso d'Este e Montecchio, 1578).

Fernándes de Cordoba, Duke of Sessa, were the order of the day both in Naples and in Sessa. In 1548 *Mirzia*, a comedy by Epicurus, had a representation in Naples, again in the Prince of Salerno's palace, and in June of 1549 an eclogue by G. B. Testa was presented in Sessa, where also in September of that same year a comedy of Plautus was recited by a group of youths.[8] Such literary-musical events were undoubtedly witnessed by the young Giaches—he probably participated in some of them. Though nothing is known of his early training, it is certain that he knew Brancaccio, the famous basso and military man, and Scipione della Palla (who later removed to Florence and whom Caccini acknowledged to have been his teacher), as well as the two Dentices.

From this point we must again conjecture. Giaches was very likely in the service of the Marchesa as a singer until his voice changed, which would have been about 1549 or 1550. At that time there would have been a decision to make as to his future; undoubtedly he had shown great promise and therefore merited further musical training. Where would he have been sent for such training if not to a court that had a fine musical establishment and one with which the Cardona-Este ménage had a connection? The logical place was Ferrara. But so far there has been no evidence that Giaches was ever at Ferrara. Examination of the payrolls of the Estense court for the years 1550–54 showed only one Giaches, and that is Giaches Organista, or Jacques Brumel. However, in Luigi Dentice's *Duo dialoghi della musica* of 1553 there is mention of a concert that took place in Naples shortly before that time, a concert which included the Marchesa della Padula, who "sang divinely," Leonardo dell'Arpa, Perino from Florence, a certain Giambattista siciliano, and Giaches da Ferrara, whom André Pirro identified as Wert.[9] This identification has been disputed hitherto on the basis that Giaches da Ferrara could only have been Giaches [Jacques] Brumel. I am inclined now, however, to think Pirro was right and that the Marchesa's youthful musician had been brought from Ferrara, for the connections are many and obvious.

Let us assume that about 1549 or 1550 Giaches was indeed sent to Ferrara for further training under the famous Cipriano de Rore. He would have been about 14 or 15 years old at the time, unable to serve as a singer. What then might he have been doing at Ferrara? Most likely he became one of the Duke's household—a page, a minor servitor, per-

[8] A. Fuscolillo, *Cronica*, in: *Archivio storico per le provincie napoletane*, I (1876), 625–27.

[9] André Pirro, *Histoire de la musique de la fin du XIVe siècle à la fin du XVIe* (Paris 1940), p. 325.

haps assisting with copying music or some such thing, receiving for his services lodging and keep and musical training. This explains why his name would not appear on any list of stipendiaries. After a few years of training there and after his voice had settled and he was again able to sing (for he was a singer), he was then ready to seek a post of his own.

Proceeding on this hypothesis, the next problem was to find supporting evidence. Uncovering no further documentary proof in Modena, I began my search in Novellara, where Giaches had served as maestro di cappella before 1558. Novellara is a sleepy little city about 40 miles from Modena, between Reggio and Mantua, and looks much the same today as it did several hundred years ago. The castle still stands—the moat is dry, however, and the fortifications are no longer operative. The "Rocca," as the castle is called, is used today to house municipal offices, the library, a music school, and various activities in the public interest. There is also a small, badly kept archive. I was most cordially received by the archivist (who is also the librarian and the sanitary inspector) and given every assistance. The records concerning Alfonso I di Novellara are meagre; only three large *buste* of letters to the Count exist; none from him and no payrolls or records of any kind. The prospect looked very discouraging, but we made a start. One package of letters was from the Bishop of Reggio, very lively and entertaining, but of no value for my purpose. Another consisted of letters from Alfonso's agent in Rome, with details of many transactions and business matters. The third packet contained miscellaneous letters from various minor officials concerning a number of properties owned by the Counts of Novellara and including information of all kinds sent from nearby courts. It was here that I found the hoped-for document—the following letter. (See Pl. 3b.) It is dated 30 October 1553, addressed to Count Alfonso, and sent by a certain Pollonice in Ferrara, evidently a representative maintained at that court, for the Counts of Novellara were feudatories of the Duke of Ferrara and therefore closely connected. The letter reads:

Illustrissimo Signore Mio—
Mando a V. S. per il presente staffiere questi madrigali, di Messer Cipriano, insieme con uno suo, li quali son certo che gli sarano carissimi, perche sono buoni; offerendo anche lui a servitio di V. S. per quanto esso m'ha imposto, sì come gli offersi e diede per suo, Messer Jacomo, il quale son certo gli farà honore. M'ha detto anchor che sempre farà cosa alcuna di nuova, vuole che lei sia de' primi, a che ne faccia parte, siche V. S. sarà de' buoni.
Il corno Nicchetto ancor non è venuta, si ne metti però all'ordine ogni cosa così pian piano, che subito venuto, non c'harà da far altro, se

non montar a Cavallo. Si ragiona di lunè o martedì prossimo che viene, ma non se ne ha certezza. Questa mattina si fa la festa del ladro che rubbò in Comaradonia, sia col farlo morire alla Forcha. Messer Nicolo Centurione, che già stava in casa, se non è ritornato a servitù del Rev^{mo} Card^{le} Monsignore, essendosi riconosciuto, et pentito dell'errore fecce, quando si partì, per quanto s'ha udito, basciandosi la mano et ragionando esso con sua S. Rev^{mo}, il che ha dato molto da ragionare alla corte. Et con questa fine, basciandole la mano, non havendo altro che gli dirò, a Voi mi racomando.

Di Ferrara il 30 dì d'ottobre del 1553.

Di V. S. S^{re} affettionatiss^{mo}
Il Pollonice

My most illustrious Signore—
I am sending to you by this footman the madrigals from Messer Cipriano, together with one of his own; I am sure you will like them very much because they are good. He enjoins me to say that he, too, offers to serve your lordship, just as Messer Jacomo, who I am certain will bring you honor, offers and dedicates himself to you. He [Rore] has told me again that whenever he does something new, he wants you to be one of the first to know about it, so that your lordship will be well-informed.

The trumpeter Nicchetto still has not arrived; however everything is being put in order so that as soon as he comes he will have only to mount his horse. There is talk that he will arrive next Monday or Tuesday, but it is not certain. Today there will be a public spectacle of the thief that was caught in Comaradonia; he will be put to death on the gallows. Messer Niccolo Centurione, who was formerly part of the household, has not returned to the service of the Most Reverend Monsignore Cardinal; having recognized and repented of his error, when he left he kissed the hand of the Cardinal and talked with him, according to hearsay. This has caused a lot of talk in the court. And with this, having nothing else to tell you, I come to a close and recommend myself to Your Lordship. From Ferrara the 30 day of October, 1553.

Most affectionate servitor of Your Excellency,
Pollonice

This gossipy letter contains several points of extreme interest. First, it appears that Cipriano di Rore had sent a package of madrigals to Alfonso, and included one of his own in it.[10] Next, Rore also made

---

[10] From two other letters in the Archivio di Novellara, it is evident that Alfonso was eager to be kept *au courant* of musical events in Italy and to receive the latest compositions of outstanding composers. One, from a certain Andrea Violo of Mirandolo (21 Nov. 1553) refers to some copies of madrigals he was to make or have made to be sent to the Count; the other, dated 10 Jan. 1554, to Alfonso from one Giovanni de Satz, is as follows:

Non ho mai scritto a V. S. perchè di qui non m'è occorse nuove degne di lei. Di nuovo al presente non le do altro che questo alegato motetto, compositione di M. Vincenzo Ruffo, il quale a questi giorni lo mandò al Rev. Mon. Sfrondato. E per essere nuovo et bello ho pigliato baldanza anzi prosunzione di mandarlo a V. S., supplicandola si degni d'accettarlo, e credo che li piacerà. Ho copiato

the gesture of offering his services to the Count and promised to send him new works whenever he composed something. Most important is the reference to "Messer Jacomo," who "offers and dedicates himself" to the Count. This can refer only to Wert. The next phrase—"I am certain he will bring you honor"—makes it clear that Giaches had promised to come to Novellara to enter Alfonso's service. Apparently he was soon to come to Novellara, and Pollonice's statement was made to reassure Alfonso in his choice. Alfonso had only recently returned to Novellara from Rome (where he had been "cameriere segreto" to Pope Paul III) in order to take up his duties as ruler of the Contea of Novellara.[11] Being a prince of the Church, he would undoubtedly have been concerned with establishing a musical cappella as soon as possible and was very likely in the process of forming one and finding a maestro to take charge of it. He would logically have turned to Ferrara and have asked the advice of Rore, who probably suggested the young composer. Wert was then just 18 years old, on the threshold of a career, and would have welcomed such an offer. He did come to Novellara and was there at least until 1558.

As to the form of his name—"Jacomo"—it fits in the picture perfectly. The two earliest existing references to Wert refer to him thus: one, in the *II° libro delle muse* of 1558,[12] lists his madrigal *Chi salirà per me* as being by "Jacomo Wert"; the other, the first letter in the Gonzaga archives referring to him, speaks of him as "Messer Jacomo, M. di cappella."[13] "Jacomo" is the Italian equivalent of James and Jacques; after 1565 Wert consistently uses "Giaches," the transliteration of the French "Jacques," for there is no such word in Italian, and his name never appears in any other form. The stubborn insistence upon the form "Giaches" would seem to indicate that he came from a French-speaking part of Flanders.[14]

assai belle cose in quelli libri che io feci fare a Roma, ma per non esser in luogo dove si exerciti le virtù, poche volte li adoperiamo . . .

[11] Between the years 1550–53, though ruler of Novellara, Alfonso spent a good portion of his time in Rome. There, in addition to his duties at the papal court he was occupied with business matters left unfinished by his uncle, Giulio Cesare Gonzaga, Patriarch of Alexandria, who died at Tivoli in the villa of his dearest friend Cardinal Ippolito d'Este. Alfonso also was concerned with marble decorations commissioned for his uncle's tomb in S. Spirito in Sassia and several paintings he had commissioned for that church. See G. Campori, *Gli Artisti italiani e stranieri negli stati estensi* (Modena 1855), p. 2ff.

[12] Rome, Antonio Barre.

[13] Mantua, Archivio di Stato, B 2944. 19 February 1565: "Con la venuta di Messer Jacomo, maestro di cappella, mando a V. S. una lettera . . ."

[14] Not once does the form "Jacob van Werth" appear in any letter or publication. This incorrect spelling of his name is based on a quite gratuitous assumption by several lexicographers that because Wert came from Flanders his name was Flemish or German.

The remainder of the letter recounts the latest events in the court. The Nicchetto referred to may very well have been Niccolò del Cornetto, who did actually spend some time in Ferrara during the years in question. In 1555 we hear of him leaving Ferrara, together with Gian Francesco dal Trombone, to go to Trent, where he had been engaged to serve the Cardinal Cristoforo Madruzzi.[15]

The discovery of this letter enables us to say with certainty that after his service as singing boy in the cappella of Maria di Cardona, Wert came to Ferrara for a period of time—perhaps as long as three years— where he was associated with Cipriano de Rore,[16] Alfonso della Viola, and Giaches Brumel, three of the leading musicians of the day, from whom he learned much. From Ferrara he went to Novellara to enter upon a long and brilliant career.

[15] Renato Lunelli, *Contributi trentini alle relazioni musicali fra l'Italia e la Germania nel Rinascimento*, in: *Acta musicologica*, XXI (1949), 56–57.

[16] This letter also justifies Einstein's guess, based on similarities of style, that Wert had been a pupil of Rore.

JANEQUIN: REWORKINGS OF
SOME EARLY CHANSONS

by A. TILLMAN MERRITT

THE NEW use of older musical materials and ideas by composers in a great variety of ways is as old as the history of music itself. It ranges from an almost literal use of the older materials to the use of only a fragment or single idea to build a new structure.

Different versions of four program chansons by Clément Janequin demonstrate a use more related to the first of these extremes, in that they show how he, and in one other case another composer, recomposed pieces that he had written earlier, without changing essentially their character. For the purpose of this essay no attention will be given to the arrangement of these pieces for lute or other instrumental media, or to their use as the basis of other types of works, such as the Mass Janequin himself wrote on his own *La Guerre*. The discussion will be focused on these four pieces which were rewritten to a greater or lesser extent, using the same musical ideas, harmonies, and texts, and remaining vocal compositions of the same genre as the originals.

Janequin was for many years widely known for several of his earliest published program chansons, to judge by the frequency of their reappearance. In one version or other they are to be found again and again, even into the 17th century, not only in a variety of publications by different publishers, but also in manuscripts. These four chansons, *Le Chant des oyseaux*, *La Guerre*, *La Chasse*, and *L'Alouette* were all published together for the first time in 1528 as *Chansons de maistre Clement Janequin nouvellement et correctement imprimeez par Pierre Attaingnant*, one of the first two publications of music by this first Parisian music publisher.[1] A fifth chanson, *Las povre cueur*, also appeared in this volume, but it was not a program chanson, it was relatively short, being

---

[1] This volume appears complete in transcription in *Les Maîtres musiciens de la renaissance française*, ed. Henry Expert, VII (Paris 1898). The same compositions will appear in vol. I of a complete edition of the chansons of Janequin by François Lesure and the present writer.

only 35 bars in length,[2] and it gained no fame, but remained at the starting post, while its four companions went far.

THERE IS no way to establish priority among the four program chansons in regard to chronology of composition, although as far as publication in one form or another is concerned *L'Alouette* came first.

In his *Chansons a troys,* dated at Venice, 15 October 1520,[3] Antico included a three-part chanson, *Or sus or sus vous dormez trop madame jolyette.* It, like all the other pieces in this volume, is not attributed to any composer. But practically the same piece appears in Attaingnant's 1528 publication as a four-part chanson by Janequin, and entitled *L'Alouette.* It is not especially unusual to find some publishers of this period mis-attributing works to well-known composers, although Attaingnant seems not to have indulged knowingly in the practice. It is not unusual, moreover, to find composers appropriating a composition and adding a part or two. It is possible, then, that Janequin took this three-part chan-son of 98 breves or measures in length, the work of another composer, re-arranged it slightly, adding a fourth voice, and offered it for publication to Attaingnant as his own four-part composition of 102 measures in length.

In any event, many years later Janequin seems clearly to have claimed the whole work as his own, with no hint that anyone else had had any part in it. Le Roy & Ballard's *Verger de musique* (1559) is a volume de-voted entirely to the works of Janequin. In this book, of which the title page tells us that the music was "revuez et corrigez par luy mesme" (that is, which Janequin himself edited), we find *Le Chant de l'alouette* exactly as it was in the 1528 version. It seems likely, although by no means cer-tain, that Janequin as the editor considered this volume a kind of official respository of the final versions of some of his most famous chansons. *La Guerre,* for instance, appears *à 4,* but *"avec la cinquiesme partie adjoutée par Verdelot sans y rien changer."* Here proper credit is given to Verdelot, but silence still reigns in regard to *L'Alouette.* Thus, the original authorship of the Antico three-part version of this piece remains uncertain. Until another composer can be proved, or convincingly sub-stituted, it will have to be assumed that Janequin is the unnamed com-poser. The date 1520 is entirely possible.

It happens that only two partbooks, those containing the outer voices, of Antico's 1520 *Chansons a troys* are presently known. For-

---

[2] Throughout this essay references to measure numbers apply to the transcrip-tions of these chansons as found in Expert.

[3] RISM 1520[6].

tunately, practically the identical three-part version is to be found complete in Florence, B. N. Magl. XIX. 117, fols. 8ᵛ–10. It is a singular coincidence that this version is the same length as the 1528 version. And it is interesting to note that the same four measures that are lacking in Antico are to be found in the other two versions, and in precisely the same place. They simply consist of repetitions of immediately preceding measures: bars 51 and 52 of the longer version repeat 49 and 50 of the shorter, while bars 72 and 92 of the former repeat 71 and 91 respectively of the latter.

Allowing for the fact that it is common to find variants, more or less small, in different editions and manuscripts of the same piece in music of this and earlier periods, it is difficult to say which two of the three versions most resemble each other, aside from the small difference in length. The superius and bass of all three are surely the same voice. It is true, to cite one very small instance, that the 1528 bass tarries in measure 88 on a semibreve and therefore gets one minim behind the MS and Antico bass, but catches up five measures later by not repeating a minim found in the two three-part versions. The tenors of Florence and Antico are basically the same; and, presumably, the missing middle voice of Antico agrees more or less with them.

The contratenor, aside from the fact that it is new in 1528, gives evidence of being the last voice composed: although skillfully enough handled it does not participate in the opening imitation; it does not start with the text of the other voices, but enters only with "madame jolyette"; it has a slight tendency to move faster than the other three parts; and it introduces phrases of text that do not occur in the other voices, snatches of Latin and mild profanity that are so typical of Janequin in chansons with texts of this general tone. These versions, then, do not indicate any major rewriting, since they all agree basically. The only change is the addition of a new contratenor in 1528.

But the curious case of *L'Alouette* does not end with the 1528 version and all those subsequent editions that agree with it. Jacques Moderne of Lyon also published a rather large volume containing nothing but Janequin chansons, *Le Difficile des chansons. Premier livre . . . contenant xxii chansons nouvelles a quatre parties en quatre livres de la facture & composition de . . . Janequin* (no date).[4] The fact that Moderne calls these chansons "nouvelles" is of no consequence; similar statements, particularly by certain publishers, were often made when they were simply reprinting, nay pirating, works that had appeared previously.

---

[4] The *Second livre* of *Le Difficile* was published in 1544. It is not likely that the *Premier livre* appeared before 1528, at least.

Moderne's statement is patently false, for every one of the chansons contained herein had been published before by Attaingnant. The four program chansons under discussion all appear among the 22 compositions.

Only the altus partbook of this volume of *Le Difficile* survives. Examination of the voices in it shows that they are the same as the contratenor parts of the same pieces in Attaingnant, and at first sight the absence of the three other partbooks would seem to be of little significance, as the pieces are all complete in Attaingnant editions. But this proves to be a false assumption when one examines *L'Alouette* on pages 29 and 30. Here a new contratenor (altus) of this piece appears, to be found by the present writer in no other source so far except the Bourdenay-Pasche manuscript.[5] This Moderne altus fits perfectly the other three parts as they appear in all other editions.[6] In several ways it is superior to the 1528 contratenor. It begins after a rest of two breves and a minim in imitation of the other voices and with the same text, "Or sus or sus." Moreover, the text continues to agree with that of the other voices far more consistently than the 1528 contratenor; departure from the sense of the text of the other voices of the 1528 version, mentioned above, does not take place. Phrases such as "Te rogamus, audi nos. Saincte teste Dieu" do not occur. Not only is the text more consistent, but the voice part itself carries out imitations throughout and feels much more at home with the other three voices than the 1528 contratenor.

In view of this more fitting altus that we find in Moderne it is curious that even Janequin continued to use the 1528 contratenor in the *Verger* of 1559. And it is also curious why the scribe of the Bourdenay-Pasche manuscript copied the Moderne altus instead of the original Attaingnant contratenor. An obvious mistake has been made by the scribe near the end of the piece when he apparently becomes confused and omits two measures. But this does not alter the fact that he copied the Moderne altus, or some other source from which it comes. Being surely an Italian he may have known only the Moderne print. Did Janequin, when Moderne was compiling this volume of *Le Difficile*, decide to furnish him with a newly written contratenor? If he did, why did he not use it himself in the *Verger*, for instance? Did François de Layolle or some other composer, not completely happy with the Janequin contratenor, decide to replace it with one of his own in this edition without mentioning himself as the composer of it? Verdelot, as we have observed, is still given credit in the *Verger* for his added fifth voice of *La Guerre*.

[5] Paris, B. N. Rés. Vm[a] 851.

[6] A wrong clef sign appears at the beginning of the first line of music at the bottom of p. 29, but is corrected at the top of p. 30.

Two questions concerning *L'Alouette* remain, therefore: the authorship of the original (?) three-part version, and that of the new contratenor (altus) in *Le Difficile*.

LA GUERRE, often called *La Bataille* and popularly known as *La Bataille de Marignan*, had a somewhat different and less puzzling career as a chanson. The actual battle of Marignan took place in 1515, soon after the assumption of the kingship by François I, and resulted in a splendid victory for him. The date of the composition and the immediate reason for its being written are not known, but the first publication of this *pièce d'occasion* took place 13 years later, surprisingly late in view of the great fame it and its composer acquired in the years to come. It is in two *parties*, 120 and 161 measures long respectively. It saw many editions by various publishers, and was copied in a number of manuscripts that still exist. And, although it underwent various transformations, as stated above, even as a program chanson it did not remain completely the same.

In 1545 Susato of Antwerp published *Le dixiesme Livre* [of chansons] *contenant la battaille a quatre de Clement Jannequin, avec cinquiesme partie de Phili. Verdelot si placet.*[7] This added fifth voice by Verdelot shows both that he must have been an admirer of the piece and that he himself was a master musician. Not a single note did he change in the original four voices of Janequin. But the voice he inserted between the contratenor and the bass adds great richness to the original texture, and is able to participate in a superb way both in the use of musical material and text, to the extent that it is almost indistinguishable in importance from the original four.

In this version *à 4* and *à 5 La Guerre* carried on in all editions with no alterations in the original writing, until the last edition of Janequin's works to be prepared during his lifetime. Le Roy & Ballard's *Verger de musique* (1559), the volume already mentioned, in which the "excellents labeurs de M. C. Janequin" were "revuez et corrigez par luy mesme," begins with *Le Chant des oyseaux*, followed by *Le Chant du rossignol, Le Chant de l'alouette, La Prinse et reduction de Boulogne, La Bataille à 4 avec la cinquiesme partie par Verdelot sans y rien changer* and *Le Siege de Metz*. But, after *Le Siege de Metz*, which is another battle piece by Janequin, even longer than the original *La Guerre*, we find still another *La Bataille*, this time *à 5*. This piece proves in essence to be the original one, but with differences other than those caused by the simple addition of a fifth voice.

The *Verger*, according to the title page, was printed in five partbooks.

[7] RISM 1545[17].

Most unfortunately no copy of the volume containing the fifth parts of the five-part compositions in this book of chansons has come to light. On account of its absence not only this version of *La Guerre* cannot be completed, but also *Le Siege de Metz* does not exist complete. Another battle piece by Janequin, *La Guerre de Renty*, is *à 4* and is thus unaffected by the lack of the fifth partbook. All other five-part pieces in the book exist complete in other editions.

The existence of four voices of *La Guerre à 5* are quite sufficient to show the differences between it and the original, and consequently the five-part Janequin-Verdelot version. The *première partie* of this version has 114 measures as against 120 of the old, and the *seconde partie* has 152 measures compared to 161 of the old. The four existing voices begin the new version precisely as they did the old. There is no way of knowing for sure in what measure the fifth voice entered, nor exactly where it lay in the texture, although there are signs, including the cadences, that it lay between the contratenor and the tenor.

In any case, this superius begins to diverge from the 1528 version in measure 8, the contratenor and tenor in measure 9 and the bass in measure 10. Each successive divergence leads to still others, and it is obvious that by measure 10 the fifth voice must be singing, as the other voices have opened up to provide air for it and are omitting chord tones for it to sing. The 42 measures preceding the first large hemiolia section have been reduced to 41 measures, and various small details have been rearranged, though the two versions do not differ greatly in basic conception. Neither the first hemiolia section nor the section following it has been changed in length, although there are varying details of rewriting, such as the elimination of hemiolia figures in the contratenor and bass in measures 89–92. The second hemiolia section, measures 95–120, has been shortened by three measures, and notes rearranged in detail, but the original four voices are still recognizable in the four new ones, and the fifth voice must be considered as essentially an added one.

The *seconde partie* of the new version reproduces faithfully that of the old for a longer time than the *première partie*. But once it begins to diverge, beginning slightly in measure 47, and more distinctly after 51, where Janequin suppresses five measures almost immediately, the progress of the new version takes place as a mild paraphrase of the old. The hemiolia section toward the end remains the same length in both versions and practically the same musically, while the final section is shortened by two more measures.

The text of the two versions is essentially the same, although there are a few interesting differences. In the 1528 version the "noble roy

François" is obviously the leading character; no other person is mentioned. Nor, in fact, is any particular enemy named. The words depict exhortation to courage, patriotism, and excitement to win, and imitate the sounds of hoof beats, roar of guns, sounding of trumpets and bugles, and such battle noises. There is little to suggest animosity toward the opposing enemy, but rather good, if dangerous, sportsmanship, such as we find in the text of La Chasse. The text of 1559 on the whole retains all the 1528 sentiment and sounds. "Le noble roy François" has become "le grand roy des François, premier du nom"; the "gentils Gascons" are as brave as ever. But the enemy are now named as "ces mutins Bourguignons, aussi ses Hennuyers" (natives of Hainault province; the locale has apparently changed!), and instead of cries of "à mort" to a nameless adversary in 1528 the soldiers of 1559 are encouraged to "mettre à mort ces Bourguignons." Even the strategy of battle has become a bit more precise: "Ne vous faittes plus canonner, la place faut abandonner."

The fifth voice of this version of La Guerre would, when or if it comes to light, complete an interesting slightly different version of it.

LA CHASSE underwent a less interesting experience than that of La Guerre. Although it inspired similar compositions by other composers such as Gombert it exists in only two versions itself, both by Janequin. Like La Guerre it is in two long parties, the first of which is 168 measures long, the second 144. In the second version, which appeared in 1537,[8] Janequin suppressed measures 8 to 11 of the première partie of 1528, but with this exception the two complete versions are exactly the same length, and no further changes were made either in construction, writing or text. Moreover, aside from the four measures that were suppressed, no change whatever was made in the 1537 version of the première partie.

But, to the four original voices of the seconde partie Janequin added three new ones, making a seven-part piece. The added voices are a "secundus superius," inserted just below the superius, a "secundus contratenor," inserted between the secundus superius and the contratenor, and a "secundus tenor," inserted between the tenor and the bass. None of the three voices starts at the beginning of the partie: the secundus tenor enters in measure 28, the secundus superius in measure 29 and the secundus contratenor in measure 30. By this time the original voices have completed the introductory text and music concerned with setting the scene of the hunt, and have just entered into the noise and excitement

---

[8] Les Chansons de La guerre, La chasse, Le chant des oyseaux, Lalouette, La rossignol composees par maistre clement Jennequin reimprimees par Pierre Attaingnant et Hubert Julet . . . Mense Mayo M. D. xxxvii.

of it, with imitations in text and music of the sounds of panting dogs and excited commands to them. The typical semiminims in a kind of patter, with little attempt at dissonance or much harmonic change, set in at this point, to continue with no relenting until almost the end.

Janequin's insertion of the three new voices does not, then, present much of a compositional problem. They are stuffed into holes where the texture was a bit thin to begin with; they do not even have to sing any meaningful text, but can echo syllables and commands already employed by the other voices; and there is no melodic imitation to speak of with which to cope. The main problem is to keep them from duplicating any of the other voices in moving consecutive fifths and octaves and to alternate them rhythmically with the other voices as much as possible, sometimes in a fashion reminiscent of hocketing. The new version of the *seconde partie*, and of that only, appears as a more dressed-up rendition of the old, perhaps suggesting the excitement of a larger band of hunters. This does not involve the process of recomposition. The *Verger* contains the seven-part version.

THE EXPERIENCE of the last of the four program chansons is far more drastic, and in some ways more interesting. *Le Chant des oyseaux* appeared in 1528 in five sections, which we shall call A, B, C, D, and E. The A section is 15 measures long, the B 37, the C 45, the D 57, and the E 54. Each section comes to an end with a full cadence and double bar.

In the 1537 edition the division into separate sections has disappeared, and the whole is now one single piece, 113 measures long instead of the original 208. The cutting down of the composition to little more than half its original length was made possible by the construction of the first version.

The 1528 version has a kind of rondo-like form. The A section never develops musically, or textually, beyond the initial two melodic ideas, the first set to "Reveillez vous cueurs endormis" and the second to "le dieu d'amour vous sonne"; it serves, in effect, as an introduction to the whole piece. The music, moreover, serves also as the ending of each of the following sections, the final E section using even the same text. The end of the B section sets different words to it: "vous serez tous en joye mis, car la saison est bonne"; that of the C section uses "rire et gaudir c'est mon devis, chacun si habandonne"; and the D section uses "fuiez regretz pleurs et soucis, car la saison l'ordonne" ("est bonne" in some editions of this version). Thus the text of the A section, together with that of the endings of the following four, results in a kind of A B C B′ A effect.

These already strong rondo-like traits in music and text are heightened by the use of almost the same 12 measures of music to begin each of the last four sections. The text is different in these four repetitions, since it serves to introduce different bird songs in each of these sections. Since sections B, C, D, and E all begin with the same 12 measures of music and each of them ends with the A section the only possible place for new music is in the middle of these sections. And it is here in sections B to E that Janequin introduces his fast patter notes and the text syllables imitating the songs of birds. The composer manages to repeat previously used music with previously used text, previously used music with new text, and new music with new text in a mildly complex way, simply shown thus:

SECTION	A	B	C	D	E
TEXT	A	a birds 1–B	β birds 2–C	γ birds 3–B′	δ birds 4–A
MUSIC	A	a new A	a new A	a new A	a new A

In rewriting *Le Chant des oyseaux* Janequin abbreviated it by eliminating the rondo-like structure. He made it into a *da capo* composition by using the whole A section of the 1528 version to begin and end the 1537 version, and by fusing sections B to E to form a large central section. The earlier sections A and B are also fused by making the last measure of A serve as the first of B. Section B proceeds verbatim until it is time for it to end with the music of the A section, at which time it passes not only over these concluding fifteen or so measures of this section but also over the twelve or so measures which opened the C section of the earlier version. Thus the process is continued, with the resulting form: A (15 measures); B (83 measures); A (15 measures). By decapitating sections C, D, and E and by decaudating sections B, C, and D Janequin has amalgamated earlier sections B to E into one large central B section.

Generally speaking, the bird imitations, both in text and music, tend in the new version to follow the order in which they appeared in the old. The typical "farirariron frere ly joly" of the original B section reappears almost exactly at the beginning of the large new B section; the "ti ti chouty . . . saincte teste Dieu . . . il est temps" of the C section follows without interruption, considerably rewritten but recognizable; the "frian . . . que l'ara . . . huit . . . teo . . . ticun . . . oy ty" of the D section follows, considerable passages reappearing exactly; and "coqu . . . par trahison . . . ponnez" of the last section runs into the final *da capo* very much as it did originally.

Janequin shows his superior compositional skill in this fusion of

several sections of a larger piece into a single shorter one. There is bound
to be disagreement about the results: the rondo-like repetitions of the
1528 version have charm and furnish a better articulation of the different
bird songs; on the other hand, the elimination of unnecessary repetitions
and the unhampered progression and piling up of fast rhythms and bird
sounds lead to an uninterrupted excitement that was only spasmodic in
the earlier version. The scribe of the Bourdenay-Pasche manuscript was
apparently impressed by both versions, for he not only copied *Il Canto
delli uccelli in francese* (the 1528 version) on pages 387–89, but also *Il
Canto delli uccelli in una parte solla* on page 389.

The thorough rewriting by Janequin of his own composition was
not the last transformation this chanson underwent. Susato's *Le dixiesme
Livre contenant la battaille . . .* , mentioned above, contains a *Chant
des oyseaux a troix*, although it does not contain either of the four-part
versions of Janequin. The three-part bird composition is by Nicolas
Gombert. It is not entirely a new piece, but rather constitutes an extensive recomposition of the 1528 four-part one by Janequin, using Janequin's music and text. Gombert has reduced the original five sections to
four by eliminating the full stop between Janequin's sections A and B,
but otherwise has retained Janequin's large organization. The resulting
four sections are 43, 41, 33, and 61 measures long respectively. Composing a piece for three voices, using the Janequin text and musical ideas
as well as the Janequin rondo-like structure, with the exception of dove-
tailing the first two sections (which Janequin himself did in his second
version), Gombert has produced a piece 178 measures long compared
with 208 of his model (or 113 of the 1537 version). The lengths of sections of the two compositions compare thus:

JANEQUIN		GOMBERT	
A + B	52 measures	A	43 measures
C	45 "	B	41 "
D	57 "	C	33 "
E	54 "	D	61 "

Despite the use of so much of Janequin's materials and methods
Gombert has condensed each of the model sections, with the exception
of the last. Schmidt-Görg discusses the relation of the two pieces at some
length,[9] and points out the more skillful handling of this kind of
"Variationskunst" by Gombert.

It is reasonable to believe that Gombert, almost a generation younger

[9] Joseph Schmidt-Görg, *Nicolas Gombert, Leben und Werk* (Bonn 1938), pp.
230–34.

than the composer he emulated, was acquainted with both the 1528 and the 1537 versions of Janequin's *Song of the Birds*. Why did he choose the earlier version to emulate? His interest in Janequin is shown by another composition in the same Susato volume entitled *La Chasse du lievre a quatre*, surely a composition inspired by Janequin's *La Chasse (du cerf)*.

MUSIC IN DANTE'S
DIVINA COMMEDIA

by KATHI MEYER-BAER

I N HIS BIOGRAPHY Boccaccio writes that "Dante in his youth was
fond of singing and music. He was a friend of every one who was
a good singer or musician. Influenced by this interest he wrote
many poems around which he had woven pleasant tunes by his composer
friends." [1] Dante is seen as a lover of music who looked at music from the
point of view of a poet; and thus we recognize him in the *Divina Commedia*. It is this attitude that makes his remarks and descriptions so in-
formative; what he has to say expresses the ideas of the average man
interested in the arts and in music around 1300 in Italy.

The *Commedia* is above all a political and a theological book; besides
these fundamental aspects the vast horizon of the author includes remarks about all the other facets of culture, and not only of his time. This
richness is one of the striking features of the poem, another being that
Dante meets and talks to personalities of many periods, from antiquity to
his own time. The tremendous impact of the *Commedia* comes from the
reaction of Dante's passionate personality in all these discourses.

In the *Inferno* there are no musical performances. In the *Purgatorio*
we hear them mentioned in the last canto as Dante approaches the earthly
paradise [2] on top of the mountain of expurgation. That contrast in itself
is revealing; it shows that the poet considers music one of the beauties of
the world. The lost people, the sinners, have no music. In the *Purgatorio*
it is only the messengers from Paradise who sing, and the *Paradiso* ends
with the vision of unceasing singing and dancing of the blessed and the
angels in the highest heaven.

Dante's remarks concern the practice of music; this is true when he
describes music he hears and also when he uses it in metaphors. Only in
a few places does he speak about the philosophy of music. His remarks,
therefore, are relevant to the musicologist. They inform us on the music
making of his period. The difficulty in interpretation arises from the

[1] A. Bonaventura, *Dante e la musica* (Leghorn 1904), p. 14.
[2] The *Paradiso* is the heavenly Paradise. It is marked here throughout with a capital P to differentiate it from the earthly paradise.

vague use of terms. With the *Vita nuova*, the *Convivio*, and the *Commedia* Dante was the creator of the new Italian language,[3] yet he was not a professional musician, not a *musicus*. We see how loosely the terms are applied from the very different explanations that the many commentators and translators have suggested.

THE MUSICAL TERMS

I SHOULD like to start by listing the different meanings Dante gives to terms connected with music.[4] Many of the expressions refer to sound in general, such as *suono, sonare, sentire,* and *udire*—sound, sounding, and hearing; they refer to noises—especially in the *Inferno*—as well as to music. The terms *armonia, armonizzare,* and *accordare*—harmony, harmonize, attune—usually have a general meaning (*Purg.* 31,144; *Par.* 1,78 and 127; *Par.* 6,126; *Par.* 28,8). The word *sinfonia* is equivalent to harmony (*Par.* 21,59). We do not find the word for music. Persons who sing are called *cantor* or *psalmista* / *salmista* (*Purg.* 10,65; *Par.* 18,51; *Par.* 25,72). For the forms of vocal music we have the words: *canto, cantico, cantilena, canzone, coro, lai, letane, salmodia, nota,* and *voce*. Of these *cantico* is the large form, containing several *canti*. The *Commedia* is divided into three *cantici: Inferno, Purgatorio,* and *Paradiso*, and each of these parts has 33 *canti*. *Canto* can also mean side (*Purg.* 12,113). These terms are more often used for the poetic form, but they may stand for song. *Cantilena* emphasizes the melodic or the short song (*Par.* 32,97). The suggested derogatory meaning, comic or love song,[5] does not fit the events it describes. *Letane* and *lai* are the terms for dirges and laments (*Inf.* 5,46; *Purg.* 9,13). They are often combined with the verbs *piangere, piangendo,* or *lagrimando cantare* (*Purg.* 33,1; the 97th psalm, *salmodia,* is sung *lagrimando*). The word *lai* is used in a way different from what we are acquainted with in medieval music. Similarly, the term *lauda* has a meaning unusual for us; it stands for the crowd of the singing blessed (*Par.* 19,37). *Coro* may mean chorus or merely a group (*Par.* 10,106). *Canzone*, sometimes identical with *cantico*, and *canzonetta* mean specifically the poetic form. Casella, Dante's friend, sings a *canzone*, an occurrence I shall explain in detail later.

The terms *voce* and *nota* are unfortunately very equivocal. *Voce* can mean voice, call, or fame. In some cases a differentiation is clear, as in the expression *ad una voce*—in unison (*Purg.* 2,47). But how are we to translate *voce a voce* and *voce in voce?* We have to look for an explana-

---

[3] K. Vossler, *Italienische Literaturgeschichte* (Berlin 1916), Chaps. II and III/1.
[4] A list of the musical terms is given in Bonaventura, *Dante,* p. 325ff.
[5] R. Hammerstein, *Die Musik der Engel* (Bern 1962), p. 149.

tion of these terms in contemporary treatises on the theory of music, but these are written in Latin. *Nota* can mean note, musical sound, word, verse, sign (*Purg.* 11,34), or singing. Sometimes we can understand the meaning if *nota* is combined with another term; *cantare* with *nota* means singing with text (*Purg.* 32,63); likewise *note* with *voci* means words and tunes (*Par.* 6,124); *nota e metro* designates tune and text or rhythm (*Par.* 28,9).

THE TEXT OF THE SONGS

Most of the songs that are mentioned here have liturgical texts. In two cases Dante's poems are quoted. One occurs in the meeting with a friend of his youth, Casella (no first name), who steps out from a crowd of the blessed to console Dante, as "he was wont to do in Florence, with a love song"—*amoroso canto: Amor che nella mente mi ragione* (*Purg.* 2,112). It is the opening poem of the third chapter in Dante's *Convivio*. It is not an ordinary love song, but deals with the love and longing for wisdom and truth. Casella sings it so *dolcemente* that the softness still rings in Dante's ear. Dante and Vergil are so overcome by its sweetness that they forget to proceed in their wandering till Cato reminds them of their task. This scene fits well with Boccaccio's biography. Casella may well have been an amateur; we do not find his name in any of the musical sources. It is doubtful whether he is identical with the Casella who was composer of a madrigal by Lemmo di Pistoia.[6] In their youth Dante and Casella may have written poetry and music for their own entertainment.

The words *dolce* and *dolcezza* point to the fact that the *canzone* belongs to the *dolce stile nuovo*, a term formulated by Dante (*Purg.* 24,57). This new style, this *ars nova*,[7] was the result of the linking of the art of the Provençal troubadours with the different schools of Italian poetry. Casella is the only musician of the period mentioned in the *Commedia;* but we meet several other representatives of the new style: Bonagiunta da Lucca recites Dante's poem *Donne ch'avete intelletto d'amore*[8] (*Purg.* 24,51); the poet Sordello da Mantua talks with Vergil about the texts of his poetry, not about the tunes (*Purg.* 6,74; 7,3, and 52; 8,38–94; 9,58). Arnaut Daniel is another Provençal poet (*Purg.* 26,142). Guido Giunzelli from Bologna (*Purg.* 11,97; 26,92) and Guido Cavalcante (*Inf.* 10,63) are typical poets of the new style. They all discuss the texts of their songs only. However, of Arnaut it is said that he walks along singing (*che plor e vau cantan*); he speaks Provençal. The discus-

[6] Bonaventura, *Dante*, p. 11; H. Gmelin, *Dante. Die göttliche Komödie. Kommentar* (Stuttgart 1954–57), II, 51ff.
[7] See fn. 3.
[8] First *canzone* in Dante's *Vita nuova*.

sions with and about the Provençal poets take place in the 11th and 26th songs of the *Purgatorio*, the latter just before Dante ascends to the earthly paradise. The only secular poet in the *Paradiso* is Folquet de Marseilles (*Par.* 9,37). He became a monk in 1195 and later bishop of Toulouse. In the 11th canto of *Purgatorio* Dante also meets four painters: Giotto, Cimabue, and two illuminators; but no musician is mentioned.

THE MANNER OF PERFORMANCE

THE SPEECHES that we hear are either sung or spoken, both the longer ones which give theological, historical, or scientific instructions, and the shorter often biographical ones. The emperor Justinian sings his speech, *canto canta* (*Par.* 5,139). Piccarda Donati tells the story of the empress Costanza, mother of Frederick II, and at the end sings the Ave Maria (*Par.* 3,122). The manner of the emperor Constantine is not specified, but Dante answers him, [*io*] *cantava cotai note*, in singing (*Inf.* 19,118). Cunizza, the sister of Ezzelino of Milan, sings her story (*Par.* 9,23). Of Folquet and St. Bonaventura it is only said that they begin their speeches (*Par.* 9,83; 12,31). Saint Peter sings his benediction (*Par.* 24,151). The reports are called *nota, canto, vita*, or *storia*. The last term reminds us of the so called *historiae* of the vesper service closing the Office of the hours in which the lives of the saints or the explanation of the festival were chanted. Sometimes the speaker separates himself from the circle and chorus to which he is assigned; then the others are silent so that Dante can understand better. After finishing, the soloists rejoin their spheres.

Most of the liturgical texts are verses from the Psalms, the Song of Songs, and the Beatitudes, chosen from a special rite or from the service of the Hours. Dante's journey is divided into several definite days and hours. Thus, for events happening in the morning, verses from Matins are selected (*Purg.* 25,121, *Summa Deus clementiae*), in other cases some from the evening service (*Purg.* 7,82; 8,12, *Salve Regina* and *Te lucis ante*). When Dante is immersed in the river Lethe (*Purg.* 31,98) the verse from the 51st psalm, *Asperges me*, part of the ritual of baptism, is sung. In the last spheres of the *Paradiso* songs in honor of the Virgin prevail; here St. Bernard, the herald of the cult of St. Mary, is Dante's guide replacing Beatrice.

Dante's terms for the manner of performance are varied. He says *dicere* (*Purg.* 17,67; 20,136f.), that is, to talk or recite, or *cantare*, which means to chant. The two terms may also be combined *cantava e dicea* or *dicere cantando* (*Purg.* 27,99), which, too, can only mean chant, as one would expect for a liturgical melody; or Dante uses the expression *voce dicendo* for singing (*Purg.* 14,132). Once Dante hears a sweet song— *canto* when Beatrice spoke: *dicea il Canto* (*Par.* 26,69). Sometimes *osannare* stands for the singing of liturgical melodies (*Par.* 28,94). At other times the text is shouted, *chiamato* or *gridato*, such as the *Maria ora per noi, Dolce Maria,* and the *Gloria* (*Purg.* 13,50; 20,20 and 133).

All these terms are applied to solos as well as to singing in chorus. The manner of execution is not always clearly defined. In some cases the meaning is plain, as when Dante says that Psalm 114 is sung *ad una voce,* i.e. in unison (*Purg.* 2,47). In the *Purgatorio* the Miserere is sung *verso a verso.* This term has been explained by the commentator Olschki [9] as alternating, by the French translator Longnon [10] as one verse after the other. If Olschki is right, it would mean an antiphonal execution. The angelic orders sing the *osanna di coro in coro* (*Par.* 28,94). This may mean alternating, or does it imply polyphonic singing? In the sphere of the Sun the blessed sing so that one song joins the other: *canto a canto colse* (*Par.* 12,6). This expression, too, may mean singing in different parts. The *Te Deum* is sung so that the voice is mixed with the sweet sound: *voce mista al dolce suono* (*Purg.* 9,140). In the verse it is not stated that the *dolce suono* is an organ, but Dante adds that he has difficulty in understanding the words, as may happen when we hear singing accompanied by an organ. This combination must have been familiar to the poet.

Two instances are especially vexing. Dante, in the sphere of Venus (*Par.* 8,17), meets the souls of famous lovers "and as in a flame we can discern sparks, in a voice we can discern a second voice when one is stable and the other comes and goes" (*e come in voce si discerne quand' una è ferma e l'altra va e riède*). This simile seems to suggest the technique of a musical composition where one part holds long notes while the other part has a discant ductus. The other instance occurs at the end of the tenth canto of the *Paradiso* (*Par.* 10,143) when Dante and Beatrice are in the sphere of Mercury and see the dance of the blessed "as harmonious as is the sound of the matin with the tin tin, I (Dante) saw the glorious round turn and add voice to voice in sound and sweetness" (*indi . . . come . . . l'una parte l'altra tire ed urge tin tin sonando con si dolce nota cosi vid'io la gloriosa rota moversi e render voce a voce in tempra ed in dolcezza*). The effect of the music is so marvelous that he cannot describe it to the people on earth. This, too, may be the descrip-

[9] Dante Alighieri, *La divina commedia,* ed. Leonardo Olschki (Heidelberg 1922); Ital. edition with German commentary.

[10] Dante, *La divine comédie,* ed. Henri Longnon (Paris 1938).

tion of a partsong. Longnon, however, translates it as "chanter à l'unison"!

Before Dante leaves the earthly paradise he hears a sweet melody: *dolce suono per canto* (*Purg.* 29,36), and sees the procession of the triumphant Church coming towards him (*Purg.* 29,16). In its center is an eagle symbolic of Christ. The figure of the eagle appears again in the sphere of Mars (*Par.* 20,16), where it is formed by the dancing blessed as the finale of a huge ballet. The souls are singing in a great chorus; the eagle sings and dances: *rotando cantava e dicea.* Here the eagle is a symbol of justice, of just government in heaven as well as on earth. Injustice is the reason for Dante's sufferings, for his exile and frustration. Therefore justice is the highest virtue for Dante. The head of the eagle has six eyes or six lights on his lids, in which six just and great rulers have their seats. Dante hears the voices of the eyes talk (*parlar*) and sing (*sonar*). The effect is one sound coming out of the image: *usciva solo un suon di quelle image* (*Par.* 19,21). This voice explains the figures in the six eyes. In the center is David the singer—*cantor*—of the Holy Spirit. The others are Trajan, Hiskia, Constantine, William II of Sicily, and the Trojan Ripheus, known from the Aeneid (II,339).

Dante is astonished to hear the voice speak in the singular though it should have spoken as "we" instead of "I" (*Par.* 19,10). This remark suggests that Dante hears the six partners singing together. Before the voice starts, the eagle has silenced the voices of the chorus behind him: *agli angelici squilli.* Its song starts like "a murmuring and becomes clear like the sound or tone that starts at the neck of a lute, or like the sound that comes out of the hole of a shawm." The six personalities who are introduced to Dante seem to step forward; the reasons why the two pagan rulers have been elected are explained at the end. While going back to their seats the two blessed lighten up "their shining attuned to their words"; this "concord" reminds Dante of the harmony that exists when "a good lute player adds a trill on the strings to heighten the enjoyment of the performance of a good singer." Dante is now in the spheres where space and time, light and sound become identical. Words, sound, and light cannot be distinguished any more. This heavenly and unrealistic feature makes an explanation of the song of the six heroes so difficult. We can recognize that the song is differentiated and separated from the chorus of the angelic crowd. But is the song in unison, or are the parts different as are the figures of the six rulers? The "we" that Dante expects may point to singing in parts. If such technique is assumed we have to think of the different nationalities of the singers: David and Hiskia,

Hebrew; Constantine and Trajan would speak Latin; Ripheus, Greek; and William II, Italian or Normanic—a combination of vernaculars in one song which reminds us of compositions with the parts in different languages such as were still written in the Ars nova. Hammerstein calls the execution merely "unisono" without noticing that Dante does not use the term *ad una voce* here.[11]

The people in the *Commedia* speak Italian with the exception of the troubadour Arnaut Daniel (*Purg.* 26,140) who uses Provençal. At the end of the speech of Justinian (*Par.* 7,1) Latin and Hebrew words are mixed. The *initia* of the liturgical tunes are given in Latin, which is sometimes translated (*Purg.* 15,39) or paraphrased in Italian (*Purg.* 22,4, paraphrase of the *Beatitudes II, Matt.* 5,6).

MUSICAL INSTRUMENTS

WE DO not hear about actual instrument playing in the *Commedia*. The reference to the organ accompanying singing may be a metaphor (*Purg.* 9,140). In several places Dante uses instruments in comparisons. Many of these instruments—*tromba, trombetta, tamburo, cenno di castello*, and Nimrod's horn—are noise or signal instruments. They are mentioned in Hell (*Inf.* 22,7) when Dante and Vergil have to cross the pond of tar where the cheaters are punished. The wanderers need guides to pass a bridge. A crowd of devils undertakes the task in a mock march which reminds Dante of military bands as he had heard them in expeditions when he took part in the Florentine wars (1280–89): bands with trumpets, bells, drums, signal horns, and a wind instrument called *cenamella*. The trumpet, of course, is mentioned as giving the signal for the Last Judgment (*Inf.* 6,95; 19,5). Of the flute and the shawm Dante speaks in comparisons. The sound of these instruments passing through the holes is compared to voice and breath (*Par.* 20,14 and 24). For the sound of the flute Dante uses the term *flaillo*, derived from the old French *flavel*.

The stringed instruments as a group are called *corde*. The lute is mentioned together with the shawm. The voice of the eagle comes out of his beak as a sound starts at the neck of the lute (*cetra*) and from the hole (*pertugio*) of the shawm (*sampogna*) (*Par.* 20,24). Also mentioned together are harp and viol (*giga*). When Dante is in the sphere of Mars (*Par.* 14,118) he sees the blessed forming a cross. They enchant Dante with their singing although at first he cannot understand the words, just as "someone can enjoy the sweet harmony of harp and viol woven together by the sounds of many strings even if he does not under-

[11] Hammerstein, *Musik*, p. 184.

stand the composition (*nota*), even if he does not know the theory of music." The sound is woven together in *tempra*, a term which has been defined as tone color or tone by the commentators. Does this comparison imply a composition in several parts? We could list a large number of instruments mentioned in the *Commedia*, and from the way in which Dante refers to them we can gather that they were in popular use at his time.

In several places Dante uses names of musical instruments for ideas different from musical experience. When he wants to illustrate the feeling of longing he tells us of the sound of church bells which a traveler —on land or sea—hears before coming home (*Purg.* 8,1). Dante, when speaking of the force of imagination, explains that it can be roused by inner light or by impressions from the outside (*Purg.* 17,13). The inspiration is likened here to the song of birds; when Vergil and Dante enter the forest of the earthly paradise the rustling of the leaves forms the ground bass, the *bordone* to the song of the birds (*Purg.* 28,18).

THE DANCES

DANCING OCCURS in the *Commedia* from the end of the earthly paradise on, when the blessed are dancing in the great procession that leads the poet to Heaven. Only one dance is mentioned earlier, the *tresca* in the *Inferno* (*Inf.* 14,40), when the people who have sinned against God and Nature defend themselves against the rain of fire. They lift their arms to smother the flames as if they were dancing the *tresca*. Muratori [12] sees as the root of the word a worksong about threshing; Battisti [13] derives it from the Provençal word for dance. In the 19th century the name designated an indecent dance from the region of Naples. In the *Commedia* it means a simple folk dance. The name occurs once more (*Purg.* 10,65) in the description of the wall reliefs in the first layer of the actual *Purgatorio* to which the proud are condemned, in a scene where the "humble psalmist" dances the high *tresca*.

Apart from this popular dance, only the blessed and the angels dance. They dance rounds called *cerchio, rota, ruota, carola, giro* (*Par.* 8,26; 25,99,130 and *passim*) and *caribo* or *coribo*, an unexplained form (*Purg.* 31,132). All these terms signify that they are round or circled dances. The rounds differ greatly in their size, tempo, and direction. Sometimes people dance alone. St. Peter circles around Dante three times (*Par.* 24,151). The archangel Gabriel circles before the Virgin while singing

---

[12] L. A. Muratori and Benvenuto, quoted in the *Dizionario etimologico* by Q. Viviani included in the 4th vol. of the *Commedia* (Udine 1828).
[13] C. Battisti, *Dizionario etimologico italiano* (1950–57).

Ave Maria (*Par.* 23,103; 32,94). Sometimes groups such as the Apostles (*Par.* 23,136) and the prelates (*Par.* 21,136) dance their round. The seven virtues in the procession of the Church (*Purg.* 31,130) come out of the crowd and circle separately in groups of four (the cardinal virtues) and three (the Christian virtues) while singing alternately the 97th psalm. Another time Dante sees the host of blessed making a great circle around him (*Par.* 10,65).

The tempo of the dances varies; there are faster and slower rounds. This reminds Dante of the movement of the wheels in a watch where some wheels run faster and some slower (*Par.* 10,139; 24,13). Sometimes, when there are several rounds, only one moves while the other stands still, "like ladies who stop dancing until a new tune has begun" (*Par.* 10,79). The higher Dante climbs and the closer the dancers move around the Lord, the faster the tempo becomes (*Par.* 8,26; 31,137).

The direction of the rounds varies. Sometimes Dante sees concentric circles moving in the same direction, such as the three highest orders of angels circling around the Lord in honor of the Trinity (*Par.* 14,28 and 74). At other times concentric rounds move in opposite directions (*Par.* 13,18 and 117), or the rounds move one beside the other so that they meet and form a knot like a figure eight. In this kind of round, one can be at a standstill while the other moves: *e nel suo giro tutta non si volse prima che un'altra d'un cerchio la chiuse* (Par. 12,4).

In the 18th canto of the *Paradiso* Dante describes a kind of ballet (*Par.* 18,73), a performance "almost with the pomp of an opera." [14] Here the poet sees the blessed dancing and singing. They move singing the tune assigned to each, *a sua nota*. When they reach the place prescribed to them, they stop singing as well as dancing and stand. They first form the letter D, then I, and then L, continuing until they have spelled out *Diligite iustitiam qui iudicatis terram*. This is the first verse in the book of the wisdom of Solomon in the Vulgate. It accentuates the virtue of justice so prominent in the thoughts of Dante. Later the letters are dissolved and the dancers form the figure of an eagle which we have described above. Such kinds of ballets must have existed in Dante's time, although I did not find a reference to them anywhere else.

All the remarks on music—on singing, on instruments, and on dancing—that we have listed from the *Commedia* prove Dante to be a person interested in music, observing its usages and having a fine musical judgment. From his impressions and formulations we can draw conclusions on the musical practices of the period. The difficulty in interpretation arises from the inconsistency in the terms used. If we could compare his

[14] Gmelin, *Dante*, II, 364.

expressions with the corresponding ones by the theorists the result could not be convincing, because all the treatises are written in Latin. Garlandia and Pseudo Vitry,[15] contemporaries of Dante, say *nota contra* (or *versus*) *notam*, but can we indentify this with Dante's *voce in voce* or *coro a coro?*

MUSICAL FIGURES OF MYTHOLOGY

VERGIL IS Dante's guide through the *Inferno* and the *Purgatorio*. The Aeneid was, if not the model, then the inspiration of the *Commedia*, and many of its passages attest to Dante's thorough knowledge of Roman and Greek mythology. There are very few references to musical figures, however. The poem opens with an invocation of the Muses. Again at the beginning of the *Purgatorio*, Dante asks the help of the Muses and especially of Calliope (*Purg.* 1,9). For inspiration to compose the *Paradiso* Dante addresses himself to Apollo, later also to Polymnia (*Par.* 1,13; 23,56). In the ninth sphere of the *Inferno* the aid of the Muses is invoked; they should help the poet as they assisted Amphion when he built the walls of Thebes by playing on his kithara (*Inf.* 32,10; see also *Purg.* 29,37, where the Muses are called *sacrosancte vergine*, and *Par.* 18,82). Amphion is the only mythical musician whom Dante mentions in the *Commedia*. Orpheus appears here among the sages beside Zeno (*Inf.* 4,140), while in the *Convivio* [16] Dante introduces him as the enchanting musician. The figure of the siren occurs once in the description of the dance of the blessed (*Par.* 12,8) when their song is appraised superior to the song of the Muses and the sirens. In Dante's symbolism the Muse is the representative of poetry; the siren, of the secular song; and *tuba* [17] stands for the celestial song. In a negative sense the siren is the symbol of seduction, of magic and enchantment in Dante's confession (*Purg.* 19,19) when she appears in his dream. She sings that she is the *dolce sirena* who misguides the mariners. A heavenly messenger comes from the Paradise to destroy her false appearance and discloses her true character as the whore of the Apocalypse. In the celestial procession after his immersion into Lethe, Dante joins the four beauties in their dance, the *quattro belle*, the cardinal virtues who start their song: "here we are nymphs, in heaven we are stars" (*Purg.* 31,106). From mythology there are, of course, the names of the gods for the planets and the spheres.

These are the few references to mythological figures related to music, Amphion being the only musician mentioned. In the *Commedia* Orpheus

[15] E. de Coussemaker, *Scriptorum de musica medii aevi nova series*, III (repr. Graz 1908), 12, 23.

[16] Dante, *Convivio*, Trattato II, cap. 1.

[17] Gmelin, *Dante*, II, canto 12, 7.

is a philosopher and later Boethius is cited as the writer of theological and philosophical books but not of the treatise on liberal arts. In the *Commedia* music is not specified as part of the quadrivium, and the traditional divisions of medieval theory—*musica mundana, musica humana,* and *musica instrumentalis*—are not referred to. All the remarks that have been listed prove that Dante was interested in practical music and not in its theory.

THE MUSIC OF THE SPHERES

THE MUSIC in Dante's *Paradiso* deludes us by making us think of the music of the spheres. This is a deceiving impression. The theory of Plato and the later neoplatonic and gnostic writings connects music with the different spheres either in a detailed manner, such as certain musical intervals corresponding to the distances of the spheres, or in letting the angelic orders correspond to specific spheres. For the *Commedia* these theories are not relevant, because Dante does not relate music to the spheres in this way. Not even in the *Convivio*,[18] where he discusses the topic intensively, does he use music for linking realms or groups together. In neither the *Convivio* nor the *Commedia* do we find any term for a musical interval, not even the word *diapason* which turns up in several general writings of the 14th century for the concept of an over-all span. The term sphere (*spera*) is employed only a few times and then is identical with heaven and *rota*. Only one sentence may be understood as reflecting the music of the spheres (*Purg.* 30,92) in which the song of the angels is said to be in accordance with the eternal rounds (*giri*).

Suffice it to state that Dante's *Paradiso* is constructed in a traditional way: the combination of the seven spheres of the planets—Moon, Mercury, Venus, Sun, Mars, Jupiter, Saturn—and the fixed stars, and on top the two Christian heavens of crystal and fire, the empyrean. In the *Convivio* Dante gives a complex theory for the motion of the stars, analyzing it as a threefold process. The explanation in the *Commedia* is different, and is pertinent to us because of the danced rounds therein—*giri* or *rote*. In one traditional theory the motion is identical with the astronomical circuits. Dante's vision is outspokenly irrational; his rounds are not identical with natural motion. Beatrice makes particular note of the rounds not conforming with the astronomical rotation (*Par.* 28,46). A second theory identifies the angelic orders with the movers of the spheres; they are the independent souls, the *intelligentiae* of the stars. Beatrice gives the names of the orders in the usual manner: seraphim and cherubim, thrones, dominations, virtues, powers, princes, archangels, and

[18] *Convivio,* Trattato II, cap. 14.

angels. Dionysos the Areopagite [19] permits these orders to move the spheres but *not* to sing. In the *Commedia* they are *not* moving the spheres, but they are singing and dancing *di coro in coro* (*Par.* 28,94). Dante locates all orders in the highest heaven, the empyrean, where they are circling in concentric rounds around the Lord, singing the Hosanna (*osannando*). They never move on the paths or the borders of the spheres.

In the *Commedia* all motion leads back to the *Primum Mobile*, to the Lord as author and origin. For this idea Dante takes a traditional musical symbol, the heavenly lyre (*Par.* 23,100), on which the Lord plays and thus regulates the cosmos, an image often occurring in the writings of the Church Fathers. Dante, however, does not elaborate on this theory.

EVEN if Dante does not follow typical theories of the heavenly music, his descriptions of musical performances in the different spheres follow a definite scheme, in accordance with and emphasizing his journey from the *Inferno* to the Highest, and he succeeds in making us rise with him to the splendor of the empyrean. The path leads from silence to unceasing singing and dancing. The beauty of music is set against noise as well as silence in the *Inferno*. Without the reader noticing it, we follow from simple to very complicated forms. Music starts with the simple solo singing on the lane (*prato*) of the earthly paradise where Dante sees two women, Leah (*Purg.* 27,97) and Matilda (*Purg.* 28,40), picking flowers and singing, evoking the idea of Spring and of spiritual resurrection. On the threshold of the heavenly Paradise he meets the procession that marks the triumph of the Church. It comes from its abode in the *Paradiso* and shows us figures belonging to higher spheres. It is a foreboding of the music in the *Paradiso*. It combines the singing of a soloist, of groups, and of a chorus, with dancing. It is here that Beatrice becomes Dante's guide. She appears in a cloud of flowers and is accompanied by songs in which everybody joins. The seven virtues sing and dance in groups of three and four and lead Dante and Beatrice to the sphere of the Moon, the lowest part of the heavenly Paradise, where they hear a chorus of angels singing above. From then on in every sphere figures approach to talk to Dante. They leave their round to speak, and when they have ended rush back to continue in their *rota*. The first to sing is the emperor Justinian. After ending his speech and singing the Hosanna, he leads up to the heaven of Mercury, the second sphere. From there Dante is lifted to the heaven of Venus, the third sphere, where for the first time he tells us that he is surrounded by a circle of blessed, singing and shining (*Par.* 12,3).

[19] *Dionysos Areopagita*, in: J.-P. Migne, *Patrologia Graeca*, III.

This motif of the sacred rounds is repeated like the theme in a musical rondo in the sphere of the Sun, in the empyrean, and as Dante passes to the heaven of Mars, the fifth sphere (*Par.* 14,23 and 73; 24,10).

In the *Convivio* [20] the seven spheres of the planets are likened to the liberal arts, and the sphere of Mars is connected by Dante with music for two reasons: *il cielo di Marte si può comparare alla musica per due proprietà*. One reason is its location in the center; it is the fifth sphere among ten. The second reason is the changing light and color of the star. *E queste due proprietadi sono nella musica*, "and these two characteristics are also to be found in music where the beauty results from the relations in a composition; the more the relation (of the parts) is beautiful, the sweeter is the resulting harmony; and the glow [*vapor* or *vapore*] in music which is like the glow of Mars, attracts the human spirit which is foremost a glow of the soul." Dante here emphasizes the two approaches to music, the *musica teorica* and the *musica prattica*, the knowledge of harmony based on numbers and the enchanting impression of music. Thus, in the *Commedia* the music of the procession transports Dante into a dream (*Purg.* 32,65) as Argus is put to sleep by Mercury's playing on the syrinx (Ovid, *Met.* I, 568). I have quoted from the *Convivio* because this part explains to us the basic ideas of Dante, how he thought and felt about music.

In the heaven of Jupiter, in the sixth sphere, a climax is reached with the performance of the ballet and the complicated song of the eagle. Here dancing is combined with the singing in chorus and the solo of the head of the eagle, and perhaps with the performance of a partsong. In the heaven of Saturn, the sphere of meditation, a musical pause occurs before Dante ascends to the three highest heavens above the realm of the planets. In the sphere of the fixed stars several persons leave their rounds to give their message to Dante in songs. When the poet passes to the crystal heaven a tripartite chorus, symbol of the Trinity, sings the Gloria and moves in concentric circles. From then on everybody is singing and dancing, and the shining quality of the blessed is stronger than the effect of their voices. In the empyrean Dante sees the heavenly court in the form of a rose with the patriarchs and the saints of the Old and New Testaments. In its border (*Par.* 32,47) the souls of the children can be recognized by their high voices. The vision of the Paradise ends with the blessed dancing and singing and shining from all sides, forming their rounds around the Light, the *Primum Mobile*, "the Love which moves the sun and the other stars": *l'amore che muove il sole e l'altre stelle*.

Thus Dante has used music, too, to aggrandize the splendor from

[20] *Convivio*, see fn. 18.

heaven to heaven. In the *Commedia* it starts when the poet is approaching the *Paradiso*, and reaches the climax with the ballet and the singing of the eagle. After a pause in the sphere of Saturn the vision becomes surrealistic. In the highest realms no difference exists between time and space, nor seeing and hearing. The irrational and mystical unification of the different traditions and experiences results, however, in a harmonious whole.

I have tried to show that Dante does not follow any particular one of the common traditions completely. He uses many features from various theories and combines them with personal experiences to achieve his vision of musical bliss and splendor. It is possible that Dante's picture was influenced by the paintings and glass windows in Gothic cathedrals that he may have seen in France. His vision of the *Paradiso* enraptured every reader of the *Commedia*, and its great influence can be seen in numerous representations of the Paradise from about 1300 on. Before that, in Romanesque art, the Elders from the Apocalypse are the music makers. After Dante's *Commedia*, from the 14th century on, they are replaced by the hosts of musician angels.

THE *MUSICA* OF
ERASMUS OF HÖRITZ

by *CLAUDE V. PALISCA*

M ARIN MERSENNE closed a brief review of current books on music in 1644 with this note about an obscure author: [1] To these I add Erasmus Horicius Germanus, who offered a musical book to Cardinal Grimani which, if it is not yet published, would merit seeing the light. Although he follows the opinion of Boethius and others who still did not use the major and minor semitones, and he knows only the major tones, nevertheless he is worthy of being read. Certainly admirable is what he communicates concerning the proportions in the Third Book.

Since Mersenne saw only a recently penned copy, he would probably have been surprised to know that the treatise dated from the first decade of the 16th century. Its existence had been called to his attention by Nicolas-Claude Peiresc of Aix. Peiresc procured in 1635 a copy of what he believed was the original manuscript owned by Jacques Golius, an orientalist and professor at the University of Leyden. The copy was intended for Giovanni Battista Doni of Rome, who was holding up the printing of his *Compendio del trattato de' generi e de' modi della musica* (Rome 1635) pending its arrival.[2] Peiresc, knowing Mersenne's deep interest in music theory, invited Mersenne to scan the treatise as it passed through Paris on the way from Leyden to Aix in December of that year, cautioning him however not to keep it or mention it in his

---

[1] *Cogitata physico-mathematica, in quibus tam naturae quam artis effectus admirandi certissimis demonstrationibus explicantur* (Paris 1644), *Harmoniae Liber IV*, p. 367: "His autem addo Erasmum Horicium Germanum, qui Musicum opus Grimanno Cardinali nuncupauit, cuius liber, si nondum sit editus, meretur lucem: quamquam enim Boetii, & aliorum mentem sequatur, qui nondum tonis maioribus & minoribus, nostrisque semitoniis maioribus & minoribus vtebantur, & solos tonos maiores agnoscat, lectu [sic] tamen dignus est, quippe praeclara tradit de proportionibus libro 3. propositionibus 27."

[2] Letter from Peiresc in Aix to Monsieur de Fontenay Bouchard at the court of Cardinal Barberini in Rome, 31 Oct. 1635, in Phillippe Tamizey de Larroque, ed., *Lettres de Peiresc*, IV (Paris 1893), 148–49. Cf. also Mersenne, *Correspondance*, ed. Cornélis de Waard, V (Paris 1959), 397.

"grand ouvraige" (*L'Harmonie universelle*, 1636–37), lest Doni be offended.[3] As soon as he saw it, Mersenne advised Peiresc to have another copy drafted so that it might be available for more leisurely study. Mersenne eventually received such a copy and kept it for at least several years. He thought highly enough of the Erasmus treatise to recommend its reading to Johann Albert Ban, though he insisted it contained "nothing or little that is new." [4] Peiresc also recommended the volume to Pierre Gassendi, saying he did not wish to dispatch the copy made for Mersenne until Gassendi had had a chance to see it.[5]

In contrast to the eager curiosity and urgent correspondence it awakened in 1635 and 1636, the *Musica* of Erasmus of Höritz has been shrouded in virtual silence since that time. Of the lexicographers, only Johann Walther [6] recognized Erasmus. He owed his knowledge of him to a citation in Gerhard Johann Vossius's *De quatuor artibus populari-bus* [7] of the praise bestowed on the book by Mersenne.

The *Musica* of Erasmus of Höritz exists in an undated manuscript of 114 folios, the very copy presented to Cardinal Domenico Grimani, in the Vatican Library, Regina collection, Latinus 1245.[8] Markings on

[3] Peiresc in Aix to Mersenne, 4 Nov. 1635, *ibid*. V, 458. Cf. also V, 397, 461, 465, 499, 506, 547; VI (Paris 1960), 7, 69, 217.
[4] Mersenne in Paris to André Rivet in Leyden, 23 Jan. 1638, *ibid.*, VII (Paris 1962), 34.
[5] Peiresc in Aix to Gassendi in Digne, 9 Jan. 1636, *ibid.*, VI, 7.
[6] *Musicalisches Lexicon* (Leipzig 1732); facs. ed. Richard Schaal (Kassel 1953), p. 318.
[7] Vossius, *De quatuor artibus popularibus* (Amsterdam 1650), Ch. 22: *De musicis partibus, generibus; ac praecipuis ejus, quos habemus, scriptoribus* (p. 97).
[8] The codex contains 114 paper folios measuring 19.3 by 27.3 centimeters. The writing begins on fol. 1ᵛ in red ink with the dedication: "Reuerendissimo germanie Principi Dominico grimanno Cardinal S. Marci Ac patriarche Aquilejensi / Erasmus Horicius germanus Philosophie et medicine doctor patrono suo humillime se Commendat." The undated letter of dedication follows and continues through fol. 2ʳ. Fol. 2ᵛ is blank, and on fol. 3ʳ appears the title in green ink: "Musica Erasmi Horicij Germani pro Rᵐᵒ Cardinali Dominico Grimanno Tituli .S. Marci Ac patriarche Aquilejensij in Germanie principe." Then a subtitle begins in red ink, describing the general contents: "Librum hunc nostrum musice in octo partiales libellos propter Huiusmodi Claritatem diuidere. . ." A preamble follows on fol. 3ᵛ and 4ʳ, where Book I begins. The treatise ends on fol. 114ʳ with these words: "et non erit Labor aliquis si priores numeros Calculatos bene inspexeris. et Cum hijs finem huic Libro nostro dabimus." Throughout the manuscript the scribe has employed initial capital letters quite indiscriminately, and punctuation is erratic, consisting of occasional periods, colons and slant-bars. Otherwise the manuscript is clearly written in a humanist secretarial hand and contains very few errors in spite of the profusion of diagrams and numerical calculations.

The Vatican MS is probably not the only surviving copy of the *Musica* of Erasmus. One copy, as we have seen, was made in 1635 from an "original," perhaps the Vatican MS, then owned by Jacques Golius of Leyden. Through the courtesy of Claude Saumaise of Leyden, Peiresc had this copy made for G. B. Doni, and it was sent to him in December 1635 at the Barberini Palace in Rome. Before it was dispatched, a copy of this copy was made by Peiresc's scribe Bouis for Mersenne's

the front flyleaf and on the first folios reveal a partial pedigree of the book's owners. On fol. 1ᵛ appears "liber D. Grimani Carᶫⁱˢ S. Marci." The first front flyleaf is marked: "Ex libris M. Meibomius," and at the bottom of fol. 2ʳ is written "ex Bibliotha Regia Rom:," that is, the library of Queen Christine of Sweden. This manuscript may also be the "original" that served as the basis for the copy made for Doni, since Jacques Golius, like Marcus Meibom, lived in Holland. The first owner, Cardinal Grimani, collector of many precious Greek and Latin manuscripts, inscriptions, and other antiquities, died in Rome in 1523. Many of his books went to the Library of San Antonio di Castello, which he founded. This library later burned, and the salvaged books were dispersed. Our manuscript must have found its way to Holland, where it was eventually acquired by Meibom, possibly from Golius. Meibom, who often had to dispose of his books to raise money, must have sold it to the library of Queen Christine. He served her for a while, and it was to her that he dedicated his *Antiquae musicae auctores septem* (Amsterdam 1652).[9] On the Queen's death in 1689, her library was inherited by her friend Cardinal Decio Azzolini, who himself died later that year. Azzolini's nephew, elected Pope Alexander VIII the same year, bought the Queen's codices with his own funds and presented them to the Vatican Library.

Erasmus of Höritz has not been entirely unknown, thanks to Theodor Kroyer, who published in 1918 a brief manuscript treatise of thirty-seven folios entitled *Musica speculativa per magistrum Erasmum Heritium lecta. 1498* from a codex in Munich.[10] Its contents parallel the Vatican treatise at many points, but in a compendious form. On the other hand the most original aspects of the *Musica* are missing. Kroyer has suggested that the Munich treatise, which is in a hand different from that of the Vatican manuscript, is a compilation of lecture notes. If so, it is

use. Later, in June 1636, Saumaise requested a copy of the treatise, and Peiresc asked Jacques Dupuy to borrow Mersenne's copy to have it recopied. Thus there were surely two copies, and perhaps a third made between 1635 and 1636. I have not so far located any of these copies.

I am indebted to four students of my Pro-Seminar at Yale University in the Spring of 1964 who together transcribed and translated about one-fourth of the *Musica:* John G. Brawley, Jr., Raymond Erickson, Martha Maas, and Barbara M. Tabak. Without their help I could not have finished this article in time for inclusion in the present volume.

⁹ Meibom made no mention of Erasmus of Höritz in his book. By coincidence Isaac Vossius, son of Gerhard, was the custodian of the library of the Queen when Gerhard Vossius published his book mentioning Erasmus: A. Wilmart, *Codices reginenses latini*, I (Rome 1937), viii.

¹⁰ Munich, Universitätsbibliothek, Codex 752, ed. Kroyer, *Die Musica speculativa des Magister Erasmus Heritius*, in: *Festschrift zum 50. Geburtstag Adolf Sandberger* (Munich 1918), pp. 65–120.

nevertheless organized in Erasmus's typical style, and his characteristic terminology and method are faithfully preserved.[11]

Still another treatise, one that has not until recently been connected with Erasmus of Höritz, may now be securely attributed to him: Berlin, Deutsche Staatsbibliothek, Ms. Mus. theor. 1310. It was once believed to be by Bartholomé Ramos de Pareja, but both Hugo Riemann and Johannes Wolf doubted that he could have been its author. Riemann found in it no trace of Ramos's theoretical innovations,[12] and Wolf reasoned that if the Berlin treatise had been written by Ramos before the *Musica practica* (Bologna 1482), he would have mentioned it there; if afterwards, the manuscript would have contained some discussion of his reforms of the solmization system and the tuning of the imperfect consonances.[13] I first suggested the attribution to Erasmus in 1962,[14] after Dr. Karl-Heinz Köhler, Director of the Musikabteilung of the Deutsche Staatsbibliothek, courteously provided me a microfilm of the manuscript. The treatise begins on fol. 4[r]: "Hunc nostrum Librum Musice in duos partiales Libros diuidemus de modis musicis sensualiter deprehensis: secundus Rationis investigationem Clare docebit." [15] Hence it may be known as *Librum musicae*. The codex contains 86 folios (the first three are blank), written mainly by the same hand as the Vatican manuscript. The contents and mode of presentation are similar to the Vatican treatise, but the organization of the work is radically different in many respects. Each, moreover, contains material not in the other. The *Librum musicae*, for example, goes beyond the scope of theoretical music into rules for solmization and discant. The *Musica*, on the other hand, is more detailed and explicit in its demonstrations. The question of

[11] In the same MS 752 and in the same but smaller and hastier hand there are on fols. 95 to 114: "Annotationes in Musicen magistri Joannis de muris per magistrum Andream Perlachium accuratae traditae." Andreas Perlach or Perlacher received his doctorate of medicine at the University of Vienna in 1530 and lectured on mathematics there from 1515 to 1549, when he became Rector. Cf. Joseph Ritter von Aschbach, *Geschichte der wiener Universität im ersten Jahrhunderte ihres Bestehens*, II (Vienna 1877), 339.

[12] H. Riemann, *History of Music Theory*, transl. (from the 2d. German ed. 1920) by Raymond Haggh (Lincoln, Nebraska 1962), p. 280, fn. 1.

[13] *Musica practica Bartolomei Rami de Pareia*, in: *Publikationen der internationalen Musikgesellschaft, Beihefte* II (Leipzig 1901), xv.

[14] *Ramos*, in: MGG, X (1962), 1910. See the page from the manuscript reproduced there.

[15] It ends on fol. 86[r]: "Et hoc facto finem librj imponimus." Fétis, who described the manuscript in his article on Ramos in *Biographie universelle*, VII, 179, believed it was written in the last years of the 15th century. According to Fétis, the MS was purchased in Catania, Sicily on 3 Dec. 1817 by Johann Christian Niemeyer. He ceded it to Georg Poelchau, whose rich library was acquired by Frederick William IV of Prussia.

whether it represents an earlier or later working will not be considered here. One important feature of the Berlin MS is that besides the principal, fair hand of the Vatican MS, there appears another hand in marginal notes, calculations, and corrections, and throughout the section from folios 14^r to 21^v. This hand is hasty and employs many abbreviations, while the principal hand uses them sparingly. The last six lines of fol. 21^v are repeated by the principal hand on fol. 22^r, suggesting that the section 14^r–21^v was inserted to replace a previously copied version later rejected. The revision is probably in the hand of the author. Thus the Berlin treatise, probably partly autograph, represents a less finished work than the Vatican treatise.

Erasmus of Höritz emerges as one of the German humanists of the early 16th century most articulate on musical matters. His biography, while still full of lacunae, is fortunately not as vacant as the musical dictionaries are silent about him. All evidence points to Höritz as his place of origin. It is a small town in what was then southwest Bohemia, since made famous by its passion plays, and now called Hořice because it is within the boundaries of Czechoslovakia. It is on the road from the Czech town of Krumau, which is eight miles to the northeast, to the Austrian border, which is about the same distance to the southwest. The nearest cities are Budweis (now České Budêjorice) and Linz. Since, in spite of these facts, he considered himself a German in a generic sense, it is appropriate to call him Erasmus of Höritz.

At the head of his dedication of the *Musica*, Erasmus assumes the title of Doctor of Philosophy and Medicine. Records show that he matriculated at numerous universities, as was the custom of students and scholars at the time. The first was Ingolstadt, on 14 May 1484 as Erasmus de Heritz.[16] Next he was at Erfurt, where he matriculated as Erasmus de Erytz de Bohemia on St. Michael's day (29 September) in 1486.[17] Two years later in May he registered at Cologne in the faculty of arts as Herasmus Herics and eventually received the degree of Magister (Doctor) there.[18] In the fall of 1494 he signed in at the University of Cracow: "Magister Erasmus de Hericz universitatis Coloniensis." [19] In his matriculation at Tübingen in 1499 as Erasmus Hericius ex Bohemia he is also

[16] Kroyer, *op. cit.*, p. 70.
[17] Gerhard Pietzsch, *Zur Pflege der Musik an den deutschen Universitäten im Osten bis zur mitte des 16. Jahrhunderts*, in: *Archiv für Musikforschung*, I (1936), 433. See also Nan Cooke Carpenter, *Music in the Medieval and Renaissance Universities* (Norman, Oklahoma 1958), pp. 225, 244, 281.
[18] Pietzsch, *op. cit.*, p. 433: "Herasmus Herics; art.; iuravit et solvit. Herijchs, L., 1488 Dec. 10 determinavit sub m. Everh. de Amersfordia."
[19] *Ibid.*, p. 433. Cf. also *Album studiosorum universitatis cracoviensis, II* [1490-1551] (Cracow 1892), p. 35.

designated a Magister of Cologne. At Vienna he is entered in the registry on Easter Sunday, 14 April 1501, among the "Ungarum nacio," students of Hungarian nationality. The record reads: "Erasmus Ericius mathematicus de Horitz nihil dedit," the last words indicating that he did not pay the usual tax.[20] He later taught there but had certainly left well before 1514, as may be gathered from these words written by Thomas Resch (Velocianus) in a letter addressed to the famous mathematician Georg Tannstetter, known also as Collimitius, and published in Tannstetter's edition of the *Tabulae Eclypsium* of Georg Peuerbach (Vienna 1514):

> Truly, again and again I have myself wished to have with me both you and [Johann] Stabius of Styria, Rosinus,[21] [Johannes] Angelus, [Erasmus] Ericius, noble mathematicians, shining with much splendor of letters, so that the renowned and very precious studies of mathematics, for a while now shamefully and savagely neglected, might through them have endured and breathed and have been preserved in our German countries by the excellent and almighty God.[22]

Of those mentioned, Johannes Angelus of Bavaria had died already in 1512. Tannstetter himself left the teaching of mathematics for medicine and university administrative posts after 1510, when he was appointed physician to Kaiser Maximilian.[23] The impression given by Resch, who was Dean of the arts faculty in 1504, 1508, and 1513, is that mathematical studies suffered a decline. This may have given Erasmus a motive for going elsewhere. Tannstetter, later recalling better times, said "Johannes Eperies and Erasmus Ericius, very distinguished men, at this same time taught mathematics with the admiration of many." [24]

A manuscript from the Kloster Tegernsee near Munich, dated 1510, confers upon a certain Magister Erasmus the degree of Bachelor of Theology and Canonic Law ("sacrae theologiae et jurispontifici baccalaureus magister Erasmus"). This may well be our Erasmus.[25] Another side of his activity is probably represented by some astronomical speculations marked "Annotatio M. Erasmi," dealing mainly with Ptolemy's *Almagest*, a work Horicius claims in his *Musica* to have corrected.[26]

[20] Institut für österreichische Geschichtsforschung, *Die Matrikel der Universität Wien, II* [*1451–1518*] (Graz 1959), p. 294.

[21] Rosinus or Stefan Rösel, like Erasmus, also came to Vienna from the University of Cracow in 1501: Rudolph Kink, *Geschichte der kaiserlichen Universität zu Wien* (Vienna 1854), I, 208.

[22] The Latin original is in Pietzsch, *op. cit.*, p. 433.

[23] Aschbach, *op. cit.*, p. 272.

[24] Pietzsch, *op. cit.*, p. 433.

[25] Munich, Staatsbibliothek, Ms. Clm. 18635, cited by Kroyer, *op. cit.*, p. 71, fn. 2, and Pietzsch, *op. cit.*, p. 433.

[26] Kroyer, *op. cit.*, p. 71; *Musica*, fol. 66ʳ.

Dedication of Erasmus of Höritz, *Musica*, to Cardinal Domenico Grimani (Rome, Vatican, Regina lat. 1245, fol. 1ᵛ).

Kroyer found these among notes taken at lectures of various professors, and specifically in a series marked "Inchoauit 1 Nov. a. 1544." If Erasmus was about 20 when he matriculated at Ingolstadt in 1484, he would at this time have been 80, so the glosses were probably taken down second-hand.

The dedication (shown here) of the *Musica* to Cardinal Grimani, whom he calls his patron, suggests that Erasmus took the road to Italy after leaving Vienna. His critical remarks about both Greek and Latin authorities, among them Aristotle, Ptolemy, and Boethius, and his progressive views concerning scientific investigation strongly hint at a connection with the University of Padua. Padua was either within or close to areas of the Cardinal's jurisdiction under a number of his appointments.[27] Erasmus cites three of Grimani's titles: Cardinal of San Marco, Patriarch of Aquileia, and Prince in Germany. Domenico Grimani, himself a scholar, received a Doctor of Arts at Padua on 23 October 1487 and remained there until 1489, when he was chosen to be one of four ambassadors to escort Emperor Frederick III to north Italy at the time of the armistice between the Emperor and Matthias Corvinus of Hungary. As a reward for this service, Frederick made Grimani a Knight, and this probably accounts for the title of "Prince in Germany." [28] After entering the Roman court in 1491, Grimani advanced rapidly, being promoted to Cardinal by Alexander VI on 20 September 1493. He was made Patriarch of Aquileia in Istria on 13 September 1497, but because of local political pressure he resigned in 1517. He was named Cardinal of San Marco on 25 December 1503, a title he retained throughout his life, though he gave up the administrative duties connected with it in 1508.[29]

1504, consequently, is the earliest possible date for the *Musica*, since by then the Cardinal had earned all of the titles conferred upon him by Erasmus. The year of Grimani's resignation from Aquileia, 1517, would be the latest possible date for the treatise. But since Grimani continued to accumulate titles, it is plausible that Erasmus, in his desire to flatter his patron, would have cited those he currently held: on 22 September 1508 named Episcopus Albanensis; on 3 June 1509, transferred to Episcopus Tusculanensis; on 20 January 1511, transferred to Episcopus Portuensis et S. Rufinae, which he kept until his death; and on 29 May 1514, in addition named Bishop of Urbino.[30] Between 4 March 1507 and 1512 he was also head of the Abbey of S. Maria delle Carceri at Este in the diocese of Padua.[31] He was mainly absent from the Curia during the papacy of Leo

---

[27] Unfortunately the records of the University of Padua were not accessible to me during the period of this investigation, so that this is mere conjecture.

[28] Mario E. Cosenza, *Biographical and Bibliographical Dictionary of the Italian Humanists and of the World of Classical Scholarship in Italy, 1300–1800* (2d ed. Boston 1962), II. Cosenza's information is taken mainly from Pio Paschini, *Domenico Grimani, Cardinale di S. Marco* (Rome 1943), which was not available to me.

[29] Conrad Eubel, ed., *Hierarchia catholica medii aevi sive summorum pontificum, S.R.E. Cardinalium ecclesiarum antistitum series*, II (Regensburg 1910), 22. His first title was Cardinal of S. Nicola inter Imagines: *ibid.*, III (Regensburg 1910), 76, and briefly he was archbishop of Nicosia in Cyprus in 1495 (*ibid.*, II, 224).

[30] *Ibid.*, II, 60, 62, 63, 103, 224; III, 61, 63, 65, 73, 76, 127.

[31] Cosenza, *op. cit.*, II.

X (1513–22), with whom he was not on good terms.[32] Domenico Grimani died on 27 August 1523. The years of highest probability for the completion of the *Musica* of Erasmus, then, are between 1504 and 1508; of secondary probability are the years 1508–14. Of little probability, however, are the years 1514–17, since Bishop of Urbino is too significant a title to overlook.

The *Musica* of Erasmus belongs to the category of *musica theorica*. Following the tradition of the *De institutione musica* of Boethius, it covers the musical part of the university curriculum in the four mathematical disciplines or *quadrivium*. Like many other university-centered theorists, Erasmus is a conservative on matters affecting musical practice. Apparently unaware of the controversy raging around Ramos de Pareja's advocacy of the just tuning of imperfect consonances, Erasmus stands by the time-honored Pythagorean division of the diatonic tetrachord into two 9/8 tones and a semitone in the ratio of 256/243. He tries to reconcile this with the modern chromatic system which he recognizes has resulted from widespread employment of *musica ficta* and modal transposition. Another sign of his conservatism is that he fails to apply his very sophisticated techniques of geometry and calculation to certain practical problems, such as tempered tuning, that were awaiting solutions at the very moment his methods offered a ready path.

If Erasmus shuns the innovations of the more practically oriented theorists such as Ramos and Spataro, he is nevertheless dissatisfied with the way the classic problems of music theory were treated in the past. His quarrel with his predecessors lies mainly in the area of methodology. It is in this sphere that he makes his principal contribution, though the novelty of his method often spills over into the matter demonstrated.

The method of Erasmus is that of natural science. He first observes as accurately as possible with the senses the phenomenon under study. Then, as the astronomer does, he investigates by means of geometry and mathematics the causes behind the effects noted through the senses. This, he was fond of repeating, was the method of the ancient Greeks in all of the sciences. For example:

> It is immediately clear to the ear that there is no difference between the consonance of the diapason and the just diapente and diatessaron taken together. From ut to sol, that is from Gamma-ut to d sol re, a fifth, and from d sol re to g sol re ut, a fourth, is nothing other than the diapason. For this [diapason] is composed of the extreme terms from both, and all three [terms] are combined in a way imperceptible to the sense. Insofar as the sense can grasp them, these things are plainly known. There re-

[32] Pio Paschini, *Domenico Grimani*, in: *Enciclopedia cattolica*, IV, 1168.

mains only to confirm this by means of geometrical and arithmetical demonstrations and to investigate the truth concerning the doubt that exists between the sense and the intellect.[33]

If the senses know with certainty that an octave is the sum of a fifth and a fourth, only mathematical analysis will reveal the cause of this: that the three terms 2, 3, 4 are such that the extremes are in the ratio 2/1, and that the two ratios 3/2 and 4/3 "added" (multiplied) produce the ratio of the octave.

Of the two large treatises of Erasmus, the organization of the one in Berlin follows most faithfully the method of proceeding from sense-perception to rationalization. It devotes the first book of 19 pages, divided into 6 *canones*, to the sensory aspect; and the remaining 147 pages in 4 parts and 64 propositions to mathematical analysis. The same method, more subtly applied, is fundamental to the organization of the Vatican treatise. Here Books I, II, IV, and V deal with knowledge derived from sense perception, while Books III, VI, VII, and VIII apply mathematical demonstrations to the phenomena discovered.

The *Musica* is divided into eight Books. In Book I (fols. 4^r–6^v), Erasmus defines and demonstrates the *voces*, that is the solmization syllables ut, re, etc.; the *litterae*, namely the alphabetical letters, A, B, C, etc. designating the steps of the octave; and finally the *claves*, which are the 20 steps of the gamut identified by joining the appropriate letters and syllables, such as Gamma-ut, A-re, etc.

Book II (fols. 6^v–10^r) proceeds to the definition of the intervals (*modi*), the conventional classification of consonances into perfect and imperfect and a consideration of the usefulness of combinations of them, such as the fifth-plus-major-third.

Book III (fols. 10^v–38^r) begins to depart from the traditional procedures of musical treatises of this time. It is divided into 27 propositions, derived mainly from Euclid's *Elements*, each of which demonstrates some geometrical method useful for the study of the ratios of musical intervals. Erasmus shows how to "add" (multiply) and "subtract" (divide) proportions. He proves, for example, that in a geometric progression the ratio of the extremes is a product of all the intermediary proportions. He shows how to reduce fractions to their simplest terms,

[33] *Musica*, fol. 54^r. "Per auditum enim id clarum modo est inter diapason consonantiam nihil esse differentiae ad diapente et diatessaron iustas simul nihil aliud est de ut ad sol de Gamma-ut ad d sol re quinta, vel diapente, et de d sol re ad g sol re ut diatessaron, consonantia quam diapason, quoniam haec extremorum terminorum composita est ex duabus et omnes tres ad sensum inperceptibiliter. Quantum sensus videlicet capere potest iam cognitae sunt. Restat modo istud geometricis ac Aritmeticis demonstrationis confirmare et de dubio quod inter sensum et intellectum est investigare veritatem." (I have normalized the spelling and added punctuation.)

and how to manipulate irrational fractions or surds. All of these operations, he holds, are necessary to the proper study of consonances and
dissonances.

Book IV (fols. 39^r–42^r) returns to categories known to sense perception, specifically the three genera of the Greeks, whose differences are
considered from an aural and affective standpoint.

Book V (42^v–48^v) extends this discussion to systems of tetrachords
used in Greek and Latin (medieval) music. Here Erasmus gives an
account of the Greek *tonoi* and attempts to distinguish them from the
Western modes.

After this empirical exploration of musical systems, Erasmus is ready
to apply the operations taught in Book III to problems related to the
material presented in Books IV and V. Book VI takes up problems relating to the diatonic system in 39 propositions (fols. 49^r–93^v), while
Book VII (fols. 94^r–99^v) extends this to the chromatic and enharmonic
systems, but only briefly, in four propositions, because Erasmus sees
limited application for these genera in his own time.

The Eighth and last Book in 13 propositions (fols. 100^r–114^r) demonstrates by geometric constructions and numerical calculations some
divisions of the monochord for the three genera.

Only a few of the original contributions of the treatise can be considered here, because of limitations of space. Surely the most characteristic is the exhaustive application of the theorems of Euclid's *Elements*.
It is this comprehensive geometrical work rather than the summary
arithmetical and musical books of Boethius that serves Erasmus as his
starting point and model. Good humanist that he was, Erasmus goes back
to the Greek sources of the doctrines of Boethius. He thus communicates
to musical readers an important fruit of the revival of interest in ancient
texts.

Euclid's *Elements*, the first mathematical book of any importance to
be printed, was published in 1482 in a Latin translation by the 13th-
century mathematician Johannes Campanus.[34] This is the translation that
Erasmus specifically cites several times because of its commentary (e.g.
fol. 41^r). Erasmus's division into propositions, some with corollaries,
his manner of stating them, the style of his demonstrations and of the
diagrams: these are all modeled on Euclid, and the Latin terminology is
that of Campanus. But Erasmus does not merely parody or slavishly imitate the ancient geometer. He avoids repeating any of the proofs of
Euclid, presenting rather proofs of purely musical or musically relevant

[34] *Praeclarissimus liber elementorum Euclidis perspicacissimi in artem Geometrie*
(Augsburg: Erhard Ratdolt, 1482).

propositions. Where a step is sufficiently demonstrated by Euclid, Erasmus is content to cite book and proposition, and pass on.[35]

A striking example of the freshness of thinking often encountered in the *Musica* is Erasmus's insistence upon exploiting irrational as well as rational proportions. The Boethians dismissed the possibility of dividing equally superparticular intervals such as the octave (2/1), the fifth (3/2), or the whole tone (9/8).[36] Each of these ratios lacks a square-root expressible in integers that would provide a mean proportional between two string lengths. Since irrational numbers are condemned because of their impreciseness by the philosophers influenced by the Pythagoreans, they were neglected throughout the Middle Ages.[37] Erasmus declares:

> In this matter all the philosophers proclaim loudly, following Boethian dictates, stated hypothetically in his *Musica*, that no superparticular proportion can be divided equally. This is very false, as we shall demonstrate here. . . Once the proportion of the whole has been found, any part of it will be obtained, and the half quite readily. . . We affirm generally that any proportion, rational or irrational, of any genus, can be divided into any number of parts.[38]

These remarks serve to introduce a demonstration of the division of the 9/8 tone into two equal parts by discovering the geometric mean between 8 and 9. In Book II, Proposition 3, he showed:

> the geometric mean is obtained when such a series of three terms is given that the proportion of the first to the second is the same as that of the second to the third. For example, in the three terms a, b, c, which are continuous proportionals, and where a:b = b:c, I say b is the geometric mean.[39]

[35] The books of Euclid most frequently cited are those dealing with proportions, namely V, VII, and VIII. Among the most used propositions are V. 15: "Parts have the same ratio as the same multiples of them taken in corresponding order"; VII. 18: "If two numbers by multiplying any number make certain numbers, the numbers so produced will have the same ratio as the multipliers"; and VIII. 2: "To find numbers in continued proportion, as many as may be prescribed, and the least that are in a given ratio." These translations are from T. L. Heath, *The Thirteen Books of Euclid's Elements* (Cambridge 1908). Frequently used are also Books I, II, III, and X. It may be assumed that Erasmus had at his command the entire corpus of Greek geometrical doctrine preserved by Euclid.
[36] Boethius, *De institutione musica,* iii. 2, and iii. 11.
[37] It must be acknowledged that Erasmus too betrays a certain horror of irrational numbers, for he expresses them as integers whose roots must be found.
[38] Bk. VI, prop. 17, fols. 65ᵛ-66ʳ: "In hac re omnes philosophi clamitant, boetiana dicta sequentes, eam scilicet hipotesim in musica sua, scilicet nullam superparticularem proportionem in aequa dividi posse, quod falsissimum est, ut in hoc loco demonstrabimus . . . Et cum proportio totius iam inventa sit, dabitur eius quotacumque pars, et facilius dimidium . . . Et dicimus universaliter quod omnis proportio tam rationalis quam surda cuiuscumque generis sit potest dividi in quodlibet partes."
[39] *Ibid.,* fol. 50ᵛ: "Medietas geometrica ex proportione accipitur, scilicet, quando tribus terminis propositis eadem est proportio primi ad secundum, sicut secundi ad

He also showed there that if a and c are given, to find b, multiply a by c and take the square root of the product. Or $b = \sqrt{ac}$. He gave the example: $a = 2$, $c = 8$; then $b = \sqrt{16}$ or 4.[40] Now in Book VI, he applies the method to a number of irrational proportions, and in Proposition 17 specifically to the ratio 9/8.

Following a method, established in earlier propositions, of representing the value of a ratio by a single straight line, he proceeds as follows (see the illustration):

As in the figure let the whole [line] AB be the sesquioctave proportion divided at point C, so that AC is a minor semitone.

By I. 2 [Euclid] I cut off from point B the equal of AC, which is BD. The remainder, CD, will be the difference between the tone and two minor semitones.

If you add the mean of this to both AC and DB by means of the doctrine often given already [in preceding propositions] the whole known AB results, the half of which proportion is what is sought.

In lines, with numbers, this would be as follows. Let F be half of the proportion CD, which, expressed by lines is G:H, or in numbers 531441:524288 [the major semitone minus the minor semitone, or 2187/2048 ÷ 256/243].

Let LM:PQ and MN:QR be two minor semitones. Since they are known [both being 256/243], their sum will be known, namely the proportion LN:PR, which is 65536:59049 [i.e. $(256/243)^2$] composed of two equal and known proportions.

If you add to these the proportion G:H, which will be KL:OP, the total will be KN:OR, composed of three known proportions. Since this total itself is known by V. 15 [of Euclid], its mean proportion will be given. [The total proportion, i.e. KN:OR] is 34,828,517,376:30,958,682, 112. The half of this [i.e. the square-root] is what is sought, or in the first figure either AE or EB.[41]

Erasmus does not proceed to compute the square root. He may have felt that this is a purely arithmetical problem not requiring demonstra-

tertium. Ut sint tres termini, a, b, c, continue proportionales ita quod proportio a ad b sit sicut b ad c. Dico b esse medium geometricum."

[40] *Ibid.*, fol. 51ʳ.

[41] *Ibid.*, fols. 66ʳ–67ʳ: "Ut in exemplo sit tota AB proportio sesquioctava divisa in puncto C ita ut AC sit semitonium minus. Et per secundam primi a puncto B accipio aequalem ei quae sit BD. Erit residuum CD ipsa differentia inter tonum et duo semitonia minora. Cuius medietatem, si addideris iuxta doctrinam saepius datam, proveniet tota AB cognita, cuius dimidia proportio est quaesita. In lineis cum numeris sic. Sit F medietas proportionis C ad D, signata lineis G ad H, in numeris 531441 et 524288. Et sint duo semitonia minora LM ad PQ, et MN ad QR. Quae cum cognita sint, erit aggregatum ex eis cognitum, scilicet proportio LN ad PR, quae est inter 65536 et 59049. Et haec iam composita est ex duabus proportionibus aequalibus et cognitis. Quibus si adieceris proportionem G ad H, quae sit KL ad OP, erit tota KN ad OR composita ex tribus proportionibus cognitis. Et ipsa cognita hinc per decimaquintam quinti, eius media proportio cognita dabitur, quae est inter 34828517376 et 30958682112. Cuius medietas est quaesitum et est in prima figuratione AE vel EB."

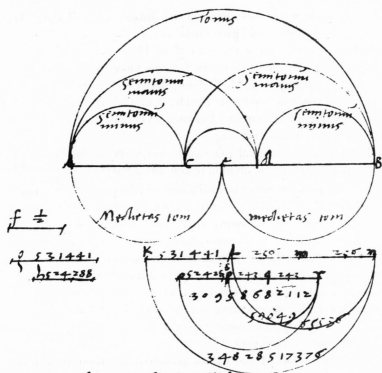

From the *Musica* of Erasmus of Höritz: diagram of the geometric division of the minor semitone (Rome, Vatican, Regina lat. 1245, fol. 66ᵛ).

tion, particularly for a student of the *quadrivium*. Certainly, throughout his treatise he shows little regard for the musician unschooled in mathematics. He also seems little aware of the practical applicability of his theorems. Having found a method for obtaining mean-semitones, Erasmus does not apply it to derive a chromatic note which would divide equally the whole tone between two diatonic steps. Between G and A, for example, this would give a note that would serve equally well G♯ and A♭, as found in the monochord of Heinrich Schreiber (Grammateus), who still deserves credit for this innovation.[42] Grammateus, however, according to J. M. Barbour, derives the mean-semitone by a geometrical construction rather than by computation.[43] It must be noted with some disappointment that Erasmus never departs from the Pythagorean minor semitone, 256/243.

Indifference to musical practice is also betrayed in the exhaustive application of geometric division to consonant intervals. Erasmus divides the octave equally to get two equal tritones in the proportion $\sqrt{144}/72$.[44] While this falls within the chromatic scale, the products of several of his other divisions—of the fourth, fifth, and minor third [45]—are purely theoretical entities. The demonstrations do lead, however, to some useful corollaries, such as the determination of the excess of the ditone over the semitone. Similarly, though we are apt to dismiss the eightfold multiplication of the ratio 9/8 to produce a whole-tone scale of eight steps [46] as an idle exercise, it does serve to prove that six such tones exceed the octave by a Pythagorean comma, or that five such tones added to two minor semitones make an octave.[47]

While Books III, VI, and VII use geometrical methods for calculating interval-ratios, the first part of Book VIII applies geometrical constructions to the division of strings without using numbers. The problem Erasmus attacks here is the very real one faced by every musician or instrument maker who wishes to divide a given string or a pipe into a certain number of equal parts. The classic method of dividing the monochord taught by Boethius and many of his successors requires the division of the string into two parts to get the octave, into three parts for the fifth, into four parts for the fourth, and into nine parts for the whole-tone 9/8.

The division into two parts is easily done, Erasmus shows. Upon a given length, B C, as a base, a triangle with 2 equal sides is constructed and a perpendicular is dropped upon this length from the opposite angle

---

[42] *Ayn new kunstlich Buech* (Nuremberg 1518). Cf. J. Murray Barbour, *Tuning and Temperament* (2d. ed. East Lansing, Michigan 1953), p. 139. Schreiber attended three of the same universities as Erasmus: Erfurt, Cracow, and Vienna, but about ten years later. The two may have known each other in Vienna, where Schreiber studied under Collimitius around 1510: Pietzsch, *op. cit.*, p. 444.

[43] Concerning this construction, see also fn. 55 below and the surrounding text.

[44] Bk. VI, prop. 13, fols. 61ᵛ–62ʳ.

[45] Bk. VI, props. 14–16, fols. 62ᵛ–65ʳ.

[46] Bk. VI, prop. 26, fols. 77ʳ–79ʳ.

[47] Bk. VI, prop. 33, fols. 86ʳ–87ʳ.

Fig. 1

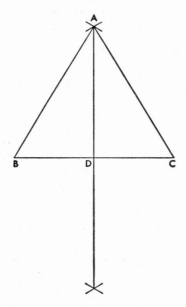

Fig. 2

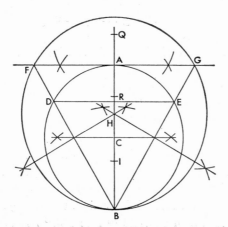

A, by Euclid I. 1. This, by Euclid I. 6, divides the length into two equal parts, B D and D C.[48]

The division of a given length into three equal parts is considerably more difficult. First, around the given length AB is constructed an equilateral triangle (see Fig. 2). This is done by bisecting AB at C, by Euclid I. 10. With C as a center, the circle of which AB is a diameter is described. AD and AE are then drawn equal to the semi-diameter AC, and D and E are joined. Then a perpendicular is drawn to AB at A. (Although he does not say so, Erasmus obviously meant this to be done by

[48] Bk. VIII, prop. 1, fol. 100ʳ–100ᵛ. This method is equivalent to Euclid I. 10.

Euclid I. 11: on AB extended find points Q and R equidistant from A and construct an equilateral triangle as in Figure. 1. Then drop a perpendicular through AB at A.) This line, by Euclid III. 18, will be a tangent. BD is now drawn and extended to F, and similarly BE to G. We now have an equilateral triangle FBG around the given line AB.[49]

About this equilateral triangle a circle is circumscribed, by Euclid IV. 5.[50] (Euclid here shows that if FB and GB are bisected, perpendiculars at the midpoints will meet in the center of the circle.) The semi-diameter of this circle is BH, and the line AB is a diameter and a half.[51] If now HI is measured off on AB equal to AH, the given length AB is divided by points H and I into three equal parts.

The division into nine equal parts, Erasmus shows,[52] can be accomplished by repeating the process just described for each of the parts, AH, HI, and IB.

Another way to accomplish the ninefold division is by the construction that divides a line into any number of equal parts.[53] This is described in Book VIII, proposition 5, of which the special case of nine parts is elaborated very briefly in proposition 6. Here I will combine the two demonstrations into one, using the figure of proposition 6, with the lettering slightly altered.

The line AB of Figure 3 is that which we wish to divide. It is extended by the addition of BC, equal to AB. BC is bisected at D. Then DC and BD are bisected at F and E. BC is thus divided into four equal parts. The line AC is now extended to H by the addition of a part equal to FC, which is 1/8 of the whole line AC. A perpendicular at A of any length is drawn to G, and GB and GH are drawn. At point C a perpendicular is raised as far as I on line GH. A line parallel to AH is extended to L on line GB. (This may be done by Euclid I. 31 and I. 23, though Erasmus omits mention of these constructions.) From L a perpendicular is drawn to line AH, by Euclid I. 12, and this will be LK. Since, by Euclid I. 29, and I. 34, LI = KC, then CH:AH = KB: AB.[54] Also, since CH is the

[49] Bk. VIII, prop. 2, fol. 101^r–101^v. I have combined the figures of Propositions 2, 3, and 4, fols. 101^r, 101^v, and 102^r, into a single figure, somewhat as Erasmus does in his *Librum musicae*, Berlin, Deutsche Staatsbibliothek, Ms. Mus. theor. 1310, Part IV, prop. 2, fol. 77^r.

[50] Bk. VIII, prop. 4, fol. 102^r.

[51] This is proved in Erasmus VIII, 3 by means of Euclid IV. 5, I. 16, I. 5, III. 3, and I. 4.

[52] Bk. VIII, prop. 6, fols. 103^v–104^r.

[53] A different solution of this problem is presented in Mersenne, *Harmonie universelle* (1636–37), First Book of String Instruments, transl. Roger E. Chapman (The Hague 1957), Prop. X, pp. 39–41.

[54] The proof of this last step is rather extended in Prop. 5, fols. 102^v–103^v, and depends on Euclid I. 32, VI. 4, and V. 11.

ninth part of AH, KB will be the ninth part of AB, and AB: AK = 9/8.

It may appear strange that in this section on geometric constructions Erasmus overlooks one of the most useful—that for finding the mean proportional between two lines. This construction, based on Euclid VI. 9 and VI. 13, was already published in a musical book by Jacques Lefèvre d'Etaples in 1496.[55] Erasmus did not omit it out of ignorance, for he cites the basic proposition of Euclid in his Book VI, Proposition 3, which deals with the finding of geometric means, though he erroneously refers to Euclid VI. 13 as VI. 16. Why he failed to describe the construction in Book VIII can be easily explained. This Book develops the division of the monochord according to the Pythagorean tuning, and for this no mean proportional needs to be found.

Fig. 3

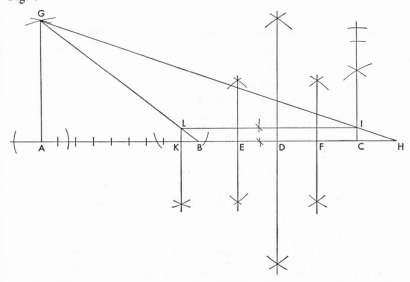

The *Musica* of Erasmus is not so oblivious of contemporary practices as this adherence to the Pythagorean tuning suggests. Like others in his time, he sought to come to terms with the proliferation of *musica ficta*. Erasmus recognizes two systems or *scalae* of "real" music: that "of the six modes," I, II, III, IV, VII, and VIII, which spans the range from Gamma-ut to EE-la, analogous to our G to e^2; and the system "of modes V and VI," which goes from Gamma-ut to EE-fa, or from our G to e♭^{2}. These two systems, found also in other German theorists of this time, seem to have been postulated in imitation of the Greek greater

perfect and lesser perfect systems respectively, of which they are extensions. The system of modes V and VI, for example, in its three lowest
conjunct tetrachords from B to d^1, is identical to the synemmenon
system of the Greeks. This is extended upward by two conjunct tetrachords from e^1 to d^2, to which is added a note $e\flat^2$ at the top. The notes
A and G are similarly added at the bottom.[56]

Fig. 4 *Scala quinti et sexti toni*

G A B c d e f g a b♭ c¹ d¹ e¹ f¹ g¹ a¹ b♭¹ c² d² e²

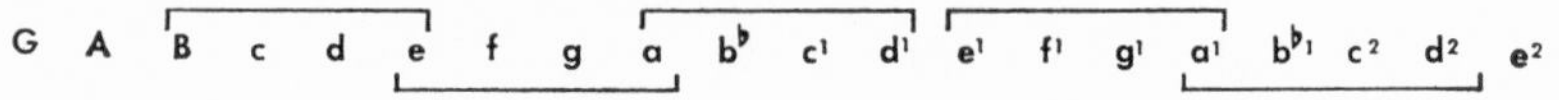

To these two fundamental systems Erasmus adds two more, both
branches from the *scala quinti et sexti toni*. These he calls *scala ficta* and
scala ficta universalis. They both require an additional tone F below
Gamma-ut, but they proceed at the other extremity like the *scala quinti
et sexti toni* to EE-fa (or $e\flat^2$).[57]

The *scala ficta* contains three conjunct tetrachords from A to c^1 and
two more conjunct tetrachords from d^1 to c^2, with extra tones d^2 and
$e\flat^2$ at the top and G and F at the bottom. All the tetrachords are sung
la-sol-fa-mi descending and are figured 9/8, 9/8, 256/243, producing in
the *scala ficta* an equivalent of the E♭-major scale from $e\flat^2$ down to
B♭, with A, G, F, added at the bottom.

Fig. 5 *Scala ficta*

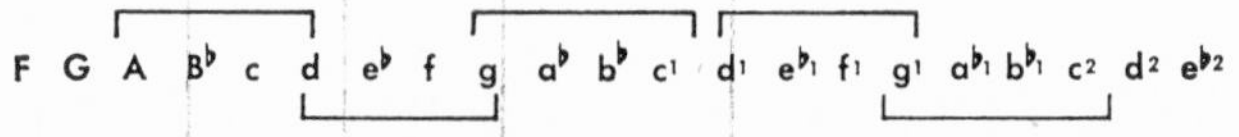

F G A B♭ c d e♭ f g a♭ b♭ c¹ d¹ e♭¹ f¹ g¹ a♭¹ b♭¹ c² d² e♭²

Whereas the *scala ficta* provides a path for mutations from the *scala
quinti et sexti toni*, the *scala ficta universalis* permits mutations from the
scala ficta. Thus b♭, which is sol in the *ficta* tetrachord c^2-b♭^{1}-a♭^{1}-g^1,
becomes la in the *universalis* tetrachord b♭^{1}-a♭^{1}-g♭^{1}-f^1. Similarly, e♭,
which is fa in the tetrachord g-f-e♭-d of the *ficta* system, now becomes
la in the tetrachord e♭-d♭-c♭-b♭ of the *universalis*. A byproduct of this
last system, then, is to provide "a minor semitone between any *claves*,"

---

[56] *Musica*, Bk. VI, prop. 28, fols. 79ᵛ–80ᵛ. Erasmus presents his scales in several
charts which show the pitches descending from top to bottom. For each step are
given string-length, solmization syllable, and clavis. In my simplified figures 4, 5, and
6, the scales are shown in terms of a standard modern alphabetical notation ascending
from left to right. All tetrachords, which are marked by brackets, are formed of the
ratios 9/8–9/8–256/243.

[57] Bk. VI, prop. 29, fol. 81ᵛ. The string-length 2304, which in the *scala quinti et
sexti toni* represented dd-la or our d^2, now represents cc-la, or our c^2. However, it
would be wrong to see these scales as transpositions upward by a whole-tone of the
scale of modes V and VI simply because cc-la has moved from 2592 to 2304. The
string-lengths do not represent absolute pitch but are merely numbers found convenient for computing relative pitch-distances.

that is any two diatonic steps.⁵⁸ It should be observed, however, that this is a minor semitone only when the fictitious note is used as a flat; employing the fictitious note as a sharp, as in the succession d-d♭-d, produces a major semitone, 2187/2048.

Fig. 6 *Scala ficta universalis*

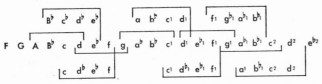

Erasmus has throughout these systems ignored the tradition established by Hermannus Contractus in the 11th century of constructing tetrachords by ascending tone-semitone-tone. He prefers to form them, like the Greeks, by descending tone-tone-semitone. This is in keeping with his evident desire to form the *scala quinti et sexti toni* on the model of the ancient synemmenon system.⁵⁹ The *scala ficta* then becomes a modern counterpart of a Greek *tonos*, since it transposes the *scala quinti et sexti toni* down a whole tone. For the *ficta* tone of disjunction, between c¹ and d¹, is a whole tone lower than that of the *scala quinti et sexti toni*, between d¹ and e¹. Erasmus knew that the system of Greek *tonoi* was a means for transposing to various levels a single scale. However imperfectly he understood other aspects of the *tonoi*, he must have incorporated this simple parallel quite consciously.

These few samples of his thought show how Erasmus of Höritz confronted the perennial challenge faced by Renaissance theory: to point the way to "the ancient music reduced to the modern practice." The theoretical doctrine that reached Erasmus, rooted in ancient thought but fitted to medieval western music, was neither true to the Greek writings nor congruent with the musical systems in use. Returning to ancient sources, Erasmus sought to restore the perennial laws of harmonics and at the same time to correct them, make them more accessible, and render their application easier. But, like his predecessors, he played the game of grafting convenient aspects of Greek theory to modern practice. So he found it expedient to revive the *tonoi* and the tetrachordal method of constructing scales. As a reconciliation of ancient theory and modern practice, his solutions were neither more nor less successful than

⁵⁸ Bk. VI, prop. 30, fol. 82ʳ.
⁵⁹ This does not apply to the Berlin treatise, however, where the *scala quinti et sexti toni* is represented on fol. 62ᵛ as proceeding from F-ut to e-mi with B♭ throughout. The Vatican treatise uses B♮ in the lowest tetrachord, as shown in Figure 4, in keeping with Greek practice.

parallel attempts by Glareanus or Vicentino. Perhaps less relevant than theirs to the contemporary musical situation, his were better founded in classical learning and objective facts.

It is not possible at this time to assess the influence his theory may have had on musical thought in his time. Echoes of his doctrines appear in Rhau, Ornithoparcus, Spangenberg, and Bogentanz, to cite a few of his own countrymen. Whether this resonance is owed to Erasmus or to a common doctrine that he happened to expound, his unpublished work was not a solitary flash. It bears witness to the fertile soil existing in Germany for the flowering music theory enjoyed there in the first half of the 16th century.

A RENAISSANCE MUSIC
MANUAL FOR CHOIRBOYS

by CARL PARRISH

THERE IS ALWAYS a special interest attached to treatises of a past age that are written primarily from a practical point of view, with a minimum of theoretical explanation and with the objective of treating a subject so that its principles may be put directly into actual use. These works often offer insights of an intimate kind into the spirit as well as the practice of an art such as are not to be found in the more formal and comprehensive presentations of learned theorists. Such is the case of the *Enchiridion utriusque musicae practicae* ("Handbook of of both kinds of musical practice") by Georg Rhau (1488–1548), the distinguished pedagogue and printer of the Reformation period. Rhau, after studies at Erfurt and Wittenberg, was for a time Cantor at the *Thomaskirche* in Leipzig, and in 1524, as a disciple of Luther, set up his printing shop in the service of the new church at Wittenberg. His products included books in regular typography (including the first printing of many of Luther's writings), partbooks of music, and books containing musical examples. Rhau's interest in "die gemeine Schule" prompted him to write and publish an *Enchiridion* in 1517. This volume dealt only with *musica plana*, but three years later he published a second *Enchiridion*, this being an instructor in *musica mensuralis*.[1] The two little volumes (*libelli*, as he called them) were usually bound together, and went through several editions, the only addition to them in their several reprintings being a dedicatory preface to Johannes Bugenhagen in 1531,[2] and a title page and monitory address to the boys of the Wittenberg

---

[1] The first of Rhau's two little handbooks, in the edition of 1538, has been published in facsimile by Hans Albrecht (Kassel 1951). Albrecht's *Nachwort* to this edition stated that the second handbook, on mensural music, would be published in the near future, also in a facsimile edition, but it has not yet appeared. A copy of the second book is in the Sibley Library of the Eastman School of Music. The references to the folio numbers (in capitals) of Volume I in this article are to the 1538 edition; those of Volume II (in lower case) are to the 1531 edition.

[2] Bugenhagen (1485–1558), a distinguished Lutheran theologian, a close friend of Luther, and a helper in the latter's translation of the Bible, was a skilful and zealous organizer of the Reformed Church. He is best known for his *Interpretatio in librum psalmorum* (1523).

Latin School in 1536. In addition to the dates mentioned above, editions of this pair of volumes were also printed in 1532, 1538, 1546, and—posthumously—in 1553.

Rhau's manuals are in a line of such works of the Luther period that began with those of his friend Martin Agricola (1488–1556) of Magdeburg (several of whose didactic works Rhau printed), and other such excellent musicians as Sebald Heyden (1488–1561) of Nuremberg and Heinrich Faber (d. 1552) of Naumberg.[3] The use of Latin by Rhau and his contemporaries for a manual of music intended for choirboys was part of a general plan of instruction; it was "for the practice of the students in that language," as Luther himself said.[4] The inclusion of music and Latin in the school curriculum was a tradition that went back to the 9th century. In the Lutheran schools of the Renaissance, an hour a day was devoted to music, with additional instruction in some schools. Instruction in music began at the age of eight and continued until 18. Emphasis in music teaching naturally stressed the practical side, for the students were important to the community for their performances at weddings, funerals, banquets, and other occasions, as well as for their regular church singing.[5]

This, then, was the general background that determined in part the the character of Rhau's *libelli*. The author's own personality comes through in them from time to time, especially in the hortative sections with their revelation of his attitude toward the readers to whom his book is addressed. His tone is warm and fatherly—belying the stern, forbidding impression given by the portrait that appears in several of his printed works [6]—and he stresses the moral and spiritual values inherent in the study of music. The Preface disclaims the need for any lengthy explanatory foreword, the principal matter of concern being the subject itself, and Rhau promises that through this book boys may arrive at a profound knowledge of the art; but he warns them that the achievement of this depends entirely upon their own diligence in study. Such precepts are not confined to the forepart of the book, though; during the course of explaining the syllables, for instance, Rhau departs from his subject to

[3] Other works of this nature are listed in Frederick Sternfeld's article, *Music in the Schools of the Reformation*, in: *Musica disciplina*, II (1948), 113–14.

[4] Luther often stressed this point. For example, in his *Deutsche Messe und Ordnung des Gottesdienst* (1526) he wrote: "I in no wise desire that the Latin language be dropped entirely from the services of worship. I say this in the interest of our youth."

[5] Sternfeld, *Schools*, p. 109ff.

[6] The portrait, a woodcut, is reproduced in F. Blume, *Die evangelische Kirchenmusik* (Potsdam 1931), p. 43.

remind the boys that they can attain the highest goals only by "daily use and continual exercise," and he holds up learning as something that can be acquired only by "toil and sweat." The riches of the spirit, he says, are more valuable than jewels and gold, and he likens a boy who has the opportunity to learn, but who wastes his time, to a merchant who invests his money unwisely and has nothing to show for it. He paints a miserable picture of such a boy who, once the opportunity has gone past, spends a wretched life—"ignorant, inglorious, saddened with regret" (fol. B vii).

Occasionally, Rhau uses picturesque turns of speech to indicate his impatience with long-winded discussions that are of only theoretical interest, and to emphasize the practical nature of his book. Concerning the endings of the psalm tones, for example, he says it is not worthwhile to devote long study to them since they are not the same in all the tones. "What purpose will it serve," he asks, "if one pours out so many gallons of *differentiae* that a ship could not carry them, when each is used with its own proper formula?" (fol. F iii verso). Again, in his book on mensural music, Rhau observes that great controversy exists among musicians in the interpretation of meter signs, and that sometimes unusual signs are used that may be confusing to a beginner. He restricts his teaching, therefore, to the most used signs, not including every variety, "for I prefer to teach the boys that it is silly to take a roundabout way—to follow a stream to the sea—when the road lies straight in another direction" (fol. b vii verso).

On the other hand, like most treatise writers, Rhau seems unable to abstain from a certain show of learning. In the Preface to the book on mensural music, for example, he uses such pompous terms as these: "The *materiala* of music is divided into the *positiva* and the *privativa*," which is merely a pretentious way of saying that music consists of sounds and silences (fol. a iii). Similarly, the measuring of notes is said to consist of the *essentialis*—the given properties of mode, time, and prolation—and the *accidentalis*—the inflection given them through alteration, imperfection, ligature, and proportion (fol. a iii). The aura of learning is also conveyed by the use of an occasional Greek word or phrase.

For the edification of his young audience, Rhau had what he calls "elegant little verses" made for each of the two books. Intended as mnemonic aids to the student, each verse briefly summarized the chief point treated in each chapter, "so that I might aid your memory in learning the elements of this art." As an example, the second chapter in the first book, which explains the hexachord system, concludes with this verse (fol. C ii):

On c begins the natural, on f the soft, and on g the hard;
Within the gamut I triple the hard hexachord but double the others;
E ends the hard, a the natural, and d the soft.[7]

The verses in the first book are said to be by one Wenceslas.[8] Those in the second, by Christoph Hegendorf,[9] appear at the beginning rather than the end of each chapter, thus serving to introduce rather than to summarize the subject discussed.

In turning to the musical content of the two little volumes, it will be noted that the general plan of the materials presented follows the usual arrangement of Renaissance books on music, with some interesting exceptions. In the volume devoted to *musica plana*, consisting of 98 pages arranged into eight chapters, the principal subject treated is, of course, solmization. This is taken up methodically and with thoroughness, beginning with the syllables in the gamut, their formation into the three hexachords, hexachord mutation, and musica ficta. Also treated are melodic intervals, modes, psalm tones, Magnificat tones, and reciting tones. Many of these, such as the examples of the modes and tones, are set in four-part harmonizations that are thought to have been made by Rhau himself.

A significant aspect of the solmization teaching is the absence of any reference to the Guidonian hand. This is all the more remarkable in that the hand is ubiquitous in musical treatises of the Renaissance, large or small, that have to do with solmization. Rhau's omission of it, which must almost certainly be considered deliberate, is an interesting reflection of his practical approach to the subject. It is likely that he regarded it as a cumbersome method of learning the syllables, and one that placed an added and needless burden on the boys in learning a system that was complicated enough to begin with.

Another unusual feature of the book is the use of various types of notation for the different styles of music treated. The author states in the introductory part of the two handbooks that he will treat exhaus-

---

[7] In c natural, f bmol, gque bdural
Bdurum triplico, reliquos cantus geminabo
E durum finit, a natural, dque bmollem.

[8] This may have been Wenceslas (or Wenzel) Linck (or Link) (1488–1547), a friend of Luther and Vicar of the German Congregation of the Augustinian Monks at Wittenberg, who also taught theology at the University of Wittenberg. Wenceslas is also quoted in the second book in a verse concerning distant imperfection (fol. c iv).

[9] Hegendorf (1500–40), a learned humanist, theologian, and jurist, was active in Leipzig and Lüneburg. He edited works of Greek and Latin authors and wrote poems, satires, and two comedies, of which the *Comoedia nova* (Leipzig 1520) was frequently performed. There were some pieces in it which may have been composed by Hegendorf himself.

tively of the music called *choralis*, which, as he says, is also called *plana*, as well as "Gregorian" and "old." (Mensural music, he states, is also called "figural" or "new.") He defines it as "that which keeps an even measuring in its notes, without a lengthening or shortening of note-values." Among the more than 50 examples in the book, however, there are very few examples of plainsong in monophonic style. Actually, the only monophonic examples consist of two exercises to illustrate mutation—these are seen in Figures 1 (fol. C verso) and 2 (fol. C iiii verso)—separate inter-

Fig. 1   Georg Rhau, *Enchiridion*, I (Wittenberg 1518), fol. C verso

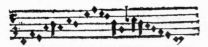

Hic hexachordū naturale leuatur a ♮durali, & contra ♭durale a bmolli,& bmolle iterum a naturali.

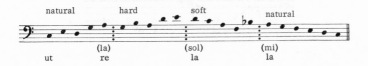

Fig. 2   *Enchiridion*, I, fol. C iiii verso

vals (fols. D v and D v verso), the traditional *tonarium* of Hermannus Contractus for teaching intervals (fol. D vi, almost identical with the version in Schering, *Geschichte der Musik in Beispielen*, No. 7), and psalm tone endings (fols. F iii verso and F iiii). These examples are all written in Gothic neumes (the so-called "Hufnagelschrift"), usually with no distinction between the use of *punctum* and *virga*, and with an occasional, though inconsistent, use of a *strophicus* to indicate lengthening at the end of a phrase, as in Figures 1 and 2. A few examples of the Gothic *clivis* occur (as in Fig. 4, alto voice, fol. C viii).

Gothic notation is also used in several four-part settings in note-against-note style, each part being in uniform note values. These include an arrangement of *Ut queant laxis* (fol. B iiii), two examples to illustrate musica ficta (fol. C viii and fol. C viii verso; see Figs. 4 and 5), exercises to illustrate intervals and hexachords (fols. B vi and B vii verso), and certain psalm tones, including the *tonus peregrinus* (fols. F vi–G).

A very unusual type of notation which might be called "quasi-

Fig. 3 *Enchiridion*, I, fol. E iv

TENOR.

Hic quíntus & fextus funt permíxti,

DISCANTVS.

ALTVS.

BASSVS.

Hic quintus et sextus sunt permixti

Here the fifth and sixth (modes) have been intermingled.

mensural" also appears in several four-part examples, namely an exercise in the use of syllables (fol. B viii), examples of the mixed mode (fol. E iii verso) and the imperfect mode (the former is seen in Figure 3, fol. E iv), another hexachord exercise (fol. B viii), certain psalm tones (fols. F iiii verso, F v, and F v verso), and all the Magnificat tones (fols. G verso–G v). These are written in predominantly uniform values, but with an occasional "half-beat," indicated by an ascending or descending stem, distinguished from the stem of the Gothic *virga* by its comparative thinness. When as many as four of these shorter notes occur in succession, they are connected with a beam (e.g. as in fol. B viii).

Strangely enough, the book on *musica plana* contains a few musical examples in white mensural notation, used in further illustration of hexachords (fol. B viii verso) and mutation (fol. C vi verso), also of the use of the ledger line (fol. D iii verso). No explanation is given as to why this notation was employed in a book dealing with plainsong, but a not unreasonable speculation would be that Rhau never originally intended to write a book on *musica mensuralis*, but felt that a few examples of such notation ought to appear in his treatise; otherwise he would most likely have kept all examples of mensural notation for the second book.

To this list of different kinds of notation used in the first volume must be added yet another which is still more unusual: a combination— in a four-part piece—of white mensural notation (in discantus, altus, and bassus) with Gothic notation (in the tenor), which is used in an example to illustrate clef-transposition (fol. D ii verso–D iii verso).

Rhau's exposition of mutation (Chap. III) and musica ficta (Chaps. III and VII) is of special interest because of its very direct approach to the problems involved, and its illustrations of them through examples written expressly to demonstrate them. His discussion is summarized in the following paragraphs.

Mutation is the change of one syllable to another on the same pitch, a procedure made necessary by the small number of syllables and the large number of tones in the gamut. It is done both *explicitly*, in which case both syllables are sounded, and *implicitly*, in which case one syllable is sung and the other is understood mentally. The latter is far more suitable than the former on both aesthetic and practical grounds: in mensural music, for example, the short duration of the smallest notes does not permit singing the two syllables. Explicit mutation is tolerable only if the mutation happens to occur on a repeated note.

Mutation from the hard to the soft hexachord, and vice versa, is normally avoided, although it is sometimes necessary (as in Fig. 1; see also fn. 10). In the solmization of the ascending gamut with b♮, the mutations occur on D and A, *re* being taken on both these notes. In the solmization of the ascending gamut with B♭, the mutations occur on D and G, *re* being taken on both these notes. In descending, mutations are made on D and A, *la* being taken on both these notes.

Rhau has a special exercise to show how a melody can go quickly through all three hexachords in succession (see Fig. 1,[10] fol. C verso); changes of hexachords, and the mutations used to effect these changes, are also shown in Figure 1.

Whether B♮ or B♭ is to be taken is usually indicated by a flat or natural sign, but this is chiefly determined by the mode of the piece. All modes have B♮ excepting five and six; in them, sometimes B♭ is taken, sometimes B♮. In a melody in the first or second mode that goes only one

---

[10] Translation of the text below the example: "Here, the natural hexachord is taken up by the hard, then the hard by the soft, and the soft once again by the natural."

PARRISH

degree higher than the highest syllable of the natural hexachord (*la*) and then returns, *fa* (i.e. B♭) is always sung. (This is the old rule: *Una nota supra la semper est canendum fa.*) But if the melody ascends a third above *la*, then *mi* (i.e. B♮) should be sung. Both these cases are illustrated in Figure 2 (fol. C iiii verso).

In plainsong, melodies cannot go below *Gamma ut* (G) nor above *eela* (e²); hence, syllables are not provided for them in the gamut. But in mensural music these limits are often exceeded, in which case the syllable names are taken from the octaves of these notes. Such notes are called "musica ficta." This term is also used in referring to notes not in the gamut, such as e♭ and a♭, and f♯ and c♯, although musica ficta may be brought about on any note in the gamut by transposition of the hexachord syllables. In the case of lowered notes, the syllable *fa* is sung, while *mi* is sung on raised notes. In leaps of the fourth and fifth, *mi-mi* or *fa-fa* may be sung, just as in leaps of the octave, in order to avoid the tritone. Musica ficta is allowed both on account of the needs of the music and because of its pleasantness. ("Admittuntur autem coniunctae, cum propter cantus necessitatem, tum iucunditatem"—fol. D viii verso).

In treating of the modes (Chap. VIII), Rhau follows the usual explanations of their various aspects, such as the ambitus, tenors (*repercussiones*), mode recognition, and mode transposition. A personal touch is added, however, when he gives the practical warning that singers should note carefully whether a piece is in an authentic, plagal, or other mode (such as mixed, or imperfect), since the range makes a great difference in performance. He notes the various ill effects that may result from improper judgment in choosing the pitch: bellowing (*rudere*), falsetto (*factitia*), dropping the voice so that the singers can hardly hear themselves (*vix a seipsis exaudiri*), and going off into a kind of throat-clearing (*in screatum quendam*). The discussion of the modes ends with the admission that it is not always possible to recognize the mode of a piece as being either plagal or authentic; that this is often conjectural. ("Nam inter tonum autenticum et plagalem non semper potest absoluta et exacta haberi cognitio et differentia, imo ex coniectura saepe cantus tono autentico vel plagali attribuitur"—fol. F iii.)

It has been noted above that Rhau set a number of examples, including illustrations of the modes, in four parts, and in predominantly note-against-note style, with an occasional use of long and short note-values. Figure 3 (fol. E iv) shows such a setting, intended to illustrate the discussion *de tono mixto*, i.e. the use of both the authentic and plagal ranges of any one mode-pair in a melody. Rhau's use of such settings of psalm tones and the like is an early but not a unique phenomenon in

German music of the Renaissance. The style appears to have had its origins in the settings of Classical poetry that appeared in Latin school dramas.[11] This style also proved to be useful for the daily psalmody, as seen in Rhau's settings of the psalm tones, and for similar items in his book, such as the setting of *Ut queant laxis*, and even for pieces without a cantus prius factus, such as that in Figure 3. (The Magnificat tones are set more elaborately, making use of free imitations.) In every case, the original melody, or the principal part in the specially composed examples, is in the tenor. About a decade after Rhau's first book appeared, Luther himself firmly sanctioned this style in the Preface to the *Geystliches Gesangk Buchleyn* (1529): "The music is arranged in four parts. I desire this particularly in the interest of young people . . ." A little more than half a century after that, when Osiander, in his *50 geistliche Lieder und Psalmen* (1586), shifted the main melody to the upper voice, the Protestant chorale was at hand.

Rhau's discussion of the syllables and their use in the hexachords is a reflection of a certain interesting stage in the evolution from the hexachord system to the system of octave scales and of major-minor feeling that was taking place in German musical theory during the 16th century. In considering the hexachord syllables, he states that they are divided into three pairs: *ut-fa*, *re-sol*, and *mi-la*. Each of these pairs, he claims (referring presumably to the tetrachords defined by each pair), gives a different effect, the first being "soft," the second "hard," and the third "natural." This classification of the syllables themselves within the hexachord seems actually to have first appeared in print only one year before Rhau's *Musica plana* in Ornithoparcus's *Musicae activae micrologus*, published at Leipzig in 1516.[12] The verse in which Rhau summarizes this concept is as follows (fol. B vi verso):

> *Ut* with *fa* is the soft syllable [-pair], because it softens the melodies;
> *Mi* with *la* is the hard, for it brings about hard songs;
> *Sol* with *re* is the natural (since it makes neither the one nor the other).[13]

The difference in each tetrachord arises from the different position of the half-step within each one, and the "softening" effect referred to in the verse comes from the fact that the note below *fa* is a half-step (in the

[11] Sternfeld, *Schools*, pp. 106–09.
[12] Ornithoparcus was connected with the University of Wittenberg at this time, when Rhau was still there. His classification of the solmization syllables may be the first to have appeared in print, but a somewhat similar syllable-division goes back as far as the *Quatuor principalia*, attributed to Simon Tunstede (d. 1369). See Coussemaker, *Scriptorum de musica*, IV, 225.
[13] *Ut* cum *fa* mollis vox est, quia canta mollit
Mi cum *la* dura est, nam duras efficit Odas
Sol naturales (quoniam neutras facit) et *re*.

other two pairs, the intervals below each note are all whole-steps), as is
the note below *ut*, if the tetrachord *ut-fa* is thought of as a continuation
of the hard hexachord. This appears to have actually been the case, so
that the hard hexachord (from G to E) had become "amalgamated," so
to speak, with the natural (from C to A). The discarding of the concept
of three different hexachords seems to have first been advanced in print
by Sebald Heyden, who wrote in his *Musicae, id est artis canendi* (Nuremberg 1537), p. 18: "How many kinds of hexachords are there? Some
say three—natural, soft, and hard—and others add a fourth kind to these,
namely the 'fictive.' But for us, for the sake of a more proper way of
teaching, let only two suffice—*b molle* and *b durum*—and every piece,
accordingly, has or does not have B♭ written at the beginning." The
examples given by him on pages 26–33 of his treatise show that he actually had major and minor in mind in this division.[14]

After the discussion of the three hexachord types, Rhau gives two
diagrams to illustrate mutations, one of which shows the gamut with B♮
throughout (fol. C iiii), the other with B♭ throughout (fol. C vi). The
first of these is described as "Scala cantus bduralis, quae docet, quoniam
pacto cantor reguliter suos cantus alternatim permutare debeat" ("The
scale of a melody using B♮, which shows that in mutation the singer
ought to change his hexachords regularly, in alternate fashion.") The
second diagram is called "Arsis et thesis omnium tonorum, fa in bfabmi
dicentium" ("The ascent and descent of all the modes, singing *fa* in
bfabmi [i.e. using B♭]"). The two diagrams merely emphasize what
Heyden claimed, namely that there were really only two kinds of scales
in the gamut—one with B♭ and one with B♮—and that the threefold
system of hexachords was obsolescent.

This explanation of the emergence in German musical thinking of the
major and minor modes out of the hexachord system, first outlined by
Adolf Aber (see footnote 14), seems to be supported by the two examples supplied by Rhau to illustrate music written *in locis ♮duralibus* as
compared to music *in locis bmollaribus*. These are illustrated in Figures 4
(fol. C viii) and 5 (fol. C viii verso).[15] The former appears to be associated with major feeling, which is emphasized in the final chord,
while minor quality is pronounced in the latter. Rhau's examples would

[14] See the article by Adolf Aber, *Das musicalische Studienheft des Wittenberger
Studenten Georg Donat (um 1543)*, in: SIM, XV (1913), 74.
[15] The meaning of the caption over Figure 4a seems to be: "A piece in a 'false
hexachord' follows, in which the syllables that represent 'fa' are in places where 'mi'
is usually sung." The caption over Figure 5a states the reverse, though more
succinctly. In the bass part of Figure 5a, the obvious error in the penultimate note
probably arose because of the ambiguous placing of the previous note, which should
be c.

Fig. 4 *Enchiridion*, I, fol. C viii

thus form an interesting parallel to Heyden's illustrations mentioned above, as well as to those of other contemporaneous German theorists, as actual demonstrations of the rise of the octave scale over the hexachord, of tonality over modality, and of practice over theory.[16]

In discussing the "forbidden intervals" (the augmented fourth, diminished fifth, and diminished octave), Rhau takes occasion to note

[16] It was difficult for German theorists to discard the threefold concept of hexachords. Johannes Spangenberg, in his *Quaestiones musicae* (Wittenberg 1536), proposed three scales built from hexachords: one with B♭, another with B♮, and a new one that he called a *scala ficta*, using A♭ and E♭. Even Agricola, in his *Duo libri musicae* (Wittenberg 1561), seriously considered such a system, but this seems to have been the last time such an idea appeared in print. With Johannes Zanger's *Practicae musicae praecepta* (Leipzig 1554) and Ambrosius Wilphlingseder's *Musica teutsch, der Jugent zu gut gestellt* (Nuremberg 1563), also published in Latin as *Erotemata practicae musicae* (Nuremberg 1563), the dual scale is permanently established.

Fig. 5 *Enchiridion*, fol. C viii verso

ALIVD EXEMPLVM DE,
clarans voces fictas in lo,
cis bmollaribus.

DISCANTVS.

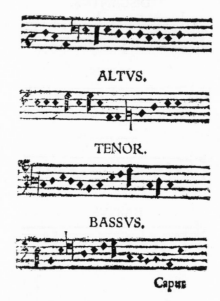

ALTVS.

TENOR.

BASSVS.

Caput

(fol. D vii verso) that the *disdiapason* (i.e. the fifteenth) is the natural limit of the human voice, and that those who go beyond that do so artificially (*factitia vox est*) and do not act wisely. Authorities from Boethius to Glareanus are quoted as supporting this opinion.

The final section of *Musica plana* (fol. G vii verso) is devoted to the "punctuation" of the Common Tones of the Mass, with illustrations of the *virgula, comma, colon,* and *interrogatio;* and explanations of their force appear in very much the same way these matters are treated in the *Liber Usualis* today.

In general, the second of Rhau's two handbooks—the *Musica mensuralis*—is of less interest than the first, although the material is perhaps laid out more logically. As before, everything unessential to the subject is avoided; only the necessary points are set forth. The exposition, in 62 pages arranged into 11 chapters, includes: notes, rests, and ligatures; mode, time, and prolation; augmentation, diminution, imperfection, and alteration; tactus, meter signs, dots, syncopation, and proportions. One might even use the book today as a practical introduction to the study of Renaissance notation. One reservation must be appended to the foregoing, however; in a couple of instances Rhau inserts complex musical examples that appear to be far beyond what a student would be expected to apprehend at this stage of his studies.

Among the noteworthy items in the book is the discussion of tactus (Chap. VII, *De tactibus*). Here, the author urges that in the signs of *dupla* proportion, "the notes ought either to be taken more quickly, or two beats ought to be taken for one" (fol. c vi). The significance of this remark lies in the indication that the appearance of the *dupla* sign in a composition did not necessarily mean an actual doubling of the tempo, but could, at the conductor's discretion, mean simply a quickening.[17] We also learn in this chapter that under all meter signs except those of the proportions the semibreve is a whole beat ("semibreve tactu mensuratur integro"), and that this is the *tactus minor*, the *tactus major* being, of course, the breve as the beat.

Also of special interest is Rhau's explanation of why rests are used in music. He gives four reasons (fol. a iiii):

1) So that the singer may take a breath
2) For the sake of making canons ("formandarum fugarum gratia")
3) To avoid the tritone and the augmented fifth
4) To give variety of sound, which, he says, is especially important "in our own period, when the outstanding composers write pieces for five . . . eight . . . or even twelve voices."

A very practical feature of the musical examples in *Musica mensuralis* is the occasional insertion of "silent" notes to indicate the actual rather than the apparent value of certain notes. In the explanation of the ligatures, for example (Chap. II, *De ligaturis*), Rhau shows graphically that the binaria with ascending stem to the left (the "opposite propriety" of the Middle Ages), which looks like a pair of two breves, is actually a pair

[17] The actual passage reads: "In huius modi signis ¢ ¢ O₂ ¢₂ aliqua mensurae pars adimitur, hinc est quod in ipsis, vel notae velotius tangi debent, vel semper duo tactus accipi pro uno." The same statement is made in Chapter VI (*De diminutione et augmentatione*, fol. b vi verso) and in Chapter V (*De signis*, fol. b viii). See Curt Sachs, *Rhythm and Tempo* (New York 1953), p. 223, for references to similar statements by contemporaneous theorists, including Glareanus.

of semibreves, as at the end of Figure 6 (fol. b ii verso).[18] This device is also employed in his examples to demonstrate the force of alteration (fol. c vii verso and c viii).

Fig. 6   *Enchiridion*, II, fol. b ii verso

Vltima afcendens à præcedente, breuis
eft, excipe ligaturam duarum femibreuium.

Like other Renaissance writers on music, Rhau makes much of the dot, and recognizes three main types—those of perfection, addition, and division. The latter type, he says, is also known as the dot of alteration, of imperfection, and transposition (*punctus transportationis*), meaning by the latter term what is more commonly called by his contemporaries the dot of syncopation. The dot of perfection is said to have been "devised for the sake of unsure singers" ("et est excogitatus propter incertos cantores"—fol. d).

The last chapter of Rhau's second book is devoted to the proportions, and here he again stresses his practicality by stating that it is not his business to write about the various kinds of proportions, since they have more to do with theoretical rather than practical music. He restricts himself, therefore, to a brief discussion, with illustrative examples, of each of the following: *dupla, tripla, quadrupla, sesquialtera, sesquitertia,* and *hemiola.* It is curious that he should make a distinction between *sesquialtera* and *hemiola,* which are generally taken to be synonymous, but Rhau defines the former as applying to minims (fol. d vi verso), the latter to semibreves (fol. d vii verso). Both numbers and coloration are used in his examples to produce the shortened values of this proportion. Rhau also explains that proportions may be shown by canons, such as *Diminitur, Decrescit in duplo,* or *Brevis sit semibrevis,* and others (fol. d v).[19]

It was indicated earlier that one aspect of *Musica mensuralis* of which one might be critical, from the standpoint of rational pedagogy, is the introduction of complicated examples too early in the book. In view of the apparent popularity and success of Rhau's *libelli,* one would be happy to know more about the actual classroom operation of a system of music

---

[18] Translation of the rubric in this example: "A final note ascending from the preceding note is a breve, with the exception of the ligature of two semibreves."

[19] Rhau defines the canon as "a fanciful precept, drawing forth a part not written from the written parts of a composition" (fol. dv verso), which is actually a description of the puzzle canon, rather than of the canon in general.

Fig. 7   *Enchiridion*, II, fol. c iiii verso and c v recto

instruction demanding that boys perform such pieces as its two three-part examples in which the parts are set in a different mensuration, maintained simultaneously throughout. One of these is in Chapter III, *De tribus musicae gradibus* ("Concerning the three levels of mensuration"), the other in Chapter VI, *De notarum imperfectione* ("Concerning imperfection of the notes"). The latter example (fol. c iv verso and c v) appears, together with its transcription into modern notation, in Figure 7. The introductory sentence reads, in translation: "An example in three parts follows, with imperfection of such notes (each in its own degree of music) as, for instance, the semibreve in perfect prolation, the long in perfect minor mode, and the breve in perfect time."

Thus these little books, though modest in dimensions and purposely limited by their author to "practical" aims, are at the same time indicative of a progressiveness that we do not ordinarily associate with works of this general character. We see the Guidonian hand disappearing, we learn that *dupla* proportion is to be freely interpreted, we are told that the pitch of a piece should be placed in a comfortable range for the singers regardless of its mode, and we are given actual exercises in mutation. Also, we see the combination of Gregorian monophony with harmony of a purely chordal kind, and a reflection of this in the joining of mensural notation to Gothic neumes, graphically presenting, in such a combination, a symbol of the union of old and new. Less tangible in the *Enchiridion*, yet stirring in it restlessly if unconsciously, is the awakening sense of major-minor tonality. The winds of change were blowing hard when Rhau lived in Wittenberg, not only from a theological but a musical quarter as well.

A LETTER OF CHARLES VIII
OF FRANCE CONCERNING
ALEXANDER AGRICOLA

by MARTIN PICKER

ALEXANDER AGRICOLA'S position as a major figure in European music at the end of the 15th and the beginning of the 16th centuries is undisputed. He was one of many Northern masters who contributed to the musical life of Renaissance Italy, mainly at Milan and Florence. His works were published in quantity during the first decade of the 16th century by Ottaviano de' Petrucci at Venice.[1] The high esteem that Agricola enjoyed among his contemporaries is reflected in the poetry of Jean Lemaire de Belges, whose work, like that of his mentor Jean Molinet, abounds in musical references. Lemaire often praises Agricola, "dont musique fait luire le nom plus cler cent fois que fin argent," and links him with the most illustrious musicians of the time.[2]

Despite Agricola's fame, his life remains shadowy to us and our knowledge of it is riddled with gaps. We are not entirely sure of the place or year of his birth. These are inferred from the *Epitaphion Alexandri Agricolae symphonistae regis Castiliae* ("Musica, quid defles?"), printed at Wittenberg by Georg Rhau in his *Symphoniae jucundae* as late as 1538, in a musical setting that is probably by his countryman and colleague, Heinrich Isaac.[3] In this text Agricola is called a "Belgian"

---

[1] Petrucci published 47 pieces in 11 different collections, plus an entire book of Masses by Agricola. This number was exceeded only for Josquin des Prez and, to a lesser extent, Loyset Compère. See Anne-Marie Bautier-Regnier, *L'Edition musicale italienne et les musiciens d'outremonts au XVIe siècle (1501–1563)*, in: *La Renaissance dans les provinces du nord*, ed. François Lesure (Paris 1956), p. 34.

[2] The passage quoted is from Lemaire's *La Plainte du désiré* (1503), ed. D. Yabsley (Paris 1932), p. 81. For a remarkable characterization of the music of his time, including that of Agricola, Josquin, Ockeghem, and Compère, see Lemaire's *La Concorde des deux langages*, ed. J. Frappier (Paris 1947), p. 18.

[3] Georg Rhau, *Musikdrucke aus den Jahre 1538 bis 1545*, ed. Hans Albrecht, III (Kassel 1959), 165. Isaac's authorship of this composition is proposed by Ludwig Finscher in his review of this edition in *Die Musikforschung*, XVI (1963), 204. The motet immediately following the *Epitaphion* in Rhau's print (*Nil prosunt lacrimae*) forms a logical *secunda pars*, both musically and textually, and the epitaph seems incomplete without it. Since Isaac is named as the composer of this piece, his authorship of the whole seems probable.

and his death is stated to have occurred from fever at Valladolid in the month of August, and when he was 60 years old. His name disappears from the records of the Burgundian court chapel after 16 August 1506, at which time the court was in Spain.[4] If we assume that Agricola's death took place in 1506, then we may set the year of his birth as 1446. Despite numerous references to Agricola in the records of his Italian service as "de Alemania" and "Germanus" the epitaph, which indicates that he was of Flemish origin, must be given credence.

The first specific date cited for Agricola's life is 1470, which is given as the year of his marriage in Florence.[5] Agricola's service from 1471 to 1474 at Milan, where Duke Galeazzo Maria Sforza had brought together a spectacular array of musicians, including Josquin des Prez, Loyset Compère, and Johannes Martini, is well documented. In 1474 Agricola received permission to leave Milan, obtaining from the Duke a letter of recommendation to Lorenzo de' Medici. The Duke also gave him a splendid testimonal of faithful service and granted him permission to seek his fortune in the Low Countries.[6] Agricola first went to Florence. From there he wrote to the Duke of Milan apologizing for his departure and recommending a young organist whom he had met in Ferrara.[7] In 1476 Agricola was among the "petits vicaires" of the Cathedral of Cambrai, having finally carried out his intention to find a position in the North.[8]

Fifteen years later, on 1 October 1491, Agricola is recorded as a singer at the Florence Cathedral, under the patronage of Lorenzo de' Medici.[9] Heinrich Isaac was also among the singers there, and the fact that the two were colleagues lends some support to the theory that in later years Isaac paid tribute to Agricola with a musical setting of the *Epitaphion*. On the way to Florence Agricola appears to have visited Mantua, al-

---

[4] This date is given by Walter H. Rubsamen in his article *La Rue*, in: MGG,VIII (Kassel 1960), 227. Concerning Agricola's service in the Netherlands court chapel, see Georges van Doorslaer, *La Chapelle musicale de Philippe le Beau*, in: *Revue belge d'archéologie et d'histoire de l'art*, IV (1934), 139.

[5] Emilio Motta, *Musici alla corte degli Sforza*, in: *Archivio storico lombardo*, ser. 2, IV (1887), 322f and 532. Extensive documentation for Agricola's service in Milan is presented here.

[6] Edmond Van der Straeten, *La Musique aux Pays-Bas avant le XIXe siècle* (Brussels 1867–1888), IV, 13.

[7] Claudio Sartori, *Organs, Organ-Builders, and Organists in Milan, 1450–1476: New and Unpublished Documents*, in: MQ, XLIII (1957), 64.

[8] André Pirro, *Jean Cornuel vicaire à Cambrai*, in: *Revue de musicologie*, X (1926), 191. Paul Müller, *Agricola*, in: MGG, I (Kassel 1949), 158, cites a reference to "magister Alexander," organist at Utrecht in 1477, who may be identical with Agricola. Müller grants that the evidence is too slender to admit this as more than a possibility.

[9] Frank A. D'Accone, *The Singers of San Giovanni in Florence during the 15th Century*, in: JAMS, XIV (1961), 344.

though there is no evidence that he served or spent any considerable time there as indicated by some biographers. The composer Johannes Martini, a former colleague of Agricola at Milan, writing from his post at Ferrara to Isabella d'Este at Mantua to explain the departure without leave in 1491 of one of her singers, Charles de Launoy, states that this musician accompanied Agricola to Florence.[10] Confirmation of this is given by the fact that Agricola and Launoy appear at the same time in the choir of the Florence Cathedral. The French musician Charles de Launoy was a brother-in-law of Isaac, their wives being daughters of a Florentine merchant.[11]

Agricola's stay in Florence was brief, for he departed on 1 June 1492.[12] The liberality of Medici patronage was sharply curtailed after Lorenzo's death in April, 1492, and Savonarola's recriminations were beginning to affect all levels of Florentine society. Agricola may have foreseen the difficult times ahead for Florence and hastened to find another situation. There were other pressures on him to quit Florence, notably from Charles VIII of France—but of this we shall have more to say presently.

Agricola's whereabouts from 1492 to 1500 are at present unknown. In 1500 he entered the court chapel of Philippe le Beau at Brussels, which numbered among its members the eminent musician Pierre de la Rue. Agricòla accompanied the court on its far-flung travels through France, Germany, and Spain. It was probably during the state visit to Spain in 1506, which was also fatal to the young King Philippe of Castile, that Agricola's death occurred, at Valladolid in late August, as stated in the epitaph.[13]

A document virtually unknown to scholars that contributes significantly to our knowledge of Alexander Agricola's career is a letter signed by (or in the name of) Charles VIII of France, dated at Poissy, 25 April (without year), addressed to Pietro de' Medici at Florence, and now in the possession of the Pierpont Morgan Library in New York City.[14] This letter, a rare Renaissance document pertaining to music in an

[10] Pietro Canal, *Della musica in Mantova*, in: *Memorie del Reale istituto veneto di scienze, lettere ed arti*, XXI (1879), 663.

[11] Frank A. D'Accone, *Heinrich Isaac in Florence: New and Unpublished Documents*, in: MQ, XLIX (1963), 469.

[12] D'Accone, *The Singers of San Giovanni*, p. 345.

[13] Uncertainty about this death date has arisen from the fact that a "cantore Allessandro Agricola" served the marquis Federigo Gonzaga at Mantua in 1521–23. The composer's age makes any activity at that date unlikely; perhaps this is a son. See Antonio Bertolotti, *Musici alla corte dei Gonzaga in Mantova dal secolo XV al secolo XVIII* (Milan 1890), p. 32; Van der Straeten, *La Musique aux Pays-Bas*, VIII, 527.

[14] It is classified among autograph letters: VR/R of F/Box I/Charles VIII/No. 4.

American collection, unequivocally informs us (1) that Agricola served in the French royal chapel, (2) that some time before April 1492 he departed thence for Florence without leave, and (3) that Charles VIII valued him highly enough to wish to reclaim him. This important document (which according to Mr. Herbert Cahoon, Curator of Autograph Manuscripts, has been in the Morgan Library for at least 50 years) has been virtually ignored in investigations of Agricola's career during the present century.

The full text of the letter (see Plate 23a), with an English translation, follows:

(Written on the reverse) A nostre cher et amé cousin, le Seigneur Pierre de Medecis.
Cher et amé cousin: Nous avons puis nagueres esté advertiz que Alexandre Agricola, chantre de nostre chappelle, et ung bon joueur de luz en sa compaignie arriverent ou temps de feu nostre cousin le Seigneur Laurens de Medecis, vostre pere, en la cité de Florence. Et pource que nous desirons singulierement recouvrer en nostre dicte chappelle icellui Alexandre, nous lui escripvons presentement qu'il s'en vienne devers nous et qu'il amene avec luy ledit joueur de luz. Si vous prions que de vostre part ne leur soit donne aucun empeschement, mais les incitez a ce qu'ilz partent le plustost que faire se pourra pour venir quelque part que soyons, en les asseurant que nous les traicterons en si bonne facon qu'ilz auront cause d'eulx bien contenter. Et vous nous ferez tresagreable plaisir. Donné a Poissy le XXV me jour d'avril.
Charles

Bohier [15]

To our dear and beloved cousin, Lord Pietro de' Medici.
Dear and beloved cousin:
We have been informed recently that Alexander Agricola, singer of our chapel, and a good lutenist in his company arrived in the city of Florence during the time of our late cousin, Lord Lorenzo de' Medici, your father. Because we particularly desire the return to our chapel of this Alexander, we are writing to him immediately, directing that he come before us and that he bring with him the said lutenist. Thus we pray that you will not hinder their departure in any way, but that on the contrary you will urge them to leave as soon as possible, so that they

[15] "Bohier" is Henry Bohier, secretary and "varlet de chambre ordinaire" to Charles VIII; see *Lettres de Charles VIII, roi de France*, ed. P. Pélicier (Paris 1898–1905), III, 302. The present letter is not published by Pélicier. It is listed in Seymour de Ricci, *Census of Medieval and Renaissance Manuscripts in the United States and Canada* (New York 1937), II, 1542. I am grateful to Mr. Frederick B. Adams, Jr., Director of The Pierpont Morgan Library, for permission to publish this document, and to Professors Alfred L. Kellogg of Rutgers University and Alfred L. Foulet of Princeton University for assistance in transcribing and translating it.

may come wherever we are to be found, assuring them that we will treat them so generously that they will have reason to be well satisfied. And (in so doing) you will give us great pleasure.
Given at Poissy, the 25th day of April.

When was this letter written? It is addressed to Pietro de' Medici, son and successor of Lorenzo *il Magnifico*. The reference to "our late cousin" places it some time after Lorenzo's death on 8 April 1492. *Terminus ad quem* is September 1494, when Charles launched his invasion of Italy. Indeed, the year 1494 is highly unlikely because Charles was at Lyon during the entire month of April.[16] Since Agricola appears to have left Florence in June 1492, it is probable that the letter was written in April of that year, while Agricola was still in Florence. If the brusque tone of the letter seems inappropriate so soon after Lorenzo's death, it may well reflect Charles's impatience and his rudely autocratic attitude. In any event, 1492 is the year to which the Morgan Library now assigns the letter.

The letter helps to fill at least one large gap in our knowledge of Agricola's life. It is clear that for part of the 15-year period between 1476 and 1491 Agricola served at the court of Charles VIII, who ruled from 1483 to 1498, this employment terminating around 1491. Perhaps Agricola returned to France after leaving Florence in 1492; but without supporting evidence this remains no more than a possibility.

The only direct reference to the letter that I have found in all the literature on Agricola occurs in J. R. Sterndale-Bennett's article for the first edition of *Grove's Dictionary of Music and Musicians* (London 1879) I, 44: "A letter of Charles VIII of France, in Mr Julian Marshall's collection, proves that he was in that king's service, and left it, without leave, for that of Lorenzo de' Medici, whence Charles reclaimed him. Charles died 1598" [sic].[17] This article was revised for subsequent editions of *Grove's Dictionary* and still serves as the basis for the entry in the recent fifth edition (1954). Unfortunately, revision has served it poorly.

---

[16] See *Lettres de Charles VIII*, IV, 36–39.
[17] After they were set in type, I discovered that the sentences quoted above do not occur in some copies (presumably the first printing) of this edition. Evidently they were inserted in a subsequent printing, still bearing the year 1879 however. The autograph letters of the Julian Marshall collection were sold at auction by Sotheby and Co. on 26 June 1884. The catalogue published for that occasion (*Catalogue of the Valuable Collection of Autograph Letters, Chiefly from or Relating to Eminent Musical Composers . . . Formed by Julian Marshall*) does not specifically list this letter. It may have been part of an odd lot, such as item 186: "Kings of France—ten docs. signed. Sold to Mr. Barker for 5 s." (I am grateful to Mr. R. A. Slade of the British Museum for this information.) Sotheby, in a communication of 9 April 1963, informs me that the firm has no record of the letter or its purchaser.

The unsubstantiated inference that Charles VIII reclaimed the composer, as well as the typographical error in the king's death-date (actually 1498), were eliminated in later editions. In their place the second edition (1904) puts the following: ". . . for that of Lorenzo de' Medici; he was at Milan till June, 1474, and after some years in the service of the Duke of Mantua, entered (about 1491) that of Philip, Duke of Austria and sovereign of the Netherlands . . ." Thus Agricola's stay in France is placed *before* his service in Milan, a chronological absurdity that is recognized by Gustave Reese in *Music in the Renaissance*.[18]

Although there are additional mis-statements in the revision—for example, evidence that Agricola actually served at Mantua is lacking, and his entry in the Netherlands court chapel took place in 1500—Sterndale Bennett's original statement was substantially correct. Yet Paul Müller's article in *Die Musik in Geschichte und Gegenwart*, the most complete biography of Agricola yet published, makes no mention of the letter or of the composer's connection with the court of France. Edward R. Lerner, in his unpublished dissertation on *The Sacred Music of Alexander Agricola* (Yale University 1958), page 28, cites the statement in *Grove's Dictionary* and laments the "loss" of Charles VIII's letter. Lerner does not refer to it in his published article on *The 'German' Works of Alexander Agricola*, in: *The Musical Quarterly*, XLVI (1960), 56, although there he treats the composer's biography in considerable detail.

At the court of Charles VIII Agricola must have served under the elderly and revered chapel-master, Johannes Ockeghem, whose death took place around 1495. On purely musical grounds Otto Gombosi, in his dissertation on the music of Obrecht, postulates a link between the work of Ockeghem and Agricola.[19] Gombosi cites Agricola as the most striking example of the "school" of Ockeghem, singling him out as a principal agent in transforming Ockeghem's rhapsodic linear polyphony into a system of ornamental motives. Agricola, in Gombosi's view, represents the increasingly rational approach of his generation as against Ockeghem's "irrational" procedures, yet one that is firmly rooted in the linear impulse that characterizes Ockeghem's style. Gombosi's insight is confirmed by the discovery that the two musicians were associates in the French royal chapel.

To be sure, the influence of Ockeghem on Agricola must antedate the latter's service in the royal chapel, as Agricola was already about 40 years of age at that time. But this influence must have received telling reinforcement through personal contact. The significance of Guillaume

[18] Gustave Reese, *Music in the Renaissance* (New York 1954), p. 208, fn. 113.
[19] Otto Gombosi, *Jacob Obrecht, eine stilkritische Studie* (Leipzig 1925), p. 12.

Crétin's *Déploration* on the death of Ockeghem deserves reëxamination in this light. Crétin calls on many composers—"Agricola, Verbonnet, Prioris, Josquin Desprez, Gaspar, Brumel, Compère"—to compose a lament for their "maistre et bon père." [20] It has been assumed that Ockeghem could not literally have been the "master" or teacher of all these musicians. However, it is noteworthy that Agricola's name heads the list. Crétin may have considered them all to be disciples or colleagues of Ockeghem, at least in a broad sense. Prioris and Compère served at the French court, and Brumel is traced at Chartres in 1483. [21]

Agricola is also linked with Ockeghem by a number of works for which he has chosen a composition of Ockeghem as model. The practice of borrowing from another composer's work was common in the Renaissance, and was generally considered an act of homage. In his bergerette *Je n'ay deuil* Agricola extracts a motive from the bass of a similarly titled rondeau by Ockeghem, developing it into an intricately textured imitative composition. [22] A setting of *Fors seulement* ascribed to "Jo. Agricola" in St. Gall, Stiftsbibliothek MS 461 is probably by Alexander. It reveals a similar transformation, incorporating the entire superius of Ockeghem's famous piece as a bass. [23] Agricola's four settings of *D'ung aultre amer*, all based on a simple, elegant rondeau by Ockeghem, provide a virtual text-book of *cantus firmus* and paraphrase techniques. [24]

In these compositions, as in his work generally, Agricola's concentration on detail, especially the interplay of rhythmic motives, prevents his polyphonic lines from achieving the soaring continuity that is so striking in Ockeghem's music. Nevertheless, Agricola's style is rooted in the polyphonic ideal of Ockeghem. Despite Agricola's early residence in Italy and his later return to the very hub of Renaissance civilization, the fruits of which were a handful of frottole and canti carnascialeschi among his works, the influence of the lucid harmonic idiom of Italian music is

[20] See Reese, MR, p. 137. The entire poem by Crétin, which names many other musicians of the royal chapel, is discussed in Michel Brenet, *Jean de Ockeghem*, in: *Musique et musiciens de la vieille France* (Paris 1911), p. 53.

[21] Reese, MR, pp. 223, 260, 263f.

[22] Ockeghem's setting is published in August Wilhelm Ambros, *Geschichte der Musik*, ed. Otto Kade, V (Leipzig 1887), 10. The setting by Agricola is found in Ottaviano de' Petrucci, *Harmonice musices Odhecaton A*, ed. Helen Hewitt & Isabel Pope (Cambridge, Mass. 1942), p. 302. Concerning the sources and original form of Ockeghem's rondeau, see my study, *The Chanson Albums of Marguerite of Austria*, in: *Annales musicologiques*, VI (1963), 167, 203, 211.

[23] Both settings are published in *Ein altes Spielbuch: Liber Fridolini Sichery*, ed. F. J. Giesbert (Mainz 1936), I, 2 and 18.

[24] Ockeghem's piece and three settings by Agricola are published in *Van Ockeghem tot Sweelinck*, ed. Albert Smijers (Amsterdam 1953-), Fasc. 1, no. 3, and Fasc. 4, nos. 27-29. A fourth setting by Agricola is cited in Howard Mayer Brown, *Music in the French Secular Theater, 1400-1550* (Cambridge, Mass. 1963), p. 209.

rarely perceptible in his music to non-Italian texts. He is far closer to Pierre de la Rue, whose entire career unfolded in the North, than he is to the Netherlanders active in Italy—Obrecht, Brumel, Compère, Gaspar, Martini, Josquin—in whose music appear such traits as functional harmonic basses, symmetrically balanced phrase-structures, and a humanistic approach to textual expression, all associated with the music written in Italy at the end of the 15th century. The experience of his service under Ockeghem must have left a profound imprint on Agricola's development, helping to counteract the pervasive Italian currents to which Agricola also had been exposed, but to which he never completely succumbed.

ON TEXT FORMS
FROM CICONIA TO DUFAY

by NINO PIRROTTA

AT THE TIME of Dufay's emergence as a composer the larger *formes fixes* of the French Ars nova were giving way to the rondeau and, to a much lesser extent, to a monostrophic type of virelai.[1] The change has to do with the trend toward a more pointed and concise style but also reflects a new relationship between poetry and music. During the previous phase ballades and virelais, whether or not set to music, had been ruled by literary standards determining the number of strophes and their organization. Repetition of similar patterns inside the strophes, originally dictated by musical exigencies, had lost much of its force in the expansion of musical expression. The shift to the rondeau and to a simpler style of music revitalized a crisper, more closely knit play of repetitions, while the shorter span placed the texts into a category of little literary pretense but that of giving occasion to music.

If we turn to settings of Italian texts during the early 15th century, we find a corresponding cultivation of the rondeau, limited, however, to a small number of examples; the ballata, usually monostrophic, maintains the predominance it had enjoyed during the preceding time. There was less need in Italy for a more specifically musical form, since already from the beginning of the 14th century a *poesia per musica* had clearly distinguished itself from the poems of purely literary significance.[2] In addition, Italian polyphonic settings of Dufay's time tend to be less compact and economically organized than their French counterparts, owing partially to the fact that most Italian composers were now provincial, old-fashioned masters, and also to the growing impact exerted on polyphony by the style of performance of some more popular type of music. The tendency toward syllabic declamation is more than counterbalanced by a prominent pattern of insistent repetition, of short broken phrases

---

[1] Gustave Reese, *Music in the Renaissance* (New York 1954), pp. 14-15.
[2] To fit the needs of the musician, for instance, ballate have usually only one strophe when their content suggests expanded melodic effusion, several strophes when a lighter tone prompts a more economical style.

673

of text or of single words, building up tension and pathos before the complete line is delivered.[3] As a result the scope of the musical setting is enlarged rather than narrowed.

Considering the virelai—for all practical purposes the formal equivalent of the ballata—Gustave Reese has remarked that it is often found in the sources "with only one set of words for section 1 and two sets for section 2,"[4] that is, with the omission of the so-called *tierce*, the residuum of text to be sung to the music of section 1. The omission may well be the fault of copyists, but it is also possible that it was encouraged by a feeling that simple repetition of the refrain after *ouvert* and *clos*, reducing the over-all musical form from *A b b a A* to *A b b A*,[5] provided a perfectly satisfactory result, at least from the point of view of music. That composers, too, may have shared this feeling is indicated by a piece in the manuscript Padua, Bibl. Universitaria 1115, *Aler m' en veus en strangne partie*. Neither Heinrich Besseler, who tentatively suggested Ciconia's authorship,[6] nor Suzanne Clercx, who confirmed it,[7] has paid attention to a detail in the virelai scheme: its refrain, AABBAAB,[8] and paired *ouvert* and *clos*, cbc'b cbc'b, are not followed by a regular *tierce*, but by a single line, a. For it the composer provided a musical phrase related to the beginning of the refrain and evidently meant to replace the intentionally omitted *tierce*.[9]

Ciconia's virelai, as we can reconstruct it through its religious contrafactum,[10] is an example of the master's predilection for free imitation—a device that also characterizes, and to a certain extent singles out in his own generation, Hugo de Lantins.[11] That Hugo, a native, like Ciconia, of the diocese of Liège, followed him on the path to the Venetian terri-

---

[3] See Ciconia's *Lizadra dona* and *O rosa bella* in Suzanne Clercx, *Johannes Ciconia* (Brussels 1960), II, 73–77, and the anonymous *Mercè, mercè, o morte*, in: *Italian Ars-Nova Music*, ed. F. Ghisi, in: *Musica disciplina*, suppl. to Vol. I (1946–47), 17–18.

[4] *Op. cit.*, p. 14.

[5] Here and henceforth italics will be used for musical schemes, each letter corresponding to a section of music, roman type for metrical schemes, each letter indicating a different rhyme; in both cases capital letters indicate refrains.

[6] Heinrich Besseler, *Studien zur Musik des Mittelalters: 1. Neue Quellen*, in: *Archiv für Musikwissenschaft*, VII (1925), 231; the Padua fragment contains only one part, ascribed to a "Johannes . . ."

[7] The music in the Padua fragment is identical to the upper voice of Ciconia's two-voice motet *O beatum incendium* in the MS Bologna, Bibl. G. Martini, Q 15 (former Liceo Musicale 37); see Clercx, *Johannes Ciconia*, I, 52, 56–57.

[8] See fn. 5.

[9] Clercx, *Johannes Ciconia*, II, 85–87; cf. measures 106–08 and 4–6. The same passage recurs, a unifying device, at measures 26–28, 64–66, 77–79.

[10] The motet (Clercx, *op. cit.*, II, 151–53) provides 12 lines of new text for each section, ignoring the virelai form; yet it preserves, quite unnecessarily, a repeat sign at the end of section 2 (*ibid.*, 33). Ciconia probably had no part in the arrangement.

[11] Charles Van den Borren, *Hugo et Arnold de Lantins*, in: *Annales de la Fédération archéologique et historique de Belgique*, XXIX (1932), 263–72; Wolfgang

tory is generally assumed on the ground that most of his works are found in the manuscript Oxford, Bodleian Library, Canonici misc. 213, which is said to come from Venice or its vicinity;[12] the assumption is confirmed by the dialectal flavor of the Italian texts he set to music, particularly by *Per amor de costei*, a ballata.[13]

Double final repetition of section 1 of music is consistently avoided in Hugo's three existing ballate; his procedure, however, is not to omit the *volta*, the equivalent of the French *tierce*, but to write new music for it. Suggestions to do so may have come from the text in the case of *Tra quante regione*, where symmetry between *ripresa* and *volta* is more apparent than real.[14] Yet the avoidance of repetition is carried even farther in the other two ballate. *Per amor de costei*, besides having new music for the *volta*, has through-composed *piedi* (section 2), lacking, that is, the usual repetition of the music of the first *piede* to the words of the second. The same result is obtained in *Io sum tuo servo* by simply suppressing the text of the second *piede*.[15]

Only one of Hugo's Italian pieces, *Mirar non posso*,[16] is a rondeau. It is impossible to decide if it is regular, since no residuum of text is preserved besides its four-line refrain. However, Hugo's Italian contemporaries, while usually fastidiously observant of the ballata form,[17] were not too orthodox in their handling of the rondeau; they favored shorter refrains than the four-line type prevailing among the French,[18] and indulged, by contrast, in some peculiar amplification handed down to them by 14th-century theorists.[19] Thus, Bartholomeo Brolo's *Vivere*

Rehm, *Lantins*, in: MGG, VIII (1960), 200–02. Hugo's secular works are published in *Pièces polyphoniques profanes de provenance liégeoise*, ed. Ch. Van den Borren (Brussels 1950).

[12] Gilbert Reaney, *The MS Oxford, Bodleian Library, Canonici misc. 213*, in: *Musica disciplina*, IX (1955), 73–104, particularly 75.

[13] *Pièces polyphoniques*, pp. 61–62. The scribe altered the last word of line 8 into "piedi"; the original "pei," which he must have judged too dialectal, is needed for the sake of the rhyme with lines 1 and 2. The metrical scheme is AA bcbc ca AA. Hugo also wrote a motet for Francesco Foscari, doge of Venice from 1423.

[14] *Ibid.*, pp. 66–69; metrical scheme to be corrected as ABB cdecde eaa ABB. The asymmetry derives from the fact that A is a proparoxytone rhyme, "mòbele"; thus lines containing 12 syllables are differently placed in *ripresa* and *volta*.

[15] *Ibid.*, pp. 64–65; correct metrical scheme: AA bc.. ca AA, or AA bcc. .a AA (dots represent the missing lines).

[16] *Ibid.*, p. 63; correct metrical scheme: ABBA.

[17] Free handling of the ballata is not without Italian precedents, however. Three late anonymous pieces, possibly all by the same poet and composer (not to mention an early example by Donato da Firenze), provide the *volta* with new music; see Nos. 2, 28, and 298 in the list of ballate of Kurt von Fischer, *Studien zur italienischen Musik des Trecento* (Bern 1956). In each case the poem is not really a ballata, but is skillfully made into one; the *ripresa* of *Omè* (No. 298), for instance, consists of this one word, borrowed from the first line of the first *piede*: "Omè, s'io gli omei sol io gli piango."

[18] Reese, MR, pp. 14–15.

[19] Antonio da Tempo, *Delle rime volgari*, ed. G. Grion (Bologna 1869), pp. 134–

et recte reminiscere [20] has a normal scheme, with a three-line refrain, up to line 8, after which recapitulation of the refrain is delayed by three additional lines. Even more irregular, the anonymous *Bianca nel negro aquilino aspecto*,[21] with a four-line refrain, follows the expected pattern up to line 10, where a new rhyme is introduced, leading to four extra lines with irregular rhymes.

Hugo's *Tra quante regione* is addressed to Cleophe Malatesta, wife of the despot of Morea and prince of Sparta, Theodore Paleologue, and the same lady for whom Dufay composed his motet *Vasilissa ergo gaude*.[22] The latter item has been taken as evidence that Dufay was already in Italy in 1420.[23] It may be observed, however, that Cleophe's brother, Pandolfo Malatesta of Pesaro, was appointed on 10 October 1418 as bishop of Coutances in Normandy, and is reported to have taken possession of his see soon after his appointment.[24] The possibility then exists that he may have met Dufay during his short stay in Normandy, or, more likely, in Paris, where he must have stopped in his trips to and from Coutances, and where we would expect to find a young cleric, like Dufay, eager to get a degree.[25] If such a connection had been established, there would be no need to assume that Dufay was in Italy at the time of Cleophe's engagement, or in 1423, when another nuptial event prompted him to compose *Resveillez vous*—a French ballade—for Cleophe's second brother, Carlo, and Vittoria Colonna, niece of Pope Martin V.[26] Nor would the dates "1425 adì 12 lujo" and "1426," appended respectively to *Je me complains piteusement*, a ballade, and

---

39, gives examples of Italian rondeaux all with refrains of 2 or 3 lines, and all having a second *additamentum:* e.g. *Mille mercedi chiero*, scheme AB aAab aAab, without indication of a final repetition of the refrain. Similar examples are given by Gidino da Sommacampagna, *Trattato dei ritmi volgari*, ed. G. B. Giuliari (Bologna 1870), pp. 124–32, where the "rotundelli" are described as consisting of *ripresa* (refrain), *seconda parte*, and *terza parte*.

[20] *Polyphonia sacra*, ed. Ch. Van den Borren (London 1932), pp. 293–94; correct metrical scheme: ABA aAaba aba ABA.

[21] MS Oxford, Bodleian Library, Canonici misc. 213, fol. 127; metrical scheme: ABBA abABac cdda ABBA.

[22] G. Dufay, *Opera Omnia*, ed. G. de Van, II (Rome 1948), 1–4.

[23] Heinrich Besseler, *Neue Dokumente zum Leben und Schaffen Dufays*, in: *Archiv für Musikwissenschaft*, IX (1952), 162.

[24] C. Eubel, *Hierarchia catholica medii aevi*, I (Münster 1913), 205; Lecanu, *Histoire du diocèse de Coutances et Avranches*, I (Coutances 1877), 380–81; R. Toustain de Billy, *Histoire ecclésiastique du diocèse de Coutances*, II (Rouen 1880), 209. Some confusion has arisen from taking Pandolfo's title, "episcopus constantiensis," as indicating Constance in Switzerland; no precise dates are given for his sojourn in Normandy.

[25] See André Pirro's review of Van den Borren's book on Dufay in *Revue musicale*, VII (1926), 321–22.

[26] Besseler, *Dokumente*, pp. 162–63.

Adieu ces bons vins de Lannoy, a rondeau,[27] imply that he was then in Italy.

One reason we may have to try to narrow down the length of Dufay's Italian sojourn is that only eight out of about ten times as many secular pieces preserved under his name have Italian texts; this is a surprisingly low number for an assumed span of about 15 years, mainly if these years included the time when a beginner should have been most eager to please and make friends.

None of the eight texts can be related to a historical or datable event. Such a possibility exists only for a ninth, nonsecular text, the sonnet in honor of St. Andrew, which provided words for triplum and motetus of *Apostolo glorioso*, a motet probably intended for the consecration in 1426 of a church of St. Andrew in Patras, restored by Pandolfo Malatesta, now archbishop of that town.[28] It seems, however, too farfetched that the piece might have been commissioned from Patras of a musician still in France. Meanwhile, another university town, Bologna, may have attracted Dufay; to place in 1426 or 1427 the beginning of his Italian career agrees with the already mentioned farewell to "the good wines of Lannoy," and with a benefit obtained about this time for Dufay by cardinal Louis Aleman, governor of Bologna.[29]

The possibility exists, of course, that Dufay had stayed for some time with one or the other member of the Malatesta family. Yet the Malatestas, often prominent in Italian politics, seldom attained the wealth and power needed to support a brilliant court with musicians who, like Dufay, were not hired men, but clerics pursuing a career not entirely dependent on their musical ability.[30] Dufay may have been a member of Pandolfo's episcopal retinue; but Pandolfo must soon have appeared too poor a chance to be taken as a patron.[31] Finally, even the early date of the motet

---

[27] MS Oxford, Bodleian Library, Canonici misc. 213, fols. 18 and 140.

[28] Besseler, *Dokumente*, pp. 163–65; the motet is in Dufay, *Opera Omnia*, II, 11–16. That the two texts (*ibid.*, XIII) belong to a sonnet is my conjecture; they consist of respectively 8 and 6 eleven-syllable lines, with the order of rhymes normally expected in a sonnet.

[29] This suggestion is not to be interpreted as a criticism of Besseler's invaluable contributions on Dufay, but as a help for the clarification of some details of his reconstruction. A stay in Paris, or at least contacts with that city, in the years up to 1426–27 would better explain Dufay's friendship with Robert Auclou as well as his exposure to English music.

[30] They were too many and their possessions—actually vicarages on Church possessions—too small; thus they traditionally employed themselves as *condottieri*. At the time under consideration, the branch of Rimini was represented by Carlo and Pandolfo, both very much in evidence during the preceding period, now in decline, that of Pesaro by their cousin Malatesta, father of Pandolfo, Carlo, Galeazzo, and Cleophe.

[31] Born c. 1390, he was probably a canon in Bologna when Alexander V and John XXIII held court there; in 1416 he was appointed as a bishop to Brescia (over

Vasilissa is questionable. Besseler's reason for placing it in 1420 is that Theodore Paleologue is only indirectly mentioned, suggesting a distant fiancé rather than an imperial husband; [32] but the argument of medieval etiquette holds only if we conceive the motet as an official piece to be performed at a public ceremony, of which evidence is lacking for this as well as for most existing motets.[33] In its stead, Hugo de Lantins's ballata congratulating Sparta for holding Cleophe and making no hint to Theodore shows that the motet *Vasilissa* might have been offered to Cleophe without breach of etiquette at any time—for instance, on Pandolfo's arrival in Patras, or even later.[34]

Of Dufay's Italian texts, only one has, under the superficial dialectal patina possibly derived from the copyists, a strong residuum of irreducible dialectal forms. This is *Donna gentil e bella*, in the Mellon Chansonnier, where "fortuna," "una," and "luna" rhyme with "corona" and "rasona"; and where the verb "stago," or "stazo," cannot be reduced to any accepted tense of "stare" without destroying the rhythm of the line. But it is difficult to say to which northern dialect the text must be related. *Invidia nimica*, in spite of a Petrarchesque incipit, has little literary pretense.[35] At the other end of the spectrum, besides Petrarch's *Vergine bella*, *Passato è il tempo omai* is also reminiscent of Petrarch in tone and general situation.

From a formal point of view, *Vergene bella*, set to a strophe of a canzone, is a unique case. Its 13 lines contain some element of repetition, but Dufay's music is through-composed and divides only into two main sections corresponding to the *frons* and *syrima*.[36] This would have made possible, at least in theory, not only the repetition of the music for any

which his older namesake ruled precariously), in 1418 to Coutances, and on 10 May 1424, to Patras (Eubel, *Hierarchia*, I, 147, 205, 394); he was certainly there in 1426. Increasing hostility on the part of Constantine and Theodore Paleologue, despots of respectively Achaea and Morea, induced him to seek help in Venice in 1428 and 1429. The financial help he obtained in 1430 in Rome came when Patras had already been conquered by Constantine Paleologue; a rescue expedition was unsuccessful. Pandolfo died, a bishop *in partibus*, in 1441. See E. Gerland, *Neue Quellen zur Geschichte des lateinischen Erzbistum Patras* (Leipzig 1903), pp. 64–68.

[32] Besseler, *Dokumente*, p. 161.

[33] More on this point and on the status of musicians is contained in a paper of mine, read at the 1963 meeting of the American Musicological Society in Seattle, not yet ready for publication.

[34] 1426 or later would suit better than 1420 the rhythmic and stylistic features of *Vasilissa*. Cleophe is reported to have come back from Greece with Pandolfo and to have died in Pesaro in 1433.

[35] In order to obtain a correct number of syllables for each line, one is frequently obliged to apply quite unusual diaereses, e.g. in the first two lines: "Invidïa nimica / Di ciascun virtüoso."

[36] In Dante's terminology, the first and second part of the *stanza*.

of the following strophes, but also the inclusion of the final *commiato*, applying to it section 2 of the music.[37]

Four pieces are ballate: *Passato è il tempo*, with a four-line *ripresa*, has the largest frame; both *L'alta belleza tua* and *La dolce vista* have a two-line *ripresa* but different arrangement of their strophes; *Invidia nimica*, a satirical text, is the only one to have more than one strophe, namely three.[38] In the music none of the formal licenses adopted by Lantins is present, nor is the Italian fashion of repetitive delivery of the text, to which Lantins's *ballate*, as well as his Italian *rondeau*, paid tribute.

Only *Donna gentil e bella* is a regular rondeau, with a four-line refrain. Two other pieces, listed as rondeaux by Besseler [39] and as ballate by Gilbert Reaney,[40] properly belong to neither form. *Dona, i ardenti rai* has four lines set to music, and a *signum congruentiae* at the end of the second that would seem to indicate a rondeau; however, the only possible solution for the residuum of text—a similar group of four lines, plus a cue to the repetition from the beginning—is to have the complete setting repeated and then resumed again with the original lines:

Dona, i ardenti rai d' i vostri ochi suavi	] *A*
che de mi tien la chiavi [41] me infiama el pecto a vera gentileza.	] *B*
Le fiame ardente ch' ài ne li ochi, nel bel fronte	] *a*
son le cason impronte ch' el cor me acese a seguir tant' alteza.	] *b*
Dona, etc.	] *AB*

Again four lines of *Quel fronte signorile* (composed, according to the source, in Rome) [42] are given with the music, although here the *signum congruentiae* is missing, and again a similar group of four lines, plus a cue for recapitulation, are given as residuum. The disturbing and unsatisfactory final cadence on G in a piece clearly set in a C mode, prevents an interpretation similar to that given for the preceding piece (see Ex. 1).

[37] Measures 40 to the end in G. Dufay, *Zwölf geistliche und weltliche Werke*, ed. H. Besseler (Wolfenbüttel 1932), pp. 7–10. The *commiato* has the metric structure of the *syrima* of the preceding strophes.

[38] All in the Oxford MS, with the exception of *La dolce vista*, a unicum in the MS Vatican, Urb. lat. 1411.

[39] MGG, III, 902.

[40] Reaney, *MS Oxford*, p. 94.

[41] MS: "la chiave," again to be restored to a less correct form for the sake of the rhyme.

[42] Reaney, *MS Oxford*, p. 94.

Ex. 1 *Quel fronte signorile,* Dufay (from *O*)

ran - do il suo bel vi - so.

ran - do il suo bel vi - - - so.

I ochi trapassa tuti d[e] i altri el viso
con si dolce armonia
che i cor nostri s' envia
pian piano in suso, i vanno in paradiso
Quel, etc.

In my opinion, the G cadence is only an *ouvert;* the verbal cue leads to a
final recapitulation of only the first line ending with a perfectly plausible
cadence on C. Dufay's own French contrafactum of the piece, *Craindre
ne vueil,* a regular rondeau with the same music expanded to a final conclusion on C (Ex. 2), supports this interpretation.[43]

Ex. 2   Final line of *Craindre ne vueil,* Dufay (from *O* and *Esc*)

Le cuer de moy tant que ie se - ray vis

[43] The piece, with the acrostic "Caterine Dufay," is transposed a fifth above in
Zwölf Werke, p. 18.

Although Dufay's style is rather remote from any popular kind of Italian music, the two settings just mentioned are, to my knowledge, the first polyphonic examples of a lighter poetic form which had come particularly into fashion at the very beginning of the 15th century. The reason we must regard such canzonette [44] by poets like Simone Serdini, alias Saviozzo, and Leonardo Giustinian as a more popular, or less artful, genre is that they consist of a large number of strophes and lend themselves only to fast recitation, either monophonic or in simple polyphony. Usually each strophe begins with a line having the same rhyme as the last of the preceding strophe, a procedure certainly originated as a help to the popular singer to remember the correct sequence of strophes. In many cases the poem ends with an isolated line,[45] for which the singer, as in the suggested interpretation of *Quel fronte signorile*, would have had to repeat the first phrase of music.

A more popular type of poem does not imply a similar attitude of the music. Art polyphonists set only a couple of such strophes at a time, or even selected individual verses, not necessarily the initial ones, from much longer poems. Toward the middle of the century the trend prevailing among composers of polyphony, now without exception non-Italian, was to write through-composed music. A good example is Dunstable's—or Bedingham's—*O rosa bella*,[46] which suggested the topic of the present note. As observed by Bukofzer, and pointed out to me by Gustave Reese, this new setting of a text already used by Ciconia disregards the ballata form and its internal repetitions;[47] a half cadence concludes section 1, where the normal formal procedure would have had the end of the piece; no residuum of text is given for section 2. The piece must therefore be considered through-composed. In the changing balance between the forces of musical functionalism and inertia—that is, tradition—the development of polyphonic music once again points away from the direction suggested by the poetic texts it uses.

[44] The tendency among modern writers to label such poems as *sirventesi* has little support in the sources, where the most common term is "canzone" or "canzonetta."

[45] E.g. Nos. III, VI, and VII in G. Ferraro, *Alcune poesie inedite del Saviozzo, etc.* (Bologna 1879).

[46] Conflicting attributions are given respectively by the MSS Vatican, Urb. lat. 1411; and Porto, Bibl. Municipal, 714. I consider the latter most authoritative, but the possibility exists that a third Englishman was the real composer.

[47] See J. Dunstable, *Complete Works*, ed. M. F. Bukofzer (London 1953), p. 186; I do not agree with Bukofzer on the reliability of the MS Vatican, Urb. lat. 1411.

THE RECENTLY DISCOVERED
COMPLETE COPY OF A. ANTICO'S
FROTTOLE INTABULATE (1517)

by DRAGAN PLAMENAC

MONG THE BASIC LANDMARKS of early instrumental
music A. Antico's *Frottole intabulate da sonare organi, Libro
primo* [1] holds a distinguished and well-defined place. The
volume has become known as the oldest printed source of Italian organ
music and—if we take into account the tablatures in Codex 117 of the
Biblioteca Comunale at Faenza, which date from about a century earlier
—the second-oldest unified collection of compositions for the keyboard
by Italian composers that has come down to us. For a long time the
existence of the Antico print remained unknown to musicological literature. Even Johannes Wolf failed to mention it in his list of early keyboard sources printed in Volume II of his *Handbuch der Notationskunde*
(1919); [2] and as late as 1939 Fausto Torrefranca persisted in calling the
Recercari Motetti Canzoni by Marco Antonio Cavazzoni (1523) the
oldest printed collection of Italian organ music.[3]

This state of affairs was primarily due to the fact that the print had
apparently survived in one single copy preserved in a private library far
from the mainstreams of musical and musicological activity: the library
of the Polesini family in the little coastal town of Parenzo (now: Poreč)
on the Istrian peninsula. But if the rare print had until quite recently
eluded many a learned scholar it had been noted with justifiable local
pride by several 19th-century writers hailing from Antico's native
region.[4] One of the earliest publications of musicological character in
which Antico's print is found mentioned was André Pirro's little volume
entitled *Les Clavecinistes* (1924). On page 33 of this volume we even
find a facsimile of the title page of Antico's print but look in vain for

---

[1] A *Libro secondo*, if it ever existed, has not been preserved.
[2] Page 272ff.
[3] *Il Segreto del quattrocento* (Milan 1939), p. 215.
[4] The titles of these publications may be found in Knud Jeppesen's work cited
below, Vol. I, pp. 47–48. The Polesini copy of the Antico print was transferred to
Milan after the last war with the library of its owners.

information concerning its whereabouts. It was only during the last war that Antico's collection received adequate attention in Knud Jeppesen's important work on Italian organ music of the early 16th century.[5]

As the title indicates, the collection contains keyboard paraphrases of polyphonic vocal frottole, which experienced a period of enormous popularity at that time. It was most probably designed to compete for public favor with collections of similar material adapted for another musical medium—a single voice with lute accompaniment—such as Ottaviano Petrucci, Antico's great Venetian rival, had published some years earlier.[6] The authors of the vocal compositions that furnished models for Antico's keyboard transcriptions were predominantly the two foremost writers of frottole, Bartolomeo Tromboncino and Marco (Marchetto) Cara. In the *Frottole intabulate* these authors are identified by the initials of their names added to the text incipits of the vocal originals at the beginning of the single pieces. The vocal versions of the compositions involved are often found in other collections published by Antico during the same period. Jeppesen gives on pages 52–53 an index of the 26 pieces included in the keyboard collection, accompanied by a tabulation of sources, printed and manuscript, that contain the vocal versions on which the organ paraphrases were based.[7] The last two pieces in the Polesini copy are incomplete, owing to the fact that folio 37 (K1) is missing. As a consequence, No. 25 (*Hor che l ciel e la terra*) lacks the final portion and No. 26 (*Cantai mentre nel core*) the initial portion of the music. No. 25 is marked at the beginning with the initials "B.T." and the attribution to Tromboncino is confirmed by the source that contains the vocal model, in this case the *Frottole Libro secondo*

---

[5] *Die italienische Orgelmusik am Anfang des Cinquecento* (Copenhagen 1943). A second revised and greatly enlarged edition in two volumes appeared in 1961. Volume I includes on pp. 47–75 a discussion of Antico's collection and on pp. 3*–25* (at the end of the volume) six selected keyboard pieces with their vocal models. In the present paper, reference is always made to the second edition of Jeppesen's work.

[6] Franciscus Bossinensis, *Tenori e contrabassi intabulati*, Book I (1509) and II (1511).

[7] One of these collections, the *Canzoni sonetti strambotti et frottole, Libro tertio*, was published in modern transcription in 1941 by Alfred Einstein, as Volume IV of the "Smith College Music Archives" series. Einstein chose for his transcription an edition of the book that he termed the "second" (dated 27 February 1518) but that really was the third (listed in RISM I under 1518). He was not aware of the fact that an older edition of the same book, dated 1513, had been preserved in the library of the late Henry Prunières. Jeppesen, on page 52 of his work, likewise failed to take notice of the 1513 edition of Antico's "Third book." This edition is found repeatedly cited in André Pirro, *Histoire de la musique de la fin du XIVe siècle à la fin du XVIe* (Paris 1940), pp. 159, 161, 162, 164, 165. The copy that was formerly in the Prunières collection is owned at present by Mme. de Chambure (G. Thibault) in Paris and is listed in RISM I under 1513^1.

(RISM I, under [1516][2]). Since the initial portion of No. 26 is absent from the Polesini copy, however, the name of the composer could only be ascertained by consulting the *Libro tertio*, the source that includes the original vocal version. Indeed, the composition is found there with an ascription to "Marcheto carra," and this suggested that in a complete copy of the *Frottole intabulate* it would be marked with the initials "M.C."[8]

The complete copy of Antico's collection for the keyboard that has recently come to the surface proved this assumption to be correct. The copy has been preserved in the Knihovna Josefa Dobrovského (Josef Dobrovský Library) in Prague (library mark: Gg. 19).[9] In my report of a visit to Eastern European libraries in the summer of 1961,[10] I already had an opportunity to point to this newly recovered source. The collection that shelters it was known before its nationalization after the last war as the library of the counts Nostitz. It is still housed in the beautiful Nostitz palace in old Prague's Maltese Square, together with the family archives and a valuable gallery of paintings; it is now being administered by the National Museum. The title page of the copy, as will be apparent from the reproduction accompanying this article (Pl. 23b), bears the signature "Otto Gf Nostitz mp.," which testifies to the fact that the volume has been kept in the Nostitz library for at least three centuries. The counts Nostitz became prominent in Bohemia during the 17th century after members of an older generation had settled there a century earlier. The outstanding members of the family at this period were the brothers Otto and Jan Hartwig. Otto, the original owner of the Antico print, was made in 1631 a member of the high nobility in the kingdom of Bohemia and died in 1664 as a privy councillor. His brother Jan Hartwig built the palace in Prague in which the library is housed and died as lord chancellor of the realm in 1683. One of the latter's descendants built in 1781 at his expense the "Theatre of the Estates" in Prague, in which Mozart's *Don Giovanni* received its memorable first performance in 1787. Toward the end of the 18th century the Nostitz mansion was a meeting place of the foremost Czech historians, philologists, and literary scholars. Among them was Josef Dobrovský (1753–1829), one of the founders of Slavic philology, who was employed in those years as an in-

---

[8] Cf. Jeppesen, *Orgelmusik*, p. 53, last column; also, Einstein's modern edition of the *Libro tertio*, pp. XVI, 61.

[9] The Prague copy is bound together in one volume with another rare 16th-century print, the *Canzoni frottole et capitoli da diversi eccellentissimi musici . . . Libro secondo de la Croce*, published by Val. Dorich in Rome, 16 September 1531, of which only a single copy in the Bologna Conservatory library had previously been known. Cf. RISM I, under 1531[4].

[10] See *Notes*, XIX (1962), p. 593.

structor in the Nostitz home. Thus, in the process of eliminating the name of the former feudal owners from the library's title, the ties that existed between the scholar and man of letters and his aristocratic patrons were not disregarded.

The bizarre woodcut on the title page of the *Frottole intabulate* was bound to attract attention and comments. A rather poor reproduction of it may be found in Jeppesen's work cited above, on page 6 of Volume I. It is obvious that this facsimile could have been made only from the Polesini copy of Antico's print, since the existence of a Prague copy was unknown in 1943, at the time the reproduction was added to the first edition of Jeppesen's work. In the lower margin of the facsimile we find the text of an *impressum* giving the name of the printer and the place and date of publication. At first glance, one might take this impressum for a part of the woodcut itself. As will be noted, however, there is no such text found on the title page of the Prague copy; consequently, it is a later addition written in by hand. The scene depicted in the wood-cut shows a young man playing a harpsichord; [11] a stand with the coat-of-arms of Pope Leo X (who granted Antico a privilege for the printing of organ tablatures) is placed on top of it. Gesturing and grimacing in the background are a young woman holding a music book and a monkey perched on the harpsichord and holding a lute. Jeppesen [12] observes: "It is not impossible that this forms an allegorical allusion to Petrucci who . . . had published transcriptions of frottole for the lute with which Antico was intent on competing." I fully agree with interpreting the woodcut as an implied reference to Antico's rival, but would describe the scene in a slightly different way. Jeppesen holds that "the girl, with a music book in her right hand, is hitting with her left hand contemptu-ously at a monkey crouching on the lid of the harpsichord and playing the lute." In my opinion, neither can the expression on the girl's face be described as "contemptuous" nor does she seem to be "hitting" at the monkey. She is turning the music book supported by her right hand downward in an apparent attempt at discarding it; and the gesture of her left hand directed at the monkey is one of dismay and frustration, in full agreement with the expression on the monkey's face. It seems, then, that the two figures are depicted as having got together to perform (or having started to perform) frottole in transcriptions for solo voice with lute accompaniment in the manner applied in the Bossinensis arrange-

[11] The fact of the representation of a harpsichord on the title page of a collection "da sonare organi" shows conclusively that the term "organo" was used at that time to designate all kinds of keyboard instruments. Cf. the wording used by P. At-taingnant on the title pages of his publications intended for the keyboard.

[12] Jeppesen, *Orgelmusik*, p. 49.

ments published by Petrucci, and then being dislodged by the youth playing Antico's transcriptions for the keyboard. The girl seems to be saying to the monkey: "What's the use? Now that this fellow has invaded the field we may as well fold up and disappear."

Since the only copy of the *Frottole intabulate* known to exist before the discovery of the Prague source lacks one leaf—folio 37—it has seemed useful to round off these lines with reproductions of the two pages missing in the Polesini copy and transcriptions of the two pieces (Nos. 25 and 26) affected by the deficiency. The final portion of No. 25 and the initial portion of No. 26 have been supplied from the complete copy in Prague. Momentary inability to locate a reproduction of the vocal version of No. 25 (printed in the *Frottole Libro secondo*, RISM I, [c. 1516][2]) is responsible for the fact that the piece appears here without its vocal prototype; in the case of No. 26, however, the addition of the vocal version has been made possible by its inclusion in A. Einstein's modern edition of Antico's *Libro tertio* (No. 34, p. 61). A comparison of the keyboard transcription with its vocal model led to changing Einstein's barring in measures 1–8 and some of the added accidentals.

Fig. 1a   End of Tromboncino's *Hor che l ciel e la terra*, from A. Antico's *Frottole intabulate* (1517), fol. 37ʳ (Prague, Dobrovský Library, Gg. 19)

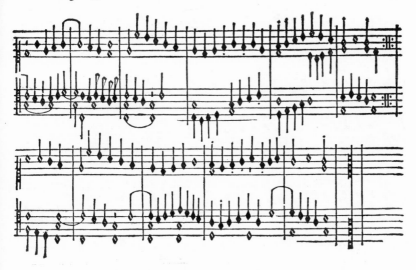

Fig. 1b   Beginning of Cara's *Cantai mentre il core*, from A. Antico's *Frottole intabulate* (1517), fol. 37ᵛ (Prague, Dobrovský Library, Gg. 19)

Ex. 1   Tromboncino, *Hor che l ciel e la terra*

Ex. 2   Cara, *Cantai mentre nel core*

Can - tai men - tre nel cor lie - to fio - ri -

[Cantai mentre nel core . . .]

[Cantai mentre nel core . . .]

[Cantai mentre nel core . . .]

(Fol. 37ᵛ)

va   De su - a - vi pen - sier   l'al - ta mia spe - ne
Hor che la man-cha o-gnor   cres - con le pe - ne

De far mi -na – za il mio do-lor e - ter - no.

KING DAVID AND HIS MUSICIANS IN SPANISH ROMANESQUE SCULPTURE

by ISABEL POPE

MONUMENTS OF ROMANESQUE architecture in Spain offer a singularly rich and varied repertory of sculptured representations of musical instruments. The representations of instruments may in general be trusted, because they possess—already—the realism that has characterized Spanish art through the centuries. One thinks immediately, of course, of the remarkable series of sculptured instruments on the *Pórtico de la Gloria* of the Cathedral of Santiago at Compostela. This portal was being planned and executed between 1168 and 1188 and therefore displays the culmination of the Spanish Romanesque style. There are earlier sculptures, however, that are of interest for the information they give concerning an earlier stage in the development of medieval instrumental types and also as a possible reflection of performance practices in the early Middle Ages. Among them are sculptured groups portraying King David with his musicians. This article will be concerned primarily with two notable examples of such groups.[1] They are to be seen on the façade above the main portal of the church of San Isidoro at Leon and on a capital at the Cathedral of Jaca in northern Aragon. These two churches were under construction during the second half of the 11th century. San Isidoro was dedicated in 1063. In this same year the cathedral at Jaca was being planned, although work probably did not begin until later. Both represent the beginnings of the Romanesque style in Spain.

Before considering the sculptures themselves a brief review of the social conditions and cultural background of Christian Spain at the midpoint of the 11th century will help to place the instruments they repre-

---

[1] The sculptures of David and musicians on the façade of the monastery church of Santa María at Ripoll (Catalonia), belonging to the later 12th century, have been so damaged by time that they can provide little sure information for the study of musical instruments. See: A. Kingsley Porter, *Romanesque Sculpture of the Pilgrimage Roads* (Boston 1923), V, Plates 562, 564, 568; Manuel Gómez Moreno, *El Arte románico español* (Madrid 1934); *Ars hispaniae* (Madrid 1948), V, 64–72.

sent in their historical perspective. At the death in 1002 of the great Almanzor, last caliph of the Omayyad dynasty in Spain, the Christian kingdoms of the North reacted vigorously. They began a rapid recovery from the series of devastating raids that Almanzor had carried out systematically against the centers of Christian power during the last years of the 10th century. The caliphate just as rapidly disintegrated; Córdoba ceased to be the political and commercial center of the Peninsula. At the same time Sancho the Great, King of Navarre (1000–1035), energetically carried forward his effort to unite northern Spain under his rule. He even endeavored to conquer the ancient kingdom of Leon, whose king was recognized as *imperator* by the other Christian kings. At the time of his death, Sancho's kingdom extended from Galicia to Catalonia. Only the king of Leon maintained his independent sway. Simultaneously Sancho initiated a policy to end Christian Spain's age-long isolation and bring it into active contact with its European neighbors.[2] He realized that the Spanish Church needed to be reformed and revitalized. To this end he invited the Benedictines of Cluny to introduce their rule in the Spanish monasteries. This reform, first carried out at the monastery of San Juan de la Peña near Jaca, spread rapidly to other monastic centers. One aspect of the Cluniac reform that had far-reaching significance was the progressive abolition of the ancient Mozarabic liturgy and the adoption, despite long and vigorous opposition, of the Roman liturgy. As a part of his revitalizing of the Church, Sancho put the great pilgrimage center of Santiago under his special protection. He carried out systematic improvements on the roads leading to Compostela. New impetus was thus given to the pilgrimage. Over these roads great throngs of pilgrims from all parts of Europe traveled to the Apostle's shrine.[3] In an effort to resettle the areas conquered from the Moslems and to stimulate the economy of the region, Sancho and his successors encouraged immigration from beyond the Pyrenees. Many French settlers, chiefly artisans and people engaged in commerce, established themselves in capitals like Jaca and Pamplona as well as in the smaller towns along the pilgrimage roads.[4]

This new orientation and all this activity stimulated the economic and social life of the region. Poor and still relatively disorganized though the area was, a new energy soon manifested itself in an artistic revival. Sancho the Great divided his domains among his three sons. At his death García, the eldest, inherited Navarre, Ferdinand, the second son, became

[2] Ramón Menéndez Pidal, *La España del Cid* (Madrid 1929), Pt. I, Cap. II.
[3] Luís Vázquez de Parga, José Ma. La Carra, Juan Uria Riu, *Las Peregrinaciones a Santiago de Compostela* (Madrid 1948), Pt. I, Cap. I.
[4] Ramón Menéndez Pidal, *Poesía juglaresca* (6th ed. Madrid 1957), pp. 256–57.

Ferdinand I of Castile, and Ramiro, the youngest, became king of the little region of northern Aragon which had remained in Christian hands.

Spanish architecture and sculpture in the 11th century displays an intermingling of influences. French Romanesque is early evident in architectural design. The sculpture displays a definite interplay of Mozarabic, Byzantine, and even antique styles with that of the new French art.

At the venerable church of San Isidoro of Leon are to be seen probably the earliest examples of sculptured musical instruments in Spain. The church proper as it stands today dates from the 12th century. It replaced, however, the church begun by Ferdinand I of Castile and finished by his widow Sancha, daughter of Alfonso V of Leon. The narthex of their church, known as the *Panteón de los Reyes*, the royal pantheon, still exists. To this church Ferdinand caused to be brought the relics of the great doctor of the Visigothic Church, St. Isidore of Seville, together with those of St. Vincent of Ávila. Here was treasured one of the most magnificent of the series of *Beatus* manuscripts. It was written and illuminated by the artist Facundo and dedicated to Ferdinand and Sancha in 1047.[5] This copy, it should be remarked, contains some of the most interesting depictions of musical instruments to be found in the whole series, which is notable for such illustrations.[6]

The royal pantheon, where Ferdinand was buried in 1065 and his widow Sancha in 1067, is embellished with sculptured capitals which archaeologists consider to be among the earliest examples of Romanesque sculpture in Spain. To approximately the same period belong the figures in high relief and statues which decorate the main portal of the church. Among them is a group representing King David and his musicians [7] (see Pl. 24a).

David is the central figure of three carved in high relief on a single block of marble. He is seated, crowned with the broad band familiar on royal heads in Byzantine mosaics. He and two of his companions are bowing fiddles (or viols). This western derivative of the Byzantine *lyra* appears in a great variety of versions in the manuscripts and sculptures of the 10th to the 12th centuries. The truly bewildering variations on

[5] Madrid, Bibl. Nac., MS B 31.

[6] Wilhelm Neuss, *Die Apokalypse des Hl. Johannes in der altspanischen und altchristlichen Bibel-Illustration* (Münster-in-Westfalen 1931): Vol. II contains photographs of the illuminations; Georgiana Goddard King, *Divagations on the Beatus*, in: *Art Studies*, VIII (1930), 1–58: illustrations from different *Beatus* manuscripts; Menéndez Pidal's *Poesía juglaresca* contains numerous fine illustrations of musical instruments drawn from different *Beatus* manuscripts.

[7] Georges Gaillard, *Les Débuts de la sculpture romane espagnole* (Paris 1938).

the basic form reflect, apparently, a period of active experimentation.[8] It is striking that each of the three instruments represented in this group is different from the others. David's fiddle is noteworthy for the exceptionally long and slender neck in proportion to the body. The pear-shaped body with typical frontal string-holder, tail-piece, and two half-moon sound holes, tapers quite abruptly to form the narrow neck which is of one piece with it. The disk shaped pegbox evidently has rear pegs. The number of strings, possibly three, cannot be definitely determined. At David's far right is a musician, seated, playing an instrument very similarly shaped but diminutive in size.[9] Again, the striking feature is the neck, long and thin in proportion to the body. Somewhat similar fiddles are to be seen in an illumination in the *Beatus* manuscript made for the Abbey of Saint-Sever at just about the time these figures were being sculptured.[10] Here the Elders of the Apocalypse are literally brandishing their fiddles in the air. Half the instruments are shown *en face;* the other half, reversed, show the backs. There are no bows. (This seems to corroborate the evidence of other representations that the western *lyra* was not always bowed.)

The other fiddle, played by the severely intent musician at David's left, is quite different in shape. It has a short rather broad neck with an angular pegbox and rear pegs. The body suggests a prow shape. The table seems to slope away on either side of the center. No sound holes are apparent. The curved bow with distinct handle is like those of the other fiddle players. The figure, not related to the group, in a circular medallion to the right plays a similarly shaped fiddle. In contrast, the companion figure in the medallion on the opposite side of the portal plays an instrument similar to David's (see Pl. 24b).

These fiddles find their beautifully developed counterpart in the sculptured instrument in the hands of King David at the Cathedral of Santiago (see Pl. 24c). This famous statue appears on the façade of the *Puerta de Las Platerías.* It belongs to a considerably earlier period than the sculptures in the *Pórtico de la Gloria.* The date is close to 1103. Here David is alone, crowned and enthroned and holding the fiddle, in a

---

[8] A drawing, labeled *lyra,* which is reproduced in Martin Gerbert's *De cantu et musica sacra* (St. Blasien 1774) from a 12th-century German manuscript (II, Tabula XXXII) may represent the paradigm. See a reproduction in H. Panum, *The Stringed Instruments of the Middle Ages* (London n.d.), Fig. 280 opposite p. 346.

[9] Note that the fingers of the player's right hand stop the strings while the bow is held in the left hand. This reversal may result, as perhaps in this case, from the exigencies of the composition. More usually it occurs when a sketch of the figure is applied face down and traced on the block to be carved.

[10] Manuscript at Paris, Bibliothèque Nationale, lat. 8878, fols. 121–22. For a photograph see Neuss, *op. cit.,* II, 126.

position of rest, in his left hand, the neck resting against his knee. In his right hand is a bow, curved, but without the handle seen on the bows at San Isidoro. The body is pear-shaped. It has the circular sound hole in the center characteristic of the Moorish *rebab* and the later European *rebec*. The body tapers to the straight, broad neck, but here the table and neck are distinct and not of one piece. The separation is marked by a horizontal ridge that indicates a difference in level between the two elements. This difference in level suggests an elementary fingerboard and at the same time provides a kind of bridge over which the strings pass. There is a clearly defined frontal string-holder from which the three strings are conducted to the tail pin. The pegbox is diamond shaped with three rear pegs. There is a nut between it and the fingerboard. The table of the instrument is edged with a narrow moulding. This instrument should also be compared with the one labeled *lyra* as reproduced by Gerbert mentioned above. The similarities and differences point up the innumerable variations which the fiddle underwent, and the interchange of the characteristic features of the Byzantine *lyra* and the Moorish *rebab* during these centuries.[11]

Let us now consider the other instruments in the ensemble at Leon. The figure standing at the extreme left is evidently playing a wind instrument. Unfortunately it has been broken off and cannot be identified. Next to the figure with the diminutive fiddle sits a musician with a harp. The small, light instrument is the typical angular harp with frontal pillar. This harp, possibly of Syrian origin, was known in Europe certainly from the 10th century.[12] It was very likely spread abroad by wandering minstrels from Britain.[13]

The most surprising instrument in the group is that held by the standing figure to the harpist's left. At first sight it might be thought to be another harp. On closer inspection it is seen to have a rear sounding board over which the strings are stretched. While the instrumentalist plucks with the fingers of the left hand, with his right he seems to be adjusting a string with a wrest applied to one of the pegs. Clearly we have to do with a type of psaltery. The instrument is held vertically against the player's chest. Its many strings—how many it is impossible to say—are stretched diagonally from the peg-board to the base. On observing the shape, that of an equilateral triangle, one is immediately reminded of the description in St. Isidore's *Etymologiae* of the *cithara*

[11] Henry George Farmer, *Studies in Oriental Musical Instruments* (London 1931), p. 56. Quotation from a 9th-century Arabic scholar: "And to them [the Byzantines] is the *lura* (lyra), and it is the *rabab* (rebec) and to it are five strings."

[12] Curt Sachs, *A History of Musical Instruments* (New York 1940), p. 263.

[13] This figure presents another example of reversal of the image.

barbarica in the shape of the Greek letter delta.[14] Isidore is here simply quoting Cassiodorus and St. Jerome, and his description of the instrument's characteristics are vague and ambiguous. Our instrument may serve to prove, however, that the frequent quotations by later medieval writers of these statements by Jerome and Isidore regarding a triangular *cithara* were not merely idle repetition. Indeed it may represent the real instrument which the strange diagrams in 10th- to 12th-century manuscripts attempt to depict. Gerbert reproduces no fewer than four of them labeled either *psalterium* or *cithara in modum delta literae.*[15]

It has been generally thought that the psaltery, both as a plucked instrument (*qanun*) and as one struck with little hammers (*santir*), was introduced into Western Europe at the time of the Crusades.[16] Curt Sachs states that the earliest examples are the two psalteries to be seen resting on the knees of two of the Elders in the *Pórtico de la Gloria* belonging to the latter part of the 12th century.[17] Here at Leon, however, we have a much earlier example. It is quite different in shape, in stringing, and in the way it is held and played. Apparently it represents a Graeco-Roman tradition rather than an Arabic importation. It is worth noting that not one of the instruments in the ensemble can be derived, despite what one would be led to expect, from the repertory of instruments brought to the peninsula by the Moslems. Like the sculpture itself, which suggests the influence of Hellenistic art, the instruments recall the Roman and Byzantine tradition which had survived from pre-Islamic times.

We may now turn our attention to an extraordinary group of sculptured instruments to be seen at the little cathedral of Jaca in northern Aragon. This church was begun by Ramiro, youngest son of Sancho the Great and half-brother of Ferdinand I of Castile and Leon. After a struggle to confirm his royal title Ramiro had established his capital at Jaca in 1054. He decided to make it also the seat of a new bishopric since the ancient bishopric of Huesca was still in Moslem hands. In 1063, the year of Ramiro's death, the new church was only just begun. Work proceeded slowly; the church was still unfinished at the close of the century.[18]

[14] Oliver Strunk, *Source Readings in Music History* (New York 1950), p. 98.

[15] Gerbert, *op. cit.,* II, *Tabulae* XXIV, No. 8; XXV, No. 10; XXIX, No. 5; XXX, No. 10.

[16] Panum, *op. cit.,* pp. 168–69 mentions the general opinion that the psaltery reached Europe through the Crusades. See, however, Farmer, *op. cit.,* p. 16: "The name and the instrument probably came through Arab Spain, and not from the East by means of the Crusades, as Fétis and Hipkins believed."

[17] Sachs, *op. cit.,* p. 292.

[18] Gaillard, *op. cit.,* pp. 87–91.

It is thus impossible to date with exactitude the exceptional sculptures which adorn this cathedral, one of the earliest Romanesque churches in Spain. Among them appears a sculptured capital that is surely the most remarkable representation in stone to be found anywhere of King David and his musicians. The capital surmounts an engaged column in the south porch. Thus the figures of David and no fewer than 11 other musicians are all grouped on the three free faces. In his book on Spanish Romanesque sculpture to which we have repeatedly referred, Georges Gaillard characterizes this ensemble as a "tour de force." He adds, "one must admire the skill which the artist has displayed in achieving a harmonious composition without any effect of heaviness and so well adapted to the general shape of the bell of the capital." [19] The observer interested in musical instruments might also add that rarely has a sculptor succeeded so well in rendering them with realism or in catching the intensity of concentration and fervor peculiar to the performing musician. On viewing the original, it is difficult not to believe that the artist has reproduced with extraordinary feeling the attitudes and gestures of players in the act of performing. The group contrasts strikingly with that at San Isidoro where, although the players are about to perform, their attitude is one of classic composure. There, it is as if the sculptor wished to portray ideally the Biblical scene as it might have been in a long distant past. At Jaca, on the contrary, all is animation; the scene is taking place here and now. The cheeks of the wind players are puffed out; the hands and fingers of the string players are in playing position; their expressions are alert and intense. (It is regrettable that because the capital is in shade beneath a portico it is impossible to observe all the details with certainty and as equally impossible to reproduce them photographically.)

King David, wearing an elaborate Byzantine crown and seated on a throne, occupies the center space of the front face of the capital (see Pls. 24d & 26a). He is bowing a fiddle, the body resting against his knee, the neck slanting away slightly from the figure. The box-like body is distinctly oval, not pear-shaped. Although the body and neck appear to be made in a single piece they are clearly distinguished one from the other. The neck forms a distinct angle with the rounded shoulders, but it curves out slightly before narrowing abruptly to the lozenge shaped pegbox. Does this outline represent a transitional stage of the fiddle from the earlier tapering shape to the later type where body and neck are independent parts? The distinct sides of the body apparently indicate a flat back. Unfortunately the surface of the stone has been damaged so that the frontal string-holder has almost disappeared. It evidently existed,

[19] Gaillard, *op. cit.*, p. 116.

however, as well as a tail-piece. The sculptor seems to have suggested three strings that are attached to rear pegs. No sound holes are indicated. The bow is far more carefully represented than is usual in painting or sculptures of the Middle Ages. It is rather broad, slightly curved and with a distinct handle. The curious bands crossing it at intervals seem somehow connected with loops that seem to hold the hairs in place at intervals. The arrangement is unusual if not unique, and puzzling from the point of view of the action.

This instrument may be compared with the viols in the hands of the Elders in the *Pórtico de la Gloria*. Its neck, differently shaped, is longer proportionately than those of instruments carved some 75 years later at Compostela. The details are more carefully shown on the later instruments. They too are box-like with sides and flat backs clearly visible. In several cases a fingerboard is apparent. Sound holes, a bridge, and frontal string-holder are evident. Although no bows appear the character of the instruments strongly suggests that they could be bowed like the one at Jaca.[20] Viols, we know, were both plucked and bowed in the Middle Ages and later.

Surely we must have an ancestor of these instruments in the one sculptured on a Roman funerary stele at Mérida (Andalusia) in the 1st century A.D. (see Pl. 25a).[21] This stele was discovered recently, lying face downward, in the course of excavations at the famous Roman site. Unfortunately only a part of the instrument is represented. We can clearly see, however, that the neck is distinct from the body and that it has a fingerboard. The four strings pass through small holes in the peg-box to rear pegs. The body obviously has parallel sides and presumably a flat back. The curve of the shoulders strongly suggests an instrument of the guitar type. It is impossible to discuss the implications of this discovery in the limited space of an article. All that can be noted here is that it provides new evidence for the history of the viol and guitar families and their relationship. The Hispanic Peninsula indeed proves to be the region where the intermingling of instrument types and significant stages in their development took place.[22]

[20] Similar instruments appear in the miniature illustrating Cantiga I of the *Cantigas de Santa Maria* (late 13th century), MS Escorial b–i–2. See Julián Ribera, *La Música de las cantigas* (Madrid 1922), last plate, unnumbered.

[21] A. Garcia y Bellido, *Lutatia Lupata, La niña del laúd*, in: *A B C* (Madrid 15 March 1959). Plate 25a is reproduced from a photograph graciously supplied by the historian, Sr. Gonzalo Menéndez Pidal.

[22] The problem of the development of the bowed and plucked instruments and their relationship has been dealt with at length by Kathleen Schlesinger in Vol. II of *The Instruments of the Modern Orchestra and Early Records of the Precursors of the Violin Family* (New York & London 1909); see also the important article by Emanuel Winternitz, *The Survival of the Kithara and the Evolution of the English Cittern*, in: *Journal of the Warburg and Courtauld Institutes*, XXIV (1961), 222–29;

The David, playing the viol at Jaca, is exchanging an intent glance with the figure to his left, as if to give the cue to strike up. This figure, standing, is holding a small, light, angular harp. It has apparently nine strings which pass over the neck to the pegs. This instrument is very similar to the harp at San Isidoro (see Pls. 25b & 26e).

At David's right stands a figure plucking a rectangular psaltery (see Pls. 24d & 26a). The sculptor has shown five strings strung vertically. They are widely spaced and so thick that it is tempting to surmise that they are the artist's abbreviation for five sets of double strings. The instrument would thus represent "the instrument of ten strings" of the Psalmist. Sachs connects it with the Phoenician zither and mentions two examples on a Phoenician ivory pyxis of the 8th century. He also surmises that this may be the "psalterium decachordum" illustrated in the famous letter attributed to St. Jerome and addressed to Dardanus.[23] Diagrams of such a psaltery are reproduced twice by Gerbert after 10th- and 12th-century manuscripts.[24] In both cases the strings are, however, strung horizontally. An instrument very similar to the one at Jaca appears in a *Beatus* manuscript of the 12th century.[25]

The psaltery at Jaca has an interesting parallel in a "double psaltery" sculptured on a metope at the little church of Artáiz in Navarre [26] (see Pl. 25c).[27] It is one of a series representing the work of a local school of sculptors in the 12th century. The rectangular instrument is very similar in size and shape to the one at Jaca. It is, however, obviously strung on both sides of a sound box. Two rows of pegs appear at the top of the instrument. The number of pegs indicates five strings on each side.

The only other stringed instrument at Jaca is a small instrument of the lute family (see Pls. 24d & 26f). The body is oval-shaped, the neck slender and bent slightly back. Since the stone has been damaged it is impossible to say whether there was a pegbox. No pegs are visible. One or perhaps two strings pass to a frontal string-holder. The table, perforated with a number of small sound holes, suggests a stretched skin. This feature and its shape and size seem to relate the instrument to the ancient Arabic *gunibri* which has survived in North Africa as a folk instrument. However, the chief characteristic of the *gunibri,* namely that the neck is a stick which passes through the body to a sound hole below

Adolfo Salazar, *La Guitarra, heredera de la kithara clásica,* in: *Nueva revista de filología hispánica,* VII (1953), num. 1–2; and Farmer, *op. cit.,* pp. 91–107: *The Origin of the Arabian Lute and Rebec.*

[23] Sachs, *op. cit.,* pp. 117–18.
[24] Gerbert, *op. cit., Tabulae* XXIV, XXX.
[25] Neuss, *op. cit.,* II, 262.
[26] On this church see: *Ars hispaniae,* V, 145.
[27] Photograph is by the courtesy of my distinguished friend, Don José E. Uranga of Pamplona, who generously made it available from his private collection.

the string-holder where it acts as a tail-piece, is certainly lacking here.[28] This instrument surely seems to represent one of the simpler of the various types of lutes which were and still are prevalent in the Moslem world.

Crouched below the lutenist is a figure activating with his left hand one of the two small triangular bellows which feed a little portative organ. It apparently has a single row of eight pipes. These have been damaged in the course of time. The keyboard is invisible. This must be one of the earliest known representations of a portative.[29] Sachs states that they are first recorded in the 12th century. The Jaca sculpture would seem to show that they were known still earlier (see Pls. 24d & 26f).

Above is a player vigorously blowing on a panpipe. His left hand is raised as if beating time (see Pls. 24d & 26c). This instrument, like that played by a musician on the opposite face of the capital, is an example of the panpipe of solid construction (see Pls. 25b & 26h). They both represent the instrument made of a flat piece of wood through which holes are drilled to make the pipes. Panpipes like these, made of box-wood, are still played in the Pyrenees.[30]

There are three figures blowing horns, curved and of medium size (see Pls. 24d, 25b, 26e, 26b). Two examples represent instruments made of animal horn. The third (Pl. 26e) suggests one made of wood. No finger holes are visible, although the fingers of the player next to the organ seem to be stopping holes. The player above the harpist obviously blows from the corner of his mouth where lip control is easiest. Instruments of similar size, already depicted in manuscripts of the 10th century, were made of metal, horn, wood, or dressed leather. They are the ancestors of the cornett or zink of the Renaissance. Gérold points to a prototype of the cornett in a French psalter of the 11th century.[31] Such instruments are still used today by shepherds and hunters in Spain.[32]

The figure between two of the horn players (see Pls. 25b & 26g) is playing a strange wind instrument that has so far defied identification. It is so long that it is bent back upon itself in a zig-zag shape to form three

---

[28] Farmer, op. cit., pp. 39–46: A North African Folk Instrument.

[29] Hans Hickmann, Das Portativ (Kassel 1936).

[30] Anthony Baines, Woodwind Instruments and their History (2nd ed. New York 1963), pp. 223–24.

[31] Théodore Gérold, Les Instruments de musique au moyen âge, in: Revue des cours et des conférences, XXIX (1927–1928), 1, 234ff (Paris, Bibl. Nat., MS lat. 11550, fol. 7); this miniature is reproduced as the frontispiece in Edward Buhle, Die musikalischen Instrumente in den Miniaturen des frühen Mittelalters, I: Die Blasinstrumente (Leipzig 1903); see also pp. 20–24; and Baines, op. cit., pp. 219–21.

[32] P. José Antonio de Donostia and Juan Tomás, Instrumentos de música popular española, in: Anuario musical, II (1947), 105–50.

sections. Each section broadens slightly toward the extremity. The carving suggests an instrument of wood loosely covered with leather. Apparently the player is blowing into a hole or mouthpiece—it is not clear which—to one side of the end of the instrument. The end itself appears to be closed. The finger of the right hand may be covering finger holes. Can this be the sculptor's attempt to represent a kind of primitive double curved cornett? Since no finger holes are evident the purpose of the broken shape remains obscure.

Below the player of this curious instrument sits another playing a small pipe with expanding conical bore. An indication of a reed and staple seems apparent at the mouth end. Since the player grasps the instrument in both hands, only two finger holes are visible at the lower end. This instrument must be a representative of the ancient family of European reed pipes,[33] called in Spanish *caramillo* (see Pls. 25b & 26d).

Whether or not it is possible to consider this lively scene as representing a real instrumental ensemble, it is worth noting that almost all the instruments belong to the class referred to in the later Middle Ages as "soft" instruments. The possible exceptions would be the horns. Yet these seem to be depicted quite regularly in early manuscripts in company with instruments of the "soft" type.

Jaca was the first stopping-place in Spain on the pilgrimage road from the direction of Toulouse; it was also a capital city. As we know, all these routes were thronged with pilgrims and other wayfarers in the late 11th and early 12th century. At such stopping-places, minstrels and other kinds of entertainers congregated.[34] Our musicians on the cathedral capital have all the appearance of such individuals drawn from life by the sculptor. Indeed some of the physiognomies as well as their hair suggest that they were perhaps Moslem *juglares* from North Africa. To be sure, the artist may have wished to give an exotic appearance to a group representing King David's musicians and chose his types from those he saw about him. It is indeed worth noting that Jewish and Saracen musicians were so common that ecclesiastical councils threatened excommunication to Christians who brought infidels with them into the churches to play and sing during nocturnal vigils.[35] This particular group, which undoubtedly performed in the little plaza beside the Cathedral, was obviously detained at the church door by the sculptor!

[33] Baines, *op. cit.*, pp. 228–30.
[34] Menéndez Pidal, *Poesía juglaresca*, provides rich documentation on the *juglares* on the Pilgrimage Roads.
[35] Frances Spalding, *Mudejar Ornament in Manuscripts* (New York 1953), p. 55. Quotation from an enactment recorded at Valladolid and appearing in an edition of *Colección de canones y de todos los concilios de la iglesia de España y de América*, ed. Juan Tejada y Ramiro (Madrid 1859), III, 500.

THE PERFORMANCE OF
MEDIEVAL MUSIC

by GILBERT REANEY

IN SPITE OF a number of useful books on musical performance in the Middle Ages, Renaissance, and Baroque,[1] the performance of medieval music remains one of the biggest problems that faces the musicologist. Strangely enough, it is too often left to the amateur who lacks the scruples of the musicologist and therefore assumes that any vocal and instrumental combination is acceptable, largely because of the variety and color of medieval instruments. Certainly one cannot blame him for wanting to hear the music, and musicologists have not given as much time to the problem as they might have. Like musica ficta, it is a thorny problem, and so is usually avoided. The result is that most recordings of medieval music show little evidence of an attempt to provide an authentic performance, though in other ways they may be excellent.

Unfortunately, medieval notation gives no indication of what voices or what instruments one should employ. Indeed, the only clue we have as to whether a line of music is vocal or instrumental is the presence of a text. And yet this factor is not lacking in ambiguity, for it is clear that a part without a text need not be instrumental in the Middle Ages, just as a part with a text might be doubled or even replaced by instruments. One of the most highly developed forms of medieval music, the organum, was composed with the idea of singing measures and measures of music to a single syllable of text. Perotin's organum *Sancte Germane* [2] begins with 43 measures of music set to the syllable *San–*. At the end of the 16th century Thomas Morley is still complaining about singers who sing music without words, "as it were a music made only for instruments." [3]

The three-part organum has been performed [4] by two solo singers

---

[1] R. Haas, *Aufführungspraxis der Musik* (Potsdam 1931); A. Schering *Aufführungspraxis alter Musik* (Leipzig 1931); R. T. Dart, *The Interpretation of Music* (London 1954).

[2] Y. Rokseth, *Les Polyphonies du XIIIe siècle*, II (Paris 1936), 24f.

[3] Thomas Morley, *A Plain and Easy Introduction to Practical Music*, ed. R. A. Harman (London 1952), p. 293.

[4] With the exception of the Machaut Mass, which was directed by Robert Craft

and an organ, with the organ playing the long-held tenor notes in support of the two lively upper voices. Of course this is just one way of arranging the piece, since all we have to go on in the original manuscripts is a three-part score with the words under the bottom line only. Why use an organ then? The truth is that the long notes that form the bottom line of the organum seem to be too long to be performed by voices. And in practice few singers admit the possibility of sustaining such notes. Even so, the study of present-day non-Western music shows that forms similar to the organum exist today and that very long notes are performed by voices, for instance on the island of Madagascar. Here then is just one example of the sort of complication that arises as soon as we begin thinking about how to perform medieval music. Nevertheless, it is by no means impossible that the drone notes of the organum tenor were sometimes doubled or replaced by an organ, the only instrument normally admitted in medieval churches.

The question might well be asked, too, how we know that voices were used for the upper voices of this organum rather than instruments. The answer is that literary sources, such as the Latin treatises of Johannes de Garlandia and Anonymous IV, tell us so. Anonymous IV also relates that instruments played a secondary part in doubling these voices in the higher octaves,[5] but this probably only occurred on special occasions. Unfortunately, literary sources are often less precise than one could wish in the Middle Ages, and references to musical performance are either all too general or completely lacking. At least Johannes de Grocheo clarifies the question whether voices perform the text in the upper parts of organa, and implicitly conductus, when he specifically indicates that the upper parts take the same text as the lowest voice.[6]

Luckily the pictorial arts are for some reason especially interested in depicting musical instruments and performers at this period. Often enough, for example, painting and manuscript illuminations are adorned with angels playing all sorts of instruments. A typical example is Matteo di Giovanni's large-scale *Madonna of the Girdle* in the National Gallery, London. The carefully drawn instruments are as follows: 2 lutes, 2 shawms, tambourine, double recorder, psaltery, portative organ, drums, fiddle, cymbals, trumpet, harp, and rebec. The 15 strings on the harp and 16 pipes on the small organ can actually be counted.

Such a picture already raises certain questions. Where is the music

from the author's score, all the pieces discussed here have been performed by the London Medieval Group under the author's direction.

[5] C.-E.-H. de Coussemaker, ed., *Scriptorum de musica medii aevi nova series 1* (Paris 1864), 362.

[6] E. Rohloff, *Der Musiktraktat des Johannes de Grocheo* (Leipzig 1943), p. 56.

for the celestial musicians? Why is there only one of each instrument in general? Why are there no voices? And above all, what connection is there between such a chamber orchestra and the medieval music still preserved in the manuscripts? In fact, there seems to be little connection at all at first. Apart from plainsong sung by small choirs or soloists, the manuscripts contain roughly three types of composition: part-music for use in church, solo secular songs without accompaniment, and an equal number of such songs with accompaniment. How does this relate to a group of instrumentalists with no music? In the first place an element of religious symbolism must be noted in paintings of angel orchestras. The Biblical call to praise God with instruments undoubtedly accounts for the widespread representation of instruments in medieval paintings.[7] Nevertheless, certain conclusions can be drawn from a painting such as the *Madonna of the Girdle*, since realistic depiction of the instruments counterbalances the religious symbolism. For one thing, it seems clear that music was very often performed without written copies in the Middle Ages. Parchment was expensive, and large manuscripts were rare. Many of them were intended as source-books rather than actual performing copies.[8] Small sheets and rolls were popular with singers in the 14th century doubtless because of their relative cheapness.[9] In any case, it is a remarkable fact that the instrumentalists are nearly always without music in medieval paintings, miniatures, and sculpture. It would be extreme to suggest that manuscripts were not used at all in performance, but the singers had priority and all read from a single codex. A fine madonna by an anonymous mid-15th-century Flemish painter shows three singers with a musical manuscript and three instrumentalists without music.[10] We actually know what the piece of music is: the popular three-part motet *Ave regina celorum* by Walter Frye.[11] Presumably the three singers each took a part, while the recorder, fiddle, and lute doubled the three parts or to some extent ornamented them. This is in fact the usual way of performing such works today.[12]

---

[7] E. Winternitz, *The Visual Arts as a Source for the Historian of Music*, in: *Report of the Eighth Congress of the International Musicological Society, New York 1961*, I (Kassel 1961), 113.

[8] Dart, *Interpretation*, p. 51, fn. 1.

[9] For example, H. Besseler, *Die Musik des Mittelalters und der Renaissance* (Potsdam 1931–34), p. 126. As far as possible, this volume will be consistently cited for illustrations (hereafter simply as Besseler).

[10] Besseler, pl. XIII.

[11] W. Frye, *Collected Works*, ed. S. W. Kenney (Tübingen 1960), No. 5.

[12] Although the music in the painting only consists of cantus and tenor parts, the absence of the contratenor is probably due to the fact that this *is* a painting. The painter did not want to indulge in even more elaborate detail work than was necessary for the depiction of two notated voices.

With accompanied solo songs we are faced with a different situation. Only one part has a text in the manuscripts, while the other parts, usually from one to three, all have no text and generally look instrumental. Even so, it is difficult to be certain that these always are instrumental parts. A drawing from a collection of accompanied solo songs, the famous late 14th-century codex Chantilly, Musée Condé, 1047, shows a number of monks singing from music on fol. 37.[13] The drawing may have nothing to do with the music—the monks may be singing plain-song—but if they *are* singing secular songs, the implication is that the accompanying parts of such songs as Galiot'*s* Le saut perilleus are vocal. At all events the consensus still seems to be that such parts without text are instrumental, and the variety of instruments to be found in the 14th and 15th centuries suggests that these were used for playing the accompanied songs which sprang up at very much the same time. The fact that paintings usually show one instrument of each kind, though occasionally more, confirms similar lists in literary works,[14] and implies that accompanied songs should not employ instruments of the same family as a general rule. The exceptions are trumpets and, more im-portantly in view of their more developed technique, members of the shawm family. It is possible to make the objection that works of art and even literature reproduce or enumerate instruments of many different kinds simultaneously for the sake of variety, but realism and actual lists of instruments confirm the general principle of employing one of a kind, though undoubtedly large collections of instruments must have been very rare.[15] As an example of the instrumentations used in performing an accompanied song, the London Medieval Group has often played the three textless parts of Machaut's Ballade *Il m'est avis* [16] on a portative organ, viol, and bassoon. The portative is a faithful reproduction of one in Memling's well-known triptych,[17] and covers two octaves above middle C. The bassoon was a necessary substitute for the more pungently colorful bass shawm.

[13] In: MGG, II, pl. 34; also F. Gennrich, *Abriss der Mensuralnotation des XIV. und der ersten Hälfte des XV. Jahrhunderts: Übertragungsmaterial* (Nieder-Modau 1948), facs. 15.
[14] For examples, see H. Abert, *Die Musikästhetik der Echecs Amoureux*, in: *Sammelbände der internationalen Musikgesellschaft*, VI (1905), 348, 354f.
[15] King John I of Aragon evidently possessed many instruments, for he was always buying new ones, and on one occasion he mentions that he has plenty of organs, harps, échiquiers, and rotes: cf. F. Pedrell, *Jean I d'Aragon, compositeur de musique*, in: *Riemann-Festschrift* (Leipzig 1909), p. 239. He also owned bagpipes, a shawm, and a bombard.
[16] Guillaume de Machaut, *Musikalische Werke*, ed. F. Ludwig, I (Leipzig 1926), 23f.; L. Schrade, *Polyphonic Music of the Fourteenth Century*, III (Monaco 1956), 98ff.
[17] Besseler, pl. XV.

As a matter of fact, it would not be altogether correct to say that instrumental music in its pure form does not exist in medieval manuscripts. Only recently an entire codex of 14th-century keyboard music came to light,[18] and a few pieces were previously known of this type.[19] They consist mainly of a highly ornamented treble part belonging to well-known partsongs, together with a single untouched lower part. It seems difficult to imagine that these pieces were played on a portative, since these instruments could only be played with one hand and they could not play in the lower registers unless the instrument were unusually large. Presumably a positive organ would be necessary if both upper and lower parts were to be played, since the left hand was used to blow the bellows on the portative. However, two factors favor the portative: (a) the possibility of using two hands while an assistant blows the bellows, and (b) the crossing of parts in many compositions. Where parts cross frequently, it would seem more reasonable to let a viol or some such instrument perform the tenor while the portative concentrates on the upper part. Even so, it may be well to bear in mind that instrumental performance often had a virtuoso character in the Middle Ages, so that the performance of both parts on one portative by one hand cannot be ruled out. Indeed, the instrumental version of Machaut's *De toutes flours*[20] has often been performed in this way by the London Medieval Group. In any case the portative was the most popular instrument of the 14th century, while the positive was less common. In the famous miniature from the Squarcialupi manuscript depicting Francesco Landini,[21] he is surrounded by many instruments which he could play—lute, psaltery, recorder, harp, and shawm—but he himself is shown playing the portative. In the last resort it may well be best to play the Faenza keyboard compositions with portative and viol, since playing both parts on the portative often necessitates transposition to the octave above, though this may be necessary even if the upper part only is played. On top of this, however, is the possibility that the lower part is given as a guide rather than as a lower part for the keyboard instrument.

This brings me to another point. In an interesting miniature from

---

[18] Cf. D. Plamenac, *Keyboard Music of the 14th Century in Codex Faenza 117*, in: JAMS, IV (1951), 179ff. Facsimile edition of the MS by A. Carapetyan, *An Early Fifteenth-Century Italian Source of Keyboard Music: The Codex Faenza, Biblioteca Comunale 117* (American Institute of Musicology 1961).

[19] Six pieces in the Robertsbridge codex; London, BM Add. 28550, facsimile edition in H. E. Wooldridge, *Early English Harmony*, I (London 1897), pls. 42–45; and two in the codex Reina: Paris, BN nouv. acq. fr. 6771.

[20] Plamenac, *Keyboard Music*, p. 189f.

[21] Besseler, pl. XI.

a Veronese picture-book of the 14th century [22] the artist shows three musicians, one singing, the other two playing portative organ and viol respectively. The caption reads: *organare cantum vel sonare*, which may be translated in two ways. It can mean "to harmonize a song," but it is more likely to mean "to accompany a song on the organ and viol." Considering that the portative plays in the treble, it seems likely that it is in some way doubling the vocal part while the viol plays the tenor.

My own theory, however, is that the organ is playing heterophonically with the voice, namely playing an ornamented version of the vocal part. The study of non-Western music suggests that this practice would be carried on in the Middle Ages, and the fact that the great majority of pre-15th-century instruments are treble ones indicates the use of heterophony, too. There are many more reasons for this theory, but suffice it to say that the existence of ornamented keyboard versions and original vocal parts of one and the same piece gives us an ideal opportunity to try out the validity of it. Dragan Plamenac, who has transcribed and indeed discovered many of the 14th-century keyboard pieces, has written out one composition, the rondeau *Jour a jour la vie*, with the original vocal part above the two instrumental parts of the keyboard arrangement.[23] In performance there is absolutely no clash between the original vocal part sung by a tenor and the ornamented version as played by the portative. An interesting parallel is furnished by the 16th-century dances for two lutes by P. P. Borrono.[24]

Of course, it is quite possible that the keyboard arrangement and the vocal original were two distinct entities, but the mysteries of medieval performance practice demand that all the possibilities suggested by the fine arts, literature, and present-day non-Western music should be investigated. One thing is clear: the contrast between vocal and instrumental performance which exists today did not exist in the Middle Ages. If voices retained a certain priority, they could easily be supported and often replaced by instruments. Machaut himself says that one of his ballades could equally well be performed by an organ, bagpipe, or other instrument, and he is obviously referring to the vocal part here.[25]

Pure instrumental music is very rare in medieval manuscripts; except

---

[22] Besseler, p. 158.
[23] Plamenac, *Keyboard Music*, p. 190ff.
[24] Cf. G. Thibault, *L'Ornementation dans la musique profane au moyen âge*, in: *Report of the Eighth Congress of the International Musicological Society, New York 1961*, I (Kassel 1961), 454.
[25] *Le Livre du Voir Dit*, ed. P. Paris (Paris 1875), p. 69 (letter 10). Cited in G. de Machaut, *Musikalische Werke*, II (Leipzig 1928), p. 55 by F. Ludwig.

for the estampies for a single instrument, there are only the three keyboard estampies in the Robertsbridge codex [26] and the three two-part
estampies in the *Sumer is icumen in* MS.[27] To be sure, these are all
dances, but they do not tell us much about performance. Are the monophonic pieces really for a single instrument, or should they be performed
heterophonically with one instrument playing the unembellished melody
while another performs an ornamented version? Generally speaking,
heterophony would seem more likely in vocal music, and certainly pictures of dances often show a single melody instrument in attendance,[28]
though there may be percussion in plenty.[29] The viol and bagpipe are
the most popular melody instruments, while the percussion may include
drums, cymbals, tambourine, handbells, clappers, etc. Even so, it is
worth pointing out that percussion is not always present.

Polyphonic dance music must have generally been improvised, for
Froissart clearly mentions the performance of estampies on shawm, bagpipe, and bombard (or trumpet),[30] and yet no French source contains
such music. But at least the different registers of the instruments indicate
that this was genuine part-music, like the 15th-century basse-danses. We
know of course that pieces like the Monk of Salzburg's two-part *Tagelied*
were "auch gut zu blasen" [31] ("also good for playing on wind instruments"), but these are primarily vocal pieces. It may be that two adjacent
pages of late 14th-century music which recently came to light in Nuremberg [32] actually contain the type of piece Froissart talks about, though
the form of the work is that of the virelai. Nevertheless, it is textless
except for the incipit *Bobik blasen* in the highest of the three parts. With
such a title the composition must be intended for wind instruments. Its
style is not only French but also very reminiscent of Guillaume de
Machaut's secular songs: the syncopated duple rhythms are particularly
characteristic and confirm the suspicion that the Machaut Rondeau *Ma
fin est mon commencement* [33] is an instrumental composition.

The performance of very early polyphony is comparatively rare,

[26] See fn. 18. The two complete estampies are transcribed in J. Handschin, *Über
Estampie und Sequenz I*, in: *Zeitschrift für Musikwissenschaft*, XII (1929–30), 14ff.
[27] Transcription in J. Wolf, *Die Tänze des Mittelalters*, in: *Archiv für Musikwissenschaft*, I (1918), 19ff.
[28] For example, Besseler, p. 120.
[29] *Ibid.*
[30] Cf. article *Froissart* in: MGG, IV (1955), 1005. There are also many illustrations of this instrumental combination, for example: Besseler, p. 142.
[31] Opening in G. Reese, MMA (New York 1940), p. 378.
[32] Nuremberg, Stadtbibliothek, CENT-V, 61.
[33] G. de Machaut, *Musikalische Werke*, I, 63f; L. Schrade, *Polyphonic Music of
the Fourteenth Century*, III (Monaco 1956), 156f.

Ex. 1 Anonymous, *Bobik blasen* (Nuremberg, Stadtbibl. CENT-V, 61, fol. 2)

and one of the obvious reasons is the difficulty of transcribing music before the Notre Dame epoch. This is unfortunate, because the four so-called St. Martial manuscripts which contain polyphonic music reveal a highly developed art that is more than a mere jumping-off point for the Notre Dame composers. The problem of course is the rhythm, but recently Bruno Stäblein has made clear the presence of modal rhythms in the melismas of St. Martial polyphonic music in a very important article.[34] I believe these rhythms are to be found in the syllabic sections too, and refer in this respect to my necessarily brief article in the Cologne congress report where I stressed the importance of consonance and the lengthening of the last note of a ligature or neume-group.[35] The use of doubled notes is in any case clear confirmation of the use of modal rhythms in St. Martial polyphony, for instance in the motet *Stirps Iesse—Benedicamus Domino* in the version of MS Paris, Bibl. Nat., fonds latin 3549, fol. 166ʳ (*StM-B*). Such notes are not present

[34] B. Stäblein, *Modale Rhythmen im Saint-Martial-Repertoire?*, in: *Festschrift Friedrich Blume* (Kassel 1963), p. 340ff.
[35] G. Reaney, *A Note on Conductus Rhythm*, in: *Kongressbericht Köln 1958* (Kassel 1959), p. 219ff.

as a general rule, unfortunately, but their importance for the style of Leonin should not be overlooked.[36] For example, shouldn't the two-part organum *Hec dies* (W1 fol. 27) begin this way?[37] The consideration of many doubled unison notes as longs in the *Magnus liber organi* may pave the way for a definitive transcription of the two-part *organa pura*.

Ex. 2   Anonymous, *Hec dies* (Wolfenbüttel, Herzog-August-Bibl. MS 628 fol. 27)

Hec   Hec

It has always been difficult for musicians to believe that music before Perotin was consistently free in rhythm. After all, it would seem reasonable to suppose that we have simply lost the key to the rhythm of these compositions rather than that they had none. The degree of rhythmic stress is another matter. Recitative-like chants were obviously the freest rhythmically, though melodies consisting of a number of notes of equal length are not lacking in rhythm.[38] In any case, it is hard to get away from the fact that, where a piece is notated in symbols that indicate rhythm clearly, the work is precise rhythmically. And then there are many early indications of strict time-beating in the arts. A very fine ivory book cover of the 9th or 10th century shows a group of singers, evidently singing the music for the Mass which is in progress, and they are *all* keeping time with their hands (not merely the conductor).[39] The miniature that opens the Florence manuscript of the Notre Dame repertory also shows conducting in progress.[40] In this case it is being carried out by the female personification of music we so often see in medieval art-works. To be sure, it is all allegorical, based on Boethius's

[36] Cf. A. Gastoué's parallel transcription of the opening of both the *StM-A* (Paris, BN fonds lat. 1139) and *StM-B* versions in *Les Primitifs de la musique française* (Paris 1922), p. 15. A facsimile of the *StM-B* version appears in MGG, IX, 642. Gastoué's transcription is unmeasured.

[37] Facsimile in J. Baxter, *An Old St. Andrews Music Book* (London 1931). Previous transcriptions in W. Apel and A. T. Davison, *Historical Anthology of Music*, I (2nd ed. Cambridge, Mass. 1949), 27ff; W. G. Waite, *The Rhythm of Twelfth Century Polyphony* (New Haven 1954), p. 120ff.

[38] According to Johannes de Grocheo, Kyries and Glorias are of this type, for the notes are all perfect longs. Cf. Rohloff, *Der Musiktraktat des Johannes de Grocheo*, p. 56.

[39] Besseler, pl. IV.

[40] Besseler, pl. I.

division of music into three types: cosmic, human, and instrumental; but because Boethius, following the ancients, believed that all things were governed by musical proportions, the direction is literally carried out with a conductor's baton.

A problem that applies to both St. Martial and Notre Dame polyphony concerns the number of performers employed. In general it may be said that most pieces of early part-music are for soloists. After all, writing in more than one part was exceptional and trained singers were needed to sing such complex works as the St. Martial *Jubilemus, exultemus* [41] or Perotin's *Alleluia Posui adiutorium*.[42] There are plenty of archival references to show that such singers were few and far between.[43] Plainsong was the normal song of the Church, and part-music was reserved for special feasts. A miniature from the Florence Notre Dame MS [44] shows three singers heading a collection of three-part conductus. Surely this suggests that this is solo music. Admittedly the miniature preceding the two-part conductus in the same sources contains four singers,[45] but even if there are two singers to a part, this is the next best thing to soloists.[46] But with three parts, the number of trained singers required is already large for the Middle Ages, even if soloists *are* used. And then another strong ground for using soloists in two-, three-, and four-part organa is the fact that polyphony occurs only in the sections that are for soloists in the original plainsong. The choral sections of organa are left as plainsong. Incidentally, it is not beyond the bounds of possibility that the choir was used for performing the long-held tenor notes of organa in the polyphonic sections. At all events, it makes sense for the same voices to continue singing the choral sections (as Rokseth indicates).[47]

The performance of monophonic music is even more puzzling than where polyphony is concerned. Plainsong is apparently mainly vocal, whether solo or choral, but the Sequence, although coming under the category of plainsong, has more in common with such a secular form as the lai than with psalms and Introits. Its origins are still disputed, but both the secular lai and the sacred trope seem to have influenced it. The

[41] Facsimile after *StM-A* fol. 41 easily available in C. Parrish, *The Notation of Polyphonic Music* (New York 1957), pl. XXI. Unmeasured transcription by J. Handschin in *Die mittelalterlichen Aufführungen in Zürich, Bern und Basel*, in: *Zeitschrift für Musikwissenschaft*, X (1927-28), 13f.

[42] Transcription in Y. Rokseth, *Les Polyphonies*, II, 31ff.

[43] Cf. F. Ll. Harrison, *Music in Medieval Britain* (London 1958), p. 114f.

[44] Fol. 201.

[45] Fol. 263.

[46] Cf. J. Handschin, *Zur Geschichte von Notre Dame*, in: *Acta musicologica*, IV (1932), 6ff.

[47] *Les Polyphonies*, II, 16ff, 24ff, 31ff.

lai is certainly instrumental as well as vocal, for references to the harp
or viol are constant in connection with lai performance.[48] Similarly the
words of Sequences often mention the effects of such instruments as
organ and bells, and it seems likely that these were the principal pro-
tagonists, together with the voices. A miniature that precedes one of the
Paris copies of the treatise of Lambertus [49] is interesting in this connection, for not only does it show the popular representation of King David
with his harp, but in the four corners are players with bells. The man at
the top left in fact has a set of eight bell-chimes which he is hitting with
small hammers. Considering the paired verses of the Sequence and the
predilection of the Middle Ages for *alternatim* performance, it seems
a very reasonable way of performing Sequences with bells to sing one
verse of a pair and play the other on a set of bell-chimes. The simplicity
of the procedure may account for its effectiveness. Many of the bell-
chimes in medieval reproductions [50] have only three or four notes, but
eight or nine notes are not infrequent and are sufficient for the performance of most Sequences. The London Medieval Group's bell-chimes
have a compass of a ninth above middle C, including B♭. This fits a work
like *Veni, sancte spiritus* [51] exactly, but a widely ranging melody such as
Lauda Sion [52] needs some adjustment. Fortunately, medieval accounts
show that this problem was solved by either moving a difficult phrase
into an octave covered by the instrument, or by transferring odd notes to
a related consonance.[53] Not everyone would of course accept the theory
that Sequences are intended to be accompanied by organs and bells just
because these instruments are mentioned in the texts, any more than
they can believe that Worcester motets like *Alleluia psallat* [54] use such
instruments, for they are also mentioned in such Sequence-like texts.
More convincing perhaps are motets like the 14th-century English
Campanis cum cymbalis [55] and the 14th-century French or German
Comes Flandrie—Rector creatorum—In cimbalis bene sonantibus from
the recently discovered Nuremberg fragments. Even these could be intended for voices imitating instruments, but surely the musicologist
should drop his mask occasionally and display the musician behind it

---

[48] Th. Gérold, *La Musique au moyen âge* (Paris 1932), pp. 375, 383.
[49] In: MGG, VIII (1960), pl. 3.
[50] Besseler, pl. VI.
[51] *Liber Usualis*, p. 880f.
[52] *Liber Usualis*, p. 945ff.
[53] J. Smits van Waesberghe, *Cymbala* (Rome 1951), p. 17f.
[54] L. Dittmer, *The Worcester Fragments* (Haarlem 1957), No. 46.
[55] L. Dittmer, *Beiträge zum Studium der Worcester-Fragmente*, in: *Die Musikfor-schung*, X (1957), 36f.

by admitting that a phrase like the following should at least be accompanied by bells.[56]

Ex. 3   Anonymous, opening of tenor of *Comes Flandrie—Rector creatorum —In cimbalis bene sonantibus* (Nuremberg, Stadtbibl. CENT-V, 61, fol. 1ᵛ)

In cimbalis bene   In   cim - ba - lis   be -

ne so - nan - ti - bus

Even the performance of troubadour and trouvère songs is not as simple as it might appear to be on the surface. In the manuscripts these works are written down without any accompaniment whatsoever. All we can find are the notes for a single voice with the words set fairly simply underneath them. And yet the more concrete evidence of literary accounts shows that the performers of these songs accompanied them on instruments, often the viol or harp as with the lais. If the accompaniment did not need writing down, it was probably fairly simple. It might have been a brief prelude, a sort of tuning-up such as we read about for the lais,[57] together with a fairly close doubling of the principal melody supported by drone strings. Drones, which today only exist on folk instruments and bagpipes, were common in the Middle Ages. In fact, it is possible that long trumpets, like those shown in a miniature from a Machaut manuscript,[58] were nothing but drones. Without a slide mechanism they could have been little more. On the viol and other stringed instruments like the rote, the drone strings would be relatively short and were fastened to the left of the peg-box. Both rote and rebec have very nasal tones almost like a woodwind instrument. Particularly the flat bridge of the rote suggests most of its strings, let alone the drones, were tuned in chords to produce a drone accompaniment, rather like the later cittern. Certain medieval songs are particularly suitable for accompaniment by a drone, for instance *Prendés i garde* by Guillaume

---

[56] In any case there is plenty of evidence that the organ and bells were the two types of instruments that managed to penetrate into the sanctuary of the church in the early Middle Ages. Cf. E. Bowles, *The Organ in the Medieval Liturgical Service*, in: *Revue belge de musicologie*, XV (1961), 15f.

[57] See fn. 41.

[58] Besseler, p. 143. It should not go unnoticed that the two bagpipes in the picture have drone pipes almost identical with the trumpets, if a little shorter.

d'Amiens [59] and *Ausi com l'unicorne* by Thibaut de Navarre.[60] Needless
to say, the drone will usually be on the final of the mode, and double or
triple drones should, if used, probably be restricted to open fifths and
octaves during the medieval period. Two other types of accompaniment
are possible in pre-14th-century solo song. One is heterophony, whereby
the accompanying instrument plays a slightly ornamented version of
the vocal melody; this type of accompaniment can of course be combined with a drone. Finally, though more sophisticated, an accompaniment in simple counterpoint to the melody is quite thinkable and works
well in performance, providing the harmonic intervals are medieval
(perfect consonances together with a few imperfect ones and a minimum of dissonances), and that instrumental usage remains in style (stepwise movement or leaps principally by perfect consonances, drones, etc.).
A piece often performed in this way by the London Medieval Group
is the anonymous *Lay des pucelles*,[61] of which the opening is given below.

Ex. 4   Anonymous, *Lay des pucelles* (Paris, BN français 12615, fol. 71)

This once again raises the question whether the piece really should be
performed in modal rhythm. Personally I have no doubts about it, even
though the notation is unmeasured. With syllabic texts the accent of
the poetry determines the rhythm. It is when note-groups lengthen that
more caution is needed, namely when the musical setting ceases to be
primarily syllabic. The opening of the *Lay des pucelles* is a characteristic
lai motif.[62] Two things are worth noticing about it: (a) the restricted

[59] F. Gennrich, *Rondeaux, Virelais und Balladen*, I (Dresden 1921), 38f.
[60] Facsimile in J. Beck, *Le Chansonnier Cangé* (Philadelphia 1927), fol. 1.
[61] See the diplomatic facsimile in A. Jeanroy, L. Brandin, and P. Aubry, *Lais et descorts français du XIIIe siècle* (Paris 1901), No. XXIII.
[62] Cf. the *Lai de la rose* in Jeanroy, Brandin, and Aubry, *Lais*, No. XXI; also the lai-like melody of the hymn *Nobilis, humilis* transcribed in W. Apel and A. T. Davison, *Historical Anthology of Music*, I, 22.

compass and (b) the repetition. I mention these points here because the motet from the Nuremberg fragments whose tenor is quoted in Ex. 4 seems to make intentional use in the upper parts of lai motifs, including the one that opens the *Lay des pucelles*. The modal rhythm is confirmed by the motet. It does seem, incidentally, that musicologists are perhaps over-cautious about accepting the evidence of later manuscripts in measured notation with reference to music originally written in un-measured notation. Obviously these later sources will have to be dis-regarded occasionally, but in my experience this is usually by way of exception rather than as a general rule.

In the 14th century, if we are to judge once again from Froissart,[63] it was the fashion to alternate vocal solos with instrumental pieces. The typical vocal solo, often quite unaccompanied, was the virelai, while the ballade and rondeau usually had written-out accompaniments by this time. It is usually assumed that the latter had become too complicated to be used for dancing. In any case Froissart's testimony confirms that the virelai often had no accompaniment when used for dancing. Machaut's 25 monophonic virelais have a folk-like simplicity for the most part which would be lost if an accompaniment were added. These compo-sitions have much in common with the later *chansons rustiques* and may well be direct ancestors of them. Like the monophonic virelais, Machaut's lais are also probably unaccompanied vocal solos, and this applies to the polyphonic lais as well as the more usual monophonic ones. However, the length of the lais as well as their wide compass does suggest that two or more soloists worked in relays. For one person to sing an entire lai with all repeats is a feat of virtuosity.

In contemporary Italy secular song composition also flourished, but generally the basic texture was that of the two-part madrigal, namely a vocal duet. Accompanied solo songs of the French type did not be-come popular until Landini wrote his three-part ballate for a single vocal part accompanied by textless tenor and contratenor. But even with Landini, the two-part texture predominates. The question must also be raised whether some of the textless parts should be provided with a text for a work like the three-part ballata *Non avra ma' pieta*,[64] which appears in three MSS with the text in the cantus only and in two with the words in both cantus and tenor.[65] This does not mean that instruments must not be employed, whether there is text or not in the lower parts, for it is clear that much medieval music can be secondarily instrumental. To

[63] Cf. my article *Froissart*, in: MGG, IV (1955), 1005.

[64] L. Schrade, *Polyphonic Music of the Fourteenth Century*, IV (Monaco 1959), 144f.

[65] Schrade, *Polyphonic Music*, IV, commentary, 117.

be sure, we do hear of virtuosos who can play two- or three-part Italian songs on the harp.[66] The result must have been that the player concentrated on the top part and simplified the lower parts to some extent, a little after the manner of the organ pieces mentioned previously. It has to be borne in mind that, like many medieval instruments, harps varied considerably in size and range. In the Middle Ages the instrument that was generally used by minstrels was relatively small, so that it was either a purely treble instrument or at most descended about an octave below middle C. There is a well-known French tapestry that shows a woman playing a harp from music.[67] The music is the cantus line of a popular 14th-century ballade by P. des Molins: *De ce que fol pense*.[68] In the existing sources the piece has at least two accompanying parts, but a small harp like this one could have played nothing but the melody. The woman player must have been of noble birth, for it was exceptional for a performer to have any music, let alone someone to hold it, and one is reminded of Valentina Visconti, wife of King Charles VI of France, for she was reputed to be an excellent harpist. From a practical point of view, the small Gothic harp can vary even apart from its size and number of strings. For example, it may be strung with wire and have a large sound-box, both features making it very sonorous, or strung with gut and built with a medium-sized sound-box; the latter specification seems to me to give a more authentic sound.

Getting back to the 14th-century Italian school, a work like Giovanni da Cascia's *O tu, cara scientia mia, musica* [69] sounds very well if the two voices sing the madrigal as it stands while a small harp plays a simplified version of both voices simultaneously. Although many medieval illustrations depict very small harps no more than an octave in range, unless one can afford the luxury of two or more instruments it is wise to have not less than about 20 strings and a compass that will take in the octave below middle C.[70] Another satisfactory way of performing two-part madrigals and ballate is to double the two vocal parts with a recorder and a bassoon.[71] If the recorder plays an octave above the upper part,

[66] S. Debenedetti, Il "Sollazzo" e il "Saporetto" con altre rime di Simone Pro-denzani d'Orvieto, in: Giornale storico della letteratura italiana, suppl. no. 15 (Turin 1913), 104 (Sonnet 25).

[67] Besseler, pl. IX.

[68] Transcription in J. Wolf, Handbuch der Notationskunde, I (1913), 357ff.

[69] N. Pirrotta, The Music of Fourteenth-Century Italy, I (Amsterdam 1954), 28ff.

[70] Machaut's Dit de la harpe mentions a harp with 25 strings, and thus a harp with about 20 strings would be neither anachronistically large nor too small to be of practical value.

[71] Purists may object to a bassoon, but after all the sound is the important factor, and it will often be necessary to choose an instrument which approximates to a medieval sound. The group that can afford to buy an example of every medieval instrument is indeed fortunate!

it will heighten the effect of the treble melody, especially if the latter is sung by a countertenor.[72] The result may be compared roughly to the addition of piccolos to flutes in the modern orchestra, and we have some justification for the procedure in the words of the medieval writer who says that wind and other instruments may be used in the upper octaves of 13th-century organa.[73] It may well be that instruments were employed far more often than we imagine in the higher octaves, either doubling or playing the higher vocal parts with ornamentation.

From the performance point of view, one of the most challenging medieval works is in fact one of the most performed, namely the Machaut Mass, and it rarely seems to come off well in practice. An invitation to produce a special score of the Mass for the Liège festival of 1958 gave me an opportunity to try out different justifiable performance procedures, though naturally it was essential in a public performance to preserve a certain homogeneity. The disposition of upper and lower voices in the Mass, as well as the textual underlay, suggest a possible use of heterophony worked out between a small group of vocalists and a modest but varied instrumental ensemble. It was necessary to employ modern instruments, but the sounds were as near to those of medieval instruments as possible. Following the lead of medieval paintings, it seemed reasonable to have only one of each type of instrument as a general principle. Oboes and cor anglais were particularly welcome for their nasal tone, rather than the flutes and recorders that too often monopolize modern performances of medieval music. The result of employing heterophony was that the voices were often given a simplified version of the music played by the instruments. The notated music is assumed to be the ornamented version of a basic vocal substructure, which is not unreasonable in view of the existence, for instance, of the ornamented keyboard versions of vocal compositions, both French and Italian. The heterophony mainly affected the upper parts, as one might expect after studying the keyboard music with its unchanged tenors. If the method is reminiscent of Schering's *Dekolorierung* technique,[74] it may be none the worse for that. Machaut himself implies that the removal of notes was common when he tells Péronne to perform his music as it is written, without adding or taking away.[75] The use of conventional ornamentation in the Middle Ages and Renaissance makes it possible to produce a simplified

[72] The purity of this kind of voice means that it is usually more effective than the typical soprano voice for performances of medieval music, though it is evident that women often performed secular music in the Middle Ages, and of course sacred music in nunneries.

[73] See fn. 5.

[74] A. Schering, *Studien zur Musikgeschichte der Frührenaissance* (Leipzig 1914), p. 79f.

[75] See fn. 24.

vocal version of the Mass rather easily, and indeed the conventional
nature of the ornaments is one justification for assuming the use of
heterophony. It might be thought that the simultaneous performance
of ornamented and unornamented versions of the same melodic line
would produce quite a lot of dissonance, but this did not prove to be
the case. At all events, here is a brief example of the simplified vocal score
with the original above and below it. It should be remembered that the
instruments played all the notes Machaut wrote when the voices were
singing a simplified version, so that the score was only changed in the
direction of heterophony. Other methods of performance used in this

Ex. 5   Machaut, *Mass*, Credo, mm. 82–89 (based on de Van's edition, Rome
        1949)

version of the Mass, apart from the usual doubling of voices by instruments, were (a) instruments in all parts and voices only in the tenor of isorhythmic sections, thus emphasizing the plainsong, and (b) voices in all parts, supported by a straightforward organ accompaniment, either stressing the main harmonies or simply doubling the lower two parts.

The general conclusion that might be drawn from this investigation of medieval performance practice is that a good deal of practical experimentation with vocal and instrumental resources is required, but it must be carried out with all due caution and discretion and backed by real knowledge of the period, musically, historically, and artistically. In this age of specialization, this probably means that the performer must proceed more carefully, while the musicologist should risk a hypothesis occasionally. The use of heterophony in medieval music is such a hypothesis, and yet it fits in so well with what we know of the history of non-Western and even Western music that it is difficult to avoid the conviction that it should be part and parcel of medieval performance practice. It certainly has as much and probably more justification than the plain doubling of voices by instruments.

THE 15th-CENTURY *CONIUNCTA:*
A PRELIMINARY STUDY

by *ALBERT SEAY*

ALTHOUGH IT now seems exceedingly doubtful that Guido of Arezzo was the sole inventor of the solmization system that bears his name, there can be no hesitation in saying that, for his time, it was an innovation of the greatest importance.[1] Designed to aid the singer in remembering where the half steps fell, the practicality of the method was such that its eventual adoption by all those concerned with the performance of plainchant was both rapid and complete. As Guido himself reported, the use of his solmization syllables allowed boys to learn in a short time what would have normally taken many weeks.[2]

The utility of Guido's procedures lay in their easy adaptation to the performance of chant, for his system of hexachords built on C, F, and G fitted well into plainchant patterns and aided in satisfying the necessity within chant to avoid what were, on both philosophical and practical grounds, considered to be harshnesses and impossibilities. With its employment, one could provide against the sounding of tritone outlines and could maintain the purity of the mode. With the introduction of the one accidental, the choosing between B♭ and B♮, both situations could be easily handled, for, by following certain fairly simple rules, one could guarantee the correct placement of the half step in its proper position; as a determinant, it was this interval, that from *mi* to *fa,* that set the mode and gave it its own characteristic arrangement.

Since the system was based upon the hexachord, six notes in its *ut* to *la* compass, those melodies which had a more extensive range presented special problems. The accommodation was made by the rather ingenious use of what were called mutations, a mutation being that process whereby solmization syllables were interchangeable between hexachords

---

[1] A full description of the Guidonian system is given in Gustave Reese, *Music in the Middle Ages* (New York 1940), pp. 149–51. The basic source for a study of Guido's accomplishments is Jos. Smits van Waesberghe, *De musico-paedagogico et theoretico Guidone Aretino* (Florence 1953); the sections on solmization, mutations, and the hand appear on pp. 94–122.

[2] See the *Epistola Guidonis Michaeli Monacho,* in: Gerbert, *Scriptores,* II, 45.

at particular points defined by rule. For example, C within that hexachord beginning on the Γ below it carried the name *fa;* if it were necessary to proceed higher than the *la* of that hexachord, an E, one might
change the name of the C from *fa* to *ut,* making it the foundation syllable
of a new hexachord and thus allowing a rise to an A (*la* in the new one).

As we have said, there were three types of these hexachords, their
names determined by whether they contained B♭, B♮, or neither. The
first group, that containing B♭, had its initial notes on F's and was known
as the *molle* (soft); the second, with B♮ and beginning on G's, was
known as the *durum* (hard); the third, containing no B's of any kind, was
that beginning on C's and was called *naturale.* The arrangements of all
three, with all their possible hexachord designations, were given the
mnemonic device known as the Guidonian hand, where each knuckle
carried the letter name of the note as well as all its possible solmization
syllables in the various hexachords; with the hand, the singer was made
capable of remembering the order of the notes, as well as where the
semitone had to fall within each of the three hexachords.

This system, briefly outlined, is that which supported the performer
of monophonic music in its development after the 10th century; indeed,
for the modern performance of plainchant, the method is ideal and is,
in many ways, more suitable than any system since devised. Although
there are some problems in chants whose range is extraordinarily large,
difficulties discussed many times by the theorists of the Middle Ages,[3] it
serves as an easily understood and effective way to insure correct performance of the chant, even by the comparatively inexperienced singer.
It requires no knowledge of the mathematical subtleties on which the
modes and their interval arrangements are based; it also makes for truer
intonation than can be gotten from modern tuning procedures, an intonation closer to that employed during the period.

With the introduction of polyphony and its simultaneous sounding
of intervals as opposed to the consecutive performance characteristic of
monophony, new problems of solmization arose, problems that were,
however, rather easily solved within the context of the system. As long
as the sole accidental allowable was that occasioned by the choice between B♭ and B♮, the older system of hexachord construction and mutation could serve equally well within the new practice. Hexachords
continued to be built on the three main notes, C, F, and G; mutations still
were made to change from one hexachord to another at appropriate

---

[3] As for example, in the *Alleluia Te martyrum,* discussed by Ugolino of Orvieto;
Ugolini urbevetani declaratio musice discipline, ed. Albert Seay (Rome 1959–1962),
I, 227–28.

places. To assist in knowing what hexachords were required, it became the usage to insert a flat before B at various points, this not to indicate a flattening of the tone in the modern sense, but to show the performer where he must sound the B♭ as with the solmization syllable *fa*, thus making the *molle* hexachord mandatory; to indicate the *durum*, a natural sign could be used, this defining the place of *mi*. With these guides, the singer would find little difficulty in the performance of the new repertoire, that of polyphony; even when these guides were omitted, and they often were, the correct pitch could be determined by simple application of the rules already learned for the introduction of mutations within monophony.[4]

With the fuller development of polyphony within the 13th century, extensions of the system were made, for, with the increasing use of transposed modes, it was found necessary to broaden the application of the flat sign as an indicator of the place of *fa*. Within the Notre Dame repertoire, there are many instances of the flat appearing before an E, again without the significance of the lowered half step, but with the then normal meaning of *fa* as the appropriate solmization syllable. Evidently, if E♭ be taken as *fa*, we have the introduction of a new hexachord, one whose *ut* will be found on B♭ and one that will thus provide a whole new set of syllables to be put by the side of those already part of the traditional three.

A second problem, arising in the Ars nova of the 14th century, was the growth of a cadential feeling, emphasized within the music by the use of a raised leading tone, the *mi-fa* relationship now acting as the determinant of a resting point. Where the older plainchant had allowed the sub-final to remain without alteration and to retain a *mi-fa* form to the final in only Modes V and VI, the new approach was to give this half step feeling to cadences in all modes, thus, in a sense, destroying certain modal characteristics in favor of the goal of cadential feeling. To achieve this *mi-fa*, the natural sign used to indicate B♮ within the hand, the normal *mi*, was no longer limited to that one isolated place. Now, it was to be used as a sign that the note before which it was placed was to be sung as

---

[4] These rules could range from the simple to the complex. An anonymous theorist of the 12th century, in speaking of the problem of B♭ or B♮, merely states that: "Where a melody sounds most harsh, B♭ is inserted stealthily instead of B♮ to temper the tritone, but where the melody returns to its normal nature, it should be removed." The complete treatise is reprinted in Albert Seay, *An Anonymous Treatise from St. Martial*, in: *Annales musicologiques*, V (1957), 7–42; the quotation is from Cap. XIII, line 9. For a more complex set of prescriptions, see Johannes Tinctoris, *Expositio manus*, in: Coussemaker, *Scriptorum*, IV, 10–14; unfortunately, most of the examples are incorrect and do not make the mutational process clear. A translation of this treatise by the present author will appear during the coming year in the *Journal of Music Theory*.

a *mi*, its immediate upper neighbor then being performed as a *fa;* thus the desired cadential effect could be achieved. This usage is defined by one Richard of Normandy, as quoted by Marchettus of Padua: "Wherever a ♮ is placed, we say the syllable *mi;* wherever, indeed, a ♭, we say the syllable *fa*." [5] Together with these two signs, Marchettus mentions a third, evidently the ♯, appearing only in measured music, one that also makes a raised semitone, a *mi;* this last is called *musica falsa* (false music), for it is a sign not part of the regular system.[6]

Evidence of the assimilation of these extensions into the music of the time is obvious, for one of the major characteristics of both French and Italian music of the Ars nova is the comparatively large number of accidentals appearing in the sources, sharps, flats, and naturals indicating the change of pitch of various notes. Raised semitones are found on C, F, and G in profusion, although lowered semitones include only those of the past, on B and E. Not every required accidental is written in the music, but, in most cases, enough are given to suggest strongly those others which should be supplied. Theorists of the Ars nova who describe the practice make no real effort to suggest that these *mi-fa* relationships imply a full series of hexachords or additions to the possible series of mutations; they are not part of the traditional scheme and are thus to be left to one side.[7]

It is only around the close of the 14th century that theorists first tried to come to grips with how to fit these divagations from the original pure modal system into the Guidonian scheme of solmization. As a first step, there had already been an attempt to denigrate the process of chromatic insertions by redefining it; thus, the stigma attached to the term "false" could be removed. To theorists, the proper term to be used in describing these chromatic insertions was now *ficta*, a term suggesting that, while necessary, they were not to be considered on the same plane as the normal unaltered pitches, or *musica recta*. A typical explanation is that of Ugolino of Orvieto, who says: "For it is called *ficta*, because such music is placed in that location where it really is not, but is pretended to be, so that the imperfection of consonances and dissonances may be filled out." [8] It cannot be called false music, for this would give the wrong connotations; it is not something to be used at the performer's will, but

---

[5] In the *Lucidarium musicae planae*, Gerbert, III, 89.

[6] *Idem*. In spite of the reference to the third sign, Marchettus never gives an example of it, save in the pertinent sections of the *Pomerium;* see *Marcheti de Padua Pomerium*, ed. Giuseppe Vecchi (Rome 1961), pp. 68–74.

[7] In spite of Marchettus's specification of the use of *mi* and *fa*, his discussion of the mutation is confined to the traditional hexachords, and none of the possibilities caused by *musica falsa* are allowed to interfere with the traditional viewpoints.

[8] Ugolino, II, 44.

is necessary. A bit later on, he states: "*Musica ficta* is the necessary placing of any syllable in a position where it is not through its own properties, for the perfection of the consonance." [9]

With these definitions, one may see something of the problems facing the theorist of the 15th century. To begin with, the new chromaticism could not be regarded as but an optional way of beautifying the musical line, for it was an integral part of the web of the music. At the same time, it had to be fitted into the system somewhere, for, with the typical medieval attitude of reference to authority, the whole scheme of solmization, so laboriously built up through the centuries and so obviously of merit in plainchant performance, could not be discarded or drastically reworked without, so theorists felt, chopping at the very roots of music itself. Yet, if one retained the solmization system and its Guidonian hand, the use of the *mi-fa* relationship in new places had to be assimilated, if only to keep some semblance of order and consistency.

The problem, however, went deeper than the mere integration of the new chromatics within the hand, for this was not just a matter of performance alone; if it had been, the solutions achieved within the 14th century, the addition of necessary accidental signs, would have been enough. The performer, seeing these signs, understood their meaning and took care of them in his performance, without regard to too many subtleties about their place in the Guidonian scheme of things. From the practical aspect, this would have been sufficient.

The obstacle came in that this level of music, the *musica instrumentalis* of Boetius's classification, was the lowest of three, standing below *musica humana* and *mundana*, serving to furnish but the physical manifestations of that on which a complete philosophical and speculative superstructure was raised. *Musica instrumentalis* was but the physical manifestation of those ratios and mathematical proportions that served, in their highest sense, to explain the beauties of the universe and the rationality behind God's creations; music reflected, in its microcosm, the perfection of the macrocosm and the order in which it was arranged.[10]

With this in mind, it is not difficult to see why theorists interested in the speculative aspects of music found it so necessary to spend much time and effort on how to make the new chromaticism not only a part of the practical scheme already long in use, but also how to fit these novelties into the elaborate mathematical system lying at the foundation of all music. One may well ask, "Why not accept these cadential for-

---

[9] *Ibid.*, II, 45.
[10] A full discussion of medieval esthetics is given by Edgar de Bruyne, *L'Esthétique du moyen âge* (Louvain 1947); for the special place of Boetius, see Leo Schrade. *Music in the Philosophy of Boetius*, in: MQ, XXXIII (1947), 188–200.

mulae and added accidentals for what they were, embellishments added for purely musical reasons?" The answer remains that it could not be so simple as this if philosophical requirements had to be satisfied as well.

To understand the difficulties, one must first recognize that the hexachord, as viewed by theorists of the late 14th and 15th centuries, was no longer merely an aid in the remembering of where the semitone fell in the outlining of the modes. It had become a way of demonstrating the mathematical ratios so important to the philosopher, where the place of each tone was calculated through the use of the monochord, that one-stringed instrument used as concrete demonstration of the various tonal proportions. The semitone was not just a note halfway in between two notes a tone apart, but had many variations in size, depending on the mathematical processes by which it was determined. As late as the time of Tinctoris, one still finds definitions of two different-sized semitones, one containing two *dieses*, the other three;[11] earlier, Marchettus speaks of three different semitones, the diatonic, enharmonic, and chromatic,[12] while Johannes Hothby gives his three forms the names, *duro*, *molle*, and *naturale*, thus relating them to the hexachord.[13] The practitioner could say, as one theorist of the 12th century did, "A semitone is a small space of rise or fall that is made from one pitch to the nearest pitch,"[14] or "One tone does not differ from any other tone, nor one semitone from another semitone."[15] The speculative musician could not and would not agree with this simplification.

Thus it is that the first attempts to coordinate the new with the old took the form of application of the principles of the old system to the extensions made by the new. The most grandiose effort seems to have been that made by Ugolino as one of the last of those to write a treatise, his *Declaratio musice discipline*, within the medieval tradition of the philosopher and speculator. His Book II, Chapter XXXIV, entitled *De ficta musica*,[16] is a magnificent attempt to bring some order out of the chaos he saw rising about him, using the ♮ and the ♭ in their traditional meanings of *mi* and *fa* to make perfect intervals that would otherwise have been imperfect. In addition, he suggests the formation of hexachords

---

[11] Tinctoris, *Expositio* (Coussemaker, IV, 15). See also Johannes Tinctoris, *Terminorum musicae diffinitorium*, ed. & transl. Carl Parrish (London 1963), pp. 56–57.

[12] *Pomerium*, pp. 69–70.

[13] Johannes Hothby, *Epistola*, Florence, Bib. Naz., Magliabecchiana XIX, 36, fols. 74ʳ–78ʳ. This treatise, together with two other treatises by Hothby, is shortly to be published by the American Institute of Musicology.

[14] Seay, *An Anonymous Treatise*, p. 15.

[15] *Ibid.*, p. 16.

[16] Ugolino, II, 44–53.

and their appropriate syllables not only on the normal C, F, and G, but also on B♭, D, and E♭. Pitches may, in this manner, now have from one to six solmization syllables, rather than a maximum of but three as in the basic Guidonian system.[17]

To make these extensions part of the mathematical complex so needed for speculative purposes, Ugolino's treatise on the monochord, coming at the close of his work,[18] uses the speculative approach to give three ways of finding pitches on that instrument, the first according to *musica recta,* the second and third in two ways, by *musica ficta.* The first division, that staying within the notes as found in Guido's original hand, is traditional in every way. The second division, that of the first way by *musica ficta,* provides for the insertion of semitones between all the tones not so provided in the *recta* division; the method here is that of inserting the minor semitone as the lower unit, the major semitone as the upper. The third division, the second in *musica ficta,* reverses the order, the major semitone falling as the lower unit. All of these are finally combined into one schematic diagram, the space between two tones being filled by, in order, one minor semitone, a comma, and a second minor semitone, the minor semitone and comma equalling together the major semitone. These could be taken in either direction, that is, the tone could be lowered or raised by either a minor or major semitone.

To none of his explanations does Ugolino attach more than the term *musica ficta,* for to him it is still something that lay outside the hand; and although much of the terminology used by Guido's solmization is retained, it is clear in Ugolino's mind that none of this is a part of the system in the same way as the original material. Ugolino's assimilation of chromaticism has been one of fitting the elements into the mathematical aspects, so that the new pitches could be determined as accurately as those of the past, by proportional division of the string of the monochord.

The final step made during the 15th century, that giving full recognition to these accretions, is the special naming of the new kinds of hexachords formed, those built on other tones than the usual three; the designation of a hexachord not found on C, F, or G is now that of a *coniuncta.* One typical definition found in several sources is: "A *coniuncta* is the intellectual transposition of one propriety or deduction

---

[17] Prosdocimus de Beldemandis, in his *Libellus monocordi* (Coussemaker, III, 248–58) precedes Ugolino in an attempt to do much the same thing, but does not carry through the discussion to the same full extent. There is more of an awareness on the part of Prosdocimus that the chromatic novelties cannot be made to fit into the earlier scheme, perhaps owing to his closer ties to the world of the university.

[18] Ugolino, III, 227–53.

from its proper place to a different place either above or below." [19] The terms *proprietas* and *deductio* here act as synonyms for the hexachord. A second definition, that of Tinctoris, is: "A *coniuncta* is when there is made of the normal tone an abnormal semitone or of the normal semitone an abnormal tone." Tinctoris gives a further definition as: "A *coniuncta* is the place of a flat or a natural in an abnormal place." In both definitions, the terms "normal" and "abnormal" mean "by rule" and "against the rule," the rule being that of the organization of the usual three hexachords and the placement of the *mi-fa* within them.[20]

The most extensive discussion of the use of the *coniuncta* is that given by Anonymous XI, in a work dating from the middle of the 15th century. He states that there are eight places in which a *coniuncta* may be found, giving for each one of the eight an example. The eight hexachords he erects as *coniunctae* are shown in the following example; the proper designation by accidental is indicated over the appropriate note:

Ex. 1   Anonymous XI (Coussemaker, III, pp. 426–29)

The *coniunctae* are to be used in both monophony and polyphony, as is shown by the particular examples used, all taken from plainchant.[21] These examples indicate that transposition of plainchant had become a fairly common practice; certain excerpts are given from the same plain-

---

[19] Anonymous XI, *Tractatus de musica plana et mensurabili* (Coussemaker, III, 426), gives the basic definition; this particular variation is found in Florentius de Faxolis, *Liber musices*, Milan, Trivulziana 2146, fol. 43ᵛ, and Rome, Vatican, Capponi 206, fol. 21ʳ. The Latin reads: "Coniuncta est alicuius proprietatis seu deductionis de loco proprio ad alienum locum sub vel supra intellectualis transpositio." We shall make further reference to both these sources later.

[20] These two definitions apear in the *Diffinitorium*, ed. Parrish, pp. 14–15. Parrish, in his note (p. 83), does not realize that the *coniuncta* is not merely a "chromatic alteration" of one tone, but is a true hexachord provided with solmization syllables.

[21] These examples may nearly all be found in present-day chantbooks, the *Liber Usualis*, *Graduale*, etc. There are intimations that chromaticism had begun to find its way into the chant, to judge from Anonymous XI's remarks, but this problem demands further investigation before definite statements can be made.

chant but taken at different pitch levels, one at the traditional pitch, the other in one of the *coniunctae.*[22] Curiously, Anonymous XI maintains the same general position as that of Ugolino, that the new use of the semitone lay outside tradition and the norm. As a footnote, he divides the types of added accidentals signified by *mi-fa* into three categories, the first including the traditional places, the second defined by *mi* on D, F, and d, the third by *fa* on E, a, and e. A chart is appended showing these placings; the alterations of the second and third categories are ". . . called improperly semitones; more properly they are *coniunctae* since they are not in the same form as what is called a semitone."[23] Evidently, the new additions had still not received a complete acceptance:

Ex. 2   Anonymous XI (Coussemaker, III, p. 429)

From this starting point, it was not long until the system of *coniunctae* was extended to hexachords beginning on other notes. The manuscript, Rome, Vatican, Capponi 206, contains two sections on the *coniuncta,* one giving a short definition of each variety with a musical example, the second in the form of a written text without examples.[24] Both are evidently derived from Anonymous XI, for the one, in explaining the term, repeats the material of the earlier source almost without change, although it gives no real definition. The other, which includes examples, begins with a definition like that of Anonymous XI, but instead of retaining the original eight places, extends the group to eleven, beginning with two hexachords whose *ut* lies outside the hand (on E♭ and F) and closing with one whose *la* is above the normal limit, E. Instead of indicating on these examples the place of *mi* or *fa,* the author uses the nomenclature of the usual three, i.e. *molle, quadrum* (an equivalent of

---

[22] Nicolaus Wollick, in his *Musica gregoriana* (Köln 1501), mentions some of the possible transpositions; see the modern edition by Klaus Wolfgang Niemöller (Köln 1955), p. 55.

[23] Anonymous XI, pp. 429–30. Curiously, in spite of the fact that a *mi* on D♯ would clearly suggest a *coniuncta* beginning on B♮, this hexachord is not given as one of the eight.

[24] The manuscript is described by William G. Waite, *Two Musical Poems of the Middle Ages,* in: *Musik und Geschichte* (Köln 1963), pp. 13–34. The particular portions on *coniunctae* come on fols. 20ʳ–22ʳ.

durum), and *natura*.[25] The reasons for these classifications are not clear, but they suggest that the *coniunctae* no longer lie outside the norm; they are now but special forms of the usual hexachord system.

A fourth statement on the *coniuncta* is given by Florentius de Faxolis in his *Liber musices* of around 1496.[26] He too bases his definition of the *coniuncta* on that of Anonymous XI, attributing it, however, to Arnaldus Dalps. His system is generally that already noted, although he gives some twelve places for the beginning of *coniunctae;* he does not use the terminology already seen, the division of these new hexachords by *molle*, *durum*, and *natura*, but indicates the place of *mi* or *fa* in each. To summarize the places on which all these new hexachords might begin, plus the older ones, we append an example here, including the letters M, D, or N to show the category given them by our Capponi Anonymous:

Ex. 3

Together with the progress seen in these writers in the expansion of the hexachord system, there is a further extension made by Johannes Hothby, who, in his various works, allowed the construction of hexachords on F♯, A♭, B♮, D♭, and E♮.[27] With these additions, practically every note of the chromatic scale as we now know it gained the potentiality of becoming a starting point for the building of a hexachord using the traditional syllables. Thus, by the latter half of the 15th century, almost every note had a multitude of possibilities for mutations, with all of the six solmization syllables present on every one.

With the confusion that this brought about, where the multiplication of hexachords was so great, it is not to be wondered that Tinctoris, in the interest of simplicity, tried to skirt the whole subject. Within his various treatises, there is no explanation of the *coniuncta* or *musica ficta*, the only appearance of the terms coming in the *Diffinitorium* and there without comment. In his discussion of the hand and how solmization syllables are to be used, found in the *Expositio manus*, there is no mention

---

[25] Bartolomeo Ramos, in his *Musica practica*, suggests that when a note is depressed from its proper place, it is then called *molle*, when raised *quadrum*. This explanation is not satisfactory, for it does not include the reason for the appellation of *natura;* in addition, by this definition the hexachord beginning on E♭ should be called *molle*. Instead, it has been labelled as *natura*. For Ramos's remarks, see the edition of Johannes Wolf (Leipzig 1901), p. 30.

[26] This treatise is completely discussed in Albert Seay, *The 'Liber Musices' of Florentius de Faxolis*, in: *Musik und Geschichte* (Köln 1963), pp. 71-95.

[27] See Gilbert Reaney, *Hothby*, in: MGG, VI, 771-82.

of any hexachord formations other than those described by Guido. His most significant remark is in Chapter III of this book, that there are many musicians who use the sign ♯ badly as a *clavis*, for this particular sign indicates a chromatic semitone.[28] This statement, together with the earlier evidence, suggests that Tinctoris recognized the difficulties brought about by the indiscriminate application of hexachord sequences on all notes; he evidently wished to make a distinction between the basic hexachords on C, F, and G, still important in the performance of plainchant, and those that had been called forth by the various chromatic additions. One may draw something of a parallel with modern conditions: the very fact that a number of accidentals may be found within a work does not necessarily imply modulation away from the central tonality; these accidentals are but additions to the basic framework. In the same way, Tinctoris believed that the chromatic tones needed for proper cadences and for the avoidance of harsh intervals were not alterations of the basic mode, but were extraneous additions that ought not to cause violent dislocations of hexachord relationships; evidently he believed that there were two kinds of functional semitones, those found in the basic three hexachords and those used for chromaticism.

While Tinctoris's difficulties with the new approach can only be deduced, those of Ramos are much more explicit. His *Musica practica* (1482) is a concentrated attack upon the failings of his own time, together with what he felt to be fitting solutions of their problems. In no area does he seem to be quite so bitter as when attacking those who had tried to graft the *coniunctae* upon the Guidonian system.

Ramos's position can be quickly summarized as one of complete opposition to the whole Guidonian approach, particularly in the perverted form caused by the massive number of mutations brought about by the overabundance of *coniunctae*. When, as Ramos says, it is possible to use six solmization syllables on any note, the number of possible mutations back and forth from any one of the six hexachords to any one of the others makes the whole process ridiculous; those who attempt to suggest that this system is logical, and their number includes Johannes Hothby as a primary target, are men who should know better.[29] The crux of their difficulty lies in the fact that, by using all these mutations, one cannot always get back to the correct pitch; with the variation in size of the semitone depending on how it is reached, from above or below, too many changes in solmization syllables will cause distinct alteration of the pitch level. In polyphony, the same problem is present, for

[28] Tinctoris, *Expositio* (Coussemaker, IV, 5).
[29] Ramos, pp. 37–38.

with too many mutations, fifths and octaves cannot remain pure and will inevitably become out of tune.

It is for this reason that Ramos introduced his famous *Psal-li-tur per vo-ces is-tas*, a solmization method with but one mutation, from *Psal-*to *-tas* and the reverse, the whole system built upon the identity of octave C's, the tone on which the solmization begins.[30] Within Ramos's system, the flat, sharp, and natural begin to take on their modern significance, without reference to the *mi-fa* relationship. To Ramos, there is no necessity for the semitone relation to be confined to the syllables *mi-fa;* this is where the followers of Guido had gone astray, with their necessity to constrict the new chromaticism within the older system.[31]

That Ramos's strictures did little or no good at the time was to be expected, for the weight of medieval authority was still strong enough to withstand pressures from the purely practical musician. To use Ramos's own phraseology, his contemporaries followed the older theorists as if they had promulgated a law of Scripture, not to be altered.[32] But, after the turn of the century, when Renaissance attitudes had had time to make themselves felt, the old necessity for continual reference to authority, for coordination of novelties within the medieval speculative framework, for the justification of innovation by fitting it into the over-all philosophical scheme, all these began to give way before the practical necessities felt by the composer. Although this process of dissolution of the Middle Ages had begun earlier, within the Ars nova, its final stage, the regarding of music as a fine art and not a liberal art within the quadrivium, was well on its way. The failure of the *coniuncta* to serve as a way of integrating the new practices with the old attitudes is but one more sign of decay.

How far the rules of *musica ficta* in the traditional sense could be taken is exemplified in the well-known *Quidnam ebrietas* of Adriano Willaert, that amazing duo in which the lower voice seemingly ends on a dissonant seventh, but, when performed by the rules of *musica ficta*, comes to a close on an octave.[33] Less known is the anonymous early 16th-century chanson, *Il estoit ung bonhomme*,[34] whose ending shows the use of *coniunctae* and solmization syllables to suggest accidentals; we give here the closing bars of the work:

[30] *Ibid.*, pp. 18–21.
[31] *Ibid.*, p. 40.
[32] For a short description of the furor aroused, see Gustave Reese, *Music in the Renaissance* (New York 1954), pp. 586–87.
[33] Discussed in Reese, MR, pp. 369–70.
[34] Published in a practical edition (ed. Albert Seay) by the Colorado College Music Press, Colorado Springs.

Ex. 4 Anonymous, *Il estoit ung bonhomme* (Paris, BN fr. 1597, fols. 59ᵛ–60ʳ)

Inspection of the text will show something of the impasse reached by the *coniuncta*, where any note could have any syllable. Only where there is a semblance of a scale do the syllables have any real meaning and then only in cases where a *mi* or *fa* can be used to indicate a semitone relationship.

Can this history of the rise and fall of the *coniuncta* have any relationship to the still unsolved problem as to why, within the music of the 15th century, there has disappeared the luxuriance of indicated accidentals seen in the music of the 14th century? It may be advanced as a partial hypothesis that one of the reasons for this change may lie in the change of the position of added chromaticism from *musica falsa* or *ficta* and an understanding of its place as outside *musica recta* to an acceptance within the over-all framework as but an extension of what had already been approved, the *coniunctae* acting merely as additional ways of making mutations. As part of the system, with well-established rules (at least according to the theorists), the now numerous chromatic insertions did not need to be notated by 15th-century musicians any more than the B♭/B♮ variation had had to be indicated by composers of the 13th century. These insertions were supposedly well taken care of by their assimilation into the already long established and well understood Guidonian system and, by that assimilation, avoided any need to be singled out as different and requiring special notational procedures.

That none of these assumptions worked out practically is obvious; yet, well into the 16th century, conservative composers continued to notate their music as if the older concepts were still valid.[35] One can

[35] A major attempt to solve all these same problems comes with the 16th-century theorist, Francesco de Brugis, who made strong attempts to cope with the objections brought up by Ramos. I have not considered his work here, since it lies outside the present topic. It has recently been published: Giuseppe Massera, *La 'Mano Musicale*

hardly help the feeling that many of them were in much the same position as that of Johannes Brahms, who, when all the rest of the world wrote for the chromatic horn, was still preparing his parts for the natural one. Medieval theory had worked well for its time, and many people still believed that it could still work in a new age. The development of the *coniuncta* is but one attempt made by 15th-century theorists to put new wine into old bottles; it could not, but in the eyes of these men, it should have succeeded.

Perfetta' di Francesco de Brugis (Florence 1963); Prof. Massera's introduction is extremely valuable, particularly for his discussion of the conservative reactions to Ramos's work.

BASSE-DANCE MUSIC IN SOME GERMAN MANUSCRIPTS OF THE 15th CENTURY

by EILEEN SOUTHERN

MUCH HAS BEEN WRITTEN about the basse dance in recent years.[1] We now know, for example, that by the middle of the 15th century, basse dances had become the most fashionable of the social dances in the aristocratic circles of western Europe, particularly in Italy and in France. The dance treatises of the time, of which more than a dozen are extant, explain in detail the various movements of the dance and the formation of the individual steps. Along with other literary sources, they inform us of the names of the most popular dances, as well as when, where, and how they were performed. From pictorial sources, we obtain additional information about dance formations and positions, the costumes of the dancers, and the kinds of instruments used to accompany them.[2]

Many contemporary paintings and engravings depict groups of three musicians playing dance music on such instruments as two shawms and a slide-trumpet; or beaked flute and drum, zink, and trombone; or lute, harp, and drum. But basse dances were performed to the music of a single player as well. Woodcuts and engravings show lutenists and harpists accompanying the dance, while literary sources mention, in addition, portative organ accompaniment. Castiglione, writing his *Il Cortegiano* in the early 16th century, undoubtedly describes an old tradition when he tells how the gathered company was entertained: Madonna Margarita

[1] See the comprehensive bibliography, with lists of primary and secondary sources, accompanying the essay of Manfred Bukofzer, *A Polyphonic Basse Dance of the Renaissance*, in: *Studies in Medieval and Renaissance Music* (New York 1950), pp. 190–216. Among the more recent studies which contain relevant information are: Otto Gombosi, *Preface to Compositione di Messer Vincenzo Capirola. Lute-book circa 1517* (Neuilly-sur-Seine 1955); Otto Kinkeldey, *Dance Tunes of the Fifteenth Century*, in: *Instrumental Music* (Cambridge 1959), pp. 3–30, 89–152; Eileen Southern, *Some Keyboard Basse Dances of the Fifteenth Century*, in: *Acta musicologica*, XXXV (1963), 114–24.

[2] Many of the studies listed in Bukofzer's bibliography include illustrations. An excellent additional source for pictorial evidence is *The Horizon Book of the Renaissance* (New York 1961).

738

nd Costanza Fregosa joined hands and danced a basse dance while
Barletto played on his instruments (probably pipe and tabor).

According to the dance manuals, the term *basse dance* refers to a
dance complex or family of dances rather than to a single dance. The
French sources distinguish between the *basse dance majeur*, the basse
dance proper, and the *basse dance mineur*, the *pas de Brabant* or *saltarello*. The Italian writers recognize four basic types, of which the first or
misura imperiale is the bassadanza proper; the *misura siconda* is the
quaternaria or *saltarello tedesco;* the *misura terza* is the *saltarello;* and the
misura quarta, the *piva* or *cacciata*.[3] These dance types differ from each
other chiefly with regard to meter and tempo, for they employ the same
basic steps, though the number of movements and the succession of steps
vary from dance to dance. The same music can be used to accompany
the different dance types, provided such music is played in the appropriate meters and tempos.

As for the dance music, it might consist of the tune or the tenor of a
favorite ballad which is "set to a basse dance."[4] In the two most important repositories of 15th-century basse dances—Brussels, Bibliothèque
royale, MS 9085 and Michel de Toulouze, *L'Art et instruction de bien
dancer* (hereafter referred to as Brussels and Toulouze)—several melodies are easily identifiable as corresponding to the tenors of popular
chansons of the period.[5] Undoubtedly, it was common practice for
dance musicians to extract tenor melodies from partsongs and turn them
into dance tenors by giving identical long-note values to the tones of
the melodies. The dance tenors were then used as cantus firmi in new
polyphonic settings with improvised upper voices or with written-out
upper voices in improvisatory style.

Some of the melodies from which the dance tenors derived, however,
may well have originated and circulated as monophonic compositions
only. Several conclusions reached in a study of two monophonic collections of the early 16th century, Paris, Bibliothèque nationale, MS fonds
fr. 9346 (*Le Manuscrit de Bayeux*), and MS fonds fr. 12744, are relevant
here.[6] The monophonic chansons in the two sources were found to differ

[3] The French term *mesure* is not exactly the same as the Italian term *misura*.
The former refers to a group of dance steps or a dance movement, several of
which constitute the dance. The latter refers to the dance type, distinguished from
other dance types by its meter, tempo, and use of typical steps.
[4] See further in Guglielmo Ebreo, *Trattato dell'arte de ballo*. Reprint by Francesco Zambrini (Bologna 1873), p. 28; Thoinot Arbeau (Jehan Tabourot), *Orchésographie* (Lengres 1588); reprint by Laura Fonta (Paris 1888), fol. 24ᵛ.
[5] The Brussels MS is published in facsimile edition by Ernest Closson, *Le Manuscrit dit des basse dances* (Brussels 1912); the Toulouze print is published in facsimile
edition by Victor Scholderer, *L'Art et instruction de bien dancer* (London 1936).
[6] See the study by Gustave Reese and Theodore Karp, *Monophony in a Group of*

from their polyphonic counterparts in significant ways, so that they should be regarded as independent pieces rather than as extractions from partsongs. As we shall see, some of the melodies associated with basse dances are extant as independent pieces as well as in polyphonic settings.

The basse-dance repertoire of the 15th century comprises, at most, less than 100 compositions, including both monophonic and polyphonic pieces. We know of only four Italian bassadanza tunes. Antonio Cornazano's manual, *Libro dell'arte del danzare*, contains three *tenori da basse-dance et saltarelli*. A fourth tune is the one that served as a model for the cantus firmi in a Mass cycle of the Italian composer Faugues, *Missa la basse dance*.

The French repertoire of dance tunes is more extensive. Brussels and Toulouze, between them, contain 56 different basse-dance melodies. Of the 59 compositions in the manuscript, 52 are basse dances. But two of the dances, *Beaulte* (No. 1) and *La verdelete* (No. 41), have identical melodies, though their titles and choreographies differ. Consequently, Brussels contributes only 51 melodies to the French repertoire. The Toulouze incunabulum contains five melodies that do not appear in Brussels. So far as I know, no one has yet called attention to the concordance of *Beaulte* and *La verdelete*. The fact that a melody receives a different title (in both Brussels and Toulouze) when associated with different choreographies is of some importance, for it suggests that the titles in the two sources indicate the names of the dances, which may or may not be identical with the titles of the original models for the dance tunes.

Some specialists regard the melodies of the so-called Namur collection as dance tunes, but the existence of a relationship between the melodies and extant dance choreographies has not yet been proved.[7] Despite a similarity between the titles of the dance tune *Je suis povere de leese* (Brussels No. 46) and the Namur tune *Je suis si pauvre de liesse*, the two melodies are not concordant. Only the opening strains show a resemblance (ten notes in the Brussels tune, eleven notes in the Namur tune); and the 42-note dance melody is much shorter than the Namur melody of 55 notes. Most of the Namur melodies are written in a non-committal stroke notation. However, one of the tunes, *Jenesse m'abuse*

Renaissance Chansonniers, in: JAMS, V (1952), 4–15. For Paris MS 9346, see *Le Manuscrit de Bayeux*, ed. Théodore Gérold (Strasbourg 1921); for Paris MS 12744, see *Chansons du XVe siècle*, ed. Gaston Paris and Auguste Gevaert (Paris 1875).

[7] I am grateful to Frederick Crane for his communication in regard to the so-called Namur collection and for his generosity in allowing me to use his micro-film of a study which includes facsimile pages of the Namur MS: Ernest Montellier, *Quatorze chansons du XVe siècle*, in: *Commission de la vieille chanson populaire. Annuaire: 1939* (Antwerp 1939), pp. 153–213.

amour, is recorded in the same kind of notation as that used to record the French dance tunes; and the middle part of another melody, *Tres belle et bonne*, is written also in black breves. It is conceivable that these two melodies are to be associated with the French basse-dance repertoire.[8]

In addition to the *Spagna* arrangements, the 15th-century repertoire of polyphonic basse dances includes settings of two other bassadanza tunes and of three French dance tunes.[9] There are also isolated examples of compositions that present all the earmarks of basse dances, but for which no monophonic models or choreographies have yet been found.[10] The main purpose of the present discussion is to reveal the existence of other polyphonic basse dances of the 15th century, heretofore unnoticed. For that, we turn to four German manuscripts written during the third quarter of the century. Some of their contents, however, date from a much earlier period.

Two of the manuscripts are devoted primarily to songs: the *Lochamer Liederbuch*, Berlin, Deutsche Staatsbibliothek, Mus. MS 40613, and the *Schedelsches Liederbuch*, Munich, Bayerische Staatsbibliothek, Cim. 351a. The Berlin source contains chiefly monophonic compositions; the Munich manuscript includes just two monophonic pieces in its repertoire of 128 compositions. The other two manuscripts are devoted primarily to keyboard music: Paumann's *Fundamentum organisandi*, bound in Berlin MS 40613 along with the *Lochamer Liederbuch*, and the *Buxheimer Orgelbuch*, Munich, Bayerische Staatsbibliothek, Cim. 352b.[11] In several studies, writers have called attention to the close interrelationship of the four manuscripts. The contents of the keyboard sources include arrangements of a large number of the repertoire items of the songbooks in the form of settings of the monophonic pieces as well as parody treatments or intabulations of the partsongs. Moreover, there are quite a few concordances among the four manuscripts.

Before discussing the newly-discovered German dances, I should like to review briefly the salient features of 15th-century basse dances as we have come to know them. Particularly is it important to distinguish

---

[8] See Montellier, *Quatorze chansons*, pp. 209, 169.

[9] The polyphonic basse dances are discussed in Bukofzer, *A Polyphonic Basse Dance* and in Southern, *Some Keyboard Basse Dances*.

[10] See further in Gombosi, *Preface*, p. xxxviii; Southern, *Some Keyboard Basse Dances*, pp. 122–23; Manfred Bukofzer, *Changing Aspects of Medieval and Renaissance Music*, in: MQ, XLIV (1958), 14–17.

[11] Berlin MS 40613 is published in facsimile edition by Konrad Ameln, *Locheimer Liederbuch und Fundamentum organisandi des Conrad Paumann* (Berlin 1925). Munich Cim. 352b is published in facsimile edition by Bertha Wallner, *Das Buxheimer Orgelbuch* (Kassel and Basel 1955), and in a modern edition by Wallner as Volumes 37–39 of *Das Erbe deutscher Musik* (Kassel 1958–59). A style-critical study of the organ book appears in Eileen Southern, *The Buxheim Organ Book* (New York 1963).

between polyphonic compositions whose tenors merely resemble basse-dance melodies and real polyphonic dances with tenors that show strict correspondence to dance tunes. Presumably, only the latter were actually used to accompany dances.

One might consider that the evolution of a basse dance comprises three stages. In the first stage, a melody or the tenor of a partsong is chosen to be "set to a basse dance." In the second stage, the dance melody emerges as an independent entity, stripped of its original melodic and rhythmic intricacies and transformed into a melodic skeleton with non-committal, equal note values. It is this melody that agrees with the dance choreography, each step-unit of the dance corresponding to a note in the melody. To be sure, we do not know which comes first, the music or the dance. Some sources indicate that dances were composed to popular tunes; others suggest that the musicians composed tunes to fit existing dances. Probably common practice included both procedures. In the third and final stage, the dance melody appears as the tenor of a polyphonic elaboration (either improvised or written out) with each of its tones receiving three, four, or six beats according to the type of dance the music is designed to accompany. Since each note of the dance tune typically occupies a full measure (or sometimes two measures) in the polyphonic realization, the number of notes in the former is generally equal to the number of measures in the latter.

Obviously, the more we are able to compare the different versions of any one melody associated with a basse dance, the more we can learn about the procedure followed in developing a melody into basse-dance music. A melody may exist, for example, in several kinds of arrangements: varying monophonic versions, varying polyphonic settings, basse-dance arrangements, and varying polyphonic settings of the basse-dance versions. Fortunately, I have been able to track several such versions of a 15th-century melody—one which must have been extremely popular in its time. The melody circulated in the form of independent monophonic chansons entitled *On doibt bien aymer l'oyselet* and in polyphonic arrangements entitled *Il fait bon aimer l'oyselet*. Related music may have been used to accompany a basse dance, *L'oyselet*, for which only the choreography exists in a 16th-century source.[12] Ex. 1 shows one of the monophonic chansons, as in Paris MS 9346, and the beginnings of four other arrangements of the melody: (1) the tenor of a three-part setting by Antoine de Févin in Cambridge, Magdalene College, MS Pepys 1760; (2) a basse-dance arrangement in Brussels, *Languir*

---

[12] See further with regard to sources Howard M. Brown, *Music in the French Secular Theater, 1400–1550* (Cambridge, Mass. 1963), pp. 228–29.

en mille destresse; (3) a monophonic version, *Virginalis flos vernalis,* in the *Lochamer Liederbuch* (hereafter referred to as Lochamer); and (4) the tenor of a basse-dance setting, *Stublin,* in the *Buxheimer Orgelbuch* (hereafter referred to as Buxheim).[13]

Ex. 1   *On doibt bien aymer l'oyselet* (after Gérold, p. 15) and beginnings of tenor of Févin's *Il fait bon aimer l'oyselet* (after Brown, p. 82), *Languis en mille destresse* (transposed; Brussels No. 40), *Virginalis flos vernalis* (Lochamer No. 45), tenor of *Stublin* (Buxheim No. 135)

[13] The monophonic chanson is taken from Gérold, *Le Manuscrit de Bayeux,* p. 13; the Févin tenor is taken from Howard M. Brown, *Theatrical Chansons of the Fifteenth and Early Sixteenth Centuries* (Cambridge 1963), p. 82. The other extracts are transcribed from the manuscripts.

A comparison of the different arrangements of the melody reveals that they agree in significant aspects. For convenience in discussion, we have indicated the phrase structure of the melody by the use of lower-case letters, *a*, *b*, . . . As the example shows, the various phrases of the melody closely resemble each other, especially in their endings. The melodic motive that appears at the end of the *a* phrases reappears at the end of the *c* phrases.[14] Among the differences between the monophonic chansons and the tenors of corresponding three-part chansons—the Févin setting and an anonymous setting in London, British Museum, MS Harley 5242—are changes in figuration, rhythm, melody, and phrase repetition. The cantus firmus of an anonymous setting *a 4* in St. Gall, Stiftsbibliothek, Cod. 462 (the *Heer Liederbuch*), varies from the monophonic chansons with regard to changes in figuration, rests, and omission of a phrase.[15]

The basse-dance arrangement *Languir en mille destresse* is obviously a melodic and rhythmic abstraction of the chanson melody. The *a* phrase of the chanson versions matches perfectly the *a* strain of the dance tune. While the opening and closing notes of the dance's *b* strain correspond to those of the chanson's *b* phrase, the middle of the dance strain includes an interpolation of notes based on a motive of the chanson's *ad* phrase. The chanson's *c* phrase is omitted entirely in the dance melody. Like the chanson tenor (and unlike the monophonic chanson), the dance tune concludes with two *a* phrases, one of them incomplete.

Except that its notes are not all of equal value, the Lochamer melody almost exactly duplicates the basse-dance tune. The second part of the song, however, labeled *Repeticio,* has no counterpart in the dance tune. Its melody seems to derive from the second part of the chanson model, phrases *ad* and *c*. Since the Buxheim polyphonic dances, Nos. 135 and 136, incorporate the Lochamer melody as cantus firmus, they too have a *Repeticio* section. The dance directions of *Languis en mille destresse* agree perfectly with the polyphonic dance music of the *Stublin* arrangements in Buxheim. Presumably, the second sections of the pieces could be choreographed as a *retour de la basse dance*.[16]

In my first explorations into the subject of the Buxheim basse dances and their monophonic models in other German manuscripts, I had overlooked several compositions written in the same style as the dances, because I had assumed that the cantus firmi in these pieces derived from German lieder and, in one instance, from an abstract solmization formula. But further investigation of the so-called lieder proved them to be contra-

---

[14] With regard to the occurrence of stereotyped motives in the monophonic chansons of Paris MS 9346 and 12744, see further Gérold, *Le Manuscrit de Bayeux*, p. xlv.

[15] For a summary of the differences between the monophonic and polyphonic versions, see Reese and Karp, *Monophony in a Group of Renaissance Chansonniers*, p. 11.

[16] With regard to the *retour de la basse dance,* see further Thoinot Arbeau, *Orchésographie*, fols. 26ʳ–28ᵛ.

Ex. 2   Beginnings of *Maitresse* (Brussels No. 18), *Ich pin pey ir* (Lochamer
         No. 22), and tenor of *Ich bin by ir* (Buxheim No. 142)

facta of French basse-dance melodies and, consequently, the polyphonic
realizations of the tunes to be polyphonic dances.

The melody *Ich pin pey ir* (Lochamer No. 22) preserves intact and with minimal embellishment the dance tune *Maitresse* (Brussels No. 18, Toulouze No. 3). The German variant moves for the most part in equal note values and so differs even rhythmically only slightly from its counterpart in the French sources. In Buxheim, the polyphonic dances (Nos. 140, 141, 142) carry the superscription *Ich bin by ir*. All three dances are triple, each note of the original dance tune receiving the value of a perfect breve. In Ex. 2, we can compare the beginnings of three versions of the *Maitresse* melody: the French dance tune, the German variant, and the tenor of one of the polyphonic dances.

As is typical in the Buxheim dances, the first note in each measure of the cantus-firmus tenor corresponds to a note in the dance tune, except in approaches to the cadences. There, it is the last note in the penultimate measure of the phrase that corresponds, leading directly to the cadence final in the following measure. (Such tones are marked by asterisks in Ex. 2.) The German variants, melody and tenors, present little melodic deviation from the dance model; they omit the third note of the dance tune and offer substitutes for five other notes. Generally, the substitutions reflect a preference for the melodic third with special emphasis on the first, third, and fifth tones of the mode. (See notes enclosed by brackets in Ex. 2.) While the Buxheim tenors appear to follow the Lochamer version, they occasionally employ notes that point directly to the French model. For example, the 14th note of the dance tune has a counterpart in the keyboard tenor but not in the Lochamer tune.

It is fairly easy to collate the dance choreography, as given in the French sources, with the polyphonic dance music in Buxheim. The dance comprises 42 notes, five *mesures*.[17] At the beginning of the dance, the gentleman is to bow to his lady or make a *reverence*. Then follows a *grande mesure*, consisting of ten steps in the order: *branle*, two *simples* (one step-unit), five *doubles*, and three *reprises*. The second group of steps, a *petite mesure*, consists of the same basic steps in the same order but in a different number. A *moyenne mesure*, another *moyenne mesure*, and a *petite mesure* conclude the dance of five *mesures*. In Ex. 3, the dance steps of the first *mesure* of *Maitresse* are applied to the appropriate music of Buxheim No. 142.

Another group of Buxheim polyphonic dances, entitled *Mi ut re ut* (Nos. 118, 119, and 212), have cantus firmi that derive from the French dance melody *Denise* (Brussels No. 52). Like the *Maitresse* settings, these dances are triple. Although the original dance melody is Dorian,

---

[17] A detailed description of the dance steps based on the dance manuals is found in Curt Sachs, *World History of the Dance* (New York 1937), pp. 302–26.

Ex. 3   Collations of dance steps of *Maitresse* (Brussels No. 18) with opening music of *Ich bin by ir* (Buxheim No. 142)

the Buxheim dances are transposed to major modes; Nos. 118 and 119
are in C and No. 212 is in F. A monophonic version of *Denise* appears
in the *Schedelsches Liederbuch* (fol. 131) as the first of two melodies
superscribed *Carmina ytalica utilia pro coreis*—there transposed also to
the C mode. It is highly probable that this melody is the direct model for
the Buxheim polyphonic dances. Ex. 4 shows the beginnings of the
dance tune, the *Liederbuch* melody, and the tenor of one of the Buxheim
pieces. These arrangements of *Denise* are not the only pieces of basse-
dance derivation in our German sources that are transposed from the
original minor mode of the model to major modes. All of the arrangements of *Une fois avant que morir* (Brussels No. 24)—a chanson-like
setting in Paumann's *Fundamentum organisandi* and nine intabulations

Ex. 4 Beginnings of *Denise* (transposed; Brussels No. 53), *Carmina ytalica* (*Schedelschen Liederbuch*, fol. 131), and tenor of *Mi ut re ut* (Buxheim No. 142)

of the setting in Buxheim—are in major modes instead of the original Dorian.[18]

Since various points of evidence indicate that a third collection of pieces in Buxheim must represent actual dance music, I include them here in our discussion of polyphonic dances, even though a dance model has not yet been located. The pieces are cantus-firmus settings in basse-dance fashion of the Lochamer melody *Was ich begynne* (No. 25). Four compositions are grouped together in the manuscript (Nos. 205, 207, 208, 209), except for the interpolation of a brief prelude (No. 206), and two others are paired (Nos. 97 and 98). In style, the pieces are similar to the other polyphonic dances in Buxheim.

Some hints of the dance origin of the *Was ich begynne* arrangements appear in their superscriptions. No. 205 presents the superscription *Was ich begynn. Scilicet duodecimum notarum.* The significance of these words becomes more apparent when they are compared to the words in the heading of No. 207, *Secunda mensura. Wass ich begynne. Quartum notarum;* in the heading of No. 208, *Tercia mensura. Wass ich begynn. Trium notarum;* and of No. 209, *Wass ich begynn. Trium notarum.* In Buxheim superscriptions, the appearance of the word *notarum* always points to the meter of the pieces. Thus, No. 207 is quadruple and Nos. 208 and 209 are triple. Of this, the tablature notation leaves no room for doubt. No. 205 is a unique example of a Buxheim piece with a superscription that includes the words *duodecimum notarum.* At first glance, the words seem to suggest $\frac{12}{4}$ meter since *quartum notarum* indicates $\frac{4}{4}$ and *trium notarum,* $\frac{3}{4}$ meter (with the semibreve as the time-unit). Actually, however, the piece calls for transcription in $\frac{6}{4}$ meter. It appears then that the words *duodecimum notarum* indicate groupings of 12 minims or eighth notes.

Let us turn now to an interpretation for the other word-pairs in the superscriptions, those including the word *mensura.* Normally, we associate the word with the musical term *measure,* in the sense of having to do with rhythmical matters. But since the superscriptions employ other words to refer to rhythmic matters, the word *mensura* apparently is used here in its choreographic sense and, consequently, is to be equated with the Italian term *misura.* In the light of our observations, the wording of the superscriptions takes on a special importance, for it suggests that the *Was ich begynn* arrangements represent examples of the four Italian *misure* (see second page of this essay). If our assumption is cor-

---

[18] The dance manuals emphasize the importance, for both the composer of dance music and the dancer, of distinguishing between the major and minor modes. See further Guglielmo Ebreo, *Trattato,* p. 27.

rect, then No. 205, with its *duodecimum notarum*, is an example of the
bassadanza proper, *regina dell'altre misure*, in which "every note is
doubled, and three are worth six and six are worth twelve." No. 207 represents the *siconda misura* or the *quaternaria*, in which there are "four
strokes for each note" and which is "most used by the Germans." No. 208
is the *terza misura*, a *saltarello* with "three strokes for every note." Although No. 209 is also triple, the piece is more likely an example of the
piva rather than a *saltarello*. Its cantus firmus is much livelier than those
of the other three pieces, suggesting a faster tempo.[19] According to the
sources, the *piva* is characterized by a very fast tempo and the use of
doubles, while the *saltarello* is not quite as fast and employs *doubles* and
contrapasso steps. The bassadanza proper moves twice as slowly as does
the *piva* and calls for the use of all the steps. The *quaternaria* has a tempo
midway between that of the bassadanza proper and the *saltarello* and
uses chiefly *simples* and *reprises*. Whether our four pieces represent independent dances or the four sections of a *ballo* is not clear. We should
assume that they are independent dances, for the extant 15th-century
ballo melodies are hardly of a length comparable to that of the combined pieces.[20] In Ex. 5, the beginnings of the tenors of the four
pieces are shown for comparison.

Ex. 5   Beginnings of *Was ich begynne* arrangements (Buxheim Nos. 205,
        207, 208, 209)

No. 205 - *bassadanza*

---

[19] The quotations are from Curzio Mazzi, *Il libro dell'arte del danzare di Antonio
Cornazano*, in: *Bibliofilia*, XVII (1915), 29. However, Cornazano agrees substantially
with the other writers, except that he lists the dance types in the order: *saltarello*,
quaternaria, *piva*, and *bassadanza*.
[20] See further Kinkeldey, *Dance Tunes*, p. 13, and consult *balli* in the Appendix,
pp. 89–151.

No. 207 - *quaternaria*

No. 208 - *saltarello*

No. 209 - *piva*

In the absence of a dance model, we have reconstructed a dance tenor based on the Buxheim cantus firmi and the Lochamer melody. The reconstructed tune corresponds remarkably to a popular 15th-century melody, *L'amour de moy* (in both Paris MS 9085 and 12744), in the same way that *Languir en mille destresse* resembles *Il fait bon aimer l'oyselet*—that is, as a melodic and rhythmic abstraction. Choreographic directions for a basse dance with a similar title appear in two dance treatises of the early 16th century, and music for chansons with the title is extant in both monophonic and polyphonic forms.[21] The differences between one of the monophonic chansons and our dance tune are typical of those which were found to exist between the melodies of the two Paris chansonniers and the tenors of parallel polyphonic chansons. Such differences include repetition of a phrase, omission of a phrase, and interpolation of extraneous materials.[22] In Ex. 6, the reconstructed dance tune is presented for comparison with the chanson melody.[23]

Ex. 6 Comparison of reconstructed dance tune based on cantus firmi of *Was ich begynne* arrangements (Buxheim Nos. 205, 207, 208, 209) and melody *Was ich begynne* (Lochamer No. 25) to monophonic chanson *L'amour de moy* (after Gérold, p. 30)

[21] The dance treatises are: Robert Copelande, *The Maner of Dauncing base Daunces* (London 1521), facsimile edition by the Pear Tree Press (Sussex 1937); and Antonius de Arena, *Ad suos compagnones . . . bassas dansas et branlos practicantes* (Avignon 1536). With regard to sources for the music, see Brown, *Music in the French Secular Theater*, pp. 247–48.

[22] See further Reese and Karp, *Monophony in a Group of Renaissance Chansonniers*, pp. 7–8.

[23] Gérold, *Le Manuscrit de Bayeux*, p. 30.

The chanson's *a* phrase corresponds fairly closely to the *a* strain of the dance; its *b* phrase does not appear at all; its *c* phrase corresponds to the dance's second strain. In the dance melody, the third, fourth, and fifth strains seem to be variants respectively of the chanson's *a* phrase, *c* phrase, and *a* phrase. Actually, the third and fifth strains of the dance tune derive from the *a* phrase in another version of the chanson, *Jamais je n'aure envie*, in Paris MS 12744.[24]

Ex. 7   Opening of *Jamais je n'aure envie* (after Paris and Gevaert, p. 29)

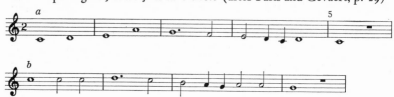

It does not appear that our investigation into the subject of 15th-century dance tunes in the four German sources, their polyphonic realizations, and their relationships to contemporary chansons is at all complete. For example, there is the case of the song *Ein gut selig jar* (Lochamer No. 29): The fact that the cantus-firmus setting of the melody (one note to a measure) in Buxheim (No. 86) is quadruple is in itself suspect, for most of the quadruple pieces in that source are associated in some way with basse dances. Now, we find that the Lochamer song and, consequently, the tenor of the Buxheim setting agree melodically with one of the Namur tunes, *Tres belle et bonne*—a melody partly recorded in basse-dance notation, as was pointed out earlier. If the Namur melody is of basse-dance origin, then the Lochamer

[24] Paris and Gevaert, *Chansons du XVe siècle*, p. 29 of the music section.

variant and the Buxheim arrangement are additions to the repertoire.

There remain many unanswered questions about basse-dance music in our sources, but they are beyond the confines of the present discussion. How did the French and Italian dance tunes find their way into the manuscripts? Who arranged the tunes? For what court circles were they written? On what occasions were they used? It is not surprising that basse-dance music should be found in manuscripts for the keyboard for, as stated earlier, 15th-century sources specifically mention organ accompaniment. At least two of the dances for which music is available in Buxheim must have been fairly popular. The poet Guillaume Coquillart, discussing basse dances in one of his works, includes in his listing of well-known dances *Ma maitresse* and *Amours* (=*L'amour de moy*).[25] And Cornazano tells us that his three basse-dance tenors, of which *Collinetto* appears in Buxheim in two arrangements, were "gli megliori et più usitati di gli altri."

[25] *Oeuvres de Coquillart*, ed. Charles d'Hericault (Paris 1857), pp. 134, 140.

THE *MISSA SI ME TENES:*
A PROBLEM OF AUTHORSHIP

by *MILTON STEINHARDT*

ON MARCH 28th of an unspecified year during the 1550s, King Maximilian of Bohemia, the future Emperor Maximilian II, wrote from Vienna to Archduke Albert V of Bavaria in Munich stating, "I have received your letter, together with the Mass *Si me tenes* which is extremely good. For this I thank you most dutifully, and assure you that I shall soon send you a Mass on *Aspice*. Whatever else I obtain that is good will always be dispatched to you." [1]

The question arises, who were the composers of the Masses referred to in this letter? The "Mass on *Aspice*" was in all probability the *Missa Aspice Domine* by Antonio Galli, a copy of which is preserved in the Nationalbibliothek of Vienna.[2] Galli served as a chaplain to the court of Maximilian, who refers to him in another letter of this period dealing with musical matters.[3]

The authorship of the *Missa Si me tenes* is more difficult to determine. For although only one Mass of this name is extant,[4] it appears with diverse attributions: in some manuscripts to Orlando di Lasso, in others to Jacobus Vaet, and in one source to both of these composers. Now that complete editions of the works of both Lasso and Vaet are in progress, it is necessary to attack this problem and, if possible, to resolve it.

I

THE *Missa Si me tenes* is known to us from six sources, most of them incomplete, and two of them not presently available and probably lost.

---

[1] Munich, Allgemeines Staatsarchiv, *Auswärtige Staaten, Oesterreich*, Lit. 1, tom. 6, fol. 15ʳ. The passage is printed in Adolf Sandberger, *Beiträge zur Geschichte der bayerischen Hofkapelle unter Orlando di Lasso*, III (Leipzig 1895) 305.

[2] Codex 15950, fol. 12ᵛ.

[3] Quoted in Sandberger, *loc. cit.* Galli is one of five chaplains listed in Maximilian's court register of 1 January 1554, now in Vienna, Haus- Hof- und Staatsarchiv, OMeA. Sr 182. This fact supplements the biographical information in Van den Borren's article "Galli" in MGG, IV (1955), 1281. There one reads, "Von diesem Zeitpunkt [1550] an ist jede Spur von ihm verschwunden."

[4] By contrast to the *Missa Aspice Domine*. Masses so titled were written, not only by Galli, but also by Ruffo, Morales, Monte, Palestrina, and Baccusi.

The oldest seems to be that in the Ratsschulbibliothek of Zwickau, MS 742, dated about 1560 in Vollhardt's catalogue of the collection.[5] It is a set of partbooks, of which the sextus, or second tenor voice, is lacking. In two of the books no composer is named; the other three contain ascriptions to Jacobus Vaet.

About 1573 the Mass was included in a codex [6] compiled for the Church of St. Egidius in Nuremberg. This choirbook is the only source to contain the Mass complete in all its voice parts and movements; it is the most carefully inscribed source; and, with respect to authorship, it is the most mystifying one. Above the first folios of music appears, in the hand of the original scribe, the title, "Missa super: Si me tenes. Orlandus di Lassus" (Pls. 27a–c) but a later, different hand has crossed out the name of the composer in order to substitute for it "Jacobi Vaët." (Pl. 27b). To compound the confusion, this Mass is preceded by a page inscribed "Missa Sex vocum. Facta ad imitationem Cantilena: Si me tenes etc: Autore Jacobo Vaet" (Pl. 27c).

Only the Zwickau and the Nuremberg manuscripts were known to Hans Jancik when, in 1929, he completed his dissertation on the Masses of Vaet.[7] He therefore assumed that the work was by this composer.

Among the sources unknown to Jancik were two in the municipal library of Wrocław (Breslau), MSS 97 and 99. During the last war they disappeared from the library but, nevertheless, the *Missa Si me tenes* contained in them can be identified with our Mass, thanks to an incipit given by Emil Bohn in his catalogue of the collection.[8] According to information contained therein, these manuscripts dated from the last decade of the 16th century. MS 97 lacked the Credo, while MS 99 comprised only the altus and *vagans* partbooks. The attributions were to Orlando di Lasso.

Bohn, perhaps inadvertently, cast some doubt on the authorship of this Mass when he wrote, concerning MS 97 and its 42 Masses by various composers: "The manner of the composer ascription often leaves doubt as to whether it applies to the Mass itself, or only to the theme (motet, etc.) on which the Mass is based." [9] Bohn's remark was not repeated for MS 99; and, in any case, it would not be applicable to the *Missa Si me tenes*, for its parody model was not by Lasso.

[5] Reinhard Vollhardt, *Bibliographie der Musik-Werke in der Ratsschulbibliothek zu Zwickau* (Leipzig 1896), p. 259.

[6] Now MS Fenitzer IV, 227 of the Landeskirchliches Archiv, Nuremberg.

[7] Hans Jancik, *Die Messen des Jacobus Vaet* (Diss. Vienna 1929). I am indebted to Dr. Jancik for placing the results of his investigation at my disposal.

[8] Emil Bohn, *Die musikalischen Handschriften des XVI. und XVII. Jahrhunderts in der Stadtbibliothek zu Breslau* (Breslau 1890), p. 109.

[9] *Ibid.*

Nevertheless, this cause for doubt was quoted by Joachim Huschke when, in 1940, he questioned the authorship of seven Masses (including this one) attributed to Lasso in the Wrocław manuscripts.[10] After adding, as corroborative evidence, that none of these Masses had been printed, and that the partbooks are careless and faulty copies, he concluded: "Closer examination of the music revealed technical defects that make the authorship of Lasso very questionable. It is therefore appropriate to attribute these Masses to one or several of the East German minor masters who are well represented in the manuscripts." [11]

In so remarking, Huschke was unknowingly contradicting, insofar as the *Missa Si me tenes* is concerned, the judgment of Jancik, for the latter had praised this work as displaying a complete mastery of technique. Apparently Huschke was just as unaware of the existence of this Mass with Vaet attributions in Zwickau and Nuremberg as was Jancik of the location in Wrocław.

In addition to the sources mentioned thus far, the Mass exists in fragmentary form in two other places. A manuscript formerly in Brieg, presently MS 19 of the University Library in Wrocław, contains the tenor voice part, with an ascription to "Orlando." The Sanctus and Agnus Dei, as well as the latter part of the Credo, are lacking.

Another manuscript, formerly in Bártfa and now catalogued as Bártfa 12 of the National Library of Budapest, is a single partbook containing the *Bassus II* (*Quintus*) of the Kyrie and the greater part of the Gloria (to "cum Sancto"). It bears no composer attribution.

Neither of these two sources, relatively unimportant though they may be, has been taken into account heretofore. Including them, we may summarize as follows: of the six manuscripts containing the *Missa Si me tenes*, the three from Wrocław name Lasso as its composer; one, in Zwickau, names Vaet: one, in Nuremberg, names both men; another, in Budapest, is anonymous. On a purely numerical basis the authorship of Lasso is indicated. One cannot, however, ignore the fact (assuming Vollhardt's dating of the Zwickau collection to be correct) that the oldest source, and the only one to date from Vaet's lifetime, names the Viennese composer. The manuscript most centrally located, with respect to the activities of the composers involved, is that in Nuremberg.[12] And

[10] Joachim Huschke, *Orlando di Lassos Messen*, in: *Archiv für Musikforschung*, V (1940), 177. One of these Masses, the *Missa Confundantur*, is now known to be a Lasso work, on the evidence of a letter from Duke Ferdinand II of the Tyrol to Jacobus Vaet. The pertinent passage is quoted in Walter Senn, *Musik und Theater am Hof zu Innsbruck* (Innsbruck 1954), pp. 153–54.

[11] Huschke, *loc. cit.*

[12] The works of both men were published extensively by Berg and Neuber of that city. In addition, Lasso is known to have visited Nuremberg several times.

although the attributions in it contradict each other, it is significant that the original scribe considered the work to be by Lasso.

The evidence of the sources is so confused that it cannot lead to an unequivocal solution of the problem. Nevertheless, I believe that the scales incline slightly in favor of Orlando di Lasso.

II

RETURNING NOW to the letter of King Maximilian quoted earlier, it would seem, on the surface, to indicate rather clearly the authorship of Lasso. Maximilian thanks Albert for a Mass he has received; we know that Lasso was a member of Albert's court chapel; *ergo*, the Mass is by Lasso. The only flaw in this beautifully neat argument is the possibility that the letter was written before the arrival of Lasso in Munich in the fall of 1556.

The letter is preserved in a bound volume of the Bavarian State Archives made up of correspondence with Austria from 1551 to 1559.[13] There is, unfortunately, no way of determining whether or not the letters in this volume were assembled in a strictly chronological order. Only from folio 202 on (a communication dated November 1556) can a regular sequence be established, either because the letters are dated by year as well as month, or because their contents provide some clue. The preceding folios may or may not have been haphazardly arranged.

Our letter, dated merely March 28th, forms folio 15, occupying a place in the volume that could suggest the year 1553. It was in this year that Vaet gave first evidence of his association with the House of Hapsburg.[14] Lasso was then still in Rome. There is, however, good reason to believe that the message originated several years later than this. An analogous situation exists with respect to another of these letters, dated October 14th, and implying by its location on folio 116 the year 1554. However, it was obviously written after Lasso's arrival in Munich, for in it Maximilian requests of Albert that when Orlando di Lasso composes something it be sent to him.[15]

Even if our letter antedated the fall of 1556, it still could have referred to a Mass by Lasso, for some of his works, like his fame, had preceded him to the Munich court. We know, for example, that in the summer of that year Hans Jacob Fugger of Augsburg sent a Lasso motet to Albert V.[16]

---

[13] Munich, Bayerisches Staatsarchiv, *Oest. Sachen* (*1551–59*) *Tomus I.* I am indebted to Dr. Puchner, Director of the Archives, for supplying information concerning this source.

[14] It is his motet *Romulidum invicti*, written for the July 1553 wedding of Maximilian's sister, Catherine, to King Sigismund Augustus of Poland.

[15] The passage is printed in Sandberger, *op. cit.*, 305.

[16] Cf. Sandberger, *op. cit.*, 304.

Also, it was not unusual for composers, then as now, to send their compositions to a prospective employer.[17]

Discounting the possibility that Maximilian was referring in his letter of March 28th to some *Missa Si me tenes* that has since disappeared, the evidence seems to indicate that Lasso, rather than Vaet, was its composer. Nevertheless, to come to a decision before examining the work itself for clues to authorship would be premature.

III

The *Missa Si me tenes* is a six-voice parody Mass based on a chanson by Thomas Crecquillon. It is a fully developed work, rather than a *Missa brevis*. In both size and in general style it much resembles Lasso's five-voice *Missa Domine secundum actum meum*, a parody Mass derived from a motet by Jachet de Mantua.[18] This *Missa Domine secundum* and Lasso's five-voice plainsong Mass, *Paschalis*, have been dated somewhat before 1556. Together with an incomplete *Missa ferialis*, they form the earliest known group of his Mass compositions.[19]

How does the *Missa Si me tenes* compare with Lasso's two complete early Masses, on the one hand, and with Vaet's eight Mass Ordinaries (excluding the Requiem) on the other? Looking first at some of the more external details, we can note a number of significant relationships. The *Missa Si me tenes* comprises 16 movements; the *Missa Paschalis* contains 17, and the *Missa Domine secundum* (with its unusual feature of two Agnus Deis), 18. Vaet's Mass subdivisions, by contrast, range from 12 to 14 in number.

Another aspect of the formal construction can best be represented graphically: As the table on page 761 illustrates, the Kyrie of our Mass is about the same size as those of Lasso, but considerably shorter than those by Vaet. Furthermore, the relative lengths of paired Kyries and Glorias fall into patterns of sharp disparity in the first three Masses, as opposed to those of greater equality in the Vaet works.

A third point of resemblance (not tabulated) between the Lasso Masses and the *Missa Si me tenes* is the division of the Gloria into four movements: *Et in terra, Domine Deus, Qui tollis,* and *Cum Sancto.* This procedure contrasts with Vaet's practice of dividing the Gloria into two

---

[17] In August 1567, for example, after Vaet's death had made vacant the post of Imperial Kapellmeister, Maximilian noted in his day book, "Der Gabriel Martinengo hatt mir allerlei komposiciones zugeschickt und war gern kapelmeister." (Vienna, Haus- Hof- und Staatsarchiv, *Familien Akten, Kart. 88.*)

[18] Wolfgang Boetticher erroneously thought the model to be by Cipriano de Rore. See his *Orlando di Lasso und seine Zeit* (Kassel 1958) I, 151.

[19] *Ibid.,* p. 49. I am indebted to Dr. Siegfried Hermelink for furnishing me with photostats of these Masses.

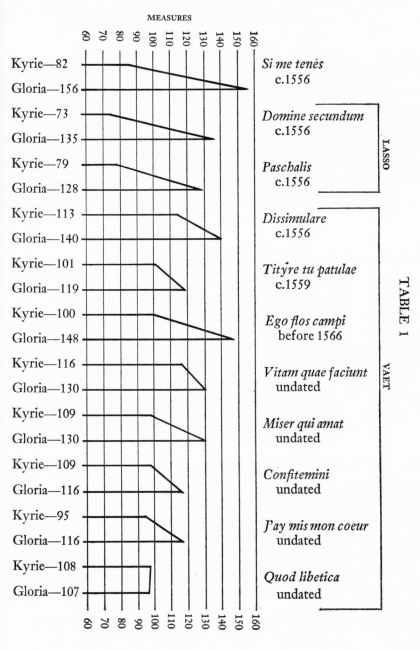

MEASURES

movements or three. The latter subdivision occurs in only two of his Masses.

The texture of the *Missa Si me tenes* is preponderantly polyphonic, with chordal or semi-chordal writing reserved either for special emphasis or for variety. In this respect it favors neither Vaet nor Lasso, and reflects the influence of Crecquillon's consistently contrapuntal chanson.

There are, however, among the passages that show no derivation from the model and hence may be considered representative of the Mass composer, a few that are distinctive. In the Credo, for example, the words, "descendit de caelis" are set as follows:

Ex. 1 *Missa Si me tenes*, Credo; mm. 71–81 (Nuremberg, Landeskirchliches Archiv, MS Fenitzer, IV, 227)

Although word-painting on such texts was common, a musical representation as graphic as this is seldom seen. Beginning in measure 74, the two
lowest voices stride downward in semibreves from d^1 to F, a distance of
almost two octaves. One is reminded of Robert Wilder's statement:
"Lasso seldom overlooks an opportunity for indulging in this con-

ventional type of word-painting; his keen sense for the dramatic, more-over, occasionally leads to exaggerated representation . . . Consistently the most emphatic of these pictorial passages is the portrayal of 'descendit de coelis,' . . . nearly always composed by Lasso as an extended passage in imitative style." [20] Wilder's words echo the judgment of Huschke, who found this trait to be more prevalent in Lasso's early works than in his later ones.[21]

Turning to Vaet, we know from a study of his motets that "he is not given to the use of madrigalistic expression of detail" and that when he does indulge in the traditional clichés, it is with some restraint.[22] Of the seven Masses by him that contain a Credo, only three set the words, "descendit de caelis" in a manner that could be considered descriptive.[23] None of them employs means as remarkable as does the *Missa Si me tenes*.

There is, however, one detail in Example 1 that recalls Vaet, rather than Lasso: the *nota cambiata* in the bassus at measure 74, appearing in its archaic form of three notes followed by a pause. Vaet used this figuration fairly frequently.[24] Lasso employed it neither in his early Masses, nor in the collection of his motets published in Antwerp in 1556. However, he was not averse to the use of other "old-fashioned" forms of the *cambiata*. Examples of this figure with an upward leap as the fourth note may be found in his motet, *Domine probasti*, as well as in the *Missa Domine secundum* (Sanctus, mm. 22–23).

A particularly striking passage in the *Missa Si me tenes* is that at the conclusion of the Agnus Dei, on the words, "miserere nobis."

[20] Robert Wilder, *The Masses of Orlando di Lasso with Emphasis on his Parody Technique* (Diss. Harvard 1952), pp. 233 and 235; published on microcards (Rochester 1959).

[21] Huschke, *op. cit.*, 173.

[22] Milton Steinhardt, *Jacobus Vaet and his Motets* (East Lansing, Mich. 1951), p. 33.

[23] The Masses *Confitemini, Ego flos campi*, and *Quodlibetica*.

[24] There are at least 13 examples in his Masses and motets.

Ex. 2   *Missa Si me tenes,* Agnus Dei; mm. 21–31 (Nuremberg, Landeskirchliches Archiv, MS Fenitzer, IV, 227)

Here, over a harmonic background that shifts on almost every quarter note of the score, the cantus sings a five-fold series of motives, descending in a quasi-sequential order, on "miserere." To stress further the poignancy of the text, the composer colored the passage with accidentals, so that it contains every chromatic tone but one, A♭.

The words of Wolfgang Boetticher describing the style of Lasso's early Masses apply to the passage above with astonishing aptness: "The harmonic rhythm is no less fluid than in Palestrina's early Masses, for Lasso loves concise motivic entries on various degrees of the scale, with the insertion of innumerable sequences. The sound-complex resembles an accumulation of root position chords of the most diverse kinds . . ."[25] Huschke was also impressed by this aspect of Lasso's style and quoted an illustrative example, analogous to ours, from his *Missa Douce memoire*.[26]

Ex. 3   Lasso, *Missa Douce memoire* (from Joachim Huschke, *Orlando di Lassos Messen*, in: AfMF V (1940), 162

[25] Boetticher, *op. cit.*, 151.
[26] Huschke, *op. cit.*, 162.

A perusal of the works of Vaet reveals only one passage that is at all comparable, a three-fold sequence on "perducam" at the conclusion of his motet, *Ego Dominus.*[27]

Taken as a whole, the characteristics of the *Missa Si me tenes,* both external and internal, show a closer kinship with Lasso's early Masses than with those of Vaet. Therefore, despite the presence of conflicting and confusing details in the sources, in King Maximilian's letter, and even in the work itself, I believe that we can state with reasonable certainty that the Mass was written by Orlando di Lasso. It should, then, be both included in the complete edition of his works and taken into account in assessing his stylistic development.

[27] Jacobus Vaet, *The Complete Works,* in: *Denkmäler der Tonkunst in Öster-reich,* Vol. 98 (Wien 1961), I, 30.

POLYPHONIC TROPERS IN
14th-CENTURY ENGLAND

by DENIS STEVENS

O F ALL THE REVEALING DISCOVERIES that emerge from a healthy concourse of scholarly disciplines, few in recent years have surpassed in number and importance the results of applying our knowledge of early liturgies to the vast repertory of medieval and Renaissance church music. The influence of plainsong upon polyphony in terms of form, texture, and performance has in many ways seemed worthy of renewed study, bringing into being what is virtually a new and almost boundless area of investigation. Apparently isolated and epigrammatic motets are now known to form an integral part of larger structures, and when it is seen that they fit as the hand in the glove or the jewel in its rightful setting, the subtlety of the music as well as the sense of the text finally become clear both to listeners and performers. Certain motets would be better designated as polyphonic tropes, since their tenors, or sometimes inner voice-parts, make use of plainsong tropes such as *Regnum tuum solidum* and *Spiritus et alme*. Both of these are tropes to *Gloria in excelsis,* the former in honor of the Trinity, the latter for special Masses of the Blessed Virgin.[1]

The classical definition of a trope as an interpolation into a liturgical text [2] states the case in its simplest form, and with no aesthetic overtones. Doubtless intended originally as a kind of rhapsodic exegesis, or as a musico-poetical ornamentation adding stature and beauty to a plain text, these interpolations spread rapidly from the Ordinary of the Mass to the Proper and eventually to the Office. At first sentences were split and phrases inserted to amplify or modify the sense; later the same technique was applied to words, yielding such strange results as *Alle psallite cum luya* and *Benedica in seculamus Domino*. When new words and phrases were inserted, new music or repetitions of old music had to be fitted as neatly as possible.

[1] G. Reese, *Music in the Middle Ages* (New York 1940), p. 316. The present article has been prepared with the support of a grant from the American Philosophical Society.
[2] Léon Gautier, *Histoire de la poésie liturgique au moyen âge: Les Tropes* (Paris 1886), p. 1.

The speed at which tropes proliferated may be judged from the two versions of the Winchester Cantatorium,[3] which were copied within 50 or 60 years of each other. In the earlier manuscript, known as the Ethelred Troper, one of the Gloria tropes (*Laus tua Deus resonet*) has for its ninth clause or verse *Regnum tuum solidum permanebit in eternum*, with a fine jubilus on the syllable *per*. In the later manuscript, this jubilus carries a four-line text of its own beginning *Rex glorie qui es splendor ac decus ecclesie*, so that a mere half-century has produced a trope upon a trope. Gautier lists nearly 30 different tropes to *Regnum tuum solidum*, which retained its popularity in France long after it ceased to appear in English manuscripts. Fragmentary polyphonic settings are found in English sources of the late 13th or early 14th century, and the one easily available in transcription [4] shows *Regnum* with its insertion [O] *rex glorie* as tenor, and an upper voice presenting a further trope *Regnum sine termino*. Since at least one voice is missing, there may have been yet another gloss upon this apparently inexhaustible theme. Long before the era of polyphonic settings such as this, there were many who thought that tropes had gone too far. "It might have been natural to suppose that the trope-writers would have been satisfied with having introduced [nine] irrelevant clauses into the *Gloria;* but no: 'crescit indulgens sibi dirus hydrops': they set to work to make a trope on a trope." [5] Bishop Frere's considered opinion seems to echo not a few medieval criticisms.

Spiritus et alme shows a parallel tendency, and is even more important than *Regnum* because of the extreme profusion of complete examples, which range between the 13th and the 16th centuries, and geographically from Rome to London, from Barcelona to Glogau in Upper Silesia.[6] English monks seem to have had a special liking for *Spiritus et alme*, and Richard de Burgate, Abbot of Reading from 1268 to 1290, may have been one of the first to write a polyphonic setting if we accept the evidence of a well-known index of lost organa.[7] In the Sarum rite, the trope was sung within the Gloria at Saturday Masses of the B.V.M. in the Lady

[3] Oxford, Bodleian Library, Bodley 775 (written between 979 and 1016); Cambridge, Corpus Christi College 473 (c. 1050).

[4] Luther Dittmer, *The Worcester Fragments* (Haarlem 1957), p. 152, from Worcester Cathedral Library Add. MS 68, Fragment XII[v].

[5] W. H. Frere, *The Winchester Troper*, Henry Bradshaw Society, VIII (London 1884), p. xv.

[6] Apart from the anonymous settings discussed here, there are important examples (also by unknown composers) in manuscripts at Apt, Barcelona, Burgos, Gerona, Ivrea, Modena, Padua, Rome, and Trent. Among famous composers to have written Masses that use the *Spiritus et alme* trope are Anchieta, Bourgois, Chierisy, Ciconia, Dufay, Dunstable, Josquin, Pycard, Queldryk, and Nicolaus Zacharias.

[7] British Museum, Harley 978, fol. 160[v]–161. For Richard de Burgate, see Bertram Schofield, *The Provenance and Date of "Sumer is icumen in,"* in: *The Music Re-*

Chapel, also at the last Mass of the B.V.M. before Advent and before Lent, drawing upon the resources of the whole choir (*a toto choro in stallis*). In the octaves of two major feasts, however (Assumption and Nativity of the B.V.M.), the trope was sung at the choir step by three senior clerks in their surplices (*a tribus clericis de superiore gradu in superpellicis ad gradum chori*).[8]

In spite of its widespread use, the purpose, text, and music of *Spiritus et alme* have given rise to a certain amount of confusion and controversy. Polyphonic versions of the trope and its various offshoots did not of course include the chanted sections of the Gloria, which the monks would know by heart, nor was there any mention of the title *Gloria* since this too would be common knowledge.[9] The trope was always known by its incipit, and was so listed by Chevalier.[10] In a trenchant and extensive review of Chevalier's catalog, Clemens Blume complained of the presence of a prose text pure and simple among so many hymns in verse form.[11] But the case was not by any means as clear-cut as Blume imagined, for the boundary between prose and verse has occasionally been known to exhibit somewhat elastic qualities. Only a few years before Blume wrote his review, Josef Dankó had published the trope in such a way as to suggest that its first three sections at least might be said to rhyme with parts of the Gloria: [12]

Domine Fili unigenite Jesu Christe.
Spiritus et alme orphanorum paraclite.
Domine Deus Agnus Dei Filius Patris.
Primogenitus Marie virginis Matris.
Qui tollis . . . suscipe deprecationem nostram.
Ad Marie gloriam.

The last three sections afford no such opportunity for stretching of points:

view, IX (1948), 81; also Jacques Handschin, *The Summer Canon and its Background (I)*, in: *Musica disciplina*, III (1949), 91.

[8] *Graduale Sarisburiense* (London 1894), pl. 14+.

[9] Cf. Luther Dittmer, *An English Discantuum Volumen*, in: *Musica disciplina*, VIII (1954), 39: "We must reject this concordance [Bodley 384], because the compositions themselves are much later, and because the tropes are included as an appendix to a Gloria, whereas no Gloria is mentioned in the Reading list."

[10] *Repertorium hymnologicum*, No. 19312.

[11] Clemens Blume, S.J., *Kritischer Wegweiser durch U. Chevaliers Repertorium Hymnologicum*, in: *Hymnologische Beiträge*, II (1901), 289: "Was sollen diese rein prosaischen Einschiebsel in 'Gloria' an dieser Stelle? Sie gehören wohl in eine Geschichte der Tropen, aber doch nicht in ein hymnologisches Register."

[12] Josef Dankó, *Vetus hyrnarium ecclesiasticum Hungariae* (Budapest 1893), p. 314. For a typical theological commentary on the text of the trope, see J. Clichtoveus, *Elucidatorium ecclesiasticum ad officium ecclesiae pertinentia planius exponens* (Paris 1515), III, 114.

Quoniam tu solus sanctus.
Mariam sanctificans.
Tu solus Dominus.
Mariam gubernans.
Tu solus altissimus.
Mariam coronans.

As soon as the trope was troped, however, the poetic element came boldly to the fore, as may be seen in this expanded form of the first section:

Spiritus almifice
consecrans mirifice
Marie corpusculum
quo floret sacrarium
visita nos inclite
orphanos paraclite.

As with the text, so with the music. Peter Wagner, in stressing the stylistic and modal unity generally typical of the trope-melodies and their matrices, began his musical example at "Domine Fili," just a little too late to reveal the hysteron-proteron aspects of centonization techniques that were so common in the Middle Ages.[13] By going back to "gloriam tuam," the source of the trope-melody becomes clear at once:

Ex. 1   From *Gloria IX* (Graduale Sarisburiense)

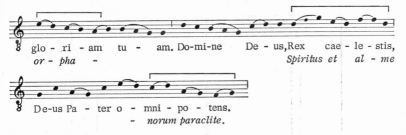

Later phrases in the trope-melody similarly echo portions of the chant, looking now forward, now backward, with "Qui sedes ad dexteram" supplying material for the trope sections immediately preceding and following.[14] The result was a closely-integrated composition, especially rich in polyphonic possibilities because of the time-honored practice of assigning the tropes to a small group of solo voices.

It may not be a coincidence that the rubric quoted above refers to

[13] Peter Wagner, *Einführung in die gregorianischen Melodien,* III (Leipzig 1895), 510.
[14] Jacques Handschin, *Zur Frage der melodischen Paraphrasierung im Mittelalter,* in: *Zeitschrift für Musikwissenschaft,* X (1927), 539.

a group of three singers, and the majority of medieval documents mentioning polyphony refer to *triplici cantu*.[15] Settings of *Spiritus et alme* in three-part harmony are far more numerous than four-part settings, especially in the 13th and 14th centuries, and it is not difficult to imagine the three senior clerks cheerfully replacing their unison chant with unified harmony. Even when an early four-part version of the trope makes its appearance, as in the 13th-century fragments that form part of Mus. c. 60 (Oxford, Bodleian Library), the texture is so clearly 3 + 1 that the soloists may well have sung the three upper parts while the choir sustained the long notes of the tenor.[16] But three-part settings were the norm throughout the 14th century in England, and a complex of fragmentary polyphonic tropers makes this clear when the evidence is pieced together, albeit from five widely scattered sources.

A 15TH-CENTURY MANUSCRIPT of Chaucer's *Canterbury Tales*, almost certainly written and bound in London,[17] and now in the Bodleian Library (Arch. Selden B.14) has for its flyleaves a Sarum Calendar, fragmentary but roughly contemporary with the body of the manuscript, and as paste-downs a pair of vellum leaves from a polyphonic troper of the 14th century. These leaves, both bifolia, now measure a little less than 14 x 9 inches thanks to the binder's knife; when fitted together in photographic facsimile, something like the true original size can be deduced:

Diagram A

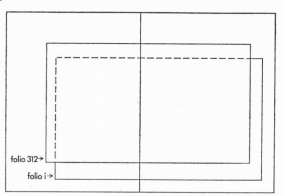

folio 312→
folio i→

---

[15] Medieval Ordinals and Customaries such as those of Westminster, Exeter, York (St. Mary's), and Norwich frequently employ this phrase or similar ones: "sollemniter in triplum," "in triplis sollemniter," "triplici melodia."

[16] For a partial transcription see Anselm Hughes, O.S.B. (ed.), *The New Oxford History of Music*, II (Oxford 1954), 375.

[17] This manuscript is not mentioned in *The New Oxford History of Music*, III (London 1960), although early English music is otherwise dealt with in detail.

Lying open on a lectern, the troper would have measured approximately 18 x 12 inches, and there were 12 staves to each page. Although much of the music has been lost or obliterated by trimming and glueing (see Pl. 28a), enough remains for a tentative catalog to be drawn up,[18] and since reference to the present foliation would become complicated (for the two bifolia must be imagined in the middle of a gathering) it seems best to refer to them by the letters *a* through *h*.

Diagram B

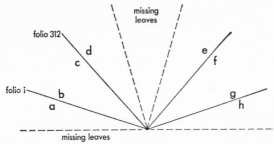

a) *Kyrie* (incipit of trope illegible; *Christe* begins *Christe dulcis amor virginum*. These are five polyphonic verses, musical form AABCC, intended to alternate with plainsong, but the text of the last verse has not been completed beyond the first word).

b) *Kyrie* (untroped, originally occupying first six staves. Found also in another Bodleian manuscript, Barlow 55, fol. 5ᵛ).

   Kyrie (untroped, but with the *Orbis factor* melody in the uppermost voice. Again for alternatim use: 1, 3 [3 = 1], 5, 7, 9; but the scribe has placed the last two verses in the wrong order).

c) *Kyrie* (with trope *Regina virginum*, presumably a Marian form of *Rex virginum amator Deus*, with musical form AAA BBB CCC, continued overleaf).

d) end of foregoing *Kyrie*.

   Kyrie (with trope *Christifera*, found also in a later and highly ornamented form in British Museum, Sloane 1210, fol. 139. Form AAA BBB CCC).[19]

Bibliographical references occur in the *Summary Catalogue of Western Manuscripts in the Bodleian Library* (No. 3360) and in Hughes, *Medieval Polyphony in the Bodleian Library* (Oxford 1951), pp. 47–48. There is a brief discussion in Ernst Apfel, *Studien zur Satztechnik der mittelalterlichen englischen Musik* (Heidelberg 1959), I, 59, and in Manfred Bukofzer, *Speculative Thinking in Mediaeval Music*, in: *Speculum*, XVII (1942), 165.

   [18] This differs in several details from Hughes and Apfel, but makes no claim to be definitive.

   [19] Partial transcription in Johannes Wolf, *Handbuch der Notationskunde* (Leipzig 1913–19), I, 269.

e) *Manens celi gloria* (ending with "gubernans," therefore trope of the fifth of six Marian verses to *Gloria in excelsis*. Followed by the sixth of these verses).

f) *Spiritus almifice* (first verse of another set of tropes, followed by the other verses, and continued on next page).

g) *graciam concinimus* (end of verse 3; followed by 4, 5, and 6).

h) *Virgo decora statu meliora* (motet).

All the texts listed above are in honor of the Virgin, but so far they have not been found in missals or graduals, nor do they appear in the great printed collections of trope texts. It must therefore be assumed that the verses were composed expressly for the musical setting, perhaps along the same lines as the *poesia per musica* of the Italian Renaissance. In its original form, the troper could have contained similar elaborations of Sanctus, Benedictus, and Agnus Dei, comparable to the many troped sections of the Ordinary of the Mass in Las Huelgas Codex.[20]

For the purposes of our present investigation, the two fragmentary Gloria tropes on pages *e, f,* and *g* are of unusual interest. *Spiritus almifice* proved amenable to reconstruction,[21] revealing music whose functional and fauxbourdonian naiveté did not exclude attractive metrical shifts harking back to the rhythmic modes of earlier times. For all his anonymity, the composer knew the subtleties of integrating plainsong within polyphony and trope within trope, as is shown by the first verse:

Ex. 2   *Spiritus almifice,* verse 1.   B

[20] Other parallels between Spanish and English sources are discussed by Handschin, *The Summer Canon and its Background (II)*, in: *Musica disciplina,* V (1951), 105; also in a very useful but little-known article by Higini Anglès, *La Música anglesa dels segles xiii–xiv als països hispànics,* in: *Analecta sacra tarraconensia,* XI (1935), 219–33.

[21] With music and text invented where necessary, this Gloria was performed at the annual concert of the Plainsong and Mediaeval Music Society in 1958.

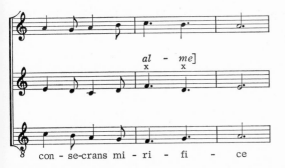

Similar in date and style is a three-part setting of the original *Spiritus et alme* text which has been known in facsimile and transcription since Coussemaker published his *Histoire de l'harmonie au moyen-âge* in 1852.[22] The source is the so-called Coussemaker Fragment, some small part of whose strange history will be briefly retraced here.

These two vellum leaves, now measuring 13½ x 9 inches, were probably flyleaves in the volume whose title has been written in an 18th-century hand, at the top of the verso of the first leaf: "Hieronymi Epistolae Ejusdem Musica, cum figuris. Saec XII" (see Pl. 28b). In the same hand is the price asked, £9.9.0, so that Coussemaker could have acquired the book on one of his visits to England, where he had links with the Society of Antiquaries. Nine guineas seems a high price to pay for two leaves; and the most likely explanation is that Coussemaker bought the entire book because of its flyleaves, which he later cut out. Since the scandalous sale of John Stafford Smith's library had taken place in 1844, and since the collection is known to have been exceptionally rich in medieval English musical manuscripts,[23] this sale or one of its offshoots may well have been the occasion for Coussemaker's purchase. In any event, he had made a diplomatic copy as well as a transcription by 1850, when the *Histoire* was being made ready for the press, and all these materials were left to the Royal Library in Brussels shortly after Coussemaker's death in 1876.

A printed description appeared in J. van den Gheyn's *Catalogue des Manuscrits de la Bibliothèque Royale de Belgique* in 1901,[24] but was not apparently known to the world of musical scholarship. When Handschin

[22] Reese, MMA, p. 404.
[23] For an account of the collection and the sale, see the article by W. H. Husk in *Grove's Dictionary* (5th ed. London 1954), VII, 856.
[24] Vol. I, p. 442, No. 714, where the shelfmark is given as II 266. This is a collection of fragments from liturgical books, presumably assembled by Coussemaker. The only polyphonic music is in fragment 10 (our source C). No. 11 is a diplomatic copy as used in Coussemaker's book, while No. 12 consists of his rough transcriptions of this material.

published his article on melodic paraphrase in 1927, he referred to Plate 33 of Coussemaker's *Histoire* but was obliged to admit that the original manuscript had disappeared.[25] He re-discovered it soon after, and reported his find in 1935, listing the contents for the first time.[26] The two leaves may originally have been joined together, but they do not form the center of a gathering, as is proved by the music and by the wormholes, which do not correspond in every instance. Assuming the possibility of a bifolium, the contents may be listed as follows, the four pages being designated by the numerals i–iv:

i) *Maria[m] sine crimine* (last two verses of *Spiritus almifice* in Arch. Selden B.14, page g).

   Spiritus et alme (the setting published by Coussemaker, and in a better transcription by Handschin.[27] Continued overleaf).

ii) *Mariam gubernans* (last two verses of foregoing trope).

   Spiritus procedens (first four verses of a troped *Spiritus et alme*. The first verse only is found, with some variants, in New College MS 362, fol. 82ᵛ; and the text, with entirely different music, in a composite collection of 13th-century leaves and photostats in the Bodleian Library: Lat. liturg. d. 20).

iii) *Salve virgo singularis* (Chevalier: *Repertorium*, No. 18304; Dreves: *Analecta hymnica*, XXXIX, 47. This polyphonic setting is found in fragmentary form in British Museum Add. 38651 fol. 48ᵛ, and the double versicles given there indicate that it was a Prose or Sequence).

   Mutato modo geniture (another Marian sequence, also found in two Cambridge MSS: Gonville & Caius 543/512, fol. 256, and Gonville & Caius 727/334, fol. 199. Fragments are also visible on some narrow strips of parchment in British Museum Add. 38651 fol. 49).

iv) [continuation and end of above-mentioned sequence] followed by: *Beata es Maria* (beginning of a Marian Sequence).

The concordance between the first item on page i of Coussemaker (C) and the *Spiritus almifice* trope in Arch. Selden B.14 (B) proves to be both useful and revealing. Even more involved is the case of *Spiritus procedens*, closely linked with New College 362 (N) and the text from

---

[25] *Zeitschrift für Musikwissenschaft*, X (1927), 543: "Nicht unwichtig für unsere Frage ist das Fragment Coussemaker, ein einst Coussemaker gehörendes, heute verschollenes Fragment . . ."

[26] *Acta musicologica*, VII (1935), 160—a brief entry under the heading "Miscellanea." No list was ever printed by Coussemaker, who mentioned only that the fragment contained a few motets in honor of the Virgin.

[27] *Zeitschrift für Musikwissenschaft*, X (1927), 543.

one of the Worcester fragments (W). These four sources will, for convenience, be referred to as C, B, N, and W. B is earlier than C by perhaps 40 years, during which time the formal hand used for the text gave way to a cramped style of writing full of abbreviations and contractions. The scribe has ventured to improve the final couplet by making a rhyme, forgetting all the time that the final word must be "coronans" because the verse is really an expansion of the two words "Mariam coronans":

B	C
Mariam laudant infera	Mariam laudant infera
colunt tellus et ethera	colunt tellus et ethera
per quem crimina condonet	per quem *nostra* crimina condonet
Christe atque nos coronans.	Christe atque nos *coronet.*

Comparable quirks occur in the music of C, which looks neat enough but contains numerous errors in copying or transmission, indicating that the scribe did not "hear" what he wrote down:

Ex. 3 *Spiritus almifice*, verse 5.

ma-trem Fi - li - o   gu - ber - nans.

Occasionally there are hints of an attempt to modernize the old-fashioned consecutive triads of B by converting them to something like fauxbourdon, but instead of $\frac{6}{3}$ chords we have a string of $\frac{6}{4}$ harmonies that are surely out of place:

Ex. 4 *Spiritus almifice*, verse 5. C

Ma - ri - am   si - ne cri - mi - ne

In one instance a sequence of four chords is bodily transposed up a tone, though not this time to the detriment of the harmony. Clearly the kind of copyist who liked to improve on the original existed in 14th-century England as in other epochs and countries.

AT FIRST GLANCE *Spiritus procedens* seems to be a torso destined to remain that way until a suitable concordance turns up. The single verse in N is of little help except to show that the trope is of earlier date than has hitherto been supposed, and that consequently the music is of a simpler, less ornamented type than the much later version in C.[28] It does however follow directly upon a polyphonic *Regnum* trope, suggesting that in some manuscripts at least it was common to group the Gloria tropes together. The same composer may even have been responsible for both, because a melodic fingerprint appears at least six times in the visible portion of the uppermost voice of *Regnum* (written in cantus collateralis) and in the verse from *Spiritus procedens*, which is set out as if it were a conductus: three staves with music, the text appearing only below the lowest stave. This memorable little melodic figure is doubled at the fourth below in the middle voice of *Spiritus procedens:*

Ex. 5   *Spiritus procedens,* verse 1.   N

or - pha - no - rum

This figure does not appear in *Spiritus almifice*, nor is it found in the plain *Spiritus et alme* published by Coussemaker. Oddly enough, it does appear in the two unattached verses of B, page *e:*

[28] Neil Ker, *Pastedowns in Oxford Bindings*, Oxford Bibliographical Society, New Series, V (Oxford 1954), 185, where the bifolium in question is said to be a wrapper for a book of accounts from Balliol College. Detailed discussion of the music may be seen in Anglès, *El Còdex musical de Las Huelgas* (I) (Barcelona 1931); Bukofzer, *Geschichte des englischen Diskants* (Strasbourg 1936); Rokseth, *Polyphonies du XIII⁰ siècle*, IV (Paris 1939); Harrison, *English Church Music in the Fourteenth Century*, in: *The New Oxford History of Music*, III (London 1960).

Ex. 6 *Manens celi gloriam,* B

Ma - ri - am

These two verses are the fifth and sixth of a set of six; and since C presents the same first verse as N, plus three more verses, it might reasonably be hoped that head, limbs, and torso could be reconstructed to form a coherent whole, especially in view of the stylistic similarity of the music. Fortunately, considerable help is provided by the one non-musical concordance, W, whose text serves to link B, C, and of course N.

Since W dates from the mid-13th century, and the other sources from the early 14th, some changes and expansions may be expected; and in fact the inevitable happens. A trope that has already been troped is further troped in its final verse:

W [29]	C, N
Spiritus procedens a patre	Spiritus procedens a patre
venis mundi regnans per aera	venis *mundo* regnans per aera [C: *ahera*]
orphanorum paraclite.	orphanorum paraclite.

	C
Primordio caren[s] primogenitus	*Primogenitus* carens *primordio*
ante secula deus et homo factus	ante secula deus et homo factus *est*
per viscera virginis ac matris.	per viscera virginis *et* matris.

A[d] matris Marie	Ad matris Marie
virginum piissime	*virginis* piissime
gloriam.	gloriam.

Mari[am] matrem	Mariam matrem dulcissimam
et virginem dulcissimam	digne sanctificans.
digne sanctificans.	

[29] Published in facsimile by Luther Dittmer, *Oxford, Latin Liturgical D 20, Publications of Mediaeval Musical Manuscripts, No. 6* (Brooklyn 1960), p. 37; and transcribed by him in *The Worcester Fragments* (Haarlem 1957), No. 43 (p. 68 of the musical section of the book). Dittmer reads *tamen* for *caren[s]*, *autem* for *ante*, *matris* for *ad matris*, *gloria* for *gloriam*, *moronans* for *coronans*.

B
Manens celi [gloriam]	Manens celi *gloria*

Manens celi [gloriam]   Manens celi *gloria*
Mariam gloriosam gubernans.   Mariam gloriosam gubernans.

Matrem quae reginam mundi   Mariam post carnis obitum
Ma[riam] coronans.   eterne glorie perducis ad thalamum
                                          quo leta residet tenens imperium
                                                ipsum magnificans
                                                pie glorificans
                                                et honorificans
                                          regni diademate ad pa . . .

In spite of the missing lower edge of B, page *e*, it might be guessed with a fair degree of accuracy that the truncated word "pa . . ." should rhyme with "imperium," and the final short line should rhyme with "honorificans"; and since this poetical peroration is a gloss on a trope of "Mariam coronans" the word ought to be, in fact, "coronans." But this helps the musical situation at the very end hardly at all, though two of the three lowest staves are just legible. The reconstruction is not quite complete. Nevertheless, the juxtaposition of these six verses from C, N, and B seems plausible, for various reasons.

The first and strongest reason is not connected with musical style but with the verbal text of the trope as preserved in W, the oldest source. However much may have been added by later scribes and poets, the pristine form of the trope can always be seen through the additional material. When *Mariam gubernans* becomes *Manens celi gloriam/ Mariam gloriosam gubernans*, it is immediately recognizable as a trope upon a trope. When the author of the final verse of B, giving free rein to a passionate outpouring of praise, singing of the eternal and joyous reign of the Queen of Heaven, permits himself to carry troping to the third degree and enlarge a mere two words to an eight-line verse, he still makes it perfectly clear that those words "Mariam coronans" dominate his thought. They are the alpha and omega of his theology, the cornerstones of his verse structure, and the inspiration of his fervent lyricism: whatever the technical shortcomings of his work, they will be more than compensated for by the spontaneity and sincerity of his utterance. Working in the dark years of the later Middle Ages, his basic text shines through from earlier and happier times. It is this text that links the fragments of B, C, and N.

The second reason for connecting these fragments is admittedly a stylistic one. Apart from the recurring phrase found in all the verses, there is a constancy of mode that fits not only with the plainsong (which is migrant, as in *Spiritus almifice*) but with the six polyphonic verses, all beginning and ending with a chord of g–d^1–g^1. Throughout the verses, sections in fauxbourdon are prominent, there is a careful and effective use of accidentals, and the composer really seems to have tried to decorate and beautify the text with musical flourishes to match. There is in this music a flowing sense of warmth and tenderness such as one perceives in the most exquisitely illuminated Books of Hours, with their many and colorful likenesses of the Virgin and the infant Jesus. If mere sound can ever approach the delights of vision, this is the music to parallel and reflect the art of the medieval illuminators.

Spiritus procedens, in spite of three concordances, still lacks its ending, and *Spiritus almifice* has a sizeable gap in its third verse. In both instances, music and text are missing, and nothing short of a new concordance— preferably including both items, as with B and C—will remedy the situation. By a twist of fate that might with some justification be called a *codex ex machina*, a new concordance did appear in 1961 in the form of a single vellum page containing parts of both sets of tropes.[30] The pleasure brought by the new discovery was, however, somewhat diminished on learning that an account and even a photographic reproduction of the source had appeared 22 years previously. Many archivists and archaeologians have been known to admit that in spite of the apparently inexhaustible wealth of documents awaiting the scholar's attention, most of the worth-while material has already been published; what they are less willing to admit is that this published information occurs in sources almost as remote as the originals. There would certainly seem to be little reason for a musicologist to consult the *Transactions of the Bristol and Gloucestershire Archaeological Society*, but there in Vol. 61 (including papers and other contributions for 1939) is a lengthy and detailed account of a cartulary from the 15th century, whose cover is the leaf referred to above.[31]

The Spillman Cartulary is a collection of late 15th-century copies of some 23 deeds originally written between the years 1218 and 1331. In all, there are five leaves measuring 14 x 8½ inches which have been folded and tied with a narrow strip into a cover. The measurements of the cover, when folded, are 12¾ x 8½ inches, and there are 15 staves to each side of the leaf. The recto begins with "Manens celi," the fifth verse of *Spiritus*

[30] Thanks are due to Dr. Frank Harrison for sending me news of his discovery, and allowing me to make use of it in the present study.
[31] The Revd. C. E. Watson, *The Spillman Cartulary*, in the journal referred to above, states that "the cover . . . declares itself to be a page from a church 'Ordinell' and is inscribed on both sides with a hymn to the Virgin, the words in red text and the accompanying Gregorian notation in black."

procedens, and goes on to the sixth verse "Mariam post carnis obitum," conveniently completing the missing portion of B:

regni diademate ad palacium
altissimi coronans.

Then follows *Spiritus almifice,* with space for an illuminated or colored initial "S," and this continues to the end of the verso, stopping short at the phrase "per quem crimina condonet/Christe atque . . ." This lack of the last section is not serious, however, since it is present in both B and C. What is important is that this Gloucester manuscript (G) supplies the missing portion of verse 3, and allows the three texts to be collated as follows:

G	B
Spiritus almifice	Spiritus almifice
consecras mirifice	consecrans mirifice
Marie corpusculum	Marie corpusculum
quo floret sacrarium	quo floret sacrarium
visita nos inclite	visita nos inclite
orphanos paraclite.	orphanos paraclite.
Prima primogeniti	Prima primogeniti
virgo mater inclite	virgo mater incliti
paris sine tedio	paris sine tedio
tanto digna filio	tanto digna filio
mater es electa patris	mater es electa patris
virgo tenens nomen matris.	virgo tenens
Ad matris memoriam	
et virginalem gloriam	
ut mereamur graciam	graciam
concinimus.	concinimus.
Mariam matrem gracie	Mariam matrem gracie
grex gregis regni glorie	rex regis regni glorie
Christe cuncta vivificans	Christe cuncta vivificans
matrem pie sanctificans.	matrem pie sanctificans.

	B, C
Mariam sine crimine	Mariam sine crimine
omni plena dulcedine	omni plena dulcedine
virgo matrem semper vernans	virgo matrem semper vernans [C: *mater*]
matrem filio gubernans.	matrem filio gubernans
Mariam laudant inferi	Mariam laudant *infera*
colunt tellus et ethera	colunt tellus et ethera
per quem crimina condonet	per quem crimina condonet [C: *nostra crimina*]
Christe atque	Christe atque nos coronans. [C: *coronet*]

The notation and text of G suggest a date slightly later than C, perhaps even as late as the early 15th century, yet there are enough significant divergencies from C and B to indicate an entirely different derivation. In its relative lack of ornamental figures, G most nearly approaches N, and the degree of its discretion may best be appreciated by comparing it with a typical flourish in the final verse of *Spiritus procedens:*

Ex. 7 *Spiritus procedens,* verse 6.

quo le - ta . re - si - det

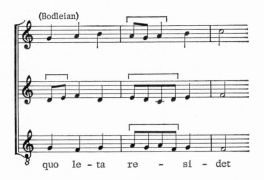

quo le - ta re - si - det

Assuming that G is a late copy of a version deriving from N (unfortunately these two sources have no verse in common with each other) would explain the frequent appearance of *puncti divisionis* between groups of two semibreves in both C and G. This phenomenon is rare in B, which has many fewer accidentals than G.[32] A tentative relationship of sources might be expressed as follows, though with due reservation in view of the difficulty of assigning dates and locations to isolated fragments of binder's waste:

[32] Other early features of B include an abundance of plicated breves and *quaternaria* groups.

Diagram C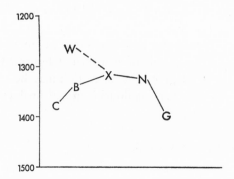

Although G may have been part of the library of the Benedictine Abbey of St. Peter at Gloucester, two fragmentary sets of Marian tropes for *Gloria in excelsis* prove very little. For the same reason it is almost impossible to guess where B, C, and N came from, since any Benedictine abbey with only a handful of polyphonic singers could have made use of material of this kind. The names of singers and composers appear not infrequently in English archives of the 15th century, but to find more than a handful of likely candidates in the 14th century is a problem of some magnitude, making it almost impossible to remove the cloak of anonymity from these unusual and fascinating compositions. The earliest and largest batch of names emerges from the Old Hall Manuscript, but it is reasonably safe to say that not even the composers of the oldest layer would bother themselves with such extravagances as a troped trope. In their day and age, the pruning operation had begun in earnest, and they were for all intents and purposes content with plain old *Spiritus et alme*.

A COMPARISON OF THE
ST. VICTOR CLAUSULAE
WITH THEIR MOTETS

by ETHEL THURSTON

TWO LARGE collections of 12th- and 13th-century polyphony [1] and a number of smaller ones have, up until now, been transcribed into modern notation, critically edited, and published. The numerous problems of medieval notation, in at least the large collections, have been solved in a remarkably masterful manner; the transcriptions are free of major errors and can convey the poetical aspects of the music. The smaller collections vary as to correctness, some needing complete revision, others only minor rectifications; and there is still a fairly large amount of 12th- and 13th-century polyphony that has not been published in transcription at all. The latter includes some of the organa, as well as some of the clausulae and conductus. One reason why this remainder has not yet appeared is that here the notation of the rhythm is more difficult to transcribe. The present study is an attempt to clarify some of these problems.

One of the most difficult problems is that of *fractio modi*, the splitting of a single beat of a rhythmic mode into two or more notes. *Fractio modi* cannot be transcribed correctly from the equivocally written square notation into modern notation without experience in comparing passages of *musica sine littera* [2] with the same music written *cum littera:* [3] this is the only means of discovering the note values in the ligatures in the contexts that the medieval theorists did not discuss. Opportunities for the largest number of *sine littera-cum littera* comparisons are provided by the collection of short melismatic pieces called clausulae, in MS Florence, Laurenziana, Plut. 29.1, known to musicologists as F. Some

---

[1] Yvonne Rokseth, *Polyphonies du XIII* siecle* (Paris 1935-39); Hans Tischler, *The Motet in Thirteenth-Century France* (Diss. Yale 1942); Tischler is preparing a *Complete Edition of the Earliest Motets, ca. 1190-1240* for publication.
[2] Literally, "music without text"; a melismatic passage set to a single syllable or to very few syllables.
[3] "Music with text"; usually one, two, or three notes to each syllable.

of these clausulae are also in W₁ and W₂.[4] The music of over one
hundred of the F clausulae is set in another part of F, as well as in other
manuscripts, to motet texts in notation *cum littera*. A second collection
offering opportunities for comparing melismatic with syllabic versions is
provided by the 40 St. Victor clausulae, 34 of which are set to motet texts
in other manuscripts. 20 of the 34 motet versions are in more than
one manuscript and 16 are in mensural notation.[5] The present study
will center on what can be learned from StV and its motets. It is fitting
enough to begin with a motet called *Douce dame sanz pitie*, which is
transcribed in my forthcoming publication aligned under its StV

Ex. 1a   Clausula and Motet 272 [5a]

[4] The following sigla will be used for the manuscripts:
Ba   Bamberg, Staatsbibliothek, C lit. 115 (mensural notation; see fn. 5 below).
Cl   Paris, Bibliothèque Nationale, nouv. acq. fr. 13521, *Chansonnier de La Clay-
       ette* (mensural notation).
F   Florence, Biblioteca Laurenziana, Plut. 29.1 (square notation).
Fauv   Paris, Bibliothèque Nationale, fr. 146 (mensural notation).
Hu   Las Huelgas (mensural notation).
Mo   Montpellier, Bibliothèque de l'Ecole de Médecine, H 196 (mensural notation).
N   Paris, Bibliothèque Nationale, fr. 12615, *Chansonnier Noailles* (square no-
       tation).
R   Paris, Bibliothèque Nationale, fr. 844, *Manuscrit du Roi* (square and men-
       sural notation).
StV   Paris, Bibliothèque Nationale, lat. 15139 (square and mensural notation).
Tu   Turin, Biblioteca Reale, Vari 42 (mensural notation).
W₁   Wolfenbüttel, Herzog August Bibliothek 677 (square notation).
W₂   Wolfenbüttel, Herzog August Bibliothek 1206 (square notation).
       This writer is preparing an edition of StV for publication.
[5] In mensural notation, the single-note longs have stems that descend from the
right, and the breves are square without stems. The single-note semibreves are
usually diamond-shaped. The shapes of the ligatures may or may not denote the
rhythmic values of their various notes.
[5a] StV and W₂ have double vertical bars that distinguish their perfect long rests
from the shorter rests, though not all perfect long rests are so designated in these
two manuscripts.

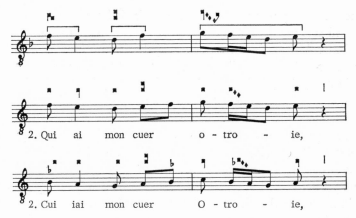

2. Qui ai mon cuer o - tro - ie,

2. Cui iai mon cuer O - tro - ie,

clausula, *Portare*, both transcriptions being accompanied by their original notation. As a motet, *Douce dame sanz pitie* appears in four sources, one of which is in mensural notation.

The first phrase of the duplum in StV has one example of *fractio modi* indicated by the quaternaria conjunctura in the first measure, which replaces a binaria in the chain of the second rhythmic mode. Without the *fractio modi*, the line would have been written as in Example 1b.

Ex. 1b

Because the tenor moves in regular patterns, one can deduce the total rhythmic value occupied by each ligature and conclude that the quaternaria, in this context, has the value of one perfect long. By knowing this value, which is the same as BL, one can then know that it replaces one of the binariae in the mode two chain. The next question is how to divide the four notes: should they begin with two semibreves, SSBB, as in Example 1c:a, end with two semibreves, BBSS, as in b, have two semibreves in the middle, BSSB, as in c, or even have some other combinations such as SSSL, as in d?

Ex. 1c

a) ♪♪♪♩ b) ♩♩♪♪ c) ♩♪♪♩ d) ♪♪♪♩

Hans Tischler, after going through all of the clausulae and the motets in W₁, W₂, and F, has verified the theory that the diamond-shaped notes of a conjunctura often replace a single beat in the modal rhythm, [5c] and this theory is confirmed here in all four of the motets, the three diamond-shaped notes representing the second beat in mode two. Furthermore, the two semibreves must come at the beginning, not the end of the modal beat. Otherwise this would involve the combination BSS on a motet syllable, a combination known to appear only in motets in much later sources than the four included here, as late as those in Tu and fascicles seven and eight of Mo. And so the solution for the quaternaria conjunctura in StV (in mode two and in this context) may be fixed definitely as BSSB. The same ligature occurs three more times in this clausula No. 35, with the rhythm confirmed in the same way; twice it is confirmed in all four of the motet versions and once in two of them.

The lack of confirmation in the last two instances (in line 11) does not in this case involve a conflicting solution, as R and N have completely different rhythms to which StV could not be adapted.

Ex. 2   Clausula and Motet 272 [5d]

[5d] The motetus of N, here, through a mistaken clef, is a second higher than in the transcription.

These are two of the many instances of ornamental or other small differences between different versions which show that one may not try to force one version to mirror another. Notice, as well, in the same line 11, that the W2 version has three diamond-shaped notes over the syllable *ne*. The first note of these may or may not be a too hastily written square note; at any rate, the ligature has the same value as the more usual one, a square followed by two diamond-shaped notes, and occurs at several other points in W2, sometimes as SSB and sometimes as SSS. The difference in ornament in N and R and the unusual ligature in W2 must both be understood as warnings that comparison can be undertaken only with the caution that results from experience with the styles and peculiarities of each of the manuscripts involved.

Upon returning to line 1, ornamental differences appear here as well. The first of these involves the note in N over *da-* of *dame*, ornamented with a plica. In deciding the note values for the StV quaternaria, this plica must be ignored, as it would bring in a fifth note. But if there were no other manuscripts with which to confirm the StV quarternaria, one might argue that the plica tone in N is just as important as the first note of the ternaria that follows it, and so one would not know the rhythm of StV. The other ornamental difference between manuscript versions in line 1 is on the second modal beat of the phrase over the syllable *-ce* of *Douce*, unornamented in StV, but ornamented in three of the motet versions by an appoggiatura; the latter is indicated by replacement of a single note with a binaria. If one did not know that the StV melisma was in the second rhythmic mode, one might be led to think that its first binaria was trochaic instead of iambic, because the pitches of the Mo, W2, and R versions form a trochaic rhythm.[6]

Now let us return to our original quarternaria conjunctura and see what becomes of it in other StV clausulae that are in mode two. It is confirmed as BSSB in No. 5, *In seculum*,[7] by the motet *Trop ma amors assailli* in W2 and Mo.[8] In No. 9, *Docebat doce*,[9] it is confirmed the same way by the motet *Pour quoi maues voz doune* three times in Mo and twice out of three times in Tu.[10] And again the same way in No. 31,

[6] Tischler transcribed the penultimate syllable of the motet *Li plusor-Se plaignant damors* (Mot. 419) in a trochaic rhythm from W2, 4, 53, fol. 236. Another version of this motet melody, Mot. 420, in W2, 2, 78, fol. 190, has notation on this next to last syllable like that on *-ce* of *Douce* in *Douce dame sanz pitie*. Rokseth, however, transcribed the penultimate syllable of *Li plusor* in an iambic rhythm. (Tischler, *op. cit.* II, 131; Rokseth, *op. cit.*, III, 201.)

[7] Fol. 288.

[8] Mot. 144: W2, 4, 79, fol. 248; Mo 6, 220, fol. 253ᵛ.

[9] Fol. 288ᵛ.

[10] Mot 353: Mo 6, 243, fol. 265ᵛ; Tu 22, fol. 27.

Go by the motet *En tel lieu sest entremis* in R and Mo.[11]

After having studied the rhythm of this ligature, one may proceed to the study of all the other ligatures in the StV clausulae, first those in mode two, then in each of the other modes. Only then is it possible to apply the knowledge to the unicum pieces in StV such as the organa and conductus, beginning with passages which have repeated rhythmic patterns in the tenor, before advancing to those which provide no control or assistance at all. Let us look at a StV organum in mode two, the beginning of the *Alleluya Magnus sanctus Paulus*, No. 8.[12]

Ex. 3a   StV second *Alleluya* from Organum 8, *Magnus sanctus Paulus*

The quarternaria conjunctura appears in the duplum just before the syllable *-le-* of *Alleluya*. Here again, because of the repeated patterns in the tenor, we can be reasonably sure that it replaces a BL binaria, and there is no reason not to conclude that it has the same rhythm that it had in the clausulae, BSSB. It is interesting to note that this ligature has always had the same rhythm in mode two, not only in the clausulae, but also, apparently, in the organa. The StV ligatures, though not completely uniform, are, on the whole, much more uniform than those in the Notre Dame manuscripts. For this reason, students who are beginning the study of transcription of 12th- and 13th-century polyphony would do well to begin with the StV clausulae before taking up the clausulae in W1, W2, and F. Furthermore, it is important that ligatures be studied one mode at a time, as the same ligature will vary in different modes. In mode one, the quaternaria conjunctura appears usually as in Example 3b, with the same values but occupying a different part of the measure.

Ex. 3b, c

[11] StV fol. 291ᵛ; Mot. 424: Mo 5, 100, and 126, fols. 140ᵛ and 172ᵛ; R 24, fol. 208.
[12] Fols. 284ᵛ–285.

It occurs this way in the clausulae Nos. 8, 17, 18, and 36 among others.[13] But in No. 15, *Et gaudebit*,[14] it is confirmed in the motetus part as BBBB in lines 8, 9, and 11 by the note forms shown in Example 3c in all of the motet versions that are precisely measured.[15] The three diamond-shaped notes no longer occupy a single modal beat, but now require two, and the whole ligature occupies three modal beats. The reason for this exception may be that clausula No. 15 parallels not only a motet in F but also a clausula in F,[16] and the F rhythm of the quaternaria conjunctura was probably written in the source from which StV was copied. In mode three, in StV, this quaternaria almost always has a total value of two perfect longs; this is confirmed in the organa Nos. 1, 5, 10, and 11,[17] in the parts which have repeated tenor patterns.

Many ligatures in *musica sine littera* can be confirmed by consulting motet versions of approximately the same historical period. But it is also extremely helpful to make use of motet versions copied at a later period, because these are in notation that is unequivocal with regard to many or even all of the notes. Late versions of earlier motets (in addition to many late motets) can be found in Ba, Hu, Tu, in fascicles 7–8 of Mo, and a number of other sources.[18] Scholars have rightfully been hesitant about consulting these later manuscripts, because they include rhythmic groupings and ornaments that do not exist in the earlier sources. A conspicuous example of such a grouping is the subdivision of the brevis recta into as many as four semibreves.[19] In the earliest motets, the brevis recta is never divided into more than two semibreves, and in the bulk of the motet repertory into no more than three, except at a final cadence on one of the last few syllables.[20] The subdivisions in the late motets combine to form an ornate style, a little different in each manuscript, and completely different from the simpler style of the earlier motets. However, if we examine the early motets in these late sources, we will find that they usually adhere in essentials to the original styles.

---

[13] Fols. 288ᵛ, 290, and 292.

[14] Fol. 289ᵛ.

[15] Mot. 317: Cl 42, fol. 380ᵛ; Mo 3, 36, fol. 63ᵛ; Ba 74, fol. 47; Hu 12, fol. 94ᵛ.

[16] Mot. 315: F. 2, 41, fol. 412ᵛ; Clausula 130, fol. 161ᵛ.

[17] Fols. 281ᵛ, 282ᵛ, 286, and 286ᵛ. The numbering here is not the same as that in Friedrich Ludwig's *Repertorium organorum recentioris et motetorum vetustissimi stili* (Halle 1910). Ludwig's 1 corresponds with 2 in the present numbering, Ludwig's 2 with the present 3, and so forth.

[18] *Qui longuement porroit joir damours*, Mot. 219: W2 3, 11, fol. 205; Mo 2, 19, fol. 24ᵛ; Cl fol. 378ᵛ; Tu 19, fol. 23. *Mal batu longuement plure*, Mot. 707: W1 4, 12, fol. 219ᵛ; Mo 5, 92, fol. 131; Cl fol. 383ᵛ; Ba 63, fol. 39ᵛ; Tu 31, fol. 40; and others.

[19] Tu 1, 4, 8, and 9, fols. 1, 5, 9ᵛ, and 11; Mo 7, 264, fol. 290ᵛ; and elsewhere.

[20] Mo 2, 33, fol. 51ᵛ; 5, 88, fol. 126ᵛ; 5, 96, fol. 136ᵛ; 5, 127, fol. 173ᵛ; and a few others.

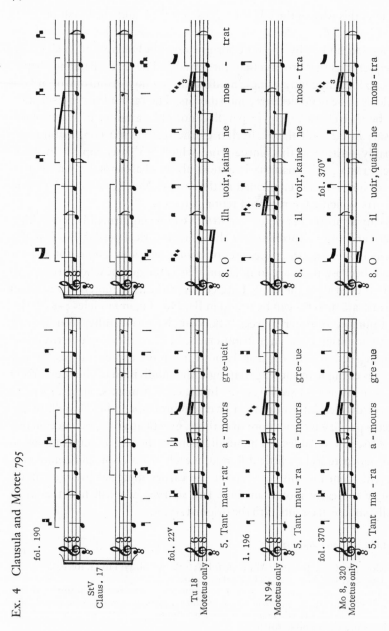

Ex. 4 Clausula and Motet 795

Line 5 in Example 4, like many other lines in motets that appear in early and late sources, is almost identical in the three motet versions. The only difference consists of an ornament at the cadence, which occurs not in the latest version, but in the earliest, N, and is notated by a trochaic binaria on the syllable -*ue* of *greue*.[21] In line 8, Tu and Mo have cadences ornamented with a trochaic binaria. On the syllable *mon-* of *monstra*, the brevis recta is divided into three semibreves in Tu and Mo, but not divided in N. However, on -*il* of *oil*, it is the N version alone which has the tripartition of the brevis. On the syllable *o-* of *oil*, the Mo version has a double appoggiatura, indicated by the ternaria *cum opposita proprietate*, on what would otherwise have been an imperfect long. This appoggiatura does not appear in N in line 8, but it appears in N in other lines of this piece quite often, including line 5.

The Tu version of this double appoggiatura, however, presents a little more of a problem, because it is written with a square followed by two diamond-shaped notes.[22] In the manuscripts in square notation and early mensural notation, this figure, when it has the total duration of an imperfect long, is SSB. But in the latest sources, including Ba, Hu, Tu, and fascicles seven and eight of Mo, SSB is written as in Example 5.

Ex. 5

So the Tu figure can here be confirmed as BSS. Notation for BSS was not needed in the earlier motets, because this rhythm evidently never appeared. In spite of the fact that Tu here has a rhythm that never occurred in the original version of this motet, one still need not be so cautious as to omit consulting the Tu version. One can incorporate the rhythms of the late manuscript insofar as these are found elsewhere in the older manuscript, preferably in the same voice of the piece in question, but at least in a piece written by the same hand. The precise notation in the late manuscripts often helps with rhythms that are current in older pieces. The matter of same voice is important, because tenors are sometimes written in a more primitive style and tripla and quadrupla in a later style than motetus parts. The matter of the same hand is important too. Because the theoretical treatises did not cover every contingency, each scribe found individual solutions in devising notes and ligatures for the rhythms he needed. Because of these individual solutions, a blind following of the theorists can result in mistakes such as writing the perfect long plica in mode two, as in Example 6a, as if it were in mode one.

[21] Concerning the trochaic binaria, see some observations by Ernest Sanders, *Duple Rhythm and Alternate Third Mode in the Thirteenth Century*, in: JAMS, XV (1962), 278ff.

[22] Tu also has LSS indicated by a ternaria beginning with a long and followed by an oblique binaria c. o. p. in *Dame de ualeur-Hei Diex*, Tr. and Mot. 363 and 361, in Tu 6, fol. 6ᵛ.

Comparison with other manuscripts in both square and mensural notation confirms the latter's rhythm as in Example 6b, in keeping with the rhythm of mode two. To return to Example 4 and the ternaria in line 8, the Tu solution causes no problem because the solution in Mo is SSB, a rhythm found frequently throughout the whole motet repertory.

Ex. 6

a) ♩ ♪   b) ♪ ♩

The solution for certain other ligatures is less obvious. Let us, for instance, consider one of the descending quaternariae in Ba, a long followed by two diamonds, and ending with a square as in Example 7a. Two examples of this quaternaria can be found in the motet, *Descendi in ortum meum*,[23] on fol. 14, which is in mode three. Are the notes in this ligature actually LSSB, or are they, like the notes in the binariae in Ba, capable of conveying several combinations? On the syllable *-um*, of *meum*, the Ba ligature coincides with Example 7b in Mo No. 7, 282; Example 7c in Mo No. 8,[24] and in LoD fol. 55ᵛ. On the penultimate syllable, *-mur* of

Ex. 7

a)   b)   c)   d)   e)

intueamur, the Ba ligature coincides with Example 7c in Mo No. 7, 282; Example 7d in Mo No. 8, 330; and 7e in LoD. In other words, the first note of the Ba quaternaria is confirmed as a long in all six cases, and the other three notes as SSB in the first four cases. This would be written in modern notation as in Example 8a, because placed in this context, the breve is altered and combines with the two semibreves to perfect the long. It is reasonable to assume that the Ba quaternaria is LSSB because the note at the end is purposely written as a square instead of as another

Ex. 8

a) ♩. ♫♩   b) ♩. ♫♩

diamond, and because many motets have this rhythm, both on a single syllable, as here, and divided between two and three syllables. The notation on the penultimate syllable in Mo No. 8, 330 and LoD is LBBB

[23] Mot. 767: Ba 25, fol. 14.
[24] Fols. 321 and 379ᵛ.

(Example 8b), often an alternate to LSSB in mode three. In Ba, LBBB is usually written as L BBB, divided into a single note and a ternaria.

Our original descending quaternaria in Ba (Example 7a) is confirmed in three other motets as LSSB by ligatures in Tu, Hu, and Fauv.[25] So we can now see whether it, in turn, will throw light on ligatures in other manuscripts. It almost always corresponds, in the old corpus of Mo (fascicles two to six), to a conjunctura made of a long followed by three diamond-shaped notes (Example 9a), this not only in mode three, but in mode one as well. And so this conjuctura in Mo should probably be transcribed as in Example 9b or 9c.

Ex. 9

The first of these rhythms occurs often in mode three, and both can occur in mode one. When the first rhythm comes in mode one, this involves one of the occasional iambic rhythms that sometimes ornament one or two perfections in a trochaic piece. Rokseth usually transcribed Example 9a (from Mo) as given in Example 9d, when in mode one, adhering to the directions of the theorists; but this is one of the contingencies that the theorists do not cover. Our descending quaternaria in Ba provides the means for finding this out.

The tracing of a particular ligature through all of the various manuscripts so often brings interesting results that it is not an exaggeration to say that before transcribing any one manuscript, one must examine each ligature in every source from W1 on through Tu and Fauv; this in addition to studying each piece in all of its sources.

Let us consider other ligatures in the StV clausula No. 35: The quinaria, in lines two and nine, is an extension of the quaternaria in line one. The square note at the end takes up an additional beat in the mode. Because this square note does not divide a modal beat with the diamond-shaped notes, and is confirmed the same way in StV clausula No. 31,[26] it is safe to transcribe it as in Example 10e in the organum No. 8, even though there is no tenor pattern underneath to confirm the total value.

[25] Tr. 85; Ba 18, fol. 9ᵛ; Tu 7, fol. 7ᵛ. Tr. and Mot. 770 and 771: Ba 5, fol. 3ᵛ; Mo 7, 285, fol. 323ᵛ; Hu 37, fol. 113ᵛ. Tr. and Mot. 598 and 599: Ba 77, fol. 49ᵛ; Fauv fol. 11ᵛ.

[26] Mot. 424, *En tel lieu sest entremis.* Confirmed in R 24, fol. 208; Mo 5, 100 and 126, fols. 141 and 173; N 47, fol. 188.

Ex. 10

Allied to this ligature is still another in the clausula No. 35, the senaria in line ten, an extension of the quinaria in line two. The two square notes at the end each have a beat in the mode, leaving the three diamond-shaped notes to divide a beat between them as in Example 10f. In mode one, the quinaria of Example 10b is confirmed as in Example 10h (LSSSL) in clausula No. 28; and the senaria of 10c as 10i (BSSBBL) in clausula No. 36. In fact almost every ligature with diamond-shaped notes confirmed by a motet is to be transcribed with the square notes having one beat each in the mode and the diamond-shaped notes sharing one or sometimes two beats between them.

With regard to the single notes in the StV clausula No. 35, almost all of the longs of the duplum have very small stems, whereas the breves have none. This differentiation is omitted in only one place, in measure seven, where the longs and breves are both without stems. However, this omission occurs after the rhythmic mode has been clearly established. In the tenor, all but one of the perfect longs have stems. The one without a stem, in measure thirteen, occurs, too, after the rhythmic pattern has been established. Both omissions involve repeated notes.

The same treatment of single notes can be found in most of the other StV clausulae. All of the notes with stems are perfect or imperfect longs and most of those without are breves, although a few without are imperfect longs. The exceptional imperfect longs without stems are written either after the rhythmic mode has been established or else in places where the rhythm could easily be deduced, such as in No. 6 at the beginning of the duplum, in Example 11. The duplum continues unequivocally

Ex. 11

in the first mode, and is confirmed by its tenor as well as by the motet *Que demandez vous* [27] in W2.

There are a few diamond-shaped single notes in the StV clausulae. These are larger than the diamond-shaped notes in the conjuncturae.

---

[27] Mot. 237: W2 4, 67, fol. 242ᵛ.

They are written only in places where repeated notes are involved and are usually breves, sometimes imperfect longs. Each of them has a rhythmic value different from that of the neighboring note of the same pitch.[28]

The single notes in W2 are nowhere near as helpful in determining rhythm, even though some of these are written with, and others without, small stems. In the W2 version of *Douce dame sanz pitie*, most of the tenor longs have stems, but a glance at the upper voice will show how unreliable the stems are in differentiating longs from breves. However, the W2 motet parts in mode six, for example in the motet *El mois dauril*,[29] have stems on the last notes of each phrase. And there are a few passages of *musica sine littera* in which the longs and breves of repeated notes are correctly differentiated by stems; one is in the *Alleluya Paraclitus spiritus sanctus* at the end of fol. 75ᵛ.[30]

Fusio modi, or the fusion of two or more values of the rhythmic mode into one note, involves few problems in the clausula-motet repertory; because of the regular patterns of rhythm in the tenor, one can usually be sure of the total duration of a note or ligature in an upper voice. In music that has no regular patterns in the tenor—the melismatic parts of organa, all the parts of conductus, and even the last few syllables of motets, where all of the voices including the tenor may slow down—problems will occur. In Example 12, for instance, the chain of ligatures in mode one (ternaria followed by several binariae) has a ternaria in the place of the second binaria.

Ex. 12   F Clausula 167

fol. 166ᵛ, beginning of duplum

According to rule, either solution 12a or 12b is possible. Familiarity with the music will develop an instinct that prefers 12b only because this sounds more like a line in an F clausula. Instinct is confirmed in this particular case, because the piece, in the first place, has regular tenor

---

[28] In clausulae 1, 2, 6, 9, 14, 15, 18, 24, 25, 28, 31, 35, and 38.
[29] Tr. 318: W2 3, 2, fol. 195.
[30] Also in the *Alleluya In conspectu*, at the bottom of fol. 79, and in the *Alleluya Posui adjutorium* at the top of fol. 84.

patterns that 12a will not fit and, in the second place, has a parallel motet.[31] In Example 13, instinct should protest loudly against the solution 13b in favor of 13a. The latter is also confirmed by tenor patterns and a motet.[32]

Ex. 13   StV Clausula 1

fol. 288, duplum, perfections 18-23

Not all choices of *fusio modi* are as clear cut from the point of view of musicality as these; however, the combination of one choice after another can involve important differences that alter the character of the music. Example 14a, for instance, is taken from William Waite's transcription of the organa in W1.[33] 14b is another transcription of the same passage, also theoretically correct, with more *fusio* and less *fractio modi*.

Ex. 14   W1 Organum, *In columbe*

fol. 18

In order to make reasonable choices in the area of *fusio* and *fractio modi*, one must first transcribe many works that have regular tenor patterns and memorize the rhythmic combinations that constantly recur. This can be done properly only by singing as much as possible of the repertory. Transcriptions have been printed that are not vocally conceived—some are not even vocally possible except at a tempo which is much too slow.

---

[31] This is the beginning of Clausula 167, F, fol. 166ᵛ; confirmed in Mot. 441, F 1, 21, fol. 394ᵛ.

[32] Clausula 1: StV, fol. 288; confirmed in Mot. 480, Hu 34, fol. 112.

[33] William Waite, *The Rhythm of Twelfth-Century Polyphony* (New Haven 1954), transcr. p. 10. From O4 *In columbe*, W1, fol. 18.

After transcribing organa or conductus, it is worth while to count the number of *fractio* and *fusio* beats and compare the result with the *fractio* and *fusio* in the clausulae of the same manuscript. The clausulae in W1, F, and W2, for instance, have many more instances of *fusio* than of *fractio*, but not the clausulae in StV, in which the proportion is the other way around. In W1, a group of clausulae in mode one, chosen at random, has 27 added notes as a result of *fractio* and 84 perfect longs or perfect long rests. The total number of perfections in this group of clausulae comes to 424.[34] Turning, then, to the first 424 perfections in Waite's transcription of W1 (not counting the parts with repeated tenor patterns), we find that he has 79 added notes as a result of *fractio* and only 67 perfect longs or perfect long rests.[35] His transcriptions, it seems to me, suffer much in this regard, even though he has made extensive and interesting discoveries in the history of the pieces and their notation. Too much *fractio modi* results in a line of considerably more tension than the lines that we find in the clausulae, the motets, or the tenor-controlled parts of the organa pura.

An interesting device in 12th- and 13th-century polyphony, which gives elegance to some of the cadences, is an alteration in rhythm, usually on the penultimate syllable. A number of trochaic pieces have one or two iambic rhythms just before the final notes. These alterations are found most often in the mensurally notated pieces but exist also in the Notre Dame pieces. In these pieces, the trochaic and iambic rhythms can occur within the same phrase and are not necessarily separated from one another by vertical bars. In Example 15, the first version is taken from Tu, as each note in this manuscript is indicated with exactness.

Ex. 15   Motet 542, *Virgo gloriosa* (last line, motetus only)

[34] W1 clausulae 15, 35, 36, 40, and 57; fols. 44, 47, 47ᵛ, and 49.
[35] *Op cit.*, transcr. pp. 1–10.

The two binariae near the end are different from one another, the first being trochaic, LB, and the other iambic, B recta B altera. In Cl and ArsA,[36] the same rhythm as that in Tu is indicated differently; the LB, the usual rhythm that has been heard throughout the piece, is conveyed by the usual binaria with square notes. An exceptional binaria, with the second note larger than the first, stands for the exceptional rhythm with the longer value on the second note. These two versions in Cl and ArsA throw light on the use of binariae with one large note. A binaria with the first note instead of the second enlarged can signify LB where BL would have been expected.[37] In Erf,[38] the two rhythms, trochaic and iambic, are distinguished by oblique and square forms. Notice, as well, that in Erf alone the group of three notes has iambic rhythm (SSB). Ba and Mo have equivocal rhythms; in Ba and in the old corpus of Mo (fascicles two through six), the binariae with square notes convey more than one combination of values. Rokseth transcribed the last binaria in Example 15 as BL,[39] and Aubry as LB.[40]

Example 16 is taken from a motet that appears in both mensural and Notre Dame sources.

Ex. 16   Tripl. or quadr. 318, *El mois davril* (line 8; same music as Tripl. 316, *Ypocrite pseudopontifices*, in F)

In Cl and Mo, the iambic rhythm on the syllables *sui tour-* is indicated by a vertical bar after the long over *part*. In F, the iambic rhythm is also indicated by a vertical bar, though without Cl and Mo, the only reason for being sure that the F rhythm on the last three syllables is not L SSS L is that tripartition of the brevis recta occurs nowhere else in this voice in F. It would be impossible to know that the iambic rhythm existed in W2 without at least one other manuscript version. The Ba version of this fragment does not have the iambic pattern.

[36] MS Paris, Bibliothèque de l'Arsenal 135 (mensural notation).
[37] For an example, see Ex. 17 below, as well as Mo 5, 165, fol. 214ᵛ, end of triplum.
[38] MS Erfurt, Bibliotheca Amploiana, fol. 169 (mensural notation).
[39] *Op. cit.* Rokseth and Tischler recognized some of the iambic cadences in their transcriptions, but the presence of Cl, discovered since their editions appeared, makes possible the finding of more.
[40] Pierre Aubry, *Cent motets du XIIIe siècle* (Paris 1908).

Example 17 is taken from the motet, *Encontre le tens pascor—Mens fidem seminat*, which appears in mensural and Notre Dame sources, and has a clausula in W1 and F.

Ex. 17   Tripl. 496, *Encontre le tens pascor* (lines 2–3; as a clausula in F)

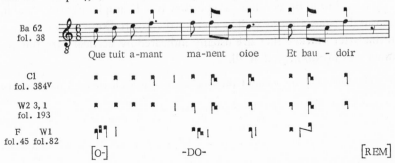

In Ba, the iambic rhythm is conveyed by the brevis followed by an oblique binaria (B BB) over the word *manent*, and later by the same note forms over *Et bau-*. In Mo, the iambic rhythm is conveyed the first time by a vertical bar after the long on the syllable *-mant* of *amant*, and the second time as in Ba. Cl and W2 also have vertical bars for the rhythm over *manent*, but their notation over *Et bau-* is equivocal. Their rhythm in the latter place was probably understood to resemble that over *manent*, since in many manuscripts the rhythm is written correctly the first time and the singer is expected to continue the same rhythm later. This fragment of the clausula is written in the same way in W1 as in F. The first vertical bar, which corresponds to the one in the motets after *amant*, is a *Silbenstrich*, coming before the syllable *-do-* of *odorem*; this vertical bar would be present regardless of the rhythm. The other

Ex. 18   Tripl. 496 (line 1)

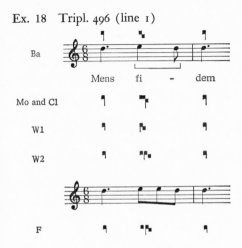

two vertical bars indicate iambic rhythm. Notice that the two forms directly over -*do*- in the F clausula can correspond in the motet either to an iambic pattern, as in Example 17, or a trochaic one, as in Example 18.

There are at least 20 examples of iambic rhythms inserted into cadences of trochaic pieces. These occur not only in the clausula and motet repertory, but in the conductus repertory too. Examples can be found in mensural manuscripts as well as each of the Notre Dame manuscripts.[41] In the latter sources, they are usually indicated by vertical bars, but are sometimes not indicated at all.

[41] The following are some of the trochaic motets with iambic rhythm at the cadences:

Mulier mysterio, Mot. 376a: Hu 8, fol. 90, last line.

In veritate comperi, Mot. 451: Hu 55, fol. 126, line 30. In many other MSS.

Je cuidai avoir Amours, Tr. 840: Ba 50, fol. 30ᵛ, line 5.

Par un matinet lautrier—Les un bosquet, Tr. 295, Mot. 296: Mo 7, 259, fol. 282; Ba 56, fol. 34ᵛ.

Amours dont ie suis espris—Lautrier au dous mois, Tr. 858, Mot. 859: Mo 7, 270, fol. 298ᵛ. The iambic binaria comes four syllables from the end and coincides with a trochaic binaria in the tenor.

Studentes conjugio—De se debent bigami, Tr. 615, Mot. 616: Mo 7, 286, fol. 324ᵛ.

The following pieces in the conductus repertory have iambic cadences:

Flos de spina: Hu 147, fol. 136ᵛ, last line. Also in W1, F, and Madrid, Biblioteca Nacional 20486.

Deus in adjutorium: Tu 2, fol. Dᵛ; Mo 8, 303, fol. 350.

Dum sigillum: Hu 152, fol. 143; F, fol. 344. The iambic binaria is in the upper voice at the end of the opening cauda.

Novus miles sequitur: Hu 102, fol. 101ᵛ; F, fol. 230; Ma, fol. 139.

PEROTINUS REVISITED

by HANS TISCHLER

OR A LONG TIME scholars have tried to amplify the bare references to the two great composers, Leonin and Perotin, made by Johannes de Garlandia and his anonymous student, the famous Anonymous IV.[1] Searching through the sources of the late 12th and early 13th centuries for possible data on these masters, Amédée Gastoué [2] and Jacques Handschin [3] at first seemed to provide some details about Perotin. The latter discussed five excerpts from GUER [4] and one from *Gallia Christiana*,[5] which refer to a Petrus Succentor and his brothers: Terricus,[6] who died as archbishop of Nicosia in Cyprus in 1211, and Johannes de Grevia, whose by-name is taken from a district of Paris at the time and seems to connect Petrus with a Philippe de Grevia, once identified with Philippe *le Chancelier* of Notre Dame, whose poetry appears in several musical settings by Perotin and who died in 1236.

This identification has long since been discarded.[7] The other material relating to the Succentor, though not exactly universally accepted as permitting a satisfactory identification of Perotin,[8] still stands as neither refuted nor solidly established. In order to identify Petrus Succentor with Perotin several conditions must be fulfilled: (1) The sources must point only to him as the possible candidate for identification. For this purpose it is necessary to survey (a) all other men of the age connected with Notre Dame and named Peter, Perotin being the diminutive of

[1] C.-E.-H. de Coussemaker, *Scriptorum de musica medii aevi nova series* (Paris 1864–76), I, 116, 342, 360.
[2] *Les Primitifs de la musique française* (Paris 1922), p. 18ff.
[3] *Zur Geschichte von Notre Dame*, in: *Acta musicologica*, IV (1932), 10ff.
[4] Benjamin Guerard, *Le Cartulaire de l'église de Notre Dame de Paris* (Paris 1850).
[5] Vol. VII (Paris 1744).
[6] For this name see Handschin (fn. 3), pp. 10f, 104.
[7] See H. Meylan, *Les "questions" de Philippe le Chancelier* (Paris 1927), p. 89ff; Yvonne Rokseth, *Polyphonies du XIIIe siècle* (Paris 1936–39), IV, 227; Hans Tischler, *New Historical Aspects of the Parisian Organa*, in: *Speculum*, XXV (1950), 25.
[8] See Rokseth (fn. 7), p. 50f; Tischler (fn. 7), p. 25ff; Hans Tischler, *The Dates of Perotin*, in: JAMS, XVI (1963), 240f.

Peter, and (b) all those who held the positions of Cantor (or Precentor) and Succentor throughout the period of Leonin and Perotin. (2) The lifetime of Perotin as deduced from other data must conform with the documented references to the Succentor, which cover the period 1208–38. (3) The office of Succentor must conform with what is otherwise known about Perotin, and here a comparison between Leonin and Perotin in this respect would be desirable. In conclusion (4) it is necessary to discuss the recent suggestion made by Heinrich Husmann that Perotin may have been connected with the church of St. Germain-l'Auxerrois, rather than with Notre Dame.

Each of these points will now be taken up in turn to assemble all that is known about Perotin. The sources on which this study is based are the cartularies and obituaries of the Parisian churches of the period and certain publications based thereon: GUER (see fn. 4), DUB, NDC, NDN, and StVA.[9] Other manuscripts have only tangential or corroborative import.

I

(a)

THE FOLLOWING MEN, named Peter and connected with Notre Dame, can be identified from the sources around 1200, where they are mentioned as indicated below; but completeness is not claimed here: [10]

1. Petrus Cancellarius, mentioned 1168–78: GUER III,439 (1168)—III,358 (1170)—II,339 (1171)—II,9 and II,176 (1173)—II,293 (1177)—II,503 (1178)—IV,14 (?).

2. Petrus Canonicus,[11] mentioned 1183–91: GUER II,501 (1183)—II,198 (1189, as Capellanus Episcopi)—I,45 (1191, as Diaconus).

3. Petrus de Corbolio (Corbeil) Canonicus: GUER I,72 (1198).

4. Petrus Cantor et Diaconus, a famous teacher and philosopher, elected to high offices in Tournai, Paris, and Reims, mentioned from 1185 to his death on 25 September 1197 (GUER IV,159 = NDN fol. 278[v], StVA fols. 799[v]–800[v] [12]): GUER II,311 (1185)

[9] DUB: Gerard Dubois, *Historia ecclesiae parisiensis*, Vol. II (Paris 1710); NDC: The Cartularies of Notre Dame (Paris, Archives Nationales, MSS LL 76 and 78); NDN: Necrologium of Notre Dame (Paris, Bibl. Nat., MS lat. 5185 cc); StVA: Annals of St. Victor (Paris, Bibl. Nat., MS lat. 14369).

[10] The datings given in GUER are not always reliable; several of them have been corrected below.

[11] According to Handschin (fn. 3), p. 104, this Petrus was a canon of St. Denis, the sister church and neighbor of Notre Dame.

[12] A eulogy inserted in 1205.

—I,398 and III,386 (1186)—II,372 (1187)—I,295, I,397, II,198, and NDC 76,657 (1189)—GUER II,400 (1190)—I,45 (1191)—II,468 (1193)—III,359 (1195)—I,57 and II,115 (1196)—I,57 and II,258 (1197).

5. Petrus Pictavensis (of Poitier) Diaconus et Cancellarius, mentioned from 1193 to his death on 3 September 1205 (GUER IV,142 = NDN fol. 267v): GUER II,468 (1193)—II,356, II,395, and III,359 (1195)—I,72 (1198)—II,69 (1201)—II,260 (1203)—II,513 (1204)—II,258 (1248, as dead).

6. Petrus II de Nemosio (Nemours), Bishop of Paris 1208-19.

7. Petrus Pulverellus:: GUER I,410 and II,517 (1236, as dead)—IV,114 (c. 1300, as dead).

8. Petrus Succentor, mentioned 1208-38: *Gallia Christiana*, VII, Instrumenta, col. 277f (1208, as not yet Succentor)—GUER I,440 (1209[13])—IV,87 = NDN fol. 219-219^v (1211[14])—GUER II,445 and II,372f (1224)—II,237 (1236)—II,422 (1238).

9. Petrus Parvus Cancellarius: GUER IV,134 = NDN fol. 262^v (as having died on 22 August c. 1245); GUER IV,142 = NDN fol. 268 (September of the same year).

10. Petrus Iuvenis Diaconus et Canonicus, mentioned 1226-59: GUER IV,46 = NDN fol. 184 (c. 1225)—GUER II,457(1226)—III,233 (1247)—IV,31 = NDN fol. 168^v (as having died on 21 March 1258?)—GUER II,67 (1259, as recently deceased).

Of all these men only Petrus Cantor (4) and Petrus Succentor (8) are connected with music. The former's musical ability is confirmed by some sources, but they stress his philosophical teaching and writing activities so much that it would be hard to believe that he was our Perotin; in fact, such an identification has been expressly rejected before.[15] Besides, the early date of his death, 1197, hardly permits this identification. The Succentor, therefore, though the sources mention

[13] The date 1208 is part of the document. Handschin thought that it was wrong, because it seemed to mention Petrus Succentor as dead and would therefore have to be corrected to 1238 or later. But both the writer of the document, Dean Hugo, who died in 1216, and Petrus were alive at the time of its writing, issuing it to set up a memorial foundation for Bishop Eude de Sully (d. 1208) apparently early in 1209; cf. Rokseth (fn. 7), p. 50.

[14] On the date see Handschin (fn. 3), p. 11.

[15] See Rudolf Ficker, *Perotinus—Organum quadruplum Sederunt principes* (Wien 1930), p. 25.

nothing of his musical achievements beyond his title, emerges as the only possible candidate for identification with Perotin. It should be added that other men named Peter, but connected with other Parisian churches, do not add any further candidates.

The sources mention many, if not all, cantors and succentors of the period. Of them some appear without dates, that is, with only month and day of death, in their obituaries, and can therefore not be placed in an orderly succession. In an alphabetic order, and omitting those hailing obviously from periods too late to concern us here, they are:

Adam Cantor, died 15 April (?) (NDN fol. 187)

Erchembaudis Succentor, died 24 March (?) (GUER IV,45f = NDN fol. 183)

Lisiernus Cantor, died 25 April (?) (GUER IV,56 = NDN fol. 194^v)

The other names can be placed in a complete or nearly complete order of cantors and succentors at Notre Dame from before 1000 to the 1250s.[16] This order incidentally shows that the office of succentor probably existed only after about 1100.

Some difficulty arises with names that appear with both titles. There is none regarding Robertus and Petrus Cantor and Succentor, separated as they are in time. But Nicholaus Cantor seems in one document to be wrongly called Succentor; for if this document of 1228 really referred to a second person, this succentor would have held office at the same time as Petrus Succentor. It further appears that Nicholaus Cantor and de Carnoto (Chartres) Cantor are the same person.

CANTORS (PRECENTORS)   SUCCENTORS

1. Adelelmus, c. 992–c. 1040:
   GUER I,326 (922)—
   I,331 (1032)—IV,166
   (died 9 October c. 1040)

2. Laudo, c. 1040–c. 1075:
   GUER III,352 (c. 1067)
   —IV,51 (died 23 April
   c. 1075)

3. Galerannus (Walerannus),
   c.1075–c.1105: GUER

[16] See for a partial presentation Rokseth (fn. 7), p. 49f.

Cantors (cont.)	Succentors (cont.)

I,280 (1076)—I,310
(c. 1092)—I,306 (1097)
—II,16 (c. 1100)—I,328,
I,373, and I,373 (1100)—
I,372, I,373, and I,448
(1101)—IV,167 =
NDN fol. 284 (died 12
October c. 1105)—IV,18
(1226, as dead)

4. Adam, c. 1105–c. 1140:
   GUER I,313 and I,386
   (1107)—I,413 (1108)—
   I,376 (1109)—I,387
   (1112)—I,375 (1117)—
   I,42 (1120)—I,382
   (c. 1120)—I,450 (1122)
   —I,334 (1124)—II,68
   (1125)—III,355
   (c. 1130)—I,337 and
   I,385 (1134)—I,384
   (c. 1134)—IV,50 (?)—
   IV,11 = NDN fol. 158
   (died 16 January c. 1140)

5. Albertus, c. 1140–c. 1177:
   NDC 76,661 (1146)—
   GUER II,360 (1147)—
   I,389 (1152)—NDC
   78,260 (after 1159)—
   GUER II,503 (1164)
   —III,439 (1168)—I,39
   (1169)—III,358
   (c. 1170)—II,339 (1171)
   —II,466f (c. 1172)—II,9
   and II,175f (1173)—
   IV,118f = NDN fol. 249
   (died 1177?)—I,398
   (c. 1188, as dead)

1. Robertus, before 1112–c. 1120:
   GUER I,387 (1112)—
   III,355 (c. 1120)

2. Girbertus, c. 1120–c. 1130:
   as Cancellarius: GUER
   I,386 and I,313f (1107)
   —I,380 and I,414 (1108)
   —I,376 (1109)
   as Archidiaconus:
   I,387 (1112)
   as Succentor: I,382
   (c. 1120)

3. Guillermus (Guillelmus),
   c. 1130–c. 1145: GUER
   III,353 (c. 1130)—IV,200
   (died 20 December before
   1146)

4. Robertus, c. 1145–c. 1175:
   GUER II,360 (1147)—I,389
   (1152)—II,503 (1164)—
   III,439 (1168)—II,339 (1171)
   —IV,19 = NDN fol. 158
   (died 14 February c. 1175)

5. Galo, c. 1175–c. 1204: [17]
   GUER II,503 (1178)—
   II,311 (1185)—I,398 and
   III,386 (1186)—II,372
   (1187)—I,397 = NDC

[17] According to Rokseth (fn. 7), p. 50, Galo probably died in 1208 and was succeeded by Petrus. But it would seem that Guillelmus must be placed between the two.

Cantors (cont.)   Succentors (cont.)

6. Galterus, 1177–c. 1184:   76,567 and II,198 (1189)—
   as Presbiter: GUER   I,45 (1191)—II,468 (1193)
   I,389 (1152)—II,339   —III,359 (1195)—II,115
   (1171)—II,175 (1173)   (1196)—I,72 = NDC
   as Cantor: II,293 (1177)   78,266ff (1198)—NDC
   —II,503 (1178)—   78,272 (1200)—GUER
   IV,31 (died 20 March   II,69 (1201)—II,260
   c. 1184)   (1203)—IV,173 (?)—IV,47
7. Petrus, c. 1184–1197 (see   = NDN fol. 185 (died 15
   above)   April 1204?)
8. Mauritius, 1197–1198:
   NDC 78,266ff (1198)
9. Robertus, 1198–c. 1215:
   GUER I,72 (1198)—
   I,429 = NDC 78,272
   (1200)—GUER II,69
   (1201)—II,260 (1203)—   6. Guillelmus, c. 1204–1208: [17]
   I,423 (1207)—IV,184   GUER IV, 120 (died
   = NDN fol. 301ᵛ (died   25 July 1220?, as once
   11 November c. 1215)   Succentor)—I,297f
10. Renaldus Bourdon, c. 1215–   (1221, as dead)
    1218: NDC 76,799   7. Petrus, 1208–c. 1245 [18] (see
    (1218)   above)
11. Nicholaus de Carnoto,   8. Henricus de Momeignia
    1218–1247: [19]   (Monmigny), 1245–c. 1270:
    as Canonicus: GUER   as Canonicus: GUER II,
    II,72 (1217)   422 (1238)—II,53 (1242)
    as Cantor: NDC 76,687   —III,394 (1244)
    (1218)—GUER II,517   as Succentor: III,229 =
    (1219)—II,74 (1221)   NDC 76,598 (1245)—
    —II,511 (1223)—   GUER III,392 and III,394
    NDC 76,671 (1228, as   (1247)—III,394 (1248)
    Succentor)—GUER   —II,53 and III,401 (1250)
    II,74 (1229)—II,74,   —IV,74 (c. 1250)—

[18] According to Rokseth (fn. 7), p. 50, Petrus assumed the office of succentor
shortly before Easter of 1209; but the reference therefor, the *Gallia Christiana*
document, shows that he already was succentor, probably since late in 1208. The
date 1245 seems necessary because the next succentor entered upon this office only
in that year.

[19] The sources also refer to another Nicholaus Cantor, who served at St. Stephen,
the sister church of Notre Dame: GUER II,90f (died c. 1204); cf. GUER II,91, fn. 1,
on the two Nicholauses.

Cantors (cont.)	Succentors (cont.)

Cantors (cont.)

II,74, and II,91 (1231)
—II,54of and II,71
(1233)—III,229 =
NDC 76,598 (1245)—
II,73f (1247)—IV,154
= NDN fol. 257ᵛ
(died 21 September
1247)

Succentors (cont.)

III,395 (1251)—III,396
(1252)—III,391 (1253)—
II,220 and II,221 (1254)
—II,88 (1255)—II,122
and III,396 (1256)—
II,186 (1257)—II,447
(1258)—II,67 and III,397
(1259)—III,401f (1262)
—II,121 and III,402
(1263)—III,402 and
III,402 (1264)—IV,152
= NDN fol. 274ᵛ (died
19 September ?)

Excepting the moot Petrus Succentor, Albertus Cantor is the only one of all these men presumed to have composed or to have had a reputation as a composer—witness the famous *Congaudeant catholici* in the *Codex Calixtinus*. And Leonin is conspicuously absent. It must, of course, be assumed that each of them was chosen to fill his office because of his musical gifts, but composing ability seems not to have been an important consideration in selecting cantors and succentors. From this point of view the identification of Perotin with Petrus Succentor therefore carries no force.

More important for the selection of such officials was their administrative ability and their family background and fortune. The latter seems to have been particularly significant in the case of Petrus. The *Gallia Christiana* document informs us that in 1208 his brother Johannes, on his leaving the Augustinian monastery of Livry and becoming a canon of the Premonstratensian Chapter of Notre Dame, gave to that monastery a considerable donation of land and money with the agreement of his brothers, Terricus and Petrus. The document appears to imply that all three brothers made the change from the Augustinian order to the stricter filial order together. Terricus became Archbishop of Nicosia, where his predecessor had just died, and he is known to have moved during his brief tenure toward reforming the Augustinians at Nicosia along Premonstratensian lines. Petrus was made Succentor at Notre Dame. This very probable interpretation of the document would make it virtually certain that he was not Perotin, since he would not have been in Paris, let alone at Notre Dame, during the master's active period, discussed in the next section.

II

THE DATES of Petrus Succentor's appearance in the sources are 1208–38, and he seems to have held his office until about 1245. It is difficult to imagine, however, that the bulk of Perotin's production, which according to Anonymous IV comprised two-, three-, and four-part organa, clausulae, and conducti, could fall that late. The Perotinian development of organum and discant clausula, taken by itself, could perhaps have occurred then; but the main body of conducti and the rise of the motet cannot be placed so late, and the latter presupposes the Perotinian clausula.

The few dates that may be connected with the early motet [20] argue for the birth of the species before 1200, since motets that obviously belong to a slightly later time than the earliest layer of such works refer to events shortly after 1200: the emergence of the Dominican and Franciscan orders (founded respectively in 1203 and 1206 and confirmed by the Pope in 1216 and 1223), the Lateran Council of 1216, and the popularity of the *Roman de Galeran* (c. 1200). Similarly, the datable Notre-Dame conducti belong to the last decades before 1200. And the only dates that can be connected with organa refer to 1198 and 1199, though Husmann has recently suggested c. 1220 for some works in the latest layer of the Magnus Liber.[21]

Let us briefly consider the dates of 1198 and 1199. Ever since Handschin published the two edicts of Bishop Eude de Sully, which refer to the feasts of Circumcision (1 January) and St. Stephen (26 December) of 1199,[22] reprinted from GUER I,72ff = DUB 217 and *Gallia Christiana*, VIII, col. 78 = DUB 218, it has been assumed that the references in both to four-part singing might refer to the two great organa quadrupla known to have been written by Perotin.[23] A careful rereading of the sources proves that the connection between the dates and works is at best tentative.

The first decree was issued for a single purpose, namely to abolish the frivolous practices of the students on the "donkey's feast" of 1 January by replacing this celebration with that of Circumcision, for which a new, dignified liturgy was instituted. It reads in part as follows:

[20] See Tischler (fn. 7), p. 29; Hans Tischler, *The Motet in 13th-Century France* (Diss. Yale University 1942), p. 255f; Tischler (fn. 8), p. 240f.
[21] Heinrich Husmann, *The Enlargement of the Magnus liber organi*, in: JAMS, XVI (1963), 186ff.
[22] Handschin (fn. 3), pp. 5ff, 7f.
[23] The other works definitely cited by Anonymous IV as being by Perotin and those tentatively ascribed to him by modern scholars are listed in Tischler (fn. 7), p. 24.

Responsorium et Benedicamus (of Vespers) *in triplo vel quadruplo vel organo poterunt decantari . . . tertium et sextum Responsorium* (of matins) *in organo vel in triplo vel quadruplo cantabuntur . . . Responsorium et Alleluya* (of matins Mass) *in triplo vel quadruplo vel organo in cappis sericis cantabuntur.*

The mention of three- and four-part singing is here so casual that it is impossible to think of it as a specific reference to a particular work then in existence or projected. It merely indicates that such works were known at the time. Indeed, many three-part organa, conducti, and motets would seem to have existed at the time of the decree, and several four-part conducti have reached us also.

When a new feast was instituted, chants from other feasts were normally pressed into service. Thus the bishop's wishes were carried out by using existing Christmas organa in the new Circumcision service.[24] The edict, a product of papal pressure upon the new bishop, was promulgated in 1198, that is, after April 1198 in our calendar. When the new feast was celebrated for the first time on the following 1 January, there had not been, it would seem, enough time to allow Perotin to compose his immense quadruplum *Viderunt* for the occasion, as has been surmised. Either it had been previously composed for Christmas, a definite possibility according to the edict, and was now applied to Circumcision, or it was written soon after the other great quadruplum, the *Sederunt*, which was destined for the next feast instituted by Bishop Eude.

That feast was to celebrate the protomartyr St. Stephen, patron saint of the cathedral's more ancient sister church, which was then being absorbed into the new edifice of Notre Dame. The *Sederunt* may well have been written during 1199, in response to the bishop's well-known intention, which took form in the second edict, reading in part as follows: ". . . *in Missa Responsum vel Alleluya in organo triplo vel quadruplo decantabunt . . .*" Incidentally, this passage settles once and for all the doubt of some scholars whether three- and four-part settings of chants may be called organa. Considering both edicts, it appears that the general term *organum* applied equally to two-, three-, and four-part works, but that in a narrower sense only the two-part arrangements were so called.[25]

Perotin's two quadrupla are accompanied in the manuscripts by a much shorter four-part organum, a single clausula of the Easter gradual

[24] See Gustave Reese, *Music in the Middle Ages* (New York 1940), p. 302; but not the *Sederunt*, as is there stated, for that work is appropriate rather for the feast of St. Stephen.
[25] See also GUER IV,6, 108, and 121.

Mors. This work exhibits a slightly later technique; it does not carry Perotin's name and is probably not by him. All three pieces are among the about one hundred organa and clausulae whose music served the oldest layer of motets. Significantly, *Mors* was turned into a triple motet, with three different texts, all related to the tenor word, whereas the Perotinian works were, in the earliest manner of motets, given single texts only, despite the rhythmic independence of their parts. The difference in age between these two works and the clausula *Mors* is thus corroborated. And we have already seen that the oldest layer of motets, which includes the work based on the latter, predates at least the second decade of the 13th century.

Thus the time sequence of the organa quadrupla is rather clear: The *Sederunt* may well be assigned to 1199; for the *Viderunt*, 1197 or 1200 would seem reasonable assumptions; and *Mors* belongs to the next decade, several years later, perhaps around 1205.

The sources make it clear that the succeeding generations recognized the two large quadrupla as great masterworks, as do modern scholars. Since Perotin also revised the two-part cycle of organa of Leonin's Magnus Liber, and composed many two-part clausulae, of which Anonymous IV proclaims him the particular master, as well as three-part organa and conducti in one, two, and three parts, he must have accomplished much of this before approaching the composition of the extraordinary quadrupla. The bulk of his work must therefore have preceded the year 1199 and succeeded the period during which Leonin composed the Magnus Liber, established the new rhythmic notation appropriate to it, differentiated between sections in organum purum and discant style, and created a vogue for the polyphonic conductus.

It is generally agreed that these Leoninian developments fall into the third quarter of the 12th century, perhaps starting some time after 1150. Many scholars start them in 1163, when the new cathedral's first stone was laid, reportedly by Pope Alexander III. To accomplish before the advent of Perotin all that has been detailed above, Leonin may well have lived and worked until 1180 or somewhat later, if he started as late as 1163. On the other hand, to accomplish before 1199 all that has been mentioned above, Perotin must have begun to compose at least a decade earlier and more probably as much as 15 years earlier, that is, in the early 1180s. Therefore, the main period of Perotin's activity is rather securely established as the last two decades of the 12th century, and the latest conceivable date for his birth would be 1155–60,[26] though

---

[26] Cf. Tischler (fn. 7), p. 25ff.

a date a decade earlier is well possible, if he worked for some time under Leonin.

The years 1208–45 would thus fall largely outside Perotin's active period. They cover mainly the development of the early motet, a species with which Anonymous IV does not connect the master, and the decline in importance of both organa and conducti. Those organa that date from this period show post-Perotinian features, well exemplified by the four-part clausula *Mors* and the clausulae of the St. Victor manuscript,[27] which are presumed to belong to the second decade of the century. Therefore, if Petrus Succentor was our Perotin, it must be assumed (a) that with the accession to his new office the composer more or less ceased to compose, and (b) that he reached the rather extraordinary age of at least 85–90 years. All this could be accepted as possible, but it is certainly improbable.

III

THE OFFICE of Succentor was the fourth highest in the Chapter of Notre Dame, ranking after the Dean, the Cantor, and three Archdeacons, and above the Cancellarius, the Penitentiary, and the fifty-two Canons. Thus a Succentor was a high administrative official, who was often called upon to witness legal documents. It was already pointed out by Rokseth [28] that it hardly goes with such a dignity for a Succentor to be called by a diminutive name by a professor of the University, John of Garland, who must have known him personally during his first stay at Paris as well as after his return there in 1232, and again by John's student, Anonymous IV, a generation after the official's death. If, as has been surmised, Perotin was the nickname of the choirboy who later grew into the composing Magister Cantus and finally into the Succentor, this diminutive would have long since been forgotten through his 30 or more years of duty as Succentor.

It is, moreover, surprising to find that no similar dignity was attained by Leonin. In fact, the latter's name does not even appear in the sources. (In all those consulted, though as stated above completeness cannot be claimed, the name Leo occurs only once during the twelfth century, in StVA fols. 98–99, under the year 1178 but referring to about 1160, a passage dedicated to the Benedictine monk of St. Victor who invented the Leonine verse.) This failure may, however, be explained by a relatively early death of Leonin, coming before he was chosen for an

---

[27] Paris, Bibl. Nat., MS lat. 15139.
[28] Rokseth (fn. 7), p. 50.

administrative office, perhaps at the age of 40–45. Such an assumption would appear well taken in any event, since his active period seems to have lasted no more than two decades. After all, Perotin is not mentioned in church records, either, except if he was the Succentor, a dignity which he would have attained at about the age of 50, as we have seen.

To the improbability that a Succentor would be called by a diminutive name may be added another one: Petrus Succentor's brother was an archbishop. Obviously this Petrus came from a good family, a fact emphasized by his various donations to the Chapter and further contradicting a diminutive appellation. It therefore seems best to heed Rokseth's suggestion that Perotin's final position was that of Magister Cantus.[29]

IV

RECENTLY HEINRICH HUSMANN has suggested that Perotin did not work at Notre Dame but rather at St. Germain-l'Auxerrois.[30] The reason: two organa, which may but need not be ascribed to the master, could be used not in the liturgy of Notre Dame but only at St. Germain. The argument is summarized by Husmann as follows: [31]

> In the . . . commune Sanctorum of (the manuscript) F [32] there is . . . one unicum, the ℞. Sancte Germane. (p. 193) . . . [As to the Saint involved] There is no choice but St. Germain of Auxerre. . . . there exists . . . a three-part organum Sancte Germane that is stylistically very close to organa . . . attributed by Anonymous IV to Perotin. Sancte Germane, consequently [!], was most likely also written by Perotin. . . . There is, understandably, no way of knowing whether the two-part organum had been composed in Notre Dame or in St. Germain itself. However, one can well imagine that Perotin was magister, not at Notre Dame, but at this old and renowned college of St. Germain. (Fn. 31, p. 194) . . . The ℞. Sancte Germane, especially its three-part version, probably [!] by Perotin, proves [!] that Perotin worked for St. Germain-l'Auxerrois . . . (p. 202).

This rather weak non-sequitur and "proof," while leading to some exciting possibilities of interpretation, is nevertheless an unwarranted assumption. Several rejoinders are rather obvious:

(1) The pieces dedicated to St. Germain need not be by Perotin: We cannot assume that all the music in the central manuscripts is exclusively the product of the two main masters; in fact, it is known that such music

---

[29] Rokseth (fn. 7), p. 5of; at the same time Mme. Rokseth there rejected Ficker's suggestion (fn. 15), p. 26, that Perotin was the Cantor Matutinorum.

[30] See Husmann, St. Germain und Notre Dame, in: Natalicia Knud Jeppesen (Copenhagen 1962), pp. 31–36.

[31] Husmann, loc. cit. (fn. 21).

[32] Florence, Bibl. Med. Laur. PL. XXIX,1.

was written at other places, such as St. Victor, Beauvais, Chartres, Britain, and elsewhere. Husmann himself argues with great finesse that some organa were written at or for Ste. Geneviève in Paris.

(2) If it is assumed that Perotin wrote his *Viderunt* and *Sederunt* c. 1197–1200 for Notre Dame, it would seem improbable that he did so while serving at St. Germain.

(3) The reference to Perotin in Anonymous IV, while not specific, does seem to point to Notre Dame as his place of activity; it follows after the mention of Leonin, whom Husmann too places at Notre Dame,[33] and relates his work to the older master's Magnus Liber, in connection with which it appears in the manuscript sources. The writer or his teacher, John of Garland, might be expected to mention Perotin's place of employment, had it been different from that of his predecessor. Their failure to do so may be cited as negative evidence.

(4) It is obvious from all sources that Notre Dame was the intellectual and musical center of the Parisian diocese. The only rivals of the cathedral during the later 12th century were at times St. Victor and St. Germain-des-Prés, though there is no mention of musical activities at either. In the obituary of St. Victor,[34] the death of Petrus Cantor is noted under 25 September and in StVA a long eulogy about him is inserted in 1205, eight years after his death. It may be assumed that besides being well known in general, he personally taught his philosophy at the abbey, whose library included copies of several of his works. The eulogy makes no mention whatever of Petrus's musical achievements. At St. Germain-des-Prés and St. Germain-l'Auxerrois, the libraries hold only very few and fragmentary sources without, it appears, any references to music.

(5) Most important, the data Husmann himself has so meticulously adduced in his recent publications, particularly in *The Enlargement of the Magnus Liber organi* (cf. fn. 21), contradict his assumption about Perotin. In his discussion of the Magnus Liber and its four historical layers he comes to the following results: The three so-called central Notre-Dame manuscripts, W1,[35] F, and W2,[36] include respectively 11, 37, and 16 Office organa and 35, 60, and 30 Mass organa in the Magnus Liber. Except for two unica which are appended to the main body of the Magnus Liber in W1 and appear to have been composed elsewhere,[37]

[33] See Husmann, *The Origin and Destination of the Magnus Liber organi*, in: MQ, XLIX (1963), 311–30; also Husmann, *St. Germain* (fn. 30), p. 36.
[34] Paris, Bibl. Nat., MS lat. 14673.
[35] Wolfenbüttel, Herzog August Bibl. 677.
[36] Wolfenbüttel, Herzog August Bibl. 1206.
[37] See Husmann, *Enlargement* (fn. 21), p. 177.

all of these come from Paris. The 10 Office organa and 24 Mass pieces common to all three manuscripts represent, according to Husmann, the original Magnus Liber as far as can be determined. A second group of six Office and six Mass organa, common only to F and W2, which seem to have been added a short time later, undoubtedly at Notre Dame, follows the original plan of the Magnus Liber. It is in the next two groups, which depart from that plan, that Husmann discovers the probability that some pieces may have been composed for, and therefore perhaps at, two other Parisian churches. Among the single Office piece and the 9 Mass organa common only to F and W1 there are two that may have been written for Ste. Geneviève rather than Notre Dame, one of them rather late, around 1220, and two others that may have been written for either, again one of them around 1220; but five point to Notre Dame as their origin. And among the 41 unica in F—19 for the Office and 22 for the Mass—7 point to Ste. Geneviève, one may have been intended for either Ste. Geneviève or Notre Dame, and one, *Sancte Germane*, points to St. Germain-l'Auxerrois.

It is this last one, or rather a three-part organum based on the same chant and extant in four manuscripts, that provides the sole basis for Husmann's conjecture. Certainly the late date that he himself assumes for the pieces intended for Ste. Geneviève, and the association of the two works here at discussion with these, render the supposition improbable. In fact, the two organa would have to be assumed to have been written before 1223, since after the death of Philip Augustus in that year Louis IX and his queen-regent mother left the Louvre, and the church of St. Germain-l'Auxerrois lost the temporary eminence as the royal parish church that it had gained after 1204, when the late king had made the Louvre his residence. It is indeed more probable to assume that they were written in the first few years of this 19-year span rather than later. A document of October 1203 [38] supports this assumption, for it shows that, in preparation for the coming eminence of St. Germain, Bishop Eude installed a cantor at that church, apparently the first one there. It may be added that the late dates, which Husmann's brilliant research leads him to propose for a few organa, connected with some probability with Ste. Geneviève, need not necessarily be taken as definitive.

In any event the overwhelming evidence of all organa points to Notre Dame as their cradle. It is not at all difficult to imagine that Perotin was requested in 1204 or 1205 to compose works for the royal parish church, though he was at Notre Dame. It is equally easy to hold—in fact, it is rather evident—that other composers soon learned from Perotin and con-

[38] GUER I,81.

tinued his work after his death; and these organa may be the works of one of these men.

It is time to tabulate the results of our search. In section I Petrus Succentor, mentioned in the sources as active from 1208 to 1238 and probably in office until about 1245, emerges as the only possible person to be identified with Perotin, but his apparent arrival at Notre Dame from Livry in 1208 renders this assumption highly improbable. In section II, the dates of Perotin's quadrupla are shown to be probably 1197–1200 and 1199, and the period after 1208 as largely unproductive years of the composer. Therefore, if Petrus Succentor was Perotin, his very long life, 1155/60–c.1245, would fall into two distinct periods, one that of the creative composer and the other that of an administrator who has abandoned creative work. In section III this second improbability is followed by a third: the persistence of a diminutive name for this dual personality through the decades of his official position and even long after his death. Section IV throws doubt, as unnecessary and improbable, on the undocumented conjecture that Perotin worked at St. Germain-l'Auxerrois rather than at Notre Dame.

In toto, then, the suggestion that Perotin may be identified with Petrus Succentor, or with any other cantor or succentor, carries no conviction. Since it does not add any information about the man as a composer, it is also unnecessary. The same may be said for the suggestion that he was connected with any church other than Notre Dame. Needless to say, this suggestion negates the first one. Thus our search leaves us without new data for Perotin's biography beyond Rokseth's guess that he may have been Notre Dame's Magister Cantus, but with a rather clear delimitation of the period of his activity as c. 1180–1200/05.

TWO COMPOSERS OF BYZANTINE MUSIC: JOHN VATATZES AND JOHN LASKARIS

by MILOŠ VELIMIROVIĆ

MODERN studies on the history of Byzantine music have seldom paid attention to the composers of Byzantine music. One of the most acceptable reasons for this is the fact that little, if anything, is known about some of these musicians, and that for a large number of them it is quite likely that they may forever remain only names in a Byzantine musical manuscript. While no critical study of the rather renowned composers exists, among those from the late Middle Ages who did attract some attention are at least two frequently mentioned musicians: John Kukuzeles and Manuel Chrysaphes.[1] As for other composers, many of them are simply listed in preliminary attempts at compilation of a catalogue of Byzantine musicians.[2] As praiseworthy as these attempts are and as rich as they may be with information about musicians from the recent past, the information about musicians of the Middle Ages is so unreliable that a fresh approach to this problem becomes a desideratum for future studies of the Byzantine chant.

[1] The most recent works on Kukuzeles are listed in MGG, VII (1958), 1888–90. Most of the Greek studies tend to place the date of Kukuzeles much too early, in the 12th century; cf. G. Papadopoulos, Συμβολαὶ εἰς τὴν ἱστορίαν τῆς παρ' ἡμῖν ἐκκλησιαστικῆς μουσικῆς (Athens 1890), with Eustratiades being the only exception known to me; cf. 'Ιωάννης ὁ Κουκουζέλης, ὁ μαΐστωρ, καὶ ὁ χρόνος τῆς ἀκμῆς αὐτοῦ, in: 'Επετηρὶς 'Εταιρείας Βυζαντινῶν Σπουδῶν [hereafter EEVS], XIV (1938), 3–27. Recent studies of Bulgarian authors place him rather late in the second half of the 14th century, while it is most likely that he was active during the early 1300s: cf. K. Levy, *A Hymn for Thursday in Holy Week*, in: JAMS, XVI (1963), 156, fn. 47. As for Chrysaphes the only study about him is that of A. Papadopoulos-Kerameus, Μανουὴλ Χρυσάφης, λαμπαδάριος τοῦ βασιλικοῦ κλήρου, in: *Vizantiĭskiĭ Vremennik*, VIII (1901), 526–45.

[2] Perhaps the most systematic attempt was that of C. Émereau published in installments in *Échos d'Orient*, XXI–XXV (1922–1926), which remained unfinished. The only effort that acquired book form was that of G. Papadopoulos, *op. cit.* Eustratiades had also compiled lists of musicians in an appendix to his *Catalogue of Greek Manuscripts in the Library of the Laura on Mount Athos, Harvard Theological Studies*, XII (Cambridge, Mass. 1925), 444–61, and in an article devoted to musicians from Thrace (see below, fn. 5). His book on composers from Jerusalem, Ποιηταὶ καὶ ὑμνογράφοι τῆς 'Ορθοδόξου Ἐκκλησίας— Α': Οἱ 'Ιεροσολυμῖται ποιηταὶ (Jerusalem 1940), was inaccessible to this writer.

The aim of this essay is to try to identify two composers of Byzantine music whose names may be encountered in some Byzantine musical manuscripts from the 15th century onwards. The following study has greatly benefited from recent Greek scholarly publications of documents in the Venetian Archives that contain a wealth of information about the period of Venetian domination over the island of Crete.[3] The documents already published contain extensive and valuable information about some singers with their full names and titles, making it thus possible to trace their activities, besides establishing the fact that at a particular period they resided on the island of Crete.

I

IT HAS BEEN A TRADITION of long standing to list several Byzantine emperors as musicians and composers. The name of one of the emperors— that of John III Vatatzes—may now be subjected to scrutiny.

The name of a John Vatatzes as a composer of Byzantine music may be found in a number of manuscripts, and it had been taken for granted that it referred to the emperor of that name, i.e. John III Vatatzes, who ruled in Nicaea from 1222–54. As a result, a number of books dealing with Byzantine music listed John Vatatzes as a composer, utilizing the biographical data about the emperor of that name.[4] It must be stressed, however, that the ambitious and indefatigable Sophronios Eustratiades had already raised some questions about these allegations, pointing out that the name of Vatatzes as a musician never carried with it the designation of imperial dignity which would have been the case had the emperor of that name been himself a musician. Much more to the point was Eustratiades's remark that this name could be found only in musical manuscripts from the 15th century onwards and not earlier, leaving thus two centuries during which an unaccountable silence existed about the artistic abilities of this person.[5]

On the basis of the recently published documents from the Venetian Archives new light may be thrown on this subject, since there is an act of confirmation of a John Vatatzes in his position as a protopsalt in Crete.[6] This act by the Venetian Doge Cristoforo Moro is addressed to the

---

[3] Crete was under Venetian domination from 1204 until 1669.

[4] Papadopoulos, *op. cit.*, pp. 267–68; see also an unsigned article Θράκες μουσικοί in the Supplement to the third volume of Θρακικά (1931), 222–24; and even Wellesz in his *A History of Byzantine Music and Hymnography* (2nd ed. Oxford 1961), p. 443.

[5] Eustratiades, Θράκες μουσικοί, in: EEVS, XII (1936), 46–48.

[6] M. I. Manoussakas, Βενετικὰ ἔγγραφα 'ἀναφερομένα εἰς τὴν 'ἐκκλησιαστικὴν 'ἱστορίαν τῆς Κρήτης τοῦ 14ου–16ου αἰώνος, in: Δελτίον τῆς 'Ιστορικῆς καὶ 'Εθνολογικῆς 'Εταιρείας τῆς 'Ελλάδος, XV (1961), 195–96.

Venetian governor of Crete, Jacob Cornaro, and is clearly dated 21 May 1465. The act simply confirms Vatatzes in the position which he was already holding at the time the document was issued. In the accompanying notes to the edition of this document, M. I. Manoussakas has pointed out that it is uncertain whether this is the same John Vatatzes whose name was recorded in Crete in 1451 for receiving financial help because he was poor. It remains unknown at what time he became protopsalt, and the only point on which certainty exists is that in 1487 another protopsalt's name appears in Venetian documents from Crete.[7]

The most important point about this document is that it ascertains that a singer by the name of John Vatatzes was recorded to have been active in Crete in the mid-60s of the 15th century, and it may be assumed that he discharged his duties for some length of time. In connection with this an important question must be raised: How old was Vatatzes at the time of his appointment?

If we glance at the manuscripts first, of the seven manuscripts in which his name has been traced (in the absence of a *Quellen-Lexikon* this number should not be considered as definitive) only one is dated, MS 2406 in the National Library in Athens, written in 1453. Another manuscript seems to date from about 1433 (No. 214 in the library of the monastery Pantocrator on Mt. Athos). Two more manuscripts are from the latter part of the 15th century, both in the National Library in Athens (Nos. 2401 and 899). The other manuscripts were written in later centuries.[8] It thus appears that Pantocrator MS 214 is the earliest so far recorded source containing any work of John Vatatzes. The Athens MS 2406 fits well between the assumed date of the Pantocrator MS and a record about a John Vatatzes on Crete, while later appearances of the name of Vatatzes have no bearing on this investigation.

If one may assume that the position John Vatatzes occupied in Crete could have been entrusted to a man in his fifties, to a man who might

---

[7] *Ibid.*

[8] The three manuscripts in the National Library in Athens were examined and studied by this writer. Although not yet described in a published catalogue, MS 2406 is already well known and has been used in recent studies, cf. Velimirović, *Liturgical Drama in Byzantium and Russia*, in: *Dumbarton Oaks Papers*, XVI (1962), 354, fn. 18. The date of the Pantocrator MS was first mentioned by H. J. W. Tillyard, *The Acclamations of Emperors in Byzantine Ritual*, in: *Annual of the British School at Athens*, XVIII (1911/12), 241 and restated by Eustratiades (see fn. 5, above). The three Athens MSS contain the same piece and it is the only piece attributed to Vatatzes in all three MSS. According to Eustratiades, the Pantocrator MS contains "several" antiphons by Vatatzes on fols. 129ᵛ-139ʳ.

The writer wishes to express his appreciation to Mr. Andreas A. Athanasopoulos, Curator of Manuscripts in the National Library in Athens, for many courtesies extended to the writer during his stay in Athens.

have spent earlier years on the mainland of Greece prior to the fall of Constantinople in 1453, when a great migration to Crete and Italy occurred,[9] it is quite possible that one of the minor composers of Byzantine music has thus been identified. As far as is known there were no legal age limitations for the position of a protopsalt in the Byzantine church practices.[10] Actually, it is precisely in Crete that one finds documentary evidence about another protopsalt who occupied this position for some 35 years,[11] and this can very easily reach into the fifties of a man's lifetime. On the basis of documents cited it thus appears that John Vatatzes the composer should be identified as a person who lived in the 15th century and for a time resided in Crete. This hypothesis appears much more plausible as an explanation of the name John Vatatzes as a composer than the hitherto held belief about the emperor-composer.

II

ANOTHER COMPOSER whose name may be encountered in Byzantine musical manuscripts of the 15th and later centuries is a John Laskaris, about whom a rather large number of documents came to light recently, and it is again thanks to the records kept by the Venetian authorities in Crete that these data are preserved. While these documents center around a court case they do contain a number of interesting data about Laskaris and some of the practices of musicians at the beginning of the 15th century. Since the full file of this court case is available in print,[12] only a brief summary will be given here with an attempt to extract pertinent information about Laskaris and the inferences that may be drawn from these data.

On 6 October 1418, in Candia, a Greek family intended to have a memorial service for one of its members in one of the local churches. Although that church had attached to it as a protopsalt a certain Emmanuel Savio,[13] whose duty it was to sing at all the services conducted there, the family summoned John Laskaris to sing on this occasion, specifying that the one who pays for the service has the right established

[9] D. Geanakoplos, *Greek Scholars in Venice* (Cambridge, Mass. 1962), p. 48ff.

[10] K. M. Rallis in his study Περὶ τοῦ ἀξιώματος τοῦ πρωτοψάλτου, in: Πρακτικὰ τῆς Ἀκαδημίας Ἀθηνῶν, XI (1936), 66–69, nowhere indicates age limitations and only lists the duties of a protopsalt: primarily to teach, to lead the singing, and to compose.

[11] See fn. 6 above, pp. 173–74 and 185–88, containing dated references to Emmanuel Savio in 1414 and 1449.

[12] Manoussakas, Μέτρα τῆς Βενετίας ἔναντι τῆς ἐν Κρήτῃ ἐπιρροῆς τοῦ πατριαρχείου Κωνσταντινουπόλεως, in: EEVS, XXX (1960/61), 85–144, with the full texts in original and a Greek translation and commentary.

[13] This is the same person mentioned in fn. 11 above.

by custom to choose the singer for the occasion. Laskaris, obviously eager to earn something and, as it also seems, holding a grudge against the singer in that church, readily obliged. As he arrived at the church after the beginning of the service, Laskaris simply started singing and switched from one mode into another, bringing the other singer to such a point of exasperation that he stopped participating in the service. The priest who performed the service appears to have felt insulted by the situation and a quarrel broke out, which finally ended in the courthouse, where depositions from both sides and witnesses were dutifully taken. According to the sentence pronounced on 26 October of the same year, Laskaris was banished from Crete and was given eight days to pack up and leave. The sentence also provided that should Laskaris at any time return to Crete, he would be punished with one year "in carceribus" after which he would again be banished.

The date of the trial in the year 1418 represents the only firm date so far known for the life of Laskaris. In the course of the proceedings a number of other points came to light, e.g. the fact that he had been living in Crete for about seven years, having come previously from Constantinople. If one is to trust the testimony of Laskaris himself, he was quite well off in Constantinople, and his stated reason for coming to Crete was that "having heard about the justice and good fame" of the Venetian authorities, he left "his goods and parents" and went to Candia. The fact that he mentioned his parents as still living makes one think that he might have been relatively young at the time of his departure from Constantinople, c. 1411.[14] This move to Crete may have been a consequence of a panic caused by the Turkish siege of Constantinople in 1411, when it may have appeared to its inhabitants that the city was about to fall into Turkish hands.[15]

Another interesting point that emerges from the testimony is that while in Crete Laskaris maintained a school (of his own?) and taught singing to boys. It was from the school that he was called to come to the church service that ended in a brawl.[16] He referred to himself as "cantor," and it appears that he had obtained a license from the Venetian

---

[14] EEVS, XXX, 116: "Excusatio Jani Laschari de Constantinopoli . . . dicit quod iste habet attinentes multos et bona in Constantinopoli et audiens justiciam et bonam famam ducalis dominationis Venetorum dereliquit sua bona et parentes suos et venit Candidam, jam sunt anni VII vel circa."

[15] G. Ostrogorski, *History of the Byzantine State* (Oxford 1956), p. 495.

[16] EEVS, XXX, 116: "et continue tenuit scolas et docebit pueros cantum." It may be of interest to mention that there was a monastic school in Candia which was "an offshoot of the famous parent monastery on the Sinai Peninsula [i.e. St. Catherine's] . . . Its curriculum consisted of Ancient Greek, theology, religious music . . . only the rudiments of these subjects were taught." See Geanakoplos, *op. cit.,* p. 46.

authorities for his singing activities in the same way that a protopsalt must have been confirmed in his position.[17] One of the points which three witnesses brought up and which by all appearances weighed heavily against Laskaris is the fact that he stated he had a license as a singer from the Constantinopolitan patriarch, while Savio (who may never have been in Constantinople) had none.

The charge against Laskaris was that he usurped the position of the protopsalt in a church service and used foul language leading to a disturbance. The defense insisted that it had the right to invite him to sing, not only because that was the custom, but because it was their wish to hear Laskaris who—and this *is* an interesting point—could sing "per artem," alleging that Savio "nescit cantare per artem." [18] According to witnesses against Laskaris, in the course of the verbal exchange Laskaris had actually boasted that he knew how to sing, while Savio did not.

The Venetian tribunal in Candia accepted the accusations and in its sentence ignored the defense statements, obviously unwilling to tolerate the presence of someone who was alleged to have mentioned the Constantinopolitan patriarch, although the Venetians had not abolished the Greek religious services in Crete. Laskaris had to leave Crete and was not heard from again.[19]

On the basis of the foregoing presentation, it would seem that John Laskaris is no longer just a name in a number of Byzantine musical manuscripts but a historically documented person and that therefore a number of musical compositions attributed to him should be dated in the first half of the 15th century. The fact that he lived in Crete is also recorded in two of the earliest known manuscripts containing his works, a circumstance that makes this identification certain beyond any reasonable doubt. The interrelationship of manuscripts and inscriptions is of help in explaining the variances in his name which, besides "John Laskaris" (with or without the specification "from Crete") is also recorded as "Laskaris Pigonitis" and "John Laskaris tou Syrpaganou."

Before proceeding with a discussion of works that can seemingly be attributed to him, it should also be pointed out that Laskaris wrote a short theoretical treatise preserved in at least two manuscripts.[20] As far

---

[17] *Ibid.*, p. 117: "dominatio fecit illum protopsalti et dominacio fecit me cantorem." See also fn. 6, above.

[18] *Ibid.*, p. 118.

[19] A certain John Laskaris was recorded as "prefect of Samothrace" at about 1453–55. See V. A. Mystakides, Λάσκαρεις in: EEVS, V (1928), 146, yet it seems unlikely that this could be our singer.

[20] Athens, Nat. Lib., MS 2401 (15th century), fols. 223ʳ–224ʳ (located by this writer) and Vallicelliana gr. 195, mentioned by L. Tardo in his *L'Antica melurgia bizantina* (Grottaferrata 1938), p. 148. For the date of this manuscript—15th

as it is possible to ascertain, this treatise has not yet been studied, nor was
its text published. In both known copies of this treatise the author's name
is simply listed as "John Laskaris." [21]

The same manuscript in Athens that contains this treatise includes a
Communion chant (*koinonikon*) of Laskaris that has been traced in an
18th-century manuscript,[22] and the same piece will undoubtedly be
found in some other yet uncatalogued manuscripts as well. The interesting point is that in this late manuscript the author's name is listed as
"Laskaris tou Pigonitou." [23]

The earliest manuscript so far known to contain the works of
Laskaris seems to be a manuscript in the library of the monastery Great
Lavra at Mt. Athos, which appears to have been written in 1436; a list of
composers whose works are to be found in this manuscript is available in
print.[24] The name of Laskaris in this manuscript appears in two forms:
"John Laskaris from Crete" and "John Laskaris Pigonitis." Three
theotokia (hymns to the Virgin) are attributed to John Laskaris "from
Crete." One of these, Ἐξέστη ἐπὶ τούτῳ, has also been traced in a manuscript written 17 years later, in 1453, the already cited Athens MS 2406.[25]
The Lavra MS also contains "some" Communion chants (unfortunately
not listed by their incipits in the article by Eustratiades) and three other
theotokia that are attributed to John Laskaris "Pigonitis": Eustratiades
added that though there is a differentiation in names, they may be the
same person. This remark of Eustratiades is now substantiated in the
Athens MS 2406 which, in addition to the already mentioned *theotokion*,
contains another from the second group of three in the Lavra MS, yet the
author is listed as John Laskaris "from Crete," and both *theotokia* are
not only attributed to the same composer but also appear in succession
in the Athens MS.[26]

In this same Athens MS, separated only by four folios from the two
theotokia, one encounters the name *John Laskaris tou Syrpaganou* as
author of texts for at least three hymns for which the music is attributed
to the lampadarios [27] of the Great Church in Constantinople (i.e. Aghia

century—see E. Martini, *Catalogo di manoscritti greci esistenti nelle biblioteche
italiane, II: Catalogos codicum graecorum qui in bibliotheca Vallicelliana Romae
adservantur* (Milan 1902), p. 219.

[21] Tardo, *loc. cit.* In the Athens MS: παρὰ Ἰωάννου τοῦ Λάσκαρι.
[22] Athens, Nat. Lib., MS 893, written in 1774, fol. 249ʳ.
[23] *Ibid.,* κὺρ Λασκάρεος τοῦ Πηγονίτου.
[24] See above, fn. 5, p. 61.
[25] See above, fn. 8.
[26] MS 2406, fols. 422ʳ and 423ʳ.
[27] On this title see Rallis, Περὶ τοῦ ἐκκλησιαστικοῦ ἀξιώματος τοῦ λαμπαδαρίου in:
Πρακτικὰ τῆς Ἀκαδημίας Ἀθηνῶν, IX (1934), 259–61. The lampadarios carried candles
during the entrances from the altar area into the church and was also a singer in the
left choir.

Sophia), John of Klada, who seems to have been active in Constantinople at the beginning of the 15th century.[28] The same combination of names, Laskaris as author of texts and Klada as composer, reappears in a manuscript in the monastery Vatopedi on Mt. Athos,[29] yet it remains unknown at the time of this writing whether the works so inscribed are identical in both of these manuscripts.

If one follows the reasoning of Ostrogorski that the prefix "syr-" is of Western origin [30] it would also appear plausible that its use, which seems to be rather rare, by implication suggests descent from a noble family (our singer may not have been immune from snobbish tendencies) and the Laskaris family is known to have played an important role in the history of Byzantium.[31] The fact that the name of John Laskaris appears twice in Athens MS 2406 in such close proximity, once with the simple addition "from Crete" and the other time with the eponym "tou Syrpaganou," suggests that this probably is the very same person.

The elimination of the prefix "syr-" leaves the surname "Paganou" which both in its corrupt pronunciation and also in its script could conceivably come close to the already mentioned designation of Laskaris as "Pigonitis." [32] One of the hypothetical explanations of this term might be that an inhabitant of the Constantinopolitan suburb αἱ Πηγαὶ (on the Pera side of the Golden Horn) could have been known as a Πηγωνίτης.[33] If such a hypothesis may be defended on linguistic grounds it would explain the origin of John Laskaris and also confirm his origin in Constantinople which, as he found out later, did not help him in establishing permanent residence in Crete.[34]

Although Laskaris's singing "per artem" seems to have had limited

[28] This is particularly clearly indicated in the Athens MS 899 (15th century) in the National Library where the following inscription may be found on fol. 327ᵛ: τὸ παρόν μέλος κράτημαν ἐστί κ. Ἰωάννου μαΐστορος τοῦ Κουκουζέλι τά δέ γράμματα κ. Ἰωάννου τοῦ λαμπαδαρίου διὰ στίχων ποιηθέντα διόρισμοῦ καὶ ζητήσεως τοῦ παναγιωτάτου καὶ οἰκουμενικοῦ πατριάρχου κ. Ματθαίου. Patriarch Matthew's years in office are 1397-1410; cf. Dictionnaire d'histoire et de géographie ecclésiastique, XIII (1956), s.v. Constantinople, pp. 629-33 for the list of names and dates of patriarchs.
[29] Eustratiades & A. Vatopedinos, Catalogue of the Greek Manuscripts in the Library of the Monastery of Vatopedi on Mount Athos, Harvard Theological Studies, XI (Cambridge, Mass. 1924), MS 1414.
[30] Ostrogorski, Pour l'histoire de la féodalité byzantine (Brussels 1954), p. 79, fn. 2.
[31] Ostrogorski, History of the Byzantine State, p. 514, for the genealogical table of the dynasty of the Lascarids.
[32] For bibliography of records of this term see EEVS, XXX, 88, fn. 1.
[33] On the location of this suburb and sources mentioning it, see R. Janin, Constantinople byzantin (Paris 1950), p. 423.
[34] A certain John Laskaris "Ryndakinos" from Adrianople and Crete [sic] was in Constantinople c.1490—see M. I. Gedeon, Χρονικά τῆς Πατριαρχικῆς Ἀκαδημίας, ἱστορικαὶ εἰδήσεις περὶ τῆς Μεγάλης τοῦ Γένους Σχολῆς, 1454-1830 (Constantinople 1883) —yet it is again most unlikely to be our singer. The designation "Ryndakinos" indicates origin from Ryndakos, a settlement on the coast of Asia Minor; cf. Mystakides, op. cit., p. 141, fn. 2.

success in Crete, his works were copied in manuscripts down to the 19th century, and from the 16th to the 18th centuries, the number of manuscripts containing his works increased substantially.[35] The following transcription of a *theotokion* by John Laskaris is offered as an example of what seems to have been a fashionable (or should one say "artistic"?) musical style in the course of the first half of the 15th century in Byzantium (see also Pl. 29). It should be pointed out, however, that this transcription is experimental and tentative. It is tentative insofar as it is prepared on the basis of only one manuscript, Athens 2406, which on the whole is a reliable and well-written manuscript. The transcription is experimental because in its preparation slight liberties have been taken in interpreting the accepted method of transcription into modern notation used in the *Monumenta musicae byzantinae*. Specifically, the neume *gorgon* (essentially designating an increase in speed) has very frequently (although not always!) been interpreted as a sign requesting that the neumes with which it is to be associated be transcribed as acciaccaturas and brief trills, rather than the conventional eighth-notes sung *accelerando*. This particular, if inconsistent, approach has made it possible to obtain in some instances rather striking figurations, such as the passages in the *teretism*,[36] which seem to intend to convey the warbling of birds —certainly a form of singing "per artem"!

[35] From the 16th century there are at least six manuscripts containing works of Laskaris: MSS 265, 269, and 271 in the library of the monastery Xeropotamou on Mt. Athos—cf. E. Xeropotaminos, Κατάλογος ἀναλυτικὸς τῶν χειρογράφων κωδίκων τῆς βιβλιοθήκης τῆς—Μονῆς τοῦ Ξηροποτάμου (Thessaloniki 1933); MS 15 in the Byzantine Museum in Athens—cf. N. Beès, Κατάλογος τῶν χειρογράφων κωδίκων τῆς Χριστιανικῆς Ἀρχαιολογικῆς Ἑταιρείας Ἀθηνῶν in: Χριστιανικὴ Ἀρχαιολογικὴ Ἑταιρεία Ἀθηνῶν, Δελτίον, VI (1906); MS 244 in the Leimon Monastery on Lesbos—cf. A. Papadopoulos-Kerameus, Μαυρογορδάτειος Βιβλιοθήκη (Constantinople 1884–88); and in Oxford, Lincoln College, MS gr. 22—cf. N. G. Wilson and D. Stefanović, *Manuscripts of Byzantine Chant in Oxford* (Oxford 1963), p. 50. From the 17th century there are seven manuscripts: MSS 261 and 273 in Xeropotamou (Xeropotaminos, *op cit.*); MS 39 in the Byzantine Museum in Athens (Beès, *op. cit.*); MS 245 at Lesbos (Papadopoulos-Kerameus, *op. cit.*,); MS Auct.T.6.1 in the Bodleian Library at Oxford (Wilson & Stefanović, *op. cit.*, p. 10); MSS Lambda 166 in the Lavra on Mt. Athos (Eustratiades, *Catalogue*) and MS 963 in the Nat. Lib. in Athens. From the 18th century there are 12 manuscripts: Xeropotamou MSS 277, 287, 307, 309, 319, and 391; Lesbos MSS 8, 230, and 238; Lavra MSS I.184 and O.154, and MS 893 in the Nat. Lib. in Athens. Only one 19th-century MS has so far been registered to contain works of Laskaris: Vatopedi 1399 (Eustratiades, *Catalogue*).

[36] These vocalizations, apparently used for display of singers' skills, were filled with nonsense syllables, e.g. re-re-rem, re-ri-re, te-te-te, ti-ti-ti, to-to-to, etc. There are no modern transcriptions so far of these *teretismata* in print. An astonishing proposition was once made by E. Vamvoudakis about the origin of these syllables. He suggested that they were in fact an abbreviation and corruption of a verse "Te regem exspectamus," which the singers were presumably singing at the end of hymns !? Cf. Τὰ ἐν τῇ Βυζαντινῇ Μουσικῇ "Κρατήματα," in: EEVS, X (1933), 353–61, especially p. 356.

In spite of the intonation sign (*martyria*)—suggesting that the reading of the neumes in the composition should start from c^2—in order to avoid excessive skips from one range of the voice to another, the initial passage has been transposed a fifth lower. The piece has consistently been centered around the *finalis* of the Third Authentic Mode (f^1) for which additional modal signatures in the course of the piece offer sufficient support.

The text of this *theotokion* may be found in the modern edition of the *Parakletike*.[37]

fol. 422ʳ

[37] ΠΑΡΑΚΛΗΤΙΚΗ (Athens 1959), p. 125, as first *theotokion* during the morning Office on Sunday morning when the "ruling" mode is the Third Authentic Mode.

καὶ τὸ ὑ-πέρ-λαμ-προν τὸ____ τῆς ἀ-γνεί-ας____

σου,____ λε----γε ὁ Γα-βρι-ἠ-

----ἠλ κα-τα---πλα-γεὶ-

ει--κει---κει-ει-ει-κει---κει-εις κα-τα-πλα-

fol. 422ᵛ

γεὶ----εἰς ἐ-βό-α____ σοι____

Θε-ο-τό------κε ἐ-βό-α____ σοι.

ὁ Γα-βρι-ἠλ κα-τα-πλα-γεὶ----εις

ἐ-βό-α____ σοι Θε-ο-τό---κε.

πα--λιν ὁ Γα-βρι-ἠλ κα-τα-πλα-

γεὶ----εις ἐ-βό-α σοι____

Θε-ο-τό-κε._____ Ποῖ--όν

JOAN qd JOHN
AND OTHER FRAGMENTS AT
WESTERN RESERVE UNIVERSITY

by *JOHN M. WARD*

". . . singing the Ballet, of *All a greene Willowe,*
to the famous Tune of *Ding, dong.*"[1]

I N 1812 John Stafford Smith published, "from an anct. MS." in his possession, what he described as "a very popular Song in the early part of Hen: 8ᵗʰˢ reign"; the piece begins: *Joan qᵈ John when wyll this be,* and has a bass part added by the editor.[2] Sometime in the 1840s Edward Rimbault printed the same melody, arranged for tenor with pianoforte accompaniment, and described his source as "an ancient vellum manuscript in the Editor's possession" which he dated from the time of Henry VIII.[3] A few years later he reprinted the words, without the music, adding to his earlier description of the source that it was "a loose sheet (perhaps torn from a book)" and that the piece had been printed, "but very imperfectly," in Smith's *Musica Antiqua*.[4] Apparently Rimbault had purchased the manuscript at the sale of Smith's library in 1844.

Who bought the vellum leaf at the sale of Rimbault's library in 1877 we do not know.[5] Perhaps it was William Chappell, who, in 1880, printed the words of *Joan qd John* in a reading different from both Smith's and Rimbault's, and referred, in a note, to the previous ownership of the manuscript, first by Smith, then by Rimbault, and to its sale at the auction of the latter's library;[6] just as plausibly, Chappell may

[1] *Laugh and lie downe* (London 1605), sig. C3.
[2] *Musica Antiqua* (London 1812), I, 32. John Stevens includes Smith's cantus in his *Index of Selected Songs,* in: *Music & Poetry in the Early Tudor Court* (London 1961), p. 443.
[3] *Ancient Vocal Music of England* (London c. 1846–49), No. XX.
[4] *A Little Book of Songs and Ballads, Gathered from Ancient Musick Books, Ms. and Printed* (London 1851), pp. 60–61.
[5] It may have formed part of lot 1381 or 1916; see the *Catalogue of the Valuable Library of the Late Edward Francis Rimbault* (London 1877).
[6] *The Roxburghe Ballads,* III (Hertford 1880), 590–92. Chappell has an earlier reference to the MS in his *Popular Music of the Olden Time,* I (London 1855), 87.

have had access to the manuscript while it belonged to Rimbault, who often made works in his library available to the author of *Popular Music of the Olden Time.*

Whatever its history, the leaf's whereabouts have not been known since 1877. It is my conjecture that, sometime after the Rimbault sale, the new owner, whoever he was, had the vellum leaf, together with a miscellaneous collection of other fragments, manuscript and printed, bound into a copy of David and Lussy's *Histoire de la notation musicale* (1882) which now, a gift from an Associate of the Libraries, belongs to Western Reserve University,[7] for a leaf in this volume provides a texted cantus of *Joan qd John* that agrees in almost every particular— text, music, and notation [8]—with the piece published by Smith in 1812, and later by Rimbault and Chappell.

If I am right, then it must be reported that none of the editors was completely successful in reproducing the original text, which should run (repetitions apart) thus: [9]

> Joan qd John when wyll this be
> tell me when wilt thow marrie me
> my cowe and eke my calf & rent
> my land and all my tenement
> saie Joan said John what wilt thow doe
> I cannot come every daie to wooe

As Rimbault and Chappell discovered, the lovers' names, the theme, and the same, or a very similar, stanza are found in many places and guises.

The names of Joan and John were commonplaces of popular song, found early in the 16th century in Richard Davy's *Jhoone is sike and ill at ease* and in the anonymous *Com kys me Johan gramercy Ione*, mentioned in Medwell's interlude of *Nature* (printed in 1530); [10] found later in *Johne, cum kis me now*, whose text—parodied in the *Gude and*

---

[7] Manfred Bukofzer first drew attention to this volume in a brief article, *A Notable Book on Music*, in: *The Broadside*, No. 1 (Nov. 1940), published for the Associates of the Libraries of Western Reserve University. In 1953 the book was included in the Toledo Museum of Art's exhibition of *Medieval and Renaissance Music Manuscripts* and a partial, somewhat inaccurate list of the 38 MS fragments given in the printed catalogue (Toledo, Ohio 1953), pp. 38-39. I should like to thank the Libraries of Western Reserve University for permission to publish several of the fragments.

[8] Smith reproduced the diamond-shaped note heads in his edition of the cantus.

[9] Apart from ordinary editorial changes, e.g. regular barring in measures of $\frac{6}{4}$, Smith made only two changes of consequence in the music: (1) the dot of augmentation at the end of m. 6 is a rest in the original; (2) the E♭ in m. 8 is editorial. The word *for*, written between *cowe* and *and*, has been canceled.

[10] The text of Davy's piece is printed in Stevens, *Music & Poetry*, pp. 377-78.

Godlie Ballatis of 1567—is lost, but whose tune remained a great favorite well into the 18th century; [11] and *Joan, come kisse me now*, a round for three voices, found in the Lant roll of 1580, Ravenscroft's *Pammelia* (1609), and the Melvill "buik off roundells" of 1612.[12]

The ballad of *John wooinge of Jone &c.* was registered with the Stationers' Company in 1592; other ballads concerning similarly named characters include: *Jone came over London bridge and told me all this geere* (1579); *Jones ale is newe* (1594); *Rocke the Babie Joane: Or, John his Petition to his loving wife Joan, to suckle the Babe that was none of her owne* (1623); and, perhaps a sequel to the last, *John for the losse of his Joane* (1633); etc.[13]

The courting dialogue—between Simon and Susan, Kit and Pegge, Jenkin the Collier and Nansie, and a host of other twain as well as Joan and John—was a stereotype of the broadside literature and, probably, of the end-piece jig performed in the public theaters after the play, though everything connected with this ill-documented genre remains conjectural.[14] Certainly the courting bumpkin, who, like John, could not come every day to woo, was a stock figure and easily turned into a character in a farce; Puttenham, or whoever wrote *The Arte of English Poesie* (1589), for example, composed an interlude, *The Wooer*, in which a country clown, grown weary of courting a city maid who gave him no answer, yea or nay, complained impatiently to her old nurse:

> Iche pray you good mother tell our young dame,
> When I am come and what is my name,
> I cannot come a woing every day.[15]

As in Ravenscroft's "wooing Song of a Yeoman of Kents Soone," dialect was added to the swain's comic accoutrements.[16]

---

[11] The Wedderburn contrafactum is printed in *A Compendious Book of Godly and Spiritual Songs,* ed. for The Scottish Text Society by A. F. Mitchell (Edinburgh 1897), pp. 158–61.

[12] Concerning the Lant MS, see Jill Vlasto, *An Elizabethan Anthology of Rounds,* in: MQ, XL (1954), 229; Ravenscroft's work has been reprinted in facsimile in *Publications of the American Folklore Society,* Bibl. & Special Series, XII (Philadelphia 1961), p. 10; and the Melvill MS has been ed. by G. Bantock & H. O. Anderton for the Roxburghe Club (1916).

[13] See Hyder E. Rollins, *An Analytical Index to the Ballad-Entries* (Chapel Hill 1924), Nos. 1299, 1287, 1288, 2318, 1298. The text of No. 2318 is printed in *The Pepys Ballads,* ed. Rollins (Cambridge, Mass. 1929), II, 213–18.

[14] Courting dialogues are discussed at length in Charles R. Baskervill's *The Elizabethan Jig* (Chicago 1929), pp. 188–200. Thomas Howell's *Arbor of Amitie* (London 1568) includes a poem in ballad meter, beginning: "Jacke shows his qualities and great good will to Jone."

[15] *The Arte of English Poesie,* ed. G. D. Willcock and A. Walker (Cambridge 1936), p. 203.

[16] The Ravenscroft piece is in *Melismata* (London 1611), No. 22; see the facs. ed. cited in fn. 12 above.

Of all the Joan and John texts, the one found with the Western Reserve fragment was probably the most familiar. It appears, sometimes by itself, other times as the first of a string of stanzas in which Joan is introduced and the details of the courtship elaborated. Thus the first stanza provides the sole text for the bass part of an anonymous setting in a British Museum manuscript of c.1600, and for the first of 11 *Joan qd John* texts set to music, apparently for three voices, by R[ichard] Nicholson.[17] The Nicholson cycle describes John's courtship; Joan's illness and John's distress thereat; her seeming death and fortunate recovery, with lamentation, then rejoicing by John; his admonishing her to take care of her health,[18] and her response:

> John, be contented, and care not for mee;
> I cannot, I will not be ruled by thee:
> Kissing and culling is lovers' delight,
> Then say what you will, John, for Joane will have right.
> Raddish and turnups, John, ladies love well,
> Though bagpipes and bellows be windie and swell:
> John, if you love mee, as love you require,
> Come kisse mee, and cull mee; such death I desire.

James Brown's description of the 11 pieces in the cycle suggests they may have formed something like a madrigal comedy; unfortunately, the two surviving partbooks discovered in 1920 and on which the description is based, seem to have disappeared again.

However, another *Joan qd John* dialogue, beginning, not with John but Joan speaking, thus: "John quoth Joane, is there such haste," was set, *a 5*, by (the same Richard?) Nicholson and is preserved complete in a set of British Museum partbooks, Add. 17786–91;[19] it may be an elaboration of one of the pieces in the cycle described by Brown (who did not print all of the texts of the *Joan qd John* pieces and none of the music from his manuscripts) or, as seems more likely, another handling of the popular theme.

A variation of the six-line Western Reserve text also occurs at the beginning of two late 17th-century broadside ballads, one of which was several times advertised as having been sung before Charles II at

[17] James Walter Brown, who owned the triplex and bass partbooks, describes them in *An Elizabethan Song-Cycle*, in: *The Cornhill Magazine*, N.S., XLVIII (1920), pp. 572–79, and *Some Elizabethan Lyrics*, in the same journal the following year, pp. 285–96. I am indebted to *The Cornhill Magazine* for permission to quote from these sources.

[18] This part begins: "Care for thy health, sweet Joane, as pearle of price," which may be a parody of the text "Care for thy soul as thing of greatest price," set by both Byrd and Pilkington.

[19] The piece was published by Peter Warlock, *The First Book of Elizabethan Songs* (London 1926), pp. 25–28.

Windsor;[20] in both ballads John's character and many of his lines remain the same, while in one ballad Joan is a decent dairymaid and in the other a "subtel slut." Two hundred years later a version of the ballad was written down, unfortunately without the music, from the singing of an Isle of Wight man; in other words, the song had entered oral tradition.[21] A long life for a simple courtship! Did it really begin "in the early part of Hen: 8ths reign"?

Smith's dating of the vellum leaf from which he took the cantus printed in *Musica Antiqua* has been accepted—*faute de mieux* since 1877—by all who have had to do with *Joan qd John*, but this dating is anything but secure. No one appears to have noted that the melody of the Western Reserve fragment (in print since 1812) is identical with the cantus of the Nicholson dialogue cited earlier, "John quoth Joane, is there such haste." Nicholson may have composed a new setting for an old voice part taken from a song of Henry VIII's time, but nothing about the piece supports such a hypothesis; the voices are completely integrated; they proceed in a typically late 16th-century manner; rather, the style favors any time between 1595 and 1639, when Nicholson was

[20] What appears to be the older of the two ballads, preserved in two different broadside editions, bears the title *The Countryman's Delight; Or, The Happy Wooing*, and is to be sung "to a New playhouse tune; or, Dolly and Molly"; see *The Roxburghe Ballads*, III, 593–96. The other ballad, entitled *The North Country lovers: Or: The plain Downright wooeing between John and Joan*, and to be sung "to a New tune, Quoth John to Joan," is in the Pepys collection and has been reprinted by Baskervill, *The Elizabethan Jig*, pp. 420–22; this and the abbreviated version printed in Tom D'Urfey's *New Collection of Songs and Poems* (London 1683), p. 48, the same editor's *Pills to Purge Melancholy* (London 1698 et seq.), III, 114–15, and elsewhere, are described as "sung before the Court at *Windsor*" or something like; see Chappell, *Popular Music of the Olden Time*, I, 87.

[21] See W. H. Long, *A Dictionary of the Isle of Wight Dialect* (London 1886), pp. 121–24. The first stanza reads:

> Zed Jan to Joan, 'Wull you hay me?
> Vor if you wull, I'll marry thee.
> I've house, and land, and cows, and swine,
> And if you likes, it med all be thine.
> Then tell me Joan if this wull do,
> Vor I can't come every day to woo.

See also David Herd, *Ancient and Modern Scottish Songs, Heroic Ballads, etc.* (Edinburgh 1776), II, 225–26, for a popular Scottish version, beginning:

> I hae layen three herring a sa't,—
> Bonie lass, gin ye'll take me tell me now,
> And I hae brow'n three pickles o' ma't—
> And I cannae cum ilka day to woo.
> To woo, to woo, to lilt and to woo,
> And I cannae cum ilka day to woo.

Recast by James Tytler, this version appears in James Johnson's *The Scots Musical Museum*, III (Edinburgh 1790), No. 244, and Ritson's *Scotish Song* (London 1794), I, 184–85.

master of the choristers of Magdalen College, and not the period of Cornysh; like Nicholson's cycle of 11 *Joan qd John* pieces, the dialogue may have been written for boys to perform, perhaps dramatically.

One question concerning the piece remains. Why does the same voice part appear on the Western Reserve leaf with one stanza of text and in Add. 17786–91 with two others? The answer is provided by Add. 17790, the sextus partbook and the only one of the five furnished with text: the two stanzas written out beneath the notes are numbered, respectively, 3 and 4; as Warlock pointed out when he edited the piece, one voice of the dialogue is missing and with it two stanzas of text. The Western Reserve leaf supplies the music and the first stanza of the missing part. When we put these three stanzas back together, the last two make more sense.

> Joan, quoth John, when wyll this be,
> Tell me when wilt thow marrie me?
> My cowe and eke my calf and rent,
> My land and all my tenement;
> Saie, Joan, said John, what wilt thow doe?
> I cannot come every daie to wooe.

> [Stanza 2 missing.]

> John, quoth Joane, is there such hast?
> Look ere you leape, least you make wast:
> If hast you have with mee to wedd,
> More belonges to a bride's bed.
> Wherefore, wherefore thus must you doo,
> Daie and night come every houre to wooe.

> John, if you will needs me have,
> This is that which I doe crave:
> To let mee have my will in all,
> And then with thee Ile never braule.
> Saie, John, saie, John, shall this be soe?
> Then you need not come every houre to wooe.

In summary: Smith's source for *Joan qd John* has been bound into a copy of David and Lussy's *Histoire de la notation musicale* now in the Libraries of Western Reserve University; his dating for the piece has been shown to be almost a century too early; and the melody he published proves to be part of a Nicholson dialogue.

II

ON THE reverse of the Western Reserve *Joan qd John* leaf is a setting of the equally well-known text:

O deathe, rocke me asleepe
bringe me to quiet rest
let passe my weary guiltles ghost
out of my carefull brest
toll on the passinge bell
ringe out my doelfull knell
let thy sounde my death tell
death doth drawe ny
there is no remidie.

Apparently Smith did not print this part of his fragment. Rimbault did publish the words, "from a MS. temp. Henry VIII, in the possession of the Editor." [22] Pointing out the manuscript's successive ownership by Smith and Rimbault, Chappell published both text and music, the latter in a much altered form and with accompaniment added.[23]

Both editors included more text than their source supplied; probably they took the additional stanzas from a version of the poem printed in 1776 by Hawkins, the text having been communicated to him by "a very judicious antiquary lately deceased" who had proposed Anne Boleyn as the author of the words, a conjecture Hawkins found not improbable.[24] Ritson, writing some years later, took exception to the suggestion—"any other state prisoner of that period having an equal claim"—and proposed as the author, perhaps ironically, not Anne, but her brother George, who had suffered a similar fate; as evidence he offered only Anthony à Wood's claim that the Viscount Rochford was reputed to be "the author of several poems, songs, and sonnets, with other things of the like nature." [25]

The poem proved popular and its anonymity continued to vex its editors. In 1838 an anonymous contributor to *Blackwood's Edinburgh Magazine*, having found *O death* to correspond "more nearly than any other piece we remember, with the unattached title of [Richard] Edwards's once celebrated 'Soul Knell'," a work mentioned by Gascoigne

[22] *A Little Book of Songs and Ballads*, pp. 65–66.
[23] *Popular Music of the Olden Time*, I, 237–39.
[24] *A General History of the Science and Practice of Music* (3rd ed. London 1875), I, 376. E. K. Chambers and F. Sidgwick drew on a different source (British Museum Add. 26737, fol. 107^v) for the five-stanza text printed in *Early English Lyrics* (London 1907), pp. 199–200. Stevens includes the song in his *Index of Selected Songs*, in: *Music & Poetry*, p. 443.
[25] *Ancient Songs from the Time of Henry the Third to the Revolution* (London 1790), p. 120. Wood's statement is in: *The Fasti;* see *Athenae Oxonienses*, ed. P. Bliss, I (London 1813), col. 99. Smith probably used the Boleyn dating of *O death* as the basis for dating its companion piece, *Joan qd John*, "in the early part of Hen: 8^{ths} reign."

in 1575 but otherwise unknown, added Edwards to the list of possible authors.[26] Rimbault thought the attribution to Edwards better than to the Boleyns, but could add nothing to the evidence. At the beginning of this century, Godfrey Arkwright included *O death* among the songs that he believed formed a distinctive part of Elizabethan choirboy plays; though this association placed the composition well past the *terminus ad quem* for a Boleyn attribution and well within the period of Edwards's activity, Arkwright saw no reason to ascribe the poem to him.[27]

However, an attribution to Edwards has its attractions. "Soul Knell" is not inappropriate as a title for the poem. Warlock thought it noteworthy that a lute-song setting of *O death* appears in an early 17th-century manuscript next to the setting of a song from Edwards's play *Damon and Pithias*.[28] Rollins discovered more compelling evidence of the same sort. In a group of poems, found at the end of a late 16th-century commonplace book, six are certainly by Edwards, another three, including *O death*, are in his vein; further, one of the pieces there ascribed to him ends: [29]

> Rocke mee asleepe in woe,
>   yow wofull Sisters three:
> Oh, cutt yo^u of my fatall threed,
>   dispatch poore Emelye.
> Why should I live, alas,
>   and linger thus in paine!
> ffarewell my life, syth that my love
>   most cruell death hath slayne.

[26] XLIV (Nov. 1838), 466. For the Gascoigne passage, see his *Posies* (1575), ed. J. W. Cunliffe (Cambridge 1907), p. 11: "What shoulde I stande much in rehersall how the *L. Vaux* his dittie (beginning thus: *I loth that I did love*) was thought by some to be made upon his death bed? and that the Soulknill of M. Edwards was also written in extremitie of sicknesse?" W. Y. Durand, *Some Errors Concerning Richard Edwards*, in: *Modern Language Notes*, XXIII (1908), 129–31, has proposed a poem, ascribed to R.E. in British Museum Cotton MS. Titus A.xxiv and beginning: "O lorde that ruleste bothe lande and seae," as the "Soulknill" referred to by Gascoigne, though there is little to support the identification.
[27] *Early Elizabethan Stage Music*, in: *The Musical Antiquary*, I (1909), 33.
[28] *The Third Book of Elizabethan Songs* (London 1926), prefatory note.
[29] See *A Note on Richard Edwards*, in: *Review of English Studies*, IV (1928), 204–06; V (1929), 55–56. Rollins's MS notes on the poems in Add. 26737, fols. 106^v–108^v, are found in a copy of L. Bradner's *The Life and Poems of Richard Edwards* now in Harvard College Library (shelf number 14453.64.50B). The nine poems are: *Come followe mee ye Nymphes*, published by Rollins, who believed it to come from Edwards's lost play *Palamon and Arcyte; In going to my naked bed; The sailing ships with joy at length; O death, rock me asleep; When women first dame nature; Out of the dungeon; When May is in his prime; Farewell my lady Mistress fair;* and *The subtle slily sleights*.

Circumstantial evidence doesn't prove Edwards to be the author, but it may help exorcise the Boleyn ghosts raised by that nameless antiquarian friend of Hawkins's, and still abroad.[30]

Who set the poem to music? For the consort song in Add. 30480–84 Arkwright thought Johnson a possible composer, since similar death songs by a Johnson are found in the same partbooks. Unfortunately, an attribution to Johnson is as good as one to Anon. for he is by turns Scotch or English, Catholic or *heretyke*, chaplain to Anne Boleyn, *peticanon of Windsore*, house musician to the Kytsons, player of wind instruments, actor, mole-catcher, and one of the Proctors of the Court of Arches, active at Kenilworth, Elvetham, and Hengrave Hall, and answers equally to the names Robert, John, and Edward. Until the Johnsons are distinguishable, it is foolhardy to ascribe music to them.[31] To a lesser degree (because there are fewer of them), similar caution should attend the attribution to Parsons tentatively put forward by Warlock; drab age music, like drab age verse, is often so neutral in tone—so like *vin ordinaire*—that making an attribution is hard work indeed.

Of course, Edwards has been proposed as the composer of the music for *O death*, since it is well known that he was a composer as well as a poet and playwright. But all that is known to remain of his music is the keyboard score of one partsong, four of the five voice parts of a Latin motet, and a setting of the Lord's Prayer, if, in fact, these are all by him: hardly enough music to support an attribution.[32] It is customary to ascribe musical settings of his own poetry to Edwards; those who do so assume, I believe, more than the evidence invites. Six of Edwards's poems

[30] See, e.g., the jacket notes to Alfred Deller's recording of the song, Bach Guild 557, and the ascription of the poem in J. W. Hebel, et al., *Tudor Poetry and Prose* (New York 1953), p. 43.

[31] The confused state of our knowledge can be judged by the Johnson entries in MGG, VII, 128–30, 131–35. See also the note to Johnson's *Defyled is my name* in the catch-all Vol. XV of *Musica Britannica:* "it has been suggested that this song was written as if from the mouth of the ill-fated Anne Boleyn, to whom Robert Johnson . . . was alleged to have been chaplain." The only "evidence" I know for this statement is the MS note at the end of the alto part of *Elissa is ye fayrest quene*, a piece written in honor of Elizabeth and found in Add. 30480, fol. 10ᵛ; the original ascription to "Mr Johnson" has been altered, in what looks like a late 18th- or early 19th-century hand, to read: "Mr E Johnson / Chaplain to / Quene Anne Bullen." The source of the information has not been found.

[32] The partsong is *O the syllye man* in the Mulliner Book (ed. D. Stevens, *Musica Britannica*, I, 59); the words are by Francis Kindlemarsh, not Edwards; see *The Paradise of Dainty Devices*, ed. Rollins (Cambridge, Mass. 1927), pp. 13–14. The motet is *Terrenum sitiens*, found in the so-called Henrician partbooks at Peterhouse, Cambridge; see the Anselm Hughes *Catalogue* (Cambridge 1953), p. 2. The setting of the Lord's Prayer is in Day's 1563 *Psalmes in foure partes*. Grattan Flood, with his accustomed largess, gratuitously credited Edwards with a Mass, other Latin motets, and a setting of Surrey's *Ye happy dames* in his *Early Tudor Composers* (London 1925), p. 114. W. H. Husk and whoever revised the Edwards article for *Grove's*, 5th ed., were equally lavish in attributing other men's work to Edwards.

are found set to music, five anonymously and one ascribed to Parsons; two appear with more than one musical setting.[33]

If, despite knowing almost nothing about Edwards as a composer, we should still be bent on attributing music for *O death* to him, which shall it be: the consort song for voice and instrumental accompaniment found in two sets of British Museum partbooks—Add. 30480–84 dating from sometime between 1560–90 and Add. 18936–39, from the first quarter of the 17th century—and edited by Warlock,[34] or the quite different setting found as a keyboard arrangement of the 1560s in Christ Church MS 371 [35] and as an arrangement for lute and voice in Add. 15117 written

[33] The six are: (1) *When May is in his prime* (*Paradise*, No. 6), set anonymously for solo voice and four accompanying instruments in Christ Church MSS 984–88 (ed. Warlock, *The Second Book of Elizabethan Songs*, pp. 1–6); the alto part, un-texted, is also found in British Museum Add. 22597, fol. 41–41^v; a different setting, cantus only, is in John Forbes's *Songs and Fancies* (Aberdeen 1662 et seq.), sig. P–P2; and what may be the bass part of still another setting is in the PRO partbook described by Denis Stevens in *Music Review*, II (1950), 169, though the Edwards text fits the music poorly; (2) *In youthfull years* (*Paradise*, No. 7), set for voice and lute, "Qd Mr Parsons," in the so-called Dallis book, Trinity College, Dublin, MS D.3.30, pp. 204–06, and, without the composer's name, in British Museum Add. 15117, fol. 14^v, the lute part quite altered; (3) *In going to my naked bed* (*Paradise*, No. 46), set anonymously *a 4*, the tenor and bass parts found in British Museum Add. 36526A, fol. 1, 6, and a keyboard arrangement in the *Mulliner Book* (the latter ed. Stevens, *Musica Britannica*, I, 60, and a reconstruction of the original partsong by Fellowes is in *The English Madrigal School*, XXXVI, last number); (4) *Where grip-ing grief* (*Paradise*, No. 57), set anonymously *a 4*, keyboard arrangement in the *Mulliner Book* (ed. Stevens, p. 83), an arrangement for lute, the cantus part omitted, in the Brogyntyn MS 27, p. 125, of the National Library of Wales, ed. Richard Newton, *The Lute Society Journal*, I (1960), 132–33; also F. W. Sternfeld, *Music in Shakespearean Tragedy* (London 1963), pp. 120–21, with a fac. of the MS source; two voice parts of another, anonymous setting are in the Taitt MS described by Walter Rubsamen, *Scottish and English Music of the Renaissance in a Newly-Discovered Manuscript*, in: *Festschrift Heinrich Besseler* (Leipzig 1961), pp. 278–79 [I am indebted to Prof. Rubsamen, who plans to publish parts of the MS, for a copy of the cantus]; another song, in two *partes*, in the Brogyntyn MS, p. 126, has the text incipit "The griping griefe that," but does not accommodate the Edwards text; (5) *When women first dame nature wrought*, set anonymously, apparently *a 4*, the three lower voices arranged for lute in the Brogyntyn MS, p. 129; (6) *Awake, ye wofull Wightes* (*Damon and Pithias*, sc. 10: "Here PITHIAS singes and the Regalles play"), set, in part, for voice and lute in British Museum Add. 15117, fol. 7 (ed. Warlock, Curwen Ed. No. 2448); the cantus, called *Damon and Pithias*, was printed on a broadside ballad of 1568 as the tune for a poem beginning: "Alas my harte doth boyle," facs. in: JAMS, X (1957), Pl. opp. p. 168; see also A. J. Sabol, *Two Unpub-lished Stage Songs for the "Aery of Children,"* in: *Renaissance News*, XIII (1960), 224, fn. 7, who identified the broadside ballad tune.

[34] *The Third Book of Elizabethan Songs*, pp. 1–3. The contratenor, in Add. 30481, fol. 40^v–41, the only texted voice of the four, is written out twice, the second time with a cento of lines taken from stanzas 2–5 of the text found in Add. 26737 and printed, from an unknown source, by Hawkins; Warlock made no use of this secunda pars in his edition.

[35] In addition to *O death*, this MS contains two songs by Philip van Wilder: the first part of *Amor me poynt* (ed. Margaret Glyn, *Early English Organ Music*, I [London 1939], 17–18, with an attribution to Tye), otherwise known only from the bass part of a 1552 Susato print; and *Fayr lady* alias *Une jeune moyne*, one of the van

down sometime after 1600? [35a] The Western Reserve cantus clearly is related to the latter, though it is not identical with the Add. 15117 voice part nor does it fit either the keyboard or lute part perfectly, as can be seen in the following music example. (A D-tuning has been used for the transcription of the lute tablature to facilitate comparison with the Christ Church piece.)

Ex. 1 Versions of O *death*

Wilder chansons printed in 1572 by Le Roy and Ballard; a third song, *Madona* (also ed. Glyn, pp. 16–17), is ascribed to van Wilder in a Tenbury MS, to Tye in another Christ Church MS, but is almost certainly by Verdelot (*Madonna somm' accorto*). The Governing Body of Christ Church, Oxford, has kindly given permission to transcribe parts of MS 371 below.

[35a] This is the well known song published by H. E. Wooldridge, in his recasting of Chappell's work, *Old English Popular Music* (London 1893), I, 111–13, and others. Add. 15117 is a motley source, indeed. It includes pieces that date well before 1600, like Byrd's *Alack, when I look back*, whose cantus (by Byrd? or Hunnis?) was printed in Hunnis's *Comfortable Dialogs* of 1583: see M. Frost, *English & Scottish Psalm & Hymn Tunes* (London 1953), p. 467, for the melody; others date from after 1600, like *Miserere, my maker*, a contrafactum of Caccini's *Amarilli mia bella;* some pieces seem to have been brought up-to-date, like Parsons's *In youthfull years;* others are freely altered, like the dialogue *Saye, fond love*, which is Dowland's *Humour, say what mak'st thou here* with a new text and a simplified lute accompaniment; sophisticated songs, like the charming (French?) *Have I caught my heavenlye jewell*, rub shoulders with artless popular pieces, like the setting of Sir Arthur Gorges's dialogue *Cumme gentle Heardman sitt with mee* to the old ballad tune of *Go from my window*: see Land, *Het Luitboek van Thysius* (Amsterdam 1889), p. 80, for the same association of text and tune. This much known, how are we to characterize Add. 15117 or to generalize about any of its contents?

dole - full knell   let thy sound my   deathe   tell

doel - full knell   let thy sounde my death   tell

let   thy sound my   deathe   tell   for   I must dye

death doth drawe   ny   there

there   is   no   re - me   -   dye

is   no re - mi-die

The kinship of the two voice parts and accompaniments is obvious; how is it to be explained? Was there a consort song of the 1560s, lost but for the Western Reserve cantus and the keyboard arrangement of the Christ Church MS, a song with the same text but quite different music from the near-contemporaneous setting edited by Warlock? Was this old (theater?) piece rearranged, sometime after 1600, by the unknown compiler of Add. 15117, an individual with a penchant for theater songs? Not only did he include songs the texts of which occur, complete or in part, in plays by Jonson and Shakespeare, but also on the recto of the *O death* leaf he copied out a lute-song setting of a stanza and a half of Edwards's *Awake, ye wofull wightes*.[35b] Perhaps, like the *Damon and Pithias* song, *O death* was also from a choirboy play—it has all the marks of the genre—and may even have come from Edwards's lost *Palamon and Arcyte*, though this is a mere guess.

However, to ascribe any of the *O death* settings to Edwards is an act more of divination than scholarship. They are best left anonymous, as they are in all the sources, and given a tentative post–1560 dating, finer distinctions to be attempted when more of the consort songs of Elizabethan England are available for study. Perhaps Edwards can be credited with the words; literary scholars must decide that question.

[35b] See fn. 33 above, item (6).

III

ANOTHER Western Reserve fragment (hereafter *WR*), one for which no Smith-Rimbault-Chappell association can be shown, provides a new source for an old refrain.

Ex. 2 Fragment, Western Reserve University Library

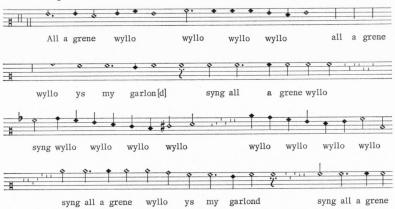

As the reader will have noted, the leaf is badly cropped at the top. Sections of an otherwise unknown song, *Bolde was ye begger & bolde was he*, fill the lower part (also cropped) of the leaf's recto and all of its verso.[36]

In physical appearance *WR* resembles a fragment (hereafter *Drexel*), discovered by Thurston Dart in the binding of a New York Public Library manuscript, described by John Stevens as an early Tudor song, and published, in facsimile and transcription, by Frederick Sternfeld.[37] I should not be surprised to learn that the two leaves come from the same manuscript. *Drexel* verso preserves twelve lines of an aging lover's complaint (beginning in medias res) and ends with the words: "for all a green willo ys [my garland]."[38] Since the same willow refrain is at the

[36] Was this, by chance, the ballad of "The bold beggar" registered 1 June 1629 with the Stationers' Company? (See Rollins, *Index*, No. 221.) Many 16th-century ballads appear to have been reprinted, some of them often, in the 17th century.

[37] New York Public Library, Drexel MS 4183, fly-leaf. Stevens, *Music & Poetry*, pp. 426–28, lists this and other Drexel fragments. Sternfeld, *Music in Shakespearean Tragedy*, pp. 49–52, publishes the willow song fragment. The New York Public Library (Mr. Philip L. Miller, Chief of the Music Division) has graciously permitted the transcription in Ex. 3.

[38] Can this be "an olde louers complaynt" registered with the Stationers' Company in 1579 and otherwise unknown? Or "the lamentation of an olde man for maryinge of a yonge mayde" registered in 1563–64? (See Rollins, *Index*, Nos. 2005, 1442.)

beginning of *WR* recto, it is tempting to surmise that the two leaves were once contiguous and that we have recovered the end of the *Drexel* voice part. However, the two willow fragments cannot be combined to form a single voice part; *Drexel* has a soprano clef and a B♭ in the signature; *WR* has a mezzo-soprano clef and no key signature, and begins with eight breves rest. And yet they are part of the same song.

 Drexel's soprano part consists of two-measure phrases set off by one or two measures of rest, a plan as striking as the anomalous rhyme scheme of its surviving text: *aaa bbbb cccc d. WR's* mezzo-soprano part, despite its cropped state, clearly consists of a like sequence of short phrases set off from one another by one or two measures of rest; in a word, *WR* complements *Drexel;* when the two are fitted together, the *Drexel* ballad recovers its refrain! The text is cast in eight-line stanzas which the composer has split between the two voices, with one refrain line of *WR* following each ballad line of *Drexel.* Reassembled, the poem runs thus:

[1]

. . . .
 Syng all a grene wyllo,
Whan I haue plesyd my lady now & tha*n*,
 Syng wyllo wyllo wyllo wyllo,   4
But now she lovyth another man,
 Wyllo wyllo wyllo wyllo,
Bycause I cannot as he can,
 Syng all a grene wyllo ys my garlond.   8

[2]

A lyttyll age but late byfell,
 Syng all a grene wyllo,
Wyche ouet of s[ervice] dyd me expell,
 Syng wyllo wyllo wyllo wyllo,   12
Now yowthe ys co*m*e t*h*at beryth t*h*e bell,
 Wyllo wyllo wyllo wyllo,
Bycause I ca*n*not do so well,
 Syng all a grene wyllo ys my garlond.   16

[3]

Now all ye lovers take hede off me,
 Syng all a grene wyllo,
For ons I was as losty as ye,
 Syng wyllo wyllo wyllo,   20
And a[s I] am all ye shalle be,
 Wyllo wyllo wyllo wyllo,
T*h*erefor come all & dau*n*ce wit*h* me,
 For all a grene wyllo ys [my garlond.]   24

WR preserves the complete refrain, written out once, with *signa congruentiae* to indicate repetition. *Drexel* preserves music for the odd-numbered lines, beginning with line 7. Both voices have words and music for line 24, though each lacks a bit of its respective ending. From a comparison of the music for stanzas 2 and 3 it becomes apparent that both are variations of the same theme (or ground). Probably the first stanza was similarly set; that its surviving text has the same scheme as corresponding lines in stanzas 2 and 3, and that line 7 is set to the same notes as line 15 supports the conjecture.

Once joined, the two voice parts prove to be related to an anonymous, textless lute piece, *All of grene willowe,* found in Folger MS

Ex. 3   Reconstruction of *Syng all a grene wyllo*

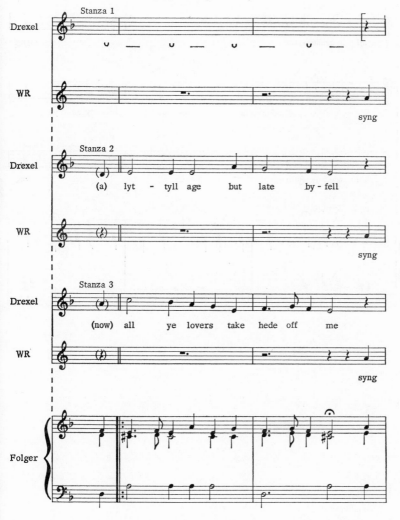

whan I have plesyd my la - dy now & than

all a grene wyllo syng

wyche ouet of s[ervice] dyd me ex - pell

all a grene wyllo syng

for ons I was as lo - sty as ye

all a grene wyllo syng

but now she lovyth an - other man

wyllo wyllo wyllo wyllo   wyllo

now yowthe ys come that ber-yth the bell

wyllo wyllo wyllo wyllo   wyllo

and a[s I] am all ye shall be

wyllo wyllo wyllo wyllo   wyllo

by - cause I can - not as he can

wyllo wyllo wyllo   syng

by - cause I can - not do so well

wyllo wyllo wyl - lo   syng

there - for come all and daunce with me for

wyllo wyllo wyl - lo   for

v.a.1.59 (formerly 448.16), fol. 19. The fit is not perfect; it should not be expected to be so; *Drexel* and *WR* probably date from the 1530s or '40s, Folger from the '70s. The difference in date makes the amount of agreement the more surprising and offers a nice confirmation of Otto Gombosi's view that the Folger willow song is "one of the oldest. . . ." [39]

In Example 3 (above, p. 847), the music for stanzas 2 and 3, and a conjectural reconstruction of stanza 1 have been placed one above the other over the Folger lute arrangement.

The binder has trimmed off so much of *WR* that an exact reading of its first line of music is impossible; therefore I have omitted this portion of *WR* from the example, though it belongs to the willow song and enables us to judge the approximate length of the original song and, consequently, how much of the *Drexel* part fell victim to the binder's shears. Just enough of the notes remain to make it clear that this section of *WR* does not fit the Folger piece. I can only guess that the original willow song began with a burden, different, in part if not wholly, from the refrain woven into the stanzas proper and sung at the beginning, perhaps also at the end, of the song. Assuming this burden to have been the same length as the succeeding stanzas—an assumption partly supported by study of the note heads and stems left on the leaf—the first line of *WR* can be reconstructed as follows:

Ex. 4

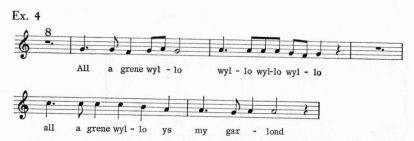

Are we to deduce from the unexpected conjugation of the greater part of *WR*, *Drexel*, and Folger that there was once a single, well-known willow song? or do the voice parts belong to an early Tudor partsong, and the lute arrangement to its vulgarization by ballad-singing Elizabethans? Evidence that more than one text may have been sung to the music (a sure sign of ballad-mongery) is provided by Master Thomas Dallis's lute arrangement of the same music (Trinity College, Dublin, MS D.3.30, p. 26, *All a greane willowe*), which he has cast in two strains

---

[39] *Renaissance News*, VIII (1955), 13. Sternfeld, *Music in Shakespearean Tragedy*, pp. 44–46, prints the Folger piece in facsimile and transcribed into modern notation.

of four measures each, a common form of the late 16th-century ballad tune and quite different from the thirteen (3 + 3 + 3 + 2 + 2) measure Folger arrangement. Perhaps we have recovered the Tudor *modo da cantare canzone del salice*, the formula for singing the many different willow songs for which we have texts and no music.[40]

IV

NEXT TO the *WR* leaf preserving the willow refrain is a second leaf (*WR2*) written in the same hand and probably cut from the same source. On one side it carries the following tenor setting of a text set to different music, also for tenor, in MS Royal Appendix 58, fol. 12ᵛ; both tenors are probably fugitives from partsongs otherwise unknown.[41]

Ex. 5 Second fragment, Western Reserve University Library

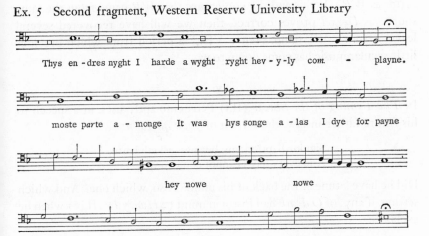

On the reverse side of *WR2* is a voice part labeled, simply, *Bassus*. It proves to be the missing voice of a puzzle-canon by Robert Fayrfax, published by Stevens from a Wells Cathedral fragment, the missing fourth voice supplied, very skilfully as we can now see, by Dart.[42] Here is the original bassus:

[40] Sternfeld, pp. 46–49, prints the Dallis piece in facsimile and transcribed into modern notation. The most famous of willow songs is, of course, that found in Add. 15117, fol. 18, beginning: *The poore soule sate sighinge by a Sickamore tree;* see Sternfeld, pp. 39–44; it is a totally different composition from that discussed in the text above.

[41] The Royal Appendix setting is No. 316 in Stevens's *Index of Selected Songs*. Both settings begin in a similar manner; thereafter they differ.

[42] *Musica Britannica*, XVIII, 43.

Ex. 6

Though I have not seen the Wells fragment which preserves the other three voices of this piece, I suspect it belonged to the same manuscript as *WR2*. If this and the conjecture that *WR* came from the same source as *Drexel* proves correct, then we will have recovered several leaves "from a MS. temp. Henry VIII," a period from which precious little secular music has come down to us.

v

In *The Taming of the Shrew* (II,i) Petruchio aptly uses, in a speech to his future father-in-law, the refrain of *Joan qd John:*

> Signior Baptista, my business asketh haste,
> And every day I cannot come to woo.

Did he have a tune at the back of his mind? If so, which one? And which setting, if any, of *O death* had Pistol in mind (*2 Henry IV*, II,iv) when he exclaims:

> What! shall we have incision? shall we imbrue?
> Then death rock me asleep, abridge my doleful days!

And which tune did the boy who played Desdemona use when he sang —or so one supposes—bits of an old willow song? Do the Western Reserve fragments provide answers?

The search for the music Shakespeare mentions or requires in his plays is often considered ended when a like-named music is found in a source more or less contemporary with the playwright. The searcher remains unaware that a choice may be available to him. Requiring a setting of *Hold thy peace* for the three catchers in *Twelfth Night* (II,iii), he may think he has found the one Shakespeare intended the actors to sing in Ravenscroft's *Deuteromelia* of 1609 and thereby ignore the elaborated version of the same catch in Melvill's 1612 *Book of Roundells* and the quite different setting in the Lant roll of 1580; [43] which is the right setting? He may assume *Greensleeves* to be a tune, like *Walsingham*, instead of a ground, and fail to note, in his annotation to *The Merry Wives of Windsor* (V,v), that no two of its discants are the same.[44] Finding a tune called *O mistress mine*, he may decide it must fit Feste's lyrics and force a marriage of syllable and note, ignoring the cautioning parallels of Parsons's *Lustie gallant* and Holborne's *Hartes ease*, neither of which fits the ballad texts associated with these tune names, and ignoring the common Elizabethan practice of associating more than one piece of music with a title or text, a practice as old Henry VIII's time, as *Thys endres nyght* and other songs prove.[45]

In other words, the Western Reserve fragments of *Joan qd John*, *O death*, and a willow song provide new difficulties for the annotator of Shakespeare's plays. For each song he is offered an *embarras de richesse* that makes him poorer by a certainty.

[43] All three are printed in the sources cited in fn. 12 above.

[44] To the versions listed by Rubsamen, *Festschrift Heinrich Besseler*, p. 274, should be added Cambridge University MSS Dd. 5.21, fol. 10 (for treble) and Dd. 5.20, fol. 6 (the *romanesca* bass). Roy Lamson, Jr., *English Broadside Ballad Tunes of the 16th and 17th Centuries*, in: *Papers Read at the International Congress of Musicology, 1939* (New York 1944), p. 118, lists versions of *Greensleeves* dating from the 16th to the 20th century.

[45] See Sydney Beck's ingenious *The Case of "O Mistresse mine,"* in: *Renaissance News*, VI (1953), 19–23; also Vincent Duckles, *New Light on "O Mistresse mine,"* in the same quarterly, VII (1954), 98–100. Parsons's piece goes by a number of names; *Lustie gallant* is the one given in Tenbury MS 389, p. 13. Holborne's almaine is called *Hartes ease* in the Cambridge University lute MS Dd. 2.11, fol. 44, and *The Honi-suckle* in the composer's *Pavans, Galliards, Almains, and Other Short Aeirs* (1597), No. 60; in Holborne's *Cittharn Schoole* (1597) it is called, simply, *Almayne*. (I am indebted to Masakata Kanazawa for the Holborne concordances.)

THE PERFORMANCE OF
AMBROSIAN CHANT IN
THE 12th CENTURY

by REMBERT G. WEAKLAND, O.S.B.

THE STUDY of medieval chant has restricted itself almost exclusively to a more accurate investigation of the melodic and rhythmic traditions. One would not question the importance of these areas as a beginning to the complex study of medieval chant, but the whole picture cannot be completed without an investigation into the many other factors that went into actual performance of the melodies. Among such factors must be listed the makeup of the choirs performing the chants, the number of participants, the chants assigned to soloists as distinct from choir chants, and all those other indications of method of performance that are not always clear from the melodic text.

In the field of Ambrosian chant one can, fortunately, obtain a somewhat clear picture of the performance practice of the metropolitan basilica at Milan at the beginning of the 12th century. Since this is also the period from which the first manuscripts of Ambrosian chant come down to us, the information in the non-musical sources from the period is vital in complementing the musical sources and adding important information concerning the actual musical performances.

Chief among the sources of Ambrosian practice is the *Ordo* written by Beroldus, the "custos et cicendelarius," as he styles himself. He states that he wrote his account of the services shortly after the death of Archbishop Olricus (1120–1125), and although his account has much information on the duties of the stewards in charge of candles that is not of musical importance, he does outline the duties of the entire personnel associated with the Milanese liturgy and of the musicians as well.[1] His concern in enumerating accurately the duties of each participant includes the remuneration each is to receive.

[1] The *Ordo* was first published in an imperfect edition by Muratori in *Antiquitates italicae medii aevi*, IV (Milan 1741) but a new critical edition was published by M. Magistretti entitled *Beroldus sive ecclesiae ambrosianae mediolanensis kalendarium et ordines saec. XII* (Milan 1894). It is the later edition that will be cited throughout the essay.

The second important source for the personnel associated with the Milanese Church and their numbers is the chronicle of Landulphus senior.[2] Although it was written some 35 years before the Beroldus account (about 1085) and has less information about the actual liturgical performances, it gives some interesting statistics on the number of performers. The chronicle of Landulphus junior, closer in time to the Beroldus *Ordo* (written about 1137), has less information about liturgical services.[3]

From these accounts and the annotations in the music manuscripts and the manuals from the 12th century one can form a rather complete picture of the usages of the metropolitan basilica at the time when the Ambrosian chant was at its apogee.

First in dignity in the Milanese church was the archbishop. His presence at the solemn liturgical functions on the greater feasts is always presupposed by Beroldus and when present, he begins the hours of the Office, says all blessings and orations. On weekdays and lesser feasts he was undoubtedly absent more often than present since Beroldus always indicates that one of the priests is to substitute for him. The first category of priests is the *sacerdotes cardinales* with their leader the archpriest. Beroldus does not give their number but Landulphus senior sets it at 24.[4] In choir they took precedence over everyone else and their presence is indicated on bigger feasts. The burden of the choir did not rest on their shoulders. The second category, the seven cardinal deacons, the first among them being called the archdeacon, formed an integral part of the ceremonies and the music. Both Beroldus and Landulphus indicate that there were seven.[5] The seven deacons were always present in choir in a section of their own and formed an integral part of the chanting of the Office and were among the principal ministers at solemn functions. In choir their chief function was that of intoning responsories and antiphons. From the account of Beroldus it is easy to see that they were not well trained in music and required the help and support of the precentor of the lectors. Their solo singing was reduced to the Gospel at Mass and an occasional respond, such as at the first nocturn of Good

---

[2] The chronicle of Landulphus senior was edited by Muratori in the *Rerum italicarum scriptores*, but this 18th-century edition has been supplanted by the edition of Alessandro Cutolo, *Landulphi senioris mediolanensis historiae libri quatuor* (Bologna 1942) in the new edition of the *Rerum italicarum scriptores*, IV, 2.

[3] In the new Bologna edition of Muratori's *Rerum italicarum scriptores* it is printed in volume V (1934).

[4] "At cum beatus Ambrosius supradictos sacerdotes Deo disponente ordinavit, visum est sibi ceteris cum fratribus, viginti quatuor sacerdotes, qui quasi cardinales essent, debere constitui." Land. sen., p. 11.

[5] Beroldus, p. 35; Land. sen., p. 12.

Friday or some of the responsories sung in the baptistery. The deacons are also listed as singing the Alleluja on some of the major feasts but this may have been limited to the intonation. On Wednesday of Holy Week (called *in authentica* by the Ambrosians) Beroldus indicates that the responsory at Vespers after the Magnificat is to be sung by the deacon "primicerio lectorum indicante sibi et cantante, si opus ei fuerit." [6] That the precentor might have to sing along with the deacon was an indication that vocal prowess was not a requirement for cardinal deacons.

The third category of choir personnel was the subdeacons. Beroldus does not give any indication of their number but only says that they had their own precentor (*primicerius*). Landulphus is misleading in his enumeration of all the personnel in book two of his chronicle. He writes: "Sacerdotes 24 ordinis majoris, diacones 7, subdiacones totidem . . . ." [7] From the context one would assume that there were seven subdeacons. From other passages, however, it can be seen that *totidem* refers to the number 24, not seven. In book one Landulphus writes: "Quos praevidens sanctus doctor Ambrosius religiose viginti quatuor subdiacones ad honorem Dei et ecclesiae suae ordinando benedixit." [8] Later in his description of the procession with the cross that took place on greater feasts he mentions that the 24 cardinal priests and many notaries stood on the eastern side while the 7 deacons and 24 subdiacones stood on the west side but turned toward the east.[9] Landulphus calls their leader an archsubdeacon rather than a precentor.

The role of the subdeacons in the choir seems to be the most ambiguous. Occasionally they are listed to sing one of the responds following the lessons at Office and naturally take a minor role in all solemn Mass functions. In this respect they functioned much like the deacons. There is no indication that proficient singing ability was required of them, but the fact that Beroldus notes that they had their own precentor shows that they sang as a group in alternation with the other sections of the choir.

Beroldus lists as a separate office the precentor of the priests (*primicerius presbyterorum*). His role was more jurisdictional than musical since he was second in power to the archbishop in the city. When the archbishop was absent, the precentor of the priests became the first dignitary in choir. Landulphus calls him a *co-episcopus*.

The two most important groups are listed next by Beroldus: the

---

[6] Beroldus, p. 89.
[7] Land. sen., p. 76.
[8] Land. sen., p. 12.
[9] Land. sen., p. 22.

notaries with their precentor (*ordo notariorum cum suo primicerio*) and the lectors (*lectores*) with their precentor (*primicerius*). Beroldus does not give the number of notaries but states that there were 16 lectors. In addition to the precentor (*primicerius*) the lectors consisted of a *secundicerius*, 4 *claricularii*, and 11 *terminarii*.[10] Landulphus also refers to these two groups but does not give a specific number for the notaries. In his enumeration in book one he simply talks of *notarios multos* and again in book two uses the same expression.[11] Landulphus lists 18 lectors: "lectores ecclesiae pondus portantes docti cantu lectione psalterio 18." [12] As he points out, this latter group carried the burden of the choir services and was trained in music. If one includes the precentor in Beroldus's group, then his number differs from Landulphus only by one.

The precentor of the lectors could rightly be called the choir-master. It was his duty to pre-intone almost everything and then to make sure that the choir took up the intonation properly. "Quis sicut rector navis regit et gubernat navem, ne pereat, sic primicerius lectorum regit chorum, ne in alliquo dilabatur vel defluat." [13] In one rather unusual passage he is described by Beroldus as using a form of chironomy in conducting his own lectors.[14] From Beroldus's description of his duties it can be seen, however, that his responsibilities involved the whole choir—not just the lectors. All the other precentors, such as the precentor of the notaries, gave pitches only within their own group.

The last category of personnel of musical importance contains the "quatuor magistri scholarum." [15] Beroldus does not mention the *pueri* of whom they were the *magistri* in his list of personnel, but he constantly mentions the role of the pueri in functions. The reason he omits them from the list is undoubtedly that they had no fixed place in choir like the other groups and were still in the training period. Beroldus mentions that the boys were to take a place in choir with their master in the winter church, but in the summer church and on certain big feasts they were to take their place "ad pedes graduum." [16] Landulphus mentions four

---

[10] Beroldus, p. 35.
[11] Land. sen., p. 22 and p. 76.
[12] Land. sen., p. 76.
[13] Beroldus, p. 38.
[14] "Tunc primicerius lectorum paululum semotus a loco suo infra chorum, incipit antiphonam in choro lectoribus circumstantibus in modum coronae, ipso meditante manu et voce descensionem antiphonae, et ascensionem et descensionem." Beroldus, p. 80.
[15] Beroldus, p. 35.
[16] Beroldus, p. 50. The use of two churches, one for winter and one for summer, is peculiar to the Milanese rite. The greater, or summer church, was under the patronage of the Virgin Mary and is now the cathedral; the lesser, or winter church, was dedicated to St. Thecla and stood at the opposite end of the piazza. It was destroyed in 1543.

scholae in the Milanese church, two of which were for music, two for philosophy.[17] Neither author gives any idea of the number of boys in the music school who participated in the services. The Latin word *pueri* is deceptive since it is sometimes interchanged with the word *clerici* and thus indicates simply those studying in the ecclesiastical school without implying that they were all *voci bianche*.[18]

The function of the *pueri* in services was an important one. They are frequently indicated by Beroldus as singing solos—especially on ferial days. It cannot be assumed that they sang easier chants than the lectors since the *psalmellus* (Roman gradual) of the Mass was always assigned to one of them and they sang the most difficult melismas of the Alleluja. They sang as a group quite frequently and sometimes in alternation with the lectors. In fact, one can see a certain rivalry between the two groups. One can assume that the *pueri* were spending more time rehearsing and thus capable of the more difficult chants.

Beroldus lists other categories of Milanese personnel such as the *custodes* and the *vetuli* but their functions were ceremonial and administrative—not musical. He also mentions a category of priests called *decumani*. In the middle of his dissertation he states that they finished their services before the solemn function began. Landulphus speaks about them at length, relating that their number had originally been 72 and that it was later increased to a hundred. They were considered as being of *minoris ordinis* compared to the *sacerdotes cardinales*. In enumerating the number of ecclesiastics serving the Milan Cathedral he lists only 12 *decumani*, whose function was mostly parochial.[19]

In each category of the musical personnel the members took turns by weeks singing the solos assigned to their category. These were called *ebdomadarii* or *septimanarii*. When two were needed, the second was called the *observator* and he was always next in line to be the *ebdomadarius*. The precentors, the archdeacon, and the archsubdeacon did not take turns but sang on the principal feasts only. The *magistri* of the *scholae* are indicated frequently as beginning chants but seldom sang alone. From the two sources cited, Beroldus and Landulphus senior, one obtains the following statistics on the Milanese choir of the 12th century:

[17] "Scholae vero, ubi cantus magistri ad docendos pueros cottidie conveniebant, in atrio ante ipsius regias duae erant . . . in atrio interiori, quod erat a latere portae respicientis ad aquilonem, philosophorum vero scholae . . . erant duae." Land. sen., p. 77.

[18] A useful discussion on the existence of similar schools attached to monastic churches such as Sant' Ambrogio is found in Monsignor Ernesto Moneta-Caglio's *I responsori 'cum infantibus' nella liturgia ambrosiana*, in: *Studi in onore di Mons. Carlo Castiglioni* (Milan 1957), pp. 494–99.

[19] Land. sen., pp. 14, 66.

24 cardinal priests, 7 cardinal deacons, 24 subdeacons, 16 lectors, many notaries, 4 masters and their students. From this it is easy to see that a choir of a hundred would not have been unusual on larger feasts.

Landulphus's account, because of its chauvinistic bias, cannot be trusted when it cites St. Ambrose as the originator of all of these categories. References to most of them, however, go back to the 9th and 10th century and show a continuous tradition. The chief source for this early witness is the *Expositio Matutini Officii*, attributed to Archbishop Theodore II (735–740), but quite erroneously. Because of the many quotations from Amalarius of Metz (c. 780–850), it could not have been written before the end of the 9th century or the beginning of the 10th.[20] Although the document is fragmentary and revels in long mystical explanations in the style of Amalarius, enough concrete references are made to existing practice to see that the functions of the deacons and subdeacons had not changed. His description and mystical analysis of the procession with the cross shows that the precentor of the lectors was then leader in the choir. He further argues that this precentor should be a priest in order to fulfill adequately his role since it is so similar to that of the good shepherd. "Let the precentor admonish his disciples to listen to the voice of the master, and to proceed, singing devoutly: and thus he should lead them as their shepherd before the cross on which the good shepherd gave up his soul for our souls: it is thus expedient that the precentor of the lectors be chosen from the ranks of the priests, because in his position he is fulfilling the office of a true priest." [21] In this same account of the procession with the cross Theodore mentions that the pueri did not take part in the procession but remained in the choir of the lectors.[22] Theodore is thus an explicit witness of the late 9th or early 10th century to all of the divisions of the Ambrosian choir except the notaries. This omission may be explained by the fragmentary nature of his account. The fluidity of this group and their secondary place and role in the choir may well indicate a later introduction into the Ambrosian church.

It was most important in the Ambrosian service that the singer intoning an antiphon or chanting a responsory do so from the proper place, a hierarchy of importance thus being created by the position the cantor took. The deacons ordinarily did not intone from their stalls but went to an elevated stand called the *stadium*. This differed from the *pulpitum*

---

[20] It was published by M. Magistretti in *Manuale ambrosianum, pars prima* (Milan 1905), pp. 114–42.
[21] *Expositio*, p. 126.
[22] *Expositio*, p. 127.

from which the deacons read the gospel and where the more elaborate solo singing took place. At times the deacon is instructed to intone from the corner of the altar (*ad cornu altaris*) or before the altar (*ante altare*). Most of the singing was done, however, in the center of the choir (*in medio chori*). In almost every case, the exact location of the singer is indicated by Beroldus and held to be significant.

Beroldus occasionally indicates the manner in which the singing is to take place, whether it should be soft (*leni voce*) or loud (*excelsa voce*). For example, he states that at the beginning of Vespers one of the lectors from the class of the *terminarii* sings the *lucernarium* softly (*leni voce*) and this is repeated softly by the master with his boys, and finally intoned by the lector and taken up by the whole choir *excelsa voce*.[23] This three-fold repetition and its proper dynamics is not indicated in the manu-scripts. Landulphus gives a description of the singing of the antiphon accompanying the procession with the cross and indicates that it was sung seven times. (This custom on the greater feasts is confirmed by Beroldus.) The sixth time it is sung in the body of the church with great noise (*magno clangore*) and the seventh in choir with high, resonant tones (*vocibus altis atque sonoris*).[24] Frequent allusions are made by Beroldus to the fact that the verses of hymns and psalms were alternated between notaries and lectors or lectors and boys. He also indicates the repetition of the same piece by another section of the choir. The amount of contrast obtained in this fashion is seen to be larger than is usually associated with chant performance.

The description that follows of the pontifical Ambrosian Mass as recorded by Beroldus, although it omits all the ceremonial details with regard to candles, incense, and the like, gives a fairly clear idea of the manner in which the different groups of the choir participated in a solemn service.[25]

In the procession as it begins from the sacristy could normally be found two deacons and three subdeacons, although some feasts call for three deacons and five subdeacons to assist the archbishop. The deacon to the right of the archbishop intoned the second processional antiphon (*psallenda*) from the night Office as the group proceeded to the high altar. It appears that the boys and their master were also in the procession, for it was their task to take up the intonation of the processional antiphon

---

[23] "Tunc terminarius lector ebdomadarius canit lucernarium . . . leni voce, et magister scholarum simili modo leni voce cum pueris suis. Deinde lector, qui incipit, et chorus qui sumit, omnes excelsa voce." Beroldus, pp. 54–55.

[24] Land. sen., p. 22.

[25] The description of the Mass and the duties of the various ministers can be found in Beroldus, pp. 46–53.

by the deacon and to repeat it after the master sang the *Gloria patri*. Having arrived at the altar, the master began the *Ingressa* (Roman Introit). The fact that on solemn feasts there was also a processional antiphon distinct from the *Ingressa* is not indicated in the manuscripts and explains why the Ambrosian *Ingressa*, although it has many features in common with the Roman Introit, is not properly a processional antiphon, lacking as it does any psalmody. All of the liturgical action—the incensations and the preliminary prayers at the foot of the altar—takes place during the singing of the *psallenda*, not the *Ingressa*.

The Kyrie of the Ambrosian Mass is sung as an addenda to the Gloria and consists of three simple Kyries. The Gloria was sung on lesser feasts in its entirety by the master of the boys; on the most solemn feasts he sang only to the "suscipe deprecationem nostram," from which point the lectors continued to the end "excelsa voce." The master and the boys added the three Kyries. It can be seen that the Gloria does not receive the prominence in the Ambrosian ceremony that it does in the Roman. The reason for this may be that it is also sung at the morning Office and its presence at Mass is a duplication.

The first lesson was sung by a lector in the pulpit unless it was one of the chief feasts of the year, in which case the leader of the subdeacons sang it. After its completion one of the pueri took a special book containing the ornate chants (similar to the Roman cantatorium but called *tabulae* by Beroldus) and sang the melismatic *psalmellus* in the pulpit. Only on rare occasions was this chant assigned to a lector and, strangely enough, to two subdeacons and two notaries on the feast of the Annunciation.

As in the Roman rite, the Epistle was sung by the subdeacon; it was considered the second lesson by the Ambrosians. Following the Epistle came the singing of the great Alleluja. The passage describing it from Beroldus hardly seems credible: "When the epistle is finished, a notary, at the bidding of his precentor, takes the *tabulae* from the altar or the ambo; having put on a surplice he sings in the pulpit the Alleluja twice before the verse. The master of the boys begins and then the lectors sing Alleluja, both the verse and the Alleluja in like manner. After the verse the same notary says Alleluja; then the master with the boys sings the *melodiae*, the lectors being silent." [26] Unless there is an error in the way Beroldus relates the manner for singing this solemn chant, it would have

[26] "Qua [epistola] finita notarius jussu primicerii sui tollit tabulas de altari vel de ambone, indutus camisio canit *Alleluja* in pulpito bis ante versum, et magister scholarum incipit, et lectores deinde canunt *Alleluja*, et versum, et *Alleluja* similiter. Post versum vero idem notarius dicit *Alleluja*, tunc magister scholarum canit melodias cum pueris suis, tacentibus lectoribus." Beroldus, p. 50.

been repeated several times with contrast between soloist, chorus, and boys. On Christmas, Epiphany, Easter, Pentecost, and the feast of the Dedication of the Church, all the deacons sang the Alleluja from the pulpit. At the beginning of Lent four boys did so.

The singing of the third lesson or gospel was the exclusive duty of the deacon. The *diaconus observator* (the one next in line to take his weekly turn) called out from the corner of the altar, "Parcite fabulis." The two *custodes* said, "excelsa voce," "Silentium habete." This need to obtain silence in the church before the reading of the gospel may have had a very practical origin. The *Antiphona post evangelium*, a peculiar feature of the Ambrosian rite, was intoned by the precentor of the lectors and sung by his group. In contrast, the *Offerenda* (Roman Offertorium) was sung by the master with the boys.

At the end of the Offertory in the Ambrosian rite—not before it as in the Roman—the Creed is sung. Beroldus stipulates that the chorus was to sing the first half to "et homo factus est" and the master with the boys to sing the second half to the end. This was the opposite of the procedure for the Gloria. The remaining chants of the Ambrosian Mass, the Sanctus, the Confractorium, and the Transitorium, were all sung by the pueri.

On weekdays most of the Mass chants were sung by the master and the boys without much solemnity. Even the Alleluja was sung by a boy who, although he held the precious *tabulae*, stood—not in the pulpit— but in the middle of the choir.

The following list of the parts of the Ambrosian Vesper service and the proper singer for each musical piece will suffice as an example of the manner in which the singing was distributed among the groups.[27]

> *Lucernarium:* lector on Sundays
>   puer on weekdays
> *Antiphona in choro:* lectors
> *Hymn:* alternation of full chorus with boys
> *Responsory:* notary on Sundays
>   lector on weekdays
> *Antiphons of psalms:* intoned by deacons, sung in alternation by all
> *Magnificat:* intoned by archbishop or priest, sung in alternation by all
> *Psallenda:* sung by deacon

The first lesson at Matins was sung by a puer, the respond by a notary; the second lesson by a notary, the respond by a lector; and the third lesson by a lector without respond. On the most solemn feasts the subdeacons and deacons took part in the reading and singing. The rubrics for the special chants that are sung on Christmas, Epiphany, Holy Week,

[27] Beroldus, pp. 53–57.

Easter, and for the many processions on the feasts of saints are given in great detail by Beroldus and show remarkable contrast between solo and chorus.

One of the most elaborate ceremonies in the Ambrosian rite was the procession with the crosses, already alluded to, that ended the morning Office on Sundays and feastdays. The *Antiphona ad crucem* that was sung during the procession was ordinarily repeated five complete times; on the Sundays of Advent, Christmas, Circumcision, and Epiphany it was sung seven times. The description given by Beroldus of this ceremony, a translation of which follows, brings to life what in the manuscripts is nothing but an ornate chant like many of the others. It cannot be seen in the manuscripts that the dramatic aspects of the ceremony were heightened with each repetition of the antiphon. It proves that for a proper aesthetic appreciation of this, and most medieval chant, a study of the single melodic line is not enough.

"On the Sundays of Advent, on Christmas and its octave, and on Epiphany the *Antiphona ad crucem* is sung seven times in the following manner. After the canticle of Deuteronomy is over, the precentor of the lectors forms a circle with the lectors in the body of the church, about a fourth of the way up from its entrance; the weekly porter stands near them with a silver cross and with three lighted candles, one of them being placed at the top of the cross. Two other crosses are carried by the porters who are to serve in the following week a short distance in front of the first cross and in a straight line with it but separated one from another. Then the precentor of the lectors begins the *antiphona ad crucem* and the lectors take it up. After it is sung once, he says the Kyrie three times and the two crosses move forward a little; the third cross moves into the place where the two crosses had been. Then the lectors sing again the antiphon in a loud voice, which finished, they say the Kyrie three times. After that, the two crosses are moved again so that they will be before the archpriest and archdeacon when these descend from the choir; the third cross moves to where the other two had been. While the lectors are singing the antiphon the members of the choir, except the archbishop, descend to a point at the middle of the pulpit. Here they arrange themselves with the priests and notaries on the north side; the others, namely the deacons and subdeacons, on the south. The archbishop then goes to the gate of the chancel of the priests, being led by the deacon of the week, as they sing the antiphon again. Then the steward in charge of the candles gives a lighted lamp to the subdeacon of the week in the sacristy and leads him to the large lamps which the subdeacon lights with his lamp, the wick being shown him by the steward. When this has been done, the steward immediately takes the lamp from the subdeacon and places it in the sacristy, leading the subdeacon through the choir to the altar. While the subdeacon remains behind the altar, the lectors come to the place where the two crosses had been and make a circle as before. The two crosses are carried to the entrance of the choir and the third progresses to where the two had been, as the lectors sing the antiphon. The rest of the singers ascend somewhat into the choir. When the lectors have finished the antiphon, the whole choir begins it. The precentor of the lectors passes through the middle of them to the major choir and there arranges the lectors at the north chancel. As the antiphon is being sung by all, as was said, the two crosses are brought behind the altar where the subdeacon is waiting, vested in his special alb, to receive them and give them to the porters to be placed in their proper places. The third cross is moved to the entrance of the choir. After the antiphon has been sung by all, the precentor of the lectors begins the *Gloria Patri et Filio et Spiritui Sancto*, and they repeat the same antiphon. When it is finished, the precentor of the lectors says to his own group: 'Pax vobis,' and the third cross is taken behind the altar. Then the subdeacon takes the candle that was on the top of this third cross and with it lights the wax candelabra and the twelve candles in the chancel of the church. In the meantime the archbishop goes to the platform, being led by his right hand by the deacon of the week, the one who had led him to the gate of the chancel. . . . Then the singers go up to the choir on the south and there arrange themselves according to their rank and sing: *Sicut erat in principio, et nunc, et semper, et in secula seculorum. Amen.* And then they sing the same antiphon again." [28]

[28] Beroldus, pp. 40–41.

THE LAST PYTHAGOREAN
MUSICIAN: JOHANNES KEPLER

by *ERIC WERNER*

> I may say with truth that whenever I consider in my thoughts the
> beautiful order, how one thing issues out of and is derived from an-
> other, then it is as though I had read a Divine Text, written into the
> world itself, not with letters but rather with essential objects, saying:
> Man, stretch thy reason hither, so that thou mayest comprehend these
> things!
>
> KEPLER (in his calendar for 1604).

SINCE HINDEMITH'S opera *The Harmony of the World* (Munich 1957), musicians have been made aware again of the conception pronounced in the title, and championed by the hero
of the work: the astronomer, mathematician, or, according to his own
preference, the "natural philosopher" Johannes Kepler. Through a
modern opera the musician and musicologist of today learns of Kepler's
profound knowledge of ancient and Renaissance music theory. For
except the solid article in *MGG*, the reference books will tell him little,
if anything, touching on Kepler and music. Otherwise his name means
practically nothing to the musical scholar. This was not always so. Aside
from the astronomer-composer Sir William Herschel, whose astronomical occupations had made him thoroughly familiar with Kepler's
writings, many students of music theory, from Mersenne to Euler, Padre
Martini, and Marpurg, were cognizant of his musical learning. When his
astronomical discoveries, epoch-making in every sense, were thrown into
the limelight of fame by Newton, the significance of his musical thinking
fell into oblivion. A few outsiders, such as A. von Thimus [1] and R. Hasenclever,[2] tried to keep his name alive in the history of music theory—
in vain! For the quadrivium, once the fertile soil of many great ideas, including Kepler's, had collapsed with the onset of particularization. Thus,
mathematics, music, and astronomy, formerly closely linked sister disciplines, were separated from each other.

In Kepler's own time, however, the quadrivial elements were still

---

[1] A. von Thimus, *Die harmonicale Symbolik des Altertums* (Cologne 1876).
[2] R. Hasenclever, *Die Grundzüge der esoterischen Harmonik* (Cologne 1870).

sufficiently close to each other to be studied together. The artificial distinction between the humanities and the sciences, of which modern culture has no reason to be proud, did not exist as yet. In particular, the concept of a philosophy of nature encompassed, as a matter of course, all cosmological speculations that had emerged in Western thought ever since Pythagoras. And many of them concerned themselves with the harmony of the spheres. It is one of history's ironical quirks that the greatest astronomer and music-theorist of antiquity, Ptolemy, was definitely refuted by Kepler, who had utilized ideas of Ptolemy. Indeed, when he studied for the first time the original Greek text of the ancient astronomer, he felt gratitude for Divine Providence, which "had the same thought about the harmonic formation turned up in the minds of two men who (though lying so far apart in time) also had devoted themselves entirely to contemplating nature." [3] These are, of course, the words of a devout and faithful Christian, and they display the distance between him and the Greek Pythagoreans better than any commentary.

This seems to be of the highest significance: without his obsession with a demonstrable harmony within the solar system, *expressible in musical notation*, Kepler would never have discovered his celebrated Third Law, the law out of which emerged Newton's concept of gravity. What makes Kepler's ideas unique is their seeming anachronism. While the Third Law was far ahead of its time—Galileo pronounced it false still in 1632, and only Newton proved it—in his way of thought Kepler harked back more than two millennia, to the Pythagoreans. Yet he demanded strictly *empirical proofs*, not speculative arguments. This Janus-faced attitude is characteristic of most pioneers of science during the late Renaissance.

We shall understand this antinomy better if we observe the status and reputation of Pythagorean thinking during the 15th and 16th centuries. Copernicus had followed certain of these conceptions, but Luther called him "the fool who went against Holy Writ," and the Holy Office of the Curia condemned his theory as heretical. Moreover, the new though self-appointed preceptor of all science, Bacon, considered the theories of Copernicus, Kepler, and Galileo all false, because they were, to him, Platonic or Pythagorean. He would have nothing of speculative or imaginative science, and the less so, the more systematic it was. "In Baconian science the bird-watcher comes into his own, while genius, ever theorizing in far places, is suspect." [4] Indeed, he had little faith in intuition—the course he proposed "leaves but little to the acuteness or

---

[3] Cf. Max Caspar, *Kepler*, transl. Doris Hellman (New York 1962), p. 276 ff.
[4] Cf. C. C. Gillispie, *The Edge of Objectivity* (Princeton 1960), p. 77.

strength of wits, but places all wits and understandings nearly on a level." [5] This sounds democratic and fair indeed, but such doctrine will never succeed in science. Yet there was reason enough for taking such a vigorous stance: the humanists of the time leaned too much toward a purely speculative cosmology, which often enough stooped to a set of esoteric, utterly uncritical fantasies. Such enlightened thinkers as the humanists Pico Della Mirandola and Johannes Reuchlin dabbled in Cabbala and Hermetics; and Kepler had to defend himself against a mixture of Cabbala, Numerology, and Rosicrucianism, represented by the Scottish nobleman Sir Robert Fludd (de Fluctibus), in the penetrating words: "I hate all cabbalists . . . Fludd takes his chief pleasure in incomprehensible picture puzzles of the reality, whereas I go forth from there, precisely to move into the bright light of knowledge the facts of nature which are veiled in darkness. The former is the subject of the chemist [here meaning an occult alchemist], followers of Hermes and Paracelsus; the latter, on the contrary, the task of the mathematician." [6] Those humanists who remained rationalistic enough to resist either Aristotelian dogmatism or Baconian pragmatism were "skeptical about the value of science, which, as they said, helped in no way toward a happy life." [7] And yet, the first definite announcement of Kepler's aim and his findings, written in a letter to his friend Wackher von Wackenfels one year before finishing the *Harmonice mundi*, has a curious ring after all: "We and the entire choir of planets revolve around the sun, subservient to him, as it were, as his own family and possession . . . As for the heavenly tones, they are to be reproduced in the usual manner of notation. The lowest note [in each case] is always the aphelion, the highest the perihelion . . . Indeed, the tones of the individual [bodies] are thus distinct, of course, with respect to the pitches, varying in height, of the musical scale." [8] (transl. E. W.)

Were it not for two references of this letter, it might be dismissed as one of the thousands of fantasies, which in past ages one scholastic divine copied from another. But these two items are novel and revolutionary indeed: Kepler promises to set down the exact notation of the tones of the planets; moreover, he identifies as the lowest tone of each

[5] *Ibid.*, p. 74.
[6] Cf. Caspar, *op. cit.*, p. 303.
[7] Cf. T. S. Kuhn, *The Copernican Revolution* (Cambridge, Mass. 1957).
[8] Johannes Kepler, *Gesammelte Werke*, ed. W. von Dyck, M. Caspar & F. Hammer, VI: *Briefe* (Munich 1940–41): "At solem et nos et omnis planetarum chorus circumimus, ei veluti famulantes, eius propria familia et peculium . . . Nam toni coelestes sunt exprimendi schematibus usitatis. Prima nota est motus aphelius, summa perihelius . . . Suntque revera sic distincti singulorum toni, diversis scilicet altitudine clavibus in scala musica" (pp. 254–55).

planet its aphelion, as the highest, its perihelion. Obviously, he meant to test and prove his amazingly concrete thesis of the celestial harmonies.

II

So FREQUENTLY has the term "harmony" been misunderstood, and so manifold are its possible applications, that we must ask quite seriously: what did "harmony" mean to Kepler? It had for him at least three different meanings, and it will be useful as well as necessary to distinguish among them: (1) Musical harmony, i.e. any interval which according to Kepler's music theory is harmonious-consonant. (2) Mathematical harmony, i.e. the division of quantities in two or more parts according to the so-called "harmonic" section. If there are two quantities, a and b, their harmonic mean or division is obtained by the formula

$$\frac{2ab}{a+b}.$$

A special case of the harmonic division is the "golden section" (*sectio aurea*) which plays an important part in classic sculpture, architecture, and music, but also in modern technology. It is represented by the equation

$$a : b = b : a + b, \quad \text{whence} \quad a = \frac{b}{2} (\sqrt{5} - 1).$$

The Pythagorean numbers of the first divisions of the monochord were also sometimes called harmonic. Finally, a sequence of numbers whose reciprocals form an arithmetic series is called a harmonic progression. Thus 1, $1/2$, $1/3$, $1/4$, $1/5$, etc. form a harmonic progression. This is a remnant of Ptolemy's theory of harmony, and has often been misunderstood.[9] (3) Occasionally the term "harmony" is used by Kepler in a sense closer to the ancient Greek meaning of that word. Then it had the general significance of something fitting, suitable, well proportioned, be it a piece of carpentry or the orbit of a planet. In this sense it was later used by Leibnitz.

Early in life Kepler intuitively but erroneously sensed the astronomical harmony of the world. Taking quite literally Copernicus's remark, "We find in this arrangement a marvelous symmetry of the

[9] Cf. C. v. Jan, *Die Harmonie der Sphaeren*, in: *Philologus*, LII (Goettingen 1894); also the article *Ptolemaios*, in: Pauly-Wissowa, *Real-Enzyklopaedie des klassischen Altertums*. Especially the harmonic division has been misunderstood, even by Riemann, *Geschichte der Musiktheorie* (2nd ed. Berlin 1920); see *infra*, text adjacent to fns. 35-36.

world and a harmony in the relationship of the motion and size of the orbits, such as one cannot find elsewhere," [10] Kepler set to work as early as 1599 to prove the harmonic character of the cosmos. He described that first brainstorm, by which he envisaged—faultily—the law of the planets, in all of its pristine enthusiasm: "The delight that I took in my discovery I shall never be able to describe in words." [11] That fundamental idea was false; yet it led, after 25 years of searching and checking, trying and rechecking, to the three laws that bear his name and made it immortal. At his time only six planets were known: Mercury, Venus, Earth, Mars, Jupiter, and Saturn. Following the Copernican theory, which envisaged the Earth as one of the planets, Kepler made the bold attempt to apply the proportions of the five so-called Platonic regular bodies to the distances between the planets. This fundamentally Pythagorean conception was first divined—though not clearly pronounced—in Plato's *Timaeus*. There it was already linked with the idea of the harmony of the spheres.[12] Kepler's first vision of geometrical proportions within the orbits of the planets was quite erroneous; and 22 years later, when he had found the correct solution, he wrote: "If my false figures came near the facts, it happened merely by chance. . . ." [13] For Kepler was never satisfied with vaguely approximate solutions, and certainly not with the ancient Platonic phantasmagorias of the cosmos: he insisted on exactitude, on proof, on numerical laws, while Plato was opposed to any kind of experimental science. Thus, in this categorical demand Kepler goes far beyond the ancients, and even more did he deny Aristotle's disclaimer of cosmic harmony: "Hence it follows: the claim that through the motions of celestial bodies harmony comes into being, in which the tones form *symphoniai*, is, though noble and original, by no means true." [14] How concretely the mature Kepler understood the phrase "cosmic harmony" may be seen from a few lines quoted from the table of contents opening the fifth book of *Harmonice mundi:*

I. De quinque solidis figuris regularibus
II. De cognitione cum iis, proportione harmonicarum
III. Summa doctrina astronomicae, necessaria ad contemplationem harmoniarum coelestium
IV. Quibus in rebus ad planetarum motus pertinentibus expressae sint

[10] Copernicus, *De revolutionibus*, I, Chap. 10.
[11] Cf. Caspar, *op. cit.*, p. 276.
[12] Cf. Plato, *Timaeus*, Loeb Classical Library (New York 1929), pp. 109ff, 126ff, 137ff.
[13] Kepler, *Mysterium cosmographicum*, Cap. 21, notes 8 and 11.
[14] Cf. Aristotle, *De coelo*, 290b (transl. E.W.). This attitude was shared by two great scholastic philosophers, Maimonides and Al-Farabi.

harmoniae simplices, et quod omnes illae in coelo reperiantur, quae in cantu insunt.[15]

V. Claves scalae musicae, seu loca systematis, et genera harmoniarum, durum et molle, a certis motibus expressa esse.

VI. Tonos seu modos musicos, singulos quodammodo a singulis planetis exprimi

VII. Contrapuncta, seu harmonias universales omnium planetarum. Easque diversas, aliam scilicet ex alia, existere posse, etc., etc.

Every astronomer or philosopher could have set forth the titles of the first four chapters. It is only thereafter that Kepler took the decisive step: he refers to *concrete musical scales* to be encountered in the movements of the planets; he speaks, later on, of the new-fangled genders of harmony, major and minor. He promises to show at least the possibility of a contrapuntal harmony among the planets, clearly notated and by no means an intellectual fantasy. Later on he will provide (Chap. IX) *a demonstratio*, an empirical and scientific proof of his thesis. And how humbly, yet proudly, does the last passage read: "Notes to this [Ptolemy's] part of the Harmonics, wherein I explain and refute the author [Ptolemy] and wherein I compare his findings and conjectures with my results." [16] Alas, this part of the appendix, so magnificently outlined, had mainly for technical, i.e. financial, reasons, to be reduced to a brief summary.

What did Kepler know about music? In sharp contrast to the vague ruminations of the Neo-Pythagoreans among the humanists, Kepler had familiarized himself with both the ancient and contemporary theory of musical harmony.

His letters contain a good many concrete musical examples, references, and questions. Through Boethius's work, which was still very much read, Kepler gained entrance to the older Greek sources, both in music and mathematics. Yet, where the Neo-Pythagoreans of his own time indulged in an esoteric numerology, Kepler wrote: "I do not wish to prove anything by the mysticism of numbers, nor do I consider it possible to do so." [17] Quite to the contrary! He wanted to encounter the "true nature of *musical* harmonics" in the world. Thus he analyzes the structure of the scale in accordance with Zarlino and Glareanus, whose

---

[15] How Kepler would have rejoiced over the discovery of the orbits of certain stars, e.g. 61 Cygni! It is sinusoidal, corresponding with the vibration of strings and tone-waves. Cf. H. Shapley, *The View from a Distant Star* (New York 1963), p. 60.

[16] J. Kepler, *Gesammelte Werke*, VI, 290: "Notas ad hanc partem harmonicarum, quibus authorem explico, refuto, eiusque vel inventa vel attentata cum meis comparo."

[17] Quoted after Caspar, *op. cit.*, p. 97 (letter, 14 September 1599, to Herward von Hohenburg).

works he had studied.[18] In a letter he gave a technical musical analysis of the sequence *Victimae paschali laudes*.[19] When he rushed to the defense of his old mother, who was accused as a witch by the Inquisition, he took with him, as reading matter, Vincenzo Galilei's *Dialogo*.[20]

III

THIS IS NOT the place to explain Kepler's line of astronomical thinking. We shall limit ourselves to demonstrating how his concern with musical harmonies aided and guided him toward his aim. Utilizing ideas and rules of music theory, Kepler attained his objective in four steps; and like a true Pythagorean, he juxtaposed mathematical and musical conceptions. Frankly, this method was not without occasional handicaps, arbitrary statements, and the like. The most difficult problem arose in identifying harmonic relations with consonant intervals. Thus the pure fourth is more harmonic, from the mathematical point of view, than the major third. But Odington and Johannes de Muris, to mention two great music theorists of the Middle Ages, considered the proportion of the Pythagorean major third, 5 : 4, as irrelevant for the musician, who would prefer the less simple but more consonant proportion $\frac{81}{64}$.[21] Moreover, misunderstandings arose concerning the harmonic progression (1, 1/2, 1/3, 1/4, 1/5, 1/6), which Zarlino considered the mathematical model of the minor scale.

Kepler dealt with six planets, including the earth, plus sun and moon, that is, with eight celestial bodies. (Uranus, Neptune, and Pluto had not been discovered at this time.) Convinced that this identity with the number of tones of the diatonic scale was not accidental, he began to search for identical properties between mathematical and musical harmonies. Under such circumstances the seventh overtone caused just as much trouble to him as to a conservative music theorist. He had to eliminate the number 7 as a member of his harmonic relations. Yet why should he stop at 6? (Octave 2, fifth 3/2, fourth 4/3, major third 5/4, minor third 6/5.) He could refer to Zarlino, whose work he knew; yet he was searching for musical as well as mathematical reasons for his self-imposed limitation. He started with a geometrical analogy: the regular polygons that can

---

[18] In *Harmonice mundi*, III, and esp. V, Chap. 5.
[19] Letter to Heydonus (May 1605), *Gesammelte Werke*, VI.
[20] *Gesammelte Werke*, VI, 479.
[21] Nonetheless, Odington is inclined to take 5 : 4 as the correct proportion of the major third. Cf. Riemann, *Geschichte der Musiktheorie* (2d ed. Berlin 1920), pp. 119–20. The Arabs knew the 5 : 4 proportion as consonant even before Odington. Cf. Riemann, *op. cit.*, p. 394.

be inscribed in a circle. He had to show that the division of a circle into equal parts by a line, a triangle, square, pentagon, and hexagon each was possible, not by a regular heptagon, which cannot be constructed by using only straight-edge and compass. This condition was and still is an inherent principle of Euclidian geometry. Kepler justifies his exclusion of the heptagon by stressing that this polygon would lead to irrational numbers ("numeri ineffabiles").[22] Yet he had to exclude other regular polygons, e.g. that of 15 sides, which can easily be constructed and does not lead to "numeri ineffabiles." We shall skip here the ingenious sophistries by which Kepler excluded such polygons; nor shall we speculate on how he might have reacted, had he known of Gauss's construction of the regular polygon of 17 sides! Thus he satisfied himself that the hexagon and octagon corresponding to the minor third and third octave are valuable and necessary, while the other polygons which exceed eight sides are not. Or in other words: "What may be constructed in geometry, is consonant in music," which in this form is absolutely untenable both from the mathematical and musical point of view.[23] And yet, even so critical a theorist as Salinas (1577) took more or less the same position as Kepler, i.e. he operated with similar sophistries as did Kepler in order to eliminate 7 from his harmonic relations.[24] It was only Mersenne (*Harmonie universelle*, 1636—after Kepler), who boldly suggested that habit might lead to considering the intervals corresponding to 6/7, 7/8, and even 5/7 as consonances.[25] Thus far all harmonics were understood as pure mathematical proportions. Yet Kepler himself turns against this very same one-sidedness in Plato, calling it a tyranny, because it violates the natural instinct of hearing.

We realize that Kepler's first step was erroneous; and yet it led him to the final correct solution. This situation repeats itself in the course of his researches. *Ducunt fata volentem* . . .

The mathematical results gained by Kepler were in full agreement with Zarlino's dictum (as Kepler had meant them to be): "Within the numbers 1: 2: 3: 4: 5: 6: all consonant harmonies are determined." [26]

[22] Kepler's "ineffabiles" is a Latinization of the Greek term *alogos*. This is pure Pythagoreanism, for he studiously avoids the word "irrational" since he had to deal with other irrational numbers rather than with quantities that could be constructed geometrically but not arithmetically, e.g. $\sqrt{2}, \sqrt{3}, \sqrt{5}$, etc.
[23] Cf. Kepler's letter to H. von Hohenburg of 14 September 1599, *Gesammelte Werke*, VI.
[24] Cf. F. Salinas, *De musica*, II (Salamanca 1577), Cap. 24, here quoted after Riemann, *op. cit.*, p. 397.
[25] Riemann, *op. cit.*, pp. 398–99, footnote.
[26] Cf. G. Zarlino, *Istitutioni harmoniche* (Venice 1558), I, Cap. 15: "Della proprietà del numero Senario et delle sue parti et come tra loro si ritrova la forma d'ogni consonanze musicale." See also *infra*, text adjacent to fns. 35–36.

Also the "harmonic" division of the fifth into the major and minor third, to be found in Zarlino, is accepted by Kepler, although he seems to have had some trifling misgivings about this division: [27]

Ex. 1

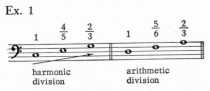

harmonic
division

arithmetic
division

Riemann has demonstrated in his *Geschichte der Musiktheorie* that Walter Odington already knew the harmonic division of the fifth into major and minor thirds.[28] Kepler's main premise consisted in excluding —both in music and mathematics—all proportions that involve the numbers 7, 11, 13, and similar primes. These proportions would (according to Kepler and all his contemporaries) produce only discordant intervals and harmonies.

Having established the mathematical "purity" of the major scale, Kepler proceeds to deduce the "melodic" intervals (*intervalla concinna*) from the principal harmonies, i.e. the whole tone (major and minor) and the two types of semitone. Then he develops out of the diatonic the chromatic scale *more mathematico*. Finally he attempts to formulate the principles of a *melopoeia* and a critique of polyphonic music; here we encounter ideas of Glareanus, S. Calvisius (*Melopoeia* 1582), A. Reinhard (*Monochordum* 1604), and G. M. Artusi (esp. his *L'Arte del contrappunto* 1586). The entire second part of Book III of the *Harmonice mundi* is yet to be evaluated by a competent musicologist; it offers ample food for thought. For here Kepler goes into musical details, quotes Josquin and Lasso, discusses various types of cadences, syncopes, good part-writing, and other problems of *musica practica*.

In his second step, Kepler finds the very same harmonic proportions that he had established in the regular polygons and in the musical scale also in the observable behavior of the planets. He lets the reader accompany him in his heuristic attempts to discover such celestial proportions;

---

[27] A modern mathematician would shrug his shoulders when considering Zarlino's harmonic and arithmetic division of the fifth and its resulting major and minor triads. For these results depend on the *direction* of the operation, upward or downward, respectively.

$$\text{Harmonic mean: } \frac{2 . 1 . \dfrac{2}{3}}{1 + \dfrac{2}{3}} = \frac{4}{5} \; ; \quad \text{arithmetic mean: } \frac{1 + \dfrac{2}{3}}{2} = \frac{5}{6}$$

[28] Riemann, *op. cit.*, p. 119.

nor is he ashamed to display his groping through a series of erroneous assumptions. Since he had constantly to resort to Tycho Brahe's and his own tables, which antedate the telescope, it is a profoundly moving spectacle to watch this honest and tenacious seeker of truth in his laborious quest. His task was now to find an equivalent for the proportion of the octave in the orbits of the planets; and after some experiments, he comes to the conclusion: "There is a distinction between the harmonies conveyed to us by the senses . . . and harmony *per se,* as abstracted from all sensuous entities . . . but in principle it is the same kind of harmony, which is defined by the proportion of 2 : 1, whether it is audible in tones, and then called octave, or visible in the beams of planets standing in opposition . . ." [29] Thereafter Kepler compares the proportions of the major axes of two planetary orbits; but in vain. Then he investigates the times of revolutions—with negative results—as well as the relations between the velocities of two planets—again without result. Then he compares the times during which two planets move the same length of an arc; here the results were inconclusive, but Kepler sensed that he had come near the solution. Finally he projects his ideal observer into the sun and calculates the extreme values of the planet's angular velocities, as seen from the sun, i.e. the planet's movement at perihelion and aphelion. And here he finds the required proportions and with them his celebrated Third Law, in modern terminology: the squares of the periods of revolution of any two planets are as the cubes of their mean distances from the sun. He proceeds to the distinction between the harmony of a planet's movement and the proportions established by a pair of planets. Immediately there occurs to him a vivid comparison with living music: "Just as the simple chant or monody which we call chorale, and which alone was known to the ancients, relates to the polyphonic, so-called figural chant, invented during the last few centuries: so also are the harmonies of a single, individual planet related to the harmonies of a pair of planets, if contemplated simultaneously [*ad harmonias junctorum*]." [30]

Such an analogy appeared natural to a man who, like Kepler, distinguished between harmonies of the senses and pure harmonies. If the soul, which recognizes and, indeed, *creates* harmony, were missing, the sensual things continue as before, but their harmony has disappeared. Why? Because harmony is a thing of reason. Hence to find and realize hidden

---

[29] This is not an exact translation of the rather intricate Latin text, but rather my paraphrase of the passage in *Harmonice mundi,* IV, Chap. 1 (*On harmonic proportions*).

[30] J. Kepler, *Gesammelte Werke,* VI, 316.

harmonics is a creative act of the soul. This train of thought is based upon an old concept that Kepler had found in Proclus's Neo-Platonic commentary on Euclid's elements. For Kepler, the celestial harmony, proof of God's transcendence, is an intellectual harmony; its finest sensual and intelligible counterpart is to be found in music and its proportions.

Following his table of contents, Kepler relates the harmonies found in the planet's elements to the proportions of the scale and to polyphonic music. He begins with the scale, placing the aphelions and perihelions in numerical sequence by a mathematical transposition of all relations into one single octave; he thus obtains (a) the major scale of G with C and C♯; and (b) a minor scale on G with E♭ and E♮:

Ex. 2   (after Kepler, *Gesammelte Werke*, VI, 319)

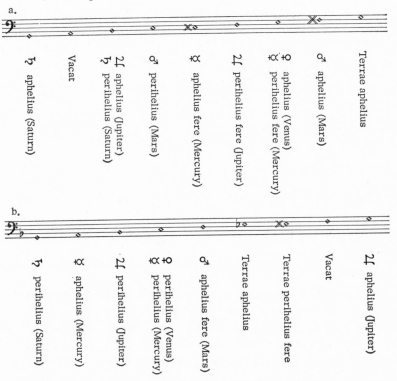

Thereto he boldly adds: "It follows that the musical scale (or the system of one octave), is doubly expressed in the sky, even according to the two *genera* of melody . . ." [31] From here he proceeds to the analysis of the scales that he just encountered "in motibus coelorum" according

[31] *Ibid.*, p. 320: "Est igitur in coelo duplici via, et in duobus quasi generibus cantus, expressa scala Musica, seu systema unius Octavae."

to the usual arrangement "per sectiones harmonicas." It is here that we meet a variety of implied assumptions pertaining to the music theory of Kepler's generation: he refers to the melodic-intervallic as well as to the polyphonic consonant relations of two or more voices, and in principle he does not make a categorical distinction between the two types of harmony—the simultaneous (vertical) and the subsequent (horizontal) one. He seems to have known the standard descriptions of harmony, especially those of Gafurius and Glareanus. Although he follows Zarlino in all essential points, he sees nothing illogical in the coexistence of the two *genera* of major and minor with the traditional octave species of the Middle Ages, for he tries to provide the necessary intervals for the *modi*. This was by no means easy; in fact, no clear *modus* is really recognizable in Kedler's attempt. Quite to the contrary, the reader is treated to a collection of melodic phrases pertaining either to the major or minor. This does not prevent Kepler from stating: "sunt ergo modi Musici inter Planetas dispertiti." He adds, in all fairness, that other and more modal distinctions are needed, which he cannot adduce. The melodic phrases assigned to the planets are:

Ex. 3

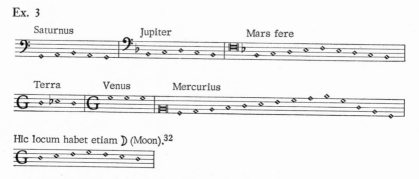

Saturnus   Jupiter   Mars fere

Terra   Venus   Mercurius

Hic locum habet etiam ☽ (Moon).[32]

In melancholic humor, he observes that the phrase assigned to the earth reads Mi—Fa—Mi, for *Miseria et Fames*.

Now Kepler is ready for the third step: the construction of the "Universal Harmony" of all planets, sounding together. He was really carried away by this conception, and opens Chapter 7 in hymnic language: "Nunc opus, Uranie, sonitu majore!" ("Now, Urania, greater sound is required!") In the subsequent paragraphs he challenges the contemporary composers to follow his lead by utilizing the specific har-

---

[32] He proceeds in the following manner: when assigning to Saturn, the most remote planet (in aphelion) the subcontra G, the most rapid motion of Mercury (at its perihelion) corresponds numerically to e⁵; reducing all proportions to one single octave, almost all notes of the diatonic major scale emerge quite naturally.

monies that he had found in the sky: "Sequimini Musici moderni remque vestris artibus, antiquitate non cogniti, causate!"[33] In the margin Kepler suggests the composition of a "celestial" motet based upon his data: "I wonder if I am not committing a turpitude by demanding from the composers of this age an artfully contrived motet for this eulogy? The Royal Psalter and other sacred books could easily provide an apt text. But hark ye, there are no more than six parts in the heavenly symphony! For the moon chants her own monody, belonging to the earth as an infant in its cradle. Assemble your notes, so that it may become a book of music for six parts, and I promise to be its diligent sponsor. For whoever will express the music of the heavens most fittingly, as described in this book, to him Clio grants the crown and Urania will give him Venus as his wife." I do not know if a composition has actually been elicited by Kepler's vision or his extravagant promises. As his laws were not generally recognized before their interpretation by Newton—even Galileo had considered them erroneous—the chances seem slim. Perhaps a Mersenne or Kircher could have written such a "cosmic motet" for six parts, but both were members of Catholic orders and had therefore to bridle their tongues and pens.

Yet Kepler was bent on demonstrating that "theoretically" the "Supreme Harmonist" himself had created the conditions necessary for a true celestial harmony of six parts. He insisted: "The heavenly motions are nothing but a continuous song for several voices . . . a music, which, through discordant tensions, through syncopes and cadences . . . progresses toward certain designated quasi six-voiced clausulae, and thereby sets landmarks in the immeasurable flow of time . . . Man wanted to reproduce the continuity of cosmic time within a short hour by an artful symphony for several voices, to obtain a sample of the delight of the Divine Creator in His works, and to partake of His joy by making music in the image of God."[34]

Yet he insisted that such a cosmic symphony is of purely intellectual, not sensual nature. In contradistinction to Galileo, for whom the physical world was an exact realization of geometrical principles, Kepler retained the ontological distinction between the ideal form as represented by mathematics, and its material realization. For him the essence of the world was spiritual, yet he maintained that it could and should be demonstrable through human senses and sciences. Thus he was aware of the slight numerical discrepancies—he calls them vices—in the planetary motions; he knew full well that a four-part harmony would occur only

[33] *Ibid.*, p. 323.
[34] *Harmonice mundi*, V, Chap. 7.

once in many centuries, because the moments when the planets stand to each other harmoniously are very rare: a six-part harmony might have occurred at the beginning of time! And here the indefatigable calculator begins to wonder if it would be possible, under such an assumption, to determine the age of the world.[35]

Kepler does not follow this tempting idea but presents at this stage a table that gives, both mathematically and musically, the values "Harmoniae Planetarum omnium seu Universales Generis Duri." Again we must ask ourselves what kind of harmony he was seeking and finding, for he speaks of *harmonia, sectio harmonica*, and the like, when he contemplates sequences such as 1, 2, 3, 5, 10, 15, 16, 20, 32, etc. It seems that he uses here a terminology, known to mathematicians and music theorists, that originated with Jamblichus's *Commentary on the Nicomachian Arithmetics*.[36] This author states that a "musical proportion" exists between two quantities a and b when the following equation is satisfied:

$$a : \frac{a+b}{2} = \frac{2ab}{a+b} : b$$

It is this equation, not the one quoted by Riemann (for Zarlino), which yields the *sectio harmonica*. Representing the c by 1, the g by 3/2, we obtain, in accordance with the above equation:

$$1 : \frac{1 + \frac{3}{2}}{2} = \frac{2.1.\frac{3}{2}}{\frac{5}{2}} : \frac{3}{2}, \text{ or } 1 : \frac{5}{4} = \frac{6}{5} : \frac{3}{2}$$

in accordance with Zarlino's and Odington's definition of the major third as the harmonic division of the fifth.

These proportions occur between planets, as Kepler admits, only under certain optimal conditions. Yet mortal man, "imitating his creator, finally invented the art of polyphonic music, unknown to antiquity; he wanted . . . to sense, as far as possible, the delight of the Divine Master in His works; he strives to experience the very same delight that such music [*imitatione Dei*] affords." [37] Here speaks not a Pythagorean, but a devout Christian.

---

[35] *Ibid.*, p. 324. Shortly before he shows that his old idea of the exact relationship between the regular bodies and the interplanetary spaces could not work.

[36] Jamblichus, *Commentaries ad Nicomach. Arithm.*, ed. Temml (Leipzig 1871), p. 168. See also F. Cajori, *History of Elementary Mathematics* (New York 1917), p. 30ff. This division seems to have originated in Babylonian astronomy.

[37] *Ibid.*, p. 328.

IV

Now LEAVING behind him all cosmological fantasies, Kepler returns to this earth and to his science. In his fourth step, he gives the rigidly observational and empirical proof of his theory, especially of his Third Law and its fundamental harmonic proportions. The numerical harmonies between the planets' angular velocities at their orbital extremes (aphelion and perihelion) were correlated with the observed mean velocities and with the time of a complete orbital revolution. Between these time values and the mean distances of the planets from the sun, the Third Law had, by induction, established a simple mathematical relation. Hence, the actual comparison of the theoretical distances with those resulting from observation constitutes the empirical test of Kepler's theories. As by-products of these calculations there emerge, again by the postulate of harmonic proportions, the correct values of the individual eccentricities for each planet. The aim that Kepler had envisaged 25 years earlier, the harmonic-geometrical laws of the solar system, had been reached, and the many bypaths, sometimes mystic, often fantastic, opened great new vistas for the genius who completed what Kepler had begun: Isaac Newton. His discernment—singling out from a jungle of hundreds of theorems and statements the Three Laws as definitive and decisive—must not be underestimated. For nowhere in Kepler's own writings do they appear together in the same treatise.[38] Yet it would not be quite fair to underrate their significance for Kepler himself, as a modern author does: "The three laws are the pillars on which the edifice of modern cosmology rests; but to Kepler they meant no more than bricks among other bricks for the construction of his baroque temple, designed by a moonstruck architect." [39]

A different judgment comes from a sober-minded historian of mathematics, the late E. T. Bell, who described the significance of the Three Laws in these words: "Kepler's laws were the climax of thousands of years of an empirical geometry of the heavens. They were discovered as the result of about 22 years of incessant calculation, *without logarithms*, one promising guess after another being ruthlessly discarded as it failed to meet the exacting demands of observational accuracy. *Only Kepler's Pythagorean faith in a discoverable mathematical harmony in nature sustained him . . .*" [40]

[38] It has been rightly stated that the Three Laws were "for Kepler simply snatches of melody in search of a symphony." (C. C. Gillispie, *op. cit.*, p. 37.)

[39] Cf. A. Koestler, *The Sleepwalkers* (New York 1959), p. 396. This book contains a magnificent biography and evaluation of Kepler, but tends too much to rhetorical hyperbole.

[40] E. T. Bell, *The Development of Mathematics* (New York 1945), p. 161; the italics are mine.

Kepler was by no means the only scholar of his time who speculated and theorized on the solar system; many others, such as Osiander, Fludd, or the Leipzig theologian Paul Nagel, had similar ambitions and even similar ideas. Yet both their methods and their aims were quite different: they wanted to prove Scripture, or to predict the future, or to interpret the numbers in the Books of Daniel and Revelation; they were not first-class mathematicians like Kepler, nor did they worry about exact empirical tests of their hypotheses; nor had any of them the bold idea of searching for numerical and musical harmonics in the Universe, although they all raved about it.[41]

In retracing Kepler's long and tortuous path, we might now single out his musical ideas. He begins by modifying Greek music theory, as expressed in Platonic doctrine and by Ptolemy: for Kepler sixths and thirds are consonances, and he endeavored to prove this unprovable axiom geometrically. He searches for harmonic progressions in the heavens; he improves Zarlino's conception of the major third as a harmonic division of the fifth; he builds his musical knowledge into his astronomical view of the world, and seeking a numerical harmony valid for *all* planets, he hits upon his Third Law. In his Faust-like urge, Kepler even starts to search for theological reasons behind the celestial harmonies. The devout Lutheran Christian, albeit a little tinged with pantheistic dreams—how could it be otherwise?—combines concepts of the Pythagoreans, of Boethius, of the great music theoreticians of the Middle Ages and the Renaissance; and he has experienced more than just a waft of the new era of empirical, not speculative, science.

And yet, his attitude toward astronomy, mathematics, music theory, and theology is still that of a great humanist: the fatal gulf between science and humanities had not opened as yet; he is much more of an artist than a mere "accountant of phenomena." [42] "We still share his belief in a mathematical harmony of the universe. It has withstood the test of ever-widening experience." [43] Thus writes a celebrated contemporary scientist. As for us, Kepler's profound understanding of musical laws and their application to the world of predictable phenomena will ever constitute a vindication of our discipline.

[41] Cf. G. Loria, *Storia della matematiche* (Milano 1950), p. 415f: "His Third Law might have been written by some superstitious fellow of the Pythagorean School . . . yet it is a proof of an extraordinary power of imagination, which would have led others to nothing but lunatic ruminations, but which guided Kepler to his great results . . ." (transl. E. W.)

[42] This striking phrase was coined by the late Lecomte de Nouy in his *Road to Reason.*

[43] H. Weyl, *Symmetry*, in: *The World of Mathematics*, ed. J. R. Newman (New York 1956), I, 720.

KEYBOARDS FOR WIND
INSTRUMENTS INVENTED
BY LEONARDO DA VINCI

by EMANUEL WINTERNITZ

I T IS ODD that the many sketches for musical instruments and
musical machines contained in the pages of Leonardo da Vinci's
notebooks have never found a thorough and systematic interpretation. It is true that some look rather fantastic, at least to us today, and
others are clearly only quick embodiments of passing ideas put down
on paper by Leonardo to aid his own memory. However, nearly all the
sketches reveal themselves as most interesting, and many as ingenious
new inventions, if they are scrutinized and analyzed in the right context,
that is, against the background of the instruments existing at Leonardo's
time, as well as with a knowledge of the mechanical devices used by
Leonardo outside the field of musical instruments, and examined in the
light of Leonardo's leading ideals for instruments, which can be distilled
from a comparison of all his drawings and from his many remarks on
music, musical aesthetics, and acoustics.

The eight sketches on the bottom of page 263 of the Arundel Codex
concern one of the crucial problems in the construction of wind instruments with sideholes: the control of fingerholes spaced wider than the
reach of human fingers. The laws of acoustics determine the distance
between fingerholes bored in the side walls of the tube of a wind instrument in order to obtain different pitches from it; [1] and the lower the
range desired, the longer the tube must be and the larger the distance
between the holes. Thus in the building of larger instruments with sideholes, a critical point is reached when a device is needed for transferring
the action of the fingers to the distant holes, in order to close them. One
device for this purpose is the key or lever, pressed on one end with the
finger and closing the fingerhole by means of a pad on the other end.

[1] There are, of course, as any player knows, other means for obtaining a variety
of tones, such as overblowing (the special combination of breath and lip pressure
to produce harmonics), mechanical devices such as slides and, since the 19th century,
valves.

Keys are used today in all so-called woodwind instruments (such as transverse flutes, clarinets, oboes, bassoons, saxophones, etc.).

Keys on woodwind instruments came into use only gradually, however. The first evidence I know of is in Sebastian Virdung's *Musica getutscht* (Basel 1511).[2] There, two of the many wind instruments illustrated in the woodcuts show one key:

Fig. 1   Sebastian Virdung. Illustrations showing a keyed shawm and a keyed recorder. From his *Musica getutscht und ausgezogen durch Sebastianum Virdung Priesters von Amberg . . . .* Basel, 1511. Facsimile ed., Robert Eitner, ed., Berlin 1882.

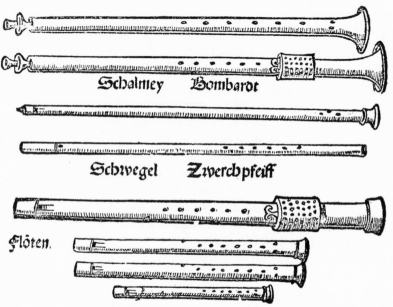

These instruments are: a bass shawm (*Schalmey*), also called a *Bombardt*, and the largest of the recorders, there called *Flöten*. In Virdung's illustration, only the upper end of the key or finger plate is visible (swallowtailed in shape for use by either the right or left hand), its lower part covered by a perforated cylinder. The purpose of this key was to control a hole placed out of reach of the little finger. The collection of ancient musical instruments in the Vienna Kunsthistorisches Museum contains several 16th-century Italian shawms with single keys (Nos. A.

[2] Facs. ed. R. Eitner (Berlin 1882); however, none of the three recorders appearing in the title woodcut of Silvestro Ganassi's *Regola Rubertina* (Venice 1542) shows a key.

191, C. 192, and C. 193 in the catalogue by Julius Schlosser, Vienna 1920). They seem, however, to come from the latter part of the 16th century.

But in earlier times it was not only woodwind instruments that had sideholes. There existed wind instruments that had mouthcups comparable to those of trumpets (and other "brass" instruments) and at the same time had sideholes: these instruments were the cornetti of the Renaissance, straight or curved tubes made of wood covered with leather or made of ivory (Pl. 30a, b). Many kinds existed, of different sizes and shapes—*curvi, diritti, muti*—and later their larger relatives, the serpents. Still later, in the second half of the 18th century and the beginning of the 19th century, a number of brass instruments with sideholes were constructed: the basshorn, ophicleide, keyed trumpet, keyed bugle, and keyed horn. They all soon became obsolete through the invention of the valve mechanism, a device employing pieces of metal tubing added to the main tube of the instrument to change its pitch.

The family of the cornetto is the only known case of a mouthcup instrument with sideholes at Leonardo's time. And while, of course, we cannot exclude with mathematical certainty the possibility that the principle of sideholes may occasionally have been transferred to the metal trumpet, it is highly unlikely. No picture, sculpture, musical treatise, or any other contemporary record represents or mentions such an instrument.

THE EIGHT SKETCHES concerning wind instruments on our page fall into two groups: four on the left dealing with the trumpet, and three on the right dealing with the pipe (*zufolo*). Evidently connected with these latter is the schematic drawing lowest on the left side; the reasons for this separation will become clear from the following analysis.

We begin with the upper left sketch (Pl. 31, No. 1), which shows a straight tube of cylindrical shape terminating in a narrowly flaring bell; six holes are clearly indicated, and they seem connected with little circles on a stick or tube that runs parallel to the main tube. The whole sketch represents a trumpet with sideholes, equipped with an auxiliary rod beneath it that carries a key mechanism for closing the sideholes. Trumpets of this shape but with no side holes abound in Italian paintings, especially of angel concerts—for instance, in Giotto's *Coronation of the Virgin* in S. Croce, Florence (Pl. 32a) and in one of the panels of Luca della Robbia's *Cantoria* (Pl. 32b). Thus, if our interpretation of Leonardo's sketch is correct, we have in it the first conception of a brass instrument with sideholes and keys; at least, no trace exists of an instrument of this kind from so early a time.[3]

The second sketch (Pl. 31, No. 2), more elaborate, shows a larger trumpet with wider bell and with seven sideholes. On the right, the tube curves upwards under the auxiliary rod and terminates in a clearly drawn mouthcup. On the right of the auxiliary rod, above rather than below the trumpet in this drawing, we see a keyboard of seven keys, marked "a b." From the auxiliary rod, seven double lines lead to the seven sideholes. The text (between drawings Nos. 3 and 4) explains, "Tasti stretti, a serrano buchi di gran distanzia infra loro, e sono al proposito della tronba prossima di sopra in a b." (Translation: "Straight keys, they close holes separated by wide distances, and belong to the trumpet drawn above and are indicated by a b.")

The auxiliary rod appears to be hollow, as we may conclude from its right end: from this opening a faint double line in loop shape appears. I should tentatively venture to guess that these lines indicate wires or threads that run inside the auxiliary rod to connect the touch piece with the closing key. Leonardo has recorded this idea quickly and very sketchily. However, perhaps the same function can be attributed to the two other sets of double lines emanating from the keyboard.

If this conjecture of mine is correct, then one may possibly go one step further and surmise that Leonardo was stimulated in the invention of this keyboard and stopping machinery by his profound knowledge of the anatomy and physiology of the human hand. The threads, then, running inside the sheath that I have called the auxiliary tube, would function like tendons conveying an impulse to the furthest point where movement is wanted, that is, the fingertips or, in terms of our wind instrument, the closing pads. Reading Leonardo's descriptions and looking at the drawings of the play of moving bones, muscles, and tendons (for example, see his *Fogli d'anatomia*, Windsor 19009, fol. A, 10[r]) one cannot help being reminded of his technical inventions. An even closer analogy between the stopping machinery and the tendons of the human finger can be found in Folio A, 10[v] of the *Fogli d'anatomia*, which is accompanied by a text that I quote only in part: "The first demonstration of the hand will be made of the bones alone . . . The fourth demonstration will be of the first set of tendons which rest upon these muscles and go to supply movement to the tips of the fingers . . ." (transl. Edward MacCurdy, *The Notebooks of Leonardo da Vinci*, London 1938, I, 107). Mechanisms observed by the dissector of the

---

[3] A keyed trumpet was first introduced publicly in Vienna by Anton Weidinger in 1801 and a keyed horn by Kölbel appeared in St. Petersburg as early as 1760.

human body would lend themselves to use by the maker of mechanical tools and machines. And, on the other hand, the experience gathered by Leonardo as a builder of machines would help him to understand more readily and profoundly the mechanisms made by nature. How conscious Leonardo was of the connection is evident from his plan to introduce his demonstration of the movement and force of man and other animals by a treatise on the elements of mechanics: "Fa che'l libro delli elementi macchinali colla sua patica vada inanti a la dimostrazione del moto e forza dell'omo e altri animali; e mediante quelli tu potrai provare ogni tua proposizione" (*Fogli d'anatomia*, fol. A, 10ʳ).

The little schematic sketch beneath the trumpet and immediately above the text (Pl. 31, No. 3) apparently gives a side view of something like a tracker mechanism, connecting the pad that closes a sidehole on the left with a key on the right. The drawing beneath the text (Pl. 31, No. 4) is a more elaborate version of No. 3: on the left, two of the closing levers are shown; on the right, the keyboard is again drawn with seven keys. Leonardo's verbal explanation, quoted under No. 2, connects this drawing with the two trumpets drawn above (Nos. 1 and 2).

WE NOW TURN from the drawings concerned with trumpet keys to the key mechanism for the *zufolo* (Pl. 31, No. 6). On top we find an elaborate keyboard of no less than ten keys whose thin stems are connected with the horizontal rods or wires that presumably lead to the sideholes. Only the lowest of these horizontal rods shows, connected with it, a bent lever which cannot be anything else than the lever with the closing pad. It is marked with a little a,[4] referring to the text on the bottom of the page, which says: "*a* entri i' loco dell-ordinarie poste che hanno i pratici ne'lor busi de'zufoli." (Translation: "*a* marks the place where normally the players have the holes in their pipes"; or, more literally: "the sketch *a* indicates what comes into the place of the ordinary locations where the players have the holes in their pipes.")

The drawing beneath this (Pl. 31, No. 7) shows the complete mechanism connecting key with closing pad: a long rod turns in loops that hold it at its left and right ends; the right end bends forward and then upward, terminating in a broad key with a square touch surface; the left end bends forward and then down, terminating in what appears to be the closing pad. If the key is depressed, the long rod rotates and

---

[4] At first glance, one may perhaps connect the a with the drawing beneath it and especially with the upright rod immediately below it; but such an interpretation would make little sense, since that rod is evidently a key shaft and far away from the closing pad which alone can be identified with the "loco dell'ordinarie poste dei busi."

turns the left end down so that the pad closes the hole.

While the rod in No. 7 is straight, the drawing beneath it (Pl. 31, No. 8) shows a rod in the form of a crankshaft. It is held by four loops near its two projecting sections; the projection on the left carries the stopping lever with the pad, and the projection on the right carries a key; still further to the right five more keys appear, inserted into what must be an auxiliary rod like that which we saw attached to the trumpet sketches, Nos. 1 and 2. A schematic sketch of this latter rod, with two projections, appears on the lower left of the page (Pl. 31, No. 5). There can hardly be any doubt that it belongs to the *zufolo* sketches, particularly to No. 8.

MANY DETAILS of the mechanisms in these sketches are not as clear as one would wish. However, the drawings are not, after all, blueprints for the workshops of instrument makers but rather are rapid records, embodiments of new ideas confided quickly to paper, to be taken up again and perhaps elaborated at some later time. Yet the gist of these drawings is quite clear—it is nothing less than the invention of a complete keyboard mechanism for wind instruments for the purpose of overcoming fundamentally, and at once, the incapacity of the player's fingers to control distant fingerholes on the tube of his instrument.

Only if we consider the fact pointed out above, that at Leonardo's time wind instruments had no keys, or perhaps at the most one single key, can we estimate the significance and novelty of his idea. A complete keywork for wind instruments, radically replacing, on principle, all finger stopping, was not introduced into instrument building before 1840. It was then based largely on the inventions of a flutist in Munich, Theobald Boehm, although Boehm incorporated ideas of some contemporaneous flute makers such as Nolan, Nicholson, and Gordon (Pl. 30c). It may not be without interest to mention here that Boehm arrived at his radical invention through an unusual combination of interests, studies, and skills: as the son of a goldsmith, he became skilled in this craft; he also learned to play the flute and built his first instrument at the age of sixteen. He became a professional flute player of wide reputation, composed many pieces for this instrument; and, combining this practical experience with a thorough knowledge of theoretical acoustics, he embarked on his reform of the flute. His invention spread immediately and, by the middle of the 19th century, revolutionized the making of all other woodwind instruments as well. Leonardo da Vinci, in the sketches discussed above, anticipated Boehm's epochal invention by three centuries and one-half.

GUSTAVE REESE:
A PARTIAL LIST OF PUBLICATIONS

Compiled by FREDERICK FREEDMAN

I BOOKS

Music in the Middle Ages (New York: W. W. Norton, 1940); Ital. ed., *La Musica nel medioevo* (Florence: Sansoni, 1960), transl. F. L. d'Ancona.
Music in the Renaissance (New York: W. W. Norton, 1954; rev. ed. 1959).
Fourscore Classics of Music Literature: A Guide to Selected Original Sources on Theory and Other Writings on Music Not Available in English, with Descriptive Sketches and Bibliographical References (New York: The Liberal Arts Press, 1957) [sponsored by The American Council of Learned Societies].

II ARTICLES

The First Printed Collection of Part-Music: The Odhecaton, in: MQ, XX (1934), 39–76.
Printing and Engraving of Music, in: Oscar Thompson, ed., *The International Cyclopedia of Music and Musicians* (New York: Dodd, Mead & Co., 1938), 1441–43.
Musicology's Service to the Composer, in: *Musical America,* LIX/14 (September 1939), 13.
42 articles on American subjects in *Grove's Dictionary of Music and Musicians,* Supplementary Volume, ed. H. C. Colles (New York: The Macmillan Co., 1940). 27 of these also appear in *Grove's Dictionary of Music and Musicians,* ed. Eric Blom (5th ed. London: Macmillan & Co., Ltd., 1954).
The Relation between the Music Librarian and the Music Publisher, in: *Notes for the Music Library Association,* Series I/14 (August 1942), 7–17 [mimeographed, Newberry Library, Chicago]. Reprinted in *Music and Libraries: Selected Papers of the Music Library Association, Presented at its 1942 Meetings,* ed. Richard S. Hill (Washington: Music Library Association, American Library Association, 1943), 46–56.
More about the Namesake, in: *A Birthday Offering to C[arl] E[ngel],* ed. Gustave Reese (New York: G. Schirmer, 1943), pp. 181–95.
A Postscript, in: MQ, XXX (1944), 368–70.
The American Musicological Society, in: *The Music Journal,* IV/6 (November–December 1946), 7, 40–42.
Maldeghem and his Buried Treasure: a Bibliographical Study, in: *Music Library Association Notes,* Series II, VI (1948), 75–117.
The Origin of the English In nomine, in: JAMS, II (1949), 7–22.
Perotinus and Machaut, in: *The Catholic Choirmaster,* XXXVII/3 (Fall 1951), 108–11, 141.

The Organist in the Sixteenth Century, in: *The Catholic Choirmaster*, XXXVII/4 (Winter 1951), 184–85.

Gustave Reese and Theodore Karp, *Monophony in a Group of Renaissance Chansonniers*, in: JAMS, V (1952), 4–15.

A Tribute to Manfred Bukofzer 1910–1955, in: JAMS, VIII (1955), 163–64.

Musical Compositions in Renaissance Intarsia, in: JAMS, X (1957), 60–62.

Four articles on the Renaissance, in: *Music and Western Man*, ed. Peter Garvie (London: Dent, 1958).

The Polyphonic Magnificat of the Renaissance as a Design in Tonal Centers, in: JAMS, XIII (1960), 68–78.

The Repertoire of Book II of Ortiz's Tratado, in: *The Commonwealth of Music*, ed. Gustave Reese and Rose Brandel (New York: Free Press, 1964), 201–07.

A Lute Manuscript of 1615 at San Francisco, in: *Musicological Essays in Honor of Dragan Plamenac* (Pittsburgh: University of Pittsburgh Press, 196–) [in preparation].

Three articles in: *The New Catholic Encyclopedia* [in preparation].

Three articles in: *Dictionary of Plainsong*, ed. Dom David Nicholson, O.S.B. (Paris: Desclée, 196–) [in preparation].

Tritonus, in: MGG [in preparation].

III REVIEWS

Ripe Fruit at Sixty: Two Reviews, in: MQ, XXVII (1941), 384–90 [reviews of Curt Sachs's *The History of Musical Instruments* and Alfred Einstein's edition of *A. Antico's Canzoni, Sonetti, Strambotti et Frottole, Libro Tertio*].

M. Schlauch and Gustave Reese, *The Hewitt Edition of the* Odhecaton, in: MQ, XXIX (1943), 257–65.

"Sumer Is Icumen In": A Revision by Manfred Bukofzer. (Berkeley and Los Angeles: University of California Press, 1944) [University of California Publications in Music, II, no. 2], in: MQ, XXXI (1945), 267–68.

Harvard Dictionary of Music by Willi Apel. (Cambridge, Mass.: Harvard University Press, 1944), in: *Saturday Review of Literature*, Jan. 20, 1945.

Studies in Medieval and Renaissance Music by Manfred Bukofzer. (New York: Norton, 1950), in: *Saturday Review of Literature*, March 31, 1951.

Willaert, Adriani. Opera Omnia. Vol. I. *Motetta IV vocum, liber primus, 1539 et 1545*. Edited by Hermann Zenck. (Rome: American Institute of Musicology in Rome, 1950) [Corpus Mensurabilis Musicae, 3], in: *Music Library Association Notes*, VIII (1951), 743–44.

Muzyka Polskiego Odrodzenia [Music of the Polish Renaissance], edited by Józef M. Chomiński and Zofia Lissa ([Cracow]: Polskie Wydawnictwo Muzyczne, 1953), in: *Renaissance News*, VII/3 (Autumn 1954), 120–21.

Annales musicologiques, moyen-âge et renaissance, Tome I (Paris: Société de musique d'autrefois, 1953), in: *Renaissance News*, VII/3 (Autumn 1954), 102–04.

John Dunstable: Complete Works, edited by Manfred F. Bukofzer (London: Stainer and Bell, Ltd., 1953) [*Musica Britannica*, VIII; published for the Royal Musical Association and the American Musicological Society], in: *Music Library Association Notes*, XI/4 (September 1954), 593–95.

The First Volume of RISM, in: *Fontes Artis Musicae*, VIII (1961), 4–7.

IV EDITOR AND COMPILER

A Birthday Offering to C[arl] E[ngel], compiled and edited by Gustave Reese (New York: G. Schirmer, Inc., 1943) [limited edition of 300 copies] .

Papers Read at the International Congress of Musicology, Held at New York, September 11th to 16th, 1939, ed. Arthur Mendel, Gustave Reese, and Gilbert Chase (New York: Published by the Music Educators' National Conference for the American Musicological Society, [1944]).

Two volumes of the *Papers* (1940, 1941), *Bulletin* No. 8 (1945), and two issues of the *Journal* (Spring, Fall 1957) of the American Musicological Society.

The Commonwealth of Music: In Honor of Curt Sachs, ed. Gustave Reese and Rose Brandel (New York: The Free Press of Glencoe, Inc., 1964) [prepared under the joint auspices of the American Musicological Society and the Society for Ethnomusicology].

V COMPOSER

Land of Freedom, words and music by Gustave Reese (New York: G. Schirmer, Inc., 1943).

VI VERSE TRANSLATOR

Twelve madrigals, in: *The Golden Age of the Madrigal*, ed. Alfred Einstein (New York: G. Schirmer, 1942).